"A new literary s
a new climate

—*C. S. Lewis*

PRAISE FOR E. R. EDDISON
AND HIS MASTERWORKS OF FANTASY

"Lavengro, Alice in Wonderland, Arabia Deserta, Gormenghast *—our literature glories in its eccentric masterpieces. E. R. Eddison is one of that company of great Outsiders whose work evades the canons and simply goes on delighting readers, generation after generation. Eddison is unequalled in the vigor, the vividness, the passionate intensity of his imagining, the brooding sadness that underlies it, and the magnificence of his language. . . . A truly strange and wonderful fantasy world."*
—Ursula K. LeGuin

"In his towering fantasy, the sweep of his invention and the grandeur of his style, I find something more than high talent—a vein of genius, setting him apart as one of the most remarkable writers of our age."
—Sir George Rostrevor Hamilton

"Eddison [does] something which no other writer has the daring or talent for. . . . His pages are living, and vivid, and noble, and are these in a sense that belongs to no other writer I know of. . . . This is the largest, most abundant, the most magnificent book of our time."
James Stephens

"[Eddison's work embodies] undiminished power and felicity of expression."
—J.R.R. Tolkien

"The reappearance of these novels restores to the library of fantasy literature a quality often missing and always in short supply: elegance—elegance of prose, of character, of vision. E. R. Eddison's opulent, sensuous, richly textured world combines the surface shimmer of gemstones with the deeper radiance of philosophy."
—Verlyn Flieger
author, *Splintered Light: Logos and Language in Tolkien's World*

Also by E. R. Eddison

THE WORM OUROBOROS

ZIMIAMVIA

A · TRILOGY

E. R. EDDISON

Introduced and Annotated by
PAUL EDMUND THOMAS

With a Foreword by
DOUGLAS E. WINTER

With an Illustration by
KEITH HENDERSON

A DELL TRADE PAPERBACK

A DELL TRADE PAPERBACK

Published by
Dell Publishing
a division of
Bantam Doubleday Dell Publishing Group, Inc.
666 Fifth Avenue
New York, New York 10103

CONTENTS

Volume Two: A Fish Dinner in Memison

Volume Three: The Mezentian Gate

BOOK 1: FOUNDATIONS

BOOK 2: UPRISING OF KING MEZENTIUS

BOOK 7: TO KNOW OR NOT TO KNOW

ACKNOWLEDGMENTS

LAST YEAR, when Dell published *The Worm Ouroboros,* I acknowledged the institutions that helped me in my research on the life and writings of E. R. Eddison, and now I have the happy task of thanking these groups again. The Parents' Association of Breck School in Minneapolis has generously given funding for my journeys to England, journeys that would not have been possible otherwise. Mrs. A. Heap and the staff of the Local History Department in the Central Library of Leeds carried heavy boxes in and out of their stacks and adjusted their working schedules so that I could work continuously for several days. Ms. Judith Priestman and the staff of the Bodleian Library of Oxford University gave me prompt and congenial assistance as I worked through their large Eddison collection beneath the aged oak beams in the golden afternoon light of the Duke Humphrey Reading Room. Mrs. Anne Hamerton and the staff of the Taylor Institution Library of Oxford took the trouble to bring Eddison's Trinity College bequest of books out of storage, and they set them out for me in the sunny Taylorian reading room. The staff of the Public Library of Marlborough gave me a quiet, comfortable place for consulting Eddison's bequest of books. I am grateful to all of the people of these institutions.

This edition of the Zimiamvian novels contains material never before published, material contained in manuscripts housed in the Bodleian Library of Oxford and in the Central Library of Leeds. These two libraries have generously allowed these materials to go into print, and I thank them.

Several people have given me advice and assistance in my work on the textual notes. Professor Verlyn Flieger, Dr. John Rateliff, and my dear departed friend Mr. Taum Santoski have given me many hours of joyful and enriching conversation about Eddison during the last six years. I wrote the notes to the cricket match completely under the guidance of my cousin Mr. Paul Hill, a passionate cricketer for more than a generation. Mr. David Miller, an enthusiast of fellwalking and of Wainwright's books, helped me find the sunken Mardale church. Mme. Susan Rhetts helped me translate the medieval French lyrics. Mr. Kenelm W. Philip illumined some of Eddison's obscure allusions for me. And, as she did with my work for *The Worm Ouroboros*, Ms. Jeanne Cavelos of Dell gave me valuable advice.

Several people have helped me through encouragement and love. My parents, Dr. John V. and Margaret B. Thomas, have shown constant cheerful enthusiasm for my work, and they generously helped fund my trips to England. My brothers and sisters have spurred me on with their curiosity for Eddison, and my oldest brother, Professor Will Thomas, read my work in draft and made many useful wisecracks about it. Five friends have helped me in innumerable ways: Ms. Michelle Kasimor, Professor John K. Severn, Mr. Timothy Rosenfield, Mr. Paul "Babe" Brashear, and Mr. Charles Fischer. My thanks and love go to these people.

And most especially, I thank E. R. Eddison's daughter, Mrs. Jean Gudrun Rücker Latham, and his granddaughter, Mrs. Anne Al-Shahi, for the kindness, hospitality, and friendship they have given me for eight years. None of my work on Eddison would have been possible without their generosity and support.

P. E. THOMAS

FOREWORD

BY

DOUGLAS E. WINTER

Is this the dream? or was that?

WORDS create worlds: Storytelling is a kind of godhood, taking the imperfect clay of language, molding it in the writer's own image and, with skill, breathing it to life. The task is a formidable one, and it is little wonder that most fiction is content with reinventing reality, safely sculpting what is known. And why not? Stories are for the most part entertainment, ephemeral, meant only for the moment. Few novels strive for life beyond their covers; few hold us in their dominion for years, fewer still for lifetimes. The words and the worlds of E. R. Eddison, which I first discovered more than twenty years ago, still intrigue me, uplift me, haunt me, today. I know that I am not alone.

Eric Rücker Eddison (1882–1945) was a civil servant at the British Board of Trade, sometime Icelandic scholar, devotee of Homer and Sappho, and mountaineer. Although by all accounts a bowler-hatted and proper English gentleman, Eddison was an unmitigated dreamer who, in occasional spare hours over some thirty years, put his dreams to paper. In 1922, just before his fortieth birthday, a small collector's edition of *The Worm Ouroboros* was published; larger printings soon followed in both England and America, and a legend of sorts was born. The book was a dark and bloodred jewel of wonder, equal parts spectacle and fantasia, labyrinthine in its intrigue, outlandish in its violence. It was also Eddison's first novel.

After writing an adventure set in the Viking age, *Styrbiorn the Strong* (1926), and a translation of *Egil's Saga* (1930), Eddison devoted the remainder of his life to the *fantastique* in a series of novels set, for the most part, in Zimiamvia, the fabled paradise of *The Worm Ouroboros*. The Zimiamvian books were, in Eddison's words, "written backwards," (p. 585) and thus published in reverse chronological order of events: *Mistress of Mistresses* (1935), *A Fish Dinner in Memison* (1941), and *The Mezentian Gate* (1958). (The final book was incomplete when Eddison died, but his notes were so thorough that his brother, Colin Eddison, and his friend George R. Hamilton were able to assemble the book for publication.) Although the books are known today as a trilogy, Eddison wrote them as an open-ended series; they may be read and enjoyed alone or in any sequence. Each is a metaphysical adventure, an intricate Chinese puzzle box whose twists and turns reveal ever-encircling vistas of delight and dread.

Eddison's four great fantasies are linked by the enigmatic character of Edward Lessingham—country gentleman, soldier, statesman, artist, writer, and lover, among other talents—and his Munchausen-like adventures in space and time. Although he disappears after the early pages of *The Worm Ouroboros,* Lessingham is central to the books that follow. "God knows," he tells us, "I have dreamed and waked and dreamed till I know not well which is dream and which is true" (p. 277). One of the pleasures of reading Eddison is that we, too, are never certain. Perhaps Lessingham is a man of our world; perhaps he is a god; perhaps he is only a dream —or a dream within a dream. And perhaps, just perhaps, he is all of these things, and more.

In a transcendent moment of *The Worm Ouroboros,* the Demonlords Juss and Brandoch Daha, searching desperately for their lost comrade-in-arms, Goldry Bluzco, ascend to the dizzying heights of Koshtra Pivrarcha. There, in the distance, they see paradise. Lord Juss speaks: "Thou and I, first of the children of men, now behold with living eyes the fabled land of Zimiamvia. Is it true, thinkest thou, which philosophers tell of that fortunate land: that no mortal foot may tread it, but the blessed souls do inhabit it of the dead that be departed, even they that were great upon earth and did great deeds when they were living, that scorned not earth and the delights and the glories thereof, and yet did justly and were not dastards nor yet oppressors?"

"Who knoweth?" answers Brandoch Daha. "Who shall say he knoweth?" *(The Worm Ouroboros* [New York: Dell, 1991] 167)

If anyone knows, it is Edward Lessingham. In the Overture to *Mistress of Mistresses,* we learn that old age has claimed him, his final hours watched over by a mysterious lover. Lord Juss's question is repeated, and the reader—like Lessingham—is taken straightaway to Zimiamvia. This is neither the biblical paradise, nor that of classical mythology, but a mad poet's dream of Northern Europe during the Renaissance. Zimiamvia is an imperfect heaven—what other kind could exist without boredom for its residents?—a Machiavellian playground for men and gods, where mystery and menace, romance and revenge, swordplay and soldiering are the natural order of things.

Three kingdoms comprise this otherworld—known, from north to south, as Fingiswold, Rerek, and Meszria—and all are ruled by the wise, firm hand of King Mezentius. In Zimiamvia, Lessingham lives on, his earthly self a duality. His namesake, Lord of Rerek, is his Apollonian half—the embodiment of reason, logic, science. Lord Lessingham is cut from the same cloth as the Demon heroes of *The Worm Ouroboros,* a demigod and bravo, a man of action and of honor with but a single stain: kinship, and thus loyalty in blood, to Horius Parry, the ambitious Vicar in Rerek. Parry, in turn, is the scheming serpent of this enigmatic Eden, a villain extraordinaire whose instinct for treachery and terror—and for surviving to scheme again another day—is worthy of the most diabolical of devils.

Lessingham's Dionysian qualities—magic, art, and madness—are found in Duke Barganax, bastard son of King Mezentius and his mistress Amalie, the Duchess of Memison. Barganax takes counsel in the aged yet ageless Doctor Vandermast, a mysterious Merlin who is given to spouting Spinoza and minding his lovely shapeshifting nymphs, Anthea and Campaspe. "My study," says Vandermast, "is now of the darkness rather which is hid in the secret heart of man: my office but only to understand, and to watch, and to wait" (p. 621).

With the deaths of King Mezentius and his only legitimate son, Styllis—in which Parry's perpetually bloody hand is suspect—the crown descends to the beautiful and doomed Queen Antiope, with whom, inevitably, Lord Lessingham will fall in love. The struggle for power, by wile and war and witchery, enwraps Zimiamvia in a web of passion and violence that is tangled by strange shifts of time.

"Time," Eddison tells us, "is a curious business" (p. 339), and in Zimiamvia it grows more and more curious. "Is this the dream?" his characters ask, "or was that?" (p. 563) These tales are not simply written backwards, they defy most novelistic notions of time. Eddison was exceptional in his embrace of the *fantastique;* in his fiction there are no logical imperatives, no concessions to cause and effect, only the elegant truths of the higher calling of myth. Characters traverse distances and decades in the blink of an eye; worlds take shape, spawn life, evolve through billions of years and are destroyed, all during a dinner of fish. These are dreams made flesh by a dreamer extraordinaire.

Ten Years: Ten Million Years: Ten Minutes. One and the same, says Eddison, and in Zimiamvia we journey beyond the pure heroic adventure of *The Worm Ouroboros* into an existential-romantic quest, a speculation on the nature of woman and man, Goddess and God, reality and dream: "it was in that moment as if he looked through layer upon layer of dream, as though veil behind veil: the thinnest veil, natural present: the next, as if a dumb-show strangely presented by art magic." (p. 134–35). Eddison's characters exist beyond time, beyond dimension, woven into a tapestry that circles and circles on itself, as abiding and eternal as its central image: the worm Ouroboros, that eateth its own tail.

"If we were Gods, able to make worlds and unmake 'em as we list, what world would we have?" (p. 518). Here is the central dilemma of *Zimiamvia*: the nature and means of creation. Worlds within worlds, stories within stories, characters within characters, phantasms within phantasms—this is a majestic maze of mythmaking, a fiction that questions all assumptions of reality. Eddison thus proves more than a dreamer; like the very best writers of the *fantastique,* he saw this fiction of (im)possibilities as the truest mirror of our lives, one that shines back brightly the depths of the human spirit as well as the surfaces of the flesh.

Eddison's prose is archaic and often difficult, an intentionally affected throwback to Elizabethan and Jacobean drama. His characters are thus eloquent but long-winded; they speak not of killing a man, but of "sending him from the shade into the house of darkness" *(The Worm Ouroboros,* p. 229). In his finest moments, Eddison ascends to a sustained poetic beauty; listen, for example, to the haunting premonition of the renegade Goblin Gro: "For as I lay sleeping betwixt the strokes of night, a dream of the night stood by my bed and beheld me with a glance so fell that I was all adrad and quaking with fear. And it seemed to me that the dream smote the roof above my bed, and the roof opened and disclosed the outer dark, and in the dark travelled a bearded star, and the night was quick with fiery signs. And blood was on the roof, and great gouts of blood on the walls and on the cornice of my bed. And the dream screeched like the screech-owl, and cried, *Witchland from thy hand, O King!*" *(The Worm Ouroboros,* p. 25).

At other times the reader is virtually overwhelmed with words. Palaces and armory were Eddison's particular vices; he describes them with such ornate grandeur that page after page is lavished with their decoration. The reader should not be deterred by the density of such passages; like a vintage wine, a taste for Eddison's prose is expensively acquired, demanding the reader's patience and perseverance—and it is worthy of its price. These are books to be savored, best read in the long dark hours of night, when the wind is against the windows and the shadows begin to walk—books not meant for the moment, but for forever.

The Zimiamvian trilogy inevitably has been compared with J.R.R. Tolkien's *Lord of the Rings,* but apart from their narrative ambition and epic sweep, the books share little in common. (Eddison, like Tolkien, disclaimed the notion that he was writing something beyond mere story: "It is neither allegory nor fable but a Story to be read for its own sake" [*The Worm Ouroboros*, p. lxiii]. But as the reader will no doubt observe, he proves much less convincing.)

If comparisons are in order, then I suggest Eddison's obvious influences—Homer and the Icelandic sagas—and that most controversial of Jacobean dramatists, John Webster, whose blood-spattered tales of violence and chaos (from which Eddison's characters quote freely) saw him chastised for subverting orthodox society and religion. The shadow of Eddison may be seen, in turn, not only in the modern fiction of heroic fantasy, but also in the writings of his truest descendants, such dreamers of the dark *fantastique* as Stephen King (whose own epics, *The Stand* and *The Dark Tower* read like paeans to Eddison) and Clive Barker (whose *The Great and Secret Show* called its chaotic forces the *Iad Ouroborous*).

Eddison would have found this line of succession, like the cyclical popularity of his books, the most natural order of events: The circle, ever turning—like the worm Ouroboros, that eateth its own tail—the symbol of eternity, where "the end is ever at the beginning and the beginning at the end for ever more" (*The Worm Ouroboros*, p. 178).

Welcome to that fabled paradise, Zimiamvia: Once you have entered these words, this world, you may never leave.

Douglas E. Winter
Alexandria, Virginia
April 1991

in memory of
Phil Grossfield

FIORINDA

INTRODUCTION

THE TWELFTH chapter of E. R. Eddison's first novel, *The Worm Ouroboros,* contains a curious episode extraneous to the main plot. Having spent nearly all their strength in climbing Koshtra Pivrarcha, the highest mountain pinnacle on waterish Mercury, the Lords Juss and Brandoch Daha stand idly enjoying the glory of their singular achievement atop the frozen wind-whipped summit, and they gaze away southward into a mysterious land never before seen:

> Juss looked southward where the blue land stretched in fold upon fold of rolling country, soft and misty, till it melted in the sky. "Thou and I," said he, "first of the children of men, now behold with living eyes the fabled land of Zimiamvia. Is that true, thinkest thou, which philosophers tell us of that fortunate land: that no mortal foot may tread it, but the blessed souls do inhabit it of the dead that be departed, even they that were great upon earth and did great deeds when they were living, that scorned not earth and the delights and the glories thereof, and yet did justly and were not dastards nor yet oppressors?"
>
> "Who knoweth?" said Brandoch Daha, resting his chin in his hand and gazing south as in a dream. "Who shall say he knoweth?"[1]

The land of Zimiamvia probably held only a fleeting and evanescent place in the minds of Eddison's readers in 1922, because this, the first and last mentioning of Zimiamvia in *Ouroboros,* flits quickly past the reader, and though it has a local habitation and a name, it does not have a place in the story. Yet in the author's mind, the name rooted itself so deeply that its engendering and growth cannot be clearly traced. Where did this name and this land come from? How and when was Zimiamvia born? How, while writing *Ouroboros* in 1921, did Eddison come to think of including this extraneous description of a land inconsequential to the story? Why did he include it?

Who knows? Who shall say he knows? No living person can answer these questions with certainty. What is certain is that Zimiamvia existed in Eddison's imagination for at least twenty-three years and that he spent much of the rare leisure time of his last fifteen years writing three novels to give tangible shape to that misty land whose existence the Lords Juss and Brandoch Daha ponder and question in those moments on the ice-clad jagged peak of Koshtra Pivrarcha.

When he finished *Ouroboros* in 1922, Eddison did not ride the hippogriff-chariot through the heavens to Zimiamvian shores directly. Instead he remained firmly earth-bound and wrote *Styrbiorn the Strong,* a historical romance based on the life of the Swedish prince Styrbiorn Starki, the son of King Olaf, who died in 983 in an attempt to usurp the kingdom from his uncle, King Eric the Victorious. Eddison finished this novel in December 1925, and on January 3, 1926, during a vacation to Devonshire, he found himself desiring to pay homage to the Icelandic sagas that had inspired so many aspects of *Ouroboros* and *Styrbiorn the Strong:* "Walking in a gale over High Peak Sidmouth . . . I thought suddenly that my next job should be a big saga translation, and that should be *Egil.*" After noting his decision, he justified it: "This may pay back some of my debt to the sagas, to which I owe more than can ever be counted."[2] Resolved on this project, he steeped himself for five years in the literary and historical scholarship requisite for translating a thirteenth-century Icelandic text into English. It was not until 1930, after *Egil's Saga* had been finished and dispatched to the Cambridge University Press, that Eddison focused his attention on the new world that had lain nearly dormant in his mind since at least 1921.

Eddison finished the first Zimiamvian novel, *Mistress of Mistresses,* in 1935. Faber & Faber published it in England; E. P. Dutton published it in America. Eddison says *Mistress of Mistresses* did not explore "the relations between that other world and our present here and now" (587), and so his ideas of those relations propelled him to write a second novel setting some scenes in Zimiamvia and others in modern Europe. Eddison finished this second novel, *A Fish Dinner in Memison,* in 1940, but the wartime paper shortage prevented Faber & Faber from publishing it, yet E. P. Dutton published it for American readers in 1941. Eddison says that writing this second novel made him "fall in love with Zimiamvia," and since "love has a searching curiosity which can never be wholly satisfied," the new ideas sprouting from his love grew into *The Mezentian Gate* (587).

Eddison never finished this third Zimiamvian novel, for he died of a sudden heart attack in 1945. He intended *The Mezentian Gate* to have thirty-nine chapters. Between 1941 and 1945, he wrote the first seven, the last four, and Chapters XXVIII and XXIX. Like many others, Eddison feared a German invasion of England, and he worried that events beyond his control would prevent his finishing *The Mezentian Gate*. So before November 1944, he wrote an Argument with Dates, a complete and detailed plot synopsis of all of the unwritten chapters. After completing the Argument and thus assuring himself that his novel's story, at least, could be published as a whole even if something happened to him, Eddison went on to write drafts for several more chapters during his last year of life. In 1958 his brother Colin Eddison, his friend Sir George Rostrevor Hamilton,[3] and Sir Francis Meynell (the founder of the Nonesuch Press and son of the poet Alice Meynell), privately published this fragmentary novel at the Curwen Press in Plaistow, West Sussex. The Curwen edition included only the finished chapters and the Argument; it did not include the substantial number of preliminary drafts for unfinished chapters that Eddison composed between January and August 1945. These drafts, extant in handwritten leaves, have lain in the darkness of manuscript boxes in the underground stacks of the Bodleian Library in Oxford, and they have been read by few since Eddison's death.

In Dell's edition, Eddison's neglected manuscript drafts for *The Mezentian Gate* have been brought into the light of print, and for the first time, the three Zimiamvian novels have been pressed within the covers of one volume and united under the title *Zimiamvia*. The book you hold in your hands is thus the most complete edition of the Zimiamvian novels that has ever been published.

I. DISTILLED ZIMIAMVIA

"How was your trip?" "What's the place like?" Travelers returning home from a faraway place are often greeted by friends with these questions. The questions are sometimes asked idly, yet if considered seriously, it is often extremely difficult to form adequate answers to them. Any description, any story, any exclamation often will only convey a small part of a vivid whole and then only a shadow of that small part. I have traveled to the land of Zimiamvia many times, and now I am hoping to persuade you to go there. The most useful thing I could do to introduce you to that faraway place is to answer those questions, but I cannot. I am not writer enough to do it. Certainly, to convey the nature of Zimiamvia in fewer and different words than Eddison used, I would need to out-Eddison Eddison: I would need to be a poet far superior to him, and I would need a form more potent and compact than his narrative prose. Happily, it has been done for me by such a man. Homer is the poet, and his "Hymn to Aphrodite" is the piece.[4] In a curious way, this mythic poem epitomizes the life and the land of Zimiamvia. If the three Zimiamvian novels could be fired to a vapor and then condensed in droplets to an essential extract, that concentrated distillation would read like Homer's Hymn. So, as a way of answering those hard questions, I offer you an abridged version of Andrew Lang's translation of the Hymn.[5] Once Homer's voice ceases, this introduction will descend from sublime verse to prosaic essay, and then I shall focus individually on significant aspects of Zimiamvia illumined by the "Hymn to Aphrodite."

The Hymn tells of the love shared by the divine Aphrodite and the mortal Anchises. With proper classical style, Homer begins by asking the Muse to sing through him; then, as the voice of the muse, the poet tells that Aphrodite has power to beguile the hearts of gods and men, and that she has manipulated Zeus by seducing him with lovely women who have borne him mortal sons. To even the score, Zeus sends "into her heart sweet desire of Anchises . . . a man in semblance like the Immortals." Smiling Aphrodite looks upon this Trojan prince, and love and "measureless desire" beat in her heart.

To prepare herself for Anchises, Aphrodite goes to her temple on the island of Cyprus:

> To Cyprus wended she, within her fragrant shrine: even to Paphos, where is her sacred garth and odorous altar. Thither went she in, and shut the shining doors, and there the Graces laved and anointed her with oil ambrosial, such as is on the bodies of the eternal Gods, sweet fragrant oil that she had by her. Then clad she her body in goodly raiment, and prinked herself with gold.

Then the goddess flies to Mount Ida near Troy, where she finds Anchises alone:

> The hero Anchises, graced with beauty from the gods . . . walked up and down, harping sweet and shrill. In front of him stood the daughter of Zeus, Aphrodite, in semblance and stature like an unwedded maid, lest he should be adread when he beheld the Goddess. And Anchises marvelled when he beheld her, her height, and beauty, and glistering raiment. For she was clad in vesture more shining than the flame of fire, and with twisted armlets and glistering earrings of flower-fashion. About her delicate neck were lovely jewels, fair and golden: and like the moon's was the light on her fair breasts, and love came upon Anchises.

Believing the maiden to be a goddess, the dazzled Anchises promises to build an altar to her; then he requests that she make him famous, that she make his life long and happy, and that she give him fair children. Aphrodite first denies immortal status and then fabricates a life's story: Otreus the Phrygian lord fathered her, and the god Hermes took her from her Trojan family to be the bride of Anchises. The words of Aphrodite bring "sweet desire" into the heart of Anchises, and he speaks his love:

> "If indeed thou art mortal and a mortal mother bore thee, and if renowned Otreus is thy father, and if thou art come hither by the will of Hermes, the immortal Guide, and art to be called my wife forever, then neither mortal man nor immortal God shall hold me from my desire before I lie with thee in love, now and anon; nay, not even if Apollo the Far-darter himself were to send the shafts of sorrow from the silver bow! Nay, thou lady like the Goddesses, willing were I to go down within the house of Hades, if but first I had climbed into thy bed."

Then Anchises takes her hand and leads her to his bed:

> It was strewn for the Prince . . . with soft garments: and above it lay skins of bears and deep-voiced lions that he had slain in the lofty hills. When then they twain had gone up into the well-wrought bed, first Anchises took from her body her shining jewels, brooches, and twisted armlets, earrings and chains: and he loosed her girdle, and unclad her of her glistering raiment, that he laid on a silver-studded chair. Then through the Gods' will and design, by the immortal Goddess lay the mortal man, not wotting what he did.

After some hours of love, Aphrodite charms Anchises to sleep and resumes her true form:

> The Goddess poured sweet sleep into Anchises, and clad herself in her goodly raiment. Now when she was wholly clad, the lady Goddess, her head touched the beam of the lofty roof: and from her cheeks shone forth immortal beauty—even the beauty of fair-garlanded Cytherea.

Then, shining in the glory of her divine form, Aphrodite awakens the bewildered Anchises:

> He started up out of slumber and was adread, and turned his eyes away when he beheld the neck and the fair eyes of Aphrodite. His goodly face he veiled again in a cloak, and imploring her, he spoke winged words:
> "Even so soon as mine eyes first beheld thee, Goddess, I

knew thee for divine: but not sooth didst thou speak to me. But by Zeus of the Aegis I implore thee, suffer me not to live a strengthless shadow among men, but pity me: for no man lives in strength that has couched with immortal Goddesses."

Aphrodite tells Anchises to take courage: he is loved by the gods, and he will be blessed by a son named Aeneas who will achieve great fame and will rule among the Trojans. She commands Anchises to keep their liaison secret; if he boasts, Zeus, she says, will strike him down with a "smoldering thunderbolt." Then the goddess ascends the clouds and vanishes.

II. MATERIAL ZIMIAMVIA

The glistening garments "more shining than the flame of fire," the twisted golden armlets, the sweet fragrant oil, the lovely jewels fair and golden, the "glistering earrings of flower-fashion," the silver-studded chair, the well-wrought bed strewn with soft garments and skins of bears and lions, the godlike body of Anchises and dazzling immortal beauty of Aphrodite: these tangible beauties of Homer's myth find a place in Eddison's Zimiamvia. Eddison loved beautiful objects, and when he constructed this imaginary land, he took the most beautiful things he knew of in this world and made Zimiamvia a world of material and sensuous splendor.

The men and women of Zimiamvia, like Anchises, are "in semblance like the Immortals." Here Eddison's great King Mezentius faces a Meszrian sunset: "Clear and smooth his brow was as the polished ivory; but the rest of his countenance, down to the beginning of the great black beard and mustachios, was weather-bitten and passion-worn with the tracings of iron resolution and of a highness of heart beyond the nature of man" (394). Here Princess Antiope, whose hair has "the colour of the young moon," stands upon a star-lit balcony, all in white: "It was as if she stood upon no firm substance but on some water-wave, the most adored beauty that ever struck amazement in the world" (166, 212). Here, with the afternoon sun "kindling to flame the native fire-colours in her hair," sits Queen Stateira on a garden bench in Rialmar: "The brightness of the sun shining from behind her obscured her features under a veiling mystery, but not to conceal an ambiency of beauty that lived in her whole frame and posture" (614). Here Duke Barganax strides to his ducal throne: "For, alike in his lithe tall frame, and in his carriage noble and debonair and of a cat-like elegance, this Duke was beautiful to look upon beyond the example of men" (42).

Splendid clothes complement the gorgeous forms of the Zimiamvians. To breakfast with the Vicar, Lord Lessingham wears "a buff-coloured kirtle of soft ribbed silk with a narrow ruff and narrow wristbands of point-lace spangled with beads of jet of the bigness of mustard seeds, and tight-fitting black silk breeches and velvet shoes" (61). At a banquet in Sestola, King Mezentius wears, over his brown doublet of rich velvet, a "collar between neck and shoulder" having links "broad as a man's hand, all in filigree of pure gold and ablaze with precious stones" (836). To another dinner party, Fiorinda wears a close-fitting black coat "woven of thousands of tiny margery pearls and yellow sapphires" (505). To conduct his weekly ducal presence in Zayana, Duke Barganax wears a kirtle "of corded silk, rose-coloured, slashed with velvet of a darker hue, and gathered about the waist with a belt of sea-horse hide happed at the edge with thread of gold and bossed with balas rubies and cat's-eye chrysoberyls" (42). And merely to walk the streets of Rialmar town, Queen Stateira wears a gown "of black sendaline edged with gold lace" (655).

Having given beautiful forms to his women and men, and having dressed them in splendid garments, Eddison does not set them to move on a barren stage. The architecture of Zimiamvia embraces a magnificence excelling that of ancient Alexandria or Rome. Three examples epitomize the character of Zimiamvian construction: the throne-room of Zayana, the Hall of Sea-horses in Rialmar Palace, and the banquet hall of Laimak castle. The walls of the Zayana throne-room are made of "pale hammered mountain gold" and "massy columns, four times a man's height, of carved black onyx with milky veins" make "caryatides in form of monstrous snakes, nine lengthwise of the hall on either side and four at either end" (35). The walls of the Hall of Sea-horses are "panelled with green jasper between pillars of lapis lazuli" (180). The walls of the huge L-shaped banquet hall in Laimak are made of "black obsidian-stone with deep mullioned windows" (113). The exotic opulence of these structures is matched by their furnishings. The priceless ducal throne of Zayana is graced by ornamental golden wings soaring up thirty feet from the throne itself: "Thousands of thousands of tiny precious stones of every sort that grows in earth or sea were inlaid upon those mighty wings, incrusting each particular quill, each little barb of each feather, so that to a man moving in that hall and looking upon the wings the glory unceasingly changed" (36). The Hall of Sea-horses has "doors all covered with leather of peacock blue, nailed all over with golden stars," and, depending from the edge of its domed ceiling, has tapestries "all of dusky stuff" glimmering in "blues or greens as the light moved," and, as its chief ornaments, has "two sea-horses rampant," which are bigger than living horses and carved "from a single stone of sea-blue rock-crystal" (181). No ordinary flame illuminates these rooms for the sensual eye. The Zayana throne-room has magical light created by Doctor Vandermast to cast no shadows: "the very light of the throne-room was . . . made misty and glamorous: brighter than twilight, gentler than the cold beams of the moon, as if the light itself were resolved into motes of radiance which, instead of darting afar, floated like snow-flakes, invisible themselves but bathing all else with their soft effulgence" (37). To light the Hall of Sea-horses "one enormous lamp swung high in the dome, of silver and topaz and yellow sapphires, shedding a radiance very warm and golden" (180). Laimak banquet hall is lighted by lamps placed upon grotesque stone heads eight feet long and carved upon the walls: "thirteen heads in all, very deformed and uglisome, laying out their tongues; and on the end of each tongue was stood a lamp brightly burning, and the eyes of the great faces were looking-glasses nicely cut up with facets to throw back the rays of the lamps, so that the whole banquetroom was lit with a brilliance of lamplight" (113).

Such people wearing such garments and traversing such rooms cannot sustain themselves on meatloaf and tuna fish casserole. On tables spread with damask, they feast upon meats "dressed in innumerable delicious ways" (516) and on "all manner of delicious fruits" (85). They drink white wines "dry and ancient . . . golden and tawny," and red wines "full of the colour of old sunsets," and sparkling wines "the foam whereof whispers of that eternal sea and of that eternal spring-time towards which all memories return and all hearts' desires for ever" (86).

In Zimiamvia, magnificence, grandeur, splendor, ceremony, opulence, and luxury surfeit the senses' and the soul's longing for material beauty. Eddison made Zimiamvia to satisfy his senses and his soul, and toward the foamy perilous waves breaking on its forlorn shores, his memories and his heart's desires returned forever through the open casements of his imagination. Like most of us, Eddison longed for a better world, and Zimiamvia is the world he built from his dreams. When Faber & Faber were considering the second Zimiamvian novel, *A Fish Dinner in Memison,* for publication in 1940, Eddison told the firm that

> Zimiamvia is a world which in all essentials—material and spiritual—resembles this world, but "moulded nearer to the heart's desire."[6]

Here Eddison uses the phrase "this world" to name his idea of European civilization. Zimiamvia resembles Europe, but not the Europe of one particular period. In a letter to an American friend named Professor Henry Lappin, Eddison describes his world:

You will not, I am sure, mistake the Zimiamvian world for a medieval one. Its roots are in Pre-Periclean Hellas, in the heroic classical age of the North, in 10th century Iceland, and—in some ways deepest of all, in the Italian and Elizabethan Renaissance. It is historically none of these, for it is an ideal age, which might have conceivably existed (but never did) on earth before gunpowder and the internal combustion engine were invented, and which might (I wish it may!) exist thousands or hundreds of years hence.[7]

To construct his ideal world, Eddison adopted an eclectic method of world-building and borrowed the things he found most beautiful from the different ages of our earthly world. From the things that attracted him most throughout the history of European civilization, Eddison molded a new world "nearer to the heart's desire." This quoted phrase Eddison took from his favorite *rubaiy* of Edward Fitzgerald's version of *The Rubaiyyat of Omar Khayyam:*

> Ah, Love! could you and I with Him conspire
> to grasp this sorry scheme of Things entire,
> Would not we shatter it to bits—and then
> Re-mould it nearer to the Heart's desire!

This *rubaiy* summarizes Eddison's motive and method for building Zimiamvia. Because he could not find his heart's desire in our flawed world, in this "sorry scheme of things entire," he conspired with the Love in himself to find the earthly things he loved most, and, taking on godlike powers of creation, he made a new world. He shattered this time-bound world to bits; he took, eclectically, fragments of things he loved from many places in many ages; he buried and compressed the most beautiful fragments in years of layering memory; he quarried them; he melted them in his imagination; and then, by casting the drossless matter, he molded Zimiamvia.

III. ZIMIAMVIA APOTHEOSIZED

Eddison first used his eclectic method of world-building in *The Worm Ouroboros,* and the sources of the dominions of Mercury that Eddison fashioned in *Ouroboros* are the same as those he used to build Zimiamvia: ancient Greece, tenth-century Scandinavia, Renaissance Italy, and Elizabethan England. Mercury and Zimiamvia share many qualities. Many parts of the Zimiamvian novels find their origin in *Ouroboros,* and readers who have slept in the Lotus Room and journeyed to Mercury will find many passages in *Zimiamvia* that ring with echoes of *Ouroboros*.

Between 1924 and 1930, while he was working on *Styrbiorn the Strong* and *Egil's Saga,* Eddison made some notes that eventually found a place in the Overture to *Mistress of Mistresses,* but on September 21, 1930, Eddison wrote on the folder containing these notes two "alternative titles" that reveal a basic difference between the world of Mercury he had constructed in *Ouroboros* and the new world then taking shape in his imagination. The first title was "Pagan Heaven." Evidently Eddison would make his new world with the same sources and the same method he used to build Mercury, but in the new world these eclectically gathered material beauties would be apotheosized.

The second title was "A Vision of Zimiamvia." A month later, on November 30, he wrote the words "far the best" next to this second potential title.[8] Since it is the first extant mentioning of the name since the paragraph in *Ouroboros,* I cannot but think that Eddison jotted down "A Vision of Zimiamvia" while thinking of the Lord Brandoch Daha, leaning his chin upon his hand and rapt in wonder while gazing into the fabled land whose existence was a matter of debate for the Mercurial philosophers. It seems that in the closing weeks of 1930, Eddison decided to call his new world Zimiamvia and to make it a heaven possessing the qualities assigned to it by Lord Juss in that brief extraneous episode in *Ouroboros*.

Although Eddison preferred the title "A Vision of Zimiamvia," the less-interesting title, "Pagan Heaven," seems more suited to the nature of Zimiamvia as Lord Juss describes it. In Juss's words, it is a world of the hereafter for immortal souls: "no mortal foot may tread it, but the blessed souls do inhabit it of the dead that be departed." Further, this heaven has a "pagan" character in Juss's description, because the Zimiamvians are not humble, self-sacrificing, Christian ascetics who treat earthly life as a journey through the vale of tears toward an abstract spiritual existence and away from a concrete material existence. Rather, Juss thinks the Zimiamvians are "they that were great upon earth and did great deeds when they were living, that scorned not earth and the delights and the glories thereof." In the context of *Ouroboros,* it seems that *earth* refers to Mercury and not to our planet Earth, so Juss is saying that Zimiamvia is the heaven in which the great Mercurians awaken after death.

As Eddison built Zimiamvia between 1930 and 1940, it maintained only some of the characteristics of Juss's description, because Eddison's idea of Zimiamvia changed and complicated while he wrote the first two novels. In *Mistress of Mistresses* and *A Fish Dinner in Memison,* Eddison never states or even implies that Zimiamvia is the heaven of the hereafter for the souls of his Mercurian heroes in

Ouroboros. But the opening sections of *Mistress of Mistresses* suggest that Zimiamvia is a special heaven, like an Elysium or a Vallhall (without exclusive male chauvinist policies for membership) for the souls of illustrious women and men who lived on our planet Earth. In the Overture the Englishman Edward Lessingham lies dead. The mysterious Señorita del Rio Amargo closes the Overture by speaking, word for word, Lord Juss's speech about Zimiamvia from Chapter XII of *Ouroboros,* and in the new context the word *earth* seemingly refers to the planet Earth. The last words from the Señorita in the Overture are "I have promised and I will perform." Then, Chapter I opens in Zimiamvia in the year 777, and Lord Lessingham is twenty-five years old. Chapter I closes with Lessingham's pausing a moment and wondering whether he truly heard a "familiar dear lost" voice whispering in his ear a moment earlier, "I have promised and I will perform." The repetition of the name *Lessingham* and the words of promise suggests that Zimiamvia is a heaven for dead earthly souls and that the Englishman Edward Lessingham is reborn in Zimiamvia as Lord Lessingham.

This interpretation, however, does not remain true in the second novel because Eddison developed a much more complicated relationship between Earth and Zimiamvia in the closing chapters of *A Fish Dinner in Memison.* It would be an atrocity against Eddison's art to reveal what actually happens during the fish dinner, but I can safely say that it becomes apparent that the Zimiamvian Lord Lessingham is not the reborn soul of the Englishman Edward Lessingham and that Zimiamvia is not a heaven of the hereafter for human souls who were great while they lived on Earth. Zimiamvia, it appears, is actually a heavenly world for immortal gods to dwell in, and the Zimiamvian women and men are gods incarnate, like Aphrodite incarnate as the daughter of Otreus and standing before the dazzled eyes of Anchises.

IV. SPIRITUAL ZIMIAMVIA

1. The Gods

To explain the life of his incarnate gods, Eddison created a "Zimiamvian myth" during the 1930s. The myth helped guide his composition of *Mistress of Mistresses* and *A Fish Dinner in Memison,* but Eddison did not set the myth in words until April 1944, when he wrote it to "to clear his mind" before beginning the final three chapters of *The Mezentian Gate.*[9]

The Zimiamvian myth is not narrative but descriptive. It is a series of assertions that describe the nature of the two Zimiamvian gods. As in Homer's Hymn, the principal gods are Zeus and Aphrodite. In the Bodleian manuscript, Eddison begins with the famous declaration twice voiced in the first Epistle of John: "God is Love" (1 John, 4:8, 16). With this sentence and its unspoken underlying assumptions as his departure point, Eddison asserts that "Love implies an object of love" because "Self-love is a loneliness, a privation, an emptiness" that "contradicts the very nature of Love." Eddison concludes the first part of the myth with the assertion that the object of love exists: "God would, therefore, be of Himself incomplete unless there existed something worth loving and yet other than God's self." The existence of the object of love is necessary for Zeus to fulfill his nature. Without the object of love, Zeus could not be love: he could not be himself.

Eddison continues the myth by dilating upon the qualities of this object of love:

> The object of omniscient and omnipotent Love must be infinitely desireable. The object must be desireable for its own sake: as end, not as means. Only a substance can be thus desireable.

The omniscient and omnipotent Zimiamvian Zeus must be capable of infinite and eternal love. Therefore, the object that is the heart's desire of Zeus must elicit infinite and eternal longing in Zeus. This object must have matter and form, like incarnate Aphrodite who stirred the desire of Anchises, and it must be the goal of desire, not an avenue to the fulfillment of another desire.

Next, Eddison asserts the location of this object of love:

> But there is only one substance, namely the Godhead. The object must therefore be within the Godhead yet other than God. That is to say, in the Unity of Godhead there is duality: Love and the Object of Love.

Here Eddison develops two paradoxes. The object of love is composed of the same substance that is Zeus, and yet it is not Zeus. Also, the object of love lies within Zeus, and yet it is separate from him.

Having created two things within one, Eddison postulates the nature of the heart's desire of Zeus, and he comes closer to naming it:

> This world is assuredly not the object: nor is any thing, idea, or person in it the Object, nor is any conceivable world or heaven. Love can only be by a person of a person. The transcendental Duality within the Godhead is therefore a Duality of Persons.

The love within Zeus is animated and personal. At this point, the myth anticipates the existence of Aphrodite, for Eddison has personified the object of desire and has created two deities who exist in a loving relationship within the godhead.

Eddison goes on to describe the qualities of each deity expressed through reciprocal love:

> Love moreover is reciprocal: on each side it has an active aspect and a passive: a masculine and a feminine. These are wed, and therefore intermingled: neither the masculine nor the feminine is ever pure. Nevertheless, in Him Power predominates (which is active and masculine), and, in Her, Beauty, (which is passive and feminine). There is God and Goddess. The Goddess I call Aphrodite, who is of Herself Beauty, both spiritual and physical.

The shared love is lively, and the qualities of the deities are in flux. The love cannot be given unilaterally because both deities love in active and passive ways, and since their ways of love are constantly intermingled, neither one can be completely passive while the other is completely active. However, even though the deities are united and their shared qualities are intermingled, they must be distinguishable to be two. So while Zeus can be passive, feminine, and beautiful, more often he is active, masculine, and powerful. And while Aphrodite can be active, masculine, and powerful, more often she is passive, feminine, and beautiful.

Having established the nature of his united gods, Zeus and Aphrodite, Power and Beauty, Eddison then describes their behavior towards each other within the Godhead. He begins with a most important declaration: "infinite Love, by means of his infinite power, creates and preserves infinite Beauty in its infinite perfection." Eddison names Zeus as Aphrodite's creator. As the omnipotent God, Zeus can create and preserve his own object of Love, his own heart's desire. It now appears that Zeus resembles neither Anchises, who holds his heart's desire for but a brief time, nor the rest of us, who search in vain for our hearts' desires through most of our lives. Zeus has perfection: his heart's desire is part of him, and it stays with him through eternity. And, because the existence of Aphrodite allows Zeus to express his nature as Love, it is Aphrodite who gives Zeus meaning and allows Zeus to be himself. If "God is Love," then, paradoxically, the creature is also the creator.

Next, Eddison describes the behavior of his two gods in more detail. His mythic design sets the gods acting in an unending cyclic pattern, and Eddison describes this pattern with the term *worm ouroboros,* the ancient Greek alchemic image of a dragon devouring its own tail so that it symbolizes a process of eternal repetition that has no clear beginning and no clear ending. Eddison discusses the specific behavior of Zeus first:

> There is a magic circle, so to speak, a Worm Ouroboros, in this divine loving: Eternal and omnipotent Love tastes delight directly caused by Her. He recognizes in the instrument of this delight (that is to say, in His Mistress) supreme Beauty. He realizes in one and the same moment that He is powerful over Her and holds Her at His mercy and by a violent antinomy, that His very power, the power of Omnipotence, is enslaved by this strengthless Beauty. In this double and paradoxical realization, He worships Her and Beauty in Her.

Zeus' behavior comprises two discoveries and a paradox. Zeus first realizes that his heart's desire is the beauty of Aphrodite. Then he realizes that even though he has power over her, she has in her beauty enough power to compel his service and worship. He then acts on his discoveries by enslaving himself to Aphrodite. The paradox is that Zeus is the creator of Aphrodite, and yet he becomes the slave of his creation because of the power of her beauty, and, to continue the paradox, this occurs within Zeus: he is himself creator and created, master and slave.

Then Eddison turns to Aphrodite and describes her behavior in detail:

> Aphrodite tastes the same delight as His, directly caused by Him. She recognizes in the instrument of this delight (that is to say, in Her lover) supreme power. She realizes in one and the same moment that Her Beauty compels worship from Him (that is to say, from Omnipotent Love), so that She experiences directly in Herself the experience of queening it over Omnipotence and by a violent antinomy, that this very Omnipotence is the eternal and only safeguard of Beauty and so of Her. In this double paradoxical realization, She gives Herself to Him, to that power in Him which She recognizes as divine. And, She finally realizes that Eternal and Omnipotent Love tastes the same delight as Hers, directly caused by Her. (And so on: the Worm's tail into the Worm's mouth)

Like Zeus, Aphrodite's attitude comprises three discoveries (two of which seemingly occur simultaneously) and a paradox. Aphrodite first realizes that her heart's desire is Zeus. Then she realizes that her beauty enslaves his love and compels him to worship her, and simultaneously, she realizes that his love is both what created her and what preserves her. The paradox is that Aphrodite submits herself to the safety of Zeus even though she knows that she has power over him.

The relationship between the two gods consists of action in "violent antinomy": their patterns of behavior contradict and make each the active master of the other and each the passive subject of the other. Aphrodite and Zeus love each other and struggle with each other simultaneously, constantly, and eternally. Their relationship is a passionate *ouroboros*, an unending cycle of concord and conflict.

The life of the Zimiamvian gods is suggested by the alternately active and passive roles played by Anchises and Aphrodite in Homer's Hymn. The concord of desire in Anchises and Aphrodite and the mutual satisfaction of that passion stand as the principal parts of the simple plot in Homer's myth, but Anchises and Aphrodite do not share love without conflict. When they first meet, Aphrodite, in the form of the maiden, tells Anchises that she was sent by Hermes to be his wife. Without agreeing to be her husband, Anchises takes an active role and declares that nothing, not even Apollo, will prevent him from making love to her immediately, and Aphrodite, who has power enough to compel his service, takes a passive role and allows him to lead her to his bed. After they have made love, Aphrodite actively intimidates Anchises by assuming her true form and by threatening him with Olympian thunderbolts, and the frightened Anchises passively asks for her pity and mercy.

Eddison's Zeus is far happier than Homer's Anchises because Zeus holds his heart's desire in his arms forever, while Anchises holds his for only a brief time. And yet, Anchises has less aggravation than Zeus because his struggle with Aphrodite lasts only a few moments, while Zeus struggles with Aphrodite through eternity. Not so happy, yet much happier: Eddison puts some human behavior into his Zimiamvian godhead because paradoxical truths often lie at the heart of relationships between men and women in our world.

2. The Gods and Zimiamvia

Homer's Hymn shows a contentious relationship between Zeus and Aphrodite upon Olympus, but then Aphrodite descends to earth and lights upon many-fountained Ida. The Zimiamvian myth shows a contentious relationship between Zeus and Aphrodite, but the gods make no descent to the mountains of Fingiswold or the gardens of Meszria: the Bodleian manuscript that contains the only extant written version of the myth closes upon the gods within the godhead and does not show their relationship to Zimiamvia.

In his Letter of Introduction to *A Fish Dinner in Memison*, written five years before the Bodleian manuscript of the Zimiamvian myth, Eddison offers the fullest extant explanation of how his Zeus and Aphrodite participate in Zimiamvian life. There he calls his gods the "ultimate reality" and declares that in Zimiamvia their divine nature is "extended to embrace the whole of Being and Becoming" (318). As the ultimate reality, united Zeus and Aphrodite exist in every Zimiamvian thing: "All men and women, all living creatures, the whole phenomenal world material and spiritual, even the very forms of Being—time, space, eternity—do but subsist in or by the pleasure of these Two, partaking, (every individual soul, we may think, in its degree), of Their divine nature" (319). The gods extend themselves throughout all of Zimiamvia. All animate and inanimate things live as partial incarnations of the gods, and each thing possesses in its substance some singular amount of the nature of the deities. Zimiamvian women and men, of course, "partake" of the divine nature more fully than other living creatures, but even among them great variation exists because each "individual soul" partakes "in its degree." As in Eddison's godhead, where the passive and active traits intermingle among the gods so that Zeus is never purely masculine and Aphrodite is never purely feminine, each person has part of Zeus and part of Aphrodite living in his or her soul. And Aphrodite does not necessarily predominate in women, nor does Zeus in men.

This general formula for divine participation in Zimiamvian life allows the gods to produce an infinite number of different incarnations of themselves. Eddison declares that because Zeus and Aphrodite are omnipotent and omniscient, they cannot have their power limited or circumscribed: they "cannot be cribbed or frozen in a single manifestation" (318). Ever-changing flux is the never-changing situation intrinsic to the godhead. And so on the surface of Zimiamvia, the gods need change and variation. They incarnate themselves, live, die, and then reincarnate themselves again in new forms in which the proportions of their divine natures are different from what they were in their previous incarnations. Zimiamvia is a heaven that the gods made for their pleasure. In this heaven's unchanging state of change, Zeus and Aphrodite thrive.

V. ZIMIAMVIA AMOROUS AND ANTAGONISTIC

Because the Zimiamvians are incarnations of the gods, and because each person partakes, in her or his degree, of the divine nature of the gods, each person exhibits, in a unique way but on a smaller scale, the behavior and characteristics of the gods. The passionate *ouroboros* of concord and conflict lives in every Zimiamvian heart. The Zimiamvians are predisposed to reenact the delightful love shared between the gods, but they are also predisposed to reenact the violent struggle for power that seethes between the gods. Zimiamvia is a heaven of loving concord and of violent conflict.

1. Zimiamvians in Concord

The hours of love shared between Anchises and Aphrodite are compressed in the concise narration of lines 166 and 167 of Homer's "Hymn to Aphrodite": "Then through the Gods' will and design, by the immortal Goddess lay the mortal man, not wotting [i.e., knowing] what he did." Eddison quotes line 167 in all three novels, and his translation is this: "—with an immortal goddess: not clearly knowing." This may have been his favorite line in the Hymn. Eddison also translates Anchises's speech of desire in *The Mezentian Gate*. Anchises is confused and somewhat intoxicated with desire for Aphrodite, and Eddison incorporated this idea into his conception of the relationship between the Zimiamvian gods and their incarnations. The Zimiamvians, although gods incarnate, are largely ignorant of their divine origins. The level of ignorance is not uniform: some characters are in complete ignorance; some characters experience (in Wordsworth's phrasing) "intimations of immortality," strange moments of insight into their true natures; and a few characters know exactly who and what they are. Eddison often manipulates this ignorance to produce fine situational irony: characters who are gods incarnate can ponder the nature of gods or speculate about what they would do if they were gods, while others, who know better, smilingly encourage their philosophical searchings. If I were to rank characters here according to their divine knowledge or name the characters awake to their own divine nature, I would be committing an injury to Eddison's art. Eddison wants the reader to be like Anchises and like the Zimiamvians while reading and experiencing the characters: "—with an immortal goddess: not clearly knowing." Unraveling the mystery of the characters and discovering who they are is part of the beauty of these novels.

This purposed ignorance of immortality makes Zimiamvia a world in which passionate love flourishes forever in new blooms. As incarnations of the gods, the Zimiamvians are born to love one another. If all the women and men were awake to their divine origins, they would recognize each other as Zeus and Aphrodite, and their love would merely be a familiar repetition of the constant and eternal "divine loving" in the godhead. But, ignorant of their divinity, the Zimiamvians experience the pleasure of discovering new love again and again. By continually incarnating themselves into temporal forms as Zimiamvian women and men, the two eternally loving gods can meet each other for the first time many times, and they can fall in love with each other for the first time many times. Because the omnipotent gods can make innumerable incarnations of themselves, the potential number of loving relationships is infinite; and, because each incarnation possesses a unique proportion of the qualities of Zeus and Aphrodite, the potential number of different loving relationships is also infinite. The gods can live many lives in Zimiamvia and enjoy each other with infinite and eternal variety.

Eddison's Zimiamvian myth provides an explanation for all kinds of loves in his pagan heaven: loves between women and men, loves between women and women, and loves between men and men. But passionate love between men and women is the most important in this pagan heaven. On an undated sheet among his early notes for *Mistress of Mistresses*, Eddison wrote that in Zimiamvia "there is no higher 'value' than the love of Man and Woman."[10] Eddison demonstrates this when he writes of the strange moments of self-knowing that come to some Zimiamvians. These "intimations of immortality" are usually propelled by an experience with a loved one, and these moments are most potent between women and men while they are falling in love and learning about each other. In this aspect, the Zimiamvian myth reflects life in our world: often by falling in love with someone we discover our true selves.

2. Zimiamvians in Conflict

On February 7, 1945, in a letter to his friend Gerald Hayes, the cartographer who drew his maps, Eddison wrote about revisions he was making to his Letter of Introduction to *The Mezentian Gate*:

> George convinced me that to say (as I had said originally) "Zimiamvia is heaven (a heaven, not the only heaven), in especial, it is Lessingham's, Mezentius's, and Barganax's" might puzzle and indeed scandalize some readers, rather than help. Better let it dawn on them gradually: as you say yourself, the earlier chapters do not ring exactly true to the hymn-book conception.[11]

George Rostrevor Hamilton persuaded Eddison that introducing, parenthetically, a belief in plural heavens would be confusing enough, but worse, saying directly that "Zimiamvia is heaven" might confuse English readers into thinking that the Zimiamvian novels portray Eddison's speculations about the heavenly hereafter for English Christians. Perhaps the most conventional notion of the Christian hereafter in heaven is that the blessed souls blissfully exist in eternal peace and joy, but as Eddison says with an impish chuckle, life in Zimiamvia does not accord with "the hymn-book conception" of the Christian heaven. No such blissful existence can be found in Zimiamvia, so perhaps it is just as well that Eddison did not imagine Zimiamvia to be a heaven of the hereafter for anyone in this world. It is a special heaven designed to be the home of Lord Lessingham and King Mezentius and Duke Barganax, particular incarnations of the Zimiamvian Aphrodite and Zeus. As the dwelling place of the incarnate gods, evil and suffering and strife have their place in it.

Eddison did not vacillate on this point. He was certain that Zimiamvia had to contain an element of evil:

> The place of evil in a perfect world is a fascinating subject for speculation. But that it must have its place, if such a world is to be, as Zimiamvia is, a heaven of *action*, seems to me beyond question.[12]

In the descriptive phrase "a heaven of action" lies the key to the reasoning behind Eddison's including evil in his heaven. Eddison's gods are active, passionate spirits, and their incarnations exhibit their characteristics. The incarnations need to challenge one another in action: some must work evil, and others must work against that evil. Without evil, says Eddison in his Letter of Introduction to *The Mezentian Gate*, Zimiamvian life would be dull: "a tedious life, surely, in the heavenly mansions, and small scope for Omnipotence to stretch its powers, were all such great eminent self-pleasuring tyrants to be banned from 'yonder starry gallery' and lodged in 'the cursed dungeon' " (586). The incarnate gods need the conflict generated by evil in order to test their powers for enacting goodness. If their heavenly home were a place of eternal peace and joy without conflict, they would grow weary of it.

Because the Zimiamvians are incarnations of the gods and display the characteristics of the gods, the behavioral standard by which the Zimiamvians act and judge acts also originates with their gods. Eddison explains this in his notes for *Mistress of Mistresses*:

> The old trinity of Truth, Beauty, and Goodness can be stated thus: the ultimate reality consists in this, that omnipotent Love is the only Power, and that that Power (which is "good") creates Beauty. Power is fundamental, in the sense that it creates and serves Beauty, which is the fundamental value. The Power that does this is the elemental Goodness, the "Love of God": indeed it would seem that all Power, except in so far as it is enslaved to Beauty must be evil.[13]

Zeus is love, and Zeus' love is goodness. Aphrodite is beauty, and beauty is good because it is the fundamental value, the most esteemed thing, the heart's desire of Zeus. The creation of Aphrodite is the first and fundamental good act, because Zeus' love, the active and masculine divine power, creates the fundamental value, beauty. Having created Aphrodite, Zeus must use his power actively to serve and preserve her, and he does so because his love of her beauty makes him her servant. Aphrodite's beauty, the passive and feminine divine power, guards against the doing of evil by ensuring that Zeus uses his power only in actions that serve and preserve her beauty. If Zeus does something to imperil Aphrodite, his act is a work of evil. The guardianship of Aphrodite's divine beauty provides the basis for Zimiamvian behavioral standards, and so in Zimiamvia, proper behavior mirrors the behavior of Zeus:

> Moral considerations belong to an imperfect world: they can have no place in Zimiamvia. The "categorical imperative"[14] there (and, perhaps, profoundly considered, everywhere) is based not on morality which alters with convention, time and place, but on beauty. The final justification of an action as good is, accordingly, that it serves or defends beauty.[15]

Like Zeus acting to serve and preserve Aphrodite within the godhead, the Zimiamvian men and women should act to serve and preserve Aphrodite incarnate in concrete beauty, and if they consciously endanger beauty, they work evil. However, in order for life in Zimiamvia to mirror the violent antinomy of the gods, some of the incarnations must actively pursue the destruction of beauty, and others must actively thwart those evil efforts with good acts that defend beauty.

Eddison erects a standard of behavior, and he even discusses it in terms of good and evil, but he resists calling it a moral law partly because he intends Zimiamvia to be an ideal and unchanging world whose values do not shift with the ages as morality has in our world, but mainly because in Zimiamvia, actions should be judged not by a moral standard but by their relationship to beauty. His standard implies that actions that some might call immoral in this world may be proper in Zimiamvia because they preserve or defend beauty. And in that preserving, the actions themselves have beauty.[16]

VI. THE ZIMIAMVIAN GATE

Near the beginning of *Mistress of Mistresses*, Edward Lessingham's friend, the narrator of the Overture, recalls his first meeting with Lessingham in the church of Mardale Green. Lessingham says, "No doubt we were both in that little place for the same reason," and then he speaks words that his friend remembers ever afterward: "The good, the true, the beautiful: within that triangle, (or rather, upon that point; for 'truth' is but to say that beauty and goodness are the ultimate reality; and goodness is servant to beauty), are not the gods protean?" Lessingham's too concise and thus darkly confusing statement of his personal theology stirs his friend's skepticism:

> Rank bad philosophy, as I soon learned when I had made some progress in metaphysics. And yet it was out of such marsh-fires that he built up in secret places of his mind . . . a palace of pleasure or house of heart's desire, a creed, a myth, a fabric of pure poetry. (14)

Eddison did not create Edward Lessingham in his own image, autobiographically, but many of Eddison's attitudes and opinions issue from Lessingham's lips. Lessingham's ambiguous theological statement contains beliefs that Eddison also maintained, and so the narrator's rebuke, "rank bad philosophy" can be directed at Eddison himself. Eddison would not deny the charge, because by the time he came to write the Zimiamvian novels, Eddison had read enough philosophy to know that some of his personal opinions about theology and existence were beliefs and not defensible arguments that could stand up to modern philosophical analysis. And yet from these beliefs, these "marsh-fires," Eddison built the heaven of Zimiamvia "in the secret places of his mind." In this concluding section, I would like to touch upon the beliefs that, as they formed, led Eddison down the way to Zimiamvia.

In 1943, while Eddison was composing *The Mezentian Gate*, he formed a friendship with C. S. Lewis, and the two men exchanged several letters. In a letter written on February 7, Eddison makes a rather surprising claim: he says that he would never have written any fiction if he had never read Immanuel Kant's *Critique of Pure Reason*.[17] With this remark, Eddison gives Kant a founding position in his intellectual and artistic development. Eddison seems to be saying that Kant's influence made him a novelist. Eddison does not elucidate this declaration in his letter to Lewis. If it were the only statement of its kind, an offhand spontaneous assertion made in a friendly letter, discretion would lead me to give it little weight, but that is not the case. Eddison made two other prominent references to Kant during the years that he wrote *The Mezentian Gate*. First, in his Letter of Introduction to *A Fish Dinner in Memison*, written three years earlier, Eddison focuses on Kant and Descartes in describing the foundation of his artistic philosophy. Second, in 1945, Eddison's friend Gerald Hayes asked Eddison about the sources of his "Zimiamvian myth," and in his response, Eddison explained his debt to Kant in more detail than he offers in the other two references. So three times in the 1940s, Eddison declares his debt to a

treatise he studied before 1905 as an undergraduate at Oxford. To
last four decades, the influence must have been a strong one, one
that cannot be dismissed.

I am not sure if a detailed analysis of Kant's influence on Eddison would even be possible, but this introductory essay is not the
place to attempt that analysis. It is sufficient here to know how Eddison thought of Kant's influence while he was composing the
Zimiamvian novels, and Eddison himself expresses this in the letter
to Gerald Hayes:

> . . . my myth owes its largeness to the crabbed little sage of
> Königsberg from whose *Critique of Pure Reason* (when I studied
> it 40 years ago) I learned the great unshaking truth that on the
> final riddles—relating to God, Beauty, Freedom, Love, Good
> and Evil, Death, Immortality—the analytic reason ceases to be a
> guide. If, speculating on these "unknowables," we try to rely on
> reason and scientific thought, we soon reach a point where
> these instruments that served us so well in the everyday busi-
> ness of life and action, become not only useless but irrelevant.
> We must upon these riddles use all our faculties,—instincts,
> choices, loves and desires,—our whole mind.[18]

In the *Critique of Pure Reason* (published in 1781), Kant attempts to
make metaphysics a more useful discipline, to give it the status of
mathematics, by determining the limits of its usefulness. Kant argues that the human faculty of reason cannot work upon matters
that can never be objects of human experience. Therefore, human
reason cannot construct metaphysical ideas about, for example,
heaven and the nature of God. Kant's arguments seem to have led
Eddison to rearrange the hierarchy of his mental faculties. It seems
that Kant gave enough power of truth to Eddison's imagination and
artistic faculties to allow them to break the controlling bonds of his
skeptical reason. While in his twenties, Eddison seems to have accepted, as a bedrock principle that he maintained for the rest of his
life, Kant's argument about the limitations of human reason, for he
calls that argument "the great unshaking truth." Eddison asserts
that other faculties ("instincts, choices, loves, and desires") are not
bound by the limitations that eventually render reason powerless,
and it is with these faculties that he could freely explore the large
questions of existence and attempt to discover the answer to the
"final riddles." Kant helped Eddison to believe that his "whole
mind" had the power to discover truth without relying mainly on
reason. When his reading of Kant led him to that point, Eddison
dropped what he calls "the scientific attitude" and adopted "the
poet's attitude." He defines this in his Letter of Introduction to *A
Fish Dinner in Memison*: "By the poet's I mean that attitude which

says that ultimate truths are to be attained, if at all, in some immediate way: by vision rather than by ratiocination" (315).

By adopting "the poet's attitude" and thus relying upon "vision" to perceive truth, Eddison came close to John Keats's ideas of the power of the imagination, close enough to merit a brief examination of Keats's position in order to illuminate Eddison's.[19] In two famous letters written at the end of 1817, Keats asserts that the imagination has more value in determining truth than the power of reason. Writing to his friend Bailey in November, Keats declares, "I am certain of nothing but of the holiness of the Heart's affections and the truth of the imagination—What the imagination seizes as Beauty must be truth—whether it existed before or not." A few sentences later, Keats says, "I have never yet been able to perceive how anything can be known for truth by consequitive reasoning." In the second letter, written to his brothers in December, Keats asserts that what makes a great writer is the quality of "negative capability": "when man is capable of being in uncertainties, Mysteries, doubts, without any irritable reaching after fact & reason." In the subsequent sentence, Keats says "with a great poet the sense of Beauty overcomes every other consideration, or rather obliterates all consideration."[20] In these letters, Keats argues that "consequitive reasoning," what Eddison calls ratiocination, is usually some system of arbitrarily constructed principles of logic, and that because the faculty of reason depends upon these artificial systems, it is a poor tool for finding the beauty that exists naturally in the world and independently of the artificial systems. Keats admires a poet like Shakespeare who, instead of relying upon consequitive reasoning, can practice negative capability: he can negate or suppress his intellectual need to reason or analyze or categorize things, a process that subjects them to the poet's own arbitrary evaluation; instead, such a poet is capable of exploring the uncertainties and mysteries of life by stretching forth the faculty of imagination and allowing it to grasp the beautiful. By such an exercise of the imagination, the poet will seize not only beauty but truth.

Once he was convinced of the eventual impotence of reason, Eddison seems to have tried to practice something like negative capability. However, he soon found that his new philosophical position had created new problems. Since he was attempting "to adopt the poet's attitude" and to use the "vision" of his "whole mind" in exploring for truth beyond the boundaries of pure reason, he realized that his faculty of reason could no longer offer him discerning judgment during these explorations, and he found himself in "a welter of disorganized fantasy . . . and no fantasy likelier than another to be true" (315–16). In trying to practice negative capability, Eddison had been lost in the mysteries and uncertainties of imaginative vision. He realized that he needed a new guide, but he also knew that he could not turn back to reason, since he had already accepted the Kantian assertion that the ultimate truths lie beyond the power of pure reason.

His search for a new guide led Eddison to question the foundation of his inquiries: why try to discover truth? In answering this basic question for himself, Eddison realized that all of his philosophical searchings had two fundamental things in common. First, an unsatisfied desire lay at the heart of all his inquiries: a longing for knowledge, for meaning, for structure, for purpose. Second, because the things he desired were ultimate truths, they seemed to have qualities in common: purity, goodness, an idealized state, perfection. These shared qualities struck his mind, as perhaps they struck Keats's, as beauty. So Eddison decided to let fundamental desire be the guide for his vision, and until he could find a more specific label for the truths he sought, he thought of them collectively as beauty. Led by his heart's desire, Eddison began an ontological search for ultimate beauty.

Ontology is the branch of metaphysics that studies existence and essence. The "ontological argument" for proving the existence of god, an argument used most famously by Descartes, is based on the belief that ideas themselves have reality and that a person can correctly conceive the objective existence of things outside the mind: finite and imperfect man can yet conceive the idea of an infinite and perfect being; therefore, this infinite and perfect being, god, must exist. Eddison knew that Kant had shattered the ontological argument when he established the limits of reason in his *Critique,* so Eddison based his ontological search for ultimate beauty not upon reason but upon the other mental faculties that had been empowered by his reading of Kant's *Critique.* Thus, even though Kant had tried to kill the ontological argument, he ironically revivified it in Eddison. Sometime before 1930, in his early notes for *Mistress of Mistresses,* Eddison expressed his conception of god:

> If I pray to Zeus conceiving him in my mind as perfect in goodness & beauty, Almighty Father, I may know that he in objective truth is & has been to all eternity as I conceive him: yes, with a beard & ambrosial locks, & with such a tone of voice (if I can conceive it), such ways, such gestures, dwelling in such an Olympus.[21]

Eddison's desire for ultimate beauty and ultimate goodness inspired his "whole mind" to envision this image of Zeus as the most perfect being. The significant part of this declaration is Eddison's belief in the truth of his image: what he envisions, if it is ultimately beautiful and good, is not only true, but it exists and has existed forever in that form. In taking such a position, Eddison approaches Keats's of the imagination's potency: "What the imagination seizes as Beauty must be truth—whether it existed before or not." Keats calls this power imagination, and Eddison calls it the poet's vision, but both men believe that by following the heart's desire for beauty, the poet can apprehend eternal truth in its eternal form.

How can anyone make such a bold assertion about the power of the mind? Eddison decided that because his particular heart's desire was guiding the vision of his "whole mind," his conception of god must be a personal truth, an individual understanding of ultimate Beauty. He knew he could not claim universality for his envisioned conception, but he nevertheless believed it to be true. His notes about the nature of god begin and end with this belief:

> All apprehensions of God, in so far as they are good & beauti-
> ful, are true. To deny anthropomorphism is to seek to impose
> limitations on God: the same applies to the denial of Polythe-
> ism. . . . God is protean. . . . In which of his manifestations
> we worship him—or them—is to be determined by our idiosyn-
> crasies, upbringing, & personal preference.[22]

Eddison believed that other people, following the guidance of their individual desires for goodness and beauty, might envision different conceptions of god, but these conceptions would be no less true than his own image. Truth, according to Eddison, has the power of the Greek god Proteus: it can appear in different forms to different people. Eddison's belief has an inherent element of religious tolera-tion, and he is confident in asserting that his "whole mind" has the power to apprehend eternal truth because he is not trying to answer "the final riddles" for anyone other than himself.

Eddison's belief in an ultimate truth that presents itself in dif-ferent forms to different minds lies behind his idea of multiple heav-ens. As he says in the letter to Gerald Hayes quoted in the last section, Zimiamvia is "a heaven, not the only heaven." Since the heart's desire varies from person to person and different minds can envision several true conceptions of god, different minds can also envision several conceptions of the dwelling place of god. Eddison carries this idea further by postulating the existence of private heav-ens. He made Zimiamvia to be a private heaven for Mezentius, Bar-ganax, and Lessingham: in Zimiamvia, these divine incarnations obtain their hearts' desires.

When he reached the point of believing in a personal appre-hension of a protean truth, Eddison began to think about the ideas and experiences that contributed to it, and new questions came to him. What moves the desire for beauty in the mind? The mind responds to the concrete experiences of life: the mind works upon information obtained by the senses from concrete experiences. Eddison realized that his envisioned conception of Zeus was obtained by his desire for beauty acting upon the concrete experiences of his life. He knew that his image was a rather conventional one: a bearded god having long hair anointed with ambrosia, having an appropriately sonorous voice, and sitting enthroned upon Olympus. Obviously, his mind had not originated this image but had generated it after his desire for beauty had collected these attributes from his concrete experiences with Greek art and poetry. Because his conception of god was based on concrete experiences of beauty, Eddison came to believe that god himself must be concrete. In his notes on the nature of god he asserts this: "He is not abstract, & by abstraction we blaspheme, seeking to belittle Him."[23] For Eddison, god, the ultimate reality that is both true and beautiful, is not disembodied: god is concrete and has tangible form.

The concreteness of god is an idea that finds a place in Eddison's Zimiamvian myth. While describing the infinite desirability of Zeus' "object of love," Eddison says that "only a substance can be thus desireable." Later he asserts that "Love can only be by a person of a person." The Zimiamvian gods, Zeus and Aphrodite, are substantial and have corporeal form.

Eddison's belief in the concrete nature of god led him to infer another belief from it. Because god has concrete nature, Eddison thought that a relationship must exist between the eternal concrete beauty of god and the temporal concrete beauty of this world. Eddison came to the belief that because his temporal experiences of beauty stirred his desire for the eternal beauty of god, therefore the eternal beauty of god must reveal itself through temporal beauty. This inferred belief was the most important of the principles that, once discovered, propelled Eddison to create Zimiamvia, and it may be called the Zimiamvian "Gate" because the archaic senses of that word embrace all that this principle meant to Eddison: his belief in the revelation of eternal concrete beauty through temporal concrete beauty was his door and his road and his way of getting to Zimiamvia.

Eddison was a man who seems to have spent considerable time thinking about beauty and god and heaven, and discovering the Zimiamvian Gate united and thus strengthened his personal theology and his art. In 1931 and again in 1933, during his work on *Mistress of Mistresses,* Eddison twice voiced his conviction and its joint implications for Zimiamvia and for his idea of the kind of heaven he would want to go to himself:

"The vine, the woman, and the rose:" these are Good, absolute Goods: on that I stake my salvation. I had rather be damned with Sappho and Egil than go to heaven with all the pale mystics that ever withered. This book must incarnate my passionate faith in these things.

The basic conception of the book is that a "mystic" or abstract or disembodied heaven is not worth a pea: & that life eternal must, if it is to be worth living, be the subsumption & apotheosis, not the disappearance, of these humble but loved particularities.[24]

Eddison begins by declaring his "passionate faith" in the importance of material beauty, epitomized here as "the vine, the woman, and the rose." Because these temporal concrete beauties both contain and reveal the eternal concrete beauty of god, they possess inestimable value, and Eddison became convinced that he must make Zimiamvia a world of material splendor stocked with the most beautiful things he had experienced. This conviction, the Zimiamvian Gate, is the unseen force that lies behind and propels every descriptive paragraph in these three novels: beauty in landscapes, in architecture, in clothing, in the physical form of women and men and also in their words and actions. Further, the Zimiamvian Gate has central importance in the Zimiamvian myth because it links the two gods with their world. In Zimiamvia, the eternal beauty is contained and revealed in the temporal beauty because the Zimiamvians are incarnations of the gods and every animate and inanimate thing in Zimiamvia partakes of the divine nature of the gods. As Eddison says above, "to deny anthropomorphism is to seek to impose limitations on God: the same applies to the denial of Polytheism."

Even though Zimiamvia is not a heaven of the hereafter but is a special heaven designed to be a dwelling place for the incarnations of the Zimiamvian gods, in the two quotations above Eddison passionately declares that a material heaven like Zimiamvia is the kind of heaven he would want to go to himself. Without being specific about the doctrines of "all the pale mystics that ever withered," Eddison sets himself against any ascetic theology that considers spiritual things to be of intrinsically greater value than material things, and that considers this worldly life as something that must be piously endured before one may shuffle it off in death and forget it forever and then find reward for that pious endurance by awaking to live in a spiritual heaven. Eddison could not embrace such an attitude toward this life in our material world, and he could not believe in an "abstract or disembodied heaven" as the place of his heart's desire. For Eddison, thoughts about the nature of heaven were inspired by experiencing the material beauty of this world, so it seemed to him contradictory that the hereafter in heaven would be a spiritual life in which those material beauties that had first given him glimpses of heaven would have no place. He could not believe that that was the truth. Eddison committed himself to believing that because material beauties contain and reveal the eternal beauty of god, therefore "these humble but loved particularities" deserve to be apotheosized and placed in the dwelling of the god whose nature they exhibit, each in its small way. Eddison decided he would rather believe in a concrete heaven that contained "the vine, the woman, and the rose" and be damned with the worldly poets he loved, Sappho and Egil Skallagrimson, than pay lip service to any conventional theology of an "abstract or disembodied" heaven.

The Zimiamvian Gate committed Eddison to an active observation of the concrete beauties in this world in order to apprehend the eternal beauty through them. His apprehension naturally elicited admiration of the source of the beauty, but it also elicited a quality requisite in any artistic disposition: his desire to create beauty. Had he been a painter, he would have frozen his inspiring apprehensions on canvas, but his intellect was better fitted to express itself in prose than in oils. Eddison had a literary mind, and even though many of his apprehensions of eternal beauty came through his experiencing the fells of the English Lake District or the fjords of Norway or the mountains of Austria or the classical Greek sculpture in the British Museum or Titians and Botticellis in Florence, he was stirred most constantly and perhaps most deeply by the poets and novelists he loved most. His apprehensions of eternal beauty through the temporal concrete beauties in their works of literature moved him to imitate them by creating his own literature that would reveal beauty to others in the same way that their works had revealed it to him. In making the revelation of beauty his chief artistic effort, Eddison takes the same position Keats took in 1817, and he says this in a letter to an American admirer:

> Keats says in one of his letters, (as I discovered only last week), "With a great poet the sense of Beauty overcomes every other consideration, or rather obliterates all consideration." I am not, alas, a great poet, but I know my aim, and those words describe with the utmost exactitude what has been my governing principle since I began to write.[25]

Eddison's art is propelled by the Zimiamvian Gate: his art is a continual striving for eternal beauty by creating temporal beauties through which the eternal ones glimmer. Perhaps the Zimiamvian Gate and the beliefs that brought him to it make for "rank bad philosophy," but this philosophical position allowed Eddison to build a world with a "fabric of pure poetry."

So in the end, it seems that Homer's "Hymn to Aphrodite" is not only distilled Zimiamvia, but distilled Eddison, because Anchises symbolizes Eddison himself. When he first gazes upon the maiden in the fiery shining garments, Anchises discerns that the maiden is actually Aphrodite. You and I know that he made this judgment before leading the goddess to his bed because Anchises confesses knowing this later when Aphrodite assumes her true form and frightens him enough to dissipate the lust that had intoxicated his mind: "Even so soon as mine eyes first beheld thee, Goddess, I knew thee for divine: but not sooth didst thou speak to me." Talking rapidly from his fear in that moment, he pleads for pity from Aphrodite, and in so doing he reveals that he knew the consequences of sharing love with an immortal before he led her to his bed: "suffer me not to live a strengthless shadow among men, but pity me: for no man lives in strength that has couched with immortal goddesses." In order to enjoy the goddess, Anchises deliberately sets aside his judgment. He ignores the sensually perceived information that his mind used to conclude that the maiden was really a goddess, and he chooses to believe her fabricated life's story. Then he chooses to let his desire guide his actions. His desire moves him to take her hand, to lead her to his bed, to undress her, and to make love with her. As he does these things, he ignores his knowledge of the dangerous consequences that could result from his actions. Anchises stops reasoning and experiences the concrete beauty of the goddess. To write the Zimiamvian novels, Eddison had to do the same thing. He had to relinquish his reason and follow his heart's desire until his philosophical searchings brought him to the Zimiamvian Gate.

However, the allegorical interpretation breaks down at this point, because Aphrodite does not symbolize the Zimiamvian novels. By Eddison's own beliefs, she cannot, because she is the eternal concrete beauty that reveals herself through the temporal concrete beauties in the books. Thus one significant difference exists between Anchises and Eddison. Anchises had enviable luck: the goddess came to him, and he held her in his arms. Not quite so lucky, Eddison had to search for her. Eddison's writing was not his heart's desire but rather his way of following his heart's desire, his way of seeking for eternal beauty, his way of hoping to experience it. The three novels of *Zimiamvia* are Eddison's hymns to Aphrodite.

PAUL EDMUND THOMAS
Minneapolis
July 1991

PREFATORY NOTE
ON THE PRONUNCIATION
OF NAMES

Proper names the reader will no doubt pronounce as he chooses. But perhaps, to please me, he will keep the *i*'s short in *Zimiamvia* and accent the third syllable; accent the second syllable in *Zayana*, give it a broad *a* (as in "Guiana"), and pronounce the *ay* in the first syllable—and the *ai* in *Laimak, Kaima,* etc., and the *ay* in *Krestenaya*— like the *ai* in "aisle"; keep the *g* soft in *Fingiswold*; let *Memison* echo "denizen" except for the *m*; accent the first syllable in *Rerek* and make it rhyme with "year"; pronounce the first syllable of *Reisma* "rays"; remember that *Fiorinda* is in origin an Italian name, *Amaury, Amalie,* and *Beroald* French, and *Antiope, Zenianthe,* and a good many others, Greek; last, regard the *sz* in *Meszria* as ornamental, and not be deterred from pronouncing it as plain "Mezria."

E. R. EDDISON

VOLUME ONE

Mistress
of
Mistresses

Mère des souvenirs, maîtresse des maîtresses,
O toi, tous mes plaisirs! ô toi, tous mes devoirs!
Tu te rappelleras la beauté des caresses,
La douceur du foyer et le charme des soirs,
Mère des souvenirs, maîtresse des maîtresses!

Les soirs illuminés par l'ardeur du charbon,
Et les soirs au balcon, voilés de vapeurs roses.
Que ton sein m'était doux! que ton coeur m'était bon!
Nous avons dit souvent d'impérissables choses
Les soirs illuminés par l'ardeur du charbon.

Que les soleils sont beaux dans les chaudes soirées!
Que l'espace est profond! que le coeur est puissant!
En me penchant vers toi, reine des adorées,
Je croyais respirer le parfum de ton sang.
Que les soleils sont beaux dans les chaudes soirées!

La nuit s'épaississait ainsi qu'une cloison,
Et mes yeux dans le noir devinaient tes prunelles,
Et je buvais ton souffle, ô douceur, ô poison!
Et tes pieds s'endormaient dans mes mains fraternelles.
La nuit s'épaississait ainsi qu'une cloison.

Je sais l'art d'évoquer les minutes heureuses,
Et revis mon passé blotti dans tes genoux.
Car à quoi bon chercher tes beautés langoureuses
Ailleurs qu'en ton cher corps et qu'en ton coeur si doux?
Je sais l'art d'évoquer les minutes heureuses!

Ces serments, ces parfums, ces baisers infinis,
Renaîtront-ils d'un gouffre interdit à nos sondes,
Comme montent au ciel les soleils rajeunis
Après s'être lavés au fond des mers profondes?
—O serments! ô parfums! ô baisers infinis!

BAUDELAIRE

THREE friends of mine I can never thank as I would: Keith Henderson, for enriching this book with decorations which in an almost magical way have caught its moods and spirit;* George Rostrevor Hamilton, for reading and rereading it in manuscript and giving me the benefit of his delicate judgment and constructive criticism on a hundred points of importance; Gerald Ravenscourt Hayes for a like assistance, and also for his delightful maps which should help readers in picturing to themselves the country where the action takes place.

I am much obliged for permission given me by Messrs. Heinemann to quote (in the Overture) from Swinburne's "Ballad of Death"; by Mr. Claude Colleer Abbott and his publishers to quote from his fascinating collection of *Early Medieval French Lyrics* (Constable, 1932); and by the Clarendon Press to use the text of Mark Alexander Boyd's "Sonet," printed in *The Oxford Book of English Verse*. For the Webster quotations I follow the text of Mr. F. L. Lucas's magnificent edition (Chatto & Windus, 4 vols., 1927). Baudelaire's "Le Balcon," which appears on a fly-leaf as a kind of motto, is so apt (even in details) to fulfill that function that it is well to note that I never read it until after this book was written. Lessingham's reference to it (*"reine des adorées"* in "Rialmar in Starlight") was added on final revision.

* The decorations drawn by Keith Henderson do not appear in the edition; they may be seen in the first edition of *Mistress of Mistresses*, published in 1935 by E. P. Dutton.

In Vandermast's aphorisms students of Spinoza will recognize that master's words, charged, no doubt, with implications which go beyond his meaning. Readers who have a holiday place, as in some isle of Ambremerine, among the rare surviving pages of Sappho, will note that, quite apart from quotations, I have not scrupled to enrich my story with echoes of her: this for the sufficient reason that she, above all others, is the poet not of "that obscure Venus of the hollow hill" but of "awful, gold-crowned, beautiful Aphrodite."

E. R. EDDISON

THE OVERTURE

*The unsetting sunset ✦ An unknown lady beside
the bier ✦ Easter at Mardale Green ✦
Lessingham ✦ Lady Mary Lessingham ✦
Meditation of mortality ✦ Aphrodite Ourania ✦
A vision of Zimiamvia ✦ A promise.*

L ET me gather my thoughts a little, sitting here alone with you for the last time, in this high western window of your castle that you built so many years ago, to overhang like a sea eagle's eyrie[1] the grey-walled waters of your Raftsund.[2] We are fortunate, that this should have come about in the season of high summer, rather than on some troll-ridden night in the Arctic winter. At least, I am fortunate. For there is peace in these Arctic July nights, where the long sunset scarcely stoops beneath the horizon to kiss awake the long dawn. And on me, sitting in the deep embrasure upon your cushions of cloth of gold and your rugs of Samarkand[3] that break the chill of the granite, something sheds peace, as those great sulphur-coloured lilies in your Ming vase shed their scent on the air. Peace; and power; indoors and out: the peace of the glassy surface of the sound with its strange midnight glory as of pale molten latoun or orichalc;[4] and the peace of the waning moon unnaturally risen, large and pink-coloured, in the midst of the confused region betwixt sunset and sunrise, above the low slate-hued cloud-bank that fills the narrows far up the sound a little east of north, where the Trangströmmen runs deep and still between mountain and shadowing

5

mountain. That for power: and the Troldtinder,[5] rearing their bare cliffs sheer from the further brink; and, away to the left of them, like pictures I have seen of your Ushba in the Caucasus, the tremendous two-eared Rulten,[6] lifted up against the afterglow above a score of lesser spires and bastions: Rulten, that kept you and me hard at work for nineteen hours, climbing his paltry three thousand feet. Lord! and that was twenty-five years ago, when you were about the age I am to-day, an old man, by common reckoning; yet it taxed not me only in my prime but your own Swiss guides, to keep pace with you. The mountains; the unplumbed deeps of the Raftsund and its swinging tideways; the unearthly darkless Arctic summer night; and indoors, under the mingling of natural and artificial lights, of sunset and the windy candlelight of your seven-branched candlesticks of gold, the peace and the power of your face.

Your great Italian clock measures the silence with its ticking: "Another, gone! another, gone! another, gone!" Commonly, I have grown to hate such tickings, hideous to an old man as the grinning *memento mori* at the feast. But now (perhaps the shock has deadened my feelings), I could almost cheat reason to believe there was in very truth eternity in these things: substance and everlasting life in what is more transient and unsubstantial than a mayfly, empirical, vainer than air, weak bubbles on the flux. You and your lordship here, I mean, and this castle of yours, more fantastic than Beckford's Fonthill,[7] and all your life that has vanished into the irrevocable past: a kind of nothingness.[8] "Another, gone! another, gone!" Seconds, or years, or aeons of unnumbered time, what does it matter? I can well think that this hour just past of my sitting here in this silent room is as long a time, or as short, as those twenty-five years that have gone by since you and I first, on a night like this, stared at Lofotveggen across thirty miles of sea, as we rounded the Landegode and steered north into the open Westfirth.[9]

I can see you now, if I shut my eyes; in memory I see you, staring at the Lynxfoot Wall: your kingdom to be, as I very well know you then resolved (and soon performed your resolve): that hundred miles of ridge and peak and precipice, of mountains of Alpine stature and seeming, but sunk to the neck in the Atlantic stream and so turned to islands of an unwonted fierceness, close set, so that seen from afar no breach appears nor sea-way betwixt them. So sharp cut was their outline that night, and so unimaginably nicked and jagged, against the rosy radiance to the north which was sunset and sunrise in one, that for the moment they seemed feigned mountains cut out of smoky crystal and set up against a painted sky. For a moment only; for there was the talking of the waves under our bows, and the wind in our faces, and, as time went by with still that unaltering scene before us, every now and again the flight and wild cry of a black-backed gull, to remind us that this was salt sea and open air and land ahead. And yet it was hard then to conceive that here was real land, with the common things of life and houses of men, under that bower of light where the mutations of night and day seemed to have been miraculously slowed down; as if nature had fallen entranced with her own beauty mirrored in that sheen of primrose light. Vividly, as it had been but a minute since instead of a quarter of a century, I see you standing beside me at the taffrail, with that light upon your lean and weather-beaten face, staring north with a proud, alert, and piercing look, the whole frame and posture of you alive with action and resolution and command. And I can hear the very accent of your voice in the only two things you said in all that four hours' crossing: first, "The sea-board of Demonland."[10] Then, an hour later, I should think, very low and dream-like, "This is the first sip of Eternity."

Your voice, that all these years, forty-eight years and a month or two, since first I knew you, has had power over me as has no other thing on earth, I think. And to-day—But why talk of to-day? Either to-day is not, or you are not: I am not very certain which. Yesterday certainly was yours, and those five and twenty years in which you, by your genius and your riches, made of these islands a brighter Hellas.[11] But to-day: it is as well, perhaps, that you have nothing to do with to-day. The fourteenth of July to-morrow: the date when the ultimatum expires, which this new government at Oslo sent you; the date they mean to take back their sovereign rights over Lofoten in order to reintroduce modern methods into the fisheries. I know you were prepared to use force. It may come to that yet, for your subjects who have grown up in the islands under the conditions you made for them may not give up all without a stroke. But it could only have been a catastrophe. You had not the means here to do as you did thirty-five years ago, when you conquered Paraguay: you could never have held, with your few thousand men, this bunch of islands against an industrialized country like Norway. Stir's, "Shall the earth-lice be my bane, the sons of Grim Kogur?"[12] They would have bombed your castle from the air.

And so, I think fate has been good to you. I am glad you died this morning.

I must have been deep in my thoughts and memories when the Señorita came into the room, for I had heard no rustle or footfall. Now, however, I turned from my window-gazing to look again on the face of Lessingham where he lay in state, and I saw that she was standing there at his feet, looking where I looked, very quiet and still. She had not noticed me, or, if she had, made no account of my presence. My nerves must have been shaken by the events of the day more than I could before have believed possible: in no other way can I explain the trembling that came upon me as I watched her, and the sudden tears that half blinded my eyes. For though, no doubt, the feelings can play strange tricks in moments of crisis, and easily confound that nice order which breeding and the common proprieties impose even on our inward thoughts, it is yet notable that the perturbation that now swept my whole mind and body was without any single note or touch of those chords which can thrill so loudly at the approach of a woman of exquisite beauty and presumed accessibility. Tears of my own I had not experienced since my nursery days. Indeed, it is only by going back to nursery days that I can recall anything remotely comparable to the emotion with which I was at that moment rapt and held. And both then as a child, and now half-way down the sixties: then, as I listened on a summer's evening in the drawing-room to my eldest sister singing at the piano what I learned to know later as Schubert's *Wohin?*, and now, as I saw the Señorita Aspasia del Rio Amargo[13] stand over my friend's deathbed, there was neither fear in the trembling that seized me and made my body all gooseflesh, nor was it tears of grief that started in my eyes. A moment before, it is true, my mind had been feeling its way through many darknesses, while the heaviness of a great unhappiness at long friendship gone like a blown-out candleflame clogged my thoughts. But now I was as if caught by the throat and held in a state of intense awareness: a state of mind that I can find no name for, unless to call it a state of complete purity, as of awaking suddenly in the morning of time and beholding the world new born.

For a good many minutes, I think, I remained perfectly still, except for my quickened breathing and the shifting of my eyes from this part to that of the picture that was burning itself into my senses so that, I am very certain, all memories and images will fall off from me before this will suffer alteration or grow dim. Then, unsurprised as one hears in a dream, I heard a voice (that was my own voice) repeating softly that stanza in Swinburne's[14] great lamentable *Ballad of Death:*

> By night there stood over against my bed
> Queen Venus with a hood striped gold and black,
> Both sides drawn fully back
> From brows wherein the sad blood failed of red,
> And temples drained of purple and full of death.
> Her curled hair had the wave of sea-water
> And the sea's gold in it.
> Her eyes were as a dove's that sickeneth.
> Strewn dust of gold she had shed over her,
> And pearl and purple and amber on her feet.

With the last cadence I was startled awake to common things, as often, startling out of sleep, you hear words spoken in a dream echo loud beyond nature in your ears. I rose, inwardly angry with myself, with some conventional apology on the tip of my tongue, but I bit it back in time. The verses had been spoken not with my tongue but in my brain, I thought; for the look on her face assured me that she had heard nothing, or, if she had, passed it by as some remark which demanded neither comment on her part nor any explanation or apology on mine.

She moved a little so as to face me, her left hand hanging quiet and graceful at her side, her right resting gently on the brow of the great golden hippogriff[15] that made the near bedpost at the foot of Lessingham's bed. With the motion I seemed to be held once again in that contemplation of peace and power from which I had these hours past taken some comfort, and at the same time to be rapt again into that state of wide-eyed awareness in which I had a few minutes since gazed upon her and Lessingham. But now, just as (they tell us) a star of earthly density but of the size of Betelgeuze would of necessity draw to it not matter and star-dust only but the very rays of imponderable light, and suck in and swallow at last the very boundaries of space into itself, so all things condensed in her as to a point. And when she spoke, I had an odd feeling as if peace itself had spoken.

She said: "Is there anything new you can tell me about death, sir? Lessingham told me you are a philosopher."

"All I could tell you is new, Doña Aspasia," I answered; "for death is like birth: it is new every time."

"Does it matter, do you suppose?" Her voice, low, smooth, luxurious, (as in Spanish women it should be, to fit their beauty, yet rarely is), seemed to balance on the air like a soaring bird that tilts an almost motionless wing now this way now that, and so soars on.

"It matters to me," I said. "And I suppose to you."

She said a strange thing: "Not to me. I have no self." Then, "You," she said, "are not one of those quibbling cheap-jacks, I think, who hold out to poor mankind hopes of some metaphysical perduration (great Caesar used to stop a bung-hole) in exchange for that immortality of persons which you have whittled away to the barest improbability?"

"No," answered I. "Because there is no wine, it is better go thirsty than lap sea-water."

"And the wine is past praying for? You are sure?"

"We are sure of nothing. Every path in the maze brings you back at last to Herakleitos if you follow it fairly; yes, and beyond him: back to that philosopher who rebuked him for saying that no man may bathe twice in the same river, objecting that it was too gross an assumption to imply that he might avail to bathe once."[16]

"Then what is this new thing you are to tell me?"

"This," said I: "that I have lost a man who for forty years was my friend, and a man great and peerless in his generation. And that is death beyond common deaths."

"Then I see that in one river you have bathed not twice but many times," she said. "But I very well know that that is no answer."

She fell silent, looking me steadfastly in the eye. Her eyes with their great black lashes were unlike any eyes that I have ever seen, and went strangely with her dark southern colouring and her jet-black hair: they were green, with enormous pupils, and full of fiery specks, and as the pupils dilated or narrowed the whole orbs seemed aglow with a lambent flame. Frightening eyes at the first unearthly glance of them: so much so, that I thought for an instant of old wild tales of lamias and vampires, and so of that loveliest of all love-stories and sweet ironic gospel of pagan love—Théophile Gautier's: of her on whose unhallowed gravestone was written:

> Ici gît Clarimonde,
> Qui fut de son vivant
> La plus belle du monde.[17]

And then in an instant my leaping thoughts were stilled, and in awed wonderment I recognized, deep down in those strange burning eyes, sixty years in the past, my mother's very look as she (beautiful then, but now many years dead) bent down to kiss her child good night.

The clock chiming the half hour before midnight brought back time again. She on the chime passed by me, as in a dream, and took my place in the embrasure; so that sitting at her feet I saw her side-face silhouetted against the twilight window, where the darkest hour still put on but such semblance of the true cloak of night as the dewdrops on a red rose might wear beside true tears of sorrow, or the faint memory of a long forgotten grief beside the bitterness of the passion itself. Peace distilled upon my mind like perfume from a flower. I looked across to Lessingham's face with its Grecian profile, pallid under the flickering candles, facing upwards: the hair, short, wavy, and thick, like a Greek God's: the ambrosial darknesses of his great black beard.[18] He was ninety years old this year, and his hair was as black and (till a few hours ago, when he leaned back in his chair and was suddenly dead) his voice as resonant and his eyes as bright as a man's in his prime age.

The silence opened like a lily, and the Señorita's words came like the lily's fragrance: "Tell me something that you remember. It is good to keep memories green."

"I remember," answered I, "that he and I first met by candlelight. And that was forty-eight years ago. A good light to meet by; and a good light for parting."

"Tell me," she said.

"It was Easter time at Mardale Green in Cumberland. I had just left school. I was spending the holidays with an aunt of mine who had a big house in the Eamont valley. On Easter Sunday after a hard day by myself on the fells, I found myself looking down on Mardale and Haweswater from the top of Kidsty Pike. It was late afternoon, and the nights still closed in early. There was leavings of snow on the tops. Beneath my feet the valley was obscure purple, the shadows of night boiling up from below while weak daylight still walked the upper air and the mountain ridges. I ran down the long spur that Kidsty Pike sends down eastwards, dividing Randale from Riggindale. I was out of breath, and half deaf too after the quick descent, for I had come down about fifteen hundred feet, I suppose, in twelve minutes by the time I came to cross the beck by the farm-house at Riggindale. Then I saw the light in the church windows through the trees. I remembered that Haweswater and all its belongings were condemned to be drowned twenty feet deep in water in order that some hive of civilization might be washed, and I thought I would go in to evening service in that little church now while I might, before there were fishes in its yew-trees instead of owls.[19] So I stumbled my way from the gathering dusk of the quiet lane through the darkness of those tremendous yews, and so by the curtained doorway under the square tower into that tiny church. I loved it at first sight, coming in from the cold and darkness outside: a place of warmth and gentle candles, with its pews of oak blackened with age, its little Jacobaean gallery, its rough whitewashed walls, simple pointed windows, low dark roof-beams: a glamorous and dazzling loveliness such as a child's eyes feed upon in its first Christmas-tree. As I found my way to a seat half-way up the aisle on the north side, I remember thinking of those little earthenware houses, white, green, and pink, that you can put a night-light inside; things I had forgotten for years, but I had one (as I remembered) long ago, in those lavender and musk-smelling days of childhood, which seemed far more distant to me then, when I was nineteen, than they do now; German things, I fancy: born of the old good German spirit of Struwwelpeter and Christmas-trees. Yes, it was those little earthenware houses that I thought of as I sat there, sensuously loving the candlelight and the moving shadows it threw: safe shadows, like those there used to be in the nursery when your nurse was still there; not the ghostly shadows that threatened and hovered when she had gone down to supper and you were left alone. And these shadows and the yellow glamour of the candles fell on kind safe faces, like hers: an old farmer with furrowed, strong, big-boned, storm-weathered features, not in his Sunday-go-to-meeting suit, but

with heavy boots nailed and plastered with mud, as if he had walked
a good distance to church, and rough strong tweed coat and
breeches. Three or four farmers, a few farm men, a few women and
girls, an old woman, a boy or two, one or two folk in the little gallery
above the door: that was all the congregation. But what pleased me
most of all was the old parson, and his way of conducting the service. He was white-haired, with a bristly moustache. He did everything himself single-handed: said the prayers, read the lessons,
collected the offertory, played the harmonium that did duty for an
organ, preached the sermon. And all these things he did methodi-
cally and without hurry or self-consciousness, as you might imagine
him looking after a roomful of friends at supper in the little rectory
across the road. His sermon was short and full of personalities, but
all kindly and gentle-humoured. His announcements of times of
services, appointments for weddings, christenings and what not,
were interspersed with detailed and homely explanations, given not
in the least *ex cathedra* but as if across the breakfast-table. One particularly I remember, when he gave out: "Hymn number one hundred and forty: the one hundred and fortieth hymn: *Jesus lives! No
longer now Can thy terrors, death, appal us.*" Then, before sitting down
to the harmonium, he looked very benevolently at his little flock
over the tops of his spectacles, and said, "I want everybody to try
and get the words right. Some people make a mistake about the first
line of this hymn, and give it quite a wrong meaning. Remember to
pause after 'lives': 'Jesus lives!' Don't do like some people do, and
say 'Jesus lives no longer now': that is quite wrong: gives quite a
wrong meaning: it makes nonsense. Now then: 'Jesus lives! No
longer now'"; and he sat down to the harmonium and began.

"It was just at that moment, as we all stood up to sing that
innocent hymn with its difficult first line, that I first saw Lessingham. He was away to my right, at the back on the south side,
and as the congregation rose I looked half round and saw him. I
remember, years later, his describing to me the effect of the sudden
view you get of Nanga Parbat from one of those Kashmir valleys;
you have been riding for hours among quiet richly wooded scenery,
winding up along the side of some kind of gorge, with nothing very
big to look at, just lush, leafy, pussy-cat country of steep hillsides
and waterfalls; then suddenly you come round a corner where the
view opens up the valley, and you are almost struck senseless by the
blinding splendour of that vast face of ice-hung precipices and soaring ridges, sixteen thousand feet from top to toe, filling a whole
quarter of the heavens at a distance of, I suppose, only a dozen
miles. And now, whenever I call to mind my first sight of Lessingham in that little daleside church so many years ago, I think of
Nanga Parbat. He stood half a head taller than the tallest man there,
but it was the grandeur of his bearing that held me, as if he had

been some great lord of the renaissance: a grandeur which seemed to sit upon every limb and feature of him with as much fitness, and to be carried with as little regard or notice from himself, as the scrubby old Norfolk jacket and breeches in which he was dressed. His jacket was threadbare, frayed at the cuffs, strapped with leather at the elbows, but it was as if lighted from within, as the flame shows in a horn lantern, with a sense of those sculptured heroes from the Parthenon. I saw the beauty of his hand where it rested on the window-sill, and the ruby burning like a coal in the strange ring he wore on the middle finger.[20] But just as, in a snow mountain, all sublimities soar upwards to the great peak in the empyrean, so in him was all this majesty and beauty and strength gathered at last in the head and face; that serene forehead, those features where Apollo and Ares seemed to mingle, the strong luxurious lines of the mouth showing between the upcurled moustache and the cataract of black beard: that mouth whose corners seemed the lurking-places of all wild sudden gleams, of delightful humour, and melancholy, and swift resolution, and terrible anger. At length his unconscious eyes met mine, and, looking through me as lost in a deep sadness, made me turn away in some confusion.

"I thought he had been quite unaware of me and my staring; but as we came out into the lane when church was over (it was starlight now, and the moon risen behind the hills) he overtook me and fell into step beside me, saying he noticed that we wore the same tie. I hardly know which was to me the more astonishing, that this man should deign to talk to me at all, or that I should find myself within five minutes swinging along beside him down the lake road, which was my way home, and talking as easily as if it had been to an intimate friend of my own age instead of a man old enough to be my father: a man too who, to all outward seeming, would have been more in his element in the company of Cesare Borgia or Gonsalvo di Cordova.[21] It was not, of course, till some time after this that I knew he traced his descent through many generations of English forefathers to King Eric Bloodaxe in York,[22] the son of Harald Hairfair,[23] that Charlemagne of the north, and, by the female line, from the greatest ruler of men that appeared in Europe in the thousand years between Charlemagne and Napoleon: the Emperor Frederick II, of whom it has been written that "the power, which in the rout of able and illustrious men shines through crannies, in him pours out as through a rift in nature." In after years I helped Lessingham a good deal in collecting material for his ten-volume *History of Frederick II*,[24] which is of course to-day the standard authority on that period, and ranks, as literature, far and away above any other history book since Gibbon.

"We talked at first about Eton; then about rowing, and riding, and then about mountains, for I was at that time newly bitten with the climbing-madness and I found him an old hand at the game, though it was not for a year or so that I discovered that he was among the best (though incomparably the rashest) of contemporary climbers. I do not think we touched on the then recent War, in which he attained great distinction, mainly in East Africa.[25] At length the wings of our talk began to take those wider sweeps which starlight and steady walking and that aptness of mind to mind which is the basis of all true friendship lead to; so that after a while I found myself telling him how much his presence had surprised me in that little church, and actually asking him whether he was there to pray, like the other people, or only to look on, like me. Those were the salad-days of my irreligious fervour, when the strange *amor mortis* of adolescence binds a panache of glory on the helmet of every unbelief, and when books like *La Révolte des Anges* or Swinburne's *Dolores*[26] send a thrill down the spine that can never be caught again in its pristine vigour when years and wisdom have taught us the true terrors of that drab, comfortless, and inglorious sinking into not-being which awaits us all at last. He answered he was there to pray. This I had not expected, though I had been puzzled at the expression on his face in church: an expression that I thought sat oddly on the face of a pagan God or an atheistical tyrant of the renaissance. I mumbled some awkwardness about his not looking to me much like a churchman. His laughter at this seemed to set the whole night a-sparkle: he stopped, caught me by the shoulder with one hand and spun me round to face him. His mouth was smiling down at me in the moonlight in a way which made me think of Pater's essay about Mona Lisa.[27] He said nothing, but I felt as if I and my half-fledged impieties shrank under that smile to something very naked and nerveless: a very immature Kapaneus posturing before Thebes;[28] a ridiculous little Aias waving a toy sword against the lightning.[29] We walked on beside the dark lake. He said nothing, neither did I. So completely had he already bound me to his chariot-wheels that I was ready, if he had informed me that he was Anabaptist or Turk, to embrace that sect. At length he spoke, words that for some reason I have never forgotten: "No doubt," he said, "we were both in that little place for the same reason. The good, the true, the beautiful: within that triangle (or rather, upon that point; for 'truth' is but to say that beauty and goodness are the ultimate reality; and goodness is servant to beauty) are not the Gods protean?" Rank bad philosophy, as I soon learned when I had made some progress in metaphysics. And yet it was out of such marsh-fires that he built up in secret places of his mind (as, from time to time in our long friendship, I have from fleeting revelations and rare partial confidences discovered) a palace of pleasure or house of heart's desire, a creed, a myth, a fabric of pure poetry, more solid in its specifications and more concrete in its strange glorious fictions and vanities beyond opium or madness than this world is, and this life that we call real. And more than that, for he moulded life to his dreams; and, besides his poems and writings "more lasting than brass," his paintings and sculptures that are scrambled for by the picture-galleries of Europe, and those other (perhaps the most astounding) monuments of his genius, the communities of men who have felt the iron and yet beneficent might of his statecraft, as here in Lofoten,—besides all these things, I know very well that he found in this Illusion of Illusions a something potent as the fabled unction of the Styx,[30] so that no earthly loss, pain, or grief, could touch him.

"It was not until after many years of friendship that I got some inkling of the full power of this consolation; for he never wore his heart for daws to peck at. The bare facts I was soon informed of: his marriage, when he was not yet twenty-six, and she barely twenty, to the beautiful and brilliant Lady Mary Scarnside,[31] and her death fifteen years later in a French railway accident along with their only child, a girl. This tragedy took place about two years before our meeting in Mardale church. Lessingham never talked of his wife. I learned that he had, soon after her death, deliberately burnt down their lovely old house in Wasdale.[32] I never saw her portrait: several, from his own brush, were destroyed in the fire; he told me, years later, that he had subsequently bought up every picture or photograph of her that he could trace, and destroyed them. Like most men who are endowed with vigorous minds and high gifts of imagination, Lessingham was, for as long as I have known him, a man of extreme attractiveness to women, and a man to whom (as to his imperial ancestor) women and the beauty of women were as mountain air and sunshine. The spectacle of the unbroken succession and variety of ladies, who crowned, like jewels, the ever increasing splendour and pomp of his existence, made me think that his marriage had been without significance, and that he never spoke of his wife because he had forgotten her. Later, when I heard about the burnt portraits, I changed my mind and supposed he had hated her. It was only when our friendship had ripened to a deep understanding in which words were scarcely needed as messengers between our minds, that I realized how things stood: that it was only his majestic if puerile belief in her personal immortality, and his own, beyond the grave, that upheld him in all the storm and peace and magnificence and high achievement of the years (fifty, as it turned out) that he was to live on without her.

"These pragmatical sophisters, with their loose psychology and their question-begging logic-chopping that masquerades as metaphysic! I would almost give them leave to gag truth and lead the world by the nose like a jackass, if they could but be men as this man, and bend error and self-deception to high and lofty imaginings as he did. For it is certain mankind would build better if they built for themselves; few can love and tender an unknown posterity. But this man, as I have long observed him, looked on all things *sub specie aeternitatis;*[33] his actions all moved (like the slow procession of this northern summer night) to slow perfection, where the common run of men spoil all in their make-shift hurry. If he followed will-o'-the-wisps in metaphysics, they proved safe lights for him in practical affairs. He was neither deceived nor alarmed by the rabble's god, mere Quantity, considering that if you inflate it big enough the Matterhorn becomes as insignificant as a grain of sand, since the eye can no longer perceive it, and that a nebula in which our whole earth would be but as a particle in a cloud of tobacco-smoke is (unless as a whetter of imagination's appetite) more unimportant than that smoke, because further divorced from life. And so, with sound wisdom, he applied all his high gifts of nature, and that sceptre which his colossal wealth set ready in his hand, not to dissipate them in the welter of the world, but to fields definite enough to show the effect. And for all his restless vigour and love of action, he withheld himself as a rule from action in the world, except where he could find conditions, as in Paraguay[34] and again in Lofoten, outside the ordinary texture of modern life. For he felt, I think, by a profound instinct, that in modern life action swallows up the individual. There is no scope for a good climber, he said, to show his powers in a quagmire. Well, it is night now; and no more climbing."

It was not until I had ended that I felt I had been making something of a fool of myself, letting my thoughts run away with my tongue. For some minutes there was silence, broken only by the solemn ticking of the clock, and now and then a sea-bird's desolate cry without. Then the Señorita's voice stole on the silence as a meteor steals across darkness: "All must pass away, all must break at last, everything we care for: lips wither, the bright brain grows dim, 'the vine, the woman, and the rose': even the names, even the mention and remembrance of created things, must die and be forgotten; until at last not these only, but death and oblivion itself must cease, dissipated in that infinite frost of illimitable nothingness of space and time, for ever and ever and ever."

I listened with that sensation of alternating strain and collapse of certain muscles which belongs to some dreams where the dreamer climbs insecurely from frame to frame over rows of pictures hung on a wall of tremendous height below which opens the abyss. Hitherto the mere conception of annihilation (when once I had imaginatively compassed it, as now and then I have been able to do, lying awake in the middle of the night) had had so much power of horror upon me that I could barely refrain from shrieking in my bed. But now, for the first time in my life, I found I could look down from that sickening verge steadfastly and undismayed. It seemed a strange turn, that here in death's manifest presence I, for the first time, found myself unable seriously to believe in death.

My outward eyes were on Lessingham's face, the face of an Ozymandias.[35] My inward eye searched the night, plunging to those deeps beyond the star-shine where, after uncounted millions of light-years' journeying, the two ends of a straight line meet, and the rays complete the full circle on themselves; so that what to my earthly gaze shows as this almost indiscernible speck of mist, seen through a gap in the sand-strewn thousands of the stars of the Lion, may be but the back view of the very same unknown cosmic island of suns and galaxies which (as a like unremarkable speck) faces my searching eye in the direct opposite region of the heavens, in the low dark sign of Capricorn.

Then, as another meteor across darkness: "Many have blasphemed God for these things," she said; "but without reason, surely. Shall infinite Love that is able to wield infinite Power be subdued to our necessities? Must the Gods make haste, for Whom no night cometh? Is there a sooner or a later in Eternity? Have you thought of this: you had an evil dream: you were in hell that night; yet you woke and forgot it utterly. Are you to-night any jot the worse for it?"

She seemed to speak of forgotten things that I had known long ago and that, remembered now, brought back all that was lost and healed all sorrows. I had no words to answer her, but I thought of Lessingham's poems, and they seemed to be, to this mind she brought me to, as shadows before the sun. I reached down from the shelf at my left, beside the window, a book of vellum with clasps of gold. "Lessingham shall answer you from this book," I said, looking up at her where she sat against the sunset. The book opened at his rondel of *Aphrodite Ourania*.[36] I read it aloud. My voice shook, and marred the reading:

"Between the sunset and the sea
  The years shall still behold Your glory,
Seen through this troubled fantasy
  Of doubtful things and transitory.

"Desire's clear eyes still search for Thee
  Beyond Time's transient territory,
  Upon some flower-robed promontory
Between the sunset and the sea.

"Our Lady of Paphos:[37] though a story
They count You: though Your temples be
  Time-wrecked, dishonoured, mute and hoary—
You are more than their philosophy.

"Between the sunset and the sea
Waiteth Your eternal glory."

While I read, the Señorita sat motionless, her gaze bent on
Lessingham. Then she rose softly from her seat in the window and
stood once more in that place where I had first seen her that night,
like the Queen of Love sorrowing for a great lover dead. The clock
ticked on, and I measured it against my heart-beats. An unreason-
ing terror now took hold of me, that Death was in the room and had
laid on my heart also his fleshless and icy hand. I dropped the book
and made as if to rise from my seat, but my knees gave way like a
drunken man's. Then with the music of her voice, speaking once
more, as if love itself were speaking out of the interstellar spaces
from beyond the mists of time and desolation and decay, my heart
gave over its fluttering and became quiet like a dove held safe in its
mistress's hand. "It is midnight now," she said. "Time to say farewell, seal the chamber, and light the pyre. But first you have leave to
look upon the picture, and to read that which was written."

At the time, I wondered at nothing, but accepted, as in a
dream, her knowledge of this secret charge bequeathed to me by
Lessingham through sealed instructions locked in a fireproof box
which I had only opened on his death, and of which he had once or
twice assured me that no person other than himself had seen the
contents. In that box was a key of gold, and with that I was at
midnight of his death-day to unlock the folding doors of a cabinet
that was built into the wall above his bed, and so leave him lying in
state under the picture that was in the cabinet. And I must seal the
room, and burn up Digermulen castle, and him and all that was in
it, as he had burnt up his house in Wasdale fifty years before. And
he had let me know that in that cabinet was his wife's picture,
painted by himself, his masterpiece never seen by living eye except
the painter's and the sitter's; the only one of all her pictures that he
had spared.

The cabinet doors were of black lacquer and gold, flush with
the wall. I turned the golden key, and opened them left and right.
My eyes swam as I looked upon that loveliness that showed doubt-
fully in the glittering candlelight and the diffused rosy dusk from
without. I saw well now that this great picture had been painted for
himself alone. A sob choked me as I thought of this last pledge of
our friendship, planned by him so many years ago to speak for him
to me from beyond death, that my eyes should be allowed to see his
treasure before it was committed, with his own mortal remains, to
the consuming element of fire. And now I saw how upon the inside
panels of the cabinet was inlaid (by his own hand, I doubt not) in
letters of gold this poem, six stanzas upon either door:

A VISION OF ZIMIAMVIA

I will have gold and silver for my delight:
  Hangings of red silk, purfled[38] and work'd in gold
With mantichores[39] and what worse shapes of fright
  Terror Antiquus spawn'd in the days of old.

I will have columns of Parian[40] vein'd with gems,
  Their capitals by Pheidias'[41] self design'd,
By his hand carv'd, for flowers with strong smooth stems,
  Nepenthe, Elysian Amaranth,[42] and their kind.

I will have night; and the taste of a field well fought,
  And a golden bed made wide for luxury;
And there—since else were all things else prov'd naught—
  Bestower and hallower of all things: I will have Thee.

—Thee, and hawthorn time. For in that new birth though all
  Change, you I will have unchang'd: even that dress,
So fall'n to your hips as lapping waves should fall:
  You, cloth'd upon with your beauty's nakedness.

The line of your flank: so lily-pure and warm:
  The globéd wonder of splendid breasts made bare:
The gleam, like cymbals a-clash, when you lift your arm;
  And the faun leaps out with the sweetness of red-gold hair.

My dear—my tongue is broken: I cannot see:
  A sudden subtle fire beneath my skin
Runs,[43] and an inward thunder deafens me,
  Drowning mine ears: I tremble.—O unpin

Those pins of anachite diamond, and unbraid
  Those strings of margery-pearls, and so let fall
Your python tresses in their deep cascade
  To be your misty robe imperial.—

The beating of wings, the gallop, the wild spate,
  Die down. A hush resumes all Being, which you
Do with your starry presence consecrate,
  And peace of moon-trod gardens and falling dew.

Two are our bodies: two are our minds, but wed.
  On your dear shoulder, like a child asleep,
I let my shut lids press, while round my head
  Your gracious hands their benediction keep.

Mistress of my delights; and Mistress of Peace:
  O ever changing, never changing, You:
Dear pledge of our true love's unending lease,
  Since true to you means to mine own self true.—

I will have gold and jewels for my delight:
  Hyacinth, ruby, and smaragd, and curtains work'd in gold
With mantichores and what worse shapes of fright
  Terror Antiquus spawn'd in the days of old.

Earth I will have, and the deep sky's ornament:
  Lordship, and hardship, and peril by land and sea.—
And still, about cock-shut time, to pay for my banishment,
  Safe in the lowe of the firelight I will have Thee.

Half blinded with tears, I read the stanzas and copied them
down. All the while I was conscious of the Señorita's presence at my
side, a consciousness from which in some irrational way I seemed to
derive an inexplicable support, beyond comprehension or comparisons. These were things which by all right judgment it was unpardonable that any living creature other than myself should have
looked upon. Yet of the rightness of her presence (more, of its deep
necessity), my sense was so lively as to pass without remark or question. When I had finished my writing, I saw that she had not
moved, but remained there, very still, one hand laid lightly on the
bedpost at the foot of the bed, between the ears of the great golden
hippogriff. I heard her say, faint as the breath of night-flowers under the stars: "The fabled land of ZIMIAMVIA. Is it true, will you think,
which poets tell us of that fortunate land: that no mortal foot may
tread it, but the blessed souls do inhabit it of the dead that be departed: of them that were great upon earth and did great deeds
when they were living, that scorned not earth and the delights and
the glories of earth, and yet did justly and were not dastards nor yet
oppressors?"[44]

"Who knows?" I said. "Who dares say he knows?"

Then I heard her say, in her voice that was gentler than the
glow-worm's light among rose-trees in a forgotten garden between
dewfall and moonrise: *Be content. I have promised and I will perform.*

And as my eyes rested on that strange woman's face, it seemed
to take upon itself, as she looked on Lessingham dead, that unsearchable look, of laughter-loving lips divine, half closed in a grave
expectancy, of infinite pity, infinite patience, and infinite sweetness,
which sits on the face of Praxiteles's Knidian Aphrodite.[45]

I

A Spring Night
in Mornagay

*A commission of peril ◆ The Three Kingdoms
masterless ◆ Policy of the vicar ◆ The promise
heard in Zimiamvia.*

B Y all accounts, 'twas to give him line only," said
Amaury; "and if King Mezentius had lived, would have
been war between them[1] this summer. Then he[2] should
have been boiled in his own syrup; and 'tis like danger
now, though smaller, to cope the son.[3] You do forget
your judgement, I think, in this single thing, save which I could
swear you are perfect in all things."

Lessingham[4] made no answer. He was gazing with a strange
intentness into the wine which brimmed the crystal goblet in his
right hand. He held it up for the bunch of candles that stood in the
middle of the table to shine through, turning the endless stream of
bubbles into bubbles of golden fire. Amaury, half facing him on his
right, watched him. Lessingham set down the goblet and looked
round at him with the look of a man awaked from sleep.

"Now I've angered you," said Amaury. "And yet, I said but
true."

As a wren twinkles in and out in a hedge-row, the demurest soft
shadow of laughter came and went in Lessingham's swift grey eyes.
"What, were you reading me good counsel? Forgive me, dear
Amaury: I lost the thread on't. You were talking of my cousin,[5] and

21

the great King, and might-a-beens; but I was fallen a-dreaming and marked you not."

Amaury gave him a look, then dropped his eyes. His thick eyebrows that were the colour of pale rye-straw frowned and bristled, and beneath the sunburn his face, clear-skinned as a girl's, flamed scarlet to the ears and hair-roots, and he sat sulky, his hands thrust into his belt at either side, his chin buried in his ruff. Lessingham, still leaning on his left elbow, stroked the black curls of his mustachios and ran a finger slowly and delicately over the jewelled filigree work of the goblet's feet. Now and again he cocked an eye at Amaury, who at last looked up and their glances met. Amaury burst out laughing. Lessingham busied himself still for a moment with the sparkling, rare, and sunset-coloured embellishments of the goldsmith's art, then, pushing the cup from him, sat back. "Out with it," he said; " 'tis shame to plague you. Let me know what it is, and if it be in my nature I'll be schooled."

"Here were comfort," said Amaury; "but that I much fear 'tis your own nature I would change."

"Well, that you will never do," answered he.

"My lord," said Amaury, "will you resolve me this: Why are we here? What waiting for? What intending?"

Lessingham stroked his beard and smiled.

Amaury said. "You see, you will not answer. Will you answer this, then: It is against the nature of you not to be rash, and against the condition of rashness not to be 'gainst all reason; yet why (after these five years that I've followed you up and down the world, and seen you mount so swiftly the degrees and steps of greatness that, in what courts or princely armies soever you might be come, you stuck in the eyes of all as the most choice jewel there) why needs must you, with the wide world to choose from, come back to this land of Rerek, and, of all double-dealers and secretaries of hell, sell your sword to the Vicar?"

"Not sell, sweet Amaury," answered Lessingham. "Lend. Lend it in cousinly friendship."

Amaury laughed. "Cousinly friendship! Give us patience! With the Devil and him together on either hand of you!" He leapt up, oversetting the chair, and strode to the fireplace. He kicked the logs together with his heavy riding-boots, and the smother of flame and sparks roared up the chimney. Turning about, his back to the fire, feet planted wide, hands behind him, he said: "I have you now in a good mood, though 'twere over much to hope you reasonable. And now you shall listen to me, for your good. You do know me: am I not myself by complexion subject to hasty and rash motions? yet I it is must catch at your bridle-rein; for in good serious earnest, you do make toward most apparent danger, and no title of advantage to be purchased by it. Three black clouds moving to a point; and here are you, in the summer and hunting-season of your youth, lying here with your eight hundred horse these three days, waiting for I know not what cat to jump, but (as you have plainly told me) of a most set obstinacy to tie yourself hand and heart to the Vicar's interest. You have these three months been closeted in his counsels: that I forget not. Nor will I misprise your politic wisdom: you have played chess with the Devil ere now and given him stalemate. But 'cause of these very things, you must see the peril you stand in: lest, if by any means he should avail to bring all things under his beck,[6] he should then throw you off and let you hop naked; or, in the other event, and his ambitious thoughts should break his neck, you would then have raised up against yourself most bloody and powerful enemies.

"Look but at the circumstance. This young King Styllis is but a boy. Yet remember, he is King Mezentius' son; and men look not for lapdog puppies in the wolf's lair, nor for milksops to be bred up for heirship to the crown and kingdom of Fingiswold. And he is come south not to have empty homage only from the regents here and in Meszria, but to take power. I would not have you build upon the Duke of Zayana's coldness to his young brother. True, in many families have the bastards been known the greater spirits; and you did justly blame the young King's handling of the reins in Meszria when (with a warmth from which his brother could not but take cold) he seemed to embrace to his bosom the lord Admiral, and in the same hour took away with a high hand from the Duke a great slice of his appanage the King their father left him. But though he smart under this neglect, 'tis not so likely he'll go against his own kindred, nor even stand idly by, if it come to a breach 'twixt the King and the Vicar. What hampers him to-day (besides his own easeful and luxurious idleness) is the Admiral and those others of the King's party, sitting in armed power at every hand of him in Meszria; but let the cry but be raised there of the King against the Vicar, and let Duke Barganax but shift shield and declare himself of's young brother's side, why then you shall see these and all Meszria stand in his firm obedience. Then were your cousin the Vicar ta'en betwixt two millstones; and then, where and in what case are you, my lord? And this is no fantastical scholar's chop-logic, neither: 'tis present danger. For hath not he for weeks now set every delay and cry-you-mercy and procrastinating stop and trick in the way of a plain answer to the young King's lawful demand he should hand over dominion unto him in Rerek?"

"Well," said Lessingham, "I have listened most obediently. You have it fully: there's not a word to which I take exceptions. Nay I admire it all, for indeed I told you every word of it myself last night."

"Then would to heaven you'd be advised by't," said Amaury. "Too much light, I think, hath made you moon-eyed."

"Reach me the map," said Lessingham. For the instant there was a touch in the soft bantering music of his voice as if a blade had glinted out and in again to its velvet scabbard. Amaury spread out the parchment on the table, and they stood poring over it. "You are a wiser man in action, Amaury, in natural and present, than in conceit; standing still, stirs your gall up: makes you see bugs and hobthrushes round every corner. Am I yet to teach you I may securely dare what no man thinks I would dare, which so by hardness becometh easy?"

Lessingham laid his forefinger on this place and that while he talked. "Here lieth young Styllis with's main head of men, a league or more be-east of Hornmere. 'Tis thither he hath required the Vicar come to him to do homage of this realm of Rerek, and to lay in his hands the keys of Kessarey, Megra, Kaima, and Argyanna, in which the King will set his own captains now. Which once accomplished, he hath him harmless (so long, at least, as Barganax keep him at arm's length); for in the south there they of the March openly disaffect him and incline to Barganax, whose power also even in this northern ambit stands entrenched in's friendship with Prince Ercles and with Aramond, spite of all supposed alliances, respects, and means, which bind 'em tributary to the Vicar.

"But now to the point of action; for 'tis needful you should know, since we must move north by great marches, and that this very night. My noble cousin these three weeks past hath, whiles he amused the King with's chaffertalk[7] of how and wherefore, opened unseen a dozen sluices to let flow to him in Owldale men and instruments of war, armed with which strong arguments (I have it by sure intelligence but last night) he means to-morrow to obey the King's summons beside Hornmere.[8] And, for a last point of logic, in case there be falling out between the great men and work no more for learned doctors but for bloody martialists, I am to seize the coastway 'twixt the Swaleback fells and Arrowfirth and deny 'em the road home to Fingiswold."

"Deny him the road home?" said Amaury. " 'Tis war, then, and flat rebellion?"

"That's as the King shall choose. And so, Amaury, about it straight. We must saddle an hour before midnight."

Amaury drew in his breath and straightened his back. "An hour to pack the stuff and set all in marching trim: and an hour before midnight your horse is at the door." With that, he was gone.

Lessingham scanned the map for yet a little while, then let it roll itself up. He went to the window and threw it open. There was the breath of spring in the air and daffodil scents: Sirius hung low in the south-west.

"Order is ta'en according to your command," said Amaury suddenly at his side. "And now, while yet is time to talk and consider, will you give me leave to speak?"

"I thought you had spoke already," said Lessingham, still at the window, looking round at him. "Was all that but the theme given out, and I must now hear point counterpoint?"

"Give me your sober ear, my lord, but for two minutes together. You know I am yours, were you bound for the slimy strand of Acheron.[9] Do but consider; I think you are in some bad ecstasy. This is worse than all: cut the lines of the King's communications northward, in the post of main danger, with so little a force, and Ercles on your flank ready to stoop at us from his high castle of Eldir and fling us into the sea."

"That's provided for," said Lessingham: "he's made friends with us for this time. Besides, he and Aramond are the Duke's dogs, not the King's; 'tis Meszria, Zayana, all their strings hold unto; north winds bring 'em the cough o' the lungs. Fear not them."

Amaury came and leaned himself too on the windowsill, his left elbow touching Lessingham's. After a while he said, low and as if the words were stones loosed up one by one with difficulty from a stiff clay soil, " 'Fore heaven, I must love you; and it is a thing not to be borne that your greatness should be made but this man's cat's-paw."

Sirius, swinging lower, touched the highest tracery of a tall ash-tree, went out like a blown-out candle behind a branch, and next instant blazed again, a quintessential point of diamond and sapphire and emerald and amethyst and dazzling whiteness. Lessingham answered in a like low tone, meditatively, but his words came light on an easy breath: "My cousin. He is meat and drink to me. I must have danger."

They abode silent at that window, drinking those airs more potent than wine, and watching, with a deep compulsive sense of essence drawn to essence, that star's shimmer of many-coloured fires against the velvet bosom of the dark; which things drew and compelled their beings, as might the sweet breathing nearness of a woman lovely beyond perfection and deeply beyond all soundings desired. Lessingham began to say slowly, "That was a strange trick of thought when I forgot you but now, and forgot my own self too, in those bubbles which in their flying upward signify not as the sparks, but that man is born for gladness. For I thought there was a voice spake in my ear in that moment and I thought it said, *I have promised and I will perform.* And I thought it was familiar to me beyond all familiar dear lost things. And yet 'tis a voice I swear I never heard before. And like a stargleam, it was gone."

The gentle night seemed to turn in her sleep. A faint drumming, as of horse-hooves far away, came from the south. Amaury stood up, walked over to the table, and fell to looking at the map again. The beating of hooves came louder, then on a sudden faint again. Lessingham said from the window, "There's one rideth hastily. Now a cometh down to the ford in Killary Bottom, and that's why we lose the sound for a while. Be his answers never so good, let him not pass nor return, but bring him to me."

II

The Duke of Zayana

Portrait of a lady ✦ *Doctor Vandermast* ✦
Fiorinda: "bitter-sweet" ✦ *The lyre that shook
Mitylene.[1]*

THE third morning after that coming of the galloping horseman north to Mornagay, Duke Barganax[2] was painting in his privy garden in Zayana in the southland: that garden where it is everlasting afternoon. There the low sun, swinging a level course at about that pitch which Antares reaches at his highest southing in an English May-night, filled the soft air with atomies of sublimated gold, wherein all seen things became, where the beams touched them, golden: a golden sheen on the lake's unruffled waters beyond the parapet, gold burning in the young foliage of the oak-woods that clothed the circling hills; and, in the garden, fruits of red and yellow gold hanging in the gold-spun leafy darkness of the strawberry-trees, a gilding shimmer of it in the stone of the carven bench, a gilding of every tiny blade on the shaven lawn, a glow to deepen all colours and to ripen every sweetness: gold faintly warming the proud pallour of Fiorinda's brow and cheek, and thrown back in sudden gleams from the jet-black smoothnesses of her hair.

"Would you be ageless and deathless for ever, madam, were you given that choice?" said the Duke, scraping away for the third time the colour with which he had striven to match, for the third time unsuccessfully, the unearthly green of that lady's eyes.

"I am this already," answered she with unconcern.

27

"Are you so? By what assurance?"

"By this most learn'd philosopher's, Doctor Vandermast."

The Duke narrowed his eyes first at his model then at his picture: laid on a careful touch, stood back, compared them once more, and scraped it out again. Then he smiled at her: "What? will you believe him? Do but look upon him where he sitteth there beside Anthea, like winter wilting before Flora in her pride. Is he one to inspire faith in such promises beyond all likelihood and known experiment?"

Fiorinda said: "He at least charmed you this garden."

"Might he but charm your eyes," said the Duke, "to some such unaltering stability, I'd paint 'em; but now I cannot. And 'tis best I cannot. Even for this garden, if 'twere as you said, madam (or worse still, were you yourself so), my delight were poisoned. This eternal golden hour must lose its magic quite, were we certified beyond doubt or heresy that it should not, in the next twinkling of an eye, dissipate like mist and show us the work-a-day morning it conceals. Let him beware, and if he have art indeed to make safe these things and freeze them into perpetuity, let him forbear to exercise it. For as surely as I have till now well and justly rewarded him for what good he hath done me, in that day, by the living God, I will smite off his head."

The Lady Fiorinda laughed luxuriously, a soft, mocking laugh with a scarce perceptible little contemptuous upward nodding of her head, displaying the better with that motion her throat's lithe strong loveliness. For a minute, the Duke painted swiftly and in silence. Hers was a beauty the more sovereign because, like smooth waters above a whirlpool, it seemed but the tranquillity of sleeping danger: there was a taint of harsh Tartarean stock in her high flat cheekbones, and in the slight upward slant of her eyes; a touch of cruelty in her laughing lips, the lower lip a little too full, the upper a little too thin; and in her nostrils, thus dilated, like a beautiful and dangerous beast's at the smell of blood. Her hair, parted and strained evenly back on either side from her serene sweet forehead, coiled down at last in a smooth convoluted knot which nestled in the nape of her neck like a black panther asleep. She wore no jewel nor ornament save two escarbuncles, great as a man's thumb, that hung at her ears like two burning coals of fire. "A generous prince and patron indeed," she said; "and a most courtly servant for ladies, that we must rot to-morrow like the aloe-flower, and all to sauce his dish with a biting something of fragility and non-perpetuity."

The Countess Rosalura, younger daughter of Prince Ercles, new-wed two months ago to Medor, the Duke's captain of the body-guard, had risen softly from her seat beside her lord on the brink of a fountain of red porphyry and come to look upon the picture with her brown eyes. Medor followed her and stood looking beside her in the shade of the great lime-tree. Myrrha and Violante joined them, with secret eyes for the painter rather than for the picture: ladies of the bedchamber to Barganax's mother, the Duchess of Memison. Only Anthea moved not from her place beside that learned man, leaning a little forward. Her clear Grecian brow was bent, and from beneath it eyes yellow and unsearchable rested their level gaze upon Barganax. Her fierce lips barely parted in the dimmest shadow or remembrance of a smile. And it was as if the low golden beams of the sun, which in all things else in that garden wrought transformation, met at last with something not to be changed (because it possessed already a like essence with their own and a like glory), when they touched Anthea's hair.

"There, at last!" said the Duke. "I have at last caught and pinned down safe on the canvas one particular minor diabolus of your ladyship's that hath dodged me a hundred times when I have had him on the tip of my brush; him I mean that peeks and snickers at the corner of your mouth when you laugh as if you would laugh all honesty out of fashion."[3]

"I laugh none out of fashion," she said, "but those that will not follow the fashions I set 'em. May I rest now?"

Without staying for an answer, she rose and stepped down from the stone plinth. She wore a coat-hardy of dark crimson satin. From shoulder to wrist, from throat to girdle, the soft and shining garment sat close like a glove, veiling yet disclosing the breathing loveliness which, like a rose in crystal, gave it life from within. Her gown, of the like stuff, revealed when she walked (as in a deep wood in summer, a stir of wind in the tree-tops lets in the sun) rhythms and moving splendours bodily, every one of which was an intoxication beyond all voluptuous sweet scents, a swooning to secret music beyond deepest harmonies. For a while she stood looking on the picture. Her lips were grave now, as if something were fallen asleep there; her green eyes were narrowed and hard like a snake's. She nodded her head once or twice, very gently and slowly, as if to mark some judgement forming in her mind. At length, in tones from which all colour seemed to have been drained save the soft indeterminate greys as of muted strings, "I wonder that you will still be painting," she said: "you, that are so much in love with the pathetic transitoriness of mortal things: you, that would smite his neck who should rob you of that melancholy sweet debauchery of your mind by fixing your marsh-fires in the sphere and making immortal for you your ephemeral treasures. And yet you will spend all your invention and all your skill, day after day, in wresting out of paint and canvas a counterfeit, frail, and scrappy immortality for some thing you love to look on, but, by your own confession, would love less did you not fear to lose it."

"If you would be answered in philosophy, madam," said the Duke, "ask old Vandermast, not me."

"I have asked him. He can answer nothing to the purpose."

"What was his answer?" said the Duke.

The Lady Fiorinda looked at her picture, again with that lazy, meditative inclining of her head. That imp which the Duke had caught and bottled in paint a while ago curled in the corner of her mouth. "O," said she, "I do not traffic in outworn answers. Ask him, if you would know."

"I will give your ladyship the answer I gave before," said that old man, who had sat motionless, serene and unperturbed, darting his bright and eager glance from painter to sitter and to painter again, and smiling as if with the aftertaste of ancient wine. "You do marvel that his grace will still consume himself with striving to fix in art, in a seeming changelessness, those self-same appearances which in nature he prizeth by reason of their very mutability and subjection to change and death. Herein your ladyship, grounding yourself at first unassailably upon most predicamental and categoric arguments in *celarent*, next propounded me a syllogism in *barbara*, the major premiss whereof, being well and exactly seen, surveyed, overlooked, reviewed, and recognized, was by my demonstrations at large convicted in fallacy of simple conversion and not *per accidens;* whereupon, countering in *bramantip*, I did in conclusion confute you in *bokardo;*[4] showing, in brief, that here is no marvel; since 'tis women's minds alone are ruled by clear reason: men's are fickle and elusive as the jack-o'-lanterns they pursue."

"A very complete and metaphysical answer," said she. "Seeing 'tis given on my side, I'll let it stand without question; though (to be honest) I cannot tell what the dickens it means."

"To be honest, madam," said the Duke, "I paint because I cannot help it."

Fiorinda smiled: "O my lord, I knew not you were wont to do things upon compulsion." Her lip curled, and she said again, privately for his own ear, "Save, indeed, when your little brother calleth the tune." Sidelong, under her eyelashes, she watched his face turn red as blood.

With a sudden violence the Duke dashed his handful of brushes to the ground and flung his palette skimming through the air like a flat stone that boys play ducks and drakes with, till it crashed into a clump of giant asphodel flowers a dozen yards away. Two or three of those stately blooms, their stems smashed a foot above the ground, drooped and slowly fell, laying pitifully on the grass their great tapering spikes of pink-coloured waxen filigree. His boy went softly after the palette to retrieve it. He himself, swinging round a good half circle with the throw, was gone in great strides the full length of the garden, turned heel at the western parapet, and now came back,

stalking with great strides, his fists clenched. The company w
stood back out of the way in an uneasy silence. Only the Lady F
orinda moved not at all from her place beside the easel of sweet
sandalwood inlaid with gold. He came to a sudden halt within a
yard of her. At his jewelled belt hung a dagger, its pommel and
sheath set thick with cabochon rubies and smaragds[5] in a criss-cross
pattern of little diamonds. He watched her for a moment, the
breath coming swift and hard through his nostrils: a tiger beside
Aphrodite's statua. There hovered in the air about her a sense-
maddening perfume of strange flowers: her eyes were averted,
looking steadily southward to the hills: the devil sat sullen and hard
in the corner of her mouth. He snatched out the dagger and, with a
savage back-handed stroke, slashed the picture from corner to corner; then slashed it again, to ribbons. That done, he turned once
more to look at her.

She had not stirred; yet, to his eye now, all was altered. As some
tyrannous and triumphant phrase in a symphony returns, against
all expectation, hushed to starved minor harmonies or borne on the
magic welling moonnotes of the horn, a shuddering tenderness, a
dying flame; such-like, and so moving, was the transfiguration that
seemed to have come upon that lady: her beauty grown suddenly a
thing to choke the breath, piteous like a dead child's toys: the bloom
on her cheek more precious than kingdoms, and less perdurable
than the bloom on a butterfly's wing. She was turned side-face towards him; and now, scarce to be perceived, her head moved with
the faintest dim recalling of that imperial mockery of soft laughter
that he knew so well; but he well saw that it was no motion of
laughter now, but the gallant holding back of tears.

"You ride me unfairly," he said in a whisper. "You who have
held my rendered soul, when you would, trembling in your hand:
will you goad me till I sting myself to death with my own poison?"

She made no sign. To the Duke, still steadfastly regarding her,
all sensible things seemed to have attuned themselves to her: a falling away of colours: grey silver in the sunshine instead of gold, the
red quince-flowers blanched and bloodless, the lush grass grey
where it should be green, a spectral emptiness where an instant
before had been summer's promise on the air and the hues of life
and the young year's burden. She turned her head and looked him
full in the eye: it was as if, from between the wings of death, beauty
beaconed like a star.

"Well," said the Duke, "which of the thousand harbours of
damnation have you these three weeks been steering for? What
murder must I enact?"

"Not on silly pictures," said she; "as wanton boys break up their
playthings; and I doubt not I shall be entreated sit for you again to-
morrow, to paint a new one."

he Duke laughed lightly. "Why there was good in that, too.
drowsy beast within me roused himself and suddenly started
making himself a horror to himself, and, now the blood's
ed, happily sleeps again."

"Sleeps!" Fiorinda said. Her lip curled.

"Come," said the Duke. "What shall it be then? Inspire my
vention. Entertain 'em all to a light collation and, by cue taken at
ine last kissing-cup, let split their weasands, stab 'em all in a moment? Your noble brother amongst them, 'tis to be feared, madam;
since him, with a bunch of others, I am to thank for these beggar-
my-neighbour sleights and cozenage beyond example. Or shall't be
a grand night-piece of double fratricide? yours and mine, spitted on
one spit like a brace of woodcock? We can proceed with the first to-
day: for the other, well, I'll think on't."

"Are you indeed that prince whom reputation told me of," said
she, "that he which did offend you might tremble with only thinking of it? And now, as hares pull dead lions by the beard—"

The Duke swung away from her a step or two, then back, like a
caged beast. His brow was thunderous again. "Ever going on beyond your possession," he said, "beyond your bounds. 'Tis well I am
of a cool judgement. There's more in't than hold up my hand, or
whistle in my fist. Content you that I have some noble great design
on foot, which in good time shall prove prodigious to 'em all: and
once holding good my advantage over them, in their fall I'll tempt
the destinies."

With an infinite slow feline grace she lifted up her head: her
nostrils widening, the flicker of a smile on her parted lips: from
beneath the shadow of long black lashes, half-moons of green lambent fire beheld him steadily. "You must not speak to me as if I were
a child or an animal," she said. "Will you swear me all this?"

"No," answered he. "But you may look back and consider of
time past: I have been so sparing to promise, that (as your ladyship
will bear me out) I have ever paid more than either I promised or
was due."

"Well," she said: "I am satisfied."

"I must to the throne-room," said the Duke. " 'Tis an hour past
the hour of audience, and I would not hold 'em too long tarrying
for me; 'tis an unhandsome part, and I use it but to curb the insolencies of some we spoke on." The Lady Fiorinda gave him at
arm's length her white hand: he bowed over it and raised it to his
lips. Standing erect again, still unbonneted before her, he rested his
eyes upon her a moment in silence, then with a step nearer bent to
her ear: "Do you remember the Poetess, madam?—

> Ἔρος δαὖτέ μ' ὁ λυσιμελης δόνει,
> γλυκυπικρον αμαχανον ορπετον."

As if spell-bound under the troublous sweet hesitation of the choriambics,[6] she listened, very still. Very still, and dreamily, and with so soft an intonation that the words seemed but to take voice-less shape on her ambrosial breath, she answered, like an echo:

"Once more Love, the limb-loosener, shaketh me:
Bitter-sweet, the dread Worm ineluctable."[7]

"It is my birthday, I am reminded," said the Duke in the same whispered quietness. "Will your ladyship do me the honour to sup with me to-night, in my chamber in the western tower that looks upon the lake, at sunset?"

There was no smile on that lady's lips. Slowly, her eyes staring into his, she bent her head. Surely all of enchantment and of gold that charged the air of that garden, its breathless promise, its storing and its brooding, distilled like the perfume of a dark red rose, as "Yes," she said. "Yes."

III

THE TABLES SET
IN MESZRIA

Presence-chamber in Acrozayana ✦ *The High
Admiral Jeronimy* ✦ *The Lord Chancellor
Beroald* ✦ *Cares that rack great statesmen* ✦
The bastard of Fingiswold ✦ *Earl Roder* ✦
Conference in the Duke's closet ✦ *King Styllis's
testament* ✦ *Rage of the Duke* ✦ *The Vicar
suspected king-killer* ✦ *League to uphold the
testament.*

M EANWHILE, for nearly two hours in the great throne-
room in Zayana had the presence begun to fill against
the Duke's appearing. Now the fashion of that hall was
that it was long, of a hundred cubits the length thereof
and the breadth forty cubits. The walls were of pale
hammered mountain gold, rough with an innumerable variety of
living things graven some in large some in little, both hairy kinds
and feathered, and scaly kinds both of land and sea, oftenest by twos
and twos with their children beside their nests or holes, and the
flowers, fruits, leaves, herbs and water-weeds native to each kind
winding in the interspaces with a conceited formal luxuriance.
Massy columns, four times a man's height, of carved black onyx with
milky veins, made caryatides in form of monstrous snakes, nine
lengthwise of the hall on either side and four at either end. These

supported on their hooded heads a frieze of tesselated jet[1] four
cubits deep, whereon were displayed poppies and blooms of the
aloe and the forgetful lotus, all in a cool frail loveliness of opals and
rose-coloured sapphires as for their several blooms and petals, and
as for their stalks and leaves of green marmolite and chalcedony.[2]
Above this great flowered frieze the roof was pitched in a vault of
tracery work of ivory and gold, so wrought that in the lower ranges
near the frieze the curls and arabesques were all of gold, then
higher a little mingling of ivory, and so more and more ivory and
the substance of the work more and more fine and airy; until in the
highest all was but pure ivory only, and its woven filaments of the
fineness of hairs to look upon, seen at that great height, and as if a
sudden air or a word too roughly spoken should be enough to
break a framework so unsubstantial and blow it clean away. In the
corners of the hall stood four tripods of dull wrought gold ten cubits
in height, bearing four shallow basins of pale moonstone. In those
basins a child might have bathed, so broad they were, and brimming
all with sweet scented essences, attar of roses and essences of the
night-lily and the hyperborean eglantine, and honey-dew from the
glades beyond Ravary,[3] and birds of paradise, gold-capped, tawny-
bodied, and with black velvet throats that scintillated with blue and
emerald fire, flitted still from basin to basin, dipping and fluttering,
spilling and spreading the sweet perfumes. The hall was paved all
over with Parian marble in flags set lozenge-wise, and pink topaz
insets in the joints; and at the northern end was the ducal throne
upon a low daïs of the same marble, and before the daïs, stretching
the whole width of the hall, a fair great carpet figured with cloud-
shapes and rainbow-shapes and comets and birds of passage and
fruits and blossoms and living things, all of a dim shifting variety of
colours, pale and unseizable like moonlight, which character came
of its cunning weaving of silks and fine wools and intermingling of
gold and silver threads in warp and woof. The throne itself was
without ornament, plainly hewn from a single block of stone, warm
grey to look on with veins of a lighter hue here and there, and here
and there a shimmer as of silver in the texture of the stone; and that
stone was dream-stone, a thing beyond price, endowed with hidden
virtues. But from behind, uplifted like the wings of a wild-duck as it
settles on the water, great wings shadowed the dream-stone; they
sprang twenty cubits high from base to the topmost feather, and
made all of gold, each particular feather fashioned to the likeness of
nature that it was a wonder to look upon, and yet with so much
awfulness of beauty and shadowing grace in the grand uprising of
the wings as made these small perfections seem but praise and worship of the principal design which gave them their life and which
from them took again fulfilment. Thousands of thousands of tiny
precious stones of every sort that grows in earth or sea were inlaid

upon those mighty wings, incrusting each particular quill, each little barb of each feather, so that to a man moving in that hall and looking upon the wings the glory unceasingly changed, as new commixtures of myriad colours and facets caught and threw back the light. And, for all this splendour, the very light in the throne-room was, by art of Doctor Vandermast, made misty and glamorous: brighter than twilight, gentler than the cold beams of the moon, as if the light itself were resolved into motes of radiance which, instead of darting afar, floated like snow-flakes, invisible themselves but bathing all else with their soft effulgence. For there was in all that spacious throne-room not a shadow seen, nor any sparkle of overbrilliance, only everywhere that veiling glamour.

Twenty-five soldiers of the Duke's bodyguard were drawn up beside the throne on either hand. Their byrnies and greaves[4] were of black iron, and they were weaponed with ponderous double-edged two-handed swords. Each man carried his helm in the crook of his left arm, for it was unlawful even for a man-at-arms to appear covered in that hall: none might so appear, save the Duke alone. They were all picked men for strength and stature and fierceness; the head of every man of them was shaven smooth like an egg, and every man had a beard, chestnut-red, that reached to his girdle. Save these soldiers only, the company came not beyond the fair carpet's edge that went the width of the hall before the throne; for this was the law in Zayana, that whosoever, unbidden of the Duke, should set foot upon that carpet should lose nothing but his life.

But in the great spaces of the hall below the carpet was such a company of noble persons walking and discoursing as any wise man should take pure joy to look upon: great states of Meszria all in holiday attire; gentlemen of the Duke's household, and of Memison; courtmen and captains out of Fingiswold holden to the lord Admiral's service or the Chancellor's or Earl Roder's, that triple pillar of the great King's power[5] in the south there, whereby he had in his life-days and by his politic governance not so much held down faction and discontents as not suffered them be thought on or take life or being. But now, King Mezentius dead, his lawful son sudden where he should be wary, fumbling where he should be resolute; his bastard slighted and set aside and likely (in common opinion) to snatch vengeance for it in some unimagined violence; and last, his Vicar in the midland parts puffed up like a deadly adder ready to strike, but at whom first none can say: these inconveniences shook the royal power in Meszria, patently, for even a careless eye to note, even here in Duke Barganax's presence-chamber.

A bevy of young lords of Meszria, standing apart under the perfume tripod in the south-eastern corner whence they might at leisure view all that came in by the great main doors at the southern end, held light converse. Said one of them, "Here comes my lord Admiral."

"Ay," said another, "main means of our lingering consumption: would the earth might gape for him."

"Nay," said a third, that was Melates of Vashtola, "I do love my Jeronimy as I love a young spring sallet: cold and safe. I will not have you blame him. Do but look: as puzzled as a cod-fish! For fancy's passion, spit upon him. Nay, Roder and Beroald are the prime blood-suckers, not he."

"Speak lower," said the Lord Barrian, he that spoke first; "there's jealous ears pricked all-wheres."

With a grave salutation they greeted the High Admiral, who with a formal bow passed on. He was somewhat heavy of build, entered a little into the decline of years; his pale hair lay lankish on the dome of his head, his pale blue eyes were straight and honest; the growth of his beard was thin, straggling over the great collar and badge of the kingly order of the hippogriff[6] that he wore about his neck; the whole aspect of the man melancholy, and as if strained with half-framed resolutions and wishes that give the wall to fears. Yet was the man of a presence that went beyond his stature, which was but ordinary; as if there hung upon him some majesty of the King's power he wielded, of sufficiency (at least in trained and loyal soldiery under arms) to have made a fair adventure to unseat the Duke upon Acrozayana, red-bearded bodyguard and all.

When he was passed by, Zapheles spake again, he that had spoken second: "Perfidiousness is a common waiter in most princes' courts. And so, in your ear, were't not for loyal obligement to a better man, I'd call it time to serve, though late, our own interest: call in him you wot of: do him obedience, 'stead of these plaguish stewards and palace-scullions that, contrary to good cupping-glasses, must affect and suck none but the best blood."

Melates looked warily round, "I taught you that, my lord: 'tis a fine toy, but in sober sadness I am not capable of it. Nor you neither, I think."

Zapheles said, " 'Twill yet bear thinking on. You have here your natural sovereign lord (o' the wrong side of the blanket may be; no matter, that's nor here nor there); you yield him service and up-holding: well. You look for quiet, therefore, and to be lord of your own, being suffered to enjoy these borders whereof you have right and particular dominion. Good: then behold your payment. He is practised upon most devilishly; even ladies will shortly scoff and prattle of it, that he is grown as tractable to't as stock-fish. You'll say that's his concernment; in the midst of idleness and deliciousness, fanned with the soft gales of his own flatterers' lips, he sitteth content. Good. But must we take cold too, 'cause he hath given his cloak away? Must I smile and sit mum (and here's a right instance hot upon me like new cakes) when that Beroald taketh up a man I ne'er saw nor heard on, took in his lordship's own private walks with a great poisoned dagger in his breeches; a pretty thing it was, and meant beyond question for my lord Chancellor; they hanged him where he stood, on a mulberry-tree; and, 'cause the vile murderer said with a lie that this was by County Zapheles his setting on, I am at short warning cited before the justiciars to answer this; and the Duke, when I appeal to him under ancient right of signiory to have the proceedings quashed under plea of *ne obstes*[7] and carried before him in person (which should but have upheld his authority, too much abridged and bridled by these hireling office-nobility), counsels me kindly waive the point of jurisdiction. And why? but that he will not be teased with these matters; which yet ensueth neither the realm's good nor his."

"To amend which," said Barrian, "you and Melates would in plain treason give over all to the Vicar?"

"Would if we were wise," replied Melates; "but for fond loyalty sake, will not. May be, too, he is loyal, and would not have us."

Zapheles laughed.

Barrian said: "Your own men would not follow you in such a bad enterprise."

" 'Tis very true," said Zapheles. "And indeed, were't otherwise, they should deserve to be hanged."

"And you and I too," said Melates.

"And you and I too. Yet in the Parry you may behold a man that knoweth at least the right trick to govern: do't through lords of land, like as we be, bounded to's allegiance, not parchment lords of's own making."

"Were the Duke but stiffened to't!" said Melates. "You are his near friend, Barrian: speak to him privately."

"Ay," said Zapheles. "Nay, I mock not: choose but the happy occasion. Say to him, 'You are Meszria: our centre whereto all lines come, all things look. Who depriveth this merchandise of reverence, defaceth all lustre of it. To it, then: out with Beroald, out with Roder and Jeronimy: throw the fowl to the Devil that hatched it.' "

"Great and thumping words," said Barrian. "But 'tis mere truth a hath not the main strength to do it and he would. But hist, here's the Chancellor."

The company by the door made way right and left with many courtesies and loutings, which the Lord Beroald acknowledged with a cold and stately smile. His gait was direct and soldierly, he carried his head like a mettled horse, and on his lean countenance, flat in the cheekbones, wide between the eyes, clean cut about the jaw, close shaven save for the bristly brown mustachios, sat that look which, as lichens grown on rock-faces, comes but with years of constant lordship over men and their long customed obedience. "See how the spongy sycophants do hang on his steps," said Zapheles. "You'd swear they feared he should have 'em called in question for simple being here in Acrozayana. And the Duke will not put down his foot, it shall soon come to this indeed; a main crime to do him this empty courtesy, attend the weekly presences, without leave asked of this great devil and his fellows. See how he and Jeronimy do draw to a point of secret mischief as the lode-stone draweth iron."

For the Chancellor, ending now his progress up the hall, was stood with the Lord Jeronimy on the great carpet before the throne. To them, as presenting in their high commission, along with Earl Roder, the King's very person and authority in Meszria, was accorded these many years the freedom of the carpet; and that was accorded to none other in all the land who was not of the Duke's own household or of the ducal line of Memison.

"I am glad to see you here, my lord Admiral," said Beroald; "and indeed it is a joy I scarcely looked for: thrice in three weeks, and you were not formerly given to great observance of this ceremony."

The Admiral looked at him with his dog-like eyes, smiled slowly, and said, "I am here to keep the peace."

"And I on the same errand," said Beroald: "and to please my lady sister. I would have you look a little more starved, as I myself do study to do. It is nought useful to remind him how we made new wood when the young King pruned away his appanage."

"There's that needs no reminding on," said Jeronimy.

"Will your lordship walk a little?" said Beroald, taking him by the arm, and, as they paced slowly to and fro, cheek by cheek for convenience of private conference: "I still do hear it opinioned that it was not without some note or touch of malice these things were brought about; and you are named in that particular, to have set the King's mind against him."

Jeronimy blew out his cheeks and shook his head. "May be I was to blame; but 'twas in the King's clear interest. I'd do it, were't to do again to-morrow."

"This country party love us the worse for it," said Beroald.

"A good housewife," answered Jeronimy, "was ever held in bad report with moths and spiders."

"We can show our teeth, and use them, if it were come to that," said Beroald. "But that were questionable policy. Too many scales stand in too uncertain balance. Roder's long tarrying in Rerek: I like it not, ha?"

"As if the King should think he needed men there."

"You have no fresh despatches?"

"Not since that I showed you, a-Thursday sennight."

"That was not so bad, methought. My lord Admiral, I have a

question I would move to you. Are we strong enough, think you, to
hold off the Vicar if need were?"

Jeronimy looked straight before him awhile; then, "Yes," he
said: "with the Duke of our side."

"You have taken me?" said Beroald. "Supposition is, things fall
out worst imaginable: war with him in Rerek, and the King's forces
overthrown. You are confident then?"

"With the Duke of our side, and with right of our side, I should
hope to do it."

"I too," said the Chancellor, "am of your opinion."

"Well, what's the matter?" The Lord Jeronimy came to a stop
in his slow deliberate pacing. A gentleman of his household waited
below the carpet: he seemed short of breath, as one that hath run a
course: with a low leg he made obeisance, drawing a packet from his
doublet. Jeronimy came to him, took it, and looked carefully at the
seal with the gold-mounted perspective-glass that hung by a fine
chain about his neck. Men marked how his sallow face turned sal-
lower. "Just," he said: "it hath all the points in it." He undid the seal
and read the letter, then handed it to Beroald; then, scowling upon
the messenger: "How hapt, ninny-hammer, that you delivered this
no sooner?"

"Lord," answered he, "his lordship, all muddied from hard
riding, did write it in your own house; and upon his sudden injunc-
tion strung with threats and filthy speeches innumerable, I did fly a-
horseback and upon admittance at the fortress gate did with such
leaps flee up the stairs as I was in point to have been laid hands on
for a madman, so had all my charge miscarried."

"Away then: to him again and say I had it, and my lord Chancellor too." Then, walking apart once more with Beroald: "We were
best act on this, albeit to see us openly on a sudden go from the
chamber may give occasion that the people may buzz and talk of it.
Yet these commends do directly say we are in peril here until he
speak with us."

"Roder," said Beroald, "is not a man to start at his own shadow.
Go we while the way's yet open."

Those two lords, presenting to curious eyes a studied show of
untroubled and careless ease, were but even come forth to the
grand staircase, when the lofty doors clanged to behind them, and
in the throne-room trumpets sounded a sennet. And now in great
pomp and splendour, an hour and a half past the just time of audience, the Duke opened the presence. There went before him, entering by a door behind the throne, six blacks with silver trumpets,
sounding to the sennet as aforesaid, and thirty peacocks, walking
two by two with their tails displayed, who, after their progress forth
and back before the throne, ranged themselves fifteen on either
hand beneath the black onyx pillars, making with their tails a screen

of shimmering green and blue and gold. Medor, Egan, and Vander-mast, and a dozen other of the Duke's household, took each his appointed station beside the throne, Medor in his bronze byrny with gorget and shoulder-pieces inlaid with silver and bearing as symbol of his office a long double-handed two-edged sword; and now the trumpets, after a long baying blast that seemed to shake the gossamer tracery of the roof, suddenly fell silent as Barganax appeared.

His kirtle was of corded silk, rose-coloured, slashed with velvet of a darker hue, and gathered about the waist with a belt of sea-horse hide lapped at the edge with thread of gold and bossed with balas rubies and cat's-eye chrysoberyls; he had thick-woven silken hose of the like rose-colour, and a long cloak of dark grey brocaded silk lined with cloth of silver; the collar of the cloak was of black cormorants' feathers cunningly sewn and fitted to make an even smoothness, cross-striped at every span with lines of rubies and fastened with golden clasps. Yet was all this but shadows in water beside the man himself. For, alike in his lithe tall frame, and in his carriage noble and debonair and of a cat-like elegance, this Duke was beautiful to look upon beyond the example of men; his skin marvellous fair and smooth, his hair the colour of burnished copper, short and curly, his nose clean cut and straight, his brow wide, his eyebrows sleek and thick and with a scarcely to be seen upward slant, that cast a quality of somewhat pensive and of somewhat faun-like across his face; his shaven chin delicate but strong, his mouth a little large, firm-lipped under daintily upcurled mustachios, sensitive, apt for sudden modulations of mood and passion; his eyes brown, contemplative, and with profound obscurities of pulsing fire. And as, with that easy simplicity of magnificence which seemed in him nature bred clean beyond the range of art, he took his seat upon the dream-stone, it was as if the richness of his jewelled apparel, the shadowing of those wings, and all the sumptuous splendours of that hall were to him but as the flower on the blackthorn or the rainbow across a mountain peak: graces wedded to a substance worthy their own unsubstantial loveliness.

Now when the ceremonial business of presentations, petitions, sealings of placets and decrees was concluded, the Duke spake to them of his council that stood beside him: "Is't not some wonder there should be no legate nor envoy here to represent the Vicar?"

"May be," answered Medor, "that he liked not your grace's sending away of Gabriel Flores a month ago."

Barganax lifted an eyebrow: " 'Twas pure charity, and indeed a compliment, to let him know I thought his honour too basely travestied by such a villain. Nor was it fit I should accept as envoy but his master of the horse, one that is besides but a patent hired intelligencer, and scarcely a gentleman by birth."

"There's one more cloud against the sun," said Egan; "so have I seen storms a-brewing. Your grace was informed ere you did enter the presence-chamber how that the Admiral and the Chancellor, that were here but a little before, were gone forth in a flutter of seeming urgency upon word brought them from without. Be advised: leave your custom, and go not to-day among the general throng below the carpet."

Barganax said, "It is seven year to-day since I did come of age and take power here in Zayana, and never yet have I omitted the custom I did that day begin."

He stood up to go, but now Medor spoke against it: "There were no harm to change it; and remember, did aught go miss, 'twere more than your own life you laid in hazard. Go not, Lord."

"Vandermast," said Barganax, "what say you?"

"They have given their reasons," answered that ancient man. "I would hear your grace's reasons on the contrary part."

"Imprimis," said the Duke, "whose turn should it serve to yerk me one under the fifth rib? Not old Jeronimy's, nor theirs that stand with him: it should raise a cloud of wasps about their ears should in three days sweep 'em out of Meszria. Nor yet our discontented lords: they cry for action, and that were a strange road, to murder me: by my soul, they can look for no other to lead 'em. The King's? True, there's some coldness betwixt us, but I'll not suspect him of things myself would not soil my hands withal. But indeed I do know all these men. Pew! I am not to begin Duke."

"Horius Parry," said Medor then, "would not stick to murder you."

"His hands are full, playing spoil-five with the King for Rerek," the Duke replied. "Come, Medor," he said: "I am minded to go my own gate;[8] and when I must skulk and beware in my own presence-chamber, then were I best slain indeed, and high time to say adieu. Attend me, Medor. But is not this right reason?" said he over his shoulder, passing by, to Doctor Vandermast. Vandermast made no reply, but as he and the Duke crossed glances it was as if two diverse wisdoms of age and of hot youth rose from their wells, recognized each his make, and clipped hands together.

Now was Duke Barganax come about three-quarters of his way down from the throne to the lower end of the chamber, walking and discoursing with this man and that, with Medor at his elbow, when there came a stir about the main doorway, as if some would have entrance but, because of the lateness and because the Duke had voided the throne, was denied. The Duke sent one to inquire and see; that one came back on the instant to say that here was the Earl Roder craved audience and would not take their no for it. "Let him come in," said the Duke, and received him where he stood.

"My lord Duke," said Roder, "I am obliged to kiss your hand;

and, ere I go further in a business which in this public place I dare not pronounce but between my teeth, I would entreat you of a matter, easy for you to grant, and condition absolute of our more large and secret conference."

"Our fashion is not curious," answered the Duke, marking his disordered countenance. "Yet do I wonder a little, if the matter crieth so loud for urgency, why you came not sooner. Or why sent you with so much parade of secrecy (for I saw it, my lord, through eyes that serve me) to fetch away the Admiral and the Chancellor, already pricked off for the presence? Or why, for a last point of wonder, you now come here without them."

"That is the condition I spoke on," answered he. "I am to beseek you confirm us, under your royal word, safe conduct and assurance all and severally of our lives and persons, which done we shall straight to the matter, but until then we may not."

To this the Duke listened with apparent wonder, then fell a-laughing. "What coil's here?" he said. "Sure, the man's frantic. What, Medor, I shall be apt to think they mean me mischief indeed, if their own sick minds do make 'em start like rabbits at such fairy-babes o' their own imagining. Howbeit, content you, Earl; I do swear you peace and grith, safe conduct to come and to go with liberty of life and of body on all lawful occasions in my dukedom of Zayana, for you and for my lord High Admiral Jeronimy and for my lord Chancellor Beroald; and unto this you have my royal word, as I do trow on the high and blessed Gods and Goddesses Who keep the wide heavens."

"I am beholden to your grace," said the Earl. "And yet, were it ask a further boon, I think they would treasure it much in writing."

The Duke's eye gleamed. "You have witnesses, my lord. And indeed, if my bond were better than my word, you might stand in some peril now."

"Forgive me," said Roder then. "We are content with your royal word, and in this I am the mouthpiece of all three of us. And truly," said he, chuckling in his beard, "I may now disclose to your grace the inwardness of my calling of 'em out: 'twas because we should not all three be in your hand afore we had ta'en assurance of our safety. But now, had you been minded to entreat me evilly, he and Beroald do stand at your doors without the citadel with enough stout lads mustered under arms as—"

The blood rushed to Barganax's face and neck, and his hand leapt to the dagger at his belt. Roder said, "I am sorry. But your grace will not forget your oath, nor you will not strike a weaponless man. Will't please you enter your closet and suffer me bring in the Admiral and the Chancellor, when we shall confer with you about matters of most weighty consequence."

"You are a brave man, Roder," said Barganax at length, folding his arms and speaking close in the Earl's face. "Bring in your friends. This circumspection of peace-pledges, and this armed alertness when we were never yet at variance, are clean past my understanding. But tell 'em, for their better counsel, 'twas well you had my oath before I knew you threatened force against me. Had I known or seen it, my answer had been pat and to the purpose."

The Earl Roder, as a man that hath escaped a danger the full menace of which he had not apprehended till the danger was past, went forth somewhat shaken from before the face of the Duke.

When they were set in Duke Barganax's closet, the lord Admiral took up the word: they were but five there, those three great officers of state, the Duke himself and Doctor Vandermast. "It was unadvisedly done," said the Admiral; "and we will first tender to your grace our large regrets and most humbly crave your pardon. Yet shall you consider, when you know all, that these be great news and sudden, and something in a manner to root up all past custom and example, so as we know not where we stand, in a manner; and albeit we do well think, my lord Duke, that it shall still lie to our interest, both yours and ours, to hold each by other, sith it well may so come about as that like dangers from the like quarter should menace us both, yet in a manner—"

"My good lord Admiral," said the Duke, "I pray you put out of mind this of the soldiers. I am satisfied: not another thought will I give it. But, for the matter in hand, we shall the more readily follow your argument if you will first tell us these news you speak on."

"Earl Roder," said Jeronimy, "hath rid from the north this morning with tidings of sudden and great import."

"Give me in a word, what is it?" said the Duke.

"Then," said Roder, "in a word: the King is dead."

"Heavy news; but 'tis ten months old."

"Nay, nay: King Styllis is dead," said Roder. "Four days since, in Rerek, in's camp a little beside Hornmere. I was by his bed, held his hand in mine when his soul took flight."

Those three lords narrowly watched the Duke who, from his late posture of careless ease, was sat upright at these tidings, his strong and delicate hands grasping the edge of the table of carved sandalwood. His eyes were on Roder's, but seemed to gaze through and beyond him: for a minute he was silent. At length he spoke, saying, "He died young. The Gods rest his soul. He was my brother, though he ne'er was good to me." He lowered his gaze and was silent again, his fingers drumming on the table. None spoke. Then, as if waking to common things, he looked up and said sharply: "Dead, by what means?"

"Eating of some venomous confection," answered Roder. He

paused an instant, then blurted out, "The common tittle-tattle doth loudly say your grace did poison him."

Barganax narrowed his eyes. He fell a-drumming once more on the table. Then, "I doubt not, my lord Admiral," said he, "you have surveyed the field anew ere you came to me with this, and perceived that it is well that you and I should have Meszria solid behind us in our next business. Were it the Vicar had took him off with poison, 'twas first to be looked for he should lay the blame to me."

None spake. Jeronimy leaned forward on the table, spreading out his hand palm upwards, and cleared his throat once and again as if in prelude to a speech. Beroald saved his embarrassments by saying, "Your grace will wish to see all the circumstances before you would determine what were best to do. It were fit you now produce the King's testament, my lord."

Roder at that word drew from his bosom a parchment sealed with the royal sign manual. The blood came and went under his swarthy skin, though there was small space to mark it, for the beard grew nigh up to his eyes, and the hair of his head, stiff like a brush, began scarce an inch above his eyebrows. Uneasily he looked at the Duke and said, "I would desire your grace have patience; and lest you should be deceived to suppose these dispositions coloured any whit by my advisements, be sure you lay your time aright: this testament was executed this fourth of April, as the King's highness' own hand under his seal doth testify, and your grace knoweth well that 'twas not till three days later I did upon commandment go to him in Rerek."

"Well, well," said the Duke, "what's this to the purpose? Let me have it; as sour as it is, my lips are primed for it."

Therewith the Lord Roder, bracing himself as a man in posture to dive into an ice-cold tarn in winter time, read out the parchment, that was writ in manner following:

"By me STYLLYS, sonne of MEZENCIUS of glorous memorye uppon whome be pece, greatt Kyng of Fingyswold and of al stattes and domynyons apparteigning thereunto, bee it by riht of guift or lawfull inheretaunce or costom of prynses or riht of conquest by the destroyenge swherde of my greatt Father or mine owne, in wycch large discrypcioun without dowbt casten or throwen uppon the fullness of the same is imbrased or con-cluded the domynyons places and pryncipalites foloing naymely that is to sayne my holle maine territorie and kyngdame of Fingyswold and the citty of Rjalmar being the capital citty thereof and prencipall sette or syedge of my statte and gouernement; and my territorie or londe of Reerec and places cytuate and plaste ther withynne being in especially but not exclusively the fortelaces or strangg houlds of Laimac, Cessary, Maegra, Caima, and Argjanna; and my marche of Ulba now gouerned undir my direccion and for my soole behoolfe and sarvys by the after naymed my Vicare of Rerec as aforn sayde; and my cuntree or lond of Mezria and the citees castills fortrasses towneshyps ballywekes herborowes[9] ylands and in a generaltie all the places there withynne buylt or unbuylt dwellid in or unhabyted, but not to exclud aught that is not naymed or emplyed in this large generaltie save and exept only the ducall apponage of Zajana whereof I doo of my brotherly loove and affectione renounse al claymes of soverainty in fauour and for enjoyment of BARRGANAX, reputed sonne of the sed Kyng Mezencius of glorous memorie vpon whome be peace, wycch sed Barrgnax I doo heereby irreuocably indue and envest and the heiers of his bodye for euer with the sayde apponage, being nycely and puntyvally limitted by the bundaries or limytts descrived or delineate on the mappe wycch by this My roialle Seall of fingyswold is made faste unto this My roialle testment—"

"Let me see it," said the Duke. He looked carefully at the map, nodded, showed it to Vandermast, then passed it back to Roder. Roder proceeded:

"I the sayde Kyng Syllys do beqwithe and giue my roiall estatt and name of Kyngdam and al my holle Realme and Pocessyons afore sed or what somever save as exepted unto my Systyr ANTIOPE Prynsace of Fingyswold being besydis myself the soole suruiuing Chylde borne in wedloke of the sayde greatt Kyng Mezencius vpon Whome bee pece. And considering how that the mortallity of kynges is subgette unto the inconsederat and fyckle stoopes and strypes of Fate noe les miserablely than comon mens mortallity, therfor in cace the sayde Prynsace Antiopy should bee in time of My deth nat yet come unto full aage of xviij yeeres, with addycyon of iij yeeres in consideracion that shee is a wommon and that I doo coumpt hir as nat fit to euse full dyscreccion and awtoritee tyll shee be full xxi years of aage, I do dyrect and wylle that the lorde HOORIUS PARRYE my wel loued and trusted servaunt being in some degrie of My kynnedred or affinitie and being heereby confirmed by Me in his estatt and roialle offyce as Vicaire on my behalve and my successours in my befoare naymed kyngdame of Reerec shalbe protectour and wardeyne of my systyr during her minorite and shall in Her name rewll the realme as Regent during that time afoare sed and shall charisshe and çare for Her diligently and louyngly in al poincts as a Father should and in al things estudie hir propper good and saftie and the inhansement of hir realme and soveraity. But as touching my sayde kyngdam of Mezria—"

"Proceed, as touching Meszria," said the Duke. " 'Tis thus far i' the bounds of reasonable surmise; though I might a looked to see my royal sister entrusted to my care sooner than to so questionable a tutor. True it is, I ne'er set eyes upon her, but I am far nearer by blood and (or I should hate myself else) far more to trust to."

"Ere I proceed," said Roder, "I would inform your grace of this; hard for me to say, but I pray bear with me. The King on's death-bed did directly say to me that though he was at odds with the Vicar, he did believe so great an honour as this is should bind him faithfully to the royal interest, but your grace he did misdoubt (as he did openly say, but I did speak against it) of a secret determination to usurp the kingdom, and so feared to entrust the Princess unto you."

"Proceed, man," said the Duke. Roder proceeded:

"As touching my sayde kyngdam of Mezria, save and exept the sayde apponage of Zayjana as heerin befoare prouided, I do point my wel beloued faythfull sarvante the Lorde Hy Amerall Ieronimy to rewill all the londe as Regent therof during my sed Systyrs minorite and therafter as Shee shall of Hir roiall wylle and pleasire determine of. And who some ere shall neglect contempne or sette on syde any dysposicion of this My Testment, lat his life haue an erly a suddant and an euill endinge and lat the Angre of the Goddes reste vpon him. Giuen under my roiall seall and under myne hande in my pauylyoun bisyde Hornmeere in Rerec this fourt day of Aprelle in the yeere of my raighne I.

Styllys R."

A silence of little ease fell on their council when Roder ended his reading of that testament. Except old Vandermast's not an eye was raised: those others shrank, in that silence, from meeting Barganax's glance: Barganax himself sat staring downward with a cat-like intention on the void table-top before him. When he spoke at last it was in a strained voice, as if he rode wrath on the curb, tight held yet ready to overleap at the least slackening of control all bounds, all reason. "You will libel me out a copy of that, my lord Chancellor, certified under your hand and under his and his," pointing with his eye at Roder and Jeronimy.

Beroald answered and said, "I will."

"I must have half an hour to consider of this ere we pursue it further," said the Duke, still with that frightening tenseness in his voice. "Vandermast, fill out Rian wines for these lords and then attend me. And to you, sirs, I will say this: I have warranted you safety and freedom in Acrozayana. But this shall you know, and consider well of it: in case you shall not wait for me in this room until I come back to talk with you, and in case I find you not here all three when I do come again, that shall be in my eyes an act of war, my lord Admiral, and I shall answer it as such." With that word, as if the reins he had held at such horrid tension had slipped on a sudden through his fingers, he leapt to his feet, smote with his dagger into the table-top so mighty a downward stabbing blow that the steel stood a hand-breadth deep in the wood and snapped off short, hurled the broken weapon in the fire-place, and in that gusty extremity of fury flung open the door, swapped it to behind him, and was gone. Doctor Vandermast, who alone of that company maintained a demeanour of detachment and imperturbability, silently set wine before them according to his master's bidding and silently departed.

"Sure, the Duke's much incensed," said Jeronimy, wiping the sweat from his brow with a silken handkercher and blowing out with his mouth.

"It was, in my conceit, a prime error in judgement," said Beroald, "not to have given him the regency. Unless I do grossly mistake him, he was ready to let go the rest had he had but that. You must pardon me, my lord Admiral; the time calls for bare truth, not glosing compliment."

"I would in pure joy give it him to-day," said the Admiral, wiping his brow anew.

Roder drank a great draught of wine, then turned square upon them as if upon revelation suddenly to announce an important truth. "Why, this is very much to the purpose, my lords. Give it him: 'tis a bargain, and he is ours."

"You do forget your gravity," said the Chancellor. "Lieth it in us to alter and set aside the King's will?"

"Ay, indeed," said Roder: "I had forgot."

" 'Tis not to be thought on," said the Admiral. "But, that provided, it is the more instant we waste not our powers in a manner with private bickerings. I am strangely puzzled. I think we be all of an accord, though, in this: that the main purport of the matter and our only thought is to uphold the young Queen as we are bound to do, and serve her wholly and throughly?"

"We be weaponless here," said Beroald, "else would I kiss my sword to that. Take up the regency, my lord Admiral, and I at least will sustain and comfort you in this 'gainst all continent impediments and unto death itself."

"Thanks, noble Beroald," said the Admiral, taking his hand

and Earl Roder's, who on the motion sware him the like upholding.
"And now, 'tis to make firm accord with the Duke if we may, and
then keep open eyes on Rerek. But there there's difficult going and
need, in a manner, to go frost-nailed, since we were much to blame
went we in aught against the King's testament, and by that testament the Vicar must have the Queen in ward and be Regent for her
in Rerek."

"Suffer me," said the Chancellor, reaching out his hand for the
document, "to peruse it again. Ha! come hither," he said: "note a
strange accident. It saith 'shall in her name rule the realm as Regent' (this of the Vicar), and then concerning you, my lord Admiral,
'to rule all the land' (that is, of Meszria) 'as Regent thereof.' It might
be nicely argued that, he being in terms named Regent of all the
realm and you but of Meszria only, effect is you shall be subject unto
him as Regent of all the realm."

" 'Twas never so intended," said Roder.

"Nay," said the Chancellor; "but 'twill be argued by the letter,
not upon supposition of intention. How came it, Roder, that you
had the original?"

"The Vicar hath it too," said he: " 'twas execute in duplicate. O
there's no doubt on't, my lords, the Vicar meaneth not sit content in
Rerek. 'Twas most observable with what a cloak of seeming loyalty
he wrapped himself withal soon as the King 'gan sicken, and with
what eagerness he did haste to wipe out of men's sight and memories all evidences of strife betwixt them. As witness, a thing I knew
by secret and most trusty intelligence: 'twas come so nigh a breach
betwixt 'em, that he had privily posted his cousin german, the great
Lord Lessingham, with near a thousand horse at Mornagay of
Rerek to hold the ways northward 'gainst the King should they
come to open differences; but straight upon the King's sickening
(for well he knew the hellish virtue of the drug that would obey no
antidote) a sent his Gabriel Flores, a close instrument of his, galloping a whole night and day, to call off Lessingham and fetch him
home again. And put it about forthright (with circumstances to be
witness in't) that 'twas Barganax in a jealous vengeful cruelty did
procure 's young brother's taking off."

"And will you say," asked Jeronimy, "that Barganax did not
indeed procure it?"

"I rest but on hearsay and what my own judgement tells me,"
answered he. "I am persuaded the Vicar did it. And hath the mind
too to use the sister as a stalk to catch birds with, and that's the
whole kingdom for's own usurping and enjoyment."

"You mind what we spoke on but now i' the throne-room?" said
Jeronimy to the Chancellor. "With right of our side, and with the
Duke of our side?"

Beroald nodded a grave assent, saying, "We need both."

The Lord Jeronimy fingered his thin beard a moment in silence: "And yet," he said, with a twitch of his mouth, "I would not trust him out of all-ho![10] His thoughts do soar too high, in a manner, for sober deed to follow. I would trust him discreetly."

The door opened, and those lords stood up in a formal deference. It was easy to read in Jeronimy's most tell-tale eyes how all his prudent and scrupulous withholdings discandied quite, only to look on Barganax that now entered to them with so lovely a taking grace as, after the foul storm he had gone out with, seemed a new man, a new day. "My lord Admiral," he said, standing in the door: "I have now thought on't. I will stand in alliance with you to uphold the King's testament unto last fulfilment. Let your scriveners draw it in form, my lord Chancellor: we'll set our hands to it. And if you will dine with me to-morrow, 'tis a pleasure I shall set store by. I'd say to-night, but—to-night I am bespoke already."

IV

ZIMIAMVIAN DAWN

Light on a dark lady

THE beginnings of new light,[1] fanned with little winds that had slept all night long on the gentle spring-time sea, entered through the wide-open windows of the Duke's private lodging in Acrozayana and so by open doors into the outer chamber and so, passing out by western windows, were lost upon distances of the hueless lake below. Upon their passage, ambrosial Night, who had first trailed her mantle of dusk and enchantery over the white damask and the wine-cups rough with jewels, and over the oysters and crayfish in hippocras, jellied ortolans, peaches, queen-apples, and strange passion-fruits filled with seeds afloat in a thin delicious juice, and had later watched, under the silver lamps, such preenings and soarings of the bird delight as even holy Night can find no name to name them, now furled plume by plume her downy wings, ready to repair for yet another diurnal span to her chambers of the west. And now morning stood awake in those rooms, loosing hand from departing Night's, even as Fiorinda, rising in a like silence, loosed her hand from her sleeping lover's late fallen asleep a little before the dawn.

Motionless at the great crystal mirror, her hands gathering behind her head the night-black heavy and scented softnesses of her unbound hair, she surveyed for a while her own naked loveliness: marvels of white, proud, Greek, modelled to the faintest half-retracted touch, pure as snows that dream out the noonday on the untrod empy-real snow-dome of Koshtra Belorn;[2] and, as in the sweet native habit of such hair, thrones whence darkness shines down darkness to the failing of vision. Compounded and made up of two things she seemed: day and sable night; only in her eyes shone that coolness of aquamarine, and as tempestuous dawns wear their rose-flowers, so she.

After a time, with a sudden melting movement, unseizable as a humming-bird's flight in its shimmer of moods and motives, voluptuous languor, half-surprised acceptance, self-surrender, disdain, she pronounced her name *Fiorinda,* delicately, as if caressing with tongue and lips the name's very beauty as she framed the syllables. She spoke it strangely, as if that name, and the looking-glass image itself, were not her own but somewhat other: somewhat of her making, it might be, as a painter should paint a picture of his heart's desire; yet not her, or at least not her complete. And, so speaking, she laughed, very light and low, all unlike to that mocking laugh that so pricked Barganax's sense, as if (by his saying yesterday) she would laugh all honesty out of fashion. For there was now in this laugh of hers a note of quality alien to all human kind, so honey-sweet it was, fancy-free, yet laughter-loving of itself: so might a sudden rift in the veil between time and eternity let through a momentary light sound of the honey-sweet imperishable laughter. On the instant, it was gone. But the memory of it remained like the ringed ripple on water where a bird has dived.

The sun rose, and shot its first beam against that lady's brow, as she turned towards the morning. And now befell a great wonder. Even as she, standing so in the first beams of day, began to put up her hair and pin it with pins of chrysolite, she seemed on the sudden grown taller by a head, to out-top the tallest of men in stature; and whereas, since there is no increase beyond perfection, the beauty of her body might not increase, yet was the substance of it as if transmuted in a moment to pure light, of a like brightness and essence with the heavenly fires of sunrise. No man could in that time have named the colour of Her eyes or of Her hair: the shifting of the dark and light was become as a blinding glory too awful for mortal eye to look upon, too swift for the mind of man to seize or read. For upon Her cheek in that hour was the beauty that belongs to fair-crowned Aphrodite; and that beauty, thus made manifest in its fulness, no eye can bear or see, not even a God's, unless it be possible for the great Father of All Who sitteth in secret, that He might behold it and know it.[3]

The rays touched Barganax's lids. He turned in his sleep: reached out a searching hand and spoke her name in his sleep. She took from the silver-studded stool where it lay her loose gown of diaphanous silken stuff spangled with silver stars and with diamonds and sapphires tiny as grains of sand, and put it about her. The marvel was overpast, as a meteor trails across heaven in the common sight of men and their lowly habitations a light never seen till now in earth or sky, and in a count of ten is gone. On the edge of the great bed upon the fair-worked lace border she sat down, placidly and gracefully as a she-leopard might sit. There was a new look in her eyes now as she watched him asleep: a simple human look, but yet as it were from above, detached and virginal, regarding as if in a tender pitiful wonder these toys of circumstance and greatness and magnificence, and him like a child asleep among them, and her own presence as part of them, sitting there. Suddenly she took his hand that lay there where it had abandoned its dreaming quest, and prisoned it, under both hers, in her bosom. The Duke opened his eyes upon her. He lay very still. Her side-face wore the cool loveliness of a windless lake at sunrise; her gaze was downward, the upper lid level and still, the eye still and wide, yet as if attending to no seen object but to some inside music. His imprisoned hand stirred: he said, under his breath, her name.

Her echo, scarce audible, upon a self-accepting Olympian faint upward nod, came with a kind of hushed assent: *Fiorinda*. And as still she sat with that downward gaze listening, the thing at the corner of her mouth, very beguiling and faun-like now, turned on its back and looked at him sideways.

V

THE VICAR OF REREK

A dog-washing in Laimak ✦ *Gabriel Flores* ✦
Amenities betwixt cousins ✦ *The curst horse feels
the bridle* ✦ *"An honest statesman to a prince."*

T HAT same eye of day, which three hours ago had
opened upon wonder in Acrozayana, was now climbed
so high in the eastern heavens as to top, fifty leagues to
the northward, the far-shadowing backbone of the
Forn, and shine clear into Owldale where, upon a little
steep hill solitary among grazing-lands betwixt mountains eastward
and westward, the hold of Laimak lay like a sleeping wolf. So steep
was that hill that it rose naked in cliffs three or four hundred feet
high on every side, and the blind walls of the fortress, built of huge
blocks quarried from the crown of the hill, followed the line of the
cliffs' brow round about. Only to the north an arched gateway broke
the walls, opening on a path hewn zig-zag up through the cliffs to
give passage for men and horses; but always upon sufferance, since
at every step the walls or towers commanded that passage way for
shooting and casting down of fire or boiling pitch; and a gatehouse
bestrode the passage way at its coming forth into the fields below,
with towers and machicolations and a portcullis of iron. Wolf-grey it
was all to look upon, as well the cliffs as the walls that frowned above
them, being of one substance of stubborn crystalline rock, of the
earth's primordial crust, wolf-grey and of an iron hardness. And this
was from antique times the castle of the Parrys, that now for thirty
generations had been lords in Rerek.[1]

57

Upon the champaign north and east under Laimak there lay in tents that army, not yet disbanded, which the Lord Horius Parry[2] had drawn to a head for dealing with the King if need were, and which, that necessity now being past, he in his prudent husbandry thought it not good too hastily to lay aside; meaning it should yet, haply for argument in the southlands, haply otherwise, nicely serve his turn.

Within the hold, thus early, he himself was up and doing, while most men yet slept. Under the mighty archway called Hagsby's Entry, that led from one of the inner courts beneath two towers into the inmost court of all, which was outer ward of the great square keep, he stood, all in dirt, stripped to the waist, aproned like a smith, with a long wooden vat or tub before him full of steaming soapy water, taking his pleasure with washing of his cursed dogs. Two or three that he had already dealt with rushed hither and thither about the narrow courtyard, yelping and barking and tumbling in a wild gladness of release; the rest skulked in shadowy corners of the archway, as hoping against hope to escape notice, yet daring not to slink away, coming each in turn when his name was called, grovelling and unwilling to his master's feet. Bushy-tailed prick-eared heavy-chested long-fanged slaver-mouthed beasts were they all, a dozen or more, some red, some black, some grey, some yellow, as big as wolves and most wolfish to look upon. Each as his turn came the Vicar seized by the scruff of the neck and by the loose skin above the haunches and, lifting it as it had been a kitten, set it in the bath. He was a huge, heavy, ugly man, nigh about fifty years of age, not tall as beside tall men, but great-thewed and broad of chest and shoulder, his neck as thick as a common man's thigh, his skin fair and full of freckons, his hair fiery red, stiff like wires and growing far down on his neck behind; he wore it trimmed short, and it had this quality that it stood upright on his head like a savage dog's if he was angry. His ears were strangely small and fine shaped, but set low; his jaw great and wide; his mouth wide with pale thin lips; his nose jutting forth with mighty side-pitched nostrils, and high and spreading in the wings; his forehead high-domed, smooth, and broad, and with a kind of noble serenity that sorted oddly with the ruffianly lines of his nose and jaw; his beard and mustachios close-trimmed and bristly; his eyebrows sparse; his eyelids heavy, not deep set. He had delicate lively hazel eyes, like the eyes of an adder. He had none of his servants by him at this dog-washing, save only his secretary, Gabriel Flores, for his mind was sprightly and busy a-mornings, and he would have the convenience to talk, if occasion were, secretly with this man, who were aptly styled (to overpass his swarthy hue, and lack of all nobleness in his softer and more bloated look) for his highness *in duodecimo*.

"Come hither, Pyewacket!" shouted the Vicar, letting go that

dog that was then in the bath and turning to peer into the shadows
of the gate. "Pyewacket! Satan's lightnings blast the bitch! Woo't
come when th'art called?" He hurled the heavy scrubbing-brush at a
brindled shadowy form that stole away in hoped obscurity: a yelp
told him that his aim was true. The great beast, her tail between her
legs, trotted away; he shouted to her again; she glanced back, a
harried reproachful glance, and trotted faster; the Vicar was upon
her with a lion-like agility; he kicked her; she laid back her ears,
snarled, and snapped at his leg; he caught her by the neck and beat
her with his fist about the ribs and buttocks till she yelped for pain;
when he had done she growled and bared her teeth; he beat her
once more, harder, then waited to see what she would do. She gave
in, and walked, but with no good grace, to the distasteful bath.
There, standing shoulder-deep in the steaming suds, grown thin to
look on beyond nature, and very pathetical, with the water's soaking
of her hair and making it cling close to the skin, she suffered sulkily
the indignities of soap and brush, and the searching erudite fingers
that (greatly indeed for her good) sought out and slew the ticks that
here and there beset her. All the while her staring eyes were sullen
with bottled-up anger, like a bull's. The Vicar's eyes had the like
look in them.

"Well," said he in a while, "is he coming? You did say I would
have speech of him, and that instantly?"

"I did give him your highness's very words," said Gabriel. He
paused: then, " 'Tis a strange folly, this tennis: racket away a hundred crowns afore breakfast,[3] and till that's done all sober business
may go hang."

"Did he not answer you?" asked the Vicar after a minute.

Gabriel smiled a crooked smile. "Not to say, answer," he said.

"What said he, then?" said the Vicar, looking up.

Gabriel said, "Faith, 'twas not for your ear intended. I were to
blame did I blab to your highness every scurvy word, spoke in un-
considerate haste, that your highness should magnify past all reason."

At that word, came Lessingham hastily towards them out of the
low dark passage that sloped upward into the long and narrow
yard, at the far, or eastern, end whereof was Hagsby's Entry where
the washing was. And at that word, whether seeing him or no, the
Vicar gave his Pyewacket a damnable slap across the nose, grabbed
her fore and aft, and flung her out in the way of Lessingham that
walked hastily to greet him. She, with the gadflies of pain and out-
raged dignity behind her and a strange man before, sprang at his
throat. Lessingham was in his shirt, tennis-racket in hand; he smote
her with the racket, across the fore-leg as she sprang: this stopped
her; she gave way, yowling and limping. "God's death!" said the
Vicar, "will you kill my brach?" and threw a long-bladed dagger at

him. Lessingham avoided it: but the singing of it was in his ear as it passed. He leapt at the Vicar and grappled him. The Vicar wrestled like a cat-a-mountain, but Lessingham held him. Gabriel, at his master's skirt, now kept off the dogs, now pleased himself with looking on the fight, ever side-stepping and dodging, like a man caught in a hill-forest in a whirlwind when the tall pines loosened at root reel and lock together and lurch, creaking and tottering, towards the last downward-tearing ruinous crash. The Vicar's breath began to come and go now in great puffs and hissings like the blowing of a sea-beast. Lessingham rushed him backwards. The edge of the wash-tub caught him behind the knees, and he fell in, body and breeches, with Lessingham a-top of him, and with that violence the tub was overturned.

They loosed hold and stood up now, and in that nick of time came Amaury into the yard. The Vicar barked out a great laugh, and held out his hand to Lessingham, who took it straight. There was in Lessingham's eye as it rested upon his cousin a singular look, as if he fingered in him a joy too fine for common capacities: such a look as a man might cast, unknowingly and because he could not help it, on his dear mistress. And indeed it was strange to consider how the Vicar, standing thus in nasty clothes, but even risen from a rude tussling-bout and a shameful fall, stood yet as clothed upon with greatness like a mantle, sunning in his majesty like adders in warm beams.

Lessingham said, "You did send for me."

"Yes," answered he: "the matter is of weight. Wash and array us, and we'll talk on't at breakfast. Gabriel, see to't."

"I'll meet you straight in my lodging, Amaury," said Lessingham.

When they were alone, "Cousin," said Lessingham, "you did throw a knife at me."

The Vicar was ill at ease under Lessingham's secure and disturbing smile. "Tush," he said, " 'twas but in sport."

"You shall find it a dangerous sport," said Lessingham. "Be advised, cousin. Leave that sport."

"You are such a quarreling, affronting—" the words ceased in his throat as his eye met Lessingham's. Like his own great hell-hound bitch a while ago, he, as for this time, bared fang yet owned his master. And in that owning, as by some hidden law, he seemed to put on again that greatness which but even now, under Lessingham's basilisk look, had seemed to fall off from him.

That was an hour later when those kinsmen brake their fast together on the roof of the great main keep, over the Vicar's lodging: a place of air and wide prospect; and a place besides of secrecy; for when the door in the northwest turret was shut, by which alone was a way up to the roof and the battlements, there was none save the fowls of the air and the huge stones of the floor and parapet to be eaves-droppers at their conference. Here in the midst of the floor was a narrow table set under the sky, with musk-millions and peaches in silver dishes, and a great haunch of cold venison, and marmalades of quince and crab-apple, and flagons of white and red hippocras, with chased gold goblets; and there were diapered linen napkins and silver-handled knives and silver forks to eat withal; all very noble and sumptuously arrayed. Two heavy arm-chairs of old black oak were set at the table; the Vicar sat at the northern side, and over against him Lessingham. They were washen now, and in fair and fine clothes. The Vicar had put on now a kirtle of dark brown velvet edged with rich embroidery of thread of gold, but frayed and dirted and rubbed with wearing; it was cut wide and low about the neck, with a flat collar of white pleated lace tied with a silken cord. Lessingham was in a buff-coloured kirtle of soft ribbed silk with a narrow ruff and narrow wristbands of point-lace span-gled with beads of jet of the bigness of mustard seeds, and tight-fitting black silk breeches and velvet shoes.

For a time they ate in silence. Every other while, the Vicar's sudden eye glinted upon Lessingham; it was as if he had a mind to propound some matter, but would be besought for it first. But Les-singham sat sphinx-like and unconcerned in his pleasant ease, as wanting nothing, desiring nothing, at peace with himself and the hour and the fresh morning. At length the Vicar spoke: "You are as unquiet and restless as an October stag: but three days here, and already I see you in a fever for some new action."

Lessingham smiled.

After a time the Vicar spoke again: "For my own part, I had as lief sit quiet now: enjoy that fortune hath given us."

"I praise your resolution," said Lessingham: "a most pious and fine humility in you, whom fortune hath so much blest, without all seconding of your proper action."

The Vicar took a peach and skinned it. "Could we but count," he said, "on others for the like temperate withholding."

Lessingham said nothing.

"The south breedeth hot bloods and hot livers like summer flies," said the Vicar after a pause. He poured out some more wine. " 'Tis that gives me stay," he said. " 'Tis that makes me think may be we should do somewhat," he said, after another mouthful.

Lessingham waited.

The Vicar smote his fist on the table. "I am master of the game, by this lucky turn," he said: "play off the fat Admiral 'gainst the Duke, and all the poppets of Meszria 'gainst each in turn: cheap as kissing, and twice as profitable. But it needs suasion, cousin, spe-cious arguments; butter 'em, tickle 'em, conycatch 'em; you must go

to 'em like coy wenches: amuse 'em, feed 'em with pathetical flim-
flams, flout 'em, then seem to forget 'em, then be somewhat bold
with 'em, laugh at 'em; last, i' the happy instant, ring up the grand
main piece. Now I, cousin, am a loose, plain, rude talker: call a
spade a spade. But you, and you would, should do this to admiration."

"I have handled such a matter ere now," said Lessingham,
"and have not spoilt things utterly."

"Cousin," said the Vicar: "harkee, I would have your head in
this. I would have you fare south and play this game for me. You
shall be my ambassador. And, so you magnify it not beyond all reason, you shall name your own reward."

"I did think you knew," said Lessingham, "that it is not my way
to do aught upon reward. Reason why, that to such things only am I
wont to set my hand as the reward thereof lieth in the doing of
'em."

" 'Twould make a dog laugh to hear such fiddle-faddle," said
the Vicar. "Go to, I shall give you wide choice of dominion and
treasure when the time comes. Will you do it?"

"I will do it," answered Lessingham: "but upon conditions."
His eyes were a-sparkle.

"Well," said the Vicar.

Lessingham said, "First is, that you uphold the King's testament."

"That," replied he, "proceedeth without question. It is my
open proclaimed policy to uphold it throughly, and if you will I'll
swear to it."

"Second is," said Lessingham, "that you own and acknowledge
to me, for my private ear only, here in this place, that 'twas by your
rede, more, your direct commandment, the King was lately thus
miserably murdered."

The Vicar laughed. " 'Las cousin, will you, too, give credit to
that slanderous rumour and obloquy now going abroad?"

"I see," said Lessingham: "you will not fulfil my second condition. Good. Get you another ambassador."

The Vicar's face was scarlet to look upon. He said, "I swear to
you by God, the very founder, furtherer, and finisher of truth—"

Lessingham brake in upon him: "Give over, cousin. Indeed, if
you be not damned already 'twere pity damn yourself for so hopeless an attempt as make me credit what I well know to be a lie. Be
not angry, cousin: here we be close as the grave: surely 'twixt you
and I 'tis stretch courtesy past use and reason to pretend I know
you not for a most approved liar and forswearer." He ate a bit of
marmalade, and leaned back in his chair. "To be open with you," he
said, "you have put me into such a gog of going, I would not stay
now for the world. Yet see the pass we stand in: if it be as hard for

you to tell the truth as for me to go back from my word, I'm sorry for it, for then all goeth miss."

"Put case it were true," said the Vicar. "Were it not rash in you to desire a knowledge might hurry you to ruin? Like to that great man's mistress, wheedled him to confess a horrid murder, which done, he swore her to silence upon a poisoned book: knowing it lay not in her to conceal his counsel, bound her to't by death."

Lessingham looked at him with the flicker of a smile in his eyes. "When I am grown so useless to you, cousin, as you should afford to lose me, I'll think it danger to receive such secrets of you. Till then, no. I'll trust no man's affections, but I trust your wisdom most securely. Most securely, cousin."

The Vicar toyed with his wine-cup. "Be that as it may," he said at last. "This you talk on is a monstrous folly. Where's the reason of the thing? I were a fine fool to a murdered the young suck-egg, when 'twas in my hand to have overthrown him with force of arms."

"There," replied Lessingham, "you do much belie your prudent mind. It had been folly indeed to stand in the eyes of the world a usurping rebel, when 'twas the readier way, with some devilish pothecary stuff,[4] stibium, henbane, I know not what, to whiffle him off and then put on your mourning and say his jealous brother did it."

"Ay, and did he," said the Vicar. "And did set too the lying tongues a-wag to say 'twas I."

Lessingham yawned and studied the back of his hand, the little silky black hairs that grew fine and smooth on the shapely finger-joints, and the heavy ancient golden worm that he wore on his middle finger, scaly, eating of its own tail, its head a cabochon ruby big as a sparrow's egg, that glowed with inward fires like the blood-red fires of sunset.

"You will go then?" said the Vicar.

"But upon condition of confession," answered he.

The Vicar lurched up from the table and began to pace about. Lessingham yawned again and played with his ring. Neither spoke. After a minute the Vicar, grinding his teeth, came and stood over against him. Lessingham looked up. "Dear cousin," he said, "how long will you stay this matter's going into action, of so much worth and moment? And how long will you seek to cast suds in my eyes that am long since satisfied of the truth, but will have it of you in friendship? You did send me out of the way to Mornagay whiles it was done. But I know it."

The Vicar laughed with anger. "Know it? Upon what evidence?" He ground his teeth. "Gabriel, that filth, was't he told you this? I'll have him hewn in pieces."

"O spare your pains," said Lessingham. "Should Gabriel tell me at noonday 'twas twelve o'clock, I'd have evidence corroborative ere I'd believe it. No, cousin, I am satisfied you did act this murder; not by your own hand, indeed: that were too simple: but yours the deed was. And since you will be so strange with me as deny the thing: well, the Gods be with you, I'll have no further hand with you."

The Vicar sat down again and leaned across the table, glowering at him awhile in silence. Lessingham returned his gaze steadily; the eyes of Lessingham were grey with brown and golden speckles. The Vicar at length turned away his gaze. "Well," he said betwixt his teeth: "I did it."

Slowly and luxuriously Lessingham stretched his arms, yawned, and then sat up. He reached out a leisurely hand to the golden flagon and filled his goblet with red hippocras. "Truth hath been long time a-coming out," he said. "I'll pledge her, so." He drank, looking over the cup at the Vicar with a slow smiling contentment, a strange, clouded look, in which came suddenly an alteration as if the red sun had glared out through a rift in the clouds. "This murder," said he, and there were now undertones and overtones in his voice that made it terrible, for all it was so quiet and came on so even and undisturbed a breath: "This murder was one of the most filthiest acts that ever was done."

The Vicar faced him like a bull of Nineveh.[5]

"You did show me the testament," said Lessingham. "Was that some fine counterfeit device of yours, or was it real and true?" The Vicar made no answer. Lessingham said, "Well, I know it was true, by tests beyond your protestations, cousin. And I remarked it very particularly, wherein it did name you vicar and viceregent of the Queen and lord protector of her minority, and did enjoin you in all points study her proper good and safety and the enhancement of her sovereign power and dominion, and tender and cherish her lovingly as a father should. You are not much practised in a father's part, I think. Since you did drive your sons away into exile. This will be hard for you."

He paused, looking the Vicar straight in the eye. It was as if across that silent table two thunder-clouds faced each other in an awful calm. Lessingham spoke: "You have promised me to uphold that testament. Well, I'll help you, as I have done before. I'll go on this embassage for you. I'll follow and uphold you as Vicar of the Queen. But this testament shall be to you as a thing enskied and holy. Which if in any jot or tittle you shall offend against, or one finger's breadth depart from it: no more, but you shall bitterly aby it."

The Vicar ran his tongue over his lips. For a minute he was silent, then in a kind of cold tart pride he said, "I were poorly paid then for my goodness and forbearance; seeing these five minutes past I have had a more than most intolerable lust to murder you, yet, I know not why, forbore." He stood up with a laugh, and with a forced pretence of jolly-scoffing bravery. "What squibs be these, for men of our kidney to tease ourselves withal of a spring morning! And, cousin, this is the maggot in the oak-apple: you are clean fallen in love with yonder little wagtail at mere hearsay."

Lessingham answered and said, "With you, cousin, I have long fallen in love."

VI

LORD LESSINGHAM'S EMBASSAGE

The Admiral and the Chancellor ✦ Discords of Lessingham's planting ✦ The Admiral much perplexed ✦ Divided politics ✦ Lessingham and Vandermast ✦ Conference in Acrozayana ✦ The Duke brought to bay ✦ A borken consort ✦ The Duke and Lessingham: strange concords.

HAT was of an evening of late May-time,[1] the fourth week after these things but now spoken of, that the Lord Beroald sat alone at the upper edge of a clearing in the oak-woods that clothe the low Darial hills south of the lake, looking northwards to Zayana. From his feet the ground fell gently away for a hundred paces or more to the bridle-path. Below that, the tree-clad face of the hill dropped sharply to the lake seven or eight hundred feet beneath. The sky was fair, and the weather smooth and calm. His horse grazed at ease, moving to and fro amid the lush grasses. Save for that munching sound, and the sound of falling water, and now and then the note of a cuckoo calling, and now and then the noise of the horse's hoof against a stone, there was silence. A marmot came out of a heap of fallen rocks behind him on his left and sat up with little fore-paws hanging down as if in a helpless soft dismay, viewing the Chancellor. She whistled and retired back to her hole when the silence was broken by a fresh noise of horse-hooves, and the lord Admiral rode up into the clearing, greeted the Chancellor, and dismounted beside him.

"It is very much," said the Lord Jeronimy, when they were sat down together upon a great stone, "that we should be fain to take counsel under the sky like owls or moor-dogs."

Beroald smiled his cold smile. "I am much beholden to your lordship for suffering this inconvenience. In the city, a flea shall not frisk forth unless his intelligencers comment upon her. And this new business both calleth for speedy action, and needs that both you and I examine and consider of it o'erheard by none."

"Will he not take my no for an answer?" said Jeronimy. "Why, what a loose hot corrupter of virtue have we here. First getteth no from me; then no from the Duke; and now sueth to your lordship to be in a manner his go-between, as if I were a silly maid to comply at last, with oftener scenting of the flower. What new conditions now then?"

"'Tis not altogether thus," said the Chancellor. "The offer is now to me in my own particular."

Jeronimy opened his lips as if to speak, but there was a moment ere the words came: "To you, my lord? Good: and upon like condition?"

"Upon like condition."

"Of suzerainty?" said Jeronimy. "Well, and do you mean to take it? No, no," he said, meeting the Chancellor's cold eye: "I meant not that. I meant, in what estate left you this business with him? did you in a manner temporize?"

Beroald answered, "I did handle the thing in such a vein as that I must give him yea or nay to-morrow."

The Admiral pulled off his black velvet cap plumed with a white estridge-feather set in a diamond brooch, mopped his head, and put on his cap again.

The Lord Beroald gazed steadily before him on Acrozayana, two or three miles away, mirrored in the glassy lake. His speech came cool and glassy, like the thing he looked on, remote and passionless as if it were his own thought speaking to itself. "It is needful," he said, "in this business, that we hold heedy guard, and reckon well our strength. Now is ten days to-day that this Lessingham, treating with full powers on behalf of the Vicar, hath dealt with us touching the Meszrian regency; and if there be any alteration made in these ten days, 'tis to their advantage, not ours. First his offer unto you, my lord Admiral, that the Vicar would receive and acknowledge you as regent in Meszria conformably in all points to the King's testament, and upon condition (which he stiffly maintained to be in that same testament supposed and implicit) that you should do him homage as, pending the Queen's minority, your overlord. That condition you did, in agreement with the Duke, with Roder, and with myself, after mature deliberation of counsel, flatly refuse. The next day after your so refusing, he did offer the regency upon like condition to the Duke, who did refuse it. That was but yesterday. And now, this very morning, did send for me and pro- pound to me the self-same offer; which I, forbearing all private closer conference, fobbed off until to-morrow. Thus standeth it, then. What follows? If I refuse" (upon that "if" the Admiral pulled out his handkerchief and mopped his head), "next move belike is overture of regency to Roder, and then, if he'll not take it, war. I like it not. The Duke I do trust but as you do, my lord: very dis- creetly. These Meszrian lords, not at all. The Vicar hath a fair solici- tor, hath got the right ear of Zapheles, and Melates, too, or I am much mistook: young fools, that have not the wit to see in all the Vicar's promises but fair sunshining, sweetly spoken and but sourly to be performed. Prince Ercles in the north, too, is not so good to rest on, even if Barganax be safe; if the Vicar make war upon the Duke and us upon pretext of enforcing of the King's testament, you shall not see Ercles nor Aramond put their finger too far in the fire o' the Duke's behalf; Lessingham, I am told, hath made friends with 'em both of late."

"That Lessingham is a subtle devil," said Jeronimy.

"This latest offer thus made to me," said the Chancellor, "hath given us the chance if need be to afterthink us. That were pity were it appear in the end that our eyes were greater than our bellies. I would remember you of this, my lord Admiral, that in point of construction the Vicar's claim of suzerainty is good in law. We are precisely bound to uphold the testament. It can be said that, going against him in this, we do merely violate it. The Parry himself none but a ninny would trust further than a might see him; but here 'tis not to deal with him direct, but through Lessingham."

"As 't should be handed us," said Jeronimy, "in a fair gilded cup, to make his poison go down the smoother."

"I see it not altogether so," said Beroald. " 'Tis a young man of most supposed abilities both in the council and a soldier of renown. I have these ten days studied him like a book, and I find no point to question, but all to confirm and justify what reputation saith of him: an honourable man, and a man with the power to hold his principal to what soever he shall stand warrant for of his behalf. And he hath, in no qualified way but at large, took it upon his honour that upon agreement made betwixt us the Vicar will perform the King's testa- ment unto the littlest letter."

Jeronimy said, "He is a subtle devil."

"It is for you, not me, to determine," said the Chancellor. "Only I would have you consider of all this, not as somewhat to be swept up with a sudden and tumultuous judgement, but as a thing of heaviest import. For you see, you may, upon this offer thus made to me, open your dealings anew with him, and take up the regency upon condition of suzerainty and upon his proper warranty of the Vicar's performance."

"And so, in a manner—" said the Admiral slowly, and fell silent. The Chancellor said no more, judging it good to give time for these matters to digest.

They sat in shadow. The sun had for some time now gone behind the hill on their left. The shadows lengthened over the lake. The horses munched on. After a while the Chancellor spoke: "Will you not change your mind?"

The Lord Jeronimy rose heavily from his seat and stood looking at him a minute in silence; then said, "No. And no more must you, my lord Chancellor."

"We stand together," said Beroald, and rose up too. "Yet remember, things worsen as time goeth by. These country lords are quite debauched by him. 'Tis time to end talking and fall to action."

The Admiral's black mare, at her lord's stirring, came to him and nuzzled her nose in his neck. He fondled and petted her. " 'Tis time indeed," he said. "Time indeed."

"Better we were not seen too much in conference to-night," said Beroald. "Better not enter the gates together."

"Will you ride first," said the Admiral, "or shall I? Truth is, I had been minded for Sestola to-night, 'bout some business of the fleet. But as things shape, I will let that go by and sleep in Zayana."

"I pray you ride first," said the Chancellor.

The Admiral came down through the wood at a walking pace, his mind heavy with thought. His men, that had waited this while in the wood with the Chancellor's, rode a score of paces or so behind him. "Lessingham," he said in himself. "A very subtle devil: a devil full of all seduction and charm. Hath a not charmed me too? Ay, but not too far: not to danger. Like to that son of mine, drowned in the Sound of Tabarey: should a been of about his years too, had he lived. Pish! 'tis foolery. And yet, 'tis in the Duke too. Lessingham: Barganax. Strange: so unlike, and yet, in a manner, so like; both of the grape, as 'twere. Red wine: white wine. Away, 'tis foolery. Still, like a shying horse: ride her up to it, let her see and examine it well as to its nature: it frighteth her not another time." His mind stood still awhile. Then he said again in himself, "Hath charmed Beroald. Nay, but that's not true neither. Nay, I trust Beroald."

He drew rein for a moment as the path rounded the verge of a jutting cliff giving a fair wide prospect over the water. An owl hooted. Jeronimy said in himself, "If he can handle Horius Parry, as folk say he can: tickle him, make him serve his turn; what wonder in the world can he not do then?" He rode on. "Beroald is a man of law. There's his element. But with me 'tis substance and intention, not form and accident. And yet indeed, a great wise man; prudent and foreseeing. Ay, 'time to afterthink us,' that's wisdom. Worse weather than that we put to sea in: ay, 'tis pure truth. There's many would take his rede and think no more on't. Safer. Safer take his rede.

"Ay, but I do know 'tis wrong. In my bones I know it." He struck spurs into the mare's flanks: she started forward violently: he leaned forward calming her, patting her neck. "No, I'll not change my mind. Nor you must not neither, my lord Chancellor. But then, what next? Action, next. An end of these talkings: 'tis time indeed." He stroked her neck again, softly, meditatively. "And I the main actor. Regent of Meszria. Lieth upon me. Well, we have long since considered on't. With right of our side; and with the Duke of our side. 'I am of your opinion,' said he. Well: now cometh this silver to the trying. Barganax: is he to trust to? 'Tis a doubt whereon hangeth all, on this one thin thread. Trust him discreetly. The word is wiser than the deed, now I consider on't. O, the down-bearing weight of this immense charge. 'Tis a fine toy, make up alliance with a royal prince on terms he must but figure bass for such a man as me to run the divisions on't; comfort and uphold me at all points whiles I sit i' the seat he looked for as his by right. If he have a spice of pride in him still (and he is made up and compounded of pride, opinion, and disdain), shall he not hate me every while, and seek but first fair occasion to ding me down and take his own back? And yet the man's mind is so noble, I'd trust him, where his word's engaged, even to breaking-point. And yet, no, 'tis mid-summer madness: 'tis but the spell of his masterful youth and grace, like t'other's. I had done with this ten minutes since: 'tis foolery. And yet, and yet: have I not proof of's loyal mind within reason: his refusing on't when Lessingham did offer it? Nay, but 'twas but stinking fish then: 'twas under suzerainty. And he of the royal ancient family of Fingiswold."

He halted, as with a sudden thought, then with a shake of the rein went on. "Of Fingiswold. Ay, and of Memison. I'll do it. Better hazard sinking there, than sink for sure where we stand. And there's some hope. Say they be corrupted indeed, these young quats, with Lessingham's words and promises: 'tis certain their corruption, even as their fealty, is but skin-deep. They'll follow their own liege sovereign prince of Meszrian blood and line a thousand times, where, were it but me, they'd take but the happy instant to throw me off and so rid them at last of the prime scourge and hate of all their liberties for years. I'll do it. Ay, I'll do it to-night."

That same night after supper the Chancellor was sat in his chamber writing out fair this letter, which being writ he signed by his name and sealed with his seal. And the letter was conceived in terms following:

> "Unto thonorable my very goode Lo. Lessynghame as wyth fulle powre and awtoritee dymysed and prorogate to speke trette and determyn on byhalve of his hyghnes Horyus Parye Lo. Protector and Vicker of the Qwene in Reyrek:
>
> I have bin carefull my Lo. to waighe and conseder of hys Highnes proposes wherewithall hys hyghnes hath honored me thorow your lops. mowth to thende that for the bettere setlying and doynge awaie of these presente diffrences I schold in myn owne persoun accept of the Regensy of Meszrya upon condicyons exposed att lardge bi your lop., and bi asspeciall thus condicyon that the Regent schalbe in al poyntes His Hyghnes subgytte and uery league man. Al whilke I hauing with carefull mind perpended and revuiewed am lefte att length wyth noe other choys that semeth to me agreable unto my propre honor and my dwte ylike to the Qwene (hoom the Goddes tender and preserue) and to thadmerall bi royalle testement named regent but bi hys hyghnes set a-syde upon refusell of condicyoun a forseyd, saue to conclud that yt is nat fytt I schold accept of the sed Regensy. Whilke resolue thus consederately taken I will vnmoueably stand upon, and wold dessire your lop. to acqweynt Hys Highnes accordynge.
>
> The Goddes leade your lop. bi the hande.
>
> I haue thonor to bee with greatt trewth and respecte your lops. most obedient humble Servaunt,
>
> BEROALD"

The ink was scarce dry and the wax yet warm when there came in a gentleman of his to say the High Admiral was here and would have speech of him. The Chancellor smiled. "That saveth me a journey," he said: "I was this instant upon going to see him;" and he bade admit him straight. When they were private, "My lord Chancellor," said Jeronimy, and his face was flushed, "I bring you good tidings. I have seen the Duke upon this matter we talked on."

The Chancellor lifted a cold eye upon him. "You have seen the Duke?"

Jeronimy's eyes took on that look that a dog's eyes have when, under a detecting gaze, he suddenly bethinks him that this eating of that bit of meat or chewing up of that bird, albeit good and reasonable in his estimation, was yet questionable in the sight of others, and fraught, may be, with consequences he till then ne'er thought upon. "I'm sorry," he said. "I am come straight from him to you. Perhaps I should a seen you first. I'm sorry, my lord."

"You are dark to me yet," said the Chancellor. "Did your lord-ship inform the Duke of this last turn: I mean this offer I told you of?"

"In a manner, yes," answered Jeronimy.

"Had I stood in your shoes, my lord Admiral," said the Chan-cellor, "I should have given you the opportunity to come with me upon such an errand."

"You and I," said the Admiral, "did conclude upon speedy ac-tion. A-riding home I did view the matter from all points, and did at last conceive in a manner but one safe way betwixt these quicksands. Brief, I did resign but now into the Duke's hand, as well for present as prospectively, the office of Regent: bade him take it up and de-fend it, and we would go through and second him."

He paused. The Chancellor's jaw set, and his lean face turned ashy. He stood up from his chair, pushed the letter across the table to Jeronimy, and stalked to the window. The Admiral took out his perspective-glass and read the letter, blowing softly with his cheeks the while. "Your lordship hath an art in drafting of such matters," he said: "'tis beyond admiration excellent." He looked cautiously up, met the Chancellor's eye, and looked away.

For a minute the Lord Beroald abode silent. When he mastered himself to speak, the words came like chips of ice clinking down an ice-slope. "Lessingham," he said, "is an able politician. You and me, my lord, he but turneth to his purpose. You have made a fine hand of it."

Jeronimy slowly shook his head. "I did play for a firm line and no stragglers," said he. "We should not have held the Duke with us had we ta'en, in a manner, the course you formerly thought on: had I complied and ta'en up the regency 'pon Lessingham's conditions."

"You have now by your act," said Beroald, "disburdened him of all conditions, and left us open to all injuries. You have, in face of dangerous enemies, set aside the law, which was our strength and our justification; you have struck wide division in our counsels, when a single mind was most needful; you have unleashed the Duke on a course may be shall prove his ruin and ours. Had you gone cap in hand to my Lord Lessingham and professed yourself ready to do his bidding so as to make fair success of his mission hither, he could a thought on no better means to bid you take than these you have taken."

Jeronimy's face became drawn and his kindly eyes darkened with anger. He rose from his chair. "This talk," he said, thickly, "doth more disgrace than it helpeth or graceth us. Let us say no more but good night, my lord Chancellor. May be morning shall bring us riper wisdom."

On the morrow towards mid-day the Lord Lessingham took horse and rode with Amaury from his lodgings in the old Leantine palace in the northern quarter down through the market-place, and so, turning right along Stonegate and Paddockgate, up into the driving-road that ran by the water-side along the top of the town wall of old red sandstone for a quarter of a mile or more; thence, turning inland at the Heugh, through some winding cobbled streets, they came out into the sunlight of the piazza of the Winds, and, crossing that from north to south, took the Way of the Seven Hundred Pillars. At a walking-pace they climbed its wide zig-zags, pleasant with the shade of ancient holm-oaks and the heavy scent of the mimosa-trees, and came at length a little before noon up to the main gate of the citadel. A guard of honour, of seven of the Duke's red-bearded swordsmen, conducted them up the shining stairs that were built of panteron stone, black green and purple, and so by many courts and colonnades to silver doors and through them to a narrow and high-roofed corridor which opened at its far end, with silver doors, upon that garden of everlasting afternoon. Here, in the low slanting rays under the tufted shade of strawberry-trees, that ancient man stood to do them welcome, Doctor Vandermast.

He said, "You are late, my lord."

Lessingham, that had not before beheld the wonder of this garden, bit in his admiration and said, "I am, on the contrary, upon the very point of noon. His grace is late, for his own time appointed."

"His grace," answered Vandermast, "is always late. That is to say, he o'errunneth the just time by an hour or so; and that is not blameworthy in a royal Duke. But here indeed is a strange impertinent jest of your lordship's, to come hither some four or five hours behind your set time, and look to find him waiting upon your pleasure."

Amaury said, "Will you make game with my lord, sir? Be more civil; for in truth you are but an old fantastical scholar, with a beard like a crow with two or three dirty straws in her mouth, going to build her nest."

"Hold your tongue, Amaury," said Lessingham. "Scandal not the reverend signior. Doctor, I heard tell ere now of this garden, that 'tis one of the wonders of the world, and that you did make it. And now I see it indeed, I am astonished."

"It is a natural garden, my lord," answered that old man. "This is very sky, and very sun, very clouds and lake, and you and I here in our bodies. You may touch, smell, walk and discourse, inhale the airs. It is natural present."

"Come," said Lessingham: "that is over high meat for my weak stomach. Why, the sun in a golden bush of glory standeth but a handbreadth above yonder woody hills beyond the water; and yet, ten minutes since, it was white noon, blazing on our heads from the meridian."

Vandermast said: "Save for birds or reremice, winged emmets, wasps, flies, and such manner of filths, there is but one only way into this garden, and it is through the lobby of the silver doors. Your lordship and this froward young man did pass the further door at noon, but the hither door some five hours after noon. It is a nice point of disputation whether you did with tortoise-like slowness transambulate that lobby, so as in five hours to proceed but twenty paces, or whether *per contra* those five hours did, with a speed whipped to ten thousand times its natural, blow by you as you walked. *Experimentum docet:*[2] you are here, and 'tis late afternoon."

"And if I shall instantly go back again?" said Lessingham. "What then?"

"You shall find it then but a little past mid-day without. The Duke expects you, my lord. He will be here ere long."

Lessingham walked and stood by the parapet, looking south. Amaury followed him. For a minute or two Lessingham abode there, then turned, leaning with an elbow on the parapet behind him, so as to face that garden. Amaury watched the look in his eyes as they wandered from yellow lily to rose and alkanet and honey-suckle, from bee-haunted lime to strawberry-tree with night-dark foliage, wine-red twisted branches, and jewel-like flower and fruit; shaven sward, porphyry seat, doves at the fountains; all in a sleepy plenitude of golden air and cool long shadows. But once in his life before had Amaury seen that look, and that was a month ago, when Lessingham had stared into the wine in Mornagay. He turned, and saw that that learned man was gazing on Lessingham with a strange intention, and that the look in the eyes of him and the look in the eyes of Lessingham were the same.

The silver doors opened in the blind northern wall, and one came to say that the council was set now in the Duke's closet and he would there receive them. As they turned to go, Lessingham halted and looked down at Doctor Vandermast. "One thing I would know," he said, "that hath strangely puzzled me since first I came hither to Zayana. What are you, old sir?"

Vandermast was silent for a moment, looking straight before him to those sunshiny hills beyond the lake, through half-closed lids, as if remarking and appraising some strange matter. He smiled. "I, my lord," he said slowly, "am one that am wont to pry beneath the unstable course and fickle flower of man's affairs. Somewhat, may be, I have digged up in my searchings. And I am an old faithful servant of the Duke of Zayana." Then, looking Lessingham in the eye, he said, "Forget not, my lord, that all things work together. If, spite all, his grace should bid you guest here this night, in Acrozayana, be very sure you do it."

So now came they to the Duke's closet. He himself sat on the north side of the table, his back to the fireplace, with the Admiral on his

right, the Chancellor on his left, and beyond the Chancellor Earl
Roder. On the Earl's left was Count Zapheles, and the Lords Melates and Barrian to the right of the Admiral. Lessingham sat mid-
most of the table over against the Duke, Amaury and Doctor
Vandermast took notes. Amaury said privately as they sat down,
"Now that we are gotten safe away, sir, out of yon sorcery-witched
garden, I'll say I'm sorry I was rude with you. I would not say it
there. I would not you should think I was afeared of you."

Vandermast answered and said, "I have an eye to find out
good, even as the margaret is found growing in the meat of certain
shell-fishes, in howsoever curious a sort it shall disguise itself.
Therefore, be at ease, young gentleman."

But even while he so spoke with Amaury, the eagle glance of
him was busy with the faces of the great men met about that table,
and most of all with the Duke's face and the Lord Lessingham's.
The Duke, under his cloak of disdainful ease, seemed as if gathered
for his spring. Lessingham, stroking his black beard, looking
through half-dropped lashes now at the Duke, now at the Admiral
or the Chancellor, and still at the Duke again, seemed waiting for
that spring should land the springer in a pit he himself had digged
for him.

"Will you speak first, my Lord Lessingham?" said the Duke.

"Willingly," answered he, with a grave inclination of the head.
"But it can but be to invite your grace to set forth the business you
have called us to consider of upon so much urgency." There was in
his voice as he spoke a lazy bantering music, full of charm, redolent
too of sleeping dangers. Amaury, that had been bred up with him to
manhood, knew it like his native air. Vandermast knew it too, but
not till now in a man's voice. For it bore, even as the troubled image
in a lake at midnight to the star it mirrors, some kinship to that
languorous mocking lazy music that awoke so often in the Lady
Fiorinda's voice; and Vandermast thought he knew, looking at the
Duke, that the Duke too felt the spell of it, albeit without recognition, as a man listening to an air which he knows yet cannot place.

"It is now going upon the eleventh day," said the Duke, "that
your lordship hath gladdened us with your company. In respect of
persons, we could wish no end to't. But in respect of matters of state
'tis not convenient."

"For your princely entertainment I am greatly beholden," answered Lessingham. "For the delays, they are none of mine. So far
forth as it lay in me to do it, all might a been done and good-bye the
first morning."

"Yet it draggeth on," said the Duke. "And thence ensueth idleness. And from idleness, mischief. My lord, I mean this offer of
yours unto my lord Chancellor: I but heard on't this morning."

"Your grace will not hold me answerable," said Lessingham,

"for this failure to tell good news round the family. Howsoever, I've not been answered yet"; and he turned to Beroald.

"There, my lord, is my answer," said Beroald; and gave it him across the table.

Lessingham took the letter: "Is it yes?"

Beroald replied, "Your lordship hath the wit to know very well 'tis no."

"That is by so much the worser answer for us all," said Lessingham, "by how much it is the shorter: by a letter. What next, then? May be your grace hath thought on some way to please us all?"

Barganax sat suddenly forward in his chair. "We shall now," said he, "play no more at fair-and-softly, or king-by-your-leave. The Vicar's offers please nobody. You are grown too bold, my lord. Or did you think I should sit content ever in my curious pretty gardens, my delicate groves, while you fob me up with fair speeches? lie sunning myself for ever, while you hawk the regency about the town to find a higher bidder? Will you not offer it to my Lord Roder next? There he is. Come, ask him."

Lessingham said nothing, but folded his arms.

Barganax said, "You shall find my patience but a gathering deadly cloud. And thus it lightens into action: These great officers of state to right and left of me, bound by old allegiance to uphold the house of Fingiswold, stand in firm league with me to say nay to the Vicar when he requireth abatement of our powers for his behoof, whom we do utterly refuse and mistrust. Under the threats and wrongfulness of whose tyranny, the lord Admiral hath solemnly resigned and given over into my hand the regency of Meszria by testament royal conferred upon him. My Lord Lessingham, I take up that regency, but under suzerainty of no man. If the Vicar will receive me as his equal, lord of Meszria as he of Rerek: good, we are at one. If not, shortest is to say to him that I will maintain my dominion in his despite: in the midst of all his bloody ruff, I'll cope with him."

Lessingham, albeit strangely surprised and put out of his reckonings by this sudden turn, yet kept his countenance, thinking swiftly with himself. He swept his gaze from one to other, facing him across that table: the Duke like a warhorse that sniffs the morning: the Chancellor, lean-visaged and inscrutable, sitting upright and staring straight before him: Jeronimy with downcast look, elbows on table, his left hand propping his chin, his right twisting and untwisting a strand of the lank spare hair above his forehead: Roder, black and scowling: Barrian with flushed countenance, playing with his pen: Zepheles with jaw thrust forward, looking steadily at the Duke: Melates, half sprawled on his folded arms upon the table, looking steadily at Lessingham. "My lord Admiral," said Lessingham at length, "what will you say to this?"

"You were best address yourself to me, my lord," said Barganax. "From henceforth it is me you have to do with."

But Lessingham said, "Under your favour, my lord Duke, I must press this. You, my lord Admiral, not his grace, are named regent in the testament."

"I have resigned it up into his grace's hand. That, in a manner, endeth it," said Jeronimy. He did not raise his eyes to meet Lessingham's levelled steely gaze.

Then said Lessingham to the Chancellor, "Your lordship did write me a letter. By his grace's leave I will read it." He spread it upon the table and read it out. "I note this," he said, "in the Chancellor's letter: that it dealeth not at all with the point of law."

Beroald said: "It did not need."

"No," said Lessingham. "Yet to have argued the thing unlawful should much have strengthened it. My lord Chancellor, did you leave out that argument, because you were satisfied that the Vicar's claim of suzerainty is right in law?"

Beroald, looking steadily before him, made no reply.

"Much lieth on this. I pray you, answer," said Lessingham.

Beroald said, "I am nowise bounden to advise your lordship on points of law."

"That is true," said Lessingham. "And it must have tried your temper very much, my lord, when they whom you do, as in duty bound, advise, do the one (I mean my Lord Jeronimy) take your advice but durst not act upon't, whiles t'other doth but put it by like idle chatter, and acteth clean contrary."

The Chancellor said in an acid voice, "By these ifs and supposings you may gather against us what proofs you list. But since your lordship hath not had my advice upon these matters, nor any authority whereby to conclude what my advice would be, your lordship's observation wanteth substance, whether in fact or probability."

"My lord, I would but have your answer on point of fact: were you, or were you not, satisfied?"

The Chancellor held his peace.

"No need to bandy words on this," said Barganax, to end it. "We will not take our law from the Vicar."

"Nor from my lord Chancellor neither, as now appeareth," said Lessingham.

Out of an angry silence, Jeronimy spoke and said, "It is, in a manner, clean 'gainst all likelihood, nay, and not to be imagined, the King should have given over clean everything unto his Vicar, seeing the unkindness there was between them. Even grant the law were in a manner doubtful—"

But Lessingham brake in upon these pleasantnesses. "My lord Duke," said he: "I stand upon the law. Be not angry if I leave velvet words and oily compliment, and talk open. You have set at naught the King's testament. You have brow-beat the High Admiral until he is become your tool. The Chancellor will not answer me, but his silence hath damned by default your rotten pretences before all the world. Be not deceived," he said, and in the pauses between his words men were ware of each other's breathing: "the beginnings of things are weak and tender; but I do very well discern your grace's end and purpose, and it is to usurp the whole kingdom 'gainst your harmless sister. It resteth with my noble kinsman, as Lord Protector, to foil you in this. Your answer to me is war. In his highness' name, the Vicar, I do defy you. And I do call upon these great officers (upon you, my lord, and you, and you) to come back to their true allegiance unto the Queen's serenity, to the overthrow of you and your unlawful usurpation."

Now ever as he spoke, for all the heat of his words and violence, his perceptive mind was cool and busy, marking how much and in what diverse ways these sayings wrought alteration in them that heard them: what jealous mutual doubtings and inward questionings arose to insinuate, like ivy-shoots betwixt the stones of some tottering wall, divisions betwixt the Duke and his sworn confederates: how, perceiving such rifts to open or but the danger of their opening, the Meszrian lords seemed to draw back and view again their own security: how in the Admiral's eyes, as in an open book, was writ in great characters the digging up again of all the old doubts he had but so lately buried, of the Chancellor's truth and of the Duke's: and how, as unkind and nipping winds will find way through every cloak, the Duke himself seemed to be touched, behind all his jaunting bravery, by such unspoken uncertainties in these that he needs must trust to. These effects Lessingham, while he spoke, conjured and swayed but with the spell now here, now there, of a justly chosen word or look; not otherwise than as a master playing on the treble viol will lead the whole consort and build up so a living presence of music: from the deep theorbo such a figure, from the recorders such, and so the treble lutes to take up the canon, and the hautboy, the dulcimer, and the rebeck, every one in his turn, and so with a ritornello, each thus and thus, and always even exact as he, leading the broken consort, would have it.[3] Even so, perceiving these motions, these ruinous doubts and questionings, leap to life at his touch, did Lessingham taste in them a delicate pleasure.

With those last words spoken he ended, and the voice of his speech was like the rattle of iron swords. The Duke, whose chin had risen little by little higher and yet higher as, with smouldering eyes fixed on Lessingham, he had hearkened to these injuries, stood up

now with the smooth and measured stateliness of a leopard rising
from sleep. With a high and noble look upon his friends to left and
right of him, "Is my hand the weaker," he said, "because it is divided into many fingers? No, 'tis the more strongly nimble." So
saying, and turning again to Lessingham, he now with a formal
courtesy unsheathed his sword, raised it point upwards till the hilt
was level with his lips, kissed the hilt, and laid it naked on the table
with the point towards Lessingham. Lessingham stood up in silence
and, going through the like ceremony, laid his bare sword beside
the Duke's, pointing towards the Duke. So for a minute they stood,
facing each other across that table, eye to eye; as if the levin-shot
dark splendour of a storm-cloud, towering from the east, faced
across listening earth the many-coloured splendour of the westering
golden sun. And when at last the Duke spoke, it was as out of that
unfathomed harmony which is at once condition of such discords
and by them conditioned; ensphered and incarnate by them to a
more diviner music. There were but two only at that table who,
hearing him so speak, were not taken with wonderment, or with
fear, or dismay: and that was Lessingham and Doctor Vandermast.

The Duke said, "My Lord Lessingham, sith our friendship
must be but a summer friendship and its leaves drop off in autumn,
let's end it as fitteth persons of our quality. Let us trust each to
other's honour until noon to-morrow: you to me, that I will do no
dastard's work against your life or freedom: I to you, that, whether
by word nor deed, you will meddle no more with these high matters
until this day's truce be past."

"My lord Duke," said Lessingham, "I am content."

Then said the Duke, "I do intend a masque to-night, and a
water banquet upon the lake. Will your lordship honour me to be
my guest, and lie to-night in Acrozayana? Until to-morrow at noon
we will expel all affairs of state, chase all difficulties from our society:
one more day to sun it in pleasures in this hot summer-blink, last
merriment 'fore winter. Then you must go. And thereafter we shall
bloodily try out by war these differences we have these ten days to so
little purpose debated."

Amaury said in Lessingham's ear, "Beware, my lord. Let us be
gone."

But Lessingham's eye still met the Duke's, and he remembered
the counsel of Doctor Vandermast. "This offer," answered he, "is
what was to be looked for in so high-minded a prince, and I embrace and accept it. I well think there is not any other prince extant
should have made me the like offer, nor at whose hand I would
have accepted of it."

VII

A NIGHT-PIECE
ON AMBREMERINE

*Zayana lake at evening ✦ Campaspe: commerce
with a water nymph ✦ Moonrise ✦ Queen of
night ✦ The philosopher speaks ✦ Song of the
faun ✦ Our lady of blindness ✦ Anthea:
commerce with an oread ✦ The nature of
dryads, naiads, and oreads ✦ The dead shadow
✦ Divine philosophy ✦ Counsel of Vandermast.*

P EACE seemed to have laid her lily over all the earth
when, that evening, eight gondolas that carried the
Duke and his company put out from the water-gate under the western tower and steered into the sunset. In
the open water they spread into line abreast, making a
shallow crescent, horns in advance, and so passed on their way,
spacing themselves by intervals of some fifty paces to be within hail
but not to the overhearing of talk within the gondolas. Three or
four hundred paces ahead of them went a little caravel, bearing
aboard of her the Duke's bodyguard and the last and most delicate
wines and meats. Her sweeps were out, for in that windless air her
russet-coloured silken sails flapped the masts. From her poop
floated over the water the music of old love-ditties, waked in the
throb of silver lute-strings, the wail of haut-boys, and the flattering
soft singing of viols.

North and north-eastward, fainter and fainter in the distance, the foot-hills took on purple hues, like the bloom on grapes. High beyond the furthest hills, lit with a rosy light, the great mountains reared themselves that shut in the habited lands on the northward: outlying sentinels of the Hyperborean snows. So high they stood, that it might have been clouds in the upper air; save that they swam not as clouds, but persisted, and that their architecture was not cloud-like, but steadfast, as of buildings of the ancient earth, wide founded, bastion upon huger bastion, buttress soaring to battlement, wall standing back upon wall, roofridge and gable and turret and airy spire; and yet all as if of no gross substance, but rather the thin spirit of these, and their grandeur not the grandeur of clouds that pass, but of frozen and unalterable repose, as of Gods reclining on heaven's brink. Astern, Acrozayana faced the warm light. On the starboard quarter, half a mile to the north, on a beach at the end of the low wooded promontory that stretches far out into the lake there towards Zayana town, two women were bathing. The sunset out of that serene and cloudless sky suffused their limbs and bodies, their reflections in the water, the woods behind them, with a glory that made them seem no women of mortal kind, but dryads or oreads of the hills come down to show their beauties to the opening eyes of night and, with the calm lake for their mirror, braid their hair.

In the outermost gondola on the northern horn was Lessingham, his soul and senses lapped in a lotus-like contentment. For beside him reclined Madam Campaspe, a young lady in whose sprightly discourse he savoured, and in the sleepy little noises of the water under the prow, a delectable present that wandered towards a yet more delectable to come.

"The seven seas," he said, answering her: "ever since I was fifteen years old."

"And you are now—fifty?"

"Six times that," answered Lessingham gravely; "reckoned in months."

"With me," she said, "reckonings go always askew."

"Let's give over reckonings, then," said he, "and do it by example. I am credibly informed that I am pat of an age with your Duke."

"O, so old indeed? Twenty-five? No marvel you are so staid and serious."

"And you, madam?" said Lessingham. "How far in the decline?"

"Nay, 'tis me to ask questions," said she: "you to answer."

Idly Lessingham was looking at her hand which rested on the cushion beside him, gloved with a black scented gauntlet with falling cuff of open-work and flower-work of yellow zircons. "I am all expectation," he said.

Campaspe stole a glance at him. Her eyes were beady, like some shy creature's of the fields or woods. Her features, considered coldly one by one, had recalled strange deformities as of frogs or spiders; yet were they by those eyes welded to a kind of beauty. So might a queen of Elfland look, of an unfair, unhuman, yet most taking comeliness. "Well," said she: "how many straws go to goose-nest?"

"None, for lack of feet."

"O, unkind! You knew it afore. That cometh of this so much faring 'twixt land and land: maketh men too knowing." After a little, she said, "Tell me, is it not better here than in your northlands?"

" 'Tis at least much hotter," said Lessingham.

"And which liketh you better, my lord, hot or cold?"

"Must I answer of airs, or of ladies' hearts?"

"You must keep order: answer of that you spoke on."

"Nay," said Lessingham, " 'tis holiday. Let me be impertinent, and answer of that I set most store by."

"Then, to be courtly, you must say cold is best," said she. "For our fashion here is cold hearts, as the easier changed."

"Ah," he said: "I see there is something, madam, you are yet to learn."

"How, my lord? i' the fashion?"

"O no. Because I am a soldier, yet have I not such numbed and so clumsy hands for't as tell a lady she's out of fashion. I meant 'tis warm hearts, not cold, are most apt to change: fire at each fresh kindling."

"Here's fine doctrine," said she. "Do you rest it, pray, upon experience?"

He smiled. " 'Tis a first point of wisdom," he replied, "to affirm nought upon hearsay."

Campaspe sat suddenly forward, with a little murmur of pleasure: "O, my friend!" addressed, as Lessingham perceived, not to him but to a lady-duck with her seven young swimming close by in column ahead. For a fleeting instant, as she leaned eagerly across to watch them, her hand, put out to steady her, touched Lessingham's knee: a touch that, sylph-like and immaterial as a dream, sent a thousand serpents through his veins. The duck and her children took fright at the gondola, and, with a scutter of feet and wings, left a little wake of troubled water which showed the better, as a foil sets off a diamond, the placid smoothness of that lake.

"And how many foolish ladies ere now," said Campaspe, very demurely, "have you found to give open ear to these schoolings?"

"There, madam," said he, "you put me to a stand. They come and go, I suppose, with the changing of the moon."

"I was a fine fool," said she, "to come into this boat with you, my lord."

Lessingham smiled. "I think," he said, "I know an argument, when we come to it, shall satisfy you to the contrary." His eyes, half veiled under their long lashes, surveyed her now with a slow and disturbing gaze. It was as if the spirit that sat in them tasted, in a profound luxurious apprehension beyond the magic of mortal vintages, the wine of its own power: tasted it doubly, in her veins as in his own, attuning blood to blood. Then, turning his gaze from her to the back of his own hand, he looked at that awhile in silence as if there were there some comic engaging matter. "Howe'er that be," he said lightly at last, "you must remember, 'tis the same moon. That were a quaint folly, for love of last month's moon at the full, to have done with moonlight for ever."

"O, you can a game beside tennis, my lord, there's n'er a doubt," she said.

"I have beat the Duke ere now at tennis," said Lessingham.

"That is hard," said she. "But 'tis harder to beat him at this."

" 'Tis but another prime article of wisdom," said Lessingham, "ne'er to let past memories blunt the fine point of present pleasures. I am skilled," he said, "to read a lady's heart from her hand. Let me try." Campaspe, laughing, struggled against him as he would have drawn off her glove. "Moist palms argue warm hearts," he said in her ear. "Is that why you wear gloves, madam?"

"Nay, but I will not. Fie, shall the gondolier see us?"

"I am discretion itself," said Lessingham.

"You must learn, my lord," she said, putting away his hands, "if you would have me to spread your table, to fall to it nicely, not swallow it like flapdragons."

Lessingham said, close at her ear, "I'll be your scholar. Only but promise."

But Campaspe said, "No promises in Zayana: the Duke hath banned them. As for performance, why, respectful service, my lord, hath its payment here as in other lands."

Her voice had taken on a new delicacy: the voice of willow-trees beside still water when the falling wind stirs them. The great flattened ball of the sun touched the western hills. Lessingham took her under the chin with his hand and turned her face towards his. "I like little water-rats," he said. Her eyes grew big and frightened, like some little fieldish thing's that sees a hawk. For a minute she abode motionless. Then, as if with a sudden resolution, she pulled off her glove: offered her bare hand, palm upwards, to his lips. The gondola lurched sideways. The lady laughed, half smothered: "Nay, no more, my lord. Nay, and you will not have patience, you shall have nought, then."

"Jenny wrens: water-rats: willow-leaves sharp against the moon like little feet. Why is your laugh like a night breeze among willows? Do I not descry you? behind your mask of lady of presence: you and your 'friend.' Are you not these? Tell me: are you not?"

Each soft stroke of the gondolier's paddle at the stern came like one more drop in the cup of enchantment, which still brimmed and still did not run over. "It is not time, my lord. O yes, these, and other besides. But see, we shall land upon the instant. I pray you, have patience. In this isle of Ambremerine is bosky glades removed, flowery headlands; in two hours the moon will ride high; and she, you know—"

"And she," said Lessingham, "is an ancient sweet suggester of ingenious pleasures." He kissed the hand again. "Let us turn the cat in the pan: say, If I have patience I shall have all, then?"

In Campaspe's beady eyes he read his passport.

Their landing was near about the south-east point of that isle, in a little natural harbour, half-moon shaped and with a beach of fine white sand. The sun had gone down, and dusk gathered on the lake; eastward, pale blue smoke hung here and there over Zayana and the citadel; the walls and the roofs and towers were grown shadowy and dim; their lamps came out like stars. In the north, the great peaks still held some light. A wide glade went up into the isle from that harbour in gently sloping lawns, shut in on all but the water side by groves of cypress-trees: pillar-like boles and dense spires so tangled, drenched, and impregnate with thick darkness that not mid-day itself might pierce nor black night deepen their elemental gloom. In the midst of that glade, on a level lawn where in their thousands daisies and little yellow cinquefoils were but now newly folded up and gone to sleep, tables were set for the feast. The main table faced south to the harbour, where the gondolas and the caravel, with their lofty stems and stern-posts and their lights, some red some green, floated graceful over their graceful images in the water. Two shorter tables ran down from that table's either end: the one faced Zayana and the night, and the other westward to the leavings of the sunset, above which the evening star, high in a pellucid heaven of pale chrysolite, burned like a diamond from Aphrodite's neck.

The tables were spread with damask, and set forth with a fish dinner: oysters and lobsters, crayfish both great and small, trout, tunny, salmon, sturgeon, lampreys and caviare, all in fair golden dishes, with mushrooms besides and sparrow-grass, cockscombs and truffles, and store of all manner of delicious fruits, and wines of all kind in great bowls and beakers of crystal and silver and gold: dry and ancient wines golden and tawny, good to sharpen the stomach and to whet the edge of wit; and red wines the heavy sweetness whereof, full of the colour of old sunsets and clinging to the goblet like blood, is able to mellow thought and steady the senses to a quiet where the inner voices may be heard; and wines the foam whereof whispers of that eternal sea and of that eternal spring-time towards which all memories return and all hearts' desires for ever. Fifty little boys, yellow-haired, clothed all in green, planted and tended torches behind the tables to give light to the feasters. Steady was the burning of those torches in the still summer air, with ever a little movement of their light, like the fall and swell of a girl's bosom; and the scent of their burning mingled in wafts with the flower scents and wood scents and the dew-laden breath of evening.

So now they made merry and supped under the sky. Scarcely was the sunset's last ember burned out westward, and night scarce well awake in the eastern heavens behind Zayana town, when from that quarter a bower of light began to spread upward, into which stepped at length, like a queen to lead night's pageant, the lady moon, and trailed her golden train across those sleeping waters. At that, their talk was stilled for a minute. Barganax, sitting in the midst of the cross table with Lessingham on his right, looked at Fiorinda, beside him on his left, as she looked at the moon. "Your looking-glass," he said, under his breath. Her face altered and she smiled, saying, with a lazy shrug of the shoulders, "One of!"

"My Lord Lessingham," said Campaspe: "imagine me potent in art magic, able to give you the thing you would. Whether would you then choose pleasure or power?"

"That question," answered he, "in such company and on such a night, and most of all by moonrise, I can but answer in the words of the poet:

"My pleasure is my power to please my mistress:
My power is my pleasure in that power."

"A roundabout answer," said the Duke: "full of wiles and guiles. Mistrust it, madam."

"Can your grace better it then?" said Campaspe.

"Most easily. And in one word: pleasure."

Fiorinda smiled.

"Your ladyship will second me," said the Duke. "What's power but for the procuring of wise, powerful and glorious pleasures? What else availeth my dukedom? 'Las, I should make very light account thereof, as being a thing of very small and base value, save that it is a mean unto that rich and sunny diamond that outlustreth all else."

"Philosophic disputations," said Fiorinda, "do still use to awake strange longings in me."

"Longings?" said the Duke. "You are mistress of our revels to-night. Breathe but the whisper of a half-shapen wish; lightning shall be slow to our suddenness to perform it."

"For the present need," said that lady, "a little fruit would serve."

"Framboises?" said the Duke, offering them in a golden dish.

"No," she said, looking upon them daintily: "they have too many twiddles in them: like my Lord Lessingham's distich."

"Will your ladyship eat a peach?" said Melates.

"I could," she said. "And yet, no. Clingstone, 'tis too great trouble: freestone, I like them not. Your grace shall give me a summer poppering."

The Duke sent his boy to fetch them from the end of the table. "You shall peel it for me," she said, choosing one.

Barganax, as drunk with some sudden exhalation of her beauty, the lazy voice, the lovely pausing betwixt torchlight and moonlight of fastidious jewelled fingers above the dish of pears, was taken with a trembling that shook the dish in his hand. Mastering which, "I had forgot," he said with a grave courtesy, "that you do favour this beyond all fruits else."

"Forgot? Is it then so long ago your grace and I reviewed these matters? And indeed I had little fault to find with your partialities, nor you I think with mine."

Lessingham, looking on at this little by-play, tasted in it a fine and curious delight; such delight as, more imponderable than the dew-sparkles on grass about sunrise or the wayward airs that lift the gossamer-spiders' threads, dances with fairy feet, beauty fitted to beauty, *allegretto scherzando*,[1] in some great master's music. Only for the whim to set such divisions a-trip again, he spoke and said: "If your ladyship will judge between us, I shall justify myself against the Duke that, would pleasure's self have had me, I should a refused to wed her. For there be pleasures base, illiberal, nasty, and merely hoggish. How then shall you choose pleasure per se?"

"By the same argument, how power per se?" replied the Duke. "What of the gardener's dog, that could not eat the cabbages in the garden and would suffer none else to do so? Call you that power good? I think I have there strook you into the hazard, my lord. Or at least, 'tis change sides and play for the chase."

"The chase is mine, then," said Lessingham. "For if power be but sometimes good, even so is pleasure. It must be noble pleasure, and the noblest pleasure is power."

Fiorinda daintily bit a piece out of her pear.

"Pray you honour us, madam, to be our umpire," said Lessingham.

She smiled, saying, "It is not my way to sit in judgement. Only to listen."

Barganax said, "But will you listen to folly?"

"O yes," answered she. "There was often more good matter in one grain of folly than in a peck of wisdom."

"Ha! that hath touched you, Vandermast," said the Duke.

That aged man, sitting at the outer end of the eastern table betwixt Anthea and the young Countess Rosalura, laughed in his beard. The Lady Fiorinda lifted her eyebrows with a questioning look first upon him, then upon the Duke, then upon Lessingham. "Is he wise?" she said. "I had thought he was a philosopher. Truly, I could listen to him a whole summer's night and ne'er tire of his preposterous nonsense."

"An old fool," said Vandermast, "that is yet wise enough to serve your ladyship."

"Does that need wisdom?" she said, and looked at the moon. Lessingham, watching her face, thought of that deadly Scythian queen who gave Cyrus his last deep drink of blood.[2] Yet, even so thinking, he was the more deeply aware, in the caressing charm of her voice, of a mind that savoured the world delicately and simply, with a quaint, amused humour; so might some demure and graceful bird gracefully explore this way and that, accepting or rejecting with an equable enjoyment. "Does that need wisdom?" she said again. And now it was as if from that lady's lips some unheard song, some unseen beauty, had stolen abroad and, taking to itself wings, mounted far from earth, far above the columnar shapes of those cypresses that, huge and erect, stood round that dim garden; until the vast canopy of night was all filled as with an impending flowering of unimagined wonder.

"There is no other wisdom than that: not in heaven or earth or under the earth, in the world phenomenal or the world noumenal, *sub specie temporali* or *sub specie aeternitatis*.[3] There is no other," said Vandermast, in a voice so low that none well heard him, save only the Countess close by on his right. And she, hearing, yet not understanding, yet apprehending in her very bowels the tenour of his words, as a reed bending before the wind might apprehend dimly somewhat of what betided in the wind-ridden spaces without to bend and to compel it, sought Medor's hand and held it fast.

There was silence. Then Medor said, "What of love?"

Vandermast said, as to himself, but the Countess Rosalura heard it: "There is no other power."

"Love," said Lessingham, cool and at ease again after the passing of that sudden light, "shall aptly point my argument. Here, as otherwhere, power ruleth. For what is a lover without power to win his mistress? or she without power to hold her lover?" His hand, as he spoke, tightened unseen about Campaspe's yielding waist. His eyes, carelessly roving, as he spoke, from face to face of that company, came to a stop, meeting Anthea's where she sat beside the learned doctor. The tawny wealth of her deep hair was to the cold beauty of her face as a double curtain of fulvid glory. Her eyes caught and held his gaze with a fascination, hard, bold, and inscrutable.

"I have been told that Love," said Fiorinda, "is a more intricate game than tennis; or than soldiership; or than politicians' games, my Lord Lessingham."

Anthea, with a little laugh, bared her lynx-like teeth. "I was remembered of a saying of your ladyship's," she said.

Fiorinda lifted an eyebrow, gently pushing her wine-cup towards the Duke for him to fill it.

"That a lover who should think to win his mistress by power," said Anthea, "is like an old dried-up dotard who would be young again by false hair, false teeth, and skilful painting of his face: thus, and with a good stoup of wine, but one thing he lacketh, and that the one thing needful."

"Did I say so indeed?" said Fiorinda. "I had forgot it. In truth, this is strange talk, of power and pleasure in love," she said. "There is a garden, there is a tree in the garden, there is a rose upon the tree.[4] Can a woman not keep her lover without she study always to please him with pleasure? Pew! then let her give up the game. Or shall my lover think with pleasing of me to win me indeed? Faugh! he payeth me then; doth he think I am for hire?"

Barganax sitting beside her, not looking at her, his shoulder towards her, his elbow on the table, his fingers in an arrested stillness touching his mustachios, gazed still before him as though all his senses listened to the last scarce-heard cadence of the music of that lady's voice.

Fiorinda, in that pause, looked across to Doctor Vandermast. Obedient to her look, he stood up now and raised a hand twice and thrice above his head as in sign to somewhat to come out of the shadows that stirred beyond the torchlight. The moon rode high now over Zayana, and out of torchbeam and moonbeam and starbeam was a veil woven that confounded earth and sky and water into an immateriality of uncertain shade and misty light. At Vandermast's so standing up, the very night seemed to slip down into some deeper pool of stillness, like the silent slipping of an otter down from the bank into the black waters. Only the purr of a nightjar came from the edge of the woods. And now on the sudden they at the tables were ware of somewhat quick, that stood in the confines of the torchlight and the shadowy region without; of man-like form, but little of stature, scarce reaching with its head to the elbow of a grown man; with shaggy hairy legs and goat's feet, and with a sprouting of horns like a young goat's upon its head; and there was in its eyes the appearance as of red coals burning. Piercing were the glances of those eyes, as they darted in swift succession from face to face (save that before Fiorinda's it dropped its gaze as if in worship),

and piercing was the music of the song it sang: the song that lovers
and great poets have ravished their hearts to hear since the world
began: a night-song, bittersweet, that shakes the heart of darkness
with longings and questionings too tumultuous for speech to fit or
follow; and in that song the listener hears echoing up the abysses of
eternity voices of men and women unborn answering the voices of
the dead.[5]

Surely, hearkening to that singing, all they sat like as amazed or
startled out of sleep. Lover clung to lover: Amaury to velvet-eyed
Violante, Myrrha to Zapheles, Bellafront to Barrian. Lessingham's
encircling arm drew closer about his Campaspe: her breast beneath
the silk under his hand was a tremulous dove: her black eyes rested
as though in soft accustomed contemplation upon the singer.
Pantasilea, with heavy lids and heavy curled lips half closed, as in
half eclipse of the outward sense, lay back sideways on Melates's
shoulder. Medor held gathered to him like a child his sweet young
Countess. Beyond them, in the outermost place of the eastern table,
Anthea sat upright and listening, her hair touching with some stray
tendrils of its glory the sleeve of old Vandermast's gaberdine where
he stood motionless beside her.

Only the Lady Fiorinda seemed to listen fancy-free to that singing, even as the cold moon, mistress of the tides, has yet no part in
their restless ebb and flow, but, taking her course serene far above
the cloudy region of the air, surveys these and all earthly things with
equal eye, divine and passionless. The Duke, sitting back, had this
while watched her from the side from under his faun-like eyebrows,
his hand moving as if with chalk or brush. He leaned nearer now,
giving over that painting motion: his right elbow on the table, his
left arm resting, but not to touch her, on the back of her chair. The
voice of the singer, that was become as the echoes of a distant music
borne on the breeze from behind a hill, now made a thin obbligato
to the extreme passionate love that spoke in the Duke's accents like
the roll of muffled thunder as, low in her ear, he began to say:

> "O forest of dark beasts about the base
>   Of some white peak that dreams in the Empyrean:
> O hare's child sleeping by a queen's palace,
>   'Mid lily-meadows of some isle Lethean:
> Barbaric, beastly, virginal, divine:
>   Fierce feral loveliness: sweet secret fire:
> Last rest and bourne of every lovely line:
>   —All these Thou art, that art the World's Desire."

The deep tones of the Duke's voice, so speaking, were hushed
to the quivering superficies of silence, beneath which the darkness
stirred as with a rushing of arpeggios upon muted strings. In the

corner of that lady's mouth, as she listened, the minor diabolus, dainty and seductive, seemed to turn and stretch in its sleep. Lessingham, not minded to listen, yet heard. Darkly he tasted in his own flesh Barganax's secret mind: in what fashion this Duke lived in that seeming woman's life far sweetlier than in his own. He leaned back to look upon her, over the Duke's shoulder. He saw now that she had glow-worms in her hair. But when he would have beheld her face, it was as if spears of many-coloured light, such light as, like the halo about the moon, is near akin to darkness, swept in an endless shower outward from his vision's centre; and now when he would have looked upon her he saw but these outrushings, and in the fair line of vision not darkness indeed but the void: a solution of continuity: nothing.

As a man that turns from the halcyon vision to safe verities, he turned to his Campaspe. Her lips invited sweetly: he bent to them. With a little ripple of laughter, they eluded him, and under his hand, with soft arched back warm and trembling, was the water-rat in very deed.

About the north-western point of that island there was a garden shadowed with oaks ten generations old and starproof cedars and delicate-limbed close-tufted strawberry-trees. Out of its leafy darknesses nightingale answered nightingale, and nightflowers, sweet-mouthed like brides in their first sleep, mixed their sweetness with the breath of the dews of night.[6] It was now upon the last hour before midnight. From the harbour to the southward rose the long slumbrous notes of a horn, swelling, drawing their heavy sweetness across the face of the night sky. Anthea stood up, slender as a moonbeam in those silent woods. "The Duke's horn," she said. "We must go back; unless you are minded to lodge in this isle tonight, my Lord Lessingham."

Lessingham stood up and kissed her hand. For a minute she regarded him in silence from under her brow, her eyes burning steadily, her chin drawn down a little: an unsmiling lip-licking look. Then giving him her arm she said, as they turned to be gone, "There is discontent in your eyes. You are dreaming on somewhat without me and beyond."

"Incomparable lady," answered he, "call it a surfeit. If I am discontented, it is with the time, that draweth me from these high pleasures to where, as cinders raked up in ashes—"

"O no nice excuses," she said. "I and Campaspe are not womankind. Truly, 'tis but at Her bidding we durst not disobey we thus have dallied with such as you, my lord."

His mustachios stirred.

"You think that a lie?" she said. "The unfathomed pride of mortals!"

Lessingham said, "My memories are too fiery clear."

They walked now under the obscurity of crowding cypresses. "It is true," said Anthea, "that you and Barganax are not altogether as the common rout of men. This world is yours, yours and his, did you but know it. And did you know it, such is the folly of mortals, you would straight be out of conceit with it and desire another. But you are well made, not to know these things. See, I tell it you, yet you believe it not. And though I should tell you from now till dawn, yet you would not believe." She laughed.

"You are pleasantly plain with me," said Lessingham after a pause. "You can be fierce. So can I. I do love your fierceness, your bites and scratches, madam. Shall I be plain too?" He looked down; her face, level with his shoulder, wore a singular look of benign tranquillity. "You," he said, "(and I must not omit Mistress Campaspe), have let me taste this night such pleasures as the heroes in Elysium, I well think, taste nought sweeter. Yet would I have more; yet, what more, I know not."

Without looking at him, she made a little mow. "In your erudite conversation, my lord, I have tasted this night such pleasures as I am by nature accustomed to. I desire no more. I am, even as always I am, contented."

"As always?" said he.

"Is 'always' a squeeze of crab-orange in your cup, my lord? 'Tis wholesome truth, howsoe'er. And now, in our sober voyaging back to Zayana, with the learn'd doctor conducting of us, I do look for no less bliss than—: but this you will think ungracious?"

She looked up, with a little pressure of her arm on his. His eyes, when he turned his face to hers, were blurred and unseeing.

The path came into the open now, as they crossed the low backbone of the island. They walked into a flood of moonlight; on their left, immeasurably far away, the great snow ranges stood like spirits in the moon-drenched air. Anthea said, "Behold that mountain, my lord, falling away to the west in saw-toothed ridges a handbreadth leftward of the sycamore-tree. That is Ramosh Arkab; and I say to you, I have dwelt there 'twixt wood and snowfield ten million years."

They were now come down to the harbour. The cypress-shadowed glade lay empty: the tables taken up where their banquet had been: the torches and the feasters gone. Far away on the water the lights of the gondolas showed where they took their course homeward to Zayana. Under an utter silence and loneliness of moonlight the lawns sloped gently to the lake. One gondola only lay by the landingstage. Beside it waited that aged man. With a grave obeisance he greeted Lessingham; they went aboard all three, loosed, and put out. There was no gondolier. Doctor Vandermast would have taken the paddle, but Lessingham made him sit beside Anthea in the seat of honour, and himself, sitting on the fore-deck with his feet in the boat's bottom, paddled her stern-foremost. So they had passage over those waters that were full of drowned stars and secret unsounded deeps of darkness. Something broke the smoothness on the starboard bow; Lessingham saw, as they neared it, that it was the round head of an otter, swimming towards Ambremerine. It looked at them with its little face and hissed. In a minute it was out of eyeshot astern.

"My beard was black once," said Vandermast. "Black as yours, my lord." Lessingham saw that the face of that old man was blanched in the moonlight, and his eyes hidden as in ocean caves or deep archways of some prison-house, so that only with looking upon him a man might not have known for sure whether there were eyes in truth within those shadows or but void eye-sockets and eclipsing darkness. Anthea sat beside him in a languorous grace. She trailed a finger in the water, making a little rippling noise, pleasant to the ear. Her face, too, was white under the moon, her hair a charmed labyrinth of moonbeams, her eyes pits of fire.

"Dryads," said Vandermast, after a little, "are in two kinds, whereof the one is more nearly consanguineous with the more madefied and waterish natures, naiads namely and nereids; but the other kind, having their habitation nearer to the meteoric houses and the cold upper borders of woods appropinquate to the snows and the gelid ice-streams of the heights, do derive therefrom some qualities of the oreads or mountain nymphs.[7] I have indulged my self-complacency so far as to entertain hopes, my lord, that, by supplying for your entertainment one of either sort, and discoursing so by turns two musics to your ear, *andante piacevole e lussurioso* and then *allegro appassionato*,[8] I may have opened a more easier way to your lordship's perfect satisfaction and profitable enjoyment of this night's revelries."

That old man's talk, droning slow, made curious harmonies with the drowsy body of night; the dip and swirl and dip again of Lessingham's paddle; the drip of water from the blade between the strokes.

"Where did your lordship forsake my little water-rat?" he asked in a while.

"She was turned willow-wren at the last," answered Lessingham.

"Such natures," said Vandermast, "do commonly suck much gratification out of change and the variety of perceptible form and corporeity. But I doubt not your lordship, with your more settled preferences and trained appetites, found her most acceptable in form and guise of a woman?"

"She did me the courtesy," answered Lessingham, "to maintain that shape for the more part of our time together."

They proceeded in silence. Vandermast spoke again. "You find satisfaction, then, in women, my lord?"

"I find in their society," Lessingham answered, "a pleasurable interlude."

"That," said that learned man, "agreeth with the conclusion whereunto, by process of ratiocination, I was led upon consideration of that stave or versicule recited by your lordship about one hour since, and composed, if I mistake not, by your lordship. Went it not thus?

> "Anthea, wooed with flatteries,
> To please her lover's fantasies,
> Unlocks her bosom's treasuries.—
> Ah! silver apples like to these
> Ne'er grew, save on those holy trees
> Tended by nymphs Hesperides."

"What's this?" said Lessingham, and there was danger in his voice.

"You must not take it ill," said Vandermast, "that this trifle, spoke for her ear only and the jealous ear of night, was known to me without o'erhearing. Yourself are witness that neither you nor she did tell it me, and indeed I was half a mile away, so scarce could a heard it. A little cold: a little detached, methought, for a love-poem. But indeed I do think your lordship is a man of deeds. Do you find satisfaction, then, in deeds?"

"Yes," answered he.

"Power," said that learned doctor: "power; which maketh change. Yea, but have you considered the power that is in Time, young man? to change the black hairs of your beard to blanched hairs, like as mine: and the last change of Death? that, but with waiting and expecting and standing still, overcometh all by drawing of all to its own likeness. Dare your power face that power, to go like a bridegroom to annihilation's bed? Let me look at your eyes."

Lessingham, whose eyes had all this while been fixed upon Vandermast's, said, "Look then."

The face of the night was altered now. A cool drizzle of rain dimmed the moon: the gondola seemed to drift a-beam, cut off from all the world else upon desolate waters. Vandermast's voice came like the soughing of a distant wind: "The hairless, bloodless, juiceless, power of silence," he said, "that consumeth and abateth and swalloweth up lordship and subjection, favour and foulness, lust and satiety, youth and eld, into the dark and slubbery mess of nothingness." Lessingham saw that the face of that old man was become now as a shrivelled death's-head, and his eyes but windows opening inwards upon the horror of an empty skull. And that lynx-eyed mountain nymph, fiercely glaring, crouching sleek and spotted beside him, was become now a lynx indeed, with her tufted slender ears erect and the whiskers moving nervously right and left of her snarling mouth. And Vandermast spake loud and hoarse, crying out and saying, "You shall die young, my Lord Lessingham. Two years, a year, may be, and you shall die. And then what help shall it be that you with your high gifts of nature did o'ersway great ones upon earth (as here but to-day you did in Acrozayana), and did ride the great Vicar of Rerek, your curst and untamed horse, till he did fling you to break your neck, and die at the last? What is fame to the deaf dust that shall then be your delicate ear, my lord? What shall it avail you then that you had fair women? What shall it matter though they contented you never? seeing there is no discontent whither you go down, my lord, neither yet content, but the empty belly of darkness enclosing eternity upon eternity. Or what shall even that vision beyond the veil profit you (if you saw it indeed tonight, then ere folk rose from table), since that is but impossibility, fiction and vanity, and shall then be less than vanity itself: less than the dust of you in the worm's blind mouth? For all departeth, all breaketh and perisheth away, all is hollowness and nothing worth ere it sink to very nothing at last."

"I saw nought," said Lessingham. "What is that Lady Fiorinda then?" His voice was level; only the strokes of his paddle came with a more steadier resolution, may be, of settled strength as that old man spoke.

The gondola lurched sideways. Lessingham turned swiftly from his outstaring of that aged man to bring her safe through a sudden turmoil of the waters that rose now and opened downward again to bottomless engulfings. Pale cliffs superimpended in the mist and the darkness, and fires burned there, with the semblance as of corpse-fires. And above those cliffs was the semblance of icy mountains, and streams that rolled burning down them of lava, making a sizzling in the water that was heard high above the voice of the waves; and Lessingham beheld walking shrouded upon the cliffs faceless figures, beyond the stature of human kind, that seemed to despair and lament, lifting up skinny hands to the earless heaven. And while he beheld these things, there was torn a ragged rift in the clouds, and there fled there a bearded star, baleful in the abyss of night. And now there was thunder, and the noise as of a desolate sea roaring upon the coasts of death. Then, as a thought steps over the threshold of oblivion, all was gone; the cloudless summer night held its breath in the presence of its own inward blessedness: the waters purred in their sleep under the touch of Anthea's idly trailing finger.

Lessingham laid down his paddle and clapped his right hand to his hip; but they had gone unweaponed to that feast. Without more ado he with an easy swiftness, scarcely to rock the boat, had gotten in his left hand the two wrists of Vandermast: his right hand slid up beneath the long white beard, and fumbled the doctor's skinny throat. "Scritch-owl," he said, "you would unman me,[9] ha? with your sickly bodings? You have done it, I think: but you shall die for't." The iron strength of his fingers toyed delicately about that old man's weasand.

Very still sat Doctor Vandermast. He said, "Suffer me yet to speak."

"Speak and be sudden," said Lessingham.

Surely that old man's eyes looked now into his with a brightness that was as the lifting up of day. "My Lord Lessingham," he said, *"per realitatem et perfectionem idem intelligo:* in my conceit, reality and perfection are one. If therefore your lordship have suffered an inconvenience, you are not to revenge it upon me: your disorder proceedeth but from partial apprehension."

"Ha! but did not you frame and present me, with fantasticoes? did not you spit your poison?" said Lessingham. "Do not mistake me: I am not afeared of my death. But I do feel within me somewhat, such as I ne'er did meet with its like aforrow, and I know not what it is, if it be not some despair. Wherefore, teach me to apprehend fully, you were best, and that presently. Or like a filthy fly I'll finger you off to hell." Upon which very word, he strangely took his fingers from the lean weasand of that old man and let go the lean wrists.

Vandermast said, as if to himself, *"Cum mens suam impotentiam imaginatur, eo ipso contristatur:* when the mind imagineth its own impotence, it by that only circumstance falleth into a deep sadness. My lord," he said, raising his head to look Lessingham in the face, "I did think you had seen. Had you so seen, these later sights I did present you, and these prognostications of decay, could not have cankered so your mind: they had been then but as fumadoes, hot and burning spices, to awake your appetite the more and prepare you for that cup whereof he that drinketh shall for ever thirst and for ever be satisfied; yea, and without it there is no power but destroyeth and murdereth itself at last, nor no pleasure but disgusteth in the end, like the stench of the dead."

"Words," said Lessingham. "The mouth jangleth, as lewd as a lamp that no light is in. I tell you, I saw nought: nought but outrushing lights and dazzles. And now, I feel my hand upon a latch, and you, in some manner I understand not, by some damned sleight, withholding me. Teach me, as you said but now, to apprehend fully. But if not, whether you be devil or demigod or old drivelling disard as I am apt to think you: by the blessed Gods, I will tear you into pieces."

Anthea widened her lips and laughed. "Now you are in a good

vein, my lord. Shall I bite his throat out?" She seemed to slaver at the mouth. "You are a lynx, go," said Lessingham. It was as if the passion of his anger was burnt out, like a fire of dead leaves kindled upon a bed of snow.

Vandermast's lean hands twisted and unclasped their fingers together in his lap. "I had thought," he said, to himself aloud, in the manner of old men, "her ladyship would have told me. O inexorable folly to think so! Innumerable laughter of the sea: ever changing: shall I never learn?"

"What is that lady?" said Lessingham.

Vandermast said, "You did command me, my lord, to learn you to apprehend fully. But here, *in limine demonstrationis,* upon the very threshold, appeareth a difficulty beyond solution, in that your lordship is instructed already in things contingent and apparent, *affectiones, actiones,* phenomenal actualities *rei politicae et militaris,* the council chamber and the camp, *puella-puellae* and matters conducive thereunto.[10] But in things substantial I find you less well grounded, and here it is beyond my art to carry you further seeing my art is the doctor's practice of reason; because things substantial are not known by reason but by perception: *perceptio per solam suam essentiam;* and *omnis substantia est necessario infinita:* all substance, in its essence, infinite."

"Leave this discourse," said Lessingham, "which, did I understand its drift, should make me, I doubt not, as wise as a capon. Answer me: of what *substantia* or *essentia* is that lady?"

Doctor Vandermast lowered his eyes. "She is my Mistress," he said.

"That, to use your gibberish, old sir, is *per accidens,*" said Lessingham. "I had supposed her the Duke's mistress: the Devil's mistress too, belike. But *per* essence, what is she? Why did my eyes dazzle when I would have looked upon her but at that moment to-night? since many a time ere then I easily enough beheld her. And why should aught lie on it, that they did so dazzle? Come, we have dealt with seeming women to-night that be nymphs of the lakes and mountains, taking at their will bird-like shapes and beastly. What is she? Is she such an one? Tell me, for I will know."

"No," said Vandermast, shaking his head. "She is not such as these."

Eastward, ahead, Lessingham saw how, with the dancings of summer lightnings, the sky was opened on a sudden behind the towers and rampires of Acrozayana. For that instant it was as if a veil had been torn to show where, built of starbeams and empyreal light, waited, over all, the house of heart's desire.

That learned man was searching now beneath the folds of his gaberdine, and now he drew forth a little somewhat and, holding it carefully in his fingers, scanned it this way and that and raised it to view its shape against the moon. Then, giving it carefully to Lessingham, "My lord," he said, "take this, and tender it as you would a precious stone; for indeed albeit but a little withered leaf, there be few jewels so hard to come by or of such curious virtue. Because I have unwittingly done your lordship an ill service to-night, and because not wisdom itself could conduct you to that apprehension you do stand in need of, I would every deal I may to serve and further you. And because I know (both of my own judgement and by certain weightier confirmations of my art) the proud integrity of your lordship's mind and certain conditions of your inward being, whereby I may, without harm to my own fealty, trust you thus, albeit to-morrow again our enemy: therefore, my Lord Lessingham, behold a thing for your peace. For the name of this leaf is called *sferra cavallo*,[11] and this virtue it hath, to break and open all locks of steel and iron. Take it then to your bed, my lord, now in the fair guest-chamber prepared for you in Acrozayana. And if, for the things you saw and for the things you saw not to-night, your heart shall be troubled, and sleep stand iron-eyed willing not to lie down with you and fold her plumes about your eyelids, then if you will, my lord, taking this leaf, you may rise and seek. What I may, that do I, my lord, giving you this. There shall, at least, no door be shut against you. But when night is done and day cometh you must by all means, (and this lieth upon your honour), burn the leaf. It is to do you good I give it unto you, and for your peace. Not for a weapon against my own sovereign lord."

Lessingham took it and examined it well in the light of the moon. Then, with a noble look to Vandermast, he put it away like a jewel in his bosom.

VIII

SFERRA CAVALLO

Pursuit of a night vision ◆ *Fiorinda on the
dream-stone* ◆ *Whirlpool* ◆ *Mistress of
Mistresses* ◆ *"North, in Rialmar."*

N THE deep and dead time of the night there went
forth a dream through the gate of horn,[1] by permission
of Her that is, and is to come. And the dream, treading
the viewless ways, came down to the land of Meszria
and to the citadel that overlooks Zayana town, and entered and stood in the fair guest-chamber at the foot of the golden
bed, the posts whereof were fashioned in the likeness of hippogriffs,
gold and with eyes of sapphire. And upon that bed was the Lord
Lessingham but even now fallen into an uncertain slumber. And the
dream put on beauty, and, to temper that beauty, the appearance of
moonlight as a gown and of a girdle as of silvery moonlight upon
snow mountains, and the appearance as of a bodice woven of those
stars which men call Berenice's Hair:[2] stars of so delicate a shimmering brightness that the gross direct look may ill perceive it, but is
best gazed on askance or indirect. But by ordainment of the Gods,
there was drawn about the head of that dream and across its face a
veil of light, as darkness inscrutable, or as wonder overwritten upon
wonder so as none might read. And the dream spake with the voice
that a sleeper may hear, too fine for waking ears (unless, indeed, for
a moment they wake and dream at once), saying: *I promised and I will
perform.*

Lessingham, hearing these words, and knowing that voice,

moved and opened his eyes and awoke to the night and the lonely chamber.

It was not as if a dream had fled: rather truth, that had stood but a moment since ready to cast off her cloak. Like a man over-taken by swift-darkening night in a bog through which a path leads, hard to find even by day and now lost though but a moment since he trod it, he seemed to plunge and stagger without a guide. Betwixt sleeping and waking, he clad himself, girt on his sword, took from beneath the pillow that little leaf, and, filled with that vision, blundered towards the door. The great iron key stood in the lock where, upon going to bed, he had turned it. With the touch of that leaf the locked door swung open before him like a door that opens in a dream. As a dreamer with hastening undirected noiseless foot-steps follows an unknown quest, Lessingham, not knowing well whether he dreamed or no, followed he knew not what, save that, may be, there was nought else in earth or heaven worth the follow-ing. And as he strode or stumbled along dim corridors, up winding shadowy stairs, across moonlit courts, still there sprang open before him both lock and bolt in a suddenness of dream-like stillness. And ever as each door opened, it opened upon emptiness: quiet empty rooms of darkness or silent moonlight.

In the mean time, not Lessingham alone waked in Acrozayana. In the spacious throne-room the wings that lifted their glory above the dream-stone seemed to quiver a little. The blackness of the great twisted pillars, the poppied frieze, the walls, the very floor of mar-ble, seemed to waver like the texture of a dream. It was as if, in that midnight hour, some deeper drowsiness of moonset, that held its breath to listen to its own stillness, hung in the perfumed air, cir-cling, tending in slow eddies ever to one centre. And there, as it had been glamour's self made flesh for a season, to be queen of all scents and furry wings, dews, and silences, and star-shimmering depths, and of all wild hearts' desires that cry to the heart of summer night, Fiorinda sat throned upon the dream-stone.

She had let fall her cloak, which lay tumbled in waves of sea-green velvet and silver about her feet and about the cushions where she sat. Her arms, bare to the shoulder, had an ivory pallour and an ivory smoothness: pillars at the temple door. Her finger-nails were as shells new-taken from some enchanted sea: the fingers as branched white coral from that sea's treasure-groves, marvellously transmuted from its native insensate elegance to be the ornament and living instrument of that lady's life and her inward thought, and wearing the livery of her own aching loveliness. Her gown was of gauzy silk coloured like moonlight, pleated with a hundred pleats and a-glitter with silver sequins and a maze of spiral tendrils made of little beads of jet. A girdle of corded silver lace curved low on her hips. Her bodice, of the like stuff save that here were diamonds instead of sequins amid the spirals, barely contained as with a double cup its warm and breathing treasures. Betwixt bodice and girdle the sweet bare interspace was a thing to shame all jewels, to make driven snow seem sullied, and magnolia petals coarse and common, beside the lily of its heavenly purity.

Upon her left, below her, a pace or so removed, Barganax sat sideways on the steps of the throne, whence he might behold all at a look her beauty: strange, complex, discordant in its elements, yet in the living whole satisfying and perfect.

"More," he said.

"I am tired of talking," answered she.

"Look at me, then," said the Duke.

She did so, with a little finical inclination of the head, as a rose might take notice of a butterfly, and looked away again.

"Were it not that I do suspect 'twas your own devilish device to trip me up, the better to flaunt your power upon me, I should be sorry," said the Duke, after a minute's silence.

"Repentance," said Fiorinda, "is a thing not easy to forgive, in a great man."

"Will you forgive the deed?" he said. "For your forgiveness, may be, shall be a sunshine to drink up these mists."

"I'll have it named first," she said.

"I'll not name it," said the Duke. "It was an abomination, a woe, a miscreative dream."

"A nameless abomination! I must pursue this." There was in her voice a voluptuous lazy languor. "And it befell—when?"

"Upon Friday of last week."

"And this is Monday!" she said. A whole masque of little gad-flies of unseizable conscient comedy danced forth in her eyes and were gone. "And yet," she said: "Anthea: one of my most happiest devisements. And yet: was it fit indeed to sup a falcon with straw?"

Barganax looked at her, and as he looked his brow lightened and his eyes grew dark. "O, you are beyond soundings," he said. "Do you laugh? or do you nurse it against me? Well, there it is: and I swear to you, there was not an instant in it but my thought and my sense were nailed to you: but only to prove for the thousandth time your power, that outparagons all.

"Well," he said: "do you know that?"

Her eyebrows, like brooding wings beyond nature long and slender of some far-flown bird, informed the serene purity of her brow with an air of permanent soft surprise touched sometimes with contemplation, and now with a faint mockery. "Yes," she said.

"Will you forgive me?"

"Yes," she said.

"I would give much," said Barganax, "but to see your mind. Do you understand, that every road I tread leads to you?"

"I have heard you say so," she said. "No doubt your grace will accept the same comforting assurance from me."

"It is true I am a proud man," said Barganax then; "yet I doubt my pride for this. For this, I must know in myself perfection."

Fiorinda smiled. It was as if the termlessness of some divinity, clear, secure, pitiless, taking its easeful pleasure in the contemplation of its own self, lay veiled in that faint Olympian smile.

"But with you," said the Duke: "no such matter. You are perfect. You know it. Most devilishly you know it."

He stood up and paced back and forth upon the carpet, then came to a stop beside her. "But no. Jealousy," he said, "is a distemper of little men. Puff! 'tis gone. I play even, madonna. And—well, I hold my own."

Slowly, after a minute, she turned her head: gave him her green eyes. As she looked they widened, and it was as if fire leapt in their deeps and then flickered down to quiet embers. She turned away, giving him now, from black hair to silver shoulder, the virginal sweet line of her bended neck; the side view of her chin, firm and proud, and of lips, where her thought seemed to rest like a lily on still water.

One foot upon the highest step of the throne, he stood looking down at her. "I have a mind," said he, "to turn sculptor: chryselephantine[3] work: no, jet and ivory: ivory and black diamonds, rather: or the old man shall conjure up from the treasure-beds of Tartarus[4] some new such thing, since earth hath nought precious enough. And I will fashion therein the likeness of each particular hair. Listen" (bending a little nearer): "I made this for you last week." And he began to speak the lines, it was as though her dark troublous beauty was turned to music in his voice. As in secret antiphone to that music, her bosom mounted and fell with a quickened breathing.

> "Some love the lily, some the rose
> Which in the summer garden blows;
> Some daisies shy, some mignonette,
> Some the sweet-breathéd violet.
> But I a statelier Flower do owe,
> Doth in a heav'nlier garden grow:
> The Lily of sphinxian mystery,
> Too fair, too perilous-sweet to see,
> With curious work of filigree
> Trac'd in a thousand crimps and rings
> On her softly spreading wings.
> Upon the mountain of delight

Bloometh my wild Flower, black like night.
Her petals, curl'd luxuriously,
Ravish the live soul forth of me.
Her perfum'd darkness sets, like wine,
My veins a-throb with fire divine.—
Fate, take all: yet leave me this:
The Flower of Flowers, my Flower-Delice."

She made no sign, but remained with her downward, listening
look. "I wonder?" Barganax said: "did I ask you, no matter what,
would you give it me? Were I bid you do, no matter what, would
you do it?"

She nodded twice or thrice, without turning her head. "All of
me," she answered softly. "What you will."

"Ah, then you shall swear this. For there is a favour you have till
now refused me."

"O," said she, and the thing that dwelt in the corner of her
mouth was awake and ready; "if you must chaffer with me for oaths
and blind bargains, I'll take back my words. We'll start fair."

"No, no," said the Duke. "No oaths, then. I'll not cheapen the
sweet bounty of your word already spoken."

"But I've taken it back," said she.

"Then," he said, "we begin again. First: will you not smile me a
thank for to-day's proceedings?"

"I'll think on't," she said. "I might. But I'll be besought more
prettily for it ere I do it."

" 'Twas but to pleasure you, so I will at least be thanked," said
the Duke. "For myself, why, I'd see the Admiral and my silly sister
and the whole bunch of cards drowned together in the Styx ere I'd
a stirred a foot in it. And so, for my payment—"

"You will unthank yourself with such talk," she said. "And besides, it is all lies."

Barganax laughed. Then, looking in hers, his eyes became dark
and masterful. "It is lies," he said. "But only because of this, that I
cannot do without you. You have taken it back?" He was suddenly
kneeled at her feet: his hands shut like shackles upon her ankles,
prisoning them. "I have never bended knee to man or woman," he
said; "and now I will have my way. At this hundredth time of asking,
will you be my Duchess in Zayana?"

She made as if to rise, but his grip tightened. He said in a low
fierce voice, "Answer." In his hands he felt her answer before she
spoke: "Never that."

"That is an old stale answer," he said. "Try again."

Fiorinda threw up her head with a little silent laugh. "If you
have your hour," she said, "to begin or to refuse, so have I mine."

"But why?" said the Duke fiercely. She looked stonily down upon him. "Why?" he said again.

"Because I had rather be my own mistress," she said. "And yours."

"Ha! and I must starve still, save at the horning of the moon? And then oft but live on supposings; and every handwhile the chance you may forsake me? By heavens, but I will have more of you, madam."

She shook her head. The Duke, letting go her feet now, clasped his arms about her below the knees. "I know you care not a rush for the ducal crown. You are not dissevered by places, nor altered by times, nor subject unto to and fro. Do it for my sake. For indeed I am most venomously in love with you," (here he buried his forehead in her lap): "were I lose you, as well tear out my heart roots."

She sat very still. Then her fingers softly stroked, the wrong way, the thick, short-cropped, coppery, curling hair at the back of his head. "O folly of men!" she whispered. "How often, my lord, have you not exclaimed against safety and enduring goods? And now will you, like a peevish boy, provoke me to dwindle into your Duchess, and poison all our bliss? I'll sit in a shed with madge howlet and catch mice first."

It was as if he had not heard her. The grip of his arms was tenser about her knees. His face, when he now looked up at her, had the look of a man dazzled from sleep. He said, "I am sick with love of you."

Fiorinda met his eyes for a minute in silence. Then she trembled: her laughter-loving imperial lips parted a little: the long black eyelashes half veiled her eyes: her eyelids quivered. With a little sudden catch of her breath, she bent forward; her chin lifted a little; her throat and bosom became in that instant the pure benediction of beauty, the opening of heaven, the coming down. "Love me, then," she answered. "I am here to be loved."

The Duke, now upon that throne beside her, had her now in his arms. As a sweet in the goblet, as pearls when the silken thread is broken, all her fierce lithe pride and queenship was unstrung: fallen loose: melted away. In the nape of her neck, where her hair was done in a knot that nestled there black and sleek like a sleeping leopard, he kissed, a dozen times, the last lowest little hairs, too young to be commanded, which, finer than gossamer-spiders' silk, shadowed the white skin with their delicately ordered growth: little hairs prophetic of all perfections. And now his bee-winged kiss, hovering below her ear, under the earring's smouldering of garnet, passed thence to where neck and shoulder join, and so to the warm throat, and so by the chin to that mocking spirit's place of slumber and provocation; until, like the bee into the honeyed oblivion of some deep flower incarnadine, it was entertained at last into the consuming heaven of that lady's lips.

Now opened the last door of all before that leaf of virtue, the high double door that led from the main staircase to the throne-room, and Lessingham, striding out of darkness into the very presence, checked in the threshold. In the first bright glimpsing, indeed, he beheld the Lady Fiorinda thus in Duke Barganax's arms; but, ere foot or hand might act on his will, shut doors and be gone, she had stood up and turned her eyes upon him: and with that he was like a man ensorcelled.[5]

For now in her, so facing him from beside the dream-stone, he beheld no longer that lady, but another. In her hair, too pale for gold, too golden for silver, braided with strings of pearls, light itself seemed fallen a-dreaming, caught and stung asleep by the thousand little twisting tendrils that floated, hovered, vanished, and glinted again, with every stir of the quiet air. Feature by feature so might have been Barganax had he been born woman: a golden girl, in the sweet holiday spring-time of her awakening beauty. Her grey eyes drew to far spaces, like the sea. On her cool lips, full, clean cut, pure of curve, every thing desirable on earth or heaven seemed delicately to slumber. As a man out of the deathlike sleep of some drug comes to his senses at first with a disordered perception, wherein familiar things stand new, with no root in time, no perfume, no promise, no echo: so Lessingham beheld her but as a vision uncurdled from the phantasmagoria of some dream: a thing which the awakening sense, making as yet no question of perduration or possession, or of a world beyond the charmed present, accepts without surprise. Then on the sudden he noted the fashion of her dress, strange, fitter for a lover's eye than for the common gaze of the court, and knew it, with a knowledge that seemed to shut fingers about his naked soul, for that very dress and garb which that dream had worn, standing but a half hour since at his bed's foot.

Up the empty hall he came to her, slowly, not to frighten away this wonder, but resolute. The Duke sprang up, his eyes shining like a lion's surprised. But Lessingham, as marking him not, was come now within ten paces of them, still with that unwavering noiseless stride, and now his foot was even upon the carpet. He halted with the prick of Barganax's sword against his chest. He stepped back a pace, and drew. For the second time in a day and a night they stood as opposites; and this time in a witched kind of stillness, wherein each leaned towards other across the kindling instant that should let them together, point and edge, like two great strokes of lightning and thunder. And for the second time, and now strangelier still, for the hotter occasion that was now than in the council chamber for bloody rages, the moment passed.

Lessingham lowered his sword. "Who you are," he said, "I know not. But I'll not fight with you."

"Nor I with you," said the Duke, yet with thunder on his brow. "Nor I with you."

With the look on the face of each of them that a man's face wears when he strives to remember some forgotten tune, each fell back yet another pace or two from the other, each staring at the other still. And so staring, both slowly put up their swords, and, with the double click of them going home in the scabbards, both turned as upon a common impulse towards Fiorinda.

Like a man's beside himself, Barganax's eyes leapt from that other to Lessingham, from him to her, and his sword was jumped half-bare from the scabbard again. "What mummery's this?" he said. "Where is my lady? God's death! speak, you were best, man, and you, woman, whoever you be."

But Lessingham, looking too at that lady, and standing as if drunk, said, in a starved voice unlike his own, "Give me her back": then bit it in and set his jaw. Barganax, with a dazed look, passed his hand across his eyes.

"My cloak, my lord," she said, turning for the Duke to put it about her shoulders. He paused a moment. Her presence, thus strangely snatched away and as strangely restored, and in so serene an unconcernment; the curve of neck and hair; her skin; the sweet smell of her: these things shook the fierce blood in him so that he scarce dared trust his hand upon her, even through the cloak. But Lessingham near her too, and more, face to face with her dark and alluring loveliness, bore himself with a cold formal courtesy.

She thanked the Duke with a look: that slow, unblinking, unsmiling, suddenly opening and then fading, stare, with which upon his birthday she had promised herself in the garden. It mastered and then steadied his senses like wine. In that moment, so near the high climacteric, his eyes looking over her shoulder met the eyes of Lessingham in a profound recognition. In Lessingham's face, the masculine of hers by many particulars, he read a promise; not indeed, as in hers, the world-dissolving epithalamion of sense and spirit, but a promise of something scarcely less deep in the blood, albeit without arrows and without fire: of brotherhood beyond time and circumstance, not to be estranged, but riveted rather together, by mutual strife upon the great stage of the world and noble great contentions.

"My Lady Fiorinda," said Lessingham, "and you my lord Duke: inconsiderate excuses are no better than accusations. I could not rest. I will say no more."

"In this world-without-end hour," said the Duke, "let us say but good night."

Fiorinda spoke: "You go north, my Lord Lessingham?"

"To-morrow, madam."

"To-day, then: it is past midnight. Ere you go, I would know a thing. Were you ever a painter of pictures?"

"No. But a doer of deeds."

"My lord the Duke painteth past admiration. Of me he hath painted forty pictures, but not yet one to's liking, and so burnt all."

"There was a man I knew did so," said Lessingham: "burnt all save one. Yet no," he said, with a strange half-waked look at her. "What was't I said?"

"It is hard, I suppose," said that lady, as if, in the enjoyment of her own thoughts' stoops and hoverings, she had no eye to note the lightless gaze with which he seemed to search inward in himself: "It is hard, I suppose, for a lover, if he be a very lover, to paint his mistress. For then that which he would paint, if he be a very lover, is not appearance, but the thing which is. How can he paint her? seeing that his picture, when it is painted, changeth then no more; but that which is, changeth unceasingly: and yet changeth not."

"And yet changeth not," said Lessingham.

"This ring of mine," she said: "see, it is wine-red tonight, but a-daytime sleepy green. And such, as Doctor Vandermast affirmeth, is beauty: ever changing, never changing. But truly it is an old prating man, and I think hardly knoweth what he prateth of."

"Ever changing, never changing," said Lessingham, as if he felt his way in the dark. Once more his gaze met the Duke's.

Her slanting green eyes, snakish, veiled with their silky dark-nesses, turned upon Barganax and then again upon Lessingham.

Lessingham, after a little silence, said, "Good night."

"And yet," said she, as he bent to kiss her hand; and surely everything of that lady, the least turn of her finger, the least falling tone of her lazy voice, was as a stirring of mists ready to blow away and open upon wonder: "what riddle was that you did ask me but now, my lord? A man's Self, said you? or his Love?"

Lessingham, who had asked no riddle, made no answer.

"I think it is both," Fiorinda said, looking steadily at him. He was ware of a settled quality of power in her face now, diamantine, older and surer than the primal crust, older than the stars: a quality that belonged most of all to her lips, and to her eyes: lips that seemed to close upon antique secrets, memories of flesh and spirit fused and transfigured in the dance of the daughters of the morn-ing; and eyes yet blurred from looking upon the very bed of beauty, and delights unconceived by the mind of man. Those eyes and those lips Lessingham knew as a child knows its mother, or as the sunset knows the sea. In a dizziness of conflicting yeas and nays, he recog-nized in her the power that had drawn him but now up the hall, on to Barganax's sword-point. Yet she who had had that power so to draw him was strangely not this woman, but another. He bethought him then of their supper under the moon, and of her *allegretto scher-zando*[6] that had then so charmed his mind. The movement was changed now to *adagio molto maestoso ed appassionato*,[7] but the charm remained; as if here were the lady and mistress of all, revealed, as his very sister, the feminine of his own self: a rare and sweet famil-iarity of friendship, but not of love; since no man can love and worship his own self.

Again she spoke: "Good night. And you are well advised to go north, my Lord Lessingham; for I think you will find there that which you seek. North, in Rialmar."

In a maze, Lessingham went from the hall.

And now Barganax and Fiorinda, standing under the shadow-ing glory of those wings, for a minute regarded one another in silence. The Duke, too, knew that mouth. He, too, knew those up-per lids with their upward slant that beaconed to ineffable sweets. He, too, knew those lower lids, of a straightness that seemed to rest upon the level infinitude of beauty, which is the laying and the consolation and the promise on which, like sleeping winds on a sleeping ocean, repose all unfulfilled desires. And now at the inner corners of those eyes, as she looked at him, something stirred, ruf-fling the even purity of that lower line as the first peep of the sun's bright limb at morning breaks the level horizon of the sea.

"Yes," she said: "you have leave to resume our conversation where it was broke off, my friend. Yet this throne-room perhaps is not the most convenientest place for us, considering the lateness; considering too the subject, which, once thus raised between us, was never, as I remember, well laid again ere morning."

IX

THE INGS[1] OF LORKAN

The Ruyar Pass ✦ *Owldale and the stringway* ✦
The Vicar prepares war; so also the Duke ✦
Lessingham invades Meszria ✦ *Burning of
Limisba* ✦ *Roder moves* ✦ *Battle of Lorkan
field* ✦ *Beroald and Jeronimy in the salimat.*

LESSINGHAM in the same hour, not to fail of his word,
burnt up that leaf. On the morrow he rode north by
way of Reisma Mere and Memison, going, as he had
come south three weeks ago, but twenty in company,
but so fast that now he was his own harbinger. So it was
that the Duke's safe conduct procured him welcome of all men and
speeding on his journey, while at less than a day's lag behind him
was shearing up of the war-arrow[2] and the countryside ablaze with
rumours of war. So by great journeys he came at evening of the
third day up through the defiles of the Ruyar to the windy stony
flats that tail away north-westward between the glacier capped cliffs
of the Hurun range on the right and Sherma on the left, and so to
where, in the cleft of the Ruyar pass where it crosses the watershed
to Outer Meszria and the north, the great work of Rumala leaves
not so much as a goat's way between cliff and towering cliff.

"This were a pretty mouse-trap," said Amaury, as they drew
rein in the cold shadow of the wall: "if he had bethought him out of
prudence, may hap, say a Monday last, soon as you broke with him,
to send a galloper whiles we dallied and gave him time for it: enjoin

109

his seneschal[3] of Rumala shut door upon us, hold us for's disposal upon further order. Had you thought on that?"

"I thought on't," said Lessingham, "when I took his offer."

"So I too," said Amaury, and loosened his sword in its scabbard. "And I think on't now."

"And yet I took his offer," said Lessingham. "And I had reason. You are prudent, Amaury, and I would have you so. Without my reason, my prudence were in you rashness. And indeed, my reason was a summer reason and would pass very ill in winter."

In Rumala they were well lodged and with good entertainment. They were up betimes. The seneschal, a gaunt man with yellow mustachios and a pale blue eye, brought them out, when they were ready after breakfast, by the northern gate to the little level saddle whence the road drops northwards into Rubalnardale.

"The Gods take your lordship in Their hand. You are for Rerek?"

"Ay, for Laimak," answered Lessingham.

"By the Salimat had been your easiest from Zayana."

"I came that way south," answered he; "and now I was minded to look upon Rumala. 'Tis as they told me; I shall not come this way again."

Amaury smiled in himself.

"You are bound by Kutarmish?" said the seneschal.

"Yes."

"I have despatches for the keeper there. If your lordship would do me the honour to carry them?"

"Willingly," said Lessingham. "Yet, if they be not of urgency, I would counsel you keep 'em till to-morrow. You may have news then shall make these stale."

The seneschal looked curiously at him. "Why what news should there be?" he said.

"How can I tell?" said Lessingham.

"You speak as knowing somewhat."

"To-morrow," said Lessingham, "was always dark to-day. To-day, is clear: so enjoy it, seneschal. Give Amaury your letters: I'll see 'em delivered in Kutarmish."

They were come now to the edge of the cliff upon the face whereof the road winds in and out for two thousand feet or more before it comes out in the bottom of Rubalnardale, plumb below the brink they stood on as a man might spit. The seneschal said, "You must walk and lead your horses, my lord, down the Curtain."

"Can a man not ride it?"

"Nor ever did, nor ever will."

Lessingham looked over and considered. "Maddalena hath carried me, and at a good racking pace, through the Hanging Corridors of the Greenbone ranges in nether Akkama: 'twas very like this." He began to mount: "Nay, touch her not: she will bite and strike with her forelegs at an unknown."

The seneschal backed away with a wry smile as Lessingham leapt astride of his dangerous-eyed red mare. With him barely in the saddle, she threw a capriole on the very verge of the precipice; tossed her mane; with a graceful turn of her head took her master's left foot daintily between her teeth; then in a sudden frozen stillness waited on his will.

"I had heard tell," said the seneschal, as the mare, treading delicately as an antelope, carried her rider down and out of sight, "that this lord of yours was a mad fighting young fellow; but never saw I the like of this. Nay," he said, as Amaury mounted and his men besides, "then give me back my letters. As well send 'em later with the party must take up your corpses."

"We shall now show you a thing: safe as flies on a wall," said Amaury.

Lessingham shouted from the bend below, " 'Tis a good road north by Rumala: a bad road south." Amaury, smiling with himself, rode over the edge, and the rest followed him man by man. The seneschal stood for a while looking down the cliff when they were gone. There was nothing to be seen: only on the ear came a jangling of bits and the uneven clatter of horse-hooves fainter and fainter from the hollows of the crags. Far below, an eagle sailed past the face of that mountain wall, a level effortless sweep on still wings brazen in the sunshine.

Dusk was confounding all distances, smoothing away all shadows, smudging with sleepy fingers the clear daylight verities of whinbush and briar and thorn, mole-hill and wayside stone, outcropping rock and grassy hummock, fern and bent, willow and oak and beech and silver birch-tree, all into a pallid oneness and immateriality of twilight, as Lessingham and Amaury came at a walking-pace over the last stretch of the long open moorland sparsely grown with trees that runs up north from Ristby, and took the road north-eastward for Owldale. The westermost outlying spur of the Forn impended in a precipitous gable on their right; beyond it, north and round to the west, gathered by the dusk into a single blue wall of crenelled and ruined towers, the Armarick peaks and the fells about Anderside and Latterdale were a vastness of peace against the windy sky. There had been showers of rain, and thunder among the hills. Great Armarick, topping the neighbouring peaks, had drawn about his frost-shattered head a coverlet of sluggish and slate-hued cloud.

They had long outridden their company. Amaury's horse was blown. Even Maddalena had quieted her fiery paces to the unrelenting plod that draws on to corn and a sweet bed and sleep at night. Lessingham in a graceful idleness rode sideways, the slacked reins in his left hand, his right flat-palmed on the crupper. Turning his head, he met Amaury's eyes regarding him through the dusk. Something in their look made him smile. "Well," he said: "grey silver aloft again, Amaury?"

"There's more in't than that," said Amaury. "You are stark mad these five days I think, since we set out north from Zayana. I cannot fathom you."

Lessingham's eyes took on their veiled inward-dreaming look and his lips their smile that had first snared Barganax's fancy, holding a mirror as it were to Fiorinda's smile. "I was never more sober in my life," he said, his hand softly stroking Maddalena's back. There was a secret beat of music in his voice, like as had been in the Duke's when, upon Ambremerine to the singing of the faun, he had spoken that stave into his mistress's ear.

They rode the next league in silence, up the deep ravine of Scandergill above which the valley spreads out into wide flats, and the road strikes across to the north side through oak-woods that turned with their overarching shade the cloudy May night to inky darkness. A drizzling rain was falling when they came out of the forest and followed the left bank of Owlswater up to the bridge above the waters-meet at Storby, where Stordale opens a gateway into the hills to the north and the Stordale Beck tumbles into Owldale white over a staircase of waterfalls. The keeper of the bridge-house took the password and came down to offer his duty to Lessingham: he flew an owl to carry tidings of their approach to the Vicar in Laimak, and another, because of the darkness, to Anguring that they should have lights to light them over the Stringway. Two hours above Storby they halted half an hour for their company, left behind in their wild riding beyond Ristby. Now the road narrowed and steepened, climbing in zig-zags under the cliffs at the base of Little Armarick and tapering at last to a four-foot ledge with the jutting rock of Anguring Combust above it and the under-cut wall of the gorge below. At the bottom of that gorge, two hundred feet beneath the road, Owlswater whitened in foam and thunder over the ruins of old Anguring castle, that twenty years ago the Lord Horius Parry had flung down there from its rock, when after a long siege he had by stratagem won it and burnt it up along with his brother and his brother's wife and their sons and daughters and all their folk, glad to have rooted out at last this tree that had stood as a shadow against the sun to mar the fair growth of his own lordship in Laimak. Then had he let build, over against it on the left bank of the gorge, his own new fortalice of Anguring, upon a backward and upward running crest, to command at close range both the road below the former castle, and the Stringway. Upon this Stringway Maddalena now delicately stepped, her soul calm, amid the flurry of winds and unseen furious waters and flare-lit darknesses, with the comfort of a familiar master-mind speaking to her through pressure of knee and through sensitive touch of bit upon lips and tongue. The gorge was here barely twenty paces broad, and a huge slab, fallen in ancient times from the mountain face above, was jammed like a platter or meat-dish caught and gripped there up on edge: one edge of the platter jammed where the road ended under old Anguring, and the other jammed against the gorge's brink where new Anguring sat perched like a preying bird. Along that slab's upturned edge ran the road: an arched footway of rock, too narrow for two horses meeting to pass one another: the inexpugnable gateway from the south into upper Owldale and the pasture lands of Laimak. Lessingham rode it unconcerned, giving Maddalena her head and letting her take her time, in the smoky glare of a dozen torches brought down to the cliff's edge out of Anguring. Amaury and the rest were fain to lead their horses across.

A little before midnight Lessingham blew horn under Laimak.

The Vicar received Lessingham by torchlight in the great main gate above the gatehouse. He advanced three steps to meet Lessingham, and embraced and kissed him on both cheeks. Lessingham said, "Your highness is to thank me indeed. I have set 'em all by the ears, and in that suspectuous squabbling insecurity declared war upon them. It resteth now but to raise force and crush them ere they run together again. I'll tell you all at large, but first I would bathe and shift me; and indeed I have not eat these eight hours, since dinnertime at Ketterby."

" 'Tis provided," said the Vicar. "Let's hold more chat over the supper table."

Half an hour past midnight supper was set in the great banquet-hall which was shapen like an L, the main member forty cubits in length and the shorter twenty-five. Amaury and they of Lessingham's company had place at the far end of the long table by the door at the end of the main body of the hall that opened on the great court. The Vicar sat with Lessingham at a little round table at the northern corner whence they might see everywhere in the hall both ways, left and right, and be out of earshot of the rest and talk at ease. The hall was of black obsidian-stone, with deep mullioned windows along its north-western wall. Devilish heads, five cubits in bigness from brow to chin, were carven in high relief along the five other walls: thirteen heads in all, very deformed and uglisome, laying out their tongues; and on the end of each tongue was stood a lamp brightly burning, and the eyes of the great faces were looking-glasses nicely cut up with facets to throw back the rays of the lamps, so that the whole banquet-room was lit with a brilliance of lamplight. It was mizzly weather, very cold for the time of year; the Vicar

bade light a fire of logs in the great hearth that stood on the inner
angle opposite their table.

Lessingham, in a pleasant ease now after nigh five days' riding,
sat eating of his supper, a neat's tongue, some jellied quails, a sallet
of endives lettuces and salsify, with hippocras and a quince pie to
end it, while the Vicar, leaning over the table at his cousin's elbow
and drinking chill wine, talked long and low in his ear. Gabriel
Flores, upon pretext of hospitable attentions, tarried by the table.
"Care not for Gabriel, he is inward in my counsels," said the Vicar.

"Not in mine," said Lessingham.

"Well, pug, begone," said the Vicar then; "we have no love for
you."

"O I do love my little Gabriel," said Lessingham; "yet sometimes he is dearest to me in absence. And that humour's on me now;
and so, Gabriel, good night." Gabriel gat him gone with an ill grace.

"Filth and damnation of these free towns in the north there!"
said the Vicar, reaching out a broad and hairy hand for the leavings
of the tongue, which he threw to a great dog that, prick-eared and
alert, watched their meal as a peri[4] should watch the things of Paradise. "I trust ere long to wash my hands in the umbles[5] of the
knaves; but all taketh time, and here's trouble upon trouble ever
since the old King died. And, like a fool, I laughed to think my
hands were untied then."

"I would you had not needed act so suddenly," said Lessingham. "These soldiers you have packed off north I could a used
to your great vantage in the south now. Tella, Lailma, Veiring, and
Abaraima, you told me, swapt up a roguish bargain with Ercles;
opened their gates to him; called him their captain?"

"Ay: 'stead of Mandricard, that held it in my interest these five
years."

"Mandricard," said Lessingham, "was never the man to serve
your turn; I told you that five years ago, cousin. Too irresolute,
fawning on the tag-rag people for favour to-day, putting 'em down
with a bloody petulance to-morrow; such an uncertain seat: such
jaggings on the bit: spoil your best of horses."

"Pah! 'twas not one man's insufficiency raised this smother,"
said the Vicar. "Hath been brewing for years. I have had my finger
on their pulses. I saw it afore yesterday. And Veiring, worst of all.
God's body! I tell you Prince Ercles' self did say to my face (when
there was less coolness 'twixt us than now-a-days befalleth): said if
they of Veiring did trouble him as they did me, he would send his
men with shovels and pickaxes and throw it into the sea."

"You have despatched Arcastus, you say, and a thousand men?"

"Twelve, no, fifteen hundred: not as upon serious action: only
to cow 'em with a show of strength: stop other sheep from following
of those through the same gate. But harkee, I have yet one good

cogging die ready upon the cast," and his voice fell to a growling whisper: "a likely lad with a good point to his knife and a well shut mouth and a good habit of miching round by unseen ways: tickled his belly with two hundred gold pieces, and five hundred more upon performance: if he but wriggle his way into Eldir—" the Vicar drank. "Gabriel procured him, and that at some third remove. My hand's not seen in't. If aught miscarry, should slander blow hitherward I can securely 'gainst all contradictions disown him."

Lessingham leaned back in his chair and stretched. He regarded his cousin with a look of profound enjoyment which, when the adder eyes met his, livened to the shadow of a smile. "I do sadly fear, cousin, this most taking simple-heartedness of yours," he said. "Consider: 'tis barely two months since the Chancellor took up one of your instruments in his garden in Zayana and hanged him there. I know 'twas given out 'twas Zapheles worked that poppet's strings, not to make too much pother of it; but in all their private counsels there was no question made but you did do it. And now Ercles: that old dog-fox is not to be caught with your springes, cousin. I would you had been in Zayana; you should a seen the labour I had untying of those bands of alliance your known ways had knit them together withal; and but for that, little enough of trust or friendship amongst 'em. My work had been easy else."

The Vicar turned upon him eyes of stone. "You have your ways," he said. "I mine."

"What strength have you in Owldale?" asked Lessingham, as a falcon leaves playing with her mate in the upper air to stoop at her proper prey. "Four thousand men?"

"Just, if you'll drink drunk and see each man double," answered he.

"Two thousand? and my own riders, eight hundred more."

"Nay, I reckoned them in," said the Vicar.

"I must have more," said Lessingham, and sprang up. "We must come down upon them like a thunderbolt ere they have time to consider too much and stick together again, else is all this work wasted."

"Softly, softly," said the Vicar. "'Tis but boys and women count to go through presently their designments a royal point; my policy runneth deeper. I'll clear my rear in the north first. Besides, I've thought on a business for you north-away; but that must wait again. For this present matter, I will first make sure of Ercles and Aramond."

Lessingham paced a dozen times to and again from the table to the fire. "Cousin," he said then, coming to a stop before the table, "you have taken my rede ere now, and have you ever fallen down by it?" The Vicar shrugged his shoulders. Lessingham's eyes were a-sparkle. "Seeing I have begun," said he, "I will stoutly go through.

You can hold Laimak and Anguring with as many men as chesnuts you could carry in two fists. Give me the rest, and your warrant to raise what more I may. Ere a month be past I'll grab you Outer Meszria in the hollow of my hand."

"You've a sweet vein in speech," the Vicar said; "but you know as well as I we cannot now lay hand on above two thousand five hundred men, and there's four or five thousand needed for such an enterprise."

"Yet shall you see me undertake it," said Lessingham. "Things least feared are least defended and observed. And remember, one great stroke i' the southlands, and these factions that vex you i' the north there shall fizzle like a lamp when the oil is out. Time enough then to sort them, put 'em to rights."

The Vicar's great spreading nostrils widened and the red blood flushed his face, as if set a-boiling with the heat of the imperious eager and resolute imaginings that burned in Lessingham's speech and bearing. He stood up now heavily, and for a minute faced Lessingham in silence. Then, clapping a heavy hand upon either shoulder of Lessingham, "We'll sleep on't," he said. "The more spacious that the tennis-court is, the more large is the hazard. And if you think, cousin, to thrust all this down my pudding-house at a gob, well, the Devil eat your soul for me then, for you are sadly mistook."

That was the twenty-seventh of May. Upon the twenty-ninth Duke Barganax, his scheme well laid now, moved north with his bodyguard of five hundred picked men-at-arms to Rumala, there to wait Barrian and Melates with the levies of Krestenaya and Memison ere he should descend into Outer Meszria and the marches. Here was good hopes, soon as the ducal banner should be shown north of the Zenner and the Vicar's garrison shut up by siege in Argyanna, that the whole March of Ulba should rise to resume their old affinities and fling off the yoke of Rerek. So upon the fifth day from Zayana, being now the second of June, came the Duke to Rumala. Upon that same day at evening the lord Admiral weighed anchor and put out from Sestola with sixteen fighting ships all manned and six ships of burden, a great and redoubtable power of men: two thousand five hundred of his own sailors, men inured to war by land as well as by sea, besides two thousand footmen of the royal garrison in Meszria and the Earl Roder himself on board with the Admiral. Roder's chosen riders, three hundred strong, veterans all of ten years' service, fared by land for lack of room a-shipboard. The like was Egan to do, with four hundred Meszrian horse. The Salimat was set for their meeting-place, of the power that went by sea, and the horse, and the Chancellor with nigh two thousand more old levies of Fingiswold. These tarried in Zayana yet a day or two for Zapheles, who was raising of forces south in Armash and Daish. All these were appointed to meet on Wednesday the seventh of June upon the Salimat, where the highway from Zayana to Ulba crosses Nephory Edge at its lowest; and that is the best vantage ground for an army to stand against an enemy faring from the north, for it gives a clear wide prospect west and north and east over the low-lying marchlands of Outer Meszria and Ulba, and the lie of the land is good for falling upon him if he will attack up the pass, and it is a strong place too to hold upon defence if need be, and a place well apt by nature for hidden ambushes and espial of any army that should fare by that road whether south or north.

The High Admiral put out upon the flood-tide from Sestola and dropped down the firth with a favouring wind. But at nightfall the wind had freshened so that it was dangerous sailing among the islands. The fleet lay up till dawn in sheltered water behind Lashoda; by then was a high sea running, and when they were come out into the open they must beat up northwards all day against a head wind and at night were glad to run for shelter in to Spruna mouth. With these delays and adverse winds it was not until the evening of the third day that they made Peraz Firth and anchored about suppertime at the head of the firth over against the town. Here were sumpter horses and mules and bullock carts to meet them, and the next day they landed the army and the stuff, and, leaving a thousand of Jeronimy's men to mind the ships, came on the morrow in a day's march up through the flowering valley of Biulmar and camped the same evening in the Salimat. Roder's three hundred horse, punctual to the day appointed, came in before night. The Meszrian horse with Egan were late: nought known of them since these had set forth without them from Zayana, after six hours' vain waiting. Roder cursed them. Of Beroald, with his two thousand, there was no sign, nor no word.

Morning rose abated with cloud and mist. A blanket of vapour rolling down the smooth rock hummocks east of the pass lay damp about the tents. The Admiral sent a man of trust east through the hills to Rumala to advertise the Duke that the Salimat was held and all well, and another to find out the Chancellor. Intelligencers had gone well a week before into Outer Meszria and the borderlands. An hour before noon came in tidings by one of these, that upon Sunday Lessingham had crossed the Zenner with no great strength of men and appeared before Fiveways: that the accursed people of that town had, against expectation, opened their gates to him: that there he lay as late as Tuesday, and there men drew to him, by twos and threes, here a score and there a score; mainly, 'twas thought, from the March, but some few, 'twas spoken, from the Meszrian border upon pretext he did owe their allegiance, bearing the Queen's warrant and upholding her right. An hour later came in others with more fresh advertisement, how but yesterday, upon their own observation, Lessingham was marched out of Fiveways, in strength some fifteen hundred foot and a thousand horse: that 'twas said seven hundred of the footmen were veterans of the Parry's, the rest raw levies: the horse mainly Lessingham's own: that with these he was turned north-east along the road by the river, as if his intents were aimed for Kutarmish. Upon which tidings, Roder took Jeronimy by the sleeve and walked out of earshot of their officers.

"What rede will you take now, my lord Admiral? One mischief never comes alone. Here you have the Chancellor a day behind time and still no news of him, and we with our powers thus clipped sit but and look on. If Kutarmish fall, then is Outer Meszria lost without a stroke, and that the richest land of all in the south here."

"Ibian will hold Kutarmish never doubt it," said the Admiral.

"Say he do," replied Roder. "Shall then these ram-cats of Meszria reap all the honour, whiles we of the Queen's true party sit quittering here? 'Twill breed discontent i' the army, too, forget not. I have felt it ere now: ears pricked up for every air that bloweth a doubt if it be we truly or these of the other party do truly uphold her interest."

"That," said Jeronimy, "is a main uncertainty of currents and shifting sands we needs must in a manner sleep and eat withal since first he was deputed overseer of her nonage, whose innocent right doth so justify his wrong."

"It lieth upon us, saving your reverence, my lord Admiral," said Roder, "not but eat and sleep only, but stand up and act. Consider: if this intelligence (and 'tis well seconded) be not all out, we be now two to one against him."

"He is strong in horse, and of great reputation in that arm," said Jeronimy.

"I redoubt him not," said Roder, "in that particular."

"All in all," said Jeronimy, "his force, be it little, is well strengthed. A little gold overvalueth much lead or iron."

Roder spat on the ground and scowled. "Were't mine alone to command," said he, after a minute, "I'd down into the flats to-day: with my new broom sweep him one swap, and sweep him out of Meszria."

The Admiral softly blew out his cheeks and shook his head. "Let us wait, my lord, till to-morrow. The Chancellor will sure be come then."

The morrow dawned fair. All the morning fog hung over the countryside to the northwards, so that it showed dull like the bloom on a black grape; above it the sky was blue and tender, and all the near stretches of the wide vale of the Zenner lay bright under the sun, but in a soft brightness, with the dwellings of men and the paleness here and there of a winding stream, and the winding empty high-road coming south across the low land till at length it breasted the slopes of these southern hills and came up to cross the

Salimat. At noon came hot news of the vicarian army marching west
again. By the third hour past noon they were in sight, coming
south-east over the brow two leagues away, above Aptyssa. The
camp in the Salimat was pitched a little to the south below the
hause, not to let it be known from the northward how strongly the
road was held. In the hause and upon the northern slope it was
jopplety ground of rock and heather: little knolls and dingles, in
which Jeronimy and Roder now disposed their army on either side
of the road, hidden and well posted for overwhelming of Lessingham should he assay the pass. He came on but slowly. It was
three hours more ere he began to drive in Jeronimy's outposts on
the Hazanat beck. Roder's patience was long since drained away,
and he was for setting upon them then and there while daylight
lasted. "Nay, we must bide fast," said Jeronimy. "Would you throw
away the advantage we do hold upon him and fight on ground of
his own choosing; aptest too for cavalry, wherein we are weakest?"

Roder drew up his lip. "Wisdom," he said, "hath her excesses,
and no less need of moderation, than folly. Take your course, my
lord; but for my own part I will not be held answerable for these
delays."

It was seen now that Lessingham halted and pitched camp in
the meadows west of Limisba, the hither side of the Hazanat, about
a mile short of where the ground began to rise. And now he arrayed
his army before the camp as if for battle. Jeronimy said, "He doth
now in a manner draw the straw before the cat. But we shall not
play withal." Roder ground his teeth and went to his quarters. Little
content it brought him to see his own summer palace of Limisba,
given him lately by King Mezentius in payment of his services in
peace and war, lie thus under the claws of Lessingham. When supper was cooked, Jeronimy bade damp out all fires, so as it should
not be known from below whether he lay there still in the Salimat or
whether he was marched away. There was yet no tidings of the
Chancellor, now full two days behind the time appointed. This lay
like an ill-digested meal on their bellies. Jeronimy chose him out a
prudent close and faithful messenger: sent him back by the Zayana
road to seek tidings. All night long Lessingham's camp-fires smoked
to the stars from glimmering points of flame. Roder said, "Are they
girl-children, then, these riff-raff of Rerek, that they must coddle by
the fire these summer nights, though we upon the hill can sleep in
the cold?" He was snoring in his tent and so saw not, an hour before
dawn, his own house of Limisba in a lowe, like Antares amid the
lesser fires of night.

At daybreak Limisba sparkled merrily, so as even here in the
Salimat a man might doubt he heard not the crackle, throwing up
vast eddying clouds of smoke that were yet but as a wreath from a
snuffed-out candle facing the clouds of the dawn. The camp-fires

burned yet, but the camp was struck. Along the winding waters towards the Zenner new fires beaconed to the sky, as if Lessingham, having done with his feint against the Salimat, would say, "Come down then and deal with me, or I will burn up all Meszria under your noses." Word was brought hastily to the generals: Roder rushed out in his shirt, sputtering a stream of blasphemies: called up the guard to summon the captains to council: gave order to strike camp and make all ready to march in posture for battle upon short warning. In the midst of which haste and fury he was met with the Lord Jeronimy with letters in his hand. "From the Chancellor: put in my hands this instant by's messenger ridden day and night," said the Admiral: "these commends express he hath had delays for cause we spoke on: doubtful allegiance 'mongst his men: but all ended now and their minds well satisfied. Doubted not to set forth from Zayana on Thursday (that's four days late)"—"Damnation of hell! what good's in that?" said Roder—"And by forced marches should be here ere to-morrow night."

"Then is our way clear," said Roder: "we wait no longer;" and he flung off to his tent to clothe himself. The lord Admiral looked after him with pursed lips and an anxious brow.

Ten minutes later was their council called in the Admiral's tent. Earl Roder came in in full battle-gear. He said, "There is first the point of policy, my lord, and that's for you and I. Pray you let's be private."

"As shall please you," said Jeronimy.

When they were private the Lord Jeronimy took him by the arm and said, "I would have you in a manner overview the thing serenely. I am no jot less eager than yourself to strike; but remember, 'tis his plain game to make us put our finger in a hole. There is hazard in't to-day. To-morrow, with the Chancellor and near another two thousand men, no hazard at all. Hasty fruits, my lord, be a pleasure for the time; but their time is but a cherry-fair."

Roder said, in a strained quietness, "Your lordship must forgive me if I speak my mind, and 'tis, of this that you have spoke now, that a lewder and feebler skill or argument can no man make: if in sober sadness you would wait till to-morrow and suffer this Lessingham slip through our fingers."

"Nay, pray you, my lord," said Jeronimy, "you must not wrest my words. Wait till to-morrow, and I will securely promise you there shall not one tail of them return again into Rerek."

"Were it speak my thought," said Roder, and grew crimson, "I should a said you did seek an argument to cloak your—nay, but I know 'tis not chicken-heartedness: I mean your pig-headedness—like a filthy fly that seeketh all over the body for a sore."

"Rude incivilities, my Lord Roder," said the Admiral, taking his hand away, "shall stand us in little stead in our search for wise counsel. In a manner, 'tis a main need for us to be of one mind in this pass we are come to: to fail of that were a ruin worth all men's pity."

"My good lord Admiral," said Roder, "give me your hand. I'm sorry my cursed words should so outrun my meaning. Only, a shame have we with so much strength at our back, when that a pawn saith to the king checkmate. Well, let him go his ways then. I reck not. And when his grace shall see, from his high vantage point of Rumala, this Lessingham fare like a king through Outer Meszria, and none to nay-say him, and we by just presumption lost or gone to sleep, he will soon down on him from Rumala, and himself do the thing we boggled at."

The Admiral listened with hands clasping and unclasping behind his back, his head bent, as if studying his own feet. At mention of the Duke he gave a little start: a deep flush overspread his countenance. "Nay, but I had forgot that," he said, after a pause. "And yet 'tis present danger, Lessingham heading east. In the mad-brain violence of his valour, to come down: cope Lessingham in the plains." Still avoiding Roder's eye, he walked slowly to the tent door and stood looking out. "Whereupon should most assuredly his too little force be incontinently overthrown and eaten up."

Roder pricked his ears. Jeronimy abode there, silent and thoughtful, twirling his gold perspective-glass on the end of its slender chain. Roder spoke: "Which if't befall, you and I should have but one shift left, my lord Admiral: that's straight go hang ourselves."

The Admiral said nothing: only ceased from twirling of his glass. Roder waited a little. Then he said, "There is yet good time to head him off, bring him to battle. After a few hours, not so easy; yet even that were better, follow at his heels through Meszria: better than sit here."

There was a long silence. Roder breathed thickly through his nose; his jowl, under the bristles of his cropped black beard, swoll above the collar of his gorget. At last, without looking round, Jeronimy spoke. "The considerations are too much different. Time: 'tis that spoils all. No time to bring word to the Duke in Rumala. And so, impulsive necessity: not your other reasons, my lord," he said, turning and coming in; " 'tis this persuadeth me to that which were else great folly. You shall have your way, my lord. Call in the rest."

"Ha! then 'tis day!" said Roder, and took him by both hands. "Now have I the bloody man upon the anvil: shall be pulp ere sundown."

Lessingham, from a rise of ground beside the Zenner where he had now halted his army, beheld at four miles' distance how Roder came down in force from the Salimat. "The Gods be praised," he said:

"here's an end of bonfires. Yet with such sluggish foxen, no way but smoke 'em out. And now we must not seem too eager, while they have yet the choice to run to earth again."

"You have roused a bed of bears, not foxen," said Amaury.

"When the bear was met with the tiger cat, then was there fur a-flying," said Lessingham. "Time is of our side. They outnumber us, but not past coping with. Give 'em time to gather all their power, we durst not stand them; but now 'tis not beyond adventure."

He issued command now, and they fell back slowly south-east-wards. The Earl turned east on this, as if to intercept them in the lava at the skirts of the hills above Nephory. After an hour's march the armies were drawn within two miles of one another. Lessingham altered his course and headed due north, hugging at last the eastern edge of the wood of Orasbieh as if he would make for the bridge at Lorkan, where the Kutarmish road running in from the north crosses the shallow and muddy river Ailyman a little above its falling into the Zenner. Here betwixt wood and river was a stretch of meadow land, firm and level: and here, resting his left upon the river a few hundred paces above the bridge and his right upon the border of Orasbieh wood, Lessingham halted and made ready for battle. Of his main battle, of footmen, he made a crescent, centre advanced, horns curving back toward the road. A great part of these were raw levies, raised, some hundreds, within the week from the countryside inland about Argyanna and seaward about Kessarey, others raised by the Vicar two months since, when he drew power to him in Owldale because of King Styllis. But nine hundred, of all the sixteen hundred foot, were veterans of the Vicar's old army, hard as bears and inured to war: these had seen service under Lessingham too ere now, seven or eight years ago when, not without discreet countenance from the princes and (as was commonly said) from Barganax, the great rebellion had shaken all Rerek nearly to the unseating of the Vicar and the conquering might of Fingiswold.[6] With some of these veteran troops Lessingham stiffened his centre, but posted them in the main upon the wings, held well back as aforesaid: ten score he kept in reserve under his own hand for more security in the dangerous purpose he did intend. Four hundred of his own horse, under command of Amaury, made his left battle, resting on the river. Three hundred more, under Brandremart, along with the squadrons lent from Argyanna, went on the right beside the wood.

When the Earl's outriders came round the south-east neb of the wood and saw these dispositions, they sent word back to let him know that Lessingham stood there in the ings of Lorkan, and in what posture, offering battle. Upon which the Earl straightway called a halt, arrayed his host as he had determined with himself before, and advanced in order of battle. He had with him the whole army that was that morning gathered in the Salimat, save only five hundred sailors from the fleet who abode still in the pass there with the High Admiral, to hold it if need were and to await the Chancellor. His main strength, of two thousand heavy-armed spearmen of Fingiswold and a thousand of Jeronimy's sailors, so far outwent in his judgement Lessingham's foot, as well in weapons and goodness as in numbers, that he made little account of the odds against him in respect of horse. With that mind, he arrayed them in deep ranks, and commanded Peropeutes, who with Hortensius and Belinus captained the foot, to throw their whole weight, upon blowing of the horn for battle, against Lessingham's centre, and break it. He himself with his three hundred picked horsemen of the Wold fared against Amaury beside the river. Egan and the Meszrian horse, but new come in that morning, went upon the left.

Earl Roder without parley let blow up the war-blast, and the banners were borne forth, and with a great and horrid shout his main battle set on at a lumbering run. Lessingham bade his folk hold their ground till it was come to handystrokes and then to hold firm on the wings at all costs. When they were come within cast, each side let at the other with twirl-spears. Upon the next instant Peropeutes and the pick of the royal guard, bearing great oblong shields and armed alternately with long thrusting-spears and two-handed swords, crashed like a battering-ram against Lessingham's centre. In the roar of that onset and the clatter of steel and grinding of edge upon edge, the levies of Rerek, under the weight of deep columns so thrown upon them, shook and bent. Many were hurt and many slain of either side in that first clash of the battle; for fair in the centre had Lessingham set with each raw young man an older fighter of the Vicar's, and these, with their short two-edged swords good for thrusting and hewing alike, and their smaller shields light but tough, made play where Roder's spearmen might scarce find weapon-room in the close mellay. With main ponderous weight of numbers thrusting in serried ranks from behind, the battle front bent northwards, until Lessingham's half-moon was clean reversed: horns reaching forward on either side, belly buckled inward. And little by little into that deepening pocket Roder's battering-ram, with ever narrowing front, crowded and battered its way.

Lessingham had under his hand a hundred picked riders and a hundred of his veteran foot, men trained to go into battle with the horsemen, holding to the stirrup when they charge. With these he hung about the backward-buckling centre as a gannet follows a shoal of mackerel. His lips were set: his eyes dancing fires. By runners and riders, where he might not see for himself, he knew minute by minute how things fared: of the Meszrian horse now broken and put to flight beside the wood: of Amaury heavily engaged with Roder on the left. For the main action, his tried troops, two hundred and fifty on either part, were now, with the passage between them of that battering-ram, posted where he would have them: upon the enemy's flanks. Even as the gannet, half closing her wings, drops like a white broad-barbed arrow to the sea, cleaving the waters with a blow that flings up spray with a swish as of a spouting whale, so, suddenly, seizing the moment, Lessingham struck.[7] Himself, with his two hundred, rushing forth now from between the ranks of the unbroken but battered and far-driven centre, turned back the advance of Roder's main front as with a blast of murdering wild-fire. In that same nick of time, the Vicar's veterans closed upon Roder's flanks like the claws of a crab. They took his right flank at open shields, so that great was the man-fall, and men cast down in heaps: some smothered under their fellows' carcases, some cut to death with their own weapons or their fellows' or ever their foes might come at them. The horse upon Lessingham's right, leaving the pursuit when they heard his horn blow up the battle-call, took a sweep south and about and fell upon the foot from flank and rear. Amaury in a last charge flung the half of Roder's famous horsemen into the river and utterly overthrew them.

The sun was a flattened ball of crimson fire touching the sea between the Quesmodian isles, when the High Admiral walked up from his tent with the Lord Beroald to a place of prospect whence they might overlook far and wide the vale of the Zenner, misty in the warm and sleepy sunset light. "Well, I have told you, I think, every tittle," he said. "And now it is the eighth hour past noon. And no news these three hours."

"And then to say he had come up with him in the ings of Lorkan?"

Jeronimy nodded his head. "Should a been more news ere now."

The Chancellor with a swift glance sideways, not to be seen, noted the Admiral's face clouded with anxious thought. "I would not think so," he said lightly.

"A cat not to be caught without mittens," said Jeronimy. He stood for a minute scanning the countryside below, then, as they turned again to their walking, "When should your main body be here?" he said.

"To-morrow night," answered Beroald.

"And Zapheles?"

Beroald's lip curled. "I will adventure upon no guesses as to that."

"To-morrow night," said Jeronimy. "And that's but lean relief, when 'tis being played out now, and for want of your army, three days dallied behind the day—nay, I blame it not on you, my lord: I know what ado you had. Nor I blame it not on myself." He met the

Chancellor's cold eye, squared his shoulders and laughed. "Your lordship must forgive me. Pah! 'tis barely sunset, and are the scritch-owls abroad already? But these land-fights, 'tis pure truth, have ever seemed a thing 'gainst nature to me, in a manner."

A studied imperturbability informed the Chancellor's lean countenance as, erect and soldier-like, he surveyed the landscape with folded arms. "The odds of strength, my lord Admiral," he said coldly, "can alone resolve you of all doubts. And Roder is no untried boy, to walk into nets or aim ere he can strike. Come, let's go to supper."

X

THE CONCORDAT OF ILKIS

Amaury before the Duke ✦ *Our lady of Cyprus*
✦ *Fiorinda in a jewelled shade* ✦ *Philommeides
Aphrodite[1]* ✦ *Her high pierian flower* ✦ *The
Duke perceives.*

DUKE BARGANAX, the second night after that battle,
sat in an upper chamber above the guard-room in
Rumala. Bolt upright he sat, in a great stone chair, back
to the wall, greaved and helmed, and in his long-
sleeved byrny, every link of which was damascened with
silver and gold. Black plumes of the bird of paradise shadowed his
helm with their shifting iridescence of green and steel-blue fires. His
hands hung relaxed over the arms of the chair. Torn and crumpled
papers lay at his feet. A lamp on the table at his left elbow lighted
the room but dimly. His face was in shadow, turned from the lamp
towards the deep-set open window and its darkness astir with starlight. He did not move at the clatter of Medor's mailed footsteps on
the stair nor at his coming in. For a full minute Medor stood before
him silent, as if afeared.

"Is he gone?"

Medor answered, "I cannot move him. He is most stubborn set
to speak with your grace."

Barganax neither spoke nor stirred.

"He will say nought to me," said Medor: "nought to any save to
your grace alone."

"Is he weary of his life?"

127

"I did instruct him at large. Yet nought will do but he shall have speech with you face to face. I have done my best."

After a pause the Duke said, "Admit him."

Thereupon was guarded into the chamber, betwixt two of the Duke's red-bearded shaven-headed men-at-arms, Amaury. He was dirted to the knee from hard riding through the marshlands. They had made him leave his weapons. "Was this well done, Amaury," said the Duke, "to come and make me your gazing-stock, and the glory of Zayana laid in the suds?"

"My lord Duke," said Amaury, "I see no such thing. If your grace will in your old used nobility meet my master, he doth most eagerly desire to treat with you, and upon such terms as shall be of more honour and advantage to you than those which he beforetime did offer, before war was betwixt you."

"Do you see that goblet?" said the Duke then. "Were you to set in it an invenomed toad and mash him to a jelly, then pour wine on't and drink it off, that were a thing likelier for your safety than come hither to insult over me with his words of peace."

Amaury flushed like a girl under his fair skin. He said, "If there is blame, blame me. Of myself, not sent, came I hither into your power; for I knew his strange and needless resolve to come himself to-morrow on the like errand, but I smelt danger in that. Therefore I came first, without leave asked, to be his taster; as great men will have the dish tasted first by another, if there be poison in it."

"Then shall he thank me," said the Duke, "for chastising of his disobedient dog. And yet," he said, "you might a known there was little danger. You might a known I should have the wit to let you go: as men use with rat-traps: there is a way in with a snap-door, but another way out: let 'em go at will, in and out, for a few nights till they have lost all fear on't; then, one night, shut the way out, catch 'em all in a bunch. Dear Gods, could I have but that Roder and that Beroald amongst 'em: mince them all!"

"But I am not a rat," said Amaury. "I can judge; and if I judge so, warn him."

The Duke's face was dark as blood. "Take him out," he said. "Tie him hand and foot and throw him down the cliff. This may somewhat ease my rage."

The guardsmen laid each a hand upon Amaury's shoulders. He turned pale. He said, "If I come not back, there is this good in it, that 'twill yet give him pause. And his life is better to me than mine."

"Make haste, as I bade you," said the Duke, starting suddenly up, deadly white, terrible, like a wounded lion. "If more come, I'll use the like liberty on them. It shall appear whether I be well tamed with the infortunity of this battle. Trokers and dastards:[2] let them know me, too late." He strode with great clanking strides to the window and stood there, stiff, his back to the room, his arms tight folded before his face and pressed against the wall, his temples pressed against the backs of his clenched fists. Medor, by a look, bade the guard stand still. Amaury waited.

"Medor," said the Duke: he was now at the window, looking out. Medor went to him.

"Keep the man till morning: out of my sight. I will think more on this."

Amaury spoke: "May I, with your grace's leave, say but a word?"

The Duke made no answer, looking still out of the window, but his frame stiffened as he stood.

"If I be not returned ere morning, there be those will tell my lord whither I am gone. He will conclude your grace hath made away with me. That ruins all."

The Duke swung round. "Have him away, ere I afterthink me." He plucked out his dagger.

"He was resolved to ride up the Curtain alone," said Amaury loudly as they led him out: "alone: in so high a trusting honour hath he held you."

"Away!" said Barganax. His left hand shut upon Medor's wrist. The soldiers hurried Amaury through the door. "O horrible ruin! was ever prince betrayed as I am? O Medor I could bathe in blood: butcher their heads off with my own hands: cut their hearts out, eat 'em raw with garlic; then sink with stink *ad Tartara Termagorum*.[3]

"Nay, that's foulness," he said, again striding up and down. "Damned Beroald: damned two-faced Zapheles: damned womanish Jeronimy: dregs of the Devil's cup. That's worst of all: I, that dared imaginarily place myself above the circle of the moon, to be the wide world's paragon, and only beauty's self to be my paramour: now baffled to extremest derision, changed to a bloody beast.

"Nay," he said, "but I'll prince it out;" and sat again in the stone chair. Medor was leaned on his elbows at the window surveying the night. "What dost think on?" said the Duke.

"On your star-like nobleness," answered he.

"What was that he said?" said the Duke suddenly: "that Lessingham would trust himself all alone to treat with me here in Rumala? That was very like a lie."

"I think it likely true," answered Medor. "He knoweth well enough your grace's firm-kept faith toward him lately in Zayana."

The Duke was silent. Then, "Why have they taken him away?" he said. "Fetch him back! Must I be betrayed by you too, to do my bidding when I'm beside myself?"

"No," replied he, and gave him a look. "I will keep my old bargain with your grace as for that."

Barganax put off his helm and set it beside him on the table with his iron gloves. The leavings of storm yet darkened and flick-

ered about his eyes and about the lines of his mouth under the
curled mustachios; but no longer so as to deform that face and brow
which, clear seen now in the upward beaming of the lamp, seemed
to contain the united sweet of heaven's graces. He said under his
breath: "Ζὰ δ' ελεξάμαν ὄναρ Κυπρογενήα. In a dream I spake
with Our Lady of Cyprus."[4]

When Amaury was come in again with Medor, "You are a brave
man, Amaury," said the Duke; "and that was to be looked for, since
you serve a brave man; and he is a man to pick out men of strength
and manliness to follow him, and men of his own bent of mind. And
now lay open your former speeches, that I may understand your
meaning."

Amaury laid it all before him point by point.

"And now," said the Duke then, "I have bethought me of this
matter betwixt me and your lord, what way it shall become. Here is
a ring," he said, and took it from his finger: "the stone of it is called
quandias: it is found in the vulture's head, and is man's friend, for it
driveth from him all things that be hurtful. Give it him from me. Say
to him, I will not be outdone by him in nobility: I'll meet with him,
but not here. I'll meet him half way, at Ilkis in Rubalnardale. To-day
'tis Monday; let it be Wednesday at noon. 'Tis best we go weaponed,
seeing the countryside may well be up in a tumult after these doings. But let there be twenty of either side, and no more. And let
truce hold, howsoe'er things fadge,[5] till Thursday midnight."

Amaury kissed Barganax's hand and took the ring. "I am so far
in my lord's counsels," he said, "that I can here confidently accept it
all on his behalf, and say that your grace's noble dealing in this
business hath opened an easy way unto honour and peace betwixt
you."

"Then fare you well, sir," said the Duke. "On Wednesday at
noonday we shall confer in Ilkis. Soldiers, conduct him: a dozen
torches down the Curtain.

"And now," said he to Medor, when Amaury was gone: "nor
you nor no man speak to me. Lights and to bed."

It was now about mid-day of Wednesday, that fourteenth day of
June. In Acrozayana, in a jewelled shade of strawberry-trees, where
the sun speckled the gravel path with moidores[6] strewn upon a
carpet of cool purple, the Lady Fiorinda rested as music rests when
the lute is laid by. Her couch was cushions of wine-dark satin on a
bench of porphyry.[7] Her gown, very soft and fine, long-sleeved,
close fitting, yellow of the pale cowslip petal and with narrow ruffs
at throat and wrist, settled at every gently taken breath to some
fresh perfection of her as she rested there, sweetly gathered up,
upon her right side, her feet along the bench. A hood of black
netted silk, rebated at the border with chrysoprases sewn upon cloth

of gold,[8] framed her face as with an aureole within which, betwixt white brow and jewelled tissue, her hair was like the mystery of night set betwixt bright sun and moon.

Below her to her left, on the step of the carved porphyry seat, sat Rosalura, her needlework fallen on the ground at her side, her hands clasped in her lap. Anthea, clothed in white, stood on the confines of the shade and the sunlight of the lawn without: the pupils of her eyes were slits against that brightness: there was in her bearing an alertness of expectancy: her hair, loosely gathered and knotted up in a disordered grace, was as fire burning. Bellafront, at the outer end of a low bench on the left, close to Anthea, caught the rays too on her coiled plaits of chestnut red. Pantasilea and Myrrha, Campaspe and Violante, reclined these upon this bench those upon that, of the two low benches to Fiorinda's left and right. All were as if listening to something afar off, or, may be, to the humming of the bees only that droned on the summer air, now louder now more dim, but never silent; listening not as hearing but rather hoping to hear some expected thing.

Doctor Vandermast, in russet-coloured gaberdine, walked in his meditation. The little arrows of sunlight, piercing the leaves, rained upon him ceaselessly in his measured walking.

Fiorinda spoke: "That was a strange freedom in so grave a scholar as you, sir, to say that I was, of myself—but indeed now I have forgot what 'twas you said."

He came to a stop at her side, looking past Anthea to the smooth sunny spaces of lawn and flower-bed beyond and, over the parapet, to mountains dim in the summer haze. "It is a principle infringible of divine philosophy," he said, "to seek an understanding of all things *sub specie quadam aeternitatis:*[9] holding them up, as to a lamp, to eternity, wherefrom they take illumination. Myself too did spend whole thirty-seven years together in studying of the Physicals and Ultramundanes,[10] proceeding therein by concatenation of axiom with proposition and so through *demonstratio, scholium, corollarium,*[11] to the union of all in a perpetual and uniform law: that vertical point above the pyramids of knowledge where the intellects may in momentary contemplation seize the truth of things. Yet was it, when all came to all, but an empty truth: *praeter verbum nihil est,*[12] a vain breath. For it supposed further, if it must stand, a reason, understanding, and platform. But whensoever, leaving these toys, I have considered of your ladyship, then is all clear daylight; and whensoever I have been put to a stound, unable to understand of this or that in nature or in time, wherefore it should be thus and not thus, I need but view it under the light of your ladyship, and in an instant I see its very worth and its necessity."

"As this late ruinous field of Lorkan?" said she, "that hath cut the ground from under his feet and sent him cap in hand to make peace with his great enemy?"

He replied: "I behold it in your ladyship as in a glass. I embrace and accept it."

"Mew!" said she, "I would plague him. That is all."

"I do discern you through a thicker cloud than that," said Vandermast, meeting her eye.

"Do you so?" said she. " 'Las! were I not somewhat high-hearted I should be scared out of my senses, as if with such a cockatrice stare the old man would unclothe me where I sit. Horror of Apollonius upon Lamia![13] are we safe indeed?"

"Apollonius," said Vandermast, "was but a very false philosopher, and had but a very superficial and poor understanding. In sum (and this was in my mind when by a trope or figure, madam, I permitted myself to liken you to *eternity*), I conclude that your ladyship is, of yourself, *omnium rerum causa immanens:* the sufficient explanation of the world."

Fiorinda did not smile. "But what needed it of explanations?" she said. "Here it is. I like it."

"Without you," said that old man, "it should fly in pieces and be gone. Like a drop of glass that I have seen, will crash instantly into dust if a man but nip its tail off."

"And, sure, you will not say there ever lived a man so wicked," said she, "as dream it could be otherwise? A world without me? or that hated me?"

"My Lady Fiorinda," said he in a low voice: *"nemo potest Deum odio habere:* no man is able to hate God. I speak not of time and place and outward habit. In Rialmar, no less constantly than in Acrozayana, you do have your siege[14] and presence. There may be more of you, three, nine, nine thousand thousand: I know not: *ex necessitate divinae naturae infinita infinitis modis sequi debent:*[15] infinite shapes and ostentations. I know, in this world, but two. And you, albeit you change, yet change not."

He fell silent. "Nay, I would have you go on," she said, in accents that seemed to draw a veil of mockery shot with starry sparkles across her thought, even as the long black lashes veiled her eyes. " 'Tis very music to me, to smooth my ear: to listen to subtleties, fantastic queries, and speculations, discoursed so by so learn'd a doctor: like as the deceiving of the senses is one of the pleasures of the senses."

Vandermast, immerst yet in his vision, and as if he had not heard her, said, "It is an open-founded doctrine, which can scarce escape the notice even of the rudest; save that they note it and pass by, not knowing fully that which they noted. As they that go to and fro in the street behold a tower, and yet there be many steps and degrees to be ascended painfully, *per scientiam,*[16] ere a man shall stand upon the top thereof and know the thing. And yet," he said, "this is to small purpose talking so, with laborious stumbling words, to your ladyship, as a child conning his lesson: to you that do know these things better than I and without all grammatication."

"You may have a nose for metaphysicals," said that lady; "but here you cry out upon no trail. I know nothing. Only, I am."

"Your ladyship doth play with me," said Vandermast.

"I play with all things," she said. It was as if that which dwelt in the corner of her mouth shot its arrow and then buried its face again for very sweetness of the place it dwelt in. Her right hand made a rest for her cheek; her left arm was thrown back and fallen behind her, behind the proud arch of her hip, as in a carelessness and divine largesse of the treasure of her body, ethereal as the scented thought of a white rose, beautiful as golden flowers, the fairness of it and the Grecian pride. "With all things," she said.

"And rightly so," said that ancient doctor, slowly, as if communing with his inward thought: "seeing that it is for you that all things, *omnia quae existunt*,[17] are kept and preserved by the sole power of God alone, *a sola vi Dei conservantur*."

The bees' drowsy note conducted on the silence. Fiorinda's voice came like honey dropping from the hive on some Elysian Hymettus,[18] saying, as in a dream, "It may be you said true. It may be I do know. The Poetess: 'σύ ἲε κᾶμος θεράπων Ἔρος.' She was charier of words than you, most reverend doctor, and yet said it all, I think: 'thou, and My servant Love.' "[19]

The Countess Rosalura, remembering Ambremerine, leaned suddenly forward to lay her head against the sandals of gold which, with broidered straps of fair Lydian work, covered Fiorinda's feet.

Fiorinda, with a little movement of her head, beckoned the learned doctor to bend nearer. "Will you credit that old tale," she said in his ear, "of their speaking with King Hakon Athelstane's-fosterling, to summon him home, when he sat there a-dying, on the bloody battle-field of Fitiar in Stord? when

> "Gondul and Skogul the Goths'-God sent
>   To choose of the kings,
> Which of Yngvi's line must with Odin fare,
>   In Valhall to won."

"And was not the king glad then, when he heard the words of the noble Valkyries, where they sat there a-horseback, and bare themselves so fairly, and sat helmed and with shield and spear?"[20]

"It is not past credit," answered Vandermast. *"Deus ex solis suae naturae legibus, et a nemine coactus agit:* God fareth according to the laws of His own nature, and under constraint of no man."

She laughed and stood up. Surely the light of her beauty was upon that old man's face, to transfigure it, as sunlight the cold frosty season of December. Every line and thought-driven furrow, the wrinkled hollows of his eye-sockets, their bristling eaves, the lean beaked nose of him, and white beard, were as lighted with her beauty from withinward; and the peace of her beauty lay upon the fragile and vein-streaked smoothness of his brow, and all his countenance was made gracious with the holy spirit and power of that lady's beauty, which stirred now and glittered in the depths of his swift and piercing eyes.

"I will look on this meeting," said she. "A man shall not need be hurt to the death, as then at Fitiar, ere he may pluck the rose acceptable to the Gods and wear it: my roses of Pieria,[21] reached tiptoe from the mere pinnacle of his hopes' defeat. Draw back the veil."

There went with that word a shadow across the sunpath, and a coolness without wind was on the air. And now it was suddenly as if trees and flowers and daisied lawns, nay the very walls and solid ground here in Acrozayana, and the stablished mountains seen beyond the parapet, far off across the lake, were thinned to a tenuous immateriality, not wavering but steady in edge and texture, as if made all of clear livid-coloured glass of the thinness of thin parchment. Through this, as through a painted window, appeared now the naked anatomy of earth, blue and cold: cliffs which swept down to fearful silences, with the tide washing against the bases of the cliffs, and a welter of drowned treasure and sea-wrack and vast worms tearing at one another in the shallows of the sea. The air between the cliffs, ruffled in mists and rawky vapours, was troubled with iron wings of chimaeras that mounted ever upwards, as bubbles mount in wine, and vanished ever in the strip of sky high up between the lips of the precipices: night sky, for all that it was day here in the natural world; and in the night a blazing star with long hairs appeared. Vandermast and those ladies were becoming even as the things about them livid and translucent, like shadows in water or fetches of the dead. She alone, in that falling away of appearance from reality, retained yet the lovely hues of life and carnal substance.

So that to the Duke, facing Lessingham across the council table in Ilkis; it was in that moment as if he looked through layer upon layer of dream, as through veil behind veil: the thinnest veil, natural present: the next, as in a dumb-show strangely presented by art magic, the dappled path beneath the strawberry-trees in his own garden in Zayana and the company there gathered: and so, the firm frame of things and a jut of rock between the abysses, and, standing upon it, that woman, clothed upon with the fires of thunder and of night. From whose eyes as from starred heavens he took knowledge of the action he now went on; and, as through them, saw it; and was content.

XI

GABRIEL FLORES

Terms of the Concordat ♦ The half-forgotten harmonies ♦ Tidings brought to the Vicar ♦ A great prince and his poor secretary ♦ A fury of dogs ♦ Entry of Lessingham into Laimak ♦ The rider thrown.

LESSINGHAM said, "I have now laid the whole matter before your grace. I hide it not, it goes better with my purpose to gather the apples this battle's lucky cast hath brought down for me and enjoy them with your grace's friendship, sooner than climb higher for more and may be break my neck. Nor can any say, who hath any forehead left, that you did draw sword and get nought by it; when you are, upon sheathing of it, seized again of your whole appanage as sovereign indefeasible, and regent besides of all Meszria, save Outer Meszria only."

"Regent," said Barganax: "and in that quality his man, vassal, and subject. Leaveth a tang upon the tongue."

"What man is not spoken of in this sense?" said Lessingham. "All are subject to the Queen of Fingiswold."

"And she," said Barganax, "to this tutor. But losers must not be choosers; and I never reared a pig but that I was ready to eat his bacon."

"My lord Duke," said Lessingham, "we have looked each other in the eye ere this. That I treat o' the Vicar's behalf, regard it not: 'tis me, not him, you deal withal. That I o'erthrew Roder in the ings of Lorkan, I have forgot it and do you, my lord, forget it. From the sweep of eagles' wings it becometh us overview the matter, and what's just and allowable of our greatness, choose that, suffering nought else in the world 'twixt that and our clear judgement."

The Duke was sat forward in his chair, his chin thrust forward a little, right elbow on the table, forearm upright, hand propping his chin; his left arm akimbo, hand upon hip with fingers spread: all with a cattish reposeful elegance. His eyes, that seemed now hawk's eyes, now a deer's, all pupil, liquid and unfathomable, now again proud, serene and relentless, like a lion's, gazed not upon Lessingham but over Lessingham's shoulder. Lessingham, sitting back, watched them in their mutations, until, with their turning at last to engage his own, it was as if from those eyes his own secret spirit faced and regarded him from without.

The Duke spoke. "Item, I subscribe my brother's testament (upon whom be peace); and sith the Admiral resigned it in my favour, take up the regency of South Meszria, doing homage therefor to my royal sister through person, during her minority, of the Lord Protector. Item, he, both for himself and for behalf of the Queen, receives me as lord of Zayana and of that whole duchy and dominion as in that testament set forth, without all suzerainty. To these I add two things further, my Lord Lessingham: first, that the Admiral is confirmed regent of Outer Meszria, 'cause 'tis in the testament so, and I'll be secured 'gainst strange fingers meddling in that pie upon my border; and secondly, the Vicar must give full amnesty to all took up weapons against him for sake of me, and especially I mean to Earl Roder and to the Chancellor."

"Let them go," said Lessingham. "They have stood your grace in little stead. 'Tis well if your dealing should measure their deserving."

"It shall rather hold measure with my own mind," replied he. "I'll not forsake them."

"Then goeth the matter out of all measure, if our agreement fall to the ground for sake of men that, with bunglings and delays—"

"My Lord Lessingham," said the Duke, "you may spare your argument. Be it the wasting and last downthrow of all my fortune, I'll not agree without this."

Then said Gabriel Flores in Lessingham's ear, from a stool at his left elbow, a little behind him, "My lord, 'twere not fit to concede this. His highness will never stand for't."

"Nature, my lord Duke, stood ever on this point," said Lessingham without heeding him: " 'Kae me, I'll kae thee.' The cushion of my cousin's throne is stuffed with thorns, and the stiffest are of your grace's stuffing in: Ercles and Aramond. He will give peace to Beroald, Roder, and Jeronimy, and all them of their following," here Gabriel put a hand upon his sleeve, but withdrew it under swift terror of Lessingham's eye-flash, "and confirm besides Jeronimy, upon homage done therefor unto his highness, in Outer Meszria, upon condition you do call off those princes from practice 'gainst him in the north there; for the world knoweth 'tis your hand works 'em, and at your bidding they can be made to do or to forbear."

"Put it in," said the Duke then: " 'tis a bargain. But you must not set me down for more than I can perform. That I will be neither aiding nor comforting and so forth: good; and that I will use all suasions: good. But if they lay deaf ear to my counselling—"

Lessingham threw out his hands. "Shall I expect your grace then with armed hand to enter their dominions? I thought of no such thing. Countenance is enough: 'tis matter of course with them, as eat and drink, meditating how they may with favour benefit you, or be wary how to offend you. Let's set down largely that you will not lend your shadow for these contrivings. Where the stream is clear, not too much scriveners' preciseness: vomit up ink to trouble the waters."

"Then 'tis fitted," said the Duke, and stood up.

"Will you appoint someone: County Medor if you please: to draw it out for us with Gabriel Flores?"

"Yes, Medor: he hath noted down all for my behalf," said Barganax. "And remember yet constantly of this," he said, walking apart with Lessingham to the pavilion door while the others gathered up their papers: " 'Tis you and I make this peace, but 'tis you must keep it. Were't the Vicar alone, I'd not waste ink and parchment 'pon a concordat I'd know he should tear, soon as advantage should wink at him to the transgressing of it. But in this I see something, that you, my Lord Lessingham, have took it upon your honour, and stand warranty unto me, that this peace shall hold."

"Here," answered Lessingham, "I must use a like licence as did your grace but now. He is not at my apron-strings as a child by his nurse. But so far as in me lies, I faithfully affirm by my solemned oath he shall in all points abide by this agreement."

Upon this, said with great grandeur by the Lord Lessingham, they two struck hand together. As they so stood, handfasted for a moment upon that peacemaking, it was as if a third stood with them: not perceivably in distinction of bodily presence, yet with a strange certitude made known to each in the other and apparent so: so that to the sense of each the other was lost, drunk up, confounded, in this new presence. So they stood, not three but two. But to the Duke the black beard and masculine presence of Lessingham were become as a cloak only, cloaking but not hiding; or as some fortress of old night, strong to preserve that which, to the Duke familiar yet ever new, unseizable as some flower dreamt of by God but not yet unfolded in Elysium, looked from its windows. So too to

Lessingham was the Duke become, but as a might of sunrise rather or of white noon; and that wonder seen at the window was for Lessingham as a forgotten music remembered again and lost again, as in that May night three weeks ago in Acrozayana.

Gabriel said at his elbow, "Pray your worship, I had rather meddle no further in this. Amaury hath a more apter hand than I for't."

Lessingham looked down coldly at him. "Belike he hath. But his highness did design your presence mainly for such work as this. You were best go through with it."

Gabriel stood uncertain. "So please you, I had rather not. So please you, I see little of his highness' design in this," he said, gathering boldness with speaking but to a shoulder. "I am a simple poor servant of his: not a great lord. May be's some trick in it; but to sell his highness' interest, I'd rather not set my pen to it, no not to the drawing of it, so please you."

"Well, begone then," said Lessingham, tartly; "for indeed I have suffered too long your impertinences in these proceedings, like a sparrow chirping and chittering to other sparrows. Begone, go."

Gabriel stood yet in doubt. "Yet, consider, my lord—"

Lessingham gave him a sudden look. "Unless you mean to be kicked," he said. "Begone."

And with great swiftness Gabriel went.

Gabriel went by chosen by-ways and with much circumspection, so that it was mid evening when he rode down through the skirts of the forest where alders and birches increase upon the oaks, and came upon the Zenner a mile below Kutarmish bridge and scarce ten miles as the crow flies from Ilkis whence he had set forth. His little brown horse swam the river, and now in another mile he turned with secure mind up into the highroad and so, 'twixt gallops and breathing times, had by nightfall left behind him the long straight causeway through the fens that runs south and north past the solitary walled bluff of Argyanna. At Ketterby he halted to bait his horse and sup at the moated house: mutton pies, tripe, cheese, and garlic, and thick black beer; would not stay, but rode on and slept in his cloak under the moon on the open heath a little this side of Ristby; saddled up again before daylight; came to Storby when folk were first astir at the bridge-house; ate breakfast at Anguring, and, galloping hard, an hour later met the Lord Horius Parry riding with a half dozen of his gentlemen in the water-meadows a league below Laimak.

"Now we shall know somewhat," said the Vicar, as Gabriel clambered down from the saddle, took his master by the foot, and with a clumsy reverence kissed it. "Chatter and surmise these two days past have fleshed us: set teeth on edge to ask for truth. Give it me in a word: good or bad?"

"Highness, 'tis very good," answered he. In the midst of the great dogs sniffing his boots and breeches he stood unbonneted, shifting from leg to leg, his eyes shifting but ever coming back to meet the Vicar's.

"That and no more?"

"I have been schooled by your highness to answer no more than your highness shall please to ask."

The Vicar looked at him piercingly for a moment, then gave a great barking laugh. "Good is enough," he said. Then, "Mandricard," he said, swinging round in his saddle so that those others, edging and craning nearer for news, drew laughably back as if upon some danger: "you and the rest go home: announce these tidings. I'll take air awhile yet, talk on some small matters concern not you. Fare you well."

"May we not know, but largely—?" Count Mandricard began to say. He was a big bacon-faced side-lipped man with the carriage of a king and a voice like the undertones of bronze, but his words withered on his lips as he met the eye of the Vicar. "Fare you well," the Vicar said, after an instant's pause. And, being that they, like Gabriel, were not without schooling, they obediently departed.

"Well?" said the Vicar. "The sum?"

He answered, "Sum is, their whole power beat in pieces in a main battle beside the Zenner, at Lorkan, a three leagues down from Kutarmish 'pon the Meszrian bank; and yonder Duke laid at your highness' disposal, ready for treading like a frog beneath your boot."

The Vicar, motionless in the saddle, head erect, gazing through half-closed eyelids down the valley, took in a breath through his nostrils, and the leather doublet creaked that encased his mighty chest. Under the freckons his face flamed like sunrise before stormy weather. "That was well done," he said. He shook the rein and turned at a walking pace east along a bridle-path that led to the mountain. Gabriel mounted and followed at his elbow.

"The Duke: ta'en, then? or how?"

Gabriel answered, "I would not have your highness fall to too sudden a conclusion. No, not ta'en; nor not like to be now. Yet was in hand to be."

"In hand to be?" said the Vicar, looking round at him. Gabriel held his peace. "When was this battle?" said the Vicar.

He answered, "Upon Saturday: five days gone." And now as they rode he told of it point by point, to the coming down of the Duke to Ilkis out of Rumala. "By the blood of Satan!" said the Vicar, "had I been there, I doubt I should a made so delicate fine-fingered a matter on't. This bastard line in Meszria springeth too rank a crop of weeds for my liking. Go, I'd a been sore tempted to take his head while God gave me opportunity; so by one gallon of blood save an ocean of cares to come."

They rode on for a few minutes in silence. "What's the end on't?" he said. "Surrender without all conditions?"

"Scarcely thus," said Gabriel.

"What then?" said the Vicar.

"Indeed," said Gabriel, and showed his teeth like a ferret, "it were fittest your highness should wait till my Lord Lessingham come home. He will resolve you of all this, ne'er a doubt on't."

Their horse-hooves, clattering among the stones as they forded a beck, measured the laden silence. Gabriel, with a sidelong glance, noted how the Vicar, bull-like and erect in an inscrutability as of hewn granite, gazed steadily between his horse's ears; only there was a duller red showed now under his fair skin between the freckons. Gabriel hazarded no more glances. A bittern boomed in the marshes far away.[1]

"Fittest I should wait?" said the Vicar in a slow purring quietness. Gabriel, biting his lip near until the blood came, rose stiff in his stirrups with head drawn back till his beard pointed skywards. The Vicar, regarding him snakishly, drew back his thin lips in a smile. "I have not taken hold of you yet, my friend," he said. His fingers like brazen clamps tightened their grip on Gabriel's elbow, while the thumbnail with an erudite cruelty searched the tissues between bone and bone, then at the one intolerable place bored in like a beak. Gabriel's leather sleeve spared him effusion of blood but not the torment. He writhed forward till his forehead hit the saddle-bow, then up again with a sudden motion as of a puppet worked by springs. "I cannot bear it," he said, "I cannot bear it."

The Vicar's hand relaxed but, like an iron gin, held him still. "I can wait?" he said, still with that low purring; "more patience than you, it seems, my little pigsnye? But I'll none of your michery; you shall lay yourself open to me, my pug, lest I open you indeed, see what colour your guts are of, as you've seen me do to others ere now. Well then, is't restore his appanage?"

"Yes," said Gabriel, "and without conditions: without suzerainty."

"If you gape upon me," said the Vicar, "I'll make dogs'-meat of you. What's done, 'tis my doing, not for such vermin as you to question or pronounce upon."

"Your highness yet needs not to eat and devour up me, that had neither hand nor part in't. For indeed there's worse to come too."

"Make haste with it," said the Vicar. " 'Tis my doing, d'ye hear? Remember that, if you would keep your belly unripped."

Gabriel said, "First there's the regency."

The Vicar reined in his horse: near threw him on his haunches. Gabriel paused, meeting his lord's eye that had the wicked look of a bull's about to charge. "God's blood! and might I not give him the regency and ne'er ask leave of thee?" For the moment Gabriel's thoughts were so intent for his proper safety that he forgot his cue to speak. "Regent of what, fool?" said the Vicar. They were bearing now down towards the road again. Gabriel answered, "Great part of Meszria: but upon your highness' suzerainty."

"Great part? What's that? The main south of Zayana, south of the neck? Memison? Doth it bar Sestola and ports besides that should give him the key to the sea? 'Twas a prime act of policy lodged the Admiral aforetime in Sestola to keep Zayana's wings clipped. Speak, fool? What part, fool?"

"All these," said he, his flesh shrinking to feel the threat of that iron grip: "all south of the mountains from Ruyar to Salimat."

"What of the north?"

"Jeronimy confirmed regent, 'pon homage done unto your highness."

"Ha, and was that well done, think you?"

" 'Twas your highness' doing: not for me to question."

"Damned measled hog, answer to the matter, or we'll cut your tongue out: was it well done to entrust my borders to this nannicock, for Zayana to make use of as the monkey do the cat's foot?"

Gabriel faced him with the boldness of a weasel driven into a corner. "Must I answer?"

"You must."

"Then," said Gabriel, "I answer your highness. Yes: it was well done."

"Why so?" said the Vicar. "Answer me, filth, you were best."

Gabriel said, "Let go my arm then, and I'll answer." The Vicar flung him off with so rude a violence, Gabriel near lost his saddle. "Because," said Gabriel then, "sith your highness had given free peace and amnesty to Beroald and Roder both, and commissioned my Lord Lessingham too to pledge you body and soul to Barganax to yield up all, as if you, not he, had been the vanquished party: a thing I would not swallow, and therefore left him—"

" 'Tis a lie," said the Vicar. "When! Pyewacket! Illmauger! Pecki'-the-crown! Loo! Loo! Hie on! Tear him! Tear him!"

Gabriel was barely in time drawing of his hanger as the dogs charged. One he slew with a down-cut, but the next in the next instant had caught his wrist of the hand that gripped the hilt. His horse reared, fell backwards: Gabriel was fallen clear, but before he was gotten upon his feet they had pulled him down and, with a hideous din, set about worrying him like a fox. The Vicar leaped from his saddle, calling them off, smiting left and right among them with his riding-switch: in a moment they were in hand again, obedient, shamefaced, waiting for his eye. All save Illmauger, that with that bite had tasted blood: he, huge, yellow-heckled, wolfish, snarling and slavering at the lips, crouched for another spring. The Vicar grabbed him by the scruff of the neck and flung him aside. He stood his ground, bristling, savage-eyed, ears laid back, growling on a deep inward-taken breath. As the Vicar made a step towards him with uplifted switch, he gathered himself and leapt at the Vicar's throat. They went down together, rolling over and over in an evil hugger-mugger as it had been of wolf and bear. The Vicar for all his bigness scarce outwent the dog in weight of bone and sinew, but it was swiftly seen that he was more deft and agile than a wolf, in strength not overmatched, and in his present mood as wolfish and as implacable. And now was an ill music of the Vicar's snarls and pants and grunts and the clashing of the great beast's teeth as he snapped at air; for the Vicar, now uppermost now under in their fight for the mastery, was never shaken nor loosened from his grasp, of his right hand iron-fast upon the throat. Little by little he tightened his grip to a better purchase, then suddenly the music changed, as his left hand found its quarry, a crueller and more ingenious hold. At length the stifled shrieks died down into a gurgling and sodden quiet. The Vicar, uppermost now, was grovelled face downwards on his adversary, and now, as a whirlwind hushes upon the centre, the leaping medley of limbs, part dog part man, began to be still. Gabriel marked how the great muscles of the Vicar's neck worked under their low-growing cropped stubble of red hair like the neck-muscles of a preying lion, and how his breath came and went, in laboured snuffs and snorts through his nostrils. At length he raised himself on his hands and knees. The dog was dead, bitten clean through the weasand.[2]

The Vicar stood up. He spat, wiped his mouth upon his sleeve, gave a hitch to his kirtle, walked to where his horse was, and climbed leisurely into the saddle. Then, gathering the reins, he with a look bade Gabriel mount too and come with him. They turned now at a walking pace toward Laimak. For a full mile they rode on without word spoken. Then, "You, my pretty pigsnye," the Vicar said: "study to be quiet and to meddle with your own business, not with matters too high for you. And remember, or I'll kill you, all these things were by my prescription and commandment to the least tittle. D'ye hear?"

"I both hear, highness, and obey," said he.

"And carry that hand of yours to the leech when we come home," said the Vicar: "toadstone is available against dog-bites and invenoming."

So, without further word spoken, they came at length, and the Vicar's great dogs beside him, through the meadows home to Laimak.

* * *

It was now afternoon, the third day after these things aforesaid.[3] Lessingham and Amaury came to a halt below the Stringway. Amaury said, "I would give all I have would you but turn back now."

Lessingham laughed.

"Had we but half the horse, your own tried men to follow you, that were security: but go alone with a bare dozen men, 'tis tempting of the Gods, stark folly: put your neck in the bear's mouth."

"What's new in that, sweet nurse-mother? Have I not lodged in my cousin's house fifty times ere now as cousins should, not as an armed enemy?"

"He had not the cause he now hath."

"'Las, is it not a fair peace I bring him home then?"

"Too fair for him that's foul."

"'Tis a peace I'll justify," said Lessingham, "'gainst all skilled advocates in the world."

"He'll say you have been open-handed at his expense. And remember, the fox his secretary ran to him first with the tale: will a put the worst face upon it."

Lessingham said, "I'd a been as open-handed with my own. And for foxes, I deal not with 'em, neither regard 'em." He touched the rein, and Maddalena stepped daintily upon the Stringway.

For a half hour beyond Anguring the road was through beechwoods mixed with chesnut and oak and sycamore, a pleasant green shade: Owlswater ran between rocky banks on their left below them as they rode. Then the woods thinned away, and the river wound gleaming through water-meadows, where in scattered droves black cows grazed or lay, smaller and smaller in the distance, and fields bounded with dry walls stretched on either hand, with here and there a white farmstead, to the rough hill-pastures and the open fell. Here and there men made hay. Smoke went up blue and still in the air where no breeze moved. All the skirts of the mountains were spotted with browsing sheep. On the right, the upper ridges of the Forn, shadowless in the afternoon sunlight, were of a delicate peach-like colour against the blue. Lessingham rode with Amaury a hundred paces or more ahead of his company. Lessingham was in his byrny of black iron, ringed with gold links about the neck and wrists. He wore a low honey-coloured ruff. He went bare-headed for pleasure of the air, and carried his helm at the saddle-bow. The folk in the fields stood up to salute him as he rode by.

They came riding now round the curve of a hill to the last house. It was built beside the road on their right. Upon the left, three sycamore-trees, old and bare of branches below, made an overarching shade before the house, so that, as they rode up, the road went as through a gateway between those trees and the house, and over the brow fell away out of sight. And through that arched way, as in a picture framed, they might see now Laimak couchant upon its rock, bare and unkind of aspect, pallid in the sunshine and with cold blue shadows; beholding which, Amaury shivered in the warm sun and, angry with himself for that, cursed aloud. And now, beyond this last farmstead, the road became but a bridleway, and there were fields no more, but moorish grounds and marsh and rank pasture with sometimes stretches of lush grass and sometimes sedges and peaty pools: the sharp squawk of a water hen, the sudden flight of wild-duck, or a heron heavily taking the air, borne swiftly on her slow flapping wings. Three black crows rose from a grassy patch on the right a hundred paces ahead and departed on furtive wing. Amaury kept his eye on the place. "Carrion," he said, as they came nearer. "One of his cursed dogs; and that's an omen," as they came alongside.

Lessingham looked and rode on. "I would have you learn a new tune, dear Amaury," he said; "not melancholy yourself to melancholy's self and die of your apprehensions."

So came they at length to the castle of the Parrys and rode north-about to the gatehouse and up by the deep hewn passage way to the main gateway, high upon the northern verge, and there was the Vicar and his men to welcome Lessingham. The Vicar was in his brown velvet kirtle, with a belt about his middle of old silver. About his shoulders was his great robe or mantle of state, of red tartarine, and upon his brow a coronal of gold. With so much unexampled show of honourable respect he received Lessingham, as offer to hold the bridle while he dismounted; then took his arms about him and kissed him. Then he made him go up with him to his private chamber in the tower above Hagsby's Entry. "Nay," he said, when they were private there, "I would hear no word from Gabriel. I would have it from your lips, cousin. And first, is it well?"

"'Tis not altogether bad," answered Lessingham, pouring out some wine.

"'Tis victory?"

"My coming home should warrant you that. Did you ever know me put up my sword with the work half done?"

"You did promise me Outer Meszria in the hollow of my hand: that in a month. 'Tis bare three weeks since then. I'm not Grizell Greedigut to ask aught past reason, but somewhat I hope you have brought me."

"Outer Meszria? Did I promise so little?" said Lessingham. "If that should content you, cousin, you shall be more than content with this when you shall have understood it and considered of it;" and with that he pulled forth from his bosom a parchment and writing sealed with seals.

"I can read," said the Vicar, "though none of the best, yet meanly," reaching out his hand for it.

"First I'll rehearse it to you at large," said Lessingham.

"Nay," said the Vicar, and took it: "if any words seem dark, you shall make it more open, cousin. I like 'em best naked: you shall put the frills and furbelows on it anon." He read it, sitting back easily in his great chair. His face as he read was open as a book, with the light full on it from the high window beside them, and Lessingham watched it, sipping his wine. There was not, as he read, so much as a passing shadow ruffled the noble serenity of the Vicar's brow or stirred the repose of those lineaments about the eyes and nose and jowl that could, upon an ill wind's blowing, wake to so much bestial ferocity. Nor was there any new note in his voice when, having read and read it again, at last he spoke. "These articles express a concordat made 'twixt me of the one part, acting within my sovereignty vicarial and as Lord Protector for the Queen, and of t'other part Duke Barganax and ('pon their by instrument accepting of it) those other scum of the world, Jeronimy, I mean, Roder, and Beroald?"

"And in case any one of them shall not within fifteen days accept it," said Lessingham, "then falleth it to the ground, and our hands free of either part. That's why I hold the army still on the Zenner. But they'll accept, ne'er fear it."

"And 'tis execute in duplicate, cousin, by you in virtue of your full powers on my behalf? And Zayana hath my seal, as I have his?"

"Yes," said Lessingham.

The Vicar let fall the parchment and clapped his hands. Six men-at-arms upon the instant leaped out upon Lessingham from behind and ere he could raise finger clamped chains upon him that shackled him, wrist and elbow, knee and foot. Lessingham saw that Gabriel Flores was come in with them and was beside his master. The Vicar started from his chair like a ravening tiger. He smote Lessingham across the face with the parchment. The countenance of Lessingham was for a moment transported with terrible anger: he neither spoke nor moved, but he became white as death. The Vicar, mastering himself, sat down again. Under the clutch of his hands the arms of his chair shook and trembled. He glared with his eyes upon Lessingham who, of his right colour again, had now in his grey eyes the steadiness of levelled steel.

The Vicar opened his mouth and said, and his words came thick and stumbling as a man's that is drunk with wine: "Overmuch have I trusted you. Yet this showed little wit, to come tell me to my face of this betrayal, that stinks more ugly in the sight of God than do all the carrion of this world. But you shall see I have a short way with such checking buzzards. A guard upon him! In an hour's time, cut his neck. Chop his carcase for the dogs, but spike up the head upon the main gate. I'll look on it before supper."

Gabriel was shivering and twitching in all his body, like a little terrier dog at the edge of a duckpond. The Vicar looked around at him, then back at Lessingham who was stood up now, taller by a head than the soldiers that held him shackled. Even upon that brink of fate and death he stood with so good a grace and presence as if a soul of iron informed him; looking upon the Vicar as from above, and in his grey eyes, keen and speckled, something very like a smile, as if he knew something that was not true. "Well," said the Vicar, "have you nothing to say?"

"Nothing but this," answered he: "that you were wont to act upon no great resolution without you first had slept upon it. It seems the Gods have infatuated your high subtle wisdom, if now you will do a wrong irrevocable both to yourself and me, and not e'en sleep upon it. Your matter hath not turned out so ill aforetime, following of my counsels."

The Vicar glowered motionless as a bull in granite; his eyes were fixed no longer on Lessingham's eyes, but below them, on his mouth or beard. The guard, obedient to a covert sign from Gabriel, made a motion to take Lessingham away. The Vicar turned suddenly and Gabriel's elbow shrank in his brazen grip. "Stay," he said. "I'll not let truth go by, albeit she were pointed out to me by a dissembling tyke. To-morrow's as good as to-day. And to make sure, unto you, Gabriel, I commit him in charge; doubt not but that I shall call to you for a strict account of your dealing with him. For his life and safe keeping your life shall answer. Here are the keys," and he threw them on the table.

Gabriel took them with a beaten scowling look.

XII

NOBLE KINSMEN IN LAIMAK

The Vicar's dream ◆ Argument of midnight ◆ Adamant grinds adamant ◆ The rider in saddle again ◆ "Policy and her true aspéct" ◆ Nuptial flight of the Peregrines ◆ Lessingham Captain-General ◆ Conceits of a lord protector ◆ Revelry; and a meeting at dawn ◆ North.

THE Lord Horius Parry awoke between midnight and cock-crow, being troubled and vexed with a certain unpleasing dream. And this was the beginning of his dream: that Gabriel sat at his knee reading in a book of the *Iliad* wherein was told the fate of the lady Simë that she was (and here Gabriel, not knowing the meaning of the Greek word, asked him the meaning). And though upon waking he knew not the word, and knew besides that in the *Iliad* is no such tale and no such lady, it seemed to him in his dream that the word meant "gutted like a dog." Thereupon in his dream the Vicar was remembered of that old tale of Swanhild, Gudrun's daughter, wed in the old time to King Jormunrek, and by him, upon lying slanders of Bikki, adjudged to die and be trod with horses in the gate; but, for the loveliness of her eyes that looked upon them, the horses would not tread upon her, but still swerved and reared and spared her, until Bikki let do a sack about her head, hiding her eyes, and she

149

was trodden so and so slain.[1] And now was the dream troubled and made unclear, as a breeze ruffles water and does away the reflected shapes and colours; and when it cleared, there was a wide plain lay amid mountains, all in a summer's evening and pleasant sunshine air, and in the midst upon a little rise of ground a table, and before the table three thrones. And the Vicar thought he saw himself sitting upon the left-hand throne, and he thought he knew in his dream that he was a king; and the plain was filled with people assembled as for some occasion, and they waited there in silence in their multitude, innumerable as the sands of the sea. And the Vicar looked upon himself, upon the king, and saw that he was both in feature and in apparel like to the Assyrian kings in the great stone likenesses carved of them of old, and his beard long was tightly frizzed and curled, and his belted robe incrusted with every kind of precious stone, so that it glittered green and purple and with sparkles of fiery red; and he was cruel and fell to look upon, and with white glinting teeth. And behold there walked a woman before the thrones, fair as the moon, clothed in a like glittering garment as the king's; and he knew in his dream that this was that lady Simë, and when he beheld her steadfastly he saw (yet without mazement, as in dreams the singularest and superlative wonder, impossibilities and fictions beyond laughter, will seem but trivial and ordinary) that she was Lessingham. It seemed to him that this she Lessingham did obeisance to the king, and took her seat on the right-hand throne; and immediately upon the third throne he beheld the queen that sat there betwixt them, as it had been a queen of hell. She was attired in a like garment of precious stones; her hair was the colour of wet mud, her eyes like two hard pebbles, set near together, her nose straight and narrow, her lips thin and pale, her face a lean sneak-bill chitty-face;[2] she had a waiting, triumphing look upon her face; and he loathed her. And now went men before the thrones, bearing on a great stand or easel a picture framed, and showed it to that bright lady; and it seemed to the Vicar that she gave a terrible cry and covered her eyes; and the men turned the picture that all might see, and he could not discern the picture to understand it; but only the writing upon it, in great letters: UT COMPRESSA PEREAT.[3] And he thought the whole multitude in their thousands took up those words and howled them aloud with a howling like the howling of wolves. And he shouted and leapt awake, sitting up in the dark in his great canopied bed in Laimak, all shaking and sweating.

For a minute he sat so, listening to the darkness, which was as if some vast body had been flung into the pool of night and made waves upon it that were his own blood-beats. Then with an obscene and blasphemous oath he felt for tinder, struck a light, and lighted the candles on the table by his bed in the silver candlesticks that stood there, and his sword beside them, and a goblet, and wine in a great-bellied bottle of green glass with a stopper of gold. As the new-kindled candleflames shrank dim in the moment before the melting of the tallow, questionable shadows crouched in the recesses of the walls and vaulted ceiling. A puff of wind stirred the curtain by the window. Then the candles burned up. Pyewacket, waked by his shout, was come from the foot of the bed and laid her chin on his thigh, looking up at him with great speaking eyes in the bright beams of the candles. The Vicar poured out wine, a brimming goblet, and guzzled it down at one gulp. Then he stood up and abode for a while staring at the candleflames and as if listening. At length he clad himself in breeches and gown, buckled on his sword, took and lighted a lantern, and unbolted the door. Gabriel was in his place without, asleep on his bed made up upon the floor across the threshold. The Vicar woke him with his foot and bade him give him the keys. He gave them in silence and would have come with him, but the Vicar with a kind of snarl bade him remain. Gabriel, considering this, and his disordered looks, and the sword at his thigh, watched him go with his bitch at his heel, through the ante-room and through the further door, that led to his private chamber, and when he was gone sat down on his pallet bed again, licking his lips.

The Vicar went down by a privy passage of his own to the prison where Lessingham was mewed up; went in by means of his private key, and locked the door behind him. He held up the lantern. Lessingham lay in the far corner, with his ankles shackled to a ball of lead great as a man's two fists. His left arm was free, but the other wrist locked in a manacle with a long chain from that to his foot. His cloak of costly silken stuff was rolled for a pillow for his cheek. The Vicar came nearer. With his dream still upon him, he stood looking upon Lessingham and listening, as upon some horrid sudden doubt, for the sound of his breathing. In a deep stillness he lay there on the cobblestones, and with so much lithe strength and splendour of limb and chest and shoulder that the mould and dank of that place and the sweating walls, with trickles of wet that glistered in the lantern-light, seemed to take on an infection from his presence and put on a kind of beauty. Yet so still and without sound as he slept, had he been dead he could scarce have lain more still. Pyewacket gave a low growl. The Vicar caught her by the collar and flashed the lantern near Lessingham's face. Upon that, he sat up wide awake, and with great coolness looked upon the Vicar.

They kept silence, each waiting on the other. Lessingham's patience outstayed the Vicar's in that game, and the Vicar spoke. "I have bethought me, cousin, and if there's aught you can say may extenuate the thing, I'll hear it."

"Extenuate?" Lessingham said, and his voice was chilling as the first streak of a winter's dawn on a frozen sea. As the Vicar held the lantern, so his own face was shadowed, but the eye of Lessingham in full light: the eye of such a man that a prince would rather be afraid of than ashamed of, so much awfulness and ascendancy it lent to his aspect over other mortals. "Is it morning then, outside of this hole you have thrust me in?"

"Two hours past midnight."

"It shall at least be set down to you for a courtesy," said Lessingham, "that at this time of night you are gotten up out of your bed to make me amends. Pray you unlock." He held out his right wrist, chained: " 'Tis a kind of gewgaw I ne'er put on till now and not greatly to my liking."

"There's time to talk on that," said the Vicar. "I'll first hear if there be any good face you can put on this ill trick you have played me."

Lessingham's eye flashed. He held out his wrist, as might a queen to her tiring-woman. "An ill trick you," he said, "have played me! By heavens, you shall unlock me first, cousin. We'll talk outside."

The Vicar paused and there was a cloud in his face. "You were a more persuasive pleader for your safety but now, cousin, when you lay sleeping. Be advised, for I have cause against you enough and beyond enough; and be sure you satisfy me. For except you do, be certain you shall never go from this place alive."

"Indeed then you might a spared your sleep and mine," said Lessingham then, shaking his cloak up as if to lie down again. The Vicar began pacing to and fro like a wolf. " 'Tis simplicity or mere impudent malice to say I did betray you; and this an insolency past forgiveness, to use me so. So touching this concordat not a word will I say till I am loosed, and 'pon no conditions neither."

The Vicar stopped and stood for a minute. Then he gave a short laugh. "Let me remember you," he said in a clear soft voice, glaring in Lessingham's face by the light of the lantern, "of Prince Valero, him that betrayed Argyanna a few years since to them of Ulba and led that revolt against me. The Gods delivered him into my hand. Know you the manner of his end, cousin? No: for none knew it but only I and my four deaf mutes you wot of, that were here at the doing on't, and I have told no man of it until now. Do you see that hook in the ceiling?" and he swung the light to show it. "I'll not weary you with particulars, cousin. I fear 'twas not without some note and touch of cruelty. Such a pretty toying wit had I. But we've washed the flagstones since.[4]

"Well?" he said, after a silence.

"Well," said Lessingham, and from now he held the Vicar constantly with his steel-cold eye: "I have listened to your story. Your manner of telling of it does you credit: not so greatly the substance of it."

"Be you ware," said the Vicar with a loud sudden violence, and give him an ill look. "The case you are in, this place you lie in, which is my hidden slaying-place in Laimak: think on't. And I can make that laughing face of yours turn serious."

"I laugh not," replied he. " 'Tis not a laughing matter." They looked one another in the eye without speaking. In that game too Lessingham outstayed the Vicar.

Then Lessingham said: "Do not mistake me. If I fear you not, I am not so foolish as hold you for a man not worthy to be feared. But to threaten me with death, 'tis as the little boy that sat on a bough and would cut away from the tree the bough he sat on. I think you have more wit than do that."

In a deadly stillness, with feet planted wide apart, the Vicar stood like a colossus looking down upon him. The Vicar's own face was now in shadow, so that when, after a long time, Lessingham spoke to him again, it was as a man might speak to an impending great darkness. "I know it is a hard choice for you, cousin. Upon this side, you have no true friend in the world but me; lose me, and you stand alone amidst a world of enemies, your back bare. And yet, against this, you have done me a gross injury, and you know me for a man who, albeit I have looked upon this world for but half your span of years, have yet slain near as many men upon matter of honour alone, in single combats, as yourself have slain whether by murder or what not. I have slain a dozen, I think, in these eight years, since I was of years seventeen, not to reckon scores I have slain in battle. So, and to judge me by yourself, you must see great danger in it to release me. A hard choice. As if you must run hazard either way to lose me. And yet, my way you stand some chance of keeping me: your way, none."

There was a pause when he ended. Then said the Vicar with his face yet in darkness, "You are a strange man. Doth not death then terrify you?"

Lessingham answered, "The horror and ugsomeness of death is worse than death itself."

The Vicar said, "Is it one to you: live or die? Do you not care?"

"O yes," said Lessingham. "I care. But this choice, cousin, is in the hand of fate now: for you even as for me. And for my part, if the fall of the dice mean death: well, it was ever my way to make the best of things."

With the cadence of his voice falling away to silence, it was as if, in that quiet charnel under Laimak that knew not night nor day, scales were held and swung doubtful, now this way now that. Then the Vicar slowly, as if upon some resolution that came near to crumbling as he embraced it, turned to the door. Behind him his shadow as he went rushed up and stopped like a winged darkness shedding obscurity from wall and ceiling over half the chamber. Then he was gone, and the door locked, and all darkness; and in that darkness

Lessingham saw Pyewacket's eyes, like two coals burning. He reached out a hand to her, open, palm downwards. He could not see her, save those eyes, but he felt her sniff cautiously and then touch the back of his hand lightly with her cold nose.

The Vicar was mid-part up the stairs when he missed her. He called her by name: then stood listening. Cursing in his beard, he was about turning back; but after a few steps down, halted again, swinging his keys. Then, very slowly, he resumed his mounting of the stairs.

Betimes in the morning the Vicar let fetch out Amaury from the place where he had been clapped up: gave him in charge to Gabriel and those six close men: made these wait in the ante-chamber: gave Amaury, in private audience, keys for Lessingham's prison by the secret door: walked the room a dozen turns, eyes still bent upon the floor, then said: "You are free, lieutenant. Go to your master: conduct's provided, Gabriel and them: strike off his chains: here's keys, enlarge him. Tell him I'm sorry: a jest: went too far: he and I am friends, understand each other: therefore let us meet as if this ne'er had befallen. He and I be two proud men, tell him. I've took a long step to meet him: 'tis for him make it easy for me now."

Amaury said with flaming face, "I humbly thank your highness. I am a blunt soldier, and there is this to be said: my lord is your highness' true and noble friend. And strangely so. And a thousand times better than you deserve."

"Have you got it by rote? say it over," said the Vicar, not hearing, or choosing not to be thought to have heard, that bearding boldness. Amaury said over his message, word by word, while the Vicar paced the room. "Away then."

Lessingham woke and came forth into the air and day with as much of careless equanimity as a man might carry who rises from the accustomed bed he has slept upon, night by night, for ten years in peace. Only there sat in his eyes a private sunbeamed look, as if he smiled in himself to see, like a sculptor, the thing shape itself as he had meant and imagined it. Amaury sat with him in his chamber while he bathed and donned clean linen. "Praise be to the blessed Gods," he said, leaping from the bath where he had rinsed away the suds, for curling of my hair by nature: not as yonder paraquitos,[5] must spend an hour a day with barbers to do't by art." His skin, save where the weather had tanned or the black hair shadowed it, was white like ivory. Then, when he was well scrubbed dry with towels: "Boy! when, with orange-flower water for my beard! Foh! I smell her yet." He gave his boy kirtle, hose, ruff: all the upper clothing he had worn in prison: bade him burn it.

Amaury spoke. "What o'clock do you mean to set forward?"

"Set forward?"

"Leave this place," said Amaury: "out of his fingers: out of Rerek?"

"Not for some weeks yet. There's a mort of work I must first set in hand the conduct of."

Amaury sprang up, and began to walk the room. "You are preserved this time beyond natural reason. If a man take a snake or serpent into his handling—O he spoke true when he said you do understand each other. And there's the despair on't: and your eyes were not open to your danger, there were hope yet, by opening of 'em, to save you from it. But you do know your danger, most clearly, most perfectly and circumspectly: yet rejoice in it, and laugh at it."

"Well, that is true," said Lessingham, giving a touch to his ruff. "What shall's do then?"

The heat of the summer noonday stood over Laimak when Lessingham at length came, with Amaury and two or three of his gentlemen attending him, to meet the Vicar on that long straight paven walk that runs, shaded at that hour by the tennis-court wall, along the battlements above the north face. Their folk, of either side, hung back a little, marking, these in the one, those in the other, their looks as each faced each: the Vicar a little put out of his countenance, Lessingham, under a generous noble courtesy, a little amused. After a while Lessingham held out his hand, and they shook hands without speaking. "Give us leave," said the Vicar and took him apart.

When they had measured a few paces in silence, "I hope you slept well," said Lessingham. "It was prettily done to leave me your bitch for company."

"What's this?" said the Vicar. "The Devil damn me! I had clean forgot her."

"I had thought," said Lessingham, "you were hard put to it to make up your mind, and conceited you might cast her for the part of Fate. A chained man: 'twas a nice poising of the chances. I admired it. And you feed 'em on man's flesh now and then I think? of ill-doers and such like."

"I swear to you, cousin, you do me wrong. By all the eternal Gods in heaven, I swear I had forgot her. But let's not talk on this—"

"Waste not a thought upon't. I ne'er slept better. Being of that sort, may be 'twas that made her take to me:

"O we curl'd-haird men
Are still most kind to women.[6]

"Or how think you?"

"Cousin," said the Vicar: "this concordat." Here he took him by the arm. "I would know the whole carriage on't. I question not there's good in't, for, by my soul, you have ever done me good: but let me die bursten if I understand the good of this."

"An answer so fairly besought," said Lessingham, "should be fairly given. But first I would have you, as a politic prince who will not lay your foundations in the dirt but upon the archaean crust, refer the whole estate you are in to your highness' deliberate overviewing again. This kingdom, whiles the old King lived, was set in its seat unshakable: terrible to kings and peoples upon lengths of seas and shores.[7] A main cause was, 'twas well knit: at one unto itself. True, at the last you had been already straining at the leash in new-conquered Rerek: unwisely, to my thinking, as I plainly told you. Then the King died, and that changed all: a hard-handed young fool in the saddle 'stead of a great wise man: and that shook all from withinwards. You had experiment then, cousin, of my mind towards you: did not I stand for you at Mornagay with my eight hundred horse, as a boy with a stick 'gainst a pack of wolves? had you miscarried I mean; and that was not past likelihood. Then you took a means that both rid you of present danger and, 'cause men shrewdly guessed it, weakened you, 'cause it blasted your reputation (and a sickly browned flower was that already)—and then immediately, by direct bounty of Heaven, was all given into your lap by handfuls: named in the testament Lord Protector and Regent for the young Queen's minority. Why, 'tis all in your hand, cousin, and you will but use it. The realm is in your hand, like a sword; but all in pieces. And first is to weld the slivers: make it a sword again, like as King Mezentius had: then strip it out against Akkama, or what other heads were best plucked off that durst threaten you."

They walked slowly, step with step, the Vicar with a brooding look, silent. Lessingham hummed under his breath a lilting southern song. When they came to the corner against the wall of the round north-western tower the Vicar stopped and, resting his elbows on the battlement, stood looking over the landscape where all colour was burnt to ashes under the sunlight. Near at hand, to the northward, a little crag rose solitary, a mimic Laimak, may be fifty feet above the marsh; and on its highest rock sat a falcon-gentle all alone, turning her head sharply every now and then to look this way and that. Once and again she took a short flight, and small birds mobbed her. And now she sat again on her rock, hunched, with a discontented look, glancing about this way and that. The Vicar watched her in his meditation, spitting at whiles thoughtfully over the parapet. "Remember, I have taught 'em," said Lessingham, "first in Zayana, and now with sharp swords upon the

Zenner, there's a higher here to o'ersway them if need be. Next is to reclaim 'em, call 'em to heel, be kind to 'em. By this, eased of your present fears lest they of your own house shall pluck the chair from under you, you may frown upon the world secure."

After a while the Vicar stood up and began to walk again. Lessingham walked beside him.

Lessingham said: "Once you have the main picture, the points of my concordat are as easily seen as we can discern flies in a milkpot. I know this Duke, cousin, as you do not. He is proud and violent: will stick at no extremity if you drive him and hold him at bay. But he is given to laziness: loveth best his curious great splendours, his women, voluptuousness, and other maddish toys, delicate gardens where he doth paint and meditate. And he is an honourable man, will hold firmly by a just peace; and this peace is just."

"Will not she hound him on to some foul turn against me? that woman of his?"

"What woman?" said Lessingham.

"Why, is't not the Chancellor's sister? Zayana loveth her as his life, they say: 'can wind him to her turn, I'm told."

"Again," said Lessingham, not to follow this vein, " 'tis weapons in your hand to a won Jeronimy, Beroald and Roder to your allegiance. The point of law hath stuck, I know, in the Chancellor's gullet since the testament was first made known: by this largesse of amnesty you purchase much secureness there."

"Ay, but 'twas put in 'pon urgency of Zayana: he'll get the thanks for it when he shows it them, not I. And why needs he your warranty, cousin, as if you should compel me to abide by it? By Satan's ear-feathers! there's neither you nor any man on earth shall so compel me."

"Compel's not in it," answered he. "He knows I am in your counsels and that you would listen to me: no more. Another great good: these vexations in north Rerek should go off the boil now, when he hath called off Ercles and Aramond from that business. Brief, we are not presently strong enough to hold down by force no more than Outer Meszria, and that but with his good will. By so much the more had it been folly to a carried the war south after this victory to Southern Meszria and Zayana."

They walked the whole length of the parapet in silence, then the Vicar stopped and took Lessingham by both arms above the elbow. "Cousin," he said, and there sparkled in his eyes a most strange and unwonted kindness:

> "That Friend a Great mans ruine strongely checks,
> Who railes into his beliefe, all his defects.[8]

"You have saved me, very matter indeed. By God, your behaviour hath not deserved such doggish dealing. Ask your reward: will you be Warden of the March of Ulba? I'd told Mandricard he should have it: 'tis yours. Or will you have Megra? What you will: you shall have it."

Lessingham smiled at him with that measure of admiration, contented and undeluded, that is in a skilled skipper's eye when he marks, on a blue and sunny sea, the white laughter of breakers above a hidden skerry. "A noble offer," he said, "and fitting in so great a prince. But I will not be a lord of land, cousin. Like those birds Mamuques, that fly upon wingless wings and the air only feeds them, such am I, I think: a storm-bird, and to no place will I be tied but live by my sword. But, for such as I am I will take this good offer you have made me; and two things I will choose: one a great matter, and one little."

"Good. The great one?"

"This it is," said Lessingham: "that wheresoever I may be within the realm I bear style and dignity of Captain-General of the Queen, having at my obedience, under your sovereignty as Lord Protector, all armed levies in her behalf whether by land or sea."

The Vicar blew out with his lips.

Lessingham said, "You see I can open my mouth wide."

"Ay," said the Vicar, after a minute. "But I will fill it. To-day there's no such office, save I suppose it vesteth in me by assumption, flowing from my powers vicarial. I cannot tell where I should better employ it than on you. Conceive it done. The next?"

"Thanks, noble cousin," said Lessingham. "After so high a thing, 'tis almost churlish ask you for more. Yet this goes with it. I wish your highness will, by decree general throughout your realm of Rerek, proclaim, as for my body, like dispensation and immunity as for your own particular. By this must all attempts 'gainst me, were they by your very commandment, carry from this time forth like guilt as attempts 'gainst you and your throne and state do carry: and like punishment."

The Vicar gave a scoffing laugh. "Come, you would be witty now."

"I was never in plainer earnest," said Lessingham.

"Then 'tis a saucy claim, deserveth no answer."

Lessingham shrugged his shoulders. "Be not sudden, cousin, the matter is of weight. Indeed, it is no more than need."

"I wonder you will not ask me deliver up to you Gabriel and those six men: 'twere scarcely more monstrous."

"That were one way," said Lessingham, "But I am reasonable. That were to shake your authority: a thing you could never grant. But this, easily. And this is as good for me."

"Dear Gods!" The Vicar laughed in his anger. "If you but

heard yourself speaking with my ears! I'll tell you, cousin, you are like a kept woman: and the cost, I 'gin to think, beyond the enjoyment. Sink away to hell then, for this is a thing you could not in your senses hope for."

The falcon was perched still on the crag, alone and unmerry. At an instant suddenly out of the sky there swept down at her a little unknown, as if she were his prey: barely avoided her as he stooped, swept up again, and stooped again. She, with wings half lifted and head lowered snakelike betwixt her shoulders, faced with sudden beak each teasing stoop of his; and now she took wing, and in ever widening spirals they rose skywards above Laimak, racing for height. Lessingham, imperturbable with folded arms, watched that play. The Vicar, following his eye, noted it too. And now as they swung wide apart, the tassel-gentle from a momentary vantage in height stooped at her in midair, avoiding her by inches as he dived past, while she in the same instant turned on her back to face his onset, scrabbling in air at him with her pounces and threatening with open beak. Twice and thrice they played over this battle in the sky: then he fled high in air eastward, she pursuing, till they were lost to sight.

"I have strained a note above Ela for a device," said Lessingham upon an unruffled easy speech, "but you can scarce expect me, for safety of my person, be content with less than this. I would not, by speaking on't, move an evil that is well laid; yet partnership betwixt us can scarce hold if I must get a good guard to secure me with swords and so forth, whensoever I am to lodge in your house of Laimak."

The Vicar ground his teeth, then suddenly facing round at him, "I know not," he said, "why I do not go through and murder you."

"Why, there it is," said Lessingham. "Have you not this moment laid great trust and charge upon me, and will you sup up your words again? Have you not a thousand tokens of my love and simple meaning to your highness? Yet, like some girl ta'en with the green sickness, you will turn upon me: and as you are, so will you still persist. 'Tis pity. Our fortunes have bettered soonest, I think, when we have gone arm in arm."

She was back again, perched. And now came her mate again and stooped at her; and again they mounted and went to their sport again, high in the blue. Lessingham said, "I'll go take a walk: leave you to yourself, cousin, to employ your mind upon't."

The Vicar replied neither with word nor look. Left to himself, he leaned upon folded arms looking north from the battlements: his brow smooth and clear, his mouth set hard and grim, and his jowl, under the red bristly clipped growth of beard, as if carved out of the unyielding granite. As a film is drawn at whiles over the eyes of a hawk or a serpent, thought clouded his eyes. The tassel-gentle was fled away again into the eastward airt, and the falcon at length, returning from the pursuit, perched once more on her little rock. She looked about, but this time he came not back again. And now she sat hunched, alone, discontented.

So it was in the end, that Lessingham had his way: confirmed by letters patent, under hand of the Lord Protector and sealed with the great seal, Captain-General of the Queen, with like inviolability of person and like guilt laid upon any that should raise hand or weapon or draw plot against him, as were it the Vicar's own person in question or one of the royal blood and line of Fingiswold. With so much honour was Lessingham now entertained and princelike estate in the open eye of the world, and proclaimed so, not in Laimak only but up and down the land. And now, for certain days and weeks, he was whiles with the Vicar in Laimak, and at whiles in the March, or south beyond the Zenner, putting in order matters that were necessary for carrying out of that concordat made at Ilkis. Nor was there found any man to speak against that measure, but it was accepted of by all of them: by the High Admiral Jeronimy, and by Earl Roder, and by the Chancellor. And all they with an industrious loyalty upheld the Duke and Lessingham in the conduct of this work, in so much that, as summer wore and July was turning toward August, things were well set in order for a good peace; and that seemed like to hold, since all were contented with it. With things in such case, Lessingham came north again to Owldale, and men thought that he, that had been great before, was by all these things grown greater.

Now the Lord Horius Parry made a feast for his cousin Lessingham in the great banquet-room in Laimak, and there were there mighty men of account from all the dales and habited lands in Rerek, and they of the Vicar's household and his great officers, and Amaury and others that followed Lessingham. And now when the feast was part done, the Vicar upon a pretext rose from his seat and made Lessingham go with him privately out of the banquet-hall, and so up upon the roof of the keep. Here they had many a time taken counsel together: as upon the morrow of Lessingham's coming from Mornagay, when he wrung from the Vicar the truth touching the taking off of King Styllis and undertook that embassage to Zayana. On this secret roof they walked now under stars which shone down with a mildness like sleep and with an untwinkling steadfastness through the region air that was woven in web and woof of moonlight and where no wind stirred. Only Antares, sinking to the west above the ridges of Armarick, blinked red with sometimes a sparkle of green fire. The noise of feasting floated up faint from the banquet-hall. The hooting of owls, as they went about their occasions, sounded at whiles from the wooded hillsides and spaces of the sleeping valley afar. Breathing such airs, showered down upon with such influences, flattered with such music, that the season of sleep discourses and the ensphered peace of the summer's night, Lessingham talked with the Lord Horius Parry of men and their factions within the land and without, and of their actions and valour, and the ordering and grounding of their several estates and powers; deliberating which of these it were fit to encourage and rely upon, which were best coaxed and dallied withal, and last, which ought upon first occasion to be suddenly extinguished. After which mature deliberation they propounded to themselves this, that Lessingham should shortly go north and across the Wold to Rialmar, there to perform for a while his office of a commander, entertaining the people and assuring himself of the great men: a thing not to be done by the Vicar himself, in so much as they of those northern parts held him suspected and were not easily to be wooed to serve him faithfully or cancel that sinister opinion they had held of him. But Lessingham was not odious to them, but rather held in admiration, upon experience in late wars both by soldiers and people, for one of fair dealing, and for a man-at-arms fierce and courageous in his venturing upon and coming off from dangers.

And now while they walked, Lessingham, debating with himself of all these things, was ware that the Vicar talked now of women, and how unfit it was they should succeed to the government of states, where need was rather of princes that should be both venerable and terrible: and so forth of women in generality: "In my conceit he understood it aright that said, 'It is all but hogsflesh, varied by sauce.' And I think you too are of that opinion, cousin?"

"Yes," said Lessingham out of the starlight, as a man might answer a child: "I am of that opinion."

"And, by that, the sured man for this further purpose. Cousin, it would comfort my hand mightily could I bring this pretty ladybird and emblem of sovereignty to dwell here in Rerek. I do mistrust the folk about her in the north there. And remember, she's of manable age: wooers, I hear tell on: that Derxis for one, newly crowned in Akkama, a sweet young swanking: in Rialmar, I have't upon sure intelligence, this very instant. Phrut! the cat will after kind. Therefore, cousin, of this plain power I give you and make you commissionary: use what means you will, but bring her south to me in Laimak."

Lessingham studied a season and at last said: "In plain terms, cousin: this is not an overture of marriage?"

"Footra! I ne'er dreamed on't."

"That is well; for 'pon first bruit of that, you should incur the hatred of them all, and all our work fly again in pieces. Well, I will undertake it, if your highness will wisely give me a large discretion:

for it is a thing may seem mischievous or profitable, and whether of the two we know not till I be there to try."

"Enough: you know my mind," said the Vicar. "Try how she stands affected to me, and do what you may. And now," he said, "let us go down and drink with them. Cousin, I do love you, but by my soul you have this fault: you do drink commonly but to satisfy nature. Let's you and I this night drink 'em all speechless."

Lessingham said, "Wine measurably drunken delighteth best. But to humour you to-night, cousin, I will drink immeasurably."

So came they again to the feast, in the hall of the great carven faces of black obsidian-stone whose eyes flung back the lamplight; and straightway there began to be poured forth by command of the Vicar cup upon cup, and as a man quaffed it down so in an instant was his cup brimmed a-fresh, and the Vicar shouted at every while that men should swiftly drink. And now he bade the cup-bearers mix the wines, and still the cups were brimmed, and swiftlier drank they, and great noise there was of the sucking down of wines and clatter of cups and singing and laughing and loud boastings each against each. And now were the wits of the more part of them bemused and altered with so much bibbing and quaffing as night wore, so that some wept, and some sang, and some embraced here his neighbour, there a cup-bearer, and some quarrelled, and some danced; some sat speechless in their chairs; some rolled beneath the table; and some upon it. The heat and sweat and the breath of furious drinking hung betwixt tables and rafters like the night mist above a mere in autumn. It was ever that the Vicar and Lessingham set the pace, carousing down goblet after goblet. But now the high windows, all wide open for air, began to pale, and the lamps to burn out one by one; and not a man remained now able to drink or speak or stand but all lay senseless among the rushes, or in their seats, or sprawled forward on the table: all save the Vicar and Lessingham alone.

The Vicar now dismissed the cup-bearers, and now they two fell again to their drinking, each against each, cup for cup. The Vicar's countenance showed scarlet in the uncertain light, and his eyes puffy like an owl's disturbed at noon; he spoke no more; his breath laboured; the sweat ran down his brow and down nose and cheeks in little runlets; his neck was bloated much beyond its common size, and of the hue of a beetroot. He drank slowlier now; Lessingham drank fair with him as before, cup against cup. All that night's quaffings had lighted but a moderate glow beneath the bronze on Lessingham's cheek, and his eyes were yet clear and sparkling, when the Vicar, lurching sideways and letting fall from nerveless fingers his half-drained cup, slid beneath the table and there lay like a hog, snoring and snouking with the rest.

Two or three lamps yet burned on the walls, but with a light that weakened moment by moment before the opening dawn. Lessingham set cushions under his cousin's head and made his way to the door, picking his steps amongst bodies thus fallen ingloriously beneath the cupdin. In the darkness of the lobby a lady stood to face him, goblet in hand, quite still, clothed all in white. "Morrow, my Lord Lessingham," she said, and drank to him. "So you go north, at last, to Rialmar?"

There was a quality in her voice that swept memory like harpstrings within him: a quality like the unsheathing of claws. His eyes could not pierce the shadow more than to know her hair, which seemed to have of itself some luminosity that showed through darkness: her eyes, like a beast's eyes lit from within: a glint of teeth. "What, dear mistress of the snows?" he said, and caught her. "Under your servant's lips? Ha, under your servant's lips! And what wind blew you to Laimak?"

"Fie!" said she. "Will the man smother me, with a great beard? I'll bite it off, then. Nay and indeed, my lord," she said, as he kissed her in the mouth, "there's no such haste: I have my lodging here in the castle. And truly I'm tired, awaiting of you all night long. I was on my way to bed now."

He suffered her to go, upon her telling him her lodging, in the half-moon tower on the west wall, and giving him besides, from a sprig she had in her bosom, a little leaf like to that which Vandermast had given him in the boat upon Zayana mere, that month of May. "And it is by leaves like this," said she, "that we have freedom of all strong holds and secret places to come and go as we list and accompany with this person or that; but wherefore, and by Whose bidding, and how passing to and fro from distant places of the earth in no more time than needeth a thought to pass: these are things, dear my lord, not to be understood by such as you."

Lessingham came out now into the great court, with broadened breast, sniffing the air. In all the hold of Laimak none else was abroad, save here and there soldiers of the night-watch. Below the walls of the banquet-chamber he walked, and so past the guardhouse and Hagsby's Entry and the keep, and so across to the tenniscourt and beyond that to the northern rampire where they had had their meeting in June. Lessingham paced the rampart with head high. Not Maddalena treading the turfy uplands in the spring of the year went with a firmer nor a lighter step. The breeze, that had sprung up with the opening of day, played about him, stirring the short thick and wavy black hair about his brow and temples.

He stood looking north. It was a little past four o'clock, and the lovely face of heaven was lit with the first beams thrown upward from behind the Forn. The floor of the dale lay yet under the coverlet of night, but the mountains at the head of it caught the day. Lessingham said in himself: "His Fiorinda. What was it she said to me? 'I think you will find there that which you seek. North, in Rialmar.'

"Rialmar." A long time he stood there, staring north. Then, drawing from the bosom of his doublet the leaf of sferra cavallo: "And meanwhile not to neglect present gladness—" he said in himself; and so turned, smiling with himself, towards the half-moon tower where, as she had kindly let him know, Anthea had her lodging.

XIII

QUEEN ANTIOPE

HROUGH the wide-flung casements of the Queen's
bed-chamber in the Teremnene palace in Rialmar came
the fifteenth day of August,[2] new born. Over a bowl of
white roses it stepped, that stood on the windowsill with
dew-drops on their petals, and so into the room, touching with pale fingers the roof-beams; the milk-white figured hangings; the bottles on the white onyx table: angelica water, attar of
roses, Brentheian unguent made from the honey of Hyperborean
flowers; the jewels laid out beside them; the mirrors framed in filigree work of silver and white coral; gowns and farthingales of rich
taffety and chamblet and cloth of silver that lay tumbled on chairs
and on the deep soft white velvet carpet; all these it touched, so that
they took form, but as yet not colour. And now it touched Zenianthe's[3] bed, which was made crossways at the foot of the Queen's,

betwixt it and the windows; and her hair it touched, but not her eyes, for she was turned on her side away from the light, and slept on. But now the day, momently gathering strength, fluttered its mayfly wings about the Queen's face. And now colour came: the damask warmth of sleep on her face; her hair the colour of the young moon half an hour after sunset when the pale radiance has as yet but the faintest tinge of gold. With a little comfortable assenting sleepy noise she stirred, turning on her back. The day kissed her beneath the eyelids, a morning kiss, as a child might kiss awake its sleeping sister.

She threw back the clothes and leapt from the bed and, in her night-gown of fine lawn, stood in the window, looking out. Seventy feet beneath her the wall had its foundations in native rock, and the cliff, greatly undercut, fell away unseen. The drop from that window-sill was clear eight hundred feet to the sea of cloud, dusky, fluffed like carded wool, that overspread the river-valley of Revarm. North-westward, to her left where she stood, the walls and roofs swept down to Mesokerasin, where, in the dip between this horn Teremne and the lower horn Mehisbon, is the main of Rialmar town; horns which overhang the precipitous face north-westward, so that both the royal Teremnene palace and the houses and temples upon Mehisbon are held out over the valley dizzily in air. To her right, south-eastward, the blanket of mist hid the harbour and the river and the Midland Sea. Overhead, in a stainless sky, night still trailed a deeper intensity of blue westwards towards the zenith. The whole half circle of the horizon was filled with the forms, diamond-clear against the saffron of the dawn, of those mountains Hyperborean that are higher than all mountains else in the stablished earth. Upon all these things the Queen looked: beholding in them (but knew it not) her own image in a mirror. A lark singing mounted from height to height of air till it was level now with her window.

After a little, "Cousin," she said, without turning: "are you awake?"

"No," answered she.

"Are you asleep?"

"No."

"Get up," said the Queen.

"No," she said, and snuggled down a little more, so that the sheet was nicely arranged to cover her mouth but not her nose.

The Queen came and stood over her. "We will wake her up ourselves, then," said she, picking up from the foot of her own bed a little white cat, very hairy, with blue eyes, and dangling it so that its paws were on the sheets above Zenianthe's chin. "Now she is at our mercy. Wake up, cousin. Talk to me."

Zenianthe took the little cat into her arms. "Well, I am talking. What about?"

"You must think of something," said the Queen. "Something useful. 'How best to rid away an unwelcome guest': a lesson on that would be good now."

"You have nothing to learn from me there, cousin," said Zenianthe.

Antiope's face was serious. "I have flaunted flags enough," she said, "to show what way the wind blows. A year ago it should not have been so."

"Perhaps," said Zenianthe, "a man might think it fit to stay till he had the Lord Protector's word to bid him be gone. But you might try with your own word. And yet some would like well to hold a king, and so goodly a young gentleman besides, at their apron-strings."

"You can have him for me," said the Queen.

"I am humbly beholden to your highness; but I think he is not a man to take the sorb-apple and leave the peach on the dish."

Antiope said, "You are both naughty and dull this morning. I think I'll send you away like the rest." She surveyed her cousin's supine form, brown hair spread in sweet tangled confusion on the pillow, and morning face. "No, you're not good," she said, sitting down on the bed's edge. "And you will not help me."

"Do your hair in some nasty fashion. That may disgust him."

"Well, give me a scissors," said the Queen: "I'll cut it off, if that might serve. But no. Not that: not even for that."

"Might fetch you a back-handed stroke too, reverse the thing you played for. High squeaking voice: if he be but half a man (as you said t'other day), half a woman should be nicer to his liking than the whole."

Antiope said, "You shall not talk to me of his likings. Bad enough to go through with it; no need to think on't and talk on't: to be gazed on like a sweetmeat or a dish of caviare. Not all men, Zenianthe, fall sick of this distemper."

"But all sorts," said Zenianthe.

"As a good horse may be took with the staggers. Yes, there was—" She thought a minute. "But not all our friends go bad. Venton, Tyarchus, Orvald, Peropeutes, why, a dozen others, can ride, be merry at table, go a-hunting, lead a coranto, and ne'er spoil friendship with this moping eat-me-up folly: talk as good sense as you, cousin: better. Zenianthe," she said after a pause, "why might we not stay children? Or if not, why could I not be my own mistress, next month when I shall be of age eighteen, as my brother was? What's a Protector, that sits in Rerek two weeks' journey from us? And these great ones here, old Bodenay and the rest: nought but for their own ends: they but play chess: if they have a Queen, exchange her for a pair of castles and a pawn soon as they see their vantage." She fell silent, stroking the cat's cheeks and putting its little ears together. Then, "I believe they are playing this king against the Vicar," she said. "Do you not think so, cousin?"

Zenianthe laughed. "I should be sorry you should wed the Vicar."

"Hark to the silly talk!" said the Queen, rolling the cat on its back, this way that way with her hand, till it kicked and fought with little velvet hind-paws and made pretence to bite her. "You at least, cousin, might keep your senses, and not think but and talk but of wed, wed, wed, like a popinjay. Get up!" and she suddenly pulled the bed-clothes and the princess with them onto the floor.

The sun was high and the hour but an hour short of noon when the king of Akkama, having broken his fast on a dish of lobsters washed down with yellow wine, walked with two or three of his gentlemen out by the back stair from his lodgings in the southern wing of the palace of Teremne and so by paths he knew of round to the Queen's garden, into which he entered by a way well chosen as not observable from the windows. The garden was designed so as none should overlook it; facing eastwards and westwards, and with a great blind wall to shelter it from the north. Walls of hewn granite six cubits high shut it in, with deep wide embrasures at every few paces on the east side and on the west, to look, those upon the valley over the precipice brink and upon the great mountains afar, these upon the main garden pleasance with its silver birch-trees and fish-ponds and walks and bowers, and beyond it hills again and circling mountains, far beyond which lies Akkama. An oval pond gleamed in the midst of that little garden, with a paved walk about it of granite, and steps of granite going down to the walk from a double flight of terraces. Late-flowering lilies, creamy white and with red anthers and speckled with brown and dust of gold, filled the beds upon the terraces; there were sunflowers a-row along the northern side, lifting their faces to the noon, and little northern mountain plants, stone-crops and houseleeks and matted pinks, were in the joints of the walls and between the paving-stones; and under the east wall were chairs set out with cushions of silk, and an ivory chair for the Queen; and upon a carven pedestal rising from the middle of the water, a chryselephantine statue of Aphrodite Anadyomene.[4]

"The presence 'gins to fill," said the Lord Alquemen, throwing open the gate they entered by at the north-west corner and standing clumsily aside for the king to go in; "yet the goddess tarries."

Derxis walked moodily into the empty garden, flicking off a lily-head with his walking-stick as he passed. He was something above the middle height, well shapen and slender. His hair was straight, brushed back from the forehead, of the colour of mud: his eyes small and hard, like pebbles, set near together: his face a lean sneak-bill chitty-face, shaved smooth as a woman's, thin-lipped and with little colour about the lips, the nose straight and narrow. For all his youth (but three-and-twenty years of age), there was a deep furrow driven upright betwixt his brows. He wore a light cloak, and doublet with puffed sleeves after the Akkama fashion: loose breeches buckled below the knee: all of a sober brownish colour. There were bracelets of gold cut-work on his wrists and a linked collar of gold, broad and set with rubies between the links, hung on his chest.

Twice round that garden the king paced idly, with his gentlemen at his elbow mum as he, as if they durst not speak unbidden. "You," he said at length. "Was it not you told me this was the place?"

"I pray your highness have but a little patience," said Alquemen. "I had it by surest ways (why, 'twas from you, my Lord Esperveris?) she cometh to this place four times out of five a-mornings 'bout this hour."

"You were best get your intelligence more precise ere you serve it up to me," said Derxis. His voice was soft, too high of pitch for a man's voice, effeminate. Yet Alquemen and those other lords, hard heavy and brutal to look upon, seemed to cringe together under the reproof of that voice as boys might cringe, lighting suddenly upon some deadly poisoned serpent.

The king walked on, whistling an air under his breath. "Well," he said, after a while, "you're tedious company. Tell me some merry tale to pass away the time."

Alquemen recounted the tale of the cook that turned fisherman: a tale of a nastiness to infect the sweet garden scents and taint the lilies' petals. The king laughed. They, as if suddenly the air were freer, laughed loudlier with him.

"You have remembered me," Derxis said, "of that conceit of the three women and the lamprey. Or how went it? It was yours, Orynxis, ha?"

Orynxis recounted that story. The king laid out his tongue and laughed till the tears started. "Come, I am merry now," said he, as they walked now westward beside the sunflowers. "What's here? a toad? Give me a stone."

Alquemen picked one from the flower-bed. The king threw and missed. Kasmon proffered him another. The king's hand was up for the second throw, when Antiope entered and, seeing him, halted in the gate, fair in the line of aim.

He dropped the stone and with a low leg wished her good morrow. "I was not without hope, madam," he said with great smoothness, as she came in with her ladies and some of her officers of state, "to have had the happy fortune to have met you here. I see now 'tis a most heavenly garden; and yet but now I thought it but ordinary. Nay, 'tis plain fact: give me leave but to tear up these flowers, throw down the carven bauble standeth in the water there, you should see, gentlemen, it should seem fairer yet: you, madam, the queen-rose to grace it, and these ladies brier-roses about you to pay you honour with their meaner sweets."

"Sir, I am infinitely full of business," said the Queen. "This is my summer council-chamber. I did send to let you know there was a hunt prepared for you this morning, but my gentleman of the horse told me you were not abroad yet."

"My chamberlain was at fault, then," said Derxis. "How came it, Orynxis, you gave me not the message?"

Orynxis, that had given it punctually, excused himself that he ne'er heard of it till now: he would examine into it, and see him punished with whom the fault lay.

"See to it," Derxis said. "Cropping of the ears were too little a punishment for such oversight. Yet, for I mind me of your compassionate nature, madam, ask me to pardon it, 'tis done, forgot, at your sweet asking."

"I pray report it to my justiciar, if aught's committed needeth correction. You are my guest, sir, in Rialmar, and I hold on the King my father's way (upon whom be peace); no private justice here."

"You speak high, madam. And that becomes you."

The Queen now espied at her feet the toad, where it cowered under the broad leaf of a saxifrage. She looked direct at Derxis, then at it, then again at Derxis.

He laughed. "You did offer me a boar-hunt, madam. Praise my simple tastes, I am content with throwing at a toad."

"At a toad?" said she, without smiling. "Why?"

"For diversion, awaiting of you. It is a toad. I would kill it."

He met in her eye an Artemisian coldness and displeasure. Then, with a sudden little lovely grace picking up the toad, she made sure it was unhurt, made as if to kiss it, then put it back in a safe place on the flower-bed.

Derxis followed her as she turned away. "What a strange pitifulness is this of yours," he said, walking at her side, "that taketh compassion of malefactors and nasty paddocks, but not of him that most needeth your dear pity." He spoke low, for her ear alone. Their people, his and hers, walked behind them.

She came to a halt. "I'm sorry, sir, but I must to business."

"Then my suit standeth first in the list, so hear it."

Antiope stood silent, with face averted. Alquemen was saying to the Princess Zenianthe, "I pray you then scent this flower: can speak to your ladyship plainer words than I durst." Zenianthe moved away. Derxis noted the Queen's lips. He gritted his teeth and said, with a persuasive sweetness, "Will you not show me your garden?"

"I had thought you had seen it," she said.

"How could I see it," said Derxis, "but with your beauteous self to show it me?"

Antiope turned to him. "I have bethought me of a game," she said. "I will show you my garden, sir, for half an hour; in which time you shall not pay me compliments. That will be a new thing indeed."

"And the wager?"

"You may leave that to me."

"Ha!" said he, softly, and his eyes surveyed her with a slow appraising stare: "that raiseth hopes."

"Let them not rise too high," she said.

The lubricity that jumped pat upon Derxis's tongue he swallowed in again. He dropped a pace or so behind her for a moment, enough to say in the ear of Lord Alquemen, "See to it you manage me some privacy."

But now came into the garden a gentleman-usher and brought a packet to the Queen's chamberlain, who, reading the direction, handed it unopened to the Queen. "I pray you hold me excused, sir," she said to Derxis, "while I read it."

The king bowed assent. With a jealous sidelong look he watched her face light up as she read. "But who's the carrier?" she said, looking up: "of these letters, I mean?"

"Serene highness," answered he that brought them: "his lordship's self that writ it bare it, and waiteth on your disposals."

"O entertain him hither straight," said Antiope. Derxis's face grew dark. "It is my great kinsman's kinsman, the great Lord Lessingham, come from the south upon some matters extraordinary," she said, turning with a lovely courtly favour to Derxis. "I have your leave, sir, to bid him join our company?"

The king stood silent. Then said the knight marshal Bodenay, "Your serenity may be sure he had rather you gave him breathing-time to prepare himself: not come all clagged with mire and clay into your grace's presence."

Antiope laughed. "O court ceremonies! have we seen ne'er a man yet in riding-gear? No, he shall come now."

"Cry you mercy, madam," said the king; "I value not a courtesy hangeth long betwixt the fingers. You did engage to show me your garden. Surely this what's-his-name can wait our pleasure while you perform your engagement to me."

"I must not," she said, "be gracious with one hand and ungracious with the other. This is a stranger, not in reputation, yet in person ne'er yet known to us. That your royal estate doth outgo his rank and place, 'tis more reason I use him honourably. No, you shall see the garden, sir, and he shall see it with us. Carry him hither straight," she said, and the messenger went forth immediately.

Derxis said nothing, neither did the Queen look at him. And

truly to have looked in that moment upon that young king, even so little crossed, had been no sight of comfort.

"What's that Lessingham?" asked the Count Orynxis, privately in Alquemen's ear.

"Cousin to the Vicar of Rerek," answered he.

"Why, 'tis that same spruce youth, is't not," said Kasmon, "captained Mezentius's horse six years ago? catched you napping when all hung in hazard at the battle of Elsmo: broke up your squadrons and beat you round your own camp? was't not Lessingham?"[5]

"O hold your clack," said Alquemen. "You came not too well out of those doings."

"Came as fast as his horse could carry him," said Orynxis. "Kasmon's ride they call it now: home through the outer Corridor, and near broke his neck i' the end. You two were best hold together, lest this fellow trounce you again. Nay, but sadly, know you aught else of him, Alquemen? The Parry is a hard man, I've heard tell."

Alquemen answered, "They are two notable knaves together: both of a hair, and both cousin germans to the Devil."

The Queen sat now in her ivory chair: Zenianthe to right of her, and upon her left, standing, Bodenay. Raviamne, Paphirrhoë, and Anamnestra, ladies of honour, with half a dozen more, court-men and lords of Fingiswold, made a half circle behind her. Derxis and his troop of gentry stood a little apart upon her right. The Queen, looking round, noted how he, with an uncivil insolence, stood now with his back towards her. As moved by some sudden toy taking her in the head, she whispered Zenianthe to sit in the siege royal while she herself, spite of all protests of the old Lord Bodenay and other grave persons about her, took place among her girls behind it.

Lessingham, ushered in by the north-western gate, walked between the sunflowers and the sun, that even at cloudless mid-day made but a temperate heat in that mountain country of the north. He was bare-headed, in his mail-coat of black iron and gold, black silk hosen and black leather riding-boots, dusty from the journey. So came he towards them, with clanking silver spurs. And as he came, he gathered with the sweep of his eyes, resting with no inconvenient intensity upon this person or that, all the posture of their company: the staid elders that curiously regarded him; Derxis and his, haughty and uneasy like cattle when the dog comes towards them; Zenianthe in the chair and her companions, who lent to that stone-walled garden a delicacy, as of tender feet trampling the fine soft bloom of grass.

Now were greetings given and taken. Lessingham said, "You must pardon me, noble ladies and you my lords of Fingiswold, to a come without all ceremony and even in my riding-clothes. But the message was, the Queen was here, and did desire me come instantly to present my service."

"Well, sir," said Zenianthe, "and will you not present it? This is the siege royal."

Lessingham bowed. "You become it most excellent well, madam."

"That is strangely spoken," said she. "Or did you look then to find some rustic girl, should know not how to draw the skirt about her ankles?"

Antiope, with a hand on Raviamne's arm, watched him very demurely.

"Your ladyship shall not find me so flat nor so stupid," answered he. "No, but I can tell 'twixt the dusky lily and the white. I am not colour-blind."

Zenianthe laughed. "You have seen my picture? May be the paint had faded."

The eye-tricks and signs they bandied amongst them did not escape Lessingham. "No, madam," he answered, "I have not seen her highness's picture. But I have heard."

"Was 'dusky lily' to say, uncomely?"

"Had your ladyship hearkened more carefully, you would have noted I stressed the 'lily.'"

Antiope spoke: "It is a wonder you will not know the Queen, sir, when you see her."

He looked at them in turn: Antiope, Paphirrhoë, Zenianthe, Anamnestra, Raviamne, Antiope again. "Ah," he said, "not till she tell me I may. That were too unmannerly, find her out sooner than she meant."

They fell a-laughing, and Zenianthe, catching Antiope's eye, stood up. "The fox was near driven, your highness, when he took this muse," she said.

"A most good and courtly answer, sir," said the Queen. "And cometh from the south: none here could have turned it so. And you'll not be angry with us for this game of play?"

"Serenissime princess and my sovereign lady," said Lessingham, "humbled on my knee I kiss your grace's hand."

King Derxis, being turned about now, looked upon these actions. With an insolent stare he went over Lessingham from brow to boots and so back and so down to boots again. And now he came to them. "Pray you present to me this gentleman, madam. I were loth to lose aught of his discourse, so pleasant as it seemeth."

"Sir," said the Queen, "this is my cousin Lord Lessingham, he that must be my captain of war against my enemies. Your highness knows him by repute?"

"In my conscience, not I," said Derxis. "Yet, being your cousin, madam, should recommend a very cuckoo: by how much more a person of so much fame and nobility as my Lord—I've forgot your name, sir?"

"It is not yet so renowned," said Lessingham, "as that ignorance need disgrace your highness."

They turned to walk now, looking on the garden and the flowers that were there. Derxis held close at the Queen's elbow, and spoke to her in undertones. Lessingham by and by fell behind, and walked now with the knight marshal and the old Countess of Tasmar and four or five others, talking of his journey north from Rerek and of matters indifferent. And first they looked askance and coldly, and cold was their talk; and then that coldness began to melt to him as morning frosts in autumn to the mounting sun, that makes warm the air, and the clouds disperse and mists are drunk up and the rime on a myriad twigs and grass-blades runs together to jewels. With so expert a touch he handled them, as one that himself at ease breathes ease into all the air about him.

And yet carried he little ease within him. To have fed in his thought these three months so many lusts and longings: to have come up to this much thought-on city of Rialmar, thus strangely held out that night to his desire: to have approved it but so, a plain walled hold, cold among northern mountains under ordinary daylight, and the dwellers in it, even to the Queen's self and her maidens, but ordinary: these things were an outshedding in his mind of wormwood and darkness. In the Queen indeed, he saw a girl gay and high-hearted, and one in whom, as they talked together, he thought he touched a mind his own rode in step with, laughing at things his laughed at, leaping where his leapt. But in this was neither recompense nor echo of that which with so much wonder had been permitted to stand for a little moment and with so much aching loss had been taken and gone, upon that midnight under the winged glory in Barganax's jewelled mansion of delights. Moreover, until now he had remembered and might feed on the memory of that moment; but now, from his first looking on very Rialmar, the memory was become as the thin lost perfume dreamed in a dream, that a man knows would restore him all, might he but breathe it again, but natural present walls him from it, as day is a wall to shut out the star-shine.

The Queen now, walking with Derxis, stopped at a bed of the yellow mountain-lily with spotted flower. "Poor little lilies," said she. "I cannot please them."

Derxis shrugged and, catching the sound of Lessingham's voice, would have walked on. But the Queen waited, so that, if with no good will, he must needs retrace his step.

"My Lord Lessingham," said she: "are you a gardener? What is it hurts my lilies?"

Lessingham viewed them. His eyes and ears were opened to the

estate of more than lilies in that garden. "Not the aspect," answered
he. "Your grace hath given them sun for their faces, and these little
mezereon bushes to shade their feet, and sheltered them from the
winds."

Derxis said apart to Alquemen, in such a whisper as all might
hear, "Hast not wit to keep the fellow away, but must be thrust still
into my company? Go draw him apart."

"But how of the soil?" said Lessingham. "They have very particular likes. Mould of old oak-leaves, and—"

"A word with you," said Alquemen, close to his ear.

Lessingham's eyes crossed with the Queen's. "Or if your grace
should be troubled with land-mice, little rude beasts that gnaw your
lilies underground? I know a way with such."

His back was turned upon Alquemen, and he gave no sign that
he had heard him or was ware of his presence.

Derxis, looking at Lessingham's riding-boots, said to the
Queen, "Belike I understand not the right ceremony of your grace's
court. It is custom, is't, to come into the presence in disarray?"

Again her eyes crossed with Lessingham's: a look sudden and
gone like a kingfisher's flight between gliding water and overshadowing trees. He turned to Derxis with a grave courtesy. "My lord
the king of Akkama, I am a soldier. And it is custom, with a soldier,
to obey his sovereign's command."

The Queen had moved onwards a step or two. "A soldier?" said
Derxis. "Go, and 'tis said women will love a soldier better than all
other men?"

Lessingham lifted an eyebrow. "I know not that. But this have I
known," said he, as if talking to the flowers: "in many countries[6] of
the world I have known ladies plagued with uncivil persons have
found a soldier excellent good as doorkeeper."

With so little conscience and so leisurable a gravity had he spoken these words, the king was unready how to take it; and ere he
was resolved, Lessingham was some paces from him walking with
the Queen and them of her household. The Princess Zenianthe
alone was left: she had turned aside suddenly, handkercher to
mouth, to contemplate a bunch of water gladiole in the near corner
of the pond. Derxis turned colour, the more at the sight of Zenianthe's shaking shoulders. With a hasty glance he satisfied himself
that, save his own folk's, no eye was on him. Then with two steps he
was at her side, took her about the neck from behind, bent back her
head and kissed her upon the lips, well and strong. Alquemen flung
up his chin with a great laugh. Lessingham looked round. She,
freeing herself, took Derxis a box on the ear that he heard bells.

The Queen and her folk waited now by the sunflowers for the
king to come up. He came, twirling his walking-stick idly as he
walked, his gentlemen in his wake, his features well composed. A

poisonsome look was in his eyes. "And now, sir," said the Queen, "is my half-hour ended; and now must I be private in this garden to confer with my council 'pon matters of state."

"Madam," Derxis said: "of all cruel ladies are not you the cruellest? Is not sunlight a darkness, and every minute a year of prison, out of sight of your life-giving eyes? Well, I am your slave to obey, then; asking but that your sweet lips that speak the sentence shall give me yet some promise of more private conference; haply this afternoon?"

"I pray you give us leave. And perhaps my huntsmen may find you the means to make life bearable."

Zenianthe said with a levelled malice, "And you, my Lord Lessingham, care not: we can offer you some sport here in the garden: a toad-hunt!" Derxis, kissing the Queen's hand, turned colour again at those words. Laughter sat in the Queen's eyes, but discretion locked it there.

As they of the king's company moved off now towards the gate, Lessingham overtook them, came beside Alquemen, who walked last, and touched him on the arm. "My Lord Alquemen: this time, a word with you. Is it as it seemed to me but now, that you laughed, when a lady was put to an inconvenience?"

"Well, and if I did?" replied he, swinging round upon his heel and thrusting his face, with its full popping eyes, into Lessingham's. " 'Shall need a better than thee to check me."

King Derxis, ware of this jangling, paused in the gate and looked back. At a word from him, Kasmon, Orynxis, and Esperveris advanced menacingly towards Lessingham and stood scowling about him. Lessingham gathered their eyes with his and folded his arms. "Let us make no jarring in this presence, my lords," he said; and, to Alquemen, "can you use a sword?"

Amid their great burst of laughter Alquemen answered, with a bloody look, "It hath been thought so."

"Good," said Lessingham. "This then, and no more: You are a mannerless swine, and shall account to me for your unmannerly dealing."

Alquemen said, "A word is as good as a blow. I take you very well. My Lord Orynxis will take order for my part."

"And for mine, my lieutenant, Amaury. I'll send him, my lord, to speak with you."

The twenty-fourth day after[7] these things just told of, a little past sunset, the Princess Zenianthe stood at that same window of the Queen's bedchamber. The room was all astir with lights and shadows of a log fire that blazed and sputtered on the hearth. To the left of the fire the deep-bayed window stood wide to the evening, which entered now with a tang of autumn and a tang of mountains and

the sea. The roofs and towers of Mehisbon were a sharp screen of
dark greenish violet against the west, where motes of a rosy radiance swam and shimmered suffusing the smoky blues and purples,
and, for a last lighting to bed of day, the broad and tapering blade
of the zodiacal light slanted up from the place of settle-gang. The
beetle, winding his faint horn to Zenianthe as he travelled the paths
of opening night beside that window, saw her as some titanic figure
darkly fair against a background of fire. The firelight saw her as its
own, spirit of its spirit, dream of its dream, that which itself would
become, might it but be clothed upon with the divinity of flesh: a
presence secure, protective, glad, warm, fancy-free; and so it made
sure of her, touching with trembling sudden fingers now her
breathing bosom, now a ringlet of brown hair that rested curled on
her shoulder, now a ruby warm against her throat.

She turned as the doors swung open in the middle of the side-
wall to the left of the great bay of the window, and, with four ladies
of the bedchamber to bear the candles before her and behind, the
Queen entered, like a lily, from her bath. Surely her eyes outdanced
the shining candles as Raviamne and Paphirrhoë lighted them, a
dozen candles by the mirror that stood on the table to the right of
the fire and another dozen by the tall mirror, framed in silver and
white coral, to the right again, in the corner; surely the warmth of
her presence hushed the encircling firelight and outglowed its glow.
Zenochlide brought from a chair beside the fire, one by one, garments fine as the spider's web, fragrant, delicate as the butterfly's
wing, and the Queen put them on. Anamnestra brought her coat-
hardy of rich sarsenet, with a silver taint like a lily, yielding and
clinging, wide-skirted downward from the hips: the Queen, pointing her white arms above her head, bowed and entered it like a
diver, and like a diver came up laughing and shaking the hair from
her eyes. The silken sleeves ended an inch or two below the shoulder, continuing thence with pale blue transparent gauze cut wide,
shimmering with dust of gold, and gathered at the wrists to bracelets of fretted silver and margery-pearls. The skirt was purfled upon
its lower edge, two spans deep, with flower-work in seed-pearls and
the soft blue of turkey-stones and thread of gold, upon pale rose-
coloured silk. Raviamne brought her shoes, sewn all over with
pearls and amber.

The Queen now, standing before the mirror, took out the pins
and, with a shake of her head, let down her hair like a garment of
netted sunlight falling nearly to the purfled flounce of her dress.
Zenianthe came with the little white cat and held it out to be kissed:
"To salute your highness respectfully on your natal day, and ask you
kindly admire my birthday collar Zenianthe gave me." Antiope bent
and kissed it between the blue eyes. "And now," she said, sitting
down with it in her lap upon a long backless tapestry-cushioned seat

of sandalwood before the table and mirror, "you were best go and make ready yourselves. Zenianthe is dressed already: will help me do my hair.

"The peace of it!" she said, when they were alone, parting and combing the masses of her hair with a golden comb: hair that was like to the pallid soul of gold breathed into a mist at the foot of some waterfall. "It is most strange calm weather, cousin: i' the court, I mean."

"Peace?" said Zenianthe, fingering the jewels on the table. "Well, for a fortnight: since Lessingham's killing of those five, and the hubble-bubble that that made, and your making the whole pack of 'em lodge henceforth without Teremne; certainly it is more peacefuller now."

"Ah, but I meant from our own folk," said Antiope. "Bodenay; old Madam Tasmar; our vulpine friend Romyrus; they let me have my way now. Do they give me line, but the readier to pluck me in? I know them too well, my puss," she said, stroking it: "twisty plots, but little sense. No, I am sure 'tis this: they are altogether carried by this man; and being by him taught sense, let me alone to go my ways. And for that," she said, meeting Zenianthe's eyes in the glass with a most limpid, unconscious, and merry look, "I am much beholden to him, and but wish he'd a come here sooner."

"Must this Derxis be at your festivities to-night?" Zenianthe asked. "Planted near two months, he begins to take root I think in Rialmar. Will you wear your sapphire comb, cousin, or the turkey-stone to go with your gown? or will you have your hair low on the neck and no comb at all?"

"I'll have the little half-moon crown of flower-delices, and do it the Greek way, and with those long strings of margarets you did give me, dear cousin." She was silent a minute, a dimple coming and going near to her mouth's corner. Then, "Must have been wormwood in his mouth, that business of Alquemen."

"These little margarets tangle in your hair, cousin, as if they were fain to wind cocoons in it and sleep themselves into fire-flies, or whatever 'tis margaret-chains turn to after their sleep."

"White moths," said the Queen: "owly faces and furry wings."

Zenianthe said, "Methought I never saw so delicate playing as my Lord Lessingham's, when you did send for him after that affair, 'pon Derxis's complaint, and did confront them. So penitent and good as he bore himself toward the king, so's who could take exceptions at it? And yet never to leave you in doubt, cousin, that he knew your mind and purpose; as if he should look through his fingers and wink at it. Faith, I near gave away all by laughing, 'twas so pretty. So remorseful, cousin: 'Yes, now 'twas put so, he did see indeed 'twas hardly to be pardoned: kill five of the king's men, and all in five minutes. And yet might he be indulged a little for ignorance sake; for truly he had not understood till now that Derxis, as a royal person, had free licence to set men in the dark under archways to kill and murder whom he pleased while guesting here in Rialmar.' "

Antiope smiled. "And there the other walked so neatly into it."

"Yes," said Zenianthe. " 'By my soul, madam, I had nought i' the world to do with it!' And then you, so sweet and harmless, 'O I see, sir, then 'twas not upon your business they went then?' And while he felt about for firm ground then Lessingham again, most courtly and submissive, remembering Derxis of that former passage with Alquemen (I was the distressed lady there, cousin: the beast had laughed when Derxis did me that insolency). Precious heaven! I near burst myself keeping of my face, thinking (while Lessingham discoursed so formal and serious) of the true tale we had had of that encounter: of his snicking of the beastly fellow's wrist at the third pass and flicking the sword from his hand, contemptuous as dust away a fly: and this their notable great duellist with twenty men's deaths to's credit: and then," she lowered her voice, that shook with suppressed merriment: "and then making him put off's breeches, and slashing 'em to ribbons, and then bid him go in that pickle, and learn when and when not to laugh from henceforth—"

"O Zenianthe!" said the Queen.

"And then you," said Zenianthe: " 'O, I'm sorry, sir. I understand. You are as blameless as I am in these mischances. This Alquemen of yours I see hath broke leash, run past your controlling, and 'twas he, not you, did fee these ruffians to sit for my officer to perform his death. Shall I punish him for you?' Cousin, I never saw man so angry, nor so checkmated. Worst of all, when, 'pon pretext to avoid such pothers from henceforth, you did decree them all lodging henceforth without Teremne."

Her hair being done, Antiope stood up now. "What's good in Lessingham is right sense," she said, "and a wit so turnable for all things alike. What needs doing, this man doth it, and that often even before I knew I needed it. And best of all, a man that stands on's own feet in's own place. Not with your own self, cousin, was I ever more at ease; that I can talk to as 'twere my brother, and never shadow nor taint of that folly that ruineth all."

The Princess was silent. She fetched from the bed a girdle which Antiope now put on, of clouded pink tourmalines; and after that her outer dress of white crinkled silken gauze, transparent as an April shower. Little blue flowers of the squill and the blue-bell were worked on it here and there, and little specks of gold. Soft it was, fitting itself to every movement, even as loveliness itself. And about her delicate neck was a ruff, heart-shaped, open-cut, edged with pearls, going down to a point between her breasts where it was fastened with a flower-delice of little diamonds, so fine that it seemed to be made of mere light. "As for this tedious King," she said, "I have in mind a way to rid us of him tonight, if aught may rid him."

"What is that?"

"O, a nice and courteous point of precedence I am minded to show him. You shall see."

"And but only this morning," said Zenianthe behind her, settling the ruff, "you did directly refuse, the third time, his offer of marriage. Poor King, he must be most pitifully fallen into your highness's toils."

"Poor King. Well, shall I take him after all, Zenianthe? For indeed I am sorry for him. And indeed I find him most displeasing. And indeed it is pitiful to consider of a person so lost in the world: pleasing of himself, but displeasing of all other. Well, then, shall I take him then?—'Las, cousin, you must not prick me with that pin so!"

The great Hall of the Sea-horses in the royal palace in Rialmar was shaped like a cross: a square central hall and four others, lower of roof, opening upon it: and each of these five was well thirty paces either way. The walls were panelled with green jasper between pillars of lapis lazuli. At the northern end, facing the main doors, was a staircase all of jasper; a broad flight leading down to the floor of the northern hall, and side-flights branching up right and left from it to the gallery. Windows, five times the height of a man, filled all the space upon the end walls east and west; in the west, the moon at this time looked in, three days old, a reaping-hook of silver fire. The main doors were in the southern side of the southern hall: doorways with pointed arches, and the doors all covered with leather of peacock blue, nailed all over with golden stars, and edged with rims of rose-pink crystal. The roofs of the side-halls were flat, of a dark stone full of fiery sparkles. Slender jasper columns, two rows down the middle of each hall, dividing it so into three aisles, bare up the ceilings. But of the main middle hall the roof was domed and exceeding high, and the whole floor of the middle hall empty and without pillars. Curtains or hangings of tapestry came down from the dome and, looped up at each corner at the level of the frieze, tumbled thence in billowy masses upon the floor: all of dusky stuff that showed blues or greens as the light moved or the eye that beheld them, and with streamed stripes of ultramarine, and roses worked in pink silk here and there, and at the converging of the stripes or streamers, bosses, broader than a man's arms might span, of cushioned black silk, sewn with vast sunflowers in gold thread. One enormous lamp swung high in the dome, of silver and topaz and yellow sapphires, shedding a radiance very warm and golden: and everywhere, suspended by iron chains, were censers of bronze hammered and damascened, some in green and white enamel, some dusky bronze, some lacquered red, and in the chains were flowers twined and the verdure of creeping plants and leaves and fruits. Alternating with the censers, scores of small hanging lamps burned with a rose-red light. The floor was of inlaid work of rare and sweet-smelling woods, divers-coloured, but with a general show of redness, bare in the main middle hall for dancing, but with crimson carpets in the four outer halls. And at the ends of the balustrades of that great staircase where it came upon the floor (and from these had the hall its name), were two sea-horses rampant, with webbed feet and finny wings and scaly fish-like bodies with fishes' tails. Bigger they were than the biggest horse that ever went upon the earth, and were carved each from a single stone of sea-blue rock-crystal.

Amid this magnificence hundreds of guests were now assembled to rejoice upon Queen Antiope's eighteenth birthday. And as they walked and mingled, it was as the shining forth of the sun after long and heavy rain, when the beams suck up from a wet hedge of box or yew a mist that shimmers with rainbow colours, and the drops upon the leaves change, as the wind shakes them, from emerald to amethyst, from that to ruby, from ruby to liquid gold. King Derxis, surveying the scene with the look of one that has yet in his mouth the taste of a sour mixture, stood with his folk in the main hall. Some saluted him with a formal respect as they passed by; more went about some other way; none joined his company. Every while, the furrow betwixt his brows knit at the sight of some young lord of Fingiswold or some proper man among the company; but his eyes turned oftenest towards the stairs. "Rialmar fashions," he said under his breath at last. "I am nigh sickened of these meant discourtesies. The bitch! am I her monkey to be led in a string? Esperveris!" he said, aloud.

"Humbly to your highness's wish."

"Send in another messenger. Say the King of Akkama tarrieth, and 'tis not our custom to wait on women's leisures.

"Hold thee. Send not." Esperveris turned back. "I've changed my mind." Esperveris, bowing his obedience, had in his eyes that frightened cringing look (seen before in the little garden), of a man that has seen a sight behind the veil.

And now, turning to look towards the eastern doors, Derxis set eye for the first time that evening upon Lessingham, where he talked with old Bodenay and the Lord Romyrus, Constable in Rialmar, and some young lords about him, Orvald, Venton, and Tyarchus, and ladies besides, the Countess Heterasmene, Myrilla, daughter to the lord Admiral Jeronimy, and others. Gay and easy seemed Lessingham, and it was plain how their conversation danced to his tune and opened under his presence as flowers to a warm sun. His attire was of great richness and darkness: blacks and deep indigo blues, with figurings of silver trefoils. He wore a narrow three-double ruff, and ruffs at the wrists besides, below cuffs of silver lace. But a single jewel he wore, of the kingly order of the hippogriff, about his neck; and upon his thumb a ring in the figure of that worm *ouroboros*, that eateth his own tail.

Not with the flicker of muscle nor eyelash did the countenance of Derxis uncover his mind as he, for a full minute, steadfastly regarded Lessingham across the hall. Then in that chill unruffled lady-like voice he said to Orynxis, taking his arm, "Behold yonder woman-server, come to ruffian it out in the company of his betters. A soldier of fortune: hireth out his sword, and body too, for trash. How call you such an one, Orynxis?"

"So please your grace, how but shortly thus?" answered Orynxis: "a male harlot."

"O sweet and excellent!" said Derxis. "Go, tell him so, from me."

His eyes, like pebbles, rested upon Orynxis, noting how the blood shrank, leaving the brutal face white and pappy, then rushed to it once more as under the lash of shame: noting the fumbling of irresolute fingers for the sword-hilt that was not there, for no man was admitted armed to that presence. Squaring his shoulders, Orynxis began to go, as a condemned man towards the beheading-block. The King stayed him with his hand. "Thou fool," he said, and there was a muted evil music of laughter in his voice that cut like the east wind: "shall I unfeather me of all my friends, aids, and helps, because you are like pilled rabbits when't cometh to facing this bloody bully? Alquemen could eat up two such as thou: yet did not this fellow whip him? As I'll whip this puling girl, might I but come at her i' the happy occasion and where I would. Whip her flesh till the blood spurt."

Almost in manner of a royal progress was Lessingham's passage among the guests: not by his doing, for he seemed ever as a man whose thoughts and looks went outwards, not busied with his own self. But, as the lily of the compass is turned always towards the pole, so of that throng of great court-men and ladies in their summer beauty and others of worship from up and down the land, were eyes turned towards him. "So you live not always upon gondolas or islands?" said a light bantering voice at his elbow. He looked down into beady eyes whose strange shy gaze captured the gaze that looked on them, allowing it no liberty to look well at the face that owned them.

> " 'My pleasure is my power to please my mistress
> My power is my pleasure in that power.' "

"Are you still so roundabout in your philosophy, my Lord Lessingham?"

"I had thought, madam," said he, bowing over her small hand, gloved to above the elbow in velvet-soft brown leather that had the sharp sweet smell of summer evenings amid rush-grown sleepy waters, "that I had demonstrated to you that 'twas a philosophy agreeable to extreme directness of practice. May I have the honour to tread a measure with you when the music shall begin?"

"Please you, I'll be asked rather when that time shall come," she replied. "I know not yet what orders have gone forth for tonight. Care not, my lord: once had, you cannot lose me." As she spoke, the brown paw had slipped from his fingers, and she in her brown fur-trimmed gown was lost among the press, as if she had slid noiselessly into water, and no ripple left behind.

Lessingham, under a singular unseizable exhilaration of spirit, looked round for her awhile in vain, then went on his way. It was as if the bright lights of that hall burned brighter, and as if secret eyes watched from the lamps themselves, and from the hangings and from the golden chapiters of the pillars, and from the walls themselves: a thousand eyes, unseen, that watched and waited on some event. Lessingham, stroking his black beard, bethought him that he had drunk no wine: bethought him then that wine has no effects like these. For now a tranquillity possessed him, and a clarity of thought and vision; wherein, as he looked round upon all that company, he was aware of a new grandeur come upon them. Zenianthe, passing through the hall, acknowledged his salutation: it seemed to him that he beheld for the first time her beauty, of her that he had thought but a princess among princesses, but clothed now with the perfection of the ancient earth, as on the hills shepherds trample the hyacinth under foot, and the flower darkens on the ground. A change, not of the like quality yet of like measure, was come upon a hundred fair women that he now gazed on, so that they seemed like Galateas in marble quickened[8] to a cold stately movement of life and breathing: statuesque presences of nymphs, or of persons half divine, brought back to the visitations of the common earth, and that September evening, and the young moon setting. Yet had this alteration no character of dream nor vision: it was a hardening rather of sensual solid fact, as if some breath had passed, blowing away all dissembling mists and exhalations and leaving naked the verity of things. Lessingham now, without surprise, met, levelled at him from the reentrant corner of the southern hall to the right of the seahorse staircase, the unblinking, cat-like, stare of his oread lady, Anthea. In her, as flame held in flame remains flame still, he beheld no change. Making his way towards her, he walked across that very place where Derxis and his gentlemen were standing: walked indeed through the midst of them, knowing not that he did so, nor that they in angry astonishment gave back right and left to let him pass. For they, under that alteration, were become so unremarkable that he did not, for the while, perceive their presence.

But ere, with mind a-surge now from memories of past love-sports in Ambremerine and lately in Laimak, he might come within speaking-distance of that lady, seven silver trumpets blew to a sennet, and upon the first blast was every person in that great hall stood still, and all eyes turned to the staircase. And now in a silence, under the shadowy splendours of the looped hangings and betwixt those mighty sea-horses, Queen Antiope came down the mid stairway and, upon the last step, stood still.

The silence broke with a stir of soft music. Guests of honour were marshalled and presented before the Queen, to kiss hands upon her birthday: King Derxis first. Lessingham, from his place a little removed upon the left or eastern side, noted her face as Derxis, with a flowery ceremony, lifted her hand: her eyes caught Lessingham's in a private interchange, too slight for any else to detect it, of comic intelligence and resignation.

Upon the ending of these formalities, came a dozen waiting-men and spread a little carpet of black velvet with selvage of silver a few paces forward from the foot of the stairs, and set upon it a chair of mother-of-pearl and ivory. Thither came the Queen now, still in her cloak of dull cloth of silver, gleaming to all greys, and four little boys to bear up the train behind her, and sat in that chair, and her ladies of presence took place behind her and upon either side. Derxis came and stood at her right hand. She gave him short answers, and spoke most to Zenianthe upon her left. The company now danced the sarabande; and in this had Lessingham Madam Campaspe to his partner. Derxis craved the honour to dance it with the Queen. She answered, it was custom for her to dance but in the pavane only, since that was their royal dance. Derxis asked when would the pavane begin. She answered, "When I shall give order for it." He prayed her then give order now, soon as this dance was done, and so ease his impatient longings. "If this can any way oblige you," she said, " 'tis a simple matter to do it"; and bade her sergeant of arms see it given forth accordingly.

As the last majestic chords of the sarabande grated on the strings, and the dancers paused and sundered, Lessingham said to his Campaspe, "Dear mistress of still waters and sallows and moonshine, may we dance again? The third from this, or what, will you grant me? Or, for your warm darknesses have charms beyond these bright lights, shall's walk then in a little garden I can find for you, where a statue of the blessed Goddess Herself stands amid water and lily-flowers?"

"So's there you may explore again the mysteries of divine philosophy?" she said, laughing in his eyes. "As upon Ambremerine?

But I'll be asked later. Nay, I'll not play kiss-and-begone, my lord. Nor I'll not nurse it against you if you find other 'ployment when the time comes. For indeed," she said, very prim-mouthed and proper, her soft arm touching his above the elbow as she with tiny gloved fingers settled the pins in a loosening plait of her dark hair, "the part, as we know, is but part of the whole."

Mistress Anthea he now claimed for his partner in the stately pavane, kissing her hand (the nails whereof he noted were polished and sharpened to claw-like points) and looking across it as he did so, from under his brows, into her yellow lynx-like eyes: beacons that he had ere now learned well to steer by, into enchanted and perilous seas wherein he had approved her to be a navigator both practised and of adventurous resource. But, "Madam," he heard a man's voice say at his side; "I pray you pardon me." Then, "My Lord Lessingham, her serene highness desireth your presence."

"Madam," said Lessingham, "there's a sovereignty ruleth here higher than even yours, that you must let your servant go when that biddeth. Strengthen me to my duty by saying I may find you anon?"

"Why, here speaks a mortal truer than he knows," said she, and the cold classic features of her fair face were chilled yet the more for a certain disdain. "It must ever be an honour to me to be to your excellence—what was't you told the learned doctor?—a 'pleasurable interlude'? But indeed, to-night there are changes in the air; and, were I you, my Lord Lessingham, I would not reckon too far ahead. Not to-night, I think." The upright slits narrowed in her eyes that seemed to plunge into his own and read his thought there, and find there matter of entertainment. Then she laughed: then turned from him.

Lessingham, smoothing his tumbled thoughts and stifling in his mind, as he walked, his discontent and his disappointed designs, threaded his way in the wake of the Queen's chamberlain through couples that stood forth now for the pavane, and so came before the Queen. She, at that instant rising from her pearly chair, let fall her cloak that the little pages received as it left her shoulders, and so stood in her rich and lovely dress, mistinesses of silver and rose and faintest blue, like the new morning sky in gentle summer weather; and nobly she carried about her shoulders that which, of all raiment worn by woman, is test of a noble carriage: a shawl, of blue pale gauze, sprinkled with little diamonds and edged with a fringe of rose-pink silk. The stringed instruments began now, preluding in parts. Lessingham read in her eye swift advertisement, sudden and gone as he made his obeisance, that here was somewhat he must swiftly do for her, and be ready upon the instant to note and act it. Derxis, upon her right, turned to her with proffered arm. She, as if not seeing it, looked round upon Lessingham. "Sir," said she, "you do here in person represent the Lord Protector, who is to me *in loco parentis.*[9] In that quality pray you take place of honour in this company, and lead on for the pavane."

Derxis, watching them go, stood rigid while a man might count ten. Amaury, chancing to pass at that moment with the Lady Myrilla on his arm, saw the look in the king's eye, and, seeing it, felt a sudden deadly weakness catch him behind the knees. Lessingham, too, had sight of that look: the Queen was ware of a sudden stiffening of the strong arm where her own hand rested. For even as the gentle voice of that young prince if he were angry, so now in his countenance, pale as ashes, and in his eyes, was something, a tang, a menace, a half-raised mask, that even a brave man might sicken at, as if in the apprehended waiting presence of the damnablest of all Furies found in hell.

When Amaury, after a minute, had mastered his senses to look again, Derxis, and his lords with him, was gone from the hall.

Above measured beats, plucked, throbbing slow, from the strings of the bass viols, came now the melody of the pavane, like the unrolling of the pageant of dawn when vast clouds, bodied forth from the windy canopy of night, ride by in smouldering splendours; and the splendours take fire, and in the glimpses of the sky, rain-washed, purer than dew or awakening airs upon the hill-tops, comes the opal morn; even as that, was this music of the pavane. Lessingham, treading its rhythm with the Queen's hand in his, beheld, as a man folded ever deeper in contemplation, Anthea's face, and after a while Campaspe's, as they passed in the dance: the one cameo-like in its setting of sun-bright hair; the other the face of some little fieldish thing with features gathered to a strange charm, not beautiful but akin to beauty, by beady and coal-black eyes. In both faces he noted an air as if they, knowing somewhat, took a secret delicate delight both in it and in him and his unknowingness.

He looked at the Queen. On her face no such mystery sat. Only she smiled at him with her eyes. He bethought him of that Lady Fiorinda, Barganax's lover: in no woman's eyes save hers had he met, and now in Antiope's, that look of friendship familiar, mere, unalloyed, unconscious, fancy-free, as of his own inward self companioning him from withoutward.

Then, while their eyes rested in that untroubled regard, as adrift together upon some surgeless sea of quiet rest, suddenly he, for the first time, was ware of that music. Like a spate roaring down from some water-spout among hills it thundered upon his inner sense, blinded him, drowned him under. Well he remembered now this music, with its deep-plucked throbbing beats, above which the melody walked singing, and the thing desirable beyond all the stars of heaven trailing in its train. He looked at Antiope as he had looked, in Ambremerine, at that night-piece, of Fiorinda with glow-worms in her hair. For a moment it was again as it then had been:

her face was to him unseeable: nought save the outshowering of spears of many lights and hues of fires. A chill-cold shivering took him. But then, in memory he heard, as it had been in very presence, the lazy caress of that voice that had seemed to play with time and the world and love and change and eternity as with a toy: *I think you will find there that which you seek: north, in Rialmar;* and with that, as with the sudden opening of a window in heaven, he saw the Queen truly, as in that dream in Acrozayana he had first seen her, and, for a second time, when he walked like a sleep-walker onto Barganax's swordpoint. Almost, it may be, as a God sees her, he saw her now; with eyes refined to look on the world new born. He knew her. The web of memories which, with his first coming up to Rialmar, had been torn up and scattered, was on the sudden whole again, so that, remembering, he recognized beyond peradventure too her voice: that voice which had spoken on that May night in Mornagay, unknown, yet beyond peradventure his: his beyond all familiar things, speaking, closer than blood or sinew, out of the abysses within his mind, while, with the meditation of bubbles mounting for ever through golden wine, his thought had hung like a kestrel stilled against the wind: *Be content. I have promised and I will perform.*

In this climacteric moment a sudden quiet seized him: such a kind of quiet as Gods know, riding betwixt the worlds: iron knees clamped against flanks of lightning: all opposites whirling to one centre, where the extremity and sightlessness of down-eddying flight stoops to awful stillness. And in that stillness, he considered now circumstance, and this Queen of his, in the spring-time and morning of her life, grey eyes where delicate morning's self sat ignorant and free. And, for the look in those eyes as they met his, he clamped tighter yet the grip of his knees; so that, if the Queen felt indeed the grasp tighten of the hand that held hers, the regard that she encountered in his eye was enough to have laid to sleep in her mind any half-wakening question ere it could come near to waking. And yet behind that unnoticed pressure of hand, given without his will and that he cursed himself inwardly for the giving of, was the whole weight of his iron spirit upon the reins to check the stoop of the winged courser he bestrode, and make it bear him still on the way he chose, superb and perilous between gulf and gulf.

The melody of the pavane, which had returned, upon its last variation, to walk in a glitter of all stars and in a hum of bees and in wafts of honey-sweet fragrance sent out by flowering lime-trees, paused now and, upon two soft pizzicato throbs, entered the doors of silence. Lessingham, making his obeisance to the Queen, handed her towards her chair. On the way to it he, looking down at her as they talked, noted her glance range over the assembled company: noted the dimple hover like a humming-bird near her mouth's corner. "Cousin," she said, holding out her free hand to Zenianthe as they met: "praise my invention. It has succeeded past belief: our enemy fled to mew, and durst no more appear. What reward, Captain-General, will you ask for your share in't? For truly, till to-night, ne'er was there prince in Rialmar so yoked as I."

"Some heights there are," replied Lessingham, "that a man may but descend from. If I may yet be honoured, I'll choose the next lower height, and ask this: that your serenity will graciously be my advocate with my Lady Zenianthe for the honour of a dance."

"Well, cousin?" said the Queen; "shall I?"

" 'Tis a request," answered she, "which I think your highness may pleasantly accept. And for this next dance following."

Lessingham carried himself, through the remaining pleasures of that evening, with open face, and as a man that gives him wholly to the immediate matter: his discourse full of lively and bright sparkles and, when need was, serious opinion. So that neither to the Queen nor to Zenianthe, nor to any that was there, was aught seen in it but of example and use: so masterfully he rode that hippogriff steed within him, and upon so delicate a curb.

Night wore, and the high festival drew to a close. And now, for an ending of ceremonies, the ladies of presence and they of her council stood below stairs in waiting, while she went up in state, alone save for her train-bearers, between the sea-horses. Lessingham, watching, bethought him that not far otherwise might the foam-born Goddess Herself[10] ascend azured spaces of Her eternal sea, between sunset and the moon's rising. And then he bethought him as if all time's treasure-house should have been distilled, from eternity to eternity, into one frail pearl, and in that superlative should pass, under his eyes, beneath cliffs of night.

XIV

Dorian Mode: Full Close[1]

*Lessingham's "I will have but
upon no conditions."*

QUEEN Antiope, upon that good-night, went up to her
rest. But Lessingham, being come at length to his bedchamber, came and went betwixt window and bed and
candle and hearth in an inward strife, as if right hand
should grapple against left hand to peril of tearing in
pieces the body that owns them.

"I will have nothing upon conditions," he said at length, aloud.
He stood now, looking in the glass until, with that staring, the reflection dimmed, and only his eyes, sharpened to steel with a veiling
and confounding of all else, stood forth against him. "Conditions!"
he said; and, turning about, drew from the breast of his doublet a
little withered leaf; the same which Anthea, for better convenience,
had given him in Laimak. Upon this he looked for a while, musing;
then opened the door: went out. The corridors were as ante-cham-
bers of sleep and oblivion: night-watchmen stood to a drowsed salute upon his passage, down the stairs, through empty halls, to the
outer doors. At that leaf's touch doors opened. He came so to the
privy garden. On noiseless hinges, under that leaf of virtue, the gate
swung wide. And he began to say in himself, walking now in the
night-light under stars, and with slower tread, and with an equanimity now of breath and heart-beat whereon his riding thoughts
seemed to mount into the starred sublimities of the unceilinged

189

night: "Nothing upon conditions. Condition of wedlock, kingdom, and be answerable: No. Betrayal so of his commission: No, by my soul! Throwing over of freedom: lean on this, 'stead of ride him as I have ridden afore-time: ha! No. Or, glutton-like: smircher of—" He checked; overtaken, as a man smitten on the nape of the neck with a stick, with a blindness of thought and sense. Then he quickened his pace for a dozen steps, then swung round and, rigid as a statue, stood facing Aphrodite's statue there: of Aphrodite, white between stars and paler stars reflected in the water, and water-lilies that floated asleep about Her feet. And he thought with himself, as thought stood up again: "You are other. Even He that made You—" the night-wind moved for a moment in that sleeping garden, and in a moment was fallen again to sleep: "Your power forced Him, making of You, make the one thing desirable."

A breath from the lilies fainted from under Lessingham's nostrils. His mind stopped and stood still. So a man cloudbound upon the backbone of some high mountain stands clean lost, for the opening and shutting again of a window in the mists that has revealed, far below, a glimpse not of familiar country but of strange and unremembered: and yet embraced, upon some unseized persuasive contrariety of argument addressed to blind certitudes secure and asleep within him, for a country familiar and his own. And now, with a like alien outwardness that the inward touch denied, words which, for all their curiosity of outmoded idiom, he seemed to know for his own words drifted across his thought:

> And we, madonna, are we not exiles still?
> When first we met
> Some shadowy door swung wide,
> Some faint voice cried,
> —Not heeded then
> For clack of drawing-room chit-chat, fiddles, glittering
>   lights,
> Waltzes, dim stairs, scents, smiles of other women—yet,
> 'Twas so: that night of nights,
> Behind the hill
> Some light that does not set
> Had stirr'd, bringing again
> New earth, new morning-tide.

As a man awakening would turn back into his dream, yet with that very striving awakes; or as eyes search for a star, picked up out but now, but vanished again in the suffusing of the sky with light of approaching day; so Lessingham seized at, yet in the twinkling lost, the occasion of those lines, the thin seeming memory blown with them as if from some former forgotten life. Out of which passivity of dream, waiting on flight where no air is to bear up wings; waiting on some face but there is no seeing where all is darkness; some voice or hand-touch where all is deaf and bodiless; out of this his senses began to look abroad again only when he was come back at last now to his own chamber, and stood, where an hour ago he had stood, looking into his own eyes. And now, as the lineaments of earth are bodied to a gradual clearness under the grey of dawn, he began to see again his own face, as mountain should so at dawn look across to mountain through heights of air.

"I will have—" he said and was silent. "But upon no bargains," he said. "Conditions is blasphemy."

Shred by shred he tore up now his leaf of sferra cavallo, sprinkling it shred by shred upon the whitening embers in the fire-place; and so, with a half mocking half regretful look, stood watching till the last shred shrivelled, and burnt up, and disappeared.

XV

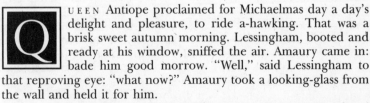

RIALMAR VINDEMIATRIX[1]

*Curbing of the Hippogriff ✦ A queen fancy-free
✦ Ride in the forest: sudden light ✦
Vandermast's wayside garden ✦ The house of
peace ✦ Naiad and dryad and oread ✦
"Sparkling-thronéd heavenly Aphrodite"[2] ✦
Spring-scents of Ambremerine ✦ Whirlpool and
a new stillness ✦ "With an immortal goddess:
not clearly knowing"[3] ✦ "Swift-flying doves to
draw you"[4] ✦ Meditation among nymphs by
firelight ✦ The rose and the adamant ✦
Summer night: Antiope ✦ Autumn dusk: the
storing and the brooding.*

Q UEEN Antiope proclaimed for Michaelmas day a day's
delight and pleasure, to ride a-hawking. That was a
brisk sweet autumn morning. Lessingham, booted and
ready at his window, sniffed the air. Amaury came in:
bade him good morrow. "Well," said Lessingham to
that reproving eye: "what now?" Amaury took a looking-glass from
the wall and held it for him.

"Is there a smudge on my nose? Is my beard awry?" He leaned
to survey himself with a mock solicitudeness.

Amaury set down the glass. "O think not I care a flea, though

193

old Bodenay and a dozen more of 'em shall be killed right out, with
your denying them all respite and very sleep. But, for your own
self—"

"Will you count how many shirts I have sweat at tennis this
week?"

"Tennis! Six weeks now, and the last three I think you're stark
mad," said Amaury. "A half-year's business thrust into twenty days:
the whole engine and governance of the Queen's strength in the
north here picked in pieces and put together good and new: a great
new body of intelligencers thrown abroad for a watch on Akkama,
till now so ill neglected: the town in act to be stocked 'gainst a twelve
months' siege if need were: works· set in hand to make sure all
defences: all things viewed, all put upon examination: the Constable
and half the officers here cashiered: three or four heads ta'en off:
every man else, by your own sole doing, manned and tamed to your
fist—"

"Well," said Lessingham, "we should think the soul was never
put into the body to stand still." He took his hat. "He that could
dine with the smoke of roast meat, Amaury, should he not soon be
rich? When I've set all in order: a week or two now: then off with
my commission, throw it by and we'll begone overseas."

Amaury followed him through the door.

Bright sun shone on Rialmar fair and beautifully as they rode
down through the market-place. By the Quiren Way they rode, and
so to the old town gate, and so out, and so, winding steeply down
the shoulder of that great hill, south-about into the levels of
Revarm. Orvald and Tyarchus led, with the guard of honour; then
the Queen in her close-bodied green riding-habit trimmed with
pearls: Anamnestra, Zenianthe, Paphirrhoë: Amaury: the Lord
Bosra, new taken for Constable in Rialmar: accipitraries,[5] seven or
eight, with spaniels and red setting-dogs; and, to bring up the rear,
with a tartaret haggard[6] hooded on his fist, Lessingham upon Maddalena, deep in counsel with the old knight marshal.

The morning they spent in the open river-meads, flying at
wildfowl. The river, meandering in mighty curves a mile and more
this way and that way, ran shallow upon great widths of shingle;
ever now and again they forded it with a plashing and a clank of
hooves among shifting stones. The dogs must swim oft at these
crossings, but nowhere was it deeper than wet the horses' bellies.
Out of the north-east the wind blew sharp from the mountains,
making sport difficult. The sun in a blue sky shone on rough blue
waves of the river and on pale swifter waves of wind-swept grass. An
hour past mid-day they rode up through lava, picking a way among
bosses and ridges of it as among stooks in a cornfield before harvest
home, and so by wide sloping stretches of black sand, a country that
seemed made of coal-dust, to a grassy saddle between two smooth

cratered hills. Here, sheltered from the wind by the breast of the hill above them, they halted to eat a little and take their ease.

"What means your highness to do this afternoon?" asked Tyarchus. "Turn back? or on over the hause and ride races on the flats there?"

"My Lord Tyarchus," said Zenianthe, "blindfold we'd know you! Your highness were best let him have his way. His eyas[7] flew ill this morning, so the sport's suddenly out of fashion."

"Be kind to him," said the Queen. " 'Twas so God made him."

"And that's why there's nought he hateth worse in the world," said the princess, "than dance, for instance."

"Now I think on't," said the Queen: "danced not one single measure upon my birthday."

"Truth is," said Tyarchus, "I am somewhat nice in matter of whom I shall dance withal."

Zenianthe laughed. "True. For you came first to me. Showed knowledge, if not judgement."

"O Zenianthe, and would you not dance with him?" said the Queen.

"Bade him try Myrilla first. So as, if he trod not upon her dress, as 'pon yours, cousin, a year ago—"

"That's unfair," said Tyarchus. "Her highness had forgot and forgiven."

Antiope seemed to have settled with this talk to a yet sweeter companionship with the green earth where she sat; and not now in her eyes only, but most subtly in all her frame and pose as she rested there, was a footing it as of little mocking faunish things, round and round, in a gaiety too smooth and too swift for eye to follow. "Most unfair," she said. "To make amends, ought I dance with you myself to-night?"

"Madam, I take that most kindly."

"But in a dress," said she, "without a train." They laughed. "But I was but thinking. No; may be, all for all, better it were you, cousin, danced with him."

"That," said Zenianthe, "I take most unkindly."

"A penance for you," replied the Queen, "for your unkindness to him."

"A penance?" Tyarchus turned to the princess. "Shall's make friends then, as both offended?"

"I know the sure way to content him," said Lessingham. "Do him that favour as to let him try this new jennet of his 'gainst your grace's Tessa."

"And to take down his pride 'pon the same motion," said Zenianthe.

"Tessa?" said Tyarchus; "was not she bred in the great horse-lands beyond the Zenner, of that race and stock your highness's father (upon whom be peace) so cherished and increased there, stablished since generations in that good land, and 'longeth now to Duke Barganax? Well, if I win, shall I have her?"

"No," said the Queen, laughing at him across her fingers that played bob together. "If you win, you shall have leave not to dance: neither me nor Zenianthe."

"A pretty forfeit! There you stand both to gain."

"You too; for do you not hate to dance? What could be fairer?"

"If your grace must be answered, thus then: choice to dance with neither or with both."

"My Lord Lessingham," the Queen said, rising, and all rose with her; "have you not your mare of that same breed? and shall she rest attemptless?"

Lessingham laughed with his eyes. "So your serene highness rode not in the race, though mine be seven year old, I doubt not mounted on her to outride any that treads on four pasterns. But let me remember that those who will eat cherries with great princes shall have their eyes dasht out with the stones. We low subjects—"

"No excuses," said the Queen. "I'll stake a jewel upon it. Come, cousin," to Zenianthe: "you and I; Lessingham, Orvald, Amaury, Tyarchus: that's six, upon well-breathed horses."

With that, they took saddle again and rode on north, over the hause and so down into woodlands of silver birch with open turfy stretches, and among the grass pallid drifts of the autumn crocus. Where the glade ran wide before them near on a mile without bend, those six took station. After some justling and curvetting, Paphir-rhoë with a wave of a white handkercher gave them the start. As they galloped, now in broad sunshine, now through airs dappled with lights and shadows, wet earth-scents flew. Rabbits that washed their faces or nibbled among the grass fled left and right to the shelter of bramble or hazel-coppice or birch-wood. Grey silver in the sun were the trunks and branches, and the twigs red as it had been copper glowing against the blue. At a mile the Queen led, out galloping Tyarchus for all his spurring. The forest ride swung west now, and after a while south-westwards, into the sun, and began to fall gently away towards a bottom of green grass. Lessingham, for the sun's glory in his eyes, scarce could see. He leaned forward, whispered Maddalena, touched her neck: in a burst of speed she carried him past Tyarchus. As by conduct of some star he rode now: a timeless chase, wherein he lost at length all wareness save of his own riding that seemed now to outswift the wind; and of Antiope ahead, on her black mare.

At a three lanes' end she drew rein. The black mare stood with head down and with heaving and smoking flanks. Lessingham too drew rein. Maddalena herself was breathed and weary: she had carried the heavier load. On either hand were wide billowing tracts of whinbushes in full flower, yellow, of a sharp, stinging scent. On either hand upon the edges of the wood, silver birches in their livery of autumn swayed in the bright air.

"We have outridden them all," Antiope said, a little breathless yet with hard riding, as she turned in the saddle to Lessingham who was halted now within hand-reach. " 'Las, and I have ridden my hair loose. Will you hold my reins while I see to it?"

She dropped reins: pulled off her gloves: began gathering with her fingers the coil of hair which, heavy, pythonlike, of the sheen of palest mountain gold, was fallen at her neck. Lessingham made no answer, neither moved. This that he looked on was become suddenly a thing to darken sight and shake the stability of nature. The wind was on that sudden fallen, and no breath stirred. On the stillness came a flutter of wings, of a wood-pigeon flapping down unseen among tree-tops. The Queen looked round into Lessingham's face. The stillness laid its finger upon her too, even to the holding in of breath. Like a lute-string strained in an air too thin to carry sound, the silence trembled. The Queen parted her lips, but no voice came.

At a grating of hinges upon the left, Lessingham swung round in his saddle to behold, with eyes startled as out of sleep and dreams, a wicket gate that opened in a low red brick wall smothered all over with dark red climbing roses. A garden close was within that gate, sweet with a hundred smells and colours of flowers, and beyond the garden a low-built old timbered house in measurable good reparations, straw-thatched, and with slender chimneys of brickwork and long low windows. A vine hung the porch with green leaves and pendulous black clusters. The wall on either hand betwixt porch and window, besides all the length betwixt the windows of the ground-floor and of the bedchambers above these, was a ripening-place for apricocks and pears and peaches trained orderly against the wall; and the slant rays of the sun turned the hanging fruits to gold, sending long shadows of them sideways on the wall, deep purple shadows against the warm and ruddy hues of the brickwork. The decline of postmeridian brought coolness to the autumn air. Homing doves rested pink feet on the roof-ridge. A smell of wood-smoke came from the house.[8] And, cap in hand upon the top step of three that led down from that wicket gate, there stood to greet them, as bidding welcome to expected guests, that same logical doctor, last seen by Lessingham in the far southlands of Zayana. Well past all mistaking Lessingham knew him: knew besides the little cat, white as new snow, that rubbed head against the skirt of that old man's gaberdine and looked ever with blue eyes upon Antiope. The sun's splendour swung at mid-evening's height above great oak-woods. These, and a high upland training across the north behind

the house, shut out all distances; not a birch was to be seen; no
whins flaunted yellow flowers; no galloping hoof drew near. Only
Tessa and Maddalena munched the wayside grass: from the roof
came the turtle dove's soft complaint: from the woodside a lowing of
cattle sounded, and nearer at hand a babble of running water.
Upon the left, to the right of the sun, a holm-oak upreared its statuesque magnificence of bough and foliage, nearly black, but with a
stir of radiance upon it like a scattering of star-dust. Doctor Vandermast was saying to Antiope, watching her face the while with most
searching gaze, "I hope, madam, that in these particularities I have
nothing forgot. I hope you shall find all perfect even as your ladyship gave in charge at my depart."

"Ladyship? Give in charge?" she said, looking on him and on
this new scene with the look of one whose senses, fresh wakened out
of sleep, stand doubtful amid things of waking knowledge and
things of dream. "Nay, you mistake, sir. And yet—"

Vandermast came down the steps: put into her hands that little
cat. It purred and snuggled its face into the warm between arm and
bosom. "I have been here before," she said, still in a slow wonder.
"That is most certain. And this learned man I have known. But
when, and where—"

The eyes of that Vandermast, watching her gaze about her and
turn in the end, with a lovely lost abandoning of the riddle, to
Lessingham, were of a lynx-like awareness. And there stirred in
them a queer, half humorous look, as of a mind that pleasantly
chews the cud of its knowledge while it beholds the sweet comedy of
others led in a maze. "If I might humbly counsel your noble grace
and excellent highness," said he, "vex not your mind with
unentangling of perplexities, nor with no back-reckonings. Please to
dismount you and come now in to your summer-house, on purpose
trimmed up for you. And you, my Lord Lessingham, to decide all
doubts be ruled by me. For I say unto you, it is a short ride hither
from Rialmar but, to-night, a far ride back. So as not to-night, no
not in ten nights' riding could you come to Rialmar on your swift
mare. Wherefore, settle your heart, my lord, and be patient. Pray
you come in."

Lessingham looked at Antiope. Her eyes said yes. He leaped
from the saddle: gave her his hand. Her hand in his was an imponderable thing: a cool flame, a deliciousness of mellifluous flowers;
her coming down, a motion to convince the sea-swallow of too dull a
grace, outparagoned by hers. Vandermast swung back the gate: Lessingham looked round: "What of the horses?"

Vandermast smiled and answered, "They will not stray: no
horse strayeth here."

"Lip-wisdom," said Lessingham, and set about taking off of
saddles and bridles. "It is my way, on the road, to see her watered

and fed ere I feed myself, not leave her to horse-boys. And I'll the same for her grace's."

"Here," answered that old man, "is water. And, for the grass of this wayside, 'tis of a singular virtue. Pastures of earth renew but the blood and animal spirits: but this of mine being grazed upon turneth in the vitals not to blood but ichor."

As one expressed with sleep, Lessingham stared upon him. But Vandermast, with that close smile, turned to Antiope. "As your lady-ship hath cited to me ere this, the Poetess's words—κοθαρὸς γὰρ ὸ χρῦσος ἴω. 'Gold is pure of rust.' "[9]

Quite lost, yet too deeply taken with the sweetness of the place to seek answers, she shook her head. Without more words, they entered; and before them went that learn'd philosopher between lupins, blue and yellow, and flaming lychnis, roses and speckled lilies and lavender and rosemary and sweet thyme and pink and white anemones, up the paven walk.

Dim was the low-ceilinged hall that now they entered from that bright garden: to the left a table of pale oak shining with age ran long and narrow under the southern windows, and places laid there for supper, and chairs with cushions of dark velvet, and at the near end an armful of white roses in a bowl of crystal. Beams, smoked black with age, ribbed the ceiling: a fire burned of logs under a great open chimney over against the door with a settle before it and deep chairs for ease. In the western end of that hall a window opened, and another, lesser, to the left of the fire. In the corner between was some instrument of music, a spinet or clavichord, and a stool to sit and play. There were pictures hung on the walls, and thick brocaded curtains drawn back between the windows. A bare oaken staircase to the right of the fire led to the upper chambers.

"If your ladyship would shift your riding-clothes before sup-per?" said the doctor. "And you, my lord? For you besides there is a chamber I have prepared, looking west, but your ladyship's is south and east." Lessingham heard, when the Queen was gone up, little cries of wonderment from above-stairs: past all mistaking, Zeni-anthe's voice laughing and joying with Antiope. He reached out a hand towards the fire: felt its warmth; then walked to the clavi-chord, opened the laburnum-wood lid and let his finger wander on the keys. The thin blade-like sweetness of the strings sprang on the air and there lay stretched, as if the first hueless streaks of a dawn which comes up seaward without wind should lie listening to their own grey stillness. He turned and was face to face with Vandermast. They looked each in the other's eye for a little without speaking. Then Lessingham said with a tartness on his tongue, "And you, signior, with your so much outward submissiveness, but (or I sadly misjudge) without that inward awfulness 't should in honesty proceed from: What in truth are you?"

"I am," answered he, "even as your excellence: a two-legged living creature, gressible, unfeathered. Will you that I conduct you to your chamber?"

Lessingham watched him for a moment through his eyelashes; then, with a slow smile, "If you please," he said. "And what house is this?" he said, when they were come up, and he beheld the fair chamber and, in a bedazzlement, his own clothes and gear laid out ready upon chest and bed.

"By your leave," said the learned doctor, fetching a boot-jack; "not to weight our presence with servants for the while, suffer me help your excellence off with your boots." Lessingham sat down: voluptuous deep cushions of sun-set-coloured silk boiled up about him like swelling water-waves. He gave a leg to Vandermast. "Well, it is, as I conceit it, the house of peace,"[10] said that old man. "And some would think this strange, that to this house should your lordship choose to come, that have the renown of a very thunder-smith and a carver in the wake of armipotent Ares."[11]

"It is part of your wisdom, I see," said Lessingham: "for a hot man cool drink."

When they were come down again and, by invitation of their host, sat at board for supper, it was with strange company and strange household folk to change the plates. The sun had set. All down the supper-table candles were burning, and on tables and chests besides and on sconces of silver on the walls. Antiope had her place in the table's midst, facing the room and the firelight; over against her sat the other ladies: upon her right hand, Doctor Vandermast; upon her left, one whose face was hard to see, but his eyes seemed large past nature and Lessingham noted of his ears that they were sharp-pricked and hairy. Of extreme litheness and soft grace was every movement he made: pricking of ears, turning of the head or shoulders, reaching hands slender and fieldish as Campaspe's own to plate or wine cup. And that was seen of his hands that they were furred or hairy, and the nails on the delicate fingers dark like tortoise-shell. Still would he be speaking whisper-talk in the Queen's ear, and ever, as she gave ear to that whispering, would a thoughtful cast over-take her countenance, as if with the swoop of some winged thing that checked and hung hovering in the sun-path of her thought; and ever, as this befell, would her glance meet Lessingham's.

Lessingham asked, "What guest is that?"

The doctor followed his eye. "That," he replied, "is a disciple of mine."

Lessingham said, "I had guessed as much."

Sitting at the table's end whence he could see all faces in the candlelight, and see, past them in the western window, the feet of day disappear under night as ankles under a skirt dropped by some lovely hand as the wearer walks by, Lessingham felt himself sink into a great peace and rest. Strange and monstrous shapes, beginning now to throng that room, astonished no more his mind. Hedgehogs in little coats he beheld as household servants busy to bear the dishes; leopards, foxes, lynxes, spider-monkeys, badgers, water-mice, walked and conversed or served the guests that sat at supper; seals, mild-eyed, mustachioed, erect on their hind flippers and robed in silken gowns, brought upon silver chargers all kind of candied conserves, macaroons, fig-dates, sweet condiments, and delicate confections of spiceries; and here were butterfly ladies seen, stag-headed men, winged lions of Sumer,[12] hamadryads[13] and all the nymphish kindred of beck and marsh and woodland and frosty mountain solitude and the blue caves of ocean: naiad and dryad and oread, and Amphitrite's brood[14] with green hair sea-garlanded and combs in their hands fashioned from drowned treasure of gold. When a sphinx[15] with dragon-fly wings sat down between the lights beyond Zenianthe and looked on Lessingham out of lustreless stone eyes, he scarce noted her: when a siren[16] opened her sea-green cloak and laid it aside, to sit bare to the waist and thence downward decently clothed in fish-scales, it seemed a thing of course: when a wyvern[17] poured wine for him he acknowledged it with that unreflective ease that a man of nice breeding gives to his thanks to an ordinary cup-bearer. He drank; and the wine, remembering in its vintage much gold molten to redness in the grape's inward parts, under the uprising, circling, and down-setting pomp of processional suns, drew itself, velvet-flanked, hot-mouthed with such memories, smoothly across his mind. And, so drawing, it crooned its lullaby to all doubts and double-facing thoughts: a lullaby which turned, as they dropped asleep, first to their passing-bell, then to their threnody, and at length, with their sinking into oblivion, to a new incongruency of pure music.

"But is this power, then?" he heard Campaspe say. "To be bitten, taken in jaws, swallowed up?"

"Suppose he should kill her indeed," said Anthea: " 'tis but an act bestial. There is no form in it: no grace, no verity. It addeth not: taketh but away. Why, I can kill. I should know." Her teeth flashed.

"It is well said," said the doctor, as if answering Lessingham's look. "In this school she is my graduate. I have nought to teach her."

Lessingham's eyes met Anthea's. It was as if, in the slits between the yellows, a light flared and was gone. "I had it," he said: "but lost again ere I could—" he saw that the room was suddenly empty of all save those seven that sat at table. But, as if with the coming and going of tiny wings, little draughts of air touched here an eyelash, there a throat, and all the candleflames were a-waver. "She is form," he said, and his eyes turned to Antiope. "She draws us. We who do, Gods be we or men, in Her is our doing. And if in this, in action, we have our only being (and by heaven, I think 'tis so), then in Her our being. She draws our actions to a shape: shapes them so, into a kind of beauty."

Campaspe, with the shadow as of moth-like wings shedding a furry and a shy and an elusive sweetness across her elfin features, said softly, " 'As the sheath is to the knife'?"

"It is good," said Vandermast; "but not enough. For the sheath is but an image of receptivity *simpliciter,* and of that which is of none effect of itself."

"Goblet to wine were nearer," said Lessingham, looking still on Antiope.

"Or eyes to the inner fire," Anthea said, leaning forward on her two elbows. Lessingham turned at her voice: faced the slits that burned and reverberated with green and yellow heat. The warm sleek redness of the wine smoothed itself against him like a lover betwixt dream and dream in the failing hour of night.

"Or," Campaspe said at his side, "weakness for strength to rest upon?" He felt the touch of her gloved fingers on his forearm: fluttering feathered bird-breast that a harsh breath might harm it.

"Goblet to wine were nearer," said that learned doctor. Lessingham turned to him: the countenance of Vandermast was mute like the irradiation of the sun behind northern mountains at night in summer on the confines of the Boreal pole.

Then Lessingham looked once more at Antiope. And slowly, as the transmutations in nature of sunset or sunrise are without the catastrophe of lesser changes, it was, as he looked, that three were subsumed to one. Not subsumed bodily, for they sat three as before, she on the left, they on the right facing her across the table; and yet now, in Antiope the lambent eyes of his oread lady, teeth of ice, clean fierce lips, breasts of snow; in Antiope, the strengthless faëry presence of his Campaspe, a rose-leaf hanging in the last near broken thread of a spider's web where the dawn-dew glitters; and in Antiope, something not these, but more than these: herself: easy to look on, fancy-free, ignorant, with a shadow like laughter's in the allurance of her lips. Her eyes, resting in his, seemed to wait betwixt believe and make-believe, then turn to hyaline gulfs where sunbeams wade trembling upon treasure inexhaustible of precious riches. "Strange talk," he heard her say. "And I remember," he heard her say, "but when, I cannot tell; nor where: but goes it not hand in hand with your saying, my Lord Lessingham—

> "Strength is not mine. Only I AM: a twilight,
> Heard between the darts of the blazing noonday;

Seen beyond loud surges: a lull: a vision:
  Peace in the spear-din.
Granite leans earthward, as a mace impending:
Butterfly wings quivering abide the shadow:
Music bitter-sweet of the Gods: Their night-song,
  Older than all worlds.

"Is She not somewhat so?"

Silence shut behind the falling wonder of her spoken words. Lessingham beheld the doctor's prick-eared disciple lift her white hand in his, that was so slender and feral in its tawny hairiness, and press it, as in a dumb worship, to his bowed forehead. This he beheld as an act beautiful and apt, and that the beholding of pleased him much as her little cat's love for her should please, issuing in some such simplicity. Only the strangeness of it, and the strangeness on her lips of words that he remembered, as if with her memory, out of some fair expired season, and that he seemed to know for his own words (though when framed, when spoken, he could not tell): these things gathered now, as a rain-drop gathers and hangs round and perfect on the point of a leaf, into the memory of that streaming up of golden bubbles through golden wine last spring in Mornagay, and of her remembered voice.

Doctor Vandermast stood up from his chair. "The night draweth in cold. Will it please you, madam, we suppose 'twere Yule-tide, and sit about the yule-log? And indeed I remember me, old customs have still pleased you from of old."

Passing by the table's end, as Vandermast and Lessingham bowed and made her way, Antiope reached a hand to Campaspe: "And you, dear, sing to us?"

"Yes, sing, dear chorister of the sleeping sallows, your May-night song," said Lessingham, "of Ambremerine. It told me more than you knew," he said, speaking to her but looking on Antiope, and so saw not the deriding "More than I knew!" in those beady eyes.

Campaspe, with swift naiad grace, was at the clavichord. She opened the lid. "May I choose my song?"

She had taken her answer, from eyes where everlastingness seemed to look, half awake, out of infinities to skyey infinities, ere the Queen's lips could frame it: "Choose: my choice is yours."

Campaspe preluded on the keys. The silence, divided with the passing of those blades of sweetness, fell together again. "My Lady Fiorinda's song?" she said: *"The nightingale my father is?"* Vandermast turned in his chair, to rest his gaze, with that veiled, wine-tasting smile of his, upon Antiope. Lessingham too watched her across the hearth from his deep chair: her face, shone upon by two candles in a sconce beside her, was lovely fair, pictured against warm darkness. Surely in the peace of her his own spirit settled, as the day settles in the west.

Campaspe sang: a bird-voice, so small and bodiless that through its faëry texture even those frail chords gleamed clear:

> "Li rosignox est mon père,
> Qui chante sor la ramee
> El plus haut boscage.
> La seraine ele est ma mere,
> Qui chante en la mere salee
> El plus haut rivage."[18]

Now there hung upon the wall, upon Lessingham's left where he sat, a looking-glass framed in tortoise-shell; and so it was that midway through her singing, with a kindling in his veins again, from that name, and from that song, of memories of Ambremerine, he chanced to look in the looking-glass. For a count of seven he stared, whether in the body, whether out of the body, he could not tell: a face, not Lessingham's but the Duke's, stared back. With the sweeping of terrible harp-strings through his blood, he sat blind.

As his blood beat steadier it seemed to him as if out of that tumult a new figure took clear shape at last of counterpoint and descant. And yet for a minute he dared not lift his eyes to where she sat beyond the hearth listening to the song. For a doubt was on him, lest he should see not the thing he would but the thing he would not: so breathing clear was his memory of what he had seemed to look on but now, when that song began that but now drew to its ending: not her, but another sitting there: a second time (as once in Acrozayana), with too near bodement of the mutability he so much affected and transience of things, as that the levin-bolt might fall not afar to gaze upon, but very here, to thunder his eyes out that gazed. He drew hand over his chin, as to sure himself of it, shaven and hard: looked in the glass: looked at last cautiously across the carpet. This was her foot: no changeling could have stole that: he knew it better than his own. "Pew!" he said in himself, "slip not the reins," and let his eyes run upward. There she sat, under the weak candles, a star between flying darknesses in a night of thunder. Side-face towards him, her chin lifted a little sideways as if, mindful of her own beautifulness, to feed his eyes a little with the silver splendour of her throat and its lovely strength, she stared in the fire through black half-closed lashes. Her head moved lazily, almost imperceptibly, as to the familiar cadence of Campaspe's song. For all else, she sat motionless: all save this, and, with each lightly taken breath, her breasts' fall and swell.

The Duke, so sitting and watching, felt sails fill and his spirit move out once more on that uncharted dangerous ever undiscovered main.

He rose: took a dish of fruit from the sideboard. Vandermast was half risen to have taken it from him, as scandalled that his great master should do handmaid-service, but the Duke prevented him with his eye, and came with the dish to where she sat. "If your ladyship will have any conceits after supper, as medlars, nuts, lady-pears?"

Very daintily she examined them, took one, and, looking at him not with eyes but with the snake-black gleams of her back hair and with the curve of white neck and shoulder, held it up for him to take and peel for her. He peeled it in silence: gave it back: her eating of it was with an air of creative awareness, as of one who carves or models: of conscious art, rather than the plain business of eating. The Duke watched her for a minute; then, behind her chair, leaned over the back and said in a low voice, "What crinkum-crankum was this?"

She leaned back her head till he could look straight down into her eyes as he bent over her, facing him as it were upside down. He looked in them; then in her mouth's corner where that thing sat at alert; then over all the imperial pitiless face of her, where a dozen warring imperfections were by some secret fire transmuted to that which is beyond flattery and beyond alchemy; then to the warm interspace where, with her leaning back, the bosom of her crimson dress strained closer; then into her eyes again. "I wonder," he said: "can the Devil outsubtle you, madonna?"

"How can I tell?" she said, with great innocence, and the thing there covered its face. "Why? Would you engage his help against me?"

"Yes. Save that I think somewhat scorn to bribe your servant."

"Is he my servant?" she asked, as who might ask an indifferent matter for information's sake: Is Vandermast your secretary? Is Campaspe a naiad?

"Or I have long been misinformed," answered the Duke. "Come, what wages do you pay him? Though I fear all the wealth I have shall scarce avail me to bid against you."

"As for me, I pay not," said that lady. "Neither am paid. Still, I have servants: perhaps him we spoke on: could at least have him if I would. And still, I am your mistress. Is not that singular?" She put up a jewelled hand, took his that rested on her chair-back, drew it secretly against her neck, then swiftly put it away again.

"The oaths you sware me," he said, close in her ear, "after that night last May, never to do it again. And yet, worse this time. By my soul, I dreamed, and I was—Lessingham."

Fiorinda said, "I have heard tell of stranger dreams than that."

"And she? that other?" he said, still lower. "Who is she?"

Fiorinda sat up and smoothed her gown. Barganax moved a

couple of paces round towards the fire so as to see her face again. "O, this large-eyed innocence," he said, "becomes your ladyship badly, who have all these things in your purse. What, is she a dress of yours?"

"I had thought you had learnt by now," she said, with a swan-like smooth motion of her hands settling the combs in her hair, "that everything that is is a dress of mine. Ever and since the world began," she said, so low as he should hear not that: but that little white cat, gazing up at her, seemed to hear it.

The Duke looked about. Campaspe at the clavichord fingered out some little lilting canon. Zenianthe had drawn her chair up beside her, and watched her as some sweet oak-tree might watch the mouse-like darts and pauses of the tree-creeper along her steadfast dream-fast limbs. The old man talked low with Anthea: that strange disciple of his was curled up on the carpet as if asleep, one arm about the little white cat that with slow blinking eyes still studied Fiorinda from a distance. "You shall know this," said the Duke: "I loved her as my life."

With that scarce perceptible little upward scoffing backward movement of her head, she laughed. "O sweetly pathetical. You mouth it, my lord, like a common play-actor."

"And would a let you, madam, go hang."

"Who would not be so lovered?" she said; and, with a flower-like grace which had yet the quality in it as of the outpeeking from flowers of a deadly poisoned adder, she stood up. "I am indeed," she said delicately, "of a most lambish patience; but I much fear, my lord, you grow tedious. Zenianthe, my cloak."

"Stay," said the Duke. "My tongue can run on patterns as well as your ladyship's. And men that be in love can ill away to have lovers appointed them by others. It was a dream."

"It was true," she replied, and her green and slanting and un-fathomable eyes held him while he took a stab from every sensuous movement of her putting on her cloak. "The first (as for loving) was true, but not the second: the second was but said in a bravado to plague me. Think, and you will remember, my friend, that I say true."

He made no reply.

"Moreover," she said, "you would not, no not even this mo-ment, let even her go hang. No, fling not off, my lord: think. You shall find I say true."

The Duke faced that lady's eyes in an arrested stillness. "Think" she said again; and he, looking now steadfastly on her lips that seemed to rest upon the antique secret memory of some condi-tion, primal and abiding, where the being of these things is alto-gether at once, which is the peculiar property of everlastingness, slowly after a pause answered and said, "Yes: but that is not to say love. For no man can love and worship his own self."

"This that you have said," said that lady, and her slow voice was like honey of roses, "I have strangely heard before. Yet not heard," she said, her eyebrows lifting with their look of permanent soft surprise as she looked down, drawing on her gloves; "for 'twas but thought, not spoken: seen, in eyes: his eyes, not yours, in Acrozayana."

"In his eyes?" said the Duke. The silence opened quivering wings above them like the wings that shadow the dream-stone.

"There have been, to say, brothers and sisters," she said. It was as if, under the ironic lazy seductive voice of her, the wings were upstrained to that ultimate throbbing tension that must dissolve the next instant in some self-consuming cataclysm of its own extremity. Then, whether upon the mere whim and fantasy: whether of her most divine discerning bounty, *bis dat quae tarde:*[19] whether but of her April mood (now lovely sunshining, now hail from a louring sky, suddenly again those stones melting at a gleam to jewelled drops on the yellow daffodils and celandines: half-fledged leaves of sallow and birch and thorn turning to green tiny flames against the sunlight: the heavens all soft and blue, and the blackthorn and wild cherry starry above new lambs): whether for all or for none of these reasons, she loosed hold. "Reverend sir, are my horses ready?"

"Truly," said the Duke, as if awake again, "I ne'er saw my—" and suddenly his eyes became veiled. "Unless—."

Vandermast came back from the door: "Madam, they are ready at the gate."

Barganax started. "What is this place? Madam, I pray you go not yet. 'Least, I'll go with you." But, out by the door that aged man held open for her, she was gone. Barganax, like a man that would pursue in a dream, but his legs, held in the woolly fetters of sleep, will not obey, stood rooted. Then the door shut.

He saw Anthea's eyes levelled upon him in a sphinxian expressionless stare. Letting that go unregarded, he stood now, back to the fire, in a study, erect, feet wide apart, one hand thrust in his jewelled girdle, the other twirling and smoothing up his mustachios. The dark fires slept and woke, glowed and slept and glowed again, in his half-closed eyes. He said in himself, "But no, dear Lady of Sakes,[20] beguiler of guiles, O you, beyond soundings: there's something there beyond that. That he hath in him something of yours, I'll not think it past credit, that am inured to marvels. Nay, I believe it: it is a lamp: shows me much was dark till now. But you are more. O you! not with the help of all the devils could I, at this day, be bobbed with such an insufficient answer."

* * *

Doctor Vandermast followed that lady through the garden: bare
beds rough with hoar-frost, and over all, hanging high in a frost-
clear heaven, the winter moon. "While you are in a condition,
madam," said he, "to understand and teach me: lest I fall out, may I
know if my part is so far justly enacted, and agreeably to your ladyship's desires?"

"Desires?" she said. "Have I desires?"

"Nay," said he, "I speak but as men speak. For I am not ignorant that *Dea expers est passionum, nec ullo laetitiae aut tristitiae affectu
afficitur:* that She Who dwelleth on high is with no affect affected,
be it of sorrow or of joy."

"How sweet a thing," said she, "is divine philosophy! And with
how taking a simplicity it speaketh, so out of your mouth, most wise
doctor, flat nays and yeas of these which were, as I had supposed,
opinable matters and disputable!"

"Oh You, Who albeit You change, change not," said that old
man: "I speak as men speak. Tell me, was there aught left undone?"

She took the reins and let Her beauty shine out for an instant,
as a blaze of fire, now bright, and now away. His eyes took light in
the light of it. "There was nought undone," She answered. "All is
perfect." And they that were harnessed took wing and, thickening
the crisp fine air with a thunder of countless wing-beats, sped with
Her in an instant high below stars through the down-shedding radiance of the frozen silvery moon. And the learned doctor, straining
eyes and ears towards heaven, followed their flight, their mounting,
circling, descending; and at length beheld them at his eastern upper
window hovering, that their driver might alight; and there like a
dream he beheld Her enter by that balcony, or like a pale moonbeam. For he saw that not as Our Lady of Sakes She entered now,
but once more Our Lady of Peace.

So now he himself turned again, came in, shut the door, and
came to the fireside again and his company.

The clock at his so coming in (as if She in that dove-drawn
flight betwixt earth and stars had swept the hours, bound to Her
chariot, to a speed beyond their customed measure), struck the last
hour before midnight. That old man came to Lessingham where he
stood yet, in a study, his back to the fire. "Sleep, my Lord Lessingham, is a surceasing of all the senses from travel. Her ladyship
that came hither with you hath this hour since ta'en her chamber.
Suffer me to conduct you now to yours."

Pausing for good-night at his chamber door, Lessingham at last
spoke. "Tell me again," he said: "what house is this?"

Vandermast answered, saying, "I have told your excellence, it is
the house of peace.

"And," he said, speaking, as old men speak, to himself, when he
was come downstairs again and stood at the open door, scenting the

April air that blew now from that garden and the scents of spring: "it is the house of heart's desire."[21]

May be for the very deepness of the peace that folded that sleeping house, so that even his own breathing and quickened heart-beats had power to keep him waking, Lessingham might not sleep. An hour past midnight he arose and dressed and softly opened his chamber door. At the head of the stair he paused, seeing lights yet in the hall both of candles and the flickering firelight. Noiselessly he came down a step or two, and stood still. On the great cushioned settle drawn up before the fire sat Doctor Vandermast. Anthea, upon the same settle, lay full length, a sleeping danger, very lovely in her sleep, her head upon the lap of that learned doctor. Zenianthe sat upon the floor, her back against his knees, staring in the fire. Campaspe knelt, sitting on her heels, her back to the fire, facing the others; Lessingham saw that she played some little game with cards on the floor, very intently, yet listening through her game to the doctor's words as he talked on in his contemplation.

"Be it but perceived and understood," said Vandermast, *"sub specie aeternitatis,* it can never be too sensual: it can never be too spiritual."

Zenianthe, smiling in the fire, slowly shook her head. "Multiplication of matterless words," said she.

"Nay, you, dear lady, should know this *per experientiam,* as from withinward. For what will a hamadryad do if her tree be cut down? What but die?"

"Can anything die?" she said. "Least of all, we, that are not of mortal race?"

"I speak," said he, "as men speak. And indeed I have thought may be there is in very deed a kind of death, as of foolish bodies who say, Tush, there is no spirit: or others, Tush, there is no sense. And have not old men ere this become dead before their time, with forgetting that this winter of their years is but a limbeck of Hers for trying of their truth and allegiance, as silver and gold are fined and tried in the fire? But, even as 'twas always that the cat winked when her eye was out, so they: 'stead of hold fast and trust in Her to bind up and bring back and give again hereafter."

"Are you, to say, old?" said Campaspe, marrying queen of spades and king of hearts.

Vandermast smiled. "I am, at least, no more fit for past youth-tricks."

"No more?"

"I speak," said he, "as of here and now."

"What else is there?" said she.

Vandermast stroked his white beard. "It may be, nothing."

"But you spoke but now," said Zenianthe, putting very gently a fresh log on the fire so that the flames crackled up, and that oread lady, with the doctor's knees for her pillow, turned in her sleep: "you spoke of 'hereafter.'"

"It may be," said Vandermast, "that 'hereafter' (and, by like process of logic, 'heretofore') is here and now."

Campaspe turned up the seven of diamonds. "What is old age?"

"What is youth, my little siren of the oozy quagmires and wood anemones in spring and sallow catkins where the puss-moth feeds at dusk of night?"

"Well, it is us," she said.

"As for old age," said Zenianthe, "the poet hath it—'My grief lies onward and my joy behind.' That for age. And for youth I would but turn the saying, and say—'My joy lies onward.'"

"Who taught you that?" said the learned doctor.

"My oak-woods," answered she.

He mused for a while in silence. Then, "It is of divine philosophy," he said, "to search lower into the most darkness and inspissation of these antinomies which are in the roots of things. I am old"; and his eyes overran the sleeping beauty of Anthea, stretched feline at her length. Scarcely to touch it, his finger followed her hair where it was pressed upwards in aureate waves from under her left brow and cheek where her head lay on his knee in the innocence of slumber. "I am old; and yet, as the Poetess—

"ἐγὼ δὲ
φιλημ' ἀβροσύναν, καί μσι τὸ
λάμπρον
ἔρος ἀελιω και τὸ κὰλον λέλογΧεν
"I love delicacy, and for me love hath
the sun's splendour and beauty."[22]

Zenianthe said, "We know, sir, who taught you that."

Still Lessingham, upon the stairs, stood and listened. Their backs were towards him. Vandermast replied: "Yes: She, ingenerable and incorruptible. Are youth and age toys of Hers? How else? seeing She plays with all things. And age, I have thought ere now, is also a part of Her wiles and guiles, to trick us into that folly which scorneth and dispraiseth the goods we can no more enjoy. Then, after leading of us as marsh-fires lead, through so many turn-agains, unveil the grace in Her eyes: laugh at us in the end."

"Love were too serious else," said Campaspe. She fetched for the queen of hearts the king of clubs: "Antiope: Lessingham."

"What is Lessingham?" Zenianthe asked the fire. "What is Barganax?"

"What am I?" asked Vandermast. "Tell me, dreamer and huntress of the ancient oak-woods, is it outside the scheme that there should be, of young men, an old age wise, unrepentant, undisillusioned? I mean not some supposititious mathematical *esse formale*,[23] as some fantastics dream, but bodied, here and now? For truly and in sadness, searching inward in myself I have not once but often times—" he fell silent.

"What is here and now?" Zenianthe said, gazing into the heart of the fire with brown dreaming eyes.

Vandermast was leaned back, his head against a cushion, his lean hands slack, palms downwards, on the seat on either side of him. He too gazed in the fire, and, may be for the hotness of it, may be for the lateness of the hour, the gleam of his eyes was softened. "As part of Her peace?" he said. "As part of Her pleasure?—O gay Goddess lustring, You Who do make all things stoop to Your lure.— Seeing all the pleasures of the world are only sparkles and parcels sent out from God? And seeing it is for Her that all things, *omnia quae existunt*,[24] are kept and preserved, *a sola vi Dei*, by the sole power of God alone?"

Zenianthe spoke: "And of lovers? Will you not think a lover has power?"

"Love," said that aged man, "is *vis Dei*.[25] There is no other power."

"And to serve Her," said Campaspe, still sitting on her heels, still playing on the floor, "(I have heard you say it): no other wisdom."

"To shine as stars into everlastingness," said that hamadryad princess, still looking in the fire.

For a few minutes none spoke, none stirred, save only for Campaspe's playing her little game. Lessingham, upon the stairs, noted how the learned doctor, as old men will, was fallen asleep where he sat. Campaspe, noting it too, softly swept up her cards. She stood for a moment looking at him so sleeping, then on tiptoe came and bent over him and, very prettily and sweetly, kissed his forehead. Anthea, turning in her sleep, put up a hand and touched his face. Lessingham very quietly came down the stairs behind them and so from the stair-foot to the door. Only Zenianthe, sitting quite still, turned her head to watch him as he passed.

Lessingham went out and shut the door behind him and stood alone with that garden and the summer night. Under stars of June he stood now, in an awareness like to that which once before he had known, upon that night of feasting in her Rialmar: as then before the pavane, a hardening of sensual reality and a blowing away of dreams. Only no hardness was in this lily-scented night: only some perfection; wherein house and slumbering garden and starry sky and the bower of radiance south-eastward where the moon, unseen, was barely risen behind Zenianthe's oak-woods, seemed now to flower into a beauty given them before all everlastingness. Slowly between sleeping flower-beds he walked to the eastern end of that garden and stood watching the top leaves of the oak-trees fill with the moon-rise. In the peace of it he remembered him of someone, not Campaspe, that had sat so a-nights upon heels before the fire, playing and talking and listening all at once: a strange accomplishment he thought now, and had thought so then: but as to speak of when, or who, the gentle night, as if it knew well but would not say the answer, held its peace in a slumbrousness of moon-dimmed stars.

He looked again at her windows. There, which had a minute before been empty, and no light within, he beheld her upon the balcony: facing the moon. From his place in the deep shade of a yew-tree, he watched her: Antiope: all in white. It was as if she stood upon no firm substance but on some water-wave, the most adored beauty that ever struck amazement in the world. Almost in disbelief, as if night had spoken, he heard her speak: "You, my lord? standing there?"

Slowly he came towards her. As spread out upon some deepening of the stillness and the blessedness, the long churr of a nightjar sounded near. It ended, purring down like the distant winding of a clock, into silence. "I could not sleep," he answered, under her window.

"Nor I," said she. All being seemed now to draw to her, as lodestones to the lode-star, or to a whirlpool's placid centre the waters which swirl round it and their floating freight, both of the quick and of the dead.

"Nor you?" said Lessingham. "What is here, to inquiet your mind?"

Her answer came as upon a catch in her breath: "Deep waters, I think."

The wistaria blossoms hung like heavy grape-bunches below her balcony: the limbs of the tree, lapped about and crushed in the grip of their own younger growths, showed gnarled and tortuous under the moon. "I think," Lessingham said, "I am broken with the fall of such as climb too high."

Again the nightjar trilled. Upon his left, sudden and silent it slipped from the branch where it had lain. He felt it circle about his head: heard the strange wild cry, *Pht! Pht!* saw it swoop and circle, its body upright as it flew, its wings, as it flew, uplifted like a great moth's that alights or like a bat's: heard the clap of its wings: heard Antiope's voice as in a dream, or as the summer night stirring in the wistaria's pendent blooms: "There is a remedy: to climb higher."

He took one step and stood quivering like a dagger struck into a table. "Ha!" he said. "If master but now, yet now am I water-weak." Then in a sudden alteration, "Tempt me not, madonna. In action I was ever a badger: where I do bite I will make my teeth meet."

He heard her say, as a star should lean to the sea, "What boots it me to be Queen? O think too," her voice faded: "—howsoever they may seem chanceful—are yet by God."

The swinging heavy blossoms, brushing his face and beard, blinded him as he came up. Standing before her in that balcony, looking down into her eyes that were unreadable in the warm and star-inwoven darkness, "Who are you?" he said in a breath without voice. "Sometimes I hardly know," she said, leaning back as if in a giddiness against the window-frame, her hands holding her breast. "Except there was a word," she said, "written inside a ring, HMETEPA—'Las," she said, "I remembered; but it is gone."

"And I remember," said Lessingham. "To say, *ours:* λμετέρα' you, ours: ημετέρα' of all things, ours: of you and me, beyond all chanceableness of fortune." Sometimes so in deep summer will a sudden air from a lime-tree in flower lift the false changing curtain, and show again, for a brief moment, in unalterable present, some mountain top, some lamp-lighted porch, some lakeside mooring-place, some love-bed, where time, transubstantiate, towers to the eternities. "'Tis gone!" he said. "But you"—her body in his arms was as the little crimple-petalled early-flowering iris that a rough breath can crush. He felt her hands behind his head: heard her say, in breaks, into his very lips, "I cannot give you myself: I think I have no self. I can give you All."

Through the wide-flung casements of Antiope's bed-chamber in that wayside house came the golden-sandalled dawn: the sky gold, and without cloud, and the sun more golden than gold in the midst of it. The Queen said, at Lessingham's side, "Thanks, my lord, I'll take my reins again." As she gathered them, the thud of galloping hooves came down the whinflower-scented air behind them, and Tyarchus and Zenianthe, knee to knee, with Amaury thundering close upon their heels swept round the turn from behind the screening birch-woods.

They were nearing Rialmar when Lessingham found means of speaking with her in private. It had been late afternoon when they turned homewards, and now, the autumn day closing in early, the sun was setting. On their right, two-horned Rialmar was lifted up dark and unassaultable against clouds that drifted down the west. The air was full of the crying of sea-mews. Southward, the wash of the sea answered from bay to bay. The blue smoke of houses and their twinking lamps showed about Rialmar town. Far as the eye could see from the eastern highlands round to Rialmar, the clouds were split level with the horizon. The dark lower layer was topped as if with breaking waves of a slate-dark purple, and in the split the sky showed pink, golden, crimson, apple-green. Above the clouds, a rosy flush thrilled the air of the western heavens, even to the zenith, where the overarching beginnings of night mixed it with dusk. The turf beneath them as they rode was a dull grey green: the whinbushes and thornbushes black and blurred. Lessingham looked at the Queen where she rode beside him: the cast of her side-bended eye: the side of her face, Greek, grave, unconscious of its own beautifulness. He said: "I had a dream."

But she, with a kind of daybreak in her eyes very soberly looking into his: "I am not learned to understand these matters; but 'twas not dreaming," she said. "I was there, my friend."

XVI

The Vicar and Barganax

"The divells quilted anvell"[1] ◆ *Apprehensions in
Kessarey* ◆ *Storms in the air* ◆ *A fief for Count
Mandricard* ◆ *"Bull tread panther"*

T HE VICAR meanwhile, sitting in his closet alone with
his cursed dogs, upon the very morrow of Lessingham's
setting out for Rialmar, sent for Gabriel Flores. "Take
ink and pen: write." Word by word he gave it him, and,
when it was written, scanned the letters; signed them:
certified them with his seal vicarial. The same hour, he took a secret
person, commanding him go with these to the High Admiral, that
lay with the fleet in Peraz Firth, and to the Chancellor in Zayana.
Another he sent to Kutarmish, to Earl Roder. That done, he summoned Count Mandricard from Argyanna, and Daiman, Thrasiline,
and Rossilion from outparts of Rerek, and had with them Arcastus
besides, that was already at hand. With these men, all five being
creatures and instruments of his, and with Gabriel, he for a full day
till supper-time held talk in secret, showing them of his mind so
much as he deemed convenient.

Now came answers again from those three great commissionaries, not concerted, for they had had no time to confer together
upon them, yet as showing one common mind; which, plainly
stripped, was readiness indeed to meet with him, but not as cattle
with the lion in the lion's lair: not in Owldale. Upon this, having
considered with himself awhile, he despatched more letters, and
first to Jeronimy in quality of regent of Outer Meszria, to the intent

that he did, as earnest of his friendship and as not unfitting to the
Admiral's charge and estate, give over and assign to him Kessarey
castle and the township and lands thereof and all the roadstead
harbour and sea-works of Kessarey, which, albeit within the March
of Ulba, yet by its situation threw far into Meszria the shadow of its
power; and now there let their conference be, in Kessarey instead of
Owldale. And, for example of friendship, he would thither come
with no more but a bodyguard; and upon such open and undoubtable terms of faith let them take counsel for the realm's good and
their own.

To Kessarey then, about middle August, came these four: Beroald, Jeronimy, and Roder, with the Vicar. There was nought given
out, that folk might have known what manner of fowl were hatched
in these layings of heads together. The Chancellor, after a day or
two, betook him home to Zayana: the Earl to Kutarmish: the Admiral settled him down in Kessarey with the fleet, and had good
strength of men both for land and sea. They parted all with manifestations of affiance and regard, the Vicar proceeding now upon a
progress through the March and Outer Meszria to take oaths of
allegiance from towns and strongholds in those parts subject to the
regent Jeronimy, like as he had taken them from the regent's self in
Kessarey, for the acknowledging and receiving him as Vicar and
Lord Protector, and owner of their fealty in peace and war. It went
not unremarked that, whereas in the great King's day had forms
and salutations upon like occasion been as unto the King's highness,
and if through viceroys, commissionaries, or other, then but
through them as middlers, and so expressed; yet now in this progress was all taken by the Vicar in person as unto himself, without
all mention made of the Queen, principal and sovereign and fount
of his authority. Which, furnishing with mischief such as will still be
tale-bearers in matter capable of reward, came, upon such tongues,
to the regent's ear in Kessarey, To such kind of talk Jeronimy listened open-eared but close-mouthed.

The Vicar, returning now to Laimak, caused Gabriel to write
him a letter to Duke Barganax as sweetly and amiably as could be
devised. To this, after not many days of waiting, the Duke answered
as pleasantly again, excusing himself from bidding the Vicar to
guest with him in Zayana (which, had it been offered, the Vicar
would, for jealousy of his own safety, have upon no conditions been
minded to accept), and proposing instead a meeting in the Salimat.
There, being that it was the border betwixt Outer and South Meszria, he would about October ceremonially receive the Vicar and do
homage to him, as vicegerent of the Queen, for the regency of
South Meszria, by the Concordat of Ilkis upon such terms of suzerainty conferred upon the Duke.

Now autumn wore, and all quiet.

* * *

In the first days of November the Chancellor came north again. Upon an afternoon he with the Admiral walked the poop of the Admiral's ship royal, at anchor in Kessarey haven. It was a tempestuous and cloudy sky, with gulls hanging in the wind, and circling intercrossing flights of sea-swallows, and sometimes the passing of a line of gannets, strong-winged, keeping their line like ships, high through that windy grey tumult of wintry weather which swept in eastwards from the high seas without. Elbow to elbow those two lords paced, cloaked and hatted against the weather and in great sea-boots, keeping to the lee side for the wind sake and spindrift.

"In Owldale," said the Admiral: "Owldale. I said, you did not carry your friendship so far as accept that inviting to go to him in Owldale."

"No. And yet that showed a certain nobility, to trust us here in Kessarey."

"The measure of his trust is but the measure of his contempt."

"For my part," said Beroald, "I will trust no man these days. Saving present company."

They took another turn or two. Then said the Admiral: "Truth is, I have it by kind to see clear and feel my power in a manner thus, with the tar smelling in my nostrils and with good oak planks and salt water a-wash beneath my feet; never so ashore. Remember," he said, after a pause, " 'tis alway stab i' the dark with him. Attempt 'gainst Ercles in September, miscarried but by accident, even as that 'gainst yourself last spring in Zayana."

Beroald said, "O I take my precautions."

Jeronimy shot a sidelong look at him. "And he is a layer of baits."

"Well?"

"Well: Sail Aninma."

The Chancellor's lip curled. "So your lordship knew of that? It was propounded to me upon terms of secrecy, and indeed I urged him keep it so. Yet in a ten days' time I found my lady sister knew it, and had inspired the Duke and his mind incensed to have made it matter of open quarrel with the Vicar. But he was not to be moved: laughed at it: said I would never take it."

"And I doubt said rightly so?"

"Such horses," said the Chancellor, "are not to be looked too near in the mouth."

"Perilous counsel. Consider Kessarey: it is good, but I am not deceived. My lord, these things are writ big, in a manner, for our instruction: that he, yes, as long since as August, I say, hath said in his heart, 'Tis time now: all lets removed: now, in the happy absence of this Lessingham, *divide et impera.*'[2] Why, the action walketh apparent, smelleth so rank a perfume of supposed seduction the gorge clean sickens at it: holding out of himself to me with such crude blandishments as disinterested noble guardian of her high-ness' rights: blackening the Duke to me with such palpable lies and wrestings of plain honest—Faugh!" he said, checking in his walk; "design is, gull and flatter us to the top of our bent: crush the Duke: that done, crush us. The wind setteth where last May it set; and 'tis that voyage over again: same lee shore, same weather, same tide-race 'twixt skerry and skerry. With the Duke of our side, and with right of our side—well; but, fail either condition—good night! My lord Chancellor, forget not that."

"I forget nothing," said Beroald. "I know the Duke. More, know my sister."

"And did your lordship foresee," said the Admiral, "upon that knowledge (as, by my soul, I think few else did), that patience and loyalty whereby he did last month do homage, meeting of him in the Salimat? 'fore all the folk assembled acknowledging him and swearing fealty? even to taking in that ceremony the Vicar's horse by the rein and humbly, while that other sat in the saddle puffed in his insolence, leading it north to south over the beck in token of submission? Did not that argue, in this loose age, a wonderful exam-pleless example of noble truth and word-keeping? But I say 'tis the blood determines it. Royal blood: and that will out."

"It was the act," answered the Lord Beroald, "of a disciplined and law-abiding person."

"Ha, and, for law-abiding, what of those late proceedings in my own vicariate, a month or so ere that? and of the Queen's highness no more mention made than had the vile murderer, by will deputed overseer of our estate, been crowned King and all?"

"That too," said the Chancellor, "is not to be forgot."

"I wish," the Admiral said, after a silence, "your lordship would, in a manner, throw back flat this offer of Sail Aninma: might give him pause, where all till now hath swum too easy."

"It handsomely becomes you, my lord Admiral, with Kessarey and the half of Meszria into your hand, to lesson me in self-sacri-fice."

"O take me not so thwart. You do know I mean not thus. More power to your hand, the better for us all. But this, a fief in South Meszria: 'tis stamp on Barganax's sore toe: 'tis wrongful, too, clean 'gainst the Concordat—"

"Not so fast," said the Chancellor. "Hath been matter of legal controversy these three generations and more, of the right status of Sail Aninma, whether of Meszria, whether a demesne apart and of itself. Do me so much right as not imagine I'd trespass one iota beyond the law."

"Then let only policy determine, and effect upon the Duke, already tried near patience's ending. You have your own man holdeth Argyanna as governor, and that is key of south Rerek, like as Kutarmish is and Kessarey of the Meszrian Marches. So, and with Roder in Kutarmish, and me in Kessarey—albeit Roder, I am sometimes apt to doubt, useth a little too much security in feeding on these morsels from the table of Laimak—"

"My good lord Admiral," said the Chancellor, "I do fear your eye so vigilant bent on Laimak importeth your too much negligence toward Zayana."

They came to a stand. The High Admiral, leaning with his elbows on the bulwark, clasping and unclasping his hands, gazed landwards. "Your lordship is known," he said, "for the flower of legists in these days. And I applaud your politics. But remember, my lord, neither to you is it given to see all and err never."

The tide was running. Like white horses ridden at barriers, now here now there all the sea-length of the mole, breakers plunged and tossed mast-high in the wind manes of spray. The castle, built of mighty blocks of sandstone mottled with lichen and sea-scurf, stood bare and square upon the seaward point of the low long shattered head-land from which the mole, built of the like stone, takes a sweep, first west and then south-about to the line of skerries, giving so a sea-mile and more of sheltered water with good anchorage and safe riding in all weathers. The ships of the fleet, a score of them besides lesser craft and a few great carracks laden with costly treasure of merchandise, lay outward from the Admiral's that was anchored scarce three hundred paces from the land. And now those two lords, looking shorewards so through that flurry of wind, saw where an eight-oarer put out from the quay under the seawall of the castle and began to row towards them. Swiftly she rowed, as upon some urgency. "Why," said Jeronimy at length, as she drew near, " 'tis his grace's friend, young Barrian"; and made ready to welcome him aboard.

When greetings were done and they three alone upon the poop, "My lord Admiral," said Barrian, "I was directed to your excellence upon matter runneth to danger. And 'tis more than common fortune I should also a found your lordship," (to the Chancellor); "Medor was sent to you, and some question where to find you. But, for the business, 'tis shortest peruse this letter, that my lord the Duke had but on Saturday evening from him we know on, out of Rerek. No forgery: the signet is knowable; and trusty for bad, if less for good. And for what his grace accounteth of it, let its plight acquaint you: ripped up the middle like a pair of breeches."

"Let's read it," said the Admiral, fumbling for his perspective-glass. He and Beroald, holding it down upon the binnacle, read it together. "Openeth very sweetly: the hand I know too (too well by now), that Gabriel Flores': unctuous sweet beginnings wont to steam up in the end into assafoetida. Ha, and there's the true whiff on't," he said, scoring it with his thumb-nail: "Mandricard to be of Al-zulma enfeoffed in fee simple. But, Alzulma? 'tis in South Meszria, broad as barn doors: in by a dozen miles. Were I his grace, I'd answer: Good; and to pay back the courtesy, I've gi'en to my Lord Barrian here Mornagay, Storby, or Anguring itself. Nay, in sadness, 'twere fair comparison: he that sits in Alzulma can say who shall pass and who pass not by the Ruyar road from Rumala to Zayana; and his saying hath currency not in weak words, but in power and deed."

They read to the end: "And so, wishing God the Father glori-ous bee your conduct, given by vertue of al powres and habilities enabling me thereunto both for mine owne Selfe and vicarially as Lord Protectoure for the Quens Highnes, HORIUS PARRY. In Laimac, thys vij daie of Novembre *anno* Z.C. 777." And then the superscription: "Unto hys Grace and Excellent Lordshipp Bar-ganax, cawld Duke of Zayana, regent under Me Meszriae Australis. So obey and perform hit. H.P."

The Chancellor, when he had read it, stood yet for a minute looking down on it, his brow a little clouded, the proud lineaments of his face a little colder drawn than of custom, with a tightening now and again about the lips especially and the wings of his nostrils. The Admiral smiled: a mirthless smile: then blew out his cheeks. "This is bull tread panther, in a manner. Are we too late?"

"His grace," answered Barrian, "hath in this bay borne himself beyond example—not nobly: when was he less than noble?—but beyond example calm. And not for lack of egging on, neither; for I and his most friends think it better that men envy him than that he should stand at reward of their pity. But was in a most happy and merry vein when this news found him; and, the first rage over and past, sent thus to you, and to you, my lord Chancellor, to call upon you both in person now to mediate his peace with the Vicar; who if he give not back from this last proud mock, the whole realm must shortly squelter with bloody wars; for this thing his grace will not swallow but thrust it down the Vicar's throat again."

The Admiral said, "Pray him for all sakes use yet a little this noble patience. Tell him I'll come to him."

"He bade me offer you this: a meeting-place halfway, in Peraz."

"Five days from to-morrow," replied the Admiral, "that's on Wednesday, expect me in Peraz, there to confer with his grace upon best means to use."

"Can I assure him," asked Barrian, "of your friendship? You will easily suppose, my lords, upon what an edge is all now poised in Zayana, and how much lieth on what I must report. 'Tell them,' he bade me (last words at parting), 'tell them I'll play fair: but tell them, by the Gods in heaven, I'll not be played with.' "

Jeronimy's eye waited on the Chancellor. The Chancellor said,

"The thing is flatly against the Concordat of Ilkis. I stand upon the law, upon that Concordat. Tell the Duke so, my lord, from me."

The Admiral said, "And the like from me, Lord Barrian."

"Your excellences are to be thanked, then. But, being thus agreed, were't not fittest act? A little slacking may all our purposes let. Sudden, and we may end it."

The Chancellor smiled. "We offer him first the law," he said; "and not till that fail use open violence."

"Ay. I have fallen down, ere this," said the Admiral, "in these civil broils; and that was always upon unripe heady action." In the dog-like open honesty of his regard there came a twinkle as it rested on Barrian. "And say to him, too, if he with his high-horsed frenzies o'erset the pot before we be met in Peraz, then am I free of my bond, to do as shall seem me fit."

Barrian, a little damped, looked from one to the other, then gripped them by the hand in turn. "I will begone back this very hour. Sleep in Ulba, thence by the Salimat: I can be in Zayana by Sunday evening. I pray you, my lord Admiral, fail not tryst."

He being gone, "When mean you to set forth for Peraz?" asked the Lord Beroald.

"Why, to-morrow, and leisurely by land, not to hazard delays in this rageous wind. Will not you come too? For 'twill need seamanship, in a manner, to handle him safely, under full sail as he is and with such young hare-brained counsellors as this, to blow him on the rocks."

The Chancellor drew up his lips and smiled. "If, with my own flesh and blood, my word could weigh as much as for my years it should," said he, "I'd instead through to Zayana. For there will she bewitch him with her beauty and dainty seductive talk till he is as wrought up as if to storm heaven, let pass Laimak, with the whirlwind inside him and flinging fiend of hell."

XVII

THE RIDE TO KUTARMISH

Peraz, and fair sunshining ♦ *A bloody
encounter* ♦ *The rose-leaf gallery in Zayana* ♦
Medor and Vandermast ♦ *Her ladyship sits* ♦
Fire-shadows from an unseen mouth ♦ *Memison
midnights* ♦ *"When such a mutual pair"*[1] ♦
Paphian stillness ♦ *Our Lady of Sakes* ♦ *Bis
dat quae tarde* ♦ *The Duke, anvil no more* ♦
The Vicar without an ally.

DULY UPON the set day was that meeting held in Peraz,
of the Duke, the Admiral, and the Chancellor. There all
was accorded as among sworn brethren; and so next
day, farewell and they parted, the Duke riding home by
easy stages, the long way, by Memison; Medor with him
and a dozen of his gentlemen. In a gay security he rode, all doubts
removed now, seeing they had sided in his behalf, Jeronimy and
Beroald both, in face of this last high-blown overweening of the
Vicar, in giving, thus wrongfully and within the Duke's dominions,
of land and licence to Count Mandricard.

The second day, about three of the afternoon, coming by the
highway round the slack of a hill where the road drops to the ford a
little beside the out-fields and muir-ground of Alzulma, they saw
where men on horseback came up from the river, and a big man in
red in the midst of them. Barganax drew rein. They were not near

enough to see faces. "Were this Mandricard," he said, "come to take delivery, that were a jest."

"Let us ride round," said Medor, "by the upper road. Your grace will not wish at this time to bandy words with them."

"They are more than we," the Duke replied. "Whoever they be, I desire no speech of them, but by God, I will not turn out of the road for them."

"This upper road is better going," said Medor.

"You should a thought on that a minute sooner. If we turn now, and if here be Mandricard indeed, they will say we were afeared to meet with them."

As they rode down, Medor said, "I pray you yet remember but my lord Chancellor's words at parting, that your grace should wait well that you take not the law into your own hand: that, that provided, all should in a few weeks be carried to a conclusion conducible unto your most contentment and honour."

The Duke laughed. "Very well: 'tis commanded, no biting of thumbs. Untie your swords, but 'pon pain of outlawry, no man speak till I speak. We will let them go by and they will."

So now they began to ride down to the ford; which when those others beheld, as though having seen it was the Duke and being willing to avoid a meeting, they turned out of the road and bare away northwards at a walking-pace towards Alzulma. But Barganax, knowing now the man in red for Mandricard, must needs, against all protestations, send a gentleman to ride after them and pray the Count turn back that they might have speech together apart from their folk. They waited now, watching the messenger overtake the other party, doff hat to Mandricard; then their talking, pointing, Mandricard as if refusing, the other pressing, Mandricard at length consenting, seeming to give command, turning his horse's head, and now riding with Barganax's man and a man of his own back towards the road. "This is to tempt the fates," said Medor. The Duke said, as merry as a magpie, " "'Tis the most fortunate good hap: a heaven-sent chance to show him I know he is here within my borders, nosing about Alzulma: that I know he hath no right to be here: that I am so good and sober a prince as will, even being dared with such an insolency as this, proceed all by law and in nought by violence. Last, to show him I count him not worth a pease, neither him nor his master."

"Stand ready, gentlemen," said Medor, as the Duke rode away. "When his heart is set thus upon a merry pin, no staying him. But stand ready, see what they will do."

The Duke when they were met bade him good morrow. "I had not heard your lordship was doing us this honour to be our guest in the south here."

Mandricard answered and said, "This meeting, my lord Duke,

may save us both some pains. His highness, I am informed, hath acquainted you of his intentions as touching me. I have here," and he drew out a parchment, "licence to have and hold this manor of Alzulma by grand sergeanty. See it, and you like: 'letters of legitimation made to the said Mandricard': 'tis sure and no question. Brief, I am here to overlook the place, and 'tis for you to give order the keys be now made over to me."

"We are indeed well met," said the Duke; "and I can save your pains. The thing you hold in your hand, my lord, you may tear up: it is not worth the parchment 'tis writ upon. The manor is mine, fiefed in the tail, and I'm sorry I have no mind to give it you."

"That will help never a dell," replied he. "The Vicar gave it me, and bade me take it up too." He spat on the ground and glowered in a dull insolency at Barganax.

"I am nowise bounden," said Barganax coldly, "to reason with his highness's servants on things that concern but me and him, well agreed as we are together, and our agreement resteth upon law. Yet, to end the matter, know that, in refusing of Alzulma to your lordship, I stand upon the law, and as read by my lord High Chancellor."

Mandricard gave him a sour look and sat there spitting and spawling. "Well, fare you well," said the Duke. "And since your lordship is not a particular friend of mine and hath besides no business here, save which is alleged by us not loisible by the treaty, I will desire you to begone north again as soon as may be."

"May be I shall find a mean to stay i' the south here."

"You stay then at your peril. Bethink you that you are now in Meszria: trust not here in the shadow of Laimak."

"I know my liripoop[2] without coming here to learn it," said Mandricard as the Duke began to move off.

Barganax turned in his saddle and drew rein. "And learn," he said, "to do after another fashion than to be thus malapertly cocking and billing with me that am your better."

Mandricard gave him a buggish word. Barganax's sword leapt from the scabbard, his face dark as blood. "Fief in the tail?" said Mandricard as he drew. "That's bungerly law, damn me else: to the bastard of Zayana!"

"Dismount and to it," said the Duke. "You are renowned to me as profoundly seen in all arts of sword-play, else would I scorn to measure swords with such a buzzardly beast."

They dismounted and went to it, *stoccata, mandritta, imbroccata*. The Duke's foot, sliding upon a stone, let Mandricard through his guard: a flesh-wound in the muscles of his sword-arm above the elbow. They stopped to bind it and stay the bleeding. His gentlemen prayed him give over now, but, as if the hurt did but exasperate his wildness and fierceness, the Duke stood forth again, his sword in his left hand.

"Have, here it is then," said Mandricard, feeling his enemy's mettle in his sword as the blades engaged, controlled one another, ground together: "it were alms you were dead. I'll spitchcock you." At the third venue Barganax with his unforeseen sudden deadly *montanto* ended the passage, sending his sword through Mandricard's throat-bole.[3]

Upon a Thursday of mid December, five weeks after these things, Count Medor, with letters in his hand, waited in the long gallery under the west tower of Acrozayana, expecting in a hot impatience audience with the Duke. The southern sealand Meszrian air, that even at Yule-time has not laid by all its summer burden, came and went through deep-mullioned sashed windows, twelve upon either hand, the length of that gallery. Rosalura, in a window-seat midway down the western side, reading her book, laid it again in her lap at whiles to look out upon the prospect: bare tree-tops of the gardens below, and beyond these Zayana lake, its face altering always between glassy expanse and patches where the wind flawed it, and beyond it the woods and ridges folded about Memison. All was white in that gallery, walls and floor and ceiling and marble frieze. Under the western windows the sun began to make patterns on the floor; through the eastern windows all was of a cold grey quietness, of the storeyed pillars of the inner court, stone balconies, and long roof-line level against the sky. "And yet best of all in summer," she said, touching hands with Medor as he paused beside her seat: "when we have rose-leaves scattered in drifts over the floor, and cool airs to stir them even in sultriest weather."

To and fro from door to door, Doctor Vandermast walked under the windows, passing at every third foot-pace from sun to shadow and so to sun again. "Four o'clock?" said Medor; "and it is now but two?"

"It was upon strictest command."

"If you knew but the urgency! Will you not go through the ante-room, knock at the door? For indeed, the fury of his grace when he shall know we let it wait may jeopard us worse than should we, as upon necessity, brave him in pure loyalty to disobey him."

"Is it matter of life and death? Or if not, shall two hours make it so? Or if, can two hours, so taken by anticipation and well plied, unmake it?"

Medor snapped his fingers.

"My Lady Fiorinda," said the learned doctor, "is but yesterday come to court. 'Tis his grace's pleasure this whole morning and till four of the afternoon to have her to himself several, painting of her likeness. Your lordship well knows that, upon such orders given, it is lawful neither for us nor no man else to prescribe or measure them in his behalf."

"Well," said Medor, taking impatiently a turn or two, "it is greatness in him: under such red and louring skies, while he waits on action, to be able to lay all by, recreate himself with swimming, tennis, painting; not sit melancholy watching for levin-bolts that, fall they or fall not, 'tis no longer in his dispensation.

"Well?" after a minute. "Are you not impatient for my news? It is at least news, when he shall hear it, to rouse and raise him from out this lethal security."

"Impatience," replied Vandermast, "is a toy of great men, but in men of mean estate a distemper. For my particular, considering how now my age draweth to its latter term, I have long eschewed impatience. And for news of so much import, not to my safe ear even could I with conscience receive or you with conscience tell it, till it be told to the Duke."

Medor looked at him. "Signior Vandermast, wholesomely have you lessoned me. Were all his mouth-friends of like temper—fie on turntippets that turn with the world and will keep their office still! Yes, you are wise: haste is our mischief. Had he but ridden somewhat slowlier home from Peraz, 'pon the morrow of that good meeting a month ago, when all was fair weather—"

Vandermast smiled, standing in the window and surveying thence, with hands clasped behind his back, chin raised, eyes half closed, the sunny vault of the sky, the lake spreading to shimmering distances. "Yet was this Mandricard," said he, "a bob which should in time have been a beetle, had the Duke not set heel on him. And yet, when destiny calleth on the event; tread down one such creeping instrument as this was, what is it but to suffer, by that very deed, another to go by that shall ascend up in due time to implement the purpose? These advertisements you have now in your mouth to speak to his grace, are they not an exemplification to approve it? No, Medor, it is a demonstrable conclusion that in haste is not our mischief, but in the commixtion rather and the opposition of divers attempts and policies, working all according to that law whereby *unaquoeque res, quantum in se est, in suo esse perseverare conatur:* everything which is, in as much as it hath being, striveth still to continue in its own proper being and so persist. 'That excellent correspondence' (saith the philosopher) 'which is between God's revealed will and His secret will, is not legible to the natural man.' I concede, had you ridden leisurely from Peraz, Mandricard belike had been gone when you came below Alzulma. But had you, contrariwise, galloped, a league or so ere your coming down, then had you been past and away ere he came thither. Had the Vicar been honest—Why, I can unwind you hypothetical probabilities and conjectures till your brain spin round, but to what purpose? for always the event is thus and not (as might have been) thus."

Medor laughed. Then, serious again, "Ah," said he, "howe'er you wind it, mischief is that bloody fact, when by forbearance we should a stood in the right with all men. Might you but know the tangle now—"

"To pass away the time," said the doctor, drawing chairs to a table between windows, "I'll to chess with you. And, to inspire a fine peril in the gambit, we'll drink old wine." Medor set out the ivory men, while Doctor Vandermast from an old Athenian amphora poured out into goblets of cut crystal. He filled them but to the half, the better to let him that should drink of it savour the fragrancy of that wine, clinging to the goblets' sides. The first cup the doctor brought to the Countess, but she gently refused it. "This wine," said he, sitting now to the chessboard and pledging Medor, "may, as I have sometimes conceited, be somewhat in kind with that which is caroused away upon high marriage nights among the Gods, when the bride is laid and the epithalamion sung, and the blessed wedding-guests, going upon the golden floor, eat and drink and renew their hearts and minds with wine not all unlike to this."

"And while they walk," said Medor, breathing in the heady perfume from his cup, "imagining some portentous birth?"

"Yes," said that aged man, touching the wine with his lips, then lifting it to gaze through against the sunlight:

> "The prophetic soul
> Of the wide world dreaming on things to come."[4]

Within, beyond the ante-chamber and beyond inner doors which, even were it against him their captain, Medor's own guardsmen barred, Duke Barganax now laid down his brush. Wrapped, as in a toga with right arm and shoulder bare, in a voluminous flowing gown of silk brocade of a creamy dun colour and edged with black fur, he sat back now in a deep chair. Before him, on the easel, was the beginnings of his picture: from it to her, from her to it, and so back again, his eye swung restlessly and as if unsatisfied.

"γλυκύπικρον ἀμάχανον ὅρπετον—You," he said. "*Bitter-sweet. You are that.*"[5]

She, bare from the waist upwards, lying on her face upon cushions of a white silken couch under the cool light of the north window, rested on folded arms, her back and shoulders flowering so, in a sleek-petalled warm paleness as of old ivory, from the dark calyx of her skirt of black silk spangled lace. From armpit to elbow her right arm, folded upon itself, swept its immaculate line. Above the lazy weight of it, midway of the upper curve, about the biceps, her nose rested daintily ruminant. From beneath the armpit, as four

serpents from some vine-shadowed lair of darkness should lay out
their necks to feel the day, the fingers showed of her left hand
bearing the soft lustre, starred about with a circle of little emeralds,
of a honey-coloured cat's-eye cymophane. Her mouth was hidden.
Only her eyes, showing their whites, looked out at him sideways.
"Yes," she said. "I am that."

"γλυκύπικρον," he said, under his breath: then suddenly
scowled, as if upon the motion to destroy his work.

" '*Post*'—" she said: "in what musty book was that written?—
'*omne animal triste.*' "[6]

"It was written," replied he, "in the book of lies."

As in the quivering of a dragon-fly's sapphired flight across the
tail of a man's vision, under the down-weighing intolerable heat of a
cloudless summer noonday, hither and back betwixt them the halcyon glance leapt, overtaking all befores and afters. The Duke rose,
went to the table in the window upon his left, opened drawers, took
out needles and a copper plate: came back to his seat.

"You have resolved then against chryselephantine work? each
hair?" she said, out of that unseen mouth. "Wisely so, I should say."

He pushed aside the easel. "Why do I make away at last every
picture I paint of you?"

"How can I tell? Easier destroy than finish, may be? A harder
question: why paint them? Having the original." Lights moved in
her green eyes like the moving lights on a river.

"Can you be still—so, a minute? Perhaps," he said, after a silence, "perhaps I try to know the original." Chin in hand, elbow on
knee, in the tenseness of a panther crouched, he watched her.

"To know?" said she, out of the long stillness. "Is it possible (if
you will credit Doctor Vandermast) to know, save that which is
dead?"

Barganax, as if body and mind were enslaved to that sole
faculty of vision, did not stir. After a while, his face relaxed: "Vandermast? Pah! he spoke but of dead knowledge. Not my way of
knowing."

"And you will know me, when, in your way of knowing? To-
day? In a week? Next hawthorn time?"

"Never."

"O, it seems then, this knowing of me is as your painting of me:
as Tom o'Bedlam would warm a slab of ice with his candle to make
him a hot plate to hold his supper?"

"That which can be done, 'twas never worth the doing."

"Attempt is all," she said.

With the overtones of a new music that cast fire-fly gleams
across the darkness of her voice, "You have much changed your
former carriage: become strangely a harper of one string," she said,
"this last year or two. Before, they tell me, there might not one of

our sect come here to court that, unless she were a very owl or an urchin for ill favour—"

"Tittle-tattle," said the Duke.

"O, some of their private, lavish, and bold discourses. That you bearded at fifteen: is that true?"

He lifted an eyebrow: "It pricketh betimes that will be a good thorn."

"Let me but fantasy myself," said she, "in your skin. Nay then, 'tis certain. I should say to myself, 'Well, she is very well, high-witted Fiorinda. But—there be others.' And yet? And why? It is a mystery: I cannot attain to it. See but Rosalura, left in your way as harmless as a might lodge his wife in some seminary. Though, to give you your due," she said, caressing delicately with the tip of her nose the smooth skin of her arm and returning so to her just pose again, "you were never a hunter in other men's preserves. Save but once, indeed," she said, browsing again in that lily-field. "And indeed I count not that, being that it was neither preserve there, nor—" she fell silent.[7]

Barganax caught her eye and smiled. "Set a candle in the sun-shine," he said.

"A courtly instance, but not new. Nay, I will have you tell me, why?"

"Pew!" he said: "a thing so plain as it needs no proof." He took up the plate as though to begin drawing, then slowly laid it down again. "Let me fantasy myself in your skin," he said, his eyes still picture-finding. " 'This Duke,' I should say, 'is one who, as in that song of mine, desireth,

> " 'por la bele étoile avoir
> k'il voit haut et cler seoir.[8]

" 'And, to show I have that same star, if I chose to give it, while others kiss with lip I'll give the cheek.' "

"To say, which is what I do? Ungrateful!"

"May be my ingratitude and your ladyship's parsimony—"

"O monstrous! and to-day, of all days!"

After a pause, "And I too," she said, "have strangely changed my fashions, since you eased me of that: cut off my train and all. Pity, since the Devil's servants must serve now without their casual-ties. Singular in me, that herebefore was almost a generalist in that regard. And yet," she said disdainishly, "not so singular; if to be given in wedlock, young, twice, to so and so, through policy. To spit in the mouth of a dog is not indecorous for a lady, and grateful too to the dog."

Like the shimmer of the sun on water, some reflection of her talk played about Barganax's eyes the while they studied her from under his faun-like eyebrows, as if he would burn first into his perception the elusive simplicities of that wherein the changing stings and perfumes and unseizable shapes and colours of her mind had their roots and being.

"Your royal father, too," she said, "(upon whom be peace), was a picker of ladies. Was it not his eye chose out my late lord for the lieutenancy of Reisma? and, that done, enforced the Duchess your mother, 'gainst all good argument she found to the contrary (for I was never in her books), receive me as one of her ladies of the bedchamber in Memison? Without which chance, I and you, may be, ne'er had met. Three years since. I was nineteen; you, I suppose, two and twenty."

"These things," said the Duke, "wait not upon chance."

There was a long silence. Then, "You took little liking for me, I think, at first meeting," said she: "upon the outterraces of her grace's summer palace: midsummer night between the last dances, after midnight: I on his arm: you with Melates, walking the terrace by moonlight and meeting us at each return. And I but the tenth week married then." She fell silent. "And his breaking away (you looked round and saw it), and running to the parapet as if to vault over it into the moat? And your saying to him, jesting, as we met at the next return, you were glad he had thought better of it, not drowned himself after all? And his laughing and saying, 'If you did but know, my lord Duke, what I was a-thinking on in that moment!' You remember?"

"And I will tell you a thing," said Barganax: "that when we were gone by, I told Melates what, as I had ne'er a doubt, the man had in truth been thinking on."[9]

"Well, and I," said she, "will tell you: that I read that easy guess in your grace's eyes. But this you did not guess: what I was a-thinking on. For besides," she said, "my eyes are my servants: trainbearers but no tale-bearers."

All the time the Duke's gaze was busied upon that unravelling quest amid many threads of knowledge and outward seeming. As if the memory of the words had risen like a slow bubble out of the marish waters of his meditation, his lips, while his eyes were busy, played now with that old sonnet which carries, even to the written page, the note of the lyre that shook Mitylene:

> "Fra bank to bank, fra wood to wood I rin,
>   Ourhailit with my feeble fantasie;
>   Like til a leaf that fallis from a tree,
> Or til a reed ourblawin with the win.
>
> "Twa Gods guides me: the ane of tham is blin,
>   Yea and a bairn brocht up in vanitie;

The next a Wife ingenrit of the sea,
And lichter nor a dauphin with her fin.

"Unhappy is the man for evermair
That tills the sand and sawis in the air;
  But twice unhappier is he, I lairn,
That feidis in his hairt a mad desire,
And follows on a woman throw the fire,
  Led by a blind and teachit by a bairn.[10]"

Their eyes met, a merry, humorous, feasting look. "You are forgetting the good there is in change, I think," she said after a silence. "For my own part, I incline much to fair hair in women. Anthea, for instance."

The Duke winced.

"I am resolved: good: dye my hair yellow."

"If you dared but even do your hair any way else but my ways—" he spoke slowly, as lost in a contemplation, his mind on drawing, not on his words.

"So, then I'll cut it off," said she.

His feeding gaze seemed to grow keener. He said on his breath, "I'd kill you."

"I should make you some sport ere that," said the lady, her mouth still hidden behind the lily smoothness of that indolent arm. "Have you forgot our first assay, laying aside of ceremonies, a month after that first meeting, three years ago next summer? I showed you then, my friend: bit a piece of flesh off your bones."

"Two minutes, my heart-dear!" He suddenly fell to drawing, line by line in swift and firm decision. There was a stillness upon that lady, while line after line traced, true and aware, its predestined furrow on the polished copper, like the stillness of a sunshine evening upon some lake in which mountain and wood and sky hang mirrored in reverse, and nothing moves save (may be with the settlings of little winged creatures) the dancing gleams, one here, one there, seven or eight at a time, of liquid golden stars coming and going upon that glassy water.

The Duke sprang up: went to the table to rub lamp-black into the lines. When he turned again, she had put on again her bodice, as it were a sleeved mail-coat made of thousands of tiny orient pearls, close fitting like a glove, and sat with her back towards him, upright on the couch. He stood for a minute looking at his drawing, then came and sat down behind her, holding the plate for both to see it. The clock struck three.

"As for painting, that was a true word you said that night to Lessingham."

"To Lessingham?" she said.

"For a lover: hard to paint the thing which is."

"O I remember: by the dream-stone."

"The One, that I still was a-hunting of in the Many, till your day; and now the Many in you." Her face was sideways towards him, looking at the dry-point. Her eyes were become Medusaean and, in its repose, her mouth snakish and cruel. "Paintings," he said: "all trash. They give me but a barren One out of your Many, and never your One that breeds those Many, as the sun breeds colours."

"But this is better, you think?"

"It is beyond comparison better; and my best."

"Of that which changeth ever, and yet, changeth not?" That lady's voice took on yet another quality of wonder, as if into the sun-warmed, cud-chewing, indolence of it were distilled all the warring elements of her divinity: fanged peril couched amid blood-red peonies: green of seawater, still and deep, above a bottom of white shell sand, or the lights in lionesses' eyes: the waved blackness of the Stygian flood[11] in the ferrying across of some soul of sweetness untimely dead: coal, snow, moonlight, the light of burning cities, eclipse, prodigious comets, the benediction of the evening star; and behind these things, a presence as of some darkness that waited, awake, shawled, and still: gravid with things past and half remembered, and things present yet not apprehended well, and with things to come: or, may be, not to come, swaying betwixt birth and the unbeing of the void.

"Of manifoldness: yes," said he, after a minute. "But of your Oneness, a shadow only: Persephone beneath the sod."[12]

She considered the picture again. "You have my mouth there, I see?"

"Ah, you can see that? though your arm hides it?"

"You have it in the eyes, and in the fingers."

"I am glad," said he: "for I meant it so."

"It came of itself I should say. I set much by mouths: especially my own."

He stood up, laid the plate on the table, turned and stood looking at her. *Omne animal triste?* she said, the devil of provocation viperine in her mouth's corner.

"I told you that was a lie," Barganax said, his eyes on hers. She settled back a little, sitting there facing him, and her eyes seemed to grow darker and larger. "It were not for every man's comfort," he said: "mate with you: a swan swimming with her wings expansed, then, whip, in a moment mew that white outward skin, soar against the sun, bring out your pounces, fly at fools and kill too. Nor for every man's capacity."

"And yet you will still be picture-making."

"O it is well," he said: "well that eagles do mate together: other else—"

"Other else," said she, "must Fiorinda have led apes in hell? or, worse, lived housewife in Reisma? Well, I like that a man should high himself even thus insufferably, so he have the pith to maintain it."

The Duke came a step towards her. "There is no middle way with you," he said: "you are all night and day: dazzling night and intolerable day."

"And roses." It was as if not she but the very stillness of her mouth had spoken. "Some red, some pink-colour."

"And eyes that are the sea. I drown in them," he said upon a sudden intake of the breath. "When I kiss you, it is as if a lioness sucked my tongue."

She leaned back with hands clasped behind her head, Valkyrie breasts breathing under that pearl-woven byrny, and above it her throat's lithe splendour and strength. "Seas are for who can swim," she said, and a sweeping of lyres was in the lazy voice of her. "White noon is for the eagle to kindle his eyes upon: the sweetness of the red rose is to be weighed down upon, to be crushed, to be scented: the wonder of darkness is lest you should despair and, numbering perfections, say, It is the sum: it is all. For am not I all, my friend? I am more than all. And when all is told and numbered and multiplied and told over again, I say to you, In my darknesses I have more. Come. Prove it again. Come."

Upon the chimes of four Doctor Vandermast knocked at the topaz-studded cedar doors of the painting-room and entered to the Duke's "Come in." The Duke, wearing no more that brocaded fur-purfled gown, but fully dressed in doublet, ruff, and hose, apprised of Medor's importunities for audience, went out to him in the gallery. The Lady Fiorinda, yet in some disarray and with her hair unbound, reclined upon the couch fanning herself with a fan of white peacock feathers twined with silver wires and set with apple-green chrysoprases in the ribs.

"Small advance, it is to be feared," she said as Vandermast surveyed the picture on the easel. "But what will you have, if two hours must be expended but in settling of my pose?" There stirred in the accents of her speech a self-mocking, self-preening, sleepy grace which, to the attentive and philosophic ear, carried some note of that silver laughter that the ageless remembering waters yet dream of, foaming disconsolate in Paphian sea-shallows.

The doctor smiled, looking on the painting but half begun; then, seeing the dry-point on the table, took it up and considered it awhile in silence. "I judge from this," he said at last, "that your ladyship has been teaching some lessons in philosophy. It is better. Nay, confine it but within its limit of purpose defined and propounded for it, there is no more to do: it is perfect."

"You will say 'Othello's occupation's gone,'[13] then? A melancholy conclusion."

"I will not say that, save after your ladyship," answered that learned man.

"Well, you must do maid-service first (these ill-appointed ways we live in): bring me the looking-glass to do my hair. Thanks, reverend sir;" she sat up, putting off in an instant her grace of languorous ease for a grace of wakefulness and speed of action, with deft sure fingers pinning into a formal court elegance her hair's braided lovelinesses, night-black, smooth-waved, with blue gleams where the light struck, like the steel-blue gleaming of certain stars, as of Vega in a moonless night in autumn. Her hands yet busied upon a last pranking of her ruff, she turned to meet Barganax's face as he strode into that room like a man that contains within his breast the whirlwind. Medor, with flushed countenance, followed at his heel.

"Here's news, and hell's fires in the tail of it," said the Duke, making with great strides towards the window and flinging himself down in his chair. "The hennardly knaves: yes, I mean your strutting stately brother, madam, with's prims and provisoes," he said, rocking from side to side: "he hath accepted Sail Aninma bestowed of him by the thundering tyrant, slick as was Mandricard to take Alzulma 'pon like offer. And Jeronimy with's cringing in the hams, licking the hand of the king-killer: if there be a badder man than that Beroald 'tis this back-starting Admiral with his thin wispy beard, ever eats with the jackals and weeps with the shepherd: now sworn new entire allegiance and obedience: given out all's o'er 'twixt them and me, our late confirmed league, 'cause of slaying of Mandricard. Damn them! after a month's digesting of it, now the meat bolketh up again. Damn them!" he said, springing up and stalking, like a beast caged, about the room: "they're all habs and nabs, foul means or fair: hearts in their hose when they catch a breath from Rerek. I almost enrage!" He caught Fiorinda's eye. "Well, will not your ladyship go join your brother in Sail Aninma? Will you not be i' the fashion, all of you, and down with me now I'm going?"

Fiorinda, in a statuesque immobility, followed him with her gaze. "What means your grace to do now?" she asked. "Paint, and let the wide world wind?"

The Duke checked and swung round upon her as if bitten. Little comfort there was in that lady's eye or in the stony curve of her lip. Yet as he looked upon her, meeting stare with outfacing stare, it was as if, like fiery molten metal in a furnace, his rage ran into some mould and cooling took shape and purpose. His jaw set. His eyes, leaving their flashes, burned steady into hers. Then there came upon all his pose and carriage that easy magnificence which best became him; and in his voice that was right antiphone for hers, bantering, careless, proud, "I'll tell you," he said: "secret, within these walls," and he looked round upon Medor and Vandermast. "Within three days I'll be man or mouse."

With a feline elegance the Lady Fiorinda rose, gathering with one white hand, not to trail them on the floor, the black shimmering flounces of her skirt, and walked to the window. There she stood, one knee upon the window-seat, her back to the room; but the Duke's eyes, as the mariner's on the cynosure amid flying cloud-rack, were fixed on her.

"Medor," he said, "you are both a count of Meszria and captain of my bodyguard. You must now for a while be my lieutenant and commissioner of my dukedom in the south here, to do all in my name: what, I shall speedily command you. Write out the commission, Vandermast: I'll sign it. For you, Medor, you are to muster up an army suddenly: Melates, Zapheles, every lord i' the south here. High master in Meszria I yet will be. But it must be suddener than move an army: take the prey with a jolly quickness, before, like water cut with a sword, they have time to join together again. Roder holds Kutarmish: by the carriage away of that, all the defenced places of Outer Meszria, and may be o' the March too, will without resistance be yielded. This then sooner of my own self than by any other middlers. I'll take with me Dioneo, Bernabo, Ansaldo, him o' the wall-eye—Friscobaldo, Fontinell: choose me out the rest: twenty-five of the most outrageousest beseen and likely men we have in the guard. I'll ride to-morrow."

"Twenty-five men?" said Medor. "Are you out of your princely wits?"

"If the gear cotton,[14] I need no more men for this dust. If not, more were useless."

Medor laughed bitterly. "Falleth not for me to question your grace's orders. But if you are thus resolute to cast your life away, let mine be in the cast too; for indeed I care not for it a pudding-prick if you miscarry."

"No, Medor. If I must be had by the back, you shall avenge me. But I know at my fingers' ends what kind of men are in that city. I do esteem this a sport." His eyes met Vandermast's. Surely the eyes of that old man were become as the thin pure radiance that suffuses the starless heavens eastward before the sun-spring of a windless dawn. Fiorinda turned. She held her head high, like a leopardess that scents the wind. "I have been anvil long enough," said the Duke: "I will now be hammer. Let all be made ready; for I've be-thought me, I'll not stay for to-morrow: I'll ride to-night.

"And now, give us leave."

When they were alone there fell a stillness. At last Barganax spoke: "So runneth the hare then. Well? and if it be farewell?" She reached out a jewelled hand: he took it in his, bowed over it, raised it to his lips, then, as with a sudden flaming of the blood, began to run with hungry kisses from palm to wrist, from wrist upwards, pushing back the sleeve till he reached the tender inner bend of the elbow, then with a stride forward seized her to him. "No," she said, withholding her mouth. "When you come back."

"That may be never." He mastered her, but her lips were lifeless under his kisses: all her body stiff and hard and unkind. "Was there ever such a venomous tyrant?" he said, letting her go at last. "All ice. And you have turned me to ice too."

"You are rightly served," replied she, "for being a glutton. The fuller fed, the greedier. This livelong morning: then more this afternoon. Well, marry Myrrha, then, or Pantasilea: some obedient commodity to all your bidding. Me you shall not have o' these terms." Leaning against the door-jamb, her hand upon the crystal knob, she watched him from under a drooped curtain of long black eyelashes while, like summer lightnings, there played about the dear beauties of hand and neck and cheek, and about the sweep of frills and ruffles and many-pleated gauzinesses of her skirt, glints of fang or claw. "Indeed," she said, "I know not why my girdle should still be at your command. Unless if it be that in you too," she said, "for all your idle plaguy ways, there is no sit still, no rest, nothing predicable. And because of that:" she suddenly paused upon a miraculous softening of every line and contour; a breath, like the sudden filling of a sail, lifting the Grecian curve of her breasts; a slowing, as if it were honey with the bee's sting lost in it, of her voice; a quivering of eyelids; an exhalation of intoxicating sweets, zephyr-like, like dark roses, in all the air about her: "because of that—I love you."

Upon which most heavenly farewell, eluding a kiss or any touch or caress, she was gone.

Barganax rode that same night. He sent up word to his mother in Memison castle as he passed next day that he intended a week's hunting of oryx and bears in the Huruns. So fast he rode that by Saturday midnight he was come up to Rumala. Here he rested horses and men till late evening of Sunday, and so at dusk came down the Curtain. They rode all night, avoiding the highway, and a mile or so south of Kutarmish, in a beech-wood of the spreading hills, waited for dawn. Twenty men, by driblets of twos and threes, he sent ahead to be ready outside the gates. At dawn the gates were opened, and there began to be coming and going of the day's traffic. The Duke with his five rode up openly; they had blue osset cloaks and common country bonnets to dissemble their warlike gear and quality. As they drew near the gates, those twenty joined them. In a moment they killed the guards and rode briskly into the town to Roder's house. Roder was upon coming forth with some men, and had but at the very instant swung himself into the saddle. Few folk

were abroad, it being thus early, and the Duke and his fared swiftlier than the hue and cry at their heels. He took Roder by the hand:
"How fares it this morning with your excellence?" In his left hand
he held a dagger, well placed, to let Roder's bare skin feel the prick
of it through his doublet, while the Duke might feel through the
pommel in his hand the leaping of Roder's heart. The face of Roder
turned dark as blood, then grey like well-thumbed parchment. His
jaw fell, and he sat still as a mouse, with dull blood-shotten bull's
eyes staring at the Duke. About the two of them the Duke's men,
swiftly casting off their cloaks, had made a circle, facing outwards
with drawn swords. People now ran together from the houses, these
in the street screeching out to those within who burst forth in heaps.
"If you love your heal, be sudden," said the Duke, "and proclaim
me. Here is your argument: hath a sharp point and a tart. If 'tis die
and go to hell now, be certain you, my lord, shall in the entrance of
this massacre be murdered: I'll send you first, show me the path. If
not, sudden, while you may."

"I am your grace's man," said the Earl then out of a dry throat,
"whatsoe'er my mouth have jangled. Aware, fellows," he shouted,
"and stand a-room: blow up your trumpets that every man of good
will shall stand 'pon his allegiance to the lord Duke of Zayana, for
whose behalf I have hold this city and do him right so."

The Duke commanded him, "Proclaim me Vicar of the Queen
in Meszria." They blew up the trumpets and so proclaimed him.

By evening was all quiet in the town, and the Duke's power well
seated. For they of his faction, that had fared this while with hidden
head while Roder held it for the Vicar, came forth upon his proclamation and set upon those of the other party. These turmoils the
Duke put down with a heavy hand without fear or favour, using the
soldiers, to the number of four or five hundred, that Roder held
the town with: not of his own private following, but of the royal
army established in the south these many years, from whom the
Duke took oath of allegiance now in the Queen's name, they accepting him sooner than accept the Vicar, after this autumn's doings, as upholder of the house of Fingiswold. But the Vicar was
proclaimed by trumpet up and down the town as traitor, usurper,
and king-killer, that every loyal subject should refuse and reject him
and receive instead, as Lord Protector and Vicegerent for the
Queen, the Duke of Zayana. And now as the day wore, and men
grew bolder, they of the town began to come with whole cart-loads
of complaints and grievances against Roder, petitioning the Duke to
deliver him up, either else punish him himself. Barganax, finding
that Roder could not bungle up but a very poor answer to these
complaints; finding besides, upon seizure of the Earl's papers, plain
proofs of wicked devices devised by him with the Vicar, upon price
of Kutarmish, for invasion of Meszria contrary to the Concordat,

and a plot drawn to murder the Duke; considering too how (and that by proof of documents) they had hatched up such bloody practices since October even and that meeting in the Salimat; accordingly next morning let lead out Roder into the market-place and there, with these proofs exposed and a man to cry them, take off his head. By which example of severity, as well as by his yesterday's insulting wild fierce and unaffrighted quick seizing of the town with so little a band of high-resolved men, men's minds were wonderfully sobered, to beware how they should make themselves as of a faction or party against him, or think to play bobfool with him.

He sent now, by chosen safe hands of men that rode with him from Zayana, to the princes in the north, Ercles and Aramond, requiring them of aid and upholding. Letters he likewise sent to Jeronimy and Beroald, in measured terms blaming them for friends unfast, and counselling them now repent and back him, rather than, for one high act by him upon bitter provocation done, forswear themselves and, to such scorned purpose, be tools for the Vicar.

And now was he within a little, while he hoped to catch a gudgeon, to have drawn up a pike.[15] For upon the twentieth of December, being but the second day after that thunder-bounce in Kutarmish, the Vicar himself chanced to come down thither with two companies of horse, having there his secret war-chest and much treasure and muniments both of weapons and horses and other things necessary for his design of Zayana; and was come well nigh within hail of the town, having, as was oft his manner because men should not have notice of his coming, fared across country to shun highways and haunts of men. But here, as the Gods would have it, was word brought him of rebellion afoot and Kutarmish lost, into which he had else entered all unknowing: wolf into trap. Nor was there given him bare five minutes law betwixt safety and undoing, for Barganax, understanding who was here, galloped out with a hundred horse to fetch him in and chased him twenty mile to the very gates of Argyanna where, in the nick of time, he went to earth, with his horses nigh foundered and himself nigh bursten with rage and furious riding. The next day, not willing, belike, to be closed within a fortress whereof, in the windings of his policy, he had lately appointed governor a creature of Beroald's, since now and amid these stounds himself and Beroald might begin, belike, to stand in very doubtful terms, he betook himself north again to Owldale. It began to be seen how, with this sudden attempt of war, the Duke was likely to make a shrewd adventure to have taken Outer Meszria from him and the March besides; for they of the Queen's upholding in the March of Ulba who had some months since begun to doubt the Vicar as the more dangerous usurper, began now openly to affect Barganax.

In a week came Melates and Barrian through the Ruyar pass with near a thousand men, to join hand with the Duke. Neither from the Admiral nor from the Chancellor had the Duke any reply as yet. But a little past the turn of the year came tidings that the Chancellor was moved eastwards in strength and sat down in Argyanna; where, because the place is both impregnable and overhangs the road that leads north from Meszria, he like a waiting hawk might cower those partridges of the march-lands and quiet their flutterings, giving Barganax besides reason of prudence not lightly to advance far out of his bridgehead beyond Kutarmish. The Duke indeed stood shortly between this and a new danger, when the regent Jeronimy, marching with an army through the Meszrian borders from the west along the Zenner, seemed to offer him battle, or if not, to menace his communications southwards. But it was as if Jeronimy, with the plain choice at last before him, yea or nay, this coming day-dawn before Kutarmish, could not find it in his heart to draw sword against a prince of King Mezentius's blood. He sent in word to the Duke, and they made peace together.

So, while the Vicar gathered force in Rerek, and while all Meszria (even such as Zapheles, who had in a discontent been used to lean towards the Vicar) rallied to Barganax as to their native lord, only Beroald waited inscrutable in Argyanna. Most men thought that he saw in this fresh war-rush of the Duke's the old danger come again that he had feared aforetime. They thought, too, that this, may be, held his hand: the opinion (that he had from the first inclined to) that in law the Vicar's claims were hardly to be assailed.

XVIII

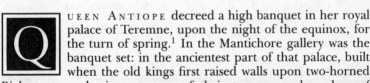

RIALMAR IN STARLIGHT

The Mantichore gallery ✦ *Design against
Akkama* ✦ *Stiff news from Rerek* ✦ *That "more
privater council-chamber"* ✦ *Antiope: the
goddess stirs* ✦ *Two ways of love* ✦ *Wastdale
distilled in Zimiamvia* ✦ *Choosing under stars
✦ Terror antiquus* ✦ *Parting at morning.*

QUEEN ANTIOPE decreed a high banquet in her royal
palace of Teremne, upon the night of the equinox, for
the turn of spring.[1] In the Mantichore gallery was the
banquet set: in the ancientest part of that palace, built
when the old kings first raised walls upon two-horned
Rialmar to make it a nursery of their tyranny and a place of
strength: hundreds of years gone, before ever they issued from
their watered valleys betwixt twin desolations of desert southward
and eagle-baffling frozen mountains on the north, or turned eyes
towards the southlands of Rerek and Meszria. Lofty was that gallery, built all of a warm grey stone having a dusky sheen like marble
and beset with black spots or strikes. The long tables and the chairs
besides were of the like stone, with silken cushions, for feasters to sit
and feast. Forty-and-four lamps wrought in silver and copper and
orichalc, and hanging by chains from the vaulted roof, went in two
rows endlong of that great gallery. Beneath, upon the tables, candles of green wax burned in candlesticks of gold, a candle to every
feaster. To the careless eye, roof and wall alike seemed plain and

without all ornament; but looked to near, they were seen to be drawn upon with narrow channelled lines as of burin or chisel. Employing which property of shining superficies and elusive graven outline, he that in former days made that gallery had by curious art brought it about so as whosoever should remain there awhile should, little by little with the altering aspects of those drawings upon the walls, seem to be ware of shadowy presences of the beast called *mantichora:* here a leonine paw or leonine shaggy mane, there a porcupine's quilly rump, a scorpion's tail, a manlike horrible face fanged and with goggling great eyes: and that is a kind of monstrous beast reputed anciently found in sandy places and gravelled in the borders of the Wold, next against the hills hitherward of Akkama.[2]

The Queen, in a dress netted and laced with gold upon a groundwork of silk, sombre orange-scarlet of bogasphodel in seeding time, and in her hair a high comb of tortoise-shell edged with balls of yellow sapphire, and about her throat a delicate cream-white ruff with setting-sticks of silver, sat in the high-seat: Lessingham upon her right as representing the Lord Protector and upon her left the old knight marshal. Beyond Lessingham the Princess Zenianthe had place, and beyond Bodenay the Countess of Tasmar: these and a few more only in place of honour upon the cross-bench and the rest of the company at the long tables, facing inwards with their backs to the walls. All the space between tables was kept clear for service of the banquet.

"Two weeks' time or three, then, Captain-General," said the Queen, "and you mean to fare south?"

"Two weeks come to-morrow, with your serene highness's leave," answered Lessingham. "My Lord Bodenay and I," he said, leaning a little forward to include the knight marshal and speaking low, not to reach the general ear, "have baked so well as we shall ask you, madam, summon a meeting to-morrow of your inner council upon the whole matter to condescend."

"And what within the pie, then, when we shall cut it?"

"A journey for me south and then, say in a three months' time, north again, upon your highness's business." He glanced carelessly about him to make sure of no eavesdropping. "In a word, madam, we shall advise you that he whose insolencies you so wittily and wisely bore with last summer is rope-ripe: so—"

"O if little cur-dogs must be whipped," said the Queen, I whipped him last September."

Bodenay shook his head. "Ah, madam, not the boy only, but that land and folk he standeth for. There is danger thence. And my Lord Lessingham will tell your serenity 'tis a maxim of great captains and men of charge: best defence is strike first."

"We will take your highness's pleasure to-morrow," said Les-

singham. "I hope you will let the thing go forward. A people that
have so soon forgot their lesson, and of an old enmity towards us,
kinged by a scorpion, unquiet as locusts: 'tis but plain prudence,
outwar and subdue them this summer and lay them to your dominion. And my mission now to raise and bring you great armies from
the south, and the Lord Protector's self (that were good if I can
compass it) to command them."

"That giveth you your date, Myrilla," said the Countess Heterasmene, holding out her fingers above a golden bowl for a waiting-
man to pour over them water of roses. "If my Lord Lessingham will
take his lieutenant into Rerek, you will have even just ten days to
become weary of your new-wedded lord."

"Yes, and you see in this, madam," said Amaury, "how well the
fates have devised for my good. For indeed I have kept me in with a
lady ere this for a month may be; and, as modest as I am, I dare
think I shall not be out with my Lady Myrilla within ten days, albeit
a week longer might strain things."

"I'll stop your mouth: no, not as you'd have it, but thus," said
Myrilla, sitting next him, and made a dab at it with a piece of
marchpane. They laughed, and Lessingham said apart to the
Queen: "Your highness was well advised to make this marriage up.
The Admiral is a man of safe anchorage. Ties of affinity 'twixt him
and Amaury will do much to settle friendships."

"Lieutenant," said the Queen, "we will set forward your wedding a day or two: see if two days more may do it."

Amaury, a little outmatched and put to silence with so many
eyes upon him, laughed as for courtesy sake, turned red, and
stroked his mustachios. From this abashment he was delivered by a
beck from Lessingham: stood up with a by-your-leave to his lady,
and went to him. The Queen's sergeant of arms was behind Lessingham's chair: "—waiteth without, and craveth instant speech
with your excellence to deliver it." "What's the fool's secret news?"
said Lessingham: "well, if it will not wait, go to him, Amaury. Be
eye, ear, conscience, for me: bid him confide in you."

In a few minutes Amaury came back. "My lord, the key fits not.
Will say nought to me save that 'tis matter of fieriest urgency, and
but for your particular ear. Hath letters too, as I suppose from the
Vicar, but these too only to be given up into your very hand."

"From Laimak?" said the Queen. "But shall we not make room
for him?"

"With respect no," Lessingham said. "I know the man: a domestic of my noble cousin's much used by him upon matters of
weight and exact import: one Gabriel Flores. If it please your serenity he be given supper in the buttery, I'll despatch his business
anon."

"See to it," said she. And the banquet proceeded.

When it was now mid-part done, and cups began to be borne round of Rian wine, and upon golden dishes macaroons, sallets of violet petals, and the conserve that is made of the flowers of marigolds confectioned with curious cookery, Lessingham upon leave given him by the Queen went from table and forth into a certain upper room, having sent word before to Gabriel to attend him there if he desired his conference. "Marked you that strange trick of the lights, cousin?" said the Queen, "how, as the Captain-General walked 'twixt table and wall, the things upon the wall seemed to wave their paws as he passed, and grin as they would have eat him?"

"It is a trick of the lights," answered that hamadryad Princess; "and your highness has seen it before."

The Queen turned now, in merry talk as before, to the old knight marshal upon her left, and to Tyarchus and Heterasmene and old Madam Tasmar.

"In what estate left you his highness?" said Lessingham, taking from Gabriel the despatch and sitting in a great oak chair with a lamp beside it while he undid the seal. Gabriel stood before him with an anxious pinched look upon his face. "I pray you read first," he said.

Lessingham read it swiftly, then turned again to the beginning and read it again, slowly, as if to confer and weigh each word; then with a delicate deliberation folded it again: with a sudden movement tossed it to lie beside him on the table, and so sat motionless for a minute, leaning forward, right hand on hip, left elbow on knee, his finger-nails drumming a marching lilt on his front teeth. In the side-shining of the lamp across Lessingham's face Gabriel could see the eyes of him in that stillness: unrevealing eyes, as if the mind behind them had sounded deep to meditate with itself. Then suddenly in those speckled grey eyes of Lessingham there danced something as if in a round of dancing girls should be glittered forth in advance some triumph.

He sat up, erect. In all his presence there dwelt that sense of abidingness, which is in the steady glitter and conflict, shining still stones and shining ever-churning ever-fleeting waves and eddies, of some watersmeet where two rivers run between green shades of oak and ash and alder, and the banks of water-worn boulders and pebbly granite shingle lie white about that murmur under the power of the sun. "Well, good pug," said he, "you are acquainted with all this?"

"It is took down from his highness's mouth, and in my own character which I think is known to your lordship."

"How comes it I am told nought of this before? Despatches two a month, good as clock-work, as if all's well, sailing fair with wind and tide: then sudden this turn: the whole boat upset; Meszria lost us and the March too: says great men hath late assembled from all the land over, offering 'pon some lying rumour of her highness's death (pray Gods forfend the omen!) the throne to her brother Barganax: Laimak close invested, and like to be smoked out of it as boys take a wasps' nest. Who heard the like? And screameth now for me to pick him out of this pot of treacle the Devil only and he know why a hath fallen in't. By my soul, I am well minded let him stay there."

"'Tis his great pride," said Gabriel. "Would not ask your help till need drove him to it. Fed you, it is true, with figments and fittons and leasings to keep you here in Fingiswold. You will belie your greatness if now in his sore need you will upon such pretexts refuse him."

"Flatter not yourself, and your master, to suppose," said Lessingham, "that I am a child, with no more means of intelligence but such advertisements as he shall think good to send me. It is true, my news is three weeks, or may be a month, behind yours: I much fear a messenger hath miscarried this last journey, fallen into Prince Ercles' claws, like enough, under Eldir. Howe'er it be, I am six weeks away, so tell me. And forget not this, my pug," said he, as Gabriel cast a sheep's eye at him, "if I shall take you lying to me or hiding aught, not you alone will smart for it."

"Well, this your excellence knows, as I judge," said Gabriel: "the bloody inrush into Kutarmish of the accursed bastard—"

"When you speak to me of great men," said Lessingham, "speak with respect, be it friend or unfriend, and with just titles of honour. I'll have you flogged else."

"The bloody inrush of his grace of Zayana," Gabriel said with a snarling look, the teeth gabbing out of his mouth. "And sweet doings there. Lord Roder ta'en and strapped in a big chair, open in the market-place, and a lad with a sword ground to a good edge: swash and away, head him like a pig, and all the sight-gazers to see it; and justly rewarded so, or why did a not hold better watch on the gates and all the treasure and goods his highness lost there? and himself too might a miscarried, intending for Kutarmish—"

"Leave particularities. I know all this."

"And the Admiral gone over, heard you that? (mid January, that was) hand and glove to the Duke's allegiance?"

"That I knew not till I read this letter," said Lessingham. "Nor, till then, of the Chancellor: last news was he yet wavered."

"Your lordship's intelligence was eight weeks stale 'pon the one, and three weeks 'pon t'other. As for my lord Chancellor, seemeth that when a had lodged himself safe in Argyanna, a sent for his learned books out of Zayana, whistled to him from all the three kingdoms a dozen doctorable men, legists, sophisters, whate'er to call 'em, and set 'em down to ferret him out colourable reasons for what, you may make no doubt, if you know a fox by's furred tail, a was all the time resolved to do. You may wager their reasons had taken water: rotten ere they might come to shore. Howso, found him the thing he asked for. Cometh out then, smooth-tongued as a dancing-madam, with item this, item that, as pretty as you could wish: conclusion, Barganax rightly called King as in male descent, and—to make all sure, if this false report of the Queen's decease, hatched up, as 'tis thought, by that Barganax"—("Have I not warned you?" said Lessingham)—"by that Duke, to give colour to his usurping: to make all sure, if this report be shown without contradiction false—some reputed law dug up out o' the dust-heaps of two centuries past to say females shall not hold kingdom in Fingiswold: thus even so securing him in's usurpation, and prefer his bastard blood before her birth noble."

Lessingham rose from his chair: took a turn or two about the room, stroking his beard. Gabriel with little swinish eyes watched him eagerly. "I was hard put to it to a come through to your excellence," he said after a while: "what with their armies set down before Laimak, and then those princes in the north that this Duke feedeth with his gold to countermind his highness' will and check his friends: do gather a power of men too. Arcastus durst not trust his nose outside Megra walls. I know not, my lord, if you have such force as that you can keep such curs in awe, to come through them?"

Lessingham stopped by the table, took up the Vicar's letter, perused it again, laid it by, then stood looking down upon Gabriel with a disturbing smile. "Your chickens, my little Gabriel, are not yet hatched. And for my intents in this pass your lord hath brought himself unto, you might more easily guess their drift if the ability were given you to look men in the eye."

"Nay," said he looking and looking away: "your worship hath an eye to shine down basilisks. I can't abear it."

Lessingham laughed. It was as if from a waiting-place above the watersmeet a sea-eagle had stooped: feinted: resumed his waiting.

Gabriel thrust out his chin and came a step nearer, looking down and tracing with one finger, while he spoke, rings and crosses on the corner of the table. "I would your noble excellence could a seen what I have seen," he said: "these six weeks. No more o' this lukewarmth then, I dare wager my head. Great men 'gainst great odds in my day have I seen, but never as this. The undutiful and traitorous affection borne against him by these lords, the more it drew men from him, made shrink his armies, disappoint his designs, the more would he give 'em still lill for loll. It is a world to see him. With but a thousand men, made a great stroke in the western Marches and then, when that Chancellor thought to a closed him in between Fiveways and the Zenner, marched sudden round his flank, then north-about by night, catched Melates 'pon a foray into

Rerek, made him eat lamb-pie. And later, shut up in Laimak with the leavings of his army, and six times his numbers barking like midden tykes at's doors but e'en so durst not come at grips: scarce a day but out he cometh with a sally, ever himself i' the front to lead it: does 'em some hurt, fetch in provisions, slay some men, what not." He ceased, his finger still fiddling on the table's corner. Suddenly he looked up, met Lessingham's eye, avoided it: with a gowked movement grabbed at Lessingham's hand and kissed it. Lessingham, as if strangely touched and ill at ease with such a homage from such a suppliant, took away his hand. "You shall have your answer to-morrow," he said; and so dismissing him returned to the banquet-chamber.

And now as Lessingham walked between table and wall, beholding the Artemisian loveliness of her where she sat sweetly talking, it was as if in the tail of his eye he saw monstrous paws brandished, and mouths of beastly great murdering teeth ready to come nigh to her.

He and she looked at one another as he resumed his seat. Amid the general talk none noted, unless it were Zenianthe and Amaury, that for a minute neither Lessingham spoke nor the Queen. Nor none guessed (unless it were these) that she and Lessingham, while they seemed for that minute but to sit silent and thoughtful at that banquet-table, had in truth retired themselves to a more privater council-chamber; where, in that which is to outward sense but the twinkling of an eye, days, weeks, and months and the changing seasons can act their slowed passage like the opening of a white rose; and thither many a time since that first night last Michaelmas had Lessingham and the Queen retired them, to pursue their noble wishes, and dwelt there in love together.

The learned doctor, standing with Zenianthe in a grassy hollow of the hill where her oak-woods upon their furthest limits face the afternoon, shaded his eyes. The sun was so far declined as barely ride clear of a fir-wood which followed the shoulder of the hill where it rose beyond the pond a stone's throw from the doctor's feet. Black against the sky was that wood, but upon the hither side of it and its cast shadow the edge of the green hill was in brilliant light. Below that band of brilliance hillside and pond were as a curtain of obfuscate golden obscurity which yet, with a hand to shade the eyes of him that looked, became penetrable to sight, revealing detail and contour and varied growth of herbage, and the pond's surface below, smooth and still. The figures of Lessingham and Antiope coming down out of the fir-trees' shadow into the band of sunshine were outlined about their edges with a smouldering golden light, so that they seemed to burn against their background of the black wood. The sound of their talk, as it became audible, seemed the translation into music of that smouldering light and of the sun and the shadows within shadows and water and green hillside about them: not into words, for words were not yet to be distinguished; nor laughter, for they did not laugh: rather the notes and rhythms that noble voices borrow from that inner vein of laughter, which enriches the easy talk of minds so well mated that each being true to the other cannot but so be true to itself.

They were come down now. Lessingham with a nod acknowledged the doctor's salutation, sat himself down upon an outcrop of stone, and there seemed fallen into a study. Anthea, erect, statuesque, with hands clasped behind her back, stared at the sun. Campaspe, in a soft clinging dress of watered chamblet coloured, like certain toadstools that grow on dead thorn-trees, of delicatest pale rose-enewed madder brown, and wearing a white lace hood, from beneath which dark curls of her hair escaping shadowed throat and cheek, and on the left her bosom, busied herself with finding flat stones to play ducks and drakes. Ever now and then the pond's still surface was broken with the scuttle and skim of her stones. Swift and dainty and mouse-like were all her movements, as a little dunlin's tripping the sky-reflecting mud-flats of tidal creeks on a sunny evening in autumn when the sea is out.

Antiope stood with the doctor and Zenianthe. Their eyes were on Lessingham, where he sat looking into the sun-path. Vandermast spoke: "You have debated all fully, then, and determined of somewhat?"

Antiope answered, "We have nothing debated, and determined all."

"That is better still," said that ancient man.

For a while, they kept silence. Vandermast saw that her gaze rested still upon Lessingham. It was as if she slept where she stood. Vandermast said, in a voice still and warm as the innermost unpierced shades of those oakwoods behind her, which outwardly the sun bathed with so lovely a splendour of golden green: "I have opined to your ladyship ere this, that there is but one wisdom. And but one power."

Antiope stood listening as if for more. "I wonder?" she said at last.

Vandermast said: "It is your own doing, this: a dress of Yours. You choose this. He chooses it with You, whether he know or not, willing it for Your sake. That loftiest of all Your roses, to pluck it for You."

She said: "I know."

Vandermast said: "For my part, I had sooner die with your ladyship than be made immortal with—"

She said, "Well? Who is my rival?"

Vandermast said, "You have none: not one: with Your starry beauties to make paragon."

She waited. The Knidian mystery lay shadowy about Her lips. *"Before the day was,"* She said.

The silence trembled.

Vandermast said: "Yours is not as our choosing, who out of many things choose this thing and not those others, because we judge this to be good. But Your choice maketh good: higheth the thing You choose, were it very nought before, to outsoar all praises."

She said: "And yet every time I pay for it. The mere condition of being, this of he and she: did I not choose it? Should not He, as easily, had I so chosen instead, have created and made Me of His omnipotence self-subsisting and self-sufficing? But this I chose rather: to be but upon terms to be loved, served, made, recreated, by that which is My servant. How were love serious else?"

Vandermast said: "Death: a lie: fairy-babes to fright children. From within, *sub specie aeternitatis,* what is it but *vox inanis,* a vain word, nothing?"

She said: "And yet, how were it possible to love entirely except some living being which liveth under the terror of those wings? Else, what needed it of love?"

Vandermast said: "And time: what evil was there ever but time sowed it, and in time it hath root and flourisheth?"

She said: "And yet, without time what were there?—the crack-brained ecstatic's blindation of undiscerning eyes upon me: the music of the spheres condensed to a caterwaul. Or how else should beauty round her day? how else should he tell my lip from my eyebrow, but in time?"

Vandermast said: "The passing and the vanishing: what else beareth witness to the eternal?"

She said: "This will-o'-the-wisp of power: that other, scorning of certainties which abide safe and endure—" Her voice vanished as, out to sea, a questing tern vanishes as the sun leaves it.

Zenianthe, with oak-leaves set round her lovely hair, said, laying a hand on the doctor's arm: "Are you part of Her? as I am?"

Vandermast said: "No, dear lady of leaves and squirrel-haunted silences. I am of that other kind."

Zenianthe said: "But if the house be part of who dwells therein? If my woods be part?"

Vandermast shook his head: made no answer.

Antiope said, startling as a sleeper wakes: "What is it, cousin? What have I spoken? You can witness, I never walked in my sleep till now?" Her eyes were troubled. She said, and her words came slowly as if with night-groping: "A black lady. I have never seen her."

Vandermast said: "Shall Self see Self?"

Antiope said: "You may better answer that: you that are a philosopher."

Vandermast said: "I can ask questions, but some I cannot answer."

Antiope said: "Has she seen me?"

Vandermast said: "I have been told so."

Antiope said: "Who told you?"

He answered: "My art."

Antiope said: "Does that speak sooth?"

Vandermast said: "How can I tell? It flares a light. I follow that, a step at a time, and so watch and wait: remembering still that, in this supermundal science concerning the Gods, determination of what Is proceedeth inconfutably and only by argument from what Ought to be. Thus far I have not been bogued."

Antiope said: "How then should she see me, if I may not see her?"

Vandermast held his peace. The words of her speech were like shadows falling. Her eyes, like a dove's, now sought Lessingham, but his face was turned from her sunwards.

Anthea said:

> I am love:
> Loving my lover,
> Love mine own self:
> For that he loveth it,
> Make it my paramour,
> Laugh in the pride of it,
> Beat in his veins:
> So, by such sharing,
> Loving prevail
> Unto self-seeing.
> —Such-like is love.

Campaspe said:

> I am love:
> Loving my lover,
> Love but his love:
> Love that arrayeth me,
> Beddeth me, wardeth me—
> Sunn'd in his noon,
> Safe under hand of him,
> Open my wild-rose
> Petals to him:

Dance in his music.
—Such-like is love.

Lessingham said: "You sit there, silent: I at the table's head,
you, Señorita Maria, at the side, as fits a guest of honour; but on my
left, as fits you. For on that side my heart is. There is no more haste
now. Peace now: *requiescat in pace:* the peace of the Gods that passeth
all understanding. Some note or flavour of it I caught now and then
even there, because of you, *madonna mia.* Do you remember?

"Mistress of my delights; and Mistress of Peace:
O ever changing, never changing, You.

"Do you remember? But the dream clouded it, and the illusion
of change and—"
"Hush!" Mary said, and trembled. "Lastingest blessednesses
are subject to end. Is this a dream? We may wake."
Lessingham said: "That was the dream. No waking again to
that. For what was it but the marred reflection, prophetic or memorial, of this present? a wind-marred image of all these things: of you
and me here alone, of those peaches, the dark wine and the golden,
the Venetian finger-bowls: a simulacrum only but half apprehended
of that Gloire de Dijon over the window, and of its perfume which is
your breath, *O reine des adorées,* perfume of love. These, and the
summer's evening leaning, with long cool shadows on the lawn, as I
towards you; and this sapphire, warm to my fingers where it sits
softly here, in this place which is of itself benediction and promise of
awakening night, and of the unveiling and the blinding and the
lotus that floats on Lethe: in this dear valley of your breast."
"Wait," she said, scarce to be heard. "Wait. It is not time."[3]
He sat back again in his chair. So sitting, he rested his eyes
upon her in silence. Then: "Do you remember the Poetess, madonna?—

"Ϝέσπερε, πάντα φέρων, ὅσα φαινολις ἐσκέδασ' αὔως,
φέρεις ὄϊν, φέρες αἴγα, φέρεις ἀπύ μάτερι παῖδα."

As if spell-bound, she listened, very still. Very still, and dreamily, and with so soft an intonation that the words seemed but to take
voiceless shape on her ambrosial breath, she answered, like an echo:

"Evening Star—gath'rer of all that the bright day-break
parted:
You gather the sheep, the goat; you gather the child safe to
the mother."[4]

The low sunbeams touched their goblets, and the beaded streams of bubbles became as upstreaming fires.

"It is things we counted most of substance," he said, after a minute, "it is those have fallen away. Those that, where all else was good, spoiled all."

"All," she said. "Even I," she said: "spoilt at last."

Lessingham started: sat rigid as if struck to stone. Then he laid out a hand palm upwards on the table: hers came, daintily under its shimmer of rings as a tame white egret to a proffered delicacy, touched with its middle finger the centre of his open palm, and escaped before it could be caught.

"Well, it was a dream," she said. "And, for my part in it, I felt nothing. No pain. No time to be frighted. It was less than a dream. For of a dream we say, It was. But this, It was not nor it is not."

"A dream," said Lessingham. "Who dreamed it?"

"I suppose, a fool."

A trick of the low sunlight in that panelled room seemed to darken the red gold of her hair even to blackness. A Medusaean glint, diamond-hard, came and went at her mouth's corner.

"Ah," he said, "we talk dream and truth till each swallow other, like as the two pythons, and nothing left. But as for that old world: it was you, Mary, said it to me in the old time, that it was as if One should have sat down alone with the chessmen and said to them, 'Live: and now see whether they can teach themselves the game.' And so wait, and watch. Time enough, in eternity. But needeth patience. More patience than for manning of a haggard,[5] madonna. More patience than mine, by heavens!"

"The patience of the Gods," said she.

"An experiment of Hers? for the mere pleasure of it, will you think? to while away a morning, as fly at the heron?" He sat silent a minute, gazing at her. Then, "I think," he said: "another painting."

"Painting? A barrenness of One? or dry-point, that shall give you, as you say, a bodiless thin Many?" They waited, as if each had heard or seen somewhat that was here and was gone. The alexandrite stone was upon her finger, water green in this light of evening, yet with a stir as of embers below the green ready to flare red when lamps should be lit.

"An experiment," said Lessingham, taking up his thread. "A breath: then no more to touch: no more but sit down and see if the meanest rude nothingness, once it be raised to being, shall not of itself in the end become the thing She chooseth. Infinite patience of the Gods. Slow perfection. The refining and refining of the Vision. —You said it, Mary. Do you remember?"

"Why will you say 'of Hers'?"

Lessingham smiled. "Why will you, 'His'?"

"Well, if it pleases me?"

They looked at one another, each with that scarcely perceptible half-mocking challenge of the head: a grace of the antlered deer. "A very good answer," said Lessingham. "I cannot better it. Unless," he said suddenly, and his voice died away as he leaned nearer, his right elbow on the table, his left arm resting, but not to touch her, on the back of her chair. It was as if from without-doors a distant music, as once upon Ambremerine, made a thin obbligato to the accents of his speech that came like the roll of muffled thunder: "unless indeed it has been with me, from the beginning, as with Anchises it was: a mortal man: not once, but many times: but many times:

"ἀθανάτη παρέλεκτο Θεᾳ βροτός, οὐ σάφα εἰδώς

" '—with an immortal Goddess: not clearly knowing.' "[6]

The deep tones of Lessingham's voice, so speaking, were hushed to the quivering superfices of silence, beneath which the darkness stirred as with a rushing of arpeggios upon muted strings. Mary nodded twice, thrice, very gently, looking down. The line of her throat and chin seen sideways was of a purity passing all purity of flowers or wind-sculptured mountain snows. "Not clearly knowing," she said; and in the corner of her mouth the minor diabolus, dainty and seductive, seemed to turn and stretch in its sleep. They sat silent. By some trick of the light, the colour of her hair seemed to change: to a gold-drained pale glory of moonlight, instead of, as her dress, red of the bog-asphodel in seed. And her eyes that had been green seemed grey now, like far sea horizons. Lessingham felt the peace of her mind enfold him like the peace of great flats of tidal bird-haunted marsh-land in a June morning looked on with the sun behind the looker: no shadows: the sky grey of the dove's breast, toning to soft blues with faint clouds blurred and indefinite: the landscape all greens and warm greys, as if it held within it a twilight which, under the growing splendour of the sun, dilutes that splendour and tames it to its own gentleness: here and there a slice of blue where the water in the creeks between wide mud-banks mirrors the sky: mirrors also boats, which, corn-yellow, white, chocolate-brown, show (and their masts) clear against sky in those reflections but less clear, against land, in nature: so, and all the air filled, as with delicate thoughts, with the voices of larks and the brilliant white and black of martins skimming, and white butterflies: drifts of horses and sheep and cattle, littler and littler in the distance, peopling the richer pastures on the right where buttercups turn the green to gold: all in a brooding loveliness, as if it could hurt nothing, and as if it scarce dared breathe for fear of waking something that sleeps and should be left to sleep because it is kind and good and deserves to be left so.

Campaspe said, at the clavichord: "You will have more?" The

bodiless tinkle of the preluding blades of sound drew like streaked clouds across the face of the stillness: then, "What shall I sing to you?" she said: "another of my Lady Fiorinda's songs?" And her naiad voice, effortless, passionless, bodiless, perfect on the note, began to sing:

> "Se j'avoie ameit un jor,
> je diroie a tous:
> bones sont amors."[7]

Lessingham leaned forward on the table, his fists to his temples. He raised his head suddenly, staring. "I have forgotten," he said. "What is this I have forgotten?"

After a minute, he sprang up. "Let us go into the garden," he said to Antiope: "settle it there. I must south. I would have you return no more to Rialmar until this tempest be overblown. You can be safe here, and my mind at ease so."

Anthea exchanged glances with Campaspe, and laughed a laugh like the crash of spears.

Lessingham followed the Queen to the door which that unnamed disciple now opened for them. They stepped out, not into that wayside garden of Vandermast's, but now, strangely, into an appearance of that Teremnene garden: the statue gracious above floating lily-leaves: terraced granite walks and steps going up from the pond: flowers asleep in the borders: the path where Derxis had thrown his stone: over all the star-dim spring night. The door shut behind them, shutting them out from the glow and the candlebeams. Antiope put a hand in his.

"Why do you tremble?" said Lessingham. "Be safe, you are now free from him."

Antiope said: "There is nought to bind you in your choice. But neither is there to bind me. Different ways you and I cannot choose. If yours to walk through dangerous and high places and to approach near steep downfalls, so mine. Or if you the safe way, so then I. And so, if you will abide by your saying and go south, then must I queen it out in Rialmar."

They looked each at other. Lessingham took a great breath. He turned to Aphrodite's statua in its cold high beauty, netted and held in the loneliness of starlight. "Let Her," he said, "choose for us."

"Be it so," said Antiope. "There is no other way of wise choosing."

"Let me look at your face," he said. She raised it to his under the stars.

After a while, he spoke in a whisper. "What mystery was this? Looking but now in your face, I have been my own love: seen myself: loved myself, being myself you for that instant, madonna: cho-

sen for you, and for me, with your love as from withinwards. Been
your love. Been—" he caught his breath: "Was that the threshold?
upon Ambremerine, with glow-worms in her hair?"

"I do not know," Antiope said, her face hidden now against his
shoulder. "But what you have seen I have seen too: I too have
chosen: been you for that instant, loving me. For a pang, and away."

For a minute they abode so, as one, motionless: then stood back
and joined hands as might two brothers before battle. "Then, this
being our choice," he said, "better it is, madonna, that you remain
in Rialmar rather than come south with me. For all Rerek and Meszria are up in war now, and my going is to put all in hazard that
must us save or spill. And well as I can answer for my cousin while I
sit in the saddle, I would not, were I to fall, leave him executor of
my trusts toward you; nor with the means to come at you. I leave
you a great army here, and the lord knight marshal: a general expert and to trust. I take but my own eight hundred horse, and may
be three hundred more. And Rialmar is by nature inexpugnable. By
heavens, they shall see lightning out of Fingiswold, and the thunder
of it shall shake Meszria and Rerek ere they shall have reckoned
with me."

Antiope said, as he kissed her hand under starlight: "We have
chosen, my friend—ἴομεν."

He raised his head again, her hand still in his. "ὦ πέπον, εἰ
μὲν γάρ—" It was as if the stars and the huge darknesses without
remembered again for their own that saying of the Lycian king to
his loved kinsman, standing forth under windly Ilios:

> Ah, lad, and were't but so: and, from this war fleeing,
> We twain, thou and I, for ever ageless and deathless
> Might endure: not then would I in the van do battle.
> Neither send forth thee to battle which maketh glorious.
> —But now—since thus serried the fates of death come nigh
> us:
> Thousands, nor is't in mortal to flee such, neither elude
> them—
> On! be it praise we become for another, or, haply, reap it.[8]

Lessingham's nostrils were like a war-horse's that hears the trumpets. Then on the sudden, in that questionable garden under stars,
he seemed to see how a change, as with eclipse or deep clouding of
the moon, overcame the beautiful face of this Queen of his, as if
night should suddenly have clothed her with the mantle, inexorable, stony, archaic, of Astarte or if there be any crueller dethroned
divinity of ages outworn: Terror Antiquus, treading the dead
mouldered faces and unfleshed skeletons of nameless forgotten

men. Then, as the silver moon with the passing of that red shadow, her beauty shone fair.

The awe of that sight darkened his voice as he spoke: "Who are you?"

Antiope trembled. "Sometimes, in such places as this," she said, "I scarcely know."

It was morning now in Doctor Vandermast's wayside house. Lessingham, booted and spurred ready for setting forth, stood beside her pillow, as debating whether to wake her or let this, awake and asleep, be the last before their returning again to action and that banquet-table. Antiope lay asleep on her side, back towards him where he stood, so that he saw, partly from behind, the line of her cheek and brow and the rose of sleep that warmed it. Lessingham said in himself: "Forgetfulness. What does it matter? Belike the old man spoke aright: that it is a precious gift of Her lap, this forgetting; in order that She may give all again, morning-new. Every momentary glimpse: every half-heard overtone in her voice: the sheet drawn so, as it always is, nicely across that mouth of mine: eyelid, virginal quiet line and long drooped lashes, closed asleep: pale dawn-like gold of that hair of mine tied back with those ribbons: I have forgotten, and even these shall be forgotten. Well: so She give it anew. Well: so that She have said: 'They are Mine: I keep them: I store them up. In time they are gone for ever, but they are Mine unto all eternity.' "

He tucked the sheet gently in behind her shoulders. She turned at the touch with a contented inarticulate little murmur and, between half-opened eyelids, as only half waking, looked up at him. "Those two songs," she said after a moment, her voice soft with the down of sleep.

"Did the little water-swallow say hers for you?" said Lessingham.

Antiope said, "Say it for me again."

Lessingham said:

> "I am love:
> Loving my lover,
> Love but his love:
> Love that arrayeth me,
> Beddeth me, wardeth me—
> Sunn'd in his noon,
> Safe under hand of him,
> Open my wild-rose
> Petals to him:
> Dance in his music.
> —Such-like is love."

Antiope said, "I like it better than that other. Say you like it better too."

"I like it best."

"Why?"

His mustachios stirred with the flicker of a smile. He paused, thoughtful, stroking his black beard. "As not my way," he said, "could I by some magic be turned to a—As not known from within. I am not Barganax."

"My brother," she said. "I have never seen him. Have you seen: that lady?"

"So far as any but he may see," answered Lessingham, "I have seen her."

"How far was that?"

He said, as if searching for words, "May be, so far as—but no: you have never seen him. What are brothers and sisters? In the main, so. But once, until I beheld nothing. Then once, until I beheld you."

"Say it again, that you like Campaspe's best."

Lessingham said again, "I like it best."

"I am glad." It was as if on her breath two shadows crossed, of laughter and tears. "I cannot, that other way."

"Because it is your way, I like it," he said. "I love you," he said, "beyond time and circumstance."

She put out an arm, and with that about his neck drew his face down to hers, warm with sleep, upon the pillow.

XIX

LIGHTNING OUT OF FINGISWOLD

*The first flash ◆ Quelling of the free towns ◆
Lessingham between pincers ◆ Battle before
Leveringay ◆ March of the Lord Jeronimy ◆
Battle of Ridinghead ◆ Peace given to the
Admiral ◆ Storm and tempest at Rivershaws ◆
The second flash ◆ Eclipse and darkness.*

ESSINGHAM came south over the Wold by great journeys and on the fifth day of April passed by the landmarch into Rerek. He had with him barely a thousand horse, but not a man of them that was not proven in war, headstrong, bloody, and violent, and of long custom bound to his obedience, not as water-spaniels but as the hand is stirred to obey the mind: of his own following, the most of them, six and seven years gone, when the great King warred down Akkama.[1] Of like temper were his captains of troops: Brandremart, Gayllard, Hortensius, Bezardes: all, like as the Captain-General's self, in the lusty flower of their youth, and such as would set no more by the life of a man, nor have no more pity thereof, than of the lives of partridges or quails which be taken in season to eat. Amaury he left in Rialmar, to be eye, ear, and hand for him in those northern parts. Gabriel Flores had set forth alone (supposed for

Laimak) in advance, the very morrow of that banquet. So now Lessingham halted in the fortress of Megra, and held counsel of war.

And first because the free towns in these outlaid parts should learn to fear him, nor trust too securely in the princes of the north, Ercles and Aramond, that still cloaked them underneath their wings, and because he would secure his rear and left flank a little ere adventure far south with an army that was all head and very little body, he rode in a sudden foray south to Abaraima. Here had Ercles last summer put down the captal[2] and other great men that held the city in the Vicar's interest, and in their rooms placed other his own creatures. But the more part of the townsfolk, who passed nothing on Prince Ercles and much less passed they on the Vicar, but desired nothing better than be let live at ease with their pleasant houses and gardens and fishponds and wives and children and delicate dogs and beasts tamed to the hand which they have *in deliciis,*[3] beholding this army suddenly at their gates, and knowing their defences weak, and hearing now the word of Lessingham that if they were taken by force they should all die and the town burnt and spoiled without mercy, upon that present terror threw open their gates to him. Lessingham, that was well served by intelligencers here as otherwhere these many months past, and judged, both from these and from his own seeing and hearing, the temper and inclination of the people, sternly withheld his soldiers from all cruelty against them so as not a man should suffer harm whether of body or goods. Only some few towers he flatted to the ground, and seized those principal persons, unquiet, busy, and high-climbing spirits, who had sided themselves and sworn to Ercles. These, to the number of seven, he caused to be brought before him in the great paven square before the courthouse, where he, armed from heel to throat in black armour and with all his soldiers arrayed under weapons about him, sat in state. Whereupon, after proclamation at large of their fault, these seven were by his command thrown down and unheaded with axes and so hanged along the wall in that place, for a warning to who would be warned. Which being done, and a baily and officers brought in and sworn in name of the Lord Horius Parry to the Queen's allegiance, Lessingham wore no more these dreadful looks but showed himself so cheerfully that within a few days' time every man in that city was joyful to behold him. Well nigh a hundred horse were added to him now, gathered of their own free will from Abaraima and the townships thereabout.

But barely seven days tarried Lessingham in Abaraima: then, for a knock of the iron gauntlet upon Aramond's door to let him know the Queen's Captain-General was afoot now and to be reckoned withal, he turned upon the sudden eastwards and in a day's hard riding came through the hills of the Mortelf down upon the rich open city of Bagort. This is the quiet heart of Aramond's country: a mediterrane or inland secret valley where not in twenty years till that day had an enemy's foot trodden; so that they listened secure to all rumours of unpeace without; and here had Prince Aramond his delicate lodge beside the salt lakes of Methmarsk. And here, in his unprepared idleness and with but a very small force at hand, the prince had but time to take boat and escape down the lake ere Lessingham's black riders were in the city. Lessingham took great store of minted money and precious stones and costly treasure besides, and took away too all weapons and armour he might come by, but the town he spared, and seeing they made no defence against him there was no man lost his life there. In Bagort he stayed three nights and refreshed his army, and upon Wednesday the eighteenth of April departed again by the same way west to Abaraima.

Upon Saturday night he stood with his army before Veiring gates. Here was Roquez nigh a twelvemonth set in power by Ercles after much strife and blood-letting: his wife a Meszrian, cousin german to the Lord Melates: she was a cruel lady, and had of late so wrought with Roquez and, through him, with them of the prince's party as that they were in purpose shortly to do somewhat against such as they loved not, that the streets should run again with blood. Lessingham sent in a herald under safe conduct to speak with them at the barriers, straitly enjoining them, on pain of their lives and goods and to be reputed enemies of the Queen's highness, that they should deliver up the town to him as Captain-General, and that within the space of one hour after the morrow's sunrise. Which Roquez denying, and speaking great words against him, there began to be a tumult in the town all night, and they of the Vicar's upholding rose up and made head against Roquez; in so much that a little before sunrise, while the issue stood yet in doubt, some suddenly surprising a gatehouse opened the gates to Lessingham. But when Lessingham and his were come in to help them, then almost nothing held against them. In that battle fell Roquez, and when they of his following knew this, in despair of speed they gave back till they were come to the keep and there shut themselves in and shot from the walls and loop-holes. Lessingham let fetch wood and firing to burn them up; so, when the fire began to take and they saw there was nought to do but surrender themselves, they came down and surrendered to his discretion.

In those days was Veiring a strong town as for walls, being by nature well postured too in a bend of the river, whereby it is from three sides hard to come at. But in length and breadth within the walls and in number of folk that dwell therein it is but as a platter to a tabletop as beside Tella or Abaraima. Lessingham made but short work, after the taking of the keep, of quieting the town. With the late ruling party he had little trouble: ready enough were they to go each to his own house and fare with hidden head, not to draw eyes which might single him out for retribution. But they that had been for the Vicar, seeing good harvest now beyond hope or dreams, and the readier because of that to make haste to cut it down and in it, began like jack sauces to jet the streets, quick to beat or kill any that should displease them or withsay anything that they would do. Even in the eye of the Captain-General's self or his own men-at-arms, as at great dogs little tykes should snar, would these flaunt their roynish fashions, their bawdry, and their insolences. To end it, Lessingham proclaimed upon trumpets through and about the town that whoso, save only soldiers of his, should after the third hour before noon be found in the streets with weapon upon him, were it but a hand-dagger, that should be his death. By noon had a score been hanged in the streets for this offence: 'twixt noon and mid-even, two more. That ended it. Of general turmoil indeed, there was none later than breakfast-time, when there gathered a band together before Roquez's house supposing to have had out his lady, who with some of her household there sought safety, and quite her for those things they thought she had devised against them. But Lessingham, riding to and about with a troop of horse, so that while yet any spark smouldered of disorder he might with his own eye see it to tread it out, came thither, as God would have it, in the nick of time when they had beat in the door and were upon dragging her forth. He, upon sight of such a beastish act against a lady, was as if taken in berserk-gang:[4] with bloody rage suddenly surprised them as he had been a wolf or a lion, and in such good coin paid them, that seven men shortly lay dead or bleeding under his feet as with one arm he bore off that lady, harmless but swooning, while in his other hand the reddened sword boded ill to any man that would nigh him near. Next morning Lessingham sent her with a conduct over land to Megra, for safety until means should offer for her faring south to Meszria to her kith and kin. He set Meron in Roquez's stead, captain of Veiring, and, because of the fury of their factions there, left him fifty horse to his bodyguard and to cow them. Three-and-thirty citizens of Ercles' faction Lessingham condemned to exile perpetual with loss of all their belongings: two hundred more to like banishment, but with leave to carry away their goods and chattels. Five he sent to be hewn of their heads in the public market-place; two of whom suffered that punishment not as traitors to the Vicar, but for divers outrages and cruelties acted by them out of private malice upon Lessingham's entry into Veiring and under cover of their espousing of his cause. It was the talk of men that Lessingham had shown by his dealings in Veiring that he was a lord both just and fearless, and wise besides and merciful, and terrible besides in season. And now was good settled peace in Veiring as had not been for many a year.

It being now near the fourth week ended since he came down from the Wold, and news of these doings flown before him about the countryside, he made haste to depart out of Veiring by the highway southward. The second of May he came to Lailma which opened gates to him: and here came word to him that Ercles himself was come down from Eldir and held the Swaleback passage by the shore of Arrowfirth. Next day Lessingham moved south, going gingerly with espials before him to feel the way, and pitched for the night a little beside Memmering, where steep and stony hills, covered all with thick-grown trackless forest, begin to close in westwards toward the sea shore. Here in the morning he had sure tidings that the prince was fallen back southwards. But while he waited to satisfy himself of this, came Daiman, ridden in huge haste from Tella upon word brought thither of Lessingham's march south, with this news now: that the lord Admiral was come round about by sea from Kessarey up to Kaima and was there disembarked the week before with a great army of as some said three thousand, others four thousand, men. Lessingham upon these tidings resolved, now that the passages of Swaleback were opened to him, swiftly and at all hazards to come through; seeing that if with so great forces they should once be closed against him he were as good pack home again to Rialmar. Upon which resolution, he struck camp and came, without sight or rumour of an enemy, through the highway past the head of the firth and pitched in strong ground rising amid open fields apt to the use of horse-soldiers some five miles west of Eldir.

He stood now in this case. Ercles, not with a handful of horse, as had at first been bruited, but with an army more than two thousand strong, was retired not to his hill fortress of Eldir but to Leveringay, seven leagues or more to the south, where, astride of the main high road southwards, he awaited Lessingham, and in the mean time burned and harried that countryside where folk yet held firm for the Vicar. Upon the other part, west-away, the Admiral was reported moving leisurely up the wide lowland vales of Fitheryside. Between these forces, each by much outnumbering his own, was Lessingham now in danger to be taken as the nut in the crackers; or if, eluding Ercles, he should escape away southwards, then to be shut in betwixt their united power and the Chancellor's that maintained siege before Laimak. All weighed, he chose to fight both; and Ercles first, the rather for two respects: the one, for that Ercles lay the nigher at hand, the other, because they that dwelt about Leveringay and Mornagay were of a tried loyalty, and, a victory once had there, they were like to take heart and flock to the Queen's banner. But now, going about to fight Ercles, he was resolved that the time and ground and manner of their fighting should be not Ercles's but his.

Lessingham struck camp in the misty early dawn of Friday, marched by the road south a mile or so, then turning suddenly north-eastward behind Proud Eldir, the little black crag that stands on the last spur of the ridge that runs south-west for two leagues or more from Eldir itself, took to the rocky upland valley of Nivararnadale and so came with his army up into the bare wild hill-country that goes up to the watershed of Swaleback. The spring was late, and there were still snowdrifts where the gills look northwards, and ice sometimes in the passes. A wind sprang up out of the north-east, bringing hail and sleet in swirls. Breath of man and horse blew misty on the ice-cold air, and the beards and mustachios of Lessingham and his men were stiffened with hoar-frost. Their march was due east among the heights till past noon, then in a sweep south-east, south, and so down south-westward from Stoopland Brink. In the failing light they rode down to the fir-wood's edge that fringes the open pasture-lands of Leveringay. The wood and the gathering darkness covered their presence: cold they supped and ill, and cold they laid them down.

Ercles's pickets came in to report no enemy this side of Eldir. None the less, as night wore, Ercles began to be ware of somewhat afoot. About the third hour after midnight he summoned his captains and upon counsel taken bade make all ready and so be in posture to join battle, if need be, at point of day. Lessingham waked all night maintaining a kind of fretting skirmishes all night long against Ercles's outposts, as if he feared nothing so much as that Ercles should carry away his army westwards ere battle could be joined, and so touch hands with Jeronimy; for, call it a fine rashness against so great odds to fight with either, Ercles or Jeronimy, to have fought with both at once had been plain madness. But Ercles and his held good espial north-westward along the high road, mindful too of these threatenings from the wood upon their right north-eastward, which yet they supposed belike (since, when the sun is set, all beasts are in the shade) sheltered but some country levies gathered to harry the prince's march and take any stragglers they might hap upon. No man was so fantastical as look that way for Lessingham, last seen at Arrowfirth head, or imagine he and his army could cross, like a flight of battle-cranes, with such suddenness and in such weather and thus early in the year, so wild a tract of mountain and surprise the prince's army upon the flank.

At spring of day Lessingham drew up his men before the wood and let blow up the war-blast. Ercles disposed his battle hastily as best he might, his main battle in the centre, the levies from the free towns upon the wings. His main battle, that had in it his own body-guard of two hundred chosen men and was all of old tried soldiers, alone outwent in numbers the whole vicarial army under Lessingham which, like a mighty storm thundering from out of the north-east, now fiercely assaulted them. Under that onslaught, this main battle alone of Ercles's held ground: the levies, beginning to be cut down in heaps, presently broke. In an hour, the field was won. Lessingham carried the pursuit to the out-fields of Mornagay and about by Shottenshaw and Hangwater and the Riddering valley. Some fled east to the fell with Brandremart at their heels: some scattered westwards: some fled into the tower of Leveringay. The prince himself escaped to Eldir. There were, by estimation, slain in that battle, and in the rout, seven or eight hundred of his army: scarce had it been more had every soldier of Lessingham's slain his man. Of Lessingham's side but three lost their lives: but one of these was Hortensius, to the Queen a servant of price.

Twelve days Lessingham rested his army after that battle. Men drew to him from the countryside, and he was now fourteen or fifteen hundred strong. Last news of the Admiral was that he had, of all arms, somewhat less than three thousand men, and lay this night, the eighteenth of May, but ten miles off, at Rangby. The next morning Lessingham said to his men, "You have come south with me upon an enterprise to throw down them that would o'erset the ancient governance of this land of Rerek, and to bring again the Queen's peace upon all this land, like as it was when we fared north last summer to Rialmar. Them that followed and obeyed Prince Ercles, when he would poll pill and shave the Queen's subjects in these parts about Leveringay and Mornagay, we have bloodily overthrown. Now there be many a hundred men here that follow me in war who have their belongings 'twixt these parts and the coastlands. For sake of these that have served me truly in every tide, loth should I be to bid 'em fare south now and leave their homes and families to the Admiral and his hired fighters out of Fingiswold or Meszria, that are not friends nor well willers of yours. Nor I like it not we should turn our back on these pick-purses: leave 'em so, when they have gotten our money, then to strike us in the brain from behind. If it be odds against us, I care not, seeing that which was seen o' Saturday two weeks. But now is no time to play the litherby now, or lazy lubber. We must on, and we must in, and we must in deep: huddle blow upon blow. And now, if there be a man had rather turn back now 'stead of follow me against the Admiral, let him stand forth. I will bid him go in peace." But the whole army roared with a great shouting that they would follow him and drive the Admiral back into the sea.

The Lord Jeronimy, considering with himself that he had force of men sufficient to crush Lessingham: that Lessingham even so was eager for battle, and moved now upon Rangby to engage him: that a patient outlengthing of delays is of good effect to wear down such rash hasty spirits: that westward the landfolk bore slacker allegiance to the house of Parry than they of these more inner parts: that being enticed westward Lessingham would be the less likely to draw to any dangerous head, and that the face of the land there, standing much in mud and ooze and much cut about with streams, was less fit for horsemen, wherein was the main power of Lessingham but the Admiral's weakness: weighing these things, the Lord Jeronimy wisely refused battle and fell back north-westwards, drawing Lessingham after him towards Tella. A little beyond Arminy he changed his course leftward and lay that night at Bank. Lessingham, willing to force battle ere the Admiral should win to Kaima, came by swift marching across to the coast-road at Minearness, three or four leagues east of Kaima castle and betwixt it and Jeronimy; but Jeronimy, still holding his enemy off, swung now south-eastward into Fitheryside again and the open marish lakelands and streamlands. Lessingham, thus drawn in a circle into this little habited and little friendly countryside, could gather little sure tidings now, save by his own men's eyes and tongues. He came at evening of the twenty-second of May to the farm at Ridinghead, that sits on a rise between the low lands of Westerwater and the Fithery. It was a dank unseasonable misty evening. The farm was deserted and no intelligence to be had. With the fall of darkness the rain began in a heavy downpour, and so settled in for the night. Lessingham supposed the Admiral heading now for Streamsteads, whither next morning he was minded to follow him. But not to be caught by any means at unawares in so thick and water-curtained a night of darkness, he threw out his sentinels and outposts far afield upon every hand with command to maintain an alert through every hour till morning.

The lord Admiral with his forward passed a bridge into Eastering Side and there lay. But as evening fell and the weather thickened, he called a council of his chief officers, whether it were not now the moment to dislodge and to draw westwards again toward Lessingham, happily to surprise him in the night and in these unhandy water-soggen ways destroy him. Which thing being by all applauded as good and forthwith put in ure, they came short of their suppose so far that Lessingham's out-sentinels brought him word of the enemy's approach in time for him to array his army to receive them.

Day broke up, grey and wet, while Lessingham posted his men for battle. The foot, between five and six hundred strong, he posted upon the right where the high ground runs down south and east beyond the steadings. Of these was Brandremart in command, and Lessingham bade him bear forth there the Queen's banner of Fingiswold, so as the enemy should think that here was the Captain-General and his main battle, and should that way throw the main weight of their assault accordingly. The steadings and outbuildings along the ridge in the middle he held lightly with but a handful of men, bidding them still make great show and din as if of numbers so as the Admiral should imagine a strength of men there and Lessingham's whole force more than the little it was. The whole main body of horse Lessingham held on purpose out of sight upon his left, behind the crest of the little hill, north or leftwards of the farmstead. Towards Fitheryside the ground falls gently to a bottom of moss and bog with a little syke running along beyond it, may be a half mile's distance from the farm. Below the steadings eastwards it is rough muirland, overrun with heather and sweet gale and here and there a dwarfed birch straggling among the blaeberry bushes and tussocks of coarse grass.

The lord Admiral drew up his battle east of the syke, and they advanced now, the main body of foot in the centre little short of three thousand strong, and upon either wing two hundred and fifty horse. But Brandremart, beholding the enemy before him cumbered (and most of all, their horse) in soft ground where they must cross the syke, forgot in that fever the orders laid down for him by Lessingham, and forgot the vantage of his position on the hill and the odds of seven to one they bare in men against him, and suddenly, unable to abide this waiting for them to attack him up the slope, came down with his five hundred, point and edge upon them. Gayllard and Bezardes stood with Lessingham at the corner of a wall north of the northernmost cow-byre whence they could overlook the whole unfolding of the battle: the fury of Brandremart's onset: the bloody brunt in the low wet bog-land: and now the weight of numbers thrusting him back south and west towards the upper ground: and great man-slaying they saw was befallen now. Both in a breath, they willed Lessingham take pity of Brandremart and his: bid the horse charge and succour them.

Lessingham stood there stiff and erect, like an arrow new-fastened in the ground from a far shot. His nostrils quivered: his eyes like wind-troubled stars stared down into the hurly-burly. "Not yet, on your life," answered he. They, knowing that look, durst not for a minute speak to him again.

"My lord," said Gayllard at length: "flesh and blood can no more. Let us in to help them. See, they are thrust backward up to the pigstyes and the hay-garths. Shall your men die like sheep? Shall my own brother Brandremart? And half of 'em butchered belike already! O 'tis past bearing!"

Lessingham, never shifting his gaze, shut his hand upon Gayllard's strong wrist like hasps of iron. "Will you lose me this battle?" he said: "you and Brandremart?" He watched the field in silence a minute: then, "He at least is about man's work—ha! see the heads fly off: cabbages under his drawing swash-blows! But hath outjumped the time: so, as he brews so must he bake. But you," he said after a while, through gritted teeth, "you and Bezardes, be still, you were best. Show me by your quietness you be men, and fit to govern an army—ha! well done, by heavens!—govern an army. Aspy the time. Then strike. Not to stand quittering like quails when the event walketh on razors' edges—" In a sudden witched stillness, his voice faded to silence: a stillness and a silence that had in that rush and tumult of outward things no proper being, save as it were of shadows thrown by the sudden stiffening of Lessingham's eye and mind to a yet tenser strain of inward readiness, while he stared across into the unequal battle, as a great beast's sinews should gather and stiffen before the spring.

"Now!" he said, letting go Gayllard's wrist. The word came as a trumpet's blare, and the face of him, suddenly facing them, as the thunder-smoke of dawn.

The lord Admiral Jeronimy, well assured now of a most complete victory, looked on the battle from a knoll upon the other side to the eastward, beholding (not without some discomfort, as at a sight his very flesh rebelled against) how the royal banner of Fingiswold staggered still backwards, with swayings and swoopings and sudden backward rushes, towards the steadings. From which contemplation he was suddenly shaken by the trumpets and shout and thundering hooves of Lessingham's horse that swept now round and down from the shoulder of the low hill on the west, and came upon his right flank like a rock-fall. The Admiral's two hundred and fifty horse were swept like a herd of goats before that onset, and the flank of his main army of footsoldiery left bare. These, taken at open shields with so well knit a body of fresh horsemen, and in the moment when they had supposed the work done, all save the slaying of Lessingham's remnant among the pigstyes, found for a time in that reeling confusion no respite and no rallying-point. Brandremart, in this breathing-while, gathered his weary and bebloodied companies where the Queen's banner still stood aloft before the steadings, and against all odds struck again. This, as the last axe-stroke when the tree creaks and totters, brought down all in havoc. The Admiral's great army was turned to a rout, which spread many miles over Fitheryside. Belike six hundred perished. Peropeutes, that fought in the centre against Brandremart, was slain, and every man that followed him. Lessingham himself was wounded, charging the Admiral's flank at the head of his men; but of his army the losses, save in Brandremart's battle, were few. Of those five hundred indeed that with Brandremart had withstood the first brunt, more than a hundred fell, and scarce a man of the four hundred that remained but took some hurt or other.

The lord Admiral, seeing this overthrow, and thinking scorn to flee when the day was lost, abode quietly in his place with sword drawn and a few about him who were of the mind to die first ere he should. Lessingham, when the flying rout began, stayed not for so much as to bind up his hurts but galloped across with his bodyguard to the Admiral to bid him peace. The Admiral, when he understood, rode down to meet Lessingham and in a noble silence offered his sword hilt foremost.

"What night-dog howled you this bad counsel, my lord Admiral," said Lessingham, "to a come and held side with her grace's enemies? Or hath God closed up the eyes of you, that you knew not the banner of the Queen's most excellent highness of Fingiswold, your lady and mistress? Upon whose commands when I fared south now, intending from Rialmar to Laimak, I looked not to find your lordship here to bar my way with an army; for in truth I was yet to learn you were a truce-breaker and a reneguer of your written word."

The Admiral reddened and said, "You do foully, my Lord Lessingham, to abraid me with either. And I will answer you in a manner thus: that I do use to look lower than banners, which be things outward and extern, but I will pry more inward. And against the Queen's highness (whom pray Gods tender and preserve) I ne'er drew sword; nor ne'er broke I word, much less broke solemn indenture. Only against your lordship's usurping cousin, that minister of mischief and sergeant of Sathanas, nuzzled in all evil, against him, 'cause of a hundred forepast proofs, I drew that sword; and against you, 'cause you sustain and aid him. And so will I do again, hability and means presented. Wherefore, if my life must answer for this, so be it. For indeed I was bred up young in King Mezentius' house and his royal father's before him (upon whom be peace), and I am over old, in a manner, to learn new tricks."

Lessingham beheld him in silence for a while, then answered and said, "Of the Concordat of Ilkis have not I taken upon me to be warranty for his highness's performance? Thus far, I one of all other, party to that concordat, have not failed of my undertaking. By God, I think I have cause against your excellency, to a sought to foin me in the belly when I go my ways south for to right things."

Jeronimy, facing him with unwavering gaze, made no reply.

"Take back your sword, my good lord Admiral," said Lessingham suddenly then, giving it again hilt foremost. "Ill it is if, within the Queen's highness's dominions in these slippery times, her faithful servants cannot agree. I pray go with me not as prisoner, but upon this only bond between us of word of honour. Bezardes, stay the pursuit: spread it abroad there's peace given and taken 'twixt me and the lord High Admiral. For the army, lie tonight at Rivershaws. And as for particulars," he said to Jeronimy, "we'll talk on 'em to-night."

"Your excellency is very pale," said the Admiral, as they took hands.

"Pah, a little too much blood-letting. I had forgot. Some, go send a leech," Lessingham swayed in the saddle: "nay, 'tis but a fleshing: 'twill mend." He steadied himself and would not dismount. Two or three galloped away: the Admiral, from a flask at his saddle-bow, poured out cordial drink. "Too much haste," he said. Lessingham, quaffing it down while they unbuckled his gorget and stopped the blood, might read in the Admiral's dog-like eyes matter that can be profoundlier discovered by such eyes as those than by noblest tongues with their traffic of words.

Lessingham made his quarters for that Wednesday night of the twenty-third of May in the old moated grange of Rivershaws, a league or more eastwards of Ridinghead in the water-meadows of the Fithery. Weary they were after that battle. Lessingham and Jeronimy supped private in an upper room in the south-western corner of the house, and after supper talked, as well as they could to speak or to be heard for the great noise of the wind which awoke now to strange fury after that rain-soaked day. Lessingham, in buff leather doublet and with Meszrian brocaded slippers to ease his feet, lay at his length on a settle drawn up near the table to the right of the fire. The Admiral sat yet at his wine, at the table, facing the fire and Lessingham.

"No," Lessingham said between the gusts: "he must first renounce the crown: no treating till then. That done, let my head redeem the promise but I will secure him all that should be his by the Concordat, and payment too for all misdone against his rights there: Sail Aninma and so forth. But to-day he standeth plain usurper, and as such I'll not treat with him save at length of weapon."

"I doubt your lordship will persuade my lord Chancellor so far," said the Admiral, "e'en and though I should second you. Many will say, mischief is that here be two usurpers, and choosing Barganax we but choose the less hurtful."

"They that will say so," replied Lessingham, "would spend their eyes to find hair upon an egg. 'Twixt the Vicar and him there's no such likeness; and were it so indeed, you shall see I shall shortly amend it."

"It was a pity," the Admiral said, "that your lordship abode not here to see to it, 'stead of go north to Rialmar."

The wind roared in the chimney, and sent with a downblow a great smother of smoke into the room. Lessingham smiled, lifting his goblet against the lamplight. "You think so?" he said, and drank slowly, as tasting some private memory. But the wine was red. And no bubbles quickened its inward parts.

He stood up and went to the western window behind his seat and, with hands for blinkers to shut out the reflections and the lamplight, peered through the glass into the darkness. The wind came in gusts that lasted two or three minutes at a time, striking the house till the solid masonry quivered: clatter of casements, squealing under the eaves and behind the wainscots, lifting of the arras, lampflames ducking and upflaring; without, trees bent and grass laid flat: a shaking, a leaping, a stamping over the hillside: then sudden silence and calm.

Lessingham, in this din, had not heard the door open behind him; and now, turning from the window, he saw stand in the threshold a man of his guard that said, upon the salute, "Lord, there attendeth your commands one that nameth himself the Lord Romyrus out of Fingiswold, new ridden from the north, and prays you admit him. And bade me say, 'tis evil tidings, as he were liever not be bearer of unto your lordship."

Lessingham bade admit him: "Nay, go not, my lord Admiral. This is our late cashiered Constable: whatso he will say, can say it as well to both of us. I trust him but little, nor his news neither."

"I like not tidings that come upon a storm," said Jeronimy.

Lessingham stroked his beard and smiled. "Omens were ever right, my lord. Let but the event answer the bodement, we say, Behold it was foretold us! If not, say, Such omens work by contraries." The windows rattled, and the door in a loud gust of wind blew open. Lessingham, standing with folded arms and unruffled brow and in a posture of idle elegance with his shoulders against the pillar of the fire-place, waited at ease, stirring not at all when Romyrus entered, save for a gracious word and movement of the head to bid him welcome.

Romyrus came in: behind him the door shut to: they regarded one another in silence a minute, Jeronimy, Lessingham, and he.

Romyrus was all spattered with mud from spurs to chest. He was like a man that has gone many nights without closing eyelid. There was ten days' growth of beard on his cheek: his face had a yellowed withered look, like a corpse's dug out of some recent grave; and he had the fear in his eyes like a hunted fox's. Lessingham took him by the hand, made him sit, poured out a great bumper of wine, and made him drink it down. "Whence come you?"

He answered, "From Rialmar."

"How then? Did her highness send you?"

He shook his head. His eyes, ringed round like an owl's, seemed now like a dead fish's eyes, goggling and charged with blood, as they looked into Lessingham's.

"What then?"

Without, the wind went whining down Fitherywater like a wounded beast.

"Speak, man," said Lessingham.

Romyrus said, "Derxis holds Rialmar." With a kind of moan he pitched forward on the table, his face buried in his hands.

The silence congealed like blood. Out of it Lessingham said, "What of the Queen?"

He answered, yet grinding his face against the table, "She is dead."

Jeronimy, that had missed these words, saw Lessingham stagger where he stood against the fire-place and turn ghastly. "Your excellence's wound," he said, starting up. But Lessingham, seeming to gather himself like a serpent coiled, as the wind again hit the house, caught out a dagger and leapt at Romyrus, shouting terribly, "A lie! and here's your death for it!" The Admiral, swift as had been praised in a man of half his years, sprang to Lessingham's armed hand, so turning the stroke, which yet ripped from the man's shoulder down to the hucklebone. Lessingham threw him off and, dropping the dagger, sank upon the settle. Romyrus slid from chair to floor with a blubbering noise. The Admiral went to him, raised him, looked to the wound. Lessingham caught the bell-rope, gave it a tang: soldiers ran in: bade them see to Romyrus, bear him out, call a chirurgeon: so sank upon the couch again and there sat bolt upright, staring as a man should stare into horror of darkness.

The wind, in its alternating fits of raging and dying, came again: first a soughing of it far off in the south-west and whistlings far away; then the return, as if some troll or evil wight should run with intermittent bursts and pauses, nearer and nearer, until with a howl of wind and huge flappings as of wings and the lashing of rain, it once more smote the house, vaulting, leading the wild round about and about as of violent waterquakes, riding the roof-tree till it was as if the roof must founder: then, in a gasp, quiet again.

Late that night Amaury, spent with long riding from the north and his horse near foundered, rode in to Rivershaws.

All night Lessingham lay upon his bed, open-eyed.

And the darkness within said: I have consumed and eat up that which was within. Forehead, indeed; but no mind inhabits behind it. Eyes, but there dwells no more anything within that might receive their message. Outward ears, servants of deafness. This throat, since I swallowed all below, is become but the shudder only, above this pit that is me within you.

And the darkness at his left hand said: Hands: fit for all noble uses. Ay, grip the bedside: is that sweet? Hands entertained for your soul's liege ambassadors, so often, into such courts: but now never again for ever.

And the darkness at his right hand laughed like a skull and said: Noble uses, as to-night! aim blade against him that ran to you, a wounded snipe to a stoat, to bring you true tidings, but you lay bloody hands upon.

And the darkness that was within said again: I strive. I will burst this shell that was you. I, that am not, will swell up like a blue poisoned corpse and burst and deflower all being.

And the darkness that was above and beneath said: I am heavy: I am fallen: I draw you: the weight and the woe for ever in your vitals of a misbegotten and never to be delivered birth.

And the darkness that was at his feet said: For then Amaury came (Lessingham looked in the darkness towards the other bed where Amaury lay unsleeping): Amaury, that would have died a hundred deaths in Rialmar to have saved her; but when she had drunk the cup—

The darkness within, and the darkness above, and the darkness beneath, sank, until the drag-hooks became an agony beyond mortal agonies.

The waning moon, in the grey latter hours, said: I wax and I wane: the sickle, the plenilune, the folding darkness. I change, and I change not. You have said it: Beyond time and circumstance. You have said: Upon no conditions.

And as the waning moon to the full, so was now the radiance as of a lunar rainbow that suffused that bedchamber upon memories, a year old that night, of Ambremerine: Vandermast's, "An old fool that is yet wise enough to serve your ladyship:" Vandermast's, "There is no other wisdom;" and again, "No other power." And that lady's, "Does that need wisdom?" as she looked at the moon.

XX

Thunder Over Rerek

The baying to Ragnarok[1] ✦ Lessingham forces peace ✦ Beroald's fore-judgement ✦ The Vicar will still play Machiavel ✦ Yet is seemingly persuaded ✦ Coming of the Parry to Argyanna ✦ Homage done by him to Barganax ✦ The Duke and his Vicar ✦ Strange brotherhood ✦ Barganax to Fiorinda.

LESSINGHAM upon that night's morrow took his way westwards with his army slowly towards Mornagay, sending word before so that all the bruit should run in all Rerek, and so through Meszria to Zayana, of this back-winter, and of need come upon all that stood now in civil strife to lay that by, and think on an enemy indeed. He had it now fully from Amaury: how Derxis, by the employment of spies, by traitors whom he had greased well in their hands, or by some other advisoes, had obtained entry for himself and some few of his men into Rialmar; where, with the chancing together of several matters which fell out well to his hand and he used them better, he had contrived his purpose so close as procure the murder, at one chop, of Bodenay and a dozen more. Which done, the Queen's power, made headless, might no longer but sever and dissolve, leaving this Derxis to be his own carver: a beast unmerciless.

Lessingham, now for two days, scarce took bite nor sup. Whether he slept none knew: only that not an hour in the night but somewhere was he to be seen about the camp, armed and in his riding-coat. Save to give orders, not a word had he for any man, neither durst any speak with him. It was, through these days, as if there rode there a man abiding indeed in his bodiness, but lapped in lead: in all else deceased, but his great heart carried him. And now began to be heard in a susurration about men's ears, the thing that in all those months past in Rialmar had not been spoke nor imagined except by Derxis, with so wise a discretion had Lessingham and the Queen refrained themselves: but now it was said, What grief was this that should so benumb a man, for but loss of his Queen? and it was answered, Past question, she loved him paramour and no other. Which coming to Amaury's ears, he was highly displeased: said to him that let fall the word, "I should slit thy tongue for chattering so wide," and by all discreet means wrought to scotch this prittle-prattle. But the rumour, once sown, ran like quitch-grass in a garden, much underground; and yet to no bad effect, knitting their hearts the closer in his service as to a man not great only, but great and unhappy. For of such kind were most that followed Lessingham, that their loves grew up as the watercresses, slowly, but with a deep root: not so ready to praise the sun at his uprising as worship him at his downgate.

The third afternoon they came to Mornagay. Lessingham would not lie here, but press on by Killary and so by the Tivots and Scorradale Heath to be in Bardardale before nightfall. Amaury rode with him, and, after the carriage beasts were well through the ford, they two drew ahead. On the great open mile-wide ridge of the heath Lessingham reined in Maddalena and, turning in the saddle, looked back northwards. The sun was set in a clear sky: the heath was become a darkness made up of all shades of blackish greens: the sky a pallour of all greys akin to blue: tarns and standing waters gleamed lighter than the sky itself, as if lit from under. From the east, little white wisps of mist came like feelers drifting from right to left over the dark heathland.

Lessingham spoke: "You were with me that night thirteen months ago, in Mornagay."

"Yes."

"Never name it again. Never name to me again aught that came of it."

"No, my lord."

"What think you, Amaury? is it true that all things have their life, their limits, their diseases, and their death?"

"All things?"

"Yes, all."

"Not all, my lord."

"What then? what hath not?"

"You have bid me never name it."

"I say, all things, Amaury. Dispute it not, else God knows I might murder you. I am in these days become a wild beast, first made fierce with tying, and then let loose. And not I alone: so is all become."

"I hope, not murder me, that loved you 'bove the world."

"Yes, you and all. Then gallop apace to my ruin."

"O, this is madness."

"No," said Lessingham, and his voice was like the muttering of distant thunder: "it is like the Twilight of the Gods: the baying of the hell-dog before Gnipa's cave: the crowing of the cocks in the three worlds: will you call that nightingales?—

"Geyr nú Garmr mjök fyrir Gnípuhelli:
Festr mun slitna, enn Freki renna!"

"Yes, Amaury: 'The fast must be loos'd, and the Wolf run free.' "[2]

Amaury sat silent, his jaw set. Those feelers had by now drawn a coverlet of mist over all the heath, hiding the ground. On the hummock where Lessingham and Amaury waited, their horses' feet were in the mist but their own heads in clear air, and the stars clear and bright above them.

Lessingham laughed. "Say over to me again, those words he used. For God knows I have dreamed and waked and dreamed till I know not well which is dream and which true."

"I dare not say it."

"Say it," said Lessingham terribly.

Amaury obeyed; "He said, 'If not to be my Queen, then you shall at least be no longer the strumpet of a soldier of fortune.' "

A full minute Lessingham neither spoke nor moved. His face, seen sideways, proud and unreadable against the May night, showed like stone or iron. There came the ring of bridles up from the Scorradale side, of the vanward nearing the brow. Lessingham shook rein, turned and rode away down before them into Bardardale. Amaury, following beside Maddalena's off hind quarter, heard him say in his teeth, "I have shut my mind against these things." Then suddenly drawing rein and staring into Amaury's eyes through the darkness: "Remember that," he said. "But remember, too, not winged horses shall prevail him to outskip my vengeance. And so, Amaury, to work."

There went messengers now, while Lessingham and the Admiral lay in Bardardale, betwixt them and the Chancellor before Laimak. By this, in a few days it was brought to a meeting betwixt them, and a charter of peace sealed with Lessingham upon provisoes and a truce to endure until the fourteenth day of June, and in the mean season counsel to be had for that matter with the Duke, late come up to Argyanna after sojourning at home awhile in Zayana. Upon the tenth of June came these lords, Lessingham, Beroald, and Jeronimy, with Amaury, to Argyanna. Here with the Duke was Count Zapheles, and the Lords Melates and Barrian and a dozen besides, men of mark. Medor, wielding by procuration the ducal power, abode yet in Zayana.

Lessingham was greatly feasted and nobly received, nor, when they fell to their business, seeking of agreement, were they slow to find sured ground: at first, common cause against Derxis, to destroy him and revenge his abomination in Rialmar: secondly, King Mezentius's lawful issue being by two murders in this short while miserably dead, there remained no colourable pretender to the throne but the Duke, whose claim thus stood waterfast. But when it was to speak of the Lord Horius Parry, and upon what terms the Duke and his would take him into their peace again, straight they lost (as for agreeing) more in a minute than they got in a day: Lessingham of the one side, all they of the other against him. The Duke required surrender without all conditions: "Which, come what will, he cannot choose but be forced unto, in a month or less. By God, I discommend your wit, my Lord Lessingham, if you think I know not a fox by his bush now, or think, now I hold him earthed in Laimak, I'll let this one wend free at your asking, to play me such another touch as last winter he did."

"He will never surrender without conditions," said Lessingham. "Why should he? Would you or I?"

"Well," said the Duke, "no more blind reckonings. This is the one sure card: soon as ever I have him, to cut off his head."

Lessingham answered, "We be all agreed that it is time we began to destroy our enemies, and first let us begin at Derxis that hath done villanies not to be spoken and threateneth our mere being. For this, we must give over even rightful quarrels amongst ourselves, else can we never achieve it. And the Vicar is a great captain not easily to be spared in the manage of so great a war as this. Besides, our folk of Rerek are stubborn and hard and can not easily digest the government of a stranger."

"They have by many a hundred rebelled against him now," said Barganax.

"That," replied Lessingham, "was when I was not by."

"They will obey you sooner than him. Let him go."

Lessingham stroked his beard. "No. If your grace take that way, I sit out."

Two days they argued it. The second, the Chancellor took Lessingham apart: said, "My Lord Lessingham, you have gotten the right ear of his grace; but in this you will not move him. This ill weed of yours, maugre your warming and watering, hath now been parched up. Only bethink you: upon what consideration, but of this man alone, should the Duke have seized power in Rerek and, by implication, in Fingiswold? 'Gainst his sister he'd ne'er a stood usurper, but 'gainst this man only that under her name cloaked his large ambitions. Your lordship hath heard how myself did in aid of that enterprise allege a law which barreth women from kingdom to the end the realm fall not into the hands of a strange prince or nation. 'Tis of questionable authority: I lent it mine, not for any quarrel with the Queen's highness (on whom be peace), but because I would not trust this man. You and he sort very ill together. If conscience will not suffer you to oppose his interest, then get you gone for a season: leave him to us. We shall speedily deal with him."

"The things," replied Lessingham, "which be main counts against his highness my cousin were done when I was beyond the Wold upon the Queen's business. For all that was then misdone I have, upon his behalf, offered atonement."

"I see your lordship will not hear reason," said Beroald. "Well, you are like to pay dear upon your bond."

"That the Gods must rule," answered he. "But remember, I am upon safe conduct here in Argyanna, and with, right upon safe conduct to return to that army I have afoot, and with that, be it little in numbers, I have ere this done somewhat. And remember the lord Admiral is upon parole to go back with me if this peace be not concluded. And if his grace will have no peace (and a hard peace for the other is this I offer you, and good for his grace), but will, as is now said, slay the Vicar, then I will promise you this: it shall be so countervenged that it shall be spoken of a hundred years hereafter."

Beroald said, "We will not talk on thunder."

"Lessingham," said the Duke, coming upon them in this: "the man is not by a noble heart such as yours in any way to be avouched or defended. Must our friendship fly in pieces for sake of such a villain?"

"If our friendship, my lord Duke (which the Gods forfend), must fly in pieces, 'tis because, to end his heroical great defence that hath so long time held you off and your armies, you will in cold blood use this same cruelty I have so oft checked in himself, of the beheading-block. But if my friendship be aught, then prove it: for I have told your grace I will, so you give him but to me, be answerable upon my honour and upon my life that he shall all repay and no more disease you."

"But to what wild purpose—?" Barganax paused silent for a minute, looking in Lessingham's eyes. There sat in them a bantering mocking look that he knew, but as belonging to other eyes: not to these speckled grey eyes of Lessingham, but to green eyes, beaconing as from every unrest and from every incertitude and peril, which things, taking on those eyes' allurance, burned high and desirable beyond all lusts and fires.

"Each to his taste," Lessingham said. "I have given you reasons enough in policy. And if you will have more, say he is a dangerous horse: say I taste a pleasure in such riding."

"Say you will break your neck, my Lord Lessingham," said the Chancellor.

But Barganax and Lessingham, like as formerly at the council-board in Ilkis, now faced one another as if, for all their company about them, they stood alone, and a third presiding: a third, perceived but by them alone; and scarcely, indeed, to be named a third, as being present strangely to the Duke in the person of Lessingham, and to Lessingham in the Duke.

Two days later, a little before noon, Lessingham rode into Laimak. It was a day of close, hazy weather, boiling up for thunderstorms. The Chancellor's armies still held siege before the castle, for the allies had no mind that the Vicar should use this truce for getting in of provision, then defy them anew and so drag on. Lessingham and his they let through with no delays, for he bare letters of credence under seal of Zayana. All the valley for a mile about the castle was wasted with fire and eaten up. The Vicar greeted Lessingham as a man might greet a son long given up for lost. He carried him to his closet in the keep, and hither was dinner brought them, poor campaigning fare indeed: bacon pies, black rye bread, cheese, and smoked fish, with a runlet of muscadine to wash it down and a little joy the heart withal.

"Are you come with a treaty in your wallet?" said the Vicar when the waiting-men had set all in order and, upon his command, left them to dine private.

Lessingham smiled. "No more treaties, cousin, of my making. I have somewhat here: but you shall sign for yourself, if it like you; and no room for cavil afterward."

"It will keep till after dinner."

"Yes. It will keep so long: not much longer."

The Vicar looked swiftly up. Lessingham's face, careless and with eyes averted, was not to be read. "You're come none too soon," said the Vicar then, and took in a great mouthful. "Rations left for seven days. Starving men make best fighters; but 'tis not a discipline fit to hold 'em to too long: though it be good to savage 'em, yet in this other 'tis as bad, that drawn out beyond a day or two it sloweth and feebleth the animal spirits. And so ninth day from this had I set for the grand carousal, warm meat and blood puddings i' the field below there, and the leavings for the crows to pick on."

"Rant it not to me as if I were a woman," said Lessingham.

"You have not sufficiency to withstand their forces: not one hour, in the open."

"Well: end so, then." He watched Lessingham through half-shut lids. "Better so than swallow another treaty like the last you crammed down my throat, cousin."

"Your highness is a great soldier," said Lessingham; "but politician, not so good. How should you now look for so good a treaty as that? which was just and equal, but you did break every article and published your every breach too from the house-tops. Be thankful if I have saved you your life, and some few false beams of your supposed honour."

"So!"

For a long while, eyeing each other, they ate and drank in silence. The Vicar's neck swelled like a puff-adder's. At length, "You've been a weary while," he said, "dallying on the door-step: more than a fortnight. Talking with those devils (the sweat and swink they've cost me!). Might a talked to me ere this, I'd have thought?"

Lessingham said nothing, only with a delicate air raised his cup and drank, regarding his cousin the while with level and thoughtful eyes. The Vicar took a gobbet of bacon-rind out of his mouth: leaned sideways to give it to Pyewacket. The play of the light revealed, as might some great master's brush, the singularity that belonged, but seldom so lively seen as now, to his strangely-sorted countenance: heavy eyelids, wide-winged jutting nose, lean lips like a snake's, delicate ears, ruffianly reddish-be-bristled jowl, serene smooth forehead, small swift-darting eyes: a singularity of brutish violence joined with some nobler element in a marriage wherein neither was ever all subdued to other, nor yet ever all distinct; so that divorce must needs have crippled a little both, as well the good as the bad. And upon Lessingham, while he so watched this renewing of a pageant he knew well, a mantle seemed to fall, enduing limb and sinew and poise of neck and head with a grander and yet more pantherine grace. And the Grecian lineaments of Lessingham, and the eyes of him thus savouring his cousin, seemed not so much to be informed now with a swift beast's majesty or an eagle's, but rather as if strength and mastery should take to itself the airy loveliness of a humming-bird, and so hang hovering on viewless wings, as the bird quivers bodiless upon air beside a flower, uncertain into which honeyed fold amid petals it shall aim its long and slender beak.

"You were ever at your best," he said after a little, "back to the wall. Trouble is, set you at your ease, you fall athinking. And that is bad for you."

"I know not, cousin, what you account good for a man. My belt's half a foot the shorter since Yule-tide."

"What dispossessed your wits," Lessingham said, "soon as my back was turned, treat this Duke as you would some poor-spirited slow boy? And did I not tell you what he is? and could you not use him accordingly?"

"That which is, is," said the Vicar, and drank and spat. "That which was, was. That which shall be, 'tis that concerneth me and you. This new turn in Rialmar," fleet as a viper's his eyebeam flashed upon Lessingham's face and away, "hath upsy-versied all, ha? Or how think you on't? Look you," he said, after a silence, and leaned forward, elbows on the table: "I will tell you a thought of mine: may be good, may be naught, howsome'er hath come me oft in mind since Kutarmish set all afire here. That Derxis. Could a been used, ha? matter of marriage, had't been nicely handled:" he paused, studying through red eyelashes Lessingham's face, inscrutable and set now as a God's likeness done in marble. "And so, using Akkama to put down Zayana, afterward—well, there be ways and means."

Lessingham toyed with his wine cup. "Ways and means!" He tossed off the wine, sprang up, walked to the window, and there stood looking down on him as in a high displeasure. "Pray talk to me of your soldiering, for there I can but admire, and even love you. But these twisting policies, I can but laugh at 'em."

"Nay, but hangeth together. My wardship's lost: so. Well, shift weight to the well-lodged foot then." He paused, sat back in his chair. Their eyes met. "I know not what this paper may say which you have in your purse, cousin; but would you'd a talked to me first ere talk to Zayana. You had not thought on this other way, ha? and yet opened fair before you: to use Derxis, I mean, as our instrument? And not too late now, neither, if rightly handled."

"What are you," said Lessingham, "but a bloody fool? Have I not told you long ago there's no way but the straight cut? the Mezentian way, not these viperine crawlings: weld all fast under Barganax now, and crush this vermin, this of Akkama. Sweet Gods in heaven, cousin, is't not your own kith and kin? (in a distant way, I grant). And as for use Derxis, I'd as soon the putrid skull of some invenomed serpent, and use't for my wine-cup."

"Go," said the Vicar, and there was the look in his eyes as of one that weigheth *pro* and *contra* as he gazed on Lessingham: "here's a talker."

Lessingham took two parchments from his doublet: tossed them before the Vicar among the dishes. "Take it or no, 'tis you to choose, cousin: but if yes, to-day's the last day: sign it or say good-bye. You may thank the kind Gods and me, that have hooked you out of this quagmire you have by your own curst mulish obstinacy rushed and stuck fast in. May be, since indeed I think you're mad now, you'll liefer choose your feast of tripes in Laimak home-mead a week hence; or t'other choice: that the Duke will give you, and please him best. Three livelong days I wrought for you, and little thanks I see for it, ere I won him to offer you this good bargain, 'stead as he would a had it: and that was, get you dead or alive, as in a month's time or less no power on earth could a letted it: head you and side you, and nail the meat up so for crows to eat on Laimak walls."

But the Vicar had snatched the parchment and was by now half-way through it, his great stubbed finger following the words as he read. When he came to the end, he read all again, this time the duplicate copy: then, without word spoken, reached pen and ink from the sideboard and signed and sealed. He then stood up: came to Lessingham beside the window, took him by both hands. "Think not I forget it, cousin, that this is by the great wit and prowess that is in you, the which I mind me well hath stood me in good stead many a time and yet shall do again."

"Good, then we're friends," said Lessingham. "You have ta'en it well, cousin, as a wise prince should do. And the sixth day from to-day, as there writ down, your highness will come to him in Argyanna, enact that ceremony? your allegiance full and perfect?"

"Ay, as a cat laps milk."

"You do well, cousin." He took up one copy of the concordat, scanning the hands and seals: the Duke's, Beroald's, Jeronimy's, and now the Vicar's. "This raiseth the siege to-day. I'll begone with it, and we meet 'pon Wednesday in Argyanna. But remember, cousin," he said upon departing: "I look for deeds from you upon this: no more false closes designed to shun a final end."

"Go, you have read me a fair lecture," answered he. "Think not I'll stumble at a straw now that I've leapt over a block. Fare you well."

The twentieth day of June was appointed a great festival and holi-day for ratifying of this peace whereby, Barganax being now in both Rerek and Meszria taken for King, the lords of those countries should in his service fare shortly with great armies north across the Wold, win back Rialmar, and so carrying the war through Akkama ravish and ruinate all the cities and people thereof and lay them under subjection, seizing above all King Derxis whom they meant to punish and kill not as befits a noble person.

Betimes that morning was the main army of the Chancellor, come down on purpose from Hornmere side and Ristby and those parts, besides the Duke's two thousand that he now held in Argyanna and thereabouts, marched under banners and with singing of war-songs and music of trumpets and drums three times round the bluff without the moat. The Duke, with fifty red-bearded men of his bodyguard bearing their great two-handed swords, had place of honour before the drawbridge. He rode upon a fierce white stallion with sweeping mane and tail and with harness all black and trappings and saddlecloth of black sendaline. Of like sad hue were the Duke's cloak and bonnet with black estridge-feathers and all his armour: black gloves upon his hands: the very ruff about his throat black, that should have been white: all this in formal sign of mourning and lamentation. The Lords Beroald and Jeronimy wore plumes of mourning in their hats and black mourning cloaks: the like tokens wore every one, high or low, man or woman, soldiers or townsfolk, that day; but the Duke alone, both for his royal estate and near kinship, that extremity of blackness.

And now, well upon the hour appointed, marching from the north down the granite-paven causeway that in a ten-mile span, laid on a foundation of thousands upon thousands of strong oaken piles, bridges the quaking-bogs in the midst of which is Argyanna, came the Vicar and his following. Twenty trumpeters on horseback headed the march: great was the flashing of their helms and trumpets, all of silver: their kirtles and hose were dyed with saffron: they had black mourning saddle-cloths and black cloaks: at every twenty paces they sounded upon their trumpets the owl-call of the house of Parry. Behind them, guarded by two score of Lessingham's black riders, went the royal banner of Fingiswold, by him brought victorious from the northland through many deadly chances and the bloody battles at Ridinghead and Leveringay. The owl of Laimak, sable, armed and beaked gules upon a field or, followed after: its motto, *Noctu noxiis noceo,* "Nightly I prey upon vermin." There went a company of veteran spearmen of Rerek four by four behind it, helmed and byrnied and with great oblong shields. The Vicar himself rode with Lessingham a score of paces behind these foot-soldiery, and a score of paces before the rest of their following: Amaury, Brandremart, Bezardes, Thrasiline, Daiman, and so horse and foot to the number of five hundred or more bringing up the rear.

Now when they were come close under Argyanna before the gates and the drawbridge, the Count Rossilion bearing the Vicar's banner rode forth with two trumpeters that blew a fanfare. And Rossilion, doffing cap to the Duke and reading from a writing in his hand, cried out with a loud voice that all might hear: "For behalf of his most excellent lordship Horius Parry I do salute the Lord Barganax, Duke of Zayana, and do receive and acknowledge him the said Duke to be great King of Fingiswold and of all states and dominions appertaining thereto, and in particular of all Meszria and the Marches and of all this territory or land of Rerek and places situate therewithin, being especially the fortresses or strong holds of Laimak, Kessarey, Megra, Kaima, and Argyanna, and of this March of Ulba. And thus saith the Lord Horius Parry: I hereby give, O

King, into the hands of your princely highness all those estates and
powers whatsoever which, whether as private-vassal and subject,
whether as Vicar of the Queen, whether as Lord Protector, I herebefore have held under kingdom of Queen Antiope of glorious
memory (upon whom be peace), hoping that your serenity may
adjudge them to have been truly and diligently by me administrated
and used, in the behoof of the weal public and the great glory of the
crown of the three kingdoms. Humbled on my knee I now kiss your
grace's hand, tendering my love and service true and perfect, and
fearfully expecting your royal commands."

The Vicar meanwhile, being dismounted from his horse, and
standing ten paces or so behind Rossilion, looked on and listened
with no outward sign save the great puffing out and great redness
of his neck. He was all armed, with a byrny of polished iron edged
at throat and wrists and skirt with links of gold; thigh-pieces and
greaves and toe-pieces and golden spurs. No weapon he bore, only
in his right hand his staff vicarial. Two boys, dressed in the russet
and purple livery of his bodyguard, bare up behind him the train of
his great black cloak.

"But look upon him," said Zapheles in the Chancellor's ear.
"What charter of peace can you contrive, my lord, but this great
devil will break it?"

Beroald shrugged his shoulders.

"Well, now a hath put his head in the lion's mouth," said Melates, as Rossilion ended, "cannot some contrive to set the King in a
fume against him? Bite it off, and all were well."

"'Tis but yonder Lessingham standeth 'twixt this and that,"
said Barrian. "A thing past man's understanding."

"That he so stands? or that his grace should heed him?"

"Both," said the Chancellor with a tart smile.

Lessingham said in the Vicar's ear, "Your highness would be
well advised, put off your bonnet: he did the like for you, if I am
told aright, in the Salimat last autumn. Besides there is about your
bonnet the diadem, which you must assume again but at his bidding."

"Let be. I'm afeared of this sun. Shall not fry my brains, concordat or no concordat."

Men noted that in the very act of homage the Parry wore still
his crown viceroyal with rich stones and orient pearl beset. Some
murmured at it: the Duke, whose eye no littlest thing might ever
escape, could not but note it, but yet let it go unremarked. Upon
kissing of hands, the trumpets of either side blew a fanfare. The
Vicar upon that, taking from off his head the coronal, presented it
to the Duke, who straightway raised it on high that all should see,
then set it again upon the head of the Vicar, saying, for all to hear:
"Be witness whom it may concern, and the blessed Gods Who keep

the wide heaven, that, upon homage thus made to me in my estate as high master of these kingdoms and agreeably to articles of peace late sealed and made betwixt us, I do hereby assign unto you, Horius Parry, the strong holds and demesnes of Laimak, Kaima, and Kessarey, and all the country and principality of old Rerek, but not Megra nor the lands north of Swaleback, and not Argyanna nor the Ulba March, to hold as my vicar or vicegerent, answerable to no man save to me, but to me to be answerable with your head. In witness whereof, receive this coronal and name of Vicar of Rerek."

This done, amid great noise of trumpets and drums and shouting of all the soldiers and people there assembled, this solemnity had its end. But first the Duke let proclaim silence, and bade the Lord Beroald say forth on his behalf this, in a great voice, that all might know: "Thus saith the most renowned and most mighty prince and lord, Barganax, great Duke of Zayana, our sovereign master and King: that it is his pleasure, even as he will change not these mourning colours till he shall have beat the outborn usurper from the land and with the Gods' help punished him with death, so will he think it scorn, and not suitable with his princely dignity, to take yet the King's name, but will first, like as all other Kings of Fingiswold, be crowned in Rialmar. At his command publish it so accordingly. God save his serene and most excellent highness, Barganax, Duke of Zayana, of the three kingdoms our sovereign lord."

They rode now in a progress once about the hold with their bodyguards, the Vicar and Barganax riding in the midst somewhat apart, jointly taking the salute from those on the walls and those in the field and all the army drawn up beside the way in double line, so as men should perceive with their eyes this new condition of peace and friendship, and the conclusion of the war and hate there had been so long betwixt them.

"This is a great pride in you, my lord Duke," the Vicar said, "not to take the style of King."

Barganax smiled. "I had thought it a great modesty."

"It was to shame me," said the Vicar. "Not clip the wings only of my vicariate, a thing I honourably endured, but make me do homage but to a ducal cap."

"'Las," said the Duke: "I fear I was thinking of my own affair, and not at all of you, my lord."

"I was gulled in it," said the Vicar. There shone in his eyes, the Duke's head being for the moment turned away to acknowledge acclamations upon his right, a most cruel, mortal, and inexorable hatred.

"Give credit, the thing ne'er entered my head," said the Duke. "But indeed," he said, "now I think on't, I can but praise your courteous carriage and affability; for indeed, God knoweth well enough without remembrancer, myself did bow as low, and to a like necessity, not a year since, i' the Salimat."

"'Tis of no moment," said the Vicar. "Only for this I thought fit to speak on't to your grace, considering we shall wisely avoid now whatsoever might diminish my estimation and authority, and so tie me shorter when we should work together for common ends."

The Duke said, "I'll not forget it. I have bespoke a banquet about noon, which I hope your highness and whom you will of your following will honour me to share with us. After that, hold council of war. Midsummer already, and much to do ere we may march in full force. And it were folly think to lead a great army over the Wold once it be turned September."

The same night, when save for the sentinels upon the walls and at the gates none was astir, Barganax and Lessingham went forth alone together to take the air and so came slowly a mile or more down the causeway from Argyanna southwards, walking and talking. The leavings of sunset, dusky orange-tawny on the horizon, crept slowly round towards the north. Bats skimmed overhead.

"A month to-day, then," said Lessingham: "that's the twentieth. In Mornagay."

"In Mornagay," said the Duke. "What shall we be? Seven thousand?"

"That's not to count the princes and the free towns."

"We shall be too many."

"A stroke that shall not miss," Lessingham said, and they fell silent.

After half an hour they came to a stand. Barganax picked up a stone and tossed it in a reed-bed to wake the reed warblers that forthwith began their chattering. He said, "What make you of that light, there in the darkest bit among the moss-hags? A pool? A broken goblet throwing back the sky? A broken sword? A whole nation of glow-worms gone astray? A chink in the saucepan lid to let us see 'tis here they brew the marsh-fires?"

"I think you shall find it but stagnant water if you go to it," said Lessingham. "Here, it might be all those things."

"A light asleep in the dark," said the Duke. "I should like to paint this night," he said, after a little. "The past: all gone. The thing to come, crouching in those obscurities of ooze and reed-bed, ready to spring. The thing present: you and me. And that is strangest of all: unpaintable, too, like as are most things worth painting."

Lessingham was silent.

"Were you a tenderer of your own safety, you'd now leave me," said the Duke. "Espousing my cause thus wholly, and enforcing this last settlement of peace upon him, you now go naked to his claws.

No argument remains of self-interest, as before most strongly served, why he should not destroy you."

"I have now a kind of freedom," said Lessingham. "I'll not give up you; nor I'll not give up him."

"Pity that savage mare of yours, who biteth and striketh all men else, will not content you."

"Would she content your grace, and you stood where I stand?"

They began to walk slowly, in their companionship of silence, back again towards Argyanna that stood squat, square, and black, against the sky to the north. They were half-way home when the Duke began to say, under his breath, as if the words had been not words but echoes only, answering the measured tread of his musing footsteps along the causeway:

> "Earth I will have, and the deep sky's ornament:
>   Lordship, and hardship, and peril by land and sea.—
> And still, about cock-shut time, to pay for my banishment,
>   Safe in the lowe of the firelight I will have Thee."

Lessingham, who had listened with breath held back lest a word should be lost, suddenly, when the stave was ended, checked in his stride. They halted and faced one another in the stillness. "Who are you?" Lessingham said at last, staring through the soft darkness into Barganax's face: so like to his sister's, save for the varying characters of he and she, that Lessingham's very being was, for that likeness, confounded within him. Barganax made no answer. The silence was full of bird-voices afar on marshes that never go quite to sleep: now a redshank's cry, now some little plover. Lessingham said, "Who made that stave?"

"That? I made it."

"You?" In the stillness a curlew whistled far away, awake in the night.

"I like it," Barganax said, "if for its very vanity."

"Its vanity!" said Lessingham, and they stood silent.

"Why did you bid me," he said then, "to your love-feast upon Ambremerine? Why that night did she draw me through doors? What changed then in your throne-room? Why did she send me to Rialmar? Who is she?" he said, last of all.

Barganax shook his head. " 'Las," he said, "I can answer none of these riddles." He met Lessingham's eyes through the dark. Inch for inch he and Lessingham stood of a height. It was as if he could not easily resolve to let loose that which was upon his tongue. At last he spoke: "Lessingham, I can, as I said, answer none of your riddles. But I will tell you this: upon Michaelmas night,[3] taking my ease in a certain house of Vandermast's, I looked in a mirror and I beheld there not my own face, but yours."

Lessingham neither spoke nor moved.

"Well," Barganax said. "What was it? Know you such a house?"

"And I beheld," said Lessingham, stare for stare, "your face, not mine. In that house. Upon Michaelmas night."

He swung round: began walking again homeward. Barganax, at his elbow, heard the gritting of his teeth upon a smothered groan, as a man might grit them with the turning of the blade in a wound. But in time, as they walked on in that commerce of mind with mind in which speech were but a troubling of the stream that else runs crystal clear, Lessingham tasted again, as upon Ambremerine, the leaning of Barganax's spirit towards that seeming woman of his; and strangely in the tasting took balm to his own mortal hurt, until his own spirit within him was borne up on high like a great violent flame of fire, as for the grand last act indeed.

The Duke wrote that night, and sent it south by safe hand betimes the next morning:

"Righte Expectable and Noble Lady, these to kiss your hands and informe you that matters occurent must hold me in the north now well till autumne. I would be sured therefore that your Ladyship will keep my private lodging as your own upon AkroZayana till these inconveniences be over past. I have todaye with the Parry sealed againe the infringible band of faith, but fear I shall never love him, nor would you, not for the honesty of his conversation neither nice in bodie but grossly sett and thick. And kinde will creep where it may not go, hee is enemy I think to all men save to such as will subject themselves to him. As for L. I doo think your Ladyship knoweth more than I of his affair, I mean not my Sisters parte which was with so much wisedome kept close as never a whisper went on it, I mean things deeper farre than that. My thoughts growe busy that some way there bee iv of us but some way ij only. O beguiler of guiles, opening of your garments, sudden flashing of your Beauty, what webs are these? But no more, it is coriander in swete wine. I shall never have done when I am once in, and never settle my self for want of lipwork in stead of penwork. O Blacke Lily one and onemost, disdainer, and hallower, of all things, blinder of sight, bedde of the dragon and the dove, robe state and crowne imperiall of my desire, in daylight acte my Cynosura, wanting you here, in my dreames I taste you, and wanting wordes to endear you, call you but Mine, me, Yours."

XXI

Enn Freki Renna[1]

Pack'd cards with Derxis ♦ *The thing laid bare
to Lessingham* ♦ *Last clash of the Adamants* ♦
Insultans tyrannus[2] ♦ *The wolf runs* ♦ *Antiope
in Mornagay.*

ESSINGHAM, being by the Duke confirmed now in his
office of Captain-General, departed next day out of
Argyanna about taking order, against the trysting-time
set for Mornagay, for yet more forces and muniments
of war. Upon which great business was he now for
weeks journeying without delays or respite through Rerek and the
Marches and Outer Meszria, cementing alliances, pacifying squab-
bles. The High Admiral was rode back to take the water again at
Kessarey and so move to Kaima; Zapheles and Melates fared south
into Meszria; the Lord Horius Parry home to Laimak. Barrian the
Duke sent in embassage to those Princes Ercles and Aramond, to
salve their wounds with estates and signiories in the north there,
carved out of that great slice which had by the peace of Argyanna
been trimmed off from the vicariate. The Duke himself, with the
Chancellor, and with Lessingham's thousand horse, lay yet in Argyanna, meaning in time to move north in great strength; and command was that all with their armies should come together the
twentieth of July at Mornagay, thence to march north to the Wold,
whence tidings now began to be had of Derxis's advance southwards, as upon a design for invasion of Rerek ere summer be too far
worn.

But the Vicar, soon as he was come again to Laimak, retired himself to his private chamber; took from the iron chest, where he kept such matters, the new concordat; sat thinking with himself an hour or two; then sent for Gabriel Flores. "Come hither, good pug, let's closely to our business. You must north again, 'to Megra,' as we'll call it: 'to Arcastus,' we'll say."

Gabriel waited obedient.

"I'll set down nought in writing, no more than I would before. This," the Vicar flicked the edge of the parchment with a finger, " 'gins smell too much of the inkhorn already. Get yonder ragman's-roll by rote ere you go: tell it him word by word. Then tell him this pointeth north to his destruction ere he shall be ready to come conquering down hitherward: that, the Queen being dead by some misfortune—how, I know not: miss not that,—and the royal line of Fingiswold come so to an end, this Zayana entirely hath now the love of all nobles, princes, and all other in the realm save mine only, to back his usurpation; and mine but in show and policy. Speak to him so: show him what stark folly 'twere in him to enterprise to seize kingdom here without some bolsterer or comforter in his deed: and for such, he may take me, whose help is worth ten armies; and so on. Speak earnestly, even till his teeth run a water. Let him understand by all means that you are sent to practise my good and his. Then let him know my easy condition: letters patent under his royal hand and seal confirming me in perpetuity, as for him and his heirs and successors, his Vicar for all Meszria and all Rerek; 'pon receipt of which by your hand, I will, in token of faith and as his loyal obedienciary, shortly send him the heads or other proofs of the taking off of the persons here most disaffected, and these the principal: Barganax, Beroald, Jeronimy. Which I shall find good opportunity to perform ere it be well onward in summer, having lulled 'em into so lethargic a sleep with this," and he flicked the parchment again, "and preparing me an occasion."

"Your highness hath forgot to name one name," said Gabriel, "will, for the king's jealous hate and spleen, weigh with him 'gainst these as gold against feathers."

"And whose is that, my pigsnye?"

"Your highness will not wish I should name it."

The Vicar's eyes narrowed upon him. "No, or may be I'd tear your tongue out." With such a sudden fury he hurled the inkpot, that Gabriel was barely in time to save his teeth, or may be an eye, by swift raising of his arm.

"Meddle not beyond your commission," said the Vicar, while Gabriel mopped the ink-splashes with his handkercher and looked to his bruised arm. "Sit down. Study your part. I'll hear it over ere you go."

Gabriel was ready to set forth that evening. The rather not to be remarked, he made himself like a peddling chapman; took a spare horse and some huckstering wares, put on coarse blue country-garb, trimmed his hair shorter, and dyed that and his beard and eyebrows with henna. Ere he took horse, he was sent for again to the Vicar's chamber. "Well, scab, are you busked and ready?"

"So please your highness."

"Come, you shall drink some malmsey[3] for stirrup-cup": he poured it out, gave it him with his own hand. He put, when Gabriel set down the cup, a great arm about his neck, drawing him to him, and so looked down into the weasel eyes of him: "I did wrong to strike at you. There," he said, holding him off at arm's length: "when, until now, said I ever to you or any man that I was sorry for aught I'd done? But truth is, you were right in reason, my pug. And truth is, I cannot well digest reason in this particular, for truly I cannot root out of me the liking I have for the man; having both already made my profit by him and wishing still so to do; and yet, little commodity I see in't, as things sort. And yet," he said, "I have a kind of love for the man."

Gabriel stood awkward, listening to these words, that seemed as the rumour of some fight conduced in the very soul of his great master.

"Fare you well, then," said the Vicar.

"Highness, farewell," said Gabriel. "And as for loving," he said, as upon a sudden bursting of the doors of speech, "be certain of this: your highness cannot now afford to bear love or liking to any: no, not even to me."

It was now upon mid July. The Vicar, with some thousand heavy-armed troops of Rerek, was come up to Mornagay. Here Gabriel, back from his mission, was two days closeted with his lord. None knew, nor none guessed nor sought to know, what might be there a-hatching between them; for in all things, in peace as in war, it was the Vicar's custom so to deal closely with this man or with Lessingham if he were at hand, but with others seldom or never.

Upon the thirteenth, Gabriel rode north again, now in a new disguise and with beard and mustachios shaved clean off. That same day, as the Gods would have it, came Lessingham riding post from Bardardale. He took day-meal; would not tarry, spite of the Vicar's wish to stay him, but saddle up again and on northward; being by appointment to meet with Barrian and Prince Ercles beyond Swaleback, for concerting of certain movements against next week's beginning of the great march north. This the pretext: but the true necessity was upon word from Barrian that this should do great good now, if Lessingham might but with the sunbeams of his countenance be finally his own peacemaker for all back-reckonings those princes yet held noted against him, as for plunder of Bagort that spring and the bad entreaty Ercles had had at Leveringay.

Lessingham rode with but five-and-twenty and Amaury. About the fifteenth mile, midway on from Leveringay to Eldir, they happed upon Gabriel, pricking fast, two or three hundred paces ahead. He, when he saw them, turned out of the road and made down towards that boggy bottom where a bridle-path, going among fields and then among woods, cuts off a large loop of the main north road. That, if the waters had not been up, had been the best way: but not so now. All saw him, but through that disguise Lessingham only knew him. Lessingham said apart to Amaury, "This jackal hath seen us: it is plain he would be glad to avoid me. I like not that." He bade the others wait while he alone galloped after Gabriel. Gabriel, when he saw he was followed and could not escape, drew rein and waited.

"If I could know you under these mumming weeds, and beard-less as a pig," Lessingham said, "you sure knew me? Why run away then? what hath so uncivil'd you?"

"Nay, by the Gods I knew not your worship."

Lessingham's glance seemed like that winter wind that will go clean through a man, clothes and body and all. "So you begin with a lie, my Gabriel? We'll talk further, then: see wherefore truth's so coy to-day." At first Gabriel's answers came pert and pat: then he began to trip amid the threads of his own invention: at last, tied up in a knot of plain contradictions, could no more, but stood ridiculous with all the tangle of his lies made manifest. Then, to cap ill with worse, he upon a swift chance struck spurs into his horse to flee. In a moment Lessingham had ridden him down: caught him by the collar. "I smell a pad in the straw: come, we'll search you." Gabriel, while this went forward, by a swift sleight crammed a crumpled paper in his mouth. Lessingham forced open his mouth: made him spit it out like a dog: took him such a cuff across the head as knocked him half-stunned from the saddle: sprang to earth, secured the paper, spread it and read it. Gabriel, standing up quakingly and gathering his senses, shrank under Lessingham's look; for there was in the countenance of Lessingham as he laid up the half-chewed paper like some jewel in his bosom, that blazing of eyes, that same deathly white paleness of terrible anger, which Gabriel had once before beheld; and that was when Lessingham, chained and under the strength of six men's hands, had been, in that helplessness, shamefully by the Vicar stricken across the face with the Concordat of Ilkis.

"This is private," said Lessingham, "'twixt your lord and me. No living soul else shall know on't. So much for your ease of mind." So saying, he caught him by the throat: shook him thrice and again until the eyes of Gabriel began to bulge from his blood-bolled chok-ing face, then threw him cruelly on the ground. "When I break my rod," he said, "it shall be on a bigger back than yours." Gabriel, may be as conceiving it safest to feign death, did not move till Lessingham was mounted again.

Lessingham rode but a score of paces to have sight again of his folk, where they waited some quarter of a mile away: made sign to Amaury he should come alone; then leisurely returned to where Gabriel stood afeared. Amaury galloped up to them: halted, looked obedient at Lessingham, then fierce at Gabriel. "Tell them, Amaury, this was but a messenger sent to seek me and had missed us in the way, so luckily overtaken, with word from my lord Chancellor upon which I must myself return for a night. You and the rest, ride forward; bring my excuses to Prince Ercles. Expect me in two days at most in Memmering." Amaury read notice, in his lord's mask of careless ease, of some great matter toward: read notice, too, not but at his peril to be called in question, that in this thing his part should be but to hear exactly and exactly to obey. Lessingham with a light word farewelled him, and turned south again at a walking-pace alone. When they were out of sight, he touched rein, whispered Maddalena: she carried him south like the wind.

In the long meadow-close below the northerner of the out-farms of Mornagay, as Lessingham rode in, were Rossilion, Thrasiline, and others, casting at the mark with javelins for their sport. "Why, 'tis like a masque," said Rossilion: "one fresh pageant after another. First, but an hour since, message to say the Duke and all his great army, seven days afore the day appointed, is come up now and shall be before sunset here in Mornagay; and now, back cometh the Captain-General."

"The eagles gather," said Thrasiline. "Sure, now shall we do somewhat."

The Vicar came by as Lessingham dismounted before the hostelry. In Lessingham's look he might read no danger, nor (knowing of old these sudden swift turns and changes of settled order) need he marvel if, set forth but three hours since for the north upon urgency and in company, Lessingham were now in great haste come south again. "Cousin, there is a business I must utter to you. Will your highness give me private audience?" The Vicar consenting with a shrug, they retired themselves to that same upper room where, more than a year ago, Lessingham and Amaury had supped that night when news came of King Styllis's death, and all the balance of affairs tipped above new deeps of peradventure: a room of beginnings and of memories.

Three of the Vicar's great dogs lay there in the rushes. There was wine upon the table, and drinking-cups: on the settle, the Vicar's armour: goose-feather pens, ink, papers, parchments, all Gabriel's writing-tackle, in a hodge-podge upon the sideboard. Lessingham said, "Who will write you your so many letters, cousin, whiles your secretary maketh up secret treaties betwixt you and Derxis?"

There was not a tremor in the Vicar's great hand, reaching the wine-jug, pouring a cupful. "Nimble and quick-silvered brains such as yours need this to settle 'em: quiddling upon such moonshine."

Lessingham struck the cup from his hand. "Did you not hear something cry thump?" he said upon the crash, as the Vicar, eyes aflame, leapt to his feet. "Come, I'll read it you: here 'tis, under your hand and seal:" he watched the Vicar, at the pulling out of the paper, change colour: 'ay, spittly and slimy too from the beast's mouth I plucked it out on. But legible."

"Go, you are a fool. Counterfeit letters. My fine device to draw him out."

"Prettily thought on," said Lessingham. "Tell me the crow is white."

The Vicar, with the table between himself and Lessingham, and eyeing him from beneath bent forehead, began to move with a side-long motion leftwards towards the door. But Lessingham, swift as a leopard, was there before him, hand upon sword-hilt. His left hand shot home the bolt behind him. "Had you been drunk so long you'd a done your estate better service. Plot treason? Is't come to this? And with this princox,[4] voice like a woman, this filth of filths, this murderer of—"

"O leave your cackling," said the Vicar, hand upon sword-hilt, head down, like a bull about to charge. "Thought you, while you played your games at put-pin, I'd sit idle for ever? I'll tell you, here's been small leisure for kissing and haking in Owldale this five month past, by the Gods!"

Lessingham's sword flamed out: the Vicar's too. "Loo! Loo! tear him! Pyewacket! Peck-i'-the-crown! tear his lights out!" As the dogs rushed in from the side, Pyewacket, as moved by a friendship strangely struck in that dungeon under Laimak, fastened her teeth in the backside of one, so that, missing of his spring, with a howl of pain he turned to fight her. Another, Lessingham stabbed dead with a dagger snatched left-handed from his belt; but, since a man's eyes look but one way, the Vicar, foining at Lessingham's middle, passed under his guard; but, by good hap, no more than a skin-wound beside the thigh. Amid the rage of the dogs yet worrying and snarling, and the charging against the door by soldiers without, whom the Vicar now in a voice of brass shouted for again and again to come and aid him, Lessingham, free now, albeit hurt, to use his swordsmanship, in a few passes sent the Vicar's weapon flying.

The Vicar, crouching like a cat-a-mountain, seemed for the instant as if he would have leapt onto Lessingham's sword-point. But the hinges began to yield under that thunder of blows, and, as lord of his mind once more, he reared himself up and, stone still and with arms folded, faced Lessingham, who, regarding him again in a high and cool carelessness that was yet alert for all mischiefs, now sheathed his sword. The door gave and fell. A dozen men armed leapt in with it. In the sudden hush of that obstreperous noise the Vicar commanded them, pointing with his finger: "Arrest me that man."

For two breaths they stood doubtful. Then, one by one as their glances met Lessingham's, so one by one they were gathered by him and held. "You have won the wager, cousin," he said, throwing with a laugh his purse of gold on the table. "And truth to tell, I feared you would. Not your own men, at your own bidding, will so far forget your highness's edict as lay hand upon the King's Captain-General."

With swift comprehension, the Vicar, bursting into a great bois-terous laugh, clapped him on the back, took the purse, tossed it up ringing in the air, caught it, and thrust it away in his bosom.

When they were alone again, "Well, fanged adder?" said Les-singham, speaking low; "so you dare try masteries with me? So you set your dogs on me, ha?" Pyewacket, looking up at him, fawned and wagged her tail; "set your men on me?"

The Vicar, sitting at the table sideways, left hand akimbo on his hip, right elbow crooked far forward on the table top, the hand a rest for his mighty jowl, looked steadily up at Lessingham. "You have forgot your part," he said, and his voice, low and quiet, came like the dank air from some grave. "And your hand is out."

To Lessingham, thus looking down into the eyes of his cousin, it was as if their hard and adamantine lustre and wicked fires should have been but the image upon a still water, in depths whereof, were no image there to veil them, deadlier matters should have been beheld. And now, as upon that surface, memories stirred like a flaw of wintry air, blurring the image: memories of a voice which, a year ago, borne up loud and hoarse over water, had unsphered a sum-mer night and withered fair flesh to a mountain-lynx's pelt and sinew and claw.

The Vicar seemed to wait. There seemed a contentment in his waiting, as of one that had weighed all and all determined. But to questioning eyes his countenance showed no answer. As well might a man, looking from the fields across to Laimak, have hoped to divine, only with such looking, the prison-houses that lay quarried in the rock's bowels: the prisoners, their names, qualities, aspects, and conditions, who rotted in those prisons: the deaths some died there.

"By God, then, I will teach you," Lessingham said. "By God, I will tread you under feet. Come, you shall be my secretary. Write," he said, thrusting from Gabriel's table the means before him, and taking out, to read from it, the damning document: "'tis well enough worded, do it out fair. 'Unto the most high king'—foh! the words foul my mouth. On then: your own invention: out with it: all the sweet persuasive points, the special trust and affiance he hath in you, as fitted by nature for rapes and treasons and all villany: let not the filth be in doubt, you are his good jade, hate us all, too, 'cause of your quondamship:[5] let him but trap you in gold, *quid pro quo,* vicariate and so forth, as here set down, and you'll have us all murdered with bodkins pat o' the eve of his coming south hither: and now, time that for Mornagay, night o' the first new moon in August. Write," he said, and it was as if the rehearsing only of the thing had blown his cooling rage to great flames again within him. "We shall be ready. O this is double treason! lure him like a polecat to the gin."

The Vicar in all this moved not at all. Only across his eyes, adder-like, resting on Lessingham, it was as if a film had been drawn, veiling the unfoldings of his thought; and along the lips of him something, the scales whereof glinted colours of mockery, gaiety, and disdain, seemed to draw its subtle length. At last, taking up the pen, he with awkward slow unclerkly fingers began to write under Lessingham's eye. When it was done he pushed it towards Lessingham, who took and read it. "Is it fit?"

Lessingham read. "It will serve."

"Reach me the wax," said the Vicar. "A candle: so." He sealed it. "What safe hand now have you to bear it? There's heading business in this were't wrongly handled. Where's Gabriel?"

"Give it to me," Lessingham said. "I'll be bearer of both." The Vicar gave it in silence. In silence their eyes engaged. Then first this paper, then that (which Gabriel had disgorged), Lessingham held in the candleflame: scornfully beheld them catch fire, curl up, flare, burn down, fall in black ashes. "Ah, cousin, am I yet to teach you," he said, "that I do that I will do, not upon condition of this and that, as use your bungerly foul plots, but in my own way, and with clean hands?"

He turned and went. The Vicar, watching his passage to the door, the sweep of his cloak, the carriage of his head, the swing of his gait to the clanking of golden spurs, narrowed his lids to a gaze serpently shrewd. So, left alone, in a sullen grandeur of storm-tormented sea-cliff against which every great wave that rides crashes and falls broken, he sat, and waited.

In the same hour came Gabriel Flores. The Vicar sat yet in his chamber. Gabriel came tiptoe to the table. "Highness, spake my Lord Lessingham aught to you of the letter I bare? Upon my soul, I would a died sooner—"; here, upon his knees he blubbered out the story.

"Well," said the Vicar when it was done: "give you your due, you did all you might. This but shows I'd better a holden to my resolve, spite of all, to put nought in writing."

"There's this," Gabriel said: "not a soul hath knowledge of the thing except you and me and his lordship. Not Amaury, I know: they spake not together but in my presence, I swear to you, and then one rode north, t'other south to you. Hath your highness the paper?"

"I have both had it and burnt it."

"Good so far," said Gabriel; then paused. His furtive gaze came again under his master's eye. "Lord, I pray you, 'tis but my love and service speaketh: be not angry. But must your highness not fear lest he will not thus leave you, nor your part in this, undiscovered?"

The Vicar looked down upon him. "The Duke," he said, "with five thousand men, will be here afore sunset." He paused. Gabriel met his eye and trembled. "And so, my nobs and cony sweet, infix your mind to virtue and prudence: employment in a work shall please your disposition, and upon a very small warning. Look you, the skies do thunder. My cousin Lessingham: let not the Duke nor any of these come at him, on your life."

Gabriel bared his teeth like a stoat. "What means shall I use?"

"All means, so nor you nor I be not seen in it. Give me notice in some secret sort when you have prepared the thing."

Gabriel gave a little laugh. There was a fell and ugly look on the face of him.

"How now?" said the Vicar, "are you afeared?"

"Of your highness somewhat. Not of aught else."

"The deed is meritorious."

"Ay. I trow it should not much go to my heart so that another did it. But would your highness would give a name to the deed. I durst not go by guess."

"Will you play bodger with me, you scurvy scrub? Is not your life mine? Standeth there aught but my might and my name 'twixt you and a hundred men that have no dearer wish than your heart were leaping in their hand? Will you traffic with me, filth?"

"Your highness knoweth my inward mind," replied he. "I would but be sure you know your own: will not repent and tear me in pieces, who did you this service, when 'tis done."

"Go, I'll tell you," said the Vicar. "There is i' the camp here, and walked from this chamber not ten minutes since, one that hath to-day with so many and vile injuries abused me and borne me such derision as, not were he set upon the inflexible purpose to destroy himself, might he a done more. I will use him no longer. Choose your instrument: let him think this is done i' the Duke's service; that there have been promises he caused to be performed in these late peace-makings to the feeblishment of the duchy; that the Duke will reward it if the person be made away."

Gabriel looked at him: ran his tongue along his lips. "I have a lad for the work, manful of mind, but as wise as a woodcock. How likes your highness this pleasantness, to do it in sight of the Duke before they may come to speech together? and I being by, soon as the stroke is struck, will, in a seeming indignation to revenge it, stab the striker, and so, sith dead men tell no tales—?"

"Enough. Away and to it. And the Devil and the whirlwind be your helpers."

Gabriel went. The Vicar, sitting awhile in his melancholy with the westering sun beginning now through the window to shine into his eyes, yielded his hand to Pyewacket's nuzzling cold nose and restfully with his fingers searched her jowl and behind her ear. "Ay, my brach," he said in himself: "I'll not blame you to a ta'en his part, all and it had been easier otherways. Dead men, quotha?" he said in himself after a minute, and the wings of his nostrils hardened suddenly. "May be, poor pug, you counselled me more wholesomely than you bargained for."

The day was near spent when the Duke with the forward of his army began their winding ascent by the Killary road towards Mornagay. The Vicar, with Lessingham and a dozen other of his gentlemen about him, came a little upon the road to bring him in with honour. Before the hostelry where they lodged, a score of trumpeters took their stand, and bagpipers wearing the Parry's livery of russet and purple, and drummers, and fifty spearmen to be a guard of honour, and bearers of the banners of Fingiswold and Rerek: all in a golden magnificence of the declining sun, and in a windless summer stillness. The Vicar was in his robes of state, and bare-headed, save for his circlet of gold: Lessingham, upon his right, went armed to the throat, but without his helm. Gabriel Flores, like a shadow, kept step with his lord, a little behind, and betwixt the two of them.

"You look merry, cousin," said the Vicar as they walked.

"Not merry," Lessingham answered: "contented."

"With that you have? or with that you look to?"

"Contented," answered Lessingham, "that all sorteth now to wished effect: power where, were it mine to give, I would give it; and our sword, not now to be escaped neither eluded, lifted up against our enemy." Upon that word, there seemed a triumph to clothe him, such as stars wear riding between clouds in a gale at sea, when all perils of night and shipwreck are become but a carpet unrolled for those flaming feet to walk on. His eye, as from that pinnacled certitude, met the Vicar's, that till now had avoided the encounter.

They halted. The Duke on his white pawing stallion, with the Chancellor upon his right and the Meszrian lords in great splendour about him, was approached now within twenty paces and still came on. Trumpeters sounded the royal salute. In Gabriel's secret ear the Vicar flung a sudden word: "I have changed my mind. Prevent it." In this, at ten paces' distance, Barganax and Lessingham met eye to eye. And even as Barganax a year ago in Acrozayana had, upon such an eye-glance, seemed to behold very incarnate in Lessingham the masculine of his own dark lady and queen of his desires, so Lessingham now, in a slow astonishment to master body and soul, beheld in Barganax the like marvel; and then, in a moment, as night is opened for a flash with lightning, not that masculine, but, as to carry perfection beyond perfection, her, very Antiope: given back, for that flash, in this world-without-end sunset hour of Mornagay, this place of beginnings and of endings.

Gabriel was too late. The murderer, shouting, "This from the great Duke of Zayana!" sent it down a foot deep into Lessingham between neck and gorget. In the same instant Gabriel, swift upon his cue, had despatched the doer of the deed beyond justification, repentance, or confession. The Vicar, amid the sudden huge turmoil, smiting left and right with his hand-mace, struck with the one stroke his kinsman's slayer, that reeled butchered already by Gabriel's sword, and with the other his last imaginable danger extant and repository of his secret treason: Gabriel Flores. Whose brains, as serviceable unto this extremity, but now no further, to the master he had so faithfully nursed and obeyed, were thus, for last warranty of that master's safety, spattered unregarded upon the grass.

But the Vicar, that had for this safety so much adventured and so much cast away, looking up, swift from these strokes, into Barganax's face, stood as a man at whose feet suddenly opens the abyss. For there glared upon him out of that face not Barganax's eyes, but eyes speckled and grey: the eyes of Lessingham.

And Barganax, in a voice like a great crack of thunder, commanded them, "Take the Vicar!"

XXII

ZIMIAMVIAN NIGHT

Antiphone to dawn[1] ✦ *Her infinite variety* ✦
"More than was promised or was due" ✦
Moonset between the worlds.

FIORINDA, in the Duke's private lodging that looks from the citadel over Zayana lake, set down her crystal, having beheld that end. The eye of day stared red now from a split in the clouds that shrouded up the evening, west over Ambremerine; in which glare of settle-gang,[2] all the element was become as a flame: tongues of it licking the folds and falls of the damask table-cloth: sparks of it in momentary death and birth upon every shining surface of knife or fork, goblet, platter, or smooth-skinned fruit: smoke of it invading the dimness of Barganax's bedchamber which, within part-opened folding doors, stood void and dream-fast as upon memories of so many sunsets, and of lamplight times, and pleasure, and sleep, and dawn, and the long interludes of clear daylight emptiness which is, for beds, their night-time and time of reposing. And in the proud pallour of that lady's brow and cheek, and in the exaltation of her carriage, the glory sat throned, gleaming again from her jet-black seat-waved hair; and of it some touch or savour was in the terrible and unfathomable eyes of her, as she stood so, and upon such tidings, gazing from that high western window into the conflagration of the west.

So she stood, while night gathered. Colour began to fail before the shades, both here in the room with its so many rarities of gold-

303

broidered curious hangings, rich and costly treasures of furniture, and lilied golden chapiters of pillars and gold-wrought ceiling; and, without, in the lake stretching dim, and in the mountains companying with clouds and frozen immensities of night, and in the flowers of Barganax's gardens folding their petals for sleep. "So falls a thundered tower," she said. From some pinebranch in the garden beneath, a nightjar thrilled. "No self—but All," she said.

She took a taper: lighted it where the fire was dying on the hearth: lighted the candles. Wine was on the table, and crystal beakers. She filled one and held it up, crowned with foam, between her eye and the candles, watching the beads mount upwards: through a golden element, atomies of golden fire. She quaffed it down and turned to the looking-glass. And now, with movements swift, yet of an easy staid nobility of sequence as when the leafage of a wood sways to the wind in summer, loosing of girdle and brooch and pin, she put off her ruby-spangled red silken dress and all raiment else, and so, in that mixed light of candles and afterglow, fronted in a stillness her own image in the glass. With a strange look she beheld it, like as a year ago last May, in that other great mirror within, at dawn she had beheld it, upon the morrow of his twenty-fifth birthday: a distant, appraising, look. With such an eye might her lover himself have considered not her, but one of those many portraitures he painted of her and had smudged then or slashed to oblivion, as being not her, or at least not her enough. But not with such lips. For that which, sleeping or waking, held licence of the lips of that lady, inhabiting the corners of her mouth: a thing once bottled by him in paint but straight let out again: this woke and viewed in the glass now its own superlative, which thence, with a sidelong look, acknowledged her.

"Fiorinda," she said. "Mary," she said. "Antiope." The names remained on the silence like ripples on still water. She took out the pins one by one, and let down in floods of blackness her hair; and so, yet gazing in the glass, settled upon a couch that faced it, her feet along the couch, her right hand making a rest for her cheek. So in the mirror she regarded for another while with flickering eyelids that which was of itself mirror of all wonders; her beauty-clad naked body, awful as mountains in the dawn, and completing and making up in its Greek perfection quintessences of night and of scented gardens and of glory of sun and moon, and, in eyes, the sea. With hands clasped behind her head, she leaned back now upon the cushions of honey-coloured silk, watching in the glass her image, which now began to change. And so watching, she named the changes by names whereof but the spoken sound is a train of fire, beauty across darkness: Pentheseleia,[3] Lydian Omphale,[4] Hypermnestra,[5] Semiramis,[6] Roxana,[7] Berenice;[8] spotless and unparagoned Zenobia,[9] Queen of Palmyra, Queen of the East, for so long time matched against the overmastering odds of imperial Rome, and in the end triumphed on yet not dishonoured; Gudrun of Laxriverdale;[10] Petrarch's Laura;[11] Boccaccio's Fiammetta;[12] Giulia Farnese,[13] Vittoria Corombona,[14] and the white and deadly blossom of the house of Borgia.[15] Even, passing all these, her for whom Trojans and well-greaved Achaians so long time suffered sorrows;[16] and, (mother of her), that Argive Queen, lovely-ankled Leda,[17] and other earth-born paramours of Olympian Zeus. And with every change, it was as if the likeness in the mirror was yet her own, or, at least, part of her.

Her left hand, lazily fallen behind the milk-white somnolent supple grandeur of her thigh, chanced between couch and cushion upon a book there, slipped down and forgotten. Drawing it forth, she opened it and knew the writing: the Greek upon the left, Barganax's Englishing of it upon the right:

ποικιλόθρον' ἀθάνατ' Αφροδιτα,
παῖ Διος, δολόπλοκε, λισσομαι σε

So far she read, softly, aloud, in a voice that took on, with the Poetess's words, a more diviner grace, as with a letting through, by some momentary rift between time and eternity, of some far-off cadence of the honey-sweet imperishable laughter:

"Sparkling-thronéd heavenly Aphrodite,
Child of God, beguilder of guiles—beseech You,
Not with sating, neither with ache and anguish,
⠀⠀⠀⠀Lady, my heart quell.

"Nay, but come down, if it be true indeed that
Once to cry of mine from a far place list'ning
You did hark and, leaving Your Father's golden
⠀⠀⠀⠀House, did come down with

"Chariot yok'd and harness'd, and so in beauty
O'er the black earth swift-flying doves did draw You,
Filling high heav'n full of the rush of wing-beats
⠀⠀⠀⠀Down the mid ether.

"Swift, and they were vanisht. But You, most blessed,
Smil'd with eyes and heavenly mouth immortal,
Asking me what suffer'd I then, or why then
⠀⠀⠀⠀Call'd I on You, and

"What, all else beyond, I desir'd befall me,
In my wild heart: 'Who shall, at My sweet suasion,

> Even thee lead into her love? Who is't, O
> Sappho, hath wrong'd thee?

> " 'For, though she fly, presently she shall seek thee;
> Ay, though gifts she'll none of, yet she shall give thee;
> Ay, and kiss not, presently she shall kiss thee,
> All and unwilling.'

> "Very now come so, and, from cares that tangle,
> Loose; and whatsoever to bring to pass my
> Heart hath thirsted, bring it to pass; and be Your-
> Self my great ally."[18]

She stood up, saying again, in Her beauty-blushing orient, those last words again:

> "Σὺ δ' αὐτα
> σύμμαχος ἔσσο'

"Yes; for so will I be petitioned," said She. "Yes; and by such great mettled and self wild hawks, which fall and perish in their height. I promise: do I not perform? O more than either was promised or was due."

Upon a table by the couch, in a golden bowl, were roses, withered and dead. She took one and held it, like Cleopatra's aspick, to the flower of Her own breast. And, as if to show upon experiment that in that place nothing but death can die and corruption self-corrupted fall like a foul garment to leave perfection bare, all the starved petals of the rose, shrivelled and brown, opened into life again, taking on again the smoothness and softness of the flesh of a living flower: a deep red rose, velvet-dark that the sense should ache at it, with a blueness in its darkest darknesses, as if the heavy perfume clung as a mist to dull the red.

As the wind whispers cool through apple-boughs, and sleep streams from their trembling leaves, She spoke again: "One day of Zimiamvia, my Lord Lessingham; one day, my lord Duke. And what is one, in My sight? Did not you say it: *Still about cock-shut time?—Safe in the lowe of the firelight:* Have not I promised it? And now is time for that.

"For now Night," She said, scarce to be heard, "rises on Zimiamvia. And after that, To-morrow, and To-morrow, and To-morrow, of Zimiamvia. And all of Me. What you will. For ever. And if it were possible for more than for ever, for ever more."

Upon the sudden, She put on Her full beauty, intolerable, that no eye can bear, but the hearts of Her doves turn cold, and they drop their wings. So the eternal moment contemplates itself anew beside the eternal sea that sleeps about the heavenly Paphos. Only She was: She, and the hueless waiting wonder of the sea at daybreak, and Her zephyrs, and Her roses, and Her hours with their frontlets of gold.

In that high western room in Acrozayana, the transfiguring glory passed. So shuts darkness behind a meteor that, sliding out of darkness silently between star and star in a splendour to outface all the great lamps of heaven, slides beneath stars silently into the darkness and is gone.

The Lady Fiorinda turned to the sideboard beyond the mirror. Its polished surface was dulled under the dust of neglect. There lay there a sword of Barganax's, a pair of her crimson gloves, a palette of his with the colours dried up on it, and a brush or two, uncleaned, with the paint clogged stiff in their bristles; and among these toys, two or three pear-shaped drops of coloured glass, one blue, another red, another purple of the nightshade, no bigger than sloes and with long thin tadpole tails, such as are called Rupert's drops. She, upon a remembrance, took one daintily and between jewelled fingers snapped off the end of its tail, and saw the drop crash instantly into dust. So she dealt with another and beheld it shatter: another, and beheld that: so, till all were ruined; and so stood for a while, looking upon their ruin, as if remembered of the saying of that old man. At last, she went to the window and stood, and so after a time sat down there in the window, upon cushions of cloth of gold. Her face, turned side-face to the room and the warmth, was outlined against night that rolled up now filthy and black. When, after a long time, She spoke as if in a dream, it might have been Her own Poetess herself speaking out of the darkness in the high between the worlds:

> "Δέδυκε μέν ά σελαννα
> και ΓΓληιαδες, μέσαι δέ
> νύκτες, παρά δ' έρΧετ' ώρα,
> έγω δέ μόνα κατεύδω.

> "The moon is set, and set are
> The Pleiades; and midnight
> Soon; so, and the hour departing:
> And I, on my bed,—alone."[19]

Motionless She sat: Her gaze downward: upper lids level and still: eyes still and wide. There was no sound now save in changeless ceaseless rhythm, through the open window of the Duke's great bedchamber and the open door that led there, the land-wash of the sea.

Seeing that Her thoughts are higher than our thoughts, it were the part of a fool to think to comprehend them, or set them down. And yet, very because that they are higher, it sorts not to man to let them go by: rather note such looks and such casts which, upon such nights, have ere this shadowed the outward seeming of Her divinity; as if that impossible were possible, and His hand had failed wherein Her weak perfections lie trembling; or as if the thunder of His power were turned an insensate thing, and His eyes seeled up, and love found but a school-name, and She (for all that nought else is of worth or of verity) found not worth much at last. And as if, under the imagination of such thoughts in Her—Who of Her vernal mere unquestioned I AM recreates and sets Him on high, the patent of Whose omnipotency is but to tender and serve Her—the very heart of the world should be closed with anguish.

As the glory, so now this agony passed, resumed so, with that glory, into Her pavilion of Night.

> Χαῖρ' ἑλικοβλέφαρε, γλυκυμείλιΧε' δὸς δ' ἐν ἀγῶνι
> νίκην τῷδε φέρεσθαι, ἐμὴν δ' ἔντυνον ἀοιδήν.
> αὐτὰρ ἐγὼ καὶ Σεῖο καὶ ἄλλης μνήσομ' ἀοιδῆς.

> —Hymn to Aphrodite

VOLUME TWO

A FISH DINNER IN
MEMISON

This divine beauty is evident, fugitive, impalpable, and homeless in a world of material fact; yet it is unmistakably individual and sufficient unto itself, and although perhaps soon eclipsed is never really extinguished: for it visits time and belongs to eternity.

GEORGE SANTAYANA

Χοόνια μέν τὰ τῶν θεῶνύῶς, πως, εις τέλος δ' ουΧ
ἀοϑενή.

EURIPIDES, *Ion*, 1615

       . . . though what if Earth
Be but the shaddow of Heav'n, and therein
Each to other like, more than on earth is thought?

MILTON, *Paradise Lost*, V. 571

Ces serments, ces parfums, ces baisers infinis,
Renaîtront-ils d'un gouffre interdit à nos sondes,
Comme montent au ciel les soleils rajeunis
Après s'être lavés au fond des mers profondes?
—O serments! ô parfums! ô baisers infinis!

BAUDELAIRE, *Le Balcon*

ελϑε μοι Χαὶ νύν, Χαλεπάν δέ λύσον
ἐΧ μεοιμνάν, ὄσσα δέ μοι τελέσσαι
ϑύμος ἱμέοοει τέλεσον Σὺ δ' αῦτα
σύμμαΧος ἔσσο.

SAPPHO, *Ode to Aphrodite*

To my son-in-law
FLYING OFFICER
KENNETH HESKETH HIGSON
who in an air fight
over Italy saved his
four companions' lives
at cost of his own
I dedicate this book
which he had twice read.

I THANK those who have helped and inspired me with their criticism, notably George Rostrevor Hamilton and Kenneth Hesketh Higson; also Gerald Ravenscourt Hayes for his excellent map, which should help readers in picturing to themselves the country where the action takes place; and I thank Edward Abbe Niles, for nearly twenty years friend and supporter of my work in our great sister-country the United States of America.

In Doctor Vandermast's aphorisms students of Spinoza may often recognize their master's words, charged, no doubt, with implications which go beyond his meaning. Lovers of the supreme poetess will note that, apart from quotations, I have not scrupled to enrich my pages with echoes of her: this for the sufficient reason that Sappho, above all others, is the poet not of "that obscure Venus of the hollow hill" but of "awful gold-crowned, beautiful Aphrodite."

E. R. EDDISON

A LETTER OF INTRODUCTION

To George Rostrevor Hamilton[1]

My dear George,

    You have, for both my Zimiamvian books, so played Pallas Athene—sometimes to my Achilles sometimes to my Odysseus[2]—counselling, inciting, or restraining, and always with so foster-brotherly an eye on the object we are both in love with, that it is to you sooner than to anyone else that this letter should be addressed. To you, a poet and a philosopher: from me, who am no poet (for my form is dramatic narrative in prose), nor philosopher either. Unless to be a humble lover of wisdom earns that name, and to concern myself as a storyteller not so much with things not of this world as with those things of this world which I take to be, because preëminently valuable, therefore preëminently real.

    The plain "daylight" parts of my story cover the years from April 1908 to October 1933; while, as for the month that runs contemporaneously in Zimiamvia (from Midsummer's Day, Anno Zayanae Conditae 775,[3] when the Duke first clapped eyes on his Dark Lady,[4] to the 25th July, when his mother, the Duchess of Memison, gave that singular supper-party), it is sufficient to reflect that the main difference between earth and heaven may lie in this: that here we are slaves of Time, but there the Gods are masters.

    There are no hidden meanings: no studied symbols or allegories. It is the defect of allegory and symbolism to set up the general above the individual, the abstract above the concrete, the idea above the person. I hold the contrary: to me the value of the sunset is not that it suggests to me ideas of eternity; rather, eternity itself acquires value to me only because I have seen it (and other matters besides) in the sunset and (shall we say) in the proud pallour of Fiorinda's brow and cheeks—even in your friend, that brutal ferocious and lionlike fox, the Vicar of Rerek—and so have foretasted its perfections.

Personality is a mystery: a mystery that darkens as we suffer our imagination to speculate upon the penetration of human personality by Divine, and vice versa. Perhaps my three pairs of lovers are, ultimately, but one pair. Perhaps you could as truly say that Lessingham, Barganax, and the King (on the one hand), Mary, the Duchess, and Fiorinda (on the other) are but two persons, each at three several stages of "awakeness," as call them six separate persons.

And there are other teasing mysteries besides this of personality. For example: Who am I? Who are you? Where did we come from? Where are we going? How did we get here? What is "here"? Were we ever not "here," and, if so, where were we? Shall we someday go elsewhere? If so, where? If not, and yet we die, what is Death? What is Time, and why? Did it have a beginning, and will it have an end? Whatever the answer to the last two questions, (i.e., that time had a beginning or that it had not: or an end) is either alternative conceivable? Are not both equally inconceivable? What of Space (on which very similar riddles arise)? Further, *Why* are we here? What is the good of it all? What do people mean when they speak of Eternity, Omnipotence, God? What do they mean by the True, the Good, the Beautiful? Do these "great and thumping words" relate to any objective truth, or are they empty rhetoric invented to cheer or impress ourselves and others: the vague expressions of vague needs, wishes, fears, appetites of us, weak children of a day, who know little of (and matter less to) the vast, blind, indifferent, unintelligible, inscrutable machine or power or flux or nothingness, on the skirts of whose darkness our brief lives flicker for a moment and are gone?

And if this is the true case of us and our lives and loves and all that we care for, then Why is it?

> Ah, Love! could you and I with Him conspire
> To grasp this sorry Scheme of Things entire,
>   Would not we shatter it to bits—and then
> Re-mould it nearer to the Heart's Desire![5]

Why not? Why is there Evil in the world?

Such, in rapid and superficial survey, are the ultimate problems of existence; "riddles of the Sphinx" which, in one shape or another, have puzzled men's minds and remained without any final answer since history began, and will doubtless continue to puzzle and elude so long as mankind continues upon this planet.

But though it is true that (as contrasted with the special sciences) little progress has been made in philosophy: that we have not to-day superseded Plato and Aristotle in the sense in which modern medicine has superseded Hippocrates and Galen: yet, on the negative side and particularly in metaphysics, definite progress has been made.

Descartes' *Cogito ergo sum*[6]—"I think; therefore I exist"—has been criticized not because its assumptions are too modest, but because they are too large. Logically it can be reduced to *cogito,* and even that has been shorn of the implied *ego.* That is to say, the momentary fact of consciousness is the only reality that cannot logically be doubted; for the mere act of doubting, being an act of consciousness, is of itself immediate proof of the existence of that which was to be the object of doubt.

Consciousness is therefore the fundamental reality, and all metaphysical systems or dogmas which found themselves on any other basis are demonstrably fantastic. In particular, materialistic philosophies of every kind and degree are fantastic.

But, because demonstrably fantastic, they are not therefore demonstrably false. We cannot, for instance, be reasonably driven to admit that some external substance called "matter" is prior to or condition of consciousness; but just as little can we reasonably deny the *possibility* of such a state of things. For, logically, denial is as inadmissible as assertion, when we face the ultimate problems of existence outside the strait moment of consciousness which is all that certainly remains to us after the Cartesian analysis. Descartes, it is true, did not leave it at that. But he had cleared the way for Hume and Kant[7] to show that, briefly, every assumption which he himself or any other metaphysician might produce like a rabbit from the hat must have been put into the hat before being brought out. In other words, the scientific method, applied to these problems and pressed to its logical implications, leads to an agnosticism which must go to the whole of experience, as Pyrrho's[8] did, and not arbitrarily stop short at selected limits, as did the agnosticism of the nineteenth century. It leads, therefore, to an attitude of complete and speechless scepticism.

If we think this conclusion a *reductio ad absurdum,* and would seek yet some touchstone for the false and the true, we must seek it elsewhere than in pure reason. That is to say (confining the argument to serious attitudes of speculation on the ultimate problems of existence), we must at that stage abandon the scientific attitude and adopt the poet's. By the poet's I mean that attitude which says that ultimate truths are to be attained, if at all, in some immediate way: by vision rather than by ratiocination.

How, then, is the poet to go to work, voyaging now in alternate peril of the Scylla and Charybdis[9] which the Cartesian-Kantian criticism has laid bare—the dumb impotence of pure reason on the one hand, and on the other a welter of disorganized fantasy through which reason of itself is powerless to choose a way since to reason (in these problems) "all things are possible" and no fantasy likelier than another to be true?

Reason, as we have seen, reached a certain bed-rock, exiguous but unshakable, by means of a criticism based on credibility: it cleared away vast superfluities of baseless system and dogma by divesting itself of all beliefs that it was possible to doubt. In the same way, may it not be possible to reach a certain bed-rock among the chaos of fantasy by means of a criticism based not on credibility but on value?

No conscious being, we may suppose, is without desire; and if certain philosophies and religions have set up as their ideal of salvation and beatitude a condition of desirelessness, to be attained by an asceticism that stifles and starves every desire, this is no more than to say that those systems have in fact applied a criticism of values to dethrone all minor values, leaving only this state of blessedness which (notwithstanding their repudiation of desire) remains as (for their imagination at least) the one thing desirable. And in general, it can be said that no religion, no philosophy, no considered view of the world and human life and destiny has ever been formulated without some affirmation, express or implied, of what is or is not to be desired: and it is this star, for ever unattained yet for ever sought, that shines through all great poetry, through all great music, painting, building, and works of men, through all noble deeds, loves, speculations, endurings and endeavours, and all the splendours of "earth and the deep sky's ornament"[10] since history began, and that gives (at moments, shining through) divine perfection to some little living thing, some dolomite wall lighted as from within by the low red sunbeams, some skyscape, some woman's eyes.

This then, whatever we name it,—the thing desirable not as a means to something else, be that good or bad, high or low (as food is desirable for nourishment; money, for power; power, as a means either to tyrannize over other men or to benefit them; long life, as a means to achievement of great undertaking, or to cheat your heirs; judgement, for success in business; debauchery, for the "bliss proposed;" wind on the hills, for inspiration; temperance, for a fine and balanced life), but for itself alone,—this, it would seem, is the one ultimate and infinite *Value*. By a procedure corresponding to that of Descartes when, by doubting all else, he reached through process of elimination something that he could not doubt, we have, after rejecting all things whose desirableness depends on their utility as instruments to ends beyond themselves, reached something desirable as an end in itself. What it is in concrete detail, is a question that may have as many answers as there are minds to frame them ("In my Father's house are many mansions"). But to deny its existence, while not a self-contradictory error palpable to reason (as is the denial of the Cartesian *cogito),* is to affirm the complete futility and worthlessness of the whole of Being and Becoming.

It is not to be gainsaid that a position of complete scepticism and complete nihilism in regard to objective truth and objective value is, logically, unassailable. But since, logically, he who takes up that position must remain speechless (for nothing, *ex hypothesi,* can be affirmed, nor does anybody exist to listen to the affirmation), must desire nothing (for there is nothing to be desired), and do nothing (for nothing is worth doing), therefore "the rest is silence."

Proceeding, then, on the alternative supposition—that is to say, accepting the fact of consciousness as our fundamental reality and this undefined but unelimenable "one thing desirable" as the fundamental value—we are free to speculate on the ultimate problems of metaphysics, using as instrument of investigation our mind at large, which includes (but is not restricted to) the analytic reason. Such speculation is what, for want of a better word, I have called *poetic.* It might (with some danger of misconception) also be called the kind of speculation appropriate to the lunatic, or to the lover! for—

> The lunatic, the lover, and the poet,
> Are of imagination all compact.[11]

Three broad considerations may here be touched on:

(1) It does not seem necessary to postulate a plurality of ultimate values. Truth, Beauty, Goodness are commonly so postulated. The claim of Truth, however, can hardly survive examination. On the one hand, the empirical truths of science or the abstract truths of mathematics are "values" either as a means to power, or else for a kind of rightness or perfection which they seem to possess: a perfection which seems to owe its value to a kind of Beauty. On the other hand, Truth in the abstract (the quite neutral judgement, "That which is, is") can have no value whatsoever: it acquires value only in so far as "that which is" is desirable in itself, and not merely on account of its "truth." If Schopenhauer's *The World as Will and Idea*[12] is a statement of the truth, then truth has, ultimately, a negative value and we are better off without it (except as a means to power, etc.). Truth, therefore, is only an ultimate value if it is good. But the "Good," again, is ambiguous, meaning both (a) good as an end to be desired, and (b) moral good. In sense (a) it is surely tautologous to speak of the "good" as distinct from the beautiful; in sense (b) it is arguable (and, as I myself hold, true) that acts are morally "good" only insofar as, in the last analysis, they tend to create, serve, or safeguard Beauty. The trinity of so-called "ultimate values" is thus reduced to one.

(2) No sane theory of values will ultimately square with the facts of this world as we know it "here and now." But ultimate value, as

we have seen, is one of the "bed-rocks": not so, however, this world, which we know only empirically and as a particular phase of our other "bed-rock" (viz. consciousness). Accordingly, the test of any metaphysic is not that it should square with the world as we know it, but that it should square with the ultimate value. (Cf. Vandermast's words—*Mistress of Mistresses*, p. 250—"In this supermundal science concerning the Gods, determination of what Is proceedeth inconfutably and only by argument from what Ought to be.")

(3) Concrete reality, whether as consciousness or as value, has two aspects which are never in fact separated or separable: the One and the Many: the Universal and the Particular: the Eternal and the Temporal: the Never Changing and the Ever Changing. It is the inseparability of these modes of Being that makes it idle to seek abstract Beauty, Truth, Goodness, apart from their particular manifestations, and equally idle (conversely) to try to isolate the particulars. The Many are understandable only as manifestations of the One: the One, only as incarnate in the Many. Abstract statements, therefore, such as have been occupying our attention in the preceeding pages, can bear no nearer relation to the concrete truths which they describe than (for example) the system of latitude and longitude bears to the solid earth we live on.

It is on these terms only, then (as an explanation of our "latitude and longitude"), that it is possible to sum up in a few lines the conception which underlies *Mistresses of Mistresses* and *A Fish Dinner in Memison*.

In that conception, ultimate reality rests in a Masculine-Feminine dualism, in which the old trinity of Truth, Beauty, Goodness is extended to embrace the whole of Being and Becoming; Truth consisting in this—That Infinite and Omnipotent Love creates, preserves, and delights in. Infinite and Perfect Beauty: *(Infinitus Amor potestate infinitâ Pulchritudinem infinitam in infinitâ perfectione creatur et conservatur).* Love and Beauty are, in this duality, coequal and coeternal; and, by a violent antinomy, Love, owing his mere being to this strengthless perfection which he holds at his mercy, adores and is enslaved by her, while Beauty (by a like antinomy) queens it over the very omnipotence which both created her and is her only safeguard.

Ultimate reality, as was said above, must be concrete; and an infinite power, creating and enjoying an infinite value, cannot be cribbed or frozen in a single manifestation. It must, on the contrary, be capable of presenting itself in an infinite number of aspects to different minds and at different moments; and every one of these aspects must be true and (paradoxically) complete, whereas no abstract statement, however profound in its analysis, can ever be either complete or true. This protean character of truth is the philosophical justification for religious toleration; for it is almost inconceivable that truth, realized in the richness of its concrete actuality, should ever present itself to two minds alike. Churches, creeds, schools of thought, or systems of philosophy are expedient, useful or harmful, as the case may fall out. But the ultimate Vision—the "flesh and blood" actuality behind these symbols and formulas—is to them as the living body is to apparel which conceals, disguises, suggests, or adorns that body's perfections.

This "flesh and blood," then, so far as it shapes itself in *Mistress of Mistresses* and is on the way to further definition in the *Fish Dinner*, shows this ultimate dualism as subsisting in the two supreme Persons, the divine and perfect and eternal He and She, *Zeus* and *Aphrodite*, "more real than living man." All men and women, all living creatures, the whole phenomenal world material and spiritual, even the very forms of Being—time, space, eternity—do but subsist in or by the pleasure of these Two, partaking (every individual soul, we may think, in its degree) of Their divine nature. "The Lord possessed Me in the beginning of His way, before His works of old. I was set up from everlasting, from the beginning, or ever the earth was . . . When He prepared the Heavens I was there: when he set a compass on the face of the depth: when He established the clouds above: when He strengthened the fountains of the deep: when He gave to the sea His decree, that the waters should not pass His commandment: when He appointed the foundations of the earth: then I was by Him, as one brought up with Him, and I was daily His delight, rejoicing always before Him . . . Whoso findeth Me findeth life, and shall obtain favour of the Lord. But he that sinneth against me wrongeth his own soul: all they that hate Me love death" (*Proverbs, VIII:* there spoken by *Wisdom;* but it is truer of a less mundane matter. For wisdom can never be an ultimate value but a means only to something beyond itself, e.g. a guide to action; whereas She (*l'inutile Beauté*) is not a means but the end and mistress of all action, the sole thing desirable for Herself alone, the *causa immanens* of the world and of very Being and Becoming:—"Before the day was, I am She.")

Mundane experience, it must be admitted, goes, broadly, against all this: it affords little evidence of omnipotent love, but much of feeble, transient, foolish loves: much of powerful hatreds, pain, fear, cruelty. "Tout passe, tout casse, tout lasse:"[13] death, disease, deformity come to mortals indiscriminately. "And captive good attending captain ill"—this and all the accusations of Shakespeare's LXVIth sonnet[14] are true of "this vain world," and always have been true. This world, to say the best of it, has always been both good and bad; to say the best of it, it is a flux, in which, on the whole, the changes compensate each other.

But (standing upon the rock—the Zeus-Aphrodite dualism) we are faced, in this imperfection of mundane experience, with the problem of Evil; and (standing upon that rock) the only solution we can accept is one that shall concede to Evil something less than reality. Lame excuses for the impotence, unskilfulness, inattentiveness, callousness, or plain malevolence of God Almighty, to which all other solutions of the problem reduce themselves, are incompatible with the omnipotence of Love, which can hardly be supposed to possess, in action, the attributes of an idiot or a devil. (It may be said, no doubt, that Love is *not* omnipotent but subject to some dark Ἀνάγχη, or necessity, that binds even a God. Obviously this can neither be proved nor disproved, but it is repugnant to my judgment. For, if true, it means that the Scheme is indeed rotten at the core.)

Sub specie aeternitatis, therefore, this present world is understandable only on the assumption that its reality is not final but partial. On two alternative hypotheses might it thus be credible—

(i) as something *in the making,* which in future aeons will become perfect;

(ii) as an instrument of ἄσχησις (a training-ground or testing place).

Both hypotheses, however, present difficulties: (i) Why need omnipotence wait for future aeons to arrive? why have imperfections at all? (ii) (The same difficulty in a different aspect) If perfection were available—and, to omnipotence, what is not?—why need omnipotence arrange for tests or trainings?

We are forced back, therefore, on the question: if illusion, *why is there this illusion?*

There seems to be no clear answer to this question; and no certain test (short of experience) of the truth of any particular experience. This world has got to be lived through, and the best way of living through it is a question for *ethics:* the science of the Good in action. A "good" action is an action of Love, i.e. (see p. 317 above) an action which serves *Beauty.* The "good" man in action is therefore doing, so far as his action is good, and so far as his power goes, what the divine eternal Masculine is doing: creating, serving, worshipping, enjoying and loving Her, the divine eternal Feminine. And, by complement, the "good" woman in action is doing, so far as in her lies, what the divine eternal Feminine is doing; completing and making up, that is to say, in her unique person, by and in her action and by and in her passivity, "whatsoever is or has been or shall be desirable, were it in earth or heaven." In action therefore, this is "All ye know on earth, and all ye need to know."[15]

But man is not πράΧτιΧος only but θεωρήτιχος—concerned not with action only but with contemplation—and the unanswered questions in the third preceding paragraph remain. May there possibly be one answer to both? viz. that there is no *necessity* for these peculiar and (to us) inconvenient arrangements, but that—for the moment—they are amusing?

That they are far from *"amusing"* to *us,* here and now—that they daily, for some or other of their helpless victims, produce woes and agonies too horrible for man to endure or even think of—is perhaps because we do not, in the bottom of our hearts, believe in our own immortality and the immortality of those we love. If, for you and me as individuals, this world is the sum, then much of it in detail (and the whole in general plan) is certainly not amusing. But to a mind developed on the lines of the Mahometan fanatic's, the Thug's, the Christian martyr's, is it not conceivable that (short, perhaps, of acute physical torture) the "slings and arrows of outrageous fortune" should be no more painful than the imagined ills of a tragic drama, and could be experienced and appraised with a like detachment? The death of your nearest and dearest, e.g., would be but a deepening of experience for you, if you could believe and know (beyond peradventure and with that immediacy which belongs to sense experience) that there *is* no death, except of the body in this transient and unsatisfactory life; that Truth rests indeed in that eternal duality whereby the One Value is created and tendered by the One Power; that the Truth is not abstract and bodiless, but concrete in all imaginable richness of spirit and sense; that the parting is therefore but for a while; and, last, that the whole of human history, and the material cosmos known to science, are but trivial occurrences—episodes invented perhaps, and then laid aside, as we ourselves might conceive and in a few minutes reject again some theory of the universe, in conversation after supper.

It may be asked, Why not suicide, then, as a way out? Is not that the logic of such an other-worldly philosophy? The answer surely is that there is a beauty of action (as the Northmen knew), and only seldom is suicide a fine act. Unless it is time to "do it in the high Roman fashion": unless we stand where Othello stood, or Cleopatra, suicide is an ignoble act, and, (as such) little to Her liking. The surer we are of Her, therefore, the less we are likely to take, in despair, that dark leap which (though not, as is vulgarly said, an act of cowardice: it demands much courage if done deliberately) is essentially a shirking of the game She sets us. And that game (as no one will doubt, who has looked in the eyes of "sparkling-thronéd heavenly Aphrodite, child of God, beguiler of guiles") is a game which, to please Her, we must play "according to its strict rules."

This book can be read as well before as after *Mistress of Mistresses*. The chief persons appear in both books, but each is a self-contained work complete in itself.

Yours affectionately,

E.R.E.

Dark Lane
Marlborough
Wiltshire
29th July, 1940

I

APHRODITE IN VERONA

CA M'AMUSE."[1] The words, indolent, indolently
fallen along the slowness of a lovely lazy voice, yet
seemed to strike night, no, Time itself, with a sudden
division; like as when that bare arrow-like three-octave
E, high on the first violin, deep on the cello, stabs suddenly the witched quietude of the *andante* in the third Rasoumoffsky
Quartet.[2] A strange trick, indeed, in a woman's voice: able so, with a
chance phrase overheard, to snatch the mind from its voyaging in
this skiff between sightless banks: snatch and translate it so, to some
stance of rock, archaean, gripping the boot-nails, high upon mountains; whence, as gathering your senses out of sleep, you should
seem to discern the true nature of the stream of things. And here,
to-night, in Verona—

Lessingham looked round, quickly enough to catch the half
mocking, half listening, inclination of her head as her lips closed
upon the lingering last syllable of that private "m'amuse." The
words had been addressed, it was clear, to nobody, for she was alone
at her table: certainly not to him: not even (curiously) to herself: to
velvet-bosomed Night, possibly, sister to sister: to the bats, the inat-
tentive stars, this buzz of Latin night-life; little white tables with
their coffee, *vino rosso, vino bianco,* carafe and wine-glass, the music
and the talk; wreaths of cigar-smoke and cigarette-smoke that hung

and dissipated themselves on airs that carried from the flower-beds of the mid piazza a spring fragrancy and, from the breathing presences of women, wafts of a more exotic and a deeper stirring sweetness. Over all, the tremendous curved façade of Diocletian's amphitheatre, ruined deep in time, stood desolate in the glare of electric arclights. In Lessingham's hand arrested on the table-top, the cigar went out. Into the stillness all these things—amphitheatre, electric lights, the Old and the New, this simple art of living, the bat-winged night, the open face of the dark—seemed to gather and, with the slow upsurging might of their rise, to reach to some time-less moment which seemed her; and which seemed as fixed, while beyond it life and the hours streamed unseizable as the unseizable down-streaming spray-motes into which water is dissipated when it falls clear over a great height. *Ça m'amuse.*

Then, even as in the *andante* the processional secular throb of the arpeggios, so Time seemed now to recover balance: catch breath: resume its inexplicable unseizable irreversible way. Not to be explained, yet upon that echo illuminated: not to be caught, yet (for that sudden) unprecedentedly submitting itself within hand-reach: not to be turned back, yet suddenly self-confessed as perhaps not worth the turning. She looked up, and their eyes met.

"Vous parlez français, madame?"

"O, depende dello soggetto: depende con cui si parla.[3] To an Englishman, English."

"Mixed with Italian?"

"Addressed to a person so mixed. Or do I not guess aright?"

Lessingham smiled and replied: "You pay me a doubtful com-pliment, signora. Is it not a saying: 'Inglese Italianato e Diavolo incarnato?'[4] And as for the subject," he said, "if the signora will permit a question: is there then a special fitness to be amused, in French?"

"Simply to be amused—perhaps, No. But to be amused at *this*—Yes."

"And *this* is?—"

Her hand, crimson-gloved, on which till now her cheek had been resting, traced, palm-upwards, a little half circle of disdain indicative of the totality of things. "There is a something logical: a something of precision, about the French, which very well fits this affair. To be polite to it, you must speak of it in French: it is the only language."

"There is in Latin, equally, a precision."

"O but certainly: and in a steam roller: but not altogether *spiri-tuel*. Il faut de l'esprit pour savourer nettement cette affaire-là,"[5] and again her hand delicately acknowledged it: "this clockwork world, this mockshow, operated by Time and the endless chain of cause and effect. Time, if you consider it," she said, "works with so ingenious a simplicity: so perfect a machine. Like a clock. Say you are God: you need but wind it up, and it proceeds with its business: no trouble at all."

"Until," said Lessingham, "you have to wind it up again?"

The lady shrugged her shoulders.

"Signora," he said, "do you remember M. d'Anquetil, at that enjoyable unrestrained supper-party in *La Rôtisserie de la Reine Pédauque?* 'Je vous confierai que je ne crois pas en Dieu.' "

"And permit me, sir," said she, "to continue the quotation from that entertaining book: 'Pour le coup, dit l'abbé, je vous blâme, monsieur.'[6] And yet I am glad; for indeed it is a regrettable defect of character in a young man, to believe in God. But suppose, sir, that you in fact were—shall I say?—endowed with that authority: would you wind it up again?"

He paused before answering, held by the look of her: the passivity of her lips, that was like the swept silences of the sky expectant of dawn, or like the sea's innumerable rippled stillness expectant of the dark after sunset: an assuredness, as native to some power that should so far transcend omnipotence as that it needs no more but merely to be and continue in that passivity, and omnipotence in action must serve it.

Like the oblique wide circle of a swift's flight, down and round and up again, between earth and sky, the winged moment swung: now twenty years backwards into earliest childhood: the tennis lawn, of a June evening, of the old peelhouse where he was born, youngest of seven, of a great border family, between the Solway and the Cumberland hills:[7] church bells, long shadows, Rose of Sharon with its sticky scent: Eton:[8] then, at eighteen (getting on for eight years ago now), Heidelberg, and that unlucky episode that cut his studies short there. Then the Paris years, the Sorbonne, the obsessed concentration of his work in Montmartre studios, ending with the duel with knives with that unsavoury Jew musician[9] to whose Spanish mistress Lessingham, with the inexperienced ardour and quixotism of youth, had injudiciously offered his protection. And so, narrowly escaping imprisonment, to Provence and his Estremaduran Amaryllis: in a few weeks their parting by mutual consent, and his decision (having overspent his allowance, and in case his late adversary, again in hospital, should die, and that be laid at his door) to enlist in the *Légion Etrangère* under an assumed name. His desertion after some months (disillusioned with such a school but pleased with the experience for the power it gave him), and escape through Morocco in Egypt. Arrival penniless at the British Agency: news that his father, enraged at these proceedings, had stopped allowances and cut him out of his will. So, work his passage home as a stoker on a P. & O.: upon his twenty-first birthday, the twenty-fourth of November, 1903, land at Tilbury, and (by his mother's means, that queen of women, seconding friendship and strong argument of flesh and blood) at one again with his father before Christmas; and so a year in England, his own master and with enough money to be trusted to do what money is meant for: look after itself, and leave its owner free. Then east, mainly India: two seasons exploring and climbing, Eastern Himalaya, Karakoram.[10] Journey home, against official advice and without official countenance, dangerously through Afghanistan and Persia: then nearly the whole year 1906 in Greece, on horseback, sailing among the islands, studying in Athens. Then—the nineteenth of December, 1906. Sixteen months ago.

The nineteenth of December: Betelgeuze on the meridian at midnight, his particular star. The beginning: dinner at his sister Anne's, and on with her party to that historic ball at the Spanish Embassy. Queer composition, to let the theme enter *pianissimo*, on muted strings, as it were; inaudible under such a blaring of trumpets. Curious to think of: towards the end of the evening, puzzling over his own scribble on his programme, "Dijon-Fiammetta," against the next waltz, and recalling at last what it stood for: "Fiammetta"—*flame:* red-gold hair, the tea-rose she wore in it, and a creamy dress like the rose's petals. Their dancing: then, afterwards, sitting out on the stairs: then, (as in mutual unspoken agreement to leave deserted partners to their devices in the glitter and heat of the ball-room, and themselves to savour a little longer this quiet), their sitting on, and so through two dances following. Whether Mary was tired, or whether minded to leave the ball of conversation to him, they had talked little. Dark girls were the trumpets in that symphony; and he had throughout the evening neither lacked nor neglected opportunity to store his mind with images of allures, Circean splendours, unstudied witty charms, manifested in several partners of that preferred complexion. The mockery! that on such hushed strings, and thus unremarked, should have been the entry of so imperial a theme. So much so, that the next morning, in idle waking recollection casting up the memories of the night before, he had forgotten her.

And yet, a week later, Christmassing with Anne and Charles at Taverford Manor, he had forgot the others but begun to remember her: first, her talking of *Wuthering Heights,* a very special book of his: then a saying of her own here and there: the very phrase and manner. She had been of few words that night, but those few singularly as if her own yet not self-regarding: pure Maryisms: daffodils or stars of the blackthorn looking on green earth or out to the sun. As for instance this (comparing Highlanders and the Tyrolese): "Mountain people seem all rather the same,—vague and butterflyish. If they lose something,—well, there it is. All ups and downs. I should think." Or this (of the smallness of human beings in an Alpine valley): "What weasels we look!" Also, there had been near the corner of her mouth, a "somewhat," that sometimes slept, sometimes stirred. He had wondered idly who she was, and whether these things took place as well by daylight. And then, next week, at the meet of the West Norfolk, his fresh introduction to her, and satisfying himself on both questions; and, as for the second, that they did.

Then, six months afterwards. Twenty-fourth of June. That river-party: that well planned, well timed, confident proposal: its rejection: (a discomfiture in which he had not been singular; rather ninth or tenth, if talk were to be trusted). And, most devastating, something in the manner of her refusal: an Artemisian quality, quiver of startled hind, which stripped scales from his eyes to let him see her as never before: as the sole thing, suddenly, which as condition absolute of continuing he must have, let the world else go hang; and, in the same thunderclap, the one sole thing denied him. And so, that feverish fortnight, ending (thank heaven) with the best terms he might make (her cousin Jim Scarnside playing honest broker): burial of that black No, upon condition he should himself leave the country and not before fifteen months come back for his answer: eighteen months, as first propounded; which he would have shortened to August year (that is harvest time); but Mary would not give ground beyond Michaelmas: "An omen too, if you were wise.—Vintage."

Vintage. *Vindemiatrix:* she who harvests the grape: the delicate star in whose house the sun sits at autumn, and with her mild beams moderates his own to a more golden and more tranquil and more procreative radiance.

Nine months gone: Dahomey, Spain, Corsica. And April now: the twenty-second of April. A hundred and fifty-nine days to go.

The back arrowed swoop of the moment swung high into the unceilinged future, ten, fifty, sixty years, may be: then, past seeing, up to that warmthless unconsidered mock-time when nothing shall be left but the memorial that fits all (except, if there be, the most unhappiest) of human kind: *I was not. I lived and loved. I am not.* Then (or was it a bat, of the bats that hawked there between the piazza lamps and the stars?) it swung near, flashing darkly past that Dark Lady's still mouth, at whose corner flickered a something: miraculously that which, asleep or awake, resided near the corner of Mary's mouth.

Queen of Hearts: Queen of Spades: "Inglese Italianato:" the conflict of north and south in his blood; the blessing of that—of all— conflict. And yet, so easily degraded. As woman's beauty, so easily degraded. The twoness in the heart of things: that rock that so many painters split on. Loathsome Renoir, with his sheep-like slackmouthed simian-browed superfluities of female flesh: their stunted tapered fingers, puffy little hands, breasts and buttocks of a pneumatic doll, to frustrate all his magic of colour and glowing air. Toulouse-Lautrec, with his imagination fed from the stews, and his canvases all hot sweat and dead beer. Etty's[11] fine sensuality coarsely bitted and bridled by a convention from without, and starved so of the spirit that should have fed it to beauty from within. Burne-Jones's[12] beauties, nipped by some frost: Rossetti's[13] weighted with undigested matter: Beardsley,[14] a whore-master, prostituting his lovely line to unlovely canker-buds. Even the great: even Titian in his *Sacred and Profane Love,* even Botticelli in his supreme Venus, were (he said in himself), by some meddling from within or without, restrained from the ultimate which I would have, and which as a painter I (Kapaneaus's,[15] θεῶν θεαόντων ἐχπέραειν πόλιν, ἤ μῆ θελόντων φησι—with God's will, or if not, against it) will attain. Did the Greeks, with their painted statues, Apelles[16] with Phryne[17] for his model, attempt it? Did they, attempting, succeed? We can never know. Do such things die, then? things of the spirit? Sappho's burnt poems? Botticelli's pictures of "beautiful naked women" of like quality, perhaps, with his Venus and his nymphs of spring?—poor consolation that he was burnt that burnt them.

Yes. They die ὁ δ' ἐν στροφάλιγγι χονίης χείτο μέγας μεγαλωστί, λελασμένος Ιπποσυνάων—half brother to man-slaying Hector, and his charioteer; under the dusty battle-din before Ilios, "mighty, mightily fallen: forgetful of his horsemanship."[18] All time past, the conflict and the heartbreak (he looked at the amphitheatre, a skeleton lifted up to witness): frozen. He looked at her: her eyes were more still than the waiting instant between the flash and the thunder. No. Not frozen; for that is death. No death here: rather the tenseness of sinew that is in the panther before the leap: Can Grande's tomb, as this morning, in broad sunshine. Below, under the Gothic canopy carved in stone, the robed figure, lying in state, of the great condottiere, submissive, supine, with pious hands clasped upon his breast as in prayer, *"requiescat in pace," "Domine, in manus tuas,"* etc., weak childhood come back like a song's refrain, sightless eyes facing upwards. But above, high upon that canopy, the demonic equestrian figure of him in the April sap of his furious youth, helmed and harnessed, sword aloft, laughing on his caparisoned horse that seems itself to be informed with a secret kindred laughter, to say ha! ha! among the trumpets: a stirring together of the warring mights and glories, prides, overthrowings, and swiftnesses, of all worlds, to one flame; which takes on, of its mere eternity and only substantiality, as ice will scorch or fire freeze, the semblance of a death-like stillness.

* * *

All this in a few seconds of time: apocalyptically.

Lessingham answered her: "Signora, if I were God Omnipotent, I should be master of it. And, being master, I would not be carried by it like a tripper who takes a ticket for a cruise. I would land where I would; put in to what ports I liked, and out again when I would; speed it up where I would, or slow it down. I would wind it to my turn."

"That," she said, "would be a very complicated arrangement. One cannot deny it would be a pleasure. But the French precision, I fear, would scarcely apply itself so fitly, were that the state of things."

"You would hardly have me do otherwise?"

Slowly drawing off her right-hand glove, she smiled her secular smile. "I think, sir, (in my present mood), that I would desire you, even so, to play the game according to its strict rules."

"O," said Lessingham. "And that, (if it is permissible to enquire), in order to judge my skill? or my patience?"

Her fingers were busied about her little gold-meshed bag, finding a lira for her wine: Lessingham brought out a handful of coins, but she gracefully put aside his offer to pay for it. "I wonder?" she said, looking down as she drew on her crimson glove again: "I wonder? Perhaps my answer is sufficient, sir, if I say—Because it amuses me." She rose. Lessingham rose too. "Is that sufficient?" she said.

Lessingham made no reply. She was tall: Mary's height to an inch as he looked down at her: incredible likenesses to Mary: little turns of neck or hand, certain looks of the eye, that matter of the mouth (a thing surely unknown before a living woman). Unlike Mary, she was dark: jet-black hair and a fair clear skin. "Good night, sir," she said, and held out her hand. As if bred up in that gracious foreign courtesy, he bowed: raised it to his lips. Strangely, he made no motion to follow her; only as she turned away, watched her gait and carriage, inhumanly beautiful, till she was vanished among the crowd. Then he put on his hat again and slowly sat down again at his table.

So he sat, half an hour more, may be: a spectator: looking at faces, imagining, playing with his imaginations: a feeling of freedom in his veins: that strange glitter of a town at night, offering boundless possibilities. In that inward-dreaming mood he was unconscious of the clouding over of the stars and the closeness of the air, until rain had begun in big drops and the whole sky was split with lightning which unleashed the loud pealing thunder. Hastening back drenched to his hotel with collar turned up and with the downpour splashing again in a million jets from the flooded pavement, he, as in a sudden intolerable hunger, said in himself: "It is long enough: I will not wait five months. Home to-morrow."

* * *

She, in the mean while (if, indeed, as between World and World it is legitimate to speak of "before" and "after"), had, in a dozen paces after Lessingham's far-drawn gaze had lost her, stepped from natural present April into natural present June—from that night-life of Verona out by a colonnade of cool purple sandstone onto a daisied lawn, under the reverberant white splendour of midsummer noonday.[19]

Memison:
King Mezentius

COMING now beyond the lawn, that lady paused at the lily-pond under a shade of poplar-trees: paused to look down for a minute into depths out of which, framed between the crimson lilies and the golden, looked up at her own mirrored face. The curves of her nostrils hardened: some primal antiquity seemed suddenly to inform the whole presence of her, as if this youth and high summer-season of her girlhood were, in her, no season at all: not a condition, bearing in its own self its own destiny to depart and make place for future ripenesses, of full bloom, fading and decay; but a state unchanging and eternal. Her throat: her arm: the line of her hair, strained back from the temples to that interweaving of darkness with sleek-limbed darkness, coiled, locked, and overlaid, in the nape of her neck: the upward growth there, daintily ordered as black pencillings on the white wings of a flower-delice, of tiny silken hairs shading the white skin; her lips, crystal-cold of aspect, clear cut, red like blood, showing the merest thread-like glint of teeth between; these things seemed to take on a perfection terrible, because timeless.

The lord Chancellor Beroald, from his seat beneath an arbour of honeysuckle leftwards some distance from where she stood, watched her unseen. In his look was nothing of that worship, which in dumb nature seemed: rather an appraising irony which, setting profession beside performance, fact beside seeming, sucks from their antic steps not present entertainment only, but knowledge that settles to power.

"Is your husband in the palace?" he said presently.

"How should I know?"

"I had thought you had come that way."

"Yes. But scarcely from taking an inventory."

"Ha, so there the wind sits?"

He stood up as she came towards him, and they faced each other in silence. Then, light as the stirring of air in the overarching roof of poplar leaves above them, she laughed: held out a hand to him, which he after a pause dutifully, and with some faint spice of irony to sauce the motion, kissed.

"Your ladyship has some private jest?"

She sat down, elegantly settling herself on the rose-coloured marble bench, and elegantly drawing down, to smell to, a spray of honeysuckle. The black lashes veiled her eyes, as she inhaled from eight little branching horns of crimson, apricot-gold, and creamy colour, the honeysuckle's sweetness. Then, letting go the trailing flower, she looked round at him sitting now beside her. "I was diverted," she said, "by your look, my noble brother. That look you had, I remember, when you enveigled me to fall in with your pretty plan touching my former husband."

"As we mount the hill," said the Chancellor, "the prospect opens more large. That was beginnings."

"O, I spoke not of beginnings: not with that Borgian look. Piazza steps in Krestenaya."[1]

"Leave this talk," said the Chancellor.

"Having yourself, before, fobbed him off on me like a base coin, to serve your own turn," said she; "and, soon as well rid of him, teased me to taking of this Morville: so much the better alliance for you, as being by some distant removes able to claim kinship with the Parrys. You think, I suppose, that, holding in me the Queen of Spades, you shall always be able to command the Ace to take knaves with?"

"Fie, sister!"

"Fie, brother! And you shall see, I'll play cards for love, not for policy. And next time you shall need to play me the King of Hearts, to be worth my Ace to trump him."

"What's this?" said the King behind them: "chancellors with kings i' their hands? That was ever ruin, sure, whether to him that held or him that was holden."

"Serene highness," said the Chancellor, rising and turning about to face his master: "you do know me: I ne'er play cards."

The King laughed. "Nor I: save now and then with the Devil; and that's now and then both good and needful." Well six foot tall stood the Chancellor, clean of build and soldier-like; but the King, in black-bearded majesty, with eagle eyes, from under his black bonnet plumed with black eagle's feathers, looked down to him. The Duchess of Memison on the King's arm was as the beauty of an autumn evening leaning on night: a beauty of clouds and fire, of red-gold effulgence of sunset shining low through pine-tops and fern-fronds, when a little mist steals along the hillside and homing wild-duck stream high against the west. That Dark Lady, still seated, still with her back towards them, had but reached a jewelled hand to the honeysuckle to draw it down again to smell to.

"My Lady Fiorinda."

She turned, saw, and rose, all duty and obedience, yet with the self-ordered unhasting haste of a foam-footed wave of the sea in calm June weather. "Your gentle pardon, not to have known your highness' voice. Madam, your grace's humble servant."

"I have pardoned worse than that," said the King, "in a Valkyrie."[2]

"In a Valkyrie? Am I that?"

"Answer her, madam."

"O," said the Duchess, "she is none of mine. Let her answer for herself."

"None of yours? and in lovely Memison? where the very birds do fly to you at your becking? By whose doing but by yours should I have met her this morning, on a white horse, galloping, at the first spring of day as I rode up through your oak-groves."

"As to speak of Valkyries," said Fiorinda: "I had supposed rather that your highness thought my horse had ta'en command of me: so swift as you rode me down and had him by the bridle."

The King met her eyes, green and hard. "It is best way," he said, "with a Valkyrie: safer treat Goddess as woman than woman as Goddess. And, as to speak of pardon: tell me not, mistress! You knew. And studied so to sit on: note whether I'd call you."

She stood silent, looking down, as a statue unconcerned save that from the faint lifting, like the wings of a sea-swallow in flight, of her slender black eye-brows and from some subtle change about her mouth, there seemed to be shed about her a coldness as of the waste between the worlds.

"I have procured a place for you," said the King: "lady of the bedchamber to the Duchess. Will you thank me for it?"

She looked up, and first at the Duchess. "I'll thank both, and offend none. And, so please your serenity, I'll ask my husband's leave first."

"No need," said the King. "That's asked and given this hour since. And now attend me, Beroald." He said apart to the Duchess, looking into her green eyes across her fingers as he raised her hand to his lips, "You see, madonna: I will do your way."

"The Chancellor? O I am glad," said she, and it was as if some benediction came and went like a breath of honeysuckle among common garden sweetnesses.

"Then, ladies, give us leave for an hour. 'Fore God, matters of state, here in Memison, serve as salt pilchards and fumadoes[3] 'twixt the wines, lest too much sweetness quite cloy us. Even as lovely Memison and your dear acquaintance, madam, are my noonday shadow and greenery in the desert of great action."

"And yourself," said the Duchess, "Lord of us all; and yet slave yourself to that same desert."

"Of one thing only, in earth or heaven, am I slave."

"And 'tis?"

"Of my own self will," said the King, laughing at her. "Come Chancellor."

They two walked away slowly, over the lawn and through under that colonnade to another lawn, a hundred and fifty paces in length, may be, and forty across, with the long eastward-facing wall of the castle to bound it on the further side. Fair in the midst of that lawn they now began to pace the full length of it back and forth with slow and deliberate strides; and whiles they talked, whiles they seemed, falling silent, to weigh the matter. Low was their talk, and in that open sun-smitten place no danger of eavesdropping; unless the blackbird that hopped before them, jerking his tail, should listen and understand their discourse; or the martin, skimming to and fro in flashes of black and silver, still coming and returning again to her nest in the colonnade.

"I have eggs on the spit, Beroald."

"I know," said the Chancellor, very soberly.

"How should you know? I never told you."

"I can smell them, even through this air of lilies."

"Beroald, I have resolved to employ you in a matter I did mean, until this morning, none should have hand in but myself only. Am I well advised, think you?"

"If your serenity mean, well advised in undertaking of the thing, how can I answer, knowing not for certain what it is?"

"I mean," said the King, and there was a tartness in his voice, "is it well advised to open, even to you, a business of so much peril and import?"

The Chancellor paused. Then, "That is a question," he said, "my Lord the King, that neither you nor I can answer. The event only can answer it."

"You say, then, the event must show whether I be a fool to trust you? whether you be, as I think, a man of mettle, and a man of judgement, and my man?"

"Your highness hath spoke my thought with your own mouth."

"As cold as that?"

"Well, there is this besides," said the Chancellor: "that you were always my furtherer; and I, having looked on this world for five times seven years, have learnt this much of wisdom, to 'bow to the bush I get bield frae.' "[4]

"A fair-weather friend could say that," said the King, searching his face. "But we are to put into a sea we cannot sound."

The Chancellor replied, "I can say no more; save that, if this be action indeed, as your highness (as I have ever known you) counteth action, then, choosing me or any other man, you have but a weak staff to lean unto."

"Enough. Beroald, my eye is on the Parry."

"So are lesser eyes."

"These four years."

"Since his crushing for you of Valero's rebellion[5] in the March of Ulba. You have taken your time."

"I would let him run on in his course of spending."

"Yet remember," said the Chancellor, "his policy is that of the duck: above water, idle and scarce seen to stir; but under water, secretly and speedily swimming towards his purpose."

The King said, "I know an otter shall pluck down yonder duck by the foot when least she doubts it."

"It will need civil war now to bring him in."

"He is my Vicar in Rerek. Will it not argue a feeble statecraft if I, that have reigned twenty-five years in troubles and disquietudes, cannot now command my own officer without I make war against him?"

"Your serenity may have information we know not of. But most certain it is that, ever since the overthrow of those attempts in the Marches made him higher crested, he hath used your royal commission as his grappling-iron to grapple to his private allegiance the whole mid kingdom 'twixt Megra and the Zenner. I say not he meaneth openly to outbeard the sovereign himself. I think not so. But waiteth his time."

They took a turn in silence. Then said the King, letting his right fore-arm, that had lain loosely about the Lord Beroald's neck, slip back till the hand shut strong upon his shoulder: "You remember we lately found a league in hand 'mongst some discontented spirits in Rerek and the Marches, which practice, though the branches on't were easily cut off, yet was it thought to have a more dangerous and secret root. I myself have since, by divers ways, as many lines meet in the dial's centre, come nearer to the truth. There be five or six, instruments of his: names, were I to name 'em you'd ne'er believe me: so many showing friends, so many unshowing enemies. I have letters, enough to satisfy me. Advise me: what shall I do?"

"Summon them before you, himself and all, and let them answer the matter. If their answer be not sufficient, take off their heads."

"What? When the cry 'Puss, puss, where are thou?' were next way to fright 'em to open rebellion? Mend your counsel, my lord Chancellor: this serves not."

"Serene highness, I am a man of law, and should meddle no further than my commission. Yet is it the platform and understanding of all law that the King, just cause arising, may lawfully act without the law? You are our great pilot, on whom all we cast our eyes and seek our safety. For security of your person, it were good this Vicar were made away. This then is my counsel: assure yourself well of your forces, and, that done, strike: and at unawares."

The King laughed in his great black beard. "You have confirmed my very resolve, and so shall it be. But with two provisoes. First, I'll not, like an unskilful boor, kill my good hawk 'cause she turns haggard: I'll tame my Horius Parry, not end him."

"I'm sorry, then," said the Chancellor. "He is a buzzard: he is of bad carry: you can make him do nothing."

"Who are you, to prescribe and measure my ability?"

"It should not be for my honesty to flatter you. Moreover, your highness hath proved him a man that neither believeth anything that another man speaketh, nor speaketh anything himself worthy to be believed."

"I say to you," said the King, "I'll bring him to lure. As some reclaim ravens, kestrels, pies,[6] what not, and man them for their pleasure, have I not so used him as my own these years and years? I would not lose him for twice the purchase of that dominion he holdeth for me."

Beroald said, "If my words be too thin to carry so tough a matter, let your serene highness be advised further: require of my lord Admiral, or Earl Roder, or old Bodenay, your knight marshall in Rialmar, their opinions; or your tributary princes in north Rerek: they'll say the same."

But the King answered him, "Not all of you, Beroald, on your bended knees, nor all my liege subjects up and down the Three Kingdoms, might move me in this. Besides," he said, halting and turning to look Beroald in the eye, "(and here's second proviso): to be King, as I have ever opinioned and ever set my course according, should be by competency, not by privilege. If I of myself be not competent of this thing to perform it, better goodnight then and a new king i' the land.

"Hearken, therefore, and note it well. 'Twas not by chance I guested with him in Laimak two weeks since in such loving-kindness, in my progress, and well forced; nor by chance that I removed thence with great show of pomp south hither into Meszria. It was to lull them. For all this I did, knowing secretly that he is to meet one night, in some convenient place remote among the upper waters of the Zenner, with five or six (the same I spoke on), there to complete and make up their plot for seizing of Rerek to be a kingdom of itself, with him king thereof. Of time, place, and other particulars of this meeting set, I expect information hourly. You and I, we two alone, will keep that tryst with 'em: wherein if I bring not the rest to destruction and him to his obedience, at least I'll die attempting it.

"Well? will you go, or bide behind?"

The Chancellor very pale and proud of mien, gazing as if into some distance, said after a minute: "I'll go, my Lord the King." The King took him by both hands and kissed him. "And yet," said the Chancellor, facing him now squarely, "I would, with your serene highness' leave, say one word."

"Say on, what thee lust."

"This, then: I think you are stark mad. And yet," he said and drew up his lip, "I may well humour my master in this, to suffer myself to be murdered along with him; for I am not afraid of my death."

The King looked strangely at him: so might some eagle-baffling mountain look upon its own steadfastness imagined dim in some lake where rufflings of the water mar the reflection: so, it may be, might Zeus the cloud-gatherer look down, watching out of Ida. "If such fate expect my life, then better so. This must be for us a master-hour, an hour that judgeth all others. I'll not turn back, Beroald."

III

A MATCH
AND SOME LOOKERS ON

TIME, you know, is a curious business," said Lord Anmering, tilting his head forward a little to let the brim of his panama hat shade his eyes; for it was tea-time, and the afternoon sun, from beyond the cricket field below, blazed out of cloudless blue full in their faces. "Love of money, we're told—root of all evil. Gad! I think otherwise. I think Time strikes deeper."

Lady Southmere replenished the vacuum with one of the more long-drawn, contemplative, and non-committal varieties of the inimitable transatlantic "Aha."

"Look at Mary," he said. "Look at me. If I wasn't her father: wasn't thirty-two years her senior. Wouldn't I know what to do with her?"

"Well, I dare say you would."

"Easy enough when they're not your own," he said, as they walked on slowly, coming to a halt at the top of two flights of shallow steps that led down to the field from the gardens. "But when they are—By Jove, that's the style!" The ball, from a magnificent forward drive,[1] sailed clean over the far fence, amid shouts of applause, for six.[2] "If you let your boy go and smash my melonhouses, knocking the bowling about like that,[3] I'll tell you, I'll have no more to do with him. We mustn't forget," he said, lower again: "she's very young. Never force the pace."

"O but don't I just agree? And the very dearest, sweetest,—"

"You know her, well as I do. No, you don't, though. Look there," putting up his eye-glass to examine the telegraph board: "eighty. Eighty: a hundred and sixty-three: that's eighty-four to win.[4] Not so bad, with only three wickets down.[5] It's that boy of yours is doing it: wonderful steady play: nice style too: like to see him make his century.[6] You know our two best bats, Chedisford and that young Macnaghten, didn't add up to double figures between 'em: Hugh's got his work cut out for him. Look at that! pretty warm bowling. A strong team old Playter's brought us over this time from Hyrnbastwick: Jove, I'd like to give 'em a whacking for a change. Well, Hugh and Jim seem settled to it. Would you like to come down over there: get a bit of shade?"

"I would like to do anything anybody tells me to. This is just too perfect." She turned, before coming down the steps, to look back for a minute to the great west front of Anmering Blunds, where it ranged beyond green lawns and flower-beds and trim deep-hued hedges of clipped box and barberry and yew: long rows of mullioned windows taking the sun, whose beams seemed to have fired the very substance of the ancient brickwork to some cool-burning airy essence of gold. This wing, by Inigo Jones, was the newest part, masking from this side the original flint-built house that had been old Sir Robert Scarnside's whom Henry VIII made first Earl of Anmering. Round to the right, in the home park, stood up, square and grey, Anmering church tower. A sheltering wood of oak, ash, beech and sycamore was a screen for hall and church and garden against the east; and all the midsummer leafage of these trees seemed, at this hour, impregnate with that golden light. Northwards, all lay open, the ground falling sharply to the creek, salt marshes and sand-dunes and thence-away, to the North Pole, the sea. Southwards and landwards, park and wood and meadow and arable rose gently to the heaths and commons: Bestarton, Sprowswood, Toftrising. Lady Southmere, waiting on the silence a minute, might hear as under-tones to the voices of the cricket field (of players and lookers on, click of wood against leather as the batsman played) the faint far-off rumour of tide-washed shingle, and, from trees, the woodpigeon's rustic, slumbrous, suddenly started and suddenly checked, discourse: *Two coos, tak' two coos, Taffy, tak' two coos, Taffy tak'*—. From golden rose to larkspur a swallowtail butterfly fluttered in the heat. "Just too perfect for words," she said, turning at last.

They came down the steps and began walking, first north, and so round by the top end of the cricket field towards the tents. "I'll make a clean breast of it," she said: "twenty-six years now I have been English and lived in the Shires; and yet, Blunds in summer, well, it gets me here: sends me downright home-sick." Just as, underneath all immediate sounds or voices, those distant sea-sounds were there for the listening, so in Lady Southmere's speech there survived some pleasant native intonations of the southern States.

"Home-sick?" said Lord Anmering. "Virginia?"

"No, no, no: just for Norfolk. Aren't I English? and isn't your Norfolk pure England as England ought to be?"

"Better get Southmere to do an exchange: give me the place in Leicestershire and you take Blunds."

"Well and would you consent to that? Can you break the entail?"

"My dear lady," he said, "there are many things I would do for you—"

"But hardly that?"

"I'm afraid, not that."

"O isn't that just too bad!" she said, as Jim Scarnside, playing forward to a yorker, was bowled middle stump.[7]

Fifty or sixty people, may be, watched the game from this western side where the tents were and garden chairs and benches, all in a cool shade of beech and chestnut and lime and sycamore that began to throw shadows far out upon the cricket field: a pleasant summer scene as any could wish, of mingled sound and silence, stir and repose: white hats and white flannels and coloured caps and blazers contrasting here and there with more formal or darker clothes: a gaiety of muslin frocks, coloured silks, gauzes and ribbons, silken parasols and picture hats: the young, the old, the middle-aged: girls, boys, men, women: some being of the house-party; some, the belongings of the eleven that had driven over with Colonel Playter from Hyrnbastwick; some, neighbours and acquaintance from the countryside: wives, friends, parents, sisters, cousins, aunts. Among these their host, with Lady Southmere, now threaded his way, having for each, as he passed, the just greeting, were it word, smile, formal salutation or private joke: the Playter girls, Norah and Sybil, fresh from school: old Lady Dilstead, Sir Oliver's mother, and his sister Lucy (engaged to Nigel Howard): young Mrs. Margesson, a niece of Lord Anmering's by marriage: Romer, the bursar of Trinity:[8] Limpenfield of All Souls':[9] General Macnaghten and his wife and son: Trowsley of the Life Guards: Tom and Fanny Chedisford: Mr. and Mrs. Dagworth from Semmering: Sir Roderick Bailey, the Admiral, whose unpredictable son Jack had made top score (fifty) for the visiting eleven that morning: the Rector and his wife: the Denmore-Benthams: Mr. and Mrs. Everard Scarnside (Jim's parents) and Princess Mitzmesczinsky (his sister): the Bremmerdales from Taverford: the Sterramores from Burnham Overy: Janet Rustham and her two little boys: Captain Feveringhay; and dozens besides.

"Sorry, uncle," said Jim Scarnside, as their paths met: he on his way to the pavilion. "Ingloriously out for three."

"I was always told," Lady Southmere said, "you ought to block a yorker."[10]

"My dear Lady Southmere, don't I know it? But (I know you won't believe this) it was all your fault."

"That's very, very interesting."

"It was."

"And please, why?"

"Well. Just as that chap Howard was walking back the way he does to get properly wound up for one of those charging-buffalo runs that terrify the life out of a poor little batsman like me—"

"Poor little six foot two!" she said.

"Just at that instant, there, on the horizon, your black and white parasol! And I remembered: Heavens! didn't Mary make me promise that Lady Southmere should have the first brew of strawberries and cream, because they're so much the best? and isn't it long past tea-time, and here she comes, so late, and they'll all be gone? So there: and Nigel Howard sends down his beastly yorker. Is it fair? Really, Uncle Robert, you ought not to allow ladies to look on at serious cricket like ours. All very well at Lord's[11] and places like that; but here, it's too much of a distraction."

"But dreadfully awkward," said she, laughing up at him, "not to have us to put the blame on? Jim!" she called after him as they parted: he turned. "It was real noble and kind of you to think about the strawberries."

"I'm off to rescue them." And, using his bat like a walking-stick, he disappeared with long galloping strides in the direction of the tea-tent.

St. John, next man in, was out first ball. This made an excitement, in expectation that Howard should do the hat-trick;[12] but Denmore-Bentham, who followed, batted with extreme circumspection and entire success (in keeping his wicket up, though not indeed in scoring).

"Who's this young fellow that's been putting up all the runs? Radford? Bradford? I couldn't catch the name?" said an old gentleman with white whiskers, white waistcoat, and that guinea-gold complexion that comes of long living east of Suez. His wife answered: "Lord Glanford, Lord Southmere's son. They're staying here at the house, I think. And that's his sister: the pretty girl in pink, with brown hair, talking now to Lady Mary."

His glance, following where hers gave him the direction, suddenly came to rest; but not upon Lady Rosamund Kirstead. For Mary, chancing at that instant to rise and, in her going, look back with some laughing rejoinder to her friends, stood, for that instant, singled; as if, sudden in a vista between trees, a white sail drawing to the wind should lean, pause, and so righting itself pass on its airy way. A most strange and singular look there was, for any perceiving eye to have read, in the eyes of that old colonial governor: as though, through these ordinary haphazard eyes, generations of men crowded to look forth as from a window.

Glanford, with a new partner, seemed to settle down now to win the match by cautious steady play, never taking a risk, never giving a chance. When, after a solid half hour of this, a hundred at last went up on the board, the more cavalierly minded among the onlookers began to give rein to their feelings. "Darling Anne," Fanny Chedisford said, arm in arm with Lady Bremmerdale, "I simply can't stick it any longer: poke, poke, poke: as soon look on at a game of draughts. For heaven's sake, let's go and drown our sorrows in croquet."

"Croquet? I thought you agreed with Mary—"

"I always do. But when?"

"When she said it was only fit for curates and dowagers, and then only if they'd first done a course in a criminal lunatic asylum."

"O we're all qualified after this. Try a foursome: here's Jim and Mr. Margesson: ask them to join in."

"Did I hear someone pronounce my name disrespectfully?" said Jim Scarnside. Fanny laughed beneath her white parasol. "Ah, it was my much esteemed and never sufficiently to be redoubted Miss Chedisford. You know," he said to Cuthbert Margesson, "Miss Chedisford hasn't forgiven us for not making it a mixed match."

"Broom-sticks for the men?" said Margesson.

"Not at all," said Fanny.

Jim said, "I should think not! Come on: Margesson's in next wicket down. It does seem rather cheek, when he's captain, but after all it's his demon bowling made him that, and his noted diplomacy. Let's take him on and coach him a bit: teach him to slog."

Anne Bremmerdale smiled: "Better than croquet." They moved off towards the nets.

"Are you a bat, Miss Chedisford? or a bowler?" said Margesson.

"Well, I can bat more amusingly than this:" Fanny cast a disparaging glance at the game. "My brothers taught me."

"All the same," Margesson said, "Glanford's playing a fine game. We shall beat you yet, Lady Bremmerdale. How is it you didn't bring your brother over to play for Hyrnbastwick?"

"Which one? I've five."

"I've only met one. The youngest. Your brother Edward, isn't it?"

"She couldn't bring him because she hasn't got him."

Fanny said, "I thought he was staying with you now at Taverford?"[13]

"Not since early May."

"He's the kind of man," said Jim, "you never know where he is."

Fanny looked surprised. "I'd have sworn," she said, "it was Edward Lessingham I saw this morning. Must have been his double."

"Antipholus of Ephesus," said Jim: "Antipholus of Syracuse."[14]

"About eight o'clock," said Fanny. "It was such a dream of a morning, all sopping with dew, I'd got up with the lark and walked the dogs right up onto Kelling Heath before breakfast. I'd swear no one in these parts had that marvellous seat on a horse that he has. So careless. My dear, I'll bet you anything you like it was he: galloping south, towards Holt!"

"Really, Fanny, it couldn't have been," said Anne.

"There are not many young men you'd mistake for him," said Fanny.

Jim said to them, "Talking of Kelling Heath, I'll tell you an idea of mine; why can't we get up a point-to-point there this autumn? What do you say, Cuthbert?"

"I'm all for it."

"I tackled Colonel Playter about it to-day at lunch: very important to get him, as M. F. H., to bless it: in fact, he really ought to take it over himself, if it's to be a real good show. He likes the idea. Did you sound Charles, Anne?"

"Yes I did: he's awfully keen on it, and means to get a word with you this evening. Of course you could have a magnificent run right over from Weybourne Heath to Salthouse Common,[15] and back the other way; pretty rough and steep, though, in places."

Fanny accepted the change of subject. May be she thought the more.

Bentham was out: caught at the wicket:[16] six wickets down for a hundred and nine, of which Glanford had made sixty off his own bat. Margesson now went in, and (not because of any eggings on of impatient young ladies—unless, indeed, telepathy was at work—for Glanford it was who did the scoring) the play began to be brisk. Major Rustham, the Hyrnbastwick captain, now took Howard off and tried Sir Charles Bremmerdale, whose delivery, slowish, erratic, deceptively easy in appearance, yet concealed (as dangerous currents in the body of smooth-seeming water) a puzzling variety of pace and length and now and again an unexpected and most disconcerting check or spin. But Glanford had plainly got his eye in: Margesson too. "We're winning, Nell," said Lord Anmering to his niece, Mrs. Margesson. "A dashed fine stand!" said Sybil Playter. "Shut up swearing," said her sister. "Shut up yourself: I'm not."

People clapped and cheered Glanford's strokes. Charles Bremmerdale now could do nothing with him: to mid-off, two: to mid-on,
two:[17] a wide:[18] a strong drive, over cover's head, to the boundary,
four:[19] to long-leg in the deep field, two—no—three, while Jack
Bailey bungles it with a long shot at the wicket: point runs after it:
"Come on!"—four: the fieldsman is on it, turns to throw in: "No!"
says Margesson, but Glanford, "Yes! come on!" They run: Bremmerdale is crouched at the wicket: a fine throw, into his hands, bails
off and Glanford run out.[20] "Bad luck!" said Jim Scarnside, standing with Tom and Fanny Chedisford at the scoring table: Glanford
had made ninety-one. "But why the devil will he always try and bag
the bowling?"[21]

Glanford walked from the field, bat under his arm, shaking his
head mournfully as he undid his batting-gloves. He went straight to
the pavilion to put on his blazer, and thence, with little deviation
from the direct road, to Mary. "I am most frightfully sorry," he said,
sitting down by her. "I did so want to bring you a century for a
birthday present."

"But it was a marvellous innings," she said. "Good heavens,
'What's centuries to me or me to centuries?' It was splendid."

"Jolly decent of you to say so. I was an ass, though, to get run
out."

Mary's answering smile was one to smoothe the worst-ruffled
feathers; then she resumed her conversation with Lucy Dilstead:
"You can read them over and over again, just as you can Jane Austen. I suppose it's because there's no padding."

"I've only read *Shagpat*,[22] so far," said Lucy.

"O that's different from the rest. But isn't it delicious? So serious. Comedy's always ruined, don't you think, when it's buffooned?
You want to live in it: something you can laugh with, not laugh at."

"Mary has gone completely and irretrievably cracked over
George Meredith," Jim said, joining them.

"And who's to blame for that?" said she. "Who put what book
into whose hand? and bet what, that who would not be able to
understand what-the-what it was all driving at until she had read
the first how many chapters how many times over?"

Jim clutched his temples, histrionically distraught. Hugh was
not amused. The match proceeded, the score creeping up now very
slowly with Margesson's careful play. General Macnaghten was saying to Mr. Romer, "No, no, she's only twenty. It is: yes: quite extraordinary; but being only daughter, you see, and no mother, she's
been doing hostess and so on for her father two years now, here and
in London: two London seasons. Makes a lot of difference."

Down went another wicket:[23] score, a hundred and fifty-three.
"Now for some fun," people said as Tom Appleyard came on the
field; but Margesson spoke a wingèd word in his ear: "Look here,

old chap: none of the Jessop business.[24] It's too damned serious now." "Ay, ay, sir." Margesson, in perfect style, sent back the last ball of the over. Appleyard obediently blocked and blocked.[25] But in vain. For one of Bremmerdale's master-creations of innocent out- ward show and inward guile sneaked round Margesson's defence and took his leg stump.[26] Nine wickets down: total a hundred and fifty-seven: last man, nine. Hyrnbastwick, in some elation, were throwing high catches round the field while Dilstead, Anmering's next (and last) man in, walked to the wicket. Margesson said to Tom Appleyard, "It's up to you now, my lad. Let 'em have it, damn slam and all if you like. But, by Jingo, we must pull it off now. Only seven to win." Appleyard laughed and rubbed his hands.

There was no more desultory talk: all tense expectancy. "If Sir Oliver gets the bowling, that puts the lid on it: never hit a ball yet."[27] "Why do they play him then?" "Why, you silly ass, because he's such a thundering good wicket-keeper." George Chedisford, about sixteen, home from Winchester because of the measles, main- tained a mature self-possession at Lord Anmering's elbow: "I wish my frater—wish my brother was in again, sir. He'd do the trick." "You watch Mr. Appleyard: he's a hitter." By good luck, that ball that had beaten Margesson was last of the over, so that Appleyard, not Dilstead, faced the bowling: Howard once more, a Polyphe- mus[28] refreshed. His first ball was a yorker, but Appleyard stopped it. The second, Appleyard, all prudent checks abandoned, stepped out and swiped. Boundary: four. Great applaudings: the parson's children and the two little Rustham boys, with the frenzy of Guelph and Ghibelline,[29] jumped up and down jostling each other. The next ball, a very fierce one, pitched short and rose at the batsman's head. Appleyard smashed it with a terrific over-hand stroke: four again—"Done it!" "Match!"[30]

Then, at the fourth ball, Appleyard slogged, missed, and was caught in the slips. And so amid great merriment, chaff and mutual congratulations, the game came to an end.[31]

"Come into the Refuge," said Jim Scarnside, overtaking Mary as they went in to dress for dinner: "just for two twos. I left my humble birthday offering in there, and I want to give it to you."

"O, but," she said, pausing and looking back, one foot on the threshold of the big French window: "I thought it was a bargain, no more birthday presents. I can't have you spending all those pennies on me." Her right hand was lifted to a loose hanger of wistaria bloom, shoulder-high beside the doorway: in her left she carried her hat, which she had taken off walking up from the garden. The slant evening sun kindled so deep a Venetian glory in her hair that every smooth-wound coil, each braid, each fine straying little curl or tendril, had its particular fire-colour, of chestnut, tongued flame, inward glow of the brown-red zircon, burnished copper, realgar, sun-bleached gold: not self-coloured, but all in a shimmer and inter-change of hues, as she moved her head or the air stirred them.

"Twenty pennies precisely," said Jim. "Can't call that breaking a bargain. Come. Please."

"All right," she smiled, and went before him through the small tea-room and its scents of pot-pourri, and through the great skin-strewn hall with its portraits and armour and trophies and old oak and old leather and Persian rugs and huge open fire-place filled at this season with roses and summer greenery, and so by a long soft-carpeted passage to the room they called the Refuge: a cosy sunny room, not belonging to Mary specially or to her father, but to both, and free besides to all dogs (those at least that were allowed in the house) that lived at Blunds, and to all deserving friends and rela-tions. Those parts of the walls that were not masked by bookcases or by pictures showed the pale reddish paper of Morris's willow pat-tern;[32] a frieze of his rich dark night-blue design of fruit, with its enrichments of orange, lemon, and pomegranate and their crimson and pallid blooms, ran around below the ceiling. There was a square table with dark green cloth and upon it a silver bowl of roses: writing things on the table and chairs about it, and big easy chairs before the fire-place: a bag of tools (saws, hammers, screw-drivers, pliers and such-like) behind the door, a leather gun-case and fish-ing-rods in this corner, walking-sticks and hunting-crops in that, a pair of field-glasses on the shelf, some dog-medicines: pipes and cigar-boxes on the mantel-piece: on a bureau a large mahogany musical-box: an early Victorian work-table, a rack full of newspa-pers, a Cotman[33] above the mantel, an ancient brass-bound chest covered with an oriental rug or foot-cloth of silk: a Swiss cuckoo-clock: a whole red row of Baedekers[34] on one of the bookshelves, yellowbacks on another: *Wuthering Heights* open on a side-table, Kipling's *Many Inventions* open on a chair, and a text of Homer on the top of it: a box of tin soldiers and a small boy's cricket bat beside them: over there a doll or two and a toy theatre, with a whole mass of woolly monkeys, some in silver-paper armour and holding pins for swords: a cocker spaniel asleep on the hearth-rug, and a little dark grey hairy dog, a kind of Skye terrier with big bat-like ears and of beguiling appearance, asleep in an armchair. There pervaded this room, not to be expelled for all the fresh garden air that came and went through its wide windows and door which opened on the garden, a scent curiously complex and curiously agreeable, as of a savoury stew compounded of this varied apparatus of the humani-ties. Plainly a Refuge it was, and by no empty right of name: a refuge from tidiness and from all engines, correctitudes, and impo-sitions of the world: in this great household, a little abbey of Thélème, with its sufficient law, "Fay ce que vouldras."[35]

Mary sat on the table while Jim unearthed from somewhere a little parcel and presented it to her, with scissors from the work-table to cut the string. "Twenty, you see, for the birthday cake," he said, as she emptied out on the green baize a handful of little coloured candles.

"You are so absurd."

"We ought to have the cake," he said. "No time for it now, though. Look: there are heaps of colours, you see. Do you know what they mean?"

"How should I know?"

"I'll show you:" he began to arrange them side by side. "They're highly symbolical. Nine white. Those are your nine first years: *tabula rasa*,[36] from my point of view. Then, you see, a red one: a red-letter day for you when you first met me."

"Was I ten then? I'd forgotten."

"La Belle Dame sans Merci,[37] always forgets. Now, look: violet, blue, green, yellow, orange, pink."

"The rainbow?"

"Haven't I charming thoughts?"

"Then three goldy ones. Gold dust in them," said she, touching them with one finger.

"Because of the presents," Jim said, "that I'd like to have given you these last three years, had I been Midas or John D. Rockefeller. Last, you observe: Black. For my own sake, because you're going to be married."

"My dear Jim, what awful nonsense! Who told you so?"

"That would be telling. Isn't it true?" He backed to the fire-place and stood looking at her.

The sudden colour in her cheek, spreading yet lower as she faced him, made her seem (if that could be) yet lovelier. " 'It is not so,' answered she. 'Nor it was not so. And, indeed, God forbid it ever should be so.' "

"O dangerous resolution. But I really think it's uncommon nice of you, Mary. Of course, for myself, I gave up hope long ago; and you'll have noticed I've even given up asking you these last—two years, is it? No, since your last birthday:" Mary gave a little start. He moved to the window, and stood not to look direct at her: "that was really when I decided, better give it up. But it does help my self-esteem to know there's no one else in the offing," he said, lightly as before, playing with the scissors. "May I tell people the good news?"

"Certainly not. Why should you go meddling with my affairs? I think it's most insolent of you."

"Well, I thought you might like me to tell—well, Glanford: just to break the news to the pore fella."

There was dead silence. He looked round. Mary's head was turned away: she seemed to be counting the little candles with her finger. Suddenly she stood up: went over to the fire-place. "Sheila's a naughty little thing," she said: the form curled up on the chair moved the tip of a feathery tail and, with a pricking and apologetic laying again of bat-like ears, cast up at Mary a most melting glance. "Ate a quarter of a pound of butter in the larder this morning; and yet now, what a little jewel she looks: as if butter wouldn't melt." She bent and kissed the little creature between the eyes, a kind of butter-fly kiss, then, erect again, confronted Jim.

"It was infernal cheek on my part," he said, "to say that. Still: between old friends—"

Mary swept up the candles. "I must fly and change." Then, over her shoulder from the doorway, where she turned for an instant, tall, light of carriage in her white dress, like a nymph of Artemis: "Thanks for a word fitly spoken, *mon ami.*"

IV

LADY MARY SCARNSIDE

THAT SOMETHING which, asleep or awake, resided near the corner of Mary's mouth peeked at itself in the looking-glass: a private interchange of intelligence between it and its reflection there, not for her to read. She turned from the dressing-table to the window. It was slack-water, and the tide in. Under the sun the surface of the creek was liquid gold. The point, with its coastguard cottage, showed misty in the distance. Landscape and waterscape departed, horizon beyond horizon, to that meeting of earth and heaven which, perhaps because of the so many more and finer gradations of air made visible, seemed far further remote in this beginning of midsummer evening than in the height of day. Mary stood for a minute looking from the window, where the airs stirred with honeysuckle scents and rose scents and salt and pungent scents of the marsh and sea.

Suddenly she moved and came back to the looking-glass. " 'Then that's settled, Señorita Maria. I carry you off to-night.'—And that," she said aloud, looking at herself with that sideways incisive mocking look that she inherited from her father, "was a piece of damned impertinence."

There was a knock at the door. "Come in. O Angier, I'll ring when I'm ready for you: ten minutes or so."

"Yes, my lady. I thought your ladyship would want me to do your hair to-night."

"Yes I'll ring," Mary said, giving her maid a smile in the looking-glass. She retired, saying, "It's nearly half past seven, my lady."

Half past seven. And half past seven this morning. Twelve hours ago. Thrown from her ring, where the sun took it, a rainbow streak of colour appeared on the carpet: her white kitten made a pounce to seize the mysterious dancing presence, now there, now gone. And then, half past seven to-morrow. Always on the go, by the look of it: everything. Nothing stays. She moved her finger, to draw the iridescent phantom again along the carpet and so up the wall, out of reach from velvet paws that pounced. And yet, you can't believe that. The whole point about a thing like this morning is that it does stay: somewhere it stays. What you want to find out how to get back to it: or forward? for it is forward, too. Or perhaps back and forward don't belong to it at all: it just is. Perhaps back and forward just aren't. Perhaps, perhaps, perhaps.

To ride her down like that: if anyone had seen them. "Unpardonable," Mary said, as she took her seat at the mirror and began to let down her hair. And Tessa is a pretty good little mare: showed him a clean pair of heels for a mile or so. Something in the shadowy backgrounds of the mirror surprisingly assumed a neat little black thoroughbred horse's face, and shockingly said to Mary: "Haven't I a perfect mouth? to have understood and slowed down the least little bit in the world just at the—"

The north-westerly sun made it hot in the dressing-room. The door was shut between this and her bedroom, to keep that cool for the night: bedroom with windows that opened north and east to let in the mornings. She was in a kind of kimono of pale blue silk after her bath, and now, for this heat, while she sat to brush her hair, she untied the sash, and with a shake of her shoulders, let the soft garment fall open and down about her hips. "Carry you off to-night." It really was a bit much. The extraordinary coolness of it all, after that dreadful scene they had had at the end of April, when he had turned up five months before his time, and she had said—well, said enough to end it for most men, one would think. And yet now, this morning, after six weeks of obedient absence and silence—. She had ridden to hounds often enough; but to be hunted like a hare! True, she had started the thing, in a way, by turning to ride off in the other direction as soon as she saw him. But still. Her bosom rose and fell with the memory of it: as if all the wide universe had suddenly run hunting-mad, and she the quarry: she and poor little Tessa with her flying feet: an excitement like darkness with sudden rollings in it like distant drums; and the trees, the solid ground, the waking buttercups and meadowsweet with the dew on them, the peggy-whitethroat on the thorn, the brier-rose at the edge of

the wood, larks trilling invisible in the blue, the very upland newness of the summer air of this birthday morning, all had seemed as
if caught up into that frenzy of flight to join in the hunt, multiplying
the galloping music of Lessingham's horse-hooves, now loud, now
dim, now loud again, to a hue and cry and a gallop of all these
things. And then the coolness of him, after this wild horse-race: the
astounding assurance of this proposition, put to her so easily and as
if it were the simplest thing in the world: and his having a motorcar,
so that they shouldn't be caught. Most monstrous of all, about the
luggage: that he had luggage for her as well, every possible thing
she could want, every kind of clothes.

How did he know? Mary laid down her brush and leaned back,
staring into her own eyes for a minute in the looking-glass. Then,
after a minute, some comical matter stirred in her eyes' inward
corners. "How did you know?" she said, addressing not her own
image but the mirrored door over its shoulder, as if someone had
come in there and stood in the doorway. Then, with eyes resting on
herself again, she said suddenly in herself: "This is how I should—.
If we were to be—If we are to be—But no, my friend. Not to be
swept up like—like a bunch of candles."

She and her looking-glass self surveyed one another for a while,
coolly, in detail, not looking any more into each other's eyes nor
over each other's shoulders to the door beyond. At length the looking-glass image said, not audibly, but to Mary's inward ear: I suppose a man sees it differently. I think I understand, partly, how he
might see it: something very delicate, easily hurt, easily broken, but
so gentle that you couldn't bear to. Like a field-mouse or some such:
or like a baby. No, for what matters about a baby is what it is going
to be; but this—here it is, full-fledged: what it is and what it ought to
be, in one: doesn't want to change: just to be. That is enough for
anybody. And its power, what all power ought to be: not to overpower the weak, but overpower the powerful. Really it hasn't any
power: except that it need only lift a finger, and every power there
is or ever could be must rise to protect it.

But that isn't true (said the looking-glass image, going over
with musing untroubled eyes the thing before it: chin, throat: gleam
of a shoulder betwixt fallen masses of flame-coloured hair: arms
whose curves had the motion of swans in them and the swan's whiteness: breasts of a Greek mould and firmness, dove-like, silver-pure,
pointing their rose-flowers in a Greek pride: and those wild delicate
little perfections, of the like flame-colour, beneath her arms): that
isn't true. And with that (perhaps for two seconds) something happened in the mirror: a two-seconds' glimpse as of some menace that
rushed upwards, like the smoke of some explosion, to yawning immensities bleak, unmeaning, unmindful of the worm that is man;
into which void there seemed, for that moment, to be sucked up all

comfort of cosy room, home, dear ones, gaiety of youthful blood, the sweet nostalgia of childhood born of the peace of that June evening, its scents, its inwardness and whispered promise: the familiar countryside that made a lap for all these: the sea, island-girdling of England: the kindly natural earth: the very backgrounds and foundations of historic time: sucked up, swallowed, brought to nought. And, naked to this roofless and universal Nothing, she: immeasurably alone, a little feminine living being, and these "little decaying beauties of the body."

But two seconds only, and blood danced again. Mary jumped to her feet: put on some clothes: rang the bell.

She was nearly ready when her father's knock came on the door: his voice, "Can I come in?"

"Come in, Father." She swam towards him with the style of a du Maurier duchess[1] and shook hands in the most extreme high-handed affectation of the moment. "So charmed you could come, Lord Anmering. So charmin' of you to spare us the time, with so much huntin' and shootin' this time of year, and the foxes eatin' up all the pear-blossom and all."

He played up; then stood back to admire her, theatrically posed for him, with sweeping of her train and manage of her point-lace fan. Her eyes danced with his. "Looking very bonnie," he said, and kissed her on the forehead. "Table arranged? I suppose you've given me Lady Southmere? and Hugh on your right?"

"O yes. Duty at dinner: pleasure afterwards."

He caught the look on her face as she turned to the dressing-table for her gloves: this and a strained something in her voice. "Not a very nice way," he said, "to talk about our friends."

Mary said nothing, busy at her looking-glass.

Lord Anmering stood at the window, trimming his nails, his back towards her. Presently he said quietly, "I'm getting a bit tired of this attitude towards Glanford."

Mary was unclasping her pearl necklace to change it for the sapphire pendant: it slipped and fell on the dressing-table. "Damn!" she said, and was silent.

"Do you understand what I said?"

"Attitude? I've none, that I'm aware of. Certainly not 'to-wards.' " She fastened the clasp at the back of her neck, turned and came to him where he stood, still turned away from her in the window: slipped her arm in his. "And I'm not going to be bullied on my birthday." His arm tightened on hers, a large reassuring pressure, as to say: Of course she shan't.

He looked at his watch. "Five past eight. We ought to be going down."

"O and, Father," she said, turning back to him half way to the door, "I don't think I told you (such a rush all day): whom do you think I met out riding this morning? and asked him to come to dinner to-night? Edward Lessingham. Only back from Italy, and I don't know where, last month."

Lord Anmering had stopped short. "You asked him to dinner?"

"Yes."

"What did you do that for?"

"Ordinary civility. Very lucky, too: we'd have been three thirteens otherwise, with Lady Dilstead turning up."

"Pah! we'd have been three thirteens with him, then, when you asked him. And it isn't so: we were thirty-eight."

"Thirty-nine with Madame de Rosas."

"My dear girl, you can't have that dancer woman sit down with us."

"Why not? She's very nice. Perfectly respectable. I think it would be unkind not to. Anybody else would do it."

"It's monstrous, and you're old enough to know better."

"Well, I've asked her, and I've asked him. You can order them both out if you want to make a scene."

"Don't talk to me like that," said her father. She shrugged her shoulders and stood looking away, very rebellious and angry. "And I thought you knew perfectly well," he said, "that I don't care for that young Lessingham about the place."

"I don't understand what you mean, 'about the place.' "

"I don't care about him."

"I can't think why. You've always liked Anne Bremmerdale. Isn't his family good enough for you? As old as ours. Older, I should think. You've hardly seen him."

"I don't propose to discuss him," said Lord Anmering, looking at her piercingly through his eye-glass: then fell silent, as if in debate whether or not to speak his mind. "Look here, my darling," he said, at last, with an upward flick of the eyebrow letting the eye-glass fall: "It's just as well to have cards on the table. It has been my serious hope that you would one day marry Hugh Glanford. I'm not going to force it or say any more. But, things being as they are, it is as well to be plain about it."

"I should have thought it had been plain enough for some time. Hanging about us all the season: most of last winter, too. People beginning to talk, I should think."

"What rubbish."

"All the same, it was nice of you to tell me, Father. Have you been plain about it to him too?"

"He approached me some time ago."

"And you gave him your—?"

"I wished him luck. But naturally he understands that my girl must decide for herself in a thing like that."

"How very kind of him." Mary began laughing. "This is delightful: like the ballad:

> "He's teld her father and mither baith,
>   As I hear sindry say,
> But he has nae teld the lass her sell,
>   Till on her wedding day."[2]

Her voice hardened: "I wish I was twenty-one. Do as I liked, then.
Marry the next man that asked me—"

"Mary, Mary—"

"—So long as it wasn't Hugh." Mary gave a little gulp and
disappeared into her bedroom, slamming the door behind her. Her
father, feet planted wide apart in the middle of her dressing room
floor, waited, moodily polishing his eye-glass with a white silk
pocket-handkerchief scented with eau de Cologne. In three minutes
she was back again, radiantly mistress of herself, with a presence of
mischief dimpling so elusively about mouth and eyes in her swimming towards him, that it were easier tell black from green in the
rifle-bird's glinting neck, than tell whether in this peace-making she
charmingly dispensed pardon or as charmingly sought it. "Happy
birthday?" she said, inclining her brow demurely for him to kiss.
"Must go down now, or people will be arriving."

Among the guests now assembling in the drawing-room Lessingham's arrival was with some such unnoted yet precise effect as
follows the passing of a light cloud across the sun, or the coming of
the sun full out again as the cloud shifts. Mary said, as they shook
hands, "You know Mr. Lessingham, Father? you remember he and
Jim were at Eton together."

There was frost in Lord Anmering's greeting. "I had forgotten
that," he said. "When was it I met you last?"

"About a year ago, sir," said Lessingham. "I've been out of
England."

"I think I remember. You've lived abroad a good deal?"

"Yes, sir: on and off, these last seven years."

"What did you come home for?"

Lessingham's eyes were grey: straight of gaze, but not easily
read, and with a smoulder in the depths of them. He answered, "To
settle up some affairs."

"And so abroad again?"

"I've not decided yet."

"A rolling stone?"

Lessingham smiled. "Afraid I am, sir."

Jim joined them: "Did I tell you, uncle, about Lessingham's
running across some of your Gurkha porters when he was in India

two or three years ago? that had climbed with you and Mr. Freshfield in Sikkim?"

"You're a climber, then?" Lord Anmering said to Lessingham, looking him up and down: very tall, perhaps six foot three, black-haired, sunburnt but, as his forehead showed, naturally white and clear of skin, and with the look of one able to command both himself and others, as is not often seen at that age of five and twenty.

"I've done a little."

"A lot," said Jim. Lessingham shook his head.

"In the Himalaya?" said Lord Anmering.

"A little, sir."

"A little!" said Jim: "just listen how these mountaineers talk to each other! Twenty-two thousand feet he did once, on—what's the name of it?—one of the cubs of Nanga Parbat. A terrific thing; and pages about it at the time in the *Alpine Journal*. Come," he said, taking Lessingham's arm, "I want to introduce you to my sister. She married a Russian: we can never pronounce the name, none of us; so please don't mind, and please don't try. You're taking her in to dinner: that's right, Mary?"

Mary smiled assent. For a flash, as she turned to welcome the Denmore-Benthams who had just come in, her glance met Lessingham's. And, unless seen by him and by her, then to every living eye invisible, something (for that flash) danced in the air between them: "But, after dinner—"

Dinner was in the picture gallery (where later they were also to dance), the only room big enough and long enough to take forty people comfortably at one table. A fine room it was, eighty feet perhaps by twenty-five, with a row of tall low-silled windows going the whole length of its western wall. These, left uncurtained when dinner began, and with their lower sashes thrown up to admit the evening air, were filled with the sunset. Dozens of candles, each from under its rose-coloured little prim hat of pleated silk, beamed down clear upon the white of the table-cloth, the glass, the silver and the china and the flowers of Mary's choosing and delicate trailers of greenery; imbuing besides with a softer, a widelier diffused and a warmer glow the evening dresses, the jewels, the masculine black and white, the faces, hosts' or guests': faces which, young old or of doubtful date, were yet all by this unity of candlelight brought into one picture, and by the yet airier but deeper unity that is in pleasant English blood, secure, easy, gay, fancy-free. And, (as for proof that England were to wrong her own nature did she fail to absorb the exotic), even the Spanish woman, midway down the table between Jim Scarnside and Hesper Dagworth, was assimilated by that solvent, as the sovereign alkahest[3] will subdue and swallow up all refractory elements and gold itself.

Conversation, like a ballet of little animals (guests at Queen Alice's looking-glass party when things began to happen), tripped, paused, footed it in and out, pirouetted, crossed and returned, back and forth among the faces and the glasses and the dresses and the lights. For a while, about the head of the table, the more classic figures revolved under the direction of Lord Anmering, Mr. Romer, General Macnaghten and Mr. Everard Scarnside. Lady Rosamund Kirstead, on the skirts of this Parnassus, her back to the windows, tempered its airs with visions of skiing-slopes above Villars that February (her first taste of winter sports), and so succeeded at last in enveigling Anne and Margesson and Mr. Scarnside from those more intellectual scintillations (which Anne excelled in but Rosamund found boring) down to congenial common ground of Ascot, Henley, Lord's, the Franco-British Exhibition, in prospect and retrospect: what to wear, what not to wear: August, September, grouse-moors and stalkers' paths of Invernesshire and Sutherland.[4]

Lessingham, further down on the same side of the table, held a three-cornered conversation with Amabel Mitzmesczinsky on his right and Fanny on his left: here the talk danced to merrier and stranger tunes, decking itself out as if the five continents and all past and present were its wardrobe. Into its vortex were drawn Tom Chedisford and Mrs. Bentham from across the table, till Jack Bailey sat marooned; for, while Mrs. Bentham, his rightful partner, who had hitherto displayed a most comforting interest in things within the grasp of his understanding, unfeelingly began to ignore him for the quattrocento, Lucy Dilstead on his other side conducted an esoteric conversation, not very vocal, with her fiancé. Jack, hearing at last in this loneliness a name he knew (of Botticelli's *Primavera*), took advantage of a lull in the talk to say, with honest philistine conviction, "And *that's* a *nasty* picture." Jim and Hesper Dagworth experimented by turns, Hesper with his own Spanish, Jim with the lady's English, on Madame de Rosas, who thus became a distraction in the more serious discussions carried on by Bremmerdale, Colonel Playter, and Jim on the subject of point-to-points. Appleyard with his funny stories kept the Playter girls in fits of boisterous laughter, till finally they took to bombarding him with bread-pills: an enterprise as suddenly ended as suddenly begun, under the horrified reproof of the parson's wife and the more quelling glare of the paternal eye upon them.

At the foot of the table Mary, as hostess, seemed at first to have her hands full: with Hugh on her right, rather sulky, scenting (may be) an unfavorable climate for his intended proposal, and becoming more and more nervous as time went by; and, on her left, the breezy Admiral, flirting outrageously with Mrs. Dagworth who seemed, however, a little distrait, with her eye on Hesper and the de Rosas woman. But Mary's witty talk and the mere presence of her worked as lovely weather in spring, that can set sap and blood and the whole world in tune.

Lessingham and Mary, breaking off from the dance as it brought them alongside the door, went out quickly and through the tea-room and so out from the music and the stir and the glitter to the free air of the terrace, and there stood a minute to taste it, her arm still in his, looking both into the same enbowered remoteness of the dark and the star-shine: the fragrant body of night, wakeful but still.

Mary withdrew her arm.

Lessingham said, "Do you mean to make a practice of this? For the future, I mean?"

"Of what?"

"What you've been doing to me to-night?"

"I don't know. Probably."

"Good."

Mary was fanning herself. Presently he took the fan and plied it for her. The music sounded, rhythmic and sweet, from the picture gallery. "That was rather charming of you," she said: "to say 'good.'"

"Extremely charming of me, if I was a free agent. But you may have noticed, that I'm not."

Mary said, "Do you think I am?"

"Completely, I should say. Completely free, and remarkably elusive."

"Elusive? Sometimes people speak truer than they guess."

"You've eluded me pretty successfully all the evening," Lessingham said, as she took back the fan. The music stopped. Mary said, "We must go in."

"Need we? You're not cold?"

"I want to." She turned to go.

"But, please," he said at her elbow. "What have I done? The only dance we've had, and the evening half over—"

"I'm feeling—ratty."

Lessingham said no more, but followed her between the sleeping flower-borders to the house. In the doorway they encountered, among others, Glanford coming out. He reddened and looked awkward. Mary reddened too, but passed in, aloof, unperturbed. She and Lessingham came now, through the tea-room and the great galleried hall, to the drawing-room, where, since dinner, at the far end a kind of platform or stage had been put up, with footlights along the front of it, and in all the main floor of the room chairs and sofas arranged as for an audience. Shaded lamps on standards or on tables at the sides and corners of the room made a restful, uncertain, golden light.

"You've heard the castanets before, I suppose?" said Mary.

"Yes. Only once properly: in Burgos."

"Castanets and cathedrals go rather well together, I should think."

"Yes," he said. "I never thought of that before; but they do. A curious mix up of opposites: the feeling of Time, clicking and clicking endlessly away; and the other—well, as if there were something that did persist."

"Like mountains," Mary said; "and the funny little noise of streams, day after day, month after month, running down their sides."

Lessingham said, under his breath, "And sometimes, an avalanche."

They were standing now before the fire-place, which was filled with masses of white madonna lilies. Over the mantel-piece, lighted from above by a hidden electric lamp, hung an oil painting, the head-and-shoulders portrait of a lady with smooth black hair, very pale of complexion, taken nearly full-face, with sloping shoulders under her gauzy dress and a delicate slender neck (ἁπαλήοειή, as Homer has it in the hymn). Her forehead was high: face long and oval: eyebrows arched and slender: nose rather long, very straight, and with the faintest disposition to turn up at the end, which gave it a certain air of insolent but not unkindly disdainfulness. Her eyes were large, and the space wide between them and between lid and eyebrow: the lid of each, curving swiftly up from the inner corner, ended at the outer corner with another sudden upward twist: a slightly eastern cast of countenance, with a touch perhaps of the Japanese and a touch of the harsh Tartar.

"Reynolds," said Lessingham, after a minute's looking at it in silence.

"Yes."

"An ancestress?"

"No. No relation. Look at the name."

He leaned near to look, in the corner of the canvas: *Anne Horton 1766*.[5]

"Done when she was about nineteen," said Mary. There seemed to come, as she looked at that portrait, a subtle alteration in her whole demeanour, as when, some gay inward stirrings of the sympathies, friend looks on friend. "Do you like it?"

On Lessingham's face, still studying the picture, a like alteration came. "I love it."

"She went in for fatty degeneration later on, and became Duchess of Cumberland. Gainsborough painted her as that, several times, later."

"I don't believe it," he said. He looked round at Mary. "Neither the fat," he said, "nor the degeneration. I think I know those later paintings, and now I don't believe them."

"They're not interesting," Mary said. "But in this one, she's certainly not very eighteenth-century. Curiously outside all dates, I should say."

"Or inside."

"Yes: or inside all dates."

Lessingham looked again at Mrs. Anne Horton—the sideways inclination of the eyes: the completely serene, completely aware, impenetrable, weighing, look: lips as if new-closed, as in Verona, upon that private *ça m'amuse*. He looked quickly back again at Mary. And, plain for him to see, the something that inhabited near Mary's mouth seemed to start awake or deliciously to recognize, in the picture, its own likeness.

It recognized also (one may guess) a present justification for the *ça m'amuse*. Perhaps the lady in the picture had divined Mary's annoyance at Glanford's insistent, unduly possessive, proposal, at her own rather summary rejection of it, and at Lessingham's methods that seemed to tar him incongruously with the same brush (and her father, too, not without a touch of that tar): divined, moreover, the exasperation in Mary's consciousness that she overwhelmingly belonged to Lessingham, that she was being swept on to a choice she did not want to make, and that Lessingham unpardonably (but scarcely unnaturally, not being in these secrets) did not seem to understand the situation.

Mary laughed. It was as if all the face of the night was cleared again.

The room was filling now. Madame de Rosas, in shawl and black mantilla, took her place on the platform, while below, on her right, the musicians began to tune up. Lessingham and Mary had easy chairs at the back, near the door. The lamps were switched out, all except those that lighted the pictures, and the footlights were switched on. "And my Cyprus picture over there?" Lessingham said in Mary's ear. "Do you know why I sent it you?"

Mary shook her head.

"You know what it is?"

"Yes: you told me in your letter. Sunrise from Olympus. It is marvellous. The sense of height. Windy sky. The sun leaping up behind you. The cold shadows on the mountains, and goldy light on them. Silver light of dawn. And that tremendous thrown shadow of Olympus himself and the kind of fringe of red fire along its edges: I've seen that in the Alps."

"Do you know what that is, there: where you get a tiny bit of sea, away on the left, far away over the ranges?"

"What is it?"

"Paphos. Where Aphrodite is supposed to have risen from the sea. I camped up there, above Troodos, for a fortnight: go up with my things about four o'clock every morning to catch the sunrise and paint it. I'll tell you something," he said, very low: "I actually almost came to believe that story, the whole business, Homeric hymn,[6] Botticelli's picture in the Uffizi,[7] everything: almost, in a queer way, when I was looking across there, alone, at daybreak. —But," he said. The strings burst into the rhythm of an old seguidilla[8] of Andalusia: the Spanish woman took the center of the stage, swept her shawl about her shoulders and stood, statuesque, motionless, in the up-thrown brilliance of the footlights. Lessingham looked up at her for a moment, then back at Mary. Mary's eyes had left picture for stage; but his, through the half-light, fed only upon Mary: the profile of her face, the gleam of the sapphired pendant that in so restful a sweet unrest breathed with her breathing. "But," he said, "it was you." The dusky sapphire stood still for an instant, then, like a ship from the trough of the sea, rose and, upon the surge, down again.

"It would be a foolish myth if it could have been anyone else but you," he whispered. And the castanets began softly upon a flutter or rumour of sound, scarce heard.

An Andalusian dance, done by a hired woman to please the guests at an English country house in this year of Our Lord 1908. And yet, through some handfasting of music with landscape and portrait painted and their embarking so, under the breath of secular deep memories in the blood, upon that warmed sapphire rocked on so dear a sea, the rhythms of the dance seemed to take to themselves words:

Αιδοιην χουσοστέφανον χαλήν 'Αφροδιτην—

Awful, gold-crowned, beautiful, Aphrodite—and so to the ending:

> Hail, You of the flickering eyelids, honey-sweet! and
> vouchsafe me in this contest to bear victory; and do
> You attune my song. Surely so will I too yet re-
> member me of another song to sing You.[9]

The castanets, on a long-drawn thinness of sound, as of grasshoppers on a hot hillside in summer, trembled down to silence. Then a burst of clapping: smiles and curtseys of acknowledgement from the platform: talk let loose again in a buzz and chatter, cleft with the tuning of the strings: under cover of which, Mary said softly, with her eye on the Cyprus picture, "You didn't really believe it?"

"No. Of course I didn't."

"And yet perhaps, for a moment," she said: "with that burning on the edge of the shadow? for a moment, in the hurry to paint it?"

Lessingham seemed to answer not her but the mystery, in the half-light, of her face that was turned towards his. In mid speech, as if for the sweet smell of her, the living nearness of her, his breath caught and his words stumbled. "I think there's part of one," he said, "believes a lot of queer things, when one is actually painting or writing."

"Part? And then, afterwards, not believe it any more?"

In a mist, under his eyes the sapphire woke and slept again as, with the slight shifting of her posture, the musk-rose milk-white valley narrowed and deepened.

She said, very softly, "Is that how it works? with everything?"

"I don't know. Wish I did."

V

QUEEN OF HEARTS AND QUEEN OF SPADES

A HALF MILE north-east from the summer palace at Memison, out along the backbone of the hill, a level place, of the bigness of a tennis-court, overhangs like a kestrel's nest the steeps that on that side fall abruptly to the river-mouth of Zeshmarra, its water-meadows and bird-haunted marshlands. Here, years ago, when King Mezentius made an end of the work or raising about the little old spy-fortalice of Memison halls and chambers of audience, and lodging for twenty-score soldiers and for the folk of all degree proper to a princely court besides, and brought to completion the great low-built summer palace, with groves and walks and hanging gardens and herb-gardens and water-gardens and colonnades, so that there should be no season of the year nor no extreme of weather but, for each hour of the day, some corner or nook of these garden pleasances should be found to fit it, and gave it all, with patent of the ducal name and dignity, to Amalie, his best-beloved; here, on this grassy shelf, turning to that use a spring of clear water, he had devised for her her bath, as the divine Huntress's,[1] in a shade of trees. A rib of rock, grown over with rock roses and creeping juniper, shut it from sight from the castle and gardens, and a gate and stairs through the rock led down to it. Upon the other side oaks and walnut-trees and mimosa-trees and great evergreen magnolias

365

made a screen along the parapet with vistas between of Reisma Mere and, away leftwards, of the even valley floor, all cut into fields with hedgerows and rounded shapes of trees, clustering here and there to a billowy mass of coppice or woodland. And there were farmsteads here and there, and here and there wreathings of smoke, and all the long valley blue with the midsummer dusk, the sun being settled to rest, and the mountains east and north-east dark blue against a quiet sky. All winds had fallen to sleep, and yet no closeness was on the air; for in this gentle climate of the Meszrian highlands, as there is no day of winter but keeps some spice of June in it, so is no summer's day so sun-scorched but some tang of winter sharpens it, from mountain or sea. No leaf moved. Only, from the inner side of that pool, the bubbling up of the well from below sent across the surface ring after widening ring: a motion not to be seen save as a faint stirring, as mirrored in the water, of things which themselves stood motionless: pale roses, and queenly flower-delices of dark and sumptuous hues of purple and rust of gold. In that perfect hour all shadows had left earth and sky, and but form and colour remained: form, as a differing of colour from colour, rather than as a matter of line and edge (which indeed were departed with the shadows); and colour differing from colour not in tone but in colour's self, rich, self-sufficing, undisturbed: the olive hue of the holm-oak, the green-black bosky obscurities of the pine, cool white of the onyx bench above the water, the delicate blues of the Duchess's bathing-mantle of netted silk; incarnadine purities, bared or half-veiled, of arm, shoulder, thigh; her unbound hair full of the red-gold harmonies of beechwoods in strong spring sunshine; and (hard to discern in this uncertain luminosity or gloam of cockshut time) her face. Her old nurse, white-haired, with cheeks wrinkled like a pippin and eyes that seemed to hold some sparkles blown from her mistress's beauty, was busy about drying of the Duchess's feet, while she herself, resting her cheek on her right hand with elbow propped upon cushions of dove-grey velvet, looked south-ward across the near water to the distant gleam of the mere, seen beyond the parapet, and to woods and hills through which runs the road south to Zayana.

"The sun is down. Your grace will not feel the cold?"

"Cold to-night?" said the Duchess, and something crossed her face like the dance, tiny feathered bodies upright hovering, wings a-flutter, downward-pointing tails flirting fan-like, of a pair of yellow wagtails that crossed the pool. "Wait till to-morrow: then, perhaps, cold indeed."

"His highness but goeth to come again, as ever was."

"To come again? So does summer. But, as we grow old, we learn the trick to be jealous of each summer departing; as if that were end indeed, and no summer after."

"In twenty years' time I'll give your beauteous excellence leave to begin such talk, not now: I that had you in cradle in your side-coats, and nor kings nor dukes to trouble us then."

"In twenty years?" said the Duchess. "And I to-day with a son of two and twenty."

"Will his grace of Zayana be here to-night?" Myrrha said, sitting on the grass at the Duchess's feet with Violante, ladies of honour.

"Who can foretell the will-o'-the-wisp?"

"Your grace, if any," said the old woman; "seeing he is as like your grace as you had spit him."

"Hath his father in him, too," said the Duchess: "for masterfulness, at least, pride, opinion and disdain, and ne'er sit still: turn day in night and night in day. And you, my love-birds, be not too meddling in these matters. I am informed what mad tricks have been played of late in Zayana. Remember, a spaniel puts up many a fowl. Brush my hair," she said to the nurse: "so. It is not we, nurse, that grow old. We but sit: look on. And birth, and youth, the full bloom, the fading and the falling, are as pictures borne by to please or tease us; or as seasons to the earth. Earth changes not: no more do we. And death but the leading on to another summer."

"Sad thoughts for a sweet evening," the old nurse said, brushing.

"Why not? unless (and I fear 'tis true) shades are coveted in summer, but with me 'tis fall of the leaf. Nay, I am young, surely, if sad thoughts please me. Yet, no; for there's a taint of hope sweetens the biting of this sad sauce of mine; I can no more love it unalloyed, as right youth will do. Grow old is worse than but be old," she said, after a pause. "Growing-pains, I think."

"I love your hair in summer," the nurse said, lifting the shining tresses as it had been something too fair and too fine for common hand to touch. "The sun fetches out the gold in it, where in winter was left but red-hot fire-colours."

"Gold is good," said the Duchess. "And fire is good. But pluck out the silver."

"I ne'er found one yet," said she. "So the Lady Fiorinda shall have the Countess's place in the bedchamber? I had thought your grace could never abide her?"

The Duchess smiled, reaching for her hand-glass of emerald and gold. "To-day, just upon the placing of the breakfasting-covers, I took a resolve to choose my women as I choose gowns. And black most takingly becomes me. Myrrha, what scent have you brought me?"

"The rose-flower or Armash."

"It is too ordinary. Tonight I will have something more strange, something unseasonable; something springlike to confound mid-

summer. Wood-lilies: that were good: in the golden perfume-sprin-
kler. But no," she said, as Myrrha arose to go for these: "they are
earthy. Something heaven-like for to-night. Bring me wood gentians: those that grow many along one stem, so as you would swear
it had first been Solomon's seal but, with leaving to hang its pale
bells earthward, and with looking skywards instead through a roof
of mountain pines, had turned blue at last: colour of the heaven it
looked to."

"Madam, they have no scent."

"How can you know? What is not possible, to-night? find me
some. But see: no need," she said. "Fiorinda! This is take to your
duties as an eagle's child to the wind."

"I am long used to waiting on myself," said that lady, coming
down the steps out of an archway of leafy darknesses, stone pine
upon the left and thick-woven traceries of an old gnarled strawberry-tree on the right, her arms full of blue wood gentians, and
with two little boys in green coats, one bearing upon a tray hippocras in a flagon and golden globlets, and the other apricots and
nectarines on dishes of silver.

"Have they scent indeed?" said the Duchess, taking the gentians.

"Please your grace to smell them."

The Duchess gathered them to her face. "This is magic."

"No. It is the night," said Fiorinda, bidding the boys set down
and begone. The shadow of a smile passed across her lips in the
meeting of green eye-glances, hers and the Duchess's, over the barrier of sky-blue flowers. "Your grace ought to kiss them."

The Duchess did so. Again their glances met. The scent of those
woodland flowers, subtle and elusive, spoke a private word as into
the inward and secretest ear of her who inhaled that perfume: as to
say, privately, "I have ended the war. Five months sooner than I
said, my foot is on their necks. And so, five months before the time
appointed,—I will have you, Amalie." She caught her breath; and
that perfume lying so delicate on the air that no sense but hers
might savour it, said privately again to Amalie's blood, "And that
was in that room in the tower, high upon Acrozayana, with great
windows that take the sunset, facing west over Ambremerine, but
the bedchamber looks east over the sea: the rooms where to-day
Barganax your son has his private lodging. And that was this very
night, of midsummer's day, three-and-twenty years ago." She dismissed her girls, Myrrha and Violante, with a sign of the hand, and,
while the nurse braided, coiled and put up her hair, kissed the
flowers again, smoothed her cheek against them as a beautiful cat
will do, gathered them to her throat. "Dear Gods!" she said, "were it
not blasphemy, I could suppose myself the Queen of Heaven in Her
incense-sweet temple in Cyprus, as in the holy hymm, choosing out

there My ornaments of gold and sweet-smelling soft raiment, and so upon the wind to Ida, to that princely herdsman,

"ὅς τότ ἐν ἀχροπόλοις ὅρεσιν πολυπιδάχου Ἴδης,
βουχολέεοχεν βούς, δέμας ἀϑανάτοισιν ἑοιχως·

"Who, on the high-running ranges of many-fountain'd Ida,
Neat-herd was of neat, but a God in frame and seeming."[2]

"Blasphemy?" said Fiorinda. "Will you say the Gods were e'er angered at blasphemy? I had thought it was but false gods that could take hurt from that."

"Even say they be not angered, I would yet fear the sin in it," said the Duchess: "the old sin of ὕβρις—[3] man to make himself equal with God."

Fiorinda said, "I question whether there be in truth any such matter as sin."

The Duchess, looking up at her, abode an instant as if bedazzled and put out of her reckonings by some character, alien and cruel and unregarding; that seemed to settle with the dusk on the cold features of that lady's face. "Give me my cloak," she said then to the nurse, and standing up and putting it about her, "go before and see all fit in my robing-room. Then return with lights. We'll come thither shortly." Then, the nurse being gone, "I will tell you an example," she said. "It is a crying and hellish sin, as I conceive it, to have one's husband butchered with bodkins on the piazza steps in Krestenaya."

Fiorinda raised her eyebrow in a most innocent undisturbed surprise. "That? I scarce think Gods would fret much at that. Besides, it was not my doing. Though, truly," she said, very equably, and upon a lazy self-preening cadence of her voice, " 'twas no more than the quit-claim due to him for unhandsome usage of me."

"It was done about the turn of the year," said the Duchess; "and but now, in May, we see letters patent conferring upon your husband the lieutenancy of Reisma: the Lord Morville, your present, second, husband, I mean. What qualification fitted Morville for that office?"

"I'll not disappoint your grace of your answer. His qualification was, being husband of mine; albeit then but of three weeks' standing."

"You are wisely bent, I find. Tell me: is he a good husband of his own honour?"

"Truly," answered she, "I have not given much thought to that. But, now I think on't, I judge him to be one of those bull-calves that have it by nature to sprout horns within the first year."

"A notable impudency in you to say so. But it is rifely reported you were early schooled in these matters."

Fiorinda shrugged her shoulders. "The common people," she said, "were ever eager to credit the worst."

"Common? Is that aimed at me?"

"O no. I never heard but that your grace's father was a gentleman by birth."

"How old are you?" said the Duchess.

"Nineteen. It is my birthday."

"Strange: and mine. Nineteen: so young, and yet so very—"

"Your grace will scarcely set down my youth against me as a vice, I hope: youth, and no stomach for fools,—"

"O I concern not myself with your ladyship's vices. Enough with your virtues: murder, and (shall we say?) *poudre agrippine.*"[4]

Fiorinda smoothed her white dress. "The greater wonder," she said, with a delicate air, "that your grace should go out of your way to assign me a place at court, then."

"You think it a wonder?" the Duchess said. "It is needful, then, that you understand the matter. It is not in me to grudge a friend's pleasures. Rather do I study to retain a dozen or so women of your leaven about me, both as foils to my own qualities and in case ever, in an idle hour, he should have a mind for such highly seasoned sweetmeats."

The Lady Fiorinda abode silent, looking down into the water at her feet. The full moon was rising behind a hill on the far side of the valley, and two trees upon the sky-line stood out clear like some little creature's feet held up against the moon's face. A bat flittered across the open above the pool, to and again. High in the air a heron went over, swiftly on slow wing-beats, uttering three or four times his wild harsh cry. There was a pallour of moonlight on that lady's face, thus seen sideways, downward-gazing, and on her arm, bare to the shoulder, and on the white of her gown that took life from every virginal sweet line of her body, standing so, poised in that tranquillity; and the black of her hair made all the awakening darknesses of the summer night seem luminous. And now, with the lifting of her arm to settle the pins in her back hair, there was a flash of black lightning that opened from amid those pallours and in a flash was hidden, leaving upon the air a breathlessness and a shudder like the shudder of the world's desire. At length, still side-face to the Duchess, still gazing into that quiet water, she spoke: "A dozen? Of my leaven? Must they be like me to look upon? or is it enough that they be—? but I will not borrow your grace's words."

Something seemed to stir in the warm air, with the falling tones of her voice: a languorous opening, rising and falling and closing again, of some Olympian fan. As it should have been sunset beholding the going up of Night, the Duchess stood and beheld her, as to say: You and I are one: the same common sky: one air: beauty, colour, fire. Night is young, rising in her ascendant while sunset dies: Night, kirtled with blackness and a steely glitter of stars: bat-wings; owl-wings soundless as the feathered wings of sleep; and, coming and going in unplumbed pools of gloom, pairs of eyes, bodi-less, like green moons, and the soft breathing of snakes that glide by invisible. So Night enters on her own, bitter-sweet with a passion of nightingales; and all presences of earth and air and water cover their faces before her: young (young enough, the Duchess said in herself, to have been my daughter), yet far older than all these: older than light: older than the Gods. But sunset, too, has her cli-macteric, renewed at every down-going: flowering into unimagined fire-shadows, as of some conflagration of the under-skies where all dead splendours and lovelinesses past and gone are burnt up with their own inward fire, and the red smoke of it is thrown upward in rays among incandescent mists, and overhead heaven is mottled like a kingfisher's wings, turquoise and gold and greenish chrysolite more transparent than air; and the sea spreads to a vast duskiness of purple on which, as on the dear native bosom of their rest, all winds fall asleep.

Fiorinda looked suddenly in the Duchess's face, through the deepening dusk, with eyes that seemed washed to the very hue of that chrysolite of the sky. "Words!" she said. "Will your noble grace abdicate your sovereignty to words: to-night, of all nights? Have words so much power? In Memison? O open your eyes, and wake."

For an instant the Duchess seemed to hold her breath. Then, with a high and noble look, "Put away your displeasure," she said, "and pardon me. The mistress of a great house hath many melan-cholies, and so it fareth with me to-night: not for aught concerns you. I bit the hand was nearest."

"Your grace has done me that honour to be open with me. I will be open too. I am not a commodity, not for any man."

"No," said the Duchess, searching Fiorinda's face. "I think that is true." She paused: then, "What are you?" she said. The dusk seemed to deepen.

"That is a question your grace must ask yourself."

"How? ask myself what am I myself? Or ask what you are?"

"Which you will. The answer fits."

"Well," said the Duchess: "as for myself, I am a woman."

"I have been told the same. And will that content you?"

"And with some beauty?"

"That is most certain."

"Yet it answers me not."

"No," said Fiorinda. "It is words."

The Duchess said, "I will search lower."

"Do, as the lady said to her gallant. You shall find a thing worth the finding."

"We are both, to say, in love."

"O unhandsomest and most unrevealing word of all. And of me —to say, in love!"

"Shall I tell you, then," said the Duchess, "who it is you are taken in love with?"

"I dearly wish your grace will do so."

"With your own self."

Whether for the failing light that veiled their faces, or because the thought behind each withdrew as a bird behind leafage until the intermittent flutter only and the song remains, their faces were become harder to read now and the beauty of each less a thing of itself and more a thing of like substance with the beauty (so unagreeable and contrarious to itself) which it looked upon. Of all their unlikes, unlikest were the mouths of those ladies: Amalie's with clear clean Grecian lines which gave strength and a certain inner heat of pride and resolution to what had else been over-sweetness: but Fiorinda's settling itself, when at rest, to a quality more hard and kinless than is in stone, or in the grey dawn at sea in winter, or in the lip of a glacier seen at a great height against frozen airs under the moon. And yet, near the corner of each mouth, bringing a deep likeness to these unlikes, dwelt a somewhat: a thing now still, now trailing a glitter of scales along the contours of lips that were its nesting-place and secret intricate playground of its choice. This thing, alert suddenly at the corner of the Duchess's mouth, beheld now as in a mirror, its second self in the curl of Fiorinda's lip, as, with a little luxurious silent laugh, she threw up her head, saying, "And with whom else indeed should one be in love?"

"Why, with all else," replied the Duchess, "sooner than with that."

Fiorinda drew nearer. "Let me consider your grace, then, and try: suppose you skin-changed to the purpose: rid away the she in you: more bone in the cheekbones: harder about the forehead: this dryad cast of your eyebrows masculated to a faun: up-curled mustachios: more of the wolf about the mouth:—no, truly, I think there is something in a woman's mouth is lost in a man's. Kiss me."

The Duchess, freeing herself from that embrace, stood half dazed and trembling, as one who, caught up and set on some pinnacle without the limits of the world, has thence taken one eye-sweep, one inward catch of the breath, and a headlong stoop back again to the common voices of earth: the thrush's note and the wren's, the talking of running water beneath alder and sallow, faint tinkle of cow-bells from hill pastures about Memison.

There was a sound of footsteps: the guard's challenge: opening of the gate beyond the trees: a swinging of lights among the leaves.

Six little boys came with torches and took their station in a half circle above the pool; so that those ladies stood in the torches' pulsing lowe, but the shadows, rushing together on the confines of that warmth and brightness, made darkness where before had been but translucent ultramarines and purples of the chambered dusk. And now, down those steps from the arched shade of pine-tree and strawberry-tree, came the King. "Leave us the lights, and begone," he said. The boys set the torches on their stands and retired, the way they came. Fiorinda, with an obeisance, took her leave, departing up the steps in a mingled light of the torchlight which is never at rest and the silver-footed still radiance of the moon.

"Word is come," said the King, as they turned from watching her: " 'The foxen be at play.' "

"That is the word you waited on?"

The King nodded, Ay.

"We have not even to-night, then?"

"The horses are saddled."

"But will you not stay supper?"

He shook his head. "Too much hangeth on it. The foil must be in their bosom when they thought it a yard off."

"Well," she said, and took hands with him; her grip less like a love-mate's than a fellow commander's: "your right hand find out all that you have hated, my friend."

The King sat down now on the deep-cushioned bench of onyx-stone, she standing beside him, her hand still in his, too close held to have escaped, even and it would. Presently she raised her eyes from their sidelong downward gazing and met the King's eyes, dark, looking up at her. "How chance you go not?" she said.

"Because I stand upon a just order in all things." With that, he drew her down to him on the bench, saying behind her ear, on a breath that came starry as the alighting of thistle-down, yet, as his hands possessed her, resistless as the rising tide of the sea: "Amalie, I chose you and loved you in my happiest times."

The Duchess spoke: "This be farewell. I'll not bring you on your way. Better fall from this than, i' the manner of the world, walk down again.—And tell me," she said, after a pause, as they stood now, her cheek against his, for she was tall, and his head bent to hers as he held her yet in his arms: "If we were Gods, able to make worlds as we chose, then fling 'em away like out-of-fashion garments, and renew them when we pleased: what world would we have, my friend?"

And the King answered her and said: "This world, and none other: as a curst beast, brought by me to hand; with lovely Memison, for a jewel of mine about its neck; and you, my love, my dove, my beautiful, for its rose, there set in adamant."

VI

CASTANETS BETWIXT THE WORLDS

ESSINGHAM sat iron-still. The music started once more: a bolero. Madame de Rosas, with bare arms braceletted with garnets above the elbow, bare-headed, and with one scarlet camellia in her hair, began upon an extremely slow, extremely smooth, swaying and rolling of the hips. Not to look at the sapphire, he looked at her: the red of her mouth, the whites of her black eyes. But immediately it was not she but the sapphire that, on the platform there, moved to these swaying rhythms; while the air of Mary's presence, fining gross flesh to the pure spirit of sense, raised it to some estate where flesh and spirit put on one another.

Slowly, and upon disparate faint clicks of wood with wood, scarce distinguishable even through the pale texture of the now muted strings, the castanets awoke again; then, softlier still, quickened their beat, and in a most tense graduality began to gather strength, as if horse-hooves should begin to draw nearer and nearer at a gallop from very far away. Here, no doubt, in this present drawing-room of Anmering Blunds, was the physical sound of them: the production, in natural air, of certain undulations which struck upon the tympanum of this ear or of that with varied effect, noted or ignored by this brain or that, winding strange horns, letting loose swift hunting-dogs, wild huntsmen, in as many shadowy

375

fields as minds there were to take the infection of this old clicking music dear to the goat-footed wood-god. But the inward springs or being of that music took a further reach; even as the being of some deep-eddying river-spate shapes and steers (not is shaped or steered by) these motions of leaf, twig, drowned flower-petal, water-fly, bubble, streak of foam, purling ripple, uprooted floating water-weed, which, borne by on its surface, swirling to its swirl, do but dimly portend the nature of the power that bears them.

Northward twenty miles beyond Memison, in the low valleys of the Ruyar, King Mezentius rode with the Chancellor, knee to knee. Now they breathed their horses: now put them to a walking-pace, breasting the long upward training of meadowland north of Mavia: now quickened to a hand-gallop in the dewy pastures of Terainsht. Iron-still was the King's countenance under the moon, and with a look upon it as if he had some hammers working in his head. But his seat in saddle was free and jaunting, as if he and the great black horse he bestrode shared but one body between them. So rode the King and Beroald, without word spoken; and in the beat of their horsehooves, irking the soft summer night, was the beat of the castanets, dear to goat-footed Pan.[1]

But in lovely Memison, where, seated with her women about her, the Duchess looked upon the revels held under the sky that night, this inside secret music touched the sense less unpeaceably, as it had been the purr of some great sleepy cat that rested as she rested.

And now that same peace, quiet as summer star-shine in a night without wind, settled too about Mary, whether through the music, or through the opening, like night-flowers when the sun is down, of the innermost heart and mind within her, or through some safety that came of Lessingham's nearness: of his coat-sleeve touching, light as a moth, her bare arm between shoulder and elbow.

"Go, my Violante," said the Duchess: "bid them lay a little table for his grace here beside me and bring a light collation, caviar, and then what you will, and framboises to finish with; and Rian wine. For that is royal wine, and best fits to-night: red wine of the Rian."

Violante went, lightly in both hands gathering her gown, down the half-dozen steps which, wide, shallow, made of panteron stone and carpeted in the midst with a deep-piled carpet of a holly-leaf green, led from this gallery down to the level where the dancing was. The summer palace in Memison is in plan like the letter T, and all along the main limb of it (which faces south) and along the shorter limb (which faces west) this gallery runs, with doors giving upon it and great windows, and with columns of some smooth white stone with silvery sparkles in it: these, set at fifteen-foot intervals, carry the roof above, and the upper rooms of the palace. A grass-plat, a hundred paces or more in length by sixty broad, lies below the gallery, with a formal garden of clipped ancient yew to bound it on the southern side, and a tall thick hedge of the same dark growth upon the western; and on the grass, in the north-west corner of this quadrangle, was an oaken floor laid down on purpose that night to dance on, with hanging lamps and flamboys and swinging lanterns round about on every side of it to give light to the dancers. Fifty or sixty couples now footed the coranto, in such a shifting splendour of jewels and colour of tissue in doublet, kirtle, lady's gown, rich-wrought fan and ornament, as is seen in some cascade that comes down a wide wall of rock in steep woods facing the evening sun, and every several fringe of freshet as it falls becomes a fall of precious stones: amethyst, golden topaz, ruby, sapphire, emerald, changing and interchanging with every slightest shifting of the eye that looks on them.

But as when, with the altering of the light, some watered surface or some column of falling water among the rest suddenly throws back the radiance of the great sun itself, and these lesser jewels are dimmed, so was the coming of the Duke of Zayana among this company. He came without all ceremony, with great easy strides, so that Medor and Melates, who alone attended him, had some ado to keep up with him: without all ceremony, save that, at word gone before him, the music stopped and the dancers; and two trumpeters standing forward from their place behind the Duchess's chair, sounded a fanfare.

Duke Barganax halted upon the steps and, with a sweep of his purple cloak, stood a moment to salute the guests; then upon one knee, kissed the Duchess's hand. She raised him and, for her turn, kissed him on the forehead.

"You are late," said she, as, letting a boy take his cloak, the Duke seated himself beside her in a golden chair.

"I am sorry, my lady mother. The King, I am told, was here to-day?"

"Yes."

"And gone again? Why was that?"

She shook her head.

"Thunder in the air?"

Amalie shrugged her shoulders gracefully. "And why late?" she said. Like they seemed, she and he, one to the other, as the she-lion and her son.

"Only that I had set myself to finish a head I was painting of for a new piece I am upon, of a mural painting of Hippokleides' be-trothal feast.[2] And so, third hour past noon ere I took saddle."

" 'Hippokleides, you have danced away . . . your marriage.' A subject needing some delicacy of treatment! And whose head that you painted?"

"Why, a late lady of your own: Bellafront's."

"Bellafront? she is red: Titian: of our colour. Could you not have left it till another day, this painting?"

"She might have been dead when I came home again."

"Dead? Is she sick then?"

"No!" said the Duke, laughing. " 'Tis no more but follow my father's good maxim; when I was little, and the best strawberry saved up at the side of my plate to eat it last: told me, eat it now, since I might not live to eat it later."

"You are absurd," said Amalie: "you and your teacher both. Is it true, Count Medor?"

"I were a bad servant, to call my master absurd," replied Medor; "and a worse courtier, to contradict your beauteous excellency in your own house. Well, it is true. He is absurd. But always by choice, never upon compulsion."

"O perfect courtier! But, truly, men are absurd by nature; and were you, my noble son, less than absurd, then were you less than man. And that—faugh! it was naught of mine: whether to have bred it, or to truckle withal."[3]

Supper being done, they sat on now (Barganax, with those Lords Melates and Medor, the Duchess, with her Myrrha, Violante and others), looking on the scene, in a contented silence which awoke ever and again into some lazy bandying of contented humorous talk. Lamps above and about them shed a slumbrously inconstant light. From great stone jars, ranged along the terrace edge, orchids laid out their strange and luxurious shapes, dusky-petalled, streaked or spotted, haired, smooth-lipped, velvet-skinned, exhaling upon the warm air their heady heavy sweetness.

"Will not your grace dance to-night?" Medor said at length to the Duke.

Barganax shook his head.

"Why not?" said the Duchess. "But no: it were unkind to ask you. You are in love."

"I was never in love yet," said Barganax.

"Then all these tales are but false?"

"The Duke," said Medor, "has never been out of love: to my certain knowledge, these seven years."

"What will you say to that?" said the Duchess. "As captain of your bodyguard, he should know."

"It is a prime error in these matters," said Barganax, "to fall in love. Women are like habits: if good, they stick fast, and that becomes tedious: if bad, and you love 'em, the love will stick like a leech though the woman go. No, I have taken a leaf out of their book: treat 'em as they treat fashions: enjoy for a season, then next season cast about for a new one."

Amalie fanned herself. "This is terrible good doctrine. To hear you, one might imagine some old practitioner, bald before his time with o'er-acting of the game, spoke with your lips. If you be not secretly already in love, take care; for I think you are in a dangerous aptness to be so."

The Duke laughed. "I was never sadly in love but with you, my lady mother:" he took her hand in his and kissed it. "Nor need you to blame me, neither. Surely 'tis the part of a good son to look to's parents for example? and here's example of the highest in the land for me to point to, when I will not overmuch fret myself for aught that's second best." He was leaned back in his chair, legs crossed at full stretch before him, silent now for a minute. His fingers, of the one hand, played absently with the Duchess's, while through half-closed lips his eyes rested on the bright maze of the dance and night's blue curtain beyond. "And, for your old masters of the game, madam: no. I am too hard to please. I am a painter. But pity of it is, nothing lasts. All passes away, or changes."

"Your grace," said Medor, "is a painter. Well, a picture painted will not change."

"Give it time, dear Medor, it will rot. And long ere that, you shall find the painter has changed. That, I suppose, is why pictures are no good, soon as painted."

"And no good, certainly, before they are painted," said the Duchess. "For is it not but in the painting that a picture takes being?"

"That is certain."

Medor said, "I have long begun to think, my lord Duke, that you are an atheist."

"By no means."

"You blaspheme, at least," said Amalie, "violet-crowned Kythereia,[4] the blessed Goddess and Queen of All."

"God forbid! Only I will not flatter Her, mistake Her drifts. She changes, like the sea. She is not to be caught. We needs must believe Her fixed and eternal, for how should perfection suffer change? Yet, to mock us, She ever changes. All men in love, She mocks; and were I in love (which thanks to Her, I am not, nor will not be), I know it in my bones, She should mock me past bearing. Why, the very frame and condition of our loving, here upon earth, what is it but an instrument of Hers to mock us?"

"Is this the profundities your learned tutor taught you, the old grey-beard doctor?"

"No, madam. In this, myself taught myself."

Medor smiled:

"Tho' wisdom oft hath sought me,
   I scorn'd the lore she brought me,
      My only books

Were women's looks,
And folly's all they taught me."[5]

"Well, Medor? And what of your young lady of the north, Prince Ercles's daughter, you told me of? What has she taught you?"

Medor answered soberly: "To keep her out of such discussions."

"Forgive me," said the Duke. "I know not what pert and pricking spirit leadeth me by the sleeve to-night." He leaned forward to pluck a pallid bloom of the orchid. "Flowers," he said, slowly examining the elegant wings and falls, domed and spreading sleeknesses: raising it to his nostrils to take the perfume. "As if it had lips," he said, considering it again. He dropped it: stood up now, leaning lightly against one of those silvery-sparkled pillars, the easier to overlook the company.

"You have out-Memisoned Memison to-night, madam," he said presently. "And the half of them I ne'er saw till now. Tell me, who is she in the black gown, sequins of silver, dancing with that fox Zapheles?"

The Duchess answered, "That is Ninetta, Ibian's younger daughter, newly come to court. I had thought you had known her."

"Not I," said the Duke. "Look, Melates: for dancing: as if all from the hips downward she had never a joint, but all supple and sinuous as a mermaid. I said I will not dance to-night; but, by heavens," he said, "I am in two minds, whether not to try, in this next dance following, which will she the rather, me or Zapheles. But that were 'gainst present policy. I am taming that dog-fox now by kindness: to do him that annoyance now were the next way to spoil all."

"Well, there is Pantasilea," said the Duchess, as there now passed by in the dance a languorous sleepy beauty, heavy eyelids and mouth like a heavy crimson rose: "a friend of yours."

But the Duke's gaze (which, never so idle-seeming, not the littlest thing escaped) noted how, upon that word, Melates reddened and bit his lip.

"I retired long since," said the Duke, "in favour of a friend. Now there," he said, after a little, "is a lady, I should guess, madam, of your own choosing. There: with hair coloured like pale moonshine, done in plaits crownwise round her head: one that I could paint in a green dress for Queen of Elfland. Is she maid or wife?"

"She is indeed of my choosing: Lydia, wife to a chamberlain of mine."

"Does he use her well?"

"It is to be hoped so. I think he loves her."

The Duke sat down again. "Enough. Go, Melates. I shall not

dance: I am looker-on to-night. No, in sober sadness, I mean it. But I would have you dance. Medor too."

"I had liever keep your grace company," said Medor. Melates with a low leg departed.

"There is no hope for Medor," said the Duke. "As good as wedded already."

Amalie smiled at the Count over her peacock fan. "And looks," she said, "as who should say, 'God send it were so.'"

Their talk drifted idly on.

Below, in a pause between the dances, Mistress Pantasilea waited, on Melates's arm, for the music to begin again. "You came this evening with the Duke?"

"Yes."

"He and his father: very unlike."

Melates raised his eyebrows. "Very like, I think."

"One red: t'other black."

"Well?"

"One all for love: t'other all for doing."

"I have two spears," said Melates: "each of gold and iron: the one with main show of iron, t'other of gold. Yet are both fair to look on, and each fit for the business at need."

"This one hath a more speeding trick, I would warrant, to lay down ladies than to govern a kingdom."

"You do belie him," said Melates. "Say rather, he grounds himself thus early in a wide apprenticeship to both these noble arts."

"Come," said she: "while you defend and I accuse, mischief is we both needs must love him."

Now began, stately and slow, a pavane. Barganax, on his feet again, still idly watching, bent over now and then to his mother's ear or to Medor's or to one of her girls', to ask or answer somewhat or let fall some jest. But now, at a sudden, upon one such motion, he stopped short, hand flat-palmed against the pillar, bending forwards a little, following very intently with his eye one couple amongst the dancers. The Duchess spoke. He made no reply. She looked round: saw that he had not heard: saw the fashion of his gaze, tense, like a bowstring at stretch: saw the direction of it: followed it. For well two minutes, very discreetly not to be observed, she watched him, and, hidden behind her eyes that watched, with a smile of the mind.

"Do you remember," Mary said, "that dance at the Spanish Embassy?"

"Do I remember!" said Lessingham, while, under his gaze, the quiver of velvet darkness within the sapphire deepened to the shadow or rumour of some profounder and living presence: as of all eyes and lips that have been man's since the world began: blinding themselves there, swept down there, drowned there to a kiss.

"It was curious," Mary said, very low: "our first meeting: not to have known."

The Duke spoke, suddenly down into Medor's ear, that was nearest: "What is she?"

Medor looked where the Duke gave him the direction. Something blenched in his eye. "I cannot tell. Till now, I have never seen her."

"Find out, and tell me," said the Duke, head erect, feeding his eyes. Under the upward curl of his mustachios the lamplight rested upon the Olympian curve of lips which, unlike other men's, the hotlier blown upon in the fires of luxury the finer ever and more delicate became their contours, and the subtler and the more adamantine their masterful lines of strength and self-domain. "Go," he said. "I would be informed of name and quality of everyone here to-night: 'tis as well, that the Duchess be not put upon by outsiders and so forth. Get me particulars."

The Duchess Amalie, in the mean time, very slowly and equably fanning herself, abode (in all beseeming) utterly remote and unaware.

It was after midnight now, and between the last dances. The Duchess and her ladies were, the most of them, now retired, and most of the guests departed. The full moon, riding in her meridian but low down in Capricorn, flooded the out-terraces westwards above the moat with a still radiance of silver. The Duke with slow, measured paces came and went with Melates the length of the terrace to and fro, two hundred paces, may be, to every turn. Eastward, the lights about the summer palace glimmered beyond the yew-trees: there was no music: no sound, save the crunch of the gravel as they walked, little night-sounds in the leaves, and, from below beyond the moat, a loud singing of nightingales. The path was white under the moon: the shaven grass of the borders on either hand wet with dew: the clumps of giant pink asphodel that, at spaces of ten feet or so, rearing their lovely spikes taller than a tall man, lined the length of that terrace on either hand, were blanched too to an indeterminate immateriality of whiteness.

And now as they walked, they became ware of two other persons come upon the terrace at the further end: a man and a woman, she on his arm, moving now slowly towards them. Midway, they met and passed. That lady's smile, as she acknowledged Barganax's lifted bonnet, came like the flashing, in a vista parted between blood-red lilies, of the deadly whiteness of some uncharted sea-strait.

"Do you know that lady?" said the Duke as they walked on.

Melates answered, "I know her. But name her I cannot."

"I can tell you who she is," said the Duke. "She is young sister to my lord High Chancellor."

"Why, then, I know where 'twas I saw her. He has kept her exceeding close: never till now at court, I think: certainly I ne'er saw nor heard of her at your presences, my lord Duke, in Zayana."

"Myself," said the Duke, "I ne'er saw her till to-night I saw her dance the pavane, with this man that is, I am told, her new husband."

"Your grace will remember, there was a notorious murder.[6] True, it was never brought home where it belonged."

The Duke was silent for a minute. Then, "Your great men, Melates, have commodity for bringing to pass such-like a needful thing, when need is, without all undecent show or scandal."

"There was show enough here," said Melates: "six hired cutters to make sure of him in broad daylight, in Krestenaya marketplace. And yet none durst name my lord Chancellor in it, nor her, save in a whisper and curtains drawn: and then, as your grace knows, there were pretty tales told."

"I've heard 'em."

"And yet," said Melates, "for less matter, himself hath ere this headed or hanged, in this time, scores of common men."

"The way of the world," Barganax said. "And some will say, best way too: better a hundred such should die, than one great man's hand to be hampered."

"But, too cruelly practised," said Melates, "may breed such discontent as should pluck us down, as history hath ere now remembered."

"There was never yet great men plucked down by the common riff-raff," said the Duke, "but they had first of their own selves begun to fall from their greatness. Never in this world, Melates: nor yet in any world. For that is a condition of all possible worlds."

"Your grace speaks wisely. Did your secretary (and late your tutor) learn you this? Doctor Vandermast?"

"I have learned much from the learned doctor: as this, for example—whenever you seem to speak wisdom, never to tell who taught you. Observing which, I shall doubtless in time have got a white beard and reputation of a great wise man. Unless indeed, which is likelier, cold steel—" the Duke waited as they met and passed, now the second time, that lady on her husband's arm: the green glint of her eyes in the moonlight, looking steadily before her: the glint of the moon on her teeth as she spoke some answering word to her lord: the carriage which, lily in crystal, became itself the more for the gown that veiled it, less like to natural woman's walk than to the swaying on languid stem of some undreamed-of flower, beside those curled and sweet-smelling darknesses those orchids upon the inner terrace should seem work-a-day hedgerow weeds. "—Or unless the bite of a she-puss," said the Duke, when they were out of hearing, "should first be cause of my death."

They walked on, silent, till they came to the south end of the terrace. Here, in the shadow of a holm-oak, the Duke stood a minute, watching the moon through the leaves. "The King my father it was," he said, watching the moon, "that would needs have this woman in Memison. The Duchess would not have her at first."[7]

Melates held his peace.

"He likes it that beautiful women should be here," said the Duke. "I grant, he has an eye for them. Well," he said, looking round at Melates: "is it not fit that he should? Answer me. It is not for me to talk always and you stand mum."

"It is not for me, my lord Duke, to judge of these high matters."

"So? I think there is some devil of folly in you I must exorcize. Out with it: will you say the Duchess my mother were wiser make 'em all pack, show them the door?"

"I beseech your grace: this is not my business."

"By God," said the Duke, "I can smell your thought, Melates; and hath the stink of a common horse-boy's. I say to you, her grace, my lady mother, is a queen rose; a goddess among them. By heavens, it were give small regard to her own quality or to the King's highness' discerning judgement, were she with timorous jealous misdoubts to let overcloud the sweet weather we have here. This that I tell you is truth. Will you believe it? Study your answer: for, by God, if you will not, you are friend of mine no more."

But Melates, as who would please one that is out of his princely wits, answered and said, "Your grace hath most unjustly mistook me. I believe, and did ever believe it. How else?"

They turned to walk north again between the dewy grasses and the uncertain whispering darknesses. Before them as they walked, their cast shadows flitted, hard-edged and black against the moon-flooded pallour of the path.

"Were you ever in love, Melates?"

"I have tried to follow the fashions your grace sets us."

"Fashions in love?"

"I know not."

"Fashions to keep out of it."

Slower and slower they walked, step with step. And now, forty or fifty paces ahead, they saw those others coming towards them: saw him suddenly break from his lady, run to the parapet on the left above the moat, clap hand upon the balustrade and make as if to vault over. Then back to her, and so again arm in arm.

Encountering now once more in mid-terrace, both parties, as upon a mutual impulse, stopped. Some puckish spirit danced in

Barganax's eye. "I am glad, sir," he said, "that you thought better of it: resolved after all not to drown yourself."

The lady abode silent: motionless too, save that, upon some slow, exquisite, half amused, half in derision, little condescensions of her head, she seemed to note the words: as if here were some strayed divinity, elegantly indifferent, noting these things from above. The fingers of her hand, in the crook of her lord's arm, lay out silver-white under their shimmer of jewels: a sensitive, beautiful hand, able (by the look of it) as an artist's, with sure and erudite touch, to set deep notes a-throb, attemper them, weave them to unimagined harmonies. So she stood, leaning sideways on that man, quiet and still in the unclouded serenity of the moon: virginal-sweet to look on as a wood-lily; yet with a secret air as if, like Melusine[8] in the old story, she could at seasons be snake from the waist down.

The man smiled, meeting the Duke's bantering gaze. "If you did but know, my lord Duke," he said, "what I was in truth a-thinking on in that moment!"

And Barganax was ware suddenly of that lady's eyes resting on himself, in a weighing look, completely serene, completely impenetrable. Deeper than blood or the raging sense, it seemed to touch his face: first his cheek below the cheekbone; then from head to foot the touch of that look seemed to go over him, till at last it mounted again to his face and so to his eye, and came to rest there with the same sphinxian unalterableness of green fires that slept.

"Curious our first meeting: and not to have known." Very low Mary had said it at first; and now, this second time, so low, so withinward, that the words, like a kestrel's nestlings that flutter at the nest, unready yet to trust themselves to wings and the untried air, rested unuttered within the closure of her lips. But, "Yes," it was said now, as if by some deeper abiding self that had lain asleep till now within her: "I knew. I singled you out then, my friend, as I now remember, though at the time it was almost unconsciously: yes, completely unconsciously. I knew, my friend. And knew, too, that you did not yet know." And about the words was a shimmer like the shimmer of the sun upon the tide off Paphos, the unnumbered laughter of ocean waves.

They were departed, two and two again, on their several ways. When at last the Duke spoke, it was as a man who would obliterate and put out of memory the flaming semblant, and grapple himself safe to common waking fact. "Shall I tell you, Melates, what was in truth in the man's mind, then when like a jackanapes he ran and skipped upon the parapet? It was the thought that this instant night, within this half hour maybe, he should have that woman where he wished."

They walked on in silence. At length, "What will you call her?" said the Duke.

"Call whom?"

"Whom else do we talk on? that woman."

Melates said uncourteously, "I should call her a dog-fly."

"A dog-fly!" With the moon behind them, the Duke's face was unreadable. "Well, Goddess hath borne that word from Goddess ere this." And he began to laugh, as it were privately to himself.

They looked round and saw that the terrace was empty now, save for themselves only. "Leave me," said Barganax. "I have a business to consider with myself. I will study it here awhile alone."

But that Lady Fiorinda, walking now in an obscurity of yew-trees, with that unconsidered arm to lean upon, turned Her mind to other thoughts. At Morville's third or fourth asking, What was she meditating upon so quiet? she answered at last, "Upon certain dresses of mine."

"Dresses. Of what material? Of what colour?"

"O, of the most delicatest finest material." The man saw snicker in her mouth's corner that little thing that neither now nor ever would heed nor look at him, but seemed always as if playing devilishly apart with some secret, boding no good. "And for colour," said she (noting, from above that mantelpiece perhaps, through Anne Horton's side-bended eyes, these lovers): "of a red-gold fire-colour, as the extreme outermost tongue-tip of a flame."

"It is a colour should most excellent well become you."

"Better than this black, you think?" And that little thing, in a pretty irony not for his sharing, twinkled its eye, (comparing, perhaps, two dresses of that fire-colour, so much alike: one, near of her own age, there beside Lessingham: the other here, in Memison, older by twenty years: dresses wherein She walked as it were asleep, humble, innocent, forgetful of Her Olympian home).

"Black?" said he, laughing. "You are dreaming! You are in yellow and cloth of gold to-night."

"O most just and discerning eye! How all-knowing an estate is matrimony!" And this time, the upward curl of the corner of her lip was as a twisting of tiny scaly limbs (as the thing said perhaps, in her secret ear, that a deadly sorrow it was if such a dull owl must much longer go uncuckolded).

But presently when, with those lips which hold the world's desire, She began to speak again, it was Her own poetess's words, and in the sweet Aeolian tongue: the ageless, fadeless, lilied numbers rising again in their undead youth: not as sound, not as movement or succession: rather as some subtlety of the air, some silvered showering of darkness: that shudder of the sense which, like meteors, runs near to heaven:

"φαίνεταί μοι χῆνος ἴσος Θέοισιν
ἔμμεν ὤνηο ὄστις ἐναντίός τοι
"ἰζάνει, χαί πλασίον ἀδυ φωνεύ-
    σας ὑπαχούει

"χαὶ γελαίσας ιμεϱόεν, . . .

"Like is he, I think, to a God immortal,
That man, whosoever he be, that near you
Sits and thus to you and to your sweet talking
    Privately listens,

"And lilt of your dear laughter: a thing to send the
Heart within my bosom a-leap; for barely
So can I this brief little while behold you,
    —Speech quite forsakes me.

"Ah, my tongue is broken: a sudden subtle
Fire beneath my skin in an instant courses;
Eyesight none remains to mine eyes: mine ears roar,
    Drown'd under thunder.

"And the sweat breaks forth, and a trembling seizes
All my body: paler than grass in summer
I: in all else, scarce to be told, I think, from
    One that lay lifeless.

"Yet, to dare all—[9]

All the leaves in that Memison garden trembled. Lessingham,
too, trembled, leaning towards his dear. And Mary, lost and trembling, felt her inmost being dissolve and fail within her, under his
eyes and under those self-seeing immortal eyes of Hers that, for the
instant, borrowed his.

Midnight sounded, grave, deep-tongued, from Anmering church
tower. Mary, on Lessingham's arm, stood quite still, here at the far
seaward end of the garden terrace, listening: listening now to Lessingham's whispered "Time to go."

"Don't go. Not yet," she said.

"I don't mean to: not without you."

"O don't let's—all over again. I've told you, and told you: I
can't."

"You said you would."

"I know, but I oughtn't to have said it. I can't. I can't."

"You can. I'll look after 'can,' my darling: that's my job."

Mary shook her head. They turned and began to walk, very slowly.

"You know my trouble," said Lessingham, after a silence. "I can't do without you. Can't live, without you. You know that."

She shook her head again, saying, almost inaudibly, "No. I don't."

"I don't mean shoot myself, or any tom-foolery like that. Simply, shan't live: my dead body walking about, if I haven't you."

Her face remained unreadable.

"The devilish thing about you," he said, "is that, before, I used to think of all sorts of things I might do, and do damned well. I knew it. But since you—all that's changed. There isn't a hard thing in the world I could not do, standing on my head, with you caring about it; but without you, not a thing of them worth the doing. You don't understand," he said. "How could you understand? But will you believe it?"

She said, like the sound of a moth's fluttered wing, "Yes."

"O my beloved," he caught the hand on his arm and kissed it: a cold little hand for a June night. "Then come. Everything ready: change of shoes if it's wet crossing the paddock: a new fur coat (we can give it away to-morrow if you don't like it)—"

Mary stopped: took away her arm: stood looking down, face averted, her breath coming and going, her hands tight shut. "How dare you do these things?" she said, in a kind of whisper. "How dare you tell me about them? Why did you come? Why? I told you not to. How dare you?"

Lessingham watched her. "It's been pretty difficult," he said after a while, without moving: "waiting: all this patience and obedience." For a minute they stood so; then she took his arm, and once more they began slowly walking. "We should never forgive ourselves," he said presently: "you and I, to turn back."

"Don't ask me this, my friend. For I mustn't."

"You're mine," he said, his lips touching her hair above the ear: then very softly, "you must."

"Yes: I am yours. But I mustn't."

"You must. Why not?"

"I'm someone else's too," she said, looking towards the house and its dark upper windows.

They walked on. The silence became frightening: the stiffening of Lessingham's arm under her hand: and now, when she looked up, his face, staring down at his own feet as they moved step by step.

"Be kind?"

"You're not being very kind to me," he said. "I'm not sure I've not been a fool: not been too patient and obedient:" Mary made a little sound of incredulous dissent: "not sure," he said, "that I'm not too late."

"What on earth do you mean?"

"Don't let's be absurd."

"You mean, when I said 'somebody else's'—"

The whole night seemed to turn suddenly sultry and sullen and unfriendly.

"Can't you give me too," Mary said, "a little credit, for being patient? being obedient?"

"Obedient! a dangerous virtue."

Again she stopped, and they stood off from one another.

"Don't let us play hide-and-seek. I'm frightened when you think I would—You thought—?"

Lessingham gave no sign.

"O, good heavens!" She held out both hands to him, laughing as if he and she should enjoy a private joke together. "Shall I tell you then? I refused—why, nearly two hours ago I should think. But why should you need telling?" she said.

He took the hands in his: lifted them up and up, to bring her nearer: a tremulous and starry propinquity, in which spirit to spirit drew to close that the bodied senses of sight, touch, smell seemed (as dragon-flies newly uncased from their prisons of the pupa) to hang faint and lost in the mid condition between two modes of being. Only that little thing, to all modes acclimatized and self-conditioned, and now very impertinently awake and active, regarded him from near her lip's corners. Answering which, something laughed in Lessingham's eyes. "So that's what made him look like—By heavens, I'd like to—"

"What?"

"Break the fellow's neck," he said tartly, "for daring—But it shows: there's pressure. And you're alone."

"If people should say: if he should think: O of course, that girl: we didn't hit it off, and now, you see, on the rebound—"

"Tsh! *They say, Quhat say they? They haif said. Let thame say.*" But the moon, shining down in her classic serenity on Mary's white evening dress and on those upper windows of Anmering Blunds, seemed to discover in these thumping words a sudden and most disconcerting insufficiency: at least as applied to Mary, and by him.

He let go her hands and stood, not irresolute but as if withdrawn for the moment into some inside privateness of deliberation: a silence that began to gather danger, as if one should listen for the muffled sound of bulls horning and wrestling behind closed doors. Then Mary watched the unconscious pose of him settle to lines such as, bound to an earthly permanency of bronze or marble, are sometimes seen in a masterwork of Donatello.[10] He looked up. "May I pick one?" They were standing near the stone pillar of a pergola grown over with Gloire de Dijon roses. Mary nodded, yes. "May I give it to you?" She took it, very gentle and quiet. "Let's walk along a little," he said. "Let me think.

"Well," he said, at last: "what's to be done?"

There was no answer, unless in the presence of her hand on his arm.

"Will you marry me?"

"I've promised to."

"How can you? What if they won't let you?"

"Give me two months: perhaps three."

"O these months. What then?"

"I'll have got things right by then. And if not—"

"If not?"

"If not—well: I've promised."

"You promised to come away with me to-night," he said.

He was suddenly kneeled down, his arms about her knees, his cheek pressed against her side. Presently he felt how her hand, very gently, began to stroke, the wrong way, the short cropped hair at the back of his neck: heard her voice, very gentle and trembling: "Dear. We mustn't go to-night. I didn't realize: it's too big, this of ours: it is All. How can we say, 'Let the rest go: take this?' The rest? it's part of this. That would mean spoil this for its own sake. It would be hateful. We can't do that. Shouldn't deserve each other if we could." It was as if those moon-trod spaces of lawn and cricket field were tuned to a music bearing as under-song some life to which this is but exordial. He heard her way, "Nothing can take it from us: not if we died, I think."

"We shall die someday. What then?"

"I don't know," Mary said. "Perhaps this is only the shadow of it."

"I don't believe it. This is all." His clasp tightened: his eyes now, not his cheek, buried themselves against her side.

Suddenly Mary, so standing, very still, began to say rather breathlessly, rather brokenly: "You could, you could make me go to-night. But you won't. It would spoil everything. It would hurt me. I'd always thought you were too fond of me to do that: thought you would never want to hurt me: you, of all people." Through the hammerings of his own veins he felt the trembling of her and the failing, like the yielded body of a bird in his encircling arms: felt the touch of her hand again, on his neck: heard her voice, nearer, lower: "But I'm not going to turn back. I don't doubt you, my friend. Here I am. Your very own Mary." The summer night seemed, upon that silence, to be suddenly frozen. "All of me. Do what you like with me."

But Lessingham, in this new worst wrestling behind those doors, held fast: remained as if himself, too, were frozen: then did but this: still on his knees, catch her two hands and kiss them: kiss the Gloire de Dijon, still held in one of them: then, rising to his feet, take her in his arms. "Good night, my dear, my love, my beautiful. Too good and perfect for me, but my own. You make me ashamed. Kiss me goodnight: I'm going."

And, for last goodnight, Mary, mistress of the situation, touching with the tip of her nose the most sensitive part of his ear, whispered in it: "Didn't I say: An omen, if you were wise? Michaelmas—Vintage."

VII

SEVEN AGAINST THE KING

KING MEZENTIUS and my lord Chancellor Beroald, having refreshed them with a few hours' sleep at Rumala, rode down from the Curtain into Rubalnardale: taking thus the easternmost, the directest, and the roughest-wayed and so most unfrequented pass over the mountains out of South Meszria northwards to the marches of the Zenner. They rode armed at all points, but cloaked and hooded. They were alone, even as alone they had set forth the evening before from Memison. A little beside Ilkis they began to bear away more northerly, leaving the beaten way and giving a wide berth to Kutarmish town; meaning to strike the river ten miles or more upstream and come over it by an unfrequented ford, and thence up by forest ways to the neighbourhood of Gilgash and the place intended. The sun had topped the far snow ridges of the range of Ramosh Arkab, and flooded all the vale of the Zenner with its fresh and unclouded glory of summer morning. They came on without haste now, and with time in hand.

"Beroald," said the King, reining in his horse at the top of a slope where the moorish champaign began to fall away northwards before them in fold upon fold of heather and silver birch down to the green flats, purpled with distance, of water-meadow and woodland and winding river, "I have changed my mind concerning this undertaking."

The Chancellor, with his most saturnine smile, said, "I am glad to hear it."

"Glad? Why you know not yet what it is." The King threw back the hood of his cloak: put off his helm: suffered for a minute the wild delicate morning breeze to play about his forehead and ruffle the ambrosial curls above his brow. Clear and smooth his brow was as the polished ivory; but the rest of his countenance, down to the beginning of the great black beard and mustachios, was weather-bitten and passion-worn with the tracings of iron resolution and of a highness of heart beyond the nature of man, and of humour and a most eagly suddenness of thought and act. And now, as he laughed, it was as if the infection of some unsmotherable superfluity within that King, ever rash, ever headlong, like lightning, or like the rut and furious rage of love, fed the cold light's flame in the watching eyes of the Chancellor that watched him. "For the life of me," he said, "I cannot bring myself to permit even you, Beroald, now that I come to the pinch, to have share with me in the grand main act."

The Chancellor shook his head. "I have long given over seeking to compass your serene highness or learn your drifts. You will go alone, then?"

"Alone."

Beroald was silent.

"Come," said the King, putting on his helm and drawing the hood over it once more: "you are a politician, and yet see not reason in that?"

"I see unreason in going at all. If I had your authority, I would be so bold to unvicar him, and be done. But that case I argue no longer. Your serenity over-ruled me there."

"Remember," said the King, "I go to-night to reclaim an outrageous unstaid hawk. If I go accompanied, he may think he has high cause to fear lest this wild worm of ambition wavering in his head shall be uncased and laid open to the view of the world. That may alarm him to some unadvised violence: fall upon us then and there, and so spill all. For if he do so, then one of two things, and both evil: the worse, me and you to be slain, fighting alone against too much odds; or else (the lesser evil) slay him—as I had resolved not to do, but to reduce him."

He paused. The Chancellor but tightened his lips, thinking it folly, no doubt, to spurn against the hard wall. "You shall therefore," said the King, "await me in a place I will show you, under a wood's side, a little this side of Gilgash. If I be come not again before midnight, then must you doubt not but that the worst is befallen, and so, haste haste post haste, back to Sestola, and do thus and thus" (instructing him at large in the whole manage of affairs).

* * *

Mean time, forty miles or more north-away, in the hold of Laimak, that grey eyrie by strength insuperable upon its little hill, which had been to the Parrys since generations both refuge from the storm and seat key and sustainment of that power whereby, through long vicissitudes and whether by open means or dissembled, they swayed the middle kingdom and fattened on the land of Rerek, the Lord Horius Parry, upon this sweet morning of the twenty-fifth of June, stood a minute at his window of his private chamber: gazed south. There was a tranquillity in his gaze: a tranquillity on his unfurrowed brow. Close-sprouting as a pile of velvet, the cropped hair ran up and back over the round head of him to the large bull neck: red hair, stiff like hog's bristles, growing far down the chine. His beard, clipped short too, came to a blunt point on the chin. His light hazel-hued eyes were small, set near, like a bear's: the sharpness of their glance as the flashing of diamonds. There was about his nostrils a mobility, an expansion, a bestial eagerness, so that, to look at him, one had sworn he lashed a tail. And yet, over all, that tranquillity, as of a mind at peace with its own self: all the great frame of him reposeful as a falcon hooded, or as quiet waters above some under-suck of the sea. Broad and heavy he was of body, may be nearly fifty years of age, yet knit to that hardness that comes of the soldier's life and the hunting-field, turning to brawn all over-grossness which might else proceed from overmuch pleasuring of table or bed. He scarce reached the middle stature; and yet, for some native majesty of glance and bearing, seemed a man that could be tall without walking on tip-toe.

"For's health, a were best be gone," he said without looking round. "Have you summoned me out that squadron of horse?"

Gabriel Flores answered him, seated at the broad oak table among papers and ink and seats: "Below the main gait, half-hour from now, your highness. As for him, a will hear no reason."

"Here's a villain that would face me down. Is he mad?"

"Like enough."

"Bring him in."

"If your highness pleased, I could send two lads to souse him in the moat. That might learn him."

"Bring him in, you sucking-pig."

Gabriel went and returned. "The Lord Sorms," he said loudly, falling behind to let him precede. But the room was empty. Sorms, much too aback, turned in anger upon Gabriel.

"You must have patience, my lord. His highness will certain be here anon."

"You villain, I am tired out with patience. Where is the money I gave you?"

"Your lordship hath had money's worth, and three times told in my wise advice."

"What? that I must spend yet a week waiting on my right in Laimak? Arquez hath done me wrong. 'Tis now six months since, with leave under seal vicarial and in your hand delivered to me, I have by suit of the King's peace and in all due forms took course to right me. But in vain. There's some works strings against me. I am not grounded in lands, and the faculty is very bare. At great charges I came south. I sent three days since to the Vicar for audience, but he would not be spoken with. I spoke with Rossillion: yesterday again with you: one might as well try to collect milk from a he-goat with a sieve. I sent after to the Vicar but he could not attend it for hunting. Or I will have it this morning, or I will hunt with him, by God's leave."

He strode up and down the room. Gabriel at the table fiddled about his papers: presently looked up. "I will yet, saving your worship, say a word of wisdom to you. 'Tis clean out of the ordinary, unbidden guests in Laimak. The Vicar's highness hath matter enough in hand without you and your private differences. He is wrath already with these importunings. Were I in your lordship's shoes, out of Laimak I would go while commodity yet is for departing. Till the fury of his highness settle, come not before him."

"I'll have my right," said Lord Sorms. "If not, I am resolved to hold you all such play as you shall be weary of. And you, master secretary, I do begin to discern for as honest a man as any is in the cards if the kings were out. You and your lord too." His jaw fell as, turning to a sound behind him, he faced the Parry in person, come secretly in at a little hidden door.

"Well, my Lord Sorms," said he, with much sweetness of words and amiable countenance, "I have read your lordship's depositions. And well have I in mind the painfulness it must have been to you, abiding here so long, desirous to know whether your matter be in any wise compounded, or like to be shortly compounded, or no."

"I thank your excellency. These concerns, be they but a trifle unto you, are to me a thing of good moment and importance. The pleadings, six months now, lie before your court signorial in Leveringay. Your secretary here, since April, hath notice of appeal unto your excellency's person as Vicar General in Rerek of the King. Nought moves. And now, marvelling not a little of the very frosty coldness and slack remissness shown me, I cannot but, joining words and deeds together, thereby see that all is but finesse. I cannot but think there be practices which—"

"Ay, practices," said the Vicar gently, gently drawing near to Sorms: Gabriel's ferret eye watched his master's. "And herein is lapped up a very great secret, which 'tis but fair, perhaps, I should now make plain unto your lordship, why I have had small leisure

for your domestical concerns. Well, thus it standeth: I, of my envious covetous and vengeable disposition, do now enterprise shortly
no less than to usurp and seize, wrongfully and against all right, the
whole sovereign power of the King in Rerek. Which to keep safe in
your mouth, take this:" and, leaping like unkennelled Cerberus,[1]
stabbed him in with a dagger from his belt, first by the ear, next in
the ribs, last down by the collar-bone.

Gabriel, that was small and little of stature, leaned back against
the table, watching this business; his teeth, jagged and uneven,
showed yellowish betwixt dark beard and mustachios.

"I'll teach these little lords," said the Vicar, throwing the bloodied dagger on the floor. "Come muling to me with their ails and
plainings," he said, his breath coming and going with the exertion:
"and me so grieved with so great causes. Come hither, my mopsy."
Gabriel came: his face grey, his eyes wide with apprehension. The
Vicar grabbed his two wrists in a handful, while with the other
hand, broad as a dried haddock, freckled, shimmering in the sunlight with reddish growth of hairs, he fingered Gabriel's weasand.
"You heard what I said to the scum?"

"Yes."

"You credit it?" His eyes, searchful as needles, looked down
into Gabriel's.

"Not till your highness shall say it again to me."

"How dare you imagine it other than a lie?"

"Your highness need scarce be so rabious against me. I
daren't."

"And yet, weren't very so? What then? Speak, filth, or I'll end
you."

"Whom have I but your highness? I am yours. You can work
me like wax."

The Vicar's eyes searched his, as a knife should search a wound.
Gabriel held his breath. Suddenly the Vicar drew him to him, like a
woman: kissed him. "Even you, my little pigsnye, should find it
dangerous too surely to know my drifts. I find close habours of
discontentment: matters that may be uncunningly and indiscreetly
handled: foolish and furious designs. Go, I'll mell me with no flirta-
tions but them as end in bed. They shall see my back-parts, but my
face shall not be seen.[2] And so, walk you eared for attention in my
foot-steps, if you hope to live through these next dangerous days.
So," he said, letting go of him, "it is a careful life. Wipe up the mess.
Feed that carrion to the dogs. Then attend me at the main gate. We
must be by sun-go-down at the place you wot of."[3]

The sun was of that same day now near upon setting when Count
Mandricard drew rein, coming out of the wood onto the northern
edge of the clearing before a certain old waste and broken house

desolate among pine-forests a mile above the little village of Gilgash, that lies just within the limes of Rerek. He was a big man, dull-eyed, horse-faced, with brown leathery wrinkled skin and long straggly beard with never a curl in it. There seemed a great stillness in the clearing. Westwards, gleams of the sunset pierced here and there the purplish-greenish obscurity of pine-frondage and close-set up-right trunks. Presently he walked his horse up to the house door. Nettle-beds crowded up to the walls on either side. The windows were shuttered. He edged his horse round, and so, leaning sideways from the saddle, reached to give the door a great thump with the pommel of his sword. The stillness settled yet deeper after the sound of that blow and of the scutter of little feet (rats, may be) that followed it. Mandricard waited a minute, then, growling some ob-scenity, swung from the saddle, tried the latch, went in. The house was empty, of a displeasant odour of dry-rot and of spiders: odour of grave-mould. He spat and came out again: swung up again into saddle. Dusk was gathering swiftly and the last embers of the sunset dying between the boles: blood among gallows-trees. "Some and some is honest play," he said in himself. "Snick up. If I take heed to come to the Devil's banquet pat o' the hour appointed, why not they?" He spat. "Clavius," he said in himself: "a young sly whore-son. In all abomination of life, brisk as a body-louse, but I'd ne'er trust him unless held by the ears. Why he will use him's a wonder: having took his father's head, too, for letting himself be so bedid-dered in the Ulba enterprise,[4] and he Lord President of the Marches. Then Gilmanes. Well, a man that could betray his own brother-german to him, to be cut in pieces in Laimak dungeons, I suppose a may trust him after that. Fellow's jealous as a kite, too, of Ercles and Aramond: knows that, long as the Parry sits firm in Rerek and favors him, himself 'll be left in peace to keep his claws on Veiring and Tella which else must straight fly back to allegiance to Prince Ercles. Knows, too, should a been unlorded long since, outed of all his hopes, for's misgovernment, but the Vicar pled for him: fubbed it off. Well, a may count on Gilmanes. Stathmar—well: albeit I'd fear his goodness. No moving, though, without him. Who hath 's buttocks firm in Argyanna may with one finger sway the march-lands. Olpman: I count him but a daw. He's no starter. Arquez: I hate Arquez: what's he but a common ruffian or thief, grown fat with the usurping of others' rights? He hath used him afore, true enough; and meaneth (it is in every man's mouth) to uncastle Sorms for him.—And there's the sum. I think he hath need of better tools to make such a frame perfect."

He let the reins hang loose on the pommel. The soft measured noise of champing of grass carried in that ugly stillness a threat, as of Time's sands running out. As if it were said: How if all this were but to feel our affection to his person? Not meaning to strike, but first—having summoned us together here, in this outest corner of the realm—to choose out, snap in two, throw on the midden any blades of meaner mettle? Strange how all we cannot but entirely love and cleave unto him, like unreasoned beasts, that himself is evermore false and double. May be there's a design in these chance delays: heaven's design or his. Perilous, too, to be unobedient to the sovereign—"Howsoever, I'll think so," said Mandricard suddenly. "Pack while we may." And so, giving the reins a shake, rode away through the woods northwards.

He was departed but a few minutes when the others began to come in: Prince Gilmanes first, on a white horse: overtaking him, Count Olpman.

"Your excellence rides well armed, I see."

"You too," said the Prince.

"Whom must we meet to-night?"

"You can answer that as well as I can."

"Our host, our two selves, and four besides of his picking. How like you of those four?"

"Tell me their names first."

Olpman smiled craftily. "With your excellency's leave, I'll see 'em afore I name them."

"God's death!" said the Prince, "are we children, to beat about the bush when each knows, and each knows t'other knows? No matter: 'tis safest may be. How like you of them?"

"Trust him to pick sound."

"Trust? sounds strangely after such talk; and in the mouth of a man of law."

"When time comes for action, no moving save upon some hazard."

"I'll tell you, Olpman, wherein I'll put my trust. In hate sooner than in love, and ambition than loyalty, and commodity than either. 'Tis therefore I trust the Vicar."

"Why? because of commodity?"

"Yes. Commodity: to me in him, to him in me. You I'll trust, 'cause of the hate you bear to Beroald."

"Well, your excellency too, I think, hath small reason to love that one."

"For respect of what?"

"Yonder lecherous and bloody woman. Your nephew sticked with daggers at Krestenaya."

The Prince gave a little shrug of the shoulders. A haughty unkind cold melancholy man he seemed, not without charm of manner. "O as for that, I know not. The like occasion had egged us to the like cruelty. Yours, my lord, is the more unfallible ground: beholding this Beroald, your sometime pupil, ten years your younger, preferred, 'gainst all justice and reason, to this high place, of great Chancellor of Fingiswold. They ought not to think it strange if we shall otherwise provide for ourselves, and join with other, when we find no conformity nor towardness with them.—Here's Arquez and Clavius. 'Tis fear holds those two."

"Fear, 'cause the matter he knows against 'em?"

"Aye. And 'cause he can break them in pieces when he will.— Here's Stathmar. Good. I smell comfort in Stathmar."

In the failing light it was barely possible to know faces now, the moon yet unrisen. The Vicar himself on a great chestnut stallion rode in last: Gabriel at his elbow on a brown jennet and with a led horse in his hand laden with saddle-bags and two hogsheads of wine. "God give you good e'en," said the Vicar, leaping from horse-back and passing the reins to Gabriel. "Five. Well, go we in. Every man his own horse-boy to-night. Turn 'em into the yard behind the house: we'll take no chances where unreadiness might undo all. Gabriel, shutter the windows i' yon chamber: darken the chinks with cloaks: then light candles, set the wine on the table and the meat pies. We'll confer whiles we sup." Then, under his breath, unobserved, to Gabriel, "And forget not," he said, "the word I gave you: in case." Gabriel answered with a little swift weasel-glance, secret, gone the next instant, sufficient.

They sat about a bare trestle table: the Vicar at the near end by the door, Olpman upon his right, armoured to the throat, and Stathmar upon his left, with bold honest brown eyes, square brown beard and shaven head, a big man and a strong, may be forty years of age. Huge in bulk, upon Olpman's right, sat Arquez, with tiny pig-like eyes buried in rolls of flesh; then, at the table's end facing the Vicar, Gilmanes, with Clavius on his right, and so again Stathmar. Youngest of them by much seemed this Clavius, of a malapert and insolent carriage, fluffy yellow beard, and pale fish-like eyes. Gabriel by the Vicar's command was ever in and out, to keep watch: held his meat in one hand, his sword ready in the other, and took his sup of wine between-whiles.

The Vicar sat uncloaked now, in tanned leather jerkin armed all over with scales or sequins of polished iron and with golden buckles at neck and waist and a gorget of iron plate damascened with gold and silver. Bolt upright, his hands flat-palmed before him on the table, he went over his company man by man. "You have begun ill with me, Prince," he said for first word, thrusting out his jaw at him: "broke faith ere we be set at table."

Gilmanes changed colour. "I know not what your excellency means."

"Bring a train of soldiers with you, when I made it condition all should come alone. I saw 'em myself in Gilgash."

"I'm sorry. 'Twas but three or four only, for safety of my person."

"I can care for your person, my lord. Robbers and reivers walk not here at liberty uncorrected, in South Rerek, as in your northern parts they do use. If I am to trust a man, a shall trust me, tit for tat. Who else hath done like that? Olpman, I noted your badge on half a dozen buff jackets as I came through the village."

"Your noble excellence will pardon me, I hope," said the Count, "if I mistook the condition."

"If me no ifs. All this is against you, and shall be, till you make it good."

"I thought we were free to bring 'em up to Gilgash so we came alone hither to Middlemead."

"The Devil dirt in your beard. You deal like the fish sepia, you lawyers: ever smother your traces in voidance of too much ink.[5] Stathmar?"

"Not an one, my lord."

"There speaks a man. Clavius?"

"I dare not venture myself unmanned on the Meszrian border: by cause of Ibian."[6]

"Your old kind Meszrian host? Go, I think you've reason." The Vicar laughed, a single crack betwixt a snarl and a bark. "If I'd been so unkind as give you bound to Ibian when he asked me, go, I'd wager five firkins of muscatel 'gainst a couple of peasen you'd ne'er gone gulling again.—Arquez?"

Arquez sullenly answered, "No."

"What's no? I say you brought men, contrary to troth plighted 'twixt us. Answer me directly without colour whether it be so or not."

"I say directly, your highness, it is not so."

A combust black choler seemed to darken the Vicar's eyes glaring upon him. There was silence a minute. Then the Vicar spoke again, sitting back in his chair with folded arms. "By the ear-feathers of Sathanas! I'm heartily minded to a done with you all. My Lord Stathmar and I come hither alone, as articled:" (here Gabriel, passing in his hithers and thithers out of the door, with none to mark him, laughed in his sleeve): "the rest break faith, e'en in so slight a matter, quick as a dog will eat a pudding." Like rabbits under the menace of the stoat, those great lords sat mum, meeting one after the other the eye of him upon them. "Where's Mandricard?" None could tell. "If he hath turned tricksome,—go, they say kings have long hands: a shall find that I have longer. I'll have him cabosbed[7] like a stag and bub my wine from's brain-pan. Look you," he said, and a sudden great clattering blow of his fist on the board made all leap in their seats, "if there be any here doubteth to confide himself to me in this business, let him go home now. I'll take it upon my honour I'll bear him neither grudge nor disfavour. So only it be now o' the instant; for, after this business be opened, to turn back then shall cost a man nothing but his life."

But they, as with one mouth, with most vehement heat of oaths and promises, pledged him their fealty.

"Then," said he, "to proceed with frankness to the matter. There's not a man here but of Rerek born and bred. In this land of our fathers hath changes come about, these ten years or more. We be loyal liege subjects all unto our sovereign Lord the King (Gods send he live for ever). For all that, we feel the changes: feel the foreign hand upon us. Instance myself: Laimak since thirty generations her own mistress, but now fief royal: we must do suits and services. For the lesser fish i' the pond, where were they to-day if I had not stood 'twixt them and forfeit of their privileges? where were Mandricard? County Olpman, where were you? With the heads-man's hands already fumbling at your neckband, whose mercy, say, save mine could have availed to keep that head of yours upon your shoulders? ay, and a dozen more i' the like despaired condition, attainted after Valero's treason?[8] You, and you too, my Lord Stathmar, are witness to the sharpness of my correction of that trai-tor: to the sharpness too of my dealing with some that, seeing the realm fallen in a roar, thought it time to oppress their neighbours. But I shaved their beards right smooth and clean—insolents, o' the kidney of yonder office nobility we see puffed up now, Jeronimy, Beroald, Roder, and their kind: crammed till they belch again with the rightful sustenance of better men. So help me, I'll pluck down some or another of them too, ere I come to my grey hairs. Then you, Gilmanes. Be you remembered the King took Kaima from you, the most rich and precious stone out of your princely coronal, 'cause of this matter of your brother Valero; but by my procure-ment, was given you back again. I helped you 'gainst your neigh-bour Princes, Ercles and Aramond, that, of their long accustomed malice many years rooted, so vexed you in your borders. 'Twas thanks only to my speedy intelligence but last winter, in your little beggarly town of Veiring, that you 'scaped there unmurdered. I have still helped and upholden you in correcting of the mutiny of certain cities in your parts, which were dread in time to allure and stir the more part of the other cities to the like. To you, Arquez and Clavius, I say but this: I have in a casket matter against you enough (should you displease me) to send you to them that shall cut out the head, gammon, and flitches, and hang up the rest *pro bono publico*.[9]

"Broach some more wine, good pug," he said to Gabriel. "So much friendly exhortation marvellously dries the throat." He thrummed a morris dance on the table with his fingers while the wine was pouring. When he looked up, the thunder-clouds had left his face. "We be loyal liege subjects all," he said. "But sad 'tis and true 'tis, no King lives for ever; and 'tis mere prudence to ponder what waits us round the next turning. 'Twere no great wonder if some that have well and truly served King Mezentius should boggle if it were to come to King Styllis."

"As, by law, come it must," said Count Olpman: "to the son born in wedlock and undubitate heir."

"An untried boy," said Stathmar.

"Proud, insolent, jealous of all true merit," said Gilmanes.

"God abolish his name under heaven," said Clavius.

Arquez ground his teeth.

"Such inconveniences," said the Vicar, "are lightly by wise policy to be turned to advantage. But mischief is in his tutors. Be sure of this, my lords: come that day, you shall see a triumvirate of court sycophants, under colour of young Styllis, take power i' the Three Kingdoms: Roder, 'cause the boy clings yet to him as to's wet-nurse; the fat Admiral, 'cause of legitimacy and what has been must be; and Beroald, 'cause in the sheep's-heads o' the other two is not brains sufficient betwixt the pair of 'em to keep 'em from disaster not a sennight's space, nor resolution enough to hold to any course resolved on, but still must run to him."

"And besides all this," Stathmar said, "your excellency has to reckon with Zayana."

"Aye, I was coming to that."

"O, I redoubt not him," said Olpman. "So he have his pretty pussy to huggle withal, it forceth not. A do-little, a—"

"There your judgement, my Lord Olpman, so needle-eyed as I have known it, turns blind as a beetle," said the Vicar. "Five years now he hath shown himself, in conduct of his dukedom, high-thoughted like to's father. Because in his underage and jollity he will eat and drink and have dalliance with women, be not you so bedoted as think that the sum. Bastard blood is very bold and hurtful: the more so, come of the loins of King Mezentius. And we manage not this young Duke, he may yet prove a main part of our undoing. Styllis, Barganax, and yonder three unite and joined against us, our matter were like to go evil. But feed we but their factions and hold 'em apart (as, with him, we may use the offences Styllis hath unbrotherly committed and shall likely yet commit against him)—why, with such a policy, I dare pawn down my life, Rerek shall still find her a cloak for every rain."

There fell a silence. Under the Vicar's careless-seeming yet most discomfortably mind-searching glance, men's eyes shifted, as though each looked for other first to unrip the seals and show what underlay these unresty hints and half-spoken loose suggestions. "Let me put in your minds, if you forget," said the Vicar, "that you, not I, first sought such a conference as this is, when each severally in writing you put yourselves to my protection. And, that you may see how merely for the common weal I take hand in the thing, I'll tell you: if there be any man living you think likelier than me to help you in such perilous circumstances as but now we spoke on—show him to me. I'll give place to him, swear him fealty and upholding."

Every man of them sat mute as a fish.

"You, Prince Gilmanes: will you undertake, say?"

Amid angry murmurs, Gilmanes made haste to disclaim so ungrateful an eminence.

"Shall's let this stand adjourned, then? How if we send to Ercles in Eldir, bid him our following?"

"God strike him dead first!"

"The old keen tiger that in a wait hath lain for us so long?"

Clavius began to hum a ditty sung by Gilmanes's faction in the street of Veiring:

> The elder from Eldir
> God sent him here selder!

When he might have hearing again, Gilmanes said, "Shall Rerek speak with one man's voice, with whose if not with the Parry's?"

Gabriel Flores, eyed and footed like a weasel, went betwixt bench and wall filling first for his great master then for the rest. All drank deep. Then the Vicar spoke. "If I have given you," he said, "any sour words to-night, be satisfied 'twas but in consideration of the secret knowledge I had of my own will, and being resolved to make some difference between tried just and false friends ere I would strip off all farthingales to the bare nature of these high purposes. Let's confess it was never merry world in Rerek since Fingiswold came up. Which thing, though it be coloured *per jus regale*,[10] yet it is tyranny. Which tyranny—considering the straiter amity between me and you concluded, and considering your several private promises in writing (which, as I shall satisfy you, import an army of well five thousand men, veterans all, to be had abroad in a readiness at any time now upon ten days' notice given, resting upon Kutarmish)—why, 'twere abomination irremissible and everlasting scorn upon us if we overtopple it not." He paused. All they as they listened seemed but more and more to fan their feathers in his lime. "That is to say," he added, "occasion arising."

For a minute none spoke, man watching man. Then Gilmanes, making a cast about the table with his long pale eyes and running his tongue along his thin and bloodless lips, said, "I question but one thing, my lords. His highness said 'occasion arising.' But is not occasion instant upon us? seeing the greatness of our adversary and his infinite dominion in Rerek, that already hath gone far to work us all from princes into pages. Thinks, too, that he knoweth, I ween, some hollow hearts in Rerek; and is himself one that keepeth his displeasure in close, then, like God's severe judgement, dallieth not where to strike he doth purpose."

The air in that room seemed suddenly to have grown closer. Again man eyed man. Then, "God send him here," said Arquez with a thick gluttonish laugh, "and give me the unbowelling of him."

The Vicar looked at Arquez then sidelong at Gilmanes, through half-closed lids. "Argument: ergo, dally not we, but strike first?"

"Ay," said Clavius, "and strike him into the centre."

"Who speaks against it?" said the Vicar. "In so extreme jeopardous a work as you now propound to me, needs must each stand by all or else all go down *in solido*."[11]

"Better that," said Gilmanes, "than be still kept under like beasts and slaves."

"Who speaks against it?"

But in a confusion of high and clamorous words they cried out saying, "Strike, for Parry and Rerek!" "Death to Mezentius!" "Throw the crooked tyrant to the Devil!" "Chop him into steaks!"

"You, Stathmar?" said the Vicar, seeing him sit silent amid this rant.

"'Tis but that I will not," answered he, "be one of those who rashly before a great man enter into talk unrequired. To my thinking, it is better the sword be sheathed than unsheathed. Howsomever—"

The Vicar stroked his beard thrice. Huge as a lion he seemed, high seated in that great chair; and red as a fox; and untrusty to handle as a quick eel by the tail; and a king *in potentia*, wanting but the regal crown and sceptre; and wicked out and out. In the nick of time, ere he should speak again, the door flew open in Gabriel's face, and before them in his majesty stood the King.

All leapt to their feet, and, save the Vicar's and Gilmanes's, every man's hand to his sword-hilt. It was as if the instant moment itself leapt and hung tip-toed on an instability of movelessness, while men's minds, violently unseated, waited on direction. Only the Lord Horius Parry, as in lightning-swift apprehension of the posture of affairs, and of the choices, deeply ravelled of good and bad, of known and unknown, not to be eluded nor long put off, fateful of life and death, which it imported, seemed to face it with a mind intact and unremoved. Like the snapping of a string wound to extreme tension, Gabriel heard the silence break with the King's "Good evening, cousin": heard in the deep cadence of the King's voice, careless and secure, an almost imperceptible over-tone of irony that thrilled less upon the ear than upon the marrow that runs within the neck-bones: saw the Vicar's obeisance: saw, for one breath, their mingling of eyes together, his and the King's, as if each would craftily undergrope the other's policies.

All saluted the King now, with an unhearty greeting but yet with due humble show of allegiance, drinking to him peace, health, joy, and victory upon his enemies. The Vicar made place for him at the table's head, seating himself at the King's right, betwixt the King and Count Olpman. "Bare a fortnight since I tasted your noble entertainment, cousin, in Laimak," said the King, raising to his lips the goblet from which the Vicar had but just drunk his health, and pledging them all in turn. "And now, benighted in these woods, what luckier find than this hospitable room? or what luckier choice of loving friends and subjects to be met withal?" His eye seemed merry, as of a man set among them of his household, nothing earthly mistrusting.

"'Lack," said the Vicar, "this should seem to your serene highness a strange dog-hole, I'd a thought. And, truth to say, we be assembled here 'pon a strange business."

Wise men started, and light men laughed in themselves, at these words. But the King said, unconcerned, "I had supposed yours was, as ours, a hunting party."

"It might be named so. Your serenity has had good sport, I hope?"

"Tracked the big bear to his hole," replied the King: "but as yet not killed."

The Vicar met his eye without quinching. "As for our hunting," he said, "your serene highness will laugh at us. You have heard, may be, stories of this same farmstead: that there was of old a man dwelt alone in this place, a bonder, rich in goods and in cattle, alone save for's thralls. And these thralls, uncontented, it seems, with his hard and evil usage of 'em, one night, 'pon agreement had together, took and murdered him." Glancing round the table while he talked, he saw them sit like dumb beasts, as if afeared to meet some eye upon them were they to look up, his or another's. Only the King, idly fingering his wine-goblet, gave him look for look: idly, as one who rolls on his tongue the wine of some secret jest, the delightfuller to him because hid from all men else. The Vicar proceeded: "Since when, to this day, none durst live in the place for dread of the dead sprite which, as if said, rideth the roof a-nights, breaketh the necks of man and beast, and so forth. And is neglected so, some three generations and all fallen to ruin. Now the Prince here and my Lord Olpman, they laid me a wager, a thousand ducats, that these tales were sooth and that something bad resorteth indeed to the house; but I tell 'em is but old wives' foolishness and fiddle-faddle. Which to determine, we mean to sit out the night here, drinking and discoursing, with these four lords besides to witness whether aught beyond ordinary shall befall us."

The King smiled. "I'd a sworn there were things in this house worth the finding out. Coming but now, supposing it empty, and finding, 'pon opening of the door, this jolly company within, put me in mind of the old tale of the shepherdman's coming by night beside Holyfell in Iceland. He saw that the fell was opened on the north side, and in the fell he saw mighty fires and heard huge clamour there and the clank of drinking-horns; and he heard that there was welcomed Thorstein Codbiter and his crew.[12] He and his crew. You remember?"

"That had, that same night, as was known later, been drowned in the fishing?"

"Yes: dead men," said the King: "feasting that night in Holyfell. There's the difference: that here, at present, are all yet alive."

Furtively, as though some strange unwonted horror began to invade them, men's eyes sought the Vicar's, Gabriel Flores, watching there apart, bethought him how most things have two handles. How if one of these comates of mischief had blabbed out all to the King beforehand? How if his master, sitting so thoughtful, had the like inkling? Gabriel waited for his eye. But the Vicar, smiling to himself, played softly with the great seal-ring on his left thumb and gave eye to no man. "Your highness sees some danger, then?"

"A certain danger," replied the King lightly, yet not a man there sat at ease under the look he now swept round the table, "in meddling with such business as brought you here to-night."

The Vicar still smiling, nodded his head: still intent upon his ring. Men watched him as if they knew, how smooth soever his looks were, there was a devil in his bosom.

"In some serene highness' school well brought up," said Gilmanes, after a pause, and his teeth flashed, "we are inured to dangers."

"And yet," said the King, "there is measure in all things. Courage of the wise: courage of the fool."

"The second we know," said the Vicar. "What is the first?"

"Is it not a native part of wisdom? A wise King, for instance, that will trust his person unguarded amongst his loyal loving subjects."

Men began to shift in their seats a little, as unballasted ships are rocked and tossed. Clavius, being high with wine, shouted out, "Yes: and a hundred swords ready behind the door to secure him."

"That," replied the King, "were an unwise mistrust of them that were loyal. And yet for a jest: instance the extreme of improbability: say you were of that rank sort, here met to devise my ruin. Then I, having some wisdom, and knowing as a King should know, might come indeed, as I am come, but with a force of men without prepared to seize upon you; 'stead of (as 'tis) secure in my friends, and not so much as a man-at-arms to guard me."

Olpman whispered privately to the Vicar, "This be set forth to blear our eyes. He hath men at call. Our only safety, strike and strike suddenly."

"Quiet, fool, and wait my word," said the Vicar. He paused a moment, smiling, playing with his ring: then made sign to Gabriel to fill round the wine again. A look of intelligence passed between him and Gabriel, slight and fleeting as, at slack-water, is the beginning of the turning, this way and no longer that, of the great tide unresistible of the sea. Gabriel, when he had filled round, went out by the door. The Vicar found means to say to Olpman under cover of the general talk, "I had prepared this beforehand. We will a little play for time. When you shall hear me say to Gabriel, 'Why not the wine of Armash?' that is a sign to him to admit those that shall dispatch the King's business for him right suddenly. Pass round the word. This too: that no man, on his life, stir afore my bidding."

While Olpman was cautiously in this sense instructing Arquez, the Vicar said covertly to the King, "I entreat your highness, let's manage your faces so as none shall doubt we speak on aught but trivial matters. And if I speak unprobably, yet believe it—"

"No more," said the King, with a like secrecy and a like outward carelessness. "I'll tell it you myself. You have stumbled tonight upon a wasps'-nest. But I am come on purpose to take it. All present, you alone excepted, play underboard against my royal estate and person. I have proof: I have letters. Your charge it shall be that not a man of them escape."

"A squadron of horse, my own, distant from the farm some half mile," said the Vicar. "And these, I well guess, have twice as many against us. What profit in men-at-arms, though, when the head is off?"

The King laughed. "I am glad you are not a fool, cousin."

The Vicar, playing as before with the great ring on his thumb, said, "Go, I think there's not one here, I alone excepted, believes your serene highness is in truth come alone here and unattended."

"But you, cousin, are not a fool," said the King.

"I know now. I have put my life in your highness's hand.

"How so?"

"Sitting thus at your right hand. Your hand next my heart. And your dagger, I see, ready to your hand."

"We are neither of us slow of understanding," said the King. "And I think either would be sorry to lose the other."

They had means to speak some word or two more thus privately. Then came Gabriel Flores in again with a flesh flagon of wine. "I shall in a moment," said the Vicar, "give your serene highness proof of my love and fidelity plain and perfect." Gabriel filled first to the King, then to the Vicar, who whispered him some instruction in his ear. "And you shall see too I can play at shuttlecock with two hands," said the Vicar, under his breath to the King. "Which oft cometh well."

As Gabriel passed now behind Count Olpman's chair, his eyes met his master's, and he paused. Gilmanes, Clavius, and Stathmar were in talk, heads together, at the far end of the table. Olpman, biting his lip, had secretly, under cover of the table-top, bared his sword. The Vicar rapped out suddenly to Gabriel, "Why not the wine of Armash?" and, the word scarce out of his mouth, hurled his heavy goblet in Gilmanes's face, throwing at the same time with his other hand his dagger, which pinned Clavius's right hand (put up to save him) to his cheek. Gabriel, bringing down the wine-flagon with all his might upon the bald pate of Olpman from behind, dashed out his brains. The King was sprung to his feet, sword drawn: the Vicar beside him. Amid this broilery and fury, leaping shadows on wall and ceiling, knives thrown, chairs and benches overset, the King crossed blades with Stathmar: both notable swordsmen. Arquez threw a pie-dish at the King: grazed his cheek-bone: then a chair, but it fell short, sweeping (save one) every candle from the table. At fifth or sixth pass now in that uncertain light, Stathmar fell, run through the heart. Arquez, seeing this: seeing Olpman lie sprawled over the board, his head in a pool of blood: seeing Gilmanes stretched senseless, and Clavius wounded and in a mammering whether to fly or fight: threw another chair, that tripped up the Vicar rushing bloodily upon him: then yet another at the King. It missed. Arquez jumped for the window. The King caught the chair in mid-air, hurled it again, took him on the back-side, well nigh broke his tail-bone. Down from the window he dropped, and Gabriel, with skillfully aimed kicks and with strampling on his face and belly, soon stopped his noise.

Clavius, casting himself prostrate now under the King's feet, cried out that, might but his life be spared, he would declare all: "I was neither author nor actor: only persuaded and drawn in by Olpman and Gilmanes and by—" His speech dried up in his throat as, gazing wildly round, he saw how the Vicar beheld him with a look as fell, as venomous, and as cruel as is in the face of the death-adder.

"Tie them all up," said the King: "these three that be left alive." Gabriel tied them hand and foot with rope from the pack-saddles: set them on a bench against the wall: gathered some candles from the floor to make a better light. Gilmanes and Arquez were by now come to themselves again. Little content they seemed with their lot; seeing moreover how the King drew a sheaf of papers from his bosom. But never a word they uttered.

The King's countenance seemed as a pouring down of black darkness from the sky, where all else becomes undiscernible, even to the stars whose operations make the fortunes and the destinies of men. "Some things," he said, "be provable, some unprovable. I know not how many principal members there be and how many unprincipal. I say (and that not without sufficient evidence of your own letters) that you came hither confederated to work an utter mischief against my estate, that am your King and Lord. What reason had you for such ingratitudes and undeserved unkindness?— You, Gilmanes? that four years ago I spared your life at the suit of your grey beard, and ever since have too patiently borne with your harsh government and cruelties used against my liege-men? But your ungracious and unheard wickedness shall come down upon your own pate.—You, Arquez? in hope that, if the realm were but turmoiled and shaken, your oppressing of your neighbours might have easy scope? It will come to fifty thousand ducats that you have robbed of my good subjects; but now is your audit near.—You, Clavius? because time and again my hand has opened bounty to you, but, for all that, you have remained our well proved evil willer, and, as we see, a fool besides and a dastard.

"I bid you, therefore," he said to the Vicar, "let me see the three heads off, of Clavius, Arquez, and Gilmanes, before either any man else go from this room or come into it. Olpman's too: should have been. Second bite, after I'd pardoned him his share in Valero's rebellion: it was too much. But the rat your secretary saved us that trouble. Stathmar I'd have spared. A good man, but unfit, after this, to be in the land, considering too he held the government and sway of so high a place. Him I'd have banished. But fate, you see, hath banished him further than I could."

For a minute there was dead silence. Then the Vicar motioned to Gabriel. "Work for you to try your hand on. You have the King's warrant. Creep into them." Gabriel took up his sword and stepped forward, trying the edge with his thumb. The Vicar said again, "Creep into them, basset."

But Clavius began to scream out against the Vicar: "What of yonder cruel devil, that bred all our miseries? setter on of all this, the arch-rebel himself?—"

"Hold!" said the Vicar like a thunder-crack, and Gabriel lowered his blade, swung hastily for the blow.

"—Spoke to us, King," shouted Clavius, "ere you came in: a seditious discourse farsed full of unfitting words, bordering on such strange designs that had made me haste forth, but that in the nick of time your serene highness fortunately coming in—"

The Vicar's face was scarlet: his regard inscrutable as stone. But in the King's eyes there but flickered an ironic smile. He snapped his fingers: "Why are their heads not dealt with?" and Gabriel speedily dealt with them, having off the head first of Clavius, then of Arquez (at two strokes, for the fatness of his neck); last, of Gilmanes.

"Your secretary, I see," said the King, taking the Lord Horius

Parry by the arm now and causing him to go with him out into the open air, "hath some pretty fetches: beyond what commonly we look to a learned clerk to do. Well, a fair riddance," he said, as they stood now alone under the starry sky, their eyes not yet used to the darkness. "Such men, alive or dead, lack substantial being: are a kind of nothing. Except Stathmar (whom I slew for indeed he gave me no choice) I'll be sorry for none of them: discard 'em as not worth the holding.

"But now, as for you, cousin: procurer and speciallest contriver —nay, deny it not—of all this horrible treason. What have these done to be destroyed if you go free?"

There was a strange stillness came upon the great muscles of the Parry's arm, locked in the strong arm of the King. Out of the masking darkness he answered and said, "Your serene highness hath not a tittle of evidence there against me."

"No. I said, you are not a fool."

"And besides, it is something, I'd a thought, that I saved your highness's life."

"And why?" said the King. "Why did you that?"

They were pacing now, with slow deliberate steps, away from the house. It was as if, for a minute, under the undark summer darkness, blood talked to blood in the unquiet silence of their linked arms. Then the Vicar gave a strange awkwardish little laugh. "This is scarce the moment," he said, "to ask your serene highness to swallow gudgeons.[13] I could give you a dozen specious untrue reasons you'd disbelieve. Truth is, with the suddenness and unknownness of your coming, I know not why I did it. If I had but a little backed my hand—"

The King took him by either shoulder, and stood a minute staring down into his face. There was light enough, of starshine and that luminosity which lingers at this time of year in a kind of twilight all night long, to betray a most strange uncustomed look of the Vicar's eyes: almost such a look as himself was used to meet in the eyes of Gabriel Flores. The King began to laugh: the Vicar too. "Truth is," said the King, "thinking of the matter unappassionately, there's something so glues me and you together as neither life nor death shall unglue us. Which you, my most wolvy and most foxy sergeant major general of all the Devil's engineers, are not able to forget when my eye is upon you (according to the old saying, *ex visu amor*[14]). But when you are too much left to yourself, you are sometimes prone to forget it."

"I'll swear to your serenity," said the Vicar, "by all the dreadfullest oaths you shall require me of—"

"Spare your oaths," said the King, "and your invention. I and you do well understand each other: let it rest at that. Indeed, and more of your lies might try my temper. Send that little jackal of yours to call up your men you told me of: explain the miscarriage of these five noble persons within there how you will. Take the credit of it to yourself if you like: I grudge it you not. Good night, cousin. And ponder you well the lesson I have read you this evening. There is my horse, tied by the gate there."

"But your highness's men?" said the Vicar bringing the King's horse with his own hand.

"I told you already, I am alone." He leapt into the saddle lightly as man of five and twenty.

"Alone?" said the Vicar and stood staring. "Nay," he said, "but I thought—"

"Are you in truth, cousin," said the King, gathering his reins, "so universal a liar as you end by seeing a lie in truth herself, even presented to you stark naked? As the drunkard that swallowed the true live frog in his beer-mug, supposing it but such another fantasm as he was customed to? Good night."

"Alone?" said the Vicar again, in himself, as the hoofbeats of the King's departing died away, leaving behind here only a great stillness and the night. "Go, I believed it within there 'mong those timorous and unthankful vipers. As well, perhaps, that I did. And yet: truth unbusked and naked, considered another way—might a tickled me up to what I'd now a been sorry for. And now—thinking on't in cold blood—go, 'tis a thing not believable!"

VIII

LADY MARY LESSINGHAM

I
T WAS NOW the twenty-fourth of June, nineteen hundred and fourteen, at Wolkenstein in the Grödner Dolomites,[1] nine o'clock, and a morning without cloud. Up in the sky, beyond church-spire and river and meadow and chalet and rolling pasture and pine-forest and grass-smooth steep-going alp, hung the walls of the Sella. Seen through that haze of air and the down-shedding radiance of the sun, the millions upon millions of tons of living rock seemed as if refined away to an immateriality of aery outsides, luminous, turquoise-shadowed, paler and thinner than thin clouds, yet immovable and sharp-outlined like crystal. It was as if slab, gully, scree-slope, buttress, and mile-long train of precipice wall, cut off from all supports of earth and washed of all earthy superfluities which belong to appearances subject to secular change, stood revealed in their vast substantiality; the termless imperishable eidolon, laid up in Heaven, of all these things.

On the terrace before the inn, people were breakfasting at a dozen little tables. Here a lime-tree, there a wide umbrella striped white and scarlet, made its pool of shade upon green-and-white chequered table-cloth, gravel, and paved walk. Outside these shades, all was drenched with sunlight. Here and there, a glass ball, blue, yellow, or plain silver, the size of a man's fist and having a short bottle-neck to take the top of the bamboo stick that supported it, gleamed among the rose-trees to rebate the glance of witches. All the time, amid the clink of breakfast things, was the coming and going, strong and graceful upon their feet, of the inn-keeper's two daughters: capable, self-possessed, with a native ease of manner and an infectious laughter, charming to look at in their red petticoats, many-coloured aprons, Tyrolean blouses of white linen, and embroidered belts with clasps of silver. Underneath all the sounds and movements was an undersound of waters falling, and, closer at hand, a hum overhead of bees in the lime-trees which put out at this season their delicate sweet-smelling pendant flowers. And, an intoxication of lilies to make eddies of these simplicities, sat Mary: by herself at an outer table, part in sun part in shadow.

There seemed a morning coolness, dew upon an ungathered lily, to rest upon her sitting there, unconscious, to all appearance, of the many pairs of eyes that having once looked could not but look again, as bees drawn (fly where they can) still to the honey-dropping of Aganippe's fount. Unregarding these looks, she now ate a piece of bread and honey; now (as if the little girl awoke anew in her to usurp the woman) dipped sugar in her coffee, and sucked and dipped and sucked again; now shaded her eyes to look up to the pale tremendous outlines afar of those dolomite walls under the sun.

Upon the sound from indoors of a voice among the many voices, she looked up. To a careless eye's beholding, scarcely she seemed to move the least lineament of her face. Yet to Lessingham, making his way across to her table from the clematis-shadowed door of the coffee-room, there was in some hardly perceptible quickening of her body and its every seen or unseen half-suggested grace, a private welcome that thrilled upwards as the lark ascending welcomes day. He took a chair and sat down facing her, himself in the full glare of the sun. He was in his traveling-clothes. They both laughed. "My dear Señorita, how extraordinary to run across you here, of all places!"

"Most extraordinary. And *most* embarrassing!"

"Of course I can understand that this is the last place in the world you'd expect to see me."

"The last in the world. So metropolitan. Much more natural to meet you in that shocking Georgian village in Suanetia: years ago—you remember? the year after I was married."

"You? married? How distressing! Did I know it at the time?"

"Behaved as if you didn't."

"O I shall always do that. Do you mind?"

"I think I prefer it," Mary said, and her foot touched his under the table. "We must be careful what we say—Don't look round—the gentleman behind you, with not one blade of hair on him: I'm a great puzzle to him. I'm sure this will make him draw the worst conclusions. A German gentleman, I think. He was in the train two days ago, coming up from Bozen. Had a curious stammer, and every time he stammered he spat. His wife has quite decided I'm the scarlet woman: shameless English hussy gadding about like this alone."

The elder of the girls brought Lessingham's coffee: "*And* a large cup," she said, putting it down with a flourish.

"What a memory you have, Paula!"

"O well, but some things one remembers."

"Are we to have the schuhplattler dance[2] to-night?" said Mary. "You and Andreas? I expect you've got all the steps now?"

The girl laughed. "To-morrow, it may be. To-night, no, no. To-night, some dancers from Vienna. We do not like them. But father say they can come once."

"Why don't you like them?"

Paula screwed up her nose and shook herself. "They are not as should be," she said. "Too saucy.—I must get you some more butter: some more honey." She went about it, direct as a water-hen hastens across a lawn to fetch food for its young.

"Herr Birkel is a pet," said Mary. "Fearful excitement when I arrived. Took my hand in both his. 'Welcome, *My Lady*. You are taller, I think, than ever'—and then, ever so confidential and intense—'*And* prettier!' "

"Perfectly true. Even in ten days."

"Ten days! It seems like ten months. Or—some ways—ten minutes.—You look very spry and wide awake after your all-night journey."

"Slept my berserk sleep out at Waidbruck: thirty-one hours solid. Hadn't had a wink for five nights.[3] Woke up about midnight: dined, or rather breakfasted, on soup, an omelette, Wiener schnitzel, a bit of Hansl and Gretl cake, red wine, coffee: made them produce a chariot: and here I am."

"I was so glad of your telegram," said Mary. "So all went well in Paris?"

"In the end. Only way—wear them down. Thing wanted tidying up: two years now since poor Fred went, and still hanging about with loose ends. So I just had to hold their noses to it till they signed what I wanted: just to get rid of me. Quite as amusing as fighting the Bulgarians.[4] Much more amusing than Berlin in nineteen-twelve.—Hullo, who's this?"—as a tiny white kitten clambered up the wooden balustrade and so onto Mary's lap.

"Mitzi," said she, handing it across the table to Lessingham. "—The fact is, you like to be in charge."

"I wrote to your father from Paris as soon as the thing was through; and to Jim, as your trustee. Told him there's two sums of twelve hundred thousand to go into trust: one under our marriage settlement, the other for you personally. Together, about a third of the whole. That's in case some day I go crazy with all this money business: take to high finance and burn my fingers. Do you think it's some Jew blood coming out?"

Mary smiled. "There's never any telling! The Medici blood,[5] reason enough, I should think."

"Sounds nicer. Still, if it has the same effect? You know, I wouldn't really like to spend my life money-grubbing. Not really," Lessingham said, holding up the kitten in his right hand where it sat as if in an armchair, and bringing it nearer and nearer to his face. "Not really, really, really." Mitzi, as if mesmerized, kept very still, staring at him out of eyes of that dawn-like blue that belongs to the eyes of little kittens; then, when he was near enough, put out a hesitating velvety paw to touch Lessingham on the cheek. "Have we the same room as then?"

"Haven't you been to look?"

"Do you think I'd waste time on that, when they told me you were on the terrace?"

"Well, we have," she said. "And your dressing-room next door."

"Do they blow the horn still at half past six, for them to open the doors for the beasts to go out to pasture?"

"Yes. And one microscopic child to drive them!"

"Want your wuzz again?"

She held out both hands: took the little creature. Lessingham lighted a cigar. They said no more for a few minutes; using perhaps the mountains, and the village life about them, and the bodily sight of each other sitting there as a directer medium than overt speech.

After a while, he spoke. "Have you ever felt double inside?"

"No," she answered, upon a note part mocking part caressing in her voice, as though "No" were washed with honey-water.

"One half all *Ambitioso:* set the whole world to rights and enslave mankind. The other half, all *Lussurioso* and *Supervacuo:*[6] makes me want to abduct you to some undiscovered south sea-island of the blest, and there, paint, write, live on sweetmeats: spend the whole course of everlasting time in the moving and melancholy meditation that man's life is as unlasting as a flower. Instead of either of which," he said, getting up from the table, "how about taking our lunch up to the Sella Pass?"

Doctor Vandermast, a learned man, present secretary and foretime tutor to the Duke of Zayana, was walking at break of day under Memison, by a trodden path south-eastward along the lake's edge, a mile or so on the way toward Reisma. It was between three and four o'clock: the twentieth morning after that secret master-stroke of the

King's in Rerek.[7] Reisma Mere, smooth like polished steel, spread to cool distances veiled in mist. Water, meadow-land, oakwood and beechwood and birch and far-off mountain ranges showed as but varying depths of that indeterminate grey, having a tremulousness within it as of awakening blue, which filled the whole sky. Only in the north-east the great peaks began to shape themselves to a gradual crystalline sharpness and to take on a more cold and azured tinge as the sky behind them became streaked with saffron, and at length, above the saffron, one or two little clouds (invisible till now) began to show purple, and to burn underneath with fire of gold. A delicate primrose-coloured light began to infuse all the east and to mirror itself in the still lake; and now, for first voice of day, the cuckoo replied to the owl's last hoot. The learned doctor, alone with the moment while other mortals slept, stayed it by his art: made it, as he walked, tarry for him awhile to his more perfect satisfaction and enjoyment.

He had years on his back four score. And yet, being spare of build as a dragon-fly, all eyes and leanness, he carried himself erect and without old age's infirmity. Hollowed with thought were his eye-sockets under their bristling eaves, and wan and lanked with thought was his cheek, but not to take away the fire-edge of that spirit which burned in his eyes. His white beard fell to his girdle. He was clad in a flowing gaberdine, ginger colour, and upon his head a scarlet bonnet of linsey-woolsey. Suffering, by his art, time to resume its course, he paused at a footbridge across a stream that, grown up with waterweeds, barely trickled toward the lake. Under the further bank, where a thicket of alder overhung that stream, was a water-rat, sitting in a ball, holding in her little hands a bit of weed and eating it prettily, like a squirrel. The doctor bade her "Good morrow, mouse;" and she, with a shy glance of beady black eyes set in her round head between small short rounded ears, greeted him again, in a tiny reed-like voice but with human speech.

"Where is Madam Anthea?" said the doctor.

"She passed by this way, reverend sir, about midnight on her way to the snows. Frighted me, me being in this dress and she in her teeth and claws."

"What, frighted of your sister? How shall we call this, but the most gross unknowing of God? She could not hurt you, my Campaspe, even if she would."

"It is not fit she should come in her dresses when I am in mine. Hers are too rough: mine, so easily torn."

"You can take your true shape."

"I like my little dresses. One must play and be merry a little: not duty and service all the time." She whisked across from the weedy raft she had rested on and so up the bank, and sat there washing her face and ears. "O we are all in our humours: grown a little restless, as you may conceive, sir, with all these doings."

Under Vandermast's nose the little nymphish creature changed in the twinkling of an eye her fur dress for feathers: for the silk-smooth brownish green dress, creaming to greenish buff in the under-parts, of a peggy-whitethroat: fluttered her wings, and was gone. From a hiding-place among the branches she ran him a descant, sweet falling notes of her woodland warble. His eye followed the sound to a flicker in the alderleaves; and there she was with her eyebrows. "There's been double-dealings of late," she said; "where neither of them had seen the other, nor none of them knew other's person, nor knew of other's coming." She hopped from twig to twig; daintily picked an insect or two. "Tell me, who is this King then? And this son of his, this Duke?"

"That question," said Vandermast, "raiseth problems of high dubitation: a problem *de natura substantiarum*,[8] a problem of selfness. Lieth not in man to resolve it, save so far as to peradventures, and by guess-work."

"And what is your guess?" She perched now in the tip-most leaves of the alder, bobbing and flirting her tail, looking down at him.

"You must be content with your own guesses, my little lovebird: I with mine."

"Why?"

She paused on the spray a moment; then flew down into the grass before his feet. "Well, I will tell you my guess so far," she said: "that they are one and the same, even as She in Her shapes is one and the same; and yet other. And this world his world: even as it is the King's. And by Her giving."

All the whole arch of day above them widened and rose moment by moment to new infinitudes of dawn-washed golden light. That old man resumed his walk, slowly onward.

She flew after him: settled on his finger. "Shall I take my true shape?"

"As you please. But you are very well suited thus."

"But I long to do as shall please you. You are so strange in your likes and dislikes. Why are you so?"

"Well," said Vandermast smiling, "you must remember, for one thing, I am very orderly in years."

"Do you choose, then."

"Your little dresses? there's none prettier, I think, than my water-rat."

She ran along his sleeve to the crook of his elbow and sat there eyeing him, while she washed her face with her paws. "Why?"

"In these matters, is but one answer why."

"Our Lady? She likes me thus?"

"Surely."

"She likes me all ways. We are part of Her empiredom. Is it not so?"

"Please Her," said the learned doctor, "it is so."

"There was a word in your mouth the other day: *deificatio*. What is that?"

"It is," answered the doctor, "a term of art, signifying a condition we can sooner imagine than understand: the fusing and merging of God and the soul into each other."

"Why?" The mouse-like hand and arm of Campaspe, suddenly in her own shape now, gloved to the elbow with soft brown leather that gave out a sharp odour of water-plants under a hot sun, rested light as air on his sleeve. Her grown of pale satin wrought all over with carnation silk made, as she walked, little summer-noises as of wind coming and going among reeds and willows. "Why?"

Vandermast smiled and shook his head. "Naiad: dryad," he began to say, slowly: "hamadryad: oread: nymphs of the woods and of gentle waters and of the kinless mountain, what can you learn by me? For you know all that is needful to know: know it as to the knowing born, without knowing that you know it: knowing it from within. Whereas I, that am but a looker on from withoutward—"

Campaspe looked up into his face with her bead-like eyes. "But who are you, then?" she said, and her hand tightened on his arm.

As from a window in the clouds a shaft of sunlight passes over the cold sea, so seemed for a moment the thought-furrowed lean countenance of Vandermast. "I am, I suppose," answered he, "an old man that am yet in love with youth."

"I had not thought of youth. Why with youth?" she said. "What is youth?"

But that learned philosopher, armed with so questionable a she-disciple, but came his way in silence.

Mary, walking ahead up the pass (a practice grounded, by tacit agreement, in two sufficient reasons: to feed the eyes behind her, and to leave it to her to set the pace), paused now in the shortening shadow of a pine. They were by this time come up a thousand feet from the floor of the valley, to where the hollow mountain side is a maze of hills and dells, with wide turfy stretches starred all over with flowers, and on every hand little water-courses: some alive with beck or waterfall, some but dry beds where water comes down after rain. And at every turn, with the winding upwards of that intermittent and stony path, the cliffs of the Sella constantly changed their aspect, lying back in ever more and more forced distortions of perspective as the way led nearer their roots, and thrusting up in succession ever a fresh spur of foot-stool to eclipse by its nearness the loftier summits behind it, and, in a vast illusion of instability, lean out from the body of the mountain. Under the gathering power of the sun the whole hillside was alive with grass-hoppers both great and small, taking hither and thither their low criss-cross flights, some with scarlet wings some with orange some with blue, and filling the air with the hot metallic thrill of their chirping. Lessingham, halting a few paces below her in the open, shaded his eyes to see her where she stood looking upwards to the thin roof made by the pine-tree fronds. Air stirred in the branches, sending ever changing tesselated patterns of white sunshine and amethystine luminous shadow across Mary's upturned face: her beautiful fire-red hair, done in the beautiful Austrian way, gleamed where the sun caught it, like polished metal; and every loose tendril floating on the air was at one instant invisible, the next instant a trembling of flame.

"The stillness of the trunk," she said, "Incessant little movements in the top branches. Do you think the world has its roots in heaven, and its branches spread out earthwards?"

Lessingham sat himself down on a rock at her feet.

"What a blessing," she said, "to have you real lazy, for once. The first proper lazy holiday we shall have had, for over three years. Never since Egypt, that last winter before Janet was born."

"We've not done badly. Honey-moon in Greece, nineteen hundred and eight. Caucasus, nineteen-nine: pure laze—"

He looked up at her: the Grecian profile, sweet serene forehead, very slight depression between brow and nose: eyebrows sweeping upward from the nose, then levelling: nose finely modelled, straight, pointed, with an almost imperceptible tilt up rather than down: cheekbones just sufficiently showing their presence to bring strength to the dove-like contours of her cheek: chin firm, throat and neck lithe, tender and strong: lips like the lips of a Goddess, tranquil and cool, yet of a most quicksilver mobility to fit every thought, mood, and feeling, as now a kind of satirical merry luxury of self-pleasuring comedy that blesses where it strikes, as she said, "The indolence of it, that Caucasus expedition! Nothing at all to show for it—except Ushba, of course, and about five virgin peaks!"

"Well and then next year, nineteen-ten," he said, "in the yacht to Lofoten in the early summer—true, I did dart across to Stockholm about those statues they wanted me to do for them. But, on the whole, pure lazes, both that and the month on the Italian lakes in the autumn. Still, I'll promise to be bone-lazy now for a bit. First instalment: I wrote and told brother Eric the other day (from Paris) to go to the devil, about the Parliament question. Too many jobs that want doing without that."

"O I am so glad!" said she.

"And I didn't give him an address. I'm very fond of Eric, and very fond of Jacqueline; but really we don't want them butting in again like that on our voyage to Kythera, as they did at Avignon."

They went on again, Mary ahead; maintaining for the best part of an hour a companionship of silence in which, the deeplier for no word spoken, presence quiveringly underfelt presence. From the top of the pass a ten minutes' pull up over steep grass and scree brought them to a shoulder of flowerclad alp, whence, out of sight of the path, you look east to the square-cut Towers of the Sella and west, further away beyond the hollow of the pass, to the rose-coloured wild fantastical spires and ridges of the Langkofel massif; Langkofel, Plattkofel, and Fünffingerspitze:[9] a spectacle at first blush unbelievable, unveiling at that moment above breaking clouds in the broad unreached sky.

"Like nectar!" she said, taking in through eye and deep-drawn breath the thing before her. "Don't you love to get up?"

"Up to a point."

"Where would you stop?"

"Here."

Mary drank the air again, standing tip-toe in an eagerness and poise liker to some creature of the woods and hills that is so fitted to its body that every changing motion expresses wholly and subtly, as music, the inward mood. Such a carriage, may be, had those swan maidens, king's daughters, flown from the south through Mirkwood to fulfil their fates; whom Weyland Smith and his brethren surprising at their upland bath, stole the swan-skin dresses of, and caught them so, and wedded them, and for a time sat in peace so.[10] "O I would not stop. I would go always higher. Wouldn't you come with me?"

"Would I, do you think?"

"Have to!"

"Well, but, say, twenty thousand feet: that might stop us. Heights above that, I've climbed at in the Himalaya. Can't breathe properly, lose your strength, can't sleep. And an awful depression: the sense of something watch, watch, watching you, always from behind. Like an oyster might feel, if it has an imagination, when the cook opens the shell with an oyster-knife and looks at it."

"I know. But we'd choose to be creatures that can enjoy it.—I'd like to be that," she said, pointing, as a party of choughs, glossy black plumage and yellow beaks, glided, dived, and soared below the edge of the hill, balancing on air, uttering their soft rippling cries.

She came and sat beside him: began to investigate and spread out the lunch which Lessingham produced from his rucksack. "Mass of eggs: I hope they've ducked them in cold water so that they'll peel properly. Rolls with ham in them. Chicken: I asked for that instead of veal to-day. All these snippety bits of sausage. Peaches. Plums—O you've squashed them! with your great coarse camera jabbing against them! A great wodge of butter.—Shall we ever grow old?" she said, as they began eating.

"No."

"We shall. I'm twenty-six to-day. You'll be thirty-two in November. We'll have to start being middle-aged. Thirty-three is a generation."

"You haven't given me my birthday present yet." Lessingham said, when they had finished and buried the remains.

"Do you want it?"

"It's part of the bargain."

"O stupid bargain."

"I like to go on with it. I like outward and visible signs."

"So do I. But this part of it—I mean the taking off—has lost its meaning. My dear, my dear, it has. The first time: even the second: but after that—"

"Well, you must think it a kind of exercise—a kind of ἄσχησις —for me. Come. Only once a year."

"Very well." She took off her wedding-ring and gave it him.

" 'Ours,' " he said, examining it: reading the Greek cut deeply on the inside of the ring. "HMETEPA. Feminine singular. Neuter plural. Mine, and yours."

Their eyes, turned together, rested in each other a minute, grave, uncommunicative, as with the straining between them of some secret chain in nature.

"Suppose," said Lessingham after a long pause, "one of us were to die. Do you think then there could still be any question of 'ours'?"

It was as if dogs howled on the shore. Mary looked away: across to the pale precipices of the Langkofel, rearing skyward above fans of scree that opened downward to the vast scatter of fallen boulders which fills the hollow below, called the Steinerne Stadt. "What makes you say that?" she said.

"To hear you say Yes. I wish I could say *credo quia absurdum,* as you can."

"I don't. I do believe. But not because it's absurd."

Between Langkofel and Plattkofel, lower but more venomous to look at than either, with its knife-edged reddish pinnacles, stands the Fünffingerspitze. "I climbed that thing twice; before I had a Mary," he said. "Alone, both times, like a lunatic. By the Schmidt Kamin. Deserved to be killed. No, it's not absurd," he said: "what we were talking about. But it's not believable. Not to me." He ground his nailed boot into the earth. "And the alternative," he said, "is, unfortunately, not absurd. And I find it unbearable: the mere thought, unbearable."

She shivered a little, still looking at those mountains. "I don't think we really know what we mean," she said, very low, "when we speak of Death."

"I don't think we do," said Lessingham. "But all philosophizing on that subject comes back to an earth of wretchedness and of darkness. The Red King's dream in *Alice*.[11] Go out—bang!—just like a candle."

"I don't like it when you talk like that."

"I used not to mind. Now I do."

They sat silent. He began considering the ring once more, turning it about in the sun, fitting it on his little finger first of his right hand then of his left: it would not pass the second joint. At last, offering it to her with a grave courtliness of manner, "Señorita," he said, "will you accept it back again?"

But Mary was stood up now, against the sky, looking down on him from above. And now, that minor diabolus twisting in its sleep there near her mouth's corner as if in the sweet unbusked luxury of some naughty dream, she replied, "No. I shall not. By your own stubbornness you've unmarried yourself. I'll think it over in cooler blood: possibly answer your proposal to-morrow."

"I'll come for the answer to-night," he said.

"You'll find the door locked."

"I'll get in at the window when you're asleep."

"You won't. I'll scream: create an appalling scandalismos! No, I mean it."

"You're a cruel wicked girl."

"If you're not nice to me, it'll be the day after tomorrow."

He stood up, safely pocketing the ring. "Well. Couldn't I even have a kiss?"

Sideways, tentatively, as she was used to do in the days before the era of grace, Mary submitted a very sweet but very Artemisian cheek. His lips nearly cornered the little horned thing in its bed; but Mary jumped away. And now as they stood and laughed at each other, the thing said privately to Lessingham: "Yes. A cruel wicked girl. Unpardonable. But what poverty of riches if she wasn't!"

It was ten of the clock in the forenoon, of Wednesday the fifteenth of July, in the lieutenant's house at Reisma. The master of the house was from home. The home-men and women were out in the fields along the lakeside, making hay. Under the sun's heat the house stood deserted, save only for its mistress, lazing herself on a bench of precious asterite stone under the cool of an open trellis of vines before the fore-court. Cushions made soft the bench for her reclining. Campaspe sat at her feet, holding up to her a mirror framed in pale mountain-gold garnished with sparks of small diamonds, sparks of aquamarines, and sparks of emeralds. Anthea, sitting sideways on the back of the bench, was fanning her mistress with a fan of white peacock-feathers which, at every to and fro, altered their sheen like a halo about the moon. The fingernails of Anthea tapered to claws: her hair seemed as lighted from within with a sun-like glory: white-skinned she was, of a classic cold perfection of form and feature, yet with eyes the pupils of which were upright slips opening to some inside hotness of fire, and with scarlet lips which disclosed, when she smiled, teeth of a mountain lynx. Behind Campaspe, there leaned against a pillar of the trellis-work that ancient doctor, resting, as in the contemplation of things of a higher strain than earth's, his regard upon the lady of the house.

"Signor Vandermast," said she, "it is now well onward in summer, and the days are hot and long. The Duke of Zayana, his eyes over-gazed in my excellencies, ceases not to solicit me in the unlawful purpose. My jealous husband sleeps dog-sleeps. Cool me a little, I pray you, with your unemptiable fountain of wisdom, and tell me why must I (being that I am) be teased with these inconveniences?"

"Why will your ladyship ask me such a question?" replied the doctor, "to which You (being that you are) are Yourself the alonely one and unsoilable answer."

"That answer," said she, "I could have had at any time this fortnight past, and without the asking; from his grace, who, as my true lover and humble servitor unguerdoned, is become to be as melancholy as a gib-cat. But I will not have lovers' answers, nor courtiers' answers, but an answer in philosophy."

"Mine was an answer in philosophy, madam; not sustentable, indeed, in the very point of logic, but as by fingerly demonstration: as we term it, a probation ostensive. And it is the only answer."

"Which, being unhooded, is to retort the whole upon poor me?" She reached an idle hand to pluck one of the moonlight-coloured feathers from Anthea's fan; considered curiously for a minute its shifting sheen. "O wherefore hath nature made the lawful undelightful?"

"There," replied the learned doctor, "I can none otherways but reject your major premise, which is but the empiric's judgement of imperfect laws, imperfect delights. When we have justly conceived the infinite nature or being of the Godhead—*infinitam Die atque Deae existentiam*—conceived it, that is to say, *sub specie aeternitatis,* we see that it doth altogether transcend this nice and frivolous distinction of the good and the beautiful. In this world, the good is that which serves the beautiful. And if there be any world where it is not so, then that is a bad world."

"I could imagine such a world," she said, stroking the feather to and fro softly across her knees. "You, signor, who are reputed perfect in your knowledge of all sciences and disciplines, able by your wisdom to unwrap the hid causes of things, and are besides a severe man, eschewing all sensual pleasures—can you unriddle me this: why must I, being that I am, have a body?" The silence hovered, listening to a bee's intermittent buzz and stillness among the jessamine blooms.

"I can answer but with the same answer again; desiring your ladyship but look yourself again in your self-loving glass. Some there be that have fantasied philosophical probabilities of a certain ὕλη,[12] a *prima materia* or brute matter, wherein (as they feign) do all corporeal beings consist, and of a spirit able to inform or transhape that matter to significant being. But far be it such under-age arguments should intrude themselves into God's divine mysteries; the key whereunto, to shut and unshut, is in the blessed endless duality in onehead of substance and Godhead, whereby Beauty and Omnipotency are paired together."

"Omnipotency: Beauty," said she, turning the feather this way, that way, in her fingers, watching its coruscations of pallid many-coloured fires in an ever changing changelessness glimmer and fade and gleam again: "Substance: Godhead: Duality: Matter: Spirit. A jargle of words to cast up dust betwixt us and things true and perfect, as the sun shines through white clouds unclear. Signifying (I suppose, if you will come to the point) that God Himself is not self-perfect, and therefore He made Me?"

The doctor regarded her for a minute in silence. "Yes," he said. "Schoolmen use these terms of generality as a kind of shorthand, to bear us in mind that large expression whereby it were partly possible the works of God might be comprehended in man's wit or reason. Your ladyship and that Other—He, the great Father of All—have so many countenances in Your variety that a man should as well seek to fit a garment to the moon as to set forth by enumeration of particularities the infinite nature of Gods. For instance, we speak of the Quesmodian Isles: say, 'There be nine little islands on a row.' 'Islands': it is but a pointer only: a plucking of you by the sleeve, in order that you may consider them together and severally in their manifold, unique, and undividable verity: this birch-tree, this twig, this bird on the twig, this white cloud, this breath of wind that brushes the marrams like hair, this dew-snail, this bubble in this well-spring, this grain of sand, unlike all other, and yet bearing likeness to all other. Even so, in a more august generality, we speak of Beauty; comprehending under that style all that, on this orbicular ball, is affined with your ladyship, or derived from your ladyship, or conducing to your ladyship's pleasure."

Fiorinda nodded: scarce discernible, the very shadow of a nod. "And therefore He made Me?" Her voice, suffering itself to vanish down the silence as down slow irrevocable unpathed waters of Lethe, seemed to leave on the air a perfume, a breath, a deep assurance, redolent of all lost loved things since time began, or the stars of heaven were made and the constellations thereof. "Me, created so consummately perfect that nought there is in earth or heaven that

He thinks worthy to suit Me (being so superfine) but alone to reign?
—Well, it was commendable!"

The stillness waited again on the bee in the jessamine flowers.
"I would dearly like," she said, "to be eavesdropper at some of your
discourses with the Duke your master. Have you taught him the
things a prince ought to eschew? as doting of women?"

"My Lady Fiorinda," Vandermast replied very soberly, "I have
taught him this: to know the perfect when he shall see it."

"So that his coming hither but yesterday, most peacockly
strained to the height of your philosophy and at an undue hour of
eleven o'clock in the night (my husband being from home), was with
purpose, I suppose, to have grounded me in that same lesson?—
Mew!" she said, "I sent him away with no other book to read in than
my unclasped side. Did I well so?"

"Everything that your ladyship does or ever shall do, is done
well. You cannot, of your nature, do other."

Her mouth sweetened and hardened again as she considered
herself: first, reflected in Campaspe's looking-glass, the image of her
face; next in the reposure of most soft content sweetly stretched
along that couch, the rest. "What a hell of witchcraft lies in woman's
body," she said. "Body and head together, I mean. As aqua fortis by
itself, nor vitriol by itself, hath no virtue against gold; but mix them,
you have aqua regia. And that hath a virtue to consume and dissolve
away even very gold itself."[13]

"Yet do I know a man," said the doctor, "compact of such metal
as even Your alkahest, madam, shall not dissolve nor consume. As
the ruby, which, when it cometh out of the fire uncorrupt,
becometh and remaineth of the colour of a burning coal."

"And I," said that lady, and again in the honey-sweet cadence
of each slowed word an echo sounded, faint, uncertain, full of danger, bitter-sweet: sea-sounds from a timeless shore: "And I do begin
to know him, I think, too: a man who is fingering for more of me
than God allows him. And, I do almost begin to think," said she,
"one who will gang[14] till he gets it."

Shadows were lengthening when Lessingham and Mary turned for
home. It was the time of day when the sun, no longer using the
things of earth as things to be trod under and confounded in a
general down-beating of white light from above, inclines instead
almost to a companionship with them. In that mood, the sun had
now singled out, like treasures each by itself, each tree, each broad-
eaved weather-browned chalet, each fold or wrinkle of the hillside,
each bend of each goat-track, each stone, each littlest detail of the
far-reared mountain faces, each up-turned flower; until each,
washed in golden air, rested picked out as a thing both perfect in
itself and making up with all things else in the landscape a more

large perfection: perfection bearing but this spot, endemic in all perfections of earth, that in time they pass.

They came down by a track that kept high in the sunshine under the cliffs of the Sella, then dropped steeply through woods to join their path of the morning a few minutes above the inn at Plan. The barn where, on their way up, hearing the thud of wooden flails, they had seen a young man and a girl at work threshing, stood empty now; but the dusty smell hung yet about it of corn and husk. The white walls of the inn were gay with paintings of flower-shapes and shell-shapes and, between the windows above the porch, of the Virgin and Child and holy men. A fatal accident that morning, the girl at the inn told them, on the Fünffingerspitze: a herr and his guide: in the Schmidt Kamin. The bodies had been brought down to Canazei, the far side of the pass. She had heard about it from Hansl Baumann, the chamois hunter. Herr Lessingham would remember him: had they not hunted together, a year, two years, since? Lessingham, as they went on again, felt Mary's arm twine itself in his.

Evening drew on apace. Their path crossed the bridge and joined the road, down which in a straggling slow procession cows were coming back from the alp: a dwindling procession; for at each house or turning, as they drew near the village, one or another would drop out of line of her own accord and leisurely, of her own accord, come home for milking. The goats too, undriven, came taking each her own way home. Evening was sweet with the breath of the cows, cool after the heat of the day, and full of music: a many-pitched jangling music of cow-bell and goat-bell in a hundred indeterminate drowsy rhythms. At one of the corners a child, three years old perhaps, stood expectant. A goat stopped came to him: paused while he gave her a hug with both arms about her neck: then, still in that embrace, turned with him down the path to a little poor house beside the river. Lessingham and Mary, lingering to enjoy this idyll, saw how a girl, littler even than the little boy, came from the house, staggering under the load of an open wooden box or trough which she carried in her arms and set down at last for the goat to eat. While she was eating, both these children hugged and kissed her.

Urgently, like something lost, Mary's hand felt its way into his.

"What, my darling?"

"What you said this morning: about feeling double inside."

"Yes?"

"To change suits? I believe that's part of it, don't you think?"

"Change suits?"

"Colours. King of Hearts: Queen of Spades. How silly that we can't, well—change dresses."

"Queen of Spades? Good heavens, I would never change you!"

"O yes. You'd give your soul for it sometimes. Instead of *Le Lys Rouge*, *La Tulipe Noire*.[15] When you are in that frame of mind."

"My darling, that is not me."

"Don't be too sure. Somebody else in your skin, then. O yes; and when I'm in the mood, indeed I prefer that somebody else to you, my friend!"

Lessingham was silent. Turning to go, they lingered yet a minute or two to watch the sunset on the Sella: a transformation at once more theatrical and more unearthly than that illusion of immaterial substantiality which the mountain had produced at breakfast-time. Hardly credible it seemed, that here was but, as in Alpine sunsets, an illumination of the rocks from without. Eyesight was witness against it, watching the whole vast train of storeyed precipices transformed to a single fire-opal, transparent, lighted from within by a quivering incandescence of red fire.

In a few minutes it was gone: swallowed up, as in the rising tide of a dead sea, by the rising shadow of night. Lessingham said, "Do you remember sailing up to the Westfirth, past Halogaland,[16] those sunsets on the Soundway? Not this burning inside. But they stayed."

"For a time. But they went. They went at last." The pallours that are between sunset and nightfall lay ashen on Mary's face, as on the face of the Sella. "Even the Sella," she said, "must not even that go at last? Though we ourselves go too soon and too quickly to notice it."

"Gods, I suppose, might notice it: see it, as we see the sunset go. If there were such a thing as Gods. Yes, it goes. All goes. And never comes back," he said. Adding, with a sudden tang of waspish-headed discordous humour in his voice, "How dull and savourless if it were otherwise!"

He looked round at her: saw, through the dusk, a faint lifting, like the wings of a sea-swallow in flight, of her eyebrows, and a faint mockery which, dragonflyish, here and away, darted across her lips. It was as if night and all the dark earth rose to her, upon a hunger of unassuageable desire.

Lessingham next morning opened his eyes to a greenish luminosity: spears of radiance and spears of shadowiness, all of a geometrical straightness, here vertical, there horizontal, there bent at obtuse angles and extending themselves away out of sight over his head: all very still. And all very quiet; except for a continuous undersound, like rain or like running water, saying to him, deliciously, lullingly, almost as with articulate speech: "Do not think. Do not know in what bed and in what room you are waking, or in what country. Do not wake. Shut eyes again. Snuggle the bed-clothes up round your ears: burrow your cheek into the pillow. So, with all senses abandoned to the touch of the owl-feathered wings of sleep, which, moving hoverly about you, wake what thoughts will be wakened and lull the rest, your self may taste for a while, unstrung, inert, unattached, the pure sensual beatitude of its own slumber.

"Slumber of the spirit, green and still. From depths deeper than these light-beams can wade, every now and then a bubble is released, floats upward, distinct and perfect, touches the glasslike ceiling, bursts, and is gone. So: in irregular slow procession, like cows at evening. This Tyrolean dance, gay mountain-bred, dancing to the blood: danced, it is quite true, 'too saucily' by these dancers from Vienna. Madame de Rosas rising through it, effacing it, Spanish and statuesque, upon a long tremolo of castanets: Mary listening, watching: Mary at Anmering: Mary under the pine-tree, and across her face, tesselated patterns weaving and unweaving of white sunshine and luminous jewelled shadows: grasshoppers on the hot slopes under the Sella, uttering—for whom if not for her?—their lily-like voice. Thunder-smoke of Troy burning:

"ἔσσεται ἦμαρ ὅτ' ἄν ποτ' ὀλώλῃ "Ἰλιος ἰοή
χαὶ Πρίαμος χαὶ λαὸς ἐύμελίω Ποιάμοιο"

"The day shall come when holy Ilios shall fall,
And Priam and the folk of Priam of the good ashen spear:[17]

"the slack weight in your arms beside the Struma: poor old Fred: like you, born for a fighter, berserk taint, brothers in blood: 'Strike thunder and strike loud when I farewell:'[18] thud of shells bursting, whining of them in the air: but the thinness, the shrivelled lack of actuality—was it all for this?—of the actual fact: of the end: trying to say something: bubbling of red froth between his front teeth: rattle of machine-guns—peas in a pig's bladder: no, castanets. Castanets, and the red camellia in that woman's hair: sense-maddening colubrine slow swaying and rolling of her hips: white of her eyes: smoothness of her hair: peace. Peace, in the velvet night of this single sapphire that carries in its dear unrest all these things and their swaying rhythms. It goes. All goes. All except Mary. Mary: always on the point to be caught, but never quite. Her galloping hoof-beats: like castanets. Kelling Heath and the awakening earth taking life from her life. The morning of life: the entry, upon pizzicato throbs, of that theme (which is Mary) of the Grand Variation in the C sharp minor quartet,[19] Queen of Queens, unutterable treasure of all hearts: things deep in time crowding to her, forming new earths to take their arms about her, new earths to be born and gone again and forgotten again at each throb of her footsteps.—'Perhaps my answer is sufficient, sir, if I say "Because it amuses me"?' The crimson of her mouth: crimson gloves: her white skin: that same matter which, asleep or awake, resides near the corner of Mary's mouth: Mary, but with this blackness: Ninfea di Nerezza—"[20]

So, of all these bubbles the slow last. At its touch, the glasslike ceiling trembled: tore like a garment: opened like a flower to a heaven unascended and unsullied of sunwarmed snows; and in the midst as it were a black flame to shine down the sun, and sweep up all senses in a moth-like wind-rushing blindness against that unspectable glory.

Wide awake, he leapt from his bed, flung open the green shutters, let in the white floods of sunshine. His watch on the chest of drawers said ten. He rang for his bath and, while it was getting ready, put the final touches to some lines he had written last thing before going to bed, on a half sheet of paper that lay on the top of a pile of manuscript and notes which he had been working over up till about three that morning.

Twenty minutes, and he had bathed and dressed. Then his eye fell for the first time on the envelope that lay on the bedside table. Her writing. He had slept late, and it was not his door that had been locked. Nether Wasdale paper:[21] this morning's date, twenty-fifth of June:

> Mon ami,
>   I've told Herr B. that we may or may not be back in a few days: meanwhile to keep the rooms. If you happened to be serious in the compliment you paid me yesterday on the Sella Pass, asking me to marry you, you know where to look for
>
>   Your Mary.

Lessingham, holding that letter in his hand, wore for one fleeting instant the aspect of a dog whose teasing mistress has made the motion to throw him the ball to run for, but has in fact teasingly retained it concealed in her hand. Next moment, in an up-bursting of volcanic mud-springs of black anger, his fist leapt up. He checked it in mid-air, and stood leaning his whole weight upon clenched hands on the table top: motionless, silent, only that once he growled like the Wolf fettered.[22] The audience to whom alone these naked antics were uncurtained—the four walls of that room, clothed in their wallpaper of unaspiring design, the round-seated bentwood chairs, the harmless table, the floor-boards having in their faint smell of soap a certain redolence of conscious respectability, the plain green rug by the bed, the green and white striped one by the wash-stand, and the innocent morning sunshine that pleasantly companioned them all—looked on with comfortingly unseeing gaze.

He sprang erect, the look in his eye a boy's look on a hunting morning; locked away the writing materials in his portmanteau, and kicked it back under the bed: laughed silently at himself in the look-ing-glass: flung a few things together into a suitcase; and went lei-surely down to breakfast. Within an hour he was driving down the valley to Waidbruck. And all the way, not to be shaken off, now dim, now loud, now lost for an instant, now near again, and wild hunt-ing-music, winding and swelling in secret woods and heady-scented unpathed darknesses, led the hunt through marrow and veins. He caught the train at Waidbruck; and about five o'clock that evening, thanks to his native mastery in sweeping away difficulties, to the inspired resourcefulness of Herr Birkel, and to a reckless use of telegraph and telephone, took off from Verona in a private aero-plane belonging to Jim's brother-in-law, Nicholas Mitzmesczinsky.

With neither train nor boat connexions to hamper him, nor delays of Sunday services, he landed, less than twenty-five hours after his start from Verona. His man David, instructed by telegram, was wait-ing with the car: coachman in the family like his father and grandfa-ther before him, with (of late, under protest and because needs must) part-time transformations to chauffeur. Lessingham took the wheel. It was—for a driver reckless and violent—two hours' drive home.

Evening, as the car swung in at the drive gates, was beginning with a spring-like freshness in the air after a showery day. The Wastwater Screes,[23] purplish black, stood against a confusion of grey-brown rain-clouds which blundered pell-mell southeastwards overhead. Riding higher than these and with a less precipitate haste, billowy masses of a pale indigo hue swept over from the west and north; and, like windows in heaven, rifts opened and widened one after another to quiet sublimities of white cumulus far above the turmoil and, above these again, of the ultimate sky itself; rain-washed to a purity of most limpid and tender azure: windless, im-measurably remote.

On the steps before the front door stood old Ruth: installed now as housekeeper at this manor house of Nether Wasdale, but still wearing cap and apron, as from years ago she had done, when she had had charge, as nurse, of Lessingham and of all his brothers and sisters before him.

"Well, Ruth," giving her the key of his suitcase which had gone round to the back door, "you got my telegram?"

"Yes, sir."

"Any news from her ladyship?"

"No, sir. Nothing so far."

"She'll be here to-morrow. Miss Janet asleep?"

"Ay, she is: heavenly lamb. Jessie'll put out your things, in the dressing-room as soon as I just unlock the lobby door upstairs, sir. Everything's ready there according to standing orders."

"No, I'll not sleep there to-night. The small room at the end of the west gallery to-night. O and, Ruth," he called her back. "You understand—they all understand, do they? not a word to her ladyship when she arrives, about my being here first."

"No, sir."

"Don't let there be any mistake about it."

"No, sir."

"Right. I'll dine in the Refuge."

"Yes, sir." The old woman hesitated. Something, some obscure throbbing perhaps in the air about him of that gay hunting-music, obviously eased her mind. "Please sir, if so happen her ladyship puts me the straight question, will you have me to tell her ladyship a falsehood, Mr. Edward, sir?"

"What you've got to do, my dear Ruth, is not to let on and spoil the game. If you can't do that much, without telling a downright fib, you're not the woman I've known you for."

"Mr. Edward was always one to have his joke," she said to David later.

"Ay, and her ladyship's a one too, bless her. But what beats me's his rampaging round with them there dang'd aeroplanes: hating and cursing 'em like he do, it's a caution. If he goes and breaks his neck one of these days, I'd be right sorry."

"What'd you do then, David?"

"Reckon I'd have to find a new situation."

"Like this?"

"Ay."

"Is there one, think you?"

"May be not."

"Back to Mr. Eric's at Snittlegarth?"

"Not at my time of life! Mr. Edward's a bit rough-like sometimes. But Mr. Eric, when he's in his tantrums, they do say as these days he's nobbut a stark staring madman."

"Where'd you go, then, David?"

"To that there Jackson Todd's."

"That's good! Why, he's dead now, be'n't he?"

"Another like him, then. That's your gentleman now-a-days. Got the brass, all right: but no better 'n a regular black card. I've see'd him at a shoot, over on them moors far side of Mungrisdale, afore Mr. Eric took 'em over. Did himself main well over his lunch, he did: had about a quart of champagne, he did. And there he were, a-yawkening and a-bawkening like a regular black card."

The same night Lessingham, in his way to bed, paused at the top of the wide staircase. With his master-key, that lived under the bezel of the ring on his left hand, he unlocked the lobby door on the right

there, and went in. At the end of the lobby another doorway, doorless and heavily curtained, led into the Lotus Room:[24] a room forty
or fifty feet in length, newly built out upon the east wing of this old
house. At the ends, west and east, were tall windows, and high-
mantled open fire-places between them. Since its building, three
years ago, few had set eyes on this bedchamber, or on the porphyry
and onyx bathrooms or the dressing-room or Lessingham's great
studio, upon which a door opened in the north wall, to the left of
the bed: a four-posted bed, spread wide and of great magnificence,
with hangings and coverlets of heavy bay-green figured silk and
sweet-smelling pillars of sandalwood inlaid with gold. Candles, by
scores, stood ready for lighting, upon tables and mantelshelves and
in sconces on the walls; but at present the only light in the room was
of electric bulbs, concealed in the chandeliers of crystal that, like
clusters of gigantic globular fruits, hung from the ceiling.

Pausing in the doorway, he leisurely overwent the room with
his eyes, as a man might some matter which he partly disbelieves.
The ring, key exposed, was still in his hand: Mary's wedding-pres-
ent, of massive gold having no alloy in it, in the shape of a scaled
worm, tail in mouth, and the head of the worm the bezel of the ring,
a ruby of great age and splendour: the worm Ouroboros, symbol of
eternity, the beginning of which is also the end, and the end the
beginning. And now, coming to the fire-place over against the bed,
he unlocked with that key the doors of a cabinet set in the chimney-
breast above the mantel and, gently, heedfully, as an artist traces a
curve, opened them left and right. Backing a few paces, he sat down
on the sofa at the bed's foot and considered the picture thus disclosed.

And so it was presently, as if the picture spoke. As to say: In me,
a portrait, constructed by you, upon canvas, with pigments ground
in oil, some limited perduration is in a shorthand way, given to a
fleeting moment. Looking at me, remember in your eye, in your
ear, in your nostril, in your secret blood, what was present in that
moment; and then, by all these senses under the might that is in you
forced together, remember what was not present, nor shall be.
Never present. Ever on the doorstep.—*L'Absente de tous bouquets.*[25]

To Lessingham now, sitting so in his contemplation, it was as if
in the edge of his field of vision the carved lotuses of the frieze,
under the hot flame of that picture bared, stirred slightly. The rude
hunger of the flesh was become, as wind at night sets stars a-sparkle,
the undistinguishable integument of some spiritually informing
presence: of a presence which, so in the picture as in life, with a
restful deep unrest underlay each perfection of the body. And in a
strange violent antinomy, the alone personality of Mary, that, serene and unalterable, queened it in every feature of the face—more,
in the whole deep indwelling music of body and limb—seemed, by

some fiery intermarriage of incompatibles, to take into this particular self that universal, which unhorizoned as sea-spaces at morning or as the ocean of cloud-waves overseen from on high in the faint first incarnadine of a new dawn, rested its infinity in these nakednesses of breast, of flank, of somnolent exquisite supple thigh, and in these sudden mindblinding dazzlements of curled hair shadowing the white skin. All which unspeakable whole, out of the paint and out of the awaked remembrance, said: Would you have Me otherwise? Me, always here? given you without the sweat and the agony and the birth-pang of the mind?—No, my friend. Not in Elysium even.

For, said the picture (and said the painter, to himself, out of himself), passivity is not for you: not for any man.—For a woman? Well, a species of passivity: the illusion, perhaps, of stillness, as at the maelstrom's center. A passivity that rests in its own most deep assurance of queenship over all overt power. A queenship that subsists even in its vertiginous climacteric of self-surrender:

> A quiet woman
> Is a still water under a great bridge;
> A man may shoot her safely.[26]

Mary, from her sleeping-carriage, arrived like day on the little lonely platform at Drigg[27] about half past six the next morning: the sun in her eyes, sea-swallows' voices in her ears, and heady northern sea-smells salt in her nostrils. "Leave it in the office, Tom. They'll come and fetch it this afternoon." "Yes, your ladyship," said the porter, putting her things on his barrow. He, and in turn the station-master who took her ticket, and the girl doing the steps at the inn, for each of whom she had a happy familiar word as she passed, stood a moment to gaze after her with the estranged look of woodland creatures in whose faces a fire has been brandished suddenly out of the dark.

It was a sweet morning: fields still wet, and lanes smelling all the way of wild roses and honeysuckle, with now and then heavier luscious wafts from the meadowsweet and sometimes the pungent breath of the golden whinflowers. So she walked home, seven or eight miles or so, swinging her hat in her hand for pleasure of the air.

Schooled, doubtless, to these ways, a well ordered household respectfully abstained from telling her that he was there first, and in fact now in his bath. And Mary for her part reading, doubtless, Ruth's too readable eyes, asked no questions. Only she remarked (falsely true) that the master had missed his train on Saturday morning, and would, it was to be feared, not be home till to-morrow. And so, resignedly, ordered her breakfast in the Refuge with Sheila. And was, resignedly, eating it when Lessingham came down.

And he, doubtless no less ready to take his cue, watched her for a minute, himself unseen, as, bending her white neck, she rested, chin in hand, in a beautifulness, so self-sufficing, a contemplation so remote and so chill, as it had been some corruptless and timeless divinity, having upon Her (since spirit must corporal be) the habit of woman's body, and for a small moment come down so.

IX

NINFEA DI NEREZZA[1]

I T WAS high morning beside Reisma Mere, of Tuesday the twenty-first of July, with the shadows yet long, and with heavy dews that made lace shawls of the gossamer-spiders' weavings on hedge and wayside plant. Doctor Vandermast, walking his alone, came at unawares in a turn of the path upon the Duke his master. The Duke's back was towards him; he was in riding gear, and sat, facing away from Reisma, on a trunk of a fallen ash-tree, his horse grazing untethered in the brake near at hand. He was bare-headed, and the sun lighted a smoulder as of copper heating to redness in his short crisp-waved hair. Upon the doctor's good-morrow he turned with a black look that relented in the turning.

"Your grace is become since but one short month to be as lean and as melancholic as a stag in autumn."

"Instance, then, of like effects worked by direct opposite causes."

Vandermast sat him down on the trunk, not too close but so he might at ease observe Barganax when he would: countenance and bearing. "It is but in the merest outwards and superficies that the effects are like. Inwardly, as is sufficiently demonstrated in the treatise *De Libertate Humana*,[2] *Propositio XXX*, the mind, in so far as it understandeth itself and its body *sub specie aeternitatis*, to that extent hath it of necessity an understanding of God, *scitque se in Deo esse et per Deum concipi:* knoweth itself to exist in God, and to be conceived through God. And so, by how much the zenith standeth above the nadir, by so much more excellent is it to be a man unsatisfied than a four-footed beast satisfied."

The Duke let out a bitter laugh. "I must call you mad, doctor."

"How so?"

"If you hope to reason with a madman. And, seeing you are mad, and safe so to talk nothings to, here's a piece of madman's wisdom came to me out of the suffocations that serve 'stead of air in these suburbs of hell, woman-infected watersides of Reisma, which 'cause I'm mad I turn from but still to return to, as the moth do the candleflame—

> "Answere me this You Gods above:
> What's lecherie withouten Love?—
> A thinge less maym'd (They answer'd mee)
> Than maym'd were Love sans lecherie."

"In a mad world," said the doctor, "that should be accounted madness indeed. For, albeit not so well declared as a great clerk can do, yet hath it the reach of unmutable truth; which is whole ever, and of that wholeness paradoxical, and of that paradoxicalness ever a thing that rides double. But the mad will ne'er content till he shall have patterned out to his own most mathematical likings the unpeerable inventions of God, which are the fundament and highest cornerstones of the world universal, both of the seen and of the unseen."

"Invent some business shall make it needful I go home to-day to Zayana."

Vandermast noted the proud and lovely face of him: haggard now and unspirited, as if he had watched some nights out without sleep. "If your grace hath a will to go, what (short of the King's very command) shall stay or delay you?"

"My own will, which will not will it, unless forced by some outward urgence. I will, yet will not. Unforced, I'll not go: not alone."

They sat silent. Vandermast saw the Duke's nostril widen and a strained stillness of intention overtake the bended poise of his head and face. He looked where the Duke looked. Upon a head of lychnis, that flaming herb, a yard or more beyond Barganax's foot above a bed of meadowsweet, a butterfly rested, in a quivering soft unrest, now opening now closing again her delicate wings. White and smooth were her wings, as ivory; and ever and again at their spread-eagling set forth to the gaze panther-black splashes exquisitely shaped like hearts. It was as if into the sunshine stillness of morning a heat welled up, out of the half-uncased tremulous beauties of that creature and out of the flower's scarlet lip, open amid leaves and so many frislets of tangled fragrancies.

"You in your time, I in mine," said the doctor after a while, "have wandered in the voluptuous broad way, the common labyrinth of love. We have approved by experiment the wise lesson of the Marchioness of Monferrato, when with a dinner of hens and certain sprightly words she curbed the extravagant passion of the King of France."[3]

"A dinner of hens?"

"Signifying *per allegoriam* that even as the so many divers and delectable dishes set before him were each one of them (save for variety of sauces and manner of presentation) nought but plain hen, so, in that commodity, all women are alike. It were well to be certified that it be not but that thing come up again. As the poet saith—

> "Injoy'd no sooner but dispised straight,
>   Past reason hunted, and, no sooner had,
> Past reason hated, as a swollow'd bayt
>   On purpose layd to make the taker mad;
> Mad in pursuit and in possession so;
>   Had, having, and in quest to have, extreame;
> A blisse in proofe, and, prov'd, a very wo;
>   Before, a joy propos'd; behind, a dreame."[4]

Barganax, elbow on knee, chin in hand, lips compressed, sat on so when Vandermast had ended, as if weighing it, tasting it profoundly: all very still. When at length he spoke it was softly, as to his own self retired into the secretary of his heart. "Truth's mintage," he said: "that's most certain. But that's but the reverse side. Turn the coin, so: the obverse—

> "Here, where all else is fair, I call thee fairest:
>   Were the rest foul, foulest of all thou'dst be:
> So faithfully Love's livery thou wearest,
>   Which art of all the rest the epitome.
> Virtues deifical, devils'-milk of wit,
>   Eye-bite, maidenly innocence demure—
> No proud and lovely quality but it
>   Jewels thine enchantments with its essence pure.
>   O best of best, that else were worst of worst,
>   Love's prelibation is to kiss thee first.

"—And the obverse," he said, rising to his feet to stand staring over Vandermast, like a leopard at gaze, toward Reisma and the clear-faced morning, "is where the principal design is struck." He looked down: met the doctor's eye upon him. "Well?"

Vandermast shook his head. "Nay, I find I have trained up your grace to be so good a metaphysician, there's no step further in the argument. Thesis and antithesis, these be the leaved doors of truth. Philosophy can but show us them: unlock them; may be, set them open for us; but, that being done, it is for ourselves, each soul of us alone, to pass through and see, each for himself, without all guide or perspective-glass to clear the eye if it be purblind. What should a man do with a weapon," he said after a moment's pause, "that knoweth not how to use it? There is a He and a She, and a habitude of Them both, which we would have called the love, the union, or the kindness of Them. As Their rule is infinite, Their pleasures are unconfined."

The Duke whistled his mare: she left feeding, whinnied, and came to him, delicately over the dew-bedangled grass. In the saddle he paused, then with some tormenting imp of self-mockery dancing in his eye, "You have done me no good," he said holding out a hand to the learned doctor: "left me where I was. O Vandermast," he said, gripping the hand of that old man, "I am plagued to bursting. To bursting, Vandermast."

The aged doctor, looking up at him against the blue, beheld how the hot blood suffused all his face with crimson: beheld the hammering of it in his temples and in the great veins of his neck. "And blackness," said the Duke betwixt his teeth, "is the badge of hell."

He shook his reins and rode off, a kind of unresolved unwilling pace: not the road to Zayana.

My Lady Fiorinda was abroad too that morning a-horse-back. At the footbridge by the lake, where six days ago the learned doctor had talked with his water-rat, she came face to face with the Duke. She had walked her horse down to the edge of the stream to water it: he upon the western bank did the like. Three yards of stilled water parted them, and their horses drank at the same stream.

"Fortunately met. I was come to give your ladyship the farewell."

"Farewell fieldfare?" said she upon a little eloquency of declension of her head. "But is not this an odd up-tails-all procedure: farewell at meeting?"

"No: at parting."

She rejoindered with but a satirical flicker of the nostrils.

"I purpose this day," he said, "to go home to Zayana."

"I'm sorry to hear it."

"Let's talk truth for a change."

"Pray your grace begin, then. It will amuse me to mark a difference."

"Truth is, I begin to change my mind as touching your ladyship."

"Excellent. For indeed I feared you were settling so heavily into one mind on that subject as you should be in danger to become tedious to me."

"And I do begin to think, madam, that you do think overwell of yourself." The mere bodily fact of her retorted back the words in his teeth: lily-proud poise of head and neck; smooth sea-waved blackness of parted hair which from under the bediamonded back-turned edge of her riding-bonnet overlay her brow; hands crimson-gloved, resting lightly one on the slacked rein at her horse's withers, the other on the crupper; swell and fall, as upon an undermotion of two silver apples of unvalued price, of the satin bosom of her dress; green eyes full of danger; lips that seemed apt in many a quaint unused way to play at cherry-pit with Satan; all the gems of gentleness and tiger-nursed soft graces of her, each where woman may be kissed. "I mean," he said, "as for leading me in a string. But I," in a sudden gust of rage, seeing her little silent laugh, "am not for ever to be fubbed off with lip-work."

"Pew! what an ungratefulness and unwontness the man is grown unto!"

"Nor keep-your-distance far-away future promises."

"Which your grace must think very unnatural, and therefore unwholesome, for a prince. Well? Saying is cheap. What will you do, then?"

"And again last night: coming 'pon appointment, and, of all monstrous betrayals, after long attending your leisure in the gallery, to find you private with Morville."

"With whom shall a careful housewife lawfully be private, then, if not with her lawful husband? To be honest, I was curious to observe you together: how you would behave."

"A player of mummeries, you think, for your ladyship's entertainment?"

"Why not, if I choose? The better, since you can play the Furioso[5] so lively."

"Well, good-bye," said the Duke. He gathered the reins and sat a moment, switching his boot with his riding-whip, his eyes darkling upon her.

"Good-bye," she said. "Truth is," she said, caressing thoughtfully with her right hand her horse about the crupper; and every unheeding motion of her finger seemed as a precious stone, some one of which is of more value than a whole kingdom: "truth is, I grow tired of the follies of this court."

Barganax's nostrils tightened.

"Besides, I find I am strangely falling in love with my husband."

"You think I'll credit that?"

"No," she said, and her voice lazed itself on the air in a poisony deliciousness that stings, blisters off the skin: "for indeed you are in case to become blockisher even than he. Blockish in the way you make suit to me: in the presumption of your unmatchableness, chat of love. As if (like as your Bellafronts, Pantasileas, I know not what little loose-legged hens of the game) it should need but a 'Madam, undress you and come now to bed.'"

Barganax, as struck doubly in the face betwixt such accordances to discord, but caught in his breath and remained staring at her in silence.

"You put me to forget a lady's manners. But indeed and you shall find, my lord Duke (were it to come to that indeed), loving of me is not a play nor a prittle-prattle."

The fine thread of continual flickering provocations seemed to strain and prevail past all supposed breaking-points between him and that seeming woman: a twine or twist-line, alternate of gold and fire, made fast with little grappling-hooks sharp and harder than diamond-stone to the web, secret within him of blood and spirit. "Well," said he. "When next I see your ladyship I shall look to find you in a more tractable mood."

"You will not find me. I too purpose to go away."

"And whither, if it be permissible to inquire?"

"If I answered that, where were the good of going?" The thing that nested by her imperial lips set up its horns at him, special pricks and provokements to ecstasy and anguish.

The blood left his face. "Go, then," he said. "And the Devil tear you in pieces." He jagged at his mare's mouth, who, uncustomed to such usage, swerved, spun round upon her hindlegs full circle, and bore him away at a gallop.

The lady, for her part, sat on for a minute, watching till the last glimpse of him vanished in trees at a quarter-mile's distance. Mean time the Lord Morville, himself conveniently aspying her from a hiding-place among the alders, had ocular proof how that thing, which had not in all those fourteen weeks of unmatrimonial matrimony so much as cast him a chipping, sat up now to gaze after Barganax in a veiled merriment that seemed to accept as by nature some secret league betwixt them, what unbefits a mind to search into. As amid great fireballs of lightning he sat mute.

But violet-crowned Kythereia, Daughter of Zeus,[6] turned Her thoughts to other things. May be She noted his presence, may be not. Gathering her reins, she turned homeward, guiding her horse not to trample a flower that grew at the shady foot of the bank

beside her: a kind of hill poppy, having a saffronish mounded centre and frosty-furred leaves, and the petals of it delicate frills of that
pallid yellow that tinges the moon when first it begins to take colour
after sunset.

X

The Lieutenant of
Reisma

MORVILLE, his lady being gone, fetched his horse that
he had tethered in a spinney hard by, and, as best for
the unbenumbing of his thoughts, came his way at a
slow walking-pace not homeward but north-westward
toward Memison. A big man and strong he was and of
good carriage, may be five and twenty years of age, proud of eye,
clean shaven, with enough of boniness about his features to import
masculinity in what had else been almost feminine for its transparency of skin, flaming red now as with furying of inward passions.

Coming upon the highway where it runs north under Memison
castle and south toward Zayana, he was met with a courier on horseback who off-capped to him and handed him a letter. "From my
lord High Admiral, my lord, new come up but yestermorn from
Sestola to Zayana and expected hourly to-day in Memison. I have
delivered five more at the palace yonder."

"To whom?" said Morville, undoing the seal.

"Count Medor. The lords Melates, Zapheles, and Barrian. One
for his grace of Zayana."

" 'To-day to ride north,' " said Morville in himself, reading Jeronimy's letter, " 'for meeting of the King at Rumala, and as guard of
honour to conduct him in his progress south to Sestola. That's
spend to-night in Rumala.'

"You delivered them all?" he said aloud.

"All save my lord Duke's: he was ridden forth, they said, but expected back within the hour."

Morville put up the letter, saying in himself, "The formal phrase of it is invitation; but yet, the requests of King's men can be strong commands. If the Duke must go too, what danger in my going? Besides, 'tis a notable honour. Good," he said to the messenger: "here's money. I've saved you your journey to Reisma. I'll attend my lord Admiral."

The Duchess's use it was to keep late hours in Memison. So it was that few were astir this morning when Morville rode in, save the porter at the gate and some score or so of gardeners and household folk. He gave his horse to a horse-boy and, leaving the Duchess's summer palace on his right, came by way of the great gardens to the colonnade. Here, upon sound of a known voice, rasping and full of mockery, and, most catching of all, his own name striking through his ear, he stopped quickly, stepped aside into the thick leafage of a yew-tree against the north-west corner of the wall, and from that close bushment, listened.

It was Zapheles had spoken. Now Medor: "Why might not he be called upon as fitly as you or me? He is lieutenant of Reisma."

"Just: and by what principle of merit?"

"The man is noble: in all kind of civility well brought up."

"I grant you. And a notable wise fellow until he speaks. This too I have marked: his garments do sit upon him must feater of late, since he is become the great Chancellor's brother-in-law."

"Beware lest you become a common laughing-stock," said Melates, making a third: "wearing your ill will on your sleeve so much, when 'tis know you yourself did put in for that place."

"What? of brother-in-law?"

"Of Reisma."

"I retail you but the ordinary chit-chat in Zayana. Women, Melates, are *mala necessaria*,[1] stepping-stones to fortune in this world. Unless indeed, being well wedded, we be over jealous of 'em: there can be danger in that, a were wise to consider. Our sweet young Duke was not wont of old to dwell weeks together in's mother's court. 'Tis a bye-word now how my lord Chancellor—"

"I'll leave you," said Medor shortly. Morville, withdrawn his most under the yew-tree, held in his breath while Medor flung out and past him within a yard.

The sound of their talk receded. Morville with stealth and circumspection came out of his hiding-place, and so fetching a circle back through the pleasance and round to the poplar-grove and lily-pond, waited a minute and so came openly over the lawns to the gate-house again: took horse there, and rode for home. Not so skilfully avoiding observation, howsoever, but that Medor, chancing to glance through a window on his way to the Duke's lodging, saw him go and the manner of his going.

Medor being admitted found the Duke his master sitting in his shirt, writing a letter. "Your grace means to ride to Rumala?"

"No," answered he, still writing.

Medor raised his eyebrows.

"Stand not on ceremony, good Medor, but sit you down. Eat a peach: peaches of Reisma." Medor took one from the silver dish. "They are freestone," said the Duke, who held one half-eaten in his left hand while he wrote: "easier to manage one-handed." He ended his letter: signed it. "Strike a light: I'll seal it," he said, taking off his ring. "You must take this letter, put it into the King's hand (Gods send he live for ever) with my love and duty. He will understand."

"You will stay behind?" Medor lighted a candle. "Do not."

"Reach me the sealing-wax yonder. Why?"

"Tongues are at work already. Heaven forfend I should pry into your grace's secrets; but, if you are bent as they say—"

" 'They say? What say they? They have said. Let them say.' "

"I do beseech you, dear my lord Duke, walk warily."

Barganax with a delicate precision made a round of the melted wax and sealed the letter. He looked up in Medor's eye: a laughing look, but no more than thus far to be played with. He pushed the letter across the table to Medor. "Well, well," he said, "speak on hardly. What's the matter?"

"Morville was here but now."

The Duke shrugged his shoulders.

"Slinked in a hidden corner whence he overheard Zapheles talk broadly of these conjectures. I, leaving 'em, saw him couched there at eavesdropping. I think he misdoubted not of me, but supposed himself unobserved. Is gone now in a strange haste from Memison, as myself did see by chance from a window. I think a may be expected foully bent."

"Pish!" said the Duke. "I regard him not."

"It is not for me to unease your grace. But if you are set to carry on in this course, as now the text of all talk is both here and in Zayana, I pray you think if it be not better deal with him first ere he in his raging motions let drive at you."

Barganax said in a scorning, "An eagle does not quarry upon flies. Moreover," he said, "your misgiving falls to nought by what's in that letter in your hand. Neither this nor Rumala sees me tonight. I am for Acrozayana."

Morville, soon as come down from Memison into the highway that runs here under an overarching of ancient oak-trees, put his horse to a gallop. At the outfields of his own demesne of Reisma he leapt from saddle: tethered his horse: took a turn east-about through the woods, and so to a sunk lane betwixt hedges of hazel and beech and whitehorn and sloe, all overgrown with honeysuckle and that tangling white-starred weed called love-bind: so by a gap in the hedge into the mains, and privily by way of the apple orchard and the stable yard to the back of the house: so in: search the rooms: then up the back stairs, and, with a bounce, into his lady's chamber.

She was sat before her looking-glass, in her hair, and clad but in one under-frock without sleeves, of fine white silk broidered with Meszrian lace. The lieutenant checked for an instant, one hand upon the door-latch, as reft momentarily of thought and sense by the sudden dazzle of her beauty. She looked round at him. "You might have knocked ere you came in. Leave is light."

"You are alone, it seems."

"Is that so strange?"

"I came but to acquaint you, madam, word's come this morning I must with others north to the Ruyar, to bring the King's highness with a guard of honour down to Sestola. We are to meet him, and your noble brother and the Vicar too besides, it seemeth, to-night at Rumala: to-morrow, 'tis supposed, back to Memison. I'm loth to leave you," he said, looking narrowly about the chamber. "We ride an hour before noon." He waited, then said, "Are not you glad of this?"

"Why should I be glad or sorry?"

"This is an honour, their sending for me."

"I'm glad, then."

"I had rather you said 'I care not' than such a poor frosty 'I'm glad.' "

"Since you prefer it, then, 'I care not.' "

"Has it ever bethought you," he said, standing now at the window looking out, face averted, his fingers twisting and untwisting at his belt, "seeing I love you and dote on you as the apple of my eye, that it were a small favour to wish you take some regard of me and my affairs? Even love me a little in return, perhaps, as honest wives commonly do the husband that so love and dote on them."

"I see small virtue in that: to be so amorous and besotted on me. It is merely that you cannot otherwise choose."

"It is a high and pure love," said Morville, turning with the suddenest movingest strange humility. But Fiorinda but curled her lip, that carried no trace now of that seducing mouth-dweller, keeper of the stings and sweets of darkness, that, under Morville's jealous eye that same morning, had gazed after Barganax. "A high and pure love? O manifestly so!" she said: "breeding jealousy, jars, and complaints as a dunghill breeds slugs and flies and maggots."

"Why will you be so odious and despiteful?"

"I have better cause to ask, why came you so unmannerly sudden but now into my bedchamber?"

"Why came the Duke to Reisma last night?"

"Ask him. How should I know?"

"His fashions displease. I like neither his carriage nor his company."

"Well, tell him so, if you will. It concerns not me."

"May fortune one day I will tell him. Mean time, this may concern you: had I found him in my house this morning, I would not a been in his best jerkin for twenty thousand ducats."

She fell into a laughing. "O husbands and brothers! The flattering tables of your pricings!" A flight of butterflies passed by the window on the breeze: an ever-changing curling train of seven or eight unstable scraps or motes of whiteness, wreathing and unwreathing and wreathing again on the sunlit air. "What you have, you bought," she said. "Be content with what you paid for. But you bought not me. I am not for sale: least of all to little men. What have you to do with what visits time, but belongs to eternity?"

"You are his strumpet." As if for the wasting of her heart's blood, Morville whipped out his dagger: then, as she rose up now and faced him, threw it down and stood, his countenance distort. There seemed to be shed suddenly about that lady a chill and a remoteness beside which a statue were companionable human flesh, and the dead marble's stillness kindly and human beside that stillness. He struck her across the mouth with his glove, saying, in that extreme, "Go your gait, then, you salt bitch."

Her face, all save the smouldering trail of that blow turned bloodless white. "This may be your death," she said.[2]

But Morville went from the room like a man drunk, for the galling and blistering of his eyes with broken tears; and so from the house; and so to horse.

XI

NIGHT-PIECE:
APPASSIONATO

D UKE BARGANAX, while these things were fresh at Reisma, was already gone for Zayana: his folk a mile ahead
with the baggage, himself riding alone. Every summer
sound as he came on, of wind-stirred leafage, birds
singing, becks falling, ran divisions on the tune of *Loth
to depart.* He rode at a slowed idle pace, twenty miles south now
from Memison and twenty yet before him. Whiles he shifted, as if
the saddle chafed him: whiles, cursed aloud; and then, as it were to
be spectator, not undergoer, of the comedy, laughed at himself.
Here, where the road, high above the head waters of this southernmost arm of Reisma Mere, goes level for at last half mile along the
shelf of Kephalanthe and thence rises steeply to the water-shed, he
drew to a halt. Betwixt the road and the crag's lip that overhangs
the lake, cedar-trees spread a roof, spiss, dense, high-raftered, beneath which the sun's glare entered but as attenuate pale shafts,
clear-outlined as glass, motionless to the sight, save for a drowsed
motion within them of floating specks which they kindled to dust of
gold. The Duke dismounted, loosed girths, let her go graze, and sat
down under the trees to rest. It was now the great heat of the day,
but the air hung cool under that ceiling of cedar-fronds, and of a
spice-laden sweetness. He fell asleep.

It was very still under the trees. A red mouse ran out, sat up to

451

wash his face with his little paws, and went about his affairs unconcerned, scuttering once or twice within an inch of Barganax's boot. A jennie wren scolded in the brake. As the afternoon wore, a party of long-tailed tits passed through by stages, hanging upside down on the cedar-twigs, filling the air with their tiny pipings. Two young hares came by, and stopped to play. By imperceptible slow degrees the sunbeams took a less steep incline. And now, as it drew on towards evening, two came walking between the trees from the northward as it were two nymphs of the waters and wildernesses, each with her arm about the other's waist. Their dresses, of fine gauzy stuff kilted almost to the knee, shimmered to all greys and greens of distance and whitenesses of snowfield or watersmeet. Light was their tread, scarce bending the grass beneath them; and the little things of the wild, as if knowing them familiarly, took but a hop or step aside as they passed.

"Look, sister," said she that was little and dark and with beady black eyes: "a sleeping man."

"Is it him we were sent after?"

"Are your lynx-eyes become beetle's eyes that you perceive not that?"

"His face is from us," replied the taller. Slender she was as some cattish creature of the mountains, and the colouring of her deep hair was as fire of gold. "Besides, I ne'er yet spoke with him face to face. Nor did you neither, sister."

"No, but I know him by frame and fashion: arms and legs well lengthened and strengthed after the proportions of his body, which is proportioned as a God's. And he is colour-de-roy, too: his hair at least. Come softly till we see his face: I have looked on that Duke, sister, from betwixt the bulrushes, when he little thought 'twas such as me, so innocently beholding him. Come softly. Yes, it is he, it is he."

They stood a minute looking at Barganax asleep, as reremice at the bright beams of the clear sun. Then Anthea said, "I'd have known him by his likeness to the Duchess his mother, only with a something straining or biting as ginger: more self-liked and fierce. What was the command to you?"

"When my lady's grace hath dressed this evening, to bring him to come sup at her house."

"And what to follow? Lie and look babies in one another's eyes? See, he smiles in his sleep. 'At pleasure now on stars empireth he!' "

"Sleep is a spying-hole unto man," said Campaspe. "Did you hear, sister? he spoke her name in his sleep."

"Let me consider him in his sleep, sister. You'd have thought there's more than mortal blood swells these veins. And even with the lids closed, as now, there is a somewhat betwixt his eyes, ay, in the whole countenance of him: a somewhat unfaint and durable, such as I ne'er saw till now in mortal man, but in them of our kind is never distracted either from soul or body. And firely and openly he burned with fire of love."

"See how unsettledly he searches about sideways with his hand. He speaks her name again."

"I warrant that hand," said Anthea, "is a finder of the right way to heaven."

After a little, Campaspe said, with her liquid naiad voice, "Whether think you better sport to wake him now, or give him our message while he sleeps? speak it into his dreams?"

"This is a fine toy: let's try it. We can speak wider so."

"Which shall speak it?"

"Both, by turns. Then he shall taste in his dreams the true sharps and sweets of it," said Anthea, and smiled with a white gleam of teeth.

"Which shall begin?"

"I will.—Salutation, my lord Duke. We be two waiting-maids unto my Lady Fiorinda in Reisma. And my lady said this morning that, in her seeming, red men be treacherous and full of quaintness and likened to foxes."

"But then, she said," said Campaspe, "your grace was liker a lion than a fox."

"And sitting so in her starry loveliness, with her breasts un-braced, she said: 'That would have stood the Duke of Zayana in far more stead, to have kissed the doggedness out of me, 'stead of, when I bade him go, go indeed. For I already had, truly I think, a certain smackering towards him. And such thing as man's heart is most on,' said she, 'and that these weeks past he hath made great suit unto me for, indeed I begin to think I'd liever let him have it than any man born.' "

"No, no! that was never in the patent."

Anthea laughed. "Timorous scrupulosities! 'Twas meant, if it were not said.—'And that,' said my lady, 'is why to-night I have requested his company at supper. For indeed matters stood alto-gether unadvanced 'twixt me and the Duke, until the jealous ass my husband—' "

"—'who is the miserablest young raw puttock that e'er waited slugging on his bed for day—' "

"—'this very morning, after many circumstances too long to trattle on now, gave me a smite in the face.' "

"Fie, sister! my lady would burst sooner than avouch that fact."

"I know," replied Anthea. "But is a kind of charmed sour mare's-milk very forcible to turn the brain.—'And I told him,' says my lady, 'that my lord and lover the Duke would doubtless make a capon of him therefor before he had done with him.'—Go on, sis-ter."

" 'In token whereof,' " said Campaspe, " 'I shall wear for the Duke to-night,' says she, 'my silken gown coloured of red corn-rose.' "

" 'And for the more conveniency, 'cause I think the night will be close,' says she, 'I'll wear no undergarment.' "

"O sister! We've spoke beyond our licence, and most part, I fear, untrue. This bald unjointed chat of yours![1] Will you think the Duke heard it indeed in his dream? And will he remember it when he wakes? Truly I hope not."

" 'Twill do no hurt, silly flindermouse. What skills it? so only but—

> "one desire
> May both their bloods give an unparted fire."[2]

"Sister, sister! clacketing out this nonsense, we've left the principal errand unsaid."

"What's that?"

"My lord Duke, in your dreams: we were to inform your grace directly, my lady sleeps alone to-night, the lieutenant being from home."

"O my stars, yes! that's more to the purpose than all."

"Come off, sister, and make an end. I think he's waking."

"One word of my own then, to bid him adieu.—Wear a good glove, I counsel you, my lord Duke, for your falcon-gentle straineth hard."

"Away, he opens his eyes."

Barganax sat up, wide awake on the instant, swiftly looking about him. No living thing was to be seen, save but on a branch close by, touched with the beams of the westering sun, a peggy-whitethroat trilling her sweet unbodied lay with its dying fall; and below her, in an outcropping of grey rock by a cedar's foot, an elegant lynx[3] with speckled fur, tufted ears erect, and eyes that had upright slits for pupils. The Duke leapt to his feet. Every line of his body, and every muscle of his face, seemed to tighten as with some resolve gathering weight from withinwards, unrestrainable as a great tide coming in the high sea-springs of the year. Both creatures, the one with fiery the other with timid bead-like eye, as he stood there motionless, returned him look for look. "I have dreamed of dream. Unformed stars," he said. "Small stake makes cold play. But no more of that." With a flutter of olive-yellowish breast and wing the little bird flew. The lynx in the same instant bounded away through the undergrowth, graceful in her leap as an oread in the skyish summits at point of day. Barganax whistled his mare: she came, muzzled his neck below the ear. "Come, child," he said as he tightened the girths and then jumped into the saddle, "we must ride: we must ride."

Day was near spent when the Duke came at a hand-gallop to the ford by the footbridge. Here he halted to let her drink. On the further side the land rises gradually to level stretches wooded with oak and holm-oak, through which the road winds a mile or so, and then, upon a sharp turn south-east, runs straight for a last two hundred yards in a tunnel of these trees and so out again into the open, and so down by gently sloping moory ground to the mains of Reisma. As the Duke rode into that straight, the beams shooting level through the wood from behind him struck red fire-marks on the tree-boles in front. Ahead, the end of the wood was as an arched gateway opening out of gloom upon field and champaign bathed drenched and impregnate with the red sun's glory. And seen full in that archway, in the mid distance as in a picture framed, groves of tall cypresses siding it left and right, stood the house. It shone in the last rays like a casket lifted up against the updrawing curtain of dark night, and lit by the fires of some jewel unprizable cased within it.

As Barganax drew near to that house of Reisma the sun set, and there came upon the land and air a strange uncustomed alteration. For, out of the baked earth of that evening of deep summer, smells of spring began to prick his nostrils as he rode; quinces and cherry-trees showed white through the dusk, under their traceries of pale sweet blossom; and out of short and springy turf young daffodil leaves rose excitedly like fingers, thick stiff and tense with the sap putting upward, and wet with dew. And, as the shadow of approaching night began to creep up the sky behind Reisma and the great snow ranges afar, the heavy obscurities of the strawberry-trees were filled with a passion of nightingales. In this out-of-rule mutation and unfashioning of July to April, only the heavenly bodies were some warrant of constancy, even the unsteadfast moon floating where she ought to do, all rose-colour to-night, low in the southeast among the dim stars of Sagittarius, a day or two short of her full.

The house was silent: not a light showed at door or window. The Duke, making sure of his sword, loosening it in the scabbard, rode into the forecourt past the vine-hung trellis and that bench of asterite. As he passed the empty bench, a taint or perfume as by fine and quick fingering made all his senses stand in a fire-robed expectancy. It was gone the next instant, dissipated and lost on the evening breeze.

The door stood open. He dismounted, ran up the steps, but checked at the threshold. In the profound stillness of the house sat a menace, as if the universal world were become in that sudden a city unsure, not unpregnable. It seemed suddenly to be unsufferable cold and he, standing on a bridge of thread precariously above floorless immensities, to look down between his feet to a driving

upon noiseless winds, as dead leaves are driven, earthward, skyward, and about, without path or purpose, of half-memories out of
the old age of time past, as if from other lives, other worlds. Then
natural present cleared itself again; and the Duke, loosing the grip
of his strong fingers upon the latch of the silver-studded door by
which in that turmoil he had steadied himself, crossed the threshold
into the silent house: stood listening: heard only the blood that
pounded and pounded in his ears. Then he ransacked the house,
room by room in the falling shadows that fell like slowed chords
descending of stringed instruments in ever darkening procession, as
door after door was flung wide by him and slammed to again. The
very kitchens he ransacked, store-rooms, cellars underground, sculleries, buttery, and all. And when all was searched and found void of
any living being he began again. And again everywhere, save for the
clatter of his heavy riding-boots, was silence: empty all, as last year's
nest in November. Only, as it were some intermittent rare flicker
kindling ever and again an edge of those shadows falling, came at
every while a scarce discernible tang of that most vading perfume.
Upon that faint warmth and deliciousness, as though in carnal presence she had brushed by within an inch of him and away again
unkissed and unknown, the sense was become to be no more a thing
mediate but the unshaled nakedness of the live soul, held quivering
like a bird in some titanic hand that was of itself but the bodiment of
that world-enfettering sweet hyacinthine smell. As to say: This savour, this thread-like possibility of her, is all that knits the fabric
together. Should it depart to come not again, this faint Olympian air
which is as from the very mouth of laughter-loving Aphrodite of the
flickering eyelids and violet-sweet breast, gone is then all else beside;
and you go too, and the world from your hand. Barganax, like now
to a man entering in the trembling passage of death, said in himself,
"God keep it!"

Then, in the long upper gallery that opens toward the sunset,
he was ware of her in the dusk, standing in the embrasure of a
window.

The floor rose by two steps to that embrasure, so that when she
turned at the Duke's approaching she looked down on him from
above. With her back to the light there was no reading of her face,
but she held out her hand to him. It glowed through the half-dusk,
a water-chill unsubstanced glow, like the moonstone's; but warm it
was to the touch and, as he took and kissed it, redolent, to unseating
of the wits, of that ambrosial scent. "This one too," she said, and the
self-savouring indolent voice of her came like the disclosing of dewy
roses, blood-red, underset with thorns, as she held him out the
other hand. And while he kissed that, "So you have come?" she said.

"Yes, my life-blood and my queen," said the Duke. "I have
come." Over and over again he kissed the two hands: caught them

both together to his lips, to his eyes: fell down upon his knees then
before her: seized his arms about her waist that rose slender as neck
of a Greek vase above the statuesque smooth languor of her hips
and yielding as throat or breast of some sleepy dove. His forearms,
crossing each other, were locked now behind her knees so that she
stood pinioned, backward-leaning against that window-ledge,
breathing fast, limbs unstrung. So for a fire-frozen minute, while the
Duke's forehead and eyelids pressing blindly against the folds of her
silken gown, here where it covered her flank, here her thigh, here
the dream-mounded enchanted mid region between hip and hip.

He bent lower, as if to kiss her foot. "No." she said, upon a
catch of the breath. "No. We will wait for that, my friend."

"Wait? Have I not waited long enough?" and he took her with
both hands by the waist again, drawing her down to him. "By heavens, too long."

She said, "No. You must order yourself mannerly with the
things are set before you. We will wait till after supper."

He was on his feet now beside her at the window, gripping with
his left hand the window-ledge, searching her face: her colubrine
slanting eyes with their lashes now asleep, now a-flicker: eyes en-
abled, with such a mouth, with such nostrils, to infinite allurements,
confections of sugared gall honeyed with the promise of unspeakable benedictions, unspeakable delights, or (when the Devil drives)
to the summoning of strange horrors, ice-cruel or tiger-fanged, out
of the deep. "Foh! I have dreamed dreams," he said.

She threw up her head in a little laugh, that seemed to take
flesh in her disordinate and unresty beauty. "Dreams are like an
orange. The rind is hot, and the meat within it is cold. I love a doer,
not a dreamer."

"Your ladyship sent for me. Is it not so?" He saw how her eyes,
averted now, busied no more with his, were for this once, in the fast
failing light, become softer and stiller than the eyes of a yearling
hind.

"For a wild hart wandering out of order? Well, if I did? In a
dream of my own?"

The Duke looked now where she looked, north-westward to the
lake roughened with wind, a sapphire lit from within, darker in the
distance. A little north of it, Memison showed grey against cloud-
banks of a stronger grey behind it, with a slanting smudge of pale
crimson upon a sky of yellow ochre. To the left, westward, the cloud-
bank was indigo against that yellowishness of the sky, here smirched
with brown. Hesperus, beautifullest of all stars, burned low in the
west. High over all hung that night-hue: that heaven's-blue which
holds depth beyond depth within it, and is the young unfledged
dark. Still the breath of spring persisted on the air, and the lay,
bitter-sweet, of the nightingales.

"Then you sent, and sent not? Good," he said. Leaning now his two elbows on the window-sill, he looked up at her sideways. It was as if the string of a lyre, invisible, unvibrating, strained his dark eyes to hers and tasted, in some inward contemplation of its two-fold self, the unboundlessness of music to be. "Well," he said, standing up like a man that shakes himself awake, "for the present I am content to unlace no more of these mysteries. Enough that there is a pair of us."

"And that it is supper-time."

Barganax glanced down at his dusty boots. "First I would lay off the sweat and dust I have soiled me with, hastening to this place."

"O, for that, all is laid ready for your grace within there. No, the right-hand door: this left-hand leads, I know not well whither. To heaven, perhaps. Or hell."

He looked at the doors: then at her. "Right or left, I saw neither of these two doors till now," he said. "And 'tis very certain, madam, that every door in this house I have seen and opened, twice over, before I found you here."

Surely in that Lady Fiorinda's voice were echoes of the imperishable laughter, as she answered and said, "Indeed it is true and for every door you shall open in my mansion, my lord Duke, you shall find always another yet that awaits your opening."

Curtains were drawn and the fire raked up and candles lit and supper set for two in the gallery when the Duke returned. The mistress of the house was already in her place at table. He saw now that she wore a dress of soft scarlet sendaline, flourished with gold and spangles of gold and small bone lace of gold. No jewels she wore, save but only the smaragds and diamonds of her finger-rings and, at her ears, two great escarbuncles,[4] round, smooth-cut, that each tiniest movement set aglow like two coals of fire. He saw on a chair beside her an elegant mountain lynx which she played with and caressed with her white hand luxuriously.

She made sign to him to be seated over against her. There were candles on the table in candlesticks of orichalc, and, in little bowls of Kutarmish glass coloured with rich and cloudy colours like the sunset, odoraments to smell to: rose-water, violet-flowers, balm, rose-cakes, conserves of southernwood and of cowslip. Her face in the candlelight was more beautiful than the evening star when it upsprings as forerider of the night between clouds blackened with thunder.

"I hope your grace will bear with our rude uplandish country manners this evening," she said. "Indeed I sent my servants out of the house two hours since, that our converse and business might be more free."

"But who set the table, then? Your ladyship's self?"

"It amused me."

"On my account? with such lady-soft a hand? I am ashamed, madam."

"O but indeed I did it not myself. 'Twas this mountain cat of mine did do it for me. You think that a lie?"

"I think it very like one."

"How say you to a taste of what she has set before us? What's this: a little sardine, dressed up in love-apple? May I please have that little plate to put this backbone upon."

"When next you mean to play serving-maid," said Barganax, reaching her the plate, "I hope your ladyship will let me be butler."

"I have told your grace, my creature did it. She is skilled in housewiferies of all kinds fitting."

The lynx stood up, making an arch of its back, and naughtily with her claws set to work on the edge of the chair: sat down again and, out of the upright slits of its eyes, stared at Barganax. He gave it (as at Kephalanthe) look for look, till it looked away and very coyly fell to licking its fur.

"See what a tiny bird," Fiorinda said, with a superfine daintiness taking a quail upon her fork. "A little sparrow, I think. He that shot that must surely have frighted the mother off the nest and then caught it."

Barganax smiled. "There be some things ought best to be little. Othersome, best big."

"As for instance birds," said she. "For myself, I would desire always little birds, never big ones. But dogs, always big."

"And men?"

"Truly that is a kind of cattle I find myself strangely disinclined to overbusy myself with. Of late. In their plurality. Your grace laughs?"

"Some little shrubs of pride and vanity I have in me take comfort at that 'plurality.' "

"Be not too confident."

"Faith, I am not. Should a beggar be a jetter? And yet—"

"And yet? it is better kiss a knave than to be troubled with him?"

"Ah, not that. I can tell true coin from false."

"And yet? in an undue manner the Devil coveted highness that fell not for him?"

"His hopes were dasht, then. And serve him right. Nay but the 'and yet' was mine. And, not to fall in open disobedience to your ladyship's command, it shall wait."

In soft lazy accents that wrought in the blood beyond all lovecups and enchantments, " 'Tis a good 'and yet,' " she said, "an amiable Devil, to wait so civilly. Let it not be despaired."

For a while now they ate and drank in such silence as wild hearts' desires will lie joined in, in closer lapped embraces than spoken word could fire them to: Fiorinda at every other while casting her eyes upon him, inscrutable under their curtain of long dark lashes; and he, so tall of his person, of so careless a repose of settled power in his magnificency, and with all his wilfulness and self-liking of ungoverned youth charmed asleep now, under the lynx's hot stare, and under the star of his lady's presence thus goldenly and feebly sitting before him in warrant of what transcendent fare to come.

Presently, "This is a strange wine, madam," he said, "as never in all my days I tasted. Of what sort is it? From the outlands?"

"No, it comes of the grape about Reisma."

"It is such as might be looked for at your ladyship's table. A moment ago, limpid, transparent, and still: now, restless with bubbles. Blood-red, to suit your lips, if I hold the goblet so. Then, hold it so, snake-green, seaish. Then, against the light, all paly gleams and with changing bands of colour that go and come within it as I let it swirl in the glass. How call you its name?"

"For make-believe," said she as they pledged each other, "say it is nectar."

"I could in sober truth believe that," he said. Her arm, of a lily-like smoothness and a lily-like paleness, was laid idly across the table, darkly mirrored in the polished surface, idly toying with the cup. "For make-believe," he said, sudden out of the silence, "say you are my Duchess in Zayana. Say you love me."

Some fire-worm of mockery stirred in her eyes. "But surely to say that, were a raw weak undurable and soon souring make-believe? My own I am. I stand untied."

"I too."

"You too?"

"Yes. And I am an incorrigible person, that will not be ordered."

She gathered herself sweetly back in her chair, but her eyes were unrelenting flint. "You think this is a play, then?"

"How can I tell?"

"How can I either?" said she. "Say it is a play, then; and that, in the play, you and I have forgotten, my friend, that this is the wine we drink always, you and I. And forgotten that he that drinks it with me shall return to me for ever, never altogether finding, but never altogether losing." She began to fondle the lynx and hold its head in her lap deliciously. "Is it not a play indeed, my moppet? See: riches come, and the man is not satisfied. Will he expect that freshly roasted larks shall fall into his mouth? Or is it, think you, that he came into the house but an hour ago meaning by force to ravish me, when as prevailed not, these weeks past, his fawning toys and suing tales?"

The beast fuffed at Barganax like a cat.

He laughed. "When your ladyship speaks to this lapcat it is, I suppose, in some dumb-beast tongue of its own? I understand not a word of it."

Fiorinda had bent her head, caressing softly with her cheek the lynx's fur. The bloom of her skin had an olive tinge, pallid as fields that spread their night-dews under the morning. And for apparentest outward seal of all perfections was the spider-thread fineness of her hair, seen in the prettily ordered growth of it at the temples, behind the ears, and at the nape of her neck, where it rested, coiled upon itself, a closely woven knot, superb sleek and disturbing as some sweet black hunting-beast coiled upon itself in sleep. Barganax's eyes were darkened so beholding her and his throat dried.

When she looked up again, he saw her eyes filled with tears. "There's a blindness upon me," she said, in answer to his look, "now that I have come so far."

"A blindness?"

"I know not well whether. Comed so, to the parting of two ways at night. How can I know? Talking, may be, to-morrow with your carousing toss-pot. Meszrian friends: a sweet tale, somewhat hot of the spice too, of the cozening doctor, the crafty Chancellor, and puss his sister. Indeed and indeed I could wish your grace had not gone beside your purpose: were walking even now amongst your orange-trees in Zayana. I wish you'd a stayed there. Wish most, I'd ne'er set eyes on you."

Barganax said, "This is damnable false doctrine." He came and knelt beside her, one hand on the chair-back, but not to touch her.

"Is it?" She was crying now, with little sobs, sometimes held back, sometimes coming miserably in a huddle together. "My handkerchief." She found it: a square of cambric edged with bone lace of silver, scarce big enough to cover the width of Barganax's hand. "I have seen an ugly sight. The ugly face of Nothing," she said, drying her eyes.

"But when?"

"This morning. This Tuesday morning of this instant July. No, no, no: not when you were there. Without you, I could not, O my friend, I could not, I think go on being." She avoided his eye: still stifling at every now and again a convulsive sob, while with her left hand she feverishly stroked the lynx's long back. Barganax very gently laid his cheek on her other hand which, resting on the table's edge, held her poor handkerchief, now screwed up in the fist of it like a child's; and very gently, as though it had been a child's indeed, kissed it.

A minute, so. Then she began, still trembling a little, with her finger-ends of the left hand to move caressingly over his short-cut coppery curly hair; then lapped her lovely arms about his head.

And Barganax's face, as by star-leap received up into that heaven, rested, unseen, unseeing, where, as it had been two doves, her breasts sat throned, ivory-smooth through the silk, violet-sweet, proud, and Greek.

Without word spoken, they stood up from the table. The lynx watched them from its chair out of eyes that danced with yellow fires.

That left-hand door opened upon a lobby. Fiorinda locked it behind them. At the end of the lobby they came to another doorway, doorless, curtained with rich and heavy curtains, and so to a room with tall windows at the ends west and east and, at either end between the windows, a fire-place, and the heat and movement and sweetness of fires burning of sweet cedar-logs. Scores of candles stood alight in great branched candlesticks beside the bed, and on tables and mantel-shelves and in golden sconces on the walls. The great canopied bedstead was of pure gold, throwing back fire-glitter and candlebeam, and its hangings and coverings of cramoisie silk[5] were befringed all with gold and worked in gold thread with representations as of gryphons and mantichores and flying fire-drakes[6] and many unused shapes and semblances besides, but half-divined amid the folds of the costly hangings. The floor was strewn with beast-skins, of wolves, bears, and deep-voiced mountain-lions, upon a carpet honey-coloured, very soft to walk on, silent as sleep. The walls seemed to be of a pale green marble, but with a glistening in the body of it as of gold-dust and dust of silver, and with myriads of little gems inlaid in the veins of the marble like many-coloured sparkles of fire. Betwixt wall and ceiling ran a frieze carved with lotuses, which seemed in the wobbling candlelight and the glow of the logs, now a-smolder, now shooting up tongues of flame, to swing and circle, rise and sink, as upon slumbrous slow eddies and backwashes of their native streams.

But the Duke, little regarding these marvels, regarded but his Fiorinda, standing there so close, into his hand, beautiful as golden flowers. So regarding her, surely his living self was drunk down as into the heat of a pool, deep, black-watered, full of sliding lotus-limbs: of the lotus, which yet floats so virginal-cool on the surface of the water.

As the turning of the starred sphere of night, that lady turned her head where it lay back now on his shoulder, till his eyes, close-ranged in a nearness of focus that shut out all else, rested upon her green eyes, clear-lidded, stilled, seen a little sideways: upon her nostril, which had transiently now in its cool contours as aspect most arresting, most melting, of undefended innocence: upon her cheek, firm, smooth, delicate-bloomed: last, upon her lips. It was as if, in this slowing of Time upon contemplation, Fiorinda's lips put off all particular characters which in daylight life belonged to them, as to instruments of speech, vehicles of thought, of wit, and of all self-pleasuring fierce subtle colours and musics of their mistress's mind; until, disclothed of all these, the perils and loveliness of her mouth lay naked: a vision not long tolerable in its climacteric. The tickle of her hair against his eyelids stirred his blood to ichor. Her hand, in an unbodiliness fluttering upon his, shepherded it down by small and small till it paused at the tie of her girdle. "Kiss me again," she said: "kiss the strength out of me." And then, the voice of her speech becoming as the fanning of a moth's wings, felt sooner than heard: "Unknit me this knot."

Silence swirled to down-sucking sea-floods of its own extreme, itself into itself. And Barganax, flesh and spirit as by anvil and fire-broil forged to one, beheld how She, tempering first to the capacity of mortal senses the acme and heat of the empyreal light, let slide down rustling to Her ankles Her red corn-rose dress and in the mereness of Her beauty, that wastes not neither waxeth sere, stood naked before him.

At that striking of the hour, Time, with its three-fold frustration of Past which is dead, of Future which is unborn, and of Present which before it can be seized or named is Past, was fallen away. Not as for sleepers, to leave a void: rather, perhaps, as for God and Goddess, to uncover that incandescent reality in which true things consist and have their everlastingness: a kind of flowering in which the bud is neither altered nor gone but endures yet more burningly in the full-blown rose: a kind of action which still sweeping on to new perfections retains yet the prior perfection perfect: an ecstasy that is yet stable in itself: a desire that lives on as form in the material concrete of its fulfilment. And while each succeeding moment, now as honey-fall, now thunder-shot, folded in under the hover of its wings the orb of the earth, it was as if She said:

> I am laid for you like starlight.
> As white mists
> Dispart at morning with touch of the sun,
> Look, I wait you:
> Look, I am yours:
> Secrets before unpublisht.
> A God could take no more.
>
> I am a still water:
> Come down to me.
> I am falling lights that glitter. I am these darknesses
> Panther-black,
> That scorch and unsight

At the flame of their unspher'd pride.
Make sure of me how you will.

Take me in possession.
First, kiss me, so.
Parting my sea-waved sea-strange sweet-smelling hair,
So, left and right.
I am utterly yielded, untiger'd, unqueen'd:
Have I not made me
Softer and tenderer for you than turtle's breast?

Ah, tender well my tenderness:
Life in me
Is a wing'd thing more aery than flies hemerae:
This beauty of me
More fickle and unsure
Than the rainbow'd film of a bubble, hither and gone,
On some tall cataract's lip.

Yet, O God!
Were you God indeed,
Yet, of my unstrength,
Under you, under your lips, under your mastery,
I am Mistress of you and Queen:
I hold you, my king and lord,
The render'd soul of you bar'd in my hand
To spare or kill.
God were ungodded,
The world unworlded,
Were there no Me.

Into the other and may be less perdurable Lotus Room, the night after that race home from Austria, dawn was already now beginning to creep between the curtains of the high eastern window, and the note of a blackbird in Lessingham's garden boded day. Downstairs in the Armoury the great Italian clock struck four. And Mary, between sleeping and waking turning again to him, heard between sleep and waking his voice at her ear:

"O lente, lente, currite noctis equi!
O run slow, run slow, chariot-horses of Night!"[7]

XII

SALUTE TO MORNING

ANTHEA in the mean time, left to follow her devices in that western gallery at Reisma, took her true shape, sat daintily down in her mistress's chair, and began to make her supper of the leavings. Leisurely, delicately, she ate, but playing with the food betweenwhiles after a fashion of her own: now pouring the wine from glass to glass and balancing the glasses perilously one upon another. Ossa upon Olympus, and upon Ossa, Pelion;[1] now chasing a faun hither and thither over the polished table with her finger; again, tearing a quail to pieces and arranging the pieces in little patterns, then a sudden sweeping of them all together again in a heap and begin a new figure. So, with complete contentment, for hours. At length, while she was trying her skill at picking out with her teeth special morsels from the nicely ordered mess she had made, as children play at bob-cherry, her disports were interrupted by the entrance of Doctor Vandermast.

Like a silver birch-tree of the mountains in her kirtle of white satin overlaid with network of black silk, she rose to greet him as with staid philosophic tread he came the length of the long gallery and so to the table. He kissed her brow, white as her own snows of Ramosh Arkab. "Well, my oread?" he said, touching, as a lapidary might the facets of a noble jewel, with fingers more gentle than a woman's the aureate splendours of her hair which she wore loosely knotted up and tied with a hair-band of yellow topazes. A little shamefaced now she saw his gaze come to rest on the results of her table-work, but, at the twinkle in his eye when he looked from that to her, she sprang laughing to him, hugged him about the neck and kissed him.

"Have you supped, reverend sir?"

Vandermast shook his head. "It is nearer breakfast-time than supper-time. Where is her ladyship?"

"Where the Duke would have her. In the chamber you made for them."

"It were best seal the doors," said Vandermast; and immediately by his art both those doors, the left-hand and the right, were changed to their former state, parts of the panelling of the inner wall. He stood silent a minute, his hawk-nosed face lean in the candlelight. "It is a place of delights," he said. *"Ex necessitate divinae naturae infinita infinitis modis sequi debent:* out of the necessity of the Divine nature, Her infinite variety. And now he, to the repossession of his kingdom. But let him remember, too, that She is fickle and cannot be holden against Her will." He stood at the window. "The moon is set two hours since," he said. "The night grows to waste."

"My lady sent away her servants. Paid 'em all off, every Jack and Jill of 'em."

"Yes, she intends, I think, for Memison," said the doctor. "And the Lord Morville, ridden with the cavalcade to Rumala."

Anthea bared her teeth. "Pray Gods he break his neck. There's a lust upon me for a taste of hornified cattleflesh, after supping on these kickshaws. O I could handle him with rough mittens: leave but guts and sinews for the kites. Can you think of him and not be angry as I am?"

"Yes. For God, according to His impenetrable counsel, hath made it a virtue in you to be angry; but making of me, He cooled that humour with a cooler thing more meet for it in me: I mean with the clear milk of reason which in a philosopher should ever overmaster passion. The unmistrusting man, thinking no evil, a man of common earth and clay, endued with a soul not yet unmortal, how should he wed with a great comet or blazing star, or breathe in Her heights? Doubt not that, from the beginning, he, in the opinion of his own insufficiency, poisoned the very sap should have nourished him at root, and so was become, long ere the Duke took a hand in it, but the simulacrum of a live tree, all dead touchwood or tinder within. And blasted now, under Her devilish effects, with the thunderstroke of his own jealousy."

"Why should such dirt live?"

"The egg," answered Doctor Vandermast, "is a chicken *in potentia*."

"But this was addled ere it was hatched."

The learned doctor was sat down now in Barganax's chair. Anthea came and sat sweetly on an arm of it, swinging one foot, her elbow propped on his shoulder, smiling down at him while with immemorial ancient gaze he rested in her cold classic beauty, so strangely sorted with lynx's eyes and lynx's teeth. "And my Campaspe?" he said, after a little.

"She is yonder in the leas. Some of her rattishnesses to-night, I think. Your eyes grow heavy, reverend master. Why will you sit so late?"

"Ah," said he, "in this house now-a-days I need not overmuch repose:

> "Here ripes the rare cheer-cheek Myrobalan,[2]
> Mind-gladding fruit, that can unold a man.

"And to-night, of all nights, I must not be to seek if her ladyship haply have need of me, or if he do. What of you, dear snow-maiden?"

"O it is only if I swaddle me in my humanity too thick that I grow sleepy," said she. "Besides, my lady bade me watch to-night. How were it if we played primero?"

"Well and excellent," said the doctor. "Where are the cards?"

"In the chest yonder." She fetched them, sat down, and with two sweeps of her hand cleared the remains of supper off the table and onto the floor. "The bull-fly can pick it up for himself to-morrow," she said. "We shall be gone."

They had scarce got the cards dealt when Morville came into the gallery.

"How, how, who is here?" he said. "You, old sir?"

The doctor, keeping his seat, looked up at him: saw his face pale as any lead. "My lord," he said, "I came upon urgent summons from her ladyship."

"What, in this time of night?"

"No. 'Twas about noon-time. She bade me stay."

"Ha! Did she so? For my own part, I had rather have your room as your company. To speak flatly, I have long doubted whether you wore not your woolly garment upon your wolvy back. And you, madam kiss-i'-the-dark—

> "From women light and lickerous
> Good fortune still deliver us—[3]

"Why are you not in bed?"

Anthea made no reply: only looked at him, licking her lips.

"You admire the unexpectedness of my return?" said Morville.

"Let the cat wink, and let the mouse run. It is very much if I may not for one short while turn my back, but coming home find all at large and unshut platters, dishes, and other small trashery flung so, o' the floor, with evident signs of surfeit and riot. Must I keep open household, think you, for the disordered resort and haunting of you and your kind? Where's my lady?"

Anthea gave him a bold look. "She is in bed."

"You lie, mistress. Her bed is empty. You," he said to the aged doctor, "who are in her counsels and, I am let to understand, learned in arts and studies it small befits an honest man to meddle withal, where is she?"

"My Lord Morville," replied Vandermast, "it is altogether a cross matter and in itself disagreeing, that you should expect from me an answer to such a question."

"Say you so? I expect an answer, and by God I'll have it."

"Where my lady is," said Vandermast, "is her affair. I mean you well, my lord, and where in honour I can serve you, serve you I will. But when her ladyship is concerned (even and I knew the answer) it would not be for my honesty to give it even to yourself without I first asked leave of her."

Morville came a step nearer to him: stood leaning on the table upon his clenched fists that held his riding-whip: clenched till the knuckles showed white as marble. "You are in a league against me, then? Have a care. I have means to make you tell me. I have a right, too, to know where she is."

Vandermast said, "You are master of this house. It is in your lordship's right to search and find what you may find."

"I have searched every back-nook already. She is fled. Is it not so?"

Vandermast answered never a word. His eyes, holding Morville's, were as pits umplumbed.

"She is fled with the Duke," said Morville, thrusting his face into his. "Confess 'tis so. You are his secretary. Confess, and may be I'll spare your life."

Vandermast said, "I am an old man. I am not afraid to die. But were it to forfeit my honour, I'd be sore afraid to die after that."

There was dead silence. Then Morville with a sudden unpremeditated motion swung on his heel and so to the window: stood there with his back to them, elbow crooked upon the window-sill, his forehead pressed into the crook of the arm, while his other hand beat an out-of-joint shapeless tune with his riding-whip against his riding-boot. "O God!" he said suddenly, aloud, and seemed to choke upon the word: "why came I not home sooner?" He bit the sleeve of his coat, rolling his head this way and that upon the window-ledge, still beating out the hell-march on his boot-leg, and now with an ugly blubbering sound of unremediable weeping between the bites. Doctor Vandermast, risen from his chair, began to pace with noiseless tread back and forth beside the table. He looked at Anthea. The yellow fires came and went in her strange inhuman eyes.

The Lord Morville, as with sinews tighted after that wrestling, stood up now and came to them: sat down in Vandermast's chair. "I'll put all my cards on the table," he said, looking at the doctor who, upon the word, staid his haunting walk and came to him. "There was, and ill it was there was, some semblance of falling out betwixt us this morning, and I spoke a word at her I'm sorry for: hath sticked like a fish-bone across my throat ever since. When it began to be evening, I could not face the night and us not good friends again. Devised some excuse, got leave from my lord Admiral (would to heaven it had been earlier): galloped home. And now," he said, and his teeth clicked together: "all's lost."

"Nay, this is over general," said the doctor. "It remaineth with your lordship to save what can yet be saved."

Morville shook his head. "I know not what to do. Instruct me."

"My lord," said that old man, "you have not told me the truth."

"I have told you enough."

"I can be of little avail to your lordship if you give me unsufficient premises to reason from. But worse than tell it not to me, I fear you tell it not truly to yourself."

Morville was silent.

"Fall how it may," said the doctor, "it is hard to know how I may much avail you. Only this I most dutifully urge upon your lordship: wait. A true saying it is, that that is not to be held for counsel that is taken after supper."

Morville said, "I am scalding in a lake of brimstone, and you stand on the edge and bid me wait."

"With all my heart and for all sakes' sake, yes, I bid you wait. If you fling into action now, in this uncertainty and your blood yet baked with angry passions, there's no help but 'twill be violent action and too little advised. Be you remembered, my lord, 'tis no littler thing than your whole life hangs on it; nay, for beyond the hour-glass of one man's life, your very soul, for being or for not being, is in the balance, and not for this bout only but *in saecula saeculorum*.[4] And that is a matter of far greater moment to you than whether you shall have her or no, whom when you have had you have approved yourself not able nor not worthy of such a mistress: cursed indeed with a destiny too high for you."

Morville sat still as death and with downcast look while Vandermast said these things: then jumped up like a raging wild tiger. "Would to God, then, I'd let her life out!" he said in an ear-deafening voice. "Do you take me for more than a beast that you dare to speak such words to me? Am I lustless, sexless, fireless, mute? It hath laid up revenue this month past, and I'll now take my interest. She is with her vile leman even now. I know not where; but, if in the bed of Hell, I'll seek 'em out, hew the pair of 'em into collops. For fair beginning, I'll burn this house: a place where no filthy exercise has been left unexercised. Out of my way, bawd."

He thrust Vandermast aside, so that the old man was like to have fallen. Anthea said in a low voice like the crackling of ice, "You struck her. You beetle with horns, you struck her, and spat your filth at her."

"Mew your tongue, mistress, or we'll cut it out. Void the house. You have no business here."

"I've a good pair of nails to cratch and claw with."

"Out, both of you, unless you mean to be whipped."

Anthea rose in her chair. "Shall I unpaunch him, reverend sir?"

"O be still, I charge you, be still," said the doctor. "We will go," he said to Morville, and in the same nick of time Morville struck Anthea with his riding-whip across the smooth of her neck. Like the opening of the clouds with the levin-flash she leapt into her lynx-shape and upon him: threw him plat under her.

Above the noise of their fighting on the floor, of Morville's pantings and curses, the snarls and spittings of the lynx and the doctor's calling of her off, sounded a battering upon the wall now, and the great voice of Barganax shouting from within, "Open, or I'll beat down the partition with my heels." And immediately, by art of Doctor Vandermast, the left-hand door was there, and immediately it was open, and the Duke among them, sword in hand.

That oread lady, still in her lynx-skin, in obedience to Vandermast drew back now, heckles up, still fuffing and growling, ears flattened to her head, claws out, eyes ablaze. Morville was on his feet again, his left cheek scored to the chin with four parallel furrows from which the blood ran in trickles. "Where's this whore," he said to the Duke: "this jay of Krestenaya? Your bill I'll clear first, and hers after, and," stripping out his sword, "here's coin shall pay the two of you."

"Unmannered dog," said the Duke, "fall to. And the foul word you spoke absolves me utterly."

"Ay, fall to foinery: your trade, they tell me," said Morville as they crossed blades.

They fought in silence: the most desperate foins, crossblows, *stoccata, imbroccata, rinverso,* overthwart pricks, thrusts, breaking of thrusts: sometimes closes and grips, striking with the hilts. It was well seen that each was a master in that art: Morville, may be, of the deeper grounding, but fighting as now with a less cool resolution than the Duke's and once or twice coming in with so much madness with his full career upon the body, that past belief it was how he escaped the Duke's most deadly *montanto.*[5] At last the Duke, forcing him back against the table, beat him from his best ward, mastered his weapon and, their hilts being locked now, by main strength of wrist broke it from his hand. Morville took a great fall, clean over the table backwards, on his ear and left shoulder, and lay like one dead. His sword was shot far across the room: Vandermast picked it up, gave it into the hand of the Duke. In the same moment they were ware of the Lady Fiorinda standing in that doorway.

In silence for a breath or two Barganax beheld her so stand, her nightgown of orange-colour satin fastened about her waist with a chain of pomanders and ambers and beads of pearl. Her hair, let down, untressed, freed of pins and fastenings, reached, as it had been her mantle imperial woven of all mists and stars and unpathed black darknesses of the heart of night, almost to her ankle. He said, "When he comes to, shall it go on till I kill him, madam? or shall I let him be?"

There was a glitter in her green eyes as if, from behind their careless outwardness of self-savouring languorous disdain, suddenly a lion's eyes had glared out, red, fiery, and hollow. "Your grace were as good do the one as the other. Commonly, I am told, you were the death of any that angered you." The glassy coldness of her face and of her voice was like the ice-sheathes, finger-thick, cold and transparent as glass, that enclose the live twigs and buds after a frozen thaw in winter. "If his neck be not broke already. It concerns not me," she said.

"Why, it concerns you solely," said the Duke. "Without your ladyship, where were question of choice?" Vandermast watched his master's eagle gaze, fixed upon that lady, a mariner's upon the cynosure, out of mountainous seas: watched her most sphinxian, waiting, ironic, uncommunicative, nothing-answering smile. "You and I," said the Duke at last, and fetched a deep breath: "we are not much unequals."

"No, my friend. We are not much unequals."

And now the Lord Morville, coming to, looked at her standing in such sort in that unaccustomed doorway: looked at Duke Barganax. It was as if the injuries he was about to utter shrivelled between his lips. The Duke held Morville's sword in his left hand: offered it him hilt-foremost. "Were you in my shoes, I make no doubt you'd a finished me on the floor then. May be I had been wiser do the like with you, but my way is not your way. We will now leave you and depart to Memison. Shortly there shall be set on foot a suit for a divorce to be had by the law betwixt you. And remember, I am a sure discharger of my debts to the uttermost. If you shall blab abroad, as vilely you have spoken to-night, one word against her ladyship, by all the great masters of Hell I swear I'll kill you."

"Keep it," said Morville, refusing his sword again. "From you I'll take nothing but your life. And the same of you," he said to Fiorinda: then, as if afeared of her face, strode hastily from the gallery.

Anthea, yet in her lynx dress, had marked these proceedings from a corner, herself unobserved. She now upon velvet paws, noiseless as a shadow, still unobserved, stole from the gallery on the track of Morville.

Barganax put up his sword. "O over-dearest Mistress of Mistresses and Queen of Queens," he said, "was that rightly handled?" But that Dark Lady but only smiled, as well She knows how to do when She will judge without appeal.

They saw now, through those western windows, how the whole wide champaign and wooded hills and bight of the lake, Memison upon its rock-throne, and the swift-rushing clouds of dawn, threw back the lovely lights and new-washed wide-eyed pure colours of the morning. And the scents and sounds of morning danced through the high gallery from floor to shadowy ceiling: a coolness and a freshness that held intoxications more potent than wine's. From those windows Barganax turned to her: from similitude to the self-substantial reality: her who in her alone unique person, through some uncircumscribable adorableness, seemed to complete and make up morning and evening and night besides and whatsoever is or has been or shall be desirable, were it in earth or heaven. "It is almost clear dawn," he said, and her eye-beams answered, "Almost."

"And morning," said Barganax, "were in proof the sweet of the night, might we but take upon hand to prove it."

"Your grace's archery," said that lady, and the mockery in each successive lazy word set on her lips new snares of honey and thorns, "never, I find, roves far from the mark you should level at. And indeed to-night for the once I truly think you have perhaps deserved to be humoured."

That learned doctor, alone now at the window, they being departed, abode in his meditation. "But where have you been?" he said, aware suddenly, after a long time, of Mistress Anthea a little side hand of him, very demure and morning-cool in her birch-tree kirtle. "I had forgot you, and there's a bad-cat look in your eyes. What have you been eating? What have you done?"

"I've been but gathering news," answered she, avoiding his gaze. "Nought seems newer than this of Lord Morville, eat up with wild animals in the west woods they say."

For a minute Doctor Vandermast regarded her in silence: her Greek features, so passionless, and so chill: her white skin, nails sharpened to claws, strong fierce milk-white teeth; and her yellow eyes, a little horrible now as though fires from the under-skies had but just died down in them. "Could you not learn by example of the Duke, having beheld him win a man's greatest victory, which is by feeling of his power but not using it?"

"I am not a man," answered she. "It was a most needful act. And," she said, licking her lips and looking at her finger-nails, "I won't be blamed."

Vandermast was silent. "Well," he said at length, "I, for one at least, will not blame you over much."

XIII

Short Circuit

I T WAS EASTER in England, the fifth year after, as in this world we reckon them: nineteen hundred and nineteen. The sun's limb, flashing suddenly from behind the shoulder of Illgill Head,[1] shot a dazzle of white light through the french window of the breakfast-room at Nether Wasdale and into Lessingham's eyes as, porridge-plate in hand, he came from the sideboard to his place at the table. Patterned to squares by the window-panes the light flooded the white table-cloth: danced upon silver, glowed warm through translucent yellow trumpets and green leaves of the wild daffodils which filled a great Venetian bowl in the table's centre. On the left, windows, with their lower sashes thrown up, widely let in the morning air and the view up the lake north-eastwards, of Gable, with outlines as of a wave-crest in the instant of breaking struck to stone, framed between severities of headlong scree-clad mountain sides. White clouds, blown to spidery streaks and flying dappled flecks, radiated, like the ribs and feathers of a fan, upwards from the sun against the stainless blue. Country noises, bleating of lambs, a cock crowing, a dog's bark, a cock pheasant's raucous rattling squawk, broke now and again the stillness which listened to, was never a silence but a stream of subdued sound: thin bird-voices, under-tones of water running over stones. Here in the room the fire crackled merrily with a smell of wood burning. Breakfast-smells, moving in a free fugato of fried Cumberland ham, kidneys, buttered eggs, devilled chicken-legs, steaming hot milk and the fragrancies of tea and coffee and new-made toast, came from the sideboard, where two yard-long "sluggard's friends" of burnished copper kept warm these things and the piles of hot plates for helping them.

No one else was down yet. Lessingham added first the salt then the sugar to his porridge, and was now drowning all with a rising ocean of cream, when Mary, still in her dark-green riding-habit, pattered on the glass of the garden door to be let in. "Though why all round the house and in at the window," he said, unbolting, opening, and standing aside to let her by, "when nature provided a door from the hall—"

"Hungry. Want feeding." The Terpsichorean lilt in her step as she crossed the threshold smoothed itself to a more level, more swan-maiden motion. "Look at the sun on those daffies!" she said, pausing over them a moment on her way to the sideboard. "And I saw the tree-creeper out there on the big ash. It doesn't ever go up and down the tree without little screams." As if in such mirrors the springs should be looked for of such an April morning and its pied and airy loveliness: a loveliness unfolding of itself from within, radiant ever outwards, with clear morning lids uplifted upon all but itself alone, and all eyes drawn to it, taking light from its light. As if in such broken mirrors, sooner than in Mary.

"I suppose it's the touchstone of genius," Lessingham said, while he lifted the covers one by one to show her what was underneath.

"A scrappet of ham: just half of that littlest slab," she said, pointing with her finger. "And scrambled eggs.—What is?"

He helped the dishes while Mary held out her plate. "To do what no normal person ever dreamed of doing, but do it just so; so that, soon as see it, they think: How on earth could anyone have dreamt of doing it differently!"

"Wanted just to see," she said: "see how you look from outside. Where are the others?"

"Like Sardanapalus,[2] in bed I suppose."

"Bed! How people can! this time of year."

"I'm not so sure about that. I seem to remember occasions—"

"O well, that's different.—What are you thinking about?" she said, watching him with eyes in which the question reposed itself like the shimmer of the sun on rippled water, half bantering half serene, as they took their seats at the table.

"Memories. And you, Señorita?"

"Thinking." The diamonds and emeralds blazed and slept again on her ring as she transfixed with her fork a little piece of buttered egg, applying to the action as much deliberation of raised eyebrows and exquisite precision of touch as an artist might bring to bear upon some last and crucial detail. "Thinking of you and your methods."

They went on with their breakfasts in silence. After a while Lessingham said, out of the blue, "Are you coming abroad with me?"

"Abroad?"

"Get away from it all for six months. Get into step again."

Mary opened her eyes wide and nodded three times. "Yes, I am. When?"

"The sooner the better. To-morrow. Tuesday. Wednesday."

"Very well."

"Where shall we go?" he said, keeping up the game. "South America?" Glow-worm caves I'd like to have a look for, somewhere at the back of beyond in New Zealand? Iceland? a bit too early in the year, perhaps, for Iceland. What would you like? The world's free again, and we're free. Better choose. Anywhere except German East or France."

"Some island?"

"The Marquesas? We might found a kingdom in the Marquesas. I dare say the French Government are fond enough of me to stretch a point. Freehold, with powers of life and death. I king: you queen. Jim might be lord chamberlain: Anne second lady in the land, with title of princess in her own right: Charles, lord high admiral. I'll put Milcrest on to dig out the details after breakfast."

"Better be quick, or someone will find another job for you before we can get off. We've got to make up for these missed years."

"I was thinking just now," said Lessingham: "glad my dear knew the Dolomites before the rot set in. Five years ago this summer, that last time. One moment it seems a generation: another way about five minutes."

"And you've only been home about five days. And tomorrow, it's Rob's fourth birthday."

Lady Bremmerdale came in from the hall. "Good morning, Mary," kissing her from behind: "good morning, Edward. No, no, don't bother: I'll help myself. How long have you folks been up?"

"Sunrise," said Mary.

"O come."

"Pretty nearly."

"Rode over to Wasdale Head," said Lessingham.

"Early service?"

"Back to traditions."

Anne sat down. "And here's my god-daughter."

Janet, on her best behaviour, embraced each in turn, and ensconced herself upon Anne's knee. "I had scrambly eggs for my breakfast too. Do you know, auntie, I'd a most nasty dream. All about the most horrible, but alive, sort of wuffy snakes. And a huge great dragon: much bigger nor a house. And it had a face rather like a camel."

"Had it a long neck?" said Anne.

"No. It was much more thick. A 'normous great green thing."

Lessingham said, "What did you do with it?"

"Tried to eat it up."

"And what did it do with you?"

Janet was silent.

"Anyhow, you did quite right. Always eat them up. I always do. They can't possibly hurt you then."

"Good morning everybody," said Fanny Chedisford, very smart in her new grey tweed. "Last as usual? No! no Charles yet. Saved again."

"By a short length," said Charles Bremmerdale. "My dear Mary, I apologize."

"But you know Jim's poem: 'Late for breakfast: shows your sense,' and so on? a strict rule in this household."

Janet had a piece of paper which all the time she kept on folding and unfolding. "Muvvie, I've writed a story," she said. "It's for Rob's happy birthday present. Shall I show it Father first?"

"Yes, I should," said Mary.

Janet got down: brought it to Lessingham. "Would you like to read me my story, Father? Will you read it aloud to me, please? Just you and me?"

He received it, very conspiratorially, and read it in a whisper, his cheek against hers:

"The Kitchen.—The cat has a baby kitten and the kitten is three weeks old. The parrot is grey with a red tail. 'Oh dear' said the parrot. 'I do wish cook wasn't out. 'We are not sorry' said the cat and the kitten.—Tramp! tramp! tramp! 'The cook' whispered the cat. 'Bother' said the kitten. In came the cook. She had a large bundle in her hand. Suddenly, the cat got her temper up. She rushed at the parrots cage and tried to hurt the cook. At last she managed to drive the cook out of the kitchen. 'Thank goodness' said the kitten. 'Last year' said the cat. 'I had six kittens, but the fool of a cook drowned them.' 'She realy is the limit' said the kitten. 'I tell you what' said the cat. 'I'll *eat* the parrot of I can get him. Then the cat prounced on the parrot's cage got the door open and eat it. —*The End*.

"That's the stuff," he said.

"Do you like it? really?"

"Yes, I like it," he said, going over it again as if enjoying the after-taste of some nice dish.

"Do you truly, Father? Really and truly you do?"

"I like it. There's style about it."

She laughed with pleasure. "What's that mean?"

"Never you mind." He rang the bell with his foot. "I like the way they talk and the way they do things. And I like the finish. You go on writing like that, and you'll end somewhere between Emily Brontë and Joseph Conrad when you're grown up: a twentieth century Sappho."

"Who's Emily?"

"Tell Mr. Milcrest I want to see him," he said to the servant: then to Janet, "No, not that Emily. A girl who wrote a story; and poems. Go on now, and read that to Sheila while we finish breakfast. Nothing from the post office, I suppose?" he said to the secretary.

"No, sir, nothing."

"You're satisfied your arrangements will work properly in case anything should come?"

"Absolutely."

"Good. Easter Day, just the moment they'd choose for some hurroosh. I'll be about the grounds all day, in case. Any word from Snittlegarth?"

"Yes, sir, I've just been on the phone. Mr. Eric got your letter last night. There are some matters he's anxious to talk over with you. He's riding over: started six o'clock this morning, and hoped to be with you before noon."

"It'll certainly have to be the Marquesas, at this rate," Lessingham said, with a comic look at Mary. Then to Milcrest, "Come in to the library, Jack: one or two things I want seen to." He left the room, Milcrest following.

"Eric. O my God," said Bremmerdale *sotto voce*.[3] His wife smiled at this undisguised feeling on the subject of her eldest brother.

Mary smiled too. "Never mind, Charles. You and I will flee together.—Dear, will you feed these creatures and yourself," she said to Anne. "Ring for anything you want." She collected Janet from the hearthrug and departed.

Charles shook his head. "Edward never seems to get a 'let-up:' how he goes on at this rate heaven knows I don't believe, until now, he's had four days together to call his own since the war started."

Anne said, "Quite sure he hasn't. But Edward is Edward."

"I shouldn't be surprised if they sent him off to be the military governor again of one of these comic countries somewhere, before long. He'd like that."

"I never remember names," said Fanny. "Where was it he issued stamps with his own head on them, and the Foreign Office recalled him for exceeding his instructions?"

"He always will exceed instructions," said Charles. "And the more honour to him for that. I only hope he won't kill himself with overwork before he's done."

Anne said, "We Lessinghams take quite a lot of killing."

The world, at three hundred yard's range in all directions, was apprised of Eric Lessingham's arrival by the carrying-power of his voice. Not that it was a specially loud voice, but there was in it the timbre of sounding brass; so that his inquiry, in ordinary tones at the front door, for Lady Mary, reverberated past the long west wing round to the terraces above the river, causing a thrush there to drop her worm and take to flight. Despite crooked passages and double doors, Lessingham heard it plainly in the library. At the home farm the geese screamed in the paddock.[4] Eastward in the water-gardens where, amid drifts of wild daffodil and water-blobs, the lake gives birth to the river Irt, Mary's eyebrows lifted in faint amusement and Charles Bremmerdale invoked his Maker.

"Is it really to be a holiday this time?" Anne was saying.

Mary graciously accepted a bunch of flowers presented by Lessingham's son and heir. "I don't know. I don't know. I don't know. I've learnt not to count on anything. Make no plans, and you won't have to change them.—Yes, Rob, Muvvie does like primmy-roses."

"Anyhow, brother Eric won't upset anything?"

"O dear no."

Rob said, "We put some on the grave too, like those. The bat's grave what Ruth killed in the nursery last night. I cried when it was deaded. Father buried it. We put an emptaph on the grave. Father wrote it. I tolded Father what to write: 'This bat was small.'"

"Poor little bat." said Mary.

"I'd like to have had-ed it."

"Take care. We mustn't walk on those daffodils."

"No, no, no, we mustn't, must we. Mustn't walk on those," he said, with great satisfaction and conviction.

"But how the devil, my dear fellow," Lessingham was saying to his brother as they came to the top of the three flights of steps that led down to the wild water-gardens, "was I to be expected to throw over my military and diplomatic responsibilities and come home to embark on a damned election campaign to please you? Be sensible."

"It's your duty: with all the money you've got and the brains you've got in a generation of fools."

"So you said before the war. And I told you then, that the only use of money as I conceive it is not to be a slave. And I'm not so innocent about modern politics as to want to go and get bogged in them."

Eric pushed back his hat from his broad and bony forehead and twirled his mustachios which he wore long like a viking's. For the rest, he was clean shaven. His face showed, in nose and brow and cheekbone and jawbone, a crag-like strength, and under the tan the colour came and went with every sway of his mood. His hair, darkish brown flecked with grey, was rather long at the back and about the ears: a vigorous curling growth: his ears rough and hairy. There was a demoniac twist in his eyebrows. A big man and a strong he was, of an easy six foot tall, heavy and somewhat clumsy of build, yet, for all his forty-seven years, with little sign of corpulence. He said again, "It's your duty. If everyone with you abilities took up the attitude you do, where would the country come to?"

Lessingham paused half-way down the second flight and laughed. "I don't know anyone with exactly my abilities, so your Kantian principle of the universal[5] doesn't work very well here. As for my duty, I do it according to my lights. And I think, with respect, I'm rather a better judge of it than you are."

"Well and I think, with respect, you're a damned unsatisfactory hound."

Lessingham said nothing, but his nostrils hardened. Presently, as they walked on, he said quietly, with a tang of raillery in his voice that lightened the sting of the words, "I thought you'd something important to talk about. If you've only come over to quarrel with me you'd better go home again. I've enough eggs on the spit without a dog-fight with you into the bargain."

They were on the grass now, and the others coming up from the waterside to meet them. With the magnificence of a caballero Eric swept off his hat to his sister-in-law, bent to kiss her hand, then kiss her on both cheeks. "Bless you, dear Mary," he said. "Make him do something. I can't. If he'd gone into politics when I told him to, in fourteen, might have got some of our troubles straightened out before this. If he'd do it now (Hullo, Anne. Hullo, Charles, haven't seen you for years: Taverford still standing? Going to have any pheasants this autumn? I'll come and shoot 'em for you: if I'm invited, of course)—if he'd do it now," he turned to Mary again, "he'd be Prime Minister before he's many years older, damn him. Would myself, if I'd a wife like you."

"That's the essential qualification, is it? Really, where to hide my blushes, the way you flatter me."

"Pity is," Eric said, "I had been married three times already before you and I met. And if I hadn't, he'd have cut me out all the same, before I'd a chance to start the siege. That's the trick of these younger brothers. And he's youngest, and the worst. Look at the state of the country to-day," he said: "strikes all over the place, mines, railways, the Devil knows what. Damn the lot of 'em. They want a master."

"Why don't you give them one?" said Lessingham dryly.

"It's what I'm trying to do. The trouble with your husband," he took Mary's arm, "you can take it from me, is that he was born about three hundred years too late."

Lessingham said, "Three hundred and sixty, I've always thought. Get out before the Stuarts came in: I prefer that Tudor atmosphere. Or be born, say, six hundred years ago: have a dukedom in Italy: arts of peace and art of war, both *in excelsis*.[6] War was part of the humanities as the condottieri[7] waged it, until the French and the Spaniards came down over the Alps and showed them what. I should have enjoyed myself in the skin of our maternal ancestor, Frederick II of Hohenstaufen.[8] Or go back a thousand years, to the days of our ancestor on the other side and your namesake: Eric Bloodaxe.[9] Or the Persian wars. Or Troy. But what does it matter, the time one is born in? A man can build his freedom in any age, any land. I can live as well to-day as I could have in Egil Skallagrimson's time,[10] or Sir Walter Ralegh's.[11] If I couldn't, I'd be a failure then too."

Eric snorted like a bull. "I can't understand chaps like you. Hankering already for the next war, or a revolution."

"You certainly don't understand me," said Lessingham very quietly.

Charles shook his head. " 'There ain't going to be no' next war."

"Isn't there?" said Lessingham. "Who's going to stop it?"

"I don't know. But it's got to be stopped. Or alternatively, the whole show goes west. Don't you agree, Edward? What did you and I fight for?"

Lessingham made no reply for a moment: only a myriad most slight and subtle alterations charactered the eagle in him against mountain and sky. "Fight for?" he said at last. "The motive, you mean? or the accomplished fact? I suppose we went into it because we were fighting men, and had a mind to defend what we cared for. And in the event I think we'll find we've preserved England as a land for eunuchs to dwell in, and made the world safe for short-haired females."

"That's only superficial," said Charles.

Eric gave a great guffaw. "Two distinct operations, ladies and gents; and yet, you observe, the product identical in both cases—Now I've shocked you, Mary. I do beg your pardon."

"Not in the least. I'm not shocked. It's simply that that sort of witticism doesn't frightfully amuse me. Shall we leave them to their argy-bargyings?" she said to Anne, and walked away with her toward the house.

"Superficial, my dear Charles? May be," said Lessingham. "So too is the surface of the grass-growth, seen from an aeroplane, superficial; but yet you can tell by it where the buried cities lie, accurately, street by street, feet-deep under the earth, in Mesopotamia."

"These are things that will pass. All part of the mess-up. But if they are to pass,—then, no 'next war.' Another war would put the lid on it."

"I see no early prospect of their passing," said Lessingham.

"They have hardly begun. There's a promising future for them and for what they stand for."

Charles Bremmerdale grunted. "I don't deny the danger," he said, very quiet and serious. "I think nothing will do but a real change of heart. We've said that about the enemy till one's nauseated. Got to say it now to ourselves, and do it,—or else. I do what I can. I think one's got to."

Lessingham looked at him with a queer and uncustomed tenderness in his speckled grey eyes. "Forty-five million hearts to change over?" he said. "And that's only a beginning. My dear Charles, what we're really up to is—if we can—to make the world safe for big business: for a new kind of slave state: that's the first deep current under the surface, evolution towards Hobbes's Leviathan and away from the individual. And your unhaired woman (they'll be as common as the cartway soon) and your unmasculated man, are part of the engine, worker ants, worker termites, neuters: worthless lives to themselves, which only exist to run the engine, which itself exists only to run. Until it runs down. And then sink with stink *ad Tartara Termagorum.*"

Eric's laugh came short, sharp, and harsh, like an eagle's bark. "The only true word Plato ever said," said he, the brass tenor of his voice contrasting with his brother's basso profondo, "was that the world will never go right till philosophers are kings."

"He said one or two true things besides that," said Lessingham.

"What? O yes, I can think of one: about the high-hearted man, the μεγαλόψυχος."

"That such kind of men have wrought the greatest evils both upon cities and upon private persons, and also the greatest benefits, according to their bent of mind? Yes, and then he says a weak nature can be cause of no great thing, neither of a good thing nor of an evil. Well, that's not true. Many weak natures together can be cause of the greatest evils: most of all if they are used by a scoundrel of genius as his instruments. And that is the rock on which all revolutions run to wreck."

Charles said, "Why not a man of genius to use them for good ends?"

"Because smallness of spirit," answered Lessingham, "is an apt instrument for evil: an unhandy one for good. And yet all the chat to-day is, that democratic institutions are somehow going to be the salvation of the civilized world."

"Well," said Charles, "what's your alternative?"

"I see none, on the grand scale. The folly lies not in supporting democracy as a *pis aller,*[12] but in singing hymns to it, treating it as something fundamentally good. No hard thinking, no resolute policy, even when our foot is on their neck: instead, a reiteration (like a bunch of superannuated school-ma'ams) of comfortable platitudes, with our eyes on the ballot-box. We have defeated 'Prussianism.'[13] Have we so? I thought the object in war was to defeat your enemy, not defeat some absurd abstraction. We gave him an armistice when, at the last gasp, he asked for it. Now we're going to dictate terms of peace, in Paris apparently. I'd rather have carried the war to destruction clean through Germany, defeated him bloodily beyond cavil or equivocation, let him taste it at his own fire side, and dictated peace in Berlin. If we'd lost a hundred thousand lives by doing it (and we shouldn't have: nothing like it), it would have been worth the price."

"And you one of them, perhaps?" said Charles.

"Certainly: gladly: and I one of them. For if we'd done it we could now be generous without risk of misunderstanding. As it is, I fancy we're going to be rather less than generous. And a load of mischief to come of it. Even if it doesn't cost us all the fruits of these past four years, and leave us the job to do all over again."

Eric said, "I dislike talking to you, Edward, on world politics. You depress me."

"You shouldn't be so easily depressed."

"I always remember what you said before the war, about modern war between Great Powers in Europe: what it would mean. Do you remember? Knock two chestnuts together on strings (game of conquerors): no harm done. But try that game with two expensive gold watches, and see what happens."

"The event hasn't proved that the analogy works, though," said Charles.

"Hasn't yet," said Eric. "But don't you go imagining we're out of the wood yet, my boy. Not by the hell of a long way. Edward's a cynical dog, damn him. But he talks sense."

"Edward's not a cynic," said Charles. "He's a philosopher. And a poet."

"And a painter. And a man of affairs. And a cantankerous devil. And, (to give him his due), a damn good soldier," said Eric.

Lessingham laughed. "If I'm a philosopher, I love England, and you, brother, as my real Englishman. But this is the time for looking at ourselves in foreign looking-glasses. Scaliger said, four centuries ago, 'The English are proud, savage, insolent, untruthful, lazy, inhospitable, ungainly, stupid, and perfidious.' "[14]

"Good God," said Eric. "And there's a Japanese proverb: 'When a fool spits at Heaven, the spittle falls back in his own face.' "

"Well?" said Lessingham. "Do you want to have a look at the new mistals we're building at the farm?"

As they came up upon the terrace Mary met them, with Anne Bremmerdale. She said, "Have you seen Mr. Milcrest?"

"No," said Lessingham. "And I don't desperately want to."

"He's hunting for you with some things from the post office."

"Confound them."

"Here he comes."

"What's the use of you as a secretary?" said Lessingham, as Milcrest, heated with the chase, handed him two terracotta envelopes. "Couldn't you burn the beastly things, or drown them, or lose them till to-morrow?"

"If you'll give me an indemnity in advance, sir."

"What's that you say?" Lessingham was undoing the envelope marked *Priority:* he read it through swiftly, then again slowly, then, upon a salvo of damns, began striding up and down oblivious of his company, hands in his pockets, brow black as thunder. After two or three turns, so, he opened the second telegram and, having read it, stood for perhaps twenty seconds as if withdrawn into himself. "Bad news for you, old man," he said, turning to his brother. "And for me, and the dear girl:" he looked at Anne, whose grey eyes, very like his own, waited on his words. He handed Eric the telegram. "There'll be one for you, no doubt, at Snittlegarth." Anne came and read it over Eric's shoulder: with difficulty, for his big hand shook and made the words run together. "Didn't live long to enjoy his K.C.B.,"[15] he said gruffly, almost brutally; but Mary thought she saw in the hard blue eyes of him, as he turned away, something incongruously like a tear.

Fanny Chedisford was writing letters in the drawing-room. Mary came and said to her, "You and I will have to keep each other company to-morrow." Fanny looked up brightly, but her expression changed. "We've just heard," Mary said: "my youngest brother-in-law, Will Lessingham, died suddenly in London last night. Rather a favourite."

"O Mary, I am so terribly sorry."

"Edward has to go up by the night train to-morrow in any case: some important conference suddenly called at the Foreign Office. Anne and Charles are off at once, after lunch, by car. He was a bachelor, as you know, and Anne always rather the one in the family for him. We've no details: only that he collapsed in his consulting-room in Harley Street."

"You're not going yourself?"

"No. Couldn't do anything. I don't like funerals, and Edward doesn't like them for me. I don't like them for him either. However."

Fanny was prodding at the blotting-paper with her pen. "A terrible loss to his profession. I remember him so well in the old days: always coming to stay with Anne. How old was he?"

"Eric, Frederick, Antony and Margaret, William, Anne—he came between the twins and Anne: forty-one this year, I think."

"Young."

"One used not to think forty young. Too young, certainly."

"I can't get hold of Edward," said Eric, coming in from the hall. "Seems to have locked himself into the library, and told the servants he's not to be disturbed."

"You know each other, don't you?" said Mary. "My brother-in-law,—"

"Mrs. Chedisford? I should think we do!" They shook hands. Fanny looked uncomfortable.

"Edward has shut himself up to work," Mary said. "Got to get something ready for one of his hush-hush meetings on Tuesday."

"O. Well, I'll catch him at lunch. Several things I want to suck his brains about."

"I doubt whether you'll get him at lunch. Possibly not at dinner even. You'd much better stay the night: we can fit you out. Lovely silk pyjamas. Brand new toothbrush. Everything you want. Do. To please me."

"Most awfully nice of you, Mary. Upon my word, I think I will."

"O good. We'll telephone to Jacqueline, so that she needn't be anxious about you."

"Not she. She's too well trained after fourteen years of me, to worry about where I have got to. Tell me, do you think Edward's got one of his berserk rages on him?"

"I shouldn't be surprised, from the way he got down to this job, whatever it is, in the library."

"Rolling his eyes, biting on the rim of his shield, bellowing like a bull?"

"Figuratively, yes."

"Gad. I'd have liked to have seen it. Does it often happen now-a-days?"

"Well, we haven't seen such a great deal of each other during these nightmare years. No oftener, so far as I know, than it used to do. It's a family trait, isn't it? I've always understood you had those times of, shall we say, violent inspiration followed by flop like a wrung-out dishcloth, yourself?"[16]

"Who told you that, my dear Mary? Jacqueline?"

"Perhaps."

"Secrets of the nuptial chamber: by Jove, it's monstrous. Well, I can promise you my goes are as Mother Siegel's soothing syrup compared with Edward's. Do you remember that famous occasion at Avignon, summer before the war?"

"Do I not!"

"Yes, but you only saw the working-up. I had a ring seat for the grand main act."

"What was all this?" said Fanny.

"O, that's a great story."

"Tell Miss Chedisford."

"A great story. I and my wife, Edward and Mary, all sitting enjoying ourselves in one of those open-air café places: warm summer night, lovely moon and all that, lots of chairs and tables, folks gossiping away, band playing. Table near us, pretty girl—French— and her young man: nice quiet inoffensive-looking people. Presently, hulking great rascal, sort of half-nigger, looking like one of those Yankee prize-ring johnnies, lounges up, takes a good look at the young lady, then planks himself down at their table. Well, they don't seem to value him: move away. Chap follows them: sized 'em up, apparently: got a bit of liquor on board: anyway, roots himself down on a chair and starts making up to the girl. Young man a bit rabbitish by the look of him: doesn't seem to know quite what to do. Well, Edward watches this for a minute, and his heckles begin to rise. Damn it all, he says, I'm going to put a stop to this. I tried to stop him: none of our business: don't want a scene. Not a bit of it. Up he gets, strolls over in that quiet devil-may-care way of his, stands over this tough and, I suppose, tells him to behave himself. Too far off for us to hear what they said, but evidently some backchat. At last, man ups with his arm, glass in hand, as if he meant to shy it in Edward's face: however, seems to think better of it.—You remember, Mary?"

"O dear, O dear! go on. It all comes back to me so perfectly."

"This is fun," said Fanny. "I like this."

"Next thing, both standing up; then walk away together, the fellow damned angry, blustering away, but as if under marching orders, in front, scowling and snapping over his shoulder: Edward as if treading on his heels to make him go a bit faster. By God, I said, I'm going to see this through. Left the women, and tooled along behind, keeping out of sight not to annoy Edward; but just in case. They went straight through a kind of passage there is, direction of the Palace of the Popes, till they land up at that hotel—what was it? Silver Eagle or something—and a porter in uniform standing at the door: quiet street, no one about. Poor old bruiser chap hurrying along as if he didn't know why, and didn't quite like it, but just had to: marched off like a pickpocket. Then Edward says to the porter, 'You know me?' 'Oui, monsieur.' 'Very well. You're a witness.' And he says to the chappie, 'You insulted a lady in my presence,' he says, 'and you insulted me. And when I told you to apologize, you insulted me again. Is that true?' That gets the fellow's rag out proper: wakes him out of his trance. 'Yes it is,' he says, making a face at him like a hydrophobia pig, 'yes it is, you blanky blanking blanker, and I'll blanky well blank you up the blanking blank blank': rush at him, try to kick him, the way those blackguards do; but before you could say knife, Edward grabs him somehow— too quick to see; too dark—but in about one second he has him off his feet, throws him bodily against the wall—plonk! And there he dropped."

"Threw him? do you mean threw him through the air?" said Fanny incredulously.

"Yes, like a cat. Chap weighed twelve stone[17] if he weighed an ounce. For a minute I thought he was dead: looked damned like it. Nasty mess—"

"O thank you," Mary said, "we can leave out the decorations."

Five minutes later, showing Eric his room, she said, "I ought to have told you about Fanny. She's dropped the *Mrs.*"

"What do you say? Dropped? O Lord, I made a gaff, did I? Can't be helped. What happened?"

"A great many things that had better not."

"Fellow turn out bad hat?"

"About as bad as they make them."

"Marriage of first cousins, wasn't it? and parents disapproved. Quite right too. Divorce, or what?"

"Yes."

"Quite in the fashion. Damned fool. She's a fine woman. Most people are damned fools, one way or another. I wonder what's become of that nice brother of hers, Tom Chedisford?"

Mary was silent.

"Look here, my dear Mary," he said suddenly: "you see a lot more of Anne these days than I do. Is everything going as it should there? You know what I mean."

"Absolutely, I should have said. Why?"

"That fellow Charles. Does he treat her properly?"

"Dotes on her. Always has."

"He's a dull dog. You think they're happy together?"

Mary laughed. "Good heavens, I don't know why you ask me these things. Of course they are."

"A bit hum-drum."

"Most of us get a bit hum-drum as the years go by."

"Most of us may, but some of us don't."

"Perhaps some people get on better that way. One can't lay down a *Code Napoléon* for happy marriages."

"You think she's got what she wants?"

"I certainly think so. If she hadn't we certainly couldn't give it her."

Eric wrinkled up his nose and shot out his lips. "What I don't like to see is the dear girl getting to look more and more like a spinster: kind of unattached look. Better never have married the fellow if the effect of him is to turn her into a maiden aunt. Edward hasn't done that to you. Nor I to Jacqueline."

"O dear, we're getting painfully personal. Hadn't we better stop?"

"Just as you like, my dear. But before we leave the subject I may as well tell you that you and Edward are the only married people I've ever known who always seem as if you weren't married at all, but were carrying on some clandestine affair that nobody was supposed to have wind of but yourselves. And you keep young and full of beans on it, as if you would always go on growing up, but never grow old. And if you ask me which of you deserves the honours for that, I'm inclined to think it's honours easy: between the two of you. And you can tell him from me, if you like, that that's my opinion."

It was past eleven o'clock, the same night. Lessingham was in the library among a mass of papers, books, maps, statistics, and cigar-smoke. "You'd better turn in now, Jack: be fresh for the morning. We've got most of the stuff taped and sorted now. I'll go on for a bit: get my covering memorandum into shape: that's the ticklish part of it, what the whole thing stands or falls by, and I can do it best by myself. You've got the annexes all off the roneo now, have you?"

"All but Annex V," said Milcrest.

"You'll have lots of time to finish up before lunch. You're certain they're not going to let us down about that aeroplane?"

"Certain, sir. I got the general's promise from his own mouth. Confirmation in writing too": he rummaged among the papers on the table and produced it.

"Capital. David will run you over to the aerodrome. He'll have to be back in good time to go with me to Carlisle: I start at seven o'clock sharp. All right about my sleeper?"

"Yes."

"And they know at Carlton House Terrace to expect me for bath and breakfast on Tuesday morning, and that you sleep there Monday night?"

"Yes."

"I may have to go straight on to Paris: can't tell till after Tuesday's meeting. If so, I'll want you with me. Make all arrangements on that assumption."

"Right, sir."

"Off you go to bed, then. We've done a rattling good day's work. Good night."

Lessingham, left to himself, lighted a cigar, threw up his legs on the sofa, and for a quarter of an hour sat thinking. Then he sprang up, went to the writing-table, and set to work. Two o'clock struck, and still he wrote, tossing each sheet as it was finished onto the floor beside him. At three he put down his pen, stretched his arms, went over to the side-table where, under white napkins, cold supper was appetizingly set out: chicken in aspic, green salad with radishes, and things ready for making coffee. By twenty past he was back again at work. Day began to filter through the curtains. It struck five. He drew the curtains: ate a sandwich: opened a bottle of Clicquot: collected the sheets off the floor, and sat down to go through them: checking, condensing, a rider here, a rider there, here three pages reduced to one, there an annex brought up into the body of the memorandum, or a section of the memorandum itself turned into an annex, this transposed, that deleted, the whole by pruning and compression brought down from about seven thousand words to three. Eight or nine pages, perhaps, of open-spaced typing: three foolscap pages, three and a half at most, the Foreign Office printer would make of it; apart from the annexes, which contained the real meat, the factual and logical foundation upon which the whole proposal rested. But which nobody would read, he said in himself as he snapped to the self-locking lid of the dispatch-box over the completed whole. What are the facts and what is logic? Things to play with: make a demonstration: dress your shop window with. Facts and logic can make a case for what you please. The vast majority of civilized mankind are, politically, a mongrel breed of sheep and monkey: the timidity, the herded idiocy, of the sheep: the cunning, the dissimulation, the ferocity, of the great ape. These facts are omitted in the annexes, but they are the governing facts; and policy will still be based upon them, and justified before the world as embodying the benevolent aspirations of the woolly flock together with the cleverness of the bandar-log. And the offspring of such a policy will be such as such a world deserves, that was mid-wife to it: a kind of bastard Egyptian beast-god incarnate, all ewe-lamb in the hinder parts with a gorilla's head and the sphinx's claws of brass; likely to pass away in an ungainly and displeasing hara-kiri: head and claws making a bloody havoc of their own backside and puddings, and themselves by natural consequence perishing for lack of essential organs thus unintelligently disposed of.

It was nearly half past nine when he rang the bell for Milcrest. "There it is, in the box. I don't want to see it again. Pull off copies for circulation: I rely on you to check it: wake me if there's any real doubt on any point, otherwise don't. Leave me two copies in my pouch: take the rest personally to 2 Whitehall Gardens without fail this evening. The sooner the better." He yawned and stretched. "I'm a fool," he said: "kicking against the hard wall."

Dog-tired suddenly, he went upstairs and, without enough energy to undress, flung himself on his bed just as he was. His brain had been working at full pressure for twenty-two hours on end. In less than a minute he was fast asleep. Mary peeped in at the door: came in softly: put an eider-down over him, and went out again, closing the door soundlessly behind her.

He woke late in the afternoon, had a bath, came down to tea, settled Eric's problems for him, and by seven o'clock was well on the

way to Carlisle. Old David's heart was in his mouth, between the
terrifying speed and the cool control of Lessingham's driving.

Summer night wheeled slowly above the out-terraces of Memison:
the moon up: Venus in her splendour like a young moon high in
the west. The King said, "He is returned to Acrozayana, to hold to-
morrow his weekly presence. That is well done. And you shall see
there is a back-bias shall bring him swiftly here again."

Vandermast stroked his beard.

The King said, "I am troubled in a question about God. Omnipotence, omnipresence, omniscience: having these three, what
hath He left to hope for? By my soul, did I find in myself these
swelling members grown out of form—to do all, to know all, to be all
—I swear I'd die of their tediousness."

Vandermast said, "Your serene highness may yet consider that
the greater the power, or the pleasure, the greater needeth to be
the ἄσχησις: or discipline."

The King said, "You mean that the Omniscient and Omnipotent must discipline Himself and His own power and His own
knowledge, treading, as upon a bridge of two strained ropes above
the abysses, at once the way of reason and the way of sensuality?"

Vandermast said, "Yes. Within which two ways and their per-
mutations shall be found two million ways wherein a man may live
perfectly, or a God. Or two million million ways. Or what more you
will. For who shall limit God's power, or who Her beguilings, Her
ὁολοπλοχία?"

The king said, "What is τὸ τέλος, then? What is the end and
aim of life in this world we live in?"

Vandermast said. "She is the end. Though the heaven perish,
She shall endure. A man is unmanned if he level at any lower mark.
God can reach no higher."

The King said, "But what of that dictum of the sage, *Deus se
ipsum amore intellectuali infinito amat:* God loves His own Self with an
infinite intellectual love? And is not that a higher mark?"

Vandermast said, "It is a good point of philosophy: but your
serenity hath left out of the reckoning the ultimate Duality in Oneness of the nature of God. The Self hath its being,—its cause material, its cause formal, its cause efficient, and its cause final,—wholly
in that which it loves. And yet, by unresolvable antinomy, remains it
of necessity other than that which it loves. For in love there must
needs be ever both a selfsameness and an otherness."

The King said, "Who are you, old man? winding up stars to me
out of the unbottomed well of truth, as it were myself speaking to
myself, and yet they are mysteries I never scarce cast a thought
upon until now?"

Vandermast said, "The self, as we have said, hath its being wholly in that which it loves."

And the King said, under stars in Memison, "And She too, by like argument, awful, gold-crowned, beautiful Aphrodite, loving Herself and Her own perfectnesses, loves them, I suppose, not for their own sake but because of Him that loves Her and by Her is loved."

Vandermast said, "That is undoubtable. And it is the twofold anchor-cable of truth and truth. And thus in Her and because of Her, is the supreme ἄσχησις: an infinitude of formal limits whereby the dead unformed infinite of being and becoming is made to live."

The King said, slowly, as out of a slow deep study, "So that, were it to be God: then, may be, through the mind of this horse, this fish, this slave, this sage, this queen, this conqueror, this poet, this lover, this albatross, as He or She, to open Our eyes here and there: see what manner of world this is, from inside it. And, for interest of the game, drink Lethe before so looking: be forgetful awhile of Our Olympian home and breeding. Even to look," he said after a minute's silence, "through many windows at once, many pairs of eyes. As, spill quick-silver: many shining bodies, every one outwardly reflecting all other but shut off by its own skin from all other, inwardly secret to itself: yet will join together again at the full close."

Vandermast held his peace. The King, gazing into the eyes of that old man, gazed into profundities of night: of Night, that is sister to death, but mother also of desire and mother of dreams, and between the pillars of her bed are the untravelled immensities of the interstellar spaces.

It was nineteen twenty-three, the first week in February, a gloomy sodden-souled day colourless with east wind. Mary reined up her horse at the edge of Kelling Heath. "We'd better keep to the road," she said over her shoulder to Anne Bremmerdale who had halted a yard or two behind her. "Rather dangerous, with all these old trenches. They ought to fill them up."

"Useful for the next war," Anne said.

They waited a minute, looking northwards and seawards over the heath. Mary turned in the saddle for a sweep of the eye over the country inland. All was brown and bare now and the trees unleaved; but near at hand the may-bushes were beginning to show signs of waking with their dark intricacy of thorns and their myriad tiny stars: green little balls, the first swelling of the buds, in a criss-cross twiggy heaven. No buttercups this time of year, no meadowsweet, dew-pearled, creamy and heavy-scented, no lovely falling note of the peggy-whitethroat nor lark's song mounting and mounting more golden than gold to salute the lady dawn; and yet, in this wide heathland and the turbulent sky above it, a fifteen-year-old echo of these things, and of those galloping hooves that had been as flying darkness under the morning, with muffled rollings in the heart of darkness like distant drums. "Do you think we get older?" Mary said, as they drew back into the road and at a walking-pace turned inland. "Or do you think we are like the audience at a cinema, and sit still and watch the thing go by?"

The proud lines of Anne's face hardened to a yet closer likeness to her brother Edward's. "I think we grow older," she said. "Most of us."

The wind seemed to think so too. Grow older and die. Sometimes die first. Mary said, "I think we get more awake."

And yet: to untell the days and redeem those hours? Ah, if it were possible. That had been the day of the last of those cricket matches that there used to be every year for so many years, against Hyrnbastwick. Poor Hugh, blinded in the war: at least he had his wife: probably the right one. And Lady Southmere was there, did Anne remember? Of course she did: gone long ago, both those old people. And Mr. Romer, whom Jim admired so and was so fond of up at Trinity: a great favourite of Edward's too: a man eminent in spheres usually incompatible, both as don and as man of the world: an education in itself to have known him. He died in 'fifteen. So many of those people caught by the war: Jack Bailey, killed: Major Rustham, Hesper Dagworth, Captain Feveringhay, killed, killed, killed: Norman Rustham, that delightful little boy, gone down with the *Hawke*. Nigel Howard, killed: poor Lucy. And her brother married to that—well, we won't use Edward's word for her. And Tom Chedisford, of all people, drinking himself to death, it seems: incredible: appalling. "What does Janet Rustham do now-a-days?" said Mary.

"Good works."

"And those awful Playter girls?"

Anne smiled. "One turned nun: the other's in some government job. Cuthbert Margesson captained your side that year, didn't he? I can't bear to think of Nell's never to this day knowing what became of him: too ghastly, that 'reported missing.'"

"It was worse for Amabel," Mary said, "having Nicholas murdered under her nose by those brutes in Kieff. They let her go, because she was English. But you're being dreadfully gloomy: almost making me cry, with this ugly wind and all. Remember, there have been some happy things: Tom Appleyard, an Admiral now and quite undamaged: Rosamund a full-blown marchioness: you and Charles: Edward and me: dear Jim, the salt of the earth, I don't think doomsday could change him; and Uncle Everard and Aunt Bella: and Father, so hale and hearty, though he is getting on for seventy."

"Getting on for seventy. And lonely," Anne said in her own mind.

"Lonely." To some unclothing quality in that word, the rude wind seemed to leap as to a huntsman's call, taking her breath, striking through her thick winter clothes to raise gooseflesh on her skin. She shivered and put her horse to a trot. For a while they rode in silence, each, for friendship, with the other's private ghosts for company: for Mary, Anne's dead brothers, Fred and Will Lessingham, and the only other sister, Margaret, who married that eccentric explorer man and died of yellow fever in the basin of the Orinoco; and for Anne, all Mary's three brothers, all gone: eldest and youngest killed in the war, and Maxwell, the middle one, years before that in a hunting accident. Ghosts of the past, dank and chilling. But not actively menacing as was this secret one, present to Lady Bremmerdale alone, which all the time held its ground undisturbed by her other thoughts that came and went. It held its ground with a kind of mock obsequiousness and paraded its obedience to her will: an incipient ghost, grey, obscuring with its breath the windows of the future: a ghost without distinct form, except that, like the comic man in old-fashioned pantomimes, it seemed to be perpetually removing yet another waistcoat. And at each removal, the effect was not a revealing, but an effect of ever more unmistakable and ever bleaker emptiness.

As they walked their horses up out of the dip towards Salthouse Common, she said, "Here's a general knowledge question for you, Mary dear: a point that's been teasing me a good deal lately. Would you say it was possible for two people to live successfully simply as friends? married people, I mean: so to say, a Platonic marriage?"

Mary inclined her head as if weighing the matter before she answered. "I think I would apply there Dr. Johnson's saying about the dog walking on its hind legs: it is not done well, but you are surprised to find it done at all."

"I doubt, myself, whether it is possible," said Anne. "Surely it ought to be. Not that there's any particular virtue in it: it's so obviously a matter of taste. But tastes count for a good deal when you're considering a pair of Siamese twins. I fancy differences of taste on a point like that can be unsurmountable barriers, don't you?"

Mary looked at her, but Anne's face was averted. "I don't think I ever really thought about it. Unsurmountable is a big word. I should have thought if they were fond of each other they might hit upon some *modus vivendi*."[18]

"But there might be people, of course, with such poles-asunder ideas."

"If they really cared," said Mary, "I shouldn't think ideas ought to matter much."

"Ideas about love, I meant. What it is."

"Well, if they loved each other?"

"But might it not be that, just because they do love each other, and their ideas are so different (or ideals), they settle down to a *modus vivendi* that evades these controversial ideas? And will not that lead to living on the surface: shirking the deep relationships? If you're colour-blind you can't expect to be very amusing company for someone whose whole interest is taken up with colour schemes based on red and green."

Mary said, "I wonder? Surely, when one marries one undertakes to play the game according to certain rules. Both do. It seems a bit feeble to give it up because, for one or other or for both, the rules happen to make it specially difficult."

Anne was silent for a while. Then she said, "You speak as a born mistress of the game, my beloved. I was thinking of less gifted, less fortunate, bunglers."

"Perhaps it's hard for you and me to put ourselves in their shoes," said Mary.

"Perhaps it is."

"What I'm quite sure of," said Mary, "is that if there is friction of that sort, it's much better that, of the two, the woman should be the less deeply in love."

Anne said, after a pause, "You don't believe in cutting Gordian knots,[19] then?"

"No. I don't."

"Never?"

"Never for people in the particular kind of muddle we're thinking of."

"But why never? I'd like to know why you think that."

Mary seemed to ponder a minute, stroking her horse's neck. "I expect really it is because I believe we are put into this world simply and solely to practise undoing Gordian knots." She looked at Anne, then away again: concluded very gently, "To practise undoing them: not sit down on them and pretend they aren't there."

Lady Bremmerdale sighed. "I should imagine the real trouble comes in a case where the players have themselves made the game about ten times more unplayable than it ever need have been: spoilt it, perhaps, right at the beginning, by pulling the knot into a jam there's no undoing. And then, if there is no undoing, the choice is to sit tight on the tangle and pretend it isn't there (which I think dishonest and destructive of one's self-respect), or else be honest and cut it. Or chuck it away and have done with it."

"I certainly shouldn't sit on it, myself," said Mary. "Very galling, I should think, to the sitting apparatus! But as for cutting, or throwing away," she said with a deeper seriousness, "—well, my darlin', that's against the rules." Anne said nothing: looked steadily before her. "Besides," said Mary, "I don't see how you can ever, in real life, say in advance: Here's a tangle there's no undoing."

After a long pause Anne said, "Jim takes exactly the same line as you do." She looked round, into a pair of eyes so easy to rest in, it might have been her own eyes regarding themselves from a mirror.

"O, Jim has been tried on the general knowledge paper, has he?"

"The two people I know in the world fit to be asked their opinion on such a subject."

"People talk to Jim, because he talks to nobody. I'm glad he agrees with me. Leaving out present company, I think Edward qualifies for third on your list."

"I don't count him," said Anne. "He hardly counts as another person."

Mary's silence, clearer and gentler than words could have said it, said, "I understand."

"Edward says cut it and be damned to it."

"I would agree with that," said Mary, "if there were a *tertium quid:* the vulgar triangle. There usually turns out to be, of course. Practically always. But in this hypothetical case, I gathered there was not?"

"In this hypothetical case I can promise you there isn't."

"Well then—"

It was getting late. They had fetched a circle round by Glandford and the Downs and so through Wiveton and Cley with its great church and windmill and up onto the common again and were now riding down the hill above Salthouse. The broad was alive with water-fowl. Beyond the bank they saw the North Sea like roughened lead and all the sky dark and leaden with the dusk coming on and a great curtain of cloud to northward and a sleet-storm driving over from the sea. Mary said, "I should think Charles's view might be valuable."

Lady Bremmerdale's handsome face darkened. "I haven't consulted Charles," she said, after a pause.

They came riding into Salthouse now, level with the bank. They saw how a flight of brent geese, a score or more, swept suddenly down steeply from that louring sky like a flight of arrows, to take the water: a rushing of wings, black heads and necks arrow-like pointing their path, and white sterns vivid as lightning against that murk and beginnings of winter night.

Anne said slowly, "But I think I'm inclined to agree with you and Jim."

"And we, madonna, are we not exiles still?
When first we met
Some shadowy door swung wide,

Some faint voice cried,
—Not heeded then
For clack of drawing-room chit-chat, fiddles, glittering lights,
Waltzes, dim stairs, scents, smiles of other women—yet,
'Twas so: that night of nights.
Behind the hill
Some light that does not set
Had stirr'd, bringing again
New earth, new morning-tide.

"I didn't mean that seriously, years ago when I wrote it,"
Lessingham said: "that night you were such a naughty girl at
Wolkenstein." He was working on a life-size portrait of Mary in an
emerald-green dress of singular but beautiful design, by artificial
light, between tea and dinner that same afternoon, in the old original Refuge at Anmering Blunds. "I mean, I felt it but I hadn't the
intellectual courage of my feelings. Strange how the words can come
before the thought," he talked as if half to her, half to himself, while
he worked: "certainly before the conscious thought. As if one stuck
down words on paper, or paint on canvas, and afterwards these
symbols in some obscure way have a power of coming to life and
telling you (who made them) what was in fact at the back of your
mind when you did it; though you never suspected it was there, and
would have repudiated it if you had."

Mary said, "It opens up fascinating possibilities. On that principle you might have an unconscious Almighty, saying, as He creates
the universe, *Moi, je ne crois pas en Dieu.*"[20]

"I know. I can't see why not. An atheistical Creator is a contradiction. But is not reality, the nearer you get to the heart of it,
framed of contradictions? I'm quite sure our deepest desires are."

"I'm sure they are." A comic light began to play almost imperceptibly about the corners of Mary's lips. "Really, I think I should
find an atheistical Almighty much more amusing to meet than an
Almighty who solemnly believed in Himself. Can you imagine anything more pompous and boring?"

Lessingham was silent a minute, painting with concentrated
care and intention. Then he stopped, met her eye, and laughed.
"Like an inflated Wordsworth, or Shelley, or Napoleon: prize bores
all of them, for all their genius. You can't imagine Homer, or the
man who was responsible for *Njal's Saga,* or Shakespeare, or Webster, or Marlowe, thinking like that of themselves."

Mary smiled. "Marlowe," she said: "when he was like to die,
'being persuaded to make himself ready to God for his soul, he
answered that he would carry his soul up to the top of a hill, and
run God, run devil, fetch it that will have it.' I could hug him for
that."

"So could I. They were far too deep in love with their job to bother about themselves as doers of it. They knew the stature of their own works, of course: Beethoven's saying of the *cavatina* (wasn't it?) in Op. 130, 'It will please them someday'; but that is worlds apart from the solemn self-satisfaction of these one-sided freaks, not men but sports of nature. How would you like Shelley for your *inamorato?*"

"I think I should bite his nose," Mary said.

Something danced in Lessingham's eye. He painted swiftly for a minute in silence. "Just as I know," he said, taking up the thread of his thought again, "(better than I know any of your what people call accepted scientific facts) whether a picture of mine is right when I've finished it, or whether it's worthless. It's one or the other: there's no third condition. When I've finished it. Till then, one knows nothing. This one, for instance: heaven knows whether it will come off or not. My God, I want it to."

"Yes. You used to slash them into pieces or smudge them over when they were half finished. Till you learnt better."

"Till you taught me better. You, by being Mary." He stood quickly back, to see sitter and portrait together. "You are the most intolerable and hopeless person to paint I should think since man was man. Why do I go on trying?"

"You succeeded once. Perhaps that is why. The appetite grows with feeding."

"*The Vision of Zimiamvia* portrait?[21] Yes. It caught a moment, out of your unnumerable moments: a perfect moment: I think it did. But what is one among the hundreds of millions? Besides, I want a perfect one of you that the world can see. That one is only for you and me and the Gods. O, the Devil's in it," he said, changing his brush: "it's a lunacy, a madness, this painting. And writing is as bad. And action is as bad, or worse." He stepped forward to put a careful touch on the mouth: stepped back, considered, and corrected it. "Est-ce que vous pouvez me dire, madame, quelle est la différence entre une brosse à dents et un écureuil?"[22]

Mary's response was the curiousest of little inarticulate sounds, lazy, mocking, deprecatory, that seemed, as a sleepy child might if you stroked it, or a sleepy puppy, to stretch itself luxuriously and turn over again, hiding its nose in the downy deep contentment of many beloved absurdities: how stupid you are, and yet how dear you are to be so stupid, and how cosy us two together, and how absurd indeed the world is, and how amusing to be you and me.

"Do you know the answer?" His eyes were busy.

"No," she said, in a voice that seemed to snuggle deeper yet into that downiness of honey-scented pillows.

"Quand on les mit tous les deux en dessous d'un arbre, c'est celui qui le grimpe qui est l'écureuil."[23]

"O silly riddle!"

"Do you know what you did then?" said Lessingham, painting with sudden extreme precision and certitude. "You did a kind of pussy-cat movement with your chin, as though you were smoothing it against a ruff. I know now what this picture wants. Have you got a ruffle? Can't we make one? I can see it: I could do it out of my head. But I'd like to have it in the flesh, all the same."

"Angier can make one by to-morrow. I can show her."

"Tired?"

"No."

He put down palette and brushes. "Anyhow, let's knock off and have a rest. Come and look at it. There. Aren't I right?"

Mary, standing beside him, looked at it a while in silence. "Not one of those enormous ones," she said, "like a peacock's tail."

"Good heavens, no."

"Nor the kind that swaddles one up to the chin in a sort of white concertina, as if one hadn't any neck."

"No, no. I want it quite narrow: not more than two inches deep, like Isabella d'Este's in our Titian[24] in the music-room at home. But much longer, of course, following the opening of your dress."

"When you designed this dress," said Mary, "did you mean it to be a Zimiamvian dress?"

"Pure Zimiamvian. It clothes, but does not unduly conceal: adorns, but is not silly enough to try to emulate: displays, but does not distort."

"On the principle of Herrick's *Lily in Crystal*."[25]

"Exactly. It's a Zimiamvian principle, isn't it? Up to a point."

"Or rather down."

"I should have said, down. There again: another of these antinomies at the heart of things. Every experience of pure beauty is climacteric; which means it gathers into its own being everything that has led on to it, and, conversely, all that leads on to it has value only because of that leading on. You can't live on climaxes alone."

"Words!"

He was busy selecting new brushes and setting his palette for the green. "I stand rebuked. A concrete parallel, then. Think of the climax, like all the morning stars singing together, worked up in those terrific tremolo passages towards the end of the *Arietta* in Op. 111. Played by itself, what is it but just a brilliant and extraordinarily difficult display of technique? But play it in its context, coming after the self-destroying Armageddon and Ragnarok of the *Allegro con brio ed appassionato*, and after those early unfoldings of the *Arietta* itself—"

"Ah, that little simple beginning," said Mary, "like little farms all undesecrated, and over there the sea without a blemish; and all the fields full of tiny speckets, lambs in spring."

"And so gradually, gradually, to the empyrean. Which is itself simply the ultimate essence crammed with the implications of all these things. White hot with them."

"Or a great mountain," she said. "Ushba, as we first saw him from those slopes of the Gul glen above Betsho, facing the dawn. Take away the sky: take away the roots of the mountain: the Suanetian forest about the roots—crab-apples, thorns, rowan, sweet brier and rhododendron, hornbeam and aspen and beech and oak, those monkshoods higher than your head as you rode by on horseback, and great yellow scabious eight feet tall, and further up, that riot of poppies and anemones, gentian, speedwell and ranunculus, forget-me-not, geraniums, and huge Caucasian snowdrops: take these trimmings away, you lose the size and the wonderfulness and the living glory of it, and have nothing left but a lump of ice and stone."[26]

"The unrelated climax. Dead. Nothing."

Mary was studying the picture on the easel. "You've started the hair, I see."

"Just roughed it in."

"It ought to be black. Jet-black."

"Ought it?"

"Oughtn't it? And scarlet dress?"

"Because I've captured the Queen of Spades' mood about the mouth?"

"Well, of course. Why should she be tied down to red-gold and green? She doesn't like it. Has to put up with it in this stodgy world; but, when you can paint like that, it's most unkind not to give her her own outsides sometimes. After all, she is me, just as much as I am myself. You painted her in your Valkyrie picture, but I've always felt that as fancy dress. I can't wear poppy-red, or yellow or even honey-colour. But I itch to wear them: will, too, someday. For (you and I know) there will be days there, won't there?"

"Days. And nights. How could you and I get along without them?"

"Why should we be expected to?—Well," she said, "I'm ready. An hour yet before it will be time to change for dinner."

"Head's free now," said Lessingham as he settled her pose again: "I'm only on the dress. I can't alter this now," he said, returning to his easel. "And the truth is, I couldn't bear to. But I'll do the spit image of it, if you like—same pose, same everything, but in Dark Lady form,—as soon as this is finished."

"And a self-portrait too, perhaps," said Mary, "on the same principle?"

"Very well."

"She'd like it. Personally, of course, I prefer my King suited in black rather than red. But when she gets the upper hand—and remember, she is me—"

Lessingham laughed. "It's a mercy that these Jekyll-Hyde predilections of ours don't lead to promiscuity on both sides. How is it they don't?"

"Because when longing aches you for *La Rose Noire,* it is still me you ache for. The empty body, or with someone not me behind it: what would you give for that?"

"*O madonna mia,* who sent you into this world, I wonder?"

"Who sent us?"

Lessingham painted for a while without speaking. The clock ticked, while slowly on the canvas inert pigments ground in oil gradually, through innumerable subtle relationships of form and colour, took life: gradually and painfully, like the upthrusting of daffodil blades through the hard earth in spring, became to be the material witness to the vision, seen through Lessingham's eyes, of Mary's warm and breathing body clothed in that dress which from throat to hips, like a fifteenth-century coat-hardy, fitted like a skin. Still painting, he began to say, "What happens when we get old: twenty, thirty, forty years hence? to lovers, I mean. Get old, and powers fail: blind, deaf, impotent, paralysed? Is memory enough? Even that fails. Bad to think of: a going down into fog and obscurity. All the things of the spirit belong so entirely to the body. And the body is (in our experience) matter. Time dissolves it away. What remains?"

Mary made no answer: only sat there, breathing, beautiful, desirable, while the clock ticked on.

"Some Absolute? Some universalized Being? The Self resumed like a drop of water into a river, or like the electric lamplight into the general supply of electrical energy, to be switched on again, perhaps, in new lampbulbs? Surely all these conceptions are pompous toys of the imagination, meaning the same thing—Death—from the point of view of the Me and You: from the point of view, that is to say, of the only things that have ultimate value. Futile toys, too. Abstractions. Unrealities."

"Futile toys," Mary said, under her breath.

" 'Love is stronger than Death,' " Lessingham said. "How glibly people trot out these facile optimisms, till the brutal fact pashes them to pieces. 'The spirit lives on': orthodox Christian ideals of love. Well," he said, "goodness counts." He painted in silence for a time. "And, in this world, goodness fails."

Mary half opened her lips. "Yes. It does," she said at last, in a voice that seemed to go sorrowful over seastreams to oblivion.

Lessingham's words came slower as the tempo of his painting became faster, his brushwork surer and more triumphant. "The tragedy," he said, "is in the failure of other people's goodness: to see someone you love suffer unjustly. No good man cares a snap about his own goodness' failing. Probably because, seen from inside, it is not such a good goodness after all."

Mary said, "I think we all see truest from outside."

"I hope we do."

After a silence, while the splendour of the picture grew together swiftlier and swiftlier on the canvas, he began to say, "The ideal of the non-attached. It's a compromise ideal. A sour-grapes ideal. A spiritless weak negation, to reject the goods of this world, the heaven of the senses. Sensual delight by itself is an abstraction, therefore worthless. But in its just context, it folds in the whole orb of the world: it becomes the life-blood, the beatific vision."

Mary said, "That is pure truth, *mon ami.*"

"It is the arch-truth," he said; "and of it is born the great truth of conflict and contradiction. But it is not a truth of this life. Look at the two good characters of perfection: the static and the dynamic. You must have both. But, in this life, that is just what you can't have. Evanescence in itself; the sunrise, a sheet of trembling shell-pink blossom at mid-day, bare twigs and fallen petals by evening: sunset light on the Sella (do you remember?): human birth, flowering time, decay, and death: the kitten becoming a cat: night giving place to day, day to night: all the uncertainnesses and unknownness of the future. Are not all these part of the very being of perfection? the Ever-Changing: the γλυχύπιχϱος, bitter-sweet: that which cannot be reversed: that which will never come back: that which says 'never again.' But so also, the imperishable laughter: the sun that never sets: the night that stands still for lovers: the eternal eyes of the Gods: the Never-Changing."

Mary said, "Ever-Changing: Never-Changing. You had it engraved in my alexandrite ring."

"But how reconcile them?" He squeezed out more paint. "Can you and I?"

"Only Omnipotence can do it."

"And Omnipotence is a fraud if it doesn't?"

"Dare we say that?"

"With our last breath, we must. Or be blasphemers."

After a moment's silence, "Where does that come," Mary said: *"God's adversaries are some way His own; and that ownness works patience."*?[27] Then, after another silence, "I am sometimes so taken with astonishment," she said, "at the unspeakable blessedness of some passing minute, that I could not have the heart to be unthankful even if I knew for certain there was nothing besides: nothing before that minute and nothing after it, for ever and ever and ever. And that minute, nothing too, as soon as it was over."

"And my answer to that," said Lessingham, very slowly, "is that in the pure goodness and perfectness that bred those words out of your mouth this moment, burns a reality that blows to the wind in ashes the doubt those words plead for."

She watched him painting while he spoke. "And so, you believe it?" she said at last.

Lessingham said, "Because of you."

"Literally believe it, as sober matter of fact? So firmly as to be able to die in that belief?"

"Yes," he said: "as firmly as that."

"Even at the risk of its being a false belief? And (as you used so often to say to me) how can we tell?"

"Don't you think a belief so strong that you can die in it is too strong to be false? Must it not, of its mere strength, be true?"

"I would say yes. But if it were the other to die. If you had me here dead this minute. What then?"

Lessingham painted swiftly. "Compromise," he said, "is a virtue in an imperfect world: it is the virtue of statesmanship. But in philosophy, compromise is abdication of the sovereign mind within us, and a fogging of the issue. Our love, yours and mine, is native to a perfect world, where spirit and flesh are one: where you can both eat your cake and have it. Isn't that true?" After a pause he said, very low, "And when it comes to dying, I had actually rather you went first. Not long first, I should hope; but first."

Their eyes met.

Mary said, "I know. And I know why. And, for the very same 'why' I had rather, myself, have it the other way."

She watched him awhile in silence: the Olympian grace and strength of him, the singular marriage of his bodily frame of north with south, the gyr-falcon lights in his eyes, the sensitive powerful hand that guided the brush as he painted, the great black beard. Presently he stepped back to survey his work. From half-finished portrait to original his eyes leapt, and there stayed held. Utterly unselfconscious Mary seemed, sitting there, all turned outward to the world; yet with that unselfconsciousness that accepts admiration, which is its natural atmosphere, as a flower accepts sunshine; as of course. Her hair was done low on the back of her neck, plaited so that the plaits gave a tesselated effect with ever varying shades of gold and copper and red in the tight-wound gleaming surfaces; and at the side, upon the neck behind the ear, the growth of the extreme hairs, delicate as single threads of the silkworm, rose exquisite in intricate variety of upward curve, as the lines of fire or of a fountain's upward jet blown sideways in the wind. "You say it is credible because of me," she said softly. "I suppose that must always be so: easy to see the Divine shine through in the person one loves: quite impossible to see or imagine it in oneself."

Suddenly, by a short-circuiting of the electric current, the light went out. Neither he nor she moved.

"That was a strange effect," Lessingham said out of the blackness. "My eyes were filled, I suppose, with the green of your dress, so that when the light went I still saw, for a flash, clear cut on the darkness, that dress, but flaming scarlet."

He struck a match.

"Well, here I am," Mary said, "still in my right complexion. But why scarlet?"

"The complementary colour."

"Very appropriate too, *mon ami,* after what we were talking about?"

XIV

The Fish Dinner: Praeludium

M EAN TIME in lovely Memison, (if indeed, betwixt here and yonder, there could be other than mean time), the Lady Fiorinda, pleasuring her senses with the balm-sweet breathings of the air in that Zimiamvian garden, walked, with none but her own most unexperimented thoughts for company, in the tented glory, wide-rayed, cloudless, golden, serene, of the slow July sun descending. Here, upon the Duchess's birthday, but a month ago, had she lazed herself, beneath these poplars, beside this lily-pond, but then under heat of noon: a month ago only and a day. And now, like a refrain to bring back with its presence the preluding music of that midsummer night, there came through the trees the lord Chancellor Beroald, gorgeously apparelled in doublet and hose of gold-broidered brocade.

"Good evening, good brother. Are these your mourning weeds, for your late brother-in-law?"

"No," he said. "Are these yours, for your late husband?"

"Now I think on't, they will serve." She looked down at her coat-hardy, woven of thousands of tiny margery-pearls and yellow sapphires, skin-close, clinging like a glove, and her velvet skin, black as the raven, fastened low about the hips with a broad girdle laid over with branches of honeysuckles of fine flat gold and cloudy strawberry-coloured tourmalines. "I have evened accounts with you

505

now," she said, meeting with mockery in her eyes his haughty outwardness of ironic calm. "You put on your ruffians to ease me from
the first bad card you dealt me: not out of any undue study of my
convenience, but because you thought you knew a likelier to serve
your purpose. And now I have turned your likelier second (almost
of the same suit) with the deuces and treys out of the deck."

"What course took you to destroy him?" asked Beroald equably, as it had been to ask "rode he on Tuesday to Rumala?" or such
ordinary matter.

Fiorinda laughed. "And your intelligencers have not told you
that? You, who keep a servant fee'd[1] in every man's house from
Sestola to Rialmar?"

"He was found torn in pieces in the woods hereabout," said the
Chancellor. "This is the bruit in this countryside. I know no more."

"Suffice it, he had me wronged. May be that is enough for your
lordship to know. I did not dive into your profundities in that matter of Krestenaya, thinking your most ingenious policies your affair.
You may justly use a like discretion when (as now) my private matter
is in question."

"Sometimes, my lady sister," he said, "I am almost a little
afeared of you."

Fiorinda looked at him through her fingers. "I know you are. It
is wholesome for us both you should treat me with respect. If I am
minded to lend you a hand in the otherwhile vacations of your
graver businesses, be thankful. But forget not, sweet brother, I am
not to be used for ends outside myself: not by any man: not were he
my lover even: much less by a politician such as you."

The Lord Beroald's lean lips under his short clipped mustachios stirred upon a sardonic smile. "You are all firishness and summer lightnings this afternoon. There's something unovercomable
underlies it," he said. "Howsoever, I think we have the wit to understand each other. Enough, then. I came not to speak on these trifles,
but to let you know her grace hath bid me to supper to-night, private, a fish dinner, at the summer palace. Know you who shall be
there?"

"The King. The Duke. The Parry. You. My lord Admiral (Gods
be gentle to his harmless soul). There's the sum, I think."

"No ladies?"

"Myself." All delicious pleasures and delectations worldly re-
spired about that word as she spoke it.

"No more?"

"O a one or two, for form sake." She looked at him a moment,
then said: "I will tell you a thing, now I remember me. I have been
honoured with a new proposal of marriage."

"Ha?" the Chancellor's cold eye sparkled. "I know from
whence."

"You know?"

"All Meszria knows."

"Indeed? Well, and I have refused it."

"Nay, I am put from shore then. Who was it?"

"Ask not overcuriously."

"Not the Duke of Zayana."

"The Duke of Zayana."

"But I thought so. But you jest, sister. You have refused the Duke?"

"I have refused him once, twice."

"But third time?"

"And he come to me a hundred times with such a suit, he shall have No for every time he shall ask me."

"But wherefore so? Duke Barganax?"

"I know not," said she. "Perhaps for because that I grow out of liking of this vain custom, whereby husbands have been sessed and laid upon me, as soldiers are upon subjects, against my will."

Like wind on clear water, ruffling the surface that none may see what rests below, a kind of laughter hid the deeps of her unblemishable green eyes. Beroald shrugged his shoulders. "I would know some more weighty and more serious reason why you refused so great a match."

"For a reason too nice for a man of law to unravel," she said. "Because truly and undissemblingly I wonder, sometimes, if I be not fallen, may be, a little in love with him."

Beroald looked her in the eye. "In love with him? And therefore would strain him fast and sure? And therefore not minded to dwindle into his Duchess?"

"Why truly and indeed you are my brother!" she said, and very sisterly kissed him.

The Chancellor being departed, Fiorinda resumed her walk, to and fro under the trees, from splendour to shadow and from shadow to splendour again as the arrows of gold found or missed her as she passed. There alighted upon pebbles at the pond's further brink a water ousel and began to regard her, with much dipping and bobbing of his body and much rolling up of the whites of his eyes. Whether because of her being alone, without so much as a brother's unenchanted eye to rest upon her, or for whatever cause, Her presence, in this hour of but natural beauties' composing of themselves for slumber, seemed to unsubstantiate all that was not Her. Black velvet's self and this milky way of seed-pearls and yellow sapphires: close-bodied coat, gown, and girdle: seemed as if fined to tissue of night made palpable, unveiling more than they clothed. Slowly some perfection, opening its heart like evening, began to enfold air, sky, and shadowy earth.

Presently came two little yellow wagtails to play in the air like butterflies, up and down, back and across, above the water. She held out a hand: they left playing, to perch upon her fingers, and there fell to billing and kissing of one another.

"The little silly birds too!" said Barganax, as, suddenly aware of his presence behind her, she shook them off.

"And will your grace think there is anything new in that?" said she, looking at him over her shoulder through the curtained fringes of her lids. There was something questionable coloured her mood, this evening. Her lips, where but a moment since, like the dog-star's frosted sparkle of winter-nights, the colours of her thought seemed to dance, settled suddenly to the appearance as of lips carved out of sard or cornelian: so stone-like, so suddenly unmerciless in the harsh upward curling of them, like fish-hooks at her mouth's corners. "Will you think there is anything new in that? They are grateful, I suppose, for the tricks I teach them."

"Ingenuities beyond Aretine's,"[2] he said.

She flamed crimson, cheek and neck.

"Forgive that," said the Duke. "I forgot myself. And small marvel: I find all unfirm and unstable whatever I behold out of you. But I forget not—"

Very delicately she bent, upon that hesitation and with widened nostrils, to a yellow lily that she wore pinned at the bosom of her dress. Then, with questioning eyebrows: "And what will your grace's untamed thoughts forget not?"

"Tuesday night," answered he; and watched the fires of her eyes curdle to some impenetrability of flint or ironstone.

"Well? And what will your grace wish me to say to that?"

"What you will. Worst woe in the world to me, were you ever act or speak upon order." He paused: then, "Nor, I think, need your ladyship forget it neither," he said.

The sphinxian hooks unmild hardened in the corners of her mouth. "I am yet to learn but that a night is a night, and one night as another." In the stilled silence, the blades of their eye-glances engaged: as in sword-play, feeling one another's temper.

"Shall I, for my turn," said Barganax, "to match the honesty of your conversation, madam, tell you, then, a like truth?"

"As you will. An unlawful and useless game, this truth-telling. Remember, too, you did not desire me to say truth, but say what I would."

"Know you what the wild unwise tongue of them blabbeth abroad about you, that I have it thrice in one day 'twixt here and Zayana?"

"I can conceive."

"What? that you do rustle in unpaid-for silks? live so disorderly? marry but to unmarry yourself by running away? or, the better to uncumber you of your husband, take a resolution to have him murdered."

"Fair words and good semblant."

"And fitly paid for. I'm sorry, madam, that the last, and the most mouthiest, speaker of these things—"

"A duello?"

"It was somewhat too sudden, overhearing him speak so buggishly of your ladyship: took him neck and breech, and threw him against the wall."

"And so?"

"And so." The Duke shrugged, looking at his fingernails. "Well," he said, after a moment, looking up: "that was the third. You perceive how effectual and operative your ladyship's last dealings with me were: three men's blood," he tapped his sword-hilt, "for washing out this slander-work."

She smelled once more to the lily, all the while looking up at him with a smoulder of eyes from under delicate-arching eyebrows: very slowly smiling. It was as if some string had been plucked. All little evening noises of that garden, stir of leaf, babble of running water, winding of tiny horn of gnat, beetle, or bee, seemed to put on a kind of tumultuous enormity.

"O You, unmedicinable," he said, and his voice caught: "unparagoned: ineffable: unnameable." And he said, very deep and low:

> "Nightshaded moon-still'd meadow-close,
> Where the Black Iris grows:
> The Black Musk Rose:

> "Musk-breathing, deadly sweet,
> Setting the veins a-beat
> Till eyes fail and the sense founder and fleet:

> "Imperial petals curl'd,
> Sable falls and wings deep-furl'd—
> You have drunk up the World.

> "Flow'r of unsounded Night:
> Black fire over-bright:
> Blinder of sight—

> "So, the supreme full close.
> So, drink up me, my Rose."

With unreadable grave eyes still holding his, she listened, her face still inclining above the sulphur-coloured scarlet-anthered lily-flower, where it bedded so softly, there at the sweet dividing of her breasts. Surely all the pleasures of irresolution and uncertainness, all disordinate appetites of the body and unlawful desires of the soul, the very deepest secretaries of nature, unnaturalizing itself, took flesh in their most unshelled shining mother-of-pearled proportions, in that lady's most slow and covert smile. At length she spoke:

> "Si tu m'aimes dix fois
>   Qu'une nuit de mai,
> Onziesme j'y croys
>   Que ton amour soit vrai.—[3]

"And remember, I will be wooed afresh *chaque fois, mon ami: mais chaque fois.*"[4]

The voice of her speech trailed under-tones as of ankle-rings a-clink, or as the playing of idle polished fingernails upon hanging mirrors, or the drawing of curtains to shut in the warmth and the things of heart's desire and shut out the dark. Then, like some day-drowsy sweet beast that wakes, stretches, and rises for night and action, she faced him at her full stature. "Some cannot do," she said, "but they overdo. Or did I wish your impudent grace, indeed, to meet me here to-night?"

"Chaque fois?" said the Duke, gazing at her between half-closed lids. "It has been so, and it ever shall be so, and the better so shall our tastes run in harness. I hold, not as the poet, but thus:

> "Love given unsought is good, but sought is better."

" 'Ce que femme veut, Dieu le veut'?"[5] Well?" said she. "But 'our tastes' you said? As for Meszrian grandeur, will you think, and well-shapen mustachios?"

"O and in very particular matters I have studied your ladyship's taste too."

She turned from him: then, after a step or two, upon a lazing motion full of languishing luxuriousness, paused at the pond's brim, to look down, hands lightly clasped behind her, to her own counter-shape in the cool of the water. Her hair was dressed for to-night to a new fashion of hers, close-braided in two thick tresses which, coiling each twice about her head and interwoven with strings of honey-coloured cat's-eye chrysoberyls, made her a kind of crown in the likeness of two hearts bound together; all setting back, like an aureole of polished jet, from her beautiful white brow and from the parting above it, where the black hair, albeit drawn never so demurely backward on either side, carried even so some untameable note of its own free natural habit of smooth-running waves of ocean beneath midnight unstarred. The Duke, as a man that draws tight the curb on some unrulable thing within him, stayed himself for a minute, overlooking her from that distance, twice and again, from head to foot. Without further word spoken, he came over to stand beside her, so that they looked down to their two selves, mirrored there side by side.

"I find," he said presently, "that I do begin, in you, to know my own self. My way it hath long been, born bastard and unlegitimate, to have what I have a mind to, as the whirlwind, suddenly, unresistably. But you shall find I am not a man quickly fired and quickly laid down with satisfaction." He paused. It was as if his heart's pounding were become a thing outwardly audible. "These four days," he said: "Tuesday, and now it is Saturday: back to Zayana and back again: the unfillable desire of you. Take away you out of the world," he said, "and it unworlds all."

As if bodied out of that appassionate quietude, a little owl settled on Fiorinda's shoulder. Barganax, looking round at her, met its eyes, sharp, inscrutable, staring into his. The lovely face of that lady, and lovely head inclining forward a little, showed clear, side-face in the light that began to be crimsoned now toward sun-setting: clear of the small feathered thing that perched bolt upright upon her shoulder. The whole unseizable beauty of her seemed moment by moment to suffer alteration, waxing, waning, blazing anew, as now some Greek purity of feature, now some passing favour of an unassayed sensual sweetness or, in cheekbone or nostril, some old Tartarean fierceness untreatable in the blood, wore for the instant her beauty as its own. "Another taste in common," he said: "for that fire that burneth eternally without feeding."

Utterly still she abode, save for the upward mounting of her bosom and deep fall and swell again, like the unquiet sea remembering.

Barganax said: "You are unattainable. I have proved it. The sun rising, a roundel of copper incandescent against purple cloud: you'd swear—upon witness of your senses—'tis come near, divinely come down to earth 'twixt us and that cloudbank; and yet, with the drifting of some thicker fold of that cloud 'twixt us and the sun's face,—suddenly we know. So you. Even in the extreme having of you, I had you not. The knownest and unknownest thing in the world."

"And that," said she: "is it not in the essence and very perfect nature of love?" Her words were as the plumed silence of the owl's flight that, sudden as it came, now departed, sudden from her shoulder on noiseless wing. The plague that sat dozing in her mouth's corner proked at him swiftly, an unslockened burning merry look, as she turned to him, hands behind her head, settling the plaits of her hair. "I hope it remains not unkindly with your grace that I am not one that will eat a pear unpared? Nor that there's more than but make me dress and undress because you find me pliant?"

"You and I!" said the Duke. In their stilled eye-parley, darkness trembled upon darkness. "And I think I shall carry to my grave," here he touched his left shoulder, "the print of your most eloquent teeth, madam!"

As golden bells pealing down star-lit sleep-muffled corridors of all dreaming worlds, Fiorinda laughed. "Come," she held out her hand. "Your grace may take your revenge upon this."

He took the divine white daisy-hand: took the little finger: delicately, his eyes on hers, as might a cat in play, to let feel the teeth but not to hurt, bit it.

"Your ladyship smiles."

"Perhaps. At my thought."

The hand rested soft in his. He turned it up slowly: the underpart of the wrist: that place where hand joins arm, and the bluish tracings of veins but enhance the immaculation of skin, beneath which, a bird in prison, the pulse flutters or quiets. He kissed the hand suddenly, full in the warm palm of it: then, very formally, gave it back. "At your thought? And it is—if one may know?"

"That your grace is an artist."

"You like an artist?"

"I am hard to please. I like a good servant."

"And, for you, the better artist the better servant?"

Her eyelids flickered.

"Enough. Your ladyship shall take me as servant."

" 'Las, my unpatient lord, and have I not taken," said she, and the sidelong downward halcyon-dart of her eyes was a caress, secret, precise, butterfly-fingered, mind-unthroning, "all eleven-tenths of the journey toward that consummation already?"

Barganax's glance flashed and darkened. "Ah," he said: "but I look to perpetuity. I mean, 'pon indenture."

"O no indentures. I keep my servant so long as he please me."

"And I my mistress, 'pon like terms: so unsure, both of us, what manner mind we will have to-morrow. To avoid which, madam, no remedy but we must instantly be married."

"Never. I have twice answered that."

"With answers which are not worth an egg."

"I have answered unanswerably."

"To be Duchess of mine? Your ladyship is the first woman was e'er so stubborn set as say no to that offer."

"And the first, I dare say, e'er had the offer, to say yea to or nay to?"

"Instance again, we be like-minded."

"You mean, you to offer *in extremis* a bond you'd hate to be tied withal? while I, in sheer discerning bounty, please my own self—and you—by refusing of it?"

"My life's-queen, once more your hand," said the Duke. "As for this suit, the court's up: stands adjourned—till to-morrow. But," he said, "there's measure in all things. Summer nights are but half-length. I hold me bound for to-night."

"Well, and for to-night, then," said she, letting him by her hands in his, draw her: letting herself be drawn so, from arm's-length, in a slow and level gradualness of air-light sailing motion, nearer and nearer, as a swan descending calm streams in windless July weather: "for to-night, may be, I'll not tie up all refusals fast beyond untying."

"Then, to seal the title": for all the supple strength of her striving and eluding, he kissed her in the mouth. *"Copula spiritualis."*[6] And, 'cause One is naught: 'cause all university's reckoned in Two alone: therefore"—and again, deep and long, he kissed her, pasturing his eyes, in that close-ranged nearness, on hers which, open-lidded, impersonal as a dove's eyes, still avoiding his, seemed as in soft amazement all unperceiving of outward things, their sight turned inward. "And the third: nay, then, by heaven! but 'cause I will!" From her quickened breaths new intoxications disclosed themselves and spread abroad, and from that lily, crushed in the straining of her sweet body to his, and, in that crushing, yielding up its deliciousness. " 'Cause must be must be. 'Cause blind men go by feeling. 'Cause—What's here?"

"Girls," she said, coolly disembroiling herself. "Had your grace not seen such a beast before? Mistress Anthea: Mistress Campaspe: a kind of servants too of mine." With all demureness, they made their courtesies to the Duke. "They grow," said the Lady Fiorinda, "like rosemary, in any air: despatched now with commends, most like, from her grace, to desire us go in to supper. Nay, misdoubt them not: of a most exquisite tried discretion. Will you think her grace would employ 'em else? or that I would?"

"I wager no wagers upon that," replied he. "Enough that I ne'er beheld them till now; nor e'er heard tell of 'em neither."

"And yet, since they first could prattle, have been of our lady Duchess's household. There yet remain matters hid from you, there, my lord."

Barganax looked at them. "If I should hear a cat low like an ox," he said, "that should surprise me. And so now, if I should see a pretty mountain lynx wear partlets of cobweb lawn and go gowned in peach-coloured chamlet; or see a peggy-white-throat," here he changed glances with Campaspe's shy black bead-like eyes, "with red Tyrian hair-lace, and dressed in velvet the hue of the coat of a water-rat, and with little brown musky gloves—"

Anthea laughed behind her fan. Her eyes, looking at him over the edge of it, were yellow, with upright fiery slits for pupils.

<h1 style="text-align:center">XV</h1>

<h1 style="text-align:center">THE FISH DINNER:
SYMPOSIUM</h1>

IT WAS IN HER asphodel garden, under the south wall of the old keep, overlooking Reisma Mere, that the Duchess of Memison gave supper that night to guests select and few. The table was ring-shaped, eleven or twelve foot across by outside measurement breadthways, and nine from back to front, and its top about two foot wide. Where the bezel of the ring should be, where the two ends of the table curved round to meet each other, was a gap, may be of some four-foot width, for the coming and going of serving-maids to serve the company where they sat ranged in order round about the outer side of the table. "A fish dinner," the Duchess said as they took their places: "sea-fare, in Her praise that is bred of the sea foam." Lower, for the King's ear beside her, she said, *"L'absente de tous bouquets.* You remember, my Lord?"

The great King said, "I remember."

They sat them down now: in the midst, the King in his majesty, and the Duchess at his right hand, in high-seats of sweet-smelling sandalwood cushioned with rough-plumed silver plush and inlaid with gold and ivory and all kinds of precious stones. Next to the King, Duke Barganax had his place; next to the Duke, the Vicar of Rerek; next, the lord Admiral Jeronimy; and so at the end upon that side the lord High Chancellor Beroald. Upon the other side,

515

looking across to these, sat first, on the Duchess's right, the Princess Zenianthe,[1] niece to King Mezentius and guesting as now with her grace in Memison; on Zenianthe's right, my Lady Fiorinda; and beyond her again, making ten in all, Anthea and Campaspe.

The legs of the table were of all kinds and colours of marble, massive and curiously carved, and the table top of figured yew and elm and cedarwood and its edges filleted with inlay-work of silver and lapis lazuli and panteron stone and pale mountain-gold. A lofty arbour with squared pillars of rose-pink clouded quartz partly shut out the sky above the table. From its trellised roof, over-run with ancient vines whose boles were big at the base as a man's thigh, grapes depended in a hundred clusters, barely beginning at this season of the year to turn colour: heavy sleepy-hued bunches of globed jewels hanging high on the confines of the candle-light. Three-score candles and more burned upon the table, of a warm-coloured sweet-scented wax in branched candlesticks of glittering gold. So still hung the air of the summer night, the flames of the candles were steady as sleeping crocuses: save but only for a little swaying of them now and again to some such light stirring of the air as speech or laughter made, or the passing of serving-damsels in their sleeveless Grecian gowns, some green, some sky-colour, some saffron yellow, to and fro for changing of the plates or filling out of fresh wines. Pomegranates, lemons, oranges, love-apples, peaches of the sun, made an ordered show, heaped high upon mighty dishes of silver or of alabaster at set intervals along that table. Smaller dishes held dry and wet sweetmeats; and there was store of olives, soused haberdine, cavier on toast, anchovies, botargoes, pilchards, almonds, red herrings, Parmesan cheese, red and green peppers: things in their kind to sharpen the stomach against luxurious feasting, and prepare the palate for noble wines. Cream wafers there were besides, and cream cheese; but, for the body and substance of their feasting, no meat save fish-meat alone, dressed in innumerable delicious ways and of all sorts of fishes, borne in upon great platters and chargers by turns continually: eels, lampreys, and crayfish: pickerells, salt salmon, fry of tunny; gurnards and thornbacks in muscadine sauce; barbels great and small, silver eels, basses, loaches, hen lobsters, eel-pouts, mussels, frogs, cockles, crabfish, snails and whilks; great prawns, a turtle; a sturgeon; skate, mackerel, turbot, and delicate firm-fleshed speckled trouts.

All the company were in holiday attire. The King wore a rich doublet of cloth of gold, with wine-dark velvet slashes. The linked belt about his middle was of massive gold set with emeralds and night-dark sapphires, every stone big as a thrush's egg: the buckle of the belt in the likeness of two hippogriffs wrought in gold; with wings expansed, and between the hippogriffs a lion's face, garnished with sparks of rubies, and for its eyes two escarbuncles that glowed like hot burning coals. The Duke, upon his left, was clad from throat to toe in soft-woven dark-brown satin, cut about and bepinked with broidery of silken and silver thread: close-fitting, moulding itself to his lithe strong body's grace, upon such under-rhythms as, when a panther moves or a wakening python, with sleek-gliding ripple and swell inform the smooth outward skin. His ruff and wrist-ruffs were stiffened with saffron, and his sword-belt of bull's-hide edged above and below with beads of opal and fire-opal and balas ruby: its clasps, two dark hyacinth stones cabochon, of the colour of peat-water when the sun wades deep in it. The Vicar, sitting next to him, was all in scarlet, with a gorget of dull gold about his neck. There was, when he moved, a hard look about his chest and large broad belly, witness that beneath that peaceful outward covering of weak silk he carried a privy coat, against stabbers at unawares; having, indeed, many unlovers in the land, and especially here in Meszria, and of all estates. His beard, clipped and bristly, showed red as Thor's in the candlelight. For the rest, the Chancellor went in gold-broidered brocade the colour of a moonless night in summer where the blue shows blackest: the Admiral in a loose-sleeved coat of unshorn velvet of sober green, with black brocaded cloak and white trunk hose. But as for the costly gorgeous apparel of those ladies, hardly should a man have marked it, dazzling as it was, were he come suddenly to that board, but should have stood mute amazed by their first countenance, so untranspassably lovely of themselves—breathing, moving, discoursing—without need of all adornments in this flattering candlelight: each in herself a natural heaven in which, unmanured, all pleasure lies.

Malmsey presently and muscatel, being strong sweet wines, began to circle sunwise about the board; and now free ranged their discourse, with bandyings to and fro of the ball of wit, and with disputation, and laughter, and with sparkles struck, as from flint, out of thought by thought. King Mezentius, taking, for the while, little part in the game of words, yet of his only mere presence seemed to rule it. Almost it was as if this one man sat hooded, and unbeknown looker-on at a scene of his devising, and the players thereof but creatures engendered of his hid and deep judgements out of his own secretness. In whose free persons he seemed to call into being each particularly of speech or look or thought itself, when, how, in whom and from whom, he would.

"So silent, madonna?"

The Duchess dimpled her cheek. "I was but considering how good a gift that were, to be able to stay Time, make it stand still."

"To taste the perfect moment?"

"What else?"

"But how? when Time is put to a stop and no time left to taste it in?"

"I would taste it, I think," said she, "in a kind of timeless contemplation."

"Timeless?" said the Princess Zenianthe.

"Why not?"

"Contemplation. 'Tis a long word. To say it takes time. To do it, more, I'd have thought."

"Ah, cut Time's claws, then," said the Duchess. "Let him be, for me, so he snatch not things away."

Barganax smiled. "Say I were a squirrel, sat in the fork of a nut-tree, pleasantly eating a nut. At first bite, Time stands still. Where's my second?"

The Duchess wrinkled up her nose. "Why, just! into what distemper have the Gods let decline this sweet world of ours! It is so. But need it be so? in a perfect world?"

"A perfect?" said the King.

"Now and then I have conceived of it."

"Was it like to this world?"

She nodded. "Most strangely like." And now, while the sturgeon was ushered in with music in a golden dish, she said privately, "Are you remembered, dear my Lord, of a thing I asked you: the night you rode north alone with Beroald and left me, good as fresh wed and fresh bereaved?—If we were Gods, able to make worlds and unmake 'em as we list, what world would we have?"

"Yes, I remember."

"And your answer? you remember that?"

"May be I could and I would. But natural present, *madonna mia,* should better best rememberings?"

"Your very answer!" she said. "Not word for word; but the mind behind the word." She paused. "Makes me frightened sometimes," she said, in a yet lower voice, looking down.

"Frightened?"

"When I'm alone."

"We are as the Gods fashioned us." Unseen, beneath the table, his hand closed for a moment over hers: Amalie's hand, mistress and outward symbol of so unconsumable store and incorruptible of shyest and tenderest particular wisdoms and goodnesses and nobilities of the heart, heaped through slow generations to that dear abundance, yet outwardly of so lamb-like an unprovidedness against the crude nude gluttony of the world and iniquities of time and change and death.

"There's wits enough about this table, could we unmuzzle them," he said aloud, after a moment's silence, "enough to pick the world to pieces and devise it again span new. My Lord Horius

Parry: what world will you make us, say, when we shall have granted you patent to be God Almighty?"

"Go, some have called me ere now," answered he, "and not always out of pure love of me, a man of high-vaulting ambitions. But, Satan shield us! here is a new puzzle. I ne'er looked above the moon. I can not know how to answer."

"Answer, cousin, without these protestations," said the King; "which be stale as sea-beef. I and you do know one another by this time."

"Your highness knoweth me. Would God I were sure I as thoroughly knew your highness." He guzzled down his wine, carouse: stayed toying a minute with the empty cup. "Why, as for worlds," he said, "this world fits: I ask no other. A world where the best man"—here his eye, enduring the King's, had a look less unsearchable in its depths, belike, than the looker reckoned—"a world where the best man beareth away the victory. Wine, women, war: nay, I rate it fit enough. And, upon conditions," he swept a hot bold stare round the table, "even peace," he said, "can be tolerable."

"Pax Mezentiana," said the Duke to himself.

"But peace," said the Vicar, "softeneth, womanizeth a man;" and his stare, to the disembarrassing of the ladies, singled in turn the Chancellor, the Admiral, and the Duke. Fiorinda, catching the Duke's eye, did no more but act him again a gesture of his, of an hour since in the garden: look at her finger-nails.

"In sum, my Lord the King," said the Vicar, "I am a plain man. Know my trade. Know myself. Obey my master. And, for the rest (saving present company)": he glowered, right and left, upon Duke, Admiral, and Chancellor: *"nemo me impune lacessit."*[2]

"In sum," said the King, "you like well this world and would let well alone?"

"Humbly, it is my judgement."

"Which," said the King, "your excellency may very wisely and wholesomely act upon."

It was as if, for a freezing instant, an axe had shown its mouth. The lean lines of the Chancellor's lip and nostril hardened to a sardonic smile.

"You and I," said the King, turning to the Lord Jeronimy, "are oldest here. What say you?"

"My Lord the King," answered he, "I am five years older, I think, than your serene highness. And the older I grow the more, I think, I trust my judgement, the less my knowledge. Things I thought I knew," he said, leaning an elbow on the table, finger and thumb drawing down over his forehead one strand of his lank pale hair, while he cast about the company a very kindly, very tolerant, very philosophic look, "I find I was mistaken. What in a manner were certainties, turn to doubt. In fine—" he fell silent.

"There you have, charactered in speech, the very inwardness of our noble Admiral," whispered the Duchess in Zenianthe's ear: "a man wise and good, yet in discretive niceness so over-abounding that oft when it comes to action he but runneth into a palsy, from unability to choose 'twixt two most balanced but irreconcilable alternatives."

Eyes were gentle, resting on the lord Admiral. A humorousness sweetened even Beroald's satirical smile as he said, answering the King's look, "I, too, hold by the material condition. This world will serve. I'd be loth to hazard it by meddling with the works."

The Duke shrugged his shoulders. "Unless thus far only, perhaps," he said, eyeing that Lady Fiorinda across the table: "seeing that a world should be, to say, a garment, should it not be—to fit the wearer 'twas made for—" and something momentarily ruffled the level line of her underlids as the sun's limb at point of day cuts suddenly the level horizon of the sea, "ever-changing, never-changing?"

"And is this of ours not so?" said the King, his eyes too on that lady.

"Ever-changing," the Duke said: "yes. But as for neverchanging," Campaspe heard the alteration in his voice! as the nightbreeze sudden among sallows by the margin of some forsaken lake, "I know not. Best, may be, not to know." Anthea, too, pricked ears at the alteration: scurry of sleet betwixt moraine and ice-cave when all the inside voices of the glacier are stilled by reason of the cold.

"Yes, even and were we Gods," said the King, and the stillness seemed to wait upon his words: "best, may be, not to know. Best not to know our own changelessness, our own eternal power and unspeakable majesty altogether uncircumscriptible. For there is, may be, in doubts and uncertainties a salt or savour, without which, all should be turned at last unto weariness and no zest remain. Even in that Olympus."

"Time," said the Duchess, breaking the silence. "And Change. Time, as a river: and each of us chained like Andromeda upon the bank,[3] to behold thence the everchanging treasure or mischief of our days borne past us upon the flood: things never to be seized by us till they be here: never tarrying to be enjoyed: never, for all our striving, to be eluded, neither for our longing, once gone to be had again. And, last mischief, Death."

"A just image," said the Admiral. "And, as with the falling waters of the river, no stay: no turn back."

"Yes. We may see it is so," Zenianthe said. "But how and it were other than as we see it? We on the bank, moveless at our window: Time and the world stream by. But how if the window be (though we knew it not) the windows of a caroche or litter, wherein we are borne onward with so smooth, soft, and imperceptible a motion, as floating in air, morning mists are carried beside some lake—?"

"So that we could not tell, but by descending from our chariot, whether, in a manner, the motion were in us or in the scene we look out on? 'Tis all a matter, howsoever: the masque, howsoever, of our life-days goeth by."

"Ah, but is it all a matter, my lord Admiral?" said the Duchess. "For, upon this supposition, there is not but one river only and the floating burden upon its waters: there is the wide world to move in, forth back and about, could we but command the charioteer,—"

"Or but leap from chariot and walk, as a man should, in freedom of the world," said the Duke.

The King said, "Or as God and Goddess should, in freedom of all the university of all possible worlds."

"As to say," said Barganax, *I will that it be now last Tuesday night, midnight;* and, at a word, at a thought, make it so." His eye waited on Fiorinda's, which, as in some overcast night at sea the lode-star, opened upon him momentarily green fires.

"Should need a God, I should think," said she, and some bell of mockery chimed in her lazy accents, "to devise wisely, with such infinite choice. New singular judgement, I should think, to fit your times to the high of their perfection."

The King turned to her. "Your ladyship thinks, then, 'tis as well that all is done ready to our hand, without all power whether to tarry or go back, or choose another road: much less, have done with all roads and chariots and be free?"

" 'Tis as well, I should say," the idle self-preening glance of her hovered about the Vicar: "for some of us. Your serene highness will call to mind the old tale of the goodman and his wife and the three wishes." Her brother, the Lord Beroald, stiffened: shifted in his chair. "O, ne'er imagine I'd tell it, sweet brother: plain naked words stript from their shirts—foh! yet holdeth as excellent a lesson as a man shall read any. I mean when, at their third wishing, so as to rid 'em out of the nasty pickle whereinto they had brought themselves with the two former, they were fain but to unwish those, and so have all back again as *in statu quo prius.* And here was but question of three plain wishes: not of the myriads upon myriads you should need, I suppose, for devising a world."

The King laughed in his beard. "Which is as much as to say," he looked over his left shoulder into the face of Barganax, "that a God, if He will dabble in world-making, had best not be God only but artist?"

"Because both create?" said Amalie.

Barganax smiled: shook his head. "Your artist creates not. Say I paint your grace a picture: make you a poem: that is not create. I but find, choose, set in order."

"Yet we say God created the world? Is that wrong then?" She looked from father to son. "How came the world, then?"

There fell a silence: in the midst of it, the Vicar with his teeth cracking of a lobster's claw. Amalie looked on the King, within hand's-reach upon her left. She said, as resolving her own question: "I suppose it lay in glory in His mind."

Barganax seemed to pause upon his mother's words. "And yet, so lying," he said, "is not a world yet. To be that, it must lie outside. Nor it cannot, surely, lie whole in his mind afore it be first laid also outside. So here's need to create, afore e'er you think of a world." He paused: looked at Fiorinda. "And even a God," he said, "cannot create beauty: can but discover."

"Disputing of these things," the King said, "what are we but children, who, playing on the shore, chart in childish fancy the unharvested sea? Even so, sweet is divine philosophy and a pastime at the feast.

"But to play primero you must have cards first. Grant, then, the eternity of the World (not this world: I mean all the whole university of things and beings and times). Grant God is omnipotent. Then must not that universal World be infinite, by reason of the omnipotence of God? It is the body; and the soul thereof, that omnipotence. And so, to create that universality, that infinite World, is no great matter, nor worth divinity: 'tis but the unwilled natural breath-take or blood-beat, of His omnipotence. But to make a particular several world, like this of ours: to carve that ὕλη, that *prima materia*, that gross body of chaos, and shape it to make you your World of Heart's Desire,—why, here's work for God indeed!"

"Ἐμὴν δ' ἔντυνον ἀοιδήν," said Fiorinda slowly, as if savouring the words upon her tongue: *"and do You attune my song.*—I was but remembering," she said as in answer to the King's swift look.

But Anthea, scanning, as shepherds will some red April sunrise, the shadow-play of that lady's lip and eyelash, said, for Campaspe's private ear. "Honey-dew: a certain spittle of the stars. We shall see dog-tricks to-night."

"Have I your highness's drift?" said the Duke: "that when Truth's unhusked to the kernel, every imaginable thing is real as any other? and every one of them imperishable and eternal?"

"Ay," said the King: "things past, things present, and things to come. And alike things not to come. And things imaginable and unimaginable alike."

"So that a God, walking where He will (as you, madam," to his lady mother, "in your garden, making a bunch of flowers), may gather, or note, this or this: make Him so His own particular world at choice."

The King nodded.

"And soon as made, fling it away, if not to His mind, as you your nosegay. Yet this difference: rose-bud or canker-bud, His flowers are immortal. Worlds He may create and destroy again: but not the stuff of worlds."

"Nay, there," said the King, "you go beyond me. No matter. Proceed."

"I go beyond your highness? But did not you say 'tis eternal, this stuff worlds are made of?"

"True: but who are you, to hobble the omnipotency of the most Highest? Will you deny the capacity to Almighty God with one breath to uncreate all Being, and, next breath, bring all back again pat as before?"

"To uncreate?" said the Lord Beroald: "and Himself along with it?"

"And Himself along with it. Why not, if 'tis His whim?"

"Omnipotency is able, then, on your highness's showing, to be, by very virtue of its omnipotency, also impotence? *Quod est absurdum.*"[4]

"Be it absurd: yet what more is it than to say He is able to create chaos? Chaos is a thing absurd. The condition of its existence is unreasonable. Yet it can exist."

Beroald smiled his cold smile. "Your serene highness will bear with me. In this empyreal light I am grown so owly-eyed as see but reason set to unthrone reason, and all confounded to confusion."

"You must consider of it less narrowly: *sub specie aeternitatis.* Supposition is, every conceivable bunch of circumstances, that is to say, every conceivable world, exists: but unworlded, unbunched: to our more mean capacities an unpassable bog or flux of seas, cities, rivers, lakes, wolds and deserts and mountain ranges, all with their plants, forests, mosses, water-weeds, what you will; and all manner of peoples, beasts, birds, fishes, creeping things, climes, dreams, loves, loathings, abominations, ecstasies, dissolutions, hopes, fears, forgetfulnesses, infinite in variety, infinite in number, fantasies beyond nightmare or madness. All this *in potentia.* All are there, even just as are all the particulars in a landscape: He, like as the landscape-painter, selects and orders. The one paints a picture, the Other creates a world."

"A task to decay the patience of a God!"

"No, Beroald: easy, soon done, if you be Almighty and All-knowing."

"As the poet hath it," said the Duke, and his eyes narrowed as a man's that stares up-wind searching yet more remote horizons:

"To an unfettered soules quick nimble hast
Are falling stars, and hearts thoughts, but slow pac'd."[5]

"What of Time, then?" said the Duchess.

"That is easy," said Barganax: "a separate Time for each separate world—call't earth, heaven, what you will—that He creates."

The Duchess mused. "While Himself, will you think? so dealing, moveth not in these lower, cribbed, successions which we call Time, but in a more diviner Time which we call Eternity. It must be so," she said, sitting back, gazing, herself too, as into unseen distances. "And these worlds must exist, full and actual, as the God chooses them, remaining or going back, as He neglects or destroys them, to that more dim estate which we call possibility—*These flowers, as in their causes, sleepe.*"

"All which possible worlds," said the King, "infinitely many, infinitely diverse, are one as another, being they are every one available alike to His choice."

"Except that a God," said the Duchess, "will choose the Best."

"Of an infinite number perfect, each bearing its singular and unique perfection, what is best?"

"And an infinite number imperfect?"

"How otherwise? And infinitely various and innumerable heavens. And infinitely various and innumerable hells."

"But a God," Amalie said, "will never choose one of the hells to dwell in."

"He is God, remember," said the Duke, "and can rid it away again when as the fancy takes Him."

The Vicar gave a brutal laugh. "I cannot speak as a God. But I'll stake my soul there's no man born will choose to be in the shoes of one judged to die some ill death, as (saving your presence) be flayed alive; and there's he, stripped to's buff, strapped convenient on a plank, and the hangman with's knife, split, nick, splay, roll back the skin from's belly as you'd roll up a blanket."

Zenianthe bit her knuckles. "No, no."

The King spoke, and his words came as a darkness. "As His rule is infinite, His knowing is unconfined."

"To look on at it: enough knowing so, I'd a thought," said the Parry. "Or do it. Not be done by."

"Even that," said the King, as it were thick darkness turned to speech. The eagless looked forth in Fiorinda's eyes.

"Go," said the Vicar: "I hold it plain blasphemy." Fiorinda, with unreadable gaze beholding him, drew her tongue along her lips with a strange and covert smile.

"Come, we have fallen into unhappy talk," said the King. "But I'll not disthrone and dissceptre God of His omniscience: not abridge His choice: no, not were it to become of Himself a little stinking muck of dirt that is swept out of unclean corners. For a moment. To know."

But the Duchess Amalie shivered. "Not that—that filthiness the man spoke on. God is good: will not behold evil."

"Ah, madam," the King said, "here, where this lower Time determines all our instants, and where is no turning back: here indeed is good and evil. But *sub specie aeternitatis,* all that IS is good. For how shall God, having supreme and uncontrollable authority to come and go in those infinite successions of eternity, be subject unto time, change, or death? His toys they are, not conditions of His being."

There was a pause. Then said the Duke, thoughtfully dividing with his silver fork the flesh from the bones of a red mullet, "Needs must then (so reasoneth at least my unexpert youth) that death and annihilation be real: the circle squared: square root of minus one, a real number. Needs must all particular beings, nay, spirits (if there be) unmade, without beginning or ending in time, be brought to not-being; and with these, the One unical, the only-being Being, be obliterate, put out of memory, *vox inanis,*[6] Nothing."

The Vicar, upon a swig of wine, here bedravelled both beard and cheek with his too swift up-tipping of the cup. The Lord Jeronimy, as grown suddenly a very old man, stared, slackmouthed, hollow-eyed, into vacancy, fingering tremulously the while the jewel of the kingly order of the hippogriff that hung about his neck. Zenianthe, herself too at gaze, yet bore not, as the Admiral, aught of human terror in her eye: only the loveliness of her youth seemed to settle deeper, as if rooted in the right and unjarring harmonies of some great oak-tree's being, when the rust of its leaves is melted in the incandescence of a still November sunset which feeds on summer and shines towards spring. Anthea whispered Campaspe: their nymphish glances darted from the Duchess's face to the face of her lady of honour: so, and back: so, again.

After a little, the Duchess began to say, resting her eyes the while on that Lady Fiorinda: "But there is, I think, a dweller in the innermost which yet IS, even when that immeasurable death shall have disrobed it of all being. There is that which made death, and can unmake. And that dweller, I think, is love. Nay, I question if there truly BE, in the end, aught but love and lovers; and God is the Love that unites them."

There fell a stillness. Out of which stillness, the Duke was ware of the King his Father saying, "Well? But what world, then, for us, my Amalie?"

"Answer me first," said she, "why will God this world and not that? out of this infinity of choice?"

The King answered, "For Her 'tis wrought."

"So Her choice it is?"

"Must we not think so?"

"But how is She to choose?"

"How can She choose amiss? seeing that every choice of Hers is, of Her very nature, a kind of beauty."

"But if He may so lightly and so unthriftily make and unmake, can He not make and unmake Her?"

"We must think so," said the King. "But only at cost of making and unmaking of Himself."

"My lord Chancellor smiles."

"But to observe," said the Chancellor, "how his serene highness, spite of that conclusion he hath driven upon so many reasonable principles, is enforced at last to say No to the Most Highest."

"It is Himself hast said it, not I. There is this No in His very nature, I should say," said the King. "The most single and alonely One, abiding still one in itself, though it be possible, is not a thing to be dreamed of by a God: it is poverty, parsimony, an imagination not tolerable save to unbloody and insectile creatures as far removed below men's natures as men's below Gods'."

"As the philosopher hath it," said Barganax: *"Infinitus Amor potestate infinitâ Pulchritudinem infinitam in infinitâ perfectione creatur et conservatur:* infinite Love, of His infinite power, createth and conserveth infinite Beauty in Her infinite perfection. You see, I have sat at the feet of Doctor Vandermast."

Fiorinda's uncomparable lips chilled again to the contours of the sphinx's, as she said, with accents where the bee's sting stabbed through the honey to the shuddering sense, "But whether it be more than windy words, which of us can know?"

"Which of us indeed, dear Lady of Sakes?" said the King.

"And what need we care?"

Anthea, upon a touch, feather-light, tremulous as a willow-wren's fluttered wing, of Campaspe's hand against her arm, looked round at her: with eyes feral and tawny, into eyes black and bead-like as a little water-rat's: exchanging with these a most strange, discharmed, unweariable look. And that was a look most unaccordant with the wont of human eyes: beasts' eyes, rather, wherein played bo-peep and hid themselves sudden profundities, proceeding, a learned man might have guessed, from near copulation with deity.

Amalie spoke: "It was in my mouth to answer, dear my Lord, (but I've changed my mind): 'Ah, what world if not this? But this made sure of, secured. Roses, but no thorns. Change, but no growing old. Transfiguration, but no death.'"

"A world without stoat or weasel?" cried Anthea, laughing a little wild-cat laugh, very outlandish and strange.

"I note in such a world," said the Admiral, "some breath of ʽϛυϐβη, of an overweeningness apt to tempt in a manner the jealousy of the Gods."

"I hold it flat impiety, such talk," said the Vicar, scarlet with furious feasting, and emptied his brimming cup of muscadine.

"Nay, you ought not so ungroundably," said the Chancellor, "my good lord Admiral, to imagine Gods distrained with such meaner passions as do most disbeautify mankind. Yet I see in such a world an unleefulness, and a want of logic."

"A pool without a ripple?" said Campaspe. "A sky with never at any time a hawk in it? Day, but no night?"

Again Anthea flashed lynx-like teeth. "Because She is turned virtuous, shall there be no more blood to suck?"[7]

The Duke tightened his lips.

"I could teach stoat and weasel to be gentle," the Duchess said, very low; slowly with her fan tracing little pictures on the table. "But I changed my mind."

The King waited. "What then, *madonna mia?*" he said, and opened his hand, palm upwards, on the table. The Duchess's came: daintily under its shimmer of rings touched with its middle finger the centre of his open palm: escaped before it could be caught.

"For I bethought me a little," said she, "of your highness's words awhile since, that there's a blessedness in not knowing—yes, were we God and Goddess in very deed; and a zest, and a savour. So that this world will I choose, dear my Lord, and choose it not caponed but entire. Who e'er could abide a capon unless to eat? and, for a world, 'tis not eat but live withal. And be in love withal. And time hath an art, and change too, like as the lantern of the moon, to make lovely and lovable. Beyond that, I think it best not to know."

While she so spoke, Barganax's gaze, chancing upwards, was caught by the sapphired gleam of Vega shining down through vine-leaves overhead: some purer unfadeable eye, joining with the common and unevitable mortality of these candleflames to survey the things which these surveyed and, albeit more distantly and with less flattering beams, caress them, pronounce them good. In that star's light he followed his mother's words: the honeyed accents, the owl-winged thought, the rainbow-shot web of memories, the unheard inwardness of laughter under all, as a night's dewing of grace and sweetness. Then his eye, coming down again, met with that Dark Lady's. There shone a fire there starrier than that natural star's, greener than the glow-worm's lamp, speaking, too, in articulate shudders down the spine. As to say: Yes, My friend. These words are My words: Mine to You, even just as they are Hers to Him.

"Time. And Change. But the last change," said the King: "your own word, madonna: 'last mischief, Death.'"

For a minute, the Duchess held her peace. Then she said: "I will remember you, dear my Lord, of the tragical story of the Volsungs and the Niblungs, after the battle in King Atli's hall, and they had fallen on Hogni and cut the heart out of him; but he laughed while he abode that torment. And they showed it to Gunnar, his brother, and he said, 'The mighty heart of Hogni, little like the faint heart of Hjalli, for little as it trembleth now, less it trembled whenas in his breast it lay.' And Death we know not: but without that unknown, to look it in the eye, even as did Hogni, and even as did Gunnar after, when he was cast into the worm-close:[8] without that, I wonder, could there be greatness of heart and courage in the world? No: we will have this world, and Death itself. For we will choose no world that shall not be noble."

XVI

THE FISH DINNER: CAVIAR

S O YOU AND I," said the King, "will have this world? Well, I am answered. But the game's ended ere well begun; for this world's ready made to our hand."

"If we must try tricks elsewhere, let her choose," said Amalie, looking at Fiorinda. "She is too silent. Let her speak and decide."

"Better not," he said. "She is in a contrary mood tonight. A world of her choosing, as now she is, should be a strange unlucky world indeed."

"Nay, but I am curious," said the Duchess. "Nay, I will choose her world for to-night, whatever it be. Come, you promised me."

"Well?" said the King.

In Fiorinda's eyes sat the smile, unrelentless, Olympian, fancy-free, of Her that leads at Her train the ancient golden world. "The choice is easy," she said. "I choose *That which is.*" There was a discordancy betwixt her words, so plain and so simple, and the manner of their speaking, as from an imperial lust that, being unreined, should hardly be resisted anywhere.

The King held his peace. The Duchess looked round at him, sitting so close at her left hand that sleeve brushed sleeve, yet to look on as some watch-tower removed, black and tremendous among hills: as Our Father Zeus, watching out of Ida. *"That which is?"* he said at last. "Out of your ladyship's mouth we look for meanings in such simplicities, as for colours in those shining exhalations that appear in tempests. Come, is't but this world again you mean?"

"I speak," answered she, "in honest plainness. I would wish your serene highness to receive it so."

Campaspe and Anthea laughed with one another in secret way behind their fans.

"*That which is,* then: in honest plainness what can that be," said the King, "but the ultimate Two alone? They, and the blessed Gods and Goddesses Who keep the wide heaven, of a lower reality, may be, than His and Hers, yet themselves more real than such summer-worms as men? Is this your choice, then, and the golden mansions of the Father? If: then picture it to me. Let me perceive it."

That lady smoothed her cheek, cat-like, against her ruff. To look in her eyes now was to see strange matter, as of something dancing a dance untowardly about a pit's brink. "No. No," said she. "Like as her grace, I also will change my mind too: look lower.

"Well," she said after a minute, "I have thought of a world. Will your highness create it indeed for me, as I shall specificate?" The dying fall of her voice, so languefied in its melodious faint discords, held in the very sloth of it some menace, as of one in her affections unbitted, intemperable by her estate, raging by her power.

The King beheld her so an instant in silence; then said, "I'll do my endeavour."

Fiorinda lifted her head, as a she-panther that takes the wind. "Good," she said; and her eyes, leaving the King's, rested now constantly on Duke Barganax's who gazed upon her as a man carved in stone. "And ere we begin upon our world for to-night's disport," she said, "I, as so peerlessly to be doted upon, will lay you down your terms of service, as master-builder of my worlds. Seeing I am She, I will be content with no outward shows. The wine of our loving-cup shall be the chosen butt of the chosen vintage. The very cobblers of my shoes shall be the wittiest and honestest and goodliest to look on in the world, and the best at their trade. One world shall not be enough for me. Nor one in a life-time. No, nor one a day. Aeons of unremembered ages, shall go to the making of the crumb I brush from my dress upon rising from board. Generations of mankind, innumerable as the generations of the may-fly through a hundred years, shall live and die to no purpose but to merry my senses for five minutes, if I affect for pastime before my looking-glass to untwine my tressèd hair. The slow mutations of the immemorial rocks of the ancient earth shall be but for the making ready of a soft cushion of turf for me upon some hillside, in case the fancy should one day take me there to recline myself after my walking in the mountains. Upon millions of trees millions of millions of leaves shall sprout, open, turn colour, and begin to fall, only but to give me a sweet prospect from my window some sunshiny November morning. Because of me, not Troy nor not this world only, but even the whole wide universe and giant mass of things to come at large, shall be cast away, abolished, and forgot."

Amalie's eyes, resting in the King's, read there, clear as if his lips had spoken: Yes, madonna. These words are your words: Yours to Me, even just as they are Hers to Him.

But the Duke, paler now than grass in summer, rose up, thrust back his chair, taking his stand now a little behind the King his father and his lady mother, he leaned against the bole of a strawberry-tree. Here, out of the lights, himself but hardly to be seen, he could sideways over their shoulders behold her: that mouth unparagoned, the unhealable plague of it, dark characters which who can uncypher? that moon-chilled imperial pallour of cheek and brow: all those provocations, heats, enlurings, and countermatchings, tiger's milk and enlacements of black water-snakes, which (when she turned her head) nakedly and feelingly before his eyes lay bound where, in the nape of her delicate neck, the black braids crossed and gleamed and coiled upwards: last (and unspeakable uniting together of all these), ever and again an unmasking of her eyes to meet, conscient, the burning gaze of his, constant upon her out of the shadow of darkness.

"Speak on," said the King, to Fiorinda, but his eyes always with Amalie. "All this is true and just and condition absolute of all conceivable worlds. Now to particulars."

"I will desire of you, here and now," replied that lady, "such a world as never yet was nor was thought of. And for first principle of its foundation, it shall be a world perfect and sufficient unto itself."

"Well," said the King. "What shall we frame it of?"

"You shall frame it," answered she, "of the infinities: of Time without beginning and without ending; and of Space without centre and without bourne."

"Of what fashion shall it be?"

"O I will have it of infinite fashions. But all by rule."

"But how, if you will have it of these infinities, shall it be perfect? Perfection reasoneth a limit and a bourne."

"That is easily answered. It shall be of Time and in Time: not Time in it. And in Space and of Space: not Space in it."

"So that these infinities stand not part of your world," said the King, "but it, part of them: as this bread was made of wheaten flour, yet there's wheaten flour enough and to spare, and was and shall be, other than what this bread containeth, and of other shapes too?" He dipped a piece in the gravy, and gave it to his great dog to eat that sat beside him. "Well, I have it so far," he said: "but is, so far, yet but the shadow of a world: but empty space and time."

She said, "I will desire your serene highness fill it for me."

"And what to fill it withal?"

"O, with an infinity of little entities, if you please: so tiny, a thousand at once shall dance upon the point of a needle. And even so, betwixt and between them where they dance, shall be room and to spare for another thousand."

"Another thousand? No more than so?"

"Oh, if you will, infinitely more: until you, that are tireless, tire. Crowd, if you will, infinities betwixt infinities till thought swoon at it."

Presently, "It is done," said he. "And yet remaineth, spite all this multitudinousness, a dull uniformity of a world. What then?"

"Then (with humility) is't not for you, Lord, to lay to your hand: devise, continue? Have not I required it to be of infinite fashions? And must I instruct you, the great Artificer, what way you shall do your trade?"

"You must. Nay, mistress, what is the whole matter but some upstart fancy of your own? Nay, I'll read you your mind, then. You would have me set 'em infinite dances, infinite steps and figures. Behold, then: though every dancer be like as every other, the figures or patterns of their dancing are infinitely various. Of a pavane, look, I make you gold: of a coranto, air: of a bourrée, granite: brimstone, quicksilver, lead, copper, antimony, proceed but each out of his several figure of this universal dance, yes, and the very elements of fire and water, and all minerals that compose the earth's natural body; even to this, which I have made for you of the allemande: this iron, which is the archaean dreamless soul of the world. Well?" he looked piercingly at her.

She, superciliously smiling, and with a faint delicate upward backward motion of her head, answered him, "So far, I'll allow, Lord, 'tis not so greatly amiss."

"Pshaw! it is a dead world," he said. "A dead soul."

"Nay, then, let it teem with life," said she, "if needs must. And that horribly."

"And what," said the Duchess, "is life?"

Bending with a fastidious daintiness above her plate, Fiorinda selected and held up to view upon her fork a single globule of the caviar. "In such a world," she answered, offering to her nearer inspection upon the fork's prong the little jellied fish-egg, "what else would your grace desire it to be, if not some such trash as this?"

"A fish-like world!" said the King.

"Nay, but here's a most God-given exquisite precision in it," Fiorinda said. "Life! But a new dance only, but in more complicated figures, enacted by your same little simplicities. Sort but the numbers aright, time but their steps aright, their moppings and mowings, their twirlings, curvets and caprioles—'tis done. Out of dead substance, living substance: even such a little nasty bit of sour jelly as this is. And, for the more mockery, let it arise from the sea: a very neoterical Anadyomene,[1] worthy the world it riseth on."

The King's hands, beautiful to watch in the play of their able subtle strength, were busied before him on the table. Presently he opened them slowly apart. Slowly, in even measure with their parting, the world of his making grew between them: a thing of most aery seeming substance, ensphered, glimmering of a myriad colours where the eye rested oblique on it, but, being looked to more directly, all mirk, darkling, and unsure. And within it, depth beneath depth: wherein appeared as if a seething and a churning together and apart continual of the dark and the bright. "Well, I have given it life, as you bade. Life only. Not living beings."

Fiorinda, considering it awhile in silence, nodded a soft assent. All else gazed upon it with eyes expressionless, unseeing, as though encountered, sudden out of light, with a void or a darkness: all save the Duchess only. Her eyes, beholding this toy, were wide with the innocent wonder of a child's.

"Well?" said the King of Fiorinda. "Is your ladyship content, then?"

"Your highness hath been sadly badly served of your intelligencers if you conceive I should ever be content. Generality of life, thus as you present me withal, is life indeed, but 'tis not enough."

The Duchess looked at it closely. "You have given it life, you think?" she said very softly. "What is life?"

"It is," answered he, "as you may perceive, in this world of our devising, a thing compact but of three ingredients: as, first, to feel, to wince, to answer to each intrusive touch of the outward world: second, to grow: third, to engender and give birth, like from like." His gaze, unfastening itself from her, came back to that Dark Lady, and so again to Amalie. "You," he said to both: "You, that wast with Me in the beginning of My way, before My works of old: what next?"

Fiorinda, still curiously beholding it, gave a little silent laugh. But the Duchess, shivering suddenly in the warm night air, leant back against King Mezentius as for warmth.

"I will," said the Lady Fiorinda, and each honeyed word seemed as a kissing or a handling lickerously of some new-discovered particularity of her thought: "I will that you so proceed with it, now from this beginning, as that even out of such contemptible slime as this is, shall be engendered all myriads of living creatures after their kind: little slimy polyps in the warm seas: little sea-anemones, jelly-fishes, worms, slugs, sand-hoppers, water-fleas, toadstools, grass and all manner of herbs and trees which grow. Run through all the lewd forms of them: fishes, birds, beasts even to human kind."

"Even to human kind? what, men and women, as we be?" said the Duchess.

Fiorinda, as not having marked the question, but continued; but slowlier: "I will," said she, "that this shall be the life of them, of every thing that breatheth the breath of life in this new world of ours: to be put part of the waters as it were of a whirlpool, wherein is everything for ever neither produced nor destroyed, but for ever transformed: the living substance for ever drawn in, moulded to some shape of life, and voided again as dead substance, having for that span of time yielded its strength and purpose to that common sink or cesspool of Being. So in this, my world, shall all proceed, self-made, self-sought, out of one only original: this little spittly jelly."

"A world," said the King, "of most infinite complication."

"Nay, but I give it simple laws to work by, for make-weight."

"What laws, then?"

"First, (to order perfectly my perfect world, as perfect in action), this law: that at each succeeding moment of its existence the sum and totality of my world, and all that in it is, shall be determined reasonably and inevitably by that which was the moment before."

"Sensible chaos, yet grounded in an infinite order."

"Which is," said that lady, "the strainable force of destiny. No chanceableness. Nor no meddling finger of God neither, to ruffle the serenity of my world's unfolding. As a rose-bud discloseth itself and spreadeth abroad, so shall its processions be: as inevitable as one and one is two, one and two is three, and so on for ever, *ad infinitum*. The general forms, constant, unchangeable, untransformable; but all else changing as oft as weathercock in wind. Truly a world most exquisitely well fitted to be comprehended by a man of law?" She glanced at the Lord Beroald, who, for answer, but smiled his unbelieving smile.

"But no world, sure," said the lord Admiral, "for the living beings that must live in it. What manner freedom have they, where all must be predetermined and like a clock-work?"

There was a cruel look of that lady's lips and teeth, daintily eating up the little piece of caviar. She turned upon the King eyes over the balls of which suddenly a film seemed to be drawn, as they had been the eyes of an empoisoned serpent. "I think," she said, "I will tease them a little with my laws. They shall seem indeed to themselves to have freedom; yet we, who look on, know 'tis no such matter. And they shall seem to themselves to live; yet if, 'tis a life not their own. And they shall die. Every one that knoweth life in my world shall know also death. The little simplicities, indeed, shall not die. But the living creatures shall. Die, and dissipate as children's castles in sand when the tide takes them, but the sand-grains abide.

Is it not a just and equal choice? either be a little senseless lump of jelly or of dead matter, and subsist for ever; or else be a bird, a fish, a rose, a woman, 'pon condition to fade, wax old, waste at last to carrion and corruption?"

"Men and women, as we be?" said the Duchess. "O, you have answered me! Or is it," she said under her breath, "that Myself hath answered Myself?" And again the King's gaze, unfastening itself from Fiorinda's, rested curiously on his Amalie. She was staring, as fascinated, into the teeming inwardness of the sphered thing which, motionless save for a scarce perceptible rhythmic expanding and contracting of its translucent envelope from withinward, remained balanced as it had been some heavy bubble, a foot, may be, in diameter, upon the table betwixt her and the King. There was silence for a minute, while, under the eyes of those feasters, miniature aeons trained their untermed texture of death and birth within the artificial confines of that cosmos.

Presently Fiorinda spoke, "As we be? I question that, (saving your grace). How were that possible, out of this? Is there mind in this?" Lovelier than the argent limb of the cold moon, the curve showed of that lady's arm as, chin propped on hand, she leaned pensive over the table. "Unless, indeed," she said, and the slowed music of her voice sounded to new deeps: "unless, indeed, We Ourselves will go in and enter it. Know it so. Go down—"

"Undergrope it so from within," said the King. "For a moment, We might. To know."

The Duchess trembled. It was as if, in the stillness, she had suffered his mind and thought to enter so deep into her own, that she tasted, in her inmost being and without necessity of communication, the inwardness of his: tasted how, as one awakening in a strange bed sinks back into sleep again and the place of visions, he beheld now in the baseless clearness of a dream, a meadow grey with the rime of hoar-frost that sparkled with many colours as the sun made and unmade stars of the tiny crystals. A sycamore-tree was shedding its golden leaves in a slow shower in the nearly windless air: two or three at a time it shed them, translucent gold against the rising sun, and at the foot of the tree they made a carpet of darker gold where they fell. And in that necessity of dreams, that binds together as of course things which in waking life are severed and unrelated, he perceived, in the falling of each particular leaf in that bounteousness and Danaë's shower of beauty,[2] the falling away of something that had been his. His ancient royal palace and seattown on two-horned Rialmar, his fleets, armies, great vassals, princes and counsellors and lords of the Three Kingdoms, his queens, mistresses, children, alive or dead, they of his courts and households afar or near, under his hands: all his wide dominions welded and shaped to his will, of Meszria, Rerek, and Fingiswold: lovely

Memison itself, whose balm was in his nostrils, the turf of whose garden was soft here beneath his feet: very Amalie herself, sitting and breathing now beside him: the whole of his life, this actual world he lived in, fluttered downward, unregarded, severed, golden, through that cold still air in the bright beams of the clear sun: floating scraps of memory, every one of which, even while the mind strove to grasp it, was dissipated and gone to spread deeper the bed of gold at that tree's foot.

Fiorinda but flickered an eyelid. "It moves," she said presently. "It amuses me. Always it moves. Always it changes. Yet, for all its changing, is never much the better. Nor much the worse." She paused. In the beholding of her face, thus pensive and stilled, was such unquiet pleasures as the sight of the stars gives. Then, "This amuses me, too," she began to say again: "to note how, by merest clockwork, is a kind of perfection created, brought to maturity, maintained in being." The scaled familiar gathered itself at her mouth's corner, intent, like as a lizard that espies a fly. "Amuses me to regard, as in some crooked mirror, this perfection which wanteth but one jot to be a master-work, and that jot—"

"That it be truth," said Barganax, out of the thick shadow.

It was as if a frozen blast went suddenly about that garden, come and gone in a moment of time behind the flower-sweet darknesses and the candles' soft and comfortable radiance.

Barganax and Fiorinda beheld the Duchess Amalie's hand fasten over the King's hand at her side upon the table: beheld her beauty gather itself like a serpent coiled, as she sat, level-browed, level-eyed, some high-descended Queen dreadless on the brink of fate. "The game's too much in earnest," she whispered in the King's ear. "Stay for me. You and I," she whispered: "we are noosed: we are limed. We are in it."

XVII

In What a Shadow[1]

I T WAS OCTOBER NOW, of that same year nineteen hundred and twenty-three: the nineteenth of October. Night shut down on Nether Wasdale in a great rain without wind: rain steadily falling out of the premature darkness of rain-cloud that covered the sky without a gap. There was nothing to hear but the rain: nothing to see but the appearance of trunks and leafage picked out, chalky and unsubstantial, where the glare of headlights struck the holm-oaks west of the house; these, and the rain that the cold twin beams made visible, and a feebler, more distant, luminosity as of another car waiting in the road below the drive gates.

Jim Scarnside pressed the door-bell and waited. He pressed it again: waited again: then set his thumb hard upon it and kept it there, may be for thirty seconds, while he listened to the shrill metallic whirr far away within. Then lights went up in the porch: steps sounded in the hall: turn of a key, drawing of bolts, and the door stood ajar on the chain, with old Ruth's face peering through the opening. With a little inarticulate apology, she closed the door to shoot the chain, then opened it wide. They stood silent a moment, she in the doorway, Jim over against her on the doorstep. Her face showed a death-like pallour: eyes dull and puffy.

"Master at home?" he said. He saw that her cheeks were stained with the lashing of tears.

"We don't expect him till to-morrow, at earliest."

"Nonsense. What's the car doing at the drive gates, then?"

She looked helplessly at Jim's own car, her hands, with their swollen joints and wrinkled skin, twitching at her apron.

"At the drive gates. Out in the road. It's his car. Empty, and lights on."

She brought her hand up to her mouth. "O, not that too. Please dear God, not that. And yet," she said, with a kind of sob—

"All right," said Jim. "I expect he made better time than he expected." He pulled up the collar of his mackintosh: began to run down the steps. At first step he turned. "Any man in the house?"

She shook her head: "No but me and the girls. We were shutting up for the winter, when Mr. Edward comes back all sudden-like (you know his ways, sir), and starts to, packing up and I don't know what; and then, Tuesday it was: that telegram—" she choked. "And then. Then he went," she said. "No, no man in the house. Only old David, sir, and he took David, so as he was to wait, mind the car at Dover, while the master went across to—" she broke down. "O, Mr. James, sir. Her ladyship: that telegram: it can't be true, sir: not killed: God couldn't permit it. And my Miss Janet and all. God couldn't—"

"Look here, Ruth," he said, very kind but firmly, taking her by the arms, "you and I have got to see about this: no good crying. Is the master's room ready? fires? he'll want some dinner. You get on with it: I'll be back in a few minutes."

"Yes, Mr. James, sir. That's right, sir," she said with a gulp: "that's right." Both her hands fastened on Jim's right, squeezing it. Suddenly the squeeze became tighter. He turned, looking where she looked. Their hands disengaged. Lessingham was in the porch beside them: bare-headed, in his travelling-clothes, seemingly soaked to the skin with rain.

"Jim. Good. Wait while I get the car in."

Jim, noting the steady ring of Lessingham's voice, noted too, for all the uncertain light, as it were some glint, some poise of sinew or of lineament, in the iron-seeming face of Lessingham, that stayed the impulse to offer to go too: kept him obedient in the porch. After a few minutes they saw the lights stir and creep round at the foot of the drive; then presently met the full glare of them as the car rounded the last sweep past the strawberry-trees and swung out of sight behind the house towards the garage.

"You'll be staying to dinner, sir?"

Jim shrugged his shoulders. "I don't know."

"You'd better, sir. It isn't good for Mr. Edward to be too much by his self, sir. Not just now it isn't."

"We'll see."

Lessingham's step returning, elastic and firm, crunched the gravel. "Put your car in there if you like. Ruth will get us something to eat presently. I wish I could put you up, but I may not be staying myself to-night."

Jim checked himself. "Right," he said, and got into his car.

"Well, Ruth," said Lessingham. Their eyes met for a moment. "I'm wet through, I think;" he looked down at his rain-sodden coat and trousers and muddy water-logged shoes as if he had but just discovered it.

"The luggage, sir? If you'll let me have the keys, Sally will put out your things in the dressing-room and get the bath ready and I'll be seeing about your dinner. I'll just unlock the lobby door for her, upstairs."

"No. Put the things in the Trellis Room. Here's the key of the suitcase:" he took it off his chain. "Lay for two."

"You'll have it in the dining-room?"

"No. Lay it in the Armoury. A couple of bottles of the Lafite. Careful how you decant it."

"And letters, please, sir." She handed them on the silver tray from the hall table. The tray shook a little in her hand as Lessingham rapidly went over the envelopes, took a particular one (her eye was on it, too) and put it unopened in his pocket.

"Let them wait."

The old woman put them back on the table. She hesitated for a moment, looking up at him with sad eyes like a dog's. "Nothing fresh, I suppose, sir? over there? I suppose—?"

"Nothing."

"Hope?" the word was almost inaudible.

"Nothing. Except," he said, "I've seen—" his voice hardened, "what there is to see. And that's enough for the purpose."

The hall door stood wide, lighting Jim up the steps as he returned: lighting the thin curtain of the rain. He could hear Lessingham's measured tread pacing the uncarpeted floor in the hall, the squelch of water at every foot-step. As he shut the door behind him, Ruth bustled in from the kitchen quarters with a tray: set it down on the table: tumblers, a syphon, and the curious purple bottle of Bristol glass that served as whisky-decanter. "Bath ready in ten minutes, sir. You'd better have something to warm you inside, sir: that soaked as you are."

Lessingham poured out for both. His face was unreadable: like the great rock faces, lean north crags of Mickledore, two or three miles away, three thousand feet up, alone now in the lampless darkness and the rain that turned, up there, no doubt to sleet.

As they drained the glasses, the emptiness of the house chilled

Jim Scarnside's members: took hold as with claws at the pit of his stomach.

They ate at first in silence made audible by the click of knife and fork, Ruth's quiet footsteps on the parquet floor, the faint rustle of her black dress as she came and went, the steadfast tick-tack of the great Italian clock above the door, and the crackle and hiss of the logs whenever a scutter of rain came down the chimney. Unshaded candles in Venetian silver candlesticks of the cinquecento lighted the table, and candles in sconces on the walls gleamed with sometimes a windy light on the arms and armour. Ugly shadows lengthened, shortened, trembled, or stilled themselves: shadows of these things on the walls: the pig-faced basinet dating from 1400 with its camail of chain mail: the Italian armet, late fifteenth century, an heirloom come down to Lessingham through his mother along with that morning-star[2] beside it, plated and exquisitely damascened in gold and silver, which family tradition traced back to the Prince Pier Luigi, bastard of Pope Paul III and Cellini's[3] best-hated oppressor—Signor Pier Luigi Farnese, whose portrait by Titian,[4] in black armour, black-bearded, with a wolf in each eye and bearing on his forehead and in every line of his face the brand of archangel ruined, hung over the fire-place, frighteningly like (as Jim with a new vividness of perception saw now) to Lessingham. And here were maces, war-hammers etched and gilt, pole-axes, swords by the dozen—German, Italian, French, English, Spanish: pistols, arquebuses richly wrought, a dagger of russet steel (supposed François Premier's) with gold inlaid and mother-of-pearl: the complete suit of war-harness for man and horse, a thing unique, given to Lessingham by that Arab sultan somewhere in the Middle East two or three years since, in memory of service rendered: and there, in a glass case, dark with age, notched and grown lean like a mummy, the viking sword dug up twelve years ago by Lessingham that summer they had spent carrying out excavations in Alstenö, far up the coast of Norway off Halogaland: Thorolf Kveldulfson's "Alost."[5] Dug up, at the very spot which expert conjecture pointed to as the site of the old hall at Sandness: Thorolf's house, where more than ten centuries ago he fell defending his life at hopeless odds against the great King he deserved well of. It might, for all anyone knew, have been Thorolf Kveldulfson's sword: the date was near enough: his, or one of theirs that fought beside him while the burning house scorched them from behind and King Harald Hairfair and his three hundred men set on them from before. She had loved the slow sunshiny Arctic summer: the open-air life, the far-ranging mountains, the Norse country-folk and their ways of life (so effortless, her mastery of the language), the sailing, the long drawn out processions of sunset and sunrise, the unearthly sense as of Time's clock run down. But she—Jim swallowed his second glass at a draught: the fine claret, tasteless in his mouth, at least prevented the dryness of his throat from strangling him. He saw that though Lessingham ate, his glass stood untasted. Six weeks ago they had danced in this hall; a dozen couples, in the family mostly: the old Blunds tradition. Time never touched her: that divine and lovely gift of abiding youth, no older, only maturer; a little deepening and sweetening. Six weeks: what did it mean? Dead. Killed in that railway smash in France. He looked at Lessingham who, as if unconscious of his presence, was staring before him with a stare that seemed to be blunted and forced back upon itself: turned inward.

Lessingham spoke. "Well, Jim, how do you like our post-war politics?"

"What, in this country?"

"Europe. The world."

"The Ruhr,[6] you mean? this morning's papers? I don't like them at all."

"Are you surprised at the way things are shaping?"

"Not much surprised. But sorry."

"Fear, and stupidity. The two universal counsellors and pathfinders of mankind. There's really nothing singular about it."

"I remember you saw it coming long since."

"So did you."

"When you pointed it out to me. But I don't think I honestly believed it. Just as nobody believed what you said a year ago, when a hundred marks were worth about twopence."

"What was it I said?"

"That you wouldn't discount a million of them for sixpence on twelve months' credit."

"Too optimistic, as things have turned out."

"What is it to-day? a hundred million or so to the dollar?"

"You and I have to remember," Lessingham said, "that we were born and bred up in our early youth in reposed and peaceful times almost, I suppose, without example. That led us by the sleeve: showed us but a back-eddy only in the great stream of things. Made us apt to imagine that the war was something remarkable, when it was truly no more but a ripple on the stream. You remember James Bryce's[7] saying about the Middle Ages: that never at any other time has theory, professing all the while to control practice, been so utterly divorced from it: an age ferocious and sensual, that yet worshipped humility and asceticism: never a purer ideal of love nor a grosser profligacy of life. It is a great untruth. The description is just, but it fits all human history, not merely a particular age. And as for those unhappy five years, there was nothing new in them: unless, possibly, an unusual babblery of self-righteousness."

"I'm not sure," said Jim. "Possibly there might be something a little bit new underlying just that."

"What? 'War to end war?' 'World safe for democracy?' 'A land fit for heroes to live in?' I wonder. I've more respect for old Clemenceau. He, at any rate, realized what company he was in in nineteen-nineteen, sitting between his 'sham Napoleon and sham Christ.' "

"You're unfair to them. Even the catchwords do stand for something. That they should be said at all, is something."

"I agree. And to say 'Liberté, Egalité, Fraternité' was something." Lessingham toyed with his untasted glass, his hand closing round the stem of the delicate Murano goblet, between the body of it and the foot. "A quite unimpeachable copy-book text. But (very amusingly) it turned in practice to the cutting off of people's heads with a mechanical slicer. You remember that wire puzzle made in Germany I used to bring out in school sometimes, when we were up to old Harry Broadbent in Middle Division? called *The Merry Decapitation without Trousers*?" He was smiling; but from under the smile suddenly came a sound of teeth gritted together. Jim averted his eyes: heard, as though across some solution of continuity, the ticking of the clock: then Lessingham's voice, toneless, even, and detached, resuming, as if upon an after-thought: "Women's heads, in considerable numbers." Then the clock again, intolerably loud and clear: once: twice. Then a crack, and something falling. Jim looked up quickly. The stem of the glass had snapped in Lessingham's grip and the great red stain spread wet and slow-oozing over the white cloth.

"Careless of me. Never mind. Leave it. For my own inclinations," he said after a pause, wiping his hand carefully on his dinner-napkin, "I infinitely prefer Jenghiz Khan. But then I have always favored the great carnivora rather than the monkey tribe."

They were silent. Then Jim said, "I wish you'd ring for Ruth to get a bandage or something. Your hand—"

Lessingham examined it. "It's nothing." He took out a clean handkerchief. "Give me a hand with this: that'll stop it. I'm sorry," he said, as Jim, finishing off the knot, sat back, very white. "Go on: you must finish it up." He pushed the decanter across. Jim filled, drank, and sat back once more, passing his hand with a light stroking movement from brows upwards over his forehead to the hair and so over to the back of his head. "It's purely physical," Lessingham said: "like sea-sickness, or a bad head on mountains. My father, for instance: the toughest sailor you'd find in all England; and yet, stand him on a height, he'd feel nausea: vertigo: catch behind the knees. It's the same thing."

"I suppose it is." Jim finished his glass: forced a smile. "Makes one feel a damned fool, all the same. You, of course—" he stopped.

"Yes," said Lessingham, his voice quiet and level, while Jim watched frame and feature gather by some indefinable transmutations to a yet closer likeness to the Titian on the wall: "I have. And enough, at any rate, to deaden the spice of novelty."

"You're a comfort to me, Jim," he said after a moment's silence. "You are the most perfect Tory I ever met."

"And you, the most complete and absolute Whig."

"I? I have no politics."

"You are a Whig of the Whigs. Consequently (as I've told you before) your politics are (a) damnable, and (b) completely out of date."

"I have, it is true," said Lessingham, "an interest in politics: to observe them, survey them back again: note how, under every new suit of clothes, the same body, the same soul, live on unchanged. Apparently unchangeable. An amusing study, my dear Signor Giacomo. And Machiavelli is the one philosopher who had the genius and the honesty to write down the truth about politics."

"I know what you mean. It is a limited truth, though."

"Limited to this world. I hope so."

"I limit it more narrowly than that. Besides, I've never heard you applaud our modern practitioners who live by the gospel according to Machiavelli."

"As an artist, I have a certain regard for one or two of them: always (curiously, you may think) where the field of action has been comparatively small. In the Middle East I've come across it: in the Balkans: among the Arabs, here and there."

"Yes, and you've practised it."

"Well, I have ruled 'em for their own good now and then. On the right, small, human scale."

"But the real Machiavelli: on the grand scale. You haven't much regard for him in Russia, for instance."

"The fox in the lion's skin," replied Lessingham, "is admirable up to a point. But in the bell-wether's skin, uncured and beginning to putrefy, he is no longer an impressive sight; while the mixture of stinking fox and stinking carrion—" he stopped as if he had bitten on his tongue. Jim felt his own teeth click together and a chill steal from the back of his throat down his spine: a shivering-fit blown from France.

"Mussolini?" he said quickly.

Lessingham answered with a shrug: "There is the better always, and there is the worse. But the mischief is more in the game than in the player. In mankind, not in particular men. The field, and the apparatus, are too much overgrown and sprawling."

"You know I don't wholly agree there," said Jim. "You and I never do wholly agree when it comes to fundamentals. I say the fault is in the players."

"I know you do. So do I. But not quite in the same way." He

pushed back his chair. "Have some more wine? No? Come along then, we'll smoke in the library."

"Not in the Refuge," Jim said in himself, rising to follow him. "Thank God for that, at any rate."

Lessingham, as if retired on the sudden into some secret workings of his brain, stood motionless at the table, hands in pockets, head bent on his chest, but back and shoulders straight free and majestical as some Olympian God's. Presently he began to pace slowly towards the door, pausing here and again at a weapon or a piece of harness as he passed, inspecting it narrowly, tapping it with his finger-nail. With a hand upon the door-knob, he turned, head erect now, to overrun with swift, searching gaze all four walls of that armoury. Opening the door, he laid a hand on Jim's shoulder, swinging him round so that he too might survey these things. "There's one example," he said: "death of all this. Gunpowder, the first mighty leveller." He laughed in his great black beard, while the strength of his fingers, like an iron clamp, bit into Jim's shoulder. Jim sucked from the sheer pain of it a kind of comfort; as though such vicarious hurting should be able in some faint degree to ease Lessingham's own torment: in some faint degree dilute it (as ordinary communications could not) by sharing.

"Letting go your orthodoxies and my Pyrrhonism,"[8] Lessingham said, as they passed into the library, "there does seem to be a kind of ἄτη, a kind of blindness or curse, endemic in all human affairs. A slow death. Never mind about the explanation: the facts are there, observable. After a certain stage, you see it begin: thenceforward technique, step by step as it advances, so correspondingly step by step you see it stultify itself. After a certain stage, you see dominion, as if by some inward necessity at each extension of its field, forced to take to itself more and more of what is not worth the having. So that the game becomes not worth playing. Not for a man."

"The machine age."

"It goes to more than that. The fallacy of material size and extent. Man is as unteachable a beast as can be. Take it in grand outline, the whole of human endeavour in this game of life as we know it—What will you have with your coffee, Jim? Old brandy? Grand Marnier? Kümmel?"

"Nothing, thanks."

"You must. Come: good for your digestion. Able to make exhalation, too, or smoke up into your brain. Distilled perfections of the orange: blossom and fruit." Lessingham filled a glass for him. "It used to be a ritual of ours, every time we dined on the train in France. Ever since the first: fifteen years ago."

Jim stared: durst not meet his gaze.

"Come."

"Well, if you'll join me. You've drunk nothing yourself, the whole evening."

Lessingham filled the other glass, then offered his cigar-case. "They're Partagas: your old friends. They go on, you see."

"I see they do."

There was silence while they lighted their cigars. Lessingham rose from his armchair. Jim watched him go to the writing-table, take up, without looking at it, Mary's photograph, rip it from its frame, tear it twice across, pitch it into the fire. As he sat down again, their eyes met. "I have an objection," Lessingham said, "to what the Germáns call *ersatz*."

Jim swallowed the Grand Marnier at a gulp: poured himself out a second glass: drank that. His face was expressionless as wax.

"What were we talking about?" said Lessingham. "O yes: the grand fallacy of progress. The cold lechery of *more and more*. All human endeavour, as if to play cricket, so to speak, on a pitch a hundred yards long: with a ball the size of a football: a bat to hit it with as big as a Thames punt. Good. Then, one of two things: we must either alter the whole nature of the game, or else become giants. We cannot make ourselves giants (and if we could, we should soon wish it undone again; unless indeed at the same time we altered the whole material universe—organic and inorganic, macrocosm and microcosm and all—to fit our new proportions. And then, that done, we should be precisely *in statu quo prius*:[9] indeed, being merely bigger creatures in a bigger world, I suppose we should be quite unconscious of any change at all.) And so, that door being locked, here we are busy altering, instead, the nature of the game. And in its altered nature, the game of life, the game of war, the game of politics, the game of ruling and being ruled, of merely subsisting, the whole material appurtenance and engine of our daily existence, becomes more and more a game not for men but for termites."

Jim's eyes began to smart, staring into the fire, where the last incandescent shreds of her photograph had finally disappeared. The silence hung heavy and bad-boding. "What would you have?" he said at length.

"The Greek city. I speak from experience, of course: have had it, and mean to again. Perhaps a little more; but that for the centre of your state. City and countryside: a polity the size of England—less, perhaps. And a population measured by a few tens of thousands. Beyond that, all becomes skimble-skamble."

"The Greeks made a nice mess of it."

"Because they choked themselves trying to swallow a cherry, seems a poor reason why we must guzzle down the whole pie-dish at a mouthful."

"It is an infinitely finer achievement to govern a modern state."

"I do not think so. It is not practicable, on any self-respecting interpretation of the word 'govern.' You might as well call it a finer achievement—"

"I said 'nobler,' " said Jim.

"—to skate on a pond when the ice doesn't bear than when it does. It is not more difficult: it is not an 'achievement' at all. It is merely impossible. Humans affairs conducted on the basis of megalopolitan civilization are simply not susceptible of good government. You have two choices: tyranny and mob-rule."

Jim held his tongue.

Presently Lessingham resumed, as if following some elusive thought through the floating trails of cigar-smoke: *"Wein, weib, und gesang:*[10] after all, what other thing is needful? I hate the folly, the false ends, the will-o'-the-wisps. Samuel Butler[11] knew better: said the three most important things a man has are briefly, his—(very well, my dear Jim. I'll spare your blushes), and his money, and his religious opinions."

"Yes. Like all true Whigs, you are fundamentally immoral. And unreligious."

"I have never professed to have any morals whatsoever. As for religion,—"

Jim Scarnside ground his partly-smoked cigar into the ash-tray. "What I want to know," he said violently, "is why you tore that up and threw it into the fire." And, without looking for an answer, he buried his face in his hands.

Lessingham made no sign, save for, on brow and cheekbones, a sudden paleness or discolour. Jim jumped up: met in Lessingham's eyes a flash of red-looked anger: swung away from them to lean, elbows and forehead, against the high mantelpiece. "I can bear it no more: hide and seek in the dark. I don't know what you're thinking about. Don't know what you're feeling—if you do feel. I'd better go," he said. "Only for God's sake—"

Lessingham rose. His grey eagly eyes, when Jim faced them, seemed dulled now, unproachable. However, he held out a hand: the left hand: Jim saw, as in the bright clarity of a tempera painting, the blood on the handkerchief that bandaged the right. Jim's ring, in the grip of their handshake, was driven into the flesh of his fingers like a tooth.

"It was good of you to come to me, Jim. I think you had better go now."

"I'm not sure. Not sure I ought to."

Lessingham's mustachios stirred with a sardonic smile. "You can set your mind at rest for that, my dear keeper. And in any case, I do as I please. And not all the great masters of Hell—much less you—are ever going to stop that." The cold words seemed to thin themselves on the air to a great still miasma of unfortunateness, in a loneliness of night unhandsome to work in, and (for his taking) no through-path. "I've been glad to have you," he said as, coming to the hall now, he helped Jim on with his coat.

"I wasn't much use to you."

"A little. Chiefly because you, too—"

"O, my God!"

"And yet, another ingenious device that amuses Them, I suppose (if there is any "Them"), Who look on at it all from above," said Lessingham, "is that each of us, and every living creature in the world, has to suffer alone. In the flesh, alone."

XVIII

DEEP PIT OF DARKNESS[1]

L ESSINGHAM went back to the library: rang the bell. "Take these things, Ruth. I shan't want anything else tonight. Better all get to bed early. Call me at half past five: breakfast, six fifteen sharp: I want to be off by seven. Funeral is at Anmering on Sunday. I shall come straight back. Get on with shutting up the house while I'm away. I shall only come back to finish packing: then straight abroad. Good night."

"Good night, sir. And asking your pardon for your old servant, Mr. Edward, sir, we know we are in His hand, sir; and it is written, *Our Saviour Jesus Christ hath abolished death.*"

"Yes, yes. I know. Good night, Ruth. Good night."

She had brought a pile of letters from the hall. He now sat down to them at the table and for a couple of hours dealt with them, pushing some aside to be attended to later on by Milcrest, crumpling up others and throwing them into the waste-paper basket, writing answers to some two dozen in his own hand. That done, he opened a drawer or two, burnt one or two more photographs, and so went through the hall and along the passage to the Refuge.

There was no fire here. There was her hunting-crop, on the sofa: her book-case, Meredith, Jane Austen, the Alice books, Edward Lear,[2] Ethel Sidgwick's[3] *Lady of Leisure* and *Duke Jones,* half a dozen

Conrads, Keats, Sappho, Homer: *Peter Ibbetson*—his nostrils stiffened:[4]

> Death said, I gather, and pursued his way.[5]

Here in this drawer, her account books: sweets in a tin box: sewing things, little reels of cotton and silk thread of all kinds of colours, and these little balls of wool that Mischi liked to scrabble with his white hind paws: Mischi's toy bird, with two real feathers for wings: everything in the drawer so beautifully arranged and smelling of that special French scent of hers. He shut the drawer gently: crossed over to the mantelpiece: several more photographs to burn, of various dates. He tore them up without looking at them: took from its frame and tore up also, after a moment of hesitation, that pencil drawing he had done in 1907.

It wanted a bare half-hour of midnight when he came up the leisured ascent of the great staircase, turned right, along the gallery, and stood, his back to the old oak balustrade, and before him the lobby door. Behind and beneath, in the square well of the hall, as he glanced down over his shoulder, all showed warmthless and lifeless. Against the gilded sconces unlighted candles pointed up: stiff, like dead women's fingers. The hearth stood swept and empty. A circlet of electric bulbs, high in the seven-sided lantern of the skylight—things meant but as for occasional convenience, not, as the candle-light and the lamplight, to live with—shed an unqualitied strengthless glare. He had his key in the door. A step sounded behind him: Ruth in a grey flannel dressing-gown, her hair down in plaits, a candle in her hand.

She had a scared look. "O I'm sorry, sir. I thought I heard something. Thought happen you might be wanting something, sir."

"No, thank you. I shall be turning in soon. One or two things I've got to get together in here, ready for the morning. You get along back to bed."

"Can I put a match to the fire in there? It'll be fair perishing, Mr. Edward, sir."

"I'll light it if I want it."

"It's all ready, sir, same as always at all times it was, in case—"

"I know. You go to bed, Ruth. I'll see to it."

"Very well, sir." She looked at him, and her face took on something of reassurance.

Lessingham went in and locked the door behind him. It was dark in the lobby. On the deep carpet his footfall made no sound. In half a dozen paces he came to the inner doorway leading to the Lotus Room. It had no door, but was closed with rich curtains, coloured dusky green of the moss agate, but, in this invisibility, black of the all-pervading black darkness.

At the touch of the unseen curtains, heavy, silken, smooth to the hand, and at the invading of his senses by a most faint but precise perfume which preserved within itself (as perfumes will) memories, as ephemeral winged creatures are preserved even to each tiniest particularity, unique, apparent, eternized in amber: at that touch, at the inhaling of that perfume, a memory warmed the darkness, and suddenly flamed through it to the point of hallucination. It was as if his hands, motionless in fact on the mid division of those curtains, had thrown them apart: as if the moment that was actual ten years ago were by miracle restored, and Mary, caught between the warm firelight and the glitter of the candles, sat at her dressing-table before her tortoise-shell looking-glass: her dress of sea-blue silk, webbed over with seed-pearls, as with streaks and flowers of sea-foam, fallen down billowy about her hips. It was as if she turned: gave him her face: gave him also, shadowy in the looking-glass where the candles wove ever dissolving nets of radiance, the adorable backview: the line of her cheek, seen from behind a little to one side; and the braided coils of all hues from dark chestnut through tawny Sicilian wine-gleams to hues of gold burning to redness. It was as if all the whole university of times and things sat ready in Mary's eyes. Her lips parted, but no word came.

He opened the curtains: switched on the electric light. It was as if, than this stillness, than the houselessness of this suddenly unrelated room, nothing other remained: only here, for yet a little while, the hideous bottom of the world unworlded, bearing but this last fading character—of the irrefragable irreversibility of death.

For a minute he paused there in the threshold, like a man that maintains his footing against battering great gusts of wind. Then he thrust his way into the emptiness as into some resisting substance: a substance heavy against all senses, penetrable, breathable as common air is breathable, yet too still. In a strange violent haste, he lighted the lamps now: lighted scores of candles that stood waiting on dressing-table, writing-tables, mantelpieces, walls, and beside the great canopied bed: kindled the fires of cedar-wood, in both fireplaces: then switched off the hard electric glare. Still in a deep drunkenness of the outward senses, he unlocked that cabinet that held his picture of pictures. Without looking at the picture, he cut it from the frame, rolled it up, and put it on his writing-table. Then he unlocked and threw wide the ponderous steel door of the fire-proof safe that was built into the wall behind a panel to the left of the further fireplace, pulled out of it two deed-boxes, banged the door of the safe and locked it up again, put the boxes on his writing-table, and sat down. First he unlocked the box covered with pale blue morocco leather: it was full of letters, arranged in bundles by years: hundreds, all of them of her writing, each in its original envelope, with sometimes a mark or a note on the envelope in Lessingham's own hand. He added two letters from the letter-case in his pocket, to the collection in the box: locked it again. The second box, the black one, held documents. He went through them rapidly: deeds of title, his will, Mary's will, a score perhaps in all. He tore across and across and threw into the fire the fire-insurance policy for the manor house of Nether Wasdale: tossed the rest back in the box: locked it. Last, pausing a moment as to bethink him whether anything were forgotten, he took his keys once more: opened the drawer under his right hand: took out a bunch of notes, cheque-book, pass-book, one or two Greek gems. His heavy Service revolver, box of cartridges beside it, lay in this drawer. He regarded it for a moment with a curious twitching of the nostrils, as a man might stand looking in readiness at a snarling poison-toothed jackal, then slammed the drawer and locked it.

And now, still standing at his writing-table, he began slowly and meditatively to arrange the things upon it: boxes, rolled-up canvas, tortoise-shell paper-knife, cheque-book, silver ink-stand, pass-book, rings: all to lie true with the edges of the gold-cornered black seal-skin blotter. So will a man, waiting for the next course, adjust (with his thoughts elsewhere) knife or spoon to a tangential correctitude in relation to the empty plate beside it. Suddenly he sat down in the chair, lurching forward, in a dumb beast-like extremity grinding his forehead against the table-top.

He stood up again: waited a minute, his hands flat-palmed upon the table. Slowly at last he turned: began pacing with measured steps to and about from end to end of that room, as of his cage or prison: lotus frieze, precious tapestries and hangings, carpets, priceless Eastern rugs, huge deep-reflecting mirrors, and that great bed with its carved and inlaid pillars, its golden and silken luxury. All these had a ghastliness as of things cut off, wreckage, obscene mutilations, without root or cause in reason.

He stopped presently at the far window, opened the curtains, and threw up the lower sash. Rain had long set in for the night: October downpour, that filthily, with no wind to deflect or vary it, fell out of pitch darkness into pitch darkness: gurgle of rain-gutters, intermittent plash upon soaked earth of water from some overcharged gully clogged with leaves. "What I saw at Amiens," he said in himself: "meaningless: like a dead bird: without any—" there was a horrible sudden sucking in of his breath through the nostrils —"O my queen, my heart's dear, my beautiful—thank God if that meant too quick to hurt"—He stood staring where the light from behind him was cast back in weak reflections from the face of the rain. Then, as if shaking his senses awake again, resumed his ranging walk.

"She: self-conscious as I am self-conscious." Then suddenly, out loud: "O speak to me, my dear, my dear—" and his teeth ground together.

"No," after the two or three hundredth to-and-about in that cage or room (in himself again). "No. Because this is the true material Hell.[6] Because the imagination or illusion of her which I have conceived, to my own eternal ruin, has"—Something as it had been a scorpion sitting in his brain began to speak abominations to the profanation and unhallowing both of life and death, both of body and soul, till past and present and future loomed now as transformed to tinselled tattered trappings of their own inanity, to flicker momentally between corpse-fire and charnel-house, turning the sweet air poisonous as with the sickening smell of blood.

"Alone. Punishment of the damned: an outmoded foolishness not worthy the confutation. Yet it is here. Unless," and he flung a look at the writing table, "unless that could end it. But I do not choose that."

He threw more wood on the fire near her dressing-table. "I knew. Know now. The scientific fact. Truth, like enough. But it means nothing. It may be the explanation of Edward Lessingham and Mary Scarnside: of Edward Lessingham and Mary Lessingham. No explanation whatever of Me and She." As if in utter weariness of body and mind, he flung himself into the deep armchair and sat watching the bark curl, twist, and burst into flame: the sparks fly up: disappear.

After a long time, the workings in his brain began to say: "But here—what to bank on? Empirical evidence of fact? Or the knowledge inside you that cuts and burns? Knowledge of what is perfect: of what is the unique thing desirable for itself alone. Which I have loved, had, lived with. Thought the thoughts of. Breathed the breath of. Naked in bed with."

He sprang up.

"And I will make no compromise."

He began walking again, twice, three times, back and again betwixt outmost and inmost wall. Then, as upon a sudden reminder, he took from his pocket Mary's unopened letter. It was not very long: dated from that hotel in the Champs-Elysées, Sunday, the fourteenth of October. He scanned it swiftly, sometimes skipping a line or two, sometimes stopping, as if the reading of it scalded him behind the eyeballs. He was standing at the bed's foot, the letter in his left hand. He reached out the right to take hold of the massive satinwood pillar of the bed, and so read on to the end.

As the letter fluttered from his hand onto the bed, the thin chime and answering deeper-throated strokes of the great Italian clock told four. Unstirrable as a stone he listened, bolt upright, gripping now with both hands against his chest that pillar of the wide bed, staring down at its coverlet of silk, dark green of the bay-leaf and fringed with gold:

O lente, lente, currite noctis equi!

O run slow, run slow, chariot-horses of Night!—The memory that belonged to those words stole with a quickening and down-searching of roots, lithe warm and alert, swift among secretest blood-reservoirs of the under darkness, changing suddenly to a huge unbearable pain as with the opening of him by slow incision from the roots of his belly upwards.

XIX

TEN YEARS:
TEN MILLION YEARS:
TEN MINUTES

BUT you've got to move with the times," said the little man with a square jaw. He was polishing with his handkerchief the lenses of his imitation tortoise-shell spectacles, surveying meanwhile, with that myopic blurred look common to the temporarily unspectacled, the scene before him: this spacious Piazza Brà, little white tables under the sky, music playing, laughter, people sitting, people promenading, tourists, Veronese townsfolk, habitués, birds of passage, old and young, men and women, with a good sprinkling of military uniforms here and there and the sweeping feathers of the bersaglieri:[1] smoking, drinking, in motion or at rest, grave or gay, always talking: always the persistent rhythm of the Italian tongue running like a warp through the shifting patterns of sound; and the Roman arena rearing its curved façade, huge and blind, over all. And over all was a cold illumination shed of the electric arc-lights, mundane and harsh compared with the moonlight, yet stirring to the animal spirits and the busy fancies of the mind.

"I say, Frank, what a profound observation!" said the youngest of them at the table. He had black hair, and a voice suggestive of the ping of a mosquito.

"Anyhow it's true. Ronald'll tell you that."

The eldest (by looks, perhaps five-and-thirty), was carefully rolling a cigarette. "O, it's God's truth, no doubt, my dear Michael. *Vox populi, vox Dei.*[2] And 'move with the times' has been the parrot-word of the L.C.M. of popular unintelligence since history started."

"What we were talking about was modern art" said the man with little whiskers, brown hair brushed back, and eyes like a gannet's. "I'm a modern artist myself; at any rate Willie's called me that in print, so it must be true. But I agree with Ronald that ninety-nine hundredths of it is simply fodder for engineers or eunuchs."

"Don't go away, Willie."

"I'm not going to listen to any more. It's so boring. It really is, Ronald, old man. We disagree on most things and I enjoy arguing; but on this question of art—really, I don't want to be offensive, but you don't begin to understand it and your views don't interest me."

"He's gone! never mind," said the painter.

"I'm going to take a stroll round with Willie."

"Right O, Frank. Talk to him about 'Mr. Jones.' Not too loud, or you'll both be arrested. And that would be hard luck on you, in such company: such a good little proselyte as you are of the régime. —Well, Peter. Perhaps Willie's right. Perhaps I don't understand it."

The painter shrugged his shoulders. "Wants a psychoanalyst to understand it."

"A kind of sublimation?"

"A kind of excrement."

"Of the mind? That's an attractive idea."

"By the Lord, I'm not sure it isn't true. Aristotle's *katharsis*. Always thought it rather an inadequate account of the *Agamemnon*, to compare it to a dose of calomel.[3] But our friend Daldy Roome's abortions you were talking of—"

"I'm convinced it's true," said Ronald Carwell. "Not the effect on the audience though (which Aristotle meant when he talked about purging the emotions): the effect on Roome."

"Well; I don't see he need hire a gallery to inflict them on the public, then."

"Nor I, Michael. Except that the public will every time and all the time admire what they're told they ought to admire. So that there's money in it. And we artists have to earn our living."

"So he prostitutes his art because that's what the public wants— or what Willie and the rest of 'em teach them they ought to want?"

"Not a bit of it. Roome's an artist. He hasn't the ghostliest idea why he does it. O yes, he's a very fine artist, Ronald, I assure you, as far as that goes. He's done one or two lovely things."

"Then why doesn't he do them always, instead of this patholog-ical stuff?"

"I don't know. No more does he."

"Doesn't know himself?"

"Not a bit," said the painter. "Look at Matisse, now: the nude's rather a test case, I think. Exquisite line in the abstract. But trouble is, art isn't abstract: it's concrete. Take a hundred of Matisse's nudes: I should say you'd find twenty from that point of view very much in the same boat as Roome's: another seventy, say, suffering in some degree from inappropriate distortion. Then, in the remaining ten, you'll find one or two masterpieces. As good as the best. As good as Lessingham's."

"Human form divine. If divine, why distort it?"

"To show we're cleverer than God Almighty."

The painter shook his head. "It isn't always 'divine,' you know. Even Phryne, probably, if you'd seen her in the flesh, wasn't quite as divine as the Aphrodite of Knidos."

" 'Divine'? What's the standard? A female woodlouse would be diviner than either, to a woodlouse; or, if you take a vote of negresses, a pot-bellied blubber-lipped nigger."

"There is no standard—of beauty."

"Then," said Carwell, "what do you judge by? For, by saying what you said about the Aphrodite of Knidos, you admit distortion of some kind (meaning by distortion, variation from the norm). Take your Lessingham, or take your Matisse."

"When I come to the word 'beauty,' " said Otterdale, "I put down the book. It's a perfectly infallible symptom."

"Of what?"

"Tosh. Tripe. Absence of grey matter."

"How engagingly juvenile you are, to be so frightened by a word."

"Well, it's true I'm two years younger in sin than you, Peter; but even my dawning intelligence of twenty-three summers can tell the difference between words that mean something and words that are just hot air. They don't frighten me: merely give me a pain in the tummy."

" 'Crede experto—trust one who has tried,' " said the painter, "one word goes about as near as another to explaining this business of beauty. Beauty in nature: beauty in art. It's magic. Pure magic, like the witch-doctor's. And that's all there is to it."

"So that's that."

"Hullo, Willie, back again?"

"Quite a galaxy of the great and good exercising their parasitical functions here to-night. Biggest noise, that—what's-his-name?—Lessingham. We saw him, didn't we, Frank? a few minutes ago, stalking about by himself: larger than life and about half as natural: typical nose-in-air haw-dammy look about him—"

"Shut up, Willie. There he is."

They watched. When he had passed there was a curious silence, perhaps for half a minute.

Michael Otterdale broke it, like a mosquito. "That was a good

close-up. Never seen him before, not to get a proper look at him.
What is he really, Willie?"

"An aristocratical plutocratical self-obtruding dilettante."

"He's a bit more than that," said Ronald Carwell, still chain-
smoking with cigarettes.

"How do you account for all the experts accepting him as master in their own particular line? Soldiers, as a top-notch fighting
man—I heard General Sterramore at dinner only the other night
letting himself go on that subject: called Lessingham the finest tacti-
cian in irregular warfare since Montrose.[4] Your artist cracks him up
as an artist, your writer as a writer. And so on. It's a fact. And it's
extraordinary."

"And what good has he ever done? Damn all."

"A damned sight more than you ever will."

"Depends on what you call good."

"I suppose you know he had more than any other living soul to
do, behind the scenes, with the busting up of Bela Kun's[5] tyranny in
August 'nineteen? I know. I was correspondent in Buda-Pesth at the
time."

"The East African campaign,[6] too: that fastened his reputation
as a soldier."

"And what about that amazing guerilla fighting, only two years
ago, in the Rif?"[7]

"O, an adventurer. No one denies he's a big man in a way."

"And all the while, for years, as a kind of sparetime recreation I
suppose, that colossal work on the Emperor Frederick II: out last
spring. The Cambridge pundits will tell you there's been nothing in
the same street with it since Gibbon. And a kind of philosophy of
history in itself, too, into the bargain."

"There was some sort of a romance, wasn't there? I seem to
remember—"

"Yes. Before the war. Almost before you were born, Willie. Married Anmering's daughter: a famous beauty. She died, some accident I think: that must have been ten or twelve years ago. Burnt his
house down after her death: never settled down anywhere permanently ever since."

"Burnt his house? A bit of Hollywoodish, what?"

"Great house up in Cumberland: full of treasures. The kind of
man you can't predict his acts."

"They say he destroyed all his wife's pictures after that," said
the painter: "every likeness of her he could get hold of. Masterpieces of his own among them: the famous *Green Dress* and all. Ten
years ago: nineteen twenty-three: I was a student in Paris a year or
two later: remember the sensation it made even then. A wicked
thing to do."

"Couldn't stick her, I suppose?"

"I don't know at all, my dear Michael."

There was a pause. Carwell resumed: "Funny: I can't have been more than ten: nineteen-eight, it was. This'll interest you as a Freudian, Willie. First time I consciously realized what was meant by —well, by *beauty*—in a woman—"

"Look out! you've shocked me and you've shocked our Willie. Don't use that word. You must say sex-appeal."

"I shall say Beauty. The illustrated papers were full of her at the time; and people talking, you know. Lady Mary Scarnside, she was then. Something about the name, seemed extraordinarily lovely: God knows why—Virgin Mary, Our Lady, I don't know if it's anything to do with that kind of association. Any way, I remember surreptitiously cutting out a full-page picture of her, in her riding-habit, out of the *Illustrated London News* and keeping it for months hidden away somewhere: I'd have died with shame if anyone had—"

"Dear me, Ronald! what a precocious little lounge lizard you must have been!"

"Be quiet, Michael. I want to hear this."

"Well then at Lords—I was taken because I'd a brother in the Eton Eleven that year—I saw her: quite close, in the tea tent. And, my God, Peter, I knew it was her from the pictures and I can tell you I've never seen from that day to this—All your Venuses: any other woman I've ever seen: simply not to be spoken of beside it. And, so charming too. So lovely. Classic if you like, but not cold. A kind of wildness. A kind of Ἀοτέμιδος χελαδεινῆς—swift-rushing Artemis. I never saw her again, but the impression was terrific. And permanent. Like branding. Shut my eyes, I can see her again to-day. Every detail."

"Sounds an unusual experience."

"A propitious start for you, Ronald. No. I'm not ragging."

"Extraordinarily interesting. At that age."

"It's a possession I wouldn't willingly give up," Carwell said simply.

"And the celebrated Mr. Lessingham, sitting at his table over there, looking like Sir Richard Grenville—"[8]

"Or like an up-to-date Sicilian brigand—"

"Like a God exiled from wide Heaven," said the painter.

"How bloody romantic!"

"I'm quoting his own book."

"And all the time, quite conceivably the identical same image in his mind as in yours, Ronald."

"And much more likely, quite a different one. They say he's a regular sailor. Wife in every port."

"Blast the fellow! he looks it. Must admit, takes the gilt off the romance a bit!"

"Who knows?"

A long pause: nearly a minute.

"Look there—"

With a lovely swift swaying walk, a lady was threading her way towards Lessingham's table. She was tall: black hair, slanty eyes, white fox-fur stole or collar, black hat, black dress: exquisite, vital, strong, and with a strange infection of excitement in her every motion as though she trailed like a comet, behind her as she walked, a train of fire.

Lessingham rose to greet her: kissed her hand. They sat down at his table.

"You had given me up?"

"No, signora, I knew you would come."

"How did you know, when I did not myself even?"

"I wanted you."

She looked swiftly in his face, then as swiftly away again. "Your words are suited to your eyes," she said, out of a tense little hushed silence.

"Words should say what they mean, neither less nor more. I have trained mine: good hounds: open not but where they find. You prefer vino rosso? or bianco?" He signalled to the waiter.

"The crimson rose or the gold one? O I think the crimson for to-night."

"I had thought so too, as you observe," Lessingham said as he ordered it, taking for her at the same time from a jar on the table a rose, dark as blood, that bowed down its head as with the very weight of its own sweetness. "Do you, in addition to your other accomplishments, read the Greek, signora?—

"ἦρος ἀνθεμόεντος ἐπάϊον ἀοχομένοιο."

"I heard the flowery spring beginning."[9]—So softly she echoed the words, it might have been the red rose that spoke, not her red lips as she scented it. "But this is autumn with us, not spring," she said, pinning it to her dress. "Or do you as a great man of authority command the seasons as your subjects? a forcer of them to your pleasure?"

The two tables were out of ear-shot, but within easy eye-reach. Peter Sherrill was watching that lady with his gannet-like eyes. As, upon a movement, her fur stole fell open, unapparelling the beauties of her neck and hair, he snatched the menu-card and, from his pocket, a piece of chalk: began swiftly to draw. Carwell, for his part, had all this while been staring at her as if he had forgotten where he was: like a man in a dream.

"But the advantage of complete scepticism," Lessingham was

saying, as he lighted a fresh cigar, "is that, having once reached that position, one is free: free to believe or unbelieve exactly what one pleases."

"As for example?"

"As for example, madame, that you and I were sitting in this piazza twenty-five years ago—here, in Verona, almost this very table, I think—criticizing the ways of God with men."

"Twenty-five years ago! that is not a very charmant compliment to me?"

"Private heavens are the only solution."

She was silent.

"You are not yourself yet twenty-five?"

"I am nineteen, signor."

"You are immeasurably older. You are older than the world. Older, I think, than Time."

"A strange fancy."

"Is it not true?"

"It does not sound to me very like a truth."

Lessingham watched her for a minute, in profile: this unregarding, unattached, contemplative pose: these beauties beyond the Greek, yet, in high cheek-bone and in modelling of eyelash and lip, and in the wing of the nose, something of a more rough and sharp taste, to strain the tongue; and the turning up of her hair at the nape of her neck, like a smooth beast of night coiling itself, fold upon fold, self-lovingly upon some hidden privity and unboundedness of its own desires and somnolent luxury of its own secretness. "I am not a commodity," she said, very low: "not for any man."

"I regard women," said he, "not as commodities, but as dresses of Hers."

"And who is 'She'?"

"Never mind. I have known Her. Intimately. For years and years. If you were She, signora, would you visit this earth?"

He saw something twist and elongate itself like a self-pleasing cat, in the region of her mouth and nostrils, as she replied, "Perhaps. Sometimes. If it amused me. Not often."

"And does it amuse you? 'Ça m'amuse:' did you not say that? twenty-five years ago?—"

"How should I know if I said it before I was born?"

"—This clockwork world, this mockshow, operated by Time and the endless chain of cause and effect? And the second law of thermodynamics to assure us that in time, a few million or billion years, may be, but still in time, the whole thing will have come to an end. Not dead; for to be dead implies a condition called Death, and Death itself will have ceased to be. Not forgotten either; for there will be nobody to do the forgetting. Neither forgotten nor remembered. The end laid down by the great law of entropy: the impregnable vacuity of ultimate Nothing.—Ça vous amuse, madame?"

With an almost imperceptible, half-mocking, half-listening, inclination of her head she answered, "Pour le moment—oui, monsieur. Ça m'amuse."

"Pour le moment? And next moment, drop it: bored with it: away with it and try something else. Ah, if we could."

"It is easy."

"Pistol, or over-dose of veronal?"

"But I think that way too easy."

"Needs courage. Courage of a gambler. Perhaps if people knew, beyond quibble or doubt, what was through the Door the world would be depopulated? Death, so easy, so familiar and dreadless, to a believer?"

"Does anyone, to say, know?"

"What is 'know?' Do I know whether my hotel is still where I left it after dinner?"

"Have you sometimes thought, we may have forgotten?"

"I have thought many things. Tell me, signora: when all this becomes boring, have you never thought suicide might be commendable?"

She looked at him with her green eyes: slowly smiled her secular smile. "God is not like a bee, which when she has stung cannot sting again. Also I think, Signor Lessingham (in my present mood), that I would desire you to play the game according to its strict rules."

"And we can take nothing out of the world. Is not that true?"

"Is it not rather that we can take everything worth the taking?"

"I wonder. For me, what was most worth taking is gone already. And yet, how shall I unlove this world, that has been my bosom-darling so long? And yet—this is talk, signora. Who are we, to talk? What am I? You cannot answer; if indeed you are really there to answer. For all I know, you are not there. I am, myself: but you—why, like all this, these people, this place, the times: you fly through my hands like wind ungropable, or dreams."

"Perhaps, signor, we do not sufficiently, and as much as we ought, trust the heavens with ourselves."

"You have forgotten," said Lessingham. "Then must I remember you of what you forget: how, when long ago I told you 'Je ne crois pas en Dieu,' you approved of that: called it a regrettable defect of character (in a young man) to believe in God. I am not yet an old man, signora: but I know more than in those days I did. And have borne more.

"Does that, too, amuse you?" he said suddenly: "You that go still tripping through the world in your proper form, armed and unguled?"

"Yes. Very much," she said, lifting up her chin and steadily meeting his gaze. The unfillable desire of Her, with the force as of some wind and sea-gate, seemed to set the body of night athrob.

"It is past ten o'clock," said Lessingham, after a minute, leaning nearer across the table. "Will you do me the honour, signora, to take supper with me in my rooms at the hotel that overlooks the river and the Ponte Vecchio? We can review better there the details of the portrait I am to paint of you."

May be it was not, for that moment, the eagly eyes, steel-grey and speckled, of Lessingham that she looked in; but more troublous, more faunish eyes, brown, talking directlier to the blood: eyes of Zayana. Slowly, unsmilingly, her eyes yet staring into his, she bent her head. "Yes," she answered. "Yes."

Dawn was on Verona. Lessingham, in his dressing-gown of wine-dark brocaded silk, watched from his balcony the pink glow along the brickwork of those eared battlements of the Ponte Vecchio: watched, beneath him, the tumbled waters of the Adige ceaselessly hastening from the mountains to the sea. A long while he remained there with the dewy morning lapped in the lap unspeakable of memories of the forenight: latest of all, of her sleeping face and body, as in the morning of life: of the unmasked miracle, for ever new, of he and she: the impersonality, the innocence, and the wonder of a sleeping woman: and, as the reed-like music of swans' wings, flown high, unseen in the mist, the old riddles of sleep and death.

But She, when the time came, departed at but one step from Italian autumn to summer in Zimiamvia: from this room that looked upon the Ponte Vecchio and the golden-slippered dawn, to the star-proof shade of strawberry-trees where Duke Barganax, still a silent spectator at that now silent supper-party, waited alone.

The Duke did not move: did not look at her: said but, under his breath, "Is this the dream? or was that?"

"What will you think, my friend?" The faint mockery that undersung the accents of that lady's voice seemed as a forewalker of things not of this earth.

"What will you suppose I should think of?" answered he. He felt for her in the dark: found her: drew her close.

> "χάλθ' ὄσα μαίνης μ'ἄδεα χαλλόνα—
> Come—sweet with all that beauty you mad me with!"[10]

Her waist yielded to his arm as the young night yields, drawn by sunset down to that western couch, and opens her beauties with the evening star. "You burn me," he said, "O you of many gifts."

She laughed, so, under Her servant's lips. And he, as She laughed, became aware of the music in Her laughter, that the hush of it seemed to darken sight, as with the lifting of some coverlet that had covered till now the unknowable inner things of darkness; and he was alone with those things, through Her and through that music, in their unspeakable blessedness. And, while he so held Her, the blessedness seemed to spread from the nadir up to the sightless zenith, and the heart of darkness seemed to beat faster, as, in an earthly night, the east pales in expectation of the unrisen moon; until, high beyond the dimmest ultimate scarce suspected star, the strains of that unaltering, unhastening, secret music flew and shone as sounds made visible in their white ecstasy of fire. With that, a crash went from darkness to darkness like the trumpet of God, as if the foundations of hell and heaven thundered together to fling down the shadows and blow away the times. So the eternal moment contemplates itself anew beside the eternal sea that sleeps about the heavenly Paphos.

There was silence, save for Campaspe's whisper, as the trembling of tiny waves among rushes in a windless autumn midnight: "The King of Worlds, undeadly and unsightable."

But the King, elbow on the table still, looking still from above on this curious world of his creation, waited with the pleasant idleness of one content to drowse on in that borderland where the changing of the grey light is the only reality, and that less substantial than the elusive perfume of a forgotten dream. His mustachios stirred with the flicker of a smile, as he realized how long he must have stood with his hand upon the door-handle while his mind, in the timelessness of contemplation, had been riding with that music. With an art to refine to the delicatest half-retracted touch the dawning and unveiling of an expected joy, he let go the handle, stepped backwards a pace or two, and, with his back to the old oak balustrade, stood looking at that door. Behind and beneath him, in the square well of the hall, warm gleams and warm stirring shadows pulsed and wandered, here and there a spear of radiance shooting as high as the door's dark panels, with the spurting of fresh flame as the logs settled together. He glanced down, over his shoulder. Against golden sconces a score of candles burned on the walls. On a chair was her hunting-crop thrown by: on another, things for sewing, and packets of flower-seeds (he could see the coloured pictures on the backs); and on the table in the middle of the hall were letters addressed and stamped ready for posting, and her account book and little golden pencil. On the great white bear-skin rug before the fire her Sheila, a little flat dog without much legs, iron grey and hairy and with feathery bat-like ears laid back, was stretched asleep: now and then with twitchings in her sleep, and half-smothered excited little dream-cries. Daffodils in a silver bowl in the middle of the table mixed with the candle scent and the wood scent their scent of spring.

He went to the bay-window at the end of the gallery on his left and, for a last deep draught of those airs of promise, opened it wide and stood for a minute out on the balcony. Dusk was on the garden and on the river. There were quiet noises of black-birds and thrushes settling down to roost. The Copeland hills to the west[11] were hard-outlined against the sky which low down glowed still with a waterish orange-coloured light. Higher, the bosom of the sky was neither blue nor grey nor green nor rosy but all of these at once, and yet far too pale for any of these, as if the illimitable spaces of heaven had been laid bare and found pure and perfect with the promise of alternate night and day. Across that purity, two or three vast smoky clouds drifted sea-wards; others, banked in flaky dark-ness, rested on the horizon south of the going down of the sun. The wind was falling to sleep among the apple-trees. Night, beginning to make up her jewels, set upon her forehead the evening star.

He came back, turned the handle, went in, and locked the door behind him. Before him, the lobby opened shadowy, with night-lights burning of scented wax in the embrasures of the walls to left and right. On the deep carpet his footfall made no sound; in half a dozen paces he came to the inner doorway; it had no door, but was closed with rich curtains coloured dusky green of the moss agate. Two blows of amethyst, upon tables of gold, right and left of that doorway, held immortal flowers: quiet dusky blooms of Elysian ne-penthe, drenching the air with their fragrancy.

He parted the curtains and stood on the threshold. Mary, caught between the warm firelight and the glitter of the candles, sat at her dressing-table before her tortoise-shell looking-glass.

Through a glamour blinding the eyes he beheld her stand up now: beheld her turn to him, and that sea-foam dress slide down to foam about her feet. Like the wind on the mountains falling upon the oaks, Her beauty fell upon him, intolerable, that no eye can bear. And there was a shout, terrible, all-pervading, as of a voice crying and saying that all Gods, and men, and beasts, and fowls, and fishes, and creeping things should bow down and give praise be-cause of Her; and that the sun and the moon should be glad, and the stars sing, and the winds and the mountains laugh because of Her, and the golden mansions of the Father and the desirable con-course of the Gods be open unto Her, as it was and is and ever shall be. Surely he was become as one dead, covering his face before Her on that timeless shore: he that, a mortal man, not once but ten thousand times, but ten thousand times—

ἀθανάτη παρέλεχτο Θεᾶ βροτός, οὐ σάφα εἰδώς

—with an immortal Goddess: not clearly knowing.[12] At that thought, as the heart of Her doves turns cold and they drop their wings, so he.

The King, shaking himself awake out of that study he had for these past minutes seemed lost in, sat back in his golden chair. Sidelong he regarded Her for a minute, sitting there beside him, wearing that downward inward-listening look; upper lids level and still, under lids still and wide: mouth lightly closed in a secretness cool and virginal as the inward throat of a white lily, yet with the faint flicker of some tigerness, alive but sleeping, at Her mouth's corner. He said, very low, "Well, Señorita Maria?"

With a motion scarce to be seen, she leaned nearer. The moth-like touch of her arm against his sleeve let him know she was trembling. His hand found hers, in her lap beneath the table. She said in a whisper, "It did not hurt, did it?—the coming out?"

"Not the coming out," he answered, "but the not knowing."

"The not knowing? You, that do know all? things past, present, and to come, and alike things not to come?"

"The not knowing—there—that, for you, it did not hurt. Fifty more years I endured it there,[13] remember, wanting you."

"But surely you knew, even in there, my friend?—

"And we, madonna, are we not exiles still—

"Surely you remember that?"

"Some things we knew, even in there. Some things we will remember."

"But what need to remember things true and perfect? When all of them are ours. What need to remember present good?"

The King smiled. "It is but a name, this 'remember.' "

They looked for a minute at the unsure thing on the table before them. "Fifty more years, afterwards, I wrought there," said the King: "yet here, what was it? the winking of an eyelid. And you see, it hath in itself, that world, the seeds of its own decay. Its way is not onward, but all turns in upon itself, so that every kind of being becomes there, as Time wears, ever more mongreled with the corruption of other kind. As at night all cats are grey: and as the dust of all right living things turns, mixed with bright water, to a grey mud."

"It is, what you said it should be, a strange unlucky word," he said. "Much like this real world, but crooked. The same canvas, same silks, same pattern, same colours; and yet something amiss in the working. As if a naughty child had unpicked it here and there, cut the threads, played the mischief with it." Her hand was still in the King's under the table. "You and I dreamed it: that dream.— I'm frighted," she said suddenly, and buried her face on his shoulder beside her. Under the comfort of the King's hand which ten-derly, as things too dear for hand to touch, touched now her bended neck, now the up-piled red magnificences of her hair, she was ware of Zenianthe's voice: the voice of a hamadryad, as out of the stillness of the heart of some great oak-forest:

> It was no dream; or say a dream it was,
> Real are the dreams of Gods, and smoothly pass
> Their pleasures in one long immortal dream.[14]

"Was it a dream?" the Duchess whispered, "or is this the dream? What is true?"

"That I love you," he said, "beyond dream or waking. Further than that, it is best not to know."

She raised her head. "But you. I believe you know."

"I know," he answered. "But I can forget, as you forget. It is necessary to forget."

"It is but a name, you say, this 'remember.' Shall you and I remember—?"

The King drew her closer, to say in her ear. "The Lotus Room, to-night?"

"Yes, my dear, my lover, and my friend: the Lotus Room."

"And for us, madonna," said the Duke privately to that Dark Lady, from behind, in the dark: "our Lotus Room?" As the white of her neck where her jewelled hand stroked it, smooth sleek and tender below the sleek close-wound tresses of her jet-black hair, untrodden snow is not so spotless.

"Your grace," she replied, without looking round, "may wisely unlearn to use this cast."

"What cast, dear Lady Unpeace?"

"As though you were my husband."

"Would heaven I were."

"And so foreknowledged to the estate of becco or cornuto?"[15]

"I will not hear you, wasp. He that would unwive me—well, your ladyship hath had example: he should ne'er come home un-cut."

She laughed: a sweeping of lute-strings to set all the velvet night suddenly awhirl with fire-flies. "O your grace hath a tongue to outcharm the nightingale: unsinews all my powers: is a key to unshut me quite, and leave me a poor lady uncounsellable, all o'ermastered with strawberry-water and bull-beef." Lithe as a she-leopard she eluded him, and, stepping out of the shadow, indolently approached the table. Her beauty, to the unquiet eye beholding her, seemed, spite bodice and gown's close veiling, to shine through with such pure bounty as in Titian's Venus is, naked upon her couch in that sunlit palace in Urbino:[16] a body in its most yielding swan-soft and aching loveliness more ethereal, more aery-tender, than other women's souls.

"Your promise given, you shall not unpromise it again," said the Duke at her ear, following her.

"I have not yet made up my mind. And indeed," she said, "I think, when 'tis well made up, I'll change it."

The King stood up in his majesty, the Duchess Amalie with him. All, at that, stood up from the table: all save the Vicar only, who, being untraded in philosophy, and having wisely drowned in wine the tedium of a discourse little to his taste, now slept drunk in his chair. And the King, with his Amalie's hand in his, spoke and said: "It is high time to say goodnight. For, as the poet hath sung—

"Sleep folds mountain and precipic'd ridge and steep abysm,
Wave-worn headland and deep chasm;
Creeping creatures as many as dark earth doth harbour;
Beasts too that live in the hills, and all the bee-folk;
And monsters in gulfs of the purple ocean;
Sleep folds all: folds
The tribes of the wide-wing'd birds.[17]

"And, because to-morrow the great stage of the world waits my action, and because not many such nights may we enjoy in lovely Memison, therefore we will for this night, to all who have sat at your board, madonna, wish (as Sappho of Lesbos wished) the length of our night doubled. And why we wish it," he said, secret to Amalie, "we know full well, you and I; for Night that hath the many ears calls it to us across the dividing sea."

But now, as a score of little boys, for torch-bearers, formed two lines to light them to bedward and the guests began two by two to take their stations for departing, the Lord Beroald, marking where this ensphered creation rested yet where the King had left it, said, "What of that new world there your serenity was pleased to make us?"

The King half looked round. "I had forgot it. No matter. Leave it. It will ungo of itself. For indeed," he said, with a back-cast look at Fiorinda, "rightly reading, I hope, the picture in your mind, madam, I took occasion to give it for all your little entities that compose it, this crowning law: that at every change in the figures of their dances they shall by an uneschewable destiny conform themselves more and more nearly to that figure which is, in the nature of things, their likeliest; which when they shall reach it at last, you shall find dance no more, but immobility: not Being any more, but Not-Being: end of the world and desistency of all things."

The Duchess's arm twined itself tighter in his. Fiorinda said, "I had noted that pretty kind of strategematical invention in it. And I humbly thank the King's highness and excellency for taking this pains to pleasure me."

"O, we have done with it, surely?" said the Duchess. "What began it but an unfledged fancy of hers?" Her eye-glance and Fiorinda's, like a pair of fire-flies, darted and parted: a secret dance in the air together. "Her fault it ever was made."

"For myself," said that lady. "I do begin to find no great sweetness in it. It has served its turn. And were ever occasion to arise, doubtless his serene highness could lightly make a better."

The King laughed in his black beard. "Doubtless I could. Doubtless, another day, I will. And," he said, under his breath and for that lady's ear alone, looking her sudden in the eye, "doubtless I have already. Else, O Beguiler of Guiles, how came We here?"

Anthea whispered something, inaudible save to Campaspe. Their dryad eyes, and that Princess Zenianthe's, rested now on the King, now on Barganax, now once more on the King.

And now, as the company began again to take their departure towards the Duchess's summer palace, my Lady Fiorinda, in her most languified luxuriousness lazying on Barganax's arm, idly drew from her back hair a hair-pin all aglitter with tiny anachite diamonds and idly with it pricked the thing. With a nearly noiseless fuff it burst, leaving, upon the table where it had rested, a little wet mark the size of her finger-nail. The Duke might behold now how she wore glow-worms in her hair. His eyes and hers met, as in a mutual for ever untongued understanding of his own wild unlikely surmise of Who in very truth She was: Who, for the untractable profoundness sake of his own nature and his unsatiable desires and untamed passions' sake, which safety and certitude but unhappieth, could so unheaven Herself too with dangerous elysiums, of so great frailty, such hope unsure: unmeasurable joys, may be undecayable, yet mercifully, if so, not known to be so.—Her gift: the bitter-sweet: γλυκύπικρος ἐρῶς.[18]

"Well?" she said, slowly fanning herself as they walked away, slowly turning to him once more, with flickering eyelids, Her face which is the beginning and the ending, from all unbegun eternity, of all conceivable worlds: "Well?—and what follows next, My Friend?"

VOLUME THREE

THE MEZENTIAN GATE

The Writing of *The Mezentian Gate*

ON JULY 25, 1941, E. R. Eddison wrote to George Rostrevor Hamilton and told of the birth of *The Mezentian Gate:* "After laborious lists of dates and episodes and so on, extending over many weeks, I really think the scheme for the new Zimiamvian book crystallized suddenly at 9 pm last night."[1] On September 2, Eddison was still excited about his progress and wrote to Hamilton again: "You will be glad to know that about 1500 words of the (still nameless) new Zimiamvian book are already written."[2] The opening sections, the Praeludium, which he first called "Praeludium in Excelsis" (literally, "a preface set in a high place"), and "Foundations in Rerek" alternately filled the sails of his imagination, but he decided to finish the voyage to Rerek before turning his prow toward Mount Olympus, the original setting for the Praeludium. Seven months later, on April 2, 1942, another letter to Hamilton shows that Eddison's initial swift sailing had quickly carried his imagination into the doldrums:

> I am still struggling with the opening of the new book. The "Praeludium in Excelsis" which I had written dissatisfies me: seems to be ornamental rather than profound. So I'm changing the *mise en scène* from Olympus to Lofoton, and think it will create the atmosphere I'm sniffing for. But, Lord, it comes out unwillingly and painfully.[3]

Evidently, Eddison abandoned his resolve to finish "Foundations in Rerek" first, and his imagination tacked toward Rerek and Olympus in turns, but without gaining much momentum toward either destination. Eddison eventually completed the Praeludium in July and sent it to Hamilton for a critical reading with this qualifying statement attached: "it has given me infinite trouble."[4] He did not complete "Foundations in Rerek" until October 1, 1942, fourteen months after he began it.

The two opening sections add up to about ten thousand words, and Eddison spent about 420 days composing them. On a strictly mathematical level, Eddison's average daily rate of composition was about twenty-five words. Surely a turtle's pace across the page. Such meticulous slowness seems to mark Eddison's composition: He once told Edward Abbe Niles, his consulting lawyer in America, that the ten thousand words of the thickly philosophical Chapters XV and XVI of *A Fish Dinner in Memison* took him ten months of 1937.[5] Yet in 1937, Eddison had little free time for writing because he was fully occupied with civil service as the Head of Empire Trades and Head of the Economic Division in the Department of Overseas Trade. One would expect that in 1942, three years into retired life, Eddison would be composing at a faster rate than during his working life, simply because he had more time for writing, but that is not the case. The explanation lies in our understanding the intrusion of World War II upon Eddison's life and the response of his dutiful nature to the home effort in the war.

On September 10, 1939, one week after Britain and France had declared war on Germany, Eddison speaks of his domestic preparations for wartime:

> ARP curtains, "Nox" lights, and so on have occupied most of my waking hours since the trouble began. We are well blacked out—but what a bore it is, night and morning.[6]

The annoyed tone of the last sentence is notable. Eddison's "motto" as he declared it in one letter, was "anything for a quiet life."[7] After spending most of his years in London, Eddison moved to the countryside near Marlborough to live this desired quiet life in which the breezy hours of sunshine and birdsong could be devoted to writing and reading and happy companionship with his wife and family. To have the bright hope for this life, in its first months, tangibly darkened by blackout curtains, and intangibly darkened by the fear of bombing or invasion, must have been bitterly discouraging. Time was out of joint for Eddison's retired life.

Some people in Eddison's position would have ignored the home effort in the war. Eddison could not do this: his long career in government, his interest in history and politics, his patriotism, and his keen sense of responsibility would not allow this in him. In the same letter in which he speaks of hanging the blackout curtains, Eddison tells Hamilton of his volunteering for war service:

> I've offered my services in general for any local work here that I can tackle: nothing doing so far, but that is hardly surprising. I was going to stage a "comeback" in Whitehall if war burst out a year ago; but fear it would quickly end me were I to attempt it, and that would help nobody. So, I propose to carry on to the

best of my ability till a bomb drops on me, or some other form of destruction overtakes me, or till the war comes to an end.[8]

Here is a man fifty-seven and well beyond the age parameters of active military duty, a man recently retired from public life and settled into a new house, a man who retired to devote himself to his personal literary goals, a man not in his best state of health: this man volunteers for war service during the first days of the war. Surely his action reveals a mind instinct with duty.

Only those who lived through the war years in England can truly speak about the anxieties and frustrations of carrying on daily life under the constant danger of the air raids. Living in London, Hamilton felt the German threat closely. On September 13, 1940, he wrote to say that his wife's mother had come to live at his house, for bombs had fallen perilously near to hers. Plus, Hamilton had gone to work that morning and found the floor of his office covered with shards of window glass shattered by a bomb's concussion during the previous night.[8] Because he and his family lived in Wiltshire, Eddison did not feel the threat so imminently, and he told Hamilton on September 15, 1940, that although several bombs had fallen in the countryside and one in Marlborough itself, the "total casualties and material damage is so far precisely three rabbits!"[9]

Even though the danger was not as grave in Marlborough as it was in London, Eddison's work as an air raid patrol warden continually interrupted his consciously regular life, a retired life that nevertheless maintained the structure of his working life. On October 27, 1940, Eddison told Hamilton of one incident that exemplifies these interruptions:

> I had a complete *nuit blanche* last Sunday: siren went off and woke me from my first sleep [at] 11:15 P.M.: dressed in five minutes, got here 11:25, and here we were stuck—3 men and two girls—till 5:50 A.M. Monday, when the siren sounded "raiders passed." No incidents for us to deal with, but they had it in Swindon I gather. Home to bed for 1/4 hour, and up, as usual, at 6:30. But, by 9:30 A.M. I was so dead stupid I went to bed and slept till 12:00 and even so pretty washed out for the rest of the day. I don't know how you folks stick it night after night: I suppose the adaptability of the human frame comes blessedly into play.[10]

Eddison's coming home to sleep for fifteen minutes and then rising "as usual" at 6:30 seems silly. He was living in retirement without professional responsibilities, and the scheduled hour of his rising from sleep was a demand self-imposed. The consequence of maintaining such rigid regularity on this occasion produced only weariness and inefficiency in the morning. And yet the disciplined Eddison surrendered to the needs of his body reluctantly, for he did not return to bed until three hours later.

Eddison's ARP work affected the whole of his six years of retired life, but although it was wearying and annoying to him, the ARP work was not the most demanding of the daily tasks that kept him from his writing desk. He begins the October 27 *"nuit blanche"* letter with a paragraph about gardening:

> I'm writing this in the ARP control room: my Sunday morning turn of duty. I boil my egg and have my breakfast about 7 am, and get down here by 7:45 and take charge until 11. I like it, because after that my day is free to garden; which at the moment, is a pressing occupation. I'm cleaning the herbaceous border of bindweed, a most pernicious and elusive pest: it takes about 2 hours of hard digging and sorting to do a one foot run, and there are sixty feet to do. And the things are heeled in elsewhere and waiting to be planted when my deinfestation is complete.[11]

For Eddison, gardening was not welcome physical exercise after stiff-backed hours of concentration at the writing table. Rather, gardening was his major occupation during these years; it was the work of duty that had to be done before the work of his heart's desire. Gardening is, of course, a seasonal work, and the hours Eddison spent at it surely fluctuated, but during the autumnal harvest it took up many hours every day. Eddison told Gerald Hayes in the autumn of 1943 that gardening took 42 hours per week, ARP work took 10 or 11 hours, and that he was also trying to work on *The Mezentian Gate* every day even if he could only give it one half-hour.[12]

Eddison devoted himself to gardening because the wartime food rationing in England created discomforting shortages, and Eddison wanted to be as self-sufficient as possible so that the rations could be supplemented without having to be relied on. Gardening became more important after the birth of Eddison's granddaughter Anne in November 1940, because then Eddison had another person to feed besides his wife, Winifred, his daughter Jean, his mother, Helen, when she came to visit, and himself. For Christmas in 1941, Edward Abbe Niles sent the Eddisons food parcels from New York, and on December 18, Eddison thanked him in a letter: "On the whole we don't do too badly for food. . . . One gets used (though I won't say reconciled) to short commons in things like bacon and sugar: eggs would be a severe deprivation if one had to depend on a ration, but we have six hens who keep us going with their contributions, and very lucky we are, and wise, to have started keeping them last summer."[13] Eddison's strenuous efforts in the garden, and the clucking efforts of the hens, seem to have been successful in allowing the family to live comfortably. However, Eddison's daughter Jean says that it was eventually necessary to eat all of the hens, even the ones they had become attached to as household pets.[14]

Although Eddison's many hours of gardening and ARP work filled his days and sometimes his nights, his letters from the first year and a half of the war do not have a strong tone of frustration over his lack of time for writing. Perhaps the reason is that he was between books during these months. He was busy with matters relating to *A Fish Dinner in Memison:* rewriting the cricket scene in Chapter III for an American audience unfamiliar with the game, and sending many letters to Niles in regard to the contract with Dutton. These things occupied his writing hours well into the first months of 1941. Also, perhaps he was not frustrated because he was enjoying the sweetness of having finished a work that pleased him well, and he was happily anticipating the publication of *A Fish Dinner in Memison* in May 1941.

But Eddison was never a dawdler, especially when new ideas arose like breezes to fill the sails of his imagination: only three months after *A Fish Dinner in Memison* was published, he began working on *The Mezentian Gate*. A cluster of letters from late in 1941, the period in which Eddison was working on the opening sections, shows his careworn tone and his frustration with the ability of these mundane tasks to balk his efforts to have time for writing. The two most potent letters are enough to show this wearied tone. On November 27, 1941, Eddison wrote to his Welsh friend Lewellyn Griffith:

> I too am the sport and shuttlecock of potatoes, onions, carrots, beets, turnips, and—for weeks on end—after these are laid to rest—of autumn diggings and sudden arithmetical calculations aiming at a three year rotation of crops scheme for our kitchen garden, to enable me to get on with these jobs without further thought, and learn perhaps to garden as an automaton while my mind works on the tortuous politics of the three kingdoms and the inward beings and outward actors in that play, over a period of eighty years.[15]

The second letter is to Eddison's American friend Professor Henry Lappin and was written one month after the first:

> Forgive a brief letter. I have no leisure for writing—either my next book or the letters I badly owe. For I am already whole time kitchen gardener, coal heaver, and so on, and look likely to become part time cook and housemaid into the bargain,—

this in addition to my part-time war work; and these daily jobs connected with keeping oneself and family clean, warm, and nourished, leave little enough time for the higher activities. Perhaps this is good for one,—for a time; anyway it is part of the price we all have to pay if we want to win this war.[16]

Eddison is tired of his domestic tasks, and in both letters he stresses the time they take up. He also makes a clear separation between these chores and his writing by calling his writing a "higher activity" in the second letter and by stating his mental detachment from gardening in the first letter.

Part of Eddison's frustration must have stemmed from the sheer size of The Mezentian Gate. The plot of Mistress of Mistresses covers fifteen months; that of A Fish Dinner in Memison, one month. Had he completed the sagalike Mezentian Gate, the plot would have extended over seventy-two years. Considering the number of episodes alone, Eddison's working on the "tortuous politics of the three kingdoms" over a period of seven decades was the most ambitious goal of imaginative contriving he ever attempted.

Eddison's progress on The Mezentian Gate crawled doggedly through 1942 and through most of 1943. On November 6, 1943, Eddison wrote to his new friend C. S. Lewis and said that he was feeling joyful about the new progress he was making on the novel.[17] This letter signals the beginning of a nine-month period of fruitful productivity. Though he had been at work on Chapter II, "Foundations in Fingiswold," since he had finished "Foundations in Rerek" in October 1942, Eddison completed Chapters II–VI between December 1943 and February 14, 1944.

Eddison's constant rule of composition was that he worked on whatever part of the novel made his imagination sail most confidently; he did not hold himself to a course bearing determined by the plot's chronology. In early 1944, Eddison decided to work on the end of the novel, and he wrote to Gerald Hayes on February 22 about his intention:

I am getting on with The Mezentian Gate, being now about to write the last five chapters which in the last two weeks I have roughed out on paper in scenario form, or synopsis, or by whatever absurd name it should be called. When they are written there will be in existence at least the head and tail. That is a stage I shall be glad to have reached and passed; not only because there will then be cardinal points fixed, by which to build the body of the book, but also because if I were then to be snuffed out there would remain a publishable fragment able to convey some suggestion of what the finished opus was to have been.[18]

The clause "because if I were then to be snuffed out" is a curious one because it most obviously refers to the threat of the German bombings, but it could also refer to the questionable state of Eddison's health, a matter that he held in close privacy. In any case, the sentence helps to explain why Eddison, several months later, composed such a meticulously complete synopsis of the middle twenty-six chapters.

Writing steadily over the spring and summer of 1944, Eddison completed the four final chapters and Chapter XXXIV, nearly 31,000 words, in six months. He was especially proud of the climactic chapter, "Omega and Alpha in Sestola." Eddison told Hamilton that he had spent 290 hours upon the chapter, and that it had cost him more energy than anything he had written previously.[19] By late January 1945, Eddison had completed Chapters XXVIII and XXIX, which concern Fiorinda's first appearance on the Zimiamvian stage and her ill-fated marriage to Baias. Then Eddison worked extensively on Chapter XXX, which he designed to show Fiorinda's entrance into society after the death of Baias, and especially to show the responses of the other characters to her and her somewhat tainted reputation. Many of Eddison's unfinished pieces for the chapter have a light-hearted humorous tone which is refreshing after so much Zimiamvian solemnity. The chapter's best scene shows Zapheles falling in adoration at Fiorinda's feet only to become a plaything for her amusement. In Beroald's words: "it is but one more pair of wings at the candle flame: they come and go till they be singed" (756). Eddison never completed the chapter, and it is the last part of the book that he worked on. It is a sad thing to read the unfinished pieces of this chapter, for they are confidently and sometimes exquisitely written, yet some of them date to within two weeks of his sudden death.

Another sad thing is that just before his death, Eddison was discovering a basis for a new Zimiamvian book. "I foresee the 4th beginning to shape itself," he wrote to his friend Christopher Sandford in May 1945. "I think if it materializes it will really be the fourth—an exception to my habit of writing history backwards."[20] But the book would never get its chance, for the end came quickly and unexpectedly on August 18. Winifred Eddison tells the story to George Hamilton:

> I cannot be anything but thankful that he went so quickly. He and I had been sitting outside after tea last Friday, talking most happily. I felt so strongly at the time how happy he seemed. We

fed the hens together and those of our neighbors, who are away. At about 6:30 I came in to prepare supper and at 7:00 P.M. gave the usual whistle that all was ready. There was no answer, but often the whistle didn't carry. On searching for him, I found him lying unconscious and breathing heavily— Jean came almost at once and has been the greatest help and support. The doctor said it was "a sudden and complete black-out" for him. He could have felt nothing and that is what makes me so glad. He never regained consciousness.[21]

The suddenness of the heart attack makes me wonder whether it was caused by a gradual period of declining health or by the strenuous work impressed upon Eddison by the war. If his war work brought him to his unfortunate and untimely end, he would not have changed events if he could have. He declared his views on his war service on November 24, 1942, in a letter to an American writer named William Hurd Hillyer:

> When the civilized world is agonized by a Ragnarok struggle between good and evil; when everything that can be shaken is shaken, and the only comfort for wise men is in the certitude that the things that cannot be shaken will stand; poets and artists are faced squarely with the question whether they are doing any good producing works of art: whether they had not better put it by and get on with something more useful. That is not a question that can with any honor be evaded. Nor can any man answer it for others.[22]

This philosophically minded man was dutiful and responsible; he placed the interests of his family and his community above his own. Eddison exhausted himself in the garden to ensure that his family had enough to eat. In doing this, one could say, Eddison was doing only what was necessary and what he was obliged to do as the head of the household. True, and yet the ARP work was neither necessary nor obligatory: he volunteered for it, it seems, as an alternative form of service when his doctor forbade his joining the auxiliary guard. His sense of duty made the service obligatory.

Looking at the whole of his retired years, I wonder whether Eddison took too much upon himself. He viewed his wartime tasks as work that could not be evaded without dishonor. But writing was his real work. He would have written more, and he would have lived less strenuously had there been no national crisis impinging on his retired life. Perhaps he would have lived longer, too. Part of me wants to see him as a victim, but I know that he would not want to be thought of in that way; his Scandinavian heritage was too ingrained in him for that. I think he would rather it be said that he thought of death as did Prince Styrbiorn, the hero of his historical novel *Styrbiorn the Strong:* When the Earl Strut-Harald predicts that Styrbiorn will live a short life, Styrbiorn replies "I reck not the number of my days, so they be good."[23]

PAUL EDMUND THOMAS
JULY 1991

PREFATORY NOTE BY
COLIN RÜCKER EDDISON

My brother Eric died on August 18, 1945. He had written the following note in November 1944:

> Of this book, *The Mezentian Gate*, the opening chapters (including the Praeludium) and the final hundred pages or so which form the climax are now completed. Two thirds of it are yet to write. The following "Argument with Dates" summarizes in broad outline the subject matter of these unwritten chapters. The dates are "Anno Zayanae Conditae": from the founding of the city of Zayana.
>
> The book at this stage is thus a full-length portrait in oils of which the face has been painted in but the rest of the picture no more than roughly sketched in charcoal. As such, it has enough unity and finality to stand as something more than a fragment. Indeed, it seems to me, even in its present state, to contain my best work.
>
> If through misfortune I were to be prevented from finishing this book, I should wish it to be published as it stands, together with the "Argument" to represent the unwritten parts.
>
> E. R. E.
> November 7th, 1944

Between November 1943 and August 1945 two further chapters, XXVIII and XXIX, were completed in draft and take their place in the text.

A letter written in January 1945 indicates that in the writing of Books 2 to 5, my brother might perhaps have "unloaded" some of the detail comprised in the Argument with Dates. In substance, however, there can be no doubt that he would have followed the Argument closely.

581

My brother had it in mind to use a photograph of the El Greco painting of which he writes at the end of his Letter of Introduction. I am sure that he would have preferred and welcomed the drawing by Keith Henderson which appears as a frontispiece.* The photograph has been used, by courtesy of the Hispanic Society of America, as a basis for the drawing.

We are deeply grateful to my brother's old friend Sir George Rostrevor Hamilton for his unstinted help and counsel in the preparation of *The Mezentian Gate* for publication. We also warmly appreciate the generous assistance given by Sir Francis Meynell in designing the form and typographical layout for the book. The maps were originally prepared by the late Gerald Hayes for the other volumes of the trilogy of which *The Mezentian Gate* is a part.

COLIN RÜCKER EDDISON
1958

---

* See page facing the Introduction.

WINIFRED GRACE EDDISON
To you, madonna mia,
and to my mother,
HELEN LOUISA EDDISON
and to my friends
JOHN AND ALICE REYNOLDS
and to
HARRY PIRIE-GORDON
a fellow explorer in whom (as in Lessingham)
I find that rare mixture of man of action and
connoisseur of strangeness and beauty in their
protean manifestations, who laughs where I laugh
and likes the salt that I like, and to whom I owe my
acquaintance (through the **Orkneyinga Saga***)*
with the earthly ancestress of
my Lady Rosma Parry
I dedicate this book.

E. R. EDDISON

A LETTER OF INTRODUCTION

To My Brother Colin

Dear brother:

Not by design, but because it so developed, my Zimiamvian trilogy has been written backwards. *Mistress of Mistresses,* the first of these books, deals with the two years beginning "ten months after the death, in the fifty-fourth year of his age, in his island fortress of Sestola in Meszria, of the great King Mezentius, tyrant of Fingiswold, Meszria, and Rerek." *A Fish Dinner in Memison,* the second book, belongs in its Zimiamvian parts to a period of five weeks ending nearly a year before the King's death. This third book, *The Mezentian Gate,*[1] begins twenty years before the King was born, and ends with his death. Each of the three is a drama complete in itself; but, read together (beginning with *The Mezentian Gate,* and ending with *Mistress of Mistresses*), they give a consecutive history, covering more than seventy years in a special world devised for Her Lover by Aphrodite, for whom (as the reader must suspend unbelief and suppose) all worlds are made.

The trilogy will, as I now foresee, turn to a tetralogy; and the tetralogy probably then (as an oak puts on girth and height with the years) lead to further growth. For, certain as it is that the treatment of the theme comes short of what I would, the theme itself is inexhaustible. Clearly so, if we sum it in the words of a philosopher who is besides (as few philosophers are) a poet in bent of mind and a master of art, George Santayana: "The divine beauty is evident, fugitive, impalpable, and homeless in a world of material fact; yet it is unmistakably individual and sufficient unto itself, and although perhaps soon eclipsed is never really extinguished: for it visits time and belongs to eternity." Those words I chanced upon while I was writing the *Fish Dinner,* and liked the more because they came as a catalyst to crystallize thoughts that had long been in suspension in my mind.

In this world of Zimiamvia, Aphrodite puts on, as though they were dresses, separate and simultaneous incarnations, with a different personality, a different *soul,* for each dress. As the Duchess of Memison, for example, She walks as it were in Her sleep, humble, innocent, forgetful of Her Olympian home; and in that dress She can (little guessing the extraordinary truth), see and speak with her own Self that, awake and aware and well able to enjoy and use Her divine prerogatives, stands beside Her in the person of her lady of the bedchamber.

A very unearthly character of Zimiamvia lies in the fact that nobody wants to change it. Nobody, that is to say, apart from a few weak natures who fail on their probation and (as, in your belief and mine, all ultimate evil must) put off at last even their illusory semblance of being, and fall away to the limbo of nothingness. Zimiamvia is, in this, like the sagatime;[2] there is no malaise of the soul. In that world, well fitted to their faculties and dispositions, men and women of all estates enjoy beatitude in the Aristotelian sense of ἐνεργεία κατ' ἀρετήν ἀρισγήν (activity according to their highest virtue). Gabriel Flores, for instance, has no ambition to be Vicar of Rerek: it suffices his lust for power that he serves a master who commands his dog-like devotion.

It may be thought that such dark and predatory personages as the Vicar, or his uncle Lord Emmius Parry, or Emmius's daughter Rosma, are strangely accommodated in these meads of asphodel where Beauty's self, in warm actuality of flesh and blood, reigns as Mistress. But the answer surely is (and it is an old answer) that "God's adversaries are some way his owne." This ownness is easier to accept and credit in an ideal world like Zimiamvia than in our training-ground or testing-place where womanish and fearful mankind, individually so often gallant and lovable, in the mass so foolish and unremarkable, mysteriously inhabit, labouring through bog that takes us to the knees, yet sometimes momentarily giving an eye to the lone splendour of the stars. When lions, eagles, and she-wolves are let loose among such weak sheep as for the most part we be, we rightly, for sake of our continuance, attend rather to their claws, maws, and talons than stay to contemplate their magnificences. We forget, in our necessity lest our flesh become their meat, that they too, ideally and *sub specie aeternitatis,* have their places (higher or lower in proportion to their integrity and to the mere consciencelessness and purity of their mischief) in the hierarchy of true values. This world of ours, we may reasonably hold, is no place for them, and they no fit citizens for it; but a tedious life, surely, in the heavenly mansions, and small scope for Omnipotence to stretch its powers, were all such great eminent self-pleasuring tyrants to be banned from "yonder starry gallery" and lodged in "the cursed dungeon."[3]

The Mezentian Gate, last in order of composition, is by that very fact first in order of ripeness. It in no respect supersedes or amends the earlier books, but does I think illuminate them. *Mistress of Mistresses,* leaving unexplored the relations between that other world and our present here and now, led to the writing of the *Fish Dinner;* which book in turn, at its climax, raised the question whether what took place at that singular supper party may not have had yet vaster and more cosmic reactions, quite overshadowing those affecting the fate of this planet. I was besides, by then, fallen in love with Zimiamvia and my persons; and love has a searching curiosity which can never be wholly satisfied (and well that it cannot, or mankind might die of boredom). Also I wanted to find out how it came that the great King, while still at the height of his powers, met his death in Sestola; and why, so leaving the Three Kingdoms, he left them in a mess. These riddles begot *The Mezentian Gate.*

With our current distractions, political, social and economic, this story (in common with its predecessors) is as utterly unconcerned as it is with Stock Exchange procedure, the technicalities of aerodynamics, or the Theory of Vectors. Nor is it an allegory. Allegory, if its persons have life, is a prostitution of their personalities, forcing them for an end other than their own. If they have not life, it is but a dressing up of argument in a puppetry of frigid-make-believe. To me, the persons *are* the argument. And for the argument I am not fool enough to claim responsibility; for, stripped to its essentials, it is a great eternal commonplace, beside which, I am sometimes apt to think, nothing else really matters.

The book, then, is a serious book: not a fairy-story, and not a book for babes and sucklings; but (it needs not to tell you, who know my temper) not solemn. For is not Aphrodite φιλομμειδής—"laughter-loving?" But She is also αἰδοίη— "an awful" Goddess. And She is ἑλικοβλέφαρος—"with flickering eyelids," and γλυκυμείλιχος —"honey-sweet;" and She is Goddess of Love, which itself is γλυκύπικρον ἀμάχανον ὄρπετον—"Bitter-sweet, an unmanageable Laidly Worm:" as Barganax knows. These attributes are no modern inventions of mine: they stand on evidence of Homer and of Sappho, great poets. And in what great poets tell us about the Gods there is always a vein of truth. There is an aphorism of my learned Doctor Vandermast's (a particular friend of yours), which he took from Spinoza: *Per realitatem et perfectionem idem intelligo:* "By Reality and Perfection I understand the same thing." And Keats says, in a letter: "Axioms in philosophy are not axioms until they are proved upon our pulses."

Fiorinda I met, and studied, more than fifteen years ago: not by any means her entire self, but a good enough shadow to help me to set down, in *Mistress of Mistresses* and these two later books, the quality and play of her features, her voice, and her bearing. The miniature, a photograph of which appears as frontispiece,* belongs to the Hispanic Society of America, New York: it was painted *circa* 1596 by El Greco, from a sitter who has not, so far as I know, been identified. But I think it was painted also in Memison: early July, A.Z C. 775, of Fiorinda *(aet.* 19), in her state, as lady of honour: the first of Barganax's many portraits of her. A comparison with *Mistress of Mistresses* (Chapter II especially, and—for the eyes—last paragraph but one in Chapter VIII) shows close correspondence between this El Greco miniature and descriptions of Fiorinda written and published more than ten years before I first became acquainted with it (which was late in 1944): so close as to make me hope the photograph may quicken the reader's imagination as it does mine. I record here my acknowledgements and thanks to the Hispanic Society of America for generously giving me permission to reproduce the photograph.

So here is my book: call it novel if you like: poem if you prefer. Under whatever label—

> *I limb'd this night-peece and it was my best.*[4]

Your loving brother,
E. R. E.

Dark Lane,
Marlborough,
Wiltshire.

---

* See the page facing the Introduction.

PRAELUDIUM

LESSINGHAM ON THE RAFTSUND

T WAS mid July, and three o'clock in the morning.[1] The sun, which at this time of year in Lofoten never stays more than an hour or two below the horizon, was well up, fingering to gold with the unbelievably slowed deliberation of an Arctic dawn first the two-eared peak itself and then, in a gradual creeping downward, the enormous up-thrusts of precipice that underpin that weight and bulk, of Rulten across the Raftsund. Out of the waters of that sea-strait upon its westerly side the mountains of naked stone stood up like a wall, Rulten and his cubs and, more to the north, the Troldtinder which began now, with the swinging round of the sun, to take the gold in the jags of their violent sky-line. The waters mirrored them as in a floor of smoke-coloured crystal: quiet waters, running still, running deep, and having the shadow of night yet upon them, like some-thing irremeable, like the waters of Styx.

That shadow lingered (even, as the sun drew round, seemed to brood heavier) upon this hither shore, where Digermulen castle, high in the cliffs, faced towards Rulten and the Troldfjord. The castle was of the stone of the crags on whose knees it rested, like-hued, like-framed, in its stretches of blind wall and megalithic gauntnesses of glacis and tower and long outer parapet overhanging the sea. To and fro, the full length of the parapet, a man was walking: as for his body, always in that remaining and untimely thickening dusk of night, yet, whenever he turned at this end and that, looking across the sound to morning.

It would have been a hard guess to tell the age of him.[2] Now and again, under certain effects of the light, deep old age seemed suddenly to glance out of his swift eagly eyes: a thing incongruous with that elasticity of youth which lived in his every movement as he paced, turned, or paused: incongruous with his thick black hair, clipped short but not so short as to hide the curliness of it which goes most with a gay superfluity of vigour of both body and mind that seldom outlasts the prime, and great coal-black beard. Next instant, what had shown as the ravages of the years, would seem but traces of wind and tempest, as in a man customed all his life to open weather at sea or on mountain ridges and all desolate sun-smitten places about the world. He was taller than most tall men: patently an Englishman, yet with that facial angle that belongs to old Greece. There was in him a magnificence not kingly as in ordinary experience that term fits, but deeper in grain, ignoring itself, as common men their natural motions of breathing or heart-beat: some inward integrity emerging in outward shape and action, as when a solitary oak takes the storm, or as the lion walks in grandeur not from study nor as concerned to command eyes, but from ancestral use and because he can no other.

He said, in himself: "Checkmate. And by a bunch of pawns.[3] Well, there's some comfort in that: not to be beaten by men, but the dead weight of the machine. I can rule men: have, all my life ruled them: seen true ends, and had the knack to make 'em see my ends as their own. Look at them here: a generation bred up in these five-and-twenty years like-minded with me as if I had spit 'em. Liker minded than if they had been sprung from my loins. And now?—

"the bright day is done,
And we are for the dark.

"What can a few thousand, against millions? Even if the millions are fools. It is the old drift of the world, to drabness and sameness: water, always tending by its very nature to a dead level." He folded his arms and stood looking seaward over the parapet. So, perhaps, Leonidas stood for a minute when the Persians began to close in upon the Pass.[4]

Then he turned: at a known step, perhaps: at a known perfume, like the delicate scent of the black magnolia, sharpened with spindrift and sea-foam and wafted on some air far unlike this cool northern breath of the Raftsund. He greeted her with a kind of laugh of the eyes.

"You slept?"

"At last, yes. I slept. And you, *mon ami?*"

"No. And yet, as good as slept: looking at you, feeding on you, reliving you. Who are you, I wonder, that it is the mere patent of immortality, after such a night, only to gaze upon your dear beauties asleep? and that all wisdom since life came up upon earth, and all the treasure of old time past and of eternity to come, can lie charmed within the curve of each particular hair?" Then, like the crack of a whip: "I shall send them no answer."

Something moved in her green eyes that was like the light beyond the sound. "No? What will you do, then?"

"Nothing. For the first time in my life I am come to this, that there is nothing I can do."

"That," said she, "is the impassable which little men are faced with, every day of their lives. It awaits even the greatest at last. You are above other men in this age of the world as men are above monkeys, and have so acted; but circumstance weighs at last too heavy even for you. You are trapped. In the tiger-hunts in old Java, the tiger has no choice left at last but to leap upon the spears."

"I could have told you last night," he said "(but we were engrossed with things worthier our attention), I've everything ready here: for that leap." After a pause: "They will not move till time's up: noon tomorrow. After that, with this new Government, bombers no doubt. I have made up my mind to meet them in the air: give them a keepsake to remember me by. I will have you go today. The yacht's ready. She can take you to England, or wherever you wish. You must take her as a good-bye gift from me: until we meet—at Philippi."[5]

She made no sign of assent or dissent, only stood still as death beside him, looking across at Rulten. Presently his hand found hers where it hung at her side: lifted it and studied it a minute in silence. It lay warm in his, motionless, relaxed, abandoned, uncommunicative, like a hand asleep. "Better this way than the world's way, the way of that yonder," he said, looking now where she looked; "which is dying by inches. A pretty irony, when you think of it: lifted out of primaeval seas not a mountain but a 'considerable protuberance;' then the frosts and the rains, all the infinitely slow, infinitely repeated, influences of innumerable little things, getting to work on it, chiselling it to this perfection of its maturity: better than I could have done it, or Michael Angelo, or Pheidias. And to what end? Not to stay perfect: no, for the chisel that brought it to this will bring it down again, to the degradation of a second childhood. And after that? What matter, after that? Unless indeed, the chisel gets tired of it." Looking suddenly in her eyes again: "As I am tired of it," he said.

"Of life?"

He laughed. "Good heavens, no! Tired of death."

They walked a turn or two. After a while, she spoke again. "I was thinking of Brachiano:

> "On paine of death, let no man name death to me,
>   It is a word infinitely terrible—"[6]

"I cannot remember," he said in a detached thoughtful simplicity, "ever to have been afraid of death. I can't honestly remember, for that matter, being actually afraid of anything."

"That is true, I am very well certain. But in this you are singular, as in other things besides."

"Death, at any rate," he said, "is nothing: nil, an estate of not-being. Or else, new beginning. Whichever way, what is there to fear?"

"Unless this, perhaps?—

> "Save that to dye, I leave my love alone."[7]

"The last bait on the Devil's hook. I'll not entertain it."

"Yet it should be the king of terrors."

"I'll not entertain it," he said. "I admit, though"—they had stopped. She was standing a pace or two away from him, dark against the dawn-light on mountain and tide-way, questionable, maybe as the Sphinx is questionable. As with a faint perfume of dittany afloat in some English garden at evening, the air about her seemed to shudder into images of heat and darkness: up-curved delicate tendrils exhaling an elusive sweetness: milk-smooth petals that disclosed and enfolded a secret heart of night, pantherine, furred in mystery.—"I admit this: suppose I could entertain it, that might terrify me."

"How can we know?" she said. "What firm assurance have we against that everlasting loneliness?"

"I will enter into no guesses as to how you may know. For my own part, my assurance rests on direct knowledge of the senses: eye, ear, nostrils, tongue, hand, the ultimate carnal knowing."

"As it should rightly be always, I suppose; seeing that, with lovers, the senses are the organs of the spirit. And yet—I am a woman. There is no part in me, no breath, gait, turn, or motion, but flatters your eye with beauty. With my voice, with the mere rustle of my skirt, I can wake you wild musics potent in your mind and blood. I am sweet to smell, sweet to taste. Between my breasts you have in imagination voyaged to Kythera, or even to that herdsman's hut upon many-fountained Ida where Anchises, by will and ordainment of the Gods, lay (as Homer says) with an immortal Goddess: a mortal, not clearly knowing.[8] But under my skin, what am I? A *memento mori* too horrible for the slab in a butcher's shop or the floor of a slaughter-house; a clockwork of muscle and sinew, vein and nerve and membrance, shining—blue, grey, scarlet—to all colours of corruption; a sack of offals to make you stop your nose at it. And underneath (when you have purged away these loathsomeness of the flesh), the scrannel piteous residue: the stripped bone, grinning, hairless, and sexless, which even the digestions of worm and devouring fire rebel against: the dumb argument that puts to silence all were's, maybe's, and might-have-beens."

His face, listening, was that of a man who holds a wolf by the ears; but motionless: the poise of his head Olympian, a head of Zeus carved in stone. "What name did you give when you announced yourself to my servants yesterday evening?"

"Indeed," she answered, "I have given so many. Can you remember what name they used to you, announcing my arrival?"

"The Señorita del Rio Amargo."

"Yes. I remember now. It was that."

" 'Of the Bitter River.' As though you had known my decisions in advance. Perhaps you did?"

"How could I?"

"It is my belief," he said, "that you know more than I know. I think you know too, in advance, my answer to this discourse with which you were just now exploring me as a surgeon explores a wound."

She shook her head. "If I knew your answer before you gave it, that would make it not your answer but mine."

"Well," he said, "you shall be answered. I have lived upon this earth far into the third generation. Through a long life, you have been my book (poison one way, pleasure another), reading in which I have learnt all I know: and this principally, to distinguish in this world's welter the abiding from the vading, real things from phantoms."

"Real things or phantoms? And you can credit seeing, hearing, handling, to resolve you which is which?"

"So the spirit be on its throne, I can; and answer you so out of your own mouth, madonna. But I grant you, that twirk in the corner of your lips casts all in doubt again and shatters to confusion all answers. I have named you, last night, Goddess, Paphian Aphrodite. Was that a figure of speech? a cheap poetaster's compliment to his mistress in bed? or was it plain daylight, as I discern it? Come, what do you think? Did I ever call you that before?"

"Never in so many words," she said, very low. "But I have sometimes scented in you, great man of action though you are in the world's eyes, a strange capacity to credit incredibilities."

"Let me remind you, then, of facts you seem to affect to have forgotten. You came to me—once in my youth, again once in my middle age—in Verona. In the interval, I lived with you, in our own house of Nether Wasdale and up and down the world, fifteen years, flesh of my flesh, heart of my heart. To end that, I saw you dead in the Morgue at Paris: a sight beside which your dissecting-table villainy a few minutes since is innocent nursery prattle. That was fifty years ago, next October. And now you are come again, but in your Black dress, as in Verona. For the good-bye."

She averted her face, not to be seen. "This is wild unsizeable talk. Fifty years!"

"Whether it be good sense or madhouse talk I am likely to know," he said, "before tomorrow night; or, in the alternative, to know nothing and to be nothing. If that alternative, so be it. But I hold it an alternative little worthy to be believed."

They were walking again, and came to a bench of stone. "O, you have your dresses," he said, taking his seat beside her. His voice had the notes the deeps and the power of a man's in the acme of his days. "You have your dresses: Red Queen, Queen of Hearts, *rosa mundi;* and, here and now, Black Queen of the sweet deep-curled black lily-flower, and winged wind-rushing darknesses of all hearts' desires. I envy both. Being myself, to my great inconvenience, two men in a single skin instead of (as should be) one in two. Call them rather two Devils in one bag, when they pull against one another or bite one another. Nor can I ever even incline to take sides with either, without I begin to wish t'other may win."

"The fighter and the dreamer," she said: "the doer, and the enjoyer." Then, with new under-songs of an appassionate tenderness in her voice: "What gift would you have me give you, O my friend, were I in sober truth what you named me? What heaven or Elysium, what persons and shapes, would we choose to live in, beyond the hateful River?"

His gaze rested on her a minute in silence, as if to take a fresh draft of her: the beauty that pierced her dress as the lantern-light the doors of a lantern: the parting of her hair, not crimped but drawn in its native habit of soft lazy waves, as of some unlighted sea, graciously back on either side over the tips of her ears: the windy light in her eyes. "This is the old story over again," he said. "There is but one condition for all the infinity of possible heavens: that you should give me yourself, and a world that is wholly of itself a dress of yours."

"This world again, then, that we live in? Is that not mine?"

"In some ways it is. In many ways. In every respect, up to a point. But damnably, when that point is reached, always and in every respect this world fails of you. Soon as a bud is ready to open, we find the canker has crept in. Is it yours, all of it, even to this? I think it is. Otherwise, why have I sucked the orange of this world all my life with so much satisfaction, savoured it in every caprice of fortune, waded waist-deep in this world's violences, groped in its clueless labyrinths of darkness, fought it, made treaty with it, played with it, scorned it, pitied it, laughed with it, been fawned on by it and tricked by it and be-laurelled by it; and all with so much zest? And now at last, brought to bay by it; and, even so, constrained by something in my very veins and heart-roots to a kind of love for it? For all that, it is not a world I would have you in again, if I have any finger in the plan. It is no fit habit for you, when not the evening star unnailed and fetched down from heaven, were fair enough jewel for your neck. If this is, as I am apt to suspect, a world of yours, I cannot wholly commend your handiwork."

"Handiwork? Will you think I am the Demiurge: builder of worlds?"

"I think you are not. But chooser, and giver of worlds: that I am well able to believe. And I think you were in a bad mood when you commissioned this one. The best I can suppose of it is that it may be some good as training-ground for our next. And for our next, I hope you will think of a real one."

While they talked she had made no sign, except that some scarce discernible relaxing of the poise of her sitting there brought her a little closer. Then in the silence, his right hand palm upwards lightly brushing her knee, her own hand caught it into her lap, and there, compulsive as a brooding bird, pressed it blindly down.

Very still they sat, without speaking, without stirring: ten minutes perhaps. When at length she turned to look at him with eyes which (whether for some trick of light or for some less acceptable but more groundable reason) seemed now to be the eyes of a person not of this earth, his lids were closed as in sleep. Not far otherwise might the Father of Gods and men appear, sleeping between the worlds.

Suddenly, even while she looked, he had ceased breathing. She moved his hand, softly laying it to rest beside him on the bench. "These counterfeit worlds!" she said. "They stick sometimes, like a plaster, past use and past convenience. Wait for me, in that real one, also of Your making, which, in this world here, You but part remembered, I think, and will there no doubt mainly forget this; as I, in my other dress, part remembered and part forgot. For forgetfulness is both a sink for worthless things and a storeroom for those which are good, to renew their morning freshness when, with the secular processions of sleeping and waking; We bring them out as new. And indeed, shall not all things in their turn be forgotten, but the things of You and Me?"

BOOK 1

FOUNDATIONS

I

FOUNDATIONS IN
REREK

ERTISCUS PARRY dwelt in the great moated house
beside Thundermere in Latterdale. Mynius Parry, his
twin brother, was lord of Laimak. Sidonius Parry, the
youngest of them, dwelt at Upmire under the Forn.[1]
    To Pertiscus it had long seemed against reason, and
a thing not forever to be endured, that not he but his brother
Mynius must have Laimak; which, seated upon a rock by strength
inexpugnable, had through more than twenty-five generations been
to that family the fulcrum of their power, making men regard them,
and not lightly undertake anything that ran not with their policy. In
those days, as from of old, no private man might live quiet in Rerek,
for the envies, counterplottings, and open furies of the great houses,
each against each: the house of Parry, sometimes by plain violence,
other times using under show of comity and friendship a more
mole-like policy, working ever to new handholds, new stances, on
the way up towards absolute dominion; while, upon the adverse
side, the princely lines of Eldir and Kaima and Bagort in the north
laboured by all means, even to the sinking now and then of their
mutual jealousies, to defeat these threats to their safeties and very
continuance. Discontents in the Zenner marches: emulations among
lesser lords, and soldiers of fortune: growing-pains of the free
towns, principally in the northern parts: all these were wound by

one party and the other to their turn. And always, north and south, wings shadowed these things from the outlands: eagles in the air, whose stoops none might securely foretell: Meszria in the south, and (of nearer menace, because action is of the north but the south apter to love ease and to repose upon its own) the great uneasy power of the King of Fingiswold.

So it was that the Lord Pertiscus Parry, upon the thirty-eighth birthday of him and Mynius, which fell about winter-nights, took at last this way to amend his matter: bade his brother to a birthday feast at Thundermere, and the same night, when men were bemused with wine and Mynius by furious drinking quite bereft of his senses, put him to bed to a bear brought thither on purpose, and left this to work till morning. Himself, up betimes, and making haste with a good guard to Laimak swiftlier than tidings could overtake him, was let in by Mynius's men unsuspecting; and so, without inconvenience or shedding of blood made himself master of the place. He put it about that it was the Devil had eat his brother's head off, coming in the likeness of a red bear with wings. Simple men believed it. They that thought they knew better, held their tongues.

After this, Pertiscus Parry took power in Laimak. His wife was a lady from the Zenner; their children were Emmius, Gargarus, Lugia, Lupescus, and Supervius.

Emmius, being come of age, he set in lordship at Sleaby in Susdale. Lugia he gave in marriage to Count Yelen of Leveringay in north Rerek. Gargarus, for his part simple and of small understanding, grew to be a man of such unthrifty lewd and abominable living that he made it not scrupulous to lay hand on men's daughters and lawful wives, keep them so long as suited the palate of his appetite, then pack them home again. Because of these villainies, to break his gall and in hope to soften the spite of those that had suffered by him, his father forced him to pine and rot for a year in the dungeons under Laimak. But there was no mending of his fault: within a month after his letting out of prison he was killed in a duello with the husband of a lady he had took by force in the highway between Swinedale and Mornagay. Lupescus grew up a very silent man. He lived much shut up from the world at Thundermere.

Of all Pertiscus's children the youngest, Supervius, was most to his mind, and he kept him still at his side in Laimak.

He kept there also for years, under his hand, his nephew Rasmus Parry, Mynius's only son. Rasmus had been already full grown to manhood when he had sight of his father's corpse, headless and its bowels ploughed up and the bear dead of her wounds beside it (for Mynius was a man of huge bodily strength) in that inhospitable guest-chamber at Thundermere; yet these horrid objects so much inflamed his mind that nought would he do thenceforth, day or night, save rail and lament, wishing a curse to his soul, and drink drunk. Pertiscus scorned him for a milksop, but let him be, whether out of pity or for fear lest his taking off might be thought to argue too unmanlike a cruelty. In the end, he found him house and land at Lonewood in Bardardale, and there, no great while afterwards, Rasmus, being in his drunken stupor, fell into a great vat of mead and thus, drowned like a mouse, ended his life-days.

Seventeen years Pertiscus sat secure in Laimak, begraced and belorded. Few loved him. Far fewer wᴕre those, how high soever their estate, that stood not in prudent awe of him. He became in his older years monstrously corpulent, out-bellied and bulked like a toad. This men laid to the reproach of his gluttony and gormandizing, which indeed turned at last to his undoing; for, upon a night when he was now in his fifty-sixth year, after a surfeit he had taken of a great haggis garnished with that fish called the sea-grape putrefied in wine, a greasy meat and perilous to man's body, which yet he affected beyond all other, he fell down upon the table and was suddenly dead. This was in the seven hundred and twenty-first year after the founding of the city of Zayana. In the same year died King Harpagus in Rialmar of Fingiswold, to whom succeeded his son Mardanus; and it was two years before the birth of Mezentius, son of King Mardanus, in Fingiswold.

Supervius was at this time twenty-five years of age: in common esteem a right Parry, favouring his father in cast of feature and frame of mind, but taller and without superfluity of flesh: all hardness and sinew. Save that his ears stood out like two funguses, he was a man fair to look upon: piercing pale eyes set near together, like a gannet's: red hair, early bald in front: great of jaw, and with a fiery red beard thick and curly, which he oiled and perfumed, reaching to his belt. He was of a most haughty overweeningness of bearing: hard-necked and unswayable in policy, albeit he could look and speak full smoothly: of a sure memory for things misdone against him, but as well too for benefits received. He was held for a just man where his proper interest was not too nearly engaged, and a protector of little men: open-handed, and a great waster in spending: by vulgar repute a lycanthrope: an uneasy friend, undivinable, not always to be trusted; but as unfriend, always to be feared. He took to wife, about this time, his cousin Rhodanthe of Upmire, daughter of Sidonius Parry.

Men judged it a strange thing that Supervius, being that he was the youngest born, should now sit himself down in his father's seat as though head of that house unquestioned. Prince Keriones of Eldir, who at this time had to wife Mynius's daughter Morsilla, and had therefore small cause to love Pertiscus and was glad of any disagreeings in that branch of the family, wrote to Emmius to condole his loss, styling him in the superscription *Lord of Laimak,* as with intent by that to stir up his bile against his young brother that had baulked him of his inheritance. Emmius returned a cold answer, paying no regard to this, save that he dated his letter from Argyanna. The Prince, noting it, smelt in it (what soon became generally opinioned and believed) that Supervius had prudently beforehand hatched up an agreement with his eldest brother about the heirship, and that Emmius's price for waiving his right to Laimak had been that strong key to the Meszrian marchlands: according to the old Rerek saying:

> A brace of buttocks in Argyanna
> Can swing the scales upon the Zenner.

This Lord Emmius Parry, six years older than Supervius, was of all that family likest to his mother: handsomer and finelier-moulded of feature than any else of his kindred: lean, loose-limbed, big-boned, black of hair, palish of skin, and melancholic: wanting their fire and bestial itch to action, but not therefore a man with impunity to be plucked by the beard. He was taciturn, with an ordered tongue, not a swearer nor an unreverent user of his mouth: men learned to weigh his words, but none found a lamp to pierce the profoundness of his spirit. He was a shrewd ensearcher of the minds and intents of other men: of a saturnine ironic humour that judged by deed sooner than by speech, not pondering great all that may be estimate great: saw where the factions drew, and kept himself unconcerned. No hovering temporizer, nor one that will strain out a gnat and swallow a camel, neither yet, save upon carefully weighed necessity, a meddler in such designs as can hale men on to bloody stratagems: but a patient long-sighted politician with his mind where (as men judged) his heart was, namely south in Meszria. His wife, the Lady Deïaneira, was Meszrian born, daughter to Mesanges of Daish. He loved her well, and was faithful to her, and had by her two children: Rosma the first-born, at that time a little maid seven winters old, and a son aged four, Hybrastus. Emmius Parry lived, both before at Sleaby and henceforward in Argyanna, in the greatest splendour of any nobleman in Rerek. He was good to artists of all kind, poets, painters, workers in bronze and marble and precious stones, and all manner of learned men, and would have them ever about him and pleasure himself with their works and with their discourse, whereas the most of his kin set not by such things one bean. There was good friendship between him and his brother Supervius so long as they were both alive. Men thought it beyond imagination strange how the Lord Emmius quietly put up his brother's injuries against him, even to the usurping of his place in Laimak: things which, enterprised by any other man born, he would have paid home, and with interest.

For a pair of years after Supervius's taking of heirship, nought befell to mind men of the change. Then the lord of Kessarey died heirless, and Supervius, claiming succession for himself upon some patched-up rotten arguments with more trickery than law in them, when the fruit did not fall immediately into his mouth appeared suddenly with a strength of armed men before the place and began to lay siege to it. They within (masterless, their lord being dead and all affairs in commission), were cowed by the mere name of Parry. After a day or two, they gave over all resistance and yielded up to him Kessarey, tower, town, harbour and all, being the strongest place of a coast-town between Kaima and the Zenner. Thus did he pay himself back somewhat for loss of Argyanna that he had perforce given away to his brother.

Next he drew under him Tella, a strong town in the batable lands where the territories of Kaima marched upon those subject to Prince Keriones: this professedly by free election of a creature of his as capital of Tella, but it raised a wind that blew in Eldir and in Kaima: made those two princes lay heads together. Howsoever, to consort them in one, it needed a solider danger than this of Tella which, after a few months, came to seem no great matter and was as good as forgot until, the next year, the affair of Lailma, being added to it, brought them together in good earnest.

Lailma was then but a small town, as it yet remains, but strongly seated and walled. Caunas has formerly been lord of it, holding it to the interest of Mynius Parry whose daughter Morsilla he had to wife: but some five years before the death of Pertiscus Parry, they of Lailma rose against Caunas and slew him: proclaimed themselves a free city: then, afraid of what they had done, sought protection of Eldir. Keriones made answer, he would protect them as a free commonalty: let them choose them a captain. So all of one accord assembled together and put it to voices, and their voices rested on Keriones; and so, year by year, for eight years. The Lady Morsilla, Caunas's widow, was shortly after the uproar matched to Prince Keriones; but the son of her and Caunas, Mereus by name, being at Upmire with his great-uncle Sidonius Parry and then about twelve years of age, Pertiscus got into his claws and kept him in Laimak treating him kindly and making much of him, as a young hound that he might someday find a use for. This Mereus, being grown to manhood, Supervius (practising with the electors in Lailma) now at length in the ninth year suborned as competitor of Keriones to the captainship. Faction ran high in the town, and with some bloodletting. In the end, the voices went on the side of Mereus. Thereupon the hubble-bubble began anew, and many light and unstable persons of the Parry faction running together to the signiory forced the door, came riotously into the council chamber, and there encountering three of the prince's officers, with saucy words and revilings bade them void the chamber; who standing their ground and answering threat for threat, were first jostled, next struck, next overpowered, seized, their breeches torn off, and in that pickle beaten soundly and thrown out of the window.

Keriones, upon news of this outrage, sent speedy word to his neighbour princes, Alvard of Kaima and Kresander of Bagort. The three of them, after council taken in Eldir, sent envoys to both Laimak and Argyanna, to make known that they counted the election void because of intermeddling by paid agents of Supervius Parry (acting, the princes doubted not, beyond their commission). In measured terms the envoys rehearsed the facts, and prayed the Lords Emmius and Supervius, for keeping of the peace, to join with the princes in sending of sufficient soldiers into Lailma to secure the holding of new elections soberly, so as folk might quietly and without fear of duress exercise their choice of a captain.

In both places the envoys got noble entertainment and good words; but as for satisfaction, they came bare and were sent bare away. Supervius rejected, as a just man wrongfully accused, the charges of coercion. As touching their particularities of violence done by fools, frantics and so forth, if Prince Keriones misliked it, so too did he. But 'twas no new or unheard of thing. He could rake up a dozen injuries to match it, suffered by his friends in the same town within these nine years, and upon smaller provocation; they must have respect also that many still believed (as he had heard tell) that it was not without pulling of strings from Eldir that Caunas, his kinsman-in-law, got his death. But all such things, for peace sake, it were now unproper and unprofitable to pursue, and he had very charitably passed them by. For his own part (stroking his beard), enough to say that he upheld free institutions in the free cities of the north: would uphold them by force, too, if need were.

Emmius, standing firm and unaffable in support of his brother, left the envoys in no doubt that, in case attempt were made to meddle with Lailma, he would immediately aid Mereus by force of arms. So far in audience; and this upon taking leave: "If the princes desire peace and amity, as I think they do and as we do, let's meet in some place convenient, not under either side's dominion, and hammer the thing to agreement. Tell them, if they will, I'll come and see them in Mornagay." With that, he gave them a letter to Supervius, that in their way home they might deliver it to him and (if he were of like mind) join him in this offer.

The princes sat in Eldir, last week of June, to consider of their envoys' report. Judging the business, upon examination, to be a chestnut not easy to unhusk, or with unpricked fingers, they thought fittest to accept the proffer of parley. Accordingly, after delays which all had show of reason but had origin, most of them, in Argyanna or Laimak, upon the twenty-fifth of August, in the wayside inn at Mornagay, both sides met.

The Lord Emmius Parry, arm in arm with his brother upon the stairs in their way up to the chamber where their conference should be, stayed him a moment (the others being gone before). "You took all means that the answer, on that matter of yours, should be brought hither? not miss you by going past us to Laimak?"

"All means. I am not a fool."

"I like it not, seeing, by our last intelligence 'twas directly said the letter but waited signature and should be sent you by speedy hand within twenty-four hours from them. This, in Laimak yesterday afore breakfast. A master card to deal unto them today, held we but that in our hand."

"I've plied every mean to hasten it, this two months past," said Supervius. "Much against my own nature, too: Satan sain them, sire and filly both. Ay, and I do begin to think I did ill to follow your counsel there, brother."

Emmius laughed. "I may come upon you for this hereafter."

"To cap and knee them, like some rascally suitor for a chipping; and so be thus trained. Even to putting away of my wife, too, not to miss of this golden chance, and she at the long last with child; and nought but black looks so from my uncle Sidonius, for that slight upon his daughter. 'Twas ill done. Would it were undone."

"Go, I would have you resolute and patient: not as thus, full of vertibility. Nothing was lost for asking, and this an addition most worth your waiting for."

Being set, they now fell to business. The princes, using mediocrity and eschewing all kind of provocation, first argued their case. Supervius, in answer, spoke much, full of compliment indeed but with small show of compliancy: later, when, leaving generalities, they fell to disputing of particular facts, he spoke little: Emmius, here a word and there a word. When they had thus spent near two hours but to tiffle about the matter, Prince Keriones, as a man wearied past bearing of these jugglings and equivocations, laid the question plump and fair: Were the Parry resolved to content them with nought less than leave things where they stood: Mereus in Lailma?

There was no answer. Supervius looked at the ceiling. "You are a harsh stepfather, when his own people would have him back, to wish to put him out again; and with our help, God save the mark!" Emmius raised an eyebrow, then fell to tracing with his pen-point little jags and stars on the paper before him. Keriones repeated his question. "Briefly so," said Supervius, and thrust out his jaw.

"Will you stand upon that, my Lord Emmius Parry?" said the prince. And, upon Emmius's shrugging his shoulders and saying, "At least it conveniently brings us back to a base on which we can, maybe, by further debate frame some mean toward agreement," the prince, gathering up his papers, said, "then our work is but waste work, for we will not for our part any longer endure this thing."

Supervius opened his mouth for some damageful rejoinder, but his brother, checking him with a hand upon his arm, made for both: "I pray you yet have patience awhile. Nor I nor my brother desire troubles in the land. But if, spite of that, troubles be raised, we are not unprepared; men may wisely beware how they stamp upon our peaceful stockinged feet, be it in the north there or nigher home."

"You think to cow us," said Keriones violently, "with threats of war? seeing that by fraud, art and guile you can no further? But you shall find that neither are we unprepared. Neither are we without friends to fight beside us, if needs must, in our just quarrel. Yea, friends right high and doubtable: out of Fingiswold, if you goad us to that. We will call in King Mardanus to aid us."

There was a silence. One or two startled as if a rock had fallen from the sky. The Lord Emmius smiled, drumming delicately on the table with his fingers. "Our words, of both sides," he said at last, "out-gallop our thoughts: sign we are hungry. These be not matters to be swept up in a rage, as boys end a game of marbles. Let's dine and forget 'em awhile. Then, with minds refreshed, chance our invention may devise a picture shall please us all."

Kresander said beneath his breath, but Supervius, as catching the sense of it, reddened to the ears. "He that shaketh hands with a Parry, let him count the fingers a receiveth back again."

But Keriones, his brow clearing (as though that rude discourtesy, contrariwise to its sense and purpose, wrought in him but to second Emmius's pleasant words and with potenter force than theirs), said to Emmius, "You have counselled well, my lord. Truly, he that will argue matters of state on an empty belly hath his guts in his brains."

While they waited for dinner, there were brought in spice-plates and wines. Emmius said, "I pray you do me that favour as to taste this wine. I brought it north on purpose for our entertainment. It is of Meszria, of their famousest vintage: a golden wine of Armash." With his own hand he filled round the goblets from the jewelled silver flagon. "Prince Kresander, I'll pledge you first: I know not why, unless 'tis because you and I have, of all of us, journeyed farthest to this meeting-place." With that, he drained his cup: "To our soon agreement." Kresander, flushing in the face with an awkward look, drained his. And now, carousing deep healths, the whole company pledged one another.

They dined lightly on what the inn afforded: capon, neats' tongues, bacon pies, sallets, and round white cheeses pressed in the hill-farms above Killary. These things, with much quaffing down of wine, soon warmed them to quips and merriment, so that, dinner being done, they came again, with minds cleared and blood cooled, to their chief matter subject.

"Ere we begin," said Emmius, "I would say but this. With what intent came we to this place, if not to seek agreement? Yet we spent the morning upon a dozen prickly questions, most of them not worth the reward paid to a courtesan for a night's lodging, and yet each enough by itself to stir up the gall of some or other of us and set us by the ears. How were it now if we set about it another way: talk first on those matters whereon we are at one? And, most worth of all, this: that we will have no foreign hand meddling in Rerek. That is an old tried maxim, profitably observed by us in all our private differences whatsoever, and by our fathers, and fathers' fathers."

"Your lordship has well and truly said," said Kresander; "as myself, most of all, should feel the mischief, were outlanders to come in upon us from that quarter. So much the more, then, behoveth some not to bring things to that pass that others may think it a less evil to fetch in help from without than to abide the injustices put upon them within the land."

Emmius said, "Our private differences it is for us to untangle and set in order as we have had wont to: not by war, nor by threat of war, but by wise policy, giving a little back when need be, between ourselves. They cannot, unless we have ta'en leave of our sober wits, to be let hunt counter to that cardinal trending of our politic."

"What of Kessarey?" said Keriones. "Was not that by war-stirring or war-threat? What of Tella? Nay, I cry you mercy, finish your say, my lord. I desire our agreement as much as you desire it."

"As much as that?" Alvard said, behind his hand. "Mich 'em God dich 'em! Fine agreement there, then!"

"Kessarey," replied Emmius Parry, "was anciently of Laimak; we but fetched it back where it belonged. Tella, by full franchise and liberties, chose their governor. We are here not to treat of things over and done with, but of this late unhappy accident in Lailma."

"Good," said Prince Keriones. "There's yet comfort, if you say that. Afore dinner, it seemed you would have but one way in Lailma, and that your own way."

"No, no. I never said so. I never thought so."

"My Lord Supervius said it."

Supervius shook his head. "I would not be taken altogether thus. Some way, there's ne'er a doubt, we shall patch matters together."

"As for Lailma," said Emmius, "we shall be easily set at one, so we but hold by that overruling maxim of *no foreign finger*. If we are to treat, it must be upon that as our platform. We can affirm that, my lords? that, come what may, we will have no foreign finger in Rerek?"

"I have been waiting these many minutes," said Supervius,

looking across the table with a cold outfacing stare, "to hear Prince Keriones say yea to that principle."

The prince frowned: first time since dinner. "It is a principle I have resolutely stood upon," he said, "since first I had say in the affairs of this land. And that's since I first had a beard to my chin; at which time my Lord Supervius Parry was but a year or two out of's swaddling-clothes. And will you thus ridiculously pretend that I and my friends would go about to undo this wholesome rule and practice? When in truth it is you who, seeking to perturbate these towns in our detriment and to undercreep my might and title in Lailma, hope so to drive us into a corner where we have the choice but of two things: either to give way to you at every turn and so be made at last your under-men in Rerek, either else (if we will maintain our right) to take a course which you may cry out against as violating the very principle we ourselves have made our policy and have urged upon you."

Emmius said, "Nay, pray you, my lords, let's stick to our tacklings. Mutual imputations of working underhand do but put true matters aback. Let's pledge ourselves to Prince Keriones's policy: this knotty question of Lailma we shall then easily undo. Are we accorded so far?"

"No," answered Keriones. "And, in frank plainness, for this reason. You have levies of armed men (we know this by our espials) in a readiness to march north and set upon us. I say not we are afeared of what you may do to us, but we mean not to tie our own hands and so fall in your hazard. Let's talk, if you please, of Lailma. But if in that obstinacy my Lord Supervius remains, then we sit out. And then will we assuredly bring in Fingiswold to help us, and the rebuke and damage of that will be yours, not ours."

"It will be your very deed," said Supervius, "sprung from your own fury, howsoever you colour it."

"O, no hot respectless speeches, brother," said Emmius. "These matters must be handled with clear eyes, not in a swimming of the brain."

"Prince Keriones," he said then, sharpening his eyes upon him, "this is a very peremptory sentence plumped down of you. Well, I also will speak plain, and without offence. We have offered to treat with you upon your own avouched basis of *no foreign finger*. You will not engage yourselves so far. Upon this, then, we set up our rest, I and my brother. We accept that basis. More, we are minded to enforce it. The fortress of Megra, lying upon your (and our) northern border, and longing to Fingiswold, is threat enough. It is (with all humility) for you princes to govern well your realms and give example to the cities upon your confines: so do we with ours. I have friends and affines in the southland, but I would think scorn to call upon King Kallias to prop me. If you call upon King Mardanus, I will march with my brother to defend that northern frontier thus betrayed by you. And I think we can be upon you, and deal with you, before you have time to bring in your foreign succours; as in common prudence indeed we must, since you have so threatened us, unless you give us security of peace. That is to say, material pledges: fair words, spoken or written, can by no means suffice us now.

"So much, since I would be honest, you left me no choice but to say. But surely it is not a thing unpossible or unlikely, that"—

Here Kresander could contain no longer. "We had better never have come hither," he shouted, and smote the table with his fist. "This meeting was but to mock us and dally the matter off while they sharpened their swords against us. I'm for home." He pushed back his chair and was half risen, but Kariones pulled him down again, saying, "Wait. We will hear this out."

Supervius, while his brother had been speaking, had broke the seal of a letter brought hastily in by his secretary. Keriones and Alvard watched him read it, as if themselves would read in his face something of its purport. But his face, haughty and imperturbable, showed not so much as a hairsbreadth movement of nostril or eyelid as he scanned the letter, neither at Kresander's outburst.

"Tongues can outbrawl swords," said Emmius, chilling cold of voice; "but that is for rude beasts, not for men that be reasonable. I pray you, let me finish my say. And first, by your leave," as Supervius put the letter into his hands. He read it, folded it again thoughtfully, gave it back: his face like his brother's, not to be unciphered. "Let us," he said, "as great statesmen, hold fast by our common good, of all of us, which is peace in Rerek. History hath remembered the ruins of many estates and powers which have gone down in civil strife or, albeit victorious, got in the end but a handful of smoke to the bargain. Let us live as friends. I unfeignedly wish it: so do my brothers and all that adhere to our interest. But others must do their part. This is my counsel: that we, of both sides, agree to go home, keep truce for a month, then meet again and, as I hope, determine of some new assured basis for our unluckily shaken friendship. Where shall we meet?" he said, turning to his brother.

"Why, if it shall please your excellencies to kill two birds with one stone and add merry-making to crown our peace-making," said Supervius, "what happier meeting-place than Megra? upon the twentieth day of September, which is appointed there for the feast of my betrothal"—he paused, gathering their eyes—"to the Princess Marescia of Fingiswold. Nay, read it if you please: I had it but five minutes since." And with a wolvish look he tossed the letter upon the table.

II

Foundations in Fingiswold

I T WAS eight months after that meeting in Mornagay: mid-March, and mid-afternoon.[1] Over-early spring was busy upon all that grew or breathed in the lower reaches of the Revarm. Both banks, where the river winds wide between water-meadows, were edged with daffodils; and every fold of the rising ground, where there was shelter from north and east for the airs to dally in and take warmth from the sunshine, held a mistiness of faint rose-colour: crimp-petalled blossoms, with the leaf-buds scarcely as yet beginning to open, of the early northern plum. Higher in the hillsides pasque-flowers spread their tracery of soft purple petal and golden centre. A little downstream, on a stretch of shingle that lay out from this right bank into the river, a merganser drake and his wife stood preening themselves, beautiful in their whites and bays and iridescent greens. It was here about the high limit of the tides, and from all the marshland with its slowly emptying creeks and slowly enlarging flats (for the ebb was well on its way) of mud and ooze, came the bubbling cascade of notes as curlew answered curlew amid cries innumerable of lesser shore-birds; plover and sandpiper, turnstone and spoonbill and knot and fussy redshank, fainter and fainter down the meanderings of the river to where, high upon crags which rose sudden from water-level to shut out the prospect southwards, two-horned Rialmar sat throned.

Anthea spoke: "I have examined it, honoured sir: scented it, as you bade me, from every airt."

Doctor Vandermast was sat a little above her on the rib of rock which, grown over with close-lying twigs and leaf-whorls of the evergreen creeping daphne, made for these two a dry and a cushioned resting-place. His left hand, palm-upward in white beard, propped his chin. His gaze was south, in a contemplation which seemed to look through and behind the immediate things of earth and sky, as through windows giving upon less alterable matters. Nothing moved, save when here and there, in a sparkle of black and white, a flock of shy golden-eye took wing, upstream or downstream, or a butterfly flight of terns rose and fell, drifting on air toward the unseen headwaters of the Midland Sea.

"Rialmar town?" said the doctor, at last, without shifting his gaze.

"No. This whole new world. I have quartered it over, pole to pole, so as I could (if you desired me) give you an inventory. And all since day dawning."

"What make you of it? In a word?"

"Something fair and free," she answered. "Something un-measurably old. As old as myself."

"Or as young?"

"Or as young."

"But a minute ago you called it new?" He looked down now, into this girl's staring yellow eyes: eyes whose pupils were upright slits that opened upon some inward quivering of incandescence, as of iron fired beyond redness; and his gaze grew gentle. "And you are becharmed by it: like a bee of the new brood come out to dance before the hive on a still sunshiny evening and taste open air for the first time and find your landmarks."

Anthea laughed: a momentary disclosing of pointed teeth that transshaped, as with leap and vanishing again of lightning, the classic quietude of her features. "I knew it all before," she said. "Yet for all that, it is as new and unexperimented as last night's snowfall on my high glaciers of Ramosh Arkab. A newness that makes my heckles rise. Does it not yours?"

He shook his head: "I am not a beast of prey."

"What are you, then?" she said, but without waiting for an answer. "There is a biting taste to it: a scent, a stirring: and up there, especially. In the Teremnene palace." She lifted her nose towards the royal seat-town upon its solitary heights, as if even down wind her eager sense tasted its quality.

Vandermast said, "There is a child there. You saw it no doubt? A boy."

"Yes. But no past ordinary novelty in that. Unless perhaps that when, changing my smooth skin for my furred, I slunk in and made teeth at it behind the nurse's back, it was not scared but gave me a look, so that I went out and glad to be gone. And, now I think on it, 'twas that first set me scenting this newness at every corner. Beyond all, in the Queen." She looked at him, paused, then asked suddenly. "This Queen. Who in truth is she?"

He made no reply.

"Tell me, dear master," she said, drawing herself closer by a most unhuman self-elongating of body and limbs and rubbing her cheek, as might some cattish creature, against his knee.

He said, "You must not ask questions when you know the answer."

Anthea sat back on her heels and laughed. Upon the motion, her hair, loosely bound up with a string of clouded zircon stones of that translucent blue which is in the lip of an ice-cave looked up to from within, fell, in tumbled cataracts as of very sunlight, down about her shoulders and, in one of its uncoiling fulvid streams, over her breast. "She Herself does not know the answer. I suppose, in this present dress of Hers, She is asleep?"

"In this present dress," said the ancient doctor, "She is turned outward from Herself. You may, if you choose, conceive it as a kind of sleep: a kind of forgetting. As the sunshine were to forget itself in the thing it shines on."

"In that lion-cub of hers? I cannot understand such a forgetting in Her."

"No, my oread. Nor I would not wish you able to understand it, for that were to maculate the purity of your own proper nature."

"And you would wish me be as I am?"

"Yes," answered he. "You, and all true beings else."

The girl, silent, putting up her hair, met his look unsmilingly with her unquiet, feline, burning eyes.

"We will go on," said the doctor, rising from his seat. Anthea with a lithe and sinuous grace rose to follow him.

"Whither?" she asked as they came southward.

"Up to Teremne. We will look upon these festivities."

In the old Teremnene palace which, like an eagle's nest, crowns the summit ridge of the south-eastern and loftier of the twin steep rock bastions called Teremne and Mehisbon, on and about which has grown up as by accretion of ages Rialmar town, is a little secret garden pleasaunce. It lies square between walls and the living rock, in good shelter from the unkinder winds but open to the sun, this side or that, from fore-noon till late evening. No prying windows overlook it: no intrusive noises visit it of the world's stir without: a very formal garden artificially devised with paved walks of granite trod smooth by the use of centuries, and with flights of steps going down at either side and at either end to an oval pond in the midst, and upon a pedestal in the midst of that pond a chryselephantine statue of Aphrodite as rising from the sea. At set paces there were parterres of tiny mountain plants: stonecrop, houseleek, rock madwort, mountain dryas, trefoils, and the little yellow mountain poppy; and with these that creeping evening primrose, which lifts up wavy-edged four-lobed saucers of a spectral whiteness, new every night at night-fall, to bloom through the hours of dark and fill the garden with an overmastering sharp sweetness. And at full morning they droop and begin to furl their petals, suffused now with pink colour which were white as a snowdrop's, and lose all their scent, and the thing waits lifeless and inert till night shall return again and wake it to virgin-new delicacy and deliciousness. This was Queen Stateira's garden, furnished out anew for her sake seven years ago by Mardanus her lord, who in those days made little store of gardens, but much of his young new-wedded wife.

Shadows were lengthening now, as afternoon drew towards evening. In one of the deep embrasures of the east wall which look down the precipice sheer eight hundred feet, to the river mouth and the harbour and so through skyey distances to the great mountain chains, so blanketed at this hour with cloud that hard it was to discern snowfield from cloudbank, leaned King Mardanus in close talk with two or three about him. No wind stirred in the garden, and the spring sunshine rested warm on their shoulders.

Away from them at some twenty yards remove, by the waterside, upon a bench of lapis lazuli and mother-of-pearl, sat the Queen. The brightness of the sun shining from behind her obscured her features under a veiling mystery, but not to conceal an ambiency of beauty that lived in her whole frame and posture, an easefulness and reposefulness of unselfregarding grace. The light kindled to flame the native fire-colours in her hair, and the thrown shadow of that statue touched the furred hem of her skirt and the gold-woven lace-work on her shoe.

Over against her on the same bench the Lady Marescia Parry, only child of Prince Garman of Fingiswold, and so cousin german to the King, faced the sun. She was at this time in the twenty-fourth year of her age: of a dazzling whiteness of skin: her eyes, busy, bold and eager, of a hot chestnut brown: her nose a falcon's, her yellow hair, strained back from her high forehead by a thin silver circlet garnished with stone and pearls, fell loose and untressed about her back and powerful shoulders, in fashion of a bride's.

The Queen spoke: "Well, cousin, you are wedded."

"Well wedded, but not yet bedded."

" 'Las, when mean you to give over that ill custom of yours?"

"Ill custom?"

"Ever to speak broad."

"O, between kinsfolk. Tell me unfeignedly, what thinks your highness of my Supervius? Is a not a proper man?"

"He belieth not his picture. And since 'twas his picture you fell in love with, and he with yours, I dare say you have gotten the husband of your choice."

The Princess smiled with her lips: cherry-red lips, lickerous, and masterful. "And by right of conquest," she said. "That sauceth my dish: most prickingly."

"Yet remember," said the Queen, "we wives are seldom conquerors beyond first se'nnight."

"I'll talk to your highness of that hereafter. But I spake not of conquest upon him. My blood tells me there's fire enough i' the pair of us to outburn such cold-hearth rivalries as that. Dear Gods forfend I should e'er yield myself chattel to the man I wed: but neither could I be fool enough to wed with such a man as I could bring down to be chattel of mine. Nay, I spoke of my parents; ay, and (with respect) of yourself, and of the King."

"Your conquest there," replied the Queen, "is measure of our love of you."

"Doubtless. But measure, besides, of mine own self will. Without that," here she glanced over her shoulder and leaned a little nearer, "I am apt to think your love of me (the King's, at least) had played second fiddle to more deeper policies."

The Queen said, "Well, fret not for that. You have had your way."

Marescia lifted her superb white chin and her mouth smiled. "Truly, cousin," she said, managing her voice almost to a whisper, "I think you are to thank me, all of you. Put case I had fallen in with your fine design to match me to yonder outed Prince of Akkama. The man is well enough: personable, I grant: qualified out of all ho,[2] I'd swear, to please a woman: but of what avail? With's father dead, and himself, driven away by the usurper, a landless exile still sitting on your door-step here. How shall such an one be ever a king, or lord of aught save's own empty imaginings and discontents? I swear the King (Gods send he live for ever) may get better purchase by this that, following my own natural lust o' the eye, I have brought him, than by Aktor, be he ten times prince indeed. And Rerek, far nearer us in blood and custom. Wed with yonder foreign lick-dish! God's dignity, I'd sleep in the byre sooner and breed minotaurs."

Queen Stateira laughed: honest lovely laughter, bred of sweet blood and the life-breath fancy free: "Come, you're too bitter."

"Aktor is in your highness's books, I think."

"Why think that?"

"Strange else, professing so much cousinly love to me, you should a wished me give my hand there."

The Queen looked away. "To tell you true, dear Marescia, 'twas the King's wish, and but therefore mine, as being my duty."

"Duty?" said the Princess: "to be led blindfold by your husband? Go, they'll ne'er call me perfect wife a those terms."

There was a pause. Then Marescia, sitting back again, her voice now at its ordinary strength and pitch: "What is this prognosticator by the stars, this soothsayer, your highness keeps i' the palace?"

"What do you mean? I keep none such."

"O yes: a greybeard signior: long gaberdine, and capped *magister artium*:[3] some compliment-monger, I would wager. Comes to me as I passed among the throng of guests not half an hour since on my Lord Supervius's arm, gives me a stare o' the eye turned all my backside to gooseflesh, and crieth out that I shall bear Supervius a son shall be greater than his father."

"Heaven hold fast the omen."

"And then to my Lord Emmius, whom I must now call brother-in-law: crieth out and saith that of the seed of Emmius Parry shall come both a queen of earth and a queen of heaven."

"And what will he cry out at me, think you?" said the Queen.

"Please you enter the hall of the Sea Horses, I can show him to you, and you may examine him."

"Dear my Lord," said Stateira, as the King and those about him, their business being it seemed concluded, approached her, "here's diversion for you," and told him what Marescia had said. The King bluffly humouring it as child's talk, assented.

"Yonder standeth the old man: there, that tall, lanky one," Marescia said in the Queen's ear, from behind, as they descended the great staircase into that vast hall and paused upon the last steps between the two sea-horses of dark blue rock-crystal well the height of a man's shoulder, there to take their stand and survey the company that, upon sounding of trumpets to a sennet to proclaim the King's presence, abode all motionless now and with all faces turned that way: "and the girl with beastly eyes," she said, "who is, I suppose his granddaughter. Or, may hap, his bona roba, if such a jack pudding have use or custom of such commodities."

Supervius eyed his princess with the deepening satisfaction of a skilled rider who begins to know the paces of a new high-blooded but untried mare. "Speak within door, Marescia," said her father. The King sent a little page of his of six year old that was named Jeronimy, to bring the doctor before him.

When that was done, and Vandermast made his obeisance, the King surveyed him awhile in silence: then said, "Who are you, old sir? Of my folk or an outlander?"

"I am," answered he, "your serene highness's life-long loyal faithful subject: my habitation many journeys from this, south on the Wold: my practice, that of a doctor in philosophy."

"And what make you here i' the court?"

"To pay my humble duty where most I do owe it, and to behold with mine eyes at last this place and the glory thereof."

"And to seek a pension?"

"No, Lord. Being entered now upon my ninth ten years I do find my lean patrimony sufficient to my livelihood, and in meditation of the metaphysicals food sufficient to sustain my mind. Over and above these things, I have no needs."

"A wise man," gently said the Queen, "by what he saith. For, to speak true, here is freedom indeed."

"I ne'er heard philosophy filled a man's belly," said the King, with a piercing look still regarding him. "You are bruited to me, you, to have uttered here, this instant afternoon, prognosticks and probabilities (some would call 'em improbabilities, but let that pass) touching certain noble persons, guests at our wedding feast."

Vandermast said, "I did so, my Lord and King, but in answer to interrogatives proposed to me by the persons in question."

The King raised an eyebrow at Marescia. "O yes," said she: "we did ask him."

"I gave but voice to my thoughts that came me in mind," said Vandermast. "Neither spake I unconsiderately, but such things only as upon examination with mine inward judgement seemed likely and reasonable."

The King was fallen silent a minute, glaring with his eyes into the eyes, steadfast and tranquil, of that learned doctor beneath their snow-thatched eaves, as though he would plumb some unsoundable darkness that underlay their shining and candid outward. Shifting his gaze at last, "You shall not be blamed for that," he said: then privately, to Prince Aktor, who was stood close on his right, "Here is a man I like: is able to look me in the eye without brave nor slavishness. Kings seldom have to deal but with the one or t'other."

"Your serene highness hath never, I think," replied Aktor, "had to deal with the first." He glanced across to Queen Stateira who, upon the King's left hand, wide-eyed and with lovely lips half parted, was watching Doctor Vandermast with the intent and pleasure and wonder of a child. She caught the glance and looked away.

"You have answered well," said the King to Vandermast. "These be days of mirth and rejoicing, and fitting it is folk show themselves open-handed on high holiday, to give somewhat of alms to poor needy persons, most of all when such do utter good words or in what other way soever do seem to merit it. Wear this from me," he said, taking a ring from his finger. "My grandfather's it was, King Anthyllus's upon whom be peace. 'Tis thought there be virtue in the stone, and I would not bestow it save on one in whom I seemed to smell some deserts answerable to its worth. But forget not, the law lieth very deadly against whoso shall make bold to prophesy concerning the King's person. Aim not therefore at me in your conjectures, old man, bode they good or ill, lest a worse thing overtake you."

"My Lord the King," said Vandermast, "you have commanded, and your command shall with exactness be obeyed. I have told your serenity that few and little are my possessions, and yet that there is nought whereof I do stand in want, nor will I be a taker of rewards. For it is a property universal of rewards that they can corrupt action, propounding to the actor (if the action be bad) a reason beyond the action's self, without which reason the action must have remained unacted. Because badness of itself is no reason. Contrariwise, be the action good, then the mere fact that it was acted for sake of reward can beget this bad habit in a man: to have respect to cheap, decaying, extern rewards; which enureth in the end so to debauch his inmost understanding that he becometh unable to taste or to desire the true only costly everlasting and ever satisfying reward, which hath its seat in the good action itself. But this," he said, drawing onto his finger the King's ring, "cometh not as a reward but as a gift royal, even as great Kings have from the antique times been renowned and honoured as ring-scatterers: a noble example which I find your serene highness do make your own."

"Be such as I think you to be," said the King, "and my friendship followeth the gift."

The doctor, that audience being done, came and went for a while his leisurely to and fro, within door and without, and always upon the fringes of the company, not as member thereof so much as looker on rather and listener, remarking whatsoever in any person appeared of remarkable: carriages, aspects, moods, manners, silences, little subtleties of eye, nostril, lip. And about and above him, at every succeeding step of his progress through this palace upon the southern horn of Rialmar, the greatness and the ancientness of the place hung heavier. Even as, to a climber, the mere vastness of the mountain becomes, as he goes higher, a presence, unite and palpable, built up of successive vastness of slabbed rock-face, vertiginous ice-cliff, eye-dazzling expanse of snow-field, up-soaring ultimate cornice chiselled by the wind to a sculptured perfection of line, sun-bright and remote against an infinite remoteness of blue heaven above it, so here was all gathered to an immobility of time-worn and storied magnificence: cyclopaean walls and gateways; flights of stairs six riders abreast might ride down on horseback and not touch knees; galleries, alcoves and clerestories cut from the rock; perspectives flattening the eye down distances of corbel and frieze and deep-mullioned windows six times the height of a man; colonnades with doric capitals curiously carved, supporting huge-timbered vaulted roofs; and domed roofs that seemed wide as the arch of day. All of which, apprehended in its wholeness, might cast a wise mind into oblivion not of its own self only and of all mankind but even of the everlasting mountains themselves; in the sudden apprehension that this Rialmar might be the nursery or breeding-place of a majesty and a loneliness older-rooted than theirs.

Closed in these meditations, he came once more into that presence-chamber, with its sea-horse staircase, and here was one of the Queen's chamberlains with her highness's bidding that Doctor Vandermast should attend her in the privy garden. The doctor followed him; and, passing on their way through a vaulted corridor hewn in the rock and brightly lighted with hanging lamps, they were met with a nurse leading in her hand a child yet in his side-coats, of two or three years old. The doctor viewed the boy narrowly, and the boy him. "What child was that?" he asked, when they were gone by. The chamberlain, with a skewing of his eye at him as of one smally trusting old vagrant men that were likely sprung of a stone and certainly best told nothing, as soonest mended, answered that it was one of the children of the palace, he knew not for sure which. Which answer the learned doctor let go without further remark.

"It is her highness's pleasure," said the chamberlain, at the garden gate, "to receive you in private. Be pleased to walk on:" so Vandermast entered in alone and stood before Queen Stateira.

She was sitting sideways now on the jewelled bench, her feet up, sewing a kirtle of white satin embroidered with flowers of silver. Upon the doctor's coming she but glanced up and so back to her needlework. It was yet bright sunshine, but with the wearing of the afternoon the shadow of that gold and ivory statue of our Lady of Paphos no longer touched the Queen where she sat. The air was colder, and she had a high-collared cloak about her shoulders of rich brown velvet, coloured of the pine-marten's skin in summer and lined with vair. He waited, watching her, while she with down-bended eyes plied her needle. Nought else stirred, except now and then a blazing of hot colour where her hair caught the sun, and except, where the pleated neck-ruff of her gown ran lowest, the gentle fall and swell of her breathing. After a little, she raised her eyes. "Can you guess, reverend sir, why I have sent for you?" The sun was behind her, and her countenance not to be read.

He answered, "I will not guess, for I know."

"Then tell me. For, in good sadness, I know not why I did it. Answer freely: you see we are alone."

"Because," answered he, after a moment's silence, "your highness is fugitive and homeless, therefore you did do it; vainly expecting that the will-o'-the-wisp of an old man's fallible counsel should be a lamp to light you home."

"These are strange unlikely words," she said. "I know not how to take them."

"Truth," said Vandermast gently, "was ever a strange wild-fowl."

"Truth! I that was born and bred in Rialmar, where else then shall I be at home? I that am your Queen, how should I be a fugitive, and from what?"

"To be here before your time is to be homeless. And the necessity you flee from is necessity by this cause only, that yourself (albeit I think you have forgotten) did choose it to make it so."

The violent blood suffused all her face and neck, and with the suddenness of her half-rising from her seat the rich and costly embroidery slid from her lap and lay crumpled on the ground. She sat back again: "I see you are but some phantastical sophister who with speaking paradoxically will gain the reputation of wisdom and reach. I'll listen to no more."

"I am nought else," answered that aged man, painfully upon one knee retrieving the fallen satins, "than your highness's creature and servant. You do misprize, moreover, the words I spake, referring unto one particular accident what was meant in a generality more loftily inclusive." Then, standing again in respectful reverence before her, "And yet, it fits," he said, under his breath as to himself only; but the Queen, with head bowed as before over her needle-work, seemed to shrink, as though the words touched her on a wound.

"I have lost my needle," she said. "No. Here it is." Then, after a long pause, still sewing, and as out of a deep unhappiness: "Will the gull choose, to dash herself against the Pharos light?[4] Will a seaman, where the tide runs in the wind's teeth between skerry and skerry, choose to be there in a boat without a rudder? Why should I?"

"How shall any earthly being but your highness's self answer that? Perhaps 'twas in the idle desire to feel your power."

With that, the Queen's hand stopped dead. "And you are he they tell me can read a man's destiny in his eyes? Can you not read in mine," and she raised her head to meet his gaze, "that I have no power? that I am utterly alone?"

"The King's power is your power."

She said, resuming her sewing, "I begin to dread it is not even his."

"It is yours, will you but use it."

She said, bending her white neck yet more to hide her face, "I begin to think I have lost the knack to use it." Then, scarce to be heard: "Perhaps even the wish."

Doctor Vandermast held his peace. His eyes were busied between this woman and this statue: this, more like in its outward, may be, to the unfacing reality, but of itself unreal, a mere mathematic, a superficies: that other real, but yet, save for an inner and outer loveliness, unlike, because wanting self-knowledge; and yet putting on, by virtue of that very privation, a perfection unique and sufficient unto itself albeit not belonging to the divine prototype at the fulness of Her actual; even as the great lamp of day has at sunrise and at sunset perfections of uncompleteness of transience which are consumed or blotted out in the white flame of noon.

"You are a strange secret man," she said presently, still without looking up, "that I should have spoke to you thus: things I'd a spoken to no creature else in the world. And, until today, ne'er so much as set eyes on you." Then, suddenly gathering up her needle-work, "But you give me no help. No more than the other standers by or hinderers."

He said, "There is none hath the ability to help your highness, except only your highness's self alone."

"Here's cold comfort, then. Yet against burning, I suppose, there may be some good in coldness."

She rose now and walked a turn or two in silence, coming to a stand at last under the statue; looking up at which, and with a face averted from that aged doctor, she said to him, "True it is, I did send for you in a more weightier matter than this of me. I have a son."

"Yes."

"Can you read stars and significations in the heaven?"

"Be it indeed," he replied, "that in the university of Miphraz I did seven years apply my youth to study in the Ultramundanes and the Physicals, I have long since learnt that there is no answer in the mouth of these. My study is now of the darkness rather which is hid in the secret places of the heart of man: my office but only to understand, and to watch, and to wait."

"Well, have you seen the child? What find you in him? Give me in a word your very thought. I must have the truth." She turned and faced him. "Even and the truth be evil."

"If it be truth," said the doctor, "it can in no hand be evil; according to the principle of theoric, *Quanto est, tanto bonum,* which is as much as to say that completeness of reality and completeness of goodness are, *sub specie aeternitatis,* the same. I have beheld this child like as were I to behold some small scarce discernible first paling of the skies to tomorrow's dawn, and I say to you: Here is day."

"To be King in his time?"

"So please the Gods."

"In Fingiswold, after his father?"

"So, and more. To be the stay of the whole world."

"This is heavenly music. Shall't be by power, or but by fortune?"

"By power," answered Vandermast. "And by worth."

The Queen caught a deep breath. "O, you have shown me a sweet morn after terrible dreams. But also a strange noise in my head, makes stale the morning: by what warrant must I believe you?"

"By none. You must believe not me, but the truth. I am but a finger pointing. And the nearest way for your highness (being a mortal) to believe that truth, and the sole only way for it to take body and effect in this world, is that you should act and make it so."

"You are dark to me as yet."

"I say that whether this greatness shall be or not be, resteth on your highness alone."

She turned away and hid her face. When, after a minute, she looked around at him again, she reached out her hand for him to kiss. "I am not offended with you," she said. "There was an instant, in that wild talk of ours, I could have cut your throat. Be my friend. God knows, in the path I tread, uneven, stony, and full of bogs, I need one."

Vandermast answered her, "Madam and sweet Mistress, I say to you again, I am yours in all things. And I say but again that your highness's self hath the only power able to help you. Rest faithful to that perfectness which dwelleth within you, and be safe in that."

III

NIGRA SYLVA,[1] WHERE THE DEVILS DANCE

THAT NIGHT Prince Aktor startled out of his first sleep from an evil dream that had in it nought of reasonable correspondence with things of daily life but, in an immediacy of pure undeterminable fear, horror and loss that beat down all his sense to deadness, as with a thunder of monstrous wings, hurled him from sleep to waking with teeth a-chatter, limbs trembling, and the breath choking in his throat. Soon as his hand would obey him, he struck a light and lay sweating with the bedclothes huddled about his ears, while he watched the candle-flame burn down almost to blueness then up again, and the slow strokes of midnight told twelve. After a little, he blew it out and disposed himself to sleep; but sleep, standing iron-eyed in the darkness beside his bed, withstood all wooing. At length he lighted the candle once more; rose; lighted the lamps on their pedestals of steatite and porphyry; and stood for a minute, naked as he was from bed, before the great mirror that was on the wall between the lamps, as if to sure himself of his continuing bodily presence and verity. Nor was there any unsufficientness apparent in the looking-glass image: of a man in his twenty-third year, slender and sinewy of build, well strengthened and of noble bearing, dark-brown hair, somewhat swart of skin, his face well featured, smooth shaved in the Akkama fashion, big-nosed, lips full and pleasant, and having a delicateness and a certain proudness and a certain want of resolution in their curves, well-set ears, bushy eye-brows, blue eyes with dark lashes of an almost feminine curve and longness.

Getting on his nightgown he brimmed himself a goblet of red wine from the flagon on the table at the bed-head, drank it, filled again, and this time drained the cup at one draught. "Pah!" he said. "In sleep a man's reason lieth drugged, and these womanish fears and scruples that our complete mind would laugh and away with, unman us at their pleasure." He went to the window and threw back the curtains: stood looking out a minute: then, as if night had too many eyes, extinguished the lamps and dressed hastily by moonlight, and so to the window again, pausing in the way to pour out a third cup of wine and, that being quaffed down, a fourth, which being but two parts filled left the flagon empty. Round and above him, as he leaned out now on the sill of the open window, the night listened, warm and still; wall, gable and buttress silver and black under the moonshine, and the sky about the moon suffused with a radiancy of violet light that misted the stars. Aktor said in himself, "Desire without action is poison. Who said that, he was a wise man." As though the unseasonable mildness of this calm, un-clouded March midnight had breathed suddenly a frozen air about him, he shivered, and in the same instant there dropped into that pool of silence the marvel of a woman's voice singing, light and bodiless, with a wildness in its rhythms and with every syllable clean and sharp like the tinkle of broken icicles falling:

> "Where, without the region earth,
> Glacier and icefall take their birth,
> Where dead cold congeals at night
> The wind-carv'd cornices diamond-white,
> Till those unnumbered streams whose flood
> To the mountain is instead of blood
> Seal'd in icy bed do lie,
> And still'd is day's artillery,
> Near the frost-starr'd midnight's dome
> The oread keeps her untim'd home.
> From which high if she down stray,
> On th' world's great stage to sport and play,
> There most she maketh her game and glee
> To harry mankind's obliquity."

So singing, she passed directly below him, in the inky shadow of the wall. A lilting, scorning voice it was, with overtones in it of a tragical music as from muted strings, stone-moving but as out of a stone-cold heart: a voice to send tricklings down the spine as when the night-raven calls, or the whistler shrill, whose call is a fore-tast-

ing of doom. And now, coming out into clear moonlight, she turned
about and looked up at his window. He saw her eyes, like an animal's eyes, throw back the glitter of the moon. Then she resumed
her way, still singing, toward the northerly corner of the courtyard
where an archway led to a cloistered walk which went to the
Queen's garden. Aktor stood for a short moment as if in doubt;
then, his heart beating thicker, undid his door, fumbled his way
down the stone staircase swift as he might in the dark, and so out
and followed her.

The garden gate stood open, and a few steps within it he overtook her. "You are a night-walker, it would seem, and in strange
places."

"So much is plain," said she, and her lynx-like eyes looked at
him.

"Know you who this is that do speak to you?"

"O yes. Prince by right in your own land, till your own land put
you out; and thereafter prince here, and but by courtesy. Which is
much like egg without the meat: fair outsides, but small weight and
smaller profit. I've heard some unbitted tongues say, 'princox.' "

"You are a bold little she-cat," he said. Again a shivering took
him, bred of some bite in the air. "There is frost in this garden."

"Is there? Your honour were wiser leave it and go to bed,
then."

"You must first do me this kindness, mistress. Bring me to the
old man your grandsire."

"At this time of night?"

"There is a thing I must ask him."

"You are a great asker."

"What do you mean?" he said, as might a boy caught unawares
by some uncloaking of his mind he had safely supposed well hid.

Anthea bared her teeth. "Do you not wish you had my art, to
see in the dark?" Then, with a shrug: "I heard him tell you, this
afternoon, he had no answer to questions of yours."

"I cannot sleep," said Aktor, "for want of his answer."

"There is always the choice to stay awake."

"Will you bring me to him?"

"No."

"Tell me where he sleeps, then, and I will seek him out."

Anthea laughed at the moon. "Hearken how these mortals will
ask and ask! But I am not your nurse, to weary myself with parrot-
ing of *No, no, no,* when a pettish child screams for the nightshade-
berry. You shall have it, though it poison you. Wait here till I inform
him, if so he may deign to come to you."

The prince saw her depart. As a silver birch-tree of the mountains, if it might, should walk, so walked she under the moon. And
the moon, or she so walking, or the wine that was in his veins, or the

thunder of his inward thought, wrought in him to think: "Why blame myself? Am I untrue to my friend and well-doer and dispenser of all my good, if I seek unturningly the good that seems to my incensed brain main good indeed? She is to him but an engine to breed kings to follow him. With this son bred, why, it hath long been apparent and manifest he is through with her: the pure unadulterate high perfection of all that is or ever shall be, is to him but a commodity unheeded hath served his turn. By God, what cares he for me either? That have held her today, thank the Gods (if any Gods there were, save the grand Devil perhaps in Hell that now, if flesh were or spirit were, which is in great doubt, riveth and rendeth my flesh and spirit), in my arms, albeit but for an instant only, albeit she renegued and rejected me, to know that, flesh by flesh, she must be mine to eternity? God! No, but to necessity: eternity is a trash-name. But this is now; and until my death or hers. And what of him? That, by my soul (damn my soul: for there is no soul, but only the animal spirits; and they unknown, save as the brief substance of a dream or a candle burning, that lives but and dies but in her): what surety have I (God damn me) that he meaneth not to sell me to the supplanter (I loathe him to the gallows) sits in my father's seat? Smooth words and sweet predicaments: I am in a mist. Come sight but for a lightning-flash, 'tis folly and madness to trust aught but sight. Seeing's believing. God or Hell, both unbelievable, 'tis time to believe whichever will show me firm ground indeed." He was in a muck sweat. And now, looking at that statue as an enemy, and in the ineluctable grip of indignation and love, each with the frenzy of other doubled upon it by desire, he began to say within himself: "Female Beast! Wisely was that done of men's folly, to fain you a goddess. You, who devour their brains: who ganch them on your hook by their dearest flesh till they are ready to do the abominablest treasons so only they may come at the filthy anodyne you offer them, that is a lesser death in the tasting, that breaks their will and their manhood and, being tasted, leaves them sucked dry of all save shame and emptiness only and sickness of heart. Come to life, now. Move. Turn your false lightless lustful eyes here, that you may see how your method works with me. Would they were right cockatrice's eyes, should look me dead, turn me to a stone,[2] as you are stone: to nothing, as you are nothing."

Swinging round on his heel, with his back to that image which was but as a reflection in shattered mirrors, least unsufficient in its almost changelessness, of that which is everlastingly changing and yet everlastingly perfect and the same, he came face to face with Doctor Vandermast; whose eyes, under this moonlight which has no half-tones, seemed pits of darkness in the bony sockets of a death's-head. "Wisdom," said the doctor, "is seldom in extremes. And I would wish your noble excellency consider how this mischief of blasphemy operateth not against God nor Goddess, who one while find in it diversion and matter for laughter, and another while pass it by as unworth their remark; but it operateth against the blasphemer, as an infection wonderfully deadly to the soul."

Aktor, listening to these words, looked at him aghast, and at the delicate mountain lynx who, with flaming eyes, kept at the doctor's heel. "You who can prophesy of others," he said, "I beseech you deny no longer to prophesy to me of me. The more, since I find your eyes are upon secret thoughts which, afore all things, I'd a supposed mine own and inviolate."

Vandermast answered and said, "Prince, albeit I am not wholly untraded in the noble dark science, and maybe could show you marvels should make your hair turn, I have not an art to discern men's thought; save indeed as any prudent man may discern them, which is to say, in their faces (as but even now, in yours). Neither pretend I to fore-knowledge of things to come."

Aktor said, "You did prophesy, as many can witness, this very day."

"Of whom?"

"Of these lords of Rerek."

"No," replied he. "I did but point to probabilities. It belongeth to human kind ever to desire certainties, but it belongeth as well to the world never to satisfy that desire. God, who wrought all things of nought, is doubtless able to know all things: past, present, or to come, to unbound eternity. But it shall not orderly hereupon ensure that He will elect to make actual that knowledge in very deed even in His own unscrutable inmost Mind. Whether he will so or no, is a question philosophers may wisely leave unanswered. Myself therefore, that am a humble scholar in divine wisdom and a humble seeker of truth, attempt no prophesyings of things to come. Only, observing constantly the train of the world and the bent or aptitude of the mind and heart of this man or of that, I do (so far as by conferring of act and word and outward aspect it be possible to reach some near guess or judgement thereon) now and then speak my thought. But such speech, howsoever it be addressed to unwrap the hid causes and events of things, is of likelihoods only: never of certitudes. For what, in this world, to a man or a woman, which be reasonable beasts, seemeth utterly certain and inevitable, is none the less in doubt and a thing contingent: at its highest, no higher than a probability. And this is because mortals, being that they are free movers, do daily by will or act make, transmute, or unmake again, such seeming certainties. And in action there is but one certainty, and that of God."

"For myself," said Aktor, "I tell you with open face and good conscience, I believe not in God. Nor Devil neither. But wisdom and true-heartedness I can embrace when I do see them; and I do embrace them in you. My perplexities are like to turn me into madness, and they are matters it were unsafe to give a hint of, but to mine own heart and liver, under my skin. For pity sake, speak to me. Let me entreat to know what likelihoods attend for me."

That learned man surveyed him awhile in silence. "I did constantly refuse this, for the sufficient reason that I could not understand your excellency clearly enough to speak aught save upon conjecture. But I do now understand you more thoroughly, but still I am slow to speak; because I judge your nature to be of that dangerous complexion that, hearing what I should have to tell you, you would like as not misapply it to so high a strain as should soon or late call you to a fearful audit."

Aktor said, "I swear to you, you do misjudge me."

"And yet," said Vandermast, sitting now on the bench, while the Prince waited for his words as a suitor waits before a judge for judgement, and this lynx sat elegantly on her haunches against the doctor's knee, licking her fur: "And yet, who am I to set impediments in the path of the strainable force of destiny? To hide from your excellency the matters I see, were (it might with some colour be argued) to deprive you of the chance which They who command the great wheel of things do intend for you: the chance to choose between the worser course and the better not by luck nor by sway of mood, as appetite might egg forward or timorousness hold you back, but by reasoned judgement of right and wrong. And be it that, knowing what hangeth on your choice, you must run the hazard of a wrong choice which would damn you quite and so end you, yet have you it *in potentiâ* (if your choice be noble) to make your name great and honoured among generations yet unborn. A wicked fault therefore it were in me if I should rest silent and thus, intermeddling (albeit but by abstinence) betwixt you and the unlike destinies which contend together to entertain your soul, should leave you but a weak creature uncharactered, such as of whom saith the philosopher that weak natures can attain to greatness in nothing, neither to great good nor to great evil." He paused. Those upright glowing slits, which, in the lynx's eyes staring at the Prince, were instead of pupils, pulsed with yellow fire. The frost in the garden deepened. "Know then that I seem to find in you," said the doctor: "That you are like to be in such case that, slaying your friend, you should gain a kingdom; and again, that, sparing your enemy, you should slay your only friend. Upon which matters," he said, and the voice of him was now as very frostbite in the air, "and upon whether they shall seem fit to you to be embraced and followed or (by contraries) to be eschewed and renounced, resteth (I suppose) your bliss or bale unto everlasting."

When Doctor Vandermast had so ended, Aktor, standing like a stone, seemed to consider with himself. Then, even in that moonlight, the flush of blood darkened his face, and he, that had held himself but now like a suppliant, stood like a king, his breast mightily broadened and his shoulders squared. Suddenly, glancing over his shoulder as lions do before they charge, he took a step towards the doctor, checked himself, and said, his words coming thick and stumbling like a drunken man's: "You have spoke better than you know, old man: lanced the imposthume in my breast and freed me for action, and that to the very tune I have these many weeks heard drumming in my head, but till now my fond doubts and scruples used me for their fool and rein'd me back from it. My friend: him, my seeming friend: yes, I'll kill him and be King in his place: who is my vile unshowing enemy, and to spare him were as good as go kill my only very friend in the world; and that is, her. About it, then. But 'cause you know so much, and 'cause I'll take no hazards, I'll first settle you: put you where you shall not blab."

With that he leapt at the doctor and seized him, whose tall lean body in his clutches seemed fleshless and light as the pitiful frame of a little moulted hen that seems frail as a sparrow under her sparse remnant of feathers; but the lynx bit him cruelly in the leg, that he as swiftly let go his hold upon Vandermast. His hand jumped to his belt for a weapon, but in that haste of coming down from his chamber he had forgot it. He beat her furiously about the head with his fists, but got naught for it but bloody knuckles, for she stuck like a limpet, her fore-claws deep in the fleshy parts of his thigh, her hind-claws scrabbling and gashing his calves and shins like razors. All this in a few brief moments of time, till staggering backwards, heedless of all save the bitter mischief of her teeth and claws and the agony to rid this horror which clung to his flesh like a plaster of burrowing fire, he tripped upon his heel at the pond's brink and fell plump in. His head struck the statue's plinth as he fell, which had well been the end of him, to drown there senseless in two foot depth of water. But may be the cold ducking brought him to himself; for scarce had Anthea, letting go as he fell, come out of her lynx-shape to stand, nymph once more, by the water-side, than he crawled to land again painfully, drenched and dripping.

That oread lady said to the doctor, "Shall I rip his belly open up to the chin?"

But Vandermast, lending him a hand to find his feet again, answered, "No."

Aktor, for all the ache and smart of his wounds, could not forbear to laugh. "You are of a better disposition, I see, than this hot-reined stew-pot of yours, to say nought of that hell-cat you did set upon me. Where is it?"

Mistress Anthea curled her lip: turned away from him. The classic beauty of her face, thus sideways, was like an ivory in the fireless pure glimmer of the moon.

Aktor said, " 'Twas never in my heart, learned sir, to a done you any hurt. 'Twas in a way of taste only: trying your metal."

"I am glad to hear that," replied he dryly. "As for her, 'tis a most innocent animal, howsoever nature hath armed her most magnificently: fell to action, it is true, somewhat hastily (like as did your excellency), and with no setting on by me. As well, perhaps, that she did; for fighting is an art I am scantly customed to, both by natural inclination and as being somewhat entered in years. You did take me, also, a little by surprise, bursting forth into such a sudden violence; which I hope you will henceforth be less ready unto, and will wisely bethink you beforehand, using meditations and weighings of *pro* and *contra*, afore you begin to attack men. But as for the wounds your excellency did (to consider the matter honestly), do unto yourself, here is better than any leech to their speedy healing"; and Anthea, a little impatiently at the doctor's bidding, using simples that he gave her from his purse, washed, dressed, and bound up with bandages torn from the gauze of her skirt, the evidences of her expert science in claw-work.

IV

THE BOLTED DOORS

SO ENDED the twelfth day and last, of that marriage-feast in Rialmar. Upon the morrow, guests took their farewells and departed: a few betimes (and earliest among these that ancient doctor and his questionable she-disciple); but the most part of them, suiting by just anticipation the measure to be set them by bride and bridegroom, lay till past midday. The Lord Emmius tarried but to greet his brother and sister and, for the while, bid them adieu. In mark of singular favour the King and Queen brought him to the gate, and so, parting with them in the greatest esteem and friendship, he rode off with his train by the great south road.

Supervius and his bride, it was given out, would remain yet another week in Rialmar. But when it came to the day for their departure, Marescia said she would stay yet a full week more: let her lord go now with the baggage and stuff, and see all prepared orderly against her home-coming to Laimak. This absurdly, with no further reason assigned; but folk thought it sprung of her insolency and the wish, since she was now wife, to be not only his mistress still (as were right and fitting) but her great master's master. Howe'er that might be, upon that twenty-fifth of March Supervius rode south without her.

He being gone, with the honourable leave-taking as his brother

631

had had, and the King and Queen being now returned up to Teremne, Stateira, with her hand upon her Lord's arm as he came his
way to his private chamber, prayed him gently that she might come
too. "I am infinitely full of business, madam," he said. "But come if
you must."

In that chamber, which was round and domed and with great
windows looking east to the mountains, were tables and heavy
chairs old and curiously carved, and, between the pillars of polished
marble jet-black with yellow and purple veins in it which ranged at
every two paces along the walls, presses with shelves to put books in.
Upon a hearth well fifteen foot wide a fire of sweet-scented
cedarwood was crackling and blazing, and the floor was carpeted to
within two or three feet of the walls with russet-coloured velvet that
the foot sank in, giving warmth in winter and silence all the year.
But the King, crossing to the further side, undid with his secret keys
the ponderous iron-studded doors, an outer and an inner, of his
closet, and, when she had followed him in, locked both behind
them. For here was the close work-house of his most deep-laid policies, and to it neither counsellor nor secretary had ever admittance:
not Aktor even, to whom men noted he showed, more and more
this last year or two, the kindly and dear respect due to a loved
kinsman or very son. But the Queen, it was said, was partner to all
its secrets; and a light misspeaking it was, that were she invited more
oftener to his bed and seldomer to his chancery, there were a custom all the ladies in the court could be envious of, to be owl in such
an ivy-bush.

The closet measured but five or six foot-paces either way. Cup-
boards of black iron with latches of silver lined the walls from ceiling
to floor, and here, as in the outer chamber, was the like deep-piled
velvet carpet. A long table of green prassius stone, resting on six legs
of solid gold in the semblance of hippogriffs with wings spread, was
under the window, and a great chair, hard-cushioned (seat, back,
and arms) with dark, wine-coloured silk brocade, was set at the table
to face the light. Upon that table papers and parchments lay thick as
autumn leaves: here an unsteady pile with an armoured glove for
paperweight: there another, capped with a hand-mace to keep them
together: great maps, some in scrolls, one at the far end of the table,
unrolled and held down flat with inkstands at two corners and a
heavy ivory ruler at a third. Into which seeming chaos King
Mardanus when he had thrown himself down in that chair, began
now to dig; and easy it was to see that what to the general eye were
confusion was in his capable mind no such matter, but orderly,
where whatsoever scrap or manuscript he had need of came instant
to his fingers' ends.

"Still Akkama?" said the Queen, after watching him awhile
from between table and window.

"What else?" he said, clearing a space before him by pitching a heap of letters on the floor by his chair. "Do you expect that business to be huddled up in a week or two?"

"It has trickled on for years. I wish it were ended."

"It moves," said the King. "And moves at the pace I mean it shall. There's his latest letters missive (God give him a very mischief): pressing most sweetly for the handing over of Aktor": he tossed it across the table.

She let it lie. "Well, hand him over."

King Mardanus, for the first time, looked swiftly up at her; but there was nought in his look beyond such shock as a tutor might betray, having from his chosen pupil a foolish answer.

"Nay, I meant not that," she said hastily. "But yet: poor Akkama. 'Tis a pardonable impatience, surely, seeing he broached that demand two years since. Wonder is, he does not drop it."

"No wonder in that," said the King. "I keep it alive: I mean not to let him drop it. Here's reports from two or three sure intelligencers, imports Aktor's faction puts on flesh, grows to admired purchase. Treat with the one and bolster up t'other: these two'll cut each other's throats i' the end. Then I walk in: take what I please."

The Queen said, "Yes, I know. That is our policy," and fell silent as if held in a still, strained eagerness, between the desire to ask a thing and the terror lest, asked, it should be denied, and thus leave the matter in worse posture than before. She said suddenly, "I wish, dear my Lord, you would send Aktor away."

The King stared at her.

"I wish you would."

"What, back to Akkama? That were a dastard's deed I'd be sorry for."

"Never that. But send him away from Rialmar. Let him go where he will."

"And fall in all kind of mischief? No, no. Safest here, under my hand. Besides, 'twere pure lunacy: discard the knave of trumps i' the middle of the game."

"He does no good here."

The King sat back in his chair. "Why are you so stubborn set of a sudden to be rid of him? What harm does he do to you?"

"None at all," she paused. He said nothing. "I advise you," she said, "make clean riddance of him."

Mardanus, as if troubled by some urgence in her voice that he could ill understand, looked hard in her face. But if there were characters writ in it they were in a language he was as little schooled in as was his two-year-old son in the Greek. "But why?" he said at last.

"Because I ask you."

"The best of all reasons, madam" (she interrupted, under her breath, "It used to be"): "but not a reason of state. Come, come," he said, still watching her narrowly, and his brows frowned as with some mounting anger at this insisting, without all reason, upon a thing of so small weight or moment to fool away his time withal: "Woman's nonsense. The boy wants his revenge; wants to be his own again: wants to be king. And all these are appetites make him meat for us. Why, he is the peg my whole design's hung upon. No need for you to be troubled with him; but I will for no sake let him go. Besides," he said, turning again to his papers, "I love him well. Were't but to play chess a-nights with, which is a prime merit in him, I'll not forgo his company."

Queen Stateira bit her lip. He reached for the letter from the King of Akkama, took his goose-quill pen and, slowly and awkwardly as with fingers to which such an instrument comes with less handsomeness than a sword or a spear, yet steadily without pause nor doubt, as one under no necessities to search for words to fit his clear-built purpose, fell to drafting of his reply. The Queen, noiselessly on that deep carpet, came round behind him: hovered a moment: bent, and kissed his head. He wrote on, without sign that he was any longer ware of her presence. 'I must go,' she said. The King sprang up: undid the doors for her. As she came into the outer chamber, where at a side-table the King's secretary was setting papers in order, the great iron locks clashed home behind her.

Not until she was well shut in the privacy of her own room, did she unmask. There, thrown, as on a bed of snakes, between (like enough) some drunkenness in her blood strained up by Aktor and (like enough, for the moment) a scalding indignation against the King, she let go all and wept.

V

PRINCESS MARESCIA

T HE LORD Supervius Parry, albeit with pace slowed by a long train of pack-horses laden with wedding gifts and nine-tenths of Marescia's wardrobe, came by great journeys south over the wind-scourged wastes of the Wold, and so down to Megra, and thence by Eldir and Leveringay to Mornagay. Thence, taking the bridle-path over the mountains (which is steep, dirty and dangerous, but shorter and more expeditious than the low road south-about by Hornmere and Owldale), he came, after a three-and-a-half-weeks' journey from Rialmar without stay or mishap, on the afternoon of the seventeenth of April, home to Laimak. Here were preparations already completed for his return, but for the next seven days he set all his household folk to toil and moil as if three-score devils were at their tails, labouring to turn his own private quarters above Hagsby's Entry into a fit place to lodge a bride in, to whom luxurious splendours were but the unremarkable and received frame proper to ordinary polity and civility. And doubtless it would have ill suited his intents, were his great house of Laimak to show in her eyes as little better than a rude soldier's hold, or she to suppose him content that here from hence-forward she should live like a hog. By the week's end, all was altered and nicely ordered to his liking, and the folk about the castle set agog for impatience to welcome home so great and

635

famous a lady as history hath not remembered among those that had been mistress here aforetime.

But as day followed day and yet no word or sign of the Princess, men began to wonder. Nor did they find wholesome nor comfortable their lord's thunderous silences that deepened and darkened as the days passed; nor his sometimes flashings into unforeknowable violence, which, like flashings of lightning, struck with impartial chanceableness and frightening suddenness who or what soever happed in their path at their blasting-time.

Between sunset and dark on the second day of May, it being a clear evening with the stars coming out in a rain-washed sky after a day of down-pour and tempest, Supervius was pacing to and fro in the great courtyard: slow, measured steps with a swift caged-beast turn-about at either end of the walk. Laughably in manner of a farm-lad who approaches an untethered bull of uncertain temper that may suffer him to draw near, then, without gare or beware, rush upon him and destroy him, came the captain of his bodyguard: said there was a lady below at the gate, alone and on horseback, would answer no questions as concerning her name or condition, but demanded to be brought instant before their master.

Supervius glowered at him. 'Hast seen the woman?'

'No, my lord.'

'You lewd misordered villain, why not, then? Why is she not brought to me here, if she asks that?'

'Because of your lordship's command, that no unknown person shall be admitted without your lordship's pleasure first known. 'Twas referred to me by the officer o' the guard for tonight, to learn your will, my lord, what he must do with her.'

'I would the Devil had her, and you to the bargain.'

The captain waited.

Supervius took another turn. 'Well, why is she not fetched up?'

The captain, with a low leg, departed: came again the next minute with the Princess Marescia Parry in pitiful disarray. Supervius looked at her, and the whole poise of his body seemed to stiffen. 'Leave us,' he said, resuming his to's and fro's. When they were alone he came to a halt and stood there, looking at her. Not a muscle in him stirred, save that a quick ear might catch a thickness and a tumultuousness in his breathing and a keen eye note the eyes of him in this half-light, while he watched her as a trained dog points at game. The Princess, for her part, held a like silence and a like stillness. Even in this gathering dusk it was easy to see she was as a very dowdy or slut, dirted and dishevelled with long hard riding, and hard lying may be, in the open field; and, for all she bore herself bravely enough, there was that in her that said, for all her speechlessness and the firmness of her lip, that she held it good her travels were over and she, howsoever miserably, here at last. With bull-like deliberation he began now to move towards her: then, as he came near, seized her in like sort and to like purpose (but with all unlike effect) as Tarquin seized Lucrece.[1] Marescia was a big woman and a strong, but in a twinkling he had her up in his arms and in under the huge shadowy archway of Hagsby's Entry. Thence, without pause for breath, and despite her inarticulate protests and gusts of astonished half-smothered laughter, he carried her up the dark stairs of his own chamber trimmed up on purpose for her with those sumptuous costly furnishings he had brought south with him, and there, without ceremony, and quite unregarding of the pickle she was in, rain-soaked riding-habit and muddied boots, disposed her on the bed.

'Nay, and now tell me, you sweet-breath'd monkey,' said Supervius, upon his elbow, and with his face at near range looking down at hers. She lay there supine: out-played and tamed for the while: closed eyes, half-closed lips: head turned away, exposing so into view her throat, smooth, sleek, white, like some Titan woman's, and the pulse of blood in it: one hand twining and untwining and straying and losing itself in the curled masses of his great red beard, the other yet straining down on his hand which rested upon her breast.

'Shorn of my train,' she answered presently, in a sleepy voice that seemed to taste pleasure in its own displeasure: 'tooken like a common cut-purse by my own folk: should a been clapt up in prison too, I think, and I'd not given 'em the slip. I hope you deserve me, my lord: so good faithful a wife, and a so quick contriver of means. There's this in you, that you love me impatiently. I'd ne'er stomach you less than greedy.' Then, suddenly springing up: 'In the Devil's name, how much longer must I famish here without my supper?'

'Shall be here in the flick of a cat's tail.'

'Well, but I'll dress first,' said Marescia.

'Mean time, tell me more. So far 'tis the mere chirping of frogs: terrible words I scantly believe and can make no sense of.'

'I'll dress first,' she said, opening a cupboard or two and, with some satisfaction, seeing her clothes hang there that came on before with Supervius. 'Nor not with you for looker-on, neither, my lord. Who suffers her husband in her dressing-chamber, were as good turn him off to go nest with wagtails. Where did I learn that, think you? From my mother's milk, I think. 'Tis native wisdom, certain.'

Supper was in the old banquet-hall, that was built in shape like an L, having a row of great windows in the long north-western wall, a main door, opening on the courtyard, at the far end, and a door going to the buttery and kitchens at the end of the shorter arm of the L. On the inner angle was the hearth, capacious enough to roast a neat, and a fire burning, of mighty logs. The walls were of black obsidian stone, and upon all save that which had windows were huge devilish faces, antic grotesco-work, cut in high relief, thirteen, with their tongues out, and upon each tongue's tip a lamp; and the goggling eyes of them were of looking-glass artificially cut in facets to disperse the beams of the lamplight in bushes of radiance, so that the hall was filled with light that shifted and glittered ever as the beholder moved his head. Long tables ran lengthways down the main hall, one on either side, and here the Lord Supervius's home-men were set at meat.

When the great leaved doors were flung wide and the Lady Marescia Parry, for this her first time, entered in state, gorgeously attired now in her bridal gown of white chamlet and lace of gold and with her yellow hair braided and coiled in bediamonded splendour above her brow, every man leapt from his seat and stood up to honour her and to feast his gaze upon her; while she, not a filly unridden but with the step and carriage of a war-horse and with bold chestnut eyes flashing back the bright lights, passed up between the benches on her lord's arm to take her place with him at the high table, which stood alone upon a dais in the north corner opposite the fire. Here, in sight but out of ear-shot of all other parts of that banquet hall, were covers laid for two.

'And now?' said Supervius, when they were set. He brimmed his goblet with a rough tawny wine from the March lands and drank to her, pottle-deep.

'And now?' said she, pushing her cup towards him. 'Well, pour me out to drink, then. Is these Rerek manners? a man to bib wine while's wife, out of a parched mouth, shall serve him up tittle-tattle?'

He filled. She swallowed it down at a single gulp, first savouring it curiously on her tongue. 'To go to the heart of the matter,' she said, 'as touching mine own particular, I long since took a mislike to that Aktor. The Queen I love well, albeit but cousins by affinity (not german, as I was to the King). And in this pernicious pass, with the whole land in a turmoil, besides fury and sedition of the rude people grown in the late unhappy accident, methought it likely Aktor would use her for his fool: she being caught in a forked stick betwixt doting of him (as I, of my quick sense, have precisely long suspected) and fearing for her son, and thus uncapable of firm action; while this hot-backed devil, under colour of her authority, more and more carrieth the whole sway of the court. So, to cut the Gordian knot and do for her (no leave asked) what, might she but be unbesotted, she must know to be most needful, I fled with the King before a soul could note it, meaning to have him away with me hither into Rerek. But they caught me in two days: took the child back to Rialmar, and would—'

'A burning devil take you!' said Supervius, breaking in upon this: 'what misty Tom-a-Bedlam talk have we here? of Aktor: and the Queen: and you ran with the King's highness to Rerek? are you out of your wits, woman? Are you drunk?'

Marescia stared as if stupefied at his amazement. Then, clapping down her hand on his where it grasped the table's edge, 'Why, is't possible?' she said, her sight clearing. 'I'm yet here faster than news can travel, then? Faith, I've lost all count of time i' this huggermugger, and know not what day it is. Hadn't you not heard, then, of King Mardanus's death: tenth day after our wedding?'

Supervius sat for a moment like a man stricken blind. 'Dead? On what manner? By what means?'

'Good lack, they murdered him up. By a hired rascal from Akkama stol'n into Teremne. So at least 'twas given out. But (in your secret ear) I am apt to think 'twas Aktor did it. Or by Aktor's setting on.'

The Lord Supervius drank deep. She watched him turn colour, pale then red again, and his brow became as a storm-cloud. She said, 'I see't hath troubled you near. Say you: begin you now to think that was an ill cast you threw then, when you married with me?'

'O hold your tongue with such foolishness: I think no such matter.'

'That's as well, then. I gave you credit for that.'

Supervius, as brooding darkly on this new turn, ate and drank without more words said. The Princess followed suit, now and then casting a glance at him to see, if she might, what way the wind was shifting. After a long time he looked at her and their eyes met. Marescia said, 'Yet I'm sorry they got the child Mezentius from me. Better he were here, for his and our most advantage, rather than with's mother, if Aktor must rule the roast there. And yet, 'tis a roast we may yet draw sustainment from, God turning all to the best.'

Her lord looked still at her with an unmoved stare that, from a bullish sullenness, changed by little and little to the stare of a proud ambitious man at a looking-glass that glads him with the express counter-shape of his best-loved self. 'Come sweet heart,' he said then, 'we will closely to these matters. And somewhat we'll presently devise, doubt it not, much to our good. But I'll take my brother Emmius with me, or I move one step on the road I seem to see before me.'

He bade his steward, supper now being done, dismiss all the company. And so, private in that banquet-hall, hour by hour, till the lamps began to flicker and go out and only the glow of embers on the hearth showed them each other's faces, he and she sat long into the night, talking and devising.

VI

Prospect North from Argyanna

EMMIUS PARRY had sat now more than four years in Argyanna, keeping house there in so high a style as not in all Rerek had its example, but yet to compare with Rialmar in the northlands or Zayana of the south it should have seemed no such great matter. It was thought that, need arising, he could at any time upon three days' notice set forth an army of a thousand men weaponed at all points and trained in all arts of war: this not to reckon two hundred picked men-at-arms whom he maintained under his hand at all seasons, for show of power and to keep order, and in readiness for any work he might assign them.

For three or four generations this lonely out-town, set in strength amid untranspassable fens, had been to the Parry in Laimak as a claw stretched forth southward upon the batable lands watered by the river Zenner: an armed camp, governed by the lords of Laimak through officers who were creatures of theirs and servants but never until now men of their own blood and line, in case, from the great strength of the place, it might grow to be a hand which someday, turning against the body it longed to, might break down the whole in ruin.

From Sleaby and Ketterby on the northern part and thence, west-about by the Scrowmire and east-about by the Saylings, to

Scruze and Scrightmirry on the south, the Lows of Argyanna lie ten miles long and as many in breadth. In these Lows is going neither for man nor for beast (be it more than a water-rat or an otter): only the water-fowl inhabit upon that waste of quaking-bogs. The harrier-hawks share out their dominion there by day: the owl (which the house of Laimak have for their badge or cognizance) hunts there by night, when all feathered living beings else are at roost, except the night-jar who preys on night-flying moths that breed in the fen. And through the night hobby-lanterns flicker, hither and thither in the mist and the darkness, above scores of thousands of acres, unpathed, quicksandy, squeltering in moss and slub and sedge.

In the middle of this sea of quagmire is a lone single island of sure footing and solid ground, watered with streams that have their source in a tarn of which no plummet has found the bottom: an unfailing source that puts up pure, cold and sweet from the underrocks, not surface water from the highlands of old Rerek such as feeds the marsh. The firm land stretches a five miles' length northwest to south-east, with a biggest width of about three and a half: all of rich well-husbanded grazings and ploughlands which train upwards towards the north, but nowhere to rise more than twenty foot at most above the marsh-level; except at the head of the land northwestward near the tarn where the northern scarp comes up gently to a flat of perhaps twice that height, to fall again abruptly in a low cliff on the west; and here, wholly ringed about with walls of great thickness and strength, lies Argyanna. The highway from the north, coming down by Hornmere and Ristby and so south through Susdale, strikes the Lows two miles south of Sleaby, and is carried south across them, straight as a carpenter's rule, to Argyanna and so on south to Scrightmirry, by a ten-mile causeway of granite which rests upon oaken piles through mire and ooze to bed on the rock. This road, where it crosses the tongue of land that lies out westward from the fortress, runs along the moat for several hundred paces, and so close under the walls of the main keep that, granted good natural munition and aptitude and a favouring wind from the east, a man on the battlements might spit on a passer-by. The Lord Emmius, when after his father's death he moved household and came down hither from Sleaby, built gate-houses astride of this road: one where the road comes upon the tongue, and that almost within stone-cast of the town wall, and another somewhat farther off where the road leaves land again for the marsh: this the greater and stronger of the two as a hold against the south should occasion require it. In time of peace the gates stood open, and travellers whether rich or poor had free entertainment there and a night's lodging if they would, and all with the greatest open-handedness and largesse.

* * *

Upon the fifth of May, Supervius came with his lady to Argyanna about midday and there had good welcome. When they had eaten, Emmius took them to walk in the sunshine upon the wide paved walk that runs full circle round the top of the keep between the battlements and his private lodging which stood back, full circle, in the midst of it.

'You have a fair prospect southward, lord brother-in-law,' said the Princess, shading her eyes with her hand to look across the Lows to where, between forty and fifty miles away and a little east of south, the Ruyar Pass cuts the mountain spine at the meeting of the Huron range with the peaks of Outer Meszria, carrying the great road over into Meszria itself. 'Where your fancy dallies, they tell me.'

'My wife's home. Should not that be commendation enough?'

The Lady Deïaneira smiled. She was tall: exquisite, whether in movement or at rest, as some fine-limbed shy creature of the woods: high-cheekboned, smooth-skinned and dark, and with eyes dark and lustrous that seemed as by native bent to return always, save when he was watching them, to her lord.

'And yet,' said Marescia, 'you had these tidings from the north, too, two days sooner than I could bring them.'

'I have lived in this world, dear Princess,' said Emmius lightly, 'near five times seven years, and I have learnt the need to have eyes and ears to serve me. Give me, prithee, what you saw with your own eyes. One pinch of fact outweigheth a bushel of hearsay.'

'Ay, tell it as you told it to me,' said Supervius.

Marescia said, "'Twas hear with mine ears first: a cry out of the King's bedchamber, made the gold cups ring on the shelf above my bed and the geese scream in the yard under my window.'[1]

'And that was, when?' said Emmius.

'About first light.'

'Ay, and the day?'

'Fifth morning after my lord here was ridden south. Then a noise of doors flinging open, and the Queen's voice, dreadfully, 'Marescia, Marescia.' So, on with my nightgown and scarce get the door open but her highness's self meets me there into my arms, trembling like a frightened horse: in her hair: nought but her sage-green velvet nightgown upon her: moaneth out over and over, the King's name: bringeth me thither: he on the bed, dead as a door-nail, bolled up huge as a neat, blue and grey and liver-colour, his eyes sticking out like a crab's, and his hair and his beard and his nails all bursten off him.'[2]

Deïaneira's lips pressed together till they whitened, but no sound escaped them.

The Lord Emmius had all this while of Marescia's speaking studied her face, with that gaze of his which commonly seemed, to those on whom it rested, strangely undisturbing; so free of concernment it seemed, effortless and intermittent as a star's among changing clouds, but yet as steadfast too, deep-searching, not to be eluded, and so, when they considered again of it, strangely disturbing, as able to touch and finger their privatest inward thought. He looked away now, past her, to that sun-veiled skyline in the south. 'Tell me, sister-in-law, if you can: slept she by him that night?'

'Never. Not these two years.'

'But would your ladyship a known?'

'If so they did, 'twas a thing without precedent since many months at least.'

'Truth is, we know not. Who was in the chamber when you came in, besides the Queen?'

'Not a soul. O, a woman or two o' the bedchamber I think. Then more. And then Aktor.'

'Who's that?'

'Yonder princox.'

'I remember: I caught not the name as you said it. What made he there? Was he sent for?'

The Princess changed glances with Supervius. 'I cannot tell,' she answered. 'Was in a pretty taking: weeping and lamenting: My dearest friend, my King (and so forth): author of all my good: murdered and dead.'

'In those words? Murdered: said he so?'

'A dozen times.'

'Well?'

'But at first sight of the handiwork, shouts out in a kind of fury or terror to the Queen: God grant you ha'nt touched him, madam? Go not you near, nor any person else, till leeches examine it. Here's the vile murderer's doing I sent last night to sup in Hell: woe that I should a squeezed the sting out of him but not afore he'd sown the poison.'

'What meant that gibberish?'

'Telleth us how, afore supper, he'd caught this rascally instrument of the king of Akkama (had been in Rialmar, it seems, under pretext of service in the buttery or the black guard, quite unsuspected, and for weeks biding his happy chance): Aktor caught him skulking in the private room the King and he were wonted to play chess in—'

'Slip we not there into hearsay?'

''Twas out of Aktor's mouth, in my hearing. Tells us (still in tears) how a had wrung a true tale out of this devil's-bawd—'

Here Emmius looked round at her: a comical glint in his eye. 'Is this still the Prince's words? or is't Princess's gloss?'

'Cry you mercy, 'twas my tongue slipt,' said she. 'Tells us the fellow confessed a was sent a purpose to murder the King's highness (and Aktor too if that might be compassed): says this threw him into so fierce a sweat of anger he killed the man out of hand and, not to mar our evening, huggled the dead carcase into a big box or coffer was there i' the room, to wait till morning. There was an act me thinks smelleth something oddly in this Aktor.'

'What next?'

'Next, Aktor (thinking, belike, enough made of weeping and blubbering) takes charge. Calleth for leeches: shows us the dead vermin stiff and be-bloodied in the box and with Aktor's own dagger sticking in his ribs (a pretty property for such an interlude, that, me thought).'

'Well?'

'Well, those learned men sat in inquest 'pon what was left: 'pon the dead poison-monger, 'pon the King's highness, and 'pon the chessmen. ('Twas pity Aktor thought not sooner the night before, of those chessmen.)'

'That the King and he wont to play with? Had they played with 'em that night?'

'Yes. Nay, I know not for sure. We left them to it, being bed-time.'

'And what found the leeches, then?'

'Upshot was, some nasty pothecary stuff in the King's finger and thumb: had run all over his body: same stuff on one or two chessmen, but the most of 'em pure and harmless: some more of it on the man's knife: conclusion, knife was to do the business had the chess failed.'

She ceased speaking; and Lord Emmius Parry, a cloud on his brow, looked at her in silence for almost a minute. She, with cool smile and hot chestnut eyes, met his gaze steadily as if minded to out-stare him. But as well should a printed page hope to out-stare the reader, as out-stare that eye that looked forth, cold, meditative, ambiguous, and undisturbed, from the iron yet subtle face of the Parry, and rested without distinction of kind, alike upon the landscape, or upon the stone coping of the wall, or (as for this, to her, uneasy minute) upon the challenging eye of this woman, young, fierce-blooded, masterful, who, come to a halt close under him where he halted, set the air about him afire with the agitation of all senses mixed and stirred up in the goblet of her bodily nearness and her domineering will, bent to some end as yet unrevealed. Even just as a reader, having read, looks up from his book to ruminate the matter he has read there, Lord Emmius turned now from her and, standing a little apart by the battlements, in the same remote meditation remained awhile, looking south. The Princess, left so, albeit scarcely victorious, in possession of the field, said apart to her lord, the hot blood suffusing all her fair face and brow even to the roots of the shining yellow hair that was drawn with a smaragdine fillet sleekly up from it and from behind her ears, 'Was it fitly spoken, think you?'

'Beyond admiration well,' he answered, taking his arm about her.

'No case argued, as yet.'

'No, no. It needs not.'

'He is a man I'd rather have before me than against me: your brother,' she said, and let her voluptuous weight settle closelier in the assurance of Supervius's strong encircling arm, while still she watched the Lord Emmius. Deïaneira, with a look in her sweet secret Meszrian eyes more deeplier composed, more akin to his, watched him too. A man worth their eyes he seemed, standing there: towering above them in bodily height, save Supervius, and above him for settled majesty of bearing: loose-limbed and of so much reposement of easy power, his left hand, a true Parry hand, beyond the ordinary in breadth and strength and with broad spatula-shaped fingers, yet long-fingered as a woman's, resting on the stone battlement, his right crooked in his jewelled belt. His bonnet of black velvet sat tilted across his brow: there was a set lift and downward trend of his eyebrows, betokening thought, and a breadth and heaviness in the upper lids. His nose, great, high-bridged and (like the fox's) scenting to all airts, wore a pride and a keenness of discrimination on every fine-carved surface of it: so too the lean flats of his cheek-bones and the sternness and strength of his mouth, partly veiled by a melancholy downward sweep of dark mustachios. His beard, sedulously brushed and tended, thinned to a certain sparseness of growth betwixt the mouth's corners and the chin, undiscovering so a taint of heaviness and hard implacability in his under lip.

He turned to face them now, his back against the battlement and the light behind him. 'But why, dear sister-in-law, will you think Prince Aktor the author of that deed?'

'I never said I thought so,' replied she.

'No. But it peeped from behind most every word you said.'

'Well, truly, I think it not unlikely.'

'Why disbelieve his story?' said Emmius. 'Doth anyone else? What avail to him, thus to bite the hand that fed him?'

Marescia laughed. 'Best avail of all, seeing a loveth the Queen's person to distraction. And she him.'

Emmius paused: raised an eyebrow. 'Be not discontent with me,' he said, 'if I question your ladyship somewhat sharply. The matter is of highest moment. Mean you that he acquainted himself over familiarly and unhonestly with the King's wife?'

'At a word, I do.'

'And that he and she had nothing more in their vows than his serene highness's ruin?'

'O you miss my sense abominably!' she said. 'Kill me dead at your feet if I'd e'er credit Stateira with any such wicked purpose. Him, yes.'

'Then why not her?'

''Cause I have known her since children, like a book. 'Cause it lies not in her good nature.'

'I praise your trusting affection,' said Emmius with a crooked smile. 'But remember, good qualities are easier spoilt than bad ones.'

They began to walk again, in silence till they were come more than full circle round the battlements of the great keep: Emmius with long deliberate stride, hands clasped behind him, eyes moody and lightless under half-lowered moody lids: Supervius (as if policy, counselling attend and wait, strove within him against a wolfish impatience that ill can stomach delays) opening once and again his mouth to speak, and as swiftly shutting it after a sidelong glance at his brother: the Lady Deïaneira walking as some mislaid remnant of a perfumed summer night might miraculously walk here in the face of day, between this rockish imperturbability upon her one side and that hunger for action upon the other: the Lady Marescia tasting and managing, with her bare hand linked in his, Supervius's chafing, the while she studied, all uncertainly as she must and with jealous despiteful eye, weather-signs in Emmius.

When he spoke, it was to shift no clouds. 'It is all misty stories and conjecture,' he said to Supervius. 'The one clear act was when she (as you told me at first) made to steal away the boy. But (no blame to her) that miscarried.'

Supervius said, 'Question is, what to do? And that suddenly. Whether Aktor's hand was in it or not, I account him neither fool nor weakling. He is like to seize kingdom now if we give him time to settle in his seat.'

Marescia covertly gripped his hand: whispered, 'Enough said. Better it come out of his mouth than ours: will love his own brat better than a stepchild.'

'One thing I see,' said Emmius: 'what's best not to do.' His eye, cold and direct, moved from his brother to his brother's wife, and so back again. 'Some would counsel you levy an army and ride north now, with me to back you: proclaim yourself lord Protector i' the young King's interest: or, proclaim your father-in-law, if he would undertake it. If the Queen send Aktor packing, we join force with her. If, econverse, she join with Aktor, you might look to all Fingiswold to rise and throw them out. In either event, you could hope to attain an estate and power such as you had scarce otherwise dreamed to climb up unto. For all that,' he said, and Marescia's face fell, 'I hold it were a great unwisdom in us to touch the matter.'

Supervius reddened to the ears. 'Go,' he said, 'you might a

listened to reason first, I'd think, ere condemn so good an enterprise.'

'Reason? Mine ears are yours, brother.'

'Why, 'tis a thing at the first face so wholly to be desired, it
needs no more commendations than you yourself have e'en just
now given it. What's against it, we are yet to learn.'

'First of all,' said Emmius, 'we know not whether Aktor bore
part in this business or not; neither know we the terms he is upon
with the Queen.'

Marescia let go a scoffing laugh. 'As well pretend we know not
upon what terms a drunken gallant consorteth with a stewed
whore.'

'Well,' said he, viewing her with an ironic crinkling of his under
eyelids, as if she were lit by a new light. 'You know your own kinsfolk better than can I, sweet Princess. But, be the case so, it but
strengtheneth the possibility her highness may publicly wed with
Aktor; and then what surance have you that the King's subjects will
cleave to us and not to them?'

'Good hope, at least,' replied she, 'that the better men will follow us. They will behold the Parry of Laimak, wed with a princess of
the blood, upholding the King's right against his landless outlander
hath beguiled a Queen, not of that blood at all, to's vile purposes;
and herself suspect too, though I ne'er heard it voiced till you yourself informed me—'

'Come,' said Emmius, 'you cannot argue it both ways.'

'We speak of how 'twill appear to others. For myself, I said I'd
ne'er credit the Queen with such wickedness.'

'And as for Aktor's case by itself, nobody shared your ladyship's
suspicions? Is't not so?'

''Tis so, I admit,' said Marescia and added, under her breath, a
buggish word.

'And the Prince is not ill looked on by the folk? There is, by
your own account, sister-in-law, no evidence against him sufficient
to hang a cat?'

Marescia said, very angry, 'O, some can pretend argument as
ingenuously as scritch-owls. Thank Gods for a man who will act.'

Whereupon said Supervius, loosing rein on his tongue at last:
'You are a skilful thrower down of other men's designs, brother: a
fine ruiner. But you build nothing. This was my very project, that I
came hither thinking to have your friendship in. And you, like some
pettifogging lawyer, but cavil at it and pick faults. Truly was that
said, that *Bare is back without brother behind it.*'[3]

The Lady Deïaneira's night-curtained eyes rested on Emmius,
a little uneasily. But no lineament of his cold inwardly-weighing
countenance betrayed his mind, nor no alteration in the long slow
rhythm of his walk. Presently he spoke: comfortable equable tones,

without all tang of disputation or of sarcasm: rather as a man that would reason with himself. 'States come on with slow advice, quick execution. You, brother, nobly and fortunately allied (and not without help from me there) by marriage with this illustrious lady, have your footing now as of right in the council-chambers of Rialmar. It were a rude folly to waste that vantage by menace of civil battle: foolisher still, because we can never be strong enough to win, much less keep, the victory against Fingiswold; and should besides need to purchase passageway for our army through country subject to Eldir, Kaima, and Bagort, and even so I'd never trust 'em not to break faith and upon us from behind. Our true, far, aim is clear: make friends with the lion-cub against the day he be grown a lion: I mean King Mezentius. And that must be through his mother' (here he looked at Marescia). 'In the meanwhile, prepare quietly. Strengthen us at all points. Have patience, and see.'[4]

The same day, before supper, the Lady Marescia sat in a window of Emmius's great library or study, writing a letter. Supervius, from a deep chair, watched her, stroking his flaming beard. Emmius, arms folded, stood in the window, now turning the leaves of his book, now, as in quiet thought, letting his gaze stray to far distances over the Lows and the wide woods of the Scrowmire, lit with the reddening evening-glow out of a cloudless sky. A serving-man lighted candles in branched candlesticks of mountain gold which stood on the writing-table, and so, upon a sign from Emmius, departed, leaving the rest of the room in dusky obscurity. The windows stood open, yet so calm was the evening that not a flame of the candles wavered.

The Princess signed with a flourish, laid down her pen, and sat back. 'Finished,' she said, looking first to Emmius then to her husband. 'Will it serve, think you?'

Over her shoulders, Emmius upon the right, Supervius on the left, they read the letter. It was superscribed *To the Queenes most Serene and Excellent Highnes of Fingiswold:*

> Beloved Soverayne Lady and Queene and verie dere friend and cozen in lawe, my humble dewtie remembred etc. It is to be thocht my departure from yr. highnes Court was something sodene. I am verie certaine I am abused to yr. Highnes eare by fables and foolische lyes alledging my bad meaning toward yr. highness and to the yong King his person. I beseech you believe not the sclaunders of todes, frogges and other venemous Wormes which have but a single purpose to rayse dislyke and discorde betwixte us, but believe rather that my fault was done in no wicked practise but in the horrable great coil and affricht wee then all did stagger in, and with the pure single intente to do Yr. Serene Highnes a service. For my unseemelie presump-

tuous attempte in that respecte I am trewelie penitent, and
sufficientlye punisht I hope with being clapt in goale at com-
maunde of that lewde fellow *Bodenaye,* who I am sure dealt not
as one of Your aucthorised people in using of mee thus dishon-
orable but by order of some of yr. secretories withoute your
privetie, for which his behaviour hee deserved to have beene
putt to death. I saye no more here but that I will learn wisdome
of this folly. More att large of this when I shall have the felicitie
to look upon yr. face and to kiss yr. hand. My humble suite is
that Your Serene Highness, through the olde gracious boun-
tifull affectioun wherewith you and Kinge Mardanus upon
whom bee peace did ever honor mee, wilbe plesed to receyve
mee againe and gentlie pardon my fault. Unto which ende it
willbe verye good if of yr. specyall love and kyndnes you sende
me lettres of Safe Conducte, because withoute such I do dread
lest this Bodenay whom I know to be a villain or els some other
of his kynde may out of lewdnesse and malice to meward finde
a waye to do mee the lyke disgrace or a worse.

May the Gods move Yr. Highnes hearrte to order thinges
by such a corse as wil stande with yr. Highnes dignitey and the
relief of me yr. highnes pore cozen and verye loving penitente
Servaunte,

MARESCIA

'Will it serve?' she asked, leaning back to look up into the face
first of one and then the other, when they had read it.

'Most excellent well,' said Supervius, and, bending her head yet
farther back, kissed her fiercely in the throat: adding, as he turned
away to the window, 'as the sheep-killing dog said when they
showed him the noose.'

Emmius held out his hand. The lady laid in it her own right
hand, soft, warm, dazzling white, able. He raised it to his lips and
kissed it. 'You are a good fighter, dear Marescia. And a generous
loser. Care not: you will not often lose.'

The Princess, blushing like an untutored maiden, gave him a
smile: not lip-work only, but, rare in her, a smile of her eyes. 'I can
bow to reason when I am shown it, lord brother-in-law,' said she,
and tightened her grasp on the hand that held hers. 'I bear no
grudge. For I see I was wrong.'

Supervius, stiff-necked and haughty, but serene, came from the
window. 'Yes,' he said, his gannet eyes staring in Emmius's face:
then wrung him by both hands.

BOOK 2

UPRISING OF KING MEZENTIUS

VII

ZEUS TERPSIKERAUNOS[1]

STATEIRA HAD by then reigned a full month Queen Regent in Rialmar, wielding at once that dignity and the supreme power on behalf of her infant son, King Mezentius, that was not yet three years old. She was well loved of the folk throughout that country side, nor was any lord or man of mark in all Fingiswold found to speak against her, but every man of them made haste to Rialmar to do her homage and promise her firm upholding and obedience. To all these, she made answer simply and with open countenance, as might a private lady have done to tried friends come to condole her sorrow and renew pledges of friendship; but queenly too, commanding each instantly raise forces and stand ready at time and place appointed. For she meant to let go every lesser business till she should hear reason from the King of Akkama and have of him atonement too, and sure warranty of good behaviour for the future, and punish with death every person who had took hand, were it as deviser or as executer, in this most devilish mischief, that had left her a widow in the high summer-season of her youth, and a great kingdom bereft of the strong hand that had ably ruled it: a child on the throne, and a woman to be over all, and to take order for all, and to answer for all.

Men were the better inclined, in these dark and misty matters, to follow and obey her and have confidence in her judgement and resolution, because well they knew how King Mardanus had made her secretary of his inmost intents and policies, insomuch that no lord of council nor no great officer of state had knowledge of these things so profound as she had; and they thought reasonably that her, whom so deep a politic as the great King had instructed, used, and put his trust in, they might well put their trust in too. Her council she had set up immediately under new letters patents, passing by the names of two or three but keeping all who had shown proof of their powers and weight of authority as counsellors of King Mardanus and whom he had set most store by: in especially, Mendes, the Knight Marshal: Acarnus, High Chancellor of Fingiswold: the High Admiral Psammius: Myntor, Constable in Rialmar: Prince Garman the late King's uncle and father to Marescia. The Constable she had despatched, within a week after the King's murder, upon secret embassage to Akkama with remonstrances and demands aforesaid.

Prince Aktor had throughout the whole time behaved himself with a fitness which many commended and to which none could take exceptions: bearing out a good face after the first dismay and confusion were over, and showing he had the eye of reason common with the best: never a putter forward of himself in counsel, yet, being consulted, not dasht out of countenance by any big looks: ever the first, if disagreements arose, to devise some means of concord: making himself strange always sooner than familiar with the Queen, towards whom he maintained, as well in private as under the general eye, a discreet respectuous reverence as never thinking upon other but to please her.

True it is that in the first hours, when the town was in uproar, and lie and surmise flew thick and noisy as starlings in late autumn, some shouted 'twas Aktor had slain the King in hope to ingross the kingdom to himself. Two or three voices there were that vomited out words of villany even against Queen Stateira: rhymes of *the adulterous Sargus* (which is a sea-fish, Aktor having come first to Fingiswold by sea) *courting the Shee-Goats on the grassie shore.* But a proclamation by the Lord Mendes to 'see these rumourers whipt' was so punctually put in execution by standers by, that the catchpolls running to do it found it done already; and the soundlier, as a labour of love. Since that, slanders miscoupling Aktor's name with the Queen's had no more been heard in Rialmar.

Thus these businesses rested, while the fates of peace or war swung doubtful, waiting on Akkama. But as May now passed into June, perceptive eyes in the court that had delicate discriminative minds behind them began to note, as a gardener will the beginnings of violet-buds under their obscuring leaves, signs of kindness betwixt the Queen and Aktor. The soberer among these lookers began

to think they saw, in her as in him, whenever chance or the pleasures of the court or affairs of the realm brought them together, a
drawing of curtains: a strained diligence to conceal, and that no less
jealously from each other than from the general, and more and
more diligently as the weeks passed by, his, and her, secret mind. It
was witness to the good opinion the Prince now stood in and to
men's faith in the Queen's wise discretion and loyal and noble nature, that these things, as they grew to common notice, stirred up
neither cavil nor envy, but were let alone as matter for her concern
and nobody's else.

Upon the fourth of June the Queen, as, since her assumption of the
Regency, she was wont once in every week to do, came down from
Teremne and so through the town and up to the temple of Zeus
upon Mehisbon, in which were the royal tombs and, last of them,
the tomb of King Mardanus. Without state she came, on foot,
through the wide streets and through the press of the market-place,
and thence by the triumphal way that ascends from the market-
place in broad sweeping curves, now left now right to ease the slope,
up the steep backbone of that, the north-western, horn of Rialmar.
Pillars of rose-red marble line that way on either hand, with on
every pillar a mighty cresset for lighting on nights of high festival
when, viewed from the Teremnene palace or from the town in
Mesokerasin, the road shows like the uncurling on the hill of some
gigantic fire-drake's serpentine and sinuous body, fringed with lambent flame. It was mid-afternoon, sunny, but with a hot heaviness in
the air, and on all sides an up-towering of great cloud-bastions that
darkened the horizon southwards but were of a dazzling and foaming whiteness where they took the sun. Upon her left, the Queen
led with a golden chain a black panther tamed to hand, his fur
smooth and sleek as the gown she wore of black sendaline edged
with gold lace, and upon her right a nurse wheeled the infant King
in his childish hand-carriage of sandalwood inlaid with gold and
silver. Save for an officer walking at a good distance behind with a
half-dozen men of the bodyguard, and save for this nurse and child,
she was alone and unguarded; maintaining in this the old custom of
Kings of Fingiswold, to come and go their ways in Rialmar on their
private occasions much like private folk and with scarce more ceremony: people but curtseying and capping to them as they passed.
They of the royal seat-town liked well this custom, as proof ocular
(had proof been needed) that the King thought his subjects at large
the right guards of his person, and that his greatness was not a
withered beauty that durst not be seen without ornaments of state,
but rather a freshness and a youthful halesomeness that can strip all
off if it please and be as beautiful, and majestical.

The temple of Zeus Soter, high over all the lesser temples of

Mehisbon, stands upon an outcrop of wild crag close under the peak. It is built all of jet-black marble with unpolished surfaces for the more darkness, and naked of ornament except for the carvings on the vast pediment and the sculptured frieze above the portico. Queen Stateira, when she was come to the foot of the threefold great flights of steps which, where the road ends, go up to that temple, took the child Mezentius by the hand and went on with him alone. Between the pillars of the entrance, so huge in girth that five men standing round the base of one of them might scarce touch hands, and well sixty-foot high from plinth to capital, she turned to look back across the saddle of Mesokerasin south-eastwards to the kingly palace of Teremne.

That way thunder-storms were brewing. A murky darkness of vapours, thick, leaden-hued, and oily, swoll and shouldered and mounted and spread upward till that whole quarter of the sky, east and south-east up to the zenith, was turned to the colour of black grapes. The King pulled his mother's hand and laughed, pointing to where against the black clouds the palace on that sudden appeared in an unearthly splendour, lighted by the sun which, through some window rent in the glowering and piling masses to the westward, yet shone.

There was no wind now in the lower air, but a great heat and stillness: and, with the stillness, a silence. It was as though all sound had been emptied out till not even (as in ordinary silences) the unemptiable exiguous residue remained: fall of leaf, or, immeasurably far away, in immeasurably faint echo, the unsleeping welter and surge of the sea, or stir of the market-place below. Even such shadows of sound had drowsed away to nothingness. There was left but that simulacrum of audibility born of the pulsing of living blood in the hearkening ear as it strains to catch the extreme unvoiced voice of the silence.

The Queen, still gazing on that which her son's dancing eyes still returned to, the louring gleam upon Teremne, drew him back a little under the shelter of the portico as the first thunder-drops plashed on the outer paving. Presently she began to say in herself:

> Queen of Heaven, Paphian Aphrodite,
> Let not me, too easily up-surrend'ring,
> Prove i' th'end unnoble, a common woman,
>   —Me, of like metal

> Cast with Your divinity. Nothing lower
> Dare I rate me, since that in all true lovers
> You, Who are the ultimate Fire, do burn and,
>   Burning, transmew them.

Me Your flame-tongu'd fingers, Your flick'ring lids, Your
Kisses, Your empyreal heats distraining
Soul alike and body with hapless passions,
     Long ago vanquish'd.

Yet—for Beauty dwelleth as well in action:
Not in flesh alone and the flaming semblant
(World's desire and wonder of earth and Heaven
     Warmed as jewels

'Tween Your breasts, or stars in Your hair's deep night-
shade),
But besides in mind: and in You the twain are
Undivisible even in thought, an inly
     One everlasting—

Therefore, burn me inwardly: burn my thinking
Mind, as by this lover You sweep Your fires through
This fair body, changing its blood to ichor:
     Fine me, until my

Mortal eyes behold You in very presence,
Not as feeble fantasy do conceive You,
But the truth's self, even as You Yourself be
     hold Your own Godhead.

As for answer, the storm broke on Mehisbon. A ball of eye-
blinding flame, like a falling sun, went betwixt raging sky and the
low land westward from the town; and upon its heels, with great
shakings of the air, the thunder crashed and tumbled as if in a
casting down about the temple of heavy palpable bodies toppled
from some unsighted brink of the upper heavens and falling in a
huddle amid darkness and rushing of rain. Stateira, looking down
at her child, and tightening her clasp of his hand, had now, and
now again, in the momentary livid out-leapings of the lightnings,
swift sights of his face. There was one matter only to be read in it:
not fear: not concern with her: but delight in the thunder.

ARGUMENT WITH DATES

King Mezentius Grows to Manhood
Queen Rosma
The Tragedy of Aktor
(Chapters VIII–XII)

VIII

THE PRINCE PROTECTOR

THE PLOT SYNOPSIS, EDDISON'S 'ARGUMENT WITH DATES,' BEGINS WITH THIS CHAPTER AND CONTINUES THROUGH CHAPTER XXVII. CHAPTER VIII IS THE FIRST FOR WHICH UNPUBLISHED WRITINGS EXIST. IN THIS AND SUBSEQUENT CHAPTERS, I SHALL INCORPORATE THE UNPUBLISHED DRAFTS WITH THE PUBLISHED ARGUMENT ACCORDING TO THE CHRONOLOGY OF THE STORY'S EPISODES. TO PREVENT CONFUSION WITH EDDISON'S DATES OF COMPOSITION, I HAVE MARKED ALL ZIMIAMVIAN DATES AZC (ANNO ZAYANAE CONDITAE, OR 'FROM THE FOUNDING OF THE CITY OF ZAYANA'), AND TO PREVENT CONFUSION WITH EDDISON'S WRITING, MY EDITORIAL COMMENTS HAVE BEEN SET IN THIS SMALLER TYPE. ——P. E. THOMAS

CHAPTER VIII BEGINS WITH THE ARGUMENT:

A KTOR, within a few weeks of the death of King Mardanus, utterly loathes his horrid deed. (It had been in fact not so much deed as abstention: he deliberately abstained from warning the King that the chess queens had been poisoned, and taking care not to touch his own queen, left chance to decide whether the King should touch his.) As time passes, he begins to think his crime can be 'wished' into nothingness. The Queen, so far as he can judge, suspects nothing: he begins to live in a new world, almost convincing himself that his crime never took place; the King is dead, but not through Aktor's doing or contrivance. Aktor and the Queen settle down to an Arcadian existence[1] of trust, affection, and understanding. She, feeling the alteration in him, is touched to the heart and can hardly refrain in his presence from showing her affection and passionate desire for him. However, she does refrain.

Before any reply can be received to the Queen's ultimatum, the revolution of the Nine takes place in Akkama.

IN CHAPTER VII, EDDISON NARRATES THAT QUEEN STATEIRA DISPATCHED MYNTOR THE CONSTABLE OF FINGISWOLD TO AKKAMA WITH AN ULTIMATUM REGARDING THE MURDER OF KING MARDANUS. ON JANUARY 9, 1944, EDDISON DRAFTED NOTES FOR A SCENE IN WHICH THE QUEEN RECEIVES HIS LETTERS IN LATE JULY OF 726 AZC:

Queen at work in King Mardanus's study (*not* closet).[2] Letters from Constable reporting revolt in Akkama: King and all his family thrown to the pigs (a nasty custom of the country for low-class criminals). Complete confusion, and Myntor is therefore waiting for some responsible power to crystallize with whom he can deal, and would like any new instructions. Is convinced no grave danger to him and members of their mission: Akkamites too uncertain of their position and afraid of what they've done (Aktor winces inwardly at the parallel) to bring Fingiswold into enmity against them.

Queen sends for Aktor and consults him. (Bring out relations between her and him.)

Queen: Here's news from your country. I want your head in it.
Aktor: Is't good or bad?
Queen: Doubtful. I'll read it to you: dated 20th June.
Aktor: That's quick travelling.[3]
Queen: He's been kept waiting for audience—at last given one and an interim answer. Thinks the King is raising forces. But nobles are showing signs of divided counsels. There's a strengthening of your party.

IN ADDITION TO THE NOTES ABOVE, EDDISON COMPOSED PART OF A LETTER FROM THE CONSTABLE TO QUEEN STATEIRA. THIS UNFINISHED LETTER DOES NOT MENTION THE REVOLUTION OF THE NINE, BUT IT DOES TELL OF AKKAMITE HOSPITALITY TOWARD FOREIGN AMBASSADORS:

My whole entertainment from my first arrival till towards the very end, was such as if they had devised meanes of very purpose to shew their utter disliking of the whole Fingiswold nation.

At my arriving at———there was no man to bid me well coom, not so much as to conduct me up to my lodging. After I had stayed 2 or 3 dayes to see if anie well coom or other message would coome from the King or the Lord———,[4] I sent my interpreter to the said

Lord———, to desir him to be a meanes for audience to the King.
My interpreter having attended him 2 or 3 dayes, without speaking
to him, was commanded by the Chancellour to coom no more to the
Court, nor to the house of the said Lord———. The Counsell was
commanded not to conferr with mee, nor I to send to anie of them.

When I had audience of the King in the verie entrance of my
speech I was cavilled withall by the Chancellour. . . .

The presents sent by yr. Highness to the King, and delivered to
him in his own presence, with all other writings, wear the day following retourned to mee, and very contemptuouslie cast downe before mee.

My articles of petition delivered by woord of mouth, and afterward by writing, with all other writings, wear altered and falsified by
the King's interpreter, by meanes of the Chancellour———; . . .
manie things were putt in and manie things strook out, which being
complained of and the points noted would not be redressed.

I was placed in a howse verie unhandsoom, unholsoom, of purpose (as it seemed) to doe me disgrace, and to hurt my health,
whear I was kept as prisoner, not as an ambassadour.

EDDISON MADE NO MORE NOTES UPON THE EVENTS OF THIS CHAPTER, BUT
ON JANUARY 20, 1944, HE MADE SOME NOTES ON THE GEOGRAPHY OF AKKAMA:

Akkama's capitol 300 miles from Rialmar WNW as crow flies.
1,200,000 square miles (about 500 miles greatest length and 400 N
to S, roughly bean shaped). Southern part, the Waste of Akkama,
sandy desert: Northern and central part a high tableland (? 4–5000
feet). Only practical communication with Fingiswold (except by sea)
is through passes in comparatively low country 50 miles WNW of
Rialmar between Western mountain end of mountain boundary that
encloses the fertile lowlands in horseshoe shape, of Fingiswold, and
the Bight. This way leads to the Shearbone range.[5]

FEW OF THESE PRECISE DETAILS HAVE A PLACE IN THE ARGUMENT, WHICH
BRIEFLY DESCRIBES AKKAMA AND THEN SUMMARIZES ITS HISTORY:

Akkama is a vast country lying north-west from Fingiswold: its
southern parts all sandy desert, its north and centre a high tableland. The country has a wintry climate and is sparsely inhabited by
nomads and woodmen. Five or six generations ago rebellious nobles from Fingiswold fled to Akkama and there founded a dynasty,
intermarrying with the natives and living like robber kings on Pis-
sempsco, a high rock on which sits the capital and only city of importance. With this for their hold, they lived by foray and piracy,
throwing criminals to the pigs (their chief cattle, and very fierce),
and worshipping the 'dirty gods' of the country. They vaunted

themselves rightful heirs to the throne of Fingiswold and the nobles speak the English tongue (which is common to the three kingdoms), but the natives, a cruel, base and savage people, have a gibberish of their own. The Nine represent these noble families who had fallen from power when the usurping king, Tzucho, expelled Aktor and slew the king his father. This Tzucho was a bastard of a cadet branch of the ruling family, his mother a queen of Akkama who was thrown to the pigs for adultery with a pirate of native birth.

The Nine, having slain Tzucho and set themselves in power as an oligarchy, now send an embassy to Rialmar offering every conceivable apology and atonement, short of surrender of their country. The Queen, dealing with the ambassadors in person, makes a treaty whereby Akkama promises perpetual friendship and alliance, and Aktor renounces any claim to the throne of Akkama.

It is Aktor's conduct during these negotiations that finally decides Queen Stateira to marry him. With great dignity and finesse and in a scene which does credit to them both, she in effect proposes this, and Aktor is almost frightened at the sudden fulfilment of his dearest hopes. Upon their marriage (September 726), he is proclaimed Prince Protector, making at the same time public and solemn renunciation of any higher ambition and swearing fealty to King Mezentius and to Stateira as Queen Regent.

The Queen sends for Doctor Vandermast and gives him the responsibility, under her, for the young King's upbringing. Aktor is at first in a dread lest Vandermast should disclose his secret, and meditates the doctor's destruction. But while he procrastinates he learns to trust the doctor, and soon to revere him.

With the passage of the years, Mezentius learns that he himself is King: learns too, with surprise, that he had a father other than Aktor. He shows an early instinct for command and a delight in danger for its own sake: dangerous dogs, horses, bulls, and Anthea in her lynx dress: dangerous climbing on the walls and cliffs of Rialmar. He is untirable, incredibly generous and open-handed, and in all dispute an upholder, from native inclination, of the losing side.

IX

LADY ROSMA IN ACROZAYANA

I N 7 3 2 Emmius's Meszrian policy bears fruit in the marriage of his daughter the Lady Rosma Parry, now eighteen, to King Kallias. Kallias's meaning was by this alliance to re-estate his power in the Meszrian Marches and further to aggrandize himself at the expense of Rerek. But Emmius, a more subtle and no less brutal Machiavellian, had a private understanding with Haliartes, the king's brother and heir presumptive, whereby, in case the king should die and the succession be endangered, Emmius would support Haliartes by force of arms upon condition of his immediately making Rosma his queen.

The lady, taken with a loathing for Kallias (who is forty, a gloomy tyrant, and very dissolute and debauched), murders him on his wedding-night and forthwith weds Haliartes, a weak and easy-mannered prince much more to the taste of the lords of Meszria than his self-willed, hard-driving brother. She easily persuades Haliartes to make her not his queen only but joint sovereign with himself.

665

X

STIRRING OF THE EUMENIDES[1]

I N 7 3 6 the Nine secretly offer to Aktor the throne of
Akkama. The envoy, seeing Aktor in private, explains
that this is upon condition of his first becoming King of
Fingiswold. Aktor refuses, and the matter is dropped.
He refuses mainly because of his love for the Queen (to
whom he never reveals this offer) and because of his oath of renunciation, to break which would ruin him for ever in her esteem. But
the refusal is wormwood in his soul. He grows more and more melancholic: begins to ponder whether it were not best to make away
with Mezentius who he fears may, as he grows up, find out the true
circumstances of his father's taking off: but devotion to Queen
Stateira (perhaps the one stable principle in him), seconded by a
congenital proneness to put things off, always holds him back from
this further crime. Nevertheless, the bloody secret is always a barrier
between himself and the Queen.

XI

COMMODITY OF NEPHEWS

QUEEN ROSMA,[1] grown weary after five years of the unenterprising water-gruelish Haliartes, in 738 casts her eye on his nephew Lebedes, a villainous young scoundrel five years her junior, to whom she now promises her hand in marriage if he will first kill the king his uncle. Lebedes accordingly raises rebellion and kills Haliartes in battle; but Rosma, alarmed now lest this young man prove too devilish, denies her part of the bargain and, finding ready to hand Beltran, Lebedes's elder brother, invites him to rid her of Lebedes, the consideration of which service is to be, as before, her hand in marriage. Beltran, unscrupulous but attractive, and with many saving graces, and able moreover (as no man she had before encountered) to stir faintly her affections, is madly in love and savagely jealous of his brother. He surprises Lebedes in the queen's chamber and, with a hearty good will and under her very eyes, stabs him to death. In the same hour she takes Beltran as lover, but forthwith upon a revulsion repudiates him, threatens him with death, and drives him with contumely into exile.

Rosma, now aged twenty-four, reigns henceforward as Queen of Meszria in her own right. She is a big powerful woman, dark-haired, black-eyed, dissembling, proud, grasping, perfidious, and cruel. She is handsome, and can be physically extremely alluring:

not vicious, but cold: obsessed with the lust of power. In due course, Beroald, her son by Beltran, is born in Zayana. Rosma, being by nature 'of masculine virtue,' hates to be a woman, hates her offspring, and indeed has posed, and continues to pose (with what justification none can tell) as a Virgin Queen. She conceals the birth and orders the child to be exposed on a mountain. Anthea, in her lynx dress, saves it, and, by direction of Doctor Vandermast, substitutes it for the same-aged son of the wife of a gentleman in South Meszria.

XII

ANOTHER FAIR MOONSHINY NIGHT

ING MEZENTIUS, as he approaches manhood, begins to discover justice: begins too to discover that the beauty which is in action is the necessary complement to that physical beauty which he has already learnt to worship. He shows early promise of that supreme gift of a man of action, the power to put from his mind everything except the business in hand, and develops at the same time berserk traits: fits of intense vigour and achievement which alternate with periods of moodiness, silence, lassitude, and retirement into himself. Stateira watches these things with mixed admiration and anxiety. He begins to talk to her about his father, and about Aktor, to whom (without himself knowing why) he begins to take a certain dislike. This troubles him, and his mother. And it troubles Aktor.

The closer Aktor draws to the Queen, the more he is tortured with remorse. Yet he realizes that it was in fact that wicked and secret treason that gave him his present happiness and power. His mind is thus in a perpetual conflict, and his melancholy increases upon him. Queen Stateira for her part never ceases to be under his passionate domination and grows more and more fearful lest he should someday confess to her the guilt which she never admits, even to her own secret mind, that she suspects. Deeper and nobler

671

and more Olympian is her clinging to Mezentius's future greatness (foreshadowed by Doctor Vandermast), as her sheet anchor.

In December 740, the King (aged seventeen) has been questioning his step-father about his father's murder. He does not, save in recurring moments of gnawing uneasiness and guesswork that originate in the blood rather than in the brain, suspect Aktor's complicity. Moreover, his rooted dislike for Aktor itself makes him the less ready to suspect; for it is clean against his nature to be unjust, most of all to a man personally repugnant to his sympathies. He questions Aktor now, simply because he is impatient to clear up the mystery and have done with it, and Aktor (having caught and disposed of the actual poisoner) seems to be the one person who may be able to throw any light on the thing.

The outcome of their conversation is indeterminate (as for any advancement of the King's purpose), but to Aktor, devastating. His fears, bred of a bad conscience, tell him the King has divined the secret, or been told by Vandermast. In a like agony of spirit as fourteen years ago, he comes once more at midnight to the Queen's privy garden, expecting solitude but finding Anthea there, as if waiting for him.

It is the real frost this time: the longest night of the year. That oread lady is cold, pitiless, scornful, and unkind. She knows, of course, the truth, and 'harries mankind's obliquity' in the person of the unhappy Prince Protector. Her unmercilessness, terribly seconding his own inward conscience, is in effect a means of illuminating the good (which is not inconsiderable) in Aktor, and so of awakening in an onlooker, had any been there, pity and charity on his behalf.

In this cold and this clarity induced by the scorpion sting of Anthea's scorn, he reviews the choices:

First: Kill Mezentius? But that would kill also the Queen's love for himself. And moreover, how could he hope to escape?

Second: Flee? But where to? Akkama will not have him. Besides, what profit in life without the Queen? They are by this time, it is true, scarcely more lovers than she and Mardanus had been after Mezentius's birth; but this time it is the Queen, not her lover, who has sated her passion and finds it burned out at last. But she is deeply fond of Aktor, and (as he believes in his bones) has never imagined the truth about his hand in Mardanus's murder: and to live with her, even upon terms of brother and sister, has become to him the one reason for continuance upon earth.

Third: Confess all to Mezentius, and hope he will kill him? But that, albeit quieting his conscience, would (again) hurt the Queen. Also Mezentius would tell her all, and that Aktor cannot even in imagination face.

And so, feeling he has miscooked his life (possessed his lady by unlawful means, mixed his love with ambition and, for sake of both, become a traitor, a murderer of his friend and benefactor, and a life-long liar henceforth and fugitive from truth: things which can never be reversed and never confessed but can, maybe, be expiated), and being resolved the Queen shall never know, nor Mezentius (if he does not know, or has not guessed, already), he asks Anthea to do him a single favour: the favour of silence. She scornfully, but (as Aktor by some obscure intimation realizes) with faithful meaning, assents. Aktor throws himself backwards down the eight-hundred-foot cliff that overlooks the harbour.

Anthea keeps her word. The King keeps his thoughts to himself, and refrains, with an almost feminine sympathy and intuition, from letting his mother suspect the truth, or what he guesses to be the truth.

ON DECEMBER 5, 1943, EDDISON RECORDED SOME OF HIS THOUGHTS ABOUT AKTOR'S SUICIDE:

Make Aktor's tragic end not a melodramatic retribution on a villain, but the destined expiation of a crime that demands expiation. 'What's done is done'; and in taking that way out Aktor may be thought to have redeemed himself. He is not a Morville, far less a Derxis; a man of promise, led by passion and ambition into wicked courses but in some sort reconciled at last.

BOOK 3

THE AFFAIR OF REREK

ARGUMENT WITH DATES

EMMIUS PARRY CONTINUES HIS POLICY:
LOOKING NORTH
KING MEZENTIUS GAINS REREK
(CHAPTERS XIII–XIV)

XIII

THE DEVIL'S QUILTED ANVIL[1]

I N 741 the Nine fall from power in Akkama and Melkis becomes king, being by Aktor's death the next in legitimate line of succession. After eighteen months of hesitation and diplomatic interchanges, Melkis moves to unseat King Mezentius. Supervius Parry, aged forty-six, who has now sat in Laimak twenty-one years, sends his younger son, Horius Parry (now aged sixteen), as an officer in attendance upon the general in command of a Rerek contingent in aid of King Mezentius in Fingiswold. This first meeting of Horius with the King results in a mutual interest and subtle equivocal attraction.

In the campaign which follows, the King, aged nineteen, finally repulses Akkama, who is left disgraced and licking his wounds (742).

Supervius's main concern is now to oust Gilmanes (who has succeeded his father Alvard as Prince of Kaimar) from his position of favour in Rialmar. He is jealous of Gilmanes, as of the other princes in the north (Ercles, Keriones's son and successor in Eldir, and Aramond of Bagort). Supervius is no great statesman, and is obsessed with his ambition to see Laimak received as mistress of all Rerek. He is never really loyal to his brother Emmius, as Emmius is to him for family sake and for a kind of love of him. He walks in a net so far as Emmius is concerned, and Emmius, enjoying and frustrating his brother's deep-laid and tortuous disloyalties, constantly uses him as a cat's-paw to further his own more subtle and less parochial policy.

Emmius (aged fifty-two), is preeminently by nature a user of cat's-paws: this explains his never attempting to seize Meszria for himself, but preferring to control it through his daughter Rosma. He is probably already privately toying with the notion of a marriage between her and the King. This he sees might mean the hemming in and even (if the King turns out from these beginnings a very great man) the subjection of Rerek. But if the King turns out so, this will be of little moment; for Rerek, on the doorstep of Fingiswold, could not then in any event hope to stand long against him. If, on the other hand, the King's capacities prove but mean, then the alliance would strengthen the Parry (particularly Emmius's own branch of the family), and would mean an aggrandizement of Meszria and so run with Emmius's policy, since the queen his daughter has not only married into the reigning house in Zayana but now supplanted it.

Openly, Emmius plays for time; refuses to regard Gilmanes seriously (a view justified later by the event); and prepares to use Peridor of Laveringay, his sister Lugia's son, as a thorn in Ercles's side. This project fails, however, Peridor inclining more and more to Ercles.

King Mezentius (now aged twenty), noting the uneasy balance of power in Rerek (the age-long leadership of the house of Parry counter-weighted by the loose alliance of the princes of the north, and the complicated courtship, by both sides, of the free cities), begins to think of extending his influence southwards.

His mother, Queen Stateira, mistrusting the Parry instinctively, now produces in Rialmar Ercles's sister, the Lady Anastasia, a beautiful girl whom the King easily falls in love with and marries (July 742): a further setback for Emmius Parry.

XIV

LORD EMMIUS PARRY

O PEN STRIFE breaks out next year (744) between the Parry and Ercles in Rerek. Supervius holds Megra, left to Marescia by her father's will who died a year or two ago. Ercles, feeling that this threatens his safety in Eldir, disputes the will. He prepares to besiege Megra, and Supervius, getting wind of this, sends an army to ravage the lands of Eldir itself. Ercles, thwarted, appeals to Rialmar for succour. The King refuses, telling Ercles plainly that he is not disposed to make his policy a family affair. Horius Parry (aged eighteen), shrewdly diagnosing the King's impartiality induces his father (with Emmius's approval) to agree with Ercles to a joint application to the King to arbitrate. The King establishes a just peace, confirming the Parry in Megra, but (to save the old treaty) formally as Lieutenant of the King of Fingiswold, and he must retire from Lailma pending a free election in that city.

Early in 745 Queen Anastasia dies.

In 746 a renewed attack by Akkama is bloodily thrown back by the King, demonstrating once more his armed strength in Fingiswold.

Emmius Parry now judges it the happy moment for a crucial move to bring the King into Rerek. For this purpose he successfully makes Peridor his cat's-paw (who is quite unconscious of being so used) to provoke Ercles, Gilmanes, and Aramond to assault Megra in violation of the concordat. After fruitless negotiations lasting eighteen months, during which Megra stands a siege, Supervius, as injured party, appeals to the King. The King summons a conference in Rialmar, insisting on personal attendance: no ambassadors or legates. Mainly because of stiffness on the part of Supervius and Horius, whom the princes distrust, the conference is stormy; but Emmius's diplomacy brings it at last to a joint request by all unanimously, backed by other lords of Rerek, that the King should assume the crown of Rerek as their overlord, guaranteeing all freedoms. The King accepts this (748).

Henceforth, the King's policy in Rerek is consistently *divide et impera;* and his great weapon a scrupulous fairness. His habit, all his life, is to look for (and find) the best in people. This does not mean he is never taken in, but he consistently sees the best in them, and gets the most out of them. In Horius Parry, for instance, and (later) in Rosma, he sees many bests (and many worsts). Those that disappoint him (for instance, later, Valero, and Akkama) have been wittingly tested by him, and run risks with.

BOOK 4

THE AFFAIR OF MESZRIA

ARGUMENT WITH DATES

King Mezentius Gains Meszria
Amalie
Rosma in Rialmar
(Chapters XV–XIX)

XV

QUEEN ROSMA

THE KING'S thoughts have for some years been drawn toward Meszria. This works well with Emmius Parry's long-sighted policy, who, independently and with different (but far from hostile) interests, has been steering towards the same mark: namely a nearer and still more exalted connection between the Parry (this time, of Argyanna) and the royal house of Fingiswold.

In 749 the King sends Jeronimy to ask Rosma to receive a visit from the King in person, since they are now conterminous sovereigns and ought to be friends. In late autumn the King comes to Zayana. Purely as a matter of high policy, he proposes marriage. Posing as an unscrupulous politician after her own pattern, he shows in their preliminary conversations a remarkable and detailed knowledge of her history and her polyandrous proceedings. (He is now aged twenty-six: Rosma thirty-five.)

The Queen, reflecting on these conversations, has the sensation of having been saddled and bridled: of having been made drunk with the King's personality and led by that to talk too much. However, it is not her habit to let anything except cold logic govern her actions, and by that test alone his offer is not one to be let go: by it he gains Meszria while she gains Fingiswold and Rerek. She gains, also, what is less to her taste: a master. But this inconvenience may in any case be unavoidable, since the King's overlordship in Rerek brings nearer home the danger of coercion if she is obdurate. Moreover, although their conversations have throughout been upon the explicit terms that marriage is to entail no relations between them beyond the political, she feels vaguely, as with Beltran, but now at a profounder level with King Mezentius, that here is a man for whose sake she might, if ever she should, which is to her inconceivable, make a fool of herself. After a few days' consideration, she answers that, on his present proposal, the scales are too much weighted in the King's favour as against her, since she, as a woman, gives up her independence by marrying. If, however, he will bring Akkama into the dowry, then she will accept.

XVI

LADY OF PRESENCE

MEANWHILE, the King's heart is set upon Amalie, a young lady of the Queen's bedchamber, aged sixteen, and passionately beloved by this self-willed and bloody woman. He and Amalie do not so much fall in love as have an intimation, at first looks exchanged between them and without word spoken, that they are lovers, and have been so since the beginning; and this, since not in this present (Zimiamvian) life, therefore presumably in some other world, or worlds. This echoes back to the *Praeludium:* the fifteen years 'in our own house at Nether Wasdale,' and his seeing her 'dead in the Morgue at Paris.'[1] The intimation, sometimes momentary, sometimes longer in duration, is yet fitful and unseizable. Like a perfume, it cannot be revived in memory, but, when present, has the quality of conjuring up in solid actuality of circumstance and detail all that belongs to it. He tells Amalie that he cannot offer her a crown: kings wed for policy, not for love. But he does offer her himself, and on no temporary nor no partial terms. He tells her he is going north on the Akkama business, and that in two years he means to come back, with that accomplished, for her.

In this the King is entirely open with Rosma. He will make Akkama tributary to Fingiswold, and in two years will return to Zayana to claim her hand. Their marriage is to be a purely political relationship: his wife, except in name, will be Amalie. The Queen will be free (on sole condition of avoiding public scandal) to console herself as she may please. Rosma laughs. She holds these amusements much over-rated, and is perfectly content with his proposals.

XVII

AKKAMA BROUGHT INTO THE DOWRY

T HE KING returns north, stopping a few days in Argy-
anna to confer with his future father-in-law. Preparations last far into the summer of the next year (750). In
August, he marches on Akkama with a great army of
Fingiswold levies and a powerful contingent from
Rerek under command of Supervius Parry, who has with him
Horius, his son by Marescia, aged twenty-four, and Hybrastus (Emmius's son, aged thirty-three). Ercles (aged thirty-two), and
Aramond (aged twenty-three), and Valero, Prince of Ulba (aged
twenty), are also in this expedition. Emmius had pressed personal
participation upon Supervius, both in the family interest and not to
be outweighed by the Ercles faction.

The campaign of 750 ends with a severe reverse: Supervius
Parry killed in battle: Ercles taken prisoner. But the King after a few
months retrieves all and, taking Akkama by surprise by a winter
campaign (a thing unheard of in that part of the world), crushes all
resistance after three or four big battles, the last one about mid-
February 751.

Throughout this decisive war, Horius Parry distinguishes himself both as soldier and as counsellor: an old head on young shoulders. He on land and Jeronimy at sea are (after Supervius's death)
the King's chief lieutenants. Prince Valero, a protégé of Emmius

Parry's, also does brilliant work. Seeds of ill will are sown in Horius's secret heart against Valero.

During four months' intensive work in subdued Akkama a violent quarrel comes to a head between Horius and Hybrastus Parry. Hybrastus palpably in the wrong bids his cousin to the duello and is killed. Horius, with great courage and judgement, obtains leave to go south immediately to make his peace with his uncle Emmius. He comes to Argyanna, outspeeding all rumours, armed with a letter from the King that gives the facts, and in effect offering Emmius 'self-doom.'

Emmius, partly for love of bravery in a man, partly for deep and sound reasons of policy, magnanimously forgives his son's death, but demands from Horius, by way of atonement, material guarantees in the March of Ulba, including possession of the fortress of Kessarey and the personal right to appoint a Lord President of the Marches. He appoints Count Bork. The result is that politically as well as strategically Emmius will now be all-powerful (under the King) in the whole region of the Zenner.

Horius Parry succeeds his father in Laimak. He remains on good terms with his uncle (now aged sixty) but chafes at his power, likely to be greatly increased as the King's father-in-law as well as by this new agreement. As his personal agent and intelligencer at Emmius's court in Argyanna, Horius maintains one Gabriel Flores (aged twenty-two), a low-born adventurer whom he seduced from Ercles's service a year or two back when Ercles had placed Gabriel, as his spy, in Laimak.

With his own elder half-brother, Geleron Parry, who sits like a thorn in Anguring, Horius is on terms of thinly disguised hostility. Geleron (as son to Supervius by his first wife Rhodanthe, whom Supervius put away to marry Marescia) thinks he ought by rights to have Laimak, but Supervius left it by will to Horius.

XVIII

THE SHE-WOLF TAMED
TO HAND

T H E   K I N G returns at midsummer, five months before the date appointed, to Zayana—and to Amalie. He weds Rosma, in great state and with public acclamation and rejoicings, on the terms agreed upon.

The Queen, in spite of her view of such 'amusements,' cannot upon actual experience brook Amalie's position as the King's mistress in Zayana. Her attitude in this is complex, and her grievance not' so much that Amalie is her rival in the King's affections (which she at this stage cares nothing for) as that he has taken Amalie away from her. At the Yule feast, December 751, Rosma tries to burn the King and Amalie together; but in this she is thwarted by the King, who also succeeds (almost beyond belief) in keeping the whole affair secret so far as Rosma's share in it is concerned.

After this, he tells the Queen that Meszria is not good for her, nor she for Meszria: to save her face, she had better give out (as her own proposal) that she desires a change of residence, and that the Queen of the Three Kingdoms ought to live in the chief seat-town, namely Rialmar. As underlining the fact that she must play second fiddle (politically), the King says he proposes to install Jeronimy in Meszria as Commissioner Regent.

Rosma is at first mad wroth at all this, and the King with great difficulty prevents her from hurting herself or him. However, he keeps his temper; and the end of it is that she, savouring curiously on her palate a new pleasure (of a man that can master her and also laugh at her), falls in with his plans.

This is the beginning of a closer and deeper relationship, almost of friendship, between the King and Rosma. She now resides permanently in Rialmar, while he divides his time between the three countries in turn.

XIX

THE DUCHESS OF MEMISON

THE QUEEN MOTHER, distasting the prospect of continuing in Rialmar, where she must now yield precedence to a daughter-in-law whose reputation and capabilities she reviews with dismay, resolves to leave Fingiswold. In the spring of 752 she moves south to Lornra Zombremar, in a high eastward-facing valley on the far side of the great snow ranges that enclose Meszria from the east. In this mountain retreat at the edge of the world, in a 'house of peace' built for her by art of Doctor Vandermast, she now lives retired from the busy life of courts and the restlessness of great men.

In April 752, Barganax is born in Meszria, and Amalie is made Duchess. On learning of this, the Queen offers divorce; but the King has no intention of making Amalie a queen, nor has she any ambition to be made so. From this arises a strengthening of friendship between King and Queen.

This same year Lessingham is born at Upmire, posthumous son of Romelius, a lord of Rerek who had married in 751 Eleonora, grand-daughter of Sidonius Parry. When in 726 Supervius had put away his wife Rhodanthe (Eleonora's aunt and Geleron's mother) in order to marry the Princess Marescia, this sowed enmity between his uncle Sidonius and the house of Laimak; and in that tradition Eleonora of Upmire now brings up her son.

The next few years are years of peace and consolidation, during which the personal hand of the King is felt everywhere throughout the realm.

The Queen indulges in underground political intrigues with her cousins Horius and Geleron Parry, Valero and others. She tries, more from spite than from policy, to set the King against Horius. None of these practices is hid from the King, who cannot resist teasing her; yet their queer friendship (and his and Horius Parry's) persists and grows. With unseen hand, the King fans the rivalry between the two brothers for his deep purposes.

BOOK 5

THE TRIPLE KINGDOM

ARGUMENT WITH DATES

Beltran returns

Birth of Fiorinda

End of Geleron Parry

Barganax and Styllis

Barganax and Heterasmene

Barganax Made Duke of Zayana

Prince Valero

King Mezentius and Duchess Amalie Visit

Queen Stateira:

Edward Lessingham and Lady Mary

Lessingham

Rebellion in the Marches

Overthrow of Akkama

(Chapters XX–XXVII)

XX

Dura Papilla Lupae[1]

I N AUGUST 755, Beltran (now aged forty-three) appears in Rialmar, under an assumed name and in disguise, while the King is in Memison. He discloses himself to the Queen and makes fierce love to her. Rosma, who is now forty-one and in a perilous state of boredom, is at first infuriated but at last, saying she will ne'er consent, consents. Then, in a revulsion as much savager than sixteen years ago it had been in Zayana as her present surrender has been deeper and more passionate, she murders him.

The King, returning, smells out this secret. At length Rosma, knowing herself with child and thoroughly frightened at the King's enigmatical bearing, confesses all. He receives it with so much humour and magnanimity that she is, for the time at least, bound to him as never before. His only condition is secrecy: if ever she suffers her amours to become public, that will be the end of her. Rosma thinks he means, cut her head off. The mere suggestion (of mutilation of a woman) sickens him. No; but he would make her drink a lethal draught.

On midsummer night 756, Fiorinda is born to Queen Rosma in Rialmar. This child she would have killed or exposed, but the King, employing Anthea for the purpose, and with the help of Beroald, places it, without trace of origin, with the same suppositious parents in Meszria as Beroald was foisted upon, sixteen years ago.

XXI

ANGURING COMBUST

B OUT APRIL 757, Horius Parry's feud with his half-
brother Geleron comes to a head (not without fostering
by the King's unseen hand). The immediate occasion is
Horius's discovery of foul play between his wife and
Geleron. He kills his wife and burns Anguring, destroying Geleron, Geleron's wife, and their sons and daughters. This
hellish deed both rids away, in Geleron, a turbulent and tiresome
vassal and puts Horius under yet closer obligations to the King; for
the King by a sudden swoop catches him outside his safe hold of
Laimak and by pardoning the fratricide (by law, punishable as par-
ricide) tightens the bonds of allegiance that bind Horius to the
throne, impressing him at the same time with the sense of being, as
it were, in the hand of God.

Rosma finds the King's handling of this episode after her own
heart. It brings her, at this late date, furiously in love with him,
partly because of his magnanimity, partly because she is seized with
a sudden hankering to give an heir to the Triple Throne, and with
the feeling that time is running short if this is to be done. The King,
now aged thirty-three, does not trouble himself much about this. If
he ever thinks of the succession, his attitude is coloured with the
conviction that kings must be kings by competence not by birth
merely, and with an inclination to toy with the idea of Barganax's

703

possible fitness. Constitutionally, the King is but lightly interested in posterity, intent on building his own edifice of power in his own lifetime: fate and his successors must settle what comes after.

Rosma addresses herself to fascinate him. He is at first repelled, then amused, and finally touched. He suddenly looses himself in a fierce passion for this tiger-cat of his: a kind of lustful camaraderie, involving no disloyalty to the Duchess.

In January 758, Styllis is born in Rialmar. The Queen, full of philoprogenitiveness for her first legitimate offspring, is full too of jealousy against Barganax on her son's behalf. As Styllis grows up she neglects no occasion to set him against his half-brother.

Beroald, now aged nineteen, studies law under Count Olpman.

XXII

Pax Mezentiana[1]

DURING THE next twelve years (758–770) of *Pax Mezentiana*, underground strife still smoulders in Rerek, with constant friction between the Parry and the princes, the free cities putting up their favours by auction to the highest bidder.

In 760, another child, the Princess Antiope, is born to Rosma in Rialmar.

Emmius Parry, looking ahead, in 766 makes Horius his heir. The King, disliking the prospect of so much personal power in one hand (Laimak, Argyanna, Kessarey, and the Marches), also looks ahead. He now declares Megra, Kaima, Kessarey, and Argyanna fiefs royal, but this is not to operate as regards Kaima or Argyanna so long as Gilmanes and Emmius Parry are alive. He puts his own lieutenants in the other fortresses: Arcastus in Megra, Roder in Kessarey. (Arcastus is grandson to Morsilla Parry and her first husband, Caunas, and therefore by tradition opposed to the Pertiscan branch. But Horius Parry captivates his fancy, and he always remains Horius's loyal supporter.) The fact that Emmius accepts without cavil the position as regards Kessarey, is an evidence of the strength of the friendship and understanding between Emmius and the King.

Beroald (aged twenty-seven) takes, thanks to Jeronimy's support and recommendation, a large part in advising on the administrative diplomatic and legal problems involved in this settlement. The King, much taken with his character and abilities, makes him lord of Krestenaya, and presently joins him with Jeronimy as Commissioner Regent in Meszria.

Horius Parry is not best pleased about these arrangements; but the King, admiring the way he accepts them, promises him (and confirms it under seal in his favour) inheritance under his uncle's will, except as for Argyanna which on Emmius's death will revert to the crown. Horius, when he succeeds, will thus be all-powerful in the Marches (subject however—a weighty exception—to the key fortress of Argyanna), but is deprived of Megra and (of course) of Kessarey. He (in common with most of the great vassals of Rerek and Meszria) inclines to dislike Beroald and the Admiral and Roder as 'office nobility' and upstarts.

XXIII

THE TWO DUKES

BARGANAX, at fifteen, is as big and as strong and well grown as any young man in the land three years his elder. His first love is Heterasmene, a young widow and lady of honour at the Duchess's court in Memison. Heterasmene for her part greatly enjoys this worship but, when he makes violent love to her, thinks it her duty to inform the Duchess. Amalie, judging it an admirable education for her son and making sure that the lady scoffs at the very thought of marriage with a boy half her age, rejoices that Heterasmene should at once amuse herself and bring up Barganax in the way he should go: an arrangement which works to their mutual benefit and, after a year or two, ends gradually: friendship preserved and no hearts broken. The lady, in return for this kindness, is made Countess in her own right by the King, and soon afterwards weds a lord in Rialmar.

In 770 Barganax, being now eighteen, comes of age. The King creates him Duke of Zayana, the title formerly held by heirs apparent to the old kingdom of Meszria. Rosma dislikes the implication. On Barganax's induction into his dukedom, Doctor Vandermast (hitherto his tutor) assumes the post of secretary. The King assigns to Barganax an apanage with lands extending far beyond the limits of the dukedom. Styllis, incensed at this, nurses his old jealousies and old and new grievances, which the Queen his mother does not neglect to influence.

XXIV

PRINCE VALERO

PRINCE VALERO of Ulba, who had thought he deserved one of the key fortresses in 766, has ever since been secretly busy forming a faction and endeavouring to win the confidence and support of Count Bork, Lord President of the Marches. Horius Parry, having secret intelligence of this, fosters and waters it, meaning to destroy the prince in due time and win merit thereby.

The Parry's young cousin, Lessingham, has a finger in this 'secret intelligence.' (In spite of his upbringing, Lessingham at the age of sixteen fell under the spell of Horius and became the means of reconciliation between him and Eleonora of Upmire, who, at her son's request, now allows him to reside in Laimak as page to Horius.)

Valero, now (770) in his fortieth year, is handsome and well liked, but vain, a brilliant rather than an able politician, and fundamentally dishonest. Nobody, except the King, Emmius, and Horius, sees this vital weakness. Beroald, for his part, knows Valero only by hearsay. Emmius, in this single case, suffers his predilections to blindfold his shrewd hard judgement, and is always inclined to forgive Valero and favour him. The King leaves him alone, partly to please Emmius and Rosma (whose pet he is); but he has his eye upon him, and lets Horius Parry know, pretty unmistakably, that he holds him answerable for seeing that the Prince does no serious harm.

Horius (now aged forty-four) hates Valero, but pretends friendship and does him various good turns. Valero foolishly underestimates the Parry's subtlety and reach and is in the end a complete victim to his wiles. Horius has for years maintained a most masterly patience in this business, never involving himself but always and by every means lulling Valero's suspicions, encouraging him in his grievances, flattering him, giving him rope, and pretending not so much as to dream of his having subversive intentions.

XXV

LORNRA ZOMBREMAR

UEEN STATEIRA has now for many years lived at Lornra Zombremar. The King has been her guest there more and more often as the years of *Pax Mezentiana* afford more opportunity for such pleasures of quietude; and always Doctor Vandermast is her frequent visitor, as also (of more recent years) is the King's niece Zenianthe, herself a hamadryad and friend and pupil of the learned doctor. All the nymphs, faun-kind, and half-gods, who inhabit these solitudes, are there to do Queen Stateira service. These creatures, with their pure unquestioning sight discerning the Queen Mother for who, under the disguise of wise and lovely old age, She truly is, are as children to her, loving her the more tenderly as they perceive Her inward divinity of which she for her own part is ignorant: an ignorance which is itself a grace; of equal excellence (in Vandermast's philosophic eye) with that far different but no less perfect and essential grace, of self-enjoyment and self-knowledge, that belongs to the fully conscious Godhead. She is now well entered upon her seventy-third year.

In November 770, the King and the Duchess (now aged forty-seven and thirty-seven respectively) come to see his mother in Lornra Zombremar. Amalie has never before made this journey, and it is eighteen years since she met the Queen Mother, who, then on her way from Rialmar to her new home, had been her guest in Memison. During the present visit the King and Amalie experience, in a more vivid and detailed manner than ever before, that assurance of having loved and had each other in another world (the world of the *Praeludium:* that is to say, this nineteenth- and twentieth-century world of ours): this time with the mutual knowledge that his name, there, is *Lessingham,* and hers *Mary.* They think of the Parry's young cousin whose name is Lessingham: a strange coincidence. As on other occasions, the memory (or dream?) fades and vanishes; but this time less completely in the King's mind than in the Duchess's. Even in hers, there remains a teasing sense of a forgotten or unplaceable tune, whenever she hears the name 'Lessingham.'

XXVI

REBELLION IN THE MARCHES

CHOOSING THE favourable moment when the Wold is impassable in winter and the King safe out of the way in Lornra Zombremar, King Sagartis of Akkama, in contempt of all treaties, attacks Fingiswold and invests Rialmar. Bodenay ably defends it, with the assistance of Romyrus and of Roder, what happens to be in Rialmar for the winter. Queen Rosma, in face of this deadly peril, directs and inspires the defence with politic wisdom and with the courage and fire of an Amazon.[1]

The King, on receiving the news, comes down to Sestola, and thence sails with Jeronimy in mountainous seas (830 miles from Sestola to the nearest port of Fingiswold, fifty miles from Rialmar).

Valero, as it now appears, has been in league with Sagartis, the tributary king of Akkama, who promised secretly his support to Valero's wild scheme to make himself king in Rerek. As soon as the King has sailed to the north, this traitor raises rebellion in the March of Ulba. With foolhardy courage, he has placed himself for this purpose in Argyanna, where he now attempts to seize Emmius Parry's person, his host and benefactor. Emmius, now an old man of seventy-nine, valiantly resists, but is cut down by Valero's men in Valero's presence. His wife, Deïaneira, flinging herself between Emmius and the murderers, is butchered with him. Morville, a distant cousin of the Parry, plays a part here: tries to help Emmius and, after his murder, escapes to inform Horius.

Valero fails to secure Argyanna. Horius Parry, whose agents have kept him remarkably well informed, appears swiftly and in armed strength before the fortress (too late indeed to save his uncle: enemies ask whether he really wanted to), and demands its surrender. Valero escapes by the skin of his teeth.

After several heavy battles, Horius (771) puts down the revolt. He then cleans up the rebels with merciless thoroughness and not without an eye to the interests of persons friendly to his house and supremacy in Rerek. He beheads Count Bork and a dozen other great men: spares, and so binds to his obedience, Olpman and Gilmanes (the latter, as Valero's brother thirteen years his senior, is dangerously under suspicion): punishes many more. Valero himself, fleeing for sanctuary to his brother Gilmanes in Kaima, is by him handed over to the Parry, who puts him to death in a horrible and secret manner in Laimak dungeons. Because of these severities, the Lord Horius Parry comes to be called by his ill-willers (not too loudly, and behind his back) 'the Beast of Laimak.'

Barganax, leading a small force into the Ulba March during the rebellion, wins a brilliant cavalry victory: this to the confusion of many who had until now set him down as no better than a chambering dilettante, a do-little, and a dallier with women.

With a small force the King makes a surprise landing in Akkama, defeats that power at the battle of Elsmo, and cuts the communications of the invading army, which is eventually destroyed before Rialmar, and Sagartis slain.

XXVII

THIRD WAR WITH AKKAMA

ESSINGHAM GAINS renown at the battle of Elsmo, and in his pursuit of the enemy through the Greenbone ranges. It was upon Horius Parry's recommendation that the King had taken Lessingham with him on this expedition. A mysterious and mutual attraction, as if rooted in some inward tie between them more subtle and more intimate than kinship, is privately felt both by Lessingham and by the King. The King indeed, when he looks at this young man, seems to see as in a mirror the image of his own opening manhood of thirty years ago.

In 772 the King permits Sagartis's young son Derxis (aged sixteen) to succeed his father as tributary king of Akkama, with a Fingiswold Commission of Regency to govern the country in his name, and tutors to guide him. This discontents the Queen and Styllis, who can see nothing but bravado and rashness in such action. But Barganax and the Duchess completely understand the King's settled policy of admitting even the most unhopeful and dangerous of mankind to probation, and deeply delight both in his policy and in him.

Horius Parry, since his quelling of the rising in the Marches, has enjoyed new power and exalted station as Vicar of Rerek.

Beroald is made Chancellor of Fingiswold, but continues to live at Krestenaya.

Roder, in recognition of his share in the defence of Rialmar in 771, is made an Earl.

Bodenay (aged seventy-two) is, on similar grounds, made Knight Marshal of Fingiswold.

Jeronimy, for his service at sea in this third war with Akkama, receives the kingly order of the hippogriff, hitherto conferred only upon persons of the blood royal. He, Beroald, and Roder are now joined in a triumvirate as Commissioners Regent for Meszria, exercising (in like manner as the Vicar in Rerek and Bodenay in Fingiswold) vice-regal powers during the King's absences.

Barganax is well content with his dukedom and apanage, and rules it ably and well. He is much given to women: paints, and composes poems, and is often with his mother in Memison. He becomes more and more the centre of hopes of those Meszrians whose acceptance of the King is not only because they have no choice but because he has won all hearts, and who yet resent the King's power in Meszria as embodied in the Admiral, the Chancellor, and the Earl. Of these three, Beroald is the least unpopular, because a Meszrian by birth; but they are jealous of his power and fearful of his strong hand, his pride and subtlety, and the far-laid nets of his intelligence system.

Lessingham, accompanied by his friend and lieutenant Amaury, goes abroad in 772 (aged twenty) to seek adventure as a soldier of fortune in distant countries of the world. (He does not appear again in person in this book.)

After the crushing of Akkama and the putting down of the rebellion in the Marches, the Three Kingdoms enjoy yet another five years of *Pax Mezentiana (772–6)*.

BOOK 6

LA ROSE NOIRE

XXVIII

ANADYOMENE[1]

I T W A S spring of the leaf now: mid-April of that year seven hundred and seventy-one, and these victories new in Rerek and the north. My lord Chancellor Beroald was with the King in Argyanna about the business of bringing in of Stathmar as King's Captain there, the place being devolved, since the death of Lord Emmius Parry, to estate of fief royal under like government with the other key-fortresses.

At home at Zemry Ashery the Chancellor's young sister dwelt still sweetly, quite untraded in court ceremonies or the ways of men, but in the theoric of these matters liberally grounded through daily sage expositions and informations by Doctor Vandermast, who had these four years past been to her for instructor and tutor. To try her paces and put in practice the doctor's principles and her own most will-o'-the-wisp and unexperimental embroiderings upon them, ready means lay to hand in converse with her brother: a merry war, sharping and training up the claws of her wit, and admiredly watering and firming at root the friendship between her and him, who was long become to her both father and mother in one. With the open countryside for nursery, Anthea and Campaspe for playmates, all living creatures of wood and farm and mountain for her familiars, and her fifteenth birthday at hand within a month or two, she

was beginning day by day at this season, in tune with the rising of
the world's whole sap, to put on herself fresh beauties, fresh intimations and ambiguities of awakening power, while the sun mounted
from Aries into Taurus.

In a place of her own, a backwater private beside the river
under Zemry Ashery, she was lazing herself today through the soft
spring afternoon, upon a kind of hanging bed or hammock woven
of daffodil-coloured silken cords and swung by ropes of silk from
the boughs of one of the ancient alder-trees that have their roots
deep in the marshy banks of that backwater. Overhead, these trees
spread their canopy: bare of leaf, but with gold-brown catkins dangling, gold-edged against the unclouded blue, from every mesh of
that network of tiny twigs. Ever and again a light zephyr ruffled the
stillness and made these tassels swing delicately in the spice-laden,
faintly salted, sweetness of the Meszrian spring-time. Here she
reclined, with none save the trees and the water and the little living
beings of the field to bear her company, and her own maiden
thoughts.

A heavy book lay in her lap, bound in quarto in sweet-smelling
leather with hasps of gold set with ruby and pearl. Presently she
took it up, lazily turned the leaves, and began to read in it at that
page of Homer's *Hymn to Aphrodite* where the Goddess, smitten by
Zeus with sweet desire for Anchises, a mortal man, comes to Her
own temple in Paphos and, shutting to the shining doors, makes the
Graces wash and anoint Her with olive oil,

> Immortal, such as the Gods have upon Them that live
>   forever;
> Ambrosial, fit for Her wear.

And in the fair margin of the page was all this drawn and pictured,
in colours of lapis lazuli and lamp-black and vermillion and incarnadine and leaf of gold and silver.

Idly she read on:

> Nicely upon Her skin disposing Her beautiful raiment,
> Herself with gold adorning, laughter-loving Aphrodite
> Swept on Her way toward Troy, leaving sweet-perfum'd
>   Cyprus:
> Swift so, high amid clouds, fulfilling Her journey.
> Thus came She to Ida, many-fountain'd mother of beast-kind,
> And so by straight path thorough the mountain; and here
>   about Her
> Grey wolves fawning, and lions with eyes glad-glaring,
> And bears, and fleet-footed panthers of roe-deer's flesh
>   unsatiate,

Went. She at that sight took pleasure, both bowels and spirit
    within Her.
And cast in their breasts desire, till they, of one motion,
Paired and lay with each other in shadowy mountain nest-
    beds.[2]

    Fiorinda put down her book and lay back luxuriously, clasping
her hands behind her head. Her hair, not plaited, but tied with a
single gold-lace ribbon and having for its self-colour a jet-like blackness that held, where the sun caught it, shimmerings and sparks of
heaven's blue, rumpled its dark splendours against the satin cushion. In a confusion of twists and tendrils it strayed here over the
cushion's crimson, here past ivoried smoothness of neck and arm;
one deep-convoluting tress reaching out, like as a many-headed hy-
dra, its curling ends to shadow vinelike the white silk bosom of her
gown, under which her ripening breasts gently with her breathing
rose and fell.
    After a while, the sun wheeling lower began to strike golden
between the branches, full on the back-strained pure lovely throat of
her: wrought marble to look upon, by the firmness of its contours,
were it not for the fluttering pulse of blood in it. Her eyes were
closed drooping their night-black fringes above high cheekbones
which (and also something estranged and unreinable in the very
lure of her lips, that were lightly parted now to the quickened coming and going of her breath) brought to mind, but faintly only and
distantly, as things Olympian may things of earth, the features of
her brother. Her nose, for its falcon-like keenness and mobility of
wing and nostril, was her true maternal grandfather's, Emmius's;
but delicatelier moulded, and with aphrodisian seductions en-
sweetening and ensphering to very heaven the Parry pride and
hardness.
    There was a kindling might of summer rising now, against the
common tide of nature at this hour of declining day and at this
young season of the year: an invading heat, that heightened the
musky moist scents of spring to an urgence beyond use and beyond
imagination. In that warmth and that languor, she let her right
hand reach down over the swung hammock's edge. It touched the
new growth of a narcissus: stiff, green, eager fingers, thrusting up
through grass, out of the awakening earth beneath her. With this
for hand-hold to begin with, then letting go and yielding herself to
an almost imperceptible shifting of her weight back and forth under
the gathering rhythm, she began to swing the couch she lay on: back
and forth, without all effort, yet with slowly increasing power. The
heavenly unnatured warmth, and these spring-scents stung to
drunkenness with the summer-strangeness in the air about her,
waxed and grew with the motion of that swinging till they seemed to

swallow up the whole vast universe of sense and thought and being, dissolving her like a sweet in the goblet in an overwhelming Elysian languor.

When at last she unclosed her eyelids, the sun was about setting: a flattened ball of incandescence that suffused the whole arch of the sky westwards with a blush of tremulous light. Not a breath stirred. She stood up, aery-delicate in the pallour of her silken gown, but bearing, in the light lilt and sway of her carriage, patent of some hitherto unthought-of power new born. The daybirds' voices were hushed, save for here and there the call of a water-hen going to bed, or a dabchick's trill of high bubbling notes, sweet naiad music trembling to silence. The nightingales had not yet begun their night-song. She looked about her, as to assure herself that no human presence was here to spy her solitude, then put off her shoes and stockings. Standing on the verge, her left hand upon a branch at shoulder-level to steady her, her right kilting her skirt, she dipped a foot into the darkening water. The cool of it warmed to the touch, as if some property within her had power to raise summer heats even in that inert element, home of newt and water-beetle and roach and char. Ripples travelling across the pool from her paddling foot broke the reflections. She stood back, both feet on the bank again. The ooze welled up luscious and warm between her toes through the grassroots.

The sun being gone now and the after-glow fast fading in the west, a bower of moonrise began to open from behind the hills eastward. In the midst of this presently the virgin-cold moon appeared. Yet still that unearthly warmth, spring-like in its newness, summer-like in its depth and potency, grew and strengthened. Fiorinda, as utterly surrendered up to these influences, surveyed for a while, now up, now down, the moon-drenched obscurities of land and sky, the ground and the sleepy waters at her feet, and night's thousand eyes opening one by one. Then she laughed, in herself, very low, soundlessly. All the adoring earth seemed to laugh and open its arms to her.

For the first time, with only the moon for tiring-maid, she began to put up her hair: braided it, then coiled and piled it high on her head; and finding her hair-ribbon unsufficient to hold it there, took off her girdle of white silk and margery-pearls to bind up the heavy tresses, with two brooches from the bosom of her gown to learn a new office as hair-pins. She leaned her out over the water, to have viewed herself so; but, with the moon behind her, could see nought to her purpose only but dark shadow outlined against a background of dusky blue twig-fretted sky and glimmer of star-images deep below all. Turning again, she saw where there sat, on a birch-tree's limb not a dozen paces from her, the shape of a little owl, erect, clear-outlined against the moon. Suddenly it took wing and lighted without sound, upon her proffered wrist: a being that seemed without weight or substance, and the clasp of its claws upon her tender skin harmless as those sweet smarts that are fireworkers to pleasure. She raised her arm, to look level in its round fierce eyes; but it lowered its gaze. The trembling of it, sitting there, sent little shudders up her arm and through her whole body. With her free hand she stroked its feathers, then brought it near to her lips. Gentle as a turtle-dove with his mate, it fell to billing her, trembling in the doing of it, like a young untutored lover at first kiss of his mistress: then suddenly upon noiseless downy wing departed. In that sudden she was ware of Mistress Anthea standing beside her, regarding her from eyes coruscant with yellow fire, and holding up to her a looking-glass edged about with three rows of moon-stones that shone with their own light.

Fiorinda abode motionless beholding how, from that mirror and lighted by that enchantment of stones, her own face looked out at her: a face new-wakening in a soft self-amazement, and still, perhaps, half asleep. The eyes, large, almond-shaped, set almost infinitesimally aslant, and infinitesimally at variance between themselves, altering and altering again in their sea-green deeps yet ever the same in the sweet level lines of their under-lids, gave to the slender sweep of black eyebrows and to the lovely open purity of brow above them and to the proud and unmitigable characters in nose and mouth and cheek, a bewitchment of newness and timelessness, and agelessness. Suddenly, even while she looked, the mirror was gone, and before her no longer her own face but Anthea's, staring upon her in a kind of awe and wonder. It was as though, in this creature, there stood before her but a thousandth part, perhaps, of her own self; and, in Campaspe (who waited too at hand now, ready to help her on with her cloak), another, all different, thousandth part. Taking the cloak about her, for the Meszrian spring was sobered to its natural self again, and the night-breeze came cool from the river, she said to Anthea, 'There's more difference between me of yesterday and Me tonight than between you in your girl-skin, Madam Fuff-cat, and you in your fur and claws.' At the under-musics in her voice, all the April night seemed to hold its breath and listen.

But Anthea at these words, all decencies cast aside, fell to leaping in and out of her lynx-dress, gambolling about her mistress, fawning upon her, rolling and bowling herself, rubbing her head against her, hugging and kissing her feet and ankles, till Fiorinda's hair was fallen down again about her shoulders, and herself fallen backwards on the couch, weak with laughter. Campaspe, as betwixt joy and terror at these extremes, took safety in her water-rat shape and, seated in mid-stream upon a lilyleaf, from that secure refuge awaited the riot's ending.

Fiorinda stood up: called them to heel, and then to their true shapes again: bade them, with girdle and brooches where they belonged, bring to rights her dress: last, with the hairband of gold lace, tie her hair. That performed, they soberly accompanied her, on her way homewards at last, through the open field dewy and white with moonshine.

'Men call it the star of Artemis,' Campaspe said after a while, in a whisper, gazing on the moon's face.

Fiorinda threw back her head in a slightly disdainish, half-mocking, half-caressful little motion of silent laughter. 'What is Artemis,' said she, 'but My very Sister? part of Myself: a part of Mine.'

'And Pallas,'[3] said Campaspe as, like an unbodied shadow on air, the owl floated by.

'Her too. Is a kind of engine in my soul too.'

They were come, maybe, another hundred paces in silence when Anthea spoke: very low, and with a glitter of pointed white teeth under the moon, 'And Hecate?'[4]

'Yes. But when that shall be stirring in My blood, it is time for dogs to howl, and even for the gorgons to veil their eyes and cry out for the darkness to cover them.'

The learned doctor was waiting in the castle gate. Kissing her hand, he peered closely in her face, then kissed her hand again. 'I am glad,' he said, 'that your ladyship is safe home.'

In Fiorinda's eyes looking up into his was a conscient merriment, as feasting on some secret knowledge shared by her with no person of this world save with him only and these nymphs. 'But why this new ceremoniousness of "ladyship," reverend sir?' she said.

'I think,' answered Vandermast, 'your ladyship is now awake to your very Self. And wisest now to entreat You as such.'

XXIX

Astarte[1]

P AX MEZENTIANA was begun now to rest deep on the
land: a golden age, lulled with airs blown, a man could
have believed, from Zayana, or Memison, or Lornra
Zombremar. This most of all in Meszria and Rialmar.
But even upon the factions in the Middle Kingdom,
peace strewed her poppies; under cover of which the Vicar, by firm
government, by lavishness in hospitality, and by a set policy of fastening a private hold on each man worthy his attention (laying them
under obligations to his person, or holding over them his knowledge of some secret misdoing which they would wish least of all to
see brought to light), was, without show but with patience and with
thoroughness, consolidating his power in Rerek.

The King, for his part, held by his old wont of progresses, constant so as no corner of the Three Kingdoms but had either the
fresh remembrance, or early expectation, or instant taste of his
presence; like as roosting birds should taste, familiar under their
feet, the comfort of their tree's perdurable might. His occupation
was much with merriments and light pleasures, sauced with philosophical disputations and with princely pastimes, as to see his gyr-
falcons fly at the crane, heron, and wild swan, or to hunt wolf and
bear; but greatly, amid all these doings, with overseeing of and giving order for the training up of his fighting men in all arts of war

725

and feats of endurance and might and main. Those nearest in his counsels, well thinking that lust for great performance grows with full feeding, noted how he had furnished forth that young Lord Lessingham to find out distant countries beyond seas and observe and learn their several powers, riches, and (most of all) any novel and good ways they might have devised for waging of war, and so at five years' end to come back and report to him, of these matters. They smelt, though, in his mood at this time something of that evening-sleepiness which, in skin-changers and berserks, used to follow the bouts of fury and strength and blood-shedding.[2] But well they perceived that, spite of all this unaction and sometimes seeming retirement within his own self, his sudden apprehension and piercing wits were busy as of old with every eddy and trend and deep current of the world about him; nor had they mistrust (or if any had, a word with the King, as the wind and the sun clear mists, was enough to end it) but that, whatsoever turn-about might come of these smothering times of peace, a man might as well eat hot coals as enter upon any perverse and evil dealings in hope the King should not mark him, or should wink at his misdemeanour.

Upon a May morning of the year seven hundred and seventy-four, that Lady Fiorinda being now near upon completing of the eighteenth year of her age, the Chancellor and she were ridden forth before breakfast to take the air along the sea-shore of the Korvish, south from Zemry Ashery. The tide was out, so that the whole of this silted-up southern arm of the Bishfirth, two or three miles wide upon their bridle-hand, lay dry: firm level sand, white as powdered marble, over which they galloped their horses the full six miles to the waterhead, then halted and turned homewards. Before them now, a little to the right in the far distance, the tide began to come in, with a crosswind from the east whipping it to foam. Overhead, feathery trailers of white cloud streaked the azure: a mistiness of spindrift whitened the sea-line beyond the expanse of white sands: the slopes landward, above them on the left, were misty-grey with olive trees: ahead, Zemry Ashery upon its promontory showed dusky-blue, against the more cerulean and paler hues of the great mountains afar in the north, and with edgings of gold light where the sun took its eastern walls.

They rode leisurely at a walking-pace, the horses' breaths coming in clouds on the cool morning air after that long stretch of speed. Here and there they halted to peer from the saddle into the emerald depths of some great sea-pool, sometimes with an outcrop of jade-like rock at its bottom upon which limpets had their homes, and sea-anemones; some that slept, shiny lumps of sealing-wax, scarlet or dark brown: some that waked, opening flower-like faces in hope of sea-lice and other small deer to be their breakfast. And from chinks in these drowned rocks bosky growths of sea-weed spread fans and streamers, dark green, tan-colour, orange-tawny, and rusty red, from whose shadows little iridescent fishes darted in the sunlit stillness, or a crab crept sidelong. That brother and sister, being now more than half-way home, were pleasing themselves with the contemplation of one such little seaish garden of the nereids, when they were aware of a rider coming down to them through the olive-groves. He had that seat that belongs to a man that cannot remember the first time he bestrode a horse: as though, as in the centaur-kind, man's body and horse's were engrafted and one.

'Good morrow, my Lord Baias,' said the Chancellor, returning his salute. 'I'd a mind these three weeks past to a come to greet you as our next neighbour now, which glads me for long acquaintance sake. But I've been wonderful full of business.'

Fiorinda, looking up from her pool-gazing, turned in the saddle to have sight of him. His great stone-horse, winding her little mare, threw up his head: snorted, whinnied, pawed the ground. Baias struck him with the horn handle of his riding-whip a devilish blow on the jaw, and, but for fine horsemanship, had doubtless been thrown and killed for his pains, but after a short fight brought him to order. 'I am for Krestenaya, my lord Chancellor,' he said, his eyes returning still to the vision of her where she sat, mysterious against the light, ''pon a business with your own armourer you told me of. Hath my best sword to mend. I hurt it upon a swashing fellow bade me to the *duello,* weeks since, ere I came south.'

'You hurt him worse than you hurt the sword?'

'Nay, that's certain. I hear a be dead.'

Beroald said, 'Let's ride on the way together. On a more fitting occasion you must come and see us in Zemry Ashery.'

'Joyfully,' answered he, bringing his horse up upon Fiorinda's right as they moved off. 'Have no fear, madam: he knoweth his master.'

She replied by an almost unperceptible half-scornful little backward lifting of her head, not looking at him but forward between the mare's ears. The beauty of her face, lit with morning and flushed with the wind, seemed to flicker between self-contrarying extremes: sweets and lovelinesses drawing at their train diamond-hard unswavables and that pride that binds the devils: lips whose stillness was a pool where, like lotus-buds closed under the sun's eye, delicate virginal thoughts and witty fancies seemed to slumber, but rooted, far below that shining and tranquil surface, in some elixir of darkness potent to shake man's blood.

Baias spoke: 'Your lordship has forgot to do me that honour to present me.'

'Cry you mercy. I'd forgot there was the need. This is my lady sister.'

'Your sister?' Baias bent to kiss the hand she offered him, crimson-gloved. There was here, as indeed in his every motion, a certain taking haughtiness of manner; but easeful: begotten, not court-bred. 'From what I'd heard tell,' he said to the Chancellor, 'I supposed her but a child yet. And yet, behold. You've kept her very close, my friend.'

They rode awhile in silence, Baias with eyes still upon her. When at length, turning her head, she met his gaze, he laughed merrily. 'Is your brother a blood-sucker, a troll-man, to a kept you so long time closeted up from the world?'

Faintly raising her eyebrows, that seemed of their nature to carry an air of permanent soft surprise, she said, 'I am very well content with my company, thank you.'

'He is a very secret man. I know him of old and his ways. How comes it we are never honoured with a sight of your ladyship at the presences in Zayana?'

'Some day you may live to see such a thing.'

'There is time yet,' said her brother lightly. 'Overhastiness was never a distemper in our family.'

After another silence, Baias said softly to her, 'Life's not long enough, in my seeming, to slack sail when a fair wind blows. But, for myself, to say true, I am by complexion hasty.' He paused, studying her face, sideways to him. 'I'm in hasty mood now,' he said.

Something not altogether unkind, betwixt comprehension and mockery, glinted at her mouth's corners as she said very equably, 'Then it were wrong in us to delay you further, my lord. Our horses are breathed, and I would not put them to speed again this morning.' She glanced round to her brother, who drew rein.

'Why there,' said Baias, 'spoke a true courtesy, and I'll act upon it.' They halted. In his eyes, meeting hers, sat some swift determination that seemed to stiffen the whole posture of his body and (as by infection) of the great horse's that carried him. 'But since here's parting of our ways, and delays breed loss,' said he, looking from her to Beroald and so again to her, 'I'll first, in great humility, request of your ladyship your hand in marriage.'

Save for the faintest satirical lift of eyebrows she made no response, only with great coolness regarding him.

'Was that over-sudden?' said Baias, noting the manner of her look, which was interested, meditative, removed; even just as she had looked down from above upon fishes and marauding crabs in the sea-pools' transparent deeps. 'Saw you but with my eyes, felt with my blood, you should not think so. Nay, sweet madam, take time, then, I pray you. But I pray you, for my peace sake, not too long time.'

'Your lordship were best ask my brother here, my guardian. I am not yet of full age. Besides, as he told you but now, we are not, of our family, rushers into unadvised decisions.'

'You're not offended at me, I hope?'

Fiorinda smiled: a shadowy ambiguous smile of lip and nostril, her eyes still level upon him in that studious remote intention.

'Offended because you wish to marry her?' said the Chancellor. ''Tis the best compliment he could a paid you, sister.'

'Is it?' Then, to Basias: 'O, not offended. Surprised, perhaps. Perhaps a little amused. Pity your lordship should have to wait for your answer to so natural a demand.'

'Admired and uncomparable lady, be not angry with me. I'll wait. But beseech you, not too long.'

'Depends of the answer. Too long, you may think, if answer be good; but if t'other way, you'd then have at least the comfort of delay to thank me for. We meet again?' she said, giving him her hand.

'If I thought not,' kissing it and holding it longer than need were in his, 'God for witness, I'd go stab myself.' With that, like a man unable to hold the lid longer on a boiling pot, Baias struck spurs into his stallion's flanks and, with great rearings and tossings of mane and clatter of hooves, departed.

The lady said, after a few minutes' silence as, alone together once more, they came their way: 'A turn I least looked for in you, brother. And gives me strangely to think.'

'What do you mean?'

'As good as hold me out like a piece of merchandise to this friend of yours, by I know not what fair promises made to him behind my back; and no leave asked of me.'

'You're quite mistook. I'd ne'er made mention of you.'

'Strange. If true.'

'This is the nature of him: even rash and sudden. But a man of many and remarkable virtues, and of high place in the land.'

'Does he think I am so agog for a husband, there's nought to do but whistle on his fist and I'll hop to him?'

'Come, you're too bitter. 'Tis not unpardonable in a man to know his own worth.'

'Nor in a woman. But I think he hath eyes for no other worth than his own.'

Beroald said, with an ironic twitch of his nostrils. 'You cooled any such hare-brained thought as that in him ere we parted.'

After another silence: 'I still suspect you as of his party, brother. By your talk. By your praises.'

'Well, the man is a friend of mine. And friends are useful.'

'The uses of friendship! And sisters, too, made for use?'

'I shall not answer that.' Their glances countered: a kind of merry hand-fast in the air, while that thing at the corner of Fiorinda's mouth conjured some dim earthbound shadow of itself on the Chancellor's stony lip. 'Only,' he said, cold, careless, judicial again, 'if there your fancy should chance to light, I confess 't should not displease me.'

'How old is this friend?'

'Of some five years' standing.'

'His age, I meant?'

'O, of my age, I suppose, within a year or two.'

'Old enough to have known, then, I'd have thought, that a girl's hand is to be suited for, not guttishly demanded.' She added, after a pause: 'As call for a pottle of ale in a tavern.'

They rode on, a mile or so: no word spoken, the Lord Beroald watching her. When at length their eyes met there was that in hers that seemed to hold him again at arm's-length as if, upon revolving the matter, she was not to be persuaded but that they now no longer played each other's game, but he his, she hers. Beroald smiled. 'Forget the man.'

'Pew! One needs remember in order to forget.'

'I count him but our instrument. No more but that. Forget him.'

'Alas, poor instrument! He and I have at last some fellow-feeling there, then.'

'I'll not have you think such a thought.'

'No? You are a skilful player at the chess, brother; but when you would use me for your pawn—'

'That's a wicked lie, and you know it. Where were my skill, if I knew not the difference 'twixt pawn and queen? Both in the worth and in the manage.'

'Where indeed? But I am not for your political chessboard, in whichever capacity: to be moved about. I begin to find I have an appetite,' she said, in a pensiveness now, delicately inclining to stroke her horse's neck, 'to be my own self-mover.'

That same day at evening, upon bidding goodnight, Beroald said to her, 'I will make you a promise which, until this unlucky turn this morning, I'd have thought needless between you and me. It is this: never to use you, unless of your own free motion or consent, for a means to ends of mine.'

In Fiorinda's eyes was a twinkle of the mind between sceptic caution and comical intuition, touched with a kind of love. 'Thanks, noble brother: let's make this bargain mutual. And hold me not ungracious that I do fear th' engagement may prove harder for you to abide by than for me 'twill be.'

'Come, be just to each other. For me, what is 't but stick to what hath become my natural habit since first you could prattle?'

'I think,' said she, playing with his fingers, 'you may find it less easy now.' Then, looking up, and very demurely and sweetly putting her arms about his neck: 'We understand each other?'

As a sophister should at need speak smooth words at the Sphinx, 'I think so,' said the Chancellor; and so saying, with an unbelieving twist of his lean lips, beheld shadows of things past all understanding, unmapped stars of bale and of bliss, come and go in the profundities of his young sister's eyes.

'Good,' she said, and kissed him. Laughing, they took hands, and so goodnight. He watched her go up the shining staircase; a beauty of motion that was intertangled as in counterpoint with the beams of lamplight and candlelight faintly swaying; then, with the same unbelieving smile on his lips, betook him to his study.

The Lord Baias's wooing, thus hastily begun and ever the more furiously urged and with an impatience the angrier and the sharper set as it became more manifest what dance his mistress meant to lead him, dragged and tarried through the summer. In the end (more, it was commonly suspicioned, with a mind to humour her brother than for any inordinate liking for her suitor's person), she accepted him. A few days later (early September) they were wed in Krestenaya with circumstance and ceremony befitting their noble station, and so with honour and rejoicing brought home to Masmor.

After the first month guests began to be received, and greatly was Baias envied his fair and lovely bride. Some, with more inquiring eyes and shrewd minds observing the climate, tasted uneasiness in the house, spite of all outward gaiety. It was noted moreover that Baias and his lady seldom accepted invitations in the countryside but kept much to their own society, and that she, for her part, was never seen in Zayana. Some that were very knowing said, wagging their beards, that the Chancellor's hand was in this, contriving, through Baias, to continue still his old policy of seclusion. Howsoever, it was the household folk at Masmor that had best commodiousness to acquaint themselves with these affairs, and with other little things besides. And now, as the season drew on toward mid November, it began to be merrily whispered among them that not only had her ladyship had since some time past her own chamber, but her lord was now-a-days not seldom exiled to his own bed for several nights together.

These misspeakings coming at length to Baias's ear, he took marvellous displeasure at them: let seize three of the girls deemed guilty of such tittle-tattle: duck them in the castle pond; then scissors, for well shorting and clipping away of their garments to large show of their naked thighs: for last disgrace, off with their hair; and so, in that dishonest and ugly pickle, pack them home. Whether upon suspicion of this talk's having a higher source than the mouths it had been heard drop from, or whether for a spite fed by deeper springs wholly removed from these, he now upon some slight unclear pretext sent for Anthea and Campaspe. These maidens being come before him he used very roughly, speaking doggery at them: calling them a pair of fleering slavish parasites, whose jibes behind his back (because he was not book-learned) he highly disdained any longer to endure: bade them therefore within one hour void clean out of the castle and no more resort to the same. 'Any she that disobeys, her hair goes off for it. That's blushed your cheeks, ha? And not to be compounded by a minute's perfunctory scissoring such as sufficed this morning. O, no: you ladies would be honoured with very respectful care and tendance: have it close shorn to begin with: then the razor. Fear nothing; you need but dispose yourselves as convenience of shaving may requires, and so sit still, gently re-signed up to have it taken so, with extreme particular dainty, every-where all completely off, quite and clean. Ponder on that. If you have no desire for such a needful service to be done unto you, study to meddle with your own business and obey my command. And now begone. Nay then, come you back a moment, you laughing minxes: one more word. Flatter not yourselves with the vain conceit that being gentlewomen exempts you from the barber. Were you never so noble born, upon my honour as a Meszrian lord I swear to you, it should off. Trespass you but once; clipped, soaped, and faithfully shaven you shall be, nesh and smooth as two little sea-pigs. Except your eyelashes, for I'll not be cruel, there's not one hair shall remain upon.'

My Lady Fiorinda took no overt notice of this undecent severity against her domestics nor of the dismissal of her waiting-gen-tlewomen, as though she would have it supposed that she thought it best to suffer the order of the world to manage her, for this present, without further inquisition. In truth, she herself was put to but very slight inconvenience; for Anthea and Campaspe, unshaping their bodies to their customary disguise of beast or bird, were able at all times of day or night to be present at need in Masmor. It is not to be thought that their nymphish minds misdoubted their lady's inward peace; for how (they might in their innocency question) should She, that holds in Her own self the world everlasting and unbegotten, She for whom all worlds are made, behold or know unhappiness? For all that, they scented trouble. Many a time, as the days grew shorter and the sap sunk and even in these soft sea-lands of South Meszria light ground-frosts sometimes sharpened the breath of night, Mistress Anthea licked her lips and, as frost makes the fire glow brighter in the grate, so the upright slits of her eyes burned with a more fulvid splendour. Many a time too, in her lynx-dress, she frighted her sister, chasing her for her sport. And had Baias been a man of less lion-like metal, having the ordinary aptness to obey the heart-emptying touch of fear, he were like to have been frighted too: beholding from the solitude of his bed, and not once or twice only, during these nights of the dying year in the chill betwixt midnight and dawn, those beast-eyes stare upon him out of the black and silent darkness. The third time, a little before Yule, he said to Fiorinda at breakfast that albeit she seemed, for reasons of her own, to prefer to sleep a-nights oftener with her mountain cat than with him, himself had no such preference; and unless she would promise to kennel the beast henceforth and to give him her company nightly, as of old, as a wife should, he would without further warning dispatch it with his hunting-knife. The lady listened, her green eyes cold upon him as frozen pebbles on a sea-beach under the moon. She replied: " 'First serve, syne suit,' I've heard say. But that is no maxim of yours, my lord, as I have found from the beginning, more's the pity.' With that, she left the table.

Late the same afternoon, Baias being ridden abroad upon some business and not expected home before supper-time, my Lady Fiorinda was walking her alone in the borders of those great oak-woods that train southwards along the skirts of the hills from Masmor. Here she was met with the learned doctor. After greetings they stood silent awhile, Vandermast's eyes from beneath their jutting thatch of white eyebrow searching her face in the uncertain and now fast fading light under the trees.

'Your ladyship walks alone?' he said presently. 'Where by my little disciples?'

'You must not ask me questions to which you already know the answer.'

'Nay, I worded it amiss, my mind being wholly taken up with your ladyship's affairs and forgetting that sometimes it is right and needful we attend to matters contingent. I know they are in Lornra Zombremar, having myself, by means of a certain crystal, beheld them there this morning. But I would have asked why.'

'I sent them away after breakfast, with order to dwell for a while in their true shapes, sometimes there, sometimes in Memison, and not to return, in whatever dress, until I shall send for them.'

'You are all alone, then?'

'All alone, with my lord. The time has come when it is best for us to be alone.'

Doctor Vandermast regarded her narrowly. Then he said: '*Res nullo modo neque alio ordine a Deo produci potuerunt, quam productae sunt:* Things were not able to be brought to being by God in any other manner, nor in any other order, than as they have in fact been brought. And yet this thing is, to my confined and but part-conceiving intellects, a surd: an irrational uncogitable. I mean, your ladyship's having art or part in this Baias.'

'Indeed it is certain,' she said, turning her colour and with a curl of the lip, 'he is, albeit a man of great birth and courage, very smally sensed; save in one particular and there he is a mere com-

monplace fellow and little deserving of so sanctified a gift: an en-
slaver of women, hapt in a most unlucky hour upon one he hath not
the art to enslave. The nearer known, the more unsufferable he is, I
think.'

'Beloved and honoured Mistress,' said the doctor, 'being yours
while life swayeth within me, and knowing your ladyship, may be,
better than sometimes you do know yourself, I consider not of this.
For to you there is nought uneasy to achieve. But when I consider of
these honest humble harmless children, the great offences and mis-
behavings he hath done against them as lambs voiceless before their
shearer, and abominably purposeth the like against my pretty
nymphs—'

'Mew!' said she, breaking in upon him: 'these are light occasions of small moment. But if you must know, no harm's done. My
lord Chancellor, by my request, harboureth them in Zemry Ashery:
when fit to be seen again, will be ta'en into his household there.
There are other privacies committed to my charge more troublesome and of far weightier import than these. As by proof will appear. And if you think not, reverend sir, your love towards me is not
such as our watchful friendship towards you hath deserved.'

Vandermast held his peace. For a minute in silence now, that
lady steadily beheld him. The hueless cold light of the winter sun
setting unseen behind thick cloud-banks was yet strong enough for
his eyes, gazing into hers and upon her countenance, to see, for that
minute, the truth of her: her eyes tender as a dove's: in the bird's-
wing curve of her eyebrows a timeless question that seemed to attend no answer: in her nose, a critical outward-regarding superbity
that judged without appeal, and an all-transcending power dwelling
serene in each exquisite line (carved by Him who carved the lily's
purity) of bridge and tip and wing and thought-disclosing nostril.
Her lips were lightly pursed together, as in a divine demur between
doubt and unrelenting will: their sudden up-turns at the corners
held, through these strained moments, a gravity of annealed barbed
hooks forged from a half-regretful gentleness: turtle's breast
changed to adamant by infection of some unturnable spirit that informed the strength of her underlip, clear-cut and level above the
slender firmness of her chin. Worlds' wonder and heaven's uncloy-
ing commonplace seemed, on these lips, to lie stilled in immortal
meditation; wherein, as things partly asleep, love and scorn, and a
high Olympian quintessence of inward laughter, and those hearts of
pity and ineffable sadness that throb unseen beneath all glory and
honour and beauty and beyond all worlds' endings, seemed to rest,
and, as Gods may grieve, to grieve.

'Is it not the way of Them that keep the wide heaven,' she said,
and her voice was gentle as falling shadows of night, 'to give scope
to whomsoever shall require it of Them, that none may needlessly

perish? But there cometh always an hour of decision. Lest eternity itself be parcelled out in too unprofitable leases.'

'The ways of Her are unscrutable,' said that old man, slowly and softly, after a long pause.

'Your deep discerning wisdom,' she answered, 'has never disappointed me.' She was wearing, against the wintry weather, a great cloak of rich black sables fastened at the throat with clasps of hammered silver. She opened it: flashes, under his eyes for a timeless instant, Her beauty that can by its glory darken heaven and consume to ashes all worlds: then, muffling her cloak again about her, was gone: through the trees, back to Masmor.

Left so, the aged doctor stood fixed: blinded for the while, uncertain of his direction, as a man whose light has been suddenly blown out stands lost in pitch darkness; but Vandermast, for all his darkness, stood rapt in that vision that never until today (he said to the self within himself) was vouchsafed to mortal eye.

Ten days later, upon New Year's Eve in Masmor, supper done and the guests departed, her ladyship was sat idly reading before a fire of cedar-wood in her own bower that opened off the main hall. To her left, upon a three-legged table of walnut inlaid with ivory and mother-of-pearl and arabesques of silver, nine candles in a great crystal candlestick gave a gentle and companiable light, pleasant for reading. These, and the lamplight, and the firelight, and the transmuted splendours, begotten of all three, which glowed in the inwards of the twin escarbuncles, big as gold-crest's eggs, at her ears and sparkled from the facets of the pendant of the same blood-dark stone that slumbered above her breasts, seemed to be things without substance save as part of her: part of her body's grace: visible emanations of the spirit that informed that body so that it held within itself (mixed and made one, as stillness and the extreme of ruinous power unite at a great whirlpool's centre) the ruin of worlds and the untarnishable eternity of every world's desire.

Baias, in a seeming discontent and irresolution, paced the room, his eyes returning to her as moth to candleflame. 'What were you and Melates discoursing of?' he said, coming to a stand at last over against her, his back to the fire.

'Pleasant nothings,' she answered, without looking up.

He came and sat on the arm of her chair. 'Talk some to me.'

'I pray you begin, then,' she said, continuing her reading.

''Twill be a pleasant change when you do as I wish, for once in a while,' said he: then noting the little mocking lift of her head, snatched her book and threw it on the floor. 'We might agree better that way.'

Fiorinda rose, saying under her breath, 'Oh how long? how long? It is half a death to me, this.'

'What do you mean, 'this'?'

'If you would be answered, let go of my skirt.'

'Sit down, then,' he said, letting go, and sitting himself in her chair. 'Here.'

She remained standing, looking him steadily in the eyes.

'Very well,' he said, and stood up again: thrust his face close to hers. 'You like to stand, 'cause you are more than common tall? Beware, though, how you look down on me.'

'Don't touch me, you were best.'

'I haven't, for a fortnight. That were a pleasant change, too.'

'To you, maybe. We have our several tastes in these matters.'

Upon that he seized her: mouth kissing her fiercely, her throat, her eyes, her lips, and between her breasts: hands greedy upon her: while she like a very dead thing abode in his arms, suffering all, inert, hard, and without response. After a while he desisted: swung round from her and, under the sting and fury of that flesh-enraging madness kicked the table over.

Fiorinda, standing where he had left her, hair fallen down, dress disordered, yet in an imperial immobility, looked on. 'Poor table. What had that done to be kicked? Have you hurt your toe?'

'Pick up those candles. Would you have us all burn?'

She remained without stirring. Baias, halting on his right foot, set in order table and candles again: then stood glaring upon her. 'Fut, I cannot fathom you: this strained modesty: counterfeit coyness. Or is it some prank, some new fantasticness of whorism? What end do you look of it? Are you a woman? Or a tormenting Fury, sent to make me kill you and then myself? Were we wed for that?'

'Perhaps we were. You know better than I.'

Sitting him down again in her chair, 'Get you to bed, madam,' he said, avoiding her gaze. 'I'll give you ten minutes for unreadying of yourself. Then I'll follow and make my peace; and an end so, I hope, of these jars and bickerings.'

That lady, looking down on him, searched his face for a moment, but still his eyes avoided hers. She turned and, with head bowed, walked very slowly to the door: paused there, and with head erect looked on him again. Their eyes met. 'You desire me,' she said, 'but you do not know, nor desire to know, how to make love to me.' He glowered upon her in silence, the sweat shining on his brow, the great veins standing out thick and hard on his temples. 'And,' she said, her hand behind her on the door-latch, 'so it has been from the beginning: a disableness in you, I suppose, to understand what things, and when, please me, and what displease.' She opened the door: then, turning her again to face him: 'In brief, you are a gluttonous and malignant fool.'

With that, she was gone.

Baias sat still as death. His hands, that had a sheen on the backs of them of delicate golden hair, were clamped upon the chair's arms. His eyes were on the clock. When it was a little past eleven he stood up and with firm but noiseless tread went from the room and so upstairs, and, being come to his lady's bedchamber, tried the door. It was bolted on the inside. Smoothing the accents of his voice, albeit like a hot proud horse his high blood quivered in them, 'Open,' he said, 'my love, my dew-pear, my earth's delight. Open, and I will you the order of all that I have. Let me in. I love you.'

He stood listening: not a sound from within. So still it was, he might hear the clock ticking in the hall below. He shook the door. She said, from inside, 'No opening of doors to you tonight, my lord.' And, upon his shaking it again: 'If you look for any more love-liking, in your life, betwixt you and me, importune me no more tonight.'

Baias made as if to charge against the door with his shoulder: break the bolt if he might; but, ruling himself, went away.

My Lady Fiorinda listened until the sound of her lord's foot-steps, of his going downstairs and across the hall, ceased and every-thing was still. Then, smiling, she set to to disapparel herself and, suddenly serious, stood awhile betwixt fire and mirror to contem-plate with cool appraising eye, like as that morning seven months ago she had examined from horseback the sun-lit sea-pools of the Korvish, the wonder of her own face and of all her naked beauties. Even as thought against thought, passion against passion, and all against each, made up the ever-changing bewitchments of her face: even as, throughout this other enchanted queendom, of her body, from throat to toe, from shoulder to finger-tip, some deep harmony between conflicting superlatives issued in a divine perfection: so between these two several queendoms was utter diversity in kind swept up to unity. In the face, her soul sat free: now bared, now all or in part disguised or veiled. In body's loveliness, through lively and breathing balance of form with form and of her three fair colours (white, red, and that blackness whose outbraidings are but one mode, of many divine and coequal, of the pure empyreal fire), shone the peace of Her beauty that to its eternal substance sub-sumes both earth and heaven. Each queendom by itself, face alone (incarnate soul) or body alone (incarnate spirit), were a thing ab-stracted: soul without platform or warmth or stature: spirit without understanding and without truth. But that were an impossible. Spirit, within and without, suggested this soul; and this soul spirit. Soul's beauty and spirit's were in an untimed ecstasy so steeped in each other, and by each other interpenetrated, that, without ques-tion of the outward hierarchy, each feature and lineament of her face and each particular treasure of her body, each flicker of an eyelid, each moving or stillness of swan-smooth surface, each filigree delicacy of jet-black hair was inwardly of equal honour and worth, as implicate with all the remain and, wholly as each of these, postulating and ensphering both them and Her. So that here stood She in very presence; self-exiled (doubtlessly for some such Olympian purpose as she had foreshown to Vandermast) to this house of Masmor. With a narrowing of eyes that seemed snake-like now, and with a deadly twist of some quality never, may be, noted until now even by herself, of some tigerishness and pride and unmercilessness in the contours of her lips, she smiled again. In a whisper that, to hear, should have struck chill to a man's reins and sent the blood fleeing to the heart, she said: 'Not a commodity. Not to be had by choosing or by slices, as eat a chicken. Not that, whether for man or God. And the reward of inveterate transgression, death.'

In her bower below, meanwhile, Baias threw logs on the dying fire, then sat in her chair, fidging and musing. Her book lay on the floor beside him, where he had thrown it. He picked it up. It opened at Anchises's second speech in the *Hymn to Aphrodite:*

> If mortal, then, thou beest, and woman the mother that bare
> thee;
> Otreus of name renown'd thy father, as thou averrest;
> If thou through grace of the deathless Guide be hitherward
> comen,
> Thro' Hermes, and wife of mine must be call'd to everlasting:
> Then shall none, were't whether of Gods or of men mortal,
> Me constrain nor hold, till mixt in love I have thee,
> Instant now: not were Far-darting very Apollo
> Launch from 's bow of silver the arrows that worketh
> groanings.
> Willingly I thereafter, O woman Goddess-seeming,
> So but first I mount thy bed, would sink to the House of
> Hades.[3]

'Yes,' said Baias, closing the book and with shaking hand putting it by: 'so that's the trash she reads.' "And he had, at that time, but his own imaginings to light that hot fire in him." "How much more I, that have proved and know?"

Wine and goblets stood on a side-table. He walked over to it: poured a cup: drank: returned to her chair. Quarter by quarter and hour by hour, the clock's chimes led on the watches of the night. At two o'clock, after nigh upon three hours of sitting so, he drank a second cup of wine and went upstairs again to listen. There was not a sound, save only of her breath taken peacefully in sleep. Her sleep, by native habit and suited to her years, was quiet and profound. It was dark in the passage. A faint glow of firelight showed under her door and in the chink between door and door-jamb.

Baias went to his own room, a few paces along the passage, shut the door silently, and leaned out of the window nearest hers. The night was moonless, but clear and starry. From sheer hunger for her and from hard staring to make sure that her casement stood open, as even in these winter nights was her custom so to have it, his eyes watered and smarted. He leaned out: measured the distance with his eye, window-ledge to window-ledge: said in his mind, ' 'Tis the road her cat-a-mountain took. Where that can go, there can I': stood now erect on the broad outer sill, steadying himself by hand-grip on the roll-moulded top edge of the stone architrave above his head. It was as if some unvoiced menace spoke out of the night's star-lit stillness to the proud will of him standing there: as to say, *Leap not.* He took a mighty leap sideways, face to the wall: landed with both hands clutching upon her window-sill with a jerk enough to have broken the finger-joints or dislocated the shoulders of another man, but by main strength hung on, and by the might of his arms and with scrabbling of toes against the wall pulled himself up till, half in half out of the window, he could rest at last: a thirty-foot drop below him on the outer side; but inside, the slumbrous glow from embers on the hearth: the assurance of her presence: the undisturbed sound of her sleeping, peaceful as a child's.

Next morning she rode into Zemry Ashery, gave her horse to the grooms, went up usherless to the Chancellor's study, and there found him but just finishing his breakfast. She sat her down at the far side of the table, facing him, her back to the window and the sunrise.

'An unlooked-for pleasure to begin my day with. You have breakfasted?'

She shook her head and, when he would have risen to pull the bell, prevented him with a look. He took a bit of marmalade and waited.

'I'm come home,' she said at last, looking down with the question in her eyebrows, while with one jewelled finger she moved a plate in circles before her on the sandalwood table.

'But why?'

'Decided that I do not care any longer for married life.'

A sardonic smile flickered across the granite features of the Chancellor. 'Why?' he said, and she shrugged and looked at him: a strange look. The look of a lily that has been rudely handled: but no entreaty in it, no asking for pity.

He poured out two cups of white hippocras: pushed one across the board for her. She left it untouched. He finished his breakfast in silence, as if to let her take her time. When she looked at him again her eyes were stonehard, like a snake's eyes, but, for all that, piercingly piteous now; as though here were some proud implacable thing, armed with a merciless power, come to him in its unhappiness as a hurt child to its mother.

'Is't there the wind sits?' said Beroald. 'Anchises begins to show the defects of a mortal man? A rough herdsman, albeit a prince?'

'Let's not talk Greek. There was Roman ways rather. A rape of the Sabines last night.' She gave him a steady look, then suddenly rose up and went across to the fireplace to stand there with her back to him. The curve of her neck as she looked down into the flames: back hair sitting exquisitely in the nape of it, gleaming, smooth-wound, pear-shaped, voluptuously coiling down upon itself, a black leopard, a sleeping danger: the pure and stately lines of her body, amphora-like, giving nobility to every hanging fold of her pleated skirt: as the Chancellor looked and beheld these things, his lean lips and clipped mustachios and the lines of his shaven jaw and chin seemed changed to iron.

He began a stalking up and down the room, hands clasped behind his back, and so after a turn or two placed himself to front her, a little on her right, his shoulders against the mantelpiece. 'One should not strike a woman,' he said, 'even with a flower.'

'He did not strike me.'

The Chancellor studied her face. In this shadow crosslit with the leaping fire-flames, it was like the Sphinx's. 'Shall I talk to him?' he said.

Fiorinda smoothed her dress. Very softly nodding, still looking wide-eyed into the fire, she answered in a low voice, clear and dispassionate: 'If you think it talking matter.' She looked up swiftly in his face with eyes that from their sphinxian coldness were suddenly become those of a frightened child: then bent her head for him to kiss her on the forehead. 'I was asleep,' she whispered close to his ear. 'In my own chamber, very well secured, to be from him for a while. Let himself in by the window, I suppose, without waking me. By some goatish trick, in my sleep, upon me: no help: the enemy in the gate.' She buried her face on her brother's shoulder, arms tight about his neck, sobbing and shuddering. 'I hate him. Dear Father in heaven, how I hate him.'

The next morning, not so unseasonable early as yesterday his lady, the Lord Baias came to see the Chancellor. He opened the matter with an easy frankness as between friends and brothers-in-law: a wretched inconvenience, not worth the time of day, save that it concerned her that was very dear to both of them. Main necessity was to clear with the business and stop report; and were it even for that sake alone (though he was most desirous not to hurry her) he earnestly wished her speedy return to Masmor. In this he doubted not he should have her brother's wise help, who knew as well as she did in what dear respect and love he held her. Maybe himself had been at fault too. Be that as might be, 'twere worst thing in the world were she, by tarrying over long time in Zemry Ashery, to set foolish tongues a-wagging; which, to say true, they had to his own knowledge already begun to do weeks ago, but he thought he had so far scotched that. There was nought behind it, save lovers' humours. And remember, 'twas yet but honeymoon.

At this last the Chancellor, who had listened in silence without stir of a muscle, smiled somewhat scornfully. 'For myself,' he said, 'I have never yet adventured me in the toils of wedlock, but I am enough otherwheres experienced to tell you that when a four-month honeymoon ends as this hath, 'tis time to end all. I'm sorry, my lord, but since as between kinsmen-in-law you seek my help and counsel, I can but counsel you to agree to a divorce, and that without pother or delay. Indeed, there's no choice else:' here he gave him an ill look, and added, 'unless a worser.' So saying, chill and formal again, he rose from the table.

Baias rose too: his face scarlet, but his tongue well curbed. 'This is scarce the help I looked for,' he said, 'when I came hither to you. I must take time to think on't.'

'I will give your lordship twenty-four hours,' said Beroald, 'to accept my decision.'

'You speak high, my lord Chancellor.'

'It is my custom,' replied he with great coolness, 'when the occasion demands it. Fare you well. And consider with thoughtful care what I have said to you.'

'It shall not fail. Fare you well.'

With that went Baias forth from the room, and so down the wheel-stairs in the west turret, and so through the main hall. Thence in his way out, he chanced upon his lady as she came in from the garden. She turned ashy white: checked in her walk and seemed to hesitate how she might pass him, but the passage was narrow and he blocked up the way. He unbonneted: 'I came to ask forgiveness.'

'To make your peace? i' the fashion of Wednesday night?'

Baias, as letting this pass unnoted, said, 'There's no living soul I'd accept it from but you: much less ask it. For God sake, some place with closed doors. We cannot talk here.'

'Closed doors. Upon you and me!'

'The garden, then: care not for eyes, so there be no eavesdroppers. I entreat you. I am tame. But I cannot away afore this be some way mended.'

They went, whence she had come, into the garden. After a score of paces she halted. 'This is far enough. It is past mending.'

'God forbid.'

'I have made my brother my attorney. You must talk to him.'

Lord Baias set his jaw. 'Is your pride so devilish that you cannot

be high-minded enough not to tread down mine, when like some
humble miserable suitor to his sovereign lord I come to prostrate it
before you?'

'My pride, God save the mark! when you've used me with such
outrage as I'd a supposed a scullion, perfumed with grease, would
have spared his meanest punk.'

'Must you cut my heart out? My fault was but my love for you.'

'I owe you thanks for that admission. Bear with my ignorance: I
ne'er knew man till you. And truly this halfyear's testing hath killed
my appetite for more, if you be a right example.'

'By God's lid!' said Baias, as a man whose will is seldom wonted
to be gainsaid, letting loose his passion, ''tis a perilous game you
play, mistress, and a foolish. What aim you at? are you levying faction against me? What have I done? Because your brother is the
great Chancellor and grows here to great abominable purchase,
think you by running to him with lies against me—'

'What needed lies? Truth was enough.'

'You're an ill wife. Yet hearken, for a last word: come you home
with me.'

'I will die sooner.'

'Nay, then, I have a deeper vengeance is preparing for you.
Filthy beauty. There's a man in this: men, more like. Well, 'tis Friday
morn. If by Monday you be not come back, I counsel you keep
yourself mewed in Zemry Ashery for the rest of your life. For I
swear to you by my honour, if you prove loose in the hilts I'll take
you to my fury. And I am a man that never missed of nothing yet
that I took in hand. If, being your husband, I may not have you, I'll
so deal with you as none else shall desire you. I'll slit your nose. Best
cure, as most lasting, for such as you.'

Without more for goodbye, he left her: took horse and departed.

But my Lady Fiorinda stood a full minute motionless there,
gazing after him. Upon her brow some dreadful ghastliness of old
night seemed, frowning, to rise into its throne and to shed its garment as a veil over her slanting eyes worm-glance darting, and
cover her lips, changing them for the moment to things carved out
of frozen blood. In the same hour she recounted to her brother,
word by word, these things said to her by Baias. While Beroald
listened, his lean countenance, flat in the cheekbones, wide between
the eyes, clean cut about the jaw, close shaven save for the bristly
mustachios, remained moveless as a stone. When she had done,
'Forget it,' he said, in a toneless voice, as cold and stately and as
unreadable as his face. 'And forget him.' Their eyes met, and rested
a moment together, as brother's and sister's who well understand
each other.

* * *

Next day, in the afternoon, was news brought to the Chancellor in Zemry Ashery of a horrible fact committed in Krestenaya market-place: of the Lord Baias, coming down the piazza steps there in open sight of the people and the sun shining in full splendency, set upon at unawares and stabbed in by six men with daggers: his speech and senses taken suddenly away from him, yet lived awhile, 'but the surgeons told me,' said the messenger, 'it should not be long.' Of this, some hours later, the Chancellor informed his sister; saying besides that by latest assured intelligence Baias was dead. The murderers, it seemed, were persons unknown. Except two, whom Baias had killed outright in the scuffle, they seemed to have gotten clean away. 'An act of God or the King's enemies,' said the Chancellor, looking her straight in the eye.

'An act of God,' said the lady soberly, with a like steady, uncom-municative, understanding look. 'It were wicked to be unthankful.'

ARGUMENT WITH DATES

Barganax and Fiorinda
The King and the Vicar
(Chapters XXX–XXXIII)

XXX

PHILOMMEIDES APHRODITE[1]

I THINK EDDISON FINISHED CHAPTERS XXVIII AND XXIX IN JANUARY 1945 BECAUSE ALL THE NOTES AND DRAFTS WRITTEN BETWEEN JANUARY AND AUGUST 1945, EDDISON'S LAST EIGHT MONTHS OF LIFE, SHOW HIS WORKING UPON CHAPTERS XXX–XXXIII. HERE IS HIS DRAFT FOR THE OPENING OF CHAPTER XXX:

F E W shed tears for Baias's sake. There ran a rumour that his slaying was in revenge of the strange heathenly excess of legs exposed up to mid-thigh and heads unhaired employed by him to the correction of his chamber maids; but friends and kinsfolk of these, being had before the justicier were, for want of even ocular proof, one and all pronounced guiltless. No man made so bold as alledge openly that persons in the Chancellor's service had done the thing, or by his or his sister's setting on. Any that said so, said it with circumspection and behind closed doors. Indeed, in Meszria such idle report and surmise soon died down. In the middle kingdom however it found kindlier soil and was speedily brought by busybodies expectant of reward, to Prince Gilmanes's[2] ear in Kaima. The Prince, vailing his eyelids close, heard them out: then seeming extraordinary indifferent to his nephew's unhappy ending, dashed their hopes by asking how durst they come to him: 'What a mischief mean you, to come unto me and tumble out as brainless and passionate fooleries as ever

747

I heard tell? Albeit in these lean times I be thought to hold out but small territories and little authority in respect to the whole land, or to what my fathers held aforetime, you shall see I'll not be played withal; nor made to swallow idle report and surmise what they are or how untrue. I am not justly possessed,[. . .][3] that joining great names to such black villainy standeth little with the interest of the realm or the dignity of our lord the King.'[4] With that, he gave order that they be well flogged in the market-place and then clapt up in prison: directed a writ to his chief officers, charging them see to the punishment of any that should repeat the like slanderous lies: last, with his own hand wrote privately to acquaint my lord Chancellor of these proceedings. This letter, ending with much similitude of love and good inclination, Beroald perused with a vinegar-tart smile upon his lips: then filed it in a secret box along with copies of certain two or three letters he had of recent months intercepted on their way between Baias and Gilmanes: letters having a far different importment.

The third week of January the King came down from Kessarey, where he had spent Yule-tide, to Sestola, and there held council. Business done and the council risen, he took the Chancellor apart into his closet: said he would learn more of this matter of Baias. The Chancellor recounted it at large, saying in fine, 'There, Lord, it resteth. We have, I am to confess, failed to trace the guilty persons.'

'Such a confession we have not yet learnt to expect from you, Beroald.'

'I hope your serenity will not think 'tis a failure likely to recur.'

'I think not,' said the King, steadily regarding him. 'And that is why I think now we will not let it rest.' There was a mock in this King's eye.[5] The Chancellor abode it without a blench.

'I thank your serene Highness,' he said at last, 'for your trust in me.'

'You have yourself to thank for that. If I trust you, 'tis because you are trustworthy.'

'You have copies of the letters came into my hands.'

'Yes. Fits well with certain other informations I have for your secret eye. But we will leave that affair untouched till it be nearer looked.'

'I have not mentioned aught of these things to any person else than your serene highness.'

'You have done as I would have you do. Keep it betwixt me and you alone. You have seen no sign, otherwhere, of its spreading into Meszria?'

'No sign; albeit my eyes have been busy for that.'

They sat silent for awhile in the easy and comfortable freedom of a mutuality where each can, the better for the other's presence and unvoiced comprehensions, follow his own unimpeded. Then suddenly the Chancellor was aware of his great master's eye gaze turned upon him and studying his face as it had been an open page on which some quaint matter was characterized.

'You are complained of,' said the King.

'To your highness?'

'Not directly so. But on all hands I hear you blamed.'

'Not groundably, it is to be hoped.'

'Until the other day, it is ten years since I had seen your sister. They tell me it is your fault she is never set eyes on in Zayana.'

The Chancellor gave a silent laugh. 'My fault? She is no longer in statu pupae.[6] But (for I know your highness would not have me hide my mind from you), is it not come to be a by-word now-a-days that if any woman worth notice (unless she be wed already) shall go in there it must be to the time of "Let in the maid that out a maid departed never more"?'

'What? And will you, whom rumour hath so oft maligned, be a believer of that jade?'

'Not I, Lord. I have my own means to sieve idle report from fact.'

'And how much sticks after the sieving?'

'Not too much for my taste.'

'Nor for his duchess?'

At that, Beroald's face was again unreadable. Only a momentary stiffening of his hand where it rested on the table did not escape the eye of the King. 'I do not look so high,' he cried after a pause.

'Well, you and I have this habit in common, dear Beroald: viewing the world, to stand rather with the reals than with the nominals.'

The Chancellor bent his head in a graceful assent. 'Since your serenity hath done me the honour, and her, to touch on the matter, I must remember you that, there, ladies are fashions: one commonly lasts him but a two or three months at most. There's another thing too, if the Devil must draw the tongue out of my mouth.'

'Out with it, for I've guessed it already.'

'I well believe you, for your serene highness knows me. I am an ambitious man.'

'True.'

'Ambitious as respects my sister.'

'O yes. Sisters can be ladders.'

'I think not of that. Or not only.'

'I know you are not: not beyond reason. Confess: you are yourself in honorable sort, a little in love with her?'

From betwixt half-closed eyelids, Beroald gave him a shrewd look.

' 'Tis no bad thing,' the king said, ''twixt brother and sister.' He paused. 'To say true, having beheld and spoke with her this morning, first time since ten years, I think, and then she was but a child, I can savour and appraise in my own self some whiff or draught of this penetrating humour strained brotherly affection: its very scent: something past that of friendships yet by native notion obedient to the mind's rein. Myself, I ne'er had a sister. But neither have you, I think, a daughter.'

The Chancellor's finger of his right hand had made a slow dance on the table-top before him. 'I can subtilize you points of law,' he said. 'But here your serene highness hath me out of my depth.'

'I think I know where the shoe pinches,' said the King. 'Instance of a Queen.'

The Chancellor looked swiftly at him, then lowered his eyes again. 'There be great examples,' he said very soberly, 'not necessary for everyone to follow.'

'Well, enough said for the while.' King Mezentius rose.

'A notable honour: to her and to me,' Beroald said, rising with him. Then, looking him in the eye, 'May I add this, Lord? After a sharp frost, on the heels of over-early spring, the damage comes of too sudden sun.'

'Content you,' said the King. 'I do not forget it.'

THE PASSAGE ABOVE ALLUDES TO A SCENE IN WHICH THE KING CONVERSES WITH FIORINDA. EDDISON NEVER WROTE THIS SCENE, BUT HE DESCRIBED IT IN NOTES WRITTEN ON JANUARY 26 AND 29, 1945:

The King and Fiorinda:[7] The King of course knows (secretly— no one else knows) the parentage of Beroald and Fiorinda. He is deeply impressed with her. In this scene concentrate on her wit, incalculableness, and gaiety of heart. The King laughingly asks whether she would like him to get her a new husband. She is much honored, but would prefer, after this first experience, to take her time and look round a little.

EDDISON PLANNED FOR KING MEZENTIUS TO RETURN TO THE DUCHESS AMALIE IN MEMISON AFTER CONVERSING WITH BEROALD AND FIORINDA IN SESTOLA. SOMETIME IN EARLY MAY 1945, EDDISON JOTTED DOWN SIMPLE EXPRESSIONS FOR A CONVERSATION ABOUT FIORINDA BETWEEN THE DUCHESS AND THE KING:

Duchess: I'm sorry to hear it.[8]

King: Come: that's not very reasonable—just an hearsay and fancy.

Duchess: (shrugs her shoulders)

King: I should like you to have a look at her.

Duchess: Why?

King: Because I've as good as told the Chancellor I would be glad to see her Duchess of Zayana.

Duchess: That was cruel of you, never to consult me.

King: Don't jump to conclusions: nothing's settled. He may not like her. You have a look and make up your mind.

Duchess: (angry) It's made up already.

          (later) I'm sorry I was so horrid. I'll see her.

PROBABLY USING THE SIMPLE CONVERSATIONAL NOTES ABOVE, EDDISON COMPOSED, BETWEEN MAY 15 AND 17, 1945, A MORE DETAILED SCENE BETWEEN MEZENTIUS AND AMALIE:

A night or two later, the King being in Memison, Amalie asked whether he had a true tale, among the many tales that flew: concerning Baias's taking off. He answered he had talked with the Chancellor and that clear as day it was that the Chancellor had himself procured it; but this were best not spoken of.

'She hath made a fair beginning, the she-scorpion,' said the Duchess.

The King laughed. ''Tis not to be denied it was somewhat highly handled. Yet fitted so well with greater matters I have in view, I had not the heart to blame him.'

The Duchess sat pensive. 'Barganax will be home from the west in three weeks.[9] God be thanked, not to such a wife.'

'You have seen her?'

'Never that I remember. Beroald keepeth her as formerly he did, close boxed. So Baias did while he had her. Wisely so, I should say. Stibium[10] disguised with honey. Best kept out of reach.'

'Nay, be not so unlike your dear self as fall into injustice. She was ill-served of her husband.'

'And ill rid of him, though a vile fellow indeed. Both vile together. Her reputation stinks to heaven.'

'What have you to work upon ne'er having spoke unto her, save what's prated or libelled by sluttish pamphleteers?'

'But strongly persistent. It is easy to tell by the smoke and the sparkles that there is a fire in the chimney.'

'See and speak with her before you judge.'

'Well, I'll bottle up judgment, then: I'll not judge. She concerns not me; and truly indeed, dear my lord, I've no desire to look upon her.' Amalie's fair and lovely face wore, as she spoke, its little-maid look: half-timorous, half-humorous, all self-resolved: like as when, over the pure deeps of a tarn open to the sky at evening or morn, a light breath of wind, or a stirring here and there of the glass-smooth surface stillness with the momentary alighting, immaterial as air, of some tiny winged creature, wakes ripples that seem to read, through the starred remoteness of the moment upon that profundity, to scarce-heard echoes of the innumerable laughter of the waves of ocean: a look only not to be kissed, lest that fresh enchantment break, for the while, the reign of the present.

'I'm sorry, then,' said the King. Then, answering the question in Amalie's eyes: 'Because I myself have seen her, t'other day.'

'So, indeed?'

'I liked her at first word; first glance.'

'Very strange.'

'You may think so, if you send for her. You may feel as though you were viewing your own image in that strange artificial the learned doctor fashioned and set up in Acrozayana, which mirrors, but by contrary colors. And yet, this, a greater wonder, seeing the very forms are changed. As though my Rosa Mundi should behold in this girl her own self, looking at herself, as La Rose Noire.'[11]

The Duchess sat silent. Presently he was aware of her hand finding his. 'Will you look, and tell me?'[12] he said.

'Well,' answered she, after a moment, and her hand trembled: 'I'll consider of it; sleep on it.'

IN FEBRUARY OF 775 AZC, A MONTH AFTER THE SLAYING OF BAIAS, SUITORS SEEK OUT FIORINDA IN ZEMRY ASHERY. ON JANUARY 26, 1945, EDDISON MADE SOME NOTES ON THE MEN WHO PURSUE HER AND THE TREATMENT THEY RECEIVED:

Wooers begin to line up—Barrian, Zapheles, Morville. Barrian, huffed at her rejection of him, damns her with faint praise to the Duke (a great friend of his), and is thus the means of postponing for some time any interest in her on the Duke's part.

The Zapheles episode is pointed by the fact that Zapheles is a professed misogynist and confirmed bachelor: Fiorinda very delicately and humorously pulls his leg about this, and (in spite of his cynical and embittered, backbiting, habit of mind) achieves the triumph of sending him away as her devoted and—so far as in him lies —loyal friend.

AS APRIL TURNED TO MAY IN 1945, EDDISON MADE MORE DETAILED NOTES ABOUT FIORINDA AND ZAPHELES:

Fiorinda and Zapheles:—Zapheles comes across Fiorinda alone in the countryside about Zemry Ashery. She is in her contemplation. They know each other slightly—well enough to excuse his stopping to talk with her.

He says Barrian is much upset by her rejection of his addresses: she has done a good job there: turned him into a misogynist (of Zapheles's own kidney). She mockingly questions the truth of this:

Zapheles says it is obvious; therefore, the Duke, who had shown some curiosity about her and her affairs, is quite put off by Barrian's damning her with faint praise. Moreover, Bellefront holds the fort.

She plays with Zapheles: makes further assignations with him; finally, after a few weeks, driving him to a recantation of his cynical attitude and having him at her feet with a proposal of marriage. (Make it clear that she is completely heart-free in all of this: merely enjoys the exercise of her power to twirl and turn Zapheles to her will.)

Fiorinda's attitude toward Zapheles is consistently this: any approach on his part to the role of lover sets her at arm's length. They are friends on the basis of mocking and scorning mankind (the side of her nature that lives its incarnate purity in Anthea). Zapheles soon learns to accept this, and is—on that basis—her devoted friend and admirer. (Loyal too? Well, yes—as far as in him lies!)

BETWEEN MAY 19 AND 22, 1945, EDDISON DRAFTED THE FIRST MEETING BETWEEN FIORINDA AND THE DUCHESS AMALIE:

The next Tuesday sennight the Duchess gave out that she would go down (for a week or two's tarriance and tasting of the salt breezes) to Rojuna, a little pavillion of hers beside the sea, and take but one lady along with her. Servants were sent before to open up the house and have all in a readiness; and upon the Thursday she, with Bellefront and but a groom and two serving maids to attend them, rode for Acrozayana. There they were joyfully welcomed and entertained by Medor, who for the three months of the Duke's absence was in charge there; and so next morning, took their way south eastward toward Krestenaya, meaning to cross the sands of the Korvish at ebb tide and found themselves an hour before noon under Zemry Ashery. The Duchess said, 'It is Valentine's Day, and twenty miles yet to Rojuna.[13] We will make surprise upon my lord Chancellor: bear him a morning visit.'

The Lord Beroald was sat at meat in his privy dining-chamber with his sister. Besides Anthea and Campaspe, they had no company save Zapheles only, who, having concluded some business with the Chancellor this morning, had remained a-talking with the Lady Fiorinda till dinner time. Word being brought that the Duchess of Memison was below, the Chancellor left table and went down himself to bring her in. 'Had we but had notice of your grace's intending hither,' he said, 'there should a been entertainment to offer you better fitting this happy occasion. But if you will excuse the want of preparation and partake our simple family fare (there's but Lord Zapheles here: chanced upon us like as thus, fortunately, your noble excellence hath done) 'twill be a joy to us indeed.'

'Nay, 'twas but the thought took me, passing so near your gates, to greet your lordship for friendship's sake. I am for Rojuna, and must not miss the tide for crossing of the sands. I ne'er expected to have interrupted you at dinner.'

'I pray your grace do us that honour to come in. We are now but set: our usual hour for dinner is eleven of the clock. You are already behind time for the crossing: the tide runneth in sudden and to great height, with the wind in this quarter: 'tis much too hazardous you should attempt it, and but five miles further round by land. I cannot quit you, dear madam, disappoint us not.'

Amalie smiled. 'I see you are a powerful persuader, as ever. Very well: we are persuaded.' Delicately she gave him her hand, to be helped down from her horse.

As they began to mount the stairs, a murmur of talking and laughing sounded from the dining-parlour above: now a ripple of laughter that the Duchess might know for Campaspe's: now Zapheles's known accent as that clatter of tin cans, precise, bantering, uninviting: then a burst of merriment and, as the laughter died down, one laugh that out-stayed the rest. Low-toned it was, shot with colours borrowed from the feather-soft descending cloud-gates of downiest slumber, and sun-warmed in its luxuriousness as the slow honey-dropping of those streams that have their well-spring in Mount Helicon.[14] And yet it was a light laugh, disdainful, self-enjoying, gay, fancy-free; but with harmonies in it, sudden and fleeting, that opened upon wonder, as night opens to summer-lightnings and, with the flash's passing, shuts down again upon a mystery deeper and darker than before. The Duchess, her foot on the stair, stayed herself for the instant as if, having come so far, she would yet change her mind for some panical terror bred in her by that laughter. This for the merest instant only: nobody marked it. Mistress of herself again, she, with Bellefront, followed the Chancellor.

'Please your grace that I present to you my lady sister,' said Beroald as, upon their entering the room, all rose from their seats. Fiorinda, coming from her place at the foot of the table, nearest the door, bent into a lily-like courtesy to salute the Duchess's hand. This done, and the lady standing again at her full stature, Amalie's eyes surveyed her over as though she knew not how to frame her look: a gaze so ambiguous that Fiorinda, a sudden flush overspreading the pallour of her cheek and neck, said, 'I fear your grace taketh some little dislike to see me so thus in tissue of yellow, 'stead of in widow's weeds? But truly I have a distaste for mourning colours, and especially with spring-time soon beginning.'

'Think not I'd such a thought,' said the Duchess. 'Remember we have not looked on one another till now. I was seeking for the likeness.'

'With my brother?'

'Yes, with your brother, I mean.' She added, as if to herself: 'There is not, after all, much likeness.'

To that, Fiorinda, glancing at Beroald: 'Not much likeness in looks. But more, perhaps, in likings.'

The Duchess remained for a moment in the same uneasy contemplation, which took up its rest at last on Fiorinda's sea-green eyes that now looked level into hers. Those eyes seemed to still their sea-fires, under this searching inspection, to a sweet and grave respect; but in the most imperceptible slant of them, and in the curves of the underlids, an intimation seemed to tremble on some edge of disclosure, untellable whether of fanged monsters stirring in their sleep in those green pools' deeps, or of a star that danced there unseen. Then, as if started out of dreaming, the Duchess turned to the Chancellor who had let place a chair for her on his own right, Zapheles moving down to sit by Fiorinda. Upon the other side of the table Campaspe moved closer to her sister, to let Bellefront have her seat at the Chancellor's left.

'The King's highness (Gods send he live forever) guesteth with Lord Stathmar, I learn, in Argyanna,' said Beroald. 'The Admiral showed me letters he had from him yesterday.'

'I had letters too,' said the Duchess, 'the day before, in Memison: by the same courier, doubtless.'

'Your grace means to go a-fishing at Rojuna?' said Zapheles.

'No, I love not the sport: go but to taste the spring coming in that way.'

'My lord Duke is at his fishing, 'tis said, for giant sea-pike off Quedanzar: never content but with dangerous occupation.'

'His grace told me,' said Bellefront, 'they will charge a big boat if the humour take them, supposing it to be a fish. And that human flesh they distaste, but will yet rush upon a swimmer in the water if he stir a muscle, supposing, from the motion, 'tis fish. This when they be hungry. And can at one snap take his leg off at the thigh. But I think he invented this to fright me.'

'Ay, believe not all he tells you,' Amalie said; and Bellefront reddened to the roots of her hair that, caught in a shaft of sunlight from the window, became a live fire in its heavy splendour, thick, long, close-braided on her head, and red-hot Titian colour, near the like of her mistress's own.

The Duchess saw, while they talked and jested, how Zapheles's sallow hatchet-face was at every while returning toward my Lady Fiorinda in an admiration undisguised: a strange trick in him, who was of all men noted for a soured bachelor wedded to simple life, and an inveterate back-biter of women.

'I love the comedy,' she said, laying her hand on the Chancellor's sleeve, 'of Zapheles behaving himself so unlike himself in the enemy's camp.'

Beroald shrugged. 'It is but one more pair of wings at the candle-flame,' he said under his breath. 'They come and go till they be singed.'

The Duchess's words, chancing upon a pause in the general talk, were not unheard by Zapheles. He whispered behind his hand to Fiorinda, 'She means, I have no eye for those others. Well, if it be, may I not study in what books I will?'

Fiorinda caught the Duchess's eye and said in her most languefied tones, plainly, for all to hear, 'My lord Zapheles says this behaviour is but his ordinary: that, should it appear otherwise, 'tis but that he finds me to be (as, to his thinking, all sane beings ought to be) altogether unwomanly. And therefore he would deign to take notice only of me alone. I have had left-handed compliments ere now, but this I think the curiousest.' Upon which outrageous speech, spoken with so much elegance and forced innocency of idle and lazy grace, the Duchess could not but fall a-laughing.

Zapheles, stroking his beard and putting on as good a face as he might, found no better rejoinder than say lamely to the Duchess, 'I said no such thing.'

'But you think it,' said Fiorinda.

There was a deep seduction in her voice but when he turned to her, a bed of snakes in the mockery of her lips. 'True,' replied he, 'I did think it (does that wring your withers?): until your ladyship said it. But, by your saying it (though I grant you're too deep skilled in manners to roll your eye at me), I perceive that underneath you're but as the rest.'

'Very prettily complimented. I, too, am disappointed. I had even begun to think you a remarkable man.'

'You would not find yourself alone in that opinion.'

'I was even so silly as begin to be almost persuaded there might be found in you that singularity, not to be wholly eat up with your own self-conceit.'

'Will you not speak louder? Let 'em hear how fishwifely you can rail.'

'But it was foolish in me to imagine so unnatural a monstrosity,' she said, and the same honeyedness, overlying bee-stings of silent laughter, was on every smoothly spoken word. Then, a little louder: '*Quelle est la différence, monsieur, entre un elephant et une puce?*'

He looked at her in silence, half angry, half at a loss, as a fox should look, ears down, toward some undefinable and teasing presence the menace of which is felt but hid far from view.

'*Un elephant peut avoir des puces; mais une puce ne peut pas avoir des elephants.* I sometimes question whether I be not myself an exceptional puce.'[15]

Amalie's cheek dimpled to the shadow of a smile. It passed, and her eyes still rested, sweet and dubious and searching, on Fiorinda.

Zapheles said sulkily, 'I'll talk with your ladyship more on these matters when you have not an audience to use against me.'

'Pray do my lord,' said she lightly. 'I shall heartily look forward to it.'

Dinner being done, Zapheles took his leave. The others walked awhile in the garden. Amalie, when she had Fiorinda to herself, said to her suddenly, 'Do you like Lord Zapheles? Is he a friend of yours?'

'Does your grace? Is he by chance a friend of your grace's?'

The Duchess, set then at a non plus, looked round upon her. Fiorinda was bended down as she spoke, to pluck a purple blossom of lenten rose from a great bunch which grew beside the path. She stood up again, holding the flower to her nostrils to take the scent, looking the while in the Duchess's eye with so unruffled a demeanour and into so much sweetness of pensivity on her lips that the Duchess, if she were disposed to take offence, changed her mind and but said, 'I think you are well suited to one another.'

'I am honoured by your grace's kindly interest in my affairs. 'Las it hath no scent, or I no sense of it.' She made as if to have dropped the flower: as upon second thoughts, fastened it in her bosom.

'I would not be so uncivil,' said the Duchess, 'as claim any particular interest.'

'I think he is a man. Howe'er that be, he amuses me.'

'Is that what men are made for?'

'I think probably so.'

'An illuminating answer.'

'I hope, madam, it does not scandalize you?'

'Not in the smallest. Only I understand you, and myself, better than I did.'

Fiorinda very slowly smiled. There was that in her eyes now that made Amalie, after a moment's wrestling with them, avert her own. 'If I may be permitted to speak my thought, I would guess that your noble excellence views them mainly as I do,' said she, 'And (to do justice to your beauty and other high qualities besides) with precisely as much justification.'

'I think it a hateful doctrine.'

'I am glad you should think so. Even and it be pure error, it enhances your grace's charm.'

BARGANAX'S FISHING TRIP LASTS FROM DECEMBER 774 TO MID-MARCH 775 AZC. BEFORE THE DUKE'S HOMECOMING, BEROALD AND MORVILLE MEET IN ZAYANA, AND AFTER THIS MEETING MORVILLE LEARNS OF FIORINDA IN AN IDLE CONVERSATION WITH BARRIAN, ZAPHELES, AND MELATES:

The Chancellor: (long talk with Morville in Zayana upon some question arising out of Emmius Parry's will. Some property of Deïaneira's which has been claimed by the Chancellor for the crown but the Vicar wants it to revert to him. It is complicated by being mixed up with some claims of the Duke's (the name of Alzulma?). The Chancellor is impressed with Morville's modesty and intelligent firm handling of the business) 'Fact is, until the Duke is back, my hands are full: Medor brings me dozens of difficulties unwilling to settle them uncovered. The Duke was not expected home from the West till Wednesday March 18th: but here's letters this morning saying he's advanced it to a week earlier, that's day after tomorrow, so as to hold his presence on Friday 13th. If you can divert yourself here for a while, come and see me in Zemry Ashery to-day fortnight. I think I can give you an answer then to take back to the Vicar: nothing official and binding, but enough to help him judge how the land lies.'

Morville, coming out from the Chancellor, meets Barrian, Melates, Zapheles.

Barrian: Well, what speed, my Lord Morville?

Morville: I took your advice, my Lord. The Chancellor used me very honorable: I never spoke so long with his excellence before. He is a hard man to deal with?

Zapheles: A man of iron body and mind [. . .] as full with [. . .] as a spider with poison. The devil speaks in him.

Morville: Well, I'm to see him again when he's studied the thing: Sunday March 22, in his own home.

Zapheles: Oho? Look out you be not catched there by his charmer.

Morville: What's that?

Zapheles: Barrian can tell you best.

Barrian: Pah, that's an old story. I've forgotten it.

Morville: (with self-engrossed curiosity)—I ought to know.

Melates: Enough if you remember; keep away from his treasure chamber. And be not dazzled with that diamond he keeps there. 'Twill cut you if you touch it. His (Barrian's) cut is raw yet, howso a try to pretend otherwise.

Barrian: Well, I must bid you good morning: I have an appointment.

Zapheles: But not in Zemry Ashery I hope? (exit Barrian)

Morville: I've heard the tales. But I'm not a fisher in those waters.

Zapheles: A woman-hater? I could kiss you for it!

Morville: O, no hate. I'll wed one day, for the good of the family: 'tis common practice. But women are

women, and I never had sleepless nights for any
woman, nor will neither.

Melates: Barrian was badly bit. Would've hung up his hat
there, but puss scratched him properly and sent him
away with his tail between his legs.

Zapheles: Keep off, sweet youth. Be caught by her and live
withal? Why I'd as lief go a courting of [. . .] wife.

Morville: Who's that?

Zapheles: [. . .] A beast that eateth patient husbands.

AT THE END OF FEBRUARY 775 AZC, DUKE BARGANAX COMMUNICATES WITH
HIS OFFICERS:

The month ended, and the Duke of Zayana, putting off at every
few days the date of his return, still tarried in the west at his sea-
fishing. In the first days of March came Barrian from the west:
brought commands to Medor from his Grace that they must expect
him about three weeks hence, and in the meanwhile prepare
[masques] and revels in Acrozayana against his homecoming.

ON MAY 30, 1945, EDDISON DRAFTED AN INCOMPLETE CONVERSATION IN
WHICH FIORINDA TELLS DOCTOR VANDERMAST OF HER INTENTION TO ATTEND
THE MASQUERADE BALL THAT MEDOR HAS PLANNED FOR BARGANAX'S HOMECOM-
ING. CONSIDERING FIORINDA'S HABITUALLY RECLUSIVE LIFE IN ZEMRY ASHERY,
HER DESIRE TO GO IS A CURIOUS INCLINATION:

Fiorinda with Doctor Vandermast in Zemry Ashery—

Fiorinda: Indeed my Lord Zapheles told me of these intended revels, and pestereth me still to go meet
him there and look upon them. Ladies all to go
masked.[16] It would amuse me. I gather you are to
be the master of the revels?

Vandermast: Yes, I have framed up some fantasticoes.[17]

Fiorinda: I'll go, but not tell my brother. I've heard so
much of what's done in the palace and been so
thwarted when I would see for myself, I'm resolved I'll go. Do you advise me to?

Vandermast: I always advise your ladyship to follow your own
inclinations. I can't always understand them, but
[sic]

ON MAY 25, 1945, EDDISON PLANNED THE PAIRINGS FOR CONVERSATIONS
AT THE MASQUERADE BALL THAT MEDOR PREPARES FOR MARCH 17, 775 AZC:

Fiorinda goes to masked ball in Zayana
Overhears Barrian reporting to Barganax about her ('faint praise')

—[Barrian says to the Duke: 'O no: not the mysterious lady mewed up in Zemry Ashery. I saw her when you were away: a very commonplace person. Handsome? O yes, but so so. Affected: full of herself: spiteful. No presence, like that. Voice quite different, too.']¹⁸

Duke making love to Bellefront—

Bellefront—'I like you better in this mood'

Duke—'I'm like a hunting leopard: better in my mood when starved. Starved now'

Bellefront—(bring out her mindlessness, and sensual charms: a nice good girl, but after all only one of the 'dishes of hers' served up by the Marchioness of Monferrato¹⁹)

Pantasilia—(very episodic, this): huffed by Duke's attentions to Bellefront: Melates rises on her horizon

Masked Ball: very unusual: a conceit of the Duke's

    Every guest must bring a lady with him. She is to be masked and no inquiries made as to her identity.

    Zapheles brings Fiorinda

    Melates brings Pantasilia

    Medor brings Rosalura

    Perantor brings some light-o-love of his own, who deserts him for the Duke at one stage, and causes much rage to Bellefront

    ?Vandermast there with Anthea

ON THE SAME DAY THAT HE MADE THE OUTLINE ABOVE, EDDISON REVISED SOME NOTES, FIRST WRITTEN ON APRIL 30, 1945, ABOUT BARGANAX'S RELATIONSHIPS WITH BELLEFRONT AND PANTASILIA:

Barganax's education by Heterasmene had made him have 'such a way' with women that they always fell in love with him. This in a fair way to spoil him: also to bore him with such easy preys.

Bellefront (who was in her ascendant March—June 775 [AZC]) quite unintelligent but indefatigably sensual. She is indeed the subject of the 129th Sonnet.²⁰ Barganax always 'past reason' hates her ex post facto, and always returns like moth to flame. She is stupid, tactless, unrestrained: a lovely animal, and Barganax comes back to her as the drunkard to the bottle. But her lack of artistry and her excessive 'forth comingness' grate upon him increasingly (if only intermittently and subconsciously).

Pantasilia also his mistress, but she is a restful βοῶπις ποτνια.²¹ Also, their affairs are less passionate, more sleepy and lazy. In March or (?) April he notices Melates is falling under the spell of this quiet luxurious peony-like beauty, and unobtrusively resigns in Melates's favour. (This shows his principle—never violated till the case of Morville arrives—of never hunting in another man's preserves.)

BETWEEN MAY 25 AND JUNE 1, 1945, EDDISON DRAFTED MORE DETAILED NOTES FOR THE MASQUERADE BALL:

Evening of the Masque in Zayana

Torchlight procession through the town up to the citadel, after supper. Masque is by the lady guests and Dr. Vandermast (as 'an ambassador from beyond the Hyperborean Mountains') 'presents' it. Enter to a slow music, grotescoes playing their lutes: jewels: candle-holders. Dr. Vandermast craves leave for 'their ladies to come in.'

(guests and 25 ladies)—They come in, all masked. One by one the ladies play die with the Duke: he wins in turn and gets all their money: and in turn each lady plays then against one of the guests, and wins: after which she is his partner for the evening. Bellefront at last plays and wins all his money from the Duke: he pours it out before her on the table from a golden goblet: then a little boy (as Cupid) shoots at her and then unmasks her: Bellefront is enthroned beside the Duke as Queen of the revels.

After she has won his money at dice and is seated by him as Queen of the revels, Bellefront (according to the rules) still wears her mask.

Bellefront: Are you glad it is me?

Duke: I knew you, before you spoke, spite of your visard.

Bellefront: By my lips?

Duke: Never have a painter for your lover if you mean to cheat him. He can see through taffeta as you through clear glass.

Bellefront: And you're glad of me?

Duke: Part of me is.

Bellefront: Only part?

Duke: Care not: 'tis the part your heart is on.

Bellefront: Your grace seems a little short and cynical. I hope you love me as you swore you did.

Duke: Loving goes by haps.

Bellefront: So cold as that? I'd as well a stayed in Memison. Better, with all the work I had to persuade her noble excellence give me leave for tonight.

Duke: O foolish girl. How should I know whether I love you? Give me that mouth to try (she does so). Hath that answered you?

Bellefront: Yes (much stirred). But you talk so strange.

Duke: 'Tis t'other part talks.

Bellefront: What's true then?

Duke: That you are, in all my former misled life, the

	sweetest card-conny-catcher that ever turned up ace.
Bellefront:	That's better. But how says t'other part?
Duke:	That here is the great bur again, commonly more known than commended.
Bellefront:	I hate it: and you, for so cruel a lie.
Duke:	Kiss again, then, and unsay it.
Bellefront:	No, I hate you for it. Unsay it first.
Duke:	(laughing) Come, come. If such a thing I did utter out of my distractions, 'tis easy unsaid. But your lips must help mine to unsay it. (Kisses her again.)

(Barrian comes to them)—I see your Grace is merrily disposed and sets us good example.

| Duke: | Ay, Barrian! |

All rise now and tables removed. Series of dances, in which all take part: first the lords in a line and the masked ladies facing them: then each with his lady. Dances for a time, then two by two sitting out in alcoves and lights lowered: stars of various colours wandering about in the hollow roof, like tame comets.

Barganax and Bellefront: her mindlessness and sensual charms
Pantasilia and Melates

Perantor and lady (who deserts him to talk to the Duke, to Bellefront's annoyance).

Then Car of Night enters: great crystal, colour of a black diamond: throned on it, in dusky cloak and hood, and with black mask like the rest—Night. Drawn by four beasts—unicorn, water-horse, flying bull, owl-headed tigress.

Car halts before the Duke: the lady[22] casts off her hood and cloak as the wandering stars descend and circle about her head in an aureole. She is masked with a mask of moleskin, and the green light of her eyes burns in the eyeholes. She is in a flowing gown from waist downward made all of raven's feathers and black cock's feathers, some with stag beetles' wings and spangles of ebony and jet, and a girdle of filigree silver set thick with black diamonds and black pearls. From hip to throat and from throat to finger-joints she was clad in a skin-tight garment made of the skins of black adders: her throat and neck and the lower part of her face were bared to view, of a dazzling fairness against this black and the black of her hair, that was piled high on her head and bound with enchanter's nightshade.

Beside this, the tips of her fingers alone were bared, armed with claws of gold like a lioness's claws expansed.

Fiorinda insists on going home early—before the fun becomes too fast and furious. On the way home, Zapheles proposes again, and they make their platonic pact: [She makes terms with him as cynic with cynic: he is right about women, and she too (upon her experience with Baias) right about men. 'Come then, let's be friends and mock the world together, keeping ourselves uninfested by this madness. I hate you when you begin to show signs of this common disease: as yourself—i.e. when you scorn mankind and womankind both—I delight in you.']²³

Beroald knows all about her going to Zayana: waits up for her return (not that he ever went to bed early) and cross examines her. Fiorinda gives impressions that she has had enough of this 'night-club' atmosphere and considers the Duke a mere philanderer.²⁴ Beroald decides she should marry Morville.

BEROALD'S THOUGHTS HAD BEEN IN EDDISON'S IMAGINATION FOR MONTHS BECAUSE ON FEBRUARY 13, 1945, EDDISON JOTTED DOWN THIS NOTE:

'The Chancellor begins to incline to a connexion with the Parry —for political reasons: his thoughts turn to Morville.'

ON APRIL 30 AND MAY 1, 1945, EDDISON MADE MORE NOTES ABOUT BER-OALD'S ATTITUDE TOWARD MORVILLE, STRESSING THAT BEROALD SEES MORVILLE AS A MORE ADVANTAGEOUS MATCH THAN DUKE BARGANAX FOR HIS SISTER, PARTLY BECAUSE OF THE DUCHESS'S ATTITUDE TOWARD FIORINDA:

The Duchess is prejudiced against Fiorinda (on Lewisian and Geraldian grounds²⁵) at their first (and, until her appointment at the King's instance, to be a lady of honour at Memison, only) meeting, scents the atmosphere affecting every conceivable outrageousness of opinion and behaviour.

This interview confirms the Duchess in her feeling that Fiorinda is likely to bring disaster to any man that has to do with her, and finding the King shows signs of favouring Fiorinda as a wife for Barganax, makes it perfectly clear that she will have nothing to do with such a woman, much less accept her as a daughter-in-law.

Beroald, learning (direct from the Duchess?) this attitude, dismisses any ambitions that may have formed in his mind in that direction.

Beroald thinks Morville, as a kinsman of the Parry, may be useful to him: also thinks his sister had better be married (instead of a centre of such a buzz of flies and perhaps one day a cast-off mistress of the Duke's): thus he urges the Morville connection.

MORVILLE'S FIRST GLIMPSE OF FIORINDA OCCURS WHEN SHE GOES SWIMMING IN A SECLUDED LAKE WITH ANTHEA AND CAMPASPE:

Bathing in a little mountain tarn they have just discovered: she does it rather to the scandalizing of Campaspe and enjoyment of Anthea. Morville, by chance, looks on undetected. Thinks he has Actaeon like, surprised Artemis at her bath.[26] [Anthea volunteers to slip into her lynx dress and deal with (Morville). Fiorinda decides, wait. After all, what harm?][27] He goes to Zemry Ashery (wither he is bound) and is introduced. Recognizes her at once and immediately falls in love.

ON APRIL 29 AND 30, 1945, EDDISON WROTE THAT FIORINDA TAKES ZAPHELES WITH HER TO DINNER ON THE EVENING OF MORVILLE'S ARRIVAL IN ZEMRY ASHERY, AND, PRESUMABLY, THIS DINNER FOLLOWS HER SECRET BATHING WITH ANTHEA AND CAMPASPE:

Takes him [Zapheles] with her to Zemry Ashery for dinner: there they find Morville, come on business to see the Chancellor. This is Morville's first sight of Fiorinda: Morville secretly falls in love at first sight: (Zapheles's presence gives Morville his first pangs of fatal disease—jealousy). She divines (as does Beroald too) that he has the same 'bias'—though a far different temperament and without the self-pleasing tyrannical violence and passion—as Baias.

Fiorinda, though in no way moved by Morville as a wooer, is touched by the gentleness of his methods, by contrast with Baias. She is also amused by her brother's subtle but (to her) transparent effort to steer this new boat of his into harbour. Half out of kindness, half for fun, and half because she is tired of the 'buzz' (and of the four or five with whom she has condescended to experiment—up to the hilt but with small satisfaction though doubtless with great gain to her knowledge of masculine nature and her expertise and perfection in ars amoris[28]), Fiorinda betrothes herself to Morville.

AT THIS POINT, EDDISON'S DRAFTS AND NOTES CATCH UP TO THE ARGUMENT FOR CHAPTER XXX. FIORINDA AND MORVILLE MARRY ON APRIL 20, 775 AZC:

In April, barely three months after the violent death of her first husband, she (once more, to please her brother) marries Morville, a distant cousin of the Parry. The King, seeing and talking with her for the first time in May[29] and having Barganax in mind, confers on Morville the lieutenancy of Reisma and persuades the Duchess to give Fiorinda a place at court in Memison and, later, in June, to make her lady of the bedchamber.

ON MAY 25, 1945, EDDISON WROTE A DRAFT NARRATING THE DUCHESS'S AND MEDOR'S REACTIONS TO THIS MARRIAGE AND THESE OFFICIAL APPOINTMENTS:

When the Duchess heard of this wedding she said to Medor (dining with her upon his way to Mavia about some affairs of the Duke's) 'These news are altogether good; I shall send her as my wedding gift, in token of the joy they bring me, the best white mare I have in my stables. 'Tis a match will please Lord Beroald, who is a good friend of mine. I know nought of Morville but by repute: so if he be eat up in the fashion of the former one, I need waste no tears upon it. Best of all, she will away to Rerek: a joyful departure for all concerned.'

Three weeks later, Medor bethought him of the Duchess's words. For it was in every man's mouth, and soon confirmed beyond question, that Morville was by royal letters patent appointed to the lieutenancy of Reisma, and would shortly move household and take up his abode there upon the lake, at but a short two miles distance from Memison Castle. This too, which made Medor laugh in himself: that the Duchess (yielding, it was thought, to repeated suasions from the King) had offered Fiorinda a place as one of her own ladies at the ducal court of Memison.

High summer began to draw on now in Meszria, with a great settledness of warm sunshine weather, and all quiet. It went among those that lived in the court, and more able so to note the haviour of those nearest about the Duchess, that her grace seemed somewhat better content than at first she had been with the Lady Fiorinda; but many judged that she still regarded her not without afterings of aversion and distrust. The lady for her part bore herself very demure and very respective of her honest name, and (scenting, it was supposed, her grace's mislike of any meeting or acquaintanceship prospective between her new lady of honour and Barganax) absented her always from Memison if the Duke were there or expected.[30]

IT IS FIORINDA'S 'VERY DEMURE AND VERY RESPECTIVE' BEHAVIOR THAT CHANGES THE DUCHESS'S ATTITUDE TOWARD HER, AS THE ARGUMENT TELLS:

Upon this nearer acquaintance the Duchess now changes her mind: thinks less about the reputation which, bruited by idle tongues, follows Fiorinda as a train of fire some red disastrous comet: in fine, surrenders wholly to the spell of this Dark Lady, in whose scintillating, unanalysable, and perilous perfections she seems to see (as a rose might see its own image mirrored but changed to incandescence in the surface of a pool of molten metal) a counter-image of her own inmost self: Rosa alba incarnata[31] looking upon La Rose Noire.

MEANWHILE, THE LOVE BETWEEN FIORINDA AND MORVILLE DOES NOT STAY SWEET FOR LONG. EDDISON ANALYZES THEIR PROBLEMS IN NOTES WRITTEN ON APRIL 30, MAY 1, AND MAY 25, 1945:

Make it abundantly clear that she is honest and whole hearted in her efforts to make their marriage a 'marriage of true minds'[32] (and bodies). She has, through experience and the maturity of her self knowledge, far greater power (and also, doubtless, far greater will) to do this than she had when Baias was the partner: but Morville's selfishness (in its peculiar form of weakness, self-distrust, gratuitous jealousy, fear of her beauty, of her wit, of her incalculableness, and of her abandonments) defeats her power: even Hers.

Baias had defeated her (and defeated his own ends) by selfishness in the shape of too unadulterated a masculinity: seeking to enslave her, crudely avid of his own greedy lusts, crudely obtuse to the instinctive subtleties of her innate and divine beauty, which offended him—as pearls before a swine—the perfection and acme of all unspeakable excesses.

Morville, to the contrary, defeats her by his unmanlike inability to take the lead: his timidity, self-pity, mistrustful puritanism, and self-absorption, and these at every return make him retire into his shell to brood and hatch out unworthy discontents and suspicions.

Condense all this into one great scene between them—? *al fresco*, on a perfect summer's evening (? 1st June) not far from Reisma.

1st June (see last preceding sentence): Have in mind, in writing this, the 'awakening' scene between Barganax and Fiorinda (end of Chapter XXXIII and of Book VI); and point, by juxtaposition not by disquisition, the tragic contrast—tragic because this present scene (Chapter XXX) seals Morville's fate. (It is at the end of this scene that, in fact, Fiorinda for the first time realized Morville's inescapable character and destiny that she had in mind later in Memison [*A Fish Dinner in Memison* 'Queen of Hearts and Queen of Spades'] when she said to the Duchess that Morville was 'the kind of a bull-calf that is likely to sprout horns etc., within the first year.')

Fiorinda is, for the first time in her life, in that deep content and receptiveness that (had Morville been the man to divine it and make himself part of it) might have been the unshakeable foundation (as it was later, on July 22 in Reisma, between her and Barganax) of eternal true love. In an outward-seeming idleness, but inward contemplation, she exercises her divine power of (a) making the moment stand still and be sucked like an orange, and of (b) packing the moment full of pasts and futures which thereby become presents: i.e., of tasting eternity in the interludes of time. (Some faint foretaste or instinct of this was I think in HLE's[33] habit of living happy times and episodes over again in memory: treating her memories as present possession, for present enjoyment, the past not dead, but a thing to be preserved, watered, and treasured. This must surely be part of the nature of divine Θεωρια.[34])

Morville breaks the spell by some discordant remark, which reveals his 'commonness' and unworthiness and the impassable gulf of self-centred timorous doubts and discordants which divide him from his wife.

AS THE STAR OF MORVILLE WANES, THAT OF BARGANAX WAXES. THE ARGUMENT FOR CHAPTER XXX CLOSES WITH THIS SENTENCE:

Fiorinda is passionately adored at first sight by Barganax on midsummer night, 775 [AZC], at a ball given by his mother in Memison.

XXXI

THE BEAST OF LAIMAK

THIS CHAPTER ENVELOPS CHAPTERS II, V, AND VII OF *A FISH DINNER IN MEMISON*, AND IT SHOULD BE READ WITH THEM IN MIND. ON PAGE 274 THE KING SPEAKS OF VISITING THE VICAR IN LAIMAK TWO WEEKS BEFORE MIDSUMMER, AND EDDISON PLANNED FOR THIS CHAPTER TO BEGIN WITH THAT EPISODE. ON JANUARY 27, 1945, HE WROTE NOTES FOR THIS:

T H E King's visit to the Vicar in Laimak—three nights (June 9–11, 775 [AZC])

The Vicar hastily makes Gabriel go and meet Gilmanes (who is expected to come for secret discussions on 8th) postponing his visit: he does not trust Gabriel to play a discreet part in the King's presence, and fears his presence may be suspected too by the King.

AFTER NARRATING THE EPISODE BETWEEN THE KING AND THE VICAR, EDDISON PLANNED TO TELL MORE OF THE KING'S ACTIVITIES DURING HIS DAYS IN MEMISON THAN HE TELLS IN CHAPTERS II AND V OF *A FISH DINNER IN MEMISON*. HOWEVER, EDDISON NEVER DRAFTED THESE NOTES, AND THE OUTLINE FOR THIS SECTION OF THE CHAPTER ONLY SAYS: 'THE KING IN MEMISON.' THE ARGUMENT FOR THIS CHAPTER DESCRIBES THE GROWTH OF THE VICAR'S CONSPIRACY IN REREK AND TELLS THE KING'S RESPONSE TO IT:

The Vicar (whose policy, as Beroald once said, 'is that of the duck: above water, idle and scarce seen to stir; but under water, secretly and speedily swimming towards his purpose') has ever since the rebellion been unobtrusively but with patience and thoroughness consolidating his power in Rerek. By firm government, lavishness in both promise and performance, good-fellowship, princely hospitality, a certain directness that tempts many to trust him where they had wiselier been wary of him, and by a set policy of fastening a private hold on each man worthly his attention (laying men under obligations to his person, or holding over them his knowledge of some secret misdoing which they would least of all wish to see brought to light), he has in the four years of his vicariate used the royal commission (as Beroald said) 'to grapple to his private allegiance the whole mid kingdom 'twixt Megra and the Zenner.'

The King, who has for years understood, as from inside, this 'most wolvy and most foxy sergeant major general of all the Devil's engineers,' and loves him dearly, partly for the very danger of him and for the zest of feeling his own powers stretched to their uttermost in controlling him, is well alive to these proceedings, but cannot be moved by those nearest in his counsel (Beroald, Jeronimy, Roder, Barganax) to take overt action to coerce him.

At last, this summer of 775 [AZC], the King has secret intelligence (which he partly discloses to the Chancellor and to the Duchess but to no person else) of a conspiracy to seize Rerek and set it up as a realm to itself, with the Vicar for king. The conspirators have appointed to meet one night in Middlemead, a lonely ruined farmstead on the upper waters of the Zenner; and here the King means to surprise them in person: 'wherein if I bring not the rest to destruction and him to his obedience, at least I'll die attempting it.' At the last moment he makes the Chancellor wait behind, a few miles short of Middlemead, and himself goes on, completely alone.

This incredible act of daring succeeds. The Parry, already misdoubting him of the sufficiency of these men he has assembled to be his instruments, and (which the King had with unerring insight gambled upon) coming himself to heel when faced with the King in person, accepts the King's whispered diagnosis of the situation: namely, that the Vicar has lighted by chance upon a wasps' nest which the King has come himself to take. The five rebel lords, suddenly surprised, are overcome by the King and the Vicar after a bloody fight, and their three survivors (Gilmanes, Arquez, and Clavius) are, upon the King's direction, then and there beheaded by Gabriel Flores.

TO THIS POINT, THE ARGUMENT HAS NOT REALLY EXPRESSED ANYTHING THAT HAS NOT ALREADY BEEN NARRATED IN *A FISH DINNER IN MEMISON*, BUT

THE CONCLUDING SECTION SHOWS HOW EDDISON PLANNED TO GIVE NEW TREAT-
MENT TO THE EPISODE OF MIDDLEMEAD:

This episode, treated in detail in *A Fish Dinner in Memison,* is in this present book not narrated directly but disclosed in a private and secret conversation, after the event, between the Vicar and his mother Marescia, now aged seventy-three. He has always been her favourite child, and so far as he ever opens his mind to anybody, it is to her. But even from her sympathetic ear the greater part (for example, the true extent of his implication in this conspiracy) is forever hidden.

The Vicar's personal attachment to the King not even this treason can break: in fact the outcome is an immeasurable strengthening of it. The savage dog has, for the first time, snapped at his master. But he knows he ought not to have done it, and is sorry. He will never snap at King Mezentius again; but all the more is he inwardly resolved to brook no overlordship in Rerek (were the King to die) from a young quat such as Styllis, or, for that matter, from Barganax.

Bad feeling has geen growing between the Vicar and Styllis to an extent that gives Rosma real anxiety. For the first time she comes to be ranged in a definite hostility against her cousin the Vicar, and tries, in sober earnest not in half earnest as of old, to set the King against him. But her efforts merely harden the King in his curious affection for this untameable unforseeable ravening wild beast of his, grown now so big that by no power on earth can he be safely handled but by the King's personal ascendancy alone.

IN JANUARY 1945, EDDISON DRAFTED NOTES FOR THE CONVERSATION BE-
TWEEN THE VICAR AND HIS MOTHER, AND THESE NOTES FOCUS UPON ROSMA'S
ENMITY TOWARD THE VICAR:

The Vicar and Marescia. Bring out in this conversation that fact —shrewdly suspected, and (?) revealed by some indiscretion of the questions which has come to his ear, by the Vicar—that Rosma is now definitely his enemy on account of the bad blood between him and Styllis. Also bring out fact that the Vicar (before Middlemead) began to believe that Rosma's influences had in fact turned the King against him, but the episode had now convinced him he was mistaken, and his whole mind is now cleared of that suspicion and concentrated on effecting a long-term reinsurance policy against the event of Styllis's succession to the throne.

ON MAY 25, 1945, EDDISON WROTE MORE NOTES FOR THIS CONVERSATION:

Laimak: the Vicar and Marescia

Steer round the rocks by

a) making the Vicar not reveal too much and

b) making it clear (and this can partly be done in the earlier chapters) that his relationship with his mother is strangely confidential, and that is why he can say as much as he does. Make clear at end of scene that he has not told the whole truth—not even to her (and the reader ought to realise what the whole truth is: also that the King had astutely guessed true).

XXXII

THEN, GENTLE CHEATER

THE ARGUMENT FOR THIS CHAPTER BEGINS THUS:

The stroke at Middlemead (publicly understood, with the King's connivance, to have been a signal service to the crown on the part of the Vicar) was on June 25, 775 [AZC]. During the following few weeks, Barganax's frequenting of Fiorinda's company has become matter for every scandalous breath in both Memison and Zayana.

ON JANUARY 27, 1945, EDDISON MADE NOTES FOR THE EARLY DAYS OF THE RELATIONSHIP BETWEEN BARGANAX AND FIORINDA:

Barganax, except for purposes of his weekly presences in Zayana, is now always in Memison. On polite (but never friendly) terms with Morville: paints Fiorinda's portrait (the El Greco).[1] This arranged on the Thursday, June 25—first sitting to be Sunday, June 28. This portrait painting is his very transparent stalking-horse. Morville is generally present and conversation is discreet.

June 28—Barganax begins by talking about the portrait and the difficulties. Fiorinda is very knowledgeable about this, which delights him. She also talks about his management of his dukedom, and is in her turn delighted: he is evidently not disposed to let any affair interfere with that (or with his art).

After a few days Barganax gets a private interview—in Memison, on the out-terraces, in the heat of the day (Date: Wednesday July 1st) Fiorinda very subtly and delicately begins asking him about his views on love. This talk is interrupted by Morville. He is correct in his behavior but clearly angry to find them together.

ON THE SAME DAY THAT HE MADE THE NOTES ABOVE, EDDISON DRAFTED A WORKING VERSION FOR THE PRIVATE INTERVIEW OF WEDNESDAY JULY 1, 775 AZC, ON THE OUT-TERRACES:

Barganax: The art of love is the art of pleasing women.

Fiorinda: But your grace has never been married.

Barganax: That is true, but true also, what I said.

Fiorinda: I daresay it is true. Does it mean we are harder to please?

Barganax: I think so. When you're worth pleasing: and most of you are for a time.

Fiorinda: I think if I were a man I should not bother my head —or my heart—much about the temporary cases. After all, love is a bird easily caught, if one has the right bait and nets, but to keep it is what needs art.

Barganax: The art of keeping it: a new idea to me. I wonder where it came from? What's the secret of that, do you think?

Fiorinda: For men or for women?

Barganax: For both.

Fiorinda: That one should find every morning and every night something span-new in the same person.

Barganax: A profound saying. Is it permissible to ask whether it is spoken from experience or merely from theorizing?

Fiorinda: Permissible to ask? Yes. But also permissible not to answer. I think it rather an impertinent question.

Morville clearly angry to find them together, and Fiorinda looking particularly lovely and 'wrought up' in a way he instinctively recognises but has never noted so strongly before, and the sight of her, so stirred, lights his jealously in a terrible manner. He conceals it as well as he can, but becomes boorish and unpleasant. The Duke finally departs and they go home together in silence: Morville surly and melancholy, Fiorinda singing and 'walking on flowers.'

THE ARGUMENT SUMMARIZES THE BEHAVIOR OF FIORINDA, MORVILLE, AND BARGANAX DURING THE FIRST THREE WEEKS OF JULY 775 AZC:

The lady, with every exasperation of mockery, elusiveness, and unbearable provocation, holds him on a string, but at arm's length. Morville, a simple and stupid man fatally conjoined to a wife whom he can neither win nor hold nor satisfy nor understand nor be worthy of, is wrung with jealously, while Barganax is almost driven out of his wits by a love which he can neither fulfill nor yet tear himself away from.

HIS MANUSCRIPT SHEETS ARE UNDATED, BUT EDDISON WROTE DETAILED NOTES ABOUT THE ACTIONS OF THESE THREE CHARACTERS DURING THE FIRST THREE WEEKS OF JULY 775 AZC:

After this (from Wednesday July 1 onwards), the Duke is daily with Fiorinda in Reisma or in Memison or meeting on rides, etc. (except only that on Fridays he has to be—and always is—in Zayana).

Scandal begins to grow. Fiorinda more and more, as she feels her power on him (and his on her), torments and plays with him, never of course to make a fool of him, but in a way that on the whole draws him daily deeper in her enchantments: so that now he has the heavenly certainty that she will let him have her; now again is dashed from such hopes; and the bitterness cured by some adorable new turn which draws him once more. Sometimes he is angry beyond controlling. In one of these moments he composes (and sends her) his poem (Donne's in fact) 'The Dampe.' (But even in these extreme moments of resentment and half despair his nobleness of heart keeps him from any blasphemy or grossness—such as Baias or Morville are betrayed into at times of similar exasperation.)

Morville, after about a fortnight (i.e., by July 13th or 14th) is stung into a violent scene with Fiorinda. Neither of them mentions Barganax, but Morville lets out in a spate of recriminations all his self-pity, etc., all these distresses he, of the μικροψυχια[2] of his nature, blames on her—trying by bitterness and injustice and railing to reduce her to tears which will enable him to regain some degree of ascendency in his own eyes, and make (as he thinks) a reconciliation and new start possible. But Fiorinda is not readily to be bullied into tears: she retires into her hard shell. Finally, when Morville instances his own single-eyed faithfulness, she retorts that an unfaithful husband is infinitely more tolerable than a jealous. He leaves her in a fury.

On Monday July 20 (Barganax having on the previous day been a little too possessive in his attitude, and having sent her the next morning—i.e. this Monday morning—his insolent poem 'The Dampe'), Fiorinda keeps him waiting nearly an hour attending her leisure in a gallery, then has him shown in—only to find it is a three-cornered party with Morville! Barganax behaves unexceptionally—

very nice to Morville, in strong contrast to Morville's surliness and veiled hostility. Without a single sign in all the interview giving a clue to either of them what is on her mind, Fiorinda does in her heart, definitely and irrevocably this evening at last, fall in love with Barganax and resolve to take him as her lover—i.e., recognises Him with Her Olympian insight through his Zimiamvian dress, for who in truth He is. On saying goodnight She says privately to Barganax, no use coming tomorrow evening—she is going away—doesn't know for how long. Well, may be back in a week: provincial appointment for Saturday August 1. But Barganax himself goes home in despair (in the Ninfea di Nerezza mood—*A Fish Dinner in Memison*, Chapter IX), determined to be off to Zayana next day and break with her for good and be no longer dragged, an unsatisfied spaniel-dog, at her apron strings, but have his freedom again. She is an enchantress, he thinks, and high time to be out of her toils. Morville, in a boorish way, refuses to [. . .] her and they retire to bed in their respective rooms, unreconciled. She for the first time realizes the nonentity of Morville. It is Astarte, or [? . . . Hecate . . .] (not yet—not until 10 or 11 A.M. on the morrow—21 July, Tuesday, after Morville's final blow and "salt bitch" outburst[3]—seated in her throne) that is tossing and turning in Fiorinda's bed in Reisma that night.

XXXIII

APHRODITE
HELIKOBLEPHAROS

IN ZIMIAMVIAN TIME, THE OPENING OF THIS CHAPTER FOLLOWS BY MO-
MENTS ONLY THE CONCLUSION OF CHAPTER X OF *A FISH DINNER IN MEMISON*.
ON JANUARY 28, 1945, EDDISON DRAFTED A WORKING VERSION FOR THE CON-
VERSATIONS OCCURRING IN REISMA ON THE MORNING OF MORVILLE'S STRIKING
OF FIORINDA:

Anthea and Campaspe (a little after 11:00 A.M., Tuesday, July
21st, 775 [AZC])

Anthea: Had you not better go up to her ladyship? She will
               want you to do her hair.

Campaspe: She has not rung yet.

Anthea: No. It is late. The more need to go. I liked not the
               look of the the bull-fly when he flung out of the
               house just now.

Campaspe: Thank god he's away from home tonight.

Anthea: Yes. The Admiral sent for him to ride north, meet
               the King in Rumala, and tomorrow south again.
               His serene highness is for Sestola. I hope Morville
               will break his neck. There's the bell: run you little
               flitterjack.

(Campaspe goes upstairs: finds Fiorinda sitting, in her hair and
in one underfrock without sleeves, before the mirror.

Campaspe is frightened at the expression of her face—Terror Antiquus[1]—in the looking glass: sees the mark of Morville's glove stroke on her flushed face. Seeing Campaspe, her expression changes: she is her Olympian Aphrodisian self again—reaches out her hand. Campaspe kneels and kisses it, and buries her face a moment in her mistress's lap.)

Fiorinda: Put up my hair, little warbler of mine.

Campaspe: (doing so) His lordship is gone, madam. (Fiorinda says nothing, but her whole posture is like an opening rose after a storm.)

Campaspe: What will your ladyship do today?

Fiorinda: Wait. (rings for Anthea) Anthea, go you to Memison. Find out what the Duke is about and bring me word at once.

  (exit Anthea)

        (The mark has faded now as Campaspe shows her the back view with a hand-mirror.) No. I've changed my mind. Low on my neck, as it was this morning before breakfast. (stretches her arms and leans back: the flashes of 'black lightning') And see you put out for tonight my new dress of red sendaline: the one I've never worn. I've been keeping it for a purpose.

Campaspe (wide eyed):   Yes, beloved madam.

Fiorinda: The clock has struck.

Campaspe: Will your ladyship wear with it the new silk cut-work undergarments I made?

Fiorinda: 'Twill be hot today. I'll wear no undergarment.

Campaspe: No, madam.

        (re-enter Anthea)

Anthea: His grace is set forth, baggage and all, for Zayana.

Fiorinda: 'Las, has he taken me at my word then, when I told him to go this morning? How strangely will men mistake one. Saw you him set forth?

Anthea: Yes.

Fiorinda: In what fashion went he, then? At a herd's gallop? He is a hasty man in all he undertakes. Galloped he, then?

Anthea: At a walking pace. And to the tune, methought, of 'Loth to depart.'

Fiorinda: You must overtake him: fetch him back again.

Anthea: What must we say to him?

Fiorinda: That I request his company at supper tonight, here in Reisma. And inform him—not as from me, but in kindness as from yourselves: lightly, as upon an

afterthought: that her ladyship sleeps alone to-
night, the lieutenant being from home.

THE ARGUMENT FOR THIS CHAPTER GIVES FACTS WHICH ARE FULLY NAR-
RATED IN CHAPTERS XI AND XII OF *A FISH DINNER IN MEMISON:*

On July 21, foully insulted and struck across the mouth by
Morville upon the false (or at least, premature) accusation of being
the Duke's mistress, she takes the Duke for her lover indeed.
Morville, guilty of further threats and outrage, is destroyed by
Anthea in her lynx dress.

EDDISON INTENDED TO NARRATE THE KILLING OF MORVILLE IN THIS CHAP-
TER. ON JANUARY 30, 1945, HE DRAFTED THE SCENE:

Morville walking distraught in the woods near Reisma, raging
in himself: 'Yes, I'll kill them both. . . .'

Anthea (in her own shape appearing from behind a tree) 'Good
morrow, for the second time today, my lord Morville. Is it safe for
you, think you, to wander in these woods alone and unarmed? You
are a great striker of women. I know. You struck my Lady yesterday
morning, an act that requires your death. And you struck me betwixt midnight and dawn with your riding-whip. So, upon that
great count and this small one (yet to me of itself sufficient) I have
tracked you forth and mean now to rid you of your life.'

Morville becomes numb and with clumsy fingers draws forth
his dagger.

Anthea: 'You have not the power to murder me (the dagger
drops from his fingers), but the will to do it so courts, if the cup of
your iniquities were not already full. You have been tried and found
wanting. I hate such horrified cattle as you should walk upon middle-earth: but there's one thing yet you can do: your flesh shall
make me a breakfast.'

Morville: 'Witch, deviless, I'll slay you with my hands, and then
your mistress, and then her vile leman. Then at last I'll die happy.'

Leaps upon her. She, suddenly in her lynx-dress, fastens her
teeth in the great veins of his throat: tears him bloodily in pieces,
eats her fill, takes her shape again and, beautiful and virginal, returns to Reisma.

AFTER DUELING WITH MORVILLE (A SCENE NARRATED IN CHAPTER XII OF *A*
FISH DINNER IN MEMISON), BARGANAX RETURNS WITH FIORINDA TO THE SECRET
CHAMBER WHOSE DOOR CAN BE REVEALED ONLY THROUGH DOCTOR VANDER-
MAST'S MAGIC. ON JANUARY 29, 1945, EDDISON MADE NOTES ABOUT THE EVENTS
OF JULY 22, 775 AZC:

Barganax and Fiorinda waking (for 2nd time) about 9–10 A.M., in Reisma on Wednesday morning July 22:

Barganax wakes and sees her asleep. The 'peace of her beauty.' The soul asleep in her face, but in the beauty of her naked body (the clothes thrown off and piled on the floor) the sleepless spirit awake, argus-eyed, as if returning her lover's gaze. She had fallen asleep in the crook of her arm, her cheek resting upon his heart. The black hair in deep confusion all over the pillows and bed: the white line of the parting, under his eye as he looks down on her, straight and undeviating as the right road of true love. He softly kisses it: her eyes open and she puts up her lips as though there had never been since world's beginning an awakening upon which these two had not so kissed good-morning.

That same afternoon Duke Barganax rode south to Zayana in preparation for certain knotty questions to be dealt with on Friday at his weekly presence, then, with promise to be back by Saturday. For upon Saturday his mother had appointed to give a fish dinner in the King's honour in Memison to but eight guests besides: the Vicar, the Admiral, the Chancellor, and the Duke, and for ladies, besides Fiorinda, the Princess Zenianthe, Anthea, and Campaspe. As he rode southward, he found men's mouths full of talk: how that the Lord Morville had been eat up with wild beasts in the woods near Reisma: but no word of another truth which might have tasted yet saucier to some of these blabbers, namely that a duel had been fought in Reisma in the midnight hours betwixt Morville and the Duke: neither hurt, but Morville worsted: spared by the Duke, but departed unreconciled and loudly menacing murder against both the Duke and my lady Fiorinda. Of her the Duke was not spared the hearing of much dishonest talk that day: as that she rustled in un-paid-for silks, lived very disorderly, married but to unmarry herself by running away or, the better to unencumber herself of a husband, take a resolution to have him murdered. Such talk, uttered in Barganax's presence, mixed so ill with memories in his mind and veins of the forenight, that not two but three men's blood was shed by him in that journey in [. . .] for such slander talk: two in duels: the third but seized and flung against a wall, to so good effect as dash his brains out, so that he never again spoke word.[2]

THE REST OF THE ARGUMENT FOR THIS CHAPTER SUMMARIZES THE GROW-
ING RELATIONSHIP BETWEEN FIORINDA AND BARGANAX:

The course of true love for Barganax and Fiorinda never runs smooth: their natures are too fierce, hazardous, and passion-ridden for that. But it runs always deeper and stronger and with mounting superlatives, and always morning-new. He repeatedly urges her to become Duchess of Zayana, but she as steadfastly refuses; knowing, by an insight which (in common with all her qualities) reaches perhaps beyond the strain of mortality, that it is in the core of his nature to set supreme store by unsafeties and uncertainties, dangerous elysiums, the bitter-sweet: γλνκυπικος ερ$\hat{ω}$ς.[3] And these things she gives him, unfailably, often almost unbearably, and with both hands.

The Fish Dinner
and Its Aftermath

O N J U L Y 2 5, the Duchess entertains privately at a fish dinner in
Memison the King, the Vicar, Barganax, Jeronimy, Beroald, Fiorinda, Anthea, Campaspe, and the King's niece Zenianthe.

The talk turns to divine philosophy, and so to questions of
Time and Creation: *If we were Gods, what manner of world would we
choose to make?* To this question, raised by the King, most of the
company answer, in effect: This actual world (that is to say, of
course, Zimiamvia). But my Lady Fiorinda, in a dangerously irre-
sponsible and contrary mood tonight, and speaking as if the King
were in sober truth the Almighty and she herself Aphrodite Herself,
for whom this and all conceivable worlds are made, asks him to
make for her a strange mechanical hitherto undreamed-of world
which she describes at large.

What followed, upon this request, probably none of the company but the two pairs of lovers (the King and Amalie, Barganax
and Fiorinda) fully understood. Certainly, all present, the King and
Fiorinda alone excepted, had forgotten by next morning.

The fact was this: Speculation merged into action: the King,
sitting there at supper, did in very truth create, to her specification,
this world we ourselves live in and belong to, so that they saw it
evolve, a large teeming bubble, as this whole material universe
might present itself under the eyes of the Gods, its miniature aeons
passing beneath Their immortal gaze, as millions of years condensed into, say, half an hour. More than this: the King and the
Duchess, Barganax and Fiorinda, in a desire to *know* this new world
from within, entered it and so lived out a life-time here (in our own
century), while to the other guests they merely seemed to sit gazing
in a rapt attention for a few minutes on a monstrous bubble poised
before them on the supper-table. Then the company, returning to

reality, began to break up for bed. Fiorinda, in her most languefied luxuriousness lazying on Barganax's arm, having understandably had more than enough of this not very admirable world, snuffed it out for ever as though it had never existed, by idly pricking the bubble with a bediamonded hair-pin idly drawn from her hair as she passed. In that moment the Duke, looking in Her face, which is the beginning and the ending, from all unbegun eternities, of all conceivable worlds, knew perhaps (momentarily, and with as much certainty as is good for him) Who in very truth She was.

(This theme [of our present world as a misconceived and, were it not for its nightmarish unreality and transience, unfortunate episode in the real life of the Gods] is the subject of another book, *A Fish Dinner in Memison*. In *The Mezentian Gate* that ground is not gone over again, but sufficient indications are allowed to appear of the nature and outcome of the proceedings at suppertable to enable a reader to realize the cosmic repercussions of Aphrodite's sudden 'unfledged fancy' and to be prepared for their effect upon the mind of the King. It is to be noted that he and Fiorinda alone remember next morning [and thereafter] what took place at the fish dinner after talk had passed over into action.)

This brings us to August 775. Chapter XXXIV (*The Fish Dinner: First Digestion*), dealing with the effect of the fish dinner upon the minds of the Duchess and of Barganax, is already written. The as yet unwritten Chapter XXXV (*Diet a Cause*),[1] covering the next six months or so, deals with the effects upon the King and the Vicar.

The effect on the King, of this taste in Himself of omniscience combined with omnipotence in practice, is partly disclosed in a scene between him and Vandermast.

On the Vicar, who smells a subtle change in his great master which he is at an utter loss to define or understand but which he finds profoundly disturbing, the effect is to determine him to take all further precautions against the possibility that the King may die and he himself be left to fight for his place in the sun. By all covert means the Vicar begins to build up his armed strength in Rerek to such a pitch that, if it should come to a trial of mastery between himself and Styllis, he shall prevail, even though the united forces of Fingiswold and Meszria be brought to bear against him.

The grand finale of the book (Chapters XXXVI–XXXIX: *Rosa Mundorum, Testament of Energeia, The Call of the Night-Raven,* and *Omega and Alpha in Sestola*) is already written.

E. R. E.

BOOK 7

To Know or Not to Know

XXXIV

THE FISH DINNER:
FIRST DIGESTION

U PON A morning of late August the Duchess of Memison was abroad before breakfast upon the out-terraces above the western moat. The year was turning golden to all ripenesses, of late flowers, and fruit, and (albeit yet far off) fall of the leaf. In this light of early morning the yew hedges that run beside the terraces were covered with spiders' webs wet with dew-drops, a shimmering of jewels on mantles of white lace: a beauty ever changing, and with a hint of things altogether strengthless and ephemeral. No bird-voice sounded, except twitterings of swallows in the sky or exclamations from the Duchess's white peacocks, whose plumage was like woven moonbeams, and the eyes in their tail-feathers like iridescent moons when they displayed in the slant rays of the sun.

At the far end of the terrace southwards, she was met with Duke Barganax, picking his way among the peacocks and bending, as he came towards her, to stroke now this one, now that. They drooped tails, and with an elegant, crawling, swimming, undulating gait, in its extremity of submission too abject to be called pavane, passed under his hand for the caress. 'You are up early, my lady Mother,' he said.

'Well, and what of you? And besides, is it not a virtue?'

'Depends of the occasion. For my part, I never (provided I lie alone) insult a fair morning by lying a-bed.'

'A very needful proviso. But tell me,' said she, 'while I think on't: was not that a misreckoning of mine, at our fish dinner here a month ago, not to bid you bring the learned doctor with you, 'stead of leave him to stew in his most metaphysical juices in Zayana?'

'I had not thought so. Why?'

'Might have told us now what in sober truth happened that night.'

'I can tell you that,' said the Duke. 'Noble feasting. Good discourse.'

'No more?'

'Come, you remember as well as I.'

The Duchess shook her head. 'If so, we are in one ridiculous self-same plight of forgetfulness. I remember nought past the ordinary, as you have summed it. But even next morning I woke to a discomfortable and teasing certainty that there was much forgot; and amongst it, the heart and argument of our whole proceeding.'

'What if 'twere so indeed?' said the Duke. ''Twas but pleasant talk. If unremembered, as like as not worth the remembering.'

They walked slowly on, back along the terrace, in the way of the summer palace, peacocks following them at heel. She said presently, 'More I consider of it, more am I suspicious that 'twas not talk only, but something we did. Could I call it back to mind, might give me the key to unlock certain perplexities.'

'Did you not ask the King my Father?'

'Yes. But no light there. Did but laugh at me: fub me up with quips and riddles and double meanings: made me worse.'

'Or my lord Chancellor? Or the Admiral (heaven be kind to him)? No light there? As for the Vicar—'

''Las,' said she, 'what a red lion, and what a red fox, is that! Disputations in divine philosophy are but dry hard biscuit to him.'

'And to mend the dryness, did drink drunk or the true main act of our masque were led on. And that, as myself have noted in him afore this, needeth an unconscionable, unimaginable, deal of wine.'

'The true main act: what was that?'

'Why,' said he, 'I meant when, after the rest of us (you remember this, surely?) had spoken our minds 'pon the question: What world would we choose to dwell in for ever, say we were Gods, and thus able to have our desire fulfilled into our hand soon as thought on? I meant when, after that, she, under pressure from you and from my Father, began to speak of the world which, had she that absolute sovereignty of choice, she would choose.'

'And it was—?'

Barganax had come to a stand: his gaze across the dew-drenched grass. Here, seen in the pathway of the sun, hundreds of starry lights glowed and sparkled: topaz, emerald, fire-opal, ruby, sapphire, diamond: always changing place and colour, kindling, flashing, disappearing and appearing again in least expected places, as some shift of the eye of the beholder called them into being or laid them by: tiny unsure elysiums, here and away, unreachable; and yet perfect, yet never wholly extinguished: spawned or conceived by this unsightable golden splendour of the risen sun. 'Strange. 'Tis a thing I had not thought on,' he said; 'my mind being bent on things nearer my concern. But true it is, when I try now to recall that latter part of our discourse, I am in your case: 'tis gone from me.'

'Perhaps the night put it from our minds?'

'The night?' said the Duke: no more. But when he looked round at her it was as with eyes dimmed after gazing too near at hand into a naked flame.

He began to walk up and down, the Duchess in silence watching him. Suddenly he turned heel, came straight to her where she stood, took her in his arms and kissed her. He said, still holding her, looking down into her eyes: 'Who made you such a queen-rose, my Mother?'

'I don't know,' she said, and hid her face on his shoulder, her right hand coming up to his cheek. 'I don't know. I don't know.' When she looked up, her eyes were smiling.

Taking her hands in his, 'What is this?' he said. 'You're not unhappy?'

'Something has changed since that night.' She was looking down now, playing with his fingers.

'Come, sweet Mother. You have not changed. I have not changed.'

'God be thanked, no. But—well, weather has changed.'

'Nonsense. It is set fair.'

'It is changed,' said she, 'and changing. I have a disliking for changes.'

He said, after a pause, 'I think I should die of the tediousness without them.'

The Duchess smiled. 'Everybody has a different weather, I suppose. You and I certainly. May be that is why we love each other.'

Barganax kissed her hand. She caught his and, under laughing protest, kissed it.

'My Father, then?'

She said, 'I can feel the change in him. It frightens me. I would have him never change.'

'And he you.'

'That is true, I know.'

Barganax's brow was clouded. He walked over to the parapet's edge, upon their left, and stood there silent a minute, looking over.

The Duchess followed him. 'I have not seen him since then,' he said, after a while. 'So I cannot tell.' A clump of belladonna lilies were in flower there beside them: thick strong stems, sleek and columnar, and great trumpets of a silvery rose-colour, smoothskinned as a woman's throat, cool, bedewed, exhaling a heavy sweetness. The Duke picked one. Suddenly he spoke: 'Can you remember what she said that night, when you and my Father pressed her to answer? About her world she would have?'

'Yes. That came before the things I have forgotten. She said: "The choice is easy. I choose *That which is*." '

'True. And the King took exceptions: saith, what could that be but the ultimate Two alone? They, and the lesser Gods and Goddesses who keep the wide heaven, of a lower reality, may be, than His and Hers, yet themselves more real than such summer-worms as men? And he bade her picture it to him that he might perceive it: all this and the golden mansions of the Father—I liked not that. I saw she was angry with him, thinking he mocked. She was in a strange contrary temper that evening. Answered him, "No. Like as her grace, I also will change my mind too: look lower." You remember that *Look lower*?'

The Duchess covered her face with her hands. 'When I would remember, I seem to walk on a swaying rope between darkness and darkness. What happened in truth that night?' she said, looking up again. 'Had we drunk too much wine, will you think?'

'A love-draught?' said Barganax. ''Tis not impossible.' He clasped his strong hand about his mother's shoulder and drew her to him: then, in her ear: 'Those words, *Look lower*. And with them a look in her eye I'll swear, Mother, no eye but mine hath seen or shall ever; to be seen, it needs to be loved. An unplacable look: a serpent-look.'

'The dream comes back to me,' said the Duchess, turning her fingers in his, of his hand that rested on her shoulder. ' "I have thought of a world," she said. "Will your highness create it indeed for me?" '

'Be careful,' the Duke said, in a kind of fierceness. 'It was no dream. You have brought it back alive to me, and not the words only, neither. You have caught the very accents of her voice beyond all elysiums.' Then, loosing his hold and stepping back to have full view of her: 'You remember my Father's reply? "I'll do my endeavour"?'

The Duchess was trembling. 'Since when have you, my son, had this art to speak to me, out of your own mouth, with his voice?'

'She lifted her head,' said the Duke, as if locked up alone with his inward vision, 'as a she-panther that takes the wind. By heavens!' he said, as the Duchess lifted hers; 'you have the motion. Continue, if you love me. Continue. Her eyes were on me, though she spoke as if to him. Rehearse it: act it for me, to prove it more than a dream of mine.'

And the Duchess, looking at this son of hers as it were to look through a perspective that should show her his father, her lover, began to speak: as a sleep-walker might, not her words but the Lady Fiorinda's.

When she had ended, her son abode motionless against the parapet, staring at her. Then she, as if by mere silence startled out of her sleep-walking: 'What have I said? It is gone from me: I cannot remember.'

He leaned towards her. 'For all sakes, remember. Think of me as the King my Father. He made it, that thing, that massy glistering bubble, even as she required it of him: made and fashioned it, there on the table before us, growing between his hands. What was it? Did we not behold it put on substance, mature to an inconceivable intricacy in obedience to her unbitted fancy? As though all Gods and Powers had been but ministers to her least desires (as, by my soul, they ought to be). But a clockwork only it was: a make-believe: a dead world.'

'His words,' said the Duchess, and trembled: 'his voice yet again. "A dead world. A dead soul." And she desired him then give it life: "Let it teem with life," she said; "and that horribly." So, and in that humour. Her laws for the living beings in that world: you remember? "I will tease them a little with my laws.' "

Barganax narrowed his eyelids, looking at his mother; and yet (it may be thought) not at his mother but, in her, at his Dark Lady. 'That they should seem to have freedom,' he said; 'and yet we, who look on, should know 'tis no such matter. And her law of death: "Every one that knoweth life in my world shall know also death. The little simplicities, indeed, shall not die. But the living creatures shall." Well, was she not right? "A just and equal choice: either be a little senseless lump of jelly or of dead matter, and subsist till world's ending; or else—"'

' "Or else be a bird, a fish, a rose," ' said the Duchess, as if unburying a new fragment from amongst the chaos of broken memories of that strange supper-entertainment: ' "or men and women as we be—" '

' "Upon condition to fade, wax old, waste at last to carrion and corruption."—Well? Is it so much unlike this loved world of ours?'

''Tis too much like,' the Duchess replied. 'It is the same as this world: but crooked: but spoilt.'

'Your grace needs not to tell me,' said the Duke: *et ego in Arcadiâ,*[1] and he laughed, 'but that scarce fits. "Men and women as we be." And then she said, sitting at your table here, before your summer palace, while her world-destroying beauty, pensive and stilled, shone down upon that misconceived master-work of self-thwarting perfections: "As we be? How were that possible, out of this? Is there mind in this?—Unless, indeed" (you remember), "unless We Ourselves go in and enter it. Know it so, go down—" And then my Father said: "Undergrope it from within. For a moment, We might. To know." '

'No more, I beseech you,' said the Duchess. 'What are we about?'

But Barganax had her by the hand. 'Think of me constantly now, as the King my Father. Let's try it again. You and I, this time. I begin to remember things I, too, had forgot; and I know not who I am, nor who you are. Come, we will. I will know again whether there be truth in it or but make-believe.'

'Stop!' she said, 'I cannot bear it: not a second time.'

But he, still straining her by the hand, overbore her. For a minute they stood, here in lovely Memison, as two unfleshed souls might aboard Charon's ferry, waiting to be put from shore.[2] But nothing came about: no expected half-remembered translation out of their native substantiality of life and being into a more dimmer and crippled world, in detail so like, in sum so alien: unimaginable now: a prison-life which had been, or could be, theirs, but now well forgotten; and yet half tasted in remembrances which, slight, smudged, fleeting, were now blessedly lost again, blotted out in a wreathing of mists and fog and billowing darkness. Then, as with the going of a shadow from across the sun's face, was this real world back again true and perfect: smells of wet earth and wood-smoke, the snail on the path, the wren scolding from the yews: on the glassy waters of Reisma Mere afar a rippling here and there where the morning breeze touched them: great sulphur-coloured lilies seen against the yews' darkness, distilling on the air their voluptuous sweet scent: morning light upon Memison; and breakfast-time.

The same day, Duke Barganax rode south, having appointed the day after to hold his weekly presence: receive petitions, hear suits if any there were of enough matter and moment to be pleaded before him in person, treat with men in their quarrels and set them at one, or, where that would not speed, deliver judgement and give order for its execution.

It was past supper-time when he rode up into Acrozayana. He delayed but to eat some cold collation: smoked salmon, caviar, boar's head spiced and dressed with hippocras sauce, with a flagon of Reisma wine to wash it down; then, retiring himself to the western balcony of his own privy lodging that looks on Zayana lake and Ambremerine, summoned Doctor Vandermast. 'I would have your head in a matter, honoured sir: not as my secretary, but as of old, master and teacher in the noble dark science. How came this world, think you, and other worlds if other there be?'

Vandermast answered and said, 'By God alone, that made all.'

'Good. *Ergo,* made also Himself?'

'Undoubtedly so. Your grace hath not forgotten the definitio: *Per causam sui intelligo id, cujus essentia involvit existentiam: sive id, cujus natura non potest concipi nisi existens?* Nought else save God alone is able to be cause of itself, since nought else hath such a nature as is not able to be conceived save as existing. In none else doth the Essence thereof inescapably involve also the Existence.'

The Duke sat gazing before him, as rapt with some picture in his mind. Then leaning forward to look in the doctor's eyes (as well as a man were able, under their shadowing eaves and but starlight to see by): 'But there is a Twoness,' he said, 'in the ultimate Onehead of Godhead?'

'There is a Darkness. If indeed by *God* we understand a Being absolutely infinite, that is to say, a Substance made up and compounded of infinite attributes, every particular one of which expresseth an Essence infinite and eternal.'

'And you yourself,' said the Duke, leaning nearer, eyeing him yet closelier, 'when I was but of years sixteen and did first dally with the Metaphysicals, you did ground me in that principle you name lode-star and cynosure of divine philosophy: *Per realitatem et perfectionem idem intelligo:* "Reality," that is, "and perfection are the same thing." '

'Through the monster-teeming seas of thought, ay, and in action, assaying those topless spires whence in highest majesty God looks down, that,' replied Vandermast, 'is indeed man's cynosure: the alonely certain star to steer by.'

Barganax sat back in his chair. The sky was of a soft violet-colour and full of stars whose beams showed, in those windless upper airs, a strange constancy, but the mirrored stars in Zayana lake swayed and broke in pieces and ran together again as quicksilver: a changefulness and a restlessness like as that of the dew-lights that morning in Memison. A like unrestful secretness stirred under the deep harmonies of his voice as he said, as if examining some strange unheard-of novelty in his own hidden mind: '*Realitatem: Perfectionem.* Well, I have found perfection.'

Doctor Vandermast held his peace.

The Duke said, still as to himself, almost with a tang of mockery in his accents, yet in the same slow wonder: 'Am not I therefore beyond example fortunate? What need I further, having possessed me of Perfect and Real in One?' He stretched his arms as one waking from sleep, and laughed. 'Come, you are silent. Will you envy me, old man, to have found, and in my young years, this true philosopher's stone?'[3]

'How shall any man but yourself tell whether you are to be envied or commiserated? Satiety is death. Desire is life.'

'And is not the mere quality of Perfection, this,' said the Duke, leaping to his feet to stand against the balustrade, his back to the night sky, his face in deep shadow looking down on Vandermast: 'to be infinite? Infinitely desirable, and infinitely unsupportable: explored without and within, yet ever the more terrible and the more appassionately sought in its unknowable secrets. In fiercest beauties, in supremest *deliciis*, absent, yet absent unsparable. And so, elysium beyond elysiums: here and away, yet so as a man would joyfully cut his hand off to buy off change, and when change is come, cut off t' other sooner than go back to *status quo ante*.'[4]

'*Laetitia*,' said that ancient doctor slowly, as to weigh each word, '*est hominis transitio a minore ad majorem perfectionem:* Joy is the passing of a man from the smaller to the greater perfection.'

'And (corollarium) the greater oft-times becometh greater by bringing back the smaller. Infinite change; yet infinite self-same bewitchment.'

There was a grandeur of line, beyond the use of human kind, in the lithe frame of him outlined there against stars. Vandermast watched him in silence, then spoke: 'I observed this in your grace, even at my first coming into your noble service, that alike by soul and body you are of apt temper to understand the depth of that wisdom: *Nous connaissons la vérité non seulement par la raison, mais encore par le coeur; c'est de cette dernière sorte, que nous connaissons les premières principes*.'[5]

'That is wisdom,' said Barganax. 'That is truth.' He settled himself on the stone of the balcony that was warm yet after a day of unclouded sun, and, sitting there against the sky, said: 'Our talk hath wandered somewhat beside my purpose, which concerned the making of worlds. Were I to tell you I saw one such devised and created, under my nose, a month ago, at supper-table, would you credit that?'

Doctor Vandermast paused. 'As coming from your grace, known to me for a man of keen judgement and not given to profane jesting, I should unpartially examine it.'

'I have not told you I saw it. The more I consider of it, the less know I whether I truly beheld that marvel or 'twere but legerdemain.'

'If it pleased your grace open it to me more at large—'

'Better not. I have indeed almost clean forgotten it, save the circumstances. But this I will tell you, that I seemed, when 'twas over, to have lived myself (and yet something more than myself: mixed of myself and his serene highness my Father, and, in the mixture, may be a less than him and something less too than me, as impurer; like as orange-colour hath not the pureness of red neither of yellow, being compound of both)—in that mixed self, I seemed to have lived a life-time in that world. Well,' he said, after a moment: 'I sucked its orange. But a cheap frippery of a world it was, take it for all in all: made tolerable, as I bethink me now, but by rumours and fore-savourings of this. And I seemed, besides, to have looked on from without, while untold ages passed there: first the mere ball of incandescence: then the cooling: the millennial ages through which a kind of life was brewing, in enormous wastefulness and painfulness and ever-growing interweaving of tangle, until human kind began there: slow generations, ever changing and never (on the whole) bettering, of human kind, such as we be. Ay, and I was stood by, viewing it thus from withoutward, even at the golden moment for which that defaced, gelded, exiled creation, so like the real world, yet so unlike, had from its first beginnings waited and thirsted: its dissolution. And that was when she, to pleasure whose chanceable idle soon-changed fantasy it was made, took from the braided blackness of her hair a pin starred with anachite diamonds, and as idly with it touched the bubble. And at that prick—puff! 'twas gone: nought left but the little wet mark on the table to witness it ever existed.'

Vandermast said: 'With one breath They create: with one breath uncreate.'

'I have forgot, almost,' said the Duke. Then, 'Indeed since I spoke to you even this instant moment gone, old sir, all is fled from me, like as dreams are scattered and broken at the very words we wake with on our lips to recount them. This remains (O the unsounded seas of women's bloods), that that night she wore glowworms in her hair.'

'There is danger for a man,' said Vandermast, after a silence, 'in knowing over-much.'

'Or for a God?'

'To be able to answer that with certainty,' said Vandermast, 'were, for a mortal, to know over-much.'

XXXV

Diet a Cause

EDDISON WROTE NO ARGUMENT FOR THIS CHAPTER, AND THERE ARE NO EXTANT DRAFTS FOR IT. HE DISCUSSES IT BRIEFLY IN 'THE FISH DINNER AND ITS AFTERMATH.'

XXXVI

Rosa Mundorum[1]

ELVRAZ SEBARM stands upon the lake, among orange trees and pomegranates and almonds and peaches of the south, a mile north-west over the water from Zayana town, and two miles by land: an old castle built of honey-coloured marble at the tip of a long sickle-shaped ness that sweeps round southwards, with wild gardens running down in the rocks to the water's edge, and behind the castle a wood of holm-oaks making a windbreak against the north. Here my Lady Fiorinda was keeping household in June of that next year, some few months later than these things last told of, the Duke having put it at her disposition for such times as she should not be resident in Memison or his guest in Acrozayana.

It was midsummer morning, at the half-light before the break of day. For the heat of the night, the curtains were left undrawn in the great bedchamber that looks three ways across the water: south, towards Zayana, whose towers, spires, and gables seemed in this twilight to be of no solider substance than the sky against which they rose, the reflections of them barely set moving by a ripple on the lake's placid surface: west, to the isle of Ambremerine, wooded with oak and cedar and cypress and strawberry-tree, and all misted with the radiance behind it of the setting silver moon: east, across low vineyard-clad country, to the sea at Bishfirthhead. Within that chamber the colourless luminosity of the summer night, beginning to obey at this hour some influence of the unrisen sun, partly obscured, partly revealed, shapes and presences: lustrous balls of moon-stone and fire-opal like a valance of strange fruits fringing the canopy of the great bed, which was built to the Duke's designing and by art of Doctor Vandermast, and with posts of solid gold: lamps and sconces and branched hanging candlesticks of gold and silver and crystal: pictures let into the panels of the doors of tall wardrobe presses: bookshelves filled with books between the windows: two scented lamps, filigreework of orichalc, burning for night-lights at the bed's head, one upon either side, whose beams dimly lighted a frieze, of eagles, phoenixes, chimaeras, satyrs, gorgons, winged bulls, sea-goats with fish-tailed bodies, waterhorses, butterfly-ladies, carved out of rose-coloured marble in high relief on a background of peacock green. And with the incense of the lamps was mingled a perfume more elemental and of a sweeter and more disturbing luxury: of that lady's breath and her sleeping presence.

She lay there prone, in an innocency of beauty asleep, face turned aside and pillowed in the curve of her right elbow, her left hand inshrining its smoothness between smooth right arm and cheek. All naked she slept, sheet and bed-clothes thrown off to lie in a heap upon the floor at the bedside for warmness of the night. Anthea, too, was asleep on the bed, curled up in her lynx shape at her mistress's feet.

From the gardens below the western window, the first birdsong sounded: bodiless little madrigal of a peggy-whitethroat, ending upon that falling cadence. So, and again. A third time; and the dividing notes took to themselves the articulation of human speech: Campaspe singing her morning hymn to Her that is mistress both of night and of day:

> "Our Lady, awake!
> Darkness is breaking.
> Bat wings are folded:
> Crop-full the owl.
> Night-flowers close,
> Their sweetness withhold:
> The east pales and quickens to gold:
> Night-raven and ghoul
> Flee to their make.
>
> "A breath of morning stirs on the lake.
> Colours disclose:
> Carnation, rose.
> The Worlds are waking—
> Thou, Onemost, awake!"

At the sound of that singing and at a touch of the lynx's cold nose against her foot, Fiorinda, with a little unarticulate slumbrous utterance still betwixt sleeping and waking, turned on her back. In a more slowed voluptuousness than of python uncoiling, she stretched her sleep-loosened limbs to the wide ambiency of self-oblation, and, with that, her whole body was become a source of light: sea-glitter between her opening eye-lids: a Praxitelean[2] purity, swan-white fined to tinctures of old ivory, in breast, throat, thigh, and in all the supple rondure of her hips: panther-black livery of the darkness that burned as consuming fires, blackness shining down blackness to the out-splendouring of all earthly suns. Her youth, with the lithe wild-beast strength and dove-like languor of these perfections, shadowless now, faintly incandescent, was transfigured to that ache and surquedry of beauty which great poets and great lovers, uncontented by earth's counterfeits, have strained inward eye and sense to draw down from Olympus, those things' true home; where they subsist unsmirched by times or allegiances unsubject to their sovereignty, and are not exiles bound servant to ends not theirs. Thus for a while (which whether it were of minutes or of ages, were a question barren of all result or answer) she lay: She of Herself: the verities of Her waking presence manifest, convenable to sight, touch, hearing, scent, and taste: here, in Velvraz Sebarm.

Rising at last from the golden bed, She stood to contemplate awhile, in the tall looking-glass by the growing light, the counter-image of Her own face and, at their plenilune upon which not even the eyes of a God can long bear to rest, Her ultimate beauties, from unbegun eternity lode-star, despair, and under-song, of all hearts' desires. And now, with Her standing so in deific selfknowing, everything that was not Her went out like the flame of a blown-out candle: the room, the familiarities of that Meszrian countryside, the softness of velvet carpet under Her feet, fallen to the formless ruin of oblivion.

Beneath Her, presently, some unfading dawn uncovered itself: morning of life, ancienter than worlds: saffron-hued, touching cliff and glacier to pale gold, and throwing into gullies and across snow-fields shadows of an azured transparency, chill as the winds that sprang up with day. From behind Her mountain-top where She stood,[3] the sun lept up, throwing the shadow of the mountain mile upon mile across lesser heights to the westward that were gilded with the first beams, their nearer summits bathing in primrose radiancy, their more distant in more paler, more air-softened, hues; range succeeding range to where, over the furthermost crest, day was breaking on the sea-strand and sea-foams of Paphos. Long and level in the mid distance far below Her, grey-houndish clouds drove past, trailing ever-changing shadows across the landscape of ridges and hill-tops and deep-cleft dales. Against that dawn-illumined background the great cast shadow of Olympus rested, a wide-flung wine-dark mantle of obscurity, wearing on its outermost edge a smoulder of crimson fire. Anthea and Campaspe, in their nymphish true outwards, knelt at Her feet in virgin snow. In the depths, but far above the habitations of men (if men were yet, or yet continued), a gyr-falcon, queen of the air, took her morning flight.

But She, eternal Aphrodite of the flickering eyelids and the violet-sweet breast, laughter-loving, honey-sweet, child of Zeus, She for whom all is made, spoke and said:

'Rise you worlds, made and unmade, and worship Me.

'Worship Me, women of all worlds, dresses of mine, shadows of Me in turbid water. I am the truth of you. Without those glints or keep-sakes that are in you of Me, you are nothing.

'O men, kings and lords of the ages, heroes, lovers of wisdom, great strikers, adventurers upon perilous seas, makers and doers, minds and bodies framed in His image that made you, and made Himself, and because without Me Godhead were but a trash-name, therefore, to have Me beside Him from the beginning, made Me: Rise, and worship Me. Rise and, who dares, love Me. But he that would love Me, be it God Himself, shall first kiss My feet.'

Unnumbered as motes in a sunbeam, or as the unnumbered laughter of the waves of ocean, eyes were upon Her from all remoteness of earth and sky and sea, and the rumour of them was as the rumour and rustle of starlings' wings flying in flocks of unnumbered thousands.

She said: 'Look (if your sight can face the nakedness of your hidden mind) into the sea-fire of My eyes. Look: My lips, blood-red, that can at one imperial kiss drain out the rendered soul from your body, and give it back so dyed with the taste of Me as from that now unto your death you shall seek Me ever, never finding yet never altogether losing. These jewels for snares in My hair's darkness are sleet and scourge of wild-fire. The moth-like bare touch of My hand can do away worlds or raise up the dead. In Me is the Bitter-sweet; grave, cradle, and marriage-bed of all contrairs: Rose of the Worlds: Black Lily, Black Flame, that but with the glance do stab, sear, and violently stir to one essence, spirit and sense. In all noble enterprise, in all your most fantastical desires, behold here your cynosure: this centre where all lines meet. I am She that changeth, yet changeth not. Many countenances I have, many dresses, bringing to My lover the black or the red, spade or heart, or pureness of golden flowers or a gold of waning moons at morning; and maidenhead always new. Of all that was, is, or is to come, I, even I of Myself, am end, reason, last elixir. He that loveth, and he love not Me, loveth Death. Love Me who dares. He shall be Mine, I his, for ever; and if it were possible for more than ever, then for ever more.'

She ended: terrible, lifted up above all worlds, shining down all other lights, even to the sun's.

From behind Her, eastwards, the other side from Paphos, came a roaring of avalanche and rockfall. Mists blowing upwards swallowed the mountain-top in a freezing tempest of sleet and lightnings and thundering darkness. In that void where duration can have no hour-glass, time stood still, or ceased.

Then the mists, falling apart, opened a sudden window upon Ambremerine and clear morning. Fiorinda had taken about Her lovely shoulders a robe of diaphanous black silk figured with flowerwork of gold and crimson and margery-pearls. Beside her the two nymphs, looking upon her in fearful adoration, were still kneeling.

Some three hours later, about seven o'clock, the Chancellor, riding up the Memison road a mile or so north from Zayana, had sight of her above him in the high open downland: white jennet, french hood, grass-green riding-habit, merlin on fist. She saw him and began to come down leisurely by the directest way, a steep rocky slope, slacking rein for the little mare, clever as a cat, to choose her steps amid the tangle of creeping rhododendron and daphne with boulders and stumps and old scree hidden beneath it. 'Blessings of the morning upon you, my lady sister,' said he, when they were within talking-distance. 'I am from Sestola: a message from the King's highness (Gods send he live for ever), for the Duke. You and he are commanded to supper tonight, at Sestola.'

'Excellent. Have you told his grace?'

'Not yet. I intended for Velvraz Sebarm, supposing to find him there.'

'That was a strange unlikely guess. Dwells he not in Zayana?'

'A new custom, then, when your ladyship lies in Velvraz Sebarm.'

'Have you breakfasted?'

'A bite and a sup.'

'I too. Let us breakfast together ere you go back to Acrozayana.'

They turned off from the road at a walking-pace by the path that goes to Velvraz Sebarm. Their morning shadows, still long, went before them. A heat-mist was rising from Zayana lake, and all the soft landscape westward was golden with morning. 'I would counsel you, brother,' she said, 'to stick to your politics: not pry into my domestical affairs. I too have my policies: have long ago learned, like as my Lord Barganax (as you, I thought, had likely observed), that prime article of wisdom of the learned doctor: μηδέν ἄγαν: nothing over-much.'

They rode awhile in silence.

'How like you of my little falcon? Is she not a jewel?'

The Lord Beroald perfunctorily gave it a look. 'Good for flying at vermin.'

Upon that, sourly said, she glanced sidelong at him out of her slanting green eyes. 'Clouds in your face? and so fair a morning?'

'Clouds from Rerek, may be.'

'Are but smoke-balls. Blow them away.'

'The council will sit today. By latest secret advertisements I have had, he still draweth forces to Laimak.'

'And what else indeed, then, would you look for?'

'Nought else; save now for the sequel. 'Tis time to end it.'

A satirical sumptuosity of suppressed laughter stirred at the corners of that lady's mouth. 'Heaven shield me from a condition where you and your friends swayed all. I think you would leave us no great eminent thing extant might you but avail to end it, lest by some far-fetched possibility it grow to danger perhaps your little finger.'

'I am a man of common prudence.'

'God for witness, were you that and no more, I think I'd hate you for it.'

'A quality uncommon in some quarters today.'

'Some quarters? O lawyers' equivocations! Which then?'

'Even the highest.'

'Yes, I know,' said she. 'Some safety there for unsafety, by favour of heaven.'

'Trouble not your sweet perverse heart as for that. The wolf will run: you shall see.'

'I shall see good sport, then.'

The Chancellor eyed her with a sardonic smile. 'Your ladyship was not always so chary in ending an inconvenience.'

'You think not?'

'What of your first husband? What of your second?'

'Foh!' she said. 'That was far another matter, and where there was cause why. Small nastiness, of a sort as plenty as blackberries, and thus rightly (with help of your gentle kindness, dear brother) made away.'

He laughed. 'Praise where praise is due, madam. You asked no help from me when you did up Morville.'

They were come now to the gardens, where the path leads round by the waterside to the castle gate between drifts of stately golden-eyed daisies with black-curling petals of a deep wine-purple and, at their feet, pink-coloured stonecrops on whose platter-like heads scores of butterflies sipped honey and sunned their wings. Fiorinda said, 'Because a dog grins his teeth, that means not necessarily he means to bite his master. I have known my ban-dog growl at things I could not myself neither see nor hear, much less smell.

And, 'cause my dog's a good dog, and I a good mistress, let him
growl. Like enough, hath his reasons.'

'Very well argued. But when, being bid stop growling, yet he
growleth, that is not so good.'

'O,' said she, with a little scornful backward movement of her
head, 'I follow not these subtleties. Why be so unlike your most
deep discerning self, brother? When have you known the King miss
in aught he set out to perform? Am I to tell you he hath power to
crush him we speak on, soon as crush an importunate flea, were he
so minded?'

'I dearly wish he would do it,' said the Chancellor.

'Go then, tell him to. I think you shall have the flea in your ear
for your pains. As good crush me!'

As they rode up, they beheld now before them Duke Barganax,
upon a marble bench without the gate under an arbour of climbing
roses. The involutions of their petals held every indeterminate fair
colour that lies between primrose and incarnadine: the scent of
them, the mere perfume of love. He sat there like a man altogether
given over to the influences of the time and the place, fondling the
lynx beneath the chin and sipping hippocras from a goblet of silver.
There was a merry glow in his eyes as he stood up, unbonneting, to
bid her good-morrow. Helping her down from the saddle he seized
occasion to salute her with a kiss, which she, as in a studied provoke-
ment and naughtiness, took upon a cold cheek and, when at second
attempt he would have had her lips, dexterously withheld them.

The Chancellor, dismounting, noted this by-play with ironic
unconcern. 'Fortunately met, my lord Duke,' he said, as the grooms
led away their horses. 'I was to speak with your grace, by his serene
highness's command, that you sup with him tonight in Sestola: a
farewell banquet ere they begin their progress north again to Rialmar. You are for the council, doubtless, this afternoon?'

'I fear not, my lord.'

'I'm sorry. We need our ablest wits upon't, if aught's to come of
this business.'

'I have opened all my mind to the King, and have his leave to
sit out. Truth is, there's matters on hand must detain me
otherwheres today. But as for supper, pray you say, with my duty, I
kiss his highness's hands and joyfully obey his summons.'

'I shall.'

'Strange,' said Fiorinda, 'I am bidden too.' She sat down, shedding, as some exquisite lily sheds waft by waft its luxury abroad, a
fresh master-work of seducing and sense-ensearching elegancy from
every lazy feline grace of her settling herself upon the bench: eye-
wages for the Duke.

'Is that so strange?' said he, his eyes upon her. 'I took't for granted.'

'What brings your grace hither in this hour of the morning?'

'Idleness,' answered he with a shrug of the shoulder. 'Want of a more reasonable employment. O, and now I remember me, I had these letters for your ladyship, to wish you well of your twentieth birthday.' With that, turning to the table before the bench where he had sat, he took a parchment: gave it into her hand.

She unrolled it. While she scanned it curiously, a delicate warmth of colour slowly imbued the proud pallor of her cheek. 'A dear bounty of your grace,' she said. 'I am deeply beholden. But indeed I cannot accept of it.'

'You will not be so uncivil as hand me back my gift.'

'Nay, indeed and indeed, I'll not have it. Mind you not the poet?—

> 'Nor he that still his Mistress payes,
> For she is thrall'd therefore.'

Beroald continued—

> 'Nor he that payes not, for he sayes
> Within, shee's worth no more.'

Barganax reddened to the ears. 'To the devil with your firked-up rhymes,' he said. 'Come, I give it to you freely, out of pure love and friendship. You must take it so.'

She put it into her brother's hand, who read the docket: ' "Deede of feoffment to behoof of the Ladie Fiorinda by liverie of seisin to holde in fee simple the castell of Velvraz Sebarrm and the maines therof scituate in the Roiall Appannage and Dukedome of Zayana." Why, this is princely bounty indeed.'

'Well,' said the lady, drawing down a blossom of the rose to smell to, and watching the Duke from under the drooped coal-black curtain of her eyelashes. 'Not to displeasure your grace, I'll take it. Give it me, brother: so. And now' (to the Duke) 'hereby I give it you back, i' the like truth and kindness, and for token of my devotion to your grace's person.'

'No, you anger me,' he said, snatching the parchment and flinging it, violently crumpled, on the ground. ''Tis an unheard-of thing if I may not bestow a present upon a noble lady but 'tis spat back in my face as so much muck or dirt.'

'Dear my lord, you strain too far: I intended it far otherwise. Be not angry with me, not today of all days. And before breakfast, seems in especially unkind.'

He loured upon her for a moment; then suddenly fell a-laughing.

'Nor I'll not be laughed at, neither. Come,' she said, rising and, in a divine largesse which at once sought pardon and as sweetly dispensed it, putting her arm in his, 'let's walk apart awhile while the board's a-setting.'

When they were private, 'I think,' she began to say, looking down to the jewelled fingers of her hand where it rested, a drowsed white lily for its beauty, a sleeping danger for its capacities, upon his sleeve; as hands will oftest betray in their outward some habit or essence of the soul that informs them from within: 'I think I have a kind of mistrustful jealousy against great and out-sparkling gifts. Not little gifts, of a jewel, a horse, a gown, a book: that's but innocent gew-gaws, adornments of love. But, as for greater things—'

'O madonna mia,' said Barganax, 'you have the pride of archangel ruined. What care I? For I think if God should offer you fief seignoral of Heaven itself, you'd not stoop to pick it up.'

'But surely, you and I,' she said, and the accents of her voice, summer-laden, lazy, languorous, trod measure now with his footfall and with hers as they paced in a cool of pomegranate-trees, 'we surely gave all? Body and inward sprite, yours to me, mine to you, almost a full year ago?'

'With all my heart (though I doubt 'tis not wholesome meat for you to be told so), I say ay to that.'

'To speak naked as my nail (and 'tis time, may be, to do it), I dwell in this house, have use of these lands and pleasaunces, joyfully and with a quiet mind; and why, my friend? Because they are yours, and, being yours, mine so far as need. For is not this wide world, and Heaven's mansions besides (if there be), not yours indeed, nor yet mine, but ours? Is it not graved in this ring you gave me— HIMETEPA—Ours? Feminine singular, I that am ours: neuter plural, all else whatsoever, ours. And Velvraz Sebarm, being yours, is therefore the dearer to me, who am yet more entirely yours than it. Am not I yours by blood and breathing, glued infinitely closer than had we two one body, one spirit, to make us undistinctly one? Surely a cribbed lone self-being self were no possession, no wealth, no curious mutual engine of pleasure and of love. 'Twere prison sooner.'

The Duke spoke no word: a silence that seemed to enjoin silence to itself, lest a spell break.

'But what was given already,' she said, 'and given (as it ought to be) with that reckless, unthought, uncalculated freedom as a kiss should be given—to wish now to give that again by bond and sealed instrument, 'tis unbelievable between you and me. As though you should a bethought you: 'Someday, by hap she shall be another's. Or by hap I may find (being myself too in the hot hey-day of my youth, and long wedded to variety) another mistress. And—' "

'No more of these blasphemies,' said the Duke, his voice ruled, yet as holding down some wolf within him: 'lest you be blasted.'

'Nay, you shall hear it out: "And 'cause I yet love her past remedy," you might say, "I'll give her this rich demesne: and more if need be: make my munificencies play the pander, to drug her for me, and so bind her to my bed." Heaven spare us, will you think to ensure us together by investment?'

'No more,' he said, 'for God's sake. 'Tis a filthy imagination, a horrible lie; and in your secret veins you know it. Why will you torture me?' But, even in the setting of his teeth, he clapped down his right hand upon hers where it lay, the pledge of her all-pervading presence quivering within it, along his sleeve: as not to let it go.

They walked slowly on for a while, without word spoken, unless in the unsounded commerce of minds, that can work through touch of hand on hand. Then Fiorinda said, 'We must turn back. My respected brother will think strange we should leave him so long with none but the waiting breakfast-covers for company.'

As they turned, their eyes met as in some mutual half-embraced, half-repudiate, pact of restored agreement: as if the minds behind their eyes were ware each of other's watchfulness and found there matter for hidden laughter. The Duke said, 'You spoke a while since of a token of your regard for me. I know a readier token, if your ladyship had honestly a mind to prove that.'

'O, let's not be chafferers of proofs.'

'It comes o'er my memory, my coming hither was to ask the honour of your company at supper.'

'Tonight?'

'Tonight, madam, I had dearly wished.'

'See then, how fortune makes good your wish before the asking. We sup together in Sestola.'

'Not entirely as I would, though.'

'Your grace is hard to please.'

'Is there aught new in that? 'Tis another likeness between us.'

The lady's head bent now in lazy contemplation of her own lilied hand, where it yet lay out, sunning like an adder in warm beams, along his fore-arm. Her eyes veiled themselves. Her lips, seeming to brood upon some unavowed, perhaps unconfirmed, assent, were honeyed gall. Under the coat-hardy, which from hip to throat fitted as glove fits hand, the Grecian splendours of her breasts rose and fell: restful unrestfulness of summer sea, or of two pigeons closed together on a roof. The Duke said: 'Is it permitted to ask where your ladyship means to lie tonight?'

'Truly I hope, abed. And your grace, where?'

'In heaven, I had a longing hope. It rests not with me to decide.'

The fingers of the hand on his arm began to stir: a sylph-like immateriality of touch: almost imperceptible.

'Well?' he said.

'You must not tease me. I am not in the mood to decide.'

He said, softly in her ear, 'All's hell that is not heaven, tonight. Would you have me lie in hell?'

Some seducing and mocking spirit sat up and looked at him from the corners of her mouth. 'A most furious and unreasonable observation. Nay, I am not in a mood for ayes and noes. I do entreat your favour, ask me no more.'

He stopped, and stood facing her. 'I think your ladyship is own daughter to the Devil in hell. No help for it, then: I take my leave.'

'Not in anger, I hope?' she held out her hand.

'Anger? Your body and beauty have for so long bewitched me, I am no longer capable even of the satisfaction of being angry with you.'

'Well, let's bear out a sober face 'fore the world: before my brother there. Some show of kindness. Pray your grace, kiss my hand, or he'll wonder at it.'

'You are unsupportable,' he said. He raised her hand, hot in his, to his lips: it drew a finger against his palm: then lay still. From her mouth's corner that thing eyed him, a limb-loosening equivocation of mockery, intoxicating all senses to swimmings of the brain. He kissed the hand again. 'Unsupportable,' he said: looked in her eyes, wide open suddenly now, strained to his in an unsmiling stilled intention, eyelids of the morning: beheld, in unceasing birth and rebirth through interkindling and gendering of contrarious perfects, the sea-strange unseizable beauty of her face: the power enchantment and dark extremity of her allurement now plainly spread in the brightness of the sun. He said: 'O abominable and fatal woman, why must I love you?'

'Is it, perhaps,' she replied, and the indolent muted music of her voice, distilling with the sweets of her breath on the air about him, wrought on the raging sense to upsurgings of subterranean fire: 'Is it, perhaps, because to your grace, unto whom all others your best desires, spaniel-like, do come to heel, this loving of me is the one only thing you are not able to command?'

XXXVII

TESTAMENT OF ENERGEIA

I N SESTOLA that same day toward evening, the Chancellor and Earl Roder, being come to council a little before the due time, were waiting the King's pleasure in the great stone gallery that served there as antechamber.

'Mean you by that, she has been forbid the council?' said the Earl.

'That's too rough a word.'

'Pray you amend it.'

'A bird peeped in mine ear that his serene highness graciously excuseth her from attendance today, and at her own asking.'

'Is that help to us or hindrance?'

The Lord Beroald shrugged his shoulders.

'You think unlucky?' said Roder.

'I think it of small consequence whether her highness be there or no. Yet I would she'd stayed in the north. We'd then a been spending our time in Zayana 'stead of this stony den of Sestola: fitter for a grave than for living men to dwell in.' He cast a distasteful look up at the high lancet-shaped windows whose embrasures, spacious and wide enough here withinward, narrowed to slits in the outer face of the huge main wall: slits to shoot through at assaulters from without, rather than windows to light the gallery.

'We grow customed to strange choices this twelve-month past,' Roder said.

Beroald's nostrils tightened, with a thinning of lips below close-clipped mustachios.

Roder said, 'Know you for certain what way she inclineth now, i' this thing we have in hand?'

'No. Nor much care. Strange your lordship should ask me this, who are far more in her counsels than ever I have been.'

'She is too unnatural with me of late,' said the Earl: 'too kind. Smiles at me: gives me honeyed words. Makes me afeared may be his serene highness listeneth to her more readily than he will listen to us.'

'No need to fear that.'

'No? Well, be that as may, I'm glad she cometh not to this meeting. God shield us from women on our councils of war. I never could argue with a woman. Besides, I mistrust Parry wolvishness. And bitch-wolf was ever more fell than dog-wolf, as the more uncorrigible and unforeseeable in action. Your lordship frowns? Said I not well, then?'

'Too loud. Walls have ears.'

'True. But it's commonly thought those ears are yours, my lord Chancellor.' The Earl stretched his arms with clenched fists above his head, strained wide the fingers and yawned. 'My sword is rusting in its scabbard. I hate that. What latest smelling by your blood-hounds?'

Beroald patted a bundle of dispatches under his arm. 'You shall hear all in good time, my lord.'

'Nay, I seek no favours. So it be there, well. Let it wait due audit.' He stole a look at the Chancellor's face. 'You and I are still agreed? O' the main point, I mean?'

'Surely.'

'The Admiral is with us, think you?'

'We have but the one aim,' answered Beroald: 'all three of us.'

'Ay, but 'tis readiness counts. What's aim, if blow hang i' the air?' Then, after a pause: 'I dearly wish the Duke were expected now.'

Beroald curled his lip. 'Which Duke?'

'Not Zayana.'

'I thought not,' he said dryly.

'Well, I have told your lordship at large of my talkings with Duke Styllis in April in Rialmar. It somewhat did stomach the boy to be left behind there, and this cauldron a-bubbling in the south.'

'It hath long been apparent,' said the Chancellor, 'those two agree best when farthest apart. Howsoever, no Dukes today. Lord Barganax hath leave of absence from the King.'

'I'm glad to hear it.'

'My lady Duchess,' said Beroald lightly, 'arrived today, in Zayana.'

'So. Then the King lies there tonight?'

'Like enough.'

'And cut short so our potting after supper, ha?' said the Earl, and ground his teeth. 'Women. And what comes of women. Were 't not for that, our cares were the lighter.'

'*Mala necessaria.*'

'O, if you speak law-terms, I'm a stone.'

'I but meant, my lord, where were you and I without women had bred us?'

Upon noise of a footstep, Roder looked behind him 'Here's the great lord Admiral.'

They turned to greet him, walking towards them the length of the gallery with head bent as deep in thought. 'God give you good den,' he said as they met, his eyes, candid as the day's, searching first the Chancellor's then the Earl's. 'We are to reach tonight at last, it is to be hoped, the solutions of a ticklish and tangled business. Have your lordships thought of any new mean to the unravelling of it?'

'So we be at one as for the end,' replied Beroald, 'it should be no unexampled difficulty to find out the means. Has your lordship held more talk with the King's highness in these matters?'

'None since I saw you both last night. I have been afloat all day 'pon business of the fleet. All's ship-shapen now, what-e'er be required of us in that regard. And you, Earl?'

'My folk are so well readied,' answered he, 'we are like to fall apart in rottenness, like over-ripe cheese, if we be not swiftly given the occasion to prove our worth upon't.'

'You will open the matter before the King, I take it, my lord Admiral,' said the Chancellor, 'on our behalf? His serene highness will take it kindliest from your mouth. Besides, among us three, you are *primus inter pares*.[1] And I hope you will stand resolute for action. 'Tis most needful this nettle be rooted up or it prove too late.'

'Yes, yes,' said Jeronimy, fingering his beard. ''Tis a business worth all our wits. We must not be fools, neither, to forget it toucheth the King's set policy of a lifetime's standing. Peradventure, as for this one time, he is wrong: if so be, then is it our mere duty to say so to his face. But before now, and in as weighty matters, when wise men deemed him mistook he hath turned the cat in the pan and, by the event, showed 'em fools for their pains. Well, we must ferret out the true way. And by King in council is the good stablished method so to do.'

The Earl's neck, as he listened, was swelled up red as a turkey cock's and his face, where frizz of black beard and hair disguised it not, of the like rebellious hue. The proud weather-bitten lineaments of the Lord Beroald's face wore a yet colder unpenetrable calm than before. Their eyes met. In that instant, as the Admiral ceased speaking, the door was thrown open upon his right, and the Queen, all but as red as Roder but with countenance uncipherable as the Chancellor's, came forth from the council-chamber.

Even now, when for her the winds of old age had set in, with no deadly force as yet, but enough to make her take in sail and tack against wind and tide, which with slow gathering of power drive back tall ship and feeble coracle without distinction to that hateful and treeless shore whence, against that tide and that wind, none did ever again put back to sea: even in that Novemberish raw weather of her years, some strength of lost youth, some glory, unlosable, uncrushable, indestructible, lived on. Almost might a man have believed, beholding her stand thus in the dazzle, from the open doorway behind her, of warm afternoon sun, that in these few weeks, after twenty-five years of exile, she had renewed her very body with great draughts of the fecund and lovely magic of the Meszrian highlands, over which she had so long ago, by exercise and right of her own most masculine will, made herself Queen. Here she stood: the argument of her father's dreams and policies made flesh in the daughter of his desires; and the same badge of cold ungainsayable relentlessness, more unadulterate and more openly self-proclaimed than on Emmius Parry's underlip, sat at this moment upon hers.

She looked upon the Earl's face, whose smoulder of thwarted anger mirrored, weakly may be, some locked-up passion within herself: upon the Chancellor's, that carried in its stoniness at this moment deep-seated likenesses to her own: last, upon the high Admiral's, which gave back (of any quality of hers) no reflection at all. They did obeisance to her; Roder, with a low leg, kissing her hand. 'The King is ready,' she said to them, as if speaking not to lords but to cur-dogs. 'You may go in.'

King Mezentius sat to receive them in a large chamber fairly hung with arras, the light streaming in through open western windows behind him. At this other side of the table the lords commissioners, at a sign from his hand, took their seats facing him: Jeronimy in the midst, Beroald on his right, Roder on his left. They laid out their papers. No person else was present. The table was empty before the King, neither pen, ink nor paper. 'I have commanded this council at your request,' he said. 'Speak without fear, all your mind. Gloze nothing: hold nothing back. The business, I understand, is of Rerek.'

The Admiral cleared his throat. 'My Lord the King, it needs not to say that there worketh in us but one thought and purpose, and that is to behave ourselves, waking and sleeping, as constant loyal faithful servants unto your serenity's person and, under your ordination and pleasure expressed and laid upon us, to perform (within the measure of our capacities) all that should enure to the safety of this Triple Kingdom and of the common weal thereof.'

'True, it needs not to say,' said the King. 'I know it. Proceed you therefore, my good lord Admiral, to the matter. What of Rerek?'

The Admiral paused, as a swimmer might pause upon a high bank before the plunge. His fingers toyed with the jewel of the kingly order of the hippogriff that hung by a crimson ribbon about his neck. 'For me, Lord,' he said at last, 'it is by so much the harder to urge, in a manner, this matter upon your serene highness's gracious attention (even although I hold it most crying needful), by how much it hath been my happiness to have served you and followed your fortunes since your earliest years: seen your unexampled uprising by wisdom and by might and main to this triple throne you have for yourself erected, as history remembereth not the like, so as it is become a common saying upon men's lips in these latter years, *Pax Mezentiana*. And it hath befallen me, through accident of birth and upbringing, to have longer enjoyed the high honour of your inward counsels than any here, mine equals now extant, albeit they be, I am very certain (save in this prime advantage of intimate acquaintance with your settled policy and the roots thereof) more abler men than I. Therefore I speak with due reservation'— here the Chancellor shifted slightly in his chair, and Roder, as if to shade the glare of the sun, leaned over his papers, his hand across his eyes—'I speak, in a manner, with reservation, and most of all in this business that concerneth—'

The King smiled. 'Come, noble Jeronimy: we are friends. I am not to eat you. You mean the Vicar is my not distant kinsman, and that I have, with eyes open and for reasons not perhaps beyond the guessing of those inmost in my counsels, ridden him on what you begin to think too rashly light a rein. That's common ground. You came not here to tell me (nor to learn of me) that. What of it, then?'

'I thank your highness. Well, to cut short the argument, my lord Chancellor hath here informations and reports, from divers independent intelligencers, throughly tried and not to be doubted, that (despite your plain warning to him to disband his army) he yet draweth strength to it about Laimak. Please your serenity peruse the evidences.' He turned to the Chancellor, who, rising, spread on the table befoe the King a sheaf of writings.

But the King put them aside. 'I know it. If they reported otherwise, it were an untruth. What then? You would put me in mind we may have to enforce our command?'

'By showing the whip: that at least, and at all events.'

The King glanced his eye over the papers, then, pushing them slowly and thoughtfully across the table to Beroald, shook his head. 'He will never attack me. These preparations are not against me.'

'Saving your serenity's presence,' said Roder: 'against whom, then?'

'Against the future. Which, being unknown, he prudently hath fear of. He can look round and conclude he hath many and powerful enemies.'

'Truly, my Lord the King,' said Beroald, 'I would not, for my part, gainsay him as for that. Some would say your serene highness alone standeth 'twixt him and the uniting of 'em to rid the world of him. Indeed there be some malignant grumblers—' He paused. 'Is it your pleasure I speak plain, Lord?'

'More than that: I command you.'

'With deep respect, then. There be some who murmur that your highness do play with fire may blaze out i' the end to burn their houses: think you ought to protect them, 'stead of suffer this man to grow big, run loose, and in his own time devour us all. They forget not the hellish cruelties used by him upon both small and great, and innocent persons amongst 'em ('tis not denied), upon pretext of putting down the rebellion in the Marches five years ago.'

'Was not that well done, then,' said the King, 'to put it down? Was it not his duty? You are not a child, Beroald. You were there. You need not me to tell you this realm stood never in your life-time in so fearful danger as when (I and the Admiral being held, with the main of my strength, in deadly and doubtful conflict with Akkama in the far north) Valero, following the Devil's enticements and his own wicked will and ambitious desires, raised rebellion most formidable to my great empire and obedience. By what strong hand was it if not by the Parry's alone, that the stirrers-up of those unnatural and treasonable commotions were put to the worst? And this to the evil example of all such as would hereafter attempt the like villainy. And victory is not unbloody. Are you so hardy as question my rewarding him therefore?'

'My Lord the King, you do know my whole mind in this matter,' replied the Chancellor, 'and my love and obedience.'

'But you thought I'd ne'er come back from Middlemead, a year ago?'

'I thought neither your highness nor I should ever come back. Yet must I remember you, it was bitterly against my will you enforced me to stay behind while yourself did enter that cockatrice's den[2] single-handed and alone.'

'Yet that worked?'

'It worked. And for this sole reason, because (under favour of heaven) your serene highness was there to handle it. Another than yourself, were he a man of our own day or the greatest you could choose out of times past since history began: it had been the death of him. And that you do know, Lord, in your heart, better than I.'

'To speak soberly, that is simple truth, dear Beroald,' said the

King. 'And thinking upon that, you may wisely trust me in this much lesser danger now.'

There fell a silence. Jeronimy caught the King's eye. 'I would add but this,' he said. 'There is not a man in the Three Kingdoms would trust him an inch were your highness out of the way.'

'However, I am here,' answered the King. 'You may securely leave him to me.'

Again there fell a silence. The Admiral broke it, his eyes in a dog-like fidelity fastening on his great master's and taking assurance, may be, from the half-humorous glints, sun-blink on still water, that came and went across the depths of all-swaying all-tolerant all-sufficient certitude which then looked forth upon him. 'God redeem us from omens: but we were great failers of our love and duty to your highness if we sat speechless, for want of courage to come to the kernel of the thing.'

'Which is?'

'That all men are mortal.'

The King laughed: Olympian laughter, that the whole air in that room was made heady and fresh with it. 'Why, you talk,' he said, 'as if there were no provision made. You three here in the south: Bodenay and a dozen more, seasoned captains and counsellors, to uphold the young King in Rialmar: Ercles and Aramond in north Rerek: Barganax in Zayana. Shall all these appear i' the testing-time bodgers and bunglers, at odds among themselves? Will you tell me the fleet is helpless? Or the army, Roder?'

'A prentice hand upon the tiller,' said the Admiral, 'and a storm toward, 'tis a perilous prospect, like to try all our seamanship.'

'Let me not leave your minds in doubt,' said the King. 'When I farewell, it shall not be to commit the Kingdom to a bunch of ninnies and do-littles, but to men. The Duke of Achery,[3] as legitimate heir, must look to it. He will need all his wits, and yours. I have instructed him fully, in every principle and its particular bearings, this summer, ere I came south now.'

Jeronimy said, 'The Duke of Zayana is also in question.'

'He hath his apanage. He hath no thought of claiming more than his own. You may trust him, as were he mine own younger self, to be loyal and true to's young brother (so the boy have the wisdom and common generousness to play his part), and, were Styllis to die, to be as loyal and as true to's young sister, as Queen. Let me remember you, too: his kingdom is over far other things than lands, rivers, lakes, and the bodies of men. In the camp and the council-chamber I have nurtured him up to be expert in all that a prince should be master of; but, in heart, he is poet and painter. What to Emmius Parry was second subject in the symphony, is to Barganax first subject. He is of Meszria, born and bred. If let live, he will let live. But,' said King Mezentius, his eyes upon them, 'he is my son:

therefore not a man to be mocked or teased. If forced to it, a hath that in him will make him able, and he be once set forth upon that path, to overthrow any person whatsoever who should pretend to usurp upon his right.—Well?' he said, watching them sit as men who in imagination see a load presented for them which they begin to think shall prove heavier than their powers may avail to carry. 'Tell me not you are not the men I have known you.'

The Chancellor broadened his chest and looked with resolute eye from the King to his colleagues, then again to the King. 'With deep humility,' he said, 'and I think I speak for these lords as well as for myself: your highness hath told us no new thing, but all lendeth force to the argument that 'twere prudent something be done to contain the power of the Vicar. If (which God forbid) it should someday fall to us, bereft of your serene highness, to shoulder this sackful of contending interests, that were a heavy task indeed, yet not so heavy as we should shrink from, nor doubt our ability (under heaven) to perform it as your highness would have desired and expected of us. But if the Vicar must sit by in embattled strength straddling over the middle kingdom, aspying when we were deepliest otherwhere embroiled and ready then to take us, then were we as good as—' He broke off, meeting the King's eye, keen, weighing, meditative, upon him: lifted his head like a war-horse, and set his jaw. 'What skills it to reason further?' he said, in his most chilling iron-hard voice. 'I have followed your serene highness into the mouth of destruction too many times to boggle at this.'

The King, listening, tranquil and remote, utterly at ease, made no sign. Only when his speckled grey eyes, as though by chance, came back to Beroald's, their glance was friendly.

'If it be permissible to ask,' said the Admiral; 'hath all this that your highness hath been pleased to express to us as touching his grace of Zayana been made plain to Duke Styllis?'

The King answered, 'Yes. And he is content. Hath moreover sworn oath to me to respect his brother's rights, and my will and policy.'

'Did the Duke of Zayana,' asked Roder, 'swear too?'

'It did not need.'

The commissioners began to gather up their papers. 'And we are to understand it is your highness's considered decision,' said Beroald, 'to move in no way against Rerek?'

'He keeps his vicariate,' replied the King. 'No more. No less. I may need to handle him myself in this manner of his maintaining of an army afoot by secret means. My lords Jeronimy and Roder, prepare me proposals tomorrow (and be ready to put 'em in act 'pon shortest notice) for making some show of power about Kessarey and the Marches.'

With that, he rose, liker to a man in the high summer of his youth than to one in his fifty-fourth year: 'On the far view,' he said, turning to dismiss them, 'I mean, when my day shall be over, I see no deadly danger from him, so but North and South stand firm in support of the succession. If they stand not so, that will not be my affair; but the affair of him that shall be man enough to deal with it. And now, you to your charge, I to mine.'

'What think you of this, my lord Chancellor?' said the Admiral, as they took their way across the great open quadrangel of the fortress.

Lord Beroald answered: 'I think the tide is now at high flood that began to run a year ago. And were it an ordinary man, and not our Lord the King, I should think he was fey.'[4]

'We have entered with him between the clashing rocks ere now,' said the Admiral, 'and at every tack found his dangerous courses safer than our own fears. I see no wisdom but to do so again.'

'There is no choice. And you, my Lord Roder?'

'We have no choice,' answered he in a sullen growl. 'But there's nought but ill to come of it.'

XXXVIII

THE CALL OF THE NIGHT-RAVEN

QUEEN ROSMA, observing from her window the occasion of those lords coming from the council, went to find the King. She found him alone in the empty council-chamber, seated not in his chair of state but sideways on the stone of the window-seat, seemingly wrapped in his thoughts. He showed neither by movement nor by look that he heard the opening or shutting of the door, or was aware of her waiting presence. After a while she came nearer: 'Lord, if it be your will, I would desire to speak with you in privity between us two. If this be not a fit time, I pray you appoint another.'

King Mezentius turned his eyes upon her and regarded her for a minute as a man lost in the profundities of his meditation might regard some object, table or chair or shadow thrown by the sun, which should chance within his vision.

'Let it be for another time,' she said, 'if that be better. I had thought your highness's mind being full with matters of the council, which this concerns, the occasion might be good. The thing can wait. Only I hope it must not wait too long.'

Still gazing upon her, he seemed to come back to earth. His brows cleared. 'Let it be now, madam. I am, to times, as a barber's chair that fits all buttocks. Albeit,' and he gave her a laughing look, yet as out of a louring heart, 'I think I am for the while unfit com-

pany for honest civil ladies.' He stood up and with a scenical, histri-
onical, elegance of courtliness, kissed her hand. 'But not here. I'll
breathe fresh air 'twixt this and supper or burst else. Come, I'll row
you on the firth:[1] seek variety i' the open face of the sea, since
pinched earth affordeth none. Get on your cloak, dear faithful help-
fellow of an out-worn office. When we be launched on the deep, and
but the sea-larks to overhear us, speak your fill: I shall not drown
you. I see you are come prepared. Nay, not for drowning: I mean
for plain speech. You're painted against betrayals.'

'Truly, dear my Lord, I know not what you mean. Betrayals of
what?'

'Of another kind of red very good for the cheeks. Of blushing.'

When they were come down to the water-gate, the firth lay
under the cool of the evening at the slack-water of full sea, smooth
and still as a duck-pool. Eastward and south-eastward the cliffs of
the many isles and skerries, and of the headlands that reach down
into Sestola Firth from the low-ranging jagged hills in the Neck of
Bish, were walls of gold facing the splendour of the declining sun;
and upon every sand-spit of the shore-line of Daish, under an immense peacefulness of unclouded heaven, thousands of gulls and
curlew and sea-larks and sea-pies with scarlet bills awaited the turn
of the tide. The King's boatmen held the boat against the jetty while
the Queen took her place in the stern upon a cushion of cloth of
silver. The King, facing her on the thwart amidships, took the oars,
pushed off, and with a few powerful strokes was clear of the great
shadow of the fortress. Presently, warmed with the exercise, he put
off his doublet, threw it in the bows behind him, tucked up his shirt-
sleeves of white cambric, and, settling to a slow steady stroke, held
southwards down the firth. His eyes were on Rosma, hers on him.

For a long time neither uttered word. Then the Queen broke
silence: 'Why must your highness stare upon me so strangely?'

He pulled his right, so that the sun shone full in her eyes, then,
resting on his oars, leaned forward to watch her, a kind of mockery
on his face. The water talked under the bows: a silvery babble,
voluble at first from the way given by that stroke, then dying down
to silence as the last water-drops fell from his oar-blades. 'I was
wishing,' he said, 'that you were capable to do something of your
own motion, undirected and uncontrolled by me: something I had
not foreseen in you.'

'I think,' she said, 'there is some distemper working in your
highness of late; making you brood vanities: making you, when I
ask you any question, answer without sense or reason.'

'Perhaps I am thought-sick. Who knows? But are you indeed so
ignorant as know not that you are my thing, my poppet, my creature? Whatsoever you do or enterprise, it is because I will it. You act

and think because I cause you so to do: not because you wish to. Tell me,' he said, after a pause, 'do you not find it tedious?'

'Tedious indeed, this manner of speech of your highness's which I suppose proceedeth from melancholy and filthy blood.[2] No answer upon any matter, but only putoffs.'

'Try, dear Rosma, to do something. I care not what, so but it be something that shall surprise me: hurt me or pleasure me, 'tis all a matter: do something of your own. To open my heart to you, as wedded lovers ought to do, I am sick unto weariness of for ever climbing mountains safed with a dozen ropes held by a dozen safe men: sick and weary of the remembrance that, venture how I may, I can never fall.'

He pulled a stroke or two: then let her drift. The sun was now touching the hill-tops in the north-west, a flattened red ball of incandescence. The tide had turned, and from every shore came faintly the noise of birds quarrelling and feeding on the ebb. A cool wind sprang up to blow down the firth. The Queen muffled her cormorant-feather cloak about her. She spoke: 'Was this the language your highness held to the lords in council this afternoon? Must a troubled them as it troubleth me.'

'A foolish question,' he replied, backing water, turning, and beginning to pull slowly home against wind and tide. 'I told you beforehand of my decision. And I told it to them in the like terms.'

'Comfortable words indeed. This blind drifting on the rocks in the matter of Rerek: this devilish folly in the treatment of your son.'

'My son? Which one?'

'Your son, I said. There are other names for bastards.'

'I have always admired the refinedness of your language,' said the King. "'Tis a great charm in you. Pity, though, that you are so prone to repeating of yourself. You never give me the pleasures of disappointment: even as, set a fowl's egg under a goose or a turkey, the same chick hatcheth out. Will you not modulate, merely for change sake? find some new word of opprobriousness for (shall I say?) your stepson?'

'Why would you not suffer Styllis come south with us, 'stead of leave him mewed up in Rialmar? Would a been the fitting, kingly, natural course: most of all in these days when my bloody cousin do threaten, and ('cause of your strange enduring of his packing underboard) scarce troubleth to hide the threat. You forbade me the council: shameful usage of me that am yet, by mine own right, Queen in Meszria. And that was 'cause you were stubborn-set to hold by your pernicious purpose and cram it down their throats who durst not dispute with you to question it; for you knew, had I been there, I'd not a swallowed it thus tamely. Have your heir at your side, one would a thought, ready to take the reins if by evil hap (which kind Heaven pray forfend) aught untoward should befall your highness's person.'

The King, while she so spoke, seemed sunk again into his study, watching while he rowed, as a God might watch from remote heaven, the red glory overspread the spaces of the sky from the going down of the sun. Coming now out of that contemplation, he said in mockery: 'This is your country. If there should need a successor to my throne, why might it not be you? You are hampered by no sexly weakness: as fit as any man living to undertake it. Think you not so? Better than any man, I think: except perhaps—'

As if in that unfinished sentence her mind had supplied a loathed name, the features of Rosma's face, channelled and passion-worn with the years but yet wearing uncorroded their harsh Tarta-rean beauty, took on now, in the red sunset light, a menace and a malevolence as it had been the face of the Queen of hell.

'Styllis,' said King Mezentius, still playing with her, idly, as a man might with some splendid and dangerous beast over whom he delights to feel his mastery: 'Styllis (I will say crudely to you, in case you be a little blinded by your motherly affections towards him) is as yet somewhat raw. It is a great spot to his good estimation (and I think you taught him this trick) to despise and scorn any man other than himself: an unhappy habit of mind in a king. Your Meszrian lords are proud: jealous upholders of privilege. Set him, unfledged and unexperienced, amongst 'em, and—'

Here she broke in upon him, her accents cold and level. 'Well, why delay to cut him off from the succession? One more ill deed would scarcely be noted, I should think.'

'How if I postpone his succession till he be come of years twenty-five? Make you, in that interim, Queen Regent? All's one to me. As for the world, *Post me diluvium.*'[3]

'I know,' said the Queen, 'what underlieth this michery and mummery. You are resolved in very deed, though you dare not do it by open means, to leave all to your bastard. But,' she said, the voice of her speech quivering now as with slow-burning anger, 'beware of me. Twenty-five years you have used me for your tool and chattel. But of all things there cometh an end at last.'

The King laughed in his beard. 'An end? That is vulgar, but questionable, doctrine. Howsoever,' he said, suddenly serious, so that Rosma's baleful eyes lowered their lashes and she turned aside her face, 'I will promise you this. When I die, the best man shall have the Kingdom. If that be Styllis, by proof of his abilities, good. But upon no other condition. I made this Triple Kingdom: alone, I made it: and out of worse confusion and unhandsomeness than of civil wars. It is mine to order and to dispose of how I will. And I will dispose of it into the hand of no man save into his only who shall be able to take it, and wield it, and govern it.'

'I marvel what madness or devil hath so distract your mind,' she said, slowly, looking him in the face again. 'You are likely to do a thing the whole world must weep for.'

'Care not you for that, madam. It sits awkwardly on you (I could a said unbecomingly) to pretend tenderness for the misfortunes of others. You have acted too many murders in your day, for that to ring true. And devised as many more that I have prevented your performing. Better than you, I know what I am about.'

'And I know what your bastard is about: the sole occupation he is fit for. Wallowing in his strumpet's bed in Velvraz Sebarm.'

'His private concerns are his own. Not yours. Not mine, even,' replied the King, narrowing his eyes upon her. 'But if it shall comfort you to know, I heartily commend all that he is doing. In truth, as a good Father ought, I prepared the opportunity for him myself.' He added, after a pause: 'Tonight he and my Lady Fiorinda are to sup with us in Sestola.'

Rosma drew back her head with the indignation of an adder about to strike. 'Then I keep my chamber. I have an objection to sitting at table with a whore.'

He rowed on in silence. On his left, and behind him over Sestola, night was rising fast. To larboard the sun had set in an up-piled magnificence of blood-red and iron clouds. Astern, above the Queen's head as she sat facing the rise of night, her face no longer to be discerned in this growing dusk, Antares began to open a red eye flashing with green sparkles in a rift of clear sky in the south. The wind was fallen again. The King, with eyes on that star of bale, rested on his oars: seemed to listen to the stillness.

Queen Rosma began to speak again: soberly, reining up her displeasure. 'You are wrong in many matters besides this. For example (to go back to that immediate matter which, from what you have said to me, you so lightly and so headily disposed of at the council this evening), you are deadly wrong about Rerek.'

She paused, waiting. The King made no reply, sitting motionless watching the raging lights of the Scorpion's heart.

'But sure, all's effectless when I speak to you of this,' she said. 'You never heed me.'

He began to row: meditatively, a stroke or two, to keep a little way on her against the strengthening ebbtide: then rest on the oars again: then another few strokes, and so on. They were by this time but a mile short of Sestola. 'But I am all ears,' he said, again in his baiting, scorning, humour. 'This is a business you have at least some knowledge of. He is your cousin german, and you have, in the days before I took you in hand, shown a pretty thoroughness in dealing with your kinsfolk: Lebedes: Beltran. 'Tis confessed, they were but nephews by affinity, and he of your own blood, a Parry: not a mere instrument of yours, a lover, as they were. Come, speak freely: you would have me murder him? Or, better, commission you for the kindly office? But I am not minded to let him go the way of your lesser ruffians. Me he will never bite at again. And I enjoy him. Much as, dear Rosma, I enjoy you. Or have enjoyed,' he added, with a strange unaccustomed note of sadness or longing in his voice.

'But you are mortal,' said Rosma. 'And when you shall be dead, he will bite at Styllis.'

'We are all mortal. A most profound and novel maxim.'

'I think,' she replied quietly, 'your highness is perhaps an exception. Were you of right flesh and blood, you would take some respect to the welfare or illfare of your son.'

'Do not trouble your head with the business. All is provided.'

'You are unsupportable,' she said, her anger again bursting its bonds. 'You are took with my father's disease: Meszria.'

'Well? And was it not you, madam, brought me that rich dowry?'

'Yes. But hardly foreseeing you would bestow it, and all besides, upon your bastard.'

'It was got by you with blood and horror,' said the King. 'Be reasonable. I have kept my bargain with you. I have set you in a state and in a majesty you had not before dreamed of, upon the throne of the Three Kingdoms in Rialmar. Do not fall into ingratitude.'

'O monstrous perversion. You have made me your instrument, your commodity, your beast. What profit to me though my chains be of gold, when I am kept kennelled and tied like a ban-dog?'

'You forget the benefits I have done you. I have kept your hands, these twenty-one years now, clean of blood: ever since your slaying of your lover Beltran, who begat two children upon you. This also you shall know: that them, too, I saved alive, when, being an unmerciless dam, you would a devoured them at birth.'

This he said resting on his oars. In the hush, Rosma caught her breath: then, in a shaken voice, 'You never told me this. It is a lie. They are dead.'

'They are alive, my Queen. And famous. You have spoke with them. But, like the unnatural mother you are, you know not your own whelps.'

'It is a lie.'

'When did I ever lie to you?' said the King. 'And, my dearly loved she-wolf, you have (to do you plain justice) never in all your life lied to me.'

As by tacit consent, no further word went betwixt them till they were come to land. It was almost night now. A row of cressets burning on the edge of the jetty threw a smoky glare over the welter of restless waters and up the dark face of the sea-wall of Sestola, against whose cyclopean foundations those waters, piling up with the downcome of the tide, swarmed and gurgled, surged and fell, without violence on this calm summer night, but as if in tranquil rumination of what, and they please, seas can do and wall and rock stand against. The King leapt ashore: his men steadied the boat while he reached hand to the Queen. The uncertain and palpitating glare, save where its constant shooting forth and retracting again of tongues of light touched face or form or stone or black gleaming water, made trebly dark the darkness. She stepped lightly and easily up, and stood for a minute statue-like and remote, gazing seaward, not at her Lord. Whether for the altering light, or for some cause within herself, she seemed strangely moved, for all she stood so calm and majestical: seemed, almost, a little softened of mood: as it were Persephone in dark contemplation, without regrets or hopes, overlooking her sad domain and that bitter tree of hell.[4] The King might see, in her eye, as he came closer and stood unnoted at her side, something very like the leavings of tears. 'The setting is a good foil for the jewel,' he said in her ear. 'Is this the hithermore bank of Styx? Or stand we already o' the farther side?'

Rosma silently put her arm in his and, with a dozen torches, behind and before, to light their footsteps, they took their way up the rock-hewn stairs: so to the keep and the King's privy lodging. 'I am coming in,' she said, as he paused in the entrance. The King shot a glance at her, then stepped back to let her pass. Without sound on the rich woven carpet she crossed the room and stopped, her back to him, surveying herself in the mirror by the light of two branched candlesticks that stood on the table at her either hand. 'It is near suppertime,' she said. 'We must change our clothes'; and still abode there without moving.

The King said, 'We have understood each other. Twenty-five years. A demi-jubilee. Few wedded lovers can say that, as we can. Was it because we have wisely and frugally held to our alliance as princes, and not been lovers?'

Rosma, very still and proud in her posture before the looking-glass, answered in tones startlingly gentle: almost tender: 'I do not think so.'

'No?' He was seated in a chair now, behind her, taking off his boots.

'I,' said she, 'have been a lover.'

'Well, Beltran you loved, I readily believe. None other, I think.'

' "None other" is not true.'

'Your first child by him,' said the King, 'was (to speak home) the child of your lust. The second, sixteen years later, child again of your lust, but also of your love. And, as that, the unsightable wonder of the world: of more worlds than this, could your wolf-eyes avail to look upon such glories.'

The Queen bit her lip till it slowly began to bleed.

'And there was like a diversity of conception,' he said, 'between these two children of you and me.'

With that, a great catch of her breath: then silence. The King looked up. But her back was towards him and, from where he sat, he could not see her face in the mirror. She said, in a choking voice, 'Beltran loved me. That second time, I knew it. He loved me.'

'Yes. Unluckily for him. For you devoured him. I am not for your devouring.'

The Queen, turning without a word, was on that sudden on her knees at his feet, her face hidden in his lap. 'I have loved you,' she said, 'unmovable and unreachable, since that first hour of our meeting in Zayana: a more wasteful, more unfortunate, love than ever I had for Beltran. Why could you not have let me be? You ravished me of all: kingdom, freedom, Amalie, the one living being in all the world I tendered above myself. And this I have known: that Styllis was child of your policy, or call it your more hated pity: Antiope the child of your transitory, unaccountable, late-born, soon ended, love.' She burst forth into a horrible tempestuous rage of weeping: terrible cries like a beast's, trapped and in mortal pain. The King sat like a stone, looking down upon her, there, under his hand; her bowed neck, still fair, still untouched with contagion of the hungry years: her hair still black above it as the night-raven, and throwing back gleaming lights from its heavy braided and deep-wound coils: the unwithered lovely strength of back and shoulders, strained now and shaken amid gusts of sobbing and crying. When he lifted his gaze to the spaces of the rooftimbers beyond reach of the candle-light, all the shadowy room seemed as filled with the flowering of her mind into thoughts not yet come to birth: thoughts shawled as yet, may be, from her own inmost knowledge by the unshaping shawl of doubt and terror.

She stood up: dried her eyes: with a touch or two before the mirror brought her hair to rights, then faced him. He was risen too, at his full stature (so tall she was) barely looking down into her eyes. 'You have lied to me at last,' he said. 'How dare you speak so to me of love, who do discern your secret mind, know you far better than you do know yourself, and know that you are innocent of the great name of love as is an unweaned child of wine? Nay, Rosma, I do love and delight in you for what you abidingly are: not for farding of your face with confections of love: which, in you, is a thing that is not.'

She replied upon him in a whisper scarce to be heard, as he, in their old way as between friends and allies, took her by the hand: 'I did not lie.' Then, as if the quality of that touch thrilled some poison quite to her heart, she snatched away her hand and said violently: 'And I will tell you, which you well know, that this bastard of yours is the only child of your lasting love. And for that, spite of my love and

longing, which like some stinking weed spreads the ranker underground for all my digging of it up—for that, I hate and abominate
you; and Amalie, your whore; and Barganax, that filthy spawn
whom (to your shame and mine and hers) you regard far more than
your own life and honour. My curse upon you for this. And upon
her. And upon him.'

XXXIX

OMEGA AND ALPHA IN SESTOLA

IGHT was up now over Sestola: midsummer night, but estranged with a sensible power ominously surpassing that July night's of last year, when the Duchess had entertained with a fish dinner in Memison guests select and few. The stars, by two hours further advanced than then, shone with a wind-troubled radiance dimmed by the spreading upwards of veiling obscurities between it and middle earth.[1] The moon, riding at her full in the eastern sky, gave forth spent, doubtful, and waterish rays. On the lower air hung a gathering of laid-up thunder.

Queen Rosma, being come to her own chamber, made her women bestir them to such purpose that she was dressed and waiting some while before the due time appointed for supper. Her lodgings opened upon the westernmost end of the portico which ranges, a hundred and fifty paces and more in length, above the sheer face of the fortress on its southern, oceanward, side. She dismissed her girls and the Countess Heterasmene (now lady of the bedchamber), and, hankering perhaps for fresh air after the closeness of her room and of the King's, went forth to take a turn or two on the paven way under the portico. Square pillars bear up the roof of it on either hand, both against the inner wall and upon the seaward side: at every third pace a pillar. This western half was lit only by the lamps

which, hanging betwixt each pair of outer pillars, gave barely sufficient light for a man to pick his steps by. But midway along, from
the open doors of the banqueting-chamber, there spread outwards
like a fan a brilliant patch of light, and beyond it the uncurtained
windows of the hall shed on the pavement bands of brightness,
evenly spaced with darkness. With moody, deliberate tread the
Queen came towards the light, sometimes halting, then moving onwards again. She was come within a few paces of the doors when, at
sound of footsteps approaching from the farther end, she withdrew
herself under thick shadow between wall and pillar and there
waited. The Duke of Zayana and his lady, new landed and in a
readiness for supper together in Sestola, were walking from the
east, now in full illumination, now lost again in shadow between
windows.

My Lady Fiorinda wore, over all, a hooded mantle of smoke-
black silk which, billowing as she walked, took to itself at each step
new folds, new mysteries, fire-winged with beauties and graces that
were themselves unseen. The Duke, as with every faculty strained
up to this fugato,[2] came a pace or so behind her. In the full pool of
light before the doorway she stopped, not ten feet from where
Rosma stood hid. 'Well?' she said, and her lily-honeyed voice, potent as some unvouched caress, roused whirlpools in the blood-
warm lampless sources of sense and being. 'Are you content, now
that you have driven me like a tame beast as far as this empty banquet-hall and empty deserted gallery? We're too early. What means
your grace to do now?'

'Look upon you,' said Barganax laughing. 'Talk to you. 'Tis the
only place I shall get the chance in private.'

'Well, here I am. And here are my ears to talk to.' So saying, she
threw back her hood, giving him, by turns of her head, the side-
view, either way the same. Her hair was put up in like fashion as
eleven months ago it had been, at Reisma: strained evenly back
from the parting and from those border-line fledgings, finer than
unspun silk, at the temples and at the smooth of her neck behind
her ears. And at the back of her head the great tresses were gathered and bound down, doubled and folded in themselves like
snakes lying together: a feeable stypticness of night: thunder un-
shapen to silence and, as by miracle, turned visible. These bewitchments, sitting close and exquisite in the nape of her white neck, she
thus manifested: then gave him her eyes.

Surely, thus to mingle eyes with that lady was to be drowned
under by a cataclysm that hurled out of their place the sea-gates
which divide heaven from earth, flesh from spirit, and to be swept
up so into Her oneness: into the storm and night of Her peace, who
is mistress, deviser, giver of all. Who, all being given, gives yet the
unfillable desire for more, and gives, too, eternally, that overplus to

fill it: gives in that divine giving, infinite in contradiction and variety, Her many-coloured divine self, proud with his pride which, ever as brought down by Hers, is as everlastingly, through that unsatisfiable satiety of giving, reestated. As a God might stand incarnate in fire-hot stone, so, while Barganax stared into those sea-strange intolerable Olympian eyes, the deep-throned majesty of his will rose and, as lode-stone points to lode-star, pointed out her. Like a man who gropes for words in a dream, he said: 'And, under that cloak?'

The falcon-flight of her beauty, stooping earthwards again, answered from her mouth: 'You are very inquisitive upon my affairs. See, then, how obliging I have been.' She let fall her cloak and stood before him in skin-close bodice with skirt flowing wide from the hips down, of red corn-rose sendaline: the dress she had worn for him that first night in Reisma.

'Then I am answered,' he said, surveying her slowly down from throat to emerald-spangled shoe, and thence slowly up by the same road, and so once more to her face.

Fiorinda's eyes, that were a-dance with the scents of earth again, came suddenly to rest, in a wide-open stillness of intention, on his. Her lips, bitter-sweet scarlet ministers of mockery, were grave now: lips of the Knidian Aphrodite. Then, some untameable star rising in her eyes, 'Indeed,' she said, 'it hath a happy commodity, this gown: like as your grace's jests. Remember you not so?'

'As my jests?'

'Come they not off, well and excellent?'

He bent down, one knee on the pavement, to pick up for her the fallen cloak. Being they were alone and unobserved, he locked suddenly his arms about her, his empery, his new-found-land, and for a minute abode so, crushing his shut eyes, that called in aid now a sense both more piercing and more fierier than their own particular of seeing, blindly into the pleats of her skirt. In this she remained motionless: only trembling a little, yielding a little. When the Duke was on his feet again, she had covered her face with her hands, leaving to be seen of her but these hands and arms in their immaculation of whiteness: the jet-black of her hair: this dress, sheathing her like a flame. 'O madonna, why will you look at me through your fingers?' he said, opening his arms.

As a lily leans to its reflection in still water, she came nearer: an opening of the windows of heaven to pour down blessings: nearer, till her breasts touched him about the heart, and her face was hidden on his shoulder. 'Are you still to learn that I never promise? Most of all, never to you. And this, I suppose,' she said between his kisses on her neck and hair, 'for two very ridiculous reasons: ten times more ridiculous and unreasonable when taken together. The first, because I do know you, within and without: And the second,' here, with a sudden intake of her breath, turning her head on his shoulder she gave him her lips, nectar-tongued: not without letting him taste in the end, upon a more melting, then more impetuous, closeness of insinuation of her immortal sweet body to his, a light remembrancer, between play and fierceness, of her teeth: 'And the second, because I am sometimes almost persuaded there may be no help, but you shall begin, someday, in very truth, to make me in love with you.'

Rosma, having employed her advantage to hear and narrowly observe these two lovers, and what way in their loveship they went to work, said in herself: 'So you never promise? But I promise. And most of all, to him.' With slow unsteady gait she returned privately to her chamber.

A hundred feet in length is that banquet-room in Sestola, by forty wide, and the height of it twenty foot good to the cornice and, from thence to the huge ridge-beams of the roof, of oak curiously carved and blackened with age, twenty-five foot more. Upon the walls of old red sandstone, rough-hewn, gritty to the touch, and of the deep cold purple colour of leaf-shadows on brick in hot sunshine, hung all kind of war-gear: spears and swords and daggers and twirl-spears, maces, battleaxes, morning-stars: byrnies of linked mail, helms and shields, corslets and iron gloves: some from the antique time, some new: all of them pieces of proof wrought by noted armourers, and graved or damascened with gold and silver. From the western end, under the music gallery, lofty doors open south upon the portico. These, and the tall windows spaced six foot apart along the south wall, stood wide now to the June night. Under that gallery lesser doors lead to kitchens, buttery, stillroom, larders and sculleries, and the servants' quarters. The dais, at the eastern end, was carpeted with a weave of mixed wool and silk, having a glitter of silver threads in web and woof. From the middle of it two high-seats faced down the hall, having each a table before it for eating and drinking; and outward from these in a half circle, five to the right, five to the left, stood lesser chairs of state with their tables before them. On the rush-strewn pavement of the floor below the dais a dozen long tables were set lengthways in two double rows of three and three, leaving a broad space up the body of the hall between the double rows. At the higher tables (save upon the dais, where the seats yet stood empty) the company were already assembled, lords, ladies, and gentlemen, all in holiday attire: they of most account at the four tables next below the dais and, at the next four, gentry and officers of lower estate. At the lowest tables, nearest the doors, were places set for the remainder: here (the better to assure decorum) the men on the outward, southward, side, and womenkind on the northward.

Great was the sparkle of jewels and great the splendour of rich silks and velvets of many colours under a hundred hanging lamps which, depending in four rows by long chains of bronze from the high timbers of the roof, wove with their beams between the upward gaze and those high dark empty spaces a tented canopy of air, radiant, demi-translucent, beneath which all was light and clarity of vision. These lamps, shining downward, mixed their rays with the nearer, warmer and more tendering glow of hundreds of candles set orderly in branched candlesticks of cut and polished crystal, eight candlesticks on every table.

The musicians tuned their instruments, preluded and, when the murmur of talk was stilled and the guests rising in their places turned all to face westward toward the doors, struck up a cavatina of old Meszria. A lovely, houseless, land-remembering air was this: rising, falling, returning on itself as loth to depart: even just as a linnet's child, perched with its mother on a fence, quivers its wings to be fed, then leaps fluttering over her head to perch at her other side and in quivering eagerness creeps near to her again, and so and again continually. And ever as that air hovered to full close, always it by some exquisite involution refused and rose circling again, as if end were but foil or frame to some never-ending being and unfolding, of which even the beginning was impregnate with a prophetic sadness of farewells, and the expected end held ever, and at every approach and putting-off, the more of earth-deep promise in it of renewal and spring to be. This music, bodied forth on the plangorous caressful singing of the viols, smoothed the sense of Anthea's and Campaspe's nymphish ears, as they stood listening near the head of that high table under the window close below the dais, with echoes and over-tones of a more diviner music: of my Lady Fiorinda's remembered voice, Olympian, all-beguiling, beyond all passion appassionate, yet immaculate, yet fancy-free. And beneath the ever-changing flow and wonder of that melody, plucked notes throbbed, of bass viol and theorbo, in an unchanging rhythm: deep under-march of eternity.

Now, in one tenor with that slow-throbbing plucking of strings, came a clanking of iron-shod boots from without the great doors, and a company of the King's bodyguard marched two by two up the hall. Picked men they were, deep-chested, hard, fierce of aspect, veterans of the wars in Akkama: helmed and byrnied with black iron, and in their plated gorgets and their sword-belts of black bull's-hide were studs and rivets of flashing brass. They halted in two lines, spears at salute, their backs to the tables, leaving wide clear passage-way between the lines, through which ten trumpeters resplendent in cloth of silver, each man of them with his shining trumpet at his hip, passed up now in single file and, mounting the dais, took station, five upon this side, five upon that, against the walls north and south of the great seats. Following the trumpeters came a score of waiting-maids, all in white and garlanded on their unbound hair some with bryony, some with ivyberries, some with flower of honeysuckle. Of these, some strewed roseleaves on the scented rushes of the pavement: the rest, bearing each her little silver basin, dipped their fingers as they walked and, at every step, sprinkled on this side and on that sweet-smelling perfumes. The roseleaf-scatterers when they were come up upon the dais shed petals no more, but disposed themselves orderly along either wall, their faces to the tables, their backs to the trumpeters. The sprinklers of perfume, ere joining their fellows, went twice about the whole floor of the dais, meeting and crossing, back and forth, in a sway and intricacy of movement that took time from the interlacing notes of the viols, until all the woven carpet, and, most of all, that which lay in the half-moon space before the tables, exhaled sweetness, as beds of thyme or camomile, being trod upon, send up wafts of their sharp delicate scent. And now, as the King entered in his majesty, those trumpets of silver, pointing upward to the unseen spaces of the roof, sent flight after flight of silver notes showering like meteors, riding like valkyries of the Father of Ages, through over beneath and amidst of the fine-drawn moon-stilled cloud-processions of the cavatina, which by these fanfares was neither interrupted, outmoded, nor cast in shade but, taking them into itself, was by them hardened, masculated, made to tower in climax.

His doublet was of a rich velvet of a most fine texture, revealing, as it had been his very skin, the ripple and play of the great muscles as he moved: the hue of it, warm brown of peat-water where it runs deepest between moss-hags in full sun: slashed with blue satin (wave-reflections of blue heaven on such waters), and the lips of the slashes close-broidered with wire of silver. The ruff about his neck and the lesser ruffs at his wrists were stiffened with saffron: his shoes of velveted brown leather overwrought with gold and silver thread, and their buckles set with yellow diamonds. The linked collar which he wore between neck and shoulder had every link broad as a man's hand, all in filigree of pure gold and ablaze with precious stones: sapphire and topaz, smaragd and ruby and opal, diamond and orient pearl. The belt about his middle was of black cobra-skin, studded with great diamonds in figure of stars and thunderbolts, and fastened by a clasp of pale gold carved in the image of two hippogriffs, nose to nose, wings erect, cabochon rubies for the eyes of them, and hundreds of tiny stones, topaz and burnt topaz and brown zircon and every kind of tourmaline, tracing the convolutions of their manes. Upon his head shone the crown of old Meszria, wrought with artificial semblances, in gold and jasper and pink quartz and sardonyx and jet, of poppies, flower and seed-cod of dittany, mandrake leaves, strawberry leaves, and the thornapple's prickled fruit.

For all this array, it was the majesty of the King's countenance and of his bearing that went to the marrow of folks' backbones, of those lords and ladies as they beheld him come up the hall: a majesty that seemed, tonight, no longer of this earth: holding its seat and glory chiefliest in his eyes, that showed hollow now like the eyes of lions, and terrible more for the calm that underlay the glare of them than for that all-mastering glare itself: more, even, than for the slow and consuming heat that seared the eyeballs[3] of each person meeting his regard, as though the glance of this King were able to unclothe the soul of man or woman looked upon: have it out, stripped and freezing, for him to examine, before, behind, above, below, between, in the cold betwixt the worlds.

The men of his bodyguard, two by two as he passed them, fell in and followed him with spears at salute. Upon the dais he halted and turned to overlook the hall, while these soldiers, doing obeisance before him two by two upon the steps, divided and went up past him, these to the left, those to the right, to take their stand along the east wall behind the high-seats. Earl Roder, as captain of the guard, armoured to the throat and with the ties of his sword-hilt hanging loose from the scabbard, took his stand behind the King.

Next entered the Queen, crowned and wearing a robe of black figured satin purfled with gold and lined with watermails, the train of it borne by four little blackamoors in green caps and long coats of cloth of silver. The King took her by the hand: set her in the high-seat upon his left; while two by two the guests of honour came up the mid hall, mounted the dais, did their obeisance, and took their seats in order.

The Duke sat at the King's right hand. In him, when he spoke or when he smiled, the conscience-born gaiety of a bridegroom stirred darkly tonight, fire shut in fickleforce; infusing with a kind of morning splendour both his countenance and his lithe body's strength, lovely, whether at rest or in motion, as the Hermes of Praxiteles.[4] Next to him was that old Lord Bekmar, white-haired, twi-bearded, each half of his beard falling in a diminishing spiral of twisted curls: on Bekmar's right, my lord Chancellor Beroald: then Count Medor: then, at the last of the tables on this side, the Lord Perantor. Upon him as often as Rosma's eye fell and met his gaze constant on her as on some anchorage of his prime, she looked hastily away, as from an unseasonable memento of time's iniquity gravid upon her: that this man, grown fat now, and bald, and with dewlaps on the jawy part of his face, should be, by mockery, that self-same smooth courtier and oiled-tongued suing servant whom, in the latter years of her lone queenship, by this twenty-five, thirty, years ago, she had had for lord chamberlain in Zayana.

Anthea and Campaspe, oread arm wreathed in a most unwonted protective assurance about dryad waist, watched the proceedings from their places at the highest table on the Queen's side
below the dais.

'Sister, quiet this leaping thing I find here, under your left
breast. Else I'll be sadly tempted to eat you up.'

'It will not quiet, sister, when changes are toward.'

'Little fool. Great and small can alter and change: come and go.
But we alter not. Neither can any of these shakings, that shake
nations, shake us.'

Campaspe huggled herself closer, her eyes fixed, as by fascination, upon the Queen. 'I do abhor her from my heart,' she said in a
whisper. 'As if my flesh were her meat.'

'It is her day: day of darkness and shrouded dawn. Are you
afeared, little mouse, little sparrow? We have known such days ere
now.'

'Yes. Many time, since the beginning. I fear not, dear sister. 'Tis
but only that I cannot but puff up my weak furs and feathers and
quake with the cold a little, these nights of dread.'

'They are of our Mother's milk, I think,' said that oread lady,
and snarled with her teeth. 'Fix your eye here, where it belongeth:
upon Our Lady. Doth not She fill heaven and earth?' Their pure
eyes (hunting-beast eyes of the oread: eyes of the dryad wide and
soft as a startled hind's) turned from Rosma, as from void darkness,
to that thunder-laced windrush of darkness which is the heat and
unpicturable secret centre of light's and beauty's self, the rending of
heavens, the coming down: where that Dark Lady sat, last but one
on the Queen's side, between Roder and Selmanes of Bish; and in
the trust of Her presence found their unrestful rest.

Upon the Earl's right the Countess Heterasmene had her place:
upon her right, next to the Queen, the lord Admiral Jeronimy.

With the first service brought in, and all kind of wine in great
flagons and gallipots of silver and crystal and gold, merry waxed the
talk both upon the dais and in the body of the hall. Queen Rosma,
strangely affable and amiable, said: 'You have not been to see me of
late, lord Admiral. I miss your company. And now, tomorrow, we
must bid you farewell: progress towards the north.'

'All will lament your highness's departure.'

'Not all. Myself, I shall be glad on't. I envy no man that must
inhabit in Meszria these days: least of all, foreign-born. Too many
hates and cloaked rivalries.'

'Home is good,' he said in his simplicity. 'But duty is best.'

Rosma's regard wandered from his face to rest on that Lady
Fiorinda, so that the Admiral had freedom for a minute to study her
countenance, himself unobserved. Viewing her thus, a man might
have supposed twenty years had been lifted from her natural bur-

den: as though the safe candlelight held an alchemy, transforming as lovers' eyes, to charm away and make effectless that false time which heretofore had carried her past the age of loving and being beloved. 'I laugh sometimes,' she said, an unwonted tender sadness stirring in her voice, 'to think on these turnagains we live in. Born and nursed in Sleaby: Argyanna for my salad-days: then queened here in Zayana, and for so long time wielding powers of life and death here as to mix blood with it. And yet now, no sooner come back hither, but homesick in turn for where's least my home: Rialmar.'

''Tis there your highness's state and stead. Little marvel you should desire it.'

The Queen took a sip from her goblet, set it down and sat silent a minute, gazing into the blood-dark darkness of the wine as though memories floated there; or foreshadowings. Then, turning to him with a smile: 'I think you are homesick too, for the north.'

He made no reply, toying with the dish of prawns before him.

She laid down her fork and looked at him. 'It is not hid from his serene highness nor from me,' she said, leaning sideways over the arm of her great chair, a little nearer him, to speak more privately, 'the weight of the charge we do lay on you three who now have the vogue here. To you yourself, albeit so many years set in government here in Meszria, the land's but a step-dance, and hard it is for you to contend against the jealousies that beset you.'

The Admiral shook his head thoughtfully, then looked in the Queen's face. 'Live and let live. The only way.'

'This late-discovered conspiracy against your own person, for example. We are not ignorant whence such mischiefs draw their sustainment.'

'Nay,' said the Admiral, lowering his eyes under her look, 'if your highness aim at last week's chance, of this rakehelly dissembling scrub who, being brought to my presence, would a sticked me with a dagger, 'twas no conspiracy there. No great hand behind that.'

'Judge you so indeed? I hope you are not miscast in your arithmetic.'

'Only the private discontent of a certain lord who shall be nameless. We shall make friends with him too, ere long. Mean time, the instrument i' the attempt was took and hanged.'

'Well, so far,' said the Queen. 'But you are to remember, my lord High Commissioner, there's hands behind hands in all these things. I that do, from long use, almost to the manner born know the ways of this land, would wish you have an eye to a person I bear ever in mind but will not name. Who (in your ear) may justly think a hath cause (not from you, but from your near friends),' here she

cast a covert look, not unnoted by the Admiral, on Earl Roder, 'to
fear a knife or a Spanish fig from near about you.'

'In humble honesty,' said he slowly, after a pause. 'I am troubled at your highness's gracious words. And the more, in a manner,
that I take not their meaning.'

Without looking at him, but speaking low beside his ear: 'Come
to me ere we depart tomorrow,' she said, 'and I'll speak more
openly than here were convenient. I have observed in you three,
whiles I have sojourned here, a strange carelessness touching ever-
present threats to your proper safety, and these from a high quarter
not ten miles from here I think you do least suspect. The King's
highness would not for all sakes, as I would not, see aught ill befall
you. Enough. Let's be merry. But,' said she, looking past the King
to Duke Barganax and quickly, as from some undecent sight, with-
drawing her gaze to meet the troubled eyes of Jeronimy fixed ques-
tioningly upon her: 'come to me tomorrow.'

Madam Anthea, using that *lingua franca* which half-gods and
nymphs have amongst themselves, but to human kind it is unlearn-
able and unintelligible, like the crackling of ice, or soughing of wind
among leaves, or cat-talk or bird-talk or all voices else of wood and
water and mountain solitudes, spoke saying: 'She is ill at ease, behind all this outward talk, when she looks on my Lady.'

'Will you think,' said Campaspe, in the same safe tongue, 'it
cometh her in mind of the nestling she spurned out of the nest for
dead and you bore it hither to the southlands in your mouth; by her
reckonings, twenty years ago?'

'You can read as well as I.'

'But I cannot endure to look upon her. Or if I look, thought
quite forsakes me. Lynxes' eyes are searchinger too, than water-
rats'.'"

Anthea drew back her lips, in a stealth watching the Queen.
Her left hand, slipping privily down from Campaspe's flower-soft
waist, gave her a nip where least, may be, such liberties were looked
for: made her shut together her knees with a little smothered
scream. 'She knows in her bones,' Anthea said, 'that 'tis here the
very child of her body she looks upon. Which knowledge is wormwood to her, beholding in Her her own lost (nay, never had) youth
as might have been; but she, of her own excess, fooled away the
winning hand fortune and her father dealt her, and, having mis-
played all, is left naked now and penniless, save for her hate against
everyone. Seeth my Lady's beauty: the height, the might, and the
glory of it, fed to its starriest with desire. Tasteth my Lady: almost
even as he tasteth beside whom much better men than yonder o'er-
petted swaggering Styllis of hers should suffer eclipse, meteors
beside the sun. And for that eclipse, and because of his blessed condition, as being love-drunk—from my Lady's nice teasing and

wantoning and prouding of him up this morning—and as having (as I smell this Queen do foggily sense in their eye-casts and in the under-music of their voices tonight) the world, all worlds, all Olympus, in his having of Her: because of these things, she sits crammed with stinking hellebore. Mark you, my flindermouse: we shall see the vomit ere supper well done.'

So sped the time with eating and drinking, gross meats first and finer meats afterward, and with discourse grave and gay. Bekmar, cheered by good wine and by his exalted place at table, which was above both Chancellor and Earl (this as well for respect of his white hairs as out of policy, the Queen being present, to honour especially the ancient houses of Meszria), was full of instances and remembrances of forty or fifty years' standing: better banquets then in Sestola, when Kallias was King: not a woman let come into the hall here then, save the dancing-girls. As though the memory fanned dead embers within him, a kind of corpse-light stirred in his pale eyes. 'Well,' he said, 'other times, other manners: King Haliartes put an end to those spectacles when he took kingdom in Zayana. 'Twas thought,' he said mournfully, 'that was by the Queen's setting on.'

'In that,' coldly said the Chancellor, 'I have ever thought her highness showed herself more Meszrian than our own folk of those times, Meszrians by birth. 'Tis symptom of decay in a great people nursed in civility and high gifts of learning, when they begin to make so much vulgarness of mankind's noblest pleasure as to have their courtesans dance before them stript to the buff, and so glutton on all in public.'

'I am an old man,' Bekmar replied. 'I account old things best.'

'Measure is best, my lord: ruleth all in the end.' The Chancellor, as if his own word spoken had minded him where his disquiet lay, turned his eyes, uneasy behind their mask of steely irony, on the King. In him, as he talked now with his son, burned (yet hotter and gayer than then, a year ago) that same recklessness and superfluity which, when he sent Beroald back and went on, alone with his self-sufficiency, into known instant peril of death at Middlemead, had outcountenanced the great lamp of heaven. The Lord Jeronimy, watching him too, was remembered, like enough, of that all-mastering mood the King had set out in, rashly through mountainous seas in the dead of winter, to put down Akkama. And, soon as put down, had, against all prudence and human reason, set it up again.

As the waiting storm-gatherer should speak to the lightning pent up and struggling for birth, so spoke the King now to Rosma, under his breath: 'Remember you my word. Do something. What, I care not, so it be your own.'

She became ghastly white: then red again: then, slowly turning her eyes to meet his, lowered her gaze: answered slowly in a whisper: 'Is it not a prayer commonly made to God; *Tempt me not who am mortal*?'

'But what God were that,' replied the King deep and low, as it had been the houseless mockery of old Night speaking not in her ear but unescapably in her soul: 'What God were that, that should hearken to any prayer of yours?'

The Queen put her hands under the table, in her lap, out of sight. She said, calm and equable again and with a gentleness in her voice: 'Beseech you, dear Lord, spoil not this last night's pleasure for me in mine own land. Suffer me to have good memories to carry north. Torment me no more with riddles I can neither answer nor see the sense of. Remember, if you can, that I love you.'

King Mezentius looked in her black eyes: almost a lover's look, with shadows of laughter in it but purged of all mockery: almost as a God should look, contented, upon the creature of His mind. With grave eyes she met it: then bent her head. In full view of that great company assembled, he kissed her on the forehead. 'I have told him,' he said to her, pointing, by a backward, sideways motion of his head, to Barganax, 'that I am content with him. Content that he is learning to walk without me behind him to direct his steps. I find in him wisdom.'

'I am glad,' said she, her hands still beneath the table. 'Forget, dear my Lord, what I mis-said, afore supper. I think I was sea-sick. In truth I know not what snappish devil drew out my tongue. There was no truth in it.'

'I will forget it all, my Rosma. Have forgot already. Come, now: to make game: let's read thoughts, you and I. Begin with his,' and he looked round upon Barganax, whose face was at this moment partly turned from them in courteous attention to Bekmar telling his tedious old dotterels' tales. 'Where be his thoughts tonight, think you?'

The Queen looked too, this time schooling herself not to look away: saw the Duke, while he listened, change a merry feasting glance with Fiorinda: answered, with a curl of her lip: 'Upon Monte Nero.'

Fruit was borne in now on golden dishes: peaches, dates, raisins of the sun, pomegranates, orange-apples of Zayana, and, in great bowls of gold, little wood-strawberries mixed with cream-cheeses and smothered in cream. The King spoke: 'What sweet voice have we to sing to us, for crowning of the feast? Mistress Campaspe, will you do us that delight, if madam give you leave?'

My Lady Fiorinda, the imperial lazy echoes in whose voice trained on the air perfume-laden leavings of a breeze strayed from Paphos, answered and said: 'Your serene highness's will, in little things as in great, is ours. And indeed I take a delicate pleasure to hear my gentlewoman sing.'

'What song then? You shall choose it.'

'By your serenity's gracious leave, I would have the Duke of Zayana be chooser for me tonight.'

'Then sing us,' said the Duke to Campaspe, but his eyes, darkly bright, were on her they belonged to, 'that song of *Deare love, for nothing lesse than thee*. Be it mine to choose, I'll have none other tonight.'

Campaspe, standing up in her place now like some little fieldish creature that is here and, whip, gone again in the twilight of night-fall or of dawn, but very lovely and sylph-like of posture in the faintly-moving upward glow of the candles, took her lute and began to sing. Light and immaterial was her singing as the last breath falling asleep with the falling shadows of a May evening without cloud. As the colour of red roses folding their petals as sunset ends, was the colour that softly mounted to her cheek while she sang:

"Deare love, for nothing lesse than thee
Would I have broke this happy dreame,
   It was a theame
For reason, much too strong for phantasie,
Therefore thou wakd'st me wisely; yet
My Dreame thou brok'st not, but continued'st it,
Thou art so truth, that thoughts of thee suffice
To make dreames truths; and fables histories;
Enter these armes, for since thou thought'st it best,
Not to dreame all my dreame, let's act the rest.
As lightning, or a Taper's light,
Thine eyes, and not thy noise wak'd mee;
   Yet I thought thee
(For thou lovest truth) an Angell, at first sight,
But when I saw thou sawest my heart,
And knew'st my thoughts, beyond an Angel's art,
When thou knew'st what I dreamt, when thou knew'st when
Excesse of joy would wake me, and cam'st then,
I must confesse, it could not chuse but bee
Prophane, to thinke thee any thing but thee.

"Comming and staying show'd thee, thee,
But rising makes me doubt, that now,
   Thou art not thou.
That love is weake, where feare's as strong as hee;
'Tis not all spirit, pure, and brave,
If mixture it of Feare, Shame, Honor, have.
Perchance as torches which must ready bee,
Men light and put out, so thou deal'st with mee,

Thou cam'st to kindle, goest to come; Then I
Will dreame that hope againe, but else would die."[5]

There was no sound besides in that great hall while she sang.
Eyes for the most part, rested not on the singer but on the lights, or
in high dusky spaces beyond those lights, where nought was to see
but moth-winged memories or wishes, conjured up in myriads by
that unworldly singing: moments uncatchable as the beetle's droning on the air at the half-light, or as dart of a fieldmouse amid tufted
grass: now here, now gone: lift of skirt above a known ankle, comfort of known hand, rustle of silks under the promise-laden starri-
ness of a summer's night, or sound of a known breath taken gently
in sleep: for each listener his own, her own. And each several one of
these innumerable, infinitely little, treasures of hearts' desire, in this
coming and departing and changing as smoke-wreaths change or
eddies in water, seemed yet, at every come and go, contented: save
perhaps for a fear, abysmal under all, lest such deep-contenting
changes should, by some mischieving power beyond them, ever
have end. The Duke, listening, had eyes for none of these shadows:
only for Her, in whom all that beauty comes home.

She, listening, was leant now a little forward over her table, her
right hand propping her chin. Her left arm rested in a largesse of
lazy grace across the table sideways, its hand playing with her untasted goblet of golden wine, and on its ring-finger the great eye-
refecting alexandrite-stone that changes colour from light to light,
of Barganax's ring winking and blazing. Very still was her face: the
sheen on her hair a tremble of stars on black sea at midnight. The
low-cut bosom of her dress partly gave forth to view, as she so
leaned forward, globed twin moons, plenilune at half eclipse,
lovelier in their high Grecian pride than the moon of heaven, and
holding in their warmed interspace (by patent of every Olympian
untamed contour in her countenance above them) all sweets, all
stings, all terrors, sense-furying over-weenings, doves, fire-worms,
blindings, mandragoras, velvet-sheathed claws, lionesses' teeth: all
beguilings: all incorruptibles: all keepings and waterings, returnings
and reconcilements, performance and renewal of strength: all raging powers, from everlasting, of beauty and passion of love. And, for
seeing eyes to see, between Her brows was the morning star.

Her gaze was, for this while, not upon Her lover but upon the
great King, and His on Hers: an eye-parley swift beyond stretch of
mortal sense, as though, accommodating Their large leisure to a
brief moment of time, as the wide landscape and vault of the sky will
lie mirrored in a dewdrop, God should speak with God. As if He
should say: Daughter and Sister and Mother and Lover of Mine:
Kythereia, brought up with Me from everlasting in the beginning of

My way before My works of old: what is this You have done, almost
a year ago? Why did you beguile Me to make You that false world?

And awful, gold-crowned, beautiful Aphrodite answered and
said: Because it flattered My mood that night. But I changed My
mind. Give it not a thought, My Father. It is abolished: forgot: no,
lost beyond forgetting: for how forget what never indeed existed?

He said: It is not the thing create was the mischief, but My
creating of it. In that creation I came to know what theretofore I
had blessedly (here at least, where to be is to do) not known. What
profit to be Me, when action and the springs and issues of action, in
Me, in You, in this wide world We live in, are tainted: known and
foreknown to last tittle? This world, this heavenly mansion, is
wasted and spoilt.

She said: Not for Me. I am well served. For I (through You,
there where, in what I begin to think a more wiser dress of Yours,
You do sit at Your own right hand) still find this true world a world
apt to My nature. And to Yours.

The 'Why?' in his eyes was a doubt more freezing cold than the
grave.

She said, to answer it: Because, I suppose, I can be content to
embrace this world's all: can contemplate all; desire all; possess and
receive into My being, all; and see that it is good. For I (even when I
pleasure Myself to behold Myself in the mirror of My Lover's eyes,
and so behold that which is without spot, without bridle, and without bourne) do still, in that all-seeing, limit Me to perfection: to the
perfect sum of all perfects which in Me do have their eternity. I limit
Me so to All which Is. Eschewing so (through Our common wisdom,
which do not You and I possess from the beginning?) that More
than all: which is Not; and which (seeing that all which Is, is Good;
and all which is Good, Is) is therefore Not Good.

He said: But We went down, into that misconceived misfor-
tuned world of Your passing fantasy. For a moment. To know.

She said: For a life-time's moment. Yes. It was enough.

He said: Since that night in Memison when first I tasted Mine
own infinite power: since that unchaining then in Me of this unex-
tinguishable lust of knowing: 'enough' is become to Me a noise without meaning.

She said: Our Father which watchest out of Ida, most glorious,
most great, what is this You have spoken? A dangerous saying; and
not Your own, I think. Certainly not Mine. What turn next, then?

He said: My creation-old instrument, Death.

She said: No more than so? O, You have turned up the lights
again. Your talk had put a strange thing in Me I could not give a
name to, without it were Fear.

He said: Be You not too certain sure. This lust that devours Me,
of knowing and doing, burns fiercelier than can be put out with

what mortals call Death. I could, before, by that common gate, cross Lethe: even as have not I and You, time unto time and without time, crossing it drunk oblivion? And so, with Our mind as a white paper unwritten, have refreshed Us for life and action in new mansions of this Olympus. In which are many mansions. But what soul-heal is there in that, to redeem this all-knowing knowing? Whereby they are all, here and now, present to Me already: as good go here as there, do this as that: alike it is idleness and vanity.

She said: Do not I, O My Father and My Lover, know them too? Yet there is in My knowing, no stain of this fever, of this un-peace.

He said: Who knoweth better than I, that You know All? But You are of so blest a nature as can be content to know and look on: enjoy, and not meddle: be adored, be had, rest in Your peace: the peace of that which is All, and Enough. But I, by some necessity of My nature, will to go further.

The song had ended. In the moment's silence, while folk yet sat held with the passion of it and the language and the vision, King Mezentius looked still (as Barganax too looked, but he, for his comfort, with a gaze that sounded not, as his Father's, the uttermost deeps) on that Dark Lady.

In the sea-fire eyes of laughter-loving Aphrodite, grown gentler now than a dove's eyes, seeming now to the King to be Amalie's eyes new-unmaidened in Acrozayana five and twenty years ago, but to Barganax Fiorinda's, knowledge sat, detached, tolerant, and merciful; and, by reason of its reach beyond infinitude, begat in the secret places behind the all-wielding all-seeing eyes of the King, infinite pity. Pity for Rosma, who could hate well, but not truly love: for Roder, sitting there, a man of common clay destined within a year or two for a bad end: for Styllis, foredoomed, of his rashness and stiff-necked arrogance, never to seize and hold the shining moment to be given him: for the Admiral, good faithful dog whose loyalties and self-misdoubting irresolution in action must yet withhold him from detachment alike and peace of mind: for Beroald, blinded by his own sceptic humours and intellectual ironies to the inmost natures both of Her, his sister in blood, and of the King, his master: for Heterasmene, left now with but memories of her governesship to warm her commonplace marriage: for Emmius Parry, whose greatness could as little reck of other men's pity as waste his on them: for the great Vicar of Rerek himself, not because of any warring or unhappiness in his self-perfect nature (where there was neither), but because, whereas the King and She understand from within by very feeling what it were to be this man, who all his life must, but for the master-hand upon him, have mischieved all middle earth, yet should the Vicar never understand and contain Their loves as They in a manner do his: pity for the nothings, rests and pauses and unresolved discords necessary in the symphony of this brave world, as for Fiorinda's ill-starred unsufficient husbands, as well for Valero, for Aktor, for the tragic nothings of Middlemead: for His Amalie, who must tonight be widowed and left to her motherhood and her Memisonian peace: for Queen Stateira, now to lose (except in memory) her very motherhood, and with no memories of true love and perfect, only of Mardanus's perfunctory transient love, and of her own restless, consuming, never wholly satisfied passion for Aktor: for Vandermast, albeit a contemplative that walked with God, yet exiled (unless through kindly sympathy and back-returns of the mind) from the joys and fevers of youth: for Antiope, fated, as the rock-rose's queenly blossom, to a tragic ephemeral perfection and tragic death: for Barganax even, and Lessingham, because of the limitations of their beings, not to be wholly Himself: for these nymphkind, dwelling in the superficies and so coming short of Godhead: for every man, woman, child, and living creature in Zimiamvia, because instruments, means, and ingredients to His and Her perfection in action and beatitude: even for Her, as to all eternity unable to be, were it but for a moment, He. Last, pity for that which sat conscient in Her eyes: for His love and Hers, troubled now for sake of God Himself, that He should be choked with His own omniscience and omnipotence here terribly loosed in self-emptying collision within Him: for sake of His loneliness, here where should be His home: that here, through dull privation of that doubt which alone can bring zest to omnipotency in action, He, knowing overmuch, fails of his way.

And, darkly unspoken in that commerce of eyes, a horror moved: horror not of the unknown, but of the unknowable, the impossible, the unconceivable.

King Mezentius gave command now (for ending of the revels) to bring in the Cup of Memory. A great goblet it was, of rock-crystal, egg-shaped, resting in the grasp of three feet upraised to contain between them the belly of it: feet of pure gold, one in the likeness of the pounces and talon of an eagle, another a lion's paw with claws expansed, and the third a hippogriff's hoof, all rising from a nine-sided base of hammered gold bossed with rubies and chrysoprases and hyacinth-stones and pearls. This, being brought in, went round, first at the lowest tables and so in order upwards, until every person in the body of the hall below the dais had drunk of it, each a sip. And each in turn, having drunk bowed low toward the King. The cup-bearer now, brimming it anew with ruby-dark wine of the Rian, bore it to Earl Roder, who, as captain of the guard, tasted it and with his own hand bore it to King Mezentius. Upon that, all the company below the dais stood up in their places, while the Earl returned him to his chair of state. The King, raising the cup, looked into the wine against the light, savoured it with his nostrils, and so, looking towards the company, drank deep: then said in a great voice, for all in that great banquet-chamber to hear: " 'Tis time to say goodnight. Rest well, my friends. Our banquet is sweetly ended." Upon which word all, save only the company on the dais, bowed low toward the King and so, with that for goodnight, departed. The King meanwhile, wiping the lip of the cup with his handkercher, set it down, yet three parts full, upon the Queen's table before her.

She, for her turn, lifted it in both hands: drank (as next in order of nobility) to Duke Barganax: wiped, and reached across the King's table on her right, to have passed it to the Duke. But the King, intercepting it, said lightly, 'Nay, I will break custom tonight. For good luck, since these be farewell revels, I'll pledge him too.'

Rosma laid a hand on his arm. 'Pray you, dear my Lord,' she said, smiling, but her face suddenly gone grey as ashes: 'that bringeth bad luck, not good, to drink twice ere the cup be gone round.'

King Mezentius but shifted the cup from his left hand to his right. 'Fear nothing, madam. Luck, long as I remember me, hath been my servant still. I'll go my gait, as in great things so here in little, and spite all omens.'

His eyes, while he so spoke, were met with my Lady Fiorinda's, chilling as snakes' eyes now or as stones a-glitter with heatless green fire, and saying to Him: What terrible unlawful unimagined lust is this? You are putting Us, both You and Me, and all that proceedeth from Us (or hath, or shall proceed) into deadly danger. Whither do You mean to go? What do You mean to do?

He was at the point to drink. Rosma made a movement so slight as none but his own most eagle eyes might note it, as if ready, in the open sight of the court, to have knocked the cup from his lips; but his great left hand shut, gentle but unresistible, upon her hand, pinning it to the table. He set down the goblet once more, out of her reach. 'Let's finish the evening in private. Earl, clear the hall. Let the maids and the music be gone. Set guards without all the doors, and to keep folk from the portico.'

While this was doing, those lords of Meszria and the Lady Heterasmene, in obedience to eye-signs from the King and Queen, bade goodnight, took their leaves, and departed. They being gone, Rosma said to the King: 'Lord, I beseech you, for all sakes' sakes, bear with my foolish fears. 'Tis the one boon I ask of you tonight and surely 'tis a light nothing for you to grant. There's a curse in a twice-drunk Memory-Cup. However silly I seem, to take a small matter too heavily, O, tempt no fates tonight. For my sake, Lord. And if not for mine,' she checked: then finished, looking at Barganax, 'for his.'

It was grown very close in the hall now, for all that the windows stood open. The long-gathering storm began: a great flash in dry sultry air, near overhead, and deafening peals of thunder: then pitch darkness without, as the thunder rolled away to silence. Barganax looked swiftly from Rosma to the King: from him to Fiorinda, sitting motionless as Aphrodite's statua: so to the King again. 'Lord and Father,' he said, 'pray you drink it not. The Queen's highness feareth some practice, I think. 'Twere well send for fresh wine. Let this be ta'en away and examined'; and he took hold on the goblet.

'Lay off your hand,' said the King, 'I command you.'

Barganax met his eyes: seemed to hover an instant betwixt unclear contrarious duties: then obeyed. He sat back, eyes flaming, face red as blood. Bringing his fist down upon the table before him with a blow set the plates a-leap and a-clatter, 'Yet would I give my dukedom,' he said violently, 'that your serene highness taste not this again.'

'I do not care whether you would or no. But you, as all man else i' the kingdoms, shall do my bidding.' So saying, the King, taking the great goblet betwixt his hands and looking down into the wine, swirled it about: a whirlpool in little. Presently, laughing in his black beard, 'Moonshine in water,' he said to the Duke. 'Have not she and I drunken o' this same pottle already? Were aught amiss with 't, we were both of us sped ere now.'

Queen Rosma said, and her voice shook: 'Nay then, myself, I do seem now to find, I know not what, but an after-taste in it: something sluggish in its working, may be. By heavens,' she said suddenly, 'I accuse this Roder. A meant it for Lord Barganax.'

The Earl stared at her like a startled bull.

'Come,' said the King, 'this is fits of the mother. A most strange, most unmerited, brainless accusation against a true, tried servant of ours,' he said, with a glance at Roder, whose eyes were now bolling out of his face: then turned him once more to Rosma. 'No more fooleries. A curse in a twice-drunk cup? You are much mistook, madam. This, I pledge you my kingly word for 't, is nectar.' While she sat unpowered to move or speak under the tyranny of his eyes upon her, he drank. 'To your deepest wishes, my Rosma. Which have, e'en at such times as least you dreamed it, galloped in harness with mine.'

He wiped the brim: set the half-empty cup on his table within her reach: then, his eyes meaningly and steadfastly on hers but without all note of menace or blame or resentment in them, held his handkercher to the candleflame. Being well alight, he dropped it to burn out on the table-top: of panteron stone, in some part black, in other part green, in other part purple, which is said to bolden a man, and make him invincible. The Queen, those words echoing in her ears, those things done before her eyes, that understanding in the King's eyes upon her, sat stone still.

At last, sweeping her gaze round upon Barganax, Beroald, Fiorinda, Roder, Jeronimy, to end upon the King again, 'Yes. Well,' she said, 'it is true. It is nectar': then thrust aside her table, rose to her feet and, facing him, seized the cup. 'But I meant it for that whoreson, that calleth himself Duke of Zayana.' Standing so before them, she drained it, no trickle left: turned again with a hideous cry: fell with a crash in the half-moon space before the tables, without a struggle, stone dead.

Barganax spoke silence: 'God's precious Lady be thanked then, your highness swallowed it not.'

King Mezentius gave him his eyes for an instant, undisturbed, resolute, but, save for their good will, unreadable: then, turning to the Admiral and Lord Roder, 'Take up the Queen's body,' he said. 'Sit it in her chair of state.'

When they, in a maze and rather in manner of contrived automatons than of waking men, had done his bidding, he stood up, somewhat slowly, from his high-seat and, taking from his own head the crown of Meszria, set it on hers. 'I'll view it again thus, where it belonged when first I had sight of it. Who loveth me, remember her greatness, and her father's. Put out of mind aught you may think she did amiss. She has paid for that, and as no skulking cheater, neither, nor in no false coin. Sorely tried she was, and, i' the end, no unnoble daughter of the Parry. Few there be that I shall gladlier shake by the hand, beyond the hateful river.'

He looked at Fiorinda: saw how her eyes rested constant on Barganax.

'You may see,' said the King, seated again and surveying Rosma's face, undisfigured and wearing a peace and a majesty not known there in her life-days, 'that here's no villainous discountenancing poison, to mar that which God Himself hath made, and send us aboard of Charon's ferry as puff-balls swol'n up and bursten. 'Tis a clean death, and worthy of royal Princes.'

Outside, now, a gale was raging from the west: rushings of rain, and the huge belly of darkness continually a-rumbling with near and distant thunders. The windows of the hall flickered blue with the ceaseless lightning.

'Beroald,' the King said, 'you are a brave man and a discreet, and a friend of mine. You are instantly to take boat, then saddle and ride your swiftest to Zayana. This ring,' here he took the great Worm-ring from his thumb: 'give it to her grace. She'll know the token. Say to her I have yet a few hours to live, but I am dog-weary, and it is no more in my power to turn this destiny.'

As if the forked lightning-flame had with these words leapt

among them, all, save only the King and my Lady Fiorinda, sprang to their feet. The Duke said, out of a deformed silence: 'But the counterpoisons your highness hath alway taken?'

'Without 'em, I were gone, her way, at first sip. Look to the ring on her finger: undo the bezel: so: it is empty, but for specks of this greenish dust. This was her aunt's first wedding-gift, Lugia Parry's; and 'gainst that masterpiece, wetted or ta'en by the mouth, all counterpoisons in the world are naught: save to delay. She had it in her handkercher.'

'Send for leeches.'

'They can do nothing. Begone, Chancellor: your speediest.'

'Shall I bring her noble excellence back with me?'

'No. Though my salvation hung on't, I would not hazard her safety in such a storm. But it were a hell to me to die and no word from her to speed me. Begone, Beroald, and swiftly back. Haste, haste, post haste. Worketh already, dull in my feet.

'Earl,' he said, as the Chancellor, with face like a stone, strode swiftly down the hall, 'fetch me my armour; and the triple crown; and my robes of state. Kings ought not to die lying on their backs.'

'And fetch leeches, for God's sake, quick,' said Barganax swiftly in the Earl's ear. 'All blame's mine, if 's highness mislike it.'

Within five minutes, the Chancellor put out upon the firth in the fury and height of the storm: himself at the tiller, and two boatmen to take turns at oars and bailing. There was but a mile to go, but they were not gotten half way when a tremendous sea breaking over the stern swamped the boat and left them to swim or drown. By strength and by heart, but most (it seemed) by some over-riding fate of necessity, they made land, but on a lee shore, much east beyond the right landing-place and set about with sharp rocks and skerries. On the teeth of these one of the boatmen being dashed by a wave was knocked senseless and, taken by the undersuck, no more seen. His fellow won to safety, but with 's leg broke. The Lord Beroald, bruised and cut, came aland a little farther east and, with but a tatter of soaked rags left to cover his nakedness, part walked, part ran, till he was come to the little township and fishing-harbour of Leshmar. Here the Admiral's bailiff found him dry clothes and a horse: sent, by his bidding, to bring in the wounded boatman: and so, scarce more than an hour from his leaving of the banquet-chamber, the Chancellor rode up into Acrozayana.

'Dying, and past hope of mending?' said the Duchess when he told his tale. 'God's precious Dear take mercy then of this land of Meszria, mercy of our dear son, mercy of us all. You have spoke to me killing words, noble Beroald. O, I am very sick.' And throwing herself face downward upon the great brocaded couch between the windows she fell into an unmasterable great passion of tears. The

Chancellor, that had never seen her weep, turned him away and, with folded arms and iron-lipped, unmoving as stone, stood looking on her picture above the mantel, a master-work of Barganax's painted five years ago, and so waited till this tempest should blow itself out.

Presently she stood up and dried her eyes.

He turned. 'I was to take word back from your beauteous excellency.'

'Word? You are to take me, my lord. Have you not yet given order for my horses?'

'There is a dangerous sea running in the firth tonight. The King's highness did expressly command you must not adventure it.'

'Pray you, pull me that bell-rope.'

Beroald looked at her. Something glinting in his cold eye, he went to the window, drew back the curtain, threw open the casement. The wind had dropped. Westward, over Zayana lake, was clear weather and moonlight. He came back to her beside the fireplace, reached hand to the twisted rope of honey-coloured silk and gave it a jerk. 'The Duchess intends for Sestola tonight,' he said to the waiting-woman: 'taketh but one maid and a portmanteau. Her grace's horses are at the Kremasmian gate already, waiting with mine.'

Amalie gave him her hand. 'To be great-hearted,' he said, kissing it, 'is a lovely virtue. And loveliest in woman; 'cause least of course.'

When the Duchess, with the Chancellor carrying her cloak, was come into the banquet-chamber, King Mezentius sat yet in his highseat, clad now in all his royal habiliments and ornaments of majesty. Above him were seated the Admiral, Earl Roder, Duke Barganax, and my Lady Fiorinda. The body of the Queen had been taken away to lie in state. The Duchess, very white and with eyes only for the King, came up that great empty hall almost as a woman walks in her sleep, but noble of mien and carriage as a tall ship dropping silently down the tideway at evening before a light breeze. So, mounting the dais, she stood before him.

'So, Amalie, you are come to me? and spite of my strait forbidding?'

'How could I choose?'

'Do not kiss me, sweetheart, or I shall poison you.[6] Sit where I can see you. The sands are running out. You, Beroald: thanks, and fare you well. Leave us now: you have had my commands, and you too, Jeronimy and Roder. May the Gods lead you by the hand. You too, my son: yes, but stay you. And stay you too, dear Lady of Sakes.'

When those were sorrowfully departed, the Duke set a chair for his mother and on her right another for Fiorinda, and himself took seat on his mother's left, facing the King.

The Duchess leaned forward. 'Do not kiss you?' she said. 'O yes, that you may take me with you. How can I, after so many years, bear the darkness here alone?'

'I,' said the King, 'am entering upon a darkness that was, until late ago, unthought on: darkness uncompanionable: may be, unreturnable. If there be throughway, my darling dear (and there's no man nor, I think, no God, to tell us whether), you shall find my doing was but to prepare new kingdoms for you. I' the long mean time, comfort you that My choice it was. No will but Mine could force me this gate, open it upon triumph such as eye hath not seen nor heart imagined. Or else,' he paused, and while he looked on her a film seemed to be drawn over his eyes: 'or else: upon Nothing.'

The Duchess listening, from her chair between Barganax and Fiorinda, as if to some terrible commination, seemed to miss the sense but yet to be touched, as fire touches the shrinking flesh, with the deadly import. 'I do not understand,' she said, trembling. 'Your choice? I can never forget you were my lover. I never thought you, of all people in the world, would choose to hurt me.'

He bore her look a minute in silence. Then, 'O turn your eyes away, Amalie,' he said; 'or for your dear sake I shall, at this last, fail of Myself: become less than, of My true whole nature, I must be.'

'How could you do it? O,' she cried, 'how could you do it?' and she covered her mouth with her hand, biting, for silence, at the palm.

'Remove her away for God's sake,' said the King. 'I can grapple the great death, but not with My hands tied.'

None stirred.

The Duchess, pale, but collecting herself to sit now in a selfwarranting superbity erect in her chair, said, 'I'm sorry, dear my Lord. It is brought under. I'll not, i' the last turning, become a footgin in your way.'

But that Dark Lady, Her eyes like the eyes of a lioness that gives bay to her adversaries, said to the King: 'Is she not Me, albeit she know it not? And think You I do not know Myself and, through Myself, You? It is child's play to You and Me, this world-making; and child's play to abolish and do away a world, or a million worlds. But to abolish (as You seem now, of Your furious self-feeding folly, resolved to hazard it) the very stuff of Being, which is Me and You: this seemeth to Me a greatness which, like overblown bubbles, is of its own extreme become littler than littleness.'

'Be silent, lest I strike You in pieces first with My thunderstone. We will yet see whether God be able to die.'

'Questionless, He is able. To Him is not even the impossible possible? But questionless, He will not.'

'Why not?'

'For sake of Her.'

The Duchess buried her face between Fiorinda's breasts, as if the heart-beats unquieting that violet-sweet enchanted valley were her own eternized: last core and safeguard unsure of an unbottomed world. The King, shutting his eyes not to behold her, said: 'We will see.'

'If You do Your intent, and the throw fail You,' said that Lady, 'then We shall not see. For there will be nought to see, nor eye to see it. By that unexperimented leap, in peril and blasphemy both of Yourself and Me, You may (since there be no chains to chain omnipotency run mad) at a stroke end All. End it so as not so much as a dead universe nor a dead God be left to be remembered or forgotten, but only a Nothing not to be named or thought; because in it is nor existence nor unexistence, hope nor fear nor time nor life nor God nor eternity (not even that eternity of nothing), nor truth nor untruth nor remembering nor unremembering any more: not even such last little wet mark or burnt-out ember as might rest for the uncipherable cipher: *I am not: I never was: I never shall be.'* In the honey-dropping dying music of Her voice, time, space, fate, beauty seemed let fall as a tale told, and all stings of death desirable before this horror of the void.

'Which is to deny itself,' said the Duchess, turning her head. 'Evil, which is the ultimate Nothing, so shattered at last and broken in its nothingness, as not be able even to be nothing.' She shuddered violently and, sitting up and resting a hand on Barganax's knee, 'Your way is mine,' she said to the King, in a whisper. 'The truth is, love is not able to kill love.'

'To God,' said the King, 'all things are easy. And, save one thing alone, all are accomplished.'

'You say well, my lady Mother,' said the Duke, with his hand on hers. 'But as for truth, I know not. And care not. For what's this but tilling of the sand, to talk so and question so about truth? I have small inclination for this, when this infinite which is beauty's self' (his eyes now upon Fiorinda) 'lieth open for my tilling: the only truth I know the name of, the only truth I would purchase at a flea's worth. And if God be (as I know not nor reck not whether), He is no God of mine when he ceaseth to love where I love.'

There was a long silence. Barganax, with the grace upon him of some hunting-leopard in a muse 'twixt sleeping and waking, gazed between half-shut lids now on his Father, now on Fiorinda. In her face, seen thus sideways, warring insolubles, of heart-break and heart-heal and things yet deeper in grain, not in reason adorable yet past reason adored, seemed to flicker and change with their own self-light. He saw now, like as in Memison almost a year ago but not yet seen tonight, glow-worms in her hair. Her eyes were on the

King's. He, bolt upright in his high-seat, crowned and robed and armed, looked now in them; now upon Amalie's tender neck and, smoothly drawn up from it with a high comb of tortoise-shell and inwoven to a voluptuosity of shining twists and coils on the crown of her head, the red-gold glory of her hair (her face was by this time hiding again on Fiorinda's breast); now upon the night-piece of the two of them: Queen of Spades: Queen of Hearts. Presently, as in a mirror, his speckled grey eyes, their eagle gaze unblunted yet and undimmed, met his son's.

'I leave you and the others a tangled business,' he said, 'where I could if I would have left all pat. But you'd have smally thanked me, I think: to do all beforehand and leave my after-comers with occupation gone.'

'Be you thanked as I thank you, O my Father,' said the Duke. With a catch of his breath he made as if to say more; but no words came.

Albeit midsummer, it was now turned bitter cold, in this dead time of night when the tide of man's blood runs lowest: the hour when oftenest men die. Here, under the bright lights and in the large emptiness of this banquet-chamber, scarce was a sound heard, save that of the sea with the storm-swell not yet stilled in it lapping the seawalls: this, and the breathing of those four, and the ticking of the clock. These breaths and these tickings measured out the ingredients of the stillness: hollownesses within, dulling of the spirits from sleeplessness, dulling of the brain: hands and feet grown powerless, fingers all turned to thumbs, eyelids hot and heavy. So they waited, as if for something that itself, too, held back and waited in the night without.

At length the King said, the third time: 'We will see.' Then, as in a secret gaiety which held under-stirrings of that power that moves the sun and the other stars, and which brought the Duchess on the sudden wide awake again, her name: 'Amalie.'

Upon that, Duke Barganax, looking first at his Father and then where his Father looked, beheld a great wonder. My Lady Fiorinda was stood up to her full stature: the red corn-rose dress, fallen down about Her knees, seemed water-green laced with white, sea-waves of the heavenly Paphos; and upon Her brow and cheek, and upon all Her divine body thus unveiled, was the beauty that blinds the Gods. In that great banquet-hall in Sestola was nothing now visible but that beauty, all else, for a timeless moment, put out by it as the risen sun puts out the stars. Barganax, so beholding Her, knew he beheld what his Father beheld: save only that this eternal morning wore, for his Father's eyes, an aurora of red fire, but for his own eyes that sable aurora of night: which, for him, all perfects else excels. And the face of Her, while they looked (as a finger held up before the eyes can seem now to stand against this tree in the far landscape now against that, and so alternately, as alternately right eye or left takes power) seemed now Fiorinda's, now Amalie's.

Then time and space resumed their vicegerency in Sestola; even as when the eyes, leaving to look upon the landscape and converging upon the raised finger, see it its own known self again, familiar and near again, of like flesh with the looker. That Dark Lady sat palpable and exquisite here in her chair, wearing her gown of scarlet sendaline; and on the sweet unrest of her bosom the Duchess of Memison yet laid her cheek, as if in slumber.

Barganax rising softly, came to the King's side: viewed him narrowly. Then he turned to those two. The Duchess raised her head: stood up: looked first at the King, then, as in a sudden fear at her son: saw in his eyes a new depth of power and sufficiency: new, yet far beyond all remembrance old. 'I have thought it, I think,' she said, very low, 'from the beginning: that there have been four of us. Perhaps, more than four. And yet always a twoness in that many. And that twoness so near unite to oneness as sense to spirit, yet so as not to confound to unity the very heart and being of God; who is Two in One and One in Two.'

Barganax took her hand and kissed it. 'Even and we were Gods (my Father, upon whom be peace, said it, you remember at your fish dinner last July): Even and we were Gods, best not to know. Well: thank God, I know not. Only,' he said to Fiorinda, standing within handreach, 'I believe your ladyship knows.'

In her eyes, unsounded heavens of green fire, and in the gravity that overlay the smoulder of her uncomparable lips, sweet-suggesting inviters, forcible setters-on, to the lime-bushes and labyrinthine ways of love, sat the Bitter-sweet. 'Yes,' she said. 'I know: or almost all. And indeed I suppose I have a bent of mind is able to bear with the knowledge of some matters which even to you, who are a glad man of your nature, should hardly I think be bearable.'

'Promise me this,' he said, watching her eyes, that mouth, the glow-worms in her hair: 'never to tell me.'

'It is,' answered that lady, and there was that in her voice that fetched down for him, from heaven, both the morning and the evening star, 'the one sole promise that I will ever make to your grace. And from my heart. And for love.' And she added, unspoken but read darkly, like enough, by Barganax in the comet-caging deeps of those Olympian eyes: 'for My servant, love, whose triumph We see tonight.'

FINIS

NOTES TO THE
INTRODUCTION

1. E. R. Eddison, *The Worm Ouroboros* (New York: Dell Publishing, 1991), 167.
2. SRQ 823.91 ED 23, Correspondence and Notes Relating to *Egil's Saga,* Local History Department, Reference Library, Central Library, Leeds.
3. See note 1 to the Letter of Introduction to *A Fish Dinner in Memison.*
4. This is one of several hymns, including a shorter 'Hymn to Aphrodite,' that are attributed to Homer. Whether Homer actually wrote these poems is still a matter of conjecture. Apostolos Athanassakis discusses the rather odd treatment given to the Hymns through the ages:

> Classical and even Hellenistic antiquity treated the Homeric Hymns with a considerable measure of indifference. This is rather difficult to understand, especially since they were ascribed to Homer. . . . Except for a few scattered references, chiefly by later scholiasts and antiquarians, the hymns seem to have suffered from a nearly universal literary conspiracy of silence. It is interesting that no less a writer than Thucydides obviously accepted the tradition that ascribed the hymns to Homer, but the Alexandrian grammarians and critics made up their minds that the hymns had not been composed by the poet of the *Iliad* and the *Odyssey,* and that, therefore, they did not deserve the attention lavished on Homer. . . . In modern times scholars have recognized the importance of the hymns, but students of the classics frequently by pass them for the study of the Homeric epics, and the educated public is hardly aware of their existence.

See the verse translations by Athanassakis, *The Homeric Hymns* (Baltimore: Johns Hopkins University Press, 1976).
5. I have chosen Andrew Lang's translation because Eddison, at age eleven, began reading the *Iliad* and the *Odyssey* in the translations by Lang (with W. Leaf, E. Myers, and S. H. Butcher), and this early steeping in Lang's ornate and archaic style colored Eddison's literary imagination permanently. It is possible that Eddison's first meeting with

Homer's Hymns came in the form of Lang's translations. The 'Hymn to Aphrodite' can be found in *The Homeric Hymns,* trans. Andrew Lang (London: George Allen, 1899), 166–82.

6. Ms. Eng. Lett. c. 232, fol. 3, Bodleian Library, Oxford.

7. E. R. Eddison to Henry Lappin, July 28, 1941, Ms. Eng. Lett. c. 231, fols. 145–147a, Bodleian Library, Oxford.

8. SRQ 823.91 ED 23, Manuscript Notes and Correspondence for *Mistress of Mistresses,* Local History Department, Reference Library, Central Library, Leeds.

9. All quotations in this subsection (1. The Gods) of Section IV are taken from fols. 89–92 of Ms. Eng. Misc. c. 456, Bodleian Library, Oxford.

10. SRQ 823.91 ED 23, Manuscript Notes and Correspondence for *Mistress of Mistresses,* Local History Department, Reference Library, Central Library, Leeds.

11. Eddison to Gerald Hayes, February 7, 1945, Ms. Eng. Lett. c. 230, fol. 96, Bodleian Library, Oxford.

12. Eddison to William Hurd Hillyer, November 24, 1942, Ms. Eng. Lett. c. 231, fols. 110–112, Bodleian Library, Oxford.

13. SRQ 823.91 ED 23, Manuscript Notes and Correspondence for *Mistress of Mistresses,* Local History Department, Reference Library, Central Library, Leeds.

14. This is a term used by Immanuel Kant (1724–1804) in his *Critique of Practical Reason.* A categorical imperative is the action that is universally morally correct in a particular situation and that should be enacted by all persons in those particular circumstances. For more on Kant, see the subsequent section of the Introduction and note 7 to the Letter of Introduction to *A Fish Dinner in Memison.*

15. SRQ 823.91 ED 23, Manuscript Notes and Correspondence for *Mistress of Mistresses,* Local History Department, Reference Library, Central Library, Leeds.

16. 'There is a beauty of action (as the Northmen knew),' says Eddison near the end of his Letter of Introduction to *A Fish Dinner in Memison.* By setting up beauty as the standard for evaluating behavior, Eddison imitates and borrows from the behavioral standards of the thirteenth-century Icelandic sagas. In the introduction to his translation of *Egil's Saga,* Eddison quotes Professor E. V. Gordon's description of the Icelandic behavioral values expressed in the sagas:

> Probably in no other literature is conduct so carefully examined and appraised; and the basis of the valuation is not moral, but aesthetic. In no other literature is there such a sense of the beauty of human conduct; . . . The heroes and heroines themselves had the aesthetic view of conduct; it was their chief guide, for they had a very undeveloped conception of morality, and none at all of sin. (E. R. Eddison, *Egil's Saga* [Cambridge: Cambridge University Press, 1930] xxxi–xxxii).

17. Eddison to C. S. Lewis, February 7, 1943, Ms. Eng. Lett. c. 220/2, fols. 45–46, The Letters of C. S. Lewis, Bodleian Library, Oxford.

18. Eddison to Gerald Hayes, February 24, 1945, Ms. Eng. Lett. c. 230, fols. 100–104, Bodleian Library, Oxford.

19. I am only using Keats to make Eddison's position clearer. I cannot argue for a strong influence on Eddison's personal philosophy by Keats, but some influence must have occurred since Keats stood with Donne and Swinburne as Eddison's favorite English lyric poets.

20. See *The Letters of John Keats*, ed. Robert Gittings (Oxford: Oxford University Press, 1975), 36–37, 43.

21. SRQ 823.91 ED 23, Manuscript Notes and Correspondence for *Mistress of Mistresses*, Local History Department, Reference Library, Central Library, Leeds.

22. SRQ 823.91 ED 23, Manuscript Notes and Correspondence for *Mistress of Mistresses*, Local History Department, Reference Library, Central Library, Leeds.

23. SRQ 823.91 ED 23, Manuscript Notes and Correspondence for *Mistress of Mistresses*, Local History Department, Reference Library, Central Library, Leeds.

24. The first quotation is from a 'memorandum' dated April 5, 1931; the second is from a letter Eddison wrote to George R. Hamilton on October 2, 1933. Both are contained in SRQ 823.91 ED 23, Manuscript Notes and Correspondence for *Mistress of Mistresses*, Local History Department, Reference Library, Central Library, Leeds.

25. Eddison to J. M. Howard, June 4, 1942, Ms. Eng. Lett. c. 231, fols. 130–131, Bodleian Library, Oxford.

NOTES TO
ZIMIAMVIA

A note on the Notes: I have used the following abbreviations in the textual notes:

AZC = 'Anno Zayanae Conditae' (years reckoned from the time
 of the founding of the city of Zayana)
ERE = E. R. Eddison
ES = *Egil's Saga*, trans. E. R. Eddison (Cambridge: Cambridge
 University Press, 1930)
FD = *A Fish Dinner in Memison*, the second volume of *Zimiamvia*
MG = *The Mezentian Gate*, the third volume of *Zimiamvia*
MM = *Mistress of Mistresses*, the first volume of *Zimiamvia*
SS = *Styrbiorn the Strong* (London: Jonathan Cape, 1926; New
 York: A. & C. Boni, 1926)
WO = *The Worm Ouroboros*. All references are made to the Dell
 edition published in 1991.

Quoted translations from the verse of Sappho are taken, unless otherwise indicated, from the second edition of Henry Thornton Wharton's *Sappho: Memoir, Text, Selected Renderings, and a Literal Translation* (London: John Lane, 1887). The citations of Shakespeare follow the 'Through Line Numbers' method adopted by David Bevington in his third edition of the *Complete Works of Shakespeare,* first published in 1951 by Scott, Foresman and Company in Glenview, Illinois. The quotations from John Webster's Italian tragedies are taken from *John Webster: Three Plays,* edited by D. C. Gunby and published in Harmondsworth, Middlesex, in 1972 by Penguin Books.

 I must acknowledge two places in which I have tampered with Eddison's prose. Eddison appended both *Mistress of Mistresses* and *A Fish Dinner in Memison* with a brief note in which he discussed the pronunciation of Zimiamvian names, thanked those who had helped him, and gave citations to some of the sources he quoted directly. I have incorporated Eddison's citations into my own textual notes. I combined Eddison's two paragraphs on pronunciation, and they appear near the front of *Zimiamvia* as a 'Prefatory Note on the Pronunciation of Names.' And I placed Eddison's paragraphs of thanks on the dedication pages of their respective volumes. Those desiring to see the original notes may consult the first American editions published by E. P. Dutton in 1935 and 1941.

P. E. Thomas

VOLUME ONE:
MISTRESS OF MISTRESSES

MM: **The Overture**

1. sea eagle's eyrie: The Overture is set in Lessingham's Digermulen Castle that towers from the eastern cliffs of the Raftsund (see note 2) north of the village of Digermulen on the island of Hinnoy, the southernmost island of the Vesteralen, a northeastern extension of the Lofoten Islands that stand off the northwest coast of Norway. The Lofoton chain extends about 90 miles long and is separated from mainland Norway (the region called Halogaland) by the Vestfjord, which broadens to about fifty miles at its widest span. Four main islands make up the Lofotens: Austvagoy, Vestvagoy, Moskenesoy, and Flakstadoy. The Lofotens are distinguished by smooth rock walls that drop precipitously to the sea, sometimes from heights of more than 3,000 feet. Fierce, ravenous white-tailed eagles inhabit these islands and often make their nests, or eyries, in the sheer granite cliffs above the fjords. See notes 2, 5, and 6.

2. Raftsund: This deep and narrow sea channel, walled by steep gray cliffs, separates Austvagoy, the northernmost island of the Lofoten chain, from Hinnoy, the southernmost island of the Vesteralen chain.

3. Samarkand: a city in Tadzhikistan, north of Afghanistan.

4. latoun or orichalc: Latoun (latten) is a mixed metal of a yellow color in thin sheets. Orichalc is a yellow ore or an alloy of copper. Both metals resemble brass.

5. Troldtinder: This 3,429-foot peak stands among a quartet of granite peaks on Austvagoy island. From north to south, the mountains are Store, Jaegervandstind, Trolltind, and Stortind.

6. Rulten: ERE's description of this small but magnificent mountain is accurate: it is 3,400 feet high, and it has a triple peak with two curling ridges descending like ears from the northern and southern sides of the peaks down to the sea.

7. Beckford's Fonthill: William Beckford (1759–1844) nourished the idea of living a secluded life of barbaric splendor in a gothic tower. In 1796 he employed his extreme wealth to realize his romantic dreams on the hill of Stop's Beacon in Wiltshire. The building of Fonthill lasted twenty-two years, but in December 1825, frightening cracks appeared in the lower walls of the great tower, and the structure began to sink before it burst and tumbled with an earth-shaking crash and a sun-obscuring dust cloud on December 21. Upon hearing the news, Beckford, who was traveling in Europe at the time, remarked with true panache that he only wished he had seen the fall. (Brian Fothergill, *Beckford of Fonthill* [London: Faber & Faber, 1979], 227, 255).

8. a kind of nothingness: ERE had a passionate fondness for John Webster's *The Duchess of Malfi* (published in 1623). This phrase suggests some of Bosola's final lines. This unfortunate man, spurred to violence by his own shame for having helped to betray and murder the Duchess through the direction of her brothers, becomes an instrument of retribution as he acts to knit up his tattered honor by killing the brethren. Fatally wounded, Bosola speaks jaw-clenched hatred to the Cardinal, the Duchess of Malfi's older brother:

> I do glory
> That thou, which stood'st like a huge pyramid
> Begun upon a large and ample base,
> Shalt end in a little point, a kind of nothing. (V: v: 76–79)

ERE does not make this allusion to suggest that the narrator has any of the hatred for Edward Lessingham that Bosola has for the Duchess's brother. Nevertheless, something of the abject wretchedness of Bosola's tone rings in the speaker's words because he finds that contemplating Lessingham's death tempts him to believe that life concludes in meaninglessness.

9. Landegode . . . into the open Westfirth: Edward Lessingham and his friend, the narrator, sailed from Bodo and steered north into the Westfirth (Vestfjord) after rounding Landegode, a small island south of the Lofotens and closer to mainland Norway.

10. The sea-board of Demonland: The Zimiamvian novels contain many allusions that form a dark chain mistily connecting them to *WO*. In the Induction of *WO*, in a chariot pulled by a hippogriff (see note 15), Lessingham travels to the planet Mercury. Accompanied by his guide, a footless martlet with eyes shining like stars, Lessingham travels over the Mercurial lands like a ghost 'impalpable and invisible' (*WO*, 6). The words Lessingham speaks while gazing upon the Lofotens suggest a passage in *WO* in which Lord Juss, standing aboard his homeward bound ship, gazes 'in the thunder-smoke of dawn' upon the coast of Demonland, and they also suggest that perhaps Lessingham stood unseen with Juss (*WO*, 97).

11. Hellas: The ancient Greeks called themselves Hellenes and their land Hellas.

12. Stir's "Shall the earth-lice be my bane, the sons of Grim Kogur?": ERE quotes Eirikr Magnusson's and William Morris's translation of a passage in *Landnamabok* ('the book of land-takings,' a 12th century Icelandic text) that tells the conversation between Liot the Sage and a poet named Guest Oddleifsson. Guest had the power of prophesy, so Liot asks him about his own fate:

'What will be the cause of my death?' Guest said he might not see his fate, but bade him see that he stood well with his neighbours. Asked Liot: 'What? will the earth-lice, the sons of Grim Kogr (Bantling), be my bane then?' 'Hard bites a hungry louse,' quoth Guest. (Eirikr Magnusson and William Morris, *The Saga Library*, vol. 1 [London: Bernard Quaritch, 1891], xiii–xiv)

Liot had quarreled over property boundaries with his neighbor Grim Kogr, and 'he held Grim guilty of trespass, and so they had but few dealings together.' Liot calls Grim's sons earth-lice because they were 'little men and small,' and because he held them in small regard. I do not know why ERE attributed this line to a man named "Stir"; it seems to be a simple mistake: perhaps ERE was thinking of Stirla Thordarson, the Icelandic historian who revised the *Landnamabok*.

13. Señorita Aspasia del Rio Amargo: Plutarch mentions two women named Aspasia. The more famous Aspasia was the lover of Pericles. Because this Aspasia was so renowned, Cyrus the Great (founder of the Persian dynasty) gave her name to his favorite concubine. Both women have considerable personal power: strength of will, intelligence, and physical magnetism. (See Plutarch's *Lives of the Noble Greeks and Romans*, trans. John Dryden [New York: The Modern Library, 1932] 200–201, 1267). These qualities, combined with the dubious reputation of the Periclean Aspasia, made them delightful to ERE, who admired such heroines: see notes 3–17 to Chapter XXII of *MM*. Aspasia's title means 'from the bitter river,' and so it associates her either with the river Styx, the river of deadly hatred in the Roman lower world, or with the river Acheron, the river of grief and mourning in the Roman lower world.

14. Swinburne: ERE admired Algernon Charles Swinburne enough to purchase, volume by volume between 1902 and 1914, the Chatto & Windus nineteen-volume set of his complete works. See note 26 below.

15. the great golden hippogriff: Ariosto, the great sixteenth-century Italian poet of the romantic epic *Orlando Furioso*, first used the word *ippogrifo* to label a combination of the horse and the griffin: see Canto IV, stanza 18. ERE's idea of the hippogriff differs slightly from Ariosto's description: it borrows its head from the horse rather than from the eagle.

The reference to Lessingham's bed is the second misty link in the chain connecting the Zimiamvian novels to *WO*. The hippogriff is the symbol of Demonland. The three thrones in Lord Juss's castle employ the symbol: 'At the end of the hall upon a dais stood three high seats, the arms of each composed of two hippogriffs wrought in gold, with wings spread, and the legs of the seats the legs of the hippogriffs' (*WO*, 6). The castle of Lord Brandoch Daha prominently displays hippogriffs: 'The towers and gatehouse were of white onyx like the castle itself, and on either hand before the gate was a colossal marble hippogriff . . .' (*WO*, 102). It is fitting that Lessingham should use the symbol for the posts of his bed in Digermulen Castle, for when he journeyed to

Demonland he and the martlet were 'as two dreams walking,' and perhaps Lessingham relives his journeys while asleep in his hippogriff-bed.
16. We are sure of nothing . . . he might avail to bathe once: Herakleitos, or Heraclitus, was born in Ephesus (south of modern Izmir on the coast of modern Turkey) and probably lived between 521 and 487 B.C. His reputation characterizes him as a reclusive man contemptuous of his fellow Ephesians. Plato summed up Heraclitus' beliefs as the doctrine of universal flux, *panta rhei* ('all things flow'—see Plato's dialogue *Cratylus*), and the reference made by Lessingham's friend epitomizes this belief. It is the most famous of the Heraclitean fragments and comes to us through Plutarch:

> According to Heraclitus one cannot step twice into the same river, nor can one grasp any mortal substance in a stable condition, but by the intensity and the rapidity of change it scatters and again gathers. Or rather, not again nor later but at the same time it forms and dissolves, and approaches and departs.
> (Charles H. Kahn, *The Art and Thought of Heraclitus: An Edition of the Fragments with Translation and Commentary* [Cambridge: Cambridge University Press, 1979], 168–69)

The philosopher who 'rebuked' Heraclitus was Cratylus, one of his fifth-century followers and a friend of Plato; he said that because the man himself changes even as he steps, the man cannot step into the river even once. Though this may be true, the slightly askew paraphrasing by Lessingham's friend makes a better joke.
17. Ici . . . du monde: 'Here lies Clarimonde in death, / She was, during her lifetime, / the most beautiful woman in the world' (Théophile Gautier, *La Morte Amoureuse*).
18. the ambrosial darknesses of his great black beard: ERE has in mind the bearded figures in sculptures of ancient Akkad, Assyria, and Babylon. ERE believed strongly in the beauty of the beard, and in 1930 he descried his views in an imaginative, unpublished essay called 'A Night-Piece on Hair':

> In England today the fashion of shaving is so nearly universal that you may go about for months and years without seeing a natural beard. Between the native beauty of a great beard that never was touched by razor (here I stroked my hand down the soft Assyrian blackness of my own) and the harsh stiff trimmed beards, and these as a rule, too, old men's beards, of today, there is as much difference as between the stately elm and its poor limb-lopped brothers in Kensington Gardens. So that the beard has become, from the chief ornament of manhood, the badge of a doddering age grown too idle to use the razor; and that 'bloom of youth,' the soft young growth of the beard on a young man's cheek that the Greeks so

much delighted in, is, in this country, as extinct as the osprey or the bustard.
(Ms. Eng. Misc. c. 456, fols. 74–84, Bodleian Library, Oxford)

ERE, within his narrative persona, identifies himself with the great bearded sculptures of the Assyrians that he so admired. All of the Zimiamvian heroes wear beards, and only villains like Derxis of Akkama go about clean shaven.

19. It was Easter time . . . instead of owls: ERE's geographical description in the opening section of this lengthy paragraph has precision springing from his knowledge gained through many years of fell walking in the English Lake District. The church that Lessingham's friend visits was famous locally, and it was described in 1926 in a fellwalkers' guidebook that ERE may have used:

> There is a restful calm about Mardale Chapel—an interesting little building nestling amid splendid old yews. Though small, as befits the valley, it is complete, and has every appearance of being well cared for. The door is always on the latch. The registers date from 1684 . . . The massive oak beams which support the roof are trunks of large trees, rough-hewn into shape. All this beauty and restfulness may, however, ere long be ruined by the operations of the Manchester Waterworks.
>
> (*A Pictorial and Descriptive Guide to the English Lakes,*
> [London: Ward, Lock and Co., 1926] 184).

The sentences describing this building certainly match the facts of the Ward-Lock guidebook, and they testify that ERE probably had visited this little church. In the 1930s the Manchester Waterworks dammed up the northern end of Haweswater to make it a reservoir, and in the process the Corporation condemned the village of Mardale Green to a watery grave. Since this little church now does indeed have 'fishes in its yew-trees instead of owls,' ERE's words comprise a fitting epitaph to its beauty destroyed. Since the drowning of the village occurred while ERE was composing *MM,* this contemporary event was surely in his thoughts and probably motivated him to place this tribute to the church in the mouth of his narrator. The buildings of the village are aquariums to this day, although some of the rooftops have twice reappeared above the water: in 1940 and in the dry summer of 1987 when the Haweswater level fell.

20. the strange ring he wore on the middle finger: ERE uses this motif to suggest relationships and connections between his characters. This ring has the shape of an *ouroboros,* a dragon biting its tail, and the inset ruby is the beast's head. The first mentioning of such a ring occurs on page 78 of *WO:* King Gorice XII, a sorcerer king, wears such a ring. In Zimiamvia, King Mezentius and Lord Lessingham (see note 4 to Chapter I of *MM*) wear *ouroboros* rings (850, 182). On page 433, we learn that the ring referred to here was Mary's wedding present to Edward Lessingham. (Mary Scarnside is introduced on page 15.)

21. Cesare Borgia or Gonsalvo di Cordova: The dazzling and disgusting, admirable and hateful, magnanimous and malicious, great and evil Cesare Borgia was the bastard of Rodrigo Borgia, the Pope Alexander VI, and the inspiration of Machiavelli for his famous treatise, *The Prince*. Gonsalvo Fernandez de Cordova (1453–1515) was a Spaniard and one of the greatest generals the world has known. He grew up in the house of Don Alphonso, brother to King Ferdinand. Ten years of military service in the conquest of Granada educated Gonsalvo in the arts of war, and so Queen Isabella chose him to lead a Spanish force in support of the Aragonese house of Naples and against Charles VIII of France: 'She knew that he possessed the qualities essential to success in a new and difficult enterprise,—courage, constancy, singular prudence, dexterity in negotiation, and inexhaustible fertility of resource' (W. H. Prescott, *History of the Reign of Ferdinand and Isabella the Catholic*, 3rd ed., ed. John Foster Kirk [London: Swan Sonnenschein, Lowrey & Co., 1888], 399). Gonsalvo's success in Italy earned him the governorship of Naples and the universal title of the Great Captain. Gonsalvo served Ferdinand and Isabella faithfully through his long career. His long military career glittered with successful campaigns against the French and the Turks, and these 'have made the name of Gonsalvo as familiar to his countrymen as that of the Cid' (Prescott, 689). It is ironic that Lessingham's friend speaks of Gonsalvo in the same breath as Cesare Borgia, because one of the only blemishes on Gonsalvo's honesty is his treatment of Borgia: when his father Pope Alexander VI died, Cesare lost power in Italy, but under solemn pledges from Gonsalvo, he was given safe conduct to Naples; yet, once there, Gonsalvo, by the commands of Ferdinand, arrested Cesare and sent him to Castile as a prisoner.

22. King Eric Bloodaxe in York: ERE calls Harald Hairfair (see note 23) 'that Charlemagne of the north.' James Goldman, in the play *The Lion in Winter*, compares the English King Henry II to Charlemagne when Henry, in bitter anger, sums up his life:

> My life, when it is written, will read better than it lived. Henry Fitzempress, first Plantagenet, a king at twenty-one. He led men well, he worked for justice when he could, and ruled, for thirty years, a state as great as Charlemagne's.

Both comparisons hold truth in several aspects, and one of them is that Harald, Charlemagne, and Henry II left their kingdoms to sons who could not maintain them in their full sway and magnitude. Although Eric, or Eirik, inherited his father's valiance, resourcefulness, and strength of will, he never achieved his father's success as a ruler. Eirik's reputation suffered in Icelandic tradition: *ES* characterizes him as the intemperate king of York, the enemy of Egil, and a man whose wife's personality and stature eclipsed his own. ERE describes Eirik's history in a note:

This best loved son of King Harald Hairfair succeeded him, as king of Norway, but after a stormy year or two was forced to flee the land, yielding the throne to his half-brother Hakon. Eric's mother was a Danish princess, Ragnhild, daughter of the King of Jutland. His career after he was turned out of Norway, and the date of his death (and indeed that of his turning out), are not exactly known. This much is certain, that he was a great sea-king in his youth, and also in later life: that he was sometime king in York (this is confirmed from English sources): that he was finally driven out of Northumberland, and fell (probably in 954) in a great battle in an attempt to win back that kingdom. He was 'a big man and a fair; strong and most stout of heart; a mighty warrior and victorious, fierce of mind, grim, unkind, and of few words' (quoted from the 'Saga of Harald Hairfair' in the *Heimskringla*, vol. 4–6 of *The Saga Library*, trans. Eirikr Magnusson and William Morris). 'A great soldier but a poor statesman, he was steered, like Ahab and Macbeth, by the masculine will of his wife. The rich inheritance, painfully created by his father's genius during so many years, of an undivided realm of Norway, survived for Eric but a few months, and then fell to pieces in his rude and unskillful hands.' (*ES*, 270–71)

23. Harald Hairfair: The life of this great King of Norway was, says Professor Gwyn Jones, 'heavily embroidered with folktale and legend' (*A History of the Vikings* [Oxford: Oxford University Press, 1968] 86). The most prominent facts of his life are these: he was born between 865 and 870 to Ragnhild, a princess of Ringerike (a province northwest of Oslo) and to King Halfdan the Black Gudrodarson of Vestfold (the ancient name for the region surrounding Oslo and stretching north of Oslofjord); Harald became king of the Vestfold at age ten upon the death of his father; his first years as king were spent in repelling and subjugating his father's enemies who saw him as a weak boy king and who sought to take the Vestfold from him, but with the help of his mother's brother Guthorm, Harald managed to win several battles, to slay some kings, and to conquer other provinces north of Oslofjord; between 885 and 900 he won the largest and most important battle of his life, a great sea-battle against many defiant Norwegian aristocrats in Hafrsfjord; in the years after Hafrsfjord, Harald became, if not king of all Norway, the most powerful and expansive king in Norway, and his reign lasted more than fifty years. The chief account of Harald's life appears in a saga bearing his name and contained in Snorri Sturluson's *Heimskringla*. (Literally, the title means 'the orb of the world,' and, as its title suggests, it is a work of considerable scope: it is an enormous sagalike chronicle of the lives of Norwegian kings, beginning in the Norse mythological age and continuing to 1177 in the reign of King Magnus Erlingsson: this book, written about 1225, was Snorri's greatest work, and it won him fame, for no other Icelandic historian ever attempted such a huge work; nevertheless, modern historians are skeptical of its fictional elements.) King Harald also appears in *ES*, and in his note on Harald, ERE quotes from William Morris's translation of Snorri's *Heimskringla* (in vol. 3 of *The Saga Library* of Eirikr Magnusson and William Morris [London: Bernard Quaritch, 1893], 93–95, 117):

> It is told that he wooed a maiden 'exceeding fair, and withal some-what high-minded,' who gave him this answer: 'I will not waste my maidenhood for the taking to husband of a king who has no more realm to rule over than a few Folks. But that seems to me wonder-ful,' she says, 'that there be no king who will so make Norway his own and be sole lord over it, like as hath King Gorm in Denmark, or Eric in Upsala.' Harald thereupon swore an oath never to let cut his hair or comb it till he should be sole King over all Norway. That oath he performed with the help of his mother's brother, Duke Gutthorm, and married the lady. And when he had gotten to him all the land, 'King Harald took a bath and then he let his hair be combed, and then Earl Rognvald sheared it. And heretofore it had been unshorn and uncombed for ten winters. Aforetime he had been called Shockhead [Lufa], but now Earl Rognvald gave him a by-name, and called him Harald Hairfair, and all said who saw him that that was most soothly named, for he had both plenteous hair and goodly.' (*ES*, 256)

ES tells of Harald's policy to ensure unity once 'he had gotten to him all the land':

> King Harald was much heedful, when he had gotten to him those folk-lands that were new-come under his dominion, of the landed men and powerful bonders and of all those that he had doubt of, that some uprising was to be looked for from them. Then let he every one of them do one of two things: become his servants, or get them gone out of the land; and, for a third choice, suffer hard conditions, or lose their lives else; and some were maimed either of hand or foot. King Harald gat to him in every folk-land all odal rights [i.e., family rights of land ownership] and all land, dwelt and undwelt, as well as the sea and the waters; and all dwellers therein should be his tenants, be it they that worked in the forests, or salt-carles, or all manner of hunters or fishers, both by sea and by land, these were all now made tributary unto him. But from this enslave-ment fled many men away out of the land, and then began to be settled many waste parts far and wide, both east in Jamtaland and Helsingland and in the west countries: the South-isles, Dublin's shire in Ireland, Normandy in Valland, Caithness in Scotland, the Orkneys and Shetland, the Faereys. And in that time was found Iceland. (*ES*, 6)

24. *History of Frederick II*: The quoted sentence is from the pen of Dr. M. Schipa in the *Cambridge Mediaeval History*. Edward Lessingham's

Frederick II was published in an extremely limited edition; it is now out of print, and many scholars and bibliophiles scramble to obtain it.

Frederick II of Hohenstaufen (1194–1250) was the son of Emperor Henry VI and Constance of Naples. He was named King of Germany at age two and became King of Sicily at age four, when his parents died. He lived under the Sicilian regency of Pope Innocent III until 1208. He married Constance of Aragon in 1209. In 1211, the German princes deposed Otto IV and made Frederick King of Germany, for the second time, and he was crowned in 1215. When Otto died in 1218, Frederick became the unopposed ruler of Germany, and in 1220, at the invitation of Pope Honorius III, he was crowned Holy Roman Emperor.

He was a statesman who made his mark as a legislator for Sicily and who, alone among thirteenth-century sovereigns, tried to define the relationship between the papacy and the Holy Roman Empire and to unify Germany and Italy under the dual administration of Pope and Emperor. He was a strategist who accomplished far more through diplomacy than through warfare. He spoke six languages. He promoted scholarly pursuits in all fields, both by bringing scholars to his court and by conducting correspondence with them in all parts of Europe and in the Near East. He encouraged poets and artists, and, two hundred years before the Renaissance, he took artistic inspiration from classical models. King, statesman, diplomat, legislator, soldier, scholar, scientist, poet, architect, linguist: Frederick was a man of incomparable ability. He was capable, like many princes and Popes of his age, of great generosity and great cruelty, of great virtue and great sin, but in the sheer number of his accomplishments he is unique and peerless. Some called him a bloodthirsty tyrant, and some called him the antichrist, but more called him *stupor mundi* (the wonder of the world) or *immutator mundi* (the transformer of the world). Modern historians have not skeptically or cynically disregarded these labels. E. A. Freeman claims that 'it is probable there never lived a human being with greater natural gifts,' and Thomas Curtis Van Cleve, echoing Freeman, calls Frederick a man of 'transcendent superiority' and says that he 'has no counterpart or near counterpart in history' (*The Emperor Frederick II of Hohenstaufen* [Oxford: Clarendon Press, 1972], 531, 535, 539). Lionel Allshorn boldly says 'in his tremendous intellect, in his cultured and enquiring mind, in his broad spirit of toleration, he towered far above his contemporaries . . . in genius Frederick has had no superior among the princes of the world' (*Stupor Mundi* [London: Martin Secker, 1912], 285).

25. in East Africa: Edward Lessingham fought in German East Africa (the area in which Rwanda, Burundi, and Tanzania now exist) in the last months of 1916. He was part of a British force that invaded from the south in Nyasaland and attempted to squeeze the brilliant German commander, Paul von Lettow-Vorbeck, between itself and a Belgian army invading from the west and a huge army of British and colonial troops invading from the north under the South African commander J. C. Smuts.

26. Swinburne's *Dolores*: In 1866, a bold publisher named John Camden Hotten produced Swinburne's first series of *Poems and Ballads*. The volume was sharply criticized because of its supposed tone of moral dissolution, its sensuous passions, its strong anti-Christian declarations, and its images of dark and painful sexuality. 'Dolores' is one of the most notorious poems in the volume: this pagan, passionate poem of obsessive and sadistic eroticism raised some eyebrows, speeded some pulse rates, and swelled some tightly collared necks. Swinburne calls Dolores 'our Lady of Pain' and identifies her parents as Libitina, an Italian goddess who became identified with Proserpina, and Priapus, a minor fertility god usually sculpted with an erect phallus (stanza 7). Swinburne makes Dolores a worshipful femme fatale when he writes that 'There are sins it may be to discover' (stanza 10) through her and that kissing her lips leads to these sweet sins: 'Men touch them, and change in a trice / The lilies and langours of virtue / For the raptures and roses of vice' (stanza 15). Although she brings suffering, Swinburne prefers worshipping Dolores to following the repressive doctrines of the Christian tradition: 'What ailed us, O Gods, to desert you / For creeds that refuse and restrain? / Come down and redeem us from virtue, / Our lady of Pain' (stanza 35). Lessingham's friend says that the wisdom that comes with years dampens his enthusiasm for this poem, and yet some verses anticipate what he calls the 'drab, comfortless, inglorious sinking into not-being':

> For the crown of our life as it closes
> Is darkness, the fruit thereof dust;
> No thorns go as deep as a rose's,
> And love is more cruel than lust.
> Time turns the old days to derision,
> Our loves into corpses or wives;
> And marriage and death and division
> Make barren our lives. (stanza 20)

27. Pater's essay about Mona Lisa: Walter Horatio Pater (1839–94) was a fellow of Brasenose College, Oxford; he was a friend of Swinburne and Dante Gabriel Rossetti, and he was hailed by Oscar Wilde for his writings on beauty and aesthetics. Pater achieved fame in 1873 with his book of essays called *The Renaissance: Studies in Art and Poetry*. The book included an essay, 'Leonardo Da Vinci,' which had been published in 1869, and which surveyed Da Vinci's major works. The most famous section of the essay treats the portrait of *Mona Lisa* or *La Gioconda*:

We all know the face and hands of the figure, set in its marble chair, in that cirque of fantastic rocks, as in some faint light under sea. Perhaps of all ancient pictures time has chilled it least. As often happens with works in which invention seems to reach its limit, there is an element in it given to, not invented by, the master. In that inestimable folio of drawings, once in the possession of Vasari, were certain designs by Verrocchio, faces of such impressive beauty

that Leonardo in his boyhood copied them many times. It is hard not to connect with these designs of the elder, by-past master, as with its germinal principle, the unfathomable smile, always with a touch of something sinister in it, which plays over all Leonardo's work. Besides, the picture is a portrait. From childhood we see this image defining itself on the fabric of his dreams; and but for express historical testimony, we might fancy that this was but his ideal lady, embodied and beheld at last. . . . Hers is the head upon which all 'the ends of the world are come,' and the eyelids are a little weary. It is a beauty wrought out from within upon the flesh, the deposit, little cell by cell, of strange thought and fantastic reveries and exquisite passions. Set it for a moment beside one of those white Greek goddesses or beautiful women of antiquity, and how would they be troubled by this beauty, into which the soul with all its maladies has passed? All the thoughts and experience of the world have etched and moulded there, in that which they have of power to refine and make expressive the outward form, the animalism of Greece, the lust of Rome, the reverie of the middle age with its spiritual ambition and imaginative loves, the return of the Pagan world, the sins of the Borgias. She is older than the rocks among which she sits; like the vampire, she has been dead many times, and learned the secrets of the grave; and has been a diver in deep seas, and keeps their fallen day about her; and trafficked for strange webs with Eastern merchants; and, as Leda, was the mother of Helen of Troy, and, as Saint Anne, the mother of Mary; and all this has been to her but as the sound of lyres and flutes, and lives only in the delicacy with which it has moulded the changing lineaments, and tinged the eyelids and the hands.
(Walter Pater, *The Renaissance: Studies in Art and Poetry,* 2nd ed., revised [London: Macmillan and Co., 1877], 133–36)

When you finish reading *Zimiamvia,* come back to this quotation, for Pater here suggests and echoes many of ERE's motifs and themes: the sinister but alluring smile of Mary and Fiorinda, the ideal woman embodied in flesh, a goddess incarnate, characters with traits from the traditions of Greece and Rome and medieval Europe and the pagan North and Renaissance Europe, reincarnation, supernatural female power, and timeless beauty. Also, part of ERE's Zimiamvian myth is that men and women partake of the characteristics of both Zeus and Aphrodite, that their personalities are a mixture of the archetypal masculine and feminine traits, and the unnamed narrator thinks of Pater's essay and Mona Lisa while looking at Lessingham.

28. Kapaneus posturing before Thebes: Aeschylus' *The Seven Against Thebes* (first produced in 467 B.C.) tells the tragic end of the two sons of Oedipus, Eteocles and Polyneices. After the death of the self-immolated Oedipus, his sons agree to rule Thebes in alternating administrations. Eteocles rules first, but when his term closes, he refuses to relinquish authority and with bold-faced power sweeps his brother from his sight

and into banishment. When the play begins, Polyneices is leading an
Argive army against Thebes to take the city from his usurping brother.
Kapaneus is one of seven Argive heroes who join Polyneices. The Messenger, speaking to Eteocles, describes Kapaneus as 'a giant . . . And
more than human in his arrogance':

> May god forefend his threat against our walls!
> 'God willing, or unwilling'—such his vaunt—
> 'I will lay waste this city; Pallas' self,
> Zeus' warrior maid, although she swoop to earth
> And plant her in my path, shall stay me not.' (lines 427–31)

Eteocles then derides Kapaneus' foolish pride because, 'mortal though
he be, he strains his tongue / In folly's ecstacy, and casts aloft / High
swelling words against the ears of Zeus' (lines 441–43). (Aeschylus, *The
Seven Against Thebes*, trans. E.D.A. Morshead, in *The Complete Greek
Drama*, ed. Whitney J. Oates and Eugene O'Neill, Jr. [New York: Ran-
dom House, 1938], vol. 1, 100–101).

29. little Aias . . . against the lightning: According to Proclus, who
probably lived in the fifth century A.D., two of the lost poems of the
Trojan Cycle of Epics—poems by Arctinus of Miletus and Agias of
Troezen—tell the fate of Aias, son of Oileus of Lokris. During the siege
of Troy, Aias desecrates the temple of Athena while raping Cassandra,
who, in her resistance, clings to the statue of the goddess. His actions
offend both the gods and the Greeks. The Greeks want to kill him, and
he avoids being stoned to death by taking refuge in the temple he has
defiled. Athena shows him no mercy; rather, she asks Poseidon to help
her destroy the Greeks as they sail from Troy. The two gods wreck the
fleet upon the rocks of Capherides in southern Euboea, and Athena, in
her vengeance, cleaves Aias with a thunderous levin-bolt. This Aias is
the 'lesser Aias' who fought at Troy: he is not huge Aias, the son of
Telemon.

30. the fabled unction of the Styx: According to Hesiod (eighth century B.C.), Styx was the first of the daughters of Oceanus to offer help to
Zeus in his proposed war against the Titanic gods (*Theogony*, lines 383–
403). In Homer, Zeus honors Styx by making her the 'fearful oath-river'
(*Iliad* 2:755), and the gods use her waters like a ritual unction for swearing solemn and inviolable oaths.

31. Lady Mary Scarnside: Mary makes her first appearance in the Induction to *WO*. Mary does not appear in person in *MM*, but she is a
major character in *FD*.

32. their lovely old house in Wasdale: This is yet another reference to
the Induction to *WO*, which begins with two paragraphs describing the
house, its garden, and its setting in the valley of the Wast Water.

33. *sub specie aeternitatis*: according to the form of eternity.

34. Paraguay: ERE is nowhere precise about Edward Lessingham's in-
volvement in Paraguayan affairs, but probably he participated in some
phase of the Chaco War (1932–38), a bloody dispute over boundaries in

the Chaco region between Bolivia and Paraguay, or he may have tried to help stabilize Paraguay during the violent political struggles that followed the Chaco War.

35. the face of an Ozymandias: Lessingham's friend alludes to Shelley's famous sonnet in this sentence, but which lines does he have in mind? If Lessingham's friend truly means to compare Lessingham's face to that of the fractured statue of Ozymandias, then surely the comparison produces a rather left-handed compliment, for the statue's broken face wears a frown, has 'a wrinkled lip,' and a 'sneer of cold command,' and the sculptor carved these features both in imitation and in mockery of the tyrant. Perhaps the allusion lies elsewhere. The 'conception of annihilation,' the subject of the previous two paragraphs, echoes the conclusion of this ironic sonnet, for the pedestal of the statue tells the mighty ones of earth to observe the kingdom of Ozymandias and then despair of achieving more than he, and yet 'Round the decay / of that colossal wreck, boundless and bare / The lone and level sands stretch far away.' But if this, oblivion, is the basis of the allusion, more sarcasm results because then Lessingham's friend indirectly mocks his catalog, two pages earlier, of the lasting monuments to Lessingham's genius.

36. *Aphrodite Ourania:* Aphrodite was the child of Ouranos (Uranus).

37. Our Lady of Paphos: Untraceable legend relates that the goddess Aphrodite rose from the surf-foam and came ashore at Paphos on the island of Cyprus. One of the earliest tellings of this legend appears in Hesiod's *Theogony* (eighth century B.C.). The earth-goddess Gaia, child of Chaos, gives birth to Ouranos (Uranus), the god of the sky and stars, and he becomes her lover. They produce many divine children who become the Titans. Some malevolent impulse makes Ouranos imprison some of his children; in Hesiod's version, he holds them in the womb of Gaia and causes her great pain. Because of this, enmity develops between Ouranos and his youngest son, Kronos (Saturn). Gaia later encourages Kronos to avenge himself on his father, and one night when Ouranos comes to lie with Gaia, Kronos sneaks up to him and, with a knife made of flint, dismembers the godlike virile member of Ouranos, then throws this pillar of the Titan gods into the Mediterranean. Hesiod's version of the goddess's birth from the severed organ is worth reading in full because ERE makes many allusions to this myth in *Zimiamvia*:

> But the members themselves, when Kronos
>   had lopped them with the flint,
> he threw from the mainland
>   into the great wash of the sea water
> and they drifted a great while
>   on the open sea, and there spread
> a circle of white foam
>   from the immortal flesh, and in it
> grew a girl, whose course first took her

> to holy Kythera,
> and from there she afterward made her way
>   to sea-washed Cyprus
> and stepped ashore, a modest lovely Goddess,
>   and about her
> light and slender feet the grass grew,
>   and the gods call her
> Aphrodite, and men do too,
>   and the aphro-foam-born
> goddess, and garlanded Kytheraia,
>   because from the seafoam
> she grew, and Kytheria because she had gone
>   to Kythera,
> and Kyprogeneia, because she came forth
>   from wave-washed Cyprus,
> and Philommedea, because she appeared
>   from medea, members.
>
>> (trans. Richmond Lattimore in *Great Classical Myths*,
>> ed. F.R.B. Godolphin [New York: Random House,
>> 1964], 6–7).

38. purfled: having an ornamental border; bordered with embroidery.

39. mantichores: a mythic beast who appears in Pliny's catalogs (1: 206); it has the head of a man, the body of a lion, the quills of a porcupine, and the tail of a scorpion. ERE was fond of the mantichore, and one of the most vivid passages in *WO* narrates Lord Juss's fight with one: see *WO*, 157–58.

40. Parian: a white marble highly valued by the ancient Greeks.

41. Pheidias: With the support and patronage of his friend Pericles, Pheidias made many sculptures for Athens. He produced three statues of Athena for the Acropolis, and he probably designed and supervised the relief carving of the frieze on the Parthenon.

42. Nepenthe, Elysian Amaranth: According to Greek myths, these flowers bloomed on the blessed isles of Elysium. A drug obtained from Nepenthe had the happy property of causing its user to forget sorrow. Amaranth is a fadeless flower.

43. . . . Runs: ERE borrows the first two lines of this quatrain from Sappho's 'Ode to Anactoria.' See note 9 to Chapter VI of *FD*.

44. The fabled land . . . nor yet oppressors: Here is yet another link in the shrouded chain linking *Zimiamvia* to *WO*. This passage ERE has lifted almost verbatim from the ending of Chapter XII of *WO*: see *WO*, 167.

45. Praxiteles' Knidian Aphrodite: This work was the first life-size, freely standing female nude sculpture in Greek art. Praxiteles (fourth century B.C.) made this, his most famous sculpture, for the Knidians. The body of the goddess twists, and she is shown lifting her left foot slightly as she enters her bath: these natural movements, which the stone catches in a poised moment, show Praxiteles' complete perception of the minute details of surface anatomy, and they set this sculpture apart from much of the sculpture of the fifth century B.C. Unfortunately, it exists only in Roman imitations. The best one can be seen in the Vatican Museum.

MM: Chapter I

1. war between them: Amaury speaks of the threats of war that had grown between King Mezentius and Horius Parry, the King's Vicar in Rerek. ERE dilates on this matter in Chapters XXXI, XXXVII, and XXXVIII of *MG*.

2. he: Horius Parry, the Vicar of Rerek.

3. the son: King Styllis (758–777 AZC), heir of his father, King Mezentius.

4. Lessingham: There are two Lessinghams: the Englishman Edward Lessingham (1882–1973) of the Overture to *MM*, of the Earthly chapters of *FD*, and of the Praeludium to *MG;* and the Zimiamvian Lord Lessingham (752–779 AZC). Lord Lessingham's birth is narrated in Chapter XIX of *MG*. I cannot explain the connection between them without spoiling the story of *FD*.

5. my cousin: The Vicar of Rerek is Lessingham's cousin.

6. beck: absolute power or control.

7. chaffertalk: talk of trading, buying and selling.

8. to-morrow . . . beside Hornmere: The Vicar's meeting with King Styllis is set for April 23, 777 AZC.

9. Acheron: the river of grief in the Roman lower world.

MM: Chapter II

1. the lyre that shook Mitylene: a reference to Sappho's poetic voice.

2. Duke Barganax: Four short works of fiction that ERE wrote as a child in the 1890s are extant in the Bodleian collection. The name *Barganax* began as Harry Bumbleoax in a story called 'Poniard and Morning Star.' The story is narrated by a character named Sir Roderick von Blusoe, whose name is the origin of Goldry Bluszco in *WO,* and the story also contains ERE's early use of the name *Valero,* who exists as a knight named Sir Kenneth Valero: 'Bumbleoax swung his axe & Sir Kenneth his morning star, and they began to rain down blows until Harry Bumbleoax smote Valero a crashing blow on the helm, and he fell' (from Chapter VIII of the handwritten manuscript, Ms. Eng. Misc. e. 598/3, Bodleian Library, Oxford). See also note 2 to Chapter V and note 4 to Chapter XII of *MM*.

3. laugh all honesty out of fashion: ERE has lifted this line from John Webster, who stood second to Shakespeare in his admiration. The line occurs in an early scene of *The Duchess of Malfi* in which Antonio, the Duchess's steward, describes the Duchess's two brothers, the Duke and the Cardinal, to his friend Delio:

> The Duke there? a most perverse and turbulent nature;
> What appears in him mirth, is merely outside,
> If he laugh heartily, it is to laugh
> All honesty out of fashion. (I: ii: 94–97)

4. in *celarent* **. . .** *bokardo:* These terms are used in the branch of formal logic concerning syllogisms. *Celarent* refers to an chain of reasoning like this: x is not y, and y is z, so x is not z. *Barbara* is a term used to describe a chain of reasoning like this: All animals are mortal; all men are animals; all men are mortal. The Latin phrase *per accidens* means 'as it happens'; *bramantip* describes a chain of reasoning like this: x is y, and y is z, so x is z. *Bokardo* describes a chain of reasoning like this: Some x is not y; all x is z; some z is not y.

5. cachobon . . . smaragds: The first is an adjective referring to a polished gem in its natural, uncut state; the second is another name for an emerald.

6. choriambics: a poetic foot of four syllables in which the first and fourth are stressed and the second and third are unstressed.

7. Once more . . . ineluctable: Sappho, ERE's translation of fragment 40. Here is Wharton's literal translation: 'Now Love masters my limbs and shakes me, fatal creature, bitter sweet' (Wharton, 93).

MM: Chapter III

1. tesselated jet: black polished stones in a mosaic pattern.

2. chalcedony: a transparent or translucent quartz.

3. from the glades beyond Ravary: This is another unclear reference to the Mercury of *WO*. Ravary is a mountain valley containing a vast, many-armed tarn, and significantly, it is near the Gates of Zimiamvia. In Chapter XIV of *WO*, Queen Sophonisba, the foster child of the gods, leads the lords Juss and Brandoch Daha down through a cave in the mountain Koshtra Belorn, and when they pass out of the cave's mouth, they find themselves in bright sunlight beside the lake: see *WO*, 180–81. See also note 2 to Chapter IV of *MM*.

4. byrnies and greaves: The first term refers to chain-mail coverings for the upper body; the second refers to curved plates of armor designed to protect the shins.

5. that triple pillar of the great King's power: Six years earlier, in 772 AZC, Admiral Jeronimy, Earl Roder, and Chancellor Beroald were made Commissioners Regent for Meszria by King Mezentius, to exercise viceregal powers during any absence of the King. See Chapter XXVII of *MG*.

6. the kingly order of the hippogriff: This honor was conferred upon Jeronimy in 771 AZC, after the third war with Akkama. See Chapter XXVII of *MG*.

7. *ne obstes*: no obstruction.

8. go my own gate: follow my own way, course, method, or habit.

9. ballywekes herborowes: bailiwicks (regions placed under the authority of bailiffs, king's officers) and harbors.

10. out of all-ho: beyond all proper or moderate limits.

MM: Chapter IV

1. the beginnings of new light: April 26, 777 AZC.

2. Koshtra Belorn: This mountain is a sacred and holy place whose slopes are untrodden by any except the blessed. In *WO*, after the capture of Goldry Bluzco, Lord Juss had a true dream that told him to search for his brother by inquiring in Koshtra Belorn. Juss knows that this sacred mountain cannot be ascended by any except one who first proves himself worthy by climbing Koshtra Pivrarcha, the highest peak on Mercury, and by looking down upon Koshtra Belorn from that ice-crowned pinnacle. A little talking martlet greets Juss and Brandoch Daha during their ascent of Koshtra Pivrarcha and confirms Juss's wisdom: 'No foot may tread her, save of those blessed ones to whom the Gods gave leave ages ago, till they be come that the patient years await: men like unto Gods in beauty and in power, who of their own might and main, unholpen by magic arts, shall force a passage up to her silent snows' (*WO*, 152).

3. she seemed on the sudden grown taller . . . He might behold it and know it: Here ERE paraphrases Homer's 'Hymn to Aphrodite.' See Section I of the Introduction.

MM: Chapter V

1. lords in Rerek: See Chapter I of *MG*.

2. Horius Parry: This name originates in a story called 'Europe; or the Tale of Mr. William,' which ERE wrote early in the 1890s when he was about ten. Mr. William is 'a great General of Arms' who lives in Italy. The story begins when he meets the villains:

> There came forward an ugly little man, with a heavy sword of gold & black, who didn't even trouble to take his hands from behind his back, but sauntered up & gave an ugly little bow, & stared at Mr. William in a very rude way. 'This is my friend Horius-Pareye, Mr.

William' said Mr. Henry. 'How-ow-ow do-o-o yoo-o-o-o do-o-o' said
Horius-Pareye, & turned his back & walked away.
(Ms. Eng. Misc. e. 598/2, fols. 3–4, Bodleian Library, Oxford)

3. racket away a hundred crowns afore breakfast: Gabriel's disapprov-
ing words echo lines from John Webster's *The White Devil*. Duke Brachiano, while arguing with his wife Isabella and declaring himself divorced
from her, insults Isabella's brother, the Duke of Florence:

> Because your brother is the corpulent Duke,
> That is the great Duke, 'sdeath I shall not shortly
> racket away five hundred crowns at tennis,
> but it shall rest upon record. I scorn him
> like a shav'd Polack. (II: i: 180–84)

4. with some devilish pothecary stuff: Near the end of Webster's *The
White Devil*, the Count Lodovico, who loved Isabella, avenges himself on
Isabella's husband, Brachiano, for Brachiano's mistreatment and murder of her. After poisoning Brachiano, Lodovico and his assistant Gasparo torment Brachiano by whispering in his ear the names of the
poisons they have given to him:

Gasparo: Now there's mercury—
Lodovico: And copperas—
Gasparo: And quicksilver—
Lodovico: With other devilish pothecary stuff a-melting in your
            politic brains: dost hear? (V: iii: 161–65)

5. a bull of Nineveh: ERE has in mind the sculptures of ancient Akkad
and Sumer.

MM: Chapter VI

1. an evening of late May-time: May 21, 777 AZC; twenty-five days after
the events of Chapter V.
2. *Experimentum docet:* the experience teaches it.
3. These effects . . . would have it: The treble viol is a stringed instrument resembling the violin but having a slightly different shape and
six strings rather than four: the theorbo is a lute (a stringed instrument
having a long neck and a sounding box shaped like a halved pear) with
an extra set of bass strings running outside the fingering board: a canon
is a musical form in which two instruments play the same melody beginning at different times to produce counterpoint harmony: the hautboy
is the ancestor of the modern oboe; the dulcimer has a shallow trapezoi-
dal sounding box and several strings usually played by striking them
with hammers: the rebeck has a sounding box like a halved pear and
has three strings that are played with a bow: a ritornello is a recurrent
instrumental section, like a refrain in a song.

MM: **Chapter VII**

1. *allegretto scherzando:* music played delightfully in a moderately quick tempo.

2. that deadly Scythian queen who gave Cyrus his last deep drink of blood: Herodotus (480–425 B.C.) relates this story (Xenophon [fifth century B.C.] does not include it in *Cyropaedia*) of the death, in 529 B.C., of Cyrus the Great, the conqueror of Asia Minor and Babylon and the founder of the Persian Empire. Cyrus coveted the great plain north of the Araxes River and east of the Caspian Sea, so he decided to bring war into the land and to subdue its inhabitants, the Massagetae (*History* 1: 205–15):

> The king of the Massagetae was dead, and his wife had taken over the sovereignty; her name was Tomyris. To her Cyrus sent and would have wooed her—in a word—to be his wife. But Tomyris, who understood that it was not herself that he was wooing but the kingship of the Massagetae, said no to his approaches. After this, Cyrus, since he had gained nothing by craft, drove as far as the Araxes and now openly made a campaign against the Massagetae, building bridges over the river for the passage of his army and building towers on the rafts that were to carry his men over.
>
> As he labored over all this, Tomyris sent him a herald and said: 'King of the Medes, cease to be so eager to do what you are doing; for you cannot know whether, when accomplished, it will stand you in good stead. Give it over and rule over your own people, and endure to look upon us governing ours. Still, you will not follow this advice of mine, but will do anything rather than remain at rest.'

Queen Tomyris asks Cyrus to stop his bridge construction, and she suggests that either the Persians should withdraw and allow the Massagetae to cross the Araxes, or the Massagetae should withdraw and allow the Persians to cross the river. Cyrus decides to cross the Araxes into the land of the Massagetae and, after dispatching a message to Queen Tomyris, takes two-thirds of his army across, leaving behind the sick and wounded. Spargapises, the son of Tomyris, leads one-third of the Massagetae army against the Persians who had remained behind Cyrus, and after killing them, Spargapises and his soldiers feast and then sleep. The army of Cyrus returns and attacks the sleeping Massagetae army, and they capture Spargapises. Then Tomyris writes again to Cyrus:

> 'Cyrus, insatiate of blood, be not uplifted by this thing that has happened—that with this fruit of the vine . . . because with such a powerful drug you have overmastered my son by trickery and not by strength and fighting. Now, therefore, take this proposal from me, for I advise you well. Give back my son to me now and get out

of our country, paying no penalty, although you have done violence and insolence to one-third of the army of the Massagetae. If you do not so, I swear by the sun, the lord of the Massagetae, that, for all your insatiability of blood, I will give you your fill of it.'

Cyrus does not answer her. Upon awakening, Spargapises asks to be free from his bonds, and when he gains his movement, he kills himself. Herodotus says that the battle that followed was the most severe of all of the battles fought by barbarians, and Cyrus the Great, after twenty-nine years of ruling and empire, was killed. Tomyris makes good her words after the battle:

> Tomyris sought out his corpse among the Persian dead, and, when she found it, she filled a skin with human blood and fixed his head in the skin, and, insulting over the dead, she said: 'I am alive and conqueror, but you have destroyed me, all the same, by robbing me of my son by trickery. Now it is you and I; and I will give you your fill of blood, even as I threatened.'
>
> (Herodotus, *The History,* trans. David Grene, [Chicago: University of Chicago Press, 1988], 126–30).

Here ERE, or Lessingham, describes Tomyris as a 'Scythian Queen,' and although Herodotus says that the Massagetae and the Scythians wore similar clothing and lived in similar ways, he distinguishes them (see *History* 1: 215–16). The Scythians inhabited a region generally north of the Black Sea, while the Massagetae lived north and east of the Caspian Sea.

3. the world phenomenal or the world noumenal, *sub specie temporali* **or** *sub specie aeternitatis:* In philosophy, *phenomenal* and *noumenal* are opposed terms: if a thing may be perceived through the senses, it is phenomenal, and if a thing may be perceived only through intuition, it is noumenal. The Latin phrases are opposites too: 'according to the form of measured time' and 'according to the form of eternity.' Neither phrase translates clearly into English. Spinoza used *sub specie aeternitatis* in discussing the mind's ability to perceive the essence of a thing as it exists in substance both eternal and infinite. See note 9 to Chapter X of *MM.*

4. There is . . . upon the tree: Fiorinda seems to refer to *Le Roman de la Rose,* the thirteenth-century allegorical poem by the Frenchmen Guillaume de Lorris and Jean de Meun. Much of the poem concerns romantic love and the morality of behavior in love; hence Fiorinda's allusion.

5. the song . . . the voices of the dead: At the end of this paragraph, ERE uses material he wrote in 1930 in a short poetic meditation called 'A Night-Piece on Hair':

> If you will taste the full meaning of these things, come with me this May midnight before the moonrise to a garden I shall find for you,

that goes down to a lake full of drowned stars and secret unsounded deeps of darkness. An island garden, shadowed with oaks
ten generations old and star-proof cedars and delicate-limbed close
tufted strawberry trees; and in their shadow origin night-flowers,
sweet-mouthed like brides in their first sleep, mix their sweetness
with the breath of eglantine fragrant with the dews of night. There,
out of bushy darknesses, nightingale answers nightingale with that
song that great lovers and great poets have ravished with their
hearts to hear since the world began: that night-song, bitter-sweet,
that shakes the heart of darkness with longings and questionings
too tumultuous for speech to fit or follow; and in that song the
listener hears echoing up the abysses of eternity voices of men and
women unborn answering the voices of the dead. So to you and
me, waiting on the Gods in this garden of heart's desire, strange
things may be shown. (Ms. Eng. Misc. c. 456, fols. 74–84, Bodleian
Library, Oxford)

ERE had hoped that Faber & Faber, the English publishers of *MM*,
would publish 'A Night-Piece on Hair' in a specially bound thin volume,
but this hope did not realize.

**6. About the north-western point . . . with the breath of the dews of
night:** ERE again uses material from 'A Night-Piece on Hair' in this
paragraph. See note 5 above.

7. Dryads . . . nymphs: Vandermast discourses upon the various
kinds of nymphs, all of which are minor female deities residing in specific places. Dryads live in trees, and they die when their particular trees
die. Naiads live in springs, rivers, or lakes. Nereids are sea-nymphs and
the daughters of Nereus, the wise old god of the sea. Oreads live in
mountains.

8. *andante piacevole e lussurioso . . . allegro appassionato:* music
played in a delightful, lustful, moderate tempo; music played in a fast,
passionate tempo.

9. unman me: See one of Lady Macbeth's remarks to her husband,
who displaces the banquet's mirth by gibbering hysterically when he
sees the ghost of Banquo: 'What, quite unmann'd in folly?' (*Macbeth* III:
iv: 74).

10. But here . . . thereunto: Vandermast's sentence may be paraphrased thus: 'In this situation, at the starting point of explanation, on
the very doorstep, an unsolvable problem presents itself, because you,
my Lord Lessingham, are educated only in things that you may touch
and understand with your senses: attitudes, actions, the material actualities of political and military affairs, policy debates and military strategy,
the nature of woman and women and matters that concern them.' Vandermast is asserting that Lessingham's practical education in applied
arts limits him from perceiving, as he says in the subsequent sentence,
the essence of things.

11. *sferra cavallo:* In 1916, ERE obtained a three-volume set of the
works of Sir Thomas Browne (1605–82), and he read of this magical leaf

in Browne's *Pseudodoxia Epidemica* (Enquiries into Vulgar and Common Errors):

> That *ferrum equinum,* or *sferra cavallo,* hath a virtue attractive of iron, a power to break locks and draw off the shoes of a horse that passeth over it: . . . which strange and magical conceit seems to have no deeper root in reason than the figure of its seed; for therein indeed it somewhat resembles a horse-shoe. (book 2, chapter 6, section 6)

MM: Chapter VIII

1. through the gate of horn: According to Greek mythology, true dreams come through the gate of horn, and false ones come through the gate of ivory.

2. Berenice's Hair: See note 8 to Chapter XXII of *MM.*

3. chryselephantine: a term used to describe statues overlaid with gold and ivory.

4. Tartarus: in Greek mythology, the place in the underworld where souls are punished for the wicked deeds they committed in life.

5. ensorcelled: entranced, bewitched; ERE had a fondness for this word and probably first encountered it in Sir Richard F. Burton's 'The Tale of the Ensorcelled Prince' in the first volume of his translation of *The Thousand Nights and a Night.*

6. *allegretto scherzando:* music played delightfully in a moderately quick tempo.

7. *adagio molto maestoso ed appassionato:* music played in a slow tempo, very majestically, and passionately.

MM: Chapter IX

1. Ings: meadows next to a river; here, the rivers are the Ailyman and the Zenner.

2. shearing up of the war-arrow: In the days of King Harald Hairfair of Norway (see note 23 to the Overture to *MM*), lords dispatched messengers through their lands with iron or wooden arrows to be used as symbols for a speedy call to arms. A reference to this practice occurs in Chapter III of *ES.*

3. seneschal: the officer appointed by the Duke to administer all the domestic affairs of Rumala.

4. peri: in Persian myth, a superhuman creature like a fairy or an angel.

5. umbles: the edible internal organs of a deer.

6. rebellion had shaken . . . the Vicar and . . . Fingiswold: See Chapter XXVI of *MG*. The rebellion occurred in 771 AZC.

7. Even as the gannet . . . Lessingham struck: In appropriate homage to deep-browed Homer, ERE here adopts a Homeric or epic simile to emphasize the climactic moment of his battle.

MM: Chapter X

1. Philommeides Aphrodite: This epithet of Aphrodite connotes her origin from her father's dismembered virile member, which was both cut and hurled into the sea by Kronos. See note 37 of the Overture to *MM*.

2. Trokers and dastards: The first is an obscure Scottish word for a cheater or deceiver; the second names a detestable coward.

3. *ad Tartara Termagorum:* into the region of Tartarus, within which Hecate wanders as the moon. In Greek mythology, Tartarus is the region of the lower world in which the enemies of the gods are punished. *Termagant* means 'roving three times' and refers to the moon wandering under the name Artemis in the heavens, under the name Selene on earth, and under the name Hecate in the lower world.

4. under his breath . . . Cyprus: Sappho, fragment 87. ERE uses Wharton's translation.

5. fadge: occur, happen, fall out, come off.

6. moidores: dappled light like golden coins.

7. porphyry: a purplish red granite or marble.

8. chrysoprases sewn upon cloth of gold: bright green gems on silken material containing threads of gold.

9. *sub specie quadam aeternitatis:* as far as possible according to the form of eternity. This phrase, and its near relation, *sub specie aeternitatis,* are often used by Spinoza to discuss the ability of the mind to apprehend the essences of things as they exist in eternal substantial forms. See H. F. Hallett, *Aeternitas* (Oxford: Clarendon Press, 1930), 99–104.

10. Myself . . . Physicals and Ultramundanes: material things and spiritual things (metaphysics); ERE has taken this sentence from Sir Thomas Chaloner's translation (1549) of Erasmus' *In Praise of Folly*.

11. *demonstratio, scholium, corollarium:* pointing out or showing, presenting a thesis or exposition, making an additional assertion.

12. *praeter verbum nihil est:* nothing exists beyond the words.

13. Horror of Apollonius upon Lamia: Zimiamvian libraries contain the best of terrestrial literature: Fiorinda shows some evidence of her education in English poetry. Keats found the plot for his narrative poem 'Lamia' in Robert Burton's *Anatomy of Melancholy* (see partition 3, section 2, member 1, subsection 1). Burton cites Philostratus' account of the story: a lamia (a bloodsucking vampirelike monster that takes the shape of a lovely maiden) seduces the young philosopher Lycius, and he marries her with pomp and revelry; Apollonius attends the wedding and sees through her illusions; the lamia pleads with him to hold his tongue, but he speaks out the truth, and the woman vanishes. Keats gives the moment sharpness: see 'Lamia,' II: 245–48 and 299–306.

14. siege: throne.

15. *ex necessitatae . . . debent:* out of necessity divine nature must fall into infinite shapes and kinds.

16. *per scientiam:* through knowledge.

17. *omnia quae existunt:* all things that exist.

18. Hymettus: a mountain near Athens; it is famed for its honey.

19. thou, and My servant Love: Sappho, fragment 74; ERE follows Wharton's translation. Wharton comments on the fragment: 'Sappho agreed with Diotima when the latter said to Socrates that love is not the son, but the attendant and servant of Aphrodite' (Wharton, 114).

20. Will you credit that old tale . . . sat helmed with shield and spear: Fiorinda alludes to 'The Saga of Hakon the Good' in Snorri Sturluson's *Heimskringla* (see notes 22 and 23 to the Overture to *MM*). Hakon, the son of King Harold Hairfair of Norway, was fostered by King Athelstane of England, but in the decade of the 940s he drove his brother Eirik Bloodaxe out of Norway and became King. Hakon earned the title 'the Good' through his legislation and through his defensive military policies, but, like nearly every medieval king, he had enemies. When Eirik Bloodaxe died, his wife Queen Gunnhild and his sons used the long tradition of Danish-Norwegian animosity to win the support of Gunnhild's brother, the Danish King Harald Blue-Tooth, in pressing their claims to the throne of Norway. Hakon repelled Eirik's sons twice, but in the third battle at Fitiar on the island of Stord, Hakon took a mortal wound and died soon afterward. Snorri tells that the poet Eyvind made, to commemorate Hakon, a song in which two of Odin's maiden warrior-spirits, the valkyries Gondul and Skogul, bring Hakon's soul to live in Valhalla.

21. Pieria: This region stands on the northern slopes of Mount Olympus and has been traditionally associated with the muses.

MM: Chapter XI

1. A bittern boomed in the marshes far away: The bittern is related to herons, but it is smaller in size. It is best known for the loud wailing call ('boom') it makes during its breeding season. When Dr. Watson first hears the mournful moan of the famous Hound of the Baskervilles, his companion, Stapleton, the villain of the story, compares it to the boom of the bittern.

2. All save Illmauger . . . through the weasand: Egil Skallagrimson of Burg, one of the leading figures in *ES*, is one of ERE's models for the Vicar, and his gruesome hurly-burly with his dogs was inspired by one of Egil's notable exploits. When Egil and Atli the Short cannot verbally settle a property dispute before the judges at the Gula-Thing, Egil indulges his legal right to a judicial combat, a *holmgang*, to settle the argument. Here the fight closes:

> Then Egil let go sword and shield and leapt at Atli and grabbed him with his hands. Then was known the odds of strength, and Atli fell over backwards: but Egil was crawled upon him down there, and bit asunder his weasand. There Atli lost his life. (*ES*, 158)

3. the third day after these things aforesaid: June 18, 777 AZC.

MM: Chapter XII

1. that old tale of Swanhild . . . and so slain: The fate of the unfortunate and silent Swanhild is told in chapter 40 of the *Volsunga Saga*, one of the greatest of the thirteenth-century Icelandic sagas. Swanhild is the daughter of Gudrun, the frighteningly formidable daughter of King Guiki, and of Sigurd Fafnir's-bane, the most famous of the great sons of Volsung. Swanhild grows up in the court of King Jonakr, and she becomes famous for her beauty. Jormunrek, the King of the Goths, sends his son Randver and his counselor Bikki to King Jonakr to ask for the hand of Swanhild in marriage. Jonakr cheerfully agrees to this honorable match, and he sends Swanhild with her company of servants to Randver's ship. Then Bikki manipulates Randver and Jormunrek to set in motion a destructive course of action:

> Then spake Bikki to Randver, 'How good and right it were if thou thyself had to wife so lovely a woman rather than the old man there.' Good seemed that word to the heart of the king's son, and he spake to her with sweet words, and she to him in like wise. So they came aland and go unto the king, and Bikki said unto him, 'Meet and right it is, lord, that thou shouldst know what is befallen, though hard it be to tell of, for the tale must be concerning thy beguiling, whereas thy son has gotten to him the full love of Swanhild, nor is she other than his harlot; but thou, let not the deed be unavenged.' Now many an ill rede [i.e., counsel, advice] had he given the king or [i.e., before] this, but of all his ill redes did this sting home the most; and still would the king hearken to all his evil redes; wherefor he, who might nowise still the wrath within him, cried out that Randver should be taken and tied up to the gallows-tree. . . . Bikki wrought his will, and Randver was dead-slain. And, moreover, Bikki spake, 'Against none hast thou more wrongs to avenge thee of than against Swanhild; let her die a shameful death.' 'Yea,' said the king, 'we will do after thy counsel.' So she was bound in the gate of the burg, and horses were driven at her to tread her down; but when she opened her eyes wide, then the horses durst not trample her; so when Bikki beheld that, he

bade draw a bag over the head of her; and they did so, and therewith she lost her life.
(*The Story of the Volsungs and Niblungs,* trans. Eirikr Magnusson and William Morris, The Harvard Classics, vol. 49 [New York: P. F. Collier and Son, 1910], 354–55).

Like an Icelandic Iago, Bikki seems to be propelled by a malicious jealousy of Swanhild's beauty, and he is driven to destroy her to settle his rancorous soul. This is mere speculation, and yet the text invites it because the clever author, in standard saga fashion, passes over Bikki's motives with complete silence and lets the reader interpret Bikki's character through his actions alone.

2. a lean sneak-bill chitty-face: ERE culled *sneak-bill* from the Oxford English Dictionary quotations illustrating *chitty-face,* and the rest of the phrase he borrowed from a curmudgeonly passage in Robert Burton's *Anatomy of Melancholy* (1628): 'Every Lover admires his Mistress, though she be very deformed of her self, ill-favoured, wrinkled, pimpled, pale, red, yellow, tanned, tallow-faced, have a swollen Juggler's platter-face, or a thin, lean, chitty-face' (partition 3, section 2, member 3). The sentence goes on and on with nasty descriptions.

3. UT COMPRESSA PEREAT: The word *compressa* makes this a difficult phrase. Given the varying shades of meaning, the phrase translates to something like this: 'let that pressed, constrained, dissembling woman perish' (*pereo*). This phrase, within the context of the Vicar's dream, foreshadows the closing scenes of *MM*.

4. Prince Valero . . . we've washed the flagstones since: See Chapter XXVI of *MG* for Valero's rebellion. Horius Parry and Valero are old antagonists: they first fight in 'Europe; or the Tale of Mr. William,' a story that young ERE wrote in the early 1890s.

5. paraquitos: parakeets.

6. O we curl'd-haird men / Are still most kind to women: ERE quotes John Webster's Flamineo; he speaks to taunt Vittoria Corombona, who has just called him a panderer because he helped Duke Brachiano pursue an adulterous affair with her (*The White Devil* IV: ii: 194–95).

7. upon lengths of seas and shores: This is one of two places in which ERE mentions realms beyond the three kingdoms and Akkama. In Chapter XXVII of *MG,* ERE says that when he was twenty, Lessingham went abroad 'to seek adventure as a soldier of fortune in distant countries of the world.' ERE never describes these foreign continents, and thus he never gives geographical Zimiamvia planetary shape.

8. That Friend . . . all his defects: ERE quotes John Webster's Duke Ferdinand, who spouts this sententious remark while thanking his agent Bosola for speaking plainly to him. Bosola has just told the Duke, 'you / are your own chronicle too much: and grossly / flatter yourself' (*The Duchess of Malfi* III: i: 87–93).

MM: Chapter XIII

1. but lookt to neare: ERE quotes part of a couplet spoken by Flamineo in Webster's *The White Devil:* 'Glories, like glow-worms, afar off shine bright / But look'd to near, have neither heat nor light' (V: i: 41–42). When *MM* was first published by Faber & Faber in 1935, these grouped chapter headings were page headings, and this phrase was placed above the long paragraph beginning 'And yet carried he little ease within him' (174). The paragraph describes Lessingham's mind troubling over the ordinary plainness of Rialmar and its inhabitants. Upon the dream-stone in Chapter VIII, Fiorinda kindled glories in Lessingham's imagination when she spoke of his finding his heart's desire in Rialmar. As an unseen and distant mystery of anticipation, Rialmar seemed lighted in glory to him, but once Lessingham goes there and looks closely at it, Rialmar is 'a plain walled hold' shedding 'neither heat nor light.'

2. fifteenth day of August: 777 AZC.

3. Zenianthe: The nature and identity of this lovely and quick-witted lady makes a slight crux. In *MM*, ERE first describes her as an 'oread lady' (210), like the nymphs Anthea and Campaspe, and later as a tree-nymph of royal blood: a 'hamadryad princess' (244). In *FD*, ERE describes her as 'Princess Zenianthe, niece to King Mezentius (516).' In *MG*, ERE gives her both descriptions: 'the King's niece Zenianthe, herself a hamadryad' (711). However, ERE never clearly states a familial connection that would explain her relationship to Mezentius. Besides Mezentius, ERE never mentions in *MG* any other children of King Mardanus and Queen Stateira: upon the sudden death of Mardanus, the young Mezentius becomes his undisputed successor under Stateira's regency. Mezentius seems to have no brother or sister, so he cannot have a niece, not even a niece who is a hamadryad living in a tree.

4. chryselephantine statue of Aphrodite Anadyomene: The name means 'Aphrodite rising from the sea.' Note 37 to the Overture of *MM* gives Hesiod's account of Aphrodite's birth. Chryselephantine is sculpture in gold and ivory. Usually, the main sculpted structure consists of wood, and the gold and ivory are overlaid upon it.

5. was't not Lessingham?: Lessingham served King Mezentius in the third war against Akkama. See Chapter XXVII of *MG*.

6. in many countries: Lessingham has traveled far in his short life. Chapter XXVII of *MG* relates that Lessingham, with Amaury, went abroad in 772 'to be a soldier of fortune in distant countries of the world.' And in Chapter XV of *MM*, he says he intends to travel again once he has set things in order in Rialmar: 'then off with my commission, throw it by and we'll begone overseas' (194). However, ERE never describes any Zimiamvian countries beyond the western ocean (see note 7 to Chapter XII of *MM*).

7. The twenty-fourth day after: September 8, 777 AZC.

8. Galateas in marble quickened: Book 10 of Ovid's (43 B.C.–A.D. 17) *Metamorphoses* is the source for the story of King Pygmalion and the statue that quickened with life. During the festival of Venus, Pygmalion prays to the goddess for a wife like his ivory maiden. Venus smiles at his prayers and transforms the ivory to living flesh: Not Ovid but W. S. Gilbert named the statue, in his comedy *Pygmalion and Galatea* (1871). In 1913 George Bernard Shaw translated Galatea to Eliza Doolittle and Pygmalion to Professor Henry Higgins in his *Pygmalion,* and in 1957 Lerner and Loewe wrote the musical *My Fair Lady* based on Shaw's play.

9. *in loco parentis:* in the position of the parent.

10. the foam-born Goddess Herself: Aphrodite. See note 37 to the Overture to *MM*.

MM: Chapter XIV

1. Dorian Mode: Full Close: On a piano, the ancient Grecian Dorian mode pattern can be heard by playing the white keys of the octave e'–e (low e to e above middle c). For a discussion of modes, see pages 28–34 of Donald Jay Grout's *History of Western Music* (New York: W. W. Norton, 1960).

In Book III of *The Republic*, Socrates and Glaucon discuss the place of music in the education of a warrior. After excluding the various Lydian and Ionian modes, Glaucon tells Socrates 'you've probably got the Dorian and the Phrygian left.' Then Socrates describes the modes he wants:

> Just leave that mode which would appropriately imitate the sounds and accents of a man who is courageous in warlike deeds and every violent work. . . . And, again, leave another mode for a man who performs a peaceful deed, one that is not violent but voluntary, either persuading someone of something and making a request . . . or, on the contrary, holding himself in check for someone else who makes a request or instructs him or persuades him to change. (*The Republic of Plato,* trans. Allan Bloom [New York: Basic Books, Inc., 1968] 77–78).

Lessingham, who begins the chapter in a mood of violent 'inward strife' and ends the chapter 'with a half mocking half regretful look,' has characteristics of both dispositions that Socrates describes.

MM: Chapter XV

1. Rialmar Vindemiatrix: the lady grape-harvester of Rialmar. Vindemiatrix is also the name of a star in the constellation Virgo, and the sun is in Virgo during the harvest time.

2. Sparkling-thronéd heavenly Aphrodite: ERE's translation of the opening line of Sappho's 'Hymn to Aphrodite.'

3. with an immortal goddess; not clearly knowing: See p. xxxv of the Introduction.

4. swift-flying doves to draw you: ERE's translation of a line from the third stanza of Sappho's 'Hymn to Aphrodite.'

5. accipitraries: people who catch and tame wild birds of prey.

6. tartaret haggard: The word *tartaret* signifies that this falcon comes from Barbary. A *haggard* is a falcon that has grown to adulthood in the wild before being captured and trained to hunt. It is a fact little known that migrating peregrine falcons from Barbary swoop around the cloud banks of Fingiswold.

7. eyas: falcons taken young from a nest and trained to fly and hunt.

8. the house: The description of Vandermast's wayside house echoes the splendid opening paragraphs of *WO,* in which ERE describes the house and garden of Mary and Edward Lessingham. This 'low-built old timbered house' reminds you and me of Lessingham's 'old low house in Wasdale,' and the 'low red brick wall smothered all over with dark red climbing roses' stirs our memory of the 'Climbing roses, honeysuckle, clematis, and the scarlet flame-flower' that 'scrambled up the walls' of Lessingham's house. The slanting rays of the Zimiamvian sun cast 'long shadows' and 'deep purple shadows,' which suggest the 'cool long shadows' thrown by an English sunset. Even the Zimiamvian 'Homing doves' which 'rested pink feet on the roof-ridge' have their Wasdale song mates: 'Doves murmured in the trees' (*WO,* 1). These similarities forge not a new link in the chain between Mercury and Zimiamvia, but the beginnings of a wholly new chain between England and Zimiamvia. Later, ERE gives both houses the same names: see notes 10 and 21 below.

9. Gold is pure of Rust: Sappho, fragment 109. ERE makes a conjectural translation based on the text given in *Lyra Graeca,* ed. and trans. J. M. Edmonds, Loeb Classical Library, vol. 1 (London: William Heinemann, 1922).

10. the house of peace: Here ERE strengthens the similarity between Vandermast's wayside house and Edward Lessingham's house in Wasdale. On the night of his journey to Mercury, Edward Lessingham lies alone in the Lotus Room: 'He slept soft and deep; for that was the House of Postmeridian, and the House of Peace' (*WO,* 3). See note 21 below.

11. armipotent Ares: Vandermast means that Lessingham is a warrior who wields weapons so well that he resembles the mighty Greek god of war.

12. winged lions of Sumer: ERE is imagining animate creatures like the symbolic mythological figures carved upon the massive Sumerian stone sculptures. He had a lifelong admiration for ancient art and probably went many times to see the British Museum's collection of ancient Mesopotamian sculpture.

13. hamadryads: nymphs living in trees.

14. Amphitrite's brood: She was the daughter of Nereus, Homer's benevolent sea-god, and she became the wife of Poseidon. Her children
were Triton and Rhode, but ERE seems to indicate that her 'brood' are
the mermaids or sea nymphs.

15. sphinx: a monstrous lion with a woman's head.

16. siren: a bird with a woman's head.

17. wyvern: a winged dragon having two feet like the claws of an eagle
and a long barbed tail.

18. *Li rosignox . . . rivage:* The nightingale is my father / Who sings
upon the green boughs / and from the highest grove; / The siren is my
mother / who sings from the salty sea / and from the highest shore.

19. *bis dat quae tarde:* She who gives slowly gives in two ways.

20. Lady of Sakes: This epithet refers to an aspect of the Virgin Mary;
one prays to our Lady of Sakes when one wants her help with a problem. 'Sake' can also mean strife, dispute, or conflict, and Fiorinda is
certainly capable of causing these.

21. the house of heart's desire: ERE strengthens the connection between Zimiamvian life and English life by applying to Vandermast's
wayside house another epithet he gave to Edward Lessingham's Nether
Wasdale house. When the martlet arrives to lead Edward Lessingham
to Mercury, Lessingham says he is ready to go 'For that was the House
of Heart's Desire' (*WO*, 3).

22. I love . . . beauty: Sappho, fragment 79; ERE uses Wharton's
translation.

23. *esse formale:* a formal subject; in languages, the formal rather than
the informal personal pronoun.

24. *omnia quae existunt:* all things that exist.

25. *vis Dei:* the power of the Gods.

MM: Chapter XVI

1. the Divells quilted anvell: This label for the Vicar comes from Webster's *The Duchess of Malfi*. The embittered, world-hating, and self-hating
Bosola speaks these words in reference to his master, Duke Ferdinand,
a spiteful and ruthless lord who has employed Bosola in the role of 'base
intelligencer' to spy upon his sister the duchess:

> A politician is the devil's quilted anvil,
> He fashions all sins on him, and the blows
> are never heard. (V: ii: 321–23)

2. *divide et impera:* literally, separate and control; popularly, divide
and conquer.

MM: Chapter XVII

1. when such a mutual pair: With this phrase, ERE means to compare Fiorinda and Barganax with two of their literary inspirations, Shakespeare's Antony and Cleopatra. Even though 'stiff' news comes from Rome in the play's first scene, Antony refuses to hear anything except the 'sum,' and even though the 'wrangling queen' chides him for his attitude, Antony declares his intention to indulge in an easeful life and to neglect his political and military responsibilities in Rome:

> Let Rome in Tiber melt, and the wide arch
> of the rang'd empire fall! Here is my space.
> Kingdoms are clay; our dungy earth alike
> Feeds beast as man. The nobleness of life
> Is to do thus; when such a mutual pair
> And such a twain can do't, in which I bind,
> On pain of punishment, the world to weet
> We stand up peerless. (*Antony and Cleopatra* I: i: 33–40)

In this chapter, ERE creates parallels between his plot and characters and Shakespeare's. First, Medor arrives with an urgent message at 2:00 P.M., but Vandermast, obeying by the Duke's command for privacy until 4:00 P.M., makes Medor abide the two hours. When Barganax reads the message, which has 'hell's fires in the tail of it,' Fiorinda, like the chiding Cleopatra, bites him by asking, 'What means your grace to do now? Paint, and let the wide world wind?' Barganax's reputation as an indolent man surfeited in luxury colors the opinions of many aristocrats in Zimiamvia. Even Lessingham, who knows the Duke to be an honorable man, says that he is 'given to laziness . . . women, and voluptuousness' (157). This public view of Barganax parallels the view of Antony held by some of the play's minor characters who sometimes observe the two great lovers with voyeuristic eyes. Philo opens the play by exhorting even the audience to voyeurism: 'see in him / the triple pillar of the world transform'd / into a strumpet's fool' (I: i: 11–13). ERE shatters the parallels between Barganax and Antony on page 236: there, Antony becomes a foil for the Duke when Barganax declares 'within three days I'll be man or mouse' and immediately begins to take measures in response to the news.

2. loisible . . . liripoop: lawful, permissible; a lesson, something learned or acted out.

3. They dismounted . . . Mandricard's throat-bole: A *stoccata* is a forward sword thrust; a *mandritta* is a cut from right to left; an *imbroccata* is a special thrust over the dagger when both fighters hold a rapier in their right and a dagger in their left hands, but since Barganax and Mandricard are fighting with swords only, perhaps ERE means a thrust over the left arm; a *montanto* is a quick, hard, forward thrust with the palm turned upward.

4. The prophetic soul . . . things to come: the first two lines of Shakespeare's sonnet 107.

5. Bitter-sweet: Sappho, fragment 40; see note 7 to Chapter II of *MM*.

6. *post omne animal triste:* Fiorinda pauses after saying 'post' and in discreet silence passes over the key word 'coitum' in this Latin maxim, which translates thus: 'After mating, all creatures are sad.'

7. she fell silent: Fiorinda darkly alludes to her marriage to Lord Morville, the lieutenant of Reisma, which ended two years earlier with his death during the early hours of July 22, 775 AZC. See *FD*, Chapters X–XII and *MG*, Chapters XXXII–XXXIII.

8. *por la bele . . . cler seoir:* to have that beautiful star / that he sees sitting high and clear.

9. been thinking on: See *FD*, Chapters V and VI, and *MG*, Chapter XXX.

10. Fra bank . . . bairn: by Mark Alexander Boyd (1563–1601).

11. Stygian flood: In Roman mythology, Charon, 'the grim ferryman,' carries souls whose bodies have been properly buried across the river Styx and into the nine circles of the lower world.

12. Persephone beneath the sod: Persephone was raped by Hades, she became his queen, and because she ate seven pomegranate seeds, she was condemned to divide her time between living with Hades in the lower world and living on earth. Persephone's story has sometimes been interpreted as an agricultural myth and an allegory for the growth of seeds; and this may explain Barganax's expression. See Ovid's *Metamorphoses*, book 5:491ff.

13. Othello's occupation's gone: See *Othello* III: iii: 352–62. The valiant Moor says farewell to the 'Pride, pomp, and circumstance of glorious war,' but Fiorinda, responding to Vandermast's remarking that Barganax's dry-point has achieved perfection, mockingly hints that Barganax may say farewell to brushes, palette, oils, and canvas.

14. if the gear cotton: if the effort succeeds; see the Oxford English Dictionary, definitions 9b for *gear*, and 4 for *cotton* v^1.

15. a gudgeon . . . a pike: the first is a small European freshwater fish like a minnow; the second is a general name for several large and fiercely fighting freshwater game fish.

MM: Chapter XVIII

1. the turn of spring: March 21, 778 AZC.

2. *mantichora* . . . next against the hills hitherward of Akkama: Akkama lies northwest of Fingiswold, and the mantichores are found in the borderlands between Fingiswold and Akkama. This sentence suggests a geographic link to the Mercury of *WO*, for in Chapter XII of *WO*, the Lords Juss and Brandoch Daha attempt to climb the cliffs of Ela Mantissera, the Bed of Mantichores, and within twelve miles of these cliffs stands Kostra Pivrarcha, from whose peak they gaze down into the fabled land of Zimiamvia. The great mountains, the Moruna, and the Impland of *WO* perhaps lie north or northeast of the three Zimiamvian kingdoms, but this is speculation because ERE never located them precisely and he never mentions Mercury in the Zimiamvian novels.

3. It is not time: The explicit reference to Mary links this passage to the Overture to *MM*, but other phrases on this page echo the descriptions of the house in Wasdale found in the Induction to *WO*.

4. Evening star . . . safe to the mother: Sappho, ERE's translation of fragment 95. Here is Wharton's literal translation: 'Evening, thou that bringest all that bright morning scattered; thou bringest the sheep, the goat, the child back to her mother' (Wharton, 131).

5. manning of a haggard: the long and difficult training of a hawk that has lived long enough in the wild to go through its first moulting.

6. with . . . knowing: See p. xxxv of the Introduction.

7. *Se j'avoie . . . sont amors:* If I had a lover (*ami*) for one day, / I would say to everyone: / love affairs are good. (The difficult word is *ameit:* it could be an early spelling of *a moi,* and then the first line would translate 'If I had a day to myself'; or it could be *au moins,* and then the first line would translate 'If I had at least a day.')

8. Ah, lad . . . reap it: Homer, *Iliad* 12: 322–28; translated by ERE.

MM: Chapter XIX

1. when the great King warred down Akkama: King Mezentius fought three wars with Akkama in the years 750, 771, and 772 AZC. See Chapters XVII, XXVI, and XXVII of *MG*.

2. captal: an obscure French title for captain or chief.

3. *in deliciis:* in luxury.

4. in berserk-gang: This is the first of ERE's many references to the tradition of the Icelandic berserk, so it deserves one complete explanation to serve all the references. A berserk is a warrior whose mind and body occasionally seethe with a strange and violent fury. Temporary insanity, thunderous roaring, mouth-frothing rage, insensibility to pain, iron strength, and lightning quickness seize the berserks when battle or other physical conflicts rouse them. Because these qualities swell suddenly and pass away moments later, men describe the state as a 'fit,' the 'berserk-gang.' *ES* offers an authoritative description of the berserk-gang: 'So is it said of those men that were shape-strong or of them on whom was the berserk-gang, that for so long as that held, they were so strong that there was no holding against them' . . . (*ES*, 53). Few men can contend with a berserk when the fit is on him because during the fit a berserk is not only extremely strong and quick, he is also insensible to pain. This is the idea that lies behind the disputed etymology of this Old Norse word. The term has been interpreted in two ways that emphasize a berserk's disregard for pain and injury in battle: some scholars say it derives from 'bare sark' and describes a warrior who fights without a mail coat or byrny; others say it derives from 'bear sark' and describes a warrior who fights wearing only a bearskin shirt.

The conclusion of the sentence quoted from *ES* says that when the berserk-gang dissipates, the man affected is left exhausted and weary: '. . . but forthwith when that was passed over, then were they un-mightier than of wont' (*ES*, 53). Edward Lessingham has the qualities of a berserk, and in Chapter VIII of *FD* he speaks of having his berserk sleep of thirty-one hours after going for five nights without a wink. In Chapter XIII of *FD*, Mary and Eric Lessingham talk of the berserk-gang as a family trait: 'violent inspiration followed by flop like a wrung-out dishcloth' (486). ERE uses this aspect of the berserk tradition in *WO* as well, for in Chapter II Goldry Bluzco becomes enraged, enters the berserk-gang, hurls the huge and heavy King Gorice XI over his head, and is left weakened: 'With the might of that throw Goldry's wrath departed from him and left him strengthless' (*WO*, 28).

ES continues its description by naming a particular berserk: 'And it was so with Kveldulf that, as soon as the berserk rage was gone from him, then knew he his weariness after those onslaughts he had made, and then was he altogether without might, so that he laid him down in his bed' (*ES*, 53). The name 'Kveldulf' means 'evening-wolf,' and this introduces another aspect of the berserk tradition: in berserk-gang, supposedly, the affected man sometimes transforms into a bear or a wolf. Adopting this here in *MM*, ERE compares Lessingham to a wolf and a lion. Old Norse words translating to the noun 'skin-changer' and to the adjective 'shape-strong' denote this ability to alter corporal form. In the sagas, berserks are described bellowing in battle and biting their shields like wolves, and because they become so strong and fierce and often scream from foaming mouths, other men think they are were-wolves. Men think this of Kveldulf, 'that was the talk of men, that he was exceeding shape-strong,' because he is 'evening-sleepy': 'every day when it drew toward evening, then would he begin to be sulky, so that few men might come to speech with him' (*ES*, 1). 'Evening-sleepiness' is not the exhaustion following the berserk-gang; rather, it is the gloomy state that comes upon skin-changers in the evening preceding their shape-strong change to the form of a werewolf or a predatory bear. J. R. R. Tolkien, a scholar of Old English who was also learned in Ice-landic literature, gave Kveldulf's symptoms to Beorn, the reclusive herdsman in *The Hobbit*. This skin-changer, whose name means 'bear,' shows hospitality to Gandalf's company, but late in the evening he loses interest in their stories of gold and jewels: 'When dinner was over they began to tell tales of their own, but Beorn seemed to be growing drowsy and paid little heed to them.' A few moments later, the door slams, and the evening-sleepy Beorn departs for a night of ursine prowling, and as Bilbo Baggins goes to bed, he hears the growlings of a huge scuffling animal outside the door (J. R. R. Tolkien, *The Hobbit*, 4th ed. [London: George Allen & Unwin Ltd, 1978] 111–113).

Kveldulf is a prosperous farmer whom many men respect. Beorn is admired too: Gandalf calls him 'a very great person' (*The Hobbit*, 102). However, in the sagas not all berserks have people's respect, for although kings and armies value their ferocity, they are often considered to be strange and unnatural and therefore not as brave or heroic as men who succeed in battle without relying on the temporary frenzy of the berserk-gang. Some berserks are troublesome bullies like those destroyed by the Icelandic heroes Egil (see *ES*, 153–155) and Grettir (see *The Saga of Grettir the Strong*, trans. G. A. Hight [London: J. M. Dent & Sons, Ltd, 1914] 111–112). Also, skin-changers are mocked for the indignity of their bestial transformations. Few great men in the Icelandic sagas are berserks: the brothers Skallagrim and Thorolf in *Egil's Saga*, the friends Kjartan and Bolli in *Laxdaela Saga*, and the neighbors Njal and Gunnar in *Njal's Saga* do not carry the berserk-gang traits.

MM: Chapter XX

1. The Baying to Ragnarok: In Norse mythology, a hound named Garm dwells in Niflheim, the land of the dead, and he will bark to signal Ragnarok, the destruction of the powers of the cosmos. See note 2 below.

2. Twilight of the Gods . . . the Wolf run free: This quoted couplet is from the anonymous poem *Voluspa* ('the Sibyl's prophecy'), one of the poems of the *Poetic Edda* (a collection of forty-two Old Norse poems written during the ninth and tenth centuries in simple verse forms and on ancient northern heroic and mythic subjects; the collection is also called *Saemund's Edda* or the *Elder Edda* to distinguish it from the *Snorra Edda*, the collection of myths written in prose by Snorri Sturluson early in the thirteenth century). The first part of *Voluspa* tells, in fragmentary form, the creation of the nine mythological Norse worlds, the first war of the gods, and some qualities and epithets of the gods. The second and more famous part of the poem tells the story of Ragnarok, the Old Norse term for 'the Twilight of the Gods,' the destruction of the powers of the cosmos. This couplet, appearing three times during the story of Ragnarok (see stanzas 43, 48, and 57) acts like a refrain. ERE translated these lines, and much of the *Voluspa*, for a Christmas festival recitation in his historical novel of tenth-century Sweden, *Styrbiorn the Strong* (London: Jonathan Cape, 1926):

> Garm bayeth ghastful at Gnipa's cave:
> The fast must be loos'd and the Wolf fare free

Garm is the 'hell-dog' who, until Ragnarok, remains chained at the Gnipahellir or 'cliff cave' in Niflheim, the dark and frozen land of the dead that contains the citadel of Hel. During Ragnarok, Garm and Tyr, the god of war, will kill each other. The identity of the wolf in the second line is ambiguous. *Freki* means 'greedy one,' and it is a name of one of Odin's two wolves (see stanza 19 of 'Grimnismal,' the *Poetic Edda*, trans. Lee M. Hollander, 2nd ed. [Austin: University of Texas Press, 1962], 57), but evidently the word does not refer to this wolf because he does not play a part in Ragnarok. ERE's translation suggests that he may be Fenrir, the wolf who will kill Allfather Odin and be killed by Vidar, Odin's son. Lee M. Hollander translates the lines so that the word *Freki* is an epithet for Garm: 'Garm bays loudly before Gnipa cave / breaks his fetters and freely runs' (*Poetic Edda*, 10). The most revered nineteenth-century Icelandic scholars, Gudbrand Vigfusson and York Powell, seem to agree with ERE, and they translate the lines to suggest the unleashing of Fenrir: 'Fiercely Garm [the hell-hound] bays before the cave of the Rock, the chain shall snap and the wolf range free!' (*Corpus Poeticum Boreale* [Oxford: Oxford University Press, 1883], vol.1, 198).

3. upon Michaelmas night: September 29, 777 AZC.

MM: Chapter XXI

1. *enn Freki renna:* See notes 1 and 2 to the previous chapter.
2. *insultans tyrannus:* He leaps upon the tyrant.
3. **malmsey:** a strong, sweet wine.
4. **princox:** a hot-headed young man like Tybalt in *Romeo and Juliet*.
5. **quondamship:** the state of being out of office.

MM: Chapter XXII

1. **antiphone to dawn:** An antiphony is a musical response made by one singer, or chorus of singers, to another. ERE intends this night song to be the response to Chapter IV, 'Zimiamvian Dawn.'
2. **settle-gang:** the setting of the sun; see Oxford English Dictionary, *settle*, sb[1], 6.
3. **Pentheseleia:** After Achilles kills Hector, the Amazonian queen Pentheseleia comes to aid the Trojans in their war against the Achaians. After fighting valiantly, she dies at the hands of Achilles. Achilles mourns for her lost beauty, and Thersites mocks him for loving Pentheseleia, so Achilles kills Thersites.
4. **Lydian Omphale:** This queen, the daughter of Iardanus, ruled the Maeones (Lydians) after her husband King Tmolus died. She is most famous for her association with Heracles, who allowed her to enslave him to appease the gods. Omphale made Heracles wear woman's cloth-ing and spin wool while she wore his famous fur coat, the skin of the Nemean lion, and carried his club. Omphale freed Heracles from servi-tude, married him, and had a child named Lamus by him.
5. **Hypermnestra:** Zeus loved a beautiful maiden named Io, but he

had to hide her from the jealous Hera, so he turned her into a cow. As if her bovine metamorphosis were not punishment enough for adultery, Hera tormented Io with a fly after she discovered her and stole her away from Zeus. Vexed by the fly, Io trundled off to Egypt, where, out of pity, the Egyptians worshipped her as Isis. Io bore a son named Epaphos, and he was the ancestor of two brothers, Danaus and Aegyptus. Through a virility nearly unmatched in the antique world and through an almost incredible defiance of genetic probability, Danaus had fifty daughters, and Aegyptus had fifty sons. When these brothers quarreled, Danaus and his daughters fled from Egypt to Argos, but they were pursued by the sons of Aegyptus, who forced Danaus to give his daughters in marriage to their fifty cousins. Danaus consented, and according to Pindar, the fifty women were set in a line at the end of a race course across a field. The fifty men chose their wives by running for them: a matchmaking method that Dr. Johnson would have heartily approved. Although he submitted to the marriages, a desire for revenge against his brother provoked Danaus to command his daughters to kill their new husbands on the wedding night. All the daughters obeyed their father except Hypermnestra: she saved her husband, Lynceus and helped him to escape. Horace (65–68 B.C.), in his Odes (3:11:13–52) records this much of Hypermnestra's story:

> Yet one deserved the name of bride;
> One only, who superbly lied
> To her deceitful father—Fame
> Shall ever consecrate her name.
> 'Awake!' she cried, 'my lord, my love!
> Ere from a snare thou think'st not of
> Come longer slumber! Up and go
> Before my sire and sisters know.
> Lo! they are lions, lighting on
> A herd, and rending one by one:
> But I am softer—I'll not wound
> Nor hold thee fast in prison bound.
> My sire may load me down with chains;
> Or far to Africa's domains
> May ship me, for that I, your wife,
> Was pitiful and spared thy life.
> Go, get thee gone, o'er land and flood
> While Night and Love are kind, and good
> The omens; grave upon my tomb
> One word of sorrow for my doom.'
> (translated by William Sinclair Marris)

Danaus forgave her disobedience and blessed the marriage to Lynceus, and Hypermnestra went on to have a son named Abas, the founder of the Argive dynasty. Through her willful disobedience, Hypermnestra saved herself from the ridiculous fate suffered by her sisters in Hades:

they were given jars with holes in their bottoms, and they had to try, through all eternity, to fill them with water.

6. Semiramis: In history, this woman's existence was nothing to stir a poet's pen. She was Sammu-rammat, the wife of King Shamshi-Adad V of Assyria, and she served as the Queen Regent from 811 to 808 B.C. In legend, this woman's existence is extraordinary. She was the daughter of the fertility goddess Atargatis, and after being abandoned as a baby, she was nourished by doves. A shepherd named Simmas rescued Semiramis and raised her to adulthood. A prince named Onnes married her, but the emperor Ninus fell in love with her and made her his queen, and Onnes killed himself. Semiramis later persuaded Ninus to make her the supreme ruler for five days, and on her second day of power she used her authority to order Ninus' execution. Then Semiramis ruled as empress for forty-two years. She achieved fame as an empire builder: she ordered the construction of roads, cities, and monuments in Persia and Armenia, and she built the marvelous hanging gardens of Babylon. Semiramis was also famous for her ruthless sexuality: she took many lovers during her reign, and like the black widow spider, when she wearied of a man, she had him dispatched. At the end of her life, she named her son Ninyas as her successor, and then she turned herself into a dove and flew away and was never heard from again.

7. Roxana: In the spring of 327 B.C., Alexander the Great was conquering the land of Sogdiana (in outer Iran), and he defeated the chieftain Oxyartes, who had taken refuge in a fortress on the mountain called Baisun-tau. The daughters of Oxyartes were taken captive. Among them stood a young woman, Roxana, whose name signified 'little star' and who supposedly was the most beautiful woman in all of Asia. Legend says that Alexander loved her at first sight and married her because of the force of this love. Six weeks after Alexander's death in 323 B.C., Roxana bore him a posthumous son. Both the little star and her little boy were murdered in 311 B.C. by Cassander, one of the rivals struggling for the Macedonian throne after Alexander's death.

8. Berenice: The Ptolemy dynasty ruled over Egypt after the death of Alexander and until the Roman conquest, which was completed by 30 B.C. Ptolemy III (246–221 B.C.) had a sister named Berenice, and he also married a woman named Berenice. But this did not create problems for the post office because his sister lived in Syria and was the wife of Antilochus II. When Antilochus died in 247 B.C., his former and divorced wife Laodice killed his widow Berenice, took Antilochus' estate, and Laodice's son Seleucis II was proclaimed as the successor to Antilochus. Ptolemy grew angry at these developments, so in 246 he set out for Syria to correct matters and to press his sister's rightful claims. When he left, his wife Berenice cut off a lock of her hair and dedicated it to the gods as an offering for her husband's safe return. The lock of hair disappeared mysteriously. Alexander Pope's poem *The Rape of the Lock* is based upon this story, and the Roman poet Catullus (84–54 B.C.) wrote a poem (number 66 in *Odi et Amo*) in which the shorn lock, the speaker in the poem, becomes a star.

9. Zenobia: This imperious queen succeeded her husband Odenathus as ruler of Palmyra in A.D. 266 or 267. Palmyra was a city-state in Syria that enjoyed the gentle suzerainty of the Roman Empire. Zenobia, eager to expand her dominions, invaded Egypt and Asia Minor in defiance of Rome. She was captured and deposed by Aurelian (272), and Palmyra was razed to the ground.

10. Gudrun of Laxriverdale: Probably the most famous woman in the great thirteenth-century prose epics of Iceland, Gudrun and her life's tragedy dominate the central episodes of *The Laxdaela Saga*. Gudrun meets and falls in love with the handsome and dazzling young Kjartan, the son of the illustrious Olaf the Peacock. Bolli Thorleikson, Kjartan's cousin and best friend, accompanies Gudrun and Kjartan during many of the happy times of their courtship, and he silently falls in love with Gudrun too. After a year of happy companionship, Kjartan tells Gudrun of his eagerness to go to Norway, and he asks Gudrun to wait three years for him on the promise of a marriage upon his return. Gudrun proposes that Kjartan should take her with him to Norway, but Kjartan replies that she must remain in Iceland to take care of her aged father. Gudrun makes no promise to wait for Kjartan, and the two lovers part coldly. Bolli accompanies Kjartan to Norway. Two problems develop while they are there. First, King Olaf puts pressure on the Icelanders to convert to Christianity, and even though Kjartan and his men convert to the new faith, Olaf holds Kjartan hostage as a way of putting pressure on the leading men in Iceland to consider the new faith. Second, the Princess Ingibjorg, the daughter of King Olaf Tryggvason, shows much favor to Kjartan. Bolli, who is not held hostage, returns to Iceland after three years. He tells Gudrun of Kjartan's intimate friendship with Ingibjorg, and after suggesting that Kjartan will settle in Norway, he proposes marriage to Gudrun. Although she grows angry at what she hears of Kjartan, Gudrun does not accept Bolli until her father pressures her into acceptance. The next year, having been released from King Olaf's power and having abruptly ended the affair with Ingibjorg, Kjartan returns to Iceland. Finding Gudrun married to Bolli, Kjartan hides his sorrow and marries Hrefna Asgeir's-daughter. After several petty but maddening gestures of rudeness, aggression and unkindness flourish between Kjartan and Bolli, only the strong influence of Olaf the Peacock prevents open hostility. Gudrun finally goads Bolli and his men into planning an ambush for Kjartan, and in executing it Bolli kills Kjartan. Once the feud has begun, Olaf the Peacock cannot end it; he can only delay it, and anxious peace exists for three years until Olaf dies. Then, spurred on by their mother Thorgerd, Kjartan's brothers kill Bolli.

11. Laura: The unknown lover of Petrarch (1304–1374), the great Italian poet and scholar. Petrarch first saw her in 1327, loved her distantly but passionately all his life, and he devoted most of the lyric poems in his *Canzoniere* to her. Even after her death, Petrarch wrote many sonnets to her. Laura was between sixteen and twenty-one when he first saw her. She had fair skin, blond hair, dark eyes, and heart-melting lips.

Like Fiorinda, she loved to wear jewels, and like Fiorinda, she loved her mirror.

12. Fiammetta: On March 30, 1336, Boccaccio (1313–75) went to Mass at the Church of San Lorenzo of the Franciscans, and there, in a sublimely fortuitous moment, he saw and straightway loved Maria d'Aquino. He later wrote of this moment in his *Filocolo*. He called her Fiammetta because of her hair, and in 1342–43 he wrote a prose romance that he named after her and that she narrates. See the translation by Bartholomew Yong called *Amorous Fiammetta*.

13. Giulia Farnese: This famous Italian beauty was the daughter of Pier Luigi Farnese and part of a provincially noble family. Her beauty brought fame to her family, and when she arrived in Rome she was called Giulia Bella. Cardinal Rodrigo Borgia, the ecclesiastical machiavel who became Pope Alexander VI, passionately adored her. Soon after Giulia married Orsino Orsini, the son of the niece of the Borgia, Adriana Mila, she became the Borgia's mistress and favorite concubine. Lucretia Borgia (see note 15 below) grew up in her company. See Maria Bellonci, *The Life and Times of Lucretia Borgia,* trans. Bernard Wall (London: George Weidenfeld and Nicolson, 1953).

14. Vittoria Corombona: John Webster's play *The White Devil* (1612) was based on then recent Italian history, and his heroine, who cleverly and courageously resists the manipulation and persecution of her powerful brothers, has a real counterpart in the daughter of Claudio and Tarquinia Accoramboni. Because of ERE's love of Webster's play, because of the characteristics Vittoria shares with Fiorinda and Queen Rosma in *FD* and *MG,* and because of the many resemblances between sixteenth-century Italy and Zimiamvia, Vittoria's story merits full telling. Born February 15, 1557, in Gubbio, Vittoria was a famous beauty by the age of sixteen. Although both parents had some objections, she married Francesco Peretti, the nephew of Cardinal Montalto Peretti. Quarrels soon arose between the parents because the Cardinal did not endow his nephew with the riches that the bride's family expected, and Tarquinia asked for her daughter's dowry back. Meanwhile, Tarquinia's son Marcello held the position of chamberlain to the Duke of Brachiano, Paolo Giordano Orsini. Brachiano's wife Isabella de Medici had an affair with Troilo Orsini, and as F. L. Lucas says, this affair 'ended in one of those sudden retributions which, like lightning from a clear sky, now and then shattered the careless laxities of Renaissance Italy': Isabella fell suddenly dead while washing her hair on July 14, 1576. Most believed Brachiano had strangled her; thugs sent by the Medici family shot Troilo in Paris a year later. Once Brachiano was wifeless, Marcello, perhaps through his mother's suggestion, played matchmaker between the Duke and his sister. Brachiano was ridiculously fat (he had trouble finding horses strong enough to carry him, and he had a special dispensation which excused him from having to kneel in the presence of the Pope!), and yet he and Vittoria truly loved. The only remaining obstacle was Francesco. On April 16, 1581, a late-night letter from Marcello lured Francesco from his house: the letter asked him to meet a close friend at once, and on his way to the rendezvous, Francesco was shot and stabbed to death. Within two weeks, Vittoria had secretly married Brachiano in front of a witness. The lovers spent three years avoiding persecution from Pope Gregory XIII, who refused them a marriage contract. Vittoria even attempted to throw herself out of a window because of the Pope's pressure for her to break all association with Brachiano. The Medici family probably influenced the Pope, for they had turned against Brachiano and did not want Vittoria to be stepmother to Isabella's son by Brachiano, Virginio Orsini. Brachiano later convinced several theologians that he had to marry Vittoria, and a second, public marriage took place on October 10, 1583. The Cardinal de Medici heard of the marriage, but Brachiano, brazenly denying it to his face, deceived him. Finally, the lovers had a year of peace even though Brachiano suffered from a leg ulcer, but in 1585, Cardinal Montalto was elected Pope Sixtus V upon the death of Gregory XIII, and he began an investigation into the murder of his nephew Francesco Peretti by arresting Brachiano's followers and interrogating them while they stretched upon the rack. Late in 1585, Brachiano's leg ulcer enflamed again, and he died on November 13. Vittoria tried to shoot herself. Pope Sixtus V declared Brachiano a rebel and confiscated his possessions. Vittoria surrendered some of the goods, but a skillful lawyer contrived a way for her to retain legally all of Brachiano's property in Venice. At this, Lodovico Orsini, Brachiano's young kinsman who had for years resented Vittoria and who supported Virginio's claims to Brachiano's property, plotted her death. During the revels on the eve of Santa Vittoria's Day (December 22, 1585), Lodovico's thugs, dressed in masquerade costumes, entered Vittoria's palazzo, shot down her youngest brother Flamineo who screamed a warning to her, took Vittoria at her prayers, and when she begged them to kill her clothed, tore open her dress, made vulgar jokes, and stabbed her to death. F. L. Lucas comments on her history and character:

> Vittoria remains a mystery, deeper even than most human beings, but a fascinating one. Martyr or Devil?—her own age could not agree. Her beauty and strange charm alone remained unquestioned. . . . She was accessory to the murder of a husband who loved her, after the fact, if not before; at the treacherous summons of that April night of 1581 she must have guessed, if she did not know; soon she knew, in any case, and it made no difference to her relations with her lover. Was she merely heartless and ambitious? . . . Her ambition was doubtless real; so, it would seem, was her love; so, at the last, was her piety and, always, her courage. Were it only in that, she was born for a heroine of Webster's worship. Indeed, that the world does not see more like her, is due in part to the greater kindliness, but still more to the weaker courage, of common humanity. 'Pecca fortiter,' ['sin boldly'] said Luther; there at least she did not fail.

(The Complete Works of John Webster, ed. F. L. Lucas
[London: Chatto & Windus, 1928], vol. 1, 71–85).

When reading ERE's letter of introduction to *MG,* one can certainly
hear the echo of Lucas's penultimate sentence: 'When lions, eagles, and
she-wolves are let loose among such weak sheep as for the most part we
be, we rightly, for sake of our continuance, attend rather to their claws,
maws, and talons than stay to contemplate their magnificences' (586).

15. the white and deadly blossom of the house of Borgia: A chronicler
of Ferrara describes Lucretia Borgia (1480–1519) thus: 'Lucretia is of
medium height and slim of figure; her face is a little on the long side,
her nose is well shaped and beautiful, her hair golden, her eyes pale;
her mouth, with very white teeth, is a little large; her neck is slender
and white' (Anny Latour, *The Borgias,* trans. Neil Mann [London: Elek
Books, 1963], 130). The nature of her participation in the many acts of
immorality and the many deeds of bone-chilling evil ascribed to her
brother and father has never been irrefutably elucidated. The opinions
of modern historians are so divided about her that I cannot quote any
assessment of her life and character without taking a side and thus
unfairly representing other views. The only fair treatment of her in a
textual note like this is silence, but I will mention two historians. One of
her most notable champions is the German Ferdinand Gregorovius,
and one of her harshest accusers is the Italian Giuseppe Portigliotti. As a
last word, I can say that ERE was fascinated with this lady and her
family, and part of Lucretia lives in Fiorinda.

**16. her for whom Trojans and well-greaved Achaians so long time
suffered sorrows:** The daughter of Zeus and Leda, the most lovely
Helen of Troy, was taken, some say willingly and some say unwillingly,
from her husband's home by Paris, the son of Priam. Her husband,
Menelaos, and his brother, Agamemnon, formed an alliance of Achaian
kings who sailed to Troy to recover Helen. In bloody engagement
forced upon the fields near Priam's city, Trojans and Achaians groaned
through ten years of war for the sake of this woman. Helen led a lonely
life in Troy as a kinless foreigner, befriended by the noble Hektor and
the kindly King Priam, but unloved by the mercurial man who took her
for her beauty, and held in contempt and resentment by all other
Trojans.

17. Leda: This lovely mortal, the daughter of Thestios, the king of
Aetolia, and the wife of Tyndareos, the king of Sparta, bore many illustrious children. She was an avid bird watcher, and she founded the
Avian Society of Sparta, so she was easily tricked when Zeus came to her
in the form of a swan in order to make love to her. Helen, the woman
whose face launched a thousand ships out of Achaia, was the child of
this union. Castor, the famous horse breaker, was another child who
was born to her by Zeus. Strangely, the twin brother of Castor, Pollux
the boxer, was Leda's child not by Zeus but by her husband Tyndareos.
Clytemnestra, Agamemnon's lovely wife who murdered him in his bath
when he returned from Troy, was another child of Tyndareos and Leda.

18. Sparkling-thronéd heavenly Aphrodite . . . my great ally: Sappho, 1, 'Hymn to Aphrodite,' translated by ERE.

19. The moon is set . . . alone: Sappho, fragment 52, translated by ERE. Here is Wharton's literal translation: 'The moon is set, and the Pleiades; it is midnight, the time is going by, and I sleep alone' (Wharton, 100).

VOLUME TWO:
A FISH DINNER IN MEMISON

FD: **A Letter of Introduction**

1. George Rostrevor Hamilton: Hamilton (1888–1967) was one of ERE's best friends through most of his adult life, and ERE always asked Hamilton's opinion of his work in progress (see note 2 below). As a philosopher, a literary critic, a poet, and an editor, he had an active voice in English letters during his generation. A follower of Henri Bergson, Hamilton's first work of prose was *Bergson and Future Philosophy* (1921). Two more of his influential prose works are *Poetry and Contemplation* (1937) and *The Tell Tale Article* (1949). Between 1918 and 1963, Hamilton published eighteen volumes of verse.

2. played Pallas Athene . . . to my Achilles . . . to my Odysseus: Here ERE characterizes two aspects of his authorial temperament: the suddenly inspired, furious, reckless, passionate, swift-writing aspect he calls Achilles; the clever, subtle, organized, reserved, and calculating aspect he calls Odysseus. Hamilton stood as the constant critic of ERE's literary output, so here ERE extends the metaphor to Hamilton by deifying Hamilton's critical sensibilities as Pallas Athene, the fond and friendly protector and adviser to her favorite heroes, Odysseus and Achilles. Hamilton often restrained ERE from rashly pursuing an ill-chosen course in his fiction, as Athene does when she descends from the sky and grabs Achilles by the hair to keep him from wrathfully murdering Agamemnon (*Iliad,* 1: 188–218), and he often enthusiastically encouraged ERE, as Athene does when she counsels Odysseus (*Odyssey,* 13: 287–301). ERE's placing himself among the mortals and Hamilton among the deities shows his deep respect for Hamilton's literary abilities. ERE did listen and usually obeyed his friend's advice. Their correspondence contains many examples of Hamilton's kind dissuasion followed by encouragement, and of ERE's melting stubbornness followed by gratitude.

3. Midsummer's Day, Anno Zayanae Conditae 775: the twenty-first day of June in the seven hundred and seventy-fifth year after the founding of the city of Zayana.

4. his Dark Lady: This is Fiorinda, but ERE intends the pointed comparison to the lady of Shakespeare's sonnets.

5. Ah, Love! . . . to the Heart's Desire!: This is *rubaiy* (quatrain) 99 of the fifth edition of Edward Fitzgerald's translation and transmutation of *The Rubaiyat of Omar Khayyam.*

6. Descartes' *Cogito ergo sum:* René Descartes (1596–1650) was a physicist, a mathematician, a metaphysician, and a philosopher who rejected all traditionally received philosophical and theological ideas in an effort to achieve truth based purely upon his own mental investigations. He based his method on complete skepticism: he wanted to doubt everything that could be doubted. He started with the senses and decided that sense perception is full of error and cannot be trusted. Thus, the sensually perceived world is of uncertain existence. Then he doubted the accuracy of human thought because he realized that there existed no way of telling for certain whether he was awake and thinking or asleep and dreaming. Thus he doubted his own existence. Finally, after a period of bewildering sadness in which he could find nothing unassailably certain, he realized that the mental action of doubting was something even when it was doubting his body's existence. Descartes saw this realization as the founding principle of his philosophy: *'Je pense, donc je suis.'* This principle became the Latin phrase that ERE quotes, and, as he says, it may be reduced to the mere moment of thinking: *quamdiu cogitabo.*

7. Hume and Kant: David Hume (1711–76) had one of the finest minds in Great Britain in the eighteenth century. He made significant contributions to moral philosophy, and he became famous throughout Europe as a historian. Hume's *Enquiry Concerning Human Understanding* (1748, revised 1758) contains his mature philosophical principles about the nature of human knowledge. He believed that when the mind becomes aware of objects, they take the form of impressions or ideas. Impressions are sensually gathered data, and ideas are the thoughts derived from the manipulation of impressions. Ideas are not created; they are derived. Matters of fact present themselves to the mind as formed ideas whose properties must be perceived and accepted as they are given: ice feels cold; grass looks green. Because matters of fact must be accepted by the mind, the idea of causal connections between matters of fact are derived from natural and habitual beliefs that come through experience: if I touch ice, I expect it to feel cold, and I have that thought habitually every time I touch ice. Hume asserts that these natural beliefs are universally held and that they play a large part in the thoughts of causal inference, but that these experiential beliefs prevent the human mind from clearly proving causal connections between matters of fact even when they always appear to occur in causal sequence. These are the ideas ERE has in mind when he speaks of Hume's showing that metaphysicians put rabbits into hats before bringing them out.

Immanuel Kant (1724–1804) ranks among the best thinkers who ever lived. His contributions to metaphysics, aesthetics, theology, ethics, and epistemology changed philosophical thought and influenced all subsequent philosophy. Between 1781 and 1790, Kant published his greatest works, his three critiques. The first, the *Critique of Pure Reason,* is the most important work but also the most difficult to understand.

The book attempts to make metaphysics a science comparable to mathematics by discovering its limitations. Kant first attacks the metaphysical system that prevailed in German philosophy during his day: the systems of Gottfried Wilhelm Leibniz argued that people could, through thought alone, arrive at truths about abstract concepts like human immortality and the nature of God. Kant, influenced by the skepticism of Hume, argued that the mind can know only things that it experiences, but it can never know things as they truly exist, independent of the mind, because the mind imposes its own reasoning principles upon the objects of its experience. The mind, the subject acting in an attempt to gain knowledge of a certain object, is itself mainly that object because of the reasoning principles that exist within it and which it must use in order to experience an object. In short, when we experience things that our sense and reason tell us exist outside ourselves, we are not really experiencing those external objects but rather the idea of those objects as our minds organize them for us. (ERE was highly influenced by Kant; see Section VI of the Introduction.)

8. Pyrrho: Pyrrho of Elis (365–275 B.C.) was a painter, a poet, a devoted reader of Homer and Democritus, a court philosopher to Alexander the Great, and a principal voice in Greek skeptical philosophy. Pyrrho began his philosophical argument by asking the most difficult question: What is the ultimate truth of life? Then he took three courses of action: he doubted ready explanations, he investigated and considered evidence, and he suspended his judgment. Pyrrho's skepticism was balanced by open-mindedness, so he taught his disciples to obey both civil and religious laws even when they doubted the truth of those laws, because an open mind must agree that such laws could contain truth. To describe the mental state of suspended judgment and open thinking, Pyrrho used the word *epoche*. The physical feelings corresponding to *epoche* are quietness, calmness, and tranquillity; Pyrrho described these with the term *ataraxia*. Pyrrho's emotional control and his constant *ataraxia* made him famous for his fearlessness. Because he was as openminded about death as about life, he did not set his life at a pin's fee, and he met danger with a contented smile. Supposedly he endured both a near shipwreck and a surgical operation without blanching, and yet there is a story of his disciples chiding him on an afternoon when he allowed a fierce dog to chase him up a tree. (Mary Mills Patrick, *The Greek Sceptics* [New York: Columbia University Press, 1929]).

9. Scylla and Charybdis: Poetic geographical tradition maintains that these two perils, a monster and a whirlpool, stand opposite each other in the Straits of Messina. Scylla was the daughter of Phorcys and Hecate, and she was the lover of Poseidon. A rival lover and wife of Poseidon, the nereid Amphitrite, with magic herbs turned Scylla into a sixheaded monster. Supposedly, Scylla never failed to catch six sailors, one with each head, from every passing ship. Such errorless fielding in the modern age would make even Kent Hrbek doff his cap.

10. earth . . . ornament: See Edward Lessingham's poem that closes the Overture to *MM*.

11. The lunatic . . . all compact: In scene i of act V of *A Midsummer Night's Dream,* Theseus, the Duke of Athens, speaks these lines in scornful disbelief of the strange tale told by the four lovers who have spent a night of hysterics dashing around 'in the palace wood, a mile without the town, by moonlight.'

12. *The World as Will and Idea:* This book, *Die Welt als Wille and Vorstellung* (published in 1819) is the chief philosophical work of Arthur Schopenhauer (1788–1860). Schopenhauer was a complete pessimist who saw little of value in human living; his beliefs had a deep influence on the nihilism of Friedrich Nietzsche. Schopenhauer takes the Kantian position at the beginning of his book: people cannot know things as they truly are but only as they appear to our minds, because our perceptions of things are organized by the processes in our minds when we try to understand them. He then takes the Kantian position to its most pessimistic and negative application: the entire world is merely an idea, a perceived appearance. Then Schopenhauer goes beyond Kant to assert that we do experience things as they really are through 'will,' the energetic and hungry and desperate force of life that motivates all of our passions and wishes and desires, because this life force, the will, is the irrational essence of the world and of all nature. The primordial life force splits into infinite wills incarnate in living things, and thus all human and natural activities are conflicts of insatiable wills relentlessly striving to live and producing only destruction and suffering.

13. Tout passe, tout casse, tout lasse: All things pass away, all things break, all things perish.

14. Shakespeare's LXVIth sonnet:

> Tir'd with all these, for restful death I cry:
> As, to behold desert a beggar born,
> And needy nothing trimm'd in jollity,
> And purest faith unhappily forsworn,
> And gilded honor shamefully misplac'd,
> And maiden virtue rudely strumpeted,
> And right perfection wrongfully disgrac'd,
> And strength by limping sway disabled,
> And art made tongue-tied by authority,
> And folly doctor-like controlling skill,
> And simple truth miscall'd simplicity,
> And captive good attending captain ill.
> Tir'd with all these, from these would I be gone,
> Save that, to die, I leave my love alone.

15. All . . . know: the closing line of John Keat's 'Ode on a Grecian Urn.'

FD: Chapter I

1. ça m'amuse: this amuses me.

2. the third Rasoumoffsky Quartet: Count Rasoumoffsky, the Russian Ambassador to Vienna, was the patron of and played second violin in one of the finest quartets in Europe. During his second compositional period (1802–16), Beethoven dedicated three quartets (Op. 59) to Rasoumoffsky, and he included Russian melodies as themes in two of the quartets. Beethoven incorporated several structural and thematic innovations into the pieces, and Rasoumoffsky's musicians were so struck by them that they thought Beethoven was writing musical satire. When the famous pianist Muzio Clementi remarked to Beethoven, 'Surely you do not consider these works to be music?' Beethoven supposedly countered by saying, 'Oh, they are not for you, but for a later age.' (Donald Jay Grout, *A History of Western Music*, 3d ed. [New York: W. W. Norton, 1980], 536–37).

3. Vous . . . si parla: Do you speak French, madam? Oh, that depends on the subject matter: that depends on whom I am speaking to.

4. Inglese . . . incarnato: An English Italian is a devil incarnate.

5. Il faut . . . affaire-là: It is necessary for the spirit to relish this immediate matter distinctly.

6. Je vous . . . monsieur: The first French sentence translates thus: I will confide to you that I do not believe in God. The second translates thus: This time, says the priest, I blame you, sir.

7. the Solway and the Cumberland Hills: The family estates probably lie near the northwest coast of England and slightly south of the northern city of Carlisle.

8. Eton: Founded by Henry VI in 1440, Eton College is one of England's most time-honored institutions of scholarship in preparation for a career at an English university. ERE entered Eton at age thirteen in September 1896; he studied there until the summer of 1901, and then in the autumn he went to Trinity College, Oxford.

9. that unsavoury Jew musician: ERE admired the books of George du Maurier; this small episode was probably inspired by du Maurier's *Trilby* (1895) and by that novel's compelling villain, Svengali, the musical genius who frequents the studios of painters and sculptors in Paris.

10. Karakoram: This mountain range stands in the most northern part of India. Its most famous peak is the treacherous K2.

11. Etty: As a young man, ERE probably saw William Etty's (1787–1849) work in the City Art Gallery of York, since ERE's family lived in the parish of Adel, near Leeds and less than a day's journey from York. Etty imitated Rubens and Titian, and he has been praised for his ability to paint the amorphous tones and textures of human flesh. His best known works depict female nudes and subjects from classical mythology. Lessingham's derogatory remarks echo a common negative criticism of Etty: his poor draughtsmanship. And yet Delacroix admired

Etty, and praise from Delacroix would be justification enough for any artist's work.

12. Burne-Jones: Sir Edward Coley Burne-Jones (1833–98) was a successful painter, book illustrator, and designer. Burne-Jones apprenticed himself to Dante Gabriel Rossetti in 1856, and Rossetti influenced his style more than any other artist. With Rossetti, Burne-Jones contributed to the Pre-Raphaelite movement (see note 13). Burne-Jones took his subjects mainly from medieval legends and from allegorical romances of chivalry, and he painted them as scenes both dreamlike and romantic. His compositions are marked by soft and graceful lines, detailed backgrounds, dark and deep colors, and pale and slender female figures. Looking at the women depicted in Burne-Jones's *Laus Veneris* in the Laing Art Gallery of Newcastle-upon-Tyne, Henry James described them as 'pale, sickly and wan,' and Lessingham's remark echoes James's thoughts. Burne-Jones was also a lifelong friend of William Morris: after establishing himself as a painter, he worked with Morris on the Kelmscott Press books and also designed tapestries and stained glass for Morris.

13. Rossetti: Dante Gabriel Rossetti (1828–82) founded the Pre-Raphaelite brotherhood after being trained at the Royal Academy Schools and rejecting their classical aesthetics. The seven artists and writers of the Brotherhood believed a simple aesthetic: they wanted to express serious subjects with sincere moral content in paintings that depended upon the direct observation of nature and that imitated the style of Italian painters before Raphael. Their paintings often juxtaposed vivid colors and a white background, but this practice was deplored by many, and few contemporaries admired their work. The Brotherhood did not last ten years. Rossetti temporarily abandoned oil painting and worked in watercolors after the Brotherhood broke up. In the late 1850s, Rossetti met William Morris and Burne-Jones. He then returned to work with oil paints and a second expression of the Pre-Raphaelite aesthetic. He employed both of his new friends in helping him to paint murals and frescoes of the Arthurian legends on the walls of the Oxford University Union. Jane Morris, the artist's wife, was Rossetti's favorite model in the 1860s, and he portrayed her as a large-eyed sensual figure in many romantic and allegorical paintings.

14. Beardsley: Aubrey Beardsley (1872–98) became famous as an illustrator. He first gained public notice when he drew illustrations of an 1893 edition of Sir Thomas Malory's *Le Morte d'Arthur*. He then went on in 1894 to become the art editor of a journal called *The Yellow Book*. Beardsley did not attend art school, but he developed an original style characterized by fine Art Nouveau lines of sophisticated curving calligraphy, clever contrasts of black and white, and morbid or erotic subjects. He and Oscar Wilde were the chief spokesmen for English Aestheticism, a doctrine that states that art justifies itself and does not need any social or moral purpose. Edward Lessingham's censorious remarks probably are directed not at Beardsley's *Le Morte d'Arthur,* but at his rather grotesquely sexual illustrations to an edition of the *Lysistrata*. Looking at them tends to halt conversation.

15. Kapaneau's: See note 28 to the Overture to *MM*.

16. Apelles: The ancient Greeks considered him the greatest painter of the antique world, but unfortunately none of his work has survived. And yet happily, because none of his art is extant, no one can challenge his reputation. Apelles came from Colophon and was active during the fourth century B.C. He was the court painter for Philip of Macedon and for Philip's son Alexander the Great. Supposedly, Alexander refused to sit for all portrait painters except Apelles. Apelles was reputed to be a master of vivid color, composition, and treatment of light and shadow in painting. His most famous work, Aphrodite Anadyomene, has been given a detailed description in the writings of Pliny; it pictured the goddess wringing the sea water from her hair just after she has risen up from the foam on the shore of Cyprus. Apelles' work influenced later Greek sculptors (a sculpture, dating to 350 B.C., of Aphrodite wringing her hair stands in the University Museum of the University of Pennsylvania in Philadelphia) and painters, and accounts of his work influenced Botticelli.

17. Phryne: A lovely Greek woman of the fourth century B.C. She was the model for Praxiteles when he created the Knidian Aphrodite. See note 45 to the Overture of *MM*.

18. They die . . . horsemanship: Homer, *Iliad* 16:775; translated by ERE.

19. midsummer noonday: June 24, 775 AZC.

FD: Chapter II

1. that Borgian look . . . in Krestenaya: Fiorinda speaks here and in her next words of her first husband, Lord Baias. After his mistreatment of Fiorinda, he was, by the Chancellor's contriving, murdered, like Julius Caesar, on the piazza steps of Krestenaya. Describing Beroald's face during his devising of the murder, Fiorinda compares it to that of Cesare Borgia or perhaps to that of his father, Pope Alexander VI, for both were secret men of blood notorious for political murders. (See *MG*, Chapter XXIX.)

2. Valkyrie: See note 10 to Chapter VIII of *FD*.

3. salt pilchards and fumadoes: A pilchard is a small sea fish, like a herring, seasoned in brine, and a fumado is a smoked pilchard.

4. bow to the bush I get bield frae: This is a Scottish proverb: 'I respect the shrub from which I get shelter.' The noun *bield* can mean 'help' or 'food' or 'sustenance,' but here it most strongly means 'refuge' or 'shelter.' The Oxford English Dictionary associates this proverb with another quoted by Robert Burns: 'Better a wee bush than nae bield'—'it is better to have a small shrub for shelter than no shelter at all.' (See OED, *bush*, sb,[1]: Form, *bus*.) Beroald is not obsequious, but he is certainly a careful speaker, and perhaps he refers to the King with the mildly insulting term *bush* to show that he is not a flatterer who will speak honeyed words to coax the King's generosity.

5. Valero's rebellion: See Chapters XXIV and XXVI of *MG*.

6. kestrels, pies: sparrow hawks, magpies.

FD: **Chapter III**

1. from a magnificent forward drive: Unlike baseball, in which the single batter stands at the edge of the field and must hit a 'fair ball' between the 'foul lines,' the two batsmen in cricket stand in the middle of the field and may strike the ball in any direction. Thus in baseball it would be redundant to describe a hit as a 'forward drive,' but in cricket it is necessary.

2. for six: If the batted ball crosses the field boundary without bouncing, the batsman earns six runs. Runs are normally scored by batsmen running between the two 'wickets' (see note 5 below), which stand twenty-two yards apart.

3. knocking the bowling about like that: The cricket bowler is the equivalent of the baseball pitcher. Lord Anmering's remark implies a criticism: Lady Southmere's son is batting too aggressively and thus is transgressing against cricket's sense of style by treating the bowler's bowling disrespectfully. But Anmering's words are spoken tongue-in-cheek because he praises the young man's style in the subsequent conversation.

4. the telegraph board . . . to win: Consulting the scoreboard, Lord Anmering calculates that his team needs 84 more runs to overcome the opposing team's score of 163.

5. three wickets down: A wicket consists of three wooden stakes (called stumps) driven into the ground so that they are parallel and stand about thirty inches tall. On the top of the three stakes balance two small pieces of wood called bails. A wicket has no direct parallel in baseball, but it is comparable to the strike zone because the bowler aims for it when he delivers the ball. The batsman's job is to 'defend' the wicket with his bat by keeping the ball from striking the stumps and knocking off the bails. A batsman is 'out' when he fails to defend the wicket or when his batted ball is caught on the fly. (A batsman can also be run out while trying to score as he sprints between the wickets.) In one innings, eleven men bat two at a time, so 'three wickets down' means that three of the eleven have been called out.

6. make his century: A batsman who scores 100 runs makes his century, a number that has magic inapplicable even to a score of 99, for which contribution a batsman may sometimes receive only sympathy from his teammates.

7. playing forward to a yorker, was bowled middle stump: The legal limits of cricket bowling allow the bowler great variation in delivering the ball. A bowled ball usually bounces once on its way toward the wicket, but it need not bounce at all and is then called a 'full toss,' or it may bounce more than once. A yorker is a ball cunningly delivered to bounce at the batsman's feet. It is difficult to detect and leaves the unwary batsman helpless. If the batsman 'plays forward' to a yorker by stepping toward the oncoming ball with his front leg and trying to hit the ball back toward the bowler, he will find his bat hitting nothing but air as the ball passes under it. This is what happened to Jim Scarnside, and he was called out because the ball struck the middle stump of the wicket.

8. Trinity: Trinity College, Oxford. This was ERE's college.

9. All Souls': All Souls' College, Oxford.

10. you ought to block a yorker: The accepted and the only safe way to defend the wicket against a yorker is to bring your bat down upon it and block its progress to the wicket.

11. Lord's: This is the universally recognized abbreviation for Lord's Cricket Ground in London, the accepted headquarters and the mecca for cricketers throughout the world. It is named for its founder, Thomas Lord.

12. do the hat-trick: If a bowler captures the wickets of three batsmen with successive balls, he has done the hat-trick. It is an outstanding and rare achievement, far rarer than a batsman's century. Legend records that one wealthy team captain presented an expensive hat to a bowler who had done this deed, and thus arose the name.

13. Hyrnbastwick, Taverford: These seem to be fictitious places.

14. Antipholus of Ephesus . . . Antipholus of Syracuse: In Shakespeare's *Comedy of Errors*, these men are twin brothers and sons of Egeon, a merchant of Syracuse. When Egeon's wife Emilia delivered them, 'she became / A joyful mother of two goodly sons, / And, which was strange, the one so like the other / As could not be distinguished but by names' (I: i: 49–52).

15. Kelling Heath . . . Weybourne Heath to Salthouse Common: These places are in the county of Norfolk, on the coast of the North Sea, and are connected, now, by the A 149 road. They lie within three miles of one another.

16. caught at the wicket: The catch that dismissed Bentham was made by the wicket-keeper, a quick and sure-handed specialist who wears leg pads and padded gloves and who positions himself behind the wicket.

17. to mid-off, two: to mid-on, two: Glanford has scored four runs on two strokes, the first sending the ball toward the fielder a few yards to the right of the bowler, and the second sending the ball toward the fielder a few yards to the bowler's left.

18. a wide: If the bowler bowls the ball outside the batsman's ground, which is marked with white lines, the umpire signals 'wide' to the scorer, who awards the batting team with one run.

19. a strong drive, over cover's head, to the boundary, four: The 'point' fielder stands close to the batsman and at a position almost perpendicular to the line between the bowler and the batsman; the 'cover' or 'cover-point' fielder stands between the 'point' fielder and the 'mid-off' fielder. This ball flies over the cover-point fielder's head, bounces one or more times, and crosses the boundary without being caught, and so scores four runs.

20. to long-leg . . . Glanford run out: Here Glanford has hit a long ball to the field behind his back, and Jack Bailey, the long-leg fielder, has caught it bouncing near the boundary. Glanford and Margesson go for two runs and then for three because Bailey has tried to make an out by throwing directly at the wicket instead of throwing to the wicket-keeper. Bailey's throw is poor, the ball misses the wicket, and the point fielder must run after it. Seeing this, Glanford shouts to Margesson, and they run between the wickets again. Glanford then wants to sprint for yet another run once the point fielder retrieves the ball, but Margesson thinks it is too risky, and yet the aggressive Glanford persuades him. They run, but the point fielder makes a fine throw to the bowler Brem-merdale, who runs out the overambitious Glanford by knocking off one of the wicket bails before Glanford has reached his safe ground.

21. bag the bowling: The fielding team has two bowlers: in this case, Bremmerdale and Howard. One bowler delivers a set of six balls, called an over, in sequence from one end of the field (called the pitch). Then the other bowler delivers the next over from the opposite end of the pitch. Usually, the two batsmen receive the same number of balls, but an ambitious batsman, like Glanford, can receive most of the bowling by scoring one run from the last ball of the over so that he is at the oppo-site wicket and in position to receive the first ball of the new over. Scarnside accuses Glanford of such ambitious or selfish batting.

22. *Shagpat:* George Meredith's first novel was called *The Shaving of Shagpat, an Arabian Entertainment* (1856). The book's studiously archaic, comically eccentric, and extremely artificial style made it very different from Meredith's later works. The book was a humorous literary experi-ment, and a conscious parody of Sir Richard F. Burton's *The Book of the Thousand Nights and a Night.* Mary's following comment, O that's differ-ent from the rest,' address the book's unusual character. Here is a sam-ple of what Mary calls the 'delicious' prose; this scene is the first sighting of the clothier Shagpat by Shibli Bagarag the barber:

> He who lolled there was indeed a miracle of hairiness, black with hair as he had been muzzled with it, and his head as it were a berry in a bush by reason of it. Then thought Shibli Bagarag, ' 'Tis Shagpat! If the mole could swear to him, surely can I.' So he re-garded the clothier, and there was naught seen on earth like the gravity of Shagpat as he lolled before those people, that failed not to assemble in groups and gaze at him.
> (from Chapter 1)

Certainly a touch of this found its way into ERE's style in *WO*.

23. down went another wicket: The batsman who replaced Glanford is now out. Margesson is still batting, and now Appleyard comes in as his partner.

24. none of the Jessop business: The skillful Gilbert Jessop, perhaps the most famous hitter of all time, played for England and often destroyed bowling that had defeated all his side's best batsmen. His aggressive style, much copied, unhappily requires his genius for success and is too risky for average players.

25. Appleyard obediently blocked and blocked: Margesson cautioned Appleyard against playing his natural free hitting or 'slogging' game (like Jessop) because the ten runs required for victory can be more safely gathered by waiting for bad balls that will make scoring easy. So Appleyard does no more than defend his wicket by blocking the ball. In this manner, he and Margesson score four runs before Margesson's wicket falls.

26. took his leg stump: The skillful spin-bowler Bremmerdale has delivered a bowl known as a 'leg-break.' It bounces behind Margesson's legs, spins sharply to the left, and strikes the wicket.

27. Sir Oliver . . . never hit a ball yet: Sir Oliver Dilstead replaces Margesson. Nine wickets are down, so one more is left, and Dilstead, coming in to bat with Appleyard, is the eleventh man in. On most amateur teams, the eleventh batter is the worst. Here an unnamed spectator comments that Dilstead's contributions to the team come in the field rather than at the wicket. (As the baseball phrase goes, 'good glove, no bat.') Luckily, 'the ball that had beaten Margesson was the last of the over, so that Appleyard, not Dilstead, faced the bowling.'

28. Polyphemus: He was the son of Poseidon, a man of enormous strength and stature, and the greatest of the Cyclopes. Odysseus describes him as he watches him herd his sheep:

> in truth he was a monstrous wonder made to behold, not like a man, an eater of bread, but more like a wooded peak of the high mountains seen standing away from the others.
> (*Odyssey*, trans. Richmond Lattimore [New York: Harper & Row, 1965], 142).

29. Guelph and Ghibelline: Some of the political allegory of Dante's *Divine Comedy* focuses on the thirteenth-century struggle for political power in the Florentine republic between the Guelph forces, which supported the papacy, and the Ghibelline forces, which supported the Holy Roman Emperors. The names are Italianizations of German terms: *Welf* referred to the Bavarian dukes who opposed the Hohenstaufen emperors of the Holy Roman Empire, whose ancestral castle was seated at *Weiblingen*.

30. Done it!—Match!: With two mighty strokes that bounce the ball past the boundary, Appleyard has scored eight runs, and his team has won.

31. the game came to an end: Normally, the game stops when one team wins, but this is a friendly match. Appleyard won the match on the

first two pitches of the over, but the Hyrnbastwick team, in good sports-
manship, plays on so that Appleyard and Dilstead are not deprived of
their chances to bat. Dilstead never gets a ball, however, because Appleyard makes the tenth out when he swings freely ('slogs') on the
fourth bowl and his batted ball is caught by a 'slip' fielder who stands
near the wicket on the off-side.

32. Morris's willow pattern: William Morris created several much admired and highly valued wallpaper patterns.

33. Cotman: John Sell Cotman (1782–1842) was a landscape painter
who worked in watercolors and in sepia wash (a technique using brown
ink). He was born in Norwich and studied in London, where his work
was admired by Sir George Beaumont. ERE perhaps knew and liked
Cotman's work because he toured ERE's native Yorkshire between 1803
and 1805 and painted several Yorkshire scenes. Cotman's most famous
painting, *Greta Bridge* (1805), hangs in the British Museum.

34. Baedekers: The name refers to Karl Baedeker (1801–59) and his
son, Fritz, who published a famous set of travel guide books. Their
legacy is still in print.

35. Plainly a Refuge it was . . . Fay ce que vouldras: The French
imperative clause, 'Do that which you will desire to do,' is the rule
governing behavior in the Abbey de Thélème, which François Rabelais
(1495?–1553) allows his gigantic hero to build and endow in chapters
52–58 of *Gargantua* (1535). Although the inhabitants of this utopian
abbey live according to satirically liberal standards, this simple rule
makes them incline toward virtuous thoughts and actions. The Blunds
Refuge adopts the same rule, and its furnishings promote the same
happy liberty to pursue the heart's desire in noble fashion. When ERE
was planning his retirement from the Board of Trade, he was also su-
pervising the construction of his house in Marlborough, Wiltshire. One
room on the lower level had a desk facing large curving windows so that
ERE could sit and write while overlooking his garden. He called the
room his Refuge, and though unfrequented by dogs, it had much the
same atmosphere of sublime leisure filling this room in the house of
Anmering Blunds.

36. *tabula rasa:* an erased tablet, a clean slate.

37. La Belle Dame sans Merci: Jim Scarnside alludes to John Keats's
famous ballad, written in May 1819. The poem is named for its central
character, the wild-eyed, sirenlike faerie woman of hypnotic and fatal
beauty, who lures men, unsuspecting and alone in their cars, when she
hitchhikes by the roadside. The English translation of the French title,
is, of course, 'the Beautiful Woman Without a Mercedes.'

FD: Chapter IV

1. a du Maurier duchess: It is not coincidence that Mary Scarnside
shares her Christian name and surname alliteration with Mary Seras-

kier, the Duchess of Towers, a major character in George du Maurier's first novel, *Peter Ibbetson* (1891). Mary Seraskier and Peter Ibbetson, after knowing one another as children in sunny France, meet briefly as adults in London. Ibbetson falls in love with her immediately: she becomes the one beautiful thing in his wretched life. Then he meets her in a dream that the two of them share: Mary teaches him how to dream truly, and in subsequent dreams they become companions and lovers. See also note 4 to Chapter XVIII of *FD*.

2. He's teld . . . her wedding day: From a Scottish ballad titled 'Katharine Jaffray' and found in David Herd's manuscripts called *Ancient and Modern Scottish Songs* (1776).

3. the sovereign alkahest: In alchemic theory, it was a universal solvent with the power to dissolve anything.

4. Parnassus . . . Sutherland: Parnassus is a Greek mountain (8,000 feet) sacred to Apollo and Dionysus and located north of Delphi; Villars is a ski resort in the Alps; Ascot is the famous horse-racing park located east of London in Berkshire; Henley is the famous annual rowing competition between Cambridge and Oxford; Lord's is the internationally famous professional cricket field in London; Invernesshire and Sutherland are in the Scottish Highlands.

5. *Anne Horton 1766*: ERE is fooling around with English art history in these paragraphs. Anne Horton lived from 1743 to 1808. Had Sir Joshua Reynolds painted a portrait of her in 1766, she would have been twenty-three, not nineteen. As it happens, Reynolds did paint her portrait in 1773, but then she was thirty and had been newly married to the brother of King George III, H.R.H. Henry Frederick, the Duke of Cumberland. Thomas Gainsborough, who later painted four portraits of Anne Horton as the Duchess of Cumberland, had painted his first of three portraits of the Duke in 1771 when the Duke was out of favor with his brother the king.

> This first portrait of Henry Frederick, Duke of Cumberland, one of the King's brothers, was painted when His Royal Highness was in disgrace at Court, owing to his intrigue with Lady Grosvenor. The Duke was the least popular and the most dissipated of all the Royal Family, and was continually outraging even the lax of society of the day by his escapades. Already, almost before the excitement caused by the trial of the Cumberland-Grosvenor case had subsided, he had fallen in love with the notorious Mrs. Horton, widow of the Colonel Luttrell . . . In November of the year of the exhibition of Gainsborough's first portrait of him, the Duke of Cumberland married Mrs. Horton, and went off to Calais with her, whence he informed George III of what he had done. The passing of the Royal Marriage Act in 1772 was mainly the result of this so-called *mesalliance*, though the Duke's bride seems to have been, with all her faults, far superior to her husband. The newly-married pair sat to Sir Joshua Reynolds not long after their return from their honeymoon; and it is related that the Duchess tried in vain to induce the

Duke to say something polite to the great artist. He hemmed and ha'ed and worried the painter by looking over his shoulder as he worked; but all he could think of to say was, 'What! eh, so you always begin with the head, do you?' (Mrs. Arthur Bell [n. D'Anvers] *Thomas Gainsborough* [London: George Bell & Sons, 1897] 76).

6. Homeric hymn: Lessingham's mental clutch has slipped, and he does not have the requisite volume from the Loeb Classical Library to correct the mistake. The story of the birth of Aphrodite is told in Hesiod's *Theogony* (see note 37 to the Overture to *MM*), not in Homer's 'Hymn to Aphrodite.'

7. Botticelli's picture in the Uffizi: *The Birth of Venus* (1482–84) hangs in the Uffizi in Florence.

8. an old seguidilla: a Spanish dance in a fast triple meter.

9. Awful . . . to sing You: From Homer's shorter 'Hymn to Aphrodite'; ERE's translation.

FD: Chapter V

1. the divine Huntress: Artemis; for the story of the bathing Artemis and the spying Actaeon who surprised her in her nakedness, see note 26 to Chapter XXX of *MG*.

2. Who . . . seeming: ERE translates lines 54–55 of the 'Hymn to Aphrodite.' See Section I of the Introduction to compare ERE's with Lang's.

3. ὕβρις: excessive pride in one's personal strength.

4. poudre agrippine: A poison named for Agrippina the Younger, who supposedly poisoned her second husband, the Roman emperor Claudius.

FD: Chapter VI

1. goat-footed Pan: This Greek shepherd god is best known for the story in which he invents the syrinx, or pan-flute. Syrinx was a nymph who lived in the Arcadian mountains and who was devoted to the chaste life led by Diana. When Pan saw her, desire shuddered through him, and he pursued her to the shores of the river Ladon. Reaching the shore first, Syrinx prayed to the river nymphs to change her shape so that she could avoid the lustful embrace of the goat-footed god. At the moment when Pan caught her, she became marsh reeds. As he disappointedly observed the stiff reeds that his hands clutched, the wind blew through them and made a lamenting sound. Pan cut the reeds in varying lengths, bound them together with wax, and blew melodies through them. (See Ovid, *Metamorphoses* 1: 698–712.)

2. Hippokleides' betrothal feast: Both Amalie and her son Barganax are well read in Greek literature, and they both know this funny story, which Herodotus tells in his *History,* book VI, sections 126–30. Cleisthenes, a prince of Sicyon (a city on the Peloponnesian peninsula and near the gulf of Corinth) in the sixth century B.C., won the four-horse chariot race at the Olympic games. Based on this fame, he proclaimed throughout the land that any man who thought himself worthy to marry his daughter should come to Sicyon. Prospective suitors came from all over, and Cleisthenes hosted them for a year while 'making trial of their manliness and their temper and their education and disposition.' The man Cleisthenes preferred was Hippoclides, the son of Tisander, but he decided not to make his choice known until the marriage feast. After the dinner, people began to drink, sing, and dance. Hippoclides, warmed with wine and swayed by the festive mood, began to dance furiously. Soon he was dancing upon tables, and finally he stood on his head on a table and kicked the rhythmic dance steps in the air. Cleisthenes, disgusted by this behavior, shouted to him: 'Son of Tisander, you have danced—danced away your marriage!' Still poised on his head, Hippoclides laughed and retorted, 'Not a jot cares Hippoclides!' (Herodotus, *The History,* trans. David Grene [Chicago: University of Chicago Press, 1987] 461).

3. to truckle withal: This may be paraphrased thus: 'and in addition, I would not submit to such a man.' Amalie implies that if Barganax were less than a full man, then his father Mezentius would also be less than a full man, and in that case she would never have loved Mezentius.

4. Kythereia: See note 37 to the Overture to *MM.*

5. Tho' wisdom . . . taught me: ERE quotes the closing five lines of a song by Thomas S. Moore (1870–1944). The opening five lines are these:

> The time I've lost in wooing,
> In watching and pursuing
>   The light, that lies
>   In woman's eyes,
> Has been my heart's undoing.

The poem is from Moore's *Irish Melodies* (London: Longman, Brown, Green, and Longmans), 119.

6. a notorious murder: This is another reference to the killing of Lord Baias, the first husband of Lady Fiorinda. See Chapter XXIX of *MG.*

7. The Duchess would not have her at first: See Chapter XXX of *MG.*

8. Melusine: The story of Melusine is a legend that has been associated with the Lusignan family in France. It was recorded by Jean d'Arras in 1387. A Scottish king named Elinus marries a fairy named Pressina. A condition is placed upon the marriage: He may not see Pressina while she sleeps. The couple has three daughters: Melusine, Melior, and Plantina. After the daughters are born, Elinus breaks the condition, and Pressina leaves him and returns to her native Avalon. In anger at her father, Melusine imprisons him in a mountain, yet her mother does not appreciate the vengeful act: she casts a spell that turns Melusine into a serpent from the waist down every Saturday. Pressina places a condition on her daughter's reptilian transformation: If Melusine can find a husband who will agree to stay away from her on Saturdays, she will be released from her snaky punishment. Melusine marries Count Raymond of Lusingnan and tells him that she can never spend Saturdays with him because she has joined a ladies' golf league that plays thirty-six holes every Saturday. Raymond, who, like Sean Connery, proudly maintains a low handicap, and who, also like Sean Connery, detests playing golf with women, cheerfully agrees to leave her alone for half of every weekend. The happy couple have several children, but each one is born with some monstrous birth defect. One of Raymond's brothers suspiciously whispers to him that the children are deformed because they have been fathered by some lover that Melusine sees every Saturday. Raymond suspects her caddie, and, enraged, he storms into her room, where he sees her in her serpent form. She immediately leaves, and he never sees her again. Supposedly after her death, she haunts the castle grounds, and many have testified to hearing her mournful voice weeping for her children. But the more acute listeners hear her calling 'Fore!' and weeping for a shot that she topped into the pond near the seventh green.

9. Like is he . . . to dare all: Sappho, 'Ode to Anaktoria,' translated by ERE.

10. Donatello: A principal sculptor of the Italian Renaissance, Donatello (1386–1466) imitated Roman models and produced a new taste for statuary set on pedestals that stood independent of the surrounding architecture.

FD: Chapter VII

1. unkennelled Cerberus: In Greek mythology, this beast is a monstrous dog with three heads. Cerberus is the watchdog of Hades, so in ERE's analogy, the Vicar, who has in *MM* so often been associated with dogs and wolves, becomes the dog released from the land of the dead. Appropriately, the Vicar stabs Sorms three times to complete the analogy and match Cerberus' three sets of tearing teeth.

2. They shall see my back-parts, but my face shall not be seen: In the book of Exodus, Moses listens, from chapter 25–33, to God's instructions for the construction of the tabernacle and its furnishings. At the end of chapter 33, he asks to see God's glory by looking at him. Then God responds:

Thou canst not see my face: for there shall no man see me, and live. And the Lord said, Behold, there is a place by me, and thou shalt stand upon a rock: And it shall come to pass, while my glory passeth by, that I will put thee in a clift of the rock, and will cover thee with my hand while I pass by: And I will take away mine hand, and thou shalt see my back parts: but my face shall not be seen. (Exodus 33: 20–23, King James Version)

3. you wot of: you know of.

4. bediddered in the Ulba enterprise: The Ulba enterprise was the rebellion in Rerek led by Valero, Prince of Ulba. The verb *bediddered* means 'deluded' or 'deceived,' and Mandricard wonders why the Vicar would trust Clavius after having beheaded Clavius's father who was bediddered by Valero's cunning. See Chapter XXVI of *MG*.

5. fish sepia . . . too much ink: The cuttle-fish secretes an inky substance, from which a dark brown pigment is made and used in watercolor paints.

6. by cause of Ibian: ERE never wrote a detailed narration of the events causing this animosity between Ibian and Clavius.

7. caboshed: A variation of the transitive verb *caboch*, it means to cut off the head of a deer close behind the horns.

8. Valero's treason: See *MG*, Chapters XXIV and XXVI; also *MM*, 154.

9. gammon, and flitches . . . *pro bono publico*: ham, and a side of bacon; for the good of the state.

10. *per jus regale*: through kingly law.

11. *in solido*: all together, in mass.

12. Thorstein Codbiter and his crew: This Icelander is a character in the *Eyrbyggja Saga*:

Thorstein Codbiter became a man of the greatest largesse; he had ever with him sixty freedmen; he was a great gatherer of household stuff, and was ever going a-fishing. . . . That same harvest Thorstein fared out of Hoskuldsey to fish; but on an evening of harvest a shepherd-man of Thorstein's fared after his sheep north of Holyfell; there he saw how the fell was opened on the north side, and in the fell he saw mighty fires, and heard huge clamour therein, and the clank of drinking-horns; and when he hearkened if perchance he might hear any words clear of others, he heard that there was welcomed Thorstein Codbiter and his crew, and he was bidden to sit in the high-seat over against his father. That foretoken the shepherd told in the evening to Thora, Thorstein's wife; she spake little thereon, and said that might be a foreboding of greater tidings. The morning after came men west-away from Hoskuldsey and told these tidings: that Thorstein Codbiter had been drowned in the fishing; and men thought that great scathe.

(*The Story of the Ere-Dwellers,* in *The Saga Library,* trans. Eirikr
Magnusson and William Morris [London: Bernard Quaritch,
1892], 18–19)

13. gudgeons: small freshwater fish used as bait.
14. *ex visu amor*: the English equivalent is 'out of sight, out of mind.'

FD: Chapter VIII

1. Wolkenstein in the Grödner Dolomites: The Dolomite Mountains
are part of the eastern Alps; they run from southwest to northeast on
the border of Italy and Austria. The Grödner Dolomites stand about
ninety miles northwest of Venice and extend from west to east for fifteen miles between the villages of Waidbruck, St. Peter, St. Ulrich, St.
Christina, Wolkenstein, and Campitello, which lie in the Grödner Tal
(valley).
2. schuhplattler dance: a dance in wooden clogs.
3. my berserk sleep . . . Hadn't had a wink for five nights: When the
rush of furious bodily strength symptomatic of the berserk fit burns
itself out, extreme physical exhaustion follows. See note 4 to Chapter
XIX of *MM.*
4. fighting the Bulgarians: Edward Lessingham helped the Greeks
take Thessaloniki from the Bulgarians during the second Balkan War of
the summer of 1913. It is difficult to tell what he might have been doing
in Berlin in 1912, but perhaps he was involved in the diplomatic efforts
to prevent the first Balkan War, which lasted from October to December 1912.
5. the Medici blood: This powerful banking family controlled Florence
for much of the fifteenth century.
6. *Ambitioso . . . Lussurioso . . . Supervacuo*: ambitious, lustful, su-
premely lazy.
7. twentieth morning after: July 15, 775 AZC.
8. *de natura substantiarum*: the nature of substances.
9. you look east . . . Fünffingerspitze: In this Dolomite group, which
stands four miles north of Campitello, the Langkofel rises the highest at
10,427 feet, but the Fünffingerspitze is the most famous in the group
because of its strangely sharp pinnacles and the difficulty of ascending
it.
10. those swan maidens . . . in peace so: ERE's Weland Smith is
Volund the smith in the Old Norse 'Lay of Volund,' one of the poems in
the *Poetic Edda* (see note 2 to Chapter XX of *MM*). The poem begins by
telling of three young valkyries—Hlathguth Swanwhite, Hervor Allwise,
and Olrun—who are flying through Mirkvith to find wars and adventures in which to test their powers. While resting by a lake, they meet
Volund and his brothers and fall in love with them. The three pairs of
lovers wed and spend seven happy years together. In the eighth year

the valkyries grow restless, and in the ninth year they leave their husbands to seek adventures again.

11. The Red King's dream in *Alice*: Edward Lessingham refers to the Red King in *Through the Looking Glass*. The loud snoring of the nightcapped and tasseled Red King distracts Alice from her discussion with Tweedledee and Tweedledum about the proportionate unpleasantness of the Carpenter and the Walrus. The fat twins lead Alice to him:

> 'I'm afraid he'll catch cold with lying on the damp grass,' said Alice, who was a very thoughtful little girl.
>
> 'He's dreaming now,' said Tweedledee: 'and what do you think he's dreaming about?'
>
> Alice said 'Nobody can guess that.'
>
> 'Why, about *you*!' Tweedledee exclaimed, clapping his hands triumphantly. 'And if he left off dreaming about you, where do you suppose you'd be?'
>
> 'Where I am now, of course,' said Alice.
>
> 'Not you!' Tweedledee retorted contemptuously. 'You'd be nowhere. Why, you're only a sort of thing in his dream!'
>
> 'If that there King was to wake,' added Tweedledum, 'you'd go out—bang!—just like a candle!'
>
> 'I shouldn't!' Alice exclaimed indignantly.

They never settle this debate, and Carroll does not settle it for us. At the end of the book, when Alice returns to her own world and the Red Queen turns back into Kitty, Alice tries to get the cat's opinion:

> 'Now, Kitty, let's consider who it was that dreamed it all. This is a serious question, my dear, and you should *not* go on licking your paw like that—as if Dinah hadn't washed you this morning! You see, Kitty, it *must* have been either me or the Red King. He was part of my dream, of course—but then I was part of his dream, too. *Was* it the Red King, Kitty? You were his wife, my dear, so you ought to know—Oh, Kitty, *do* help to settle it! I'm sure your paw can wait!' But the provoking kitten only began on the other paw, and pretended it hadn't heard the question.
>
> Which do *you* think it was?
>
> (Lewis Carroll, *Through the Looking Glass*).

12. ὕλη: literally, wood; here, the raw material of which things are made.

13. aqua fortis . . . gold itself: Aqua regia, which receives its kingly name from its ability to dissolve the noble metals, is a combination not of aqua fortis (nitric acid) and vitriol (sulphuric acid), but of aqua fortis and muriatic (hydrochloric) acid. As the song goes, 'Don't know much about chemistry; that's because I'm Aphrodite.'

14. gang: go on, continue, hold on tenaciously.

15. *Le Lys Rouge, La Tulipe Noire*: the red lily, the black tulip.

16. Westfirth . . . Halogaland: See note 1 to the Overture to *MM*.

17. The day . . . ashen spear: *Iliad* 6: 448; translated by ERE.

18. Strike thunder . . . when I farewell: Lessingham's inner voice, floating from thought to thought, quotes the last words of John Webster's sneering villain Flamineo, who, after describing his life as 'a black charnel,' dies rhyming: 'Let no harsh flattering bells resound my knell, / Strike thunder, and strike loud to my farewell' (*The White Devil* V: vi: 273–74).

19. quartet: Beethoven's Op. 131, written in 1825.

20. Ninfea di Nerezza: the black water lily.

21. Nether Wasdale paper: Mary and Edward Lessingham have a house in Nether Wasdale, a small village less than three miles from the Wast Water in the Lake District of England. The paper is stationery embossed with the house address.

22. the Wolf fettered: Snorri Sturluson (1179–1241) Iceland's most time-honored writer, tells the story of the binding of Fenrir in the *Prose Edda* (an anthology of Norse myths: some tell the actions of the gods and giants, some explain the creation of the nine mythic realms and their relationships, and some tell mythic stories for the purpose of illustrating the rules for writing skaldic verse). The Norse god Loki has three children with a giantess named Angrbrotha, and one of these is the wolf named Fenrir. The gods raise Fenrir in their land of Asgard, but because the rapid daily growth of the beast shocks them and the prophecies about the wolf predict he would bring doom to them, the gods decide to bind him. Fenrir easily breaks two kinds of strong fetters, so Odin sends a messenger to the dwarfs and asks them to make a fetter. The dwarfs make Gleipnir, a soft leash like a silk ribbon, from 'the noise a cat makes when it moves, the beard of a woman, the roots of a mountain, the sinews of a bear, the breath of a fish, and the spittle of a bird.' The gods trick Fenris into testing the leash, and when he rages violently against the harsh restraint, the gods shove a sword into his mouth so that the hilt rests in his lower jaw and the point jabs the roof of his mouth: 'He howls horribly, and the slaver running from his mouth forms the river called Von [i.e., expectation]. There he will lie until Ragnarok [i.e., the destruction of the cosmos].' (Snorri Sturluson, *Prose Edda*, trans. Jean I. Young [Berkeley: University of California Press, 1954], 56–59).

23. the Wastwater Screes: Scree is rock that has been shattered to bits by weather and erosion. The mountain cliffs towering in blackness from the edge of the eastern shore of the Wast Water in England's Lake District are called the Screes because their foundation slopes are glutted with jagged fragments of broken cliff-face rock. The Screes are a jagged ridge extending between Whin Rigg (1,755 feet) and Illgill Head (1,998 feet). The barren, glacial appearance of the Screes strike their observer's imagination with, as ERE's paragraph suggests, immeasurable remoteness.

24. the Lotus Room: The honey-sweet lotus fruit made Odysseus' men forget their way home and their desire to go home. (See Homer's *Odys-*

sey, book 9: 82–104.) It is from the Lotus Room that the Lessingham of *WO* leaves his home and chariots off to Mercury, a place alluring enough to make any visitor there lose the desire to go home. In the Induction to *WO*, ERE only hints darkly about the power of the Lotus Room, but it seems to be a departure point for journeys in space and time. Mary and Lessingham seem to have experienced the room's potent magic before Lessingham's journey to Mercury:

> They were silent awhile; then Lessingham said suddenly, 'Do you mind if we sleep in the east wing to-night?'
> 'What, in the Lotus Room?'
> 'Yes.'
> 'I'm too much of a lazy-bones to-night dear,' she answered.
> 'Do you mind if I go alone, then? I shall be back to breakfast. I like my lady with me; still, we can go again when next moon wanes. My pet is not frightened, is she?'
> 'No!' she said, laughing. But her eyes were a little big. Her fingers played with his watch-chain. 'I'd rather,' she said presently, 'you went later on and took me. All this is so odd still: the House, and that; and I love it so. And after all, it is a long way and several years too, sometimes, in the Lotus Room, even though it is all over next morning.' (*WO*, 2)

Lessingham confidently speaks of returning by morning, as though he were planning to take a night train, and he seems to be familiar with the room's departure schedule since it lies in conjunction with the phases of the moon. Mary, too, seems to describe the action of the Lotus Room based on several experiences. Nevertheless, Mary does not seem used to the Lotus Room: her experiences seem new and unfamiliar because they are 'so odd still.' This noted paragraph in *FD* says that the Lotus Room was 'newly built' in the east wing of the old house 'three years ago.' If Mary's words above do imply an unfamiliarity with the Lotus Room's power due to its recent building, then it may be assumed that they were spoken shortly after the construction in the east wing, and so the events of the Induction to *WO* may be placed on a cool evening in 1911.

25. *L'Absente de tous bouquets*: The woman lacking all flowers.

26. A quiet woman . . . safely: Having witnessed a bitterly jealous quarrel between the adulterous lovers Brachiano and Vittoria, Flamineo speaks these cynical lines after Brachiano attempts once again to ingratiate himself to Vittoria. Flamineo seems to want his sister to calm down and accept Brachiano's penitent words, but Vittoria responds by saying, 'O ye dissembling men!' (John Webster, *The White Devil*, IV: ii: 179–182).

27. Drigg: A town near the Cumbrian coast, about ten miles southwest of Nether Wasdale.

FD: **Chapter IX**

1. Ninfea di Nerezza: the black water lily.
2. *De Libertate Humana***:** Perhaps Spinoza's works have different names in Zimiamvia, because here Vandermast refers to proposition 30 of Spinoza's *Ethics*: 'Intellect, in function (actu) finite, or in function infinite, must comprehend the attributes of God and the modifications of God, and nothing else' (*The Chief Works of Benedict de Spinoza,* trans. R. H. M. Elwes [New York: Dover, 1951], 2: 69).
3. the Marchioness of Monferrato . . . the King of France: After hearing of the singular beauty of the wife of the Marquess of Monferrato, King Philip of France grows curious and decides to visit her while her husband is away in the Levant on a Crusade. At dinner, the King is served, according to the lady's commands, course after course of chicken. The King jokes about this, but the Marchioness replies that one chicken is like another. Her serious face and tone of voice make the King understand her implied meaning: he should seek his mistresses at home in France because the women of Monferrato are like women elsewhere, and she will not betray her husband's love. The story of this fair lady's fowl dinner is extant in very choice Italian: it is the fifth tale told on the first day in Boccaccio's *Decameron.*
4. Injoy'd no sooner . . . a dreame: Shakespeare, Sonnet CXXIX.
5. the Furioso: a man driven mad by passionate, unrequited love.
6. Daughter of Zeus: In Books 3 and 5 of the *Iliad,* Homer names Zeus and the Titan goddess Dione as the parents of Aphrodite. In this account of her birth, Homer differs from Hesiod: see note 37 to the Overture to *MM.*

FD: **Chapter X**

1. *mala necessaria***:** necessary evils.
2. 'This may be your death,' she said: ERE admired this hot-blooded scene enough to write it twice. He first used it fifteen years earlier in *Styrbiorn the Strong.* On the very night of a banquet celebrating both his impending investment with half the kingship of Sweden and his betrothal to Princess Thyri, daughter of King Harald Gormson of Denmark, Styrbiorn commits adultery with Sigrid the Haughty, Queen of Sweden and wife to Styrbiorn's uncle, King Eric the Victorious. Upon waking the next morning, Styrbiorn is nearly paralyzed with remorse and bitter regret when he realizes that he has betrayed the trust of both his uncle and his princess:

Styrbiorn moved like a blinded man towards the door; then, finding her in the way, gave back a pace. Then he said, yet with eyes averted and in alien and hard tones half-choked, 'Let me go, Sigrid.'

'I'll let thee go,' said she, 'when thou speakest to me like my noble kinsman, not like a base-born thrall.'

For a moment he paused as if doubting what were best to do, then lifted up his head and strode forward as if he were minded to thrust her aside by force. At hands'-reach he halted. The ghastliness of his look as he stood and looked upon her took from her for a minute all power of thought or motion. Then he opened his mouth and said, 'What have I to do with thee, a faithless bitch?'

With that, he turned from her, catching in his two hands the pillars of the bed. Under the grip of his hands and the weight of him flung between them the great oak pillars shook and creaked. He turned again, dazed yet with this nightmare, steadying himself yet with one hand by the pillar of the bed. He looked at her now with eyes like some dog's eyes asking to be let out: naught else matters.

But the Queen faced him, back to the door, staring. Under the injury of those words she had moved not an eyelid. But instant by instant she seemed stonier grown; her face whitened, even to the lips; and then the blood flooded back terribly. She said in a low tone, the words even and steady like water dropping and clear as the clicking of blades, 'But this shall be thy death, then.' Therewith so loud shrieked Sigrid the Queen that the cups rang on the wall and the geese screamed in the King's garth.

(*Styrbiorn the Strong* [London: Jonathan Cape, 1926] 161–2)

ERE bases the scene upon Snorri Sturluson's account of the Norwegian King Olaf Tryggvison (reigned 995–1000) contained in Snorri's highly fictive chronicle of the lives of the Norwegian kings, *Heimskringla* (see note 23 to the Overture to *MM*). ERE discusses the scene from *Heimskringla* in a historical note he composed to accompany his novel, but he severely edited the note prior to publication, and the following portion about Sigrid was not included:

. . . in her breach with Styrbiorn in Chapter IX, I have had in mind her dealings, seventeen years later, with King Olaf Tryggvison. When that admired young bayard of the north and patron saint of muscular Christianity was imposing by logic of sword and fire the blessings of his Church on Norway, he became betrothed to Queen Sigrid. Displeased, however, at her coldness toward his missionary efforts, he imprudently struck her across the mouth with his glove, saying at the same time, 'what have I to do with thee, a heathen bitch?' 'These words,' she replied, 'may likely prove thy death.' No windy menace: for her hand seems to have been in it when he fell in the great sea-fight at Svoldr under a combined attack by his enemies.

(SRQ 823.91 ED 23, Correspondence and Notes Relating to *Styrbiorn the Strong,* Local History Department, Reference Library, Central Library, Leeds)

Gwyn Jones concurs with ERE's view of Olaf Tryggvison and calls him 'the most spectacular viking of the age,' but he disagrees with ERE's assessment of Sigrid's power and influence because he believes that Sigrid the Haughty was a nonexistent woman of legend to whom Snorri gave a place in his dramatic narrative (Gwyn Jones, *A History of the Vikings* [London: Oxford University Press, 1973], 131,136).

FD: Chapter XI

1. This bald unjointed chat of yours!: Campaspe adopts a line from Hotspur's flamboyant opening speech in act I, scene iii of 1 *Henry IV,* a speech that ERE much admired. Hotspur has been explaining why he has not delivered up his prisoners from the late battle, and his excuse is his repugnance to the effeminate lord who came asking for the prisoners in the king's name: 'This bald unjointed chat of his my lord / I answered indirectly, as I said' (I: iii: 65–69).

2. one desire . . . fire: From a lyric poem by George Chapman (1559–1634). Today Chapman is perhaps best known as the translator of Homer whose images thrilled the young Keats.

3. peggy-whitethroat . . . elegant lynx: This scene has some resemblance to a scene in the *Volsunga Saga.* After slaying Fafnir, Sigurd roasts the dragon's heart over a fire. He touches the bubbling organ to see if it is cooked through, and then he puts his bloodied finger into his mouth. As soon as he tastes the dragon's blood, Sigurd can understand the songs of the birds, and the woodpeckers tell him to journey to the hall where Brynhild lies sleeping. See chapter 19 of *The Story of the Volsungs and Niblungs,* trans. Eirikr Magnusson and William Morris, in *Epics and Sagas,* vol. 49 of the Harvard Classics (New York: P. F. Collier & Son, 1938).

4. sendaline . . . smaragds . . . escarbuncles: thin silk; emeralds; rubies.

5. cramoisie silk: crimson silk.

6. gryphons and mantichores and flying fire-drakes: The first is a beast having the head, wings, and feathers of an eagle and the body of a lion; the second is a beast having a man's face, a lion's body, a porcupine's quills, and a scorpion's tail; the third is a flying fire-spewing dragon.

7. O lente . . . Night!: Christopher Marlowe's Doctor Faustus, realizing that he has 'but one bare hour to live' before he shall be 'damned perpetually' (V: ii: 143–44), does not, in his terror, forget his scholastic studies of the classics: he quotes this line from Ovid's *Amores* (1:13 and 2:39–40). A literal translation of the line would be 'O run slowly,

slowly, you horses of night,' and Marlowe uses the line as Faustus's despairing wish to postpone his damnation (V: ii: 152). The translation that appears here was done for ERE by George Rostrevor Hamilton.

FD: Chapter XII

1. Ossa . . . Pelion: In Greek mythology, two giants named Otus and Ephialtes tried to climb to heaven to make war upon the gods. They uprooted Mount Ossa and placed it upon Mount Olympus, and then they uprooted Mount Pelion and placed it upon Ossa. Zeus sighed and frowned upon such gross labors and effortlessly destroyed the giants with a thunderbolt.
2. Myrobalan: an astringent variety of plum.
3. From women . . . deliver us: In his closing note to *FD,* ERE wrote, 'I have lost the references for the two verse quotations in Chapter XII.'
4. *in saecula saeculorum*: into ages of ages.
5. *stoccata, imbrocatta, rinverso . . . montanto*: See note 3 to Chapter XVII of *MM.*

FD: Chapter XIII

1. Illgill Head: A mountain peak (1,998 feet) on the eastern shore of the Wast Water; it marks the northern end of the long precipitous ridge called the Screes. See note 23 to Chapter VIII of *FD.*
2. Sardanapalus: This ancient king of Nineveh had tremendous wealth that he kept in a treasure room securely underground. Thieves learned the plans of his palace, tunneled their way to the treasure room, stole the treasure one night while Sardanapalus was sleeping, and escaped through another tunnel to the Tigris River. See Herodotus, *History* 2: 150.
3. *sotto voce*: softly.
4. At the home farm . . . in the paddock: ERE had fondness for these descriptive clauses, which occur twice in the poems of the *Poetic Edda* (see note 2 to Chapter XX of *MM*) to describe Guthrun's lamentation, provoked by the murder of her beloved Sigurth, growing so loud that it frightens the domesticated geese:

> Then wept Guthrun,   Gjuki's daughter,
> that through her tresses   the tears did flow,
> and in the garth   the geese sang out,
> the far-famed fowl   which the fair one owned.
>   ('The First Lay of Guthrun,' stanza 16)

> Her senses lost she—   his life the king—
> her hands wrung she   so ruefully
> that in the cupboard   the beakers clinked
> and in the garth   the geese sang out.
>
>   ('The Short Lay of Sigurth,' stanza 29)
>   (*Poetic Edda,* trans. Lee M. Hollander, 2nd ed.
>   [Austin: University of Texas Press, 1962], 249, 257)

Here ERE uses the clauses for comic effect to mark the arrival of Eric Lessingham's stentorian voice, but he employs it in its original tragic setting to mark the discovery of the murder of King Mardanus in Chapter VI of *MG,* and to mark the climactic turning point in the story of Prince Styrbiorn: see note 2 to Chapter X of *FD.*

5. Kantian principle of the universal: In his *Critique of Practical Reason* (published 1788), Immanuel Kant emphasized a theoretical moral guide that he called the catagorical imperative: People should act only upon the maxim that should, in their perception, be a universal law for anyone in their situation and circumstances. See also note 7 to the Letter of Introduction to *FD.*

6. *in excelsis*: in a high degree.

7. condottieri: In fourteenth-century Italy, this term labeled mercenary soldiers who made a *condotta* or contract to wage war under fixed terms of service and payment. Employed by landed aristocrats, the captains of bands of condottieri were often aristocrats who themselves had been defeated in battle and uprooted from their estates by other bands of condottieri, while the ranks were filled with outlaws from every social class, including the clergy. Oftentimes, condottieri refused to disband once the terms of their employment had been fulfilled, and they continued to support themselves through terrorist acts of rapine, robbery, and plunder. Barbara W. Tuchman writes of them: 'Bound by no loyalties, serving for gain rather than fealty, they nourished wars for their own benefit and protracted them as long as they could, while the hapless population suffered the effects' (*A Distant Mirror* [New York: Ballantine Books, 1979], 248).

8. Frederick II of Hohenstaufen: See note 24 to the Overture to *MM.*

9. Eric Bloodaxe: See note 22 to the Overture to *MM.*

10. Egil Skallagrimson's time: In general terms, Lessingham means the colonial age and the first settled age of Iceland: from about A.D. 860 to 1000.

11. Sir Walter Ralegh: Living from 1552(?)–1618, Ralegh, or Raleigh, took part in the greatness of the political, colonial, and military power of the Elizabethan age. He knew Oxford; he saw war in France; he met Edmund Spenser in Ireland; he experienced the favor and disfavor of the Queen; he must have seen Shakespeare presenting new plays on the stage; he journeyed twice to the New World; he saw the defeat of the Spanish Armada; he sacked and burned ships in Cadiz harbor; he wrote a history of the world; he knew the disfavor of James I, and consequently he knew the gray stone walls of the Tower of London.

12. *pis aller*: a last resource, something that is better than nothing.

13. Prussianism: German militarism and imperialism.

14. Scaliger: Joseph Justus Scaliger (1540–1609) was a prominent French scholar and historian.

15. K.C.B.: Will Lessingham's work was honored by his being knighted as a Knight Commander of the Order of the Bath.

16. berserk rages . . . yourself: See note 4 to Chapter XIX of *MM*.

17. twelve stone: 168 pounds.

18. *modus vivendi*: method of living.

19. Gordian knots: An ancient oracle told the Phrygians that, during a period of civil strife, they should appoint as king the first man whom they saw approaching the temple of Zeus in a wagon. Gordius, a peasant, was chosen in this fashion. A legend grew current about the knot fixing the yoke to the wagon's pole: it was tied so cunningly that people believed the person to untie it would achieve the empire of Asia. Supposedly, Alexander the Great heard the legend, went to look upon the knot, pondered it thoughtfully for a moment, drew his sword swiftly, and cut the cords asunder.

20. *Moi . . . en Dieu*: As for me, I do not believe in God.

21. *The Vision of Zimiamvia* **portrait:** See the closing pages of the Overture to *MM*.

22. *Est-ce que . . . un écureuil*: Can it be that you are able to tell me, madam, what the difference is between a tooth-brush and a squirrel?

23. *Quand . . . l'écureuil*: When you place both of these things underneath a tree, the one that climbs the tree is the squirrel.

24. Isabella d'Este's in our Titian: This portrait is ERE's invention, but a famous portrait of Isabella, painted between 1534 and 1536, hangs in the Kunsthistorisches Museum in Vienna. Lady Isabella wears no ruff in the portrait, but she does wear a rather eyebrow-raising hat. The portrait is an official one that portrays Isabella as she ought to have looked rather than as she truly looked. Nevertheless, this woman, the childhood companion of Lucretia Borgia, was known for her beauty and known to be rather proud of her beauty.

25. Herrick's *Lily in Crystal*: Robert Herrick (1591–1674) was a Londoner by birth and at heart, but after living a few laughter-filled years of literary chatter and tankard clanking in the circle of Ben Jonson, he spent most of his productive years in what he called 'a long and dreary banishment' as the Vicar of Dean Prior in Devonshire. Although he longed for London, the quiet countryside worked on his poetic imagination and stirred his lyrics. 'The Lily in Crystal' argues for beauty quietly concealed and not splendidly revealed. His lily 'tombed in a crystal stone' shows 'more fair in this transparent case / than when it grew alone, And had but single grace.' Herrick puts forth other examples and summarizes from them:

> Thus lily, rose, grape, cherry, cream,
> And strawberry do stir
> More love when they transfer

> A weak, a soft, a broken beam,
>   Than if they should discover
> At full their proper excellence,
>   Without some screen cast over
> To juggle with the sense.

Herrick concludes by advising women to veil their bodies skillfully in silken gowns so that their 'hidden pride' may 'raise greater fires in men:' 'Thus let this crystalled lily be / A rule, how far to teach / Your nakedness must reach.' The impishness of this moral, promoting both chastity and lechery, is not unpalatable, and it seems appropriate to this laughter-loving vicar who reputedly taught his pet pig to drink beer from a cup.

26. Ushba . . . ice and stone: Mary describes a scene in the Caucasus Mountains, which lie in Georgia, east of the Black Sea.

27. God's adversaries . . . patience: Robert Harris, *Sermon*, 1642.

FD: Chapter XIV

1. keep a servant fee'd: See Macbeth's response when Lady Macbeth asks how he knows of Macduff's refusal to attend the banquet:

> There's not a one of them but in his house
> I keep a servant fee'd. (III: iv: 132–33)

2. Ingenuities beyond Aretine's: Barganax makes Fiorinda blush with indignation when he responds to her innocent remark about teaching tricks to the wagtails with a joking reference to a sixteenth-century Italian book of engraved prints showing people explicitly engaged in sexual intercourse in rather unorthodox positions requiring a gymnastic flexibility. The prints were done by Giulio Pippi and Marcantonio Raimondi, but the book became associated with Pietro Aretino (called 'the Aretine' because his birthplace was Arezzo) because he wrote a sonnet series to accompany the prints. (See Wayland Young, *Eros Denied* [New York: Grove Press, 1964], 99–116.) Aretino (1492–1556) was one of the great monsters of sixteenth-century Italy who acquired power through scandalous and corrupt practices. He was a prolific and highly independent writer who defied literary tradition and authority, and though he was capable of producing literary art, he more often used his pen to generate scandal and extort money. Although he was a notorious scoundrel, Ariosto nicknamed him 'il divino,' he was a friend of Titian's and Michelangelo's, and he was honored by Charles V and Francis I. (See Edward Hutton, *Pietro Aretino, Scourge of Princes* [London: Constable & Co., 1922].)

3. *Si tu . . . soit vrai:* If you love me ten times / During one night in May / On the eleventh time I shall believe / That your love is true.

4. *chaque . . . fois***:** on each occasion, my friend: indeed, on each occasion.

5. *Ce que . . . le veut***:** That which a woman desires, God desires.

6. *Copula spiritualis***:** a spiritual couple.

FD: **Chapter XV**

1. Zenianthe: See note 3 to Chapter XIII of *MM*.

2. *nemo . . . lacessit***:** No man irritates me with impunity.

3. Andromeda upon the bank: Her mother, Queen Cassiopeia of Ethiopia, boasted that she was more beautiful than the sea nymphs, and Poseidon, offended at this arrogance, sent a fanged and fishlike reptilian sea monster to ravage the shores of Ethiopia. Poseidon also decreed that the innocent Andromeda would have to be sacrificed to the monster's jaws to surfeit its appetite and appease its rage. King Cepheus, Andromeda's father, mournfully ordered servants to chain Andromeda to the rocks on the shore. There she lay, awaiting salty death but getting a good tan, when suddenly wing-footed Perseus flew overhead and beheld her torment. Perseus, of course, fell in love with her immediately, killed the slimy beast, and obtained the King's and Queen's permission to marry Andromeda.

4. *Quod est absurdum***:** Which is foolish.

5. To . . . pac'd: In his *Infinitati Sacrum* (1601) John Donne adopts a Pythagorean doctrine of a soul's progress through various living forms: 'the Pithagorian doctrine doth not onely carry one soule from man to man, nor man to beast, but indifferently to plants also: and therefore you must not grudge to finde the same soule in an Emperour, in a Posthorse, and in a Mucheron [i.e., mushroom].' ERE quotes the first two lines of stanza 18 of 'The Progresse of the Soule,' a song in which this doctrine is delineated. In stanza 18, the soul leaves the form of a mandrake root and enters the egg of a sparrow.

6. *vox inanis***:** an empty voice.

7. Because . . . to suck: Here Anthea darkly echoes the famous line in which Sir Toby Belch reproaches the humorless Malvolio for his self-righteous and judgmental attitude toward Sir Toby's and Sir Andrew's drunken clowning: 'Dost thou think, because thou art virtuous, there shall be no more cakes and ale?' (Shakespeare, *Twelfth Night* II: iii: 114–15).

8. Volsungs and Niblungs . . . into the worm-close: Chapters 33–38 of the *Volsunga Saga* tell of the destruction of the fair and bold sons of King Guiki. Gudrun, the daughter of King Guiki, whose first husband had been Sigurd the Volsung, takes King Atli of the Budlungs as her second husband, but 'little sweet and kind was their life together' (ch. 33). Atli, knowing that Gudrun's brothers, Gunnar and Hogni, hold all of the gold that Sigurd had achieved by killing Fafnir, invites Gunnar and Hogni to a feast with the intention of ambushing them and forcing them at sword's point to deliver Sigurd's gold to him. Gudrun warns her brothers of the conspiracy with a cunning runic message, and the wives of the Guiking brothers dream ominous images, but Gunnar shrugs off the danger with the true northern spirit of cheerful courage in the face of dark destiny: 'none may set aside the fated measure of his days, nor is it unlike that my time is short' (ch. 36). Taking the sons of Hogni, his brother-in-law Orkning, and only a few men besides, the Guikings journey to the burg of King Atli, and when they come ashore, Atli meets them with a mighty army. Gudrun straps on armor and fights stoutly beside her brothers, but the Guikings are far outnumbered, and although they gain great glory by destroying nineteen of Atli's champions, with time King Atli's men bear them down. Atli commands his men to clap fetters upon the Guikings, and then he tells them to cut out Hogni's heart. Mortally wounded already, Hogni maintains both his courage and his courtesy: 'Do according to thy will; merrily will I abide whatso thou wilt do against me; and thou shalt see that my heart is not adrad, for hard matters have I made trial of ere [i.e., before] now, and all things that may try a man was I fain to bear, whiles yet I was unhurt; but now sorely am I hurt, and thou alone henceforth will bear mastery in our dealings together.' Atli then demands that Gunnar tell him where the gold lies, but Gunnar says 'Nay, first will I behold the bloody heart of Hogni, my brother.' Then Atli's men attempt to deceive Gunnar by cutting the heart out of a thrall named Hjalli, who 'yelled and screamed or [i.e., before] ever he felt the point' of the knife. But, seeing the bloody organ, Gunnar laughs and knows it to be the timid heart of Hjalli. So, the enraged Atli commands his men to kill both brothers:

> So now they fell on Hogni even as Atli urged them, and cut the heart from out of him, but such was the might of his manhood, that he laughed while he abode that torment, and all wondered at his worth, and in perpetual memory is it held sithence.
> Then they showed it to Gunnar, and he said—
> 'The mighty heart of Hogni, little like the faint heart of Hjalli, for little as it trembleth now, less it trembled whenas in his breast it lay! But now, O Atli, even as we die so shalt thou die; and lo, I alone wot [i.e., know] where the gold is, nor shall Hogni be to tell thereof now; to and fro played the matter in my mind whiles we both lived, but now have I myself determined for myself, and the Rhine river shall rule over the gold, rather than that the Huns shall bear it on the hands of them.'
> Then said King Atli, 'Have away the bondsman'; and so they did. . . . So Gunnar was cast into a worm-close, and many worms abode him there, and his hands were fast bound; but Gudrun sent him a harp, and in such wise did he set forth his craft, that wisely he smote the harp, smiting it with his toes, and so excellently well he played, that few deemed they had heard such playing, even when the hand had done it. And with such might and power he played, that all the worms fell asleep in the end, save one adder

only, great and evil of aspect, that crept unto him and thrust its sting into him until it smote his heart; and in such wise with great hardihood he ended his life days. (*The Volsunga Saga*, translated by Erikr Magnusson and William Morris in 1888 under the title *The Story of the Volsungs and Niblungs*, now contained in *Epics and Sagas*, volume 49 of The Harvard Classics [New York: P. F. Collier & Son, 1938].)

FD: Chapter XVI

1. neoterical Anadyomene: a new world rising from the sea.
2. Danaë's shower of beauty: This lovely maiden was the daughter of King Acrisius of Argos. An oracle told Acrisius that his daughter's son would kill him, so he confined Danaë in a brass tower. Zeus loved Danaë, and in the form of a golden stream, he entered the tower and then came to life. They made love, and Perseus was born to Danaë.

FD: Chapter XVII

1. In What a Shadow: The titles of Chapters XVII and XVIII are taken from a line of John Webster's *The Duchess of Malfi*. After spending the time of the play looking for his honor first as a desperate man in need of money, then as a reluctant spy, and finally as a self-disgusted murderer, Bosola tries to regain his honor by helping Antonio obtain vengeance on the Duchess's brothers for their torturous mistreatment of their sister. Threatening in the darkness and hoping for his sword to 'fall right,' Bosola mistakenly kills Antonio. In the subsequent scene, Bosola succeeds in killing the Duchess's brothers, but he receives his own death-wound in the fray. Hearing the screams and the violence, courtiers fill the stage in the last moments of the play. One courtier demands, 'How came Antonio by his death?' and the agonizing Bosola responds, in an splendid metadramatic joke, 'In a mist: I know not how; / Such a mistake as I have often seen / in a play' (V: v: 93–96). Bosola continues, and although he expresses satisfaction with his revenge, he speaks general words tinged with particular self-reproach:

> Fare you well;
> It may be pain: but no harm to me to die
> In so good a quarrel. O this gloomy world,
> In what a shadow, or deep pit of darkness
> Doth, womanish, and fearful, mankind live? (V: v: 98–102)

2. basinet . . . camail . . . armet . . . morning-star: A basinet is a
light steel globular helmet with a rounded visor covering the whole
face. The camail is a piece of chain-mail that attaches to the lower part
of the basinet and protects the neck and shoulders. The armet replaced
the basinet in the fifteenth century; it was made of heavy iron; its visor
had thin eye-slits and angles out over the nose; it had a curved plate
protecting the back of the neck. A heavy gorget protecting the throat
and lower face was usually held on by leather straps around the back of
the neck; it was often ornamented with an elaborate head crest. A
morning star (morgenstern) is a club having a spherical iron head set
with pointed spikes.

3. Prince Pier Luigi . . . Pope Paul III . . . Cellini: Benvenuto Cellini (1500–71) was a gifted artist and a spirited writer, but he was also a
crack shot with a pistol and a man who could throw a hard right-cross
and put a dagger to its proper use. His life alternated between periods
of artistic fruition in which he created gorgeous medallions and sculptures and pieces in gold and silver, and periods when he was in banishment or on the lam due to his acts of violence. His celebrated book of
memoirs, which he began in 1558, shows him to be as talented, passionate, and arrogant as two of his famous contemporaries, Pope Paul III
and Pierluigi Farnese.

Paul III was born as Alessandro Farnese, the brother of the beautiful Giulia Farnese (see note 13 to Chapter XXII of *MM*), the mistress of
the notorious Borgia Pope, Alexander VI. Because he was devoted to
Giulia, Alexander VI made Alessandro (1468–1549) a Cardinal in 1493,
and because of his sister's influence on the Borgia Pope, Alessandro was
given the nickname 'Cardinal Petticoat' by the other Cardinals. Despite
this annoying label, Alessandro was clever and had been well educated
under the support of Lorenzo de' Medici, so he prospered and obtained allies. By unanimous election, Alessandro became Pope under
the name of Paul III in 1534 and remained in office until 1549. Paul III
encouraged art and scholarship of all kinds: most notably, he was a
patron of Michelangelo and commissioned him to paint *The Last Judgment;* also under his guidance and support, the Farnese Palace was completed in Rome. Although Paul III abused his office by using his power
in outrageous nepotism, he also did much for the Church: He recognized the need for an intelligent Catholic response to Protestantism,
and thus he worked toward the Catholic reformation; he approved the
Jesuit order; he strengthened the Cardinal College by appointing able
men to its number; he began the Council of Trent.

Perhaps Paul's most frowned-upon act of nepotism was his conferring the Duchy of Parma and Piacenza on his son (by a mistress),
Pierluigi, or Pier Luigi, Farnese (1503–47). Pierluigi became famous as a
skillful but ruthless military captain of condottieri (see note 8 to Chapter
XIII of *FD*). He did accomplish some laudable things, however: in his
duchy he helped promote better agriculture, trade, and craftsmanship.
He also punished his feudal nobility for their economic and judicial
abuses, but his severity provoked their rebellious anger. His minor

nobles rose against him, and with the support of Ferrante di Gonzago, who was appointed governor of Milan by Emperor Charles V, they conspired together and murdered Pierluigi.

4. Signor Pier Luigi Farnese . . . portrait by Titian: ERE well describes, with some romantic touches, this magnificent military portrait, which hangs in the Castello Reale in Naples. It was painted on wood in 1546, and art historians are still arguing over who actually painted it; they seem to agree, however, that it is not the work of Titian.

5. Alstenö . . . Thorolf Kveldulfson's "Alost": 'Alost' is the archaic name for the island of Alsteno, which sits in the Vefsnir firth off the northern coast of Norway. When Thorolf decides to join King Harald Hairfair (see note 23 to the Overture to *MM*), he prospers in the King's favor. Then jealous rivals, who feel that Thorolf has treated them unjustly, slander him to King Harald. Eventually these whispering slanderers convince King Harald that Thorolf plans to make himself a king in Halogaland (a coastal region in northern Norway) and a treasonous rival to Harald's authority, so King Harald takes more than three hundred men to destroy Thorolf at his house in Sandness. The King commands his men to set fire to the house, and then Thorolf leads his men in a rushing attack from the burning hall:

> Then leapt Thorolf forth and hewed on either hand; set on thitherward where the King's banner was. . . . But when Thorolf came forth so far as the shieldburg, he laid his sword through that man that bare the banner. Then spake Thorolf: 'Now come I three feet short.' There stood in him then both sword and spear, but the King himself dealt him his banewound, and Thorolf fell forward at the feet of the King. (*ES*, 40)

The King's bodyguard protects him by standing close together and forming a wall with their shields, a 'shieldburg,' in front of him. Thorolf's last words, in typically laconic Old Norse humor, refer to the space between the King and the protecting shields, the space that Thorolf cannot traverse to kill King Harald.

6. The Ruhr: In the spring of 1921, the postwar disputes about German reparations and disarmament became a crisis. On April 27, the Allied Reparations Commission gave the Germans a total reparations figure of 132 thousand million gold marks—a sum much higher than the previous German offers. On May 5, the Allies issued an ultimatum: Germany had to accept the Allied figures and payment schedule, or else the Allies would invade and occupy the Ruhr, the region of Germany's richest coal fields and industrial sites, and the region to which iron ore from Lorraine was transported for steel production. In January 1923, France's Poincaré grew tired of waiting for German compliance, and he ordered a Franco-Belgian occupation of the Ruhr. Chancellor Cuno of Germany began a policy of passive resistance to the occupation; he asked the industrial directors and workers to refuse to cooperate with the French. Although the public generally supported Cuno's policy, it strained the already weak German economy, which had suffered greatly through inflation and the growth of a huge national debt after the war, and the German mark became almost worthless. Cuno himself collapsed under the economic burdens, and he resigned in August. (See A. J. Nicholls, *Weimar and the Rise of Hitler* [London: Macmillan, 1968].) Jim Scarnside, talking here with Lessingham on the evening of October 19, refers to the morning papers. The headline of the leading article on page 12 of *The Times* for October 19, 1923, speaks of the French annoyance with the German policy of passive resistance: 'German Plan Rejected: M. Poincaré's Test: Ruhr Deliveries Essential.' The French wanted the Germans to resume normal deliveries of coke and coal before they would consider any more German proposals for war reparations: 'France will not listen to Germany until not only has the Ruhr returned to normal working order, but until the deliveries in kind to the Allies are resumed, and attain a volume equal to those made before January 11.' Another article, testifying to the poor condition of the German economy, tells of continuing food riots by unemployed workers in Mannheim and Düsseldorf.

7. James Bryce: James Viscount Bryce (1838–1922) was educated at the University of Glasgow, at Trinity College in Oxford, and at Heidelberg. For twenty-three years, he was the Regius professor of civil law at Oxford, and then he held several diplomatic posts. His most famous work, and the one from which Lessingham quotes, is *The Holy Roman Empire* (1864).

8. Pyrrhonism: See note 8 to the Letter of Introduction to *FD*.

9. *in statu quo prius*: in the situation that (existed) earlier.

10. *Wein, weib, und gesang*: wine, woman, and song.

11. Samuel Butler: A Cambridge graduate, a religious skeptic, a sheep farmer, a painter, a novelist, a philosopher, a scientific writer, a literary critic, a translator of Homer, and a musician: this man grappled with life, and, like Edward Lessingham, 'sucked the orange of this world' (594). Butler's most famous novel is *The Way of All Flesh*, published a year after his death in 1902.

FD: Chapter XVIII

1. Deep Pit of Darkness: See note 1 to Chapter XVII of *FD*.

2. Edward Lear: He lived from 1812 to 1888 and is best known for his *Book of Nonsense*, a volume of light verse and limericks illustrated by his own drawings and watercolors, published in 1845.

3. Ethel Sidgwick: This English lady flourished around the turn of the century and wrote thirteen novels, including *Laura*, *The Bells of Shoreditch*, *The Accolade*, *Hatchways*, and *Promise*.

4. *Peter Ibbetson*—his nostrils stiffened: In the second half of this novel, Peter Ibbetson and Mary Seraskier become dream-companions and share a life in their dreams during sleep. They cannot be together in waking life because Peter is a convicted murderer confined to an asylum. At the end of the book, Peter hears of Mary's death:

> I soon had the knowledge of my loss confirmed, and heard (it had been common talk for more than nine days) that the famous Mary, Duchess of Towers, had met her death at the————station of the Metropolitan Railway.

Doubtless, Lessingham's clenching of his facial muscles is the physical response to his thinking of the parallels between his own situation and that of Peter Ibbetson. But, perhaps he thinks of Peter's final hope as well:

> My hope, my certainty to be one with Mary some day—that is my haven, my heaven—a consummation of completeness beyond which there is nothing to wish for or imagine. Come what else may, that is safe, and that is all I care for.
> (George du Maurier, *Peter Ibbetson* [London: James R. Osgood, McIlvaine & Co., 1896], 342, 370).

5. Death . . . his way: ERE quotes George Meredith's *Ballad of Past Meridian,* first published in 1876:

> I. Last night returning from my twilight walk
> I met the grey mist Death, whose eyeless brow
> Was bent on me, and from his hand of chalk
> He reached me flowers as from a withered bough:
> O Death, what bitter nosegays givest thou!
>
> II. Death said, I gather, and pursued his way.
> Another stood by me, a shape in stone,
> Sword-hacked and iron-stained, with breasts of
> clay,
> And metal veins that sometimes fiery shone:
> O Life, how naked and how hard when known!
>
> III. Life said, As thou hast carved me, such am I.
> Then memory, like the nightjar on the pine,
> And sightless hope, a woodlark in night sky,
> Joined notes of Death and Life till night's decline:
> Of Death, of Life, those inwound notes are mine.

6. the true material Hell: ERE's devotion to Christopher Marlowe makes me think that ERE must have had in mind some famous lines from *Doctor Faustus* when he wrote this paragraph. In the moments following the thunderous conjuring in which he has successfully commanded Mephistophilis to appear before him, Faustus questions this fallen angel:

Faustus: Where are you damned?
Mephistophilis: In hell.
Faustus: How comes it then that thou art out of hell?
Mephistophilis: Why this is hell, nor am I out of it. (I: iii: 73–76)

Two scenes later, Marlowe, through Mephistophilis, again stresses the idea that earth itself and the world of men are part of hell because they are not part of heaven:

Faustus: First I will question with thee about hell.
                      Tell me, where is the place that men call hell?
Mephistophilis: Under the heavens.
Faustus: Ay, so are all things else; but whereabouts?
Mephistophilis: Within the bowels of these elements,
                      Where we are tortured and remain for ever.
                      Hell hath no limits, nor is circumscribed
                      In one self place. But where we are is hell,
                      And where hell is there must we ever be.
                      And to be short, when all the world dissolves
                      And every creature shall be purified,
                      All places shall be hell that is not heaven. (I: v: 118–129)

FD: Chapter XIX

1. bersaglieri: soldiers of the light infantry of the Italian army.

2. *vox populi, vox Dei:* the voice of the crowd is the voice of God.

3. a dose of calomel: The Greek term *katharsis* means purgation or the state of having been purged. Instead of taking a side in the scholarly polemic about Aristotle's use of this term, the gannet-eyed painter makes a joke about laxatives. Calomel is mercurous chloride in the form of a yellowish powder that turns gray or black when exposed to light; it is used medicinally as a mild purgative drug.

4. Montrose: James Graham, the Marquis of Montrose (1612–50), a Scottish military genius, was the greatest horseman and cavalry strategist in Britain during the great Civil War.

5. Bela Kun: When the Hungarian monarchy became impotent in 1918, King Charles IV renounced his authority on November 3. Two weeks later, the National Council declared Hungary a republic independent of Austria, and it invested Count Mihaly Karolyi, who gained national popularity as the leader of a faction of the Party of Independence, with power as the new republican president. Karolyi could not maintain his government, however, and he could not defend the country from the invasion of Serb, Czech, and Romanian troops. On March

21, 1919, Bela Kun removed Karolyi from office and established a soviet republic empowered by military intimidation. Bela Kun promised the Hungarians that Russian troops would help them against the Romanian invaders, but this promise was empty, and because Kun had antagonized the citizens, a popular revolution forced him and his party to flee Budapest.

6. East African campaign: See note 25 to the Overture to *MM*.

7. Rif: This is a mountain range on the northern coast of Morocco, and it extends along the Mediterranean for about 180 miles. The Muslim Riffians have many times tried to win independence from Morocco through guerrilla revolt, and they nearly succeeded in the 1920s under the leadership of Abdul Krim.

8. Sir Richard Grenville: He was one of the aristocratic adventurers of the Elizabethan age and one of the Queen's greatest captains. Professor Walter Raleigh calls him 'that ever-memorable and heroic fire-eater' and describes Grenville among his peers with words that would aptly serve for Edward Lessingham:

> Last of all, and among the most characteristic figures of the Elizabethan age, there are the gentlemen adventurers . . . to whom the world was their oyster, which with their sword they must open. . . . whatever their faults, these Elizabethans bear the stamp of the heroic age; they lived in an illimitable world, and had nothing about them of tame civility. They are arrogant, excessive, indomitable, inquisitive, madmen in resolution, and children at heart.
> (Walter Raleigh, *The English Voyages of the Sixteenth Century* [Glasgow: James MacLehose and Sons, 1910], 106–107).

Professor Raleigh then tells, by quoting John Huighen van Linschoten and Francis Bacon, the famous story of Grenville's death while commanding the swift and stout *Revenge* in battle near the Azores against fifteen Spanish galleons in 1591:

> The great fight of the *Revenge* was undertaken against all the rules of orthodox naval tactics, and in defiance of common sense. Its hero, says Linschoten, 'was of so hard a complexion, that as he continued among the Spanish captains, while they were at dinner or supper with him, he would carouse three or four glasses of wine, and in a bravery take the glasses between his teeth and crash them in pieces and swallow them down, so that oftentimes the blood ran out of his mouth.' (107)

9. I heard . . . beginning: Alcaios, fragment 166, *Lyra Graeca*, ed. and trans. J. M. Edmonds, the Loeb Classical Library, vol. 1 (London: William Heinemann, 1922), 423.

10. Come . . . with: Sappho, 'to Atthis,' fragment 82, *Lyra Graeca*, ed. and trans. J. M. Edmonds, the Loeb Classical Library, vol. 1 (London: William Heinemann, 1922), 239–40. ERE has taken the line from its context. Here is Edmonds's translation of the portion of the fragment ending with the quoted line:

> . . . Sappho, I swear if you come not forth I will love you no more. O rise and shine upon us and set free your beloved strength from the bed, and then like a pure lily beside the spring hold aloof your Chian robe and wash you in the water. And Cleis shall bring down from your presses saffron smock and purple robe: and let a mantle be put over you and crowned with a wreath of flowers tied about your head; and so come sweet with all the beauty with which you make me mad.

11. The Copeland hills to the west: Looking from his house in Nether Wasdale and panning his eyes from southwest to northeast on the western shore of the Wast Water, Lessingham would have seen Buckbarrow (1,410 feet), Seatallen (2,266 feet), Middle Fell (1,908 feet), and Yewbarrow (2,058 feet). A. Wainwright says that Buckbarrow 'faces the famous Screes across the Wastwater and being itself a steep and stony declivity bears some resemblance, if only in miniature.' Its parent fell, Seatallen, exhibits a steep rocky face to the north, but toward Nether Wasdale it 'shows its most innocuous slopes, extensive grass sheepwalks that descend gradually.' Middle Fell has an 'intimidating ruggedness,' because 'tier above tier of hostile crags' stand on its lakeside face, and 'steep slopes overrun by tumbled boulders' make it more formidable than its altitude would suggest. Yewbarrow looks like 'the inverted hull of a boat,' and its long ridge summit and steep sides makes it difficult to ascend, 'so that Yewbarrow is not often climbed although it is a centrepiece of magnificent fell country and commands thrilling views.' (A. Wainwright, *A Pictorial Guide to the Lakeland Fells,* vol. 7: *The Western Fells* [Kendal, Westmorland: Westmorland Gazette, 1966]).

12. with . . . knowing: See p. xxxv of the Introduction.

13. Fifty more years . . . there: See the Praeludium to *MG*.

14. It was . . . dream: John Keats, *Lamia* (June–Sept., 1819) 1:126–8.

15. becco or cornuto: Both are figurative terms for a cuckold.

16. Titian . . . Urbino: Titian painted the *Venus of Urbino* for Duke Guidobaldo della Rovere in 1538. The young Duke of Urbino wanted a nude to rival those in the collections of the d'Este family in Ferrara. Painting a nude woman in the foreground of a landscape was a stock scene for sixteenth-century Venetian painters, but in this painting Titian changed the formula by posing Venus indoors on a couch.

17. Sleep . . . birds: Alcman, fragment 36, *Lyra Graeca,* ed. and trans. J. M. Edmonds, the Loeb Classical Library, vol. 1 (London: William Heinemann, 1922), 77. ERE has made his own translation. For comparison, here is Edmonds's translation:

> Asleep lie mountain-top and mountain-gully, shoulder also and ravine; the creeping-things that come from the dark earth, the beasts

whose lying is upon the hillside, the generation of the bees, the monsters in the depths of the purple brine, all lie asleep, and with them the tribes of the winging birds.

18. γλυκύπικρος ἐρῶς: the second word is *eros*—sweetly bitter love.

VOLUME THREE:
THE MEZENTIAN GATE

Notes to the writing of *The Mezentian Gate*

1. Eddison to G. R. Hamilton, July 25, 1941, Ms. Eng. Lett. c. 233, fol. 50, Bodleian Library, Oxford.

2. Eddison to G. R. Hamilton, September 2, 1941, Ms. Eng. Lett. c. 233, fols. 51–54, Bodleian Library, Oxford.

3. Eddison to G. R. Hamilton, April 2, 1942, Ms. Eng. Lett. c. 233, fols. 62–63, Bodleian Library, Oxford.

4. Eddison to G. R. Hamilton, July 22, 1942, Ms. Eng. Lett. c. 230, fol. 192, Bodleian Library, Oxford.

5. Eddison to E. A. Niles, October 16, 1940, Ms. Eng. Lett. c. 232, fols. 60–62, Bodleian Library, Oxford.

6. Eddison to G. R. Hamilton, September 10, 1939, Ms. Eng. Lett. c. 233, fols. 19–20, Bodleian Library, Oxford.

7. Eddison to G. R. Hamilton, September 10, 1939, Ms. Eng. Lett. c. 233, fols. 19–20, Bodleian Library, Oxford.

8. G. R. Hamilton to Eddison, September 13, 1940, Ms. Eng. Lett. c. 230, fols. 169–170, Bodleian Library, Oxford.

9. Eddison to G. R. Hamilton, September 15, 1940, Ms. Eng. Lett. c. 233, fol. 29, Bodleian Library, Oxford.

10. Eddison to G. R. Hamilton, October 27, 1940, Ms. Eng. Lett. c. 233, fols. 32–33, Bodleian Library, Oxford.

11. Eddison to G. R. Hamilton, October 27, 1940, Ms. Eng. Lett. c. 233, fols. 32–33, Bodleian Library, Oxford.

12. Eddison to G. Hayes, undated (September 1943?), Ms. Eng. Lett. c. 230, fols. 57–58, Bodleian Library, Oxford.

13. Eddison to E. A. Niles, December 18, 1941, Ms. Eng. Lett. c. 232, fol. 279, Bodleian Library, Oxford.

14. Personal interview with Jean G. R. Latham, July 1986.

15. Eddison to L. W. Griffith, November 27, 1941, Ms. Eng. Lett. c. 230, fol. 125, Bodleian Library, Oxford.

16. Eddison to H. Lappin, December 29, 1941, Ms. Eng. Lett. c. 231, fol. 151, Bodleian Library, Oxford.

17. Eddison to C. S. Lewis, November 6, 1943, Ms. Eng. Lett. c. 220/2, fol. 71, Bodleian Library, Oxford.

18. Eddison to G. Hayes, February 22, 1944, Ms. Eng. Lett. c. 230, fols. 62–63, Bodleian Library, Oxford.

19. Eddison to G. R. Hamilton, January 8, 1945, Ms. Eng. Lett. c. 230, fols. 268—271, Bodleian Library, Oxford.

20. Eddison to C. Sandford, May 12, 1945, Ms. Eng. Lett. c. 231, fol. 168, Bodleian Library, Oxford.

21. Winifred G. Eddison to G. R. Hamilton, August 24, 1945, Ms. Eng. Lett. c. 233, fols. 112–113, Bodleian Library, Oxford.

22. Eddison to W. H. Hillyer, November 24, 1942, Ms. Eng. Lett. c. 231, fols. 110–112, Bodleian Library, Oxford.

23. E. R. Eddison, *Styrbiorn the Strong* (London: Jonathan Cape, 1926), 127.

MG: A Letter of Introduction

1. *The Mezentian Gate***:** ERE first thought of titling his third Zimiamvian novel *The Way of Kings,* but he later chose to focus on Mezentius because of his dominant position in the novel's political plot and because of his climactic decisions in the closing chapters. So why not *The Way of Mezentius* or *The Mezentian Way?* The chosen title has elaborate suggestiveness because it makes use of several obsolescent meanings of the word *gate.* This word means, obviously, a door or an entrance, and conversely, a barrier. But archaically it can also signify a road or pathway, the act of going on a certain path, or a particular method or fashion for doing things. King Mezentius has his own methods for ruling the triple kingdom, and he goes places, across barriers and through doors, where others do not dare go.

2. the sagatime: See note 10 to Chapter XIII of *FD.*

3. banned . . . dungeon: ERE again quotes his beloved Webster's *The White Devil.* Upon his seeing the ghost of his murdered master, the Machiavellian Flaminio, who has murdered his brother, questions the ghost about Heaven and Hell:

> In what place art thou? in yon starry gallery,
> Or in the cursed dungeon? No? Not speak?
> Pray, sir, resolve me, what religion's best
> For a man to die in? (V: v: 125–28)

4. I limb'd . . . my best: If ERE intended this line to be taken in context, it produces a grim joke about how the critics may treat ERE after reading his book. Lodovico, a banished Italian count turned adventurer and pirate in John Webster's *The White Devil,* says, as the guards take him to prison, these words in justification of his four murders:

> I do glory yet
> That I can call this act mine own. For my part,

The rack, the gallows, and the torturing wheel
Shall be but sound sleeps to me; here's my rest:
I limb'd this night-piece and it was my best.
(V: vi: 291–95)

MG: Praeludium

1. **morning:** It is mid-July in 1973, and Edward Lessingham has been the ruler of the Lofoten Islands for twenty-five years. In time, the events of the Praeludium precede those of the Overture to *MM* by only a few hours.

2. **the age of him:** Edward Lessingham is living his ninety-first year.

3. **Checkmate. . . . pawns:** The conflict, which his death prevents Edward Lessingham from facing, is explained by the unnamed narrator in the Overture to *MM*.

4. **Leonidas . . . upon the Pass:** Cyrus the Great established, in the mid-sixth century B.C., the Persian Empire in Asia Minor and in eastward lands (in modern geography: all of Turkey, Iraq, Iran, and Afghanistan). His son Cambyses, by conquering Egypt between 529 and 522 B.C., extended the empire westward and controlled all the eastern shores of the Mediterranean. Darius I, who in 521 toppled an imposter pretending to be a son of Cyrus the Great, took over the throne and attempted to protect the empire by encircling the Aegean. His first campaign was a failure, but he established the empire in Thrace (the borderland between modern Greece and Bulgaria). Darius tenaciously continued, and he subdued much of the western shore of the Aegean while aiming his campaigns at Athens, but his forces were defeated on the plains of Marathon in 490 by the Athenian commander Miltiades and a force of ten thousand Athenians. The defeat enraged Darius; he immediately began preparing a fresh assault, but a revolt in Egypt needed attention. Darius died in 485 before he could continue his war against Greece. Xerxes, the son of Darius, took up the red mantle of war and amassed enormous forces. Scholars still debate the numbers, but Xerxes may have brought to Greece an army of 400,000 and a navy of eight hundred ships. To oppose him, the Greek city-states formed an alliance under the Spartan Eurybiades, as commander of the navy, and Leonidas, the king of Sparta and descendant of Heracles, as commander of the army. Leonidas, three hundred Spartan warriors (Leonidas chose only men who were fathers: he believed that soldiers with children and wives to protect would be more committed to fighting ferociously against the foreign invader), and about six thousand Greeks from other city-states camped in the coastal mountain pass called Thermopylae ('warm gates'). The hearts of many men were distracted and not fixed on fighting, for the Persian invasion had occurred simultaneously with the Olympic festival and the Spartan harvest festival called Carnea, so when the Persians advanced, Greek courage paled. Herodo-

tus, the primary source for the Persian wars, records the moment in book 7, section 207 of the *History*:

> But the Greeks at Thermopylae, when the Persians came near the pass itself, were in sheer terror and debated whether to stay or go. The other Peloponnesians were for going to the Isthmus to guard it; but Leonidas, when the Phocians and Locrians buzzed angrily around him against this plan, gave his vote to remain where they were and to send messengers to the cities, bidding them come to their help, on the grounds that they were too few to drive off the Medes.
>
> (Herodotus, *The History*, trans. David Grene [Chicago: University of Chicago Press], 543)

Although they were vastly outnumbered, Leonidas decided to stay that day because of a prophecy given to him by the priestess of Apollo at Delphi. She told Leonidas that 'either Sparta would be destroyed by the barbarians or the king of Sparta would be destroyed' (*History*, p. 549): Leonidas knew then, as Lessingham knows at this moment, that his death will come, and that, as Hamlet says, the 'readiness is all.' Leonidas did not die on that first day of battle; the allied Greeks held off the Persians for nearly a week until they learned that the Persians had discovered a path around the mountain that would allow them to attack from two sides. Then, says Herodotus, the Greeks fell into debate, and Leonidas sent home the doubtful ones (7: 219–20):

> Thereupon the Greeks bethought them of what they ought to do, and their opinions were divided; for some were not in favor of leaving their post of battle, but there were also those of the contrary opinion. Afterwards, these split up, and some ran away and scattered, each to his own city; but there were others of them who made their preparations to stand where they were, with Leonidas. It is said that Leonidas himself sent them away, out of care that they should not die there; but for himself and his Spartiates he thought it disgraceful to quit the post they had come to guard in the first place. I am myself strongly of this opinion: that when Leonidas saw that the allies were fainthearted and unwilling to run the risk in his company, he bade them be off home, but for himself it would be dishonorable to leave. If he stood his ground, he would leave a great name after him, and the prosperity of Sparta would not be blotted out.   (*History*, 548–49)

Like Shakespeare's Henry V, Leonidas told them 'he which hath no stomach to this fight / Let him depart . . . we would not die in that man's company who fears his fellowship to die with us' (*Henry V*, IV: iii: 35–39). Unlike Henry V at Agincourt, Leonidas did not rout the larger force, yet he won glory enough to carry him through and beyond twenty-five centuries.

5. at Philippi: This ancient Greek city is near the modern city of Kavalla and inland from the Aegean island of Thasos. It seems a strange place to meet, considering that Aspasia shall have a yacht and that Philippi is not a port city. Yet Philippi was the scene of the defeat in 42 B.C. of Brutus and Cassius by Mark Antony and Octavius; perhaps ERE thought of Lessingham's similarity to Brutus, who, standing in Philippi fields, says, 'I know my hour is come. . . . Thou seest the world, Voluminus, how it goes; / our enemies have beat us to the pit' (Shakespeare, *Julius Caesar* V: v: 20–23). For both Lessingham's and Brutus' enemies, the victory will be a 'vile conquest' (V: v: 38).

6. Brachiano . . . terrible: The quoted lines are from John Webster's *The White Devil* (V: iii: 39–40). Realizing that he has been poisoned and that he shall die soon, Brachiano probably says these lines while thinking of his black sin, which cries out to heaven: he murdered his wife so that he could be with his lover, Vittoria Corombona.

7. Save . . . alone: The final line of Shakespeare's sonnet 66. See note 14 to the Letter of Introduction to *FD*.

8. Between . . . knowing: See p. xxxv of the Introduction.

MG: Chapter I

1. Pertiscus Parry dwelt . . . Forn: This, the most like a saga of the three Zimiamvian novels, begins in proper saga fashion by stating relationships and geographical locations. All the major Icelandic sagas have such beginnings. ERE began *WO* and *SS* in the same way.

MG: Chapter II

1. mid-afternoon: a March day in 725 AZC.

2. out of all ho: beyond normal limits or moderate boundaries.

3. *magister artium*: master of knowledge, letters, or art.

4. the Pharos light: Supposedly, Ptolemy II built the world's first lighthouse on the island of Pharos near Alexandria, on the northern coast of Egypt.

MG: Chapter III

1. Nigra Sylva: the dark, gloomy forest.

2. cockatrice's eyes . . . stone: ERE had a fondness for this fabulous beast, popular among the Elizabethans. In *WO*, King Gorice XII uses a cockatrice to test the courage of Lord Gro before he entrusts Gro with the task of assisting him in his dangerous conjuring practices: see *WO*, 51.

MG: Chapter V

1. Tarquin seized Lucrece: The Tarquin family and dynasty, which held power in Rome, was rooted out of the city by the other leading families in 510. According to legend, the family was expelled when Sextus Tarquinius, the son of the tyrant Tarquinius Superbus, ravished the lovely Lucretia, the wife of Collatinus. The story proved potent to English poets, for Chaucer, Gower, and Shakespeare wrote narrative poems based on the legend.

MG: Chapter VI

1. gold cups . . . my window: See note 4 to Chapter XIII of *FD*.

2. bolled up huge . . . bursten off him: Because ERE had a fascination for the Borgia family and read extensively about them, his inspiration for this repulsive image may have sprung from the accounts of the death of Rodrigo Borgia, Pope Alexander VI, who probably was poisoned, perhaps accidentally by his son Cesare, with a powerful concentration of arsenic. The Pope's face became swollen and black before his death, and in the final hours his body quickly decayed.

3. *Bare . . . behind it*: This Icelandic proverb embosses the cover of the famous translation of *Njal's Saga* by Sir George Webbe Dasent. Titled *The Story of Burnt Njal,* Dasent's translation was published by the firm of Edmonston and Douglas in Edinburgh in 1861. It is from these volumes that Mary reads to Lessingham as he smokes an after-dinner cigar on that warm evening in their Nether Wasdale house; see *WO*, 1–2.

4. Have patience, and see: On December 2, 1943, ERE drafted a factual summary of a scene between Aktor and the Akkama agent sent to assassinate King Mardanus. The next day, ERE made this note at the top of the manuscript page:

> Facts only (not to be revealed in detail—if at all—at this stage. Merely as basis for scene between Marescia, Emmius, Supervius, and Deïaneira) in Argyanna or Laimak.

The conversation of Chapter VI owes most of its energy to Emmius's gentle but precise restraining of Marescia's firmly adverse opinion of Aktor and to Emmius's cautious diligence in determining the truth from her prejudicial story that condemns Aktor beyond doubt. Allowing the reader to hear only Marescia's view of the events has other benefits than the energy it gives to the conversation: it allows ERE to develop Marescia, Emmius, and Supervius; and since Marescia's story clouds the event with ambiguity and suspense, it makes the reader think more carefully about the personalities and motives of the involved characters. The marginal note shows ERE's uncertainty about whether he would narrate the actual events of the murder from an omniscient viewpoint, but I think he definitely decided against such a clear treatment of the scene, so I have relegated it to this note rather than placing it in the text. In this draft, you and I stand with the omniscient narrator, and like ghosts, we observe the secret moments:

Aktor, wandering at night in the palace, catches a strange man in (? king's private chamber). Overpowers him, and says he will have a true tale out of him, or else kill him out of hand.

Man reveals himself as an Akkama agent, sent to spy out the land, and Aktor recognizes him as an old retainer of his father's. Man admits that he came of his own will to try and murder Mardanus and gain reward. He has been in the palace (? as part of the 'black guard') for several months. Aktor forces him to confess that he meant to kill the king if he could by an ingenious trick—poisoning the chessmen (which always stand ready in a certain room where the King plays, and are never meddled with by anyone else). Aktor (who plays chess nightly)—'Me too, then?' Man admits the soft impeachment, but asserts he was waiting for some brain wave to show a way to kill the King and spare Aktor, to whom he professes attachment. Aktor threatens him, and exacts details of his plot: a poisonous unguent smeared on the chessmen, which will poison both players. Delivers box to Aktor. Aktor—'Have you done it?' Man—'No.' Aktor—'That's a lie; I'll kill you.' Man (in terror) confesses he has done the queens. Aktor makes him touch every other one (which he does, and is evidently safe). Then—surprisingly and treacherously—Aktor kills man with his dagger: burns the poison on the fire (after first poisoning blade of man's knife): raises alarm: says man was here to kill the King, that he recognised him, forced confession, and in his extreme rage at such a villainous plot, despatched him to sup in Hell.

In course of game, Aktor exposes his queen with result that King takes her (touching her for the first time) and gives checkmate. The poison works slowly: King swells up in the night and bursts.

Doctors find identical poison on man's knife and on white queen.

(Ms. Eng. Misc. c. 456, fol. 106, Bodleian Library, Oxford)

MG: Chapter VII

1. Zeus Terpsikeraunos: Terpsichore, the muse of the arts of dancing, is the daughter of Zeus and the Titan goddess Mnemosyne (Memory). In this chapter, Zeus, as the god of thunder and lightning, dances in the heavens.

MG: Chapter VIII

1. Arcadian existence: The mountainous region in Peloponnesus called Arcadia has many mythological associations, and it may be the oldest settled region in Greece. The adjective has developed in English as a word that suggests quiet, gentle, joyful, rustic, agrarian, rural life. Sir Philip Sidney's prose romance, *The Countess of Pembroke's Arcadia*, first published in 1590 and highly popular in the subsequent generation, may be the source for this development. Here is a brief description of Sidney's Arcadia:

> There were hills which garnished their proud heights with stately trees; humble valleys whose base estate seemed comforted with re-freshing of silver rivers; meadows enamelled with all sorts of eye-pleasing flowers; thickets, which, being lined with most pleasant shade, were witnessed so to by the cheerful deposition of many well-tuned birds. . . . 'But this country where now you set your foot is Arcadia; this country being thus decked with peace and (the child of peace) good husbandry.'
> (Sir Philip Sidney, *The Countess of Pembroke's Arcadia*, ed. Maurice Evans [Harmondsworth, Middlesex: Penguin, 1982], 69–70)

2. (*not* closet): While Mardanus reigned, none but the Queen had royal permission to enter his secret closet (see Chapter IV), and ERE meant to indicate the Queen's maintenance of this tradition by empha-sizing that her conference with Aktor took place in the study.

3. quick travelling: Aktor's remark reflects the size of Akkama. Letters that arrive at Rialmar within a month of being sent from the Akkamite palace means that they traveled speedily.

4. Lord ———: I think the blanks signify names that ERE had not yet invented.

5. Shearbone range: Because neither ERE nor his friend Gerald Hayes drew a chart of Akkama, the description admits some confusion. A boundary of mountains seems to separate Fingiswold from Akkama. The passes west-northwest of Rialmar must be within miles of the sea, for on the extant map an inlet lies about fifty miles west of Rialmar across the northern part of the Wold. Perhaps the Bight is part of

Fingiswold north of Rialmar, and perhaps the Shearbone range names the mountains that lie along the Midland Sea.

MG: Chapter X

1. the Eumenides: Aktor's personality and situation share some common points with those of Claudius in *Hamlet:* both are ambitious, duplicitous, cowardly, pitiful equivocators; both have attained love, marriage, and royal position through secret murder; both must maintain these things through successfully and continually hiding the secret; both are annoyed by having authority over a prince who possesses a nature far more regal; and most important, both suffer from constant worry. When Claudius finally unpacks his heart halfway through the play, his soliloquy begins and ends emphasizing the sharp pain of his internal suffering:

> O, my offence is rank, it smells to heaven;
> It hath the primal eldest curse upon 't,
> A brother's murder. Pray can I not,
> Though inclination be as sharp as will.
> My stronger guilt defeats my strong intent. . . .
> O wretched state! O bosom black as death!
> O limed soul, that struggling to be free
> Art more engag'd!
> (*Hamlet* III: iii: 35–39, 67–69)

Claudius's suffering has a specifically Christian focus that is, of course, absent from Aktor's, but ERE has already told us that Aktor has been suffering from a loathing of his deed and from a dread fear that Vandermast will reveal his secret, and that Aktor has been trying to wish his crime away with subtle self-prevarications. This chapter, had it been written, would have shown a more melancholic Aktor suffering both from guilt and from, ironically, unfulfilled ambition because ERE says that the new thing torturing his soul is his refusal of the Akkamian throne.

The references to wormwood and to increasing melancholy hint at the reasons for the name of the chapter. *Eumenides* means 'the kindly' in Greek, and it is one of the gentler epithets referring to the Furies (Erinyes), the goddesses of vengeance in Greek and Roman mythology. In *The Oresteia* of Aeschylus, the Eumenides figure most prominently in the third play, whose title bears their name. In the beginning of the play, the Eumenides are asleep in the temple of Apollo at Delphi. They have been chasing Orestes and demanding retribution for his having killed his mother Clytemnestra, and he has taken refuge there in Apollo's guardianship. Soon the spirit of Clytemnestra comes to them and exhorts them to awaken and continue their vengeful plaguing of the son who murdered her. While she speaks, they stir and moan in their sleep. Clytemnestra's last words to these goddesses of vengeance, the words that awaken them, are these:

> Let go
> upon this man the stormblasts of your bloodshot breath,
> wither him in your wind, after him, hunt him down
> once more, and shrivel him in your vitals' heat and
> flame.
>
> (Aeschylus, *The Eumenides*, trans. Richmond Lattimore,
> in vol. 1 of *The Complete Greek Tragedies*
> [Chicago: University of Chicago Press, 1959], 136–39)

MG: Chapter XI

1. Queen Rosma: An archaeologist, explorer, and friend of T. E. Lawrence named Harry Pirie-Gordon, introduced ERE in 1938 to the Princess Ragnhild, the daughter of King Eric Bloodaxe and Queen Gunnhild of York, in the *Orkneyinga Saga* (the fictionalized prose history of the earls of the Orkney islands, written by an Icelander in the early thirteenth century). ERE paid tribute to Pirie-Gordon by dedicating *MG* to him. The Princess Ragnhild became the inspiration for ERE's fatal queen. Like her spiritual descendant, Princess Ragnhild is a Machiavellian woman of ruthless ambition and fierce will unyielding to male domination. After plotting the death of her first husband Earl Arnfinn, Ragnhild marries his brother Havard, who succeeds Arnfinn to the earldom. Soon she makes promises to Havard's nephew Einar Buttered-Bread and prods him into killing his uncle the Earl. Einar's reputation consequently suffers, so Ragnhild repudiates him and has him killed by another nephew of Havard named Einar Hard-Mouth. Then she rejects this second Einar and marries Havard's brother Ljot. Ljot later becomes the Earl, and he orders Einar Hard-Mouth to be put to death. (See Chapter 9 of *The Orkneyinga Saga*.)

MG: Chapter XIII

1. The Devil's Quilted Anvil: See note 1 to Chapter XVI of *MM*.

MG: Chapter XVI

1. at Paris: Professor Verlyn Flieger first indicated to me the chronological problem that exists here. The apocalyptic fish dinner, during which Mezentius and Amalie descend into our twentieth-century world and live lives there as Mary Scarnside and Edward Lessingham, takes place in Memison on July 25, 775 AZC. In strict Zimiamvian chronology, Mezentius and Amalie could not experience any memories of their earthly lives until after the fish dinner; but the synopsis of this chapter tells of their experiencing intimations of their earthly lives in 749 AZC, when they first meet and begin to love each other. ERE does not address this problem in any of the extant notes, and I cannot presume to suggest how he would have solved it had he lived to complete *MG*. Possibly he did not see it as a chronological problem at all.

MG: Chapter XX

1. Dura Papilla Lupae: The cruel breast of the she-wolf.

MG: Chapter XXII

1. *Pax Mezentiana*: the Mezentian peace; if ERE meant the adjective to be taken in the ablative case, the phrase implies the peace established by Mezentius.

MG: Chapter XXVI

1. an Amazon: This mythic nation of fierce female warriors lived near the Black Sea. Led by their valiant Queen Pentheseleia (see note 3 to Chapter XXII of *MM*), they fought for Troy during the Trojan War. The name *Amazon* means 'breastless' in Greek. According to legend, they burned the right breasts from their female children so that, when mature, they could draw and release a bowstring without impediment. The Amazons copulated intermittently with men solely to produce female offspring; they killed or enslaved their male children.

MG: Chapter XXVIII

1. Anadyomene: This epithet refers to the birth of Aphrodite and specifically to her first rising from the sea; see note 16 to Chapter I of *FD*.
2. Immortal . . . nest-beds: ERE translated this. See Section I of the Introduction to compare ERE's version with Lang's.
3. Pallas: No one knows what this name means, but it is an epithet for Athena.

4. Hecate: The daughter of the Titan gods Perses and Asteria, she became a Greek goddess of the underworld, of night, and of magic.

MG: Chapter XXIX

1. Astarte: Called Ashtoreth in the Bible, she was an ancient Phoenician goddess of sexuality, fertility, maternity, and war. Fruits of harvest, animals, and children were ritually sacrificed to her in worship services dedicated to increasing fertility. The cult of Astarte passed from the Phoenicians to the Greeks, and there her qualities were incorporated into the worship of Aphrodite.

2. evening-sleepiness . . . bloodshedding: See note 4 to Chapter XIX of *MM*.

3. If mortal . . . Hades: ERE translated this. See Section I of the Introduction, to compare ERE's version with Lang's.

MG: Chapter XXX

1. Philommeides Aphrodite: Laughter-loving Aphrodite was born from the severed *meides* (genitals) of her father Ouranos after Kronos lopped them off with a cruel flint knife and threw them into the Mediterranean.

2. Prince Gilmanes: Baias is the nephew of Gilmanes, Prince of Kaima, whom King Mezentius commanded to be beheaded on June 25, 775 AZC (see *FD*, Chapter VII).

3. [. . .]: The manuscript is handwritten, and a few words in this sentence are illegible. In subsequent passages, illegible words are marked with the same sign.

4. What a mischief . . . the King: Two versions of this opening section (from the first sentence up to the phrase 'with his own hand wrote privately') exist in manuscript. The first version is marked by three dates: February 4, March 2, and March 8, 1945. ERE wrote a slightly revised version on March 8, 1945. I have printed the revised version, but I have added to it Gilmanes's speech from the first version.

5. a mock in this King's eye: Between April 29 and May 1, 1945, in an outline for Chapters XXX–XXXIII, ERE made some notes on this moment between Mezentius and Beroald: 'Show the King understands (and the Chancellor understands that the King understands) the inwardness and true facts of the Baias episode.'

6. in statu pupae: in the state of girlhood.

7. The King and Fiorinda: I think ERE later decided to place the conversation between the King and Fiorinda after the conversation between the King and Beroald; on May 3, 1945, he made a Zimiamvian calendar in which he shows both conversations taking place on the same day, but the meeting with the Chancellor is listed as occurring first.

8. I'm sorry to hear it: ERE did not write the first part of the conversation. Probably, the Duchess is sorry to hear that the King likes Fiorinda and has been impressed by Fiorinda's beauty and wit.

9. in three weeks: Barganax has gone fishing for 'sea-pike.'

10. Stibium: a poison in the form of a black powder, also used as a cosmetic and called black antimony.

11. Rosa Mundi . . . Rose Noire: The rose of the world; the rose of the night (the black rose).

12. Will you look, and tell me?: Because the Curwen text contains only the Argument, it does not show the true textual situation at this point in the story. While drafting Chapter XXX in 1945, ERE changed his mind about some things he had written in 1944 in the Argument for Chapter XXX. Here are the opening sentences of the Argument:

> Until Fiorinda's marriage neither the King nor the Queen nor Barganax has ever set eyes on her. The Duchess has, and cannot abide her: probably has resolved privately that she had better not be seen by Barganax.

ERE decided that Mezentius had seen Fiorinda when she was nine years old, ten years before his conversation with Beroald in January 775. ERE also decided that Amalie has never seen Fiorinda, so he could show, in Amalie's conversation with Mezentius in January 775, that Amalie's fervent dislike of Fiorinda has its roots not in the sure evidence of actual experience with Fiorinda but in quick judgments made through her own feeling of moral outrage upon hearing the rumors of Fiorinda's dealings with Baias. ERE decided to contradict his Argument regarding Amalie and Fiorinda in May 1945, because notes he wrote at the end of April still show agreement with the Argument's statement that Amalie had seen Fiorinda:

> The King and the Duchess: the King tells her of his visit to the Chancellor and interview with Fiorinda; suggests Fiorinda should be presented to her in Memison. The Duchess accurately judges that the King has in mind a marriage between Barganax and Fiorinda. She has only once seen Fiorinda, but detests her for what she knows or hears of her, and especially took a dislike to her at first sight, Fiorinda being in her most ironic and languefied mood, and enjoying shocking the Duchess's sense of the proprieties. Barganax, she is glad to reflect, is engrossed with Bellefront.

Although ERE rejected these notes when he composed the conversation between Mezentius and Amalie on May 15, 1945, he used the ideas of the last two sentences on May 19, 1945, when he drafted the scene of the first meeting between Fiorinda and Amalie, which occurs later in Chapter XXX.

13. Zemry Ashery . . . Rojuna: ERE never indicated the exact location of these places on the map of the three kingdoms.

14. Mount Helicon: One of the places associated with the nine muses in Greek mythology.

15. Quelle . . . puce: Fiorinda poses the riddle thus: 'What is the difference, sir, between an elephant and a flea?' The answer is this: 'It is possible for an elephant to have fleas, but it is not possible for a flea to have elephants.'

16. Ladies all to go masked: On May 27, 1945, before he drafted this conversation, ERE jotted down this note: 'Fiorinda goes without the Duchess's knowledge: is recognized by her in spite of her mask.'

17. fantasticoes: Elizabethans used this word to label absurd and irrational people, but Doctor Vandermast seems to use it to name the magical illusions that he will create to entertain the guests. ERE does not mention it here, but Doctor Vandermast persuades Fiorinda to participate in his illusions by dressing up as a personification of Night.

18. [Barrian . . . too]: ERE wrote this bracketed passage on May 30, 1945; because he alludes to Barrian's words here and nowhere else, I have placed them in this outline but in brackets.

19. Marchioness of Monferrato: See note 3 to Chapter IX of *FD*.

20. 129th Sonnet: One of Shakespeare's first about the Dark Lady:

> Th' expense of spirit in a waste of shame
> Is lust in action; and till action, lust
> Is perjur'd, murd'rous, bloody, full of blame,
> Savage, extreme, rude, cruel, not to trust,
> Enjoy'd no sooner but despised straight,
> Past reason hunted, and no sooner had
> Past reason hated, as a swallowed bait
> On purpose laid to make the taker mad;
> Mad in pursuit and in possession so;
> Had, having, and in quest to have, extreme;
> A bliss in proof, and prov'd, a very woe;
> Before, a joy propos'd; behind, a dream.
> All this the world well knows; yet none knows well
> To shun the heaven that leads men to this hell.

21. βοῶπις ποτνια: 'ox-eyed queen'; ancient Greek writers used this epithet for Artemis and Aphrodite.

22. the lady: This lady, personified Night, is Fiorinda.

23. [She . . . you]: I have put the brackets around these sentences; ERE wrote them at the end of July 1945.

24. the Duke a mere philanderer: Evidently, ERE planned for Barganax to have several other parties shortly after his return to Zayana, but Fiorinda has seen enough after one. On February 21, 1945, ERE wrote this note:

Barganax in March has a series of Noctis [. . .]. Invites the Chancellor and Fiorinda, but the Chancellor excuses her on ground that she prefers to live awhile in retirement. This whets Barganax's curiosity; but Bellafront now swims over the horizon and his mind is taken up wholly with her (for three months)—painting, and more 'serious' pleasures.

25. on Lewisian and Geraldian grounds: C. S. Lewis and Gerald Hayes had little sympathy for Fiorinda. They found her to be idle, arrogant, selfish, narcissistic, manipulative, cruel, and lecherous.

26. Actaeon . . . Artemis at her bath: The story comes from Ovid. Actaeon is the grandson of Kadmus, the founder of the citadel that later became the city of Thebes. Early one morning, Actaeon goes hunting with several friends, and before noon they have much success. When the day grows too hot for hunting, Actaeon tells his friends to gather their nets, to call back the hounds, to sheath their swords, and to rest themselves in the shade. Actaeon then wanders, idly exploring the forest, but he does not know that the Fates are directing his steps toward a hidden cave and a grassy-banked, spring-fed pond where Artemis is accustomed to bathe with her nymphs. When Actaeon sees the naked goddesses, his curiosity naturally draws him ever closer, and Artemis detects his presence. The nymphs scream with embarrassment, and even Artemis blushes. Once her embarrassment converts to anger, Artemis splashes Actaeon with water and transforms him into an antlered buck. Suddenly terrified, Actaeon runs back toward his resting companions, but they see him as a magnificent beast worthy of the chase. They loose the hounds upon Actaeon, and his own skilled hunting dogs tear his throat out. See Ovid, *Metamorphoses*, book 3. Morville's self-satisfied comparing of himself with Actaeon has enough irony to make me imagine ERE's chuckling as he penned this line. Sadly, the fatefully ignorant Morville does not know the extent of Anthea's reading in the Latin classics.

27. Bathing . . . harm: ERE wrote this note on May 3, 1945. He wrote the bracketed portion on May 25, and during the interval of days he seems to have decided to follow Ovid's story in which Artemis detects the concealed observer, Actaeon.

28. Ars amoris: the art, or science, of love.

29. for the first time in May: This is actually the King's second meeting with Fiorinda in 775: he converses with her first on January 28. Here are ERE's notes, written on May 30, 1945, on this second meeting:

King in Memison: riding down Fiorinda on her white jennet. Talk with her and uncanny conviction (which his suspicions prevent his giving way to, but which he can't discuss) that she is Aphrodite. Talk about her with the Duchess.

Mezentius's intuition about Fiorinda's true nature is his motive for persuading Duchess Amalie to give Fiorinda a place in Memison.

30. When the Duchess heard . . . expected: I offer this draft even though ERE seems to have disliked it. On July 14, 1945, he wrote at the top of the manuscript page, 'not much good, any of this.'
31. rosa alba incarnata: the white rose incarnate.
32. marriage of true minds: See Shakespeare's sonnet 116.
33. HLE: ERE's mother, Helen Louisa Eddison.
34. θεωρια: contemplating, viewing, beholding, observing.

MG: Chapter XXXII

1. the El Greco: See the portrait of Fiorinda by Keith Henderson. He imitated a portrait of a noble Spanish woman painted by El Greco in 1596.
2. μικροψυχια: littleness of soul (or mind or spirit).
3. 'salt bitch' outburst: See the closing scene of Chapter X of *FD*.

MG: Chapter XXXIII

1. Terror Antiquus: ancient terror.
2. That same afternoon . . . spoke word: See Eric Lessingham's story about his brother's defense of a lady's honor in Chapter XIII of *FD*.
3. γλυκύπικρος ἐρῶς: sweetly bitter sexual love.

MG: The Fish Dinner and Its Aftermath

1. *Diet a Cause*: The title comes from partition 1, section 2, member 2, subsection 1 of Robert Burton's *Anatomy of Melancholy* (1621). In this subsection Burton argues that the food one eats can induce melancholy.

MG: Chapter XXXIV

1. *et ego in Arcadiâ*: and so I am in Arcadia; note 1 to Chapter VIII of *MG* tells of the land of Arcadia.
2. two unfleshed souls . . . from shore: Perhaps the feeling of anticipation is the same, but the situation of Barganax and Amalie is the opposite of that experienced by the unfleshed souls waiting to cross the Styx. Barganax and Amalie are in light and remembering darkness: in their eternal home, their 'native substantiality of life,' they are trying to remember earth, our 'dimmer and more crippled world.' The dead 'unfleshed souls' are in darkness and longing for light; those who have

received proper burial wait on the dismal, gloom-lit shores of Styx for the slow boat of Charon to take them across the river to their eternal dwelling places in the nine kingdoms of the lower world. See book 6 of the *Aeneid*.

3. this true philosopher's stone: Alchemists constantly searched and experimented to obtain this, the sovereign solid substance or the liquid elixir that has the ability to transform base metals into gold and silver.

4. *deliciis . . . status quo ante*: luxury; the situation that existed earlier.

5. *Nous connaissons . . . les premières principes*: We know truth not only through the faculty of reason, but also in our hearts; it is through this heart-felt truth that we know the primary principles.

MG: Chapter XXXVI

1. Rosa Mundorum: rose of the worlds.

2. Praxitelean: Praxiteles is the most famous and most praised Greek sculptor of the fourth century B.C. See note 45 to the Overture to *MM*.

3. Her mountain-top where She stood: The scene seems to have shifted, momentarily, to the Aegean, and Fiorinda is standing upon a mountain in Kythera.

MG: Chapter XXXVII

1. *primus inter pares*: first among equals.

2. cockatrice's den: See note 2 to Chapter III of *MG*.

3. Duke of Achery: Prince Styllis.

4. fey: doomed.

MG: Chapter XXXVIII

1. I'll row you on the firth: See chapter 10 of the *Volsunga Saga* (*The Story of the Volsungs and Niblungs*, trans. Eirikr Magnusson and William Morris). Mezentius, by rowing the boat, corresponds to Odin, and Rosma corresponds to both Queen Borghild and Sinfjotli. (I cannot explain the symbolic correspondence further without giving away the ending!)

2. melancholy and filthy blood: Rosma quotes Gervase Markham's *Maister-peece* (II: cxii: 404), written in 1610. Her remark reveals that her medical understanding follows the dominant medical philosophy from Chaucer's days to Milton's, when medical philosophers categorized human moods and dispositions according to the influence of the four dominant humors: blood, phlegm, yellow bile or choler, and black bile or melancholy. According to Robert Burton (1577–1640), 'a humour is a liquid or fluent part of the body, comprehended in it, for the preservation of it; and is either innate or born with us, or adventitious and acquisite.' He then describes the melancholic humor in which black bile predominates and produces either a sullen and angry person or a gloomy and sad person: 'Melancholy, cold and dry, thick, black, and sour, begotten of the more faeculent part of nourishment, and purged from the spleen, is a bridle to the other two hot humours, blood and choler, preserving them in the blood, and nourishing the bones' (*Anatomy of Melancholy,* partition I, section I, member 2, subsection 2). The idea of 'filthy blood' comes from the 'faeculent' aspect of the melancholic humor; it contains excremental matter. This remark, like many issuing from Rosma's lips, is not particularly sweet.

3. *Post me diluvium*: After I am dead, then let the flood come. (Much is implied in the sparing Latin.)

4. Persephone . . . tree of hell: In hot-blooded lust, Hades abducts Persephone and carries her off to the lower world. Ceres, her mother, appeals to Zeus to ask his brother to return the girl. Zeus agrees to allow the girl's return on the condition that she has eaten no food in the kingdom of Hades. Unfortunately, Persephone plucks a pomegranate from a drooping tree branch and eats seven of its seeds. Ascalaphus, who dwells in Acheron, sees her chewing the fruit and prevents her from returning to her mother by telling Zeus and Hades what he has seen. In vengeful anger, Ceres turns Ascalaphus into a screech owl. See Ovid, *Metamorphoses,* book 5.

MG: Chapter XXXIX

1. middle earth: This is the name for the regions of the earth inhabited by men. The term descends from the Old English word *middangeard*, which means 'earth' or 'world.' J.R.R. Tolkien discussed his use of the term in a letter in which he asserted that although he attempted to create a secondary world in his fiction, his Middle-earth is not a place separate from our world, as is ERE's Mercury in *WO:*

> 'Middle-earth,' by the way, is not a name of a never-never land without relation to the world we live in (like the Mercury of Eddison). It is just a use of Middle English *middel-erde* (or *erthe*), altered from Old English Middangeard: the name for the inhabited lands of Men 'between the seas.' And though I have not attempted to relate the shape of the mountains and land-masses to what geologists may say or surmise about the nearer past, imaginatively this 'history' is supposed to take place in a period of the actual Old World of this planet.

(*The Letters of J.R.R. Tolkien,* ed. Humphrey Carpenter and Christopher Tolkien [Boston: Houghton Mifflin, 1981], 220)

Tolkien's early ambition was to make a mythology for England, so maintaining a connection between his created world and England was essential. He designed his mythology to enter English history during the Anglo-Saxon period: he took the Anglo-Saxon name Aelfwine ('elf friend') and gave it to an English mariner who sails west to the lonely island of Tol Eressea, where he learns the history of the Valar and the Elves.

2. fugato: in the style of a fugue.

3. seared the eyeballs: See Macbeth's amazed remarks upon seeing the vision, conjured by the weird sisters, of the first two kings in the procession of eight kings descended from Banquo: 'Thou art too like the spirit of Banquo. Down! / Thy crown does sear mine eyeballs' (IV: i: 112–13).

4. the Hermes of Praxiteles: Archaeologists excavated this sculpture at Olympia (on the western coast of the Peloponnesian peninsula in Greece) in 1877. Whether the piece is an original or a marble copy of a bronze sculpture is still in dispute, but none would dispute that this piece is far and away the finest extant work of Praxiteles (active in the fourth century B.C.). The statue figures Hermes holding Dionysus, as an infant, in his left arm. The right arm, missing below the bicep, once was extended, and Hermes' right hand once dangled a tantalizing bunch of grapes before the fascinated child. The posture of Hermes resembles that of the Knidian Aphrodite and exhibits Praxiteles' perfect power of anatomical observation and rendering. The statue stands in the Archaeological Museum in Olympia.

5. Deare love . . . would die: 'The Dreame,' by John Donne.

6. Do not kiss me, sweetheart, or I shall poison you: Here Mezentius, speaking to Amalie, echoes Brachiano's tender words to his lover Vittoria Corombona: 'Do not kiss me, for I shall poison thee' (John Webster, *The White Devil* V: iii: 27). The difference is that Mezentius, perceiving the approach of death, speaks calmly out of a serene mind, while Brachiano's mind seethes with anxious guilt for his crimes.

APPENDIX A:

THE CHRONOLOGY WITHIN THE THREE VOLUMES OF *ZIMIAMVIA*

Eddison begins his Letter of Introduction to *The Mezentian Gate* with this sentence: 'Not by design, but because it so developed, my Zimiamvian trilogy has been written backwards.' He meant that the order in which he wrote the books is the opposite of the chronology of Zimiamvian years within the books; the last of the three volumes tells the earliest part of the Zimiamvian history. But Eddison's statement about writing Zimiamvian history backward does not precisely fit the actual situation: Zimiamvian time does not progress sequentially through the three books. Actually, *The Mezentian Gate* envelops *A Fish Dinner in Memison,* and *Mistress of Mistresses* follows upon the final chapters of *The Mezentian Gate.* The following scheme shows the progression of the chronology through the three novels in detail.

Zimiamvian Chronology

1) The events of Chapters I through XXIX of *The Mezentian Gate* span the years 703–774 AZC.
2) The action of Chapter XXX of *The Mezentian Gate* surrounds the action of Chapter V and the Zimiamvian sections of Chapter VI of *A Fish Dinner in Memison.* The events of these three chapters take place between January 1 and June 24, 775 AZC.
3) The action of Chapter XXI of *The Mezentian Gate* surrounds the action of Chapter VII of *A Fish Dinner in Memison,* and both chapters focus on the events of June 26, 775 AZC.
4) The action of Chapter XXXII of *The Mezentian Gate* surrounds

967

the action of the Zimiamvian sections of Chapter VIII of *A Fish Dinner in Memison*. The events of these chapters take place between June 26 and July 21, 775 AZC.

5) The events of Chapters IX and X of *A Fish Dinner in Memison* span the morning hours of July 21, 775 AZC and conclude at about 11:00 A.M.

6) The action of Chapter XXXIII of *The Mezentian Gate* surrounds the action of Chapters XI and XII of *A Fish Dinner in Memison*. The events of these chapters take place between 11:00 A.M. on July 21 and the late afternoon of July 22, 775 AZC.

7) The Zimiamvian part of Chapter XIII of *A Fish Dinner in Memison* lasts for a few moments of the evening of July 23, 775 AZC.

8) The action of Chapters XIV, XV, XVI and of the Zimiamvian part of XIX of *A Fish Dinner in Memison* occurs on July 25, 775 AZC.

9) The events of Chapters XXXIV through XXXIX of *The Mezentian Gate* take place between late August 775 and June 24, 776 AZC.

10) After a temporal hiatus of nearly ten months, the events of Chapters I through XXII of *Mistress of Mistresses* take place between April 22, 777 and July 20, 778 AZC.

The chronology of time on earth is simpler in its pattern within the books: it progresses sequentially from *A Fish Dinner in Memison* to *The Mezentian Gate* to *Mistress of Mistresses*.

Earthly Chronology

A Fish Dinner in Memison

1) The action of Chapter I occurs on April 22, 1908.

2) The events of Chapters III, IV, and the earthly parts of Chapter VI occur on one day in mid-June 1908.

3) The events of the earthly parts of Chapter VIII occur between June 24 and 27, 1914.

4) The final paragraph of Chapter XI occurs at 4:00 A.M. on June 28, 1914.

5) The events of Chapter XIII occur between Easter of 1919 and the first week of February 1923.

6) The events of Chapters XVII and XVIII take place between the evening of October 19 and 4:00 A.M. on the morning of October 20, 1923.

7) The events of the earthly section of Chapter XIX take place on two days in the autumn of 1933.

The Mezentian Gate

8) The action of the Praeludium occurs on a day in mid-July 1973.

Mistress of Mistresses

9) The action of the Overture occurs a few hours after the time of the Praeludium to *The Mezentian Gate* (mid-July 1973).

How, then, should you and I read these books? Should we read *Mistress of Mistresses* first or last? I think that all books should be read, if possible, according to Pope's maxim from *An Essay on Criticism:* 'A perfect judge will read each work of wit / with the same spirit that its author writ' (2: 233–34). Part of reading in sympathy with Eddison's spirit lies in perceiving his developing ideas. Zimiamvia and its persons did not spring from Eddison's imagination fully realized, like Athena from the head of Zeus, between 1931 and 1935; rather, many of his ideas matured slowly over twenty years, and some of them were still in the first budding stage of spring at the time of his death. I think the novels should be read in the order that they were composed, and so I have placed them in that order.

—P. E. THOMAS

APPENDIX B:

DRAMATIS PERSONAE

The list of Zimiamvian characters is arranged alphabetically according to two grouping rules: Each character is placed in her or his chronological relationship to the reign of King Mezentius, then geographically within each chronological section. If a character's dates of life are discernible from the texts, they are indicated by the numbers immediately following the colon. Within the parentheses at the end of each entry, the chapter reference indicates the first appearance of the character's name in the book; a second chapter reference, if any, indicates the first appearance of the character's name according to Zimiamvian chronology (AZC). If these appearances are the same, one chapter reference is given. Numbers in parentheses immediately following a name indicate a character who appears in more than one chronological section because her or his status changes; for these characters, life dates and chapter references are given only in the first entry. The list of English and European characters appears after the Zimiamvian list.

—P. E. Thomas

1. Before the Coming of Age of King Mezentius

Akkama
Aktor: 703–740; Prince; second husband of Stateira; Prince Protector during minority of Mezentius (*MG*–II)

Fingiswold
Acarnus: Chancellor under Mardanus (*MG*–VII)
Anthyllus: King (*MG*–II)
Garman: son of Anthyllus (*MG*–II)

Harpargus: died 721; son of Anthyllus; King (*MG*–I)

Jeronimy (1): 719–; a page in the service of Mardanus (*MM*–III; *MG*–II)

Mardanus: died 726; son of Harpargus; succeeds Harpargus as King (*MG*–I)

Marescia: daughter of Garman (*MG*–I)

Mendes: Knight Marshal under Mardanus (*MG*–VII)

Mezentius (1): 723–776; son of Mardanus (*MM*–I; *MG*–I)

Myntor: Constable in Rialmar under Mardanus (*MG*–VII)

Psammius: High Admiral under Mardanus (*MG*–VII)

Stateira: Queen of Fingiswold; wife of Mardanus (*MG*–II)

Rerek

Alvard: Prince of Kaima (*MG*–I)

Caunus: died 716; Lord of Lailma (*MG*–I)

Keriones: Prince of Eldir (*MG*–I)

Kresander: Prince of Bagort (*MG*–I)

Mereus: 712–?; son of Caunus and Morsilla Parry (*MG*–I)

Yelen: husband of Lugia Parry; Count of Leveringay (*MG*–I)

The Parry Family of Rerek

Emmius: 689–771; eldest son of Pertiscus; Lord of Sleaby in Susdale as a young man and later Lord of Argyanna (*MG*–I)

Gargarus: second son of Pertiscus (*MG*–I)

Hybrastus: 717–751; son of Emmius and Deïaneira (*MG*–I)

Lugia: the only daughter of Pertiscus (*MG*–I)

Lupescus: third son of Pertiscus; lived as a recluse at Thundermere (*MG*–I)

Morsilla: daughter of Mynius; wife of Caunus and later of Prince Keriones (*MG*–I)

Mynius: 666–704; lord of Laimak (*MG*–I)

Pertiscus: 666–721; twin brother of Mynius (*MG*–I)

Rasmus: only son of Mynius (*MG*–I)

Rhodanthe: daughter of Sidonius; wife of Supervius (*MG*–I)

Rosma (1): 714–776; daughter of Emmius and Deïaneira; marries King Kallias of Meszria; murders Kallias and marries King Haliartes and becomes joint sovereign of Meszria; becomes Queen of Meszria after death of Haliartes (*MG*–I)

Sidonius: younger brother of Mynius and Pertiscus (*MG*–I)

Supervius: 695–750; youngest son of Pertiscus; succeeds Pertiscus as Lord of Laimak (*MG*–I)

Meszria

Beltran: nephew of Haliartes (*MG*–XI)

Beroald (1): 739–?; son of Rosma Parry and Beltran (*MM*–III; *MG*–XI)

Deïaneira: ?–771; daughter of Mesanges; wife of Emmius (*MG*–I)

Haliartes: brother of Kallias; becomes King after death of Kallias; second husband of Rosma Parry (*MG*–IX)

Kallias: King; first husband of Rosma Parry (*MG*–IX)

Lebedes: nephew of Haliartes; younger brother of Beltran (*MG*–XI)

2. During the Reign of King Mezentius

Akkama

Derxis: son of Sagartis; becomes King in 772

Sagartis: King; forms treasonous alliance with Valero (*MG*–XXVI)

Fingiswold

Antiope (1): 760–778; daughter of Mezentius and Rosma (*MM*–III; *MG*–XXII)

Bodenay: 700–?; becomes Knight Marshal in 772 (*MM*–XIII; *MG*–XXVI)

Jeronimy (2): becomes the Chief Lieutenant of Mezentius in command of the fleet during war with Akkama; becomes Commissioner Regent of Meszria with Beroald under Mezentius in 766; admitted to the kingly order of the hippogriff in 772; becomes part of triumvirate of Commissioners Regent for Meszria with Beroald and Roder in 772

Mezentius (2): becomes King of Rerek in 748; becomes King of Meszria after marrying Rosma in 751

Romyrus: Lord Constable of Rialmar (*MM*–XIII; *MG*–XXVI)

Styllis (1): 758–777; son of Mezentius and Rosma; Duke of Achery (*MM*–I; *MG*–XXI)

Rerek

Anastasia: ?–745; sister of Prince Ercles; first wife of Mezentius (*MG*–XIII)

Aramond: 727–?; Prince of Bagort (*MM*–I; *MG*–XIII)

Arcastus: grandson of Morsilla Parry and Caunus; appointed Lord of Megra by Mezentius (*MG*–XXII)

Arquez: ?–775; a lord (*FD*–VII)

Bork: Lord President of the Marches (*MG*–XVII)

Clavius: ?–775; a lord (*FD*–VII)

Eleonora: granddaughter of Sidonius Parry; wife of Romelius (*MG*–XIX)

Ercles: 718–?; son of Keriones; Prince of Eldir (*MM*–I; *MG*–XIII)

Gabriel Flores: 729–778; spy and secretary for Horius Parry (*MM*–V; *MG*–XVII)

Gilmanes: ?–775; son of Alvard; Prince of Kaima; brother of Valero (*MG*–XIII)

Ibian: a lord (*FD*–VII)

Lessingham (1): 752–778; son of Romelius and Eleonora; admitted to the kingly order of the hippogriff (*MM*–I, *MG*–XIX)

Mandricard: Lord of Abaraima (*MM*–IX; *FD*–VII)

Olpman: ?–775; Count; tutor of Beroald (*FD*–VII; *MG*–XXI)

Geleron Parry: son of Supervius Parry and Rhodanthe; Lord of Anguring (*MG*–XVII)

Horius Parry: 725–?; son of Supervius Parry and Marescia; succeeds his father as Lord of Laimak; becomes Vicar of Rerek in 772 (*MM*–I; *MG*–XIII)

Morville Parry: ?–776; second husband of Fiorinda; Lieutenant of the King in Reisma (*FD*–IX; *MG*–XXVI)

Peridor: son of Lugia Parry; Prince of Laveringay (*MG*–XIII)

Roder: ?–778; appointed Lord of Kessarey by Mezentius; the King makes him an Earl in 772; becomes part of triumvirate of Commissioners Regent for Meszria with Beroald and Jeronimy in 772 (*MM*–III; *MG*–XXII)

Romelius: father of Lessingham (*MG*–XIX)

Rossillion: a lord (*FD*–VII)

Sorms: a disgruntled lord (*FD*–VII)

Stathmar: ?–775; becomes Lord of Argyanna in 772 (*FD*–VII; *MG*–XXVIII)

Valero: 730–771; son of Alvard; brother of Gilmanes; Prince of Ulba; forms treasonous alliance with King Sagartis of Akkama (*MM*–XII; *MG*–XIV)

Meszria

Amalie: 733–?; lady of the bedchamber for Queen Rosma; lover of Mezentius; appointed Duchess of Memison by Mezentius (*MM*–II; *MG*–XVI)

Baias: ?–774; Lord of Masmor; marries Fiorinda in 774 (*MG*–XXIX)

Barganax (1): 752–?; son of Mezentius and Amalie; appointed Duke of Zayana by Mezentius in 770 (*MM*–II; *MG*–XIX)

Barrian: a lord (*MM*–III; *MG*–XXX)

Bekmar: an old lord (*MG*–XXXIX)

Bellefront: a lady of honor in the court of Amalie at Memison (*MM*–VII; *MG*–XXX)

Beroald (2): appointed Lord of Krestenaya by Mezentius; becomes Commissioner Regent in Meszria with Jeronimy in 766; becomes Chancellor of Fingiswold in 772; becomes part of triumvirate of Commissioners Regent for Meszria with Roder and Jeronimy in 772

Fiorinda: daughter of Rosma and Beltran; marries Baias in 774; after death of Baias, marries Morville Parry in 775; becomes a lady of the bedchamber for Amalie in Memison (*MM*–II, *MG*–XX)

Heterasmene: a lady of honor at Amalie's court in Memison; first lover of Barganax (*MG*–XXIII)

Ibian: a lord (*MM*–IX; *FD*–VI)

Lydia: wife to one of Amalie's chamberlains (*FD*–VI)

Medor: a count; captain of Barganax's bodyguard (*MM*–II, *MG*–XXXIX)

Melates: a lord; companion of Barganax (*MM*–III; *MG*–XXX)

Myrrha: a lady of the bedchamber for Amalie in Memison (*MM*–II; *FD*–V)

Ninetta: daughter of Ibian (*FD*–VI)

the nurse of Amalie (*FD*–V)

Pantasilea: a lady of the ducal court of Zayana (*MM*–VII; *MG*–XXX)

Perantor: a lord (*MG*–XXIX)

Rosalura: a lady of the ducal court of Zayana (*MG*–XXX)

Rosma (2): becomes Queen of Fingiswold and Rerek when she marries Mezentius in 751

Selmanes: Lord of Bish (*MG*–XXXIX)

Violante: a lady of the bedchamber for Amalie in Memison (*MM*–II; *FD*–V)

Zapheles: a lord; a companion of Barganax (*MM*–III; *MG*–XXX)

3. After the Reign of King Mezentius

Akkama

Alquemen: a lord (*MM*–XIII)

Esperveris: a lord (*MM*–XIII)

Kasmon: a lord (*MM*–XIII)

Orynxis: a lord (*MM*–XIII)

Fingiswold

Anamnestra: a lady of honor in Antiope's court in Rialmar (*MM*–XIII)

Antiope (2): succeeds her brother Styllis as Queen of the triple kingdom in 777

Bosra: replaces Romyrus as Lord Constable of Rialmar (*MM*–XV)

Hortensius: ?–778; a lord; a commander in the battle of the Lorkan fields (*MM*–IX)

Jeronimy (3): named Regent of Meszria during the minority of Antiope in testament of King Styllis but resigns the office to Barganax; becomes Regent of Outer Meszria by agreement in the Concordat of Ilkis in June 777

Myrilla: daughter of Admiral Jeronimy; marries Amaury (*MM*–XIII)

Orvald: a lord (*MM*–XIII)

Paphirrhoe: a lady of honor in Antiope's court in Rialmar (*MM*–XIII)

Peropeutes: a lord; a commander in the battle of the Lorkan fields (*MM*–IX)

Raviamne: a lady of honor in Antiope's court in Rialmar (*MM*–XIII)

Styllis (2): succeeds his father Mezentius as king of the triple kingdom in 776

Countess of Tasmar: a lady of honor in Antiope's court in Rialmar (*MM*–XIII)

Tessa: Queen Antiope's horse (*MM*–XV)

Tyarchus: a lord (*MM*–XIII)

Venton: a lord (*MM*–XIII)
Zenochlide: a lady of honor in Antiope's court in Rialmar (*MM*–XIII)

Rerek

Amaury: lieutenant to Lessingham; marries Myrilla of Fingiswold (*MM*–I)
Arcastus: a lord; one of Horius Parry's military commanders (*MM*–IX)
Bezardes: one of Lessingham's military commanders (*MM*–XIX)
Brandremart: brother of Gallyard; one of Lessingham's military commanders (*MM*–IX)
Daimon: a lord (*MM*–XVI)
Gayllard: brother of Brandremart; one of Lessingham's military commanders (*MM*–XIX)
Illmauger: one of Horius Parry's dogs (*MM*–XI)
Lessingham (2): appointed Captain General of the Queen by the Lord Protector, Horius Parry, in June 777; confirmed as Captain General by Duke Barganax in 778
Horius Parry (2): becomes Regent of the triple kingdom and Lord Protector of the Queen during the minority of Antiope
Maddalena: Lessingham's horse (*MM*–IX)
Mandricard (2): made a count and Lord of Argyanna by Horius Parry
Meron: replaces Roquez as Captain of Veiring (*MM*–XIX)
Pyewacket: one of Horius Parry's dogs (*MM*–V)
Roquez: Lord of Veiring (*MM*–XIX)
Rosalura: younger daughter of Ercles; marries Medor in 777 (*MM*–II)
Seneschal of Rumala (*MM*–IX)
Thrasiline: a lord (*MM*–XVI)

Meszria

Barganax (2): reconfirmed as Duke of Zayana by King Styllis; becomes Regent of Meszria when Jeronimy resigns the office to him in May 777; becomes Regent of South Meszria by agreement in the Concordat of Ilkis in June 777; succeeds Antiope as King of the triple kingdom in June 778
Belinus: a lord; a commander in the battle of the Lorkan fields (*MM*–IX)
Bernabo: a soldier in Barganax's bodyguard (*MM*–XVII)
Beroald (3): made Lord of Sail Aninma by the Lord Protector, Horius Parry
Dioneo: a soldier in Barganax's bodyguard (*MM*–XVII)
Egan: a servant of Barganax in Zayana (*MM*–III)
Fontinell: a soldier in Barganax's bodyguard (*MM*–XVII)
Friscobaldo: a soldier in Barganax's bodyguard (*MM*–XVII)

Zimiamvian Characters Lacking Land or Lineage or Chronology

Anthea: an oread; disciple of Vandermast; servant of Fiorinda (*MM*–II; *MG*–II)

Campaspe: a dryad; disciple of Vandermast (*MM*–VII; *MG*–XXVIII)

Doctor Vandermast: studied philosophy at the University of Miphraz; tutor of Mezentius and Barganax; becomes secretary to Barganax in Zayana (*MM*–II; *MG*–II)

Zenianthe: a hamadryad; disciple of Vandermast; supposedly the niece of King Mezentius (*MM*–XIII; *MG*–XXV)

4. Characters in England and Europe

Lord Anmering, Robert Scarnside: descended from Sir Robert Scarnside, first Earl of Anmering; brother of Everard Scarnside; lives at Anmering Blunds (*FD*–I)

Appleyard, Tom: an obedient batsman (*FD*–III)

Bailey, Sir Roderick: an admiral (*FD*–III)

Bailey, Jack: son of Roderick (*FD*–III)

Bentham, Mrs.: a dinner guest at Anmering Blunds (*FD*–IV)

Birkel, Paula: a waitress at the inn in Wolkenstein (*FD*–VIII)

Bremmerdale, Anne Lessingham: sister of Edward, wife of Charles Bremmerdale (*FD*–I)

Bremmerdale, Charles: husband of Anne Lessingham (*FD*–I)

Carwell, Ronald: a young Englishman in Verona (*FD*–XIX)

Chedisford, Fanny: friend of Mary Scarnside Lessingham; marries and divorces George Chedisford (*FD*–III)

Chedisford, George: sometime husband of Fanny Chedisford (*FD*–III)

Chedisford, Tom (*FD*–III)

Dagworth, Hesper (*FD*–III)

David: Edward Lessingham's coachman and chauffeur (*FD*–VIII)

Denmore-Bentham: a consistent batsman (*FD*–III)

Dilstead, Lucy: daughter of lady Dilstead, companion of Mary Scarnside Lessingham; engaged to Nigel Howard (*FD*–III)

Dilstead, Oliver: son of Lady Dilstead (*FD*–III)

Fiorinda: converses with Lessingham in Verona (*FD*–I)

Frank: an Englisman in Verona (*FD*–XIX)

the friend of Edward Lessingham: narrator of the Overture to *MM*

Glanford, Hugh: son of Lord Southmere (*FD*–III)

Howard, Nigel: engaged to Lucy Dilstead (*FD*–III)

Jessie: a maid at Edward Lessingham's Nether Wasdale house (*FD*–VIII)

Kirkstead, Lady Rosamund: a marchioness (*FD*–III)

Lessingham, Edward: 1882–1973: husband of Mary Scarnside; governor of the Lofoton Islands (*MM*–Overture, *FD*–I)

Lessingham, Eric: older brother of Edward; lives at Snittlegarth (*FD*–VIII)

Lessingham, Janet: daughter of Edward and Mary Lessingham (*FD*–VIII)

Lessingham, Rob: son of Edward and Mary Lessingham (*FD*–X)

Limpenfield: a fellow (?) of All Souls' College, Oxford. (*FD*–III)

General Macnaughten: (*FD*–III)

Margesson, Cuthbert: (*FD*–III)

Margesson, Nell Scarnside: niece of Lord Anmering, wife of Cuthbert Margesson (*FD*–III)

Margesson, ?: the cricket captain

Milcrest, Jack: Edward Lessingham's secretary (*FD*–XIII)

Mitzmesczinsky, Princess Amabel: daughter of Everard Scarnside; married to Prince Nicholas

Mitzmesczinsky, Prince Nicholas: married to Amabel Scarnside (*FD*–VIII)

Otterdale, Michael: an English mosquito in Verona (*FD*–XIX)

Colonel Playter: coach of the Hyrnbastwick cricket team (*FD*–III)

Playter, Norah: daughter of Colonel Playter (*FD*–III)

Playter, Sybil: daughter of Colonel Playter (*FD*–III)

Romer: the bursar of Trinity College, Oxford (*FD*–III)

Madame de Rosas: a Spanish dancer (*FD*–IV)

Rustham: the Hyrnbastwick captain

Ruth: Edward Lessingham's housekeeper in Nether Wasdale (*FD*–VIII)

Scarnside, Everard: uncle of Mary Scarnside Lessingham (*FD*–III)

Scarnside, Jim: son of Everard and Bella Scarnside; cousin of Mary Scarnside Lessingham (*FD*–I)

Scarnside, Mary: 1888–1923; daughter of Lord Anmering; marries Edward Lessingham (*FD*–I)

Señorita del Rio Amargo: lover of Edward Lessingham (*MM*–Overture; *MG*–Praeludium).

Lady Southmere: lives in Norfolk, Virginia (*FD*–III)

Lord Southmere (*FD*–III)

Sterramore: a general (*FD*–III)

Trowsley (*FD*–III)

Willie: an Englisman in Verona (*FD*–XIX)

APPENDIX C:

GENEALOGICAL TABLES

THE LINE OF THI

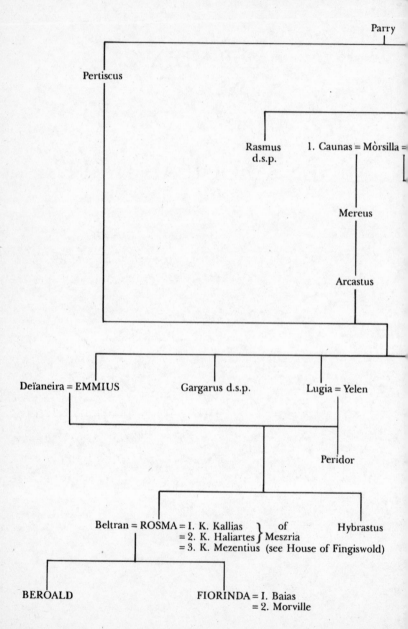

PARRY FAMILY

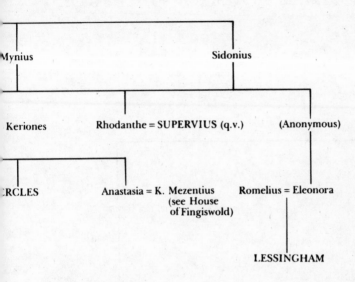

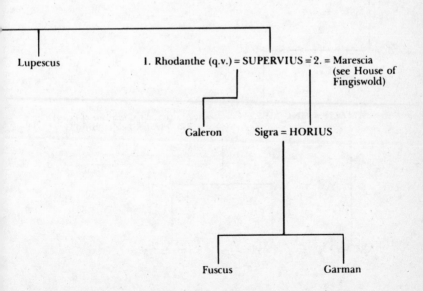

THE ROYAL HOUSE OF FINGISWOLD

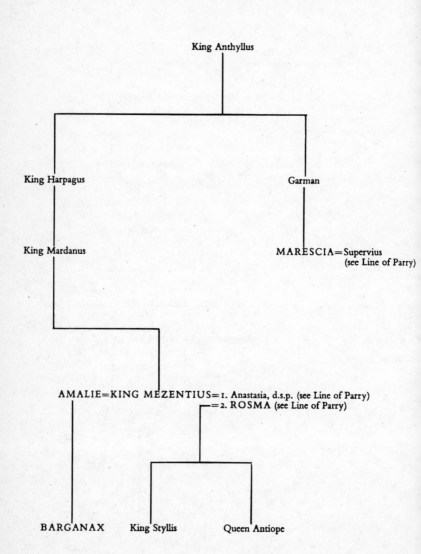

APPENDIX D:

MAPS

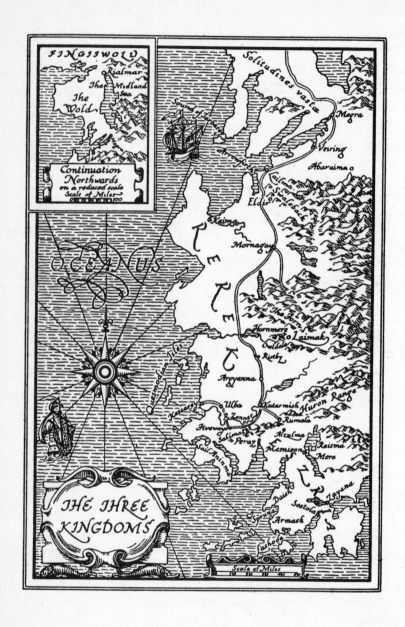

FINGISWOLD

Rialmar

The Midland Sea

The Wold

Continuation
Northwards
on a reduced scale
Scale of Miles
100

Solitudines vastæ

Magra

Veiring

Abaraima o

Eldir

OCEANUS

KEREK

Kaima

Mornagay

Thaspôn

Hornmere · Laimak

Owldale

Rietby

Argyanna

Ulba · Kutarmish · Huron Range

Zennet · Rumala

Hveweria · Aizmur

Salimat · Peraz · Reisma

Memison · Mere

ZAYANA

Daish · Argyana

Sestola

Armash

Rhoda

THE THREE
KINGDOMS

Scale of Miles

The Campaign in North Rerek
Lessingham's march ....
Jeronimy's march ------
Ercles's march ....

Lailma

Nivararnadale
Rojsbjck

Mlemmering

Camp
Proud Eldir

Eldir

Jella

Steopland Brink

Arminy

Bank

Kaima

Fithery Side

R. Fithery

Ridinghead

Rangby

Leveringay

Westerwater

Eastering Side
Rivershaws

Mornagay

The Scale of Miles

The Meszrian Border
Lessingham's march ....
Roder's pursuit ----
Gabriel Flores' ride ....

Kutarmish

The Scale of Miles

The March of Ulba

Outer Meszria

River Zenner

Ilkis

Orasbiah Hill

Lorkan Bridge

The Curtain
Rumala
Sherma

Argyssa

Nephory

Limisba

Haranot Beck

The Salimat

Nephory Edge

Alzulma